THE SANCTUM SYNDICATE
VOLUME 1

A MAFIA ROMANCE BOX SET

BY

LILITH ROMAN

Lilith Roman Books

Copyright © Lilith Roman 2024
Cover Design and Typeset by Lilith Roman copyright © Lilith Roman 2024

The Sanctum Syndicate: Volume 1
First Edition | December 2024

This is a work of fiction. References to real people, places, organizations, events, and products are intended to provide a sense of authenticity and are used fictitiously. All characters, incidents, and dialogue are drawn from the author's imagination and not to be construed as real.

Editing by Mackenzie Letson (Nice Girl Naughty Edits) and Victoria Ellis (Cruel Ink Editing)
Proofreading by Michele Ficht
Photos licensed from depositphotos.com

ISBN (eBook): 978-1-0683390-0-4
ISBN (paperback): 978-1-0683390-1-1

To find out more about the author please visit lilithromanauthor.com

AUTHOR'S NOTE

**They're feared. Powerful. Ruthless.
And they don't just love... they worship.**

Welcome to their underworld.

The Sanctum Syndicate is a mafia series of interconnected standalones, which can be read out of order, however for the best experience, I recommend starting with book 1.

This omnibus includes the first three books in the series:
- Dangerous Strokes, a dark mafia romance
- Reckless Covenant, a second chance mafia romance
- Manacled Hearts, a slow burn, age gap mafia romance

Happy reading!

Love,
Lilith

For all of you who love
your morally gray book boyfriends
adoring, obsessed, and dangerous,
Roman, Vincent, and Finnigan
are yours!

Love,
Lilith ♥ Roman.

DANGEROUS STROKES

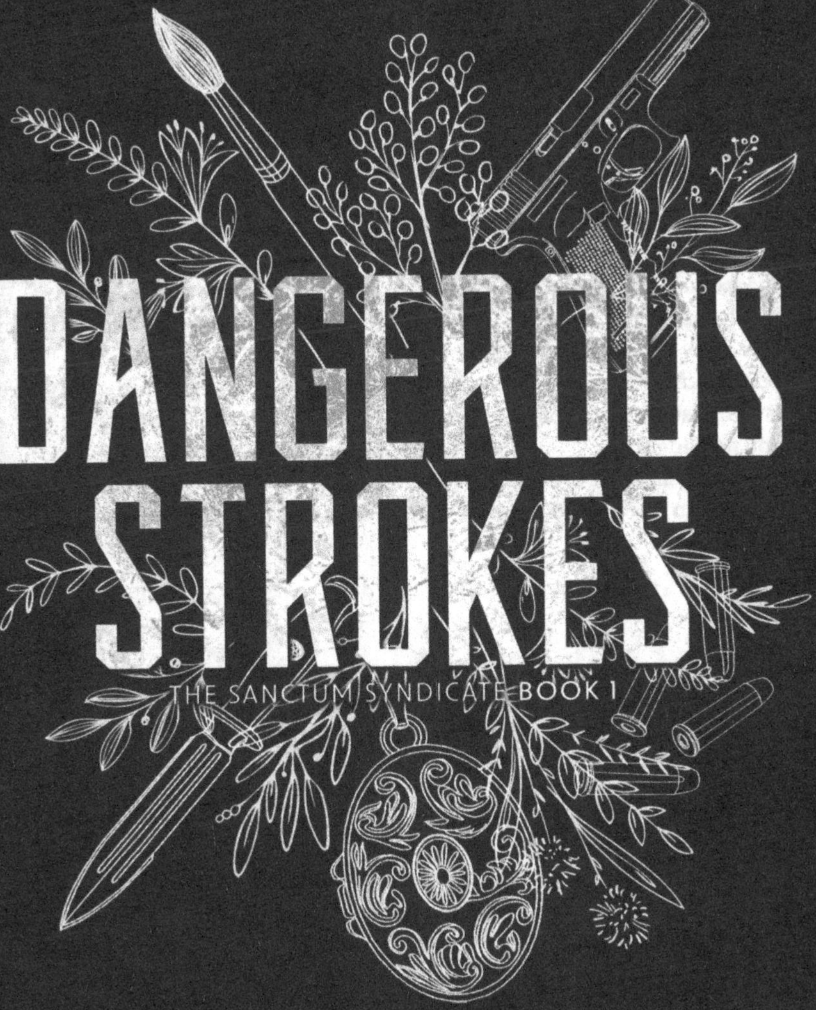

THE SANCTUM SYNDICATE BOOK 1

LILITH ROMAN

BLURB

It was supposed to be my last con.
But I didn't expect *him* to be the client.
Dangerous, powerful, and drop-dead gorgeous, Ronan Hennessey's sharp blue eyes drew me in, but it was his wicked tongue that kept me there.
As one of the leaders of his underworld, I should have been scared. Instead, I was mesmerized. Enthralled.
So I sent him an invitation made of brush strokes and riddles, tempting him to chase me. One last adventure before I vanished to my island paradise after years of crooked black-market deals.
He was only meant to be a thrill. But when he called me his *little witch*, casting his own spell on me, my heart was in trouble.
Only, I didn't know someone else was already hunting me, determined to get revenge and make me suffer for a past deceit. It was only a matter of time until this enemy found my new identity.
Meeting Ronan changed everything and mine wasn't the only life on the line anymore.
Who will get to me first? The man who makes my soul sing, or the monster who wants to burn it?

CONTENT WARNING

This is a work of fiction and should be taken as such. It contains dark themes and sensitive content that can be triggering for some including graphic violence, kidnapping, sexual assault, rape, torture, murder, loss, grief, dubious consent, unplanned pregnancy, human trafficking, psychological abuse. There is no cheating and it has a HEA. If you are easily offended or triggered by any of this content, please do not read this book. Your mental health matters.

PLAYLIST

Nikki – Worakls
Werewolf Heart – Dead Man's Bones
God Complex – VIOLENT VIRA
Left Me for Dead – Rob Dougan
Hell or High Water – From Days Gone – Billy Raffoul
Wicked Game – Chris Isaak
Change (In the House of Flies) – Deftones
PLEASE – Omido, Ex Habit
Me & My Demons – Omido, Silent Child
Love Is a Bitch – Two Feet
Vengeance – Zack Hemsey
Come Undone – Duran Duran
The Road to Hell, pt. 1 & 2 – Chris Rea
Iron Sky – Paolo Nutini
Daylight – David Kushner
Two Face (Omido Remix) – Jake Daniels, Omido
West Coast – Lana Del Rey
Love Surrounds You – Ramsey
Waking Up – MJ Cole, Freya Ridings
Sweet Dreams (Slowed + Reverb) – Ravens Rock
Nikki – Worakls
Mine – Sleep Token

CHAPTER 1
Ronan

MANY THINGS WENT through my mind the moment this woman stepped into the private garden. They're gone now, though. Replaced by one singular thought burning its way through my chest, stealing the air from my lungs—*she'll eat me alive*. Bit by bit, she'll chew me whole, spit me out, then devour me all over again.

The strange thing is that I might actually ask her to do it. Might even beg. Which is why I know she must be a witch. There's no other explanation for this paradox, this timid, delicate thing delivering such a visceral omen.

I should listen to the details of the business meeting taking place at this very moment. But her pure, deep-set eyes, trapped in a limbo between gray and blue, put a spell on me with their peculiar sparkle. Just like that porcelain skin that seems to glow in this twilight. It makes me wonder if I'm the only one seeing the creature before us, or if I'm bewitched.

There's something about her. The way she timidly peeks at me from under those thin bangs that don't fully cover her forehead. Something about the way her delicate curves stand before us. She reminds me of those precious ancient statues adorning museum halls.

Us...

My mind shifts into gear, trying to break free from this witch's charm. I focus on all the people around me—my business partners, hers, and both our security teams.

"Ronan..." My brother's tone doesn't hide the fact that he's trying to get my attention. "Meeting in two days to see the painting and close the deal sounds good to you too, yeah?"

He's going to give me a hard time after this, I just know it.

"It does. We have a warehouse in a secure location, toward the edge of the city, quiet, secluded. We can meet there." They're the first words I've spoken since the meeting started, but I only seem to direct them at *her*—Ingrid Thorp.

"Respectfully, no." The spell breaks further as Erika Brand, her business partner, replies, pulling my attention.

"No?" I question, narrowing my eyes on the brown-eyed woman.

"No offense, Mr. Hennessey, but I would prefer we meet in a place of our own choosing. Where we are a bit more... comfortable."

She means safe. She doesn't trust us, but then again, she has no reason to. We've never met before. This business deal was arranged through the dark corners of the web, where shady deals are struck, and most are for items that will never see anything but a crooked market.

Ingrid seems to share the sentiment, shifting her weight from one leg to the other, rubbing her fingers together. Her eyes nervously flash from the floor to me enough times that it gets me wondering—is it because of the meeting or... me?

A strange heat fills a part of me that has no business waking up right now.

"I believe we should all be *comfortable,* should we not?" I was expecting this. "Name the place. We'll tell you if it works for us."

Erika purses her lips and reluctantly agrees after her eyes drift briefly to my brother. "Rosenberg Hotel, in one of the private dining rooms of the restaurant. Eight in the evening, in two days—Friday."

I turn to my brother Finn, to my right, Maddox and Carter behind me, and Vincent to my left. They all nod.

"Very well. We will bring our own appraiser and continue the conversation there."

"Just a reminder, to ensure we are all on the same page. The price is no longer negotiable, and the sale will be final."

"Final? No."

"Yes," she insists.

Erika's back straightens further, her attitude grave, like until now she kept her guard low so she could offer us some sense of ease. Maybe under any other circumstances, I would be affected.

Not now. Not when my eyes drift once again to the porcelain witch standing quietly beside her, head tilted down ever so slightly. Not with that deceiving virtue painted on her lush lips, when her eyes scream of wickedness.

A bizarre desire grows inside of me, one that wants to crack her open and find out where that wickedness comes from.

"If you do not agree with the terms," Erika continues, unwavering, "we have a long list of buyers, as you well know, who would accept them in a heartbeat. Considering the... dubious provenance of the painting, surely you understand why we have to wash our hands of it right away."

"And surely you understand why three million is a lot of money to gamble with," I argue.

"If you're looking to gamble, Mr. Hennessey, I suggest visiting The Royal Casino on third street. We are seeking a business deal here." I think the air is sucked out of the atmosphere as Ingrid speaks for the first time.

Her voice distracts me from the obvious bite of her words. She sounds like a birdsong filling a meadow on a warm summer day, and I crave to be right there with her.

"Careful now, that sharp tongue and those steel eyes will get you in trouble." I lower my voice, reveling in the shock painted vividly on her parted lips. For a split moment, I forget it's not just us.

"What my partner means to say…" Erika says quickly, "is that we do not wish to waste our time or yours. We are positive that you will be pleased with the piece."

"Friday. Eight o'clock. The Rosenberg," I almost rasp, my throat constricting, my lungs close to heaving.

I'm suffocating.

That woman… she's infusing the oxygen with her seemingly innocent black magic, and I need to break the damn spell.

I have to walk past her to leave, and I can't stop myself from glancing over my shoulder. She turns her head slightly, but our gazes never connect.

I'm not sure if it makes me feel better or worse, but she's trying hard not to look at me. As I am at her.

It doesn't matter. The heat of her body as I brush past her seems to have the same effect.

* * *

We've just passed through the gates of the garden, my steps heavy and quick, eager to get the fuck out of there, when my brother gives me a forceful nudge.

"What the hell was that, man?! Do you even know what happened in that meeting?"

I roll my eyes, heading toward the driver's side of the Range Rover parked across the street, Finn falling into step behind me.

"I think we all know what happened there," Vin says, to my dismay.

Most people have an irrational fear of Vincent Sinclair's attention on them. I am no exception. It's the darkness of his black eyes that I try to avoid when I look in the rearview mirror. I swear to the gods the man can look into your soul, peel all the layers until he finds the exact information he needs to hold against you. He's five or six years younger than my twenty-seven, yet his talent doesn't show his age. He gets better the more he practices, putting the fear of God into people. Only, those people have begun calling him *The Serpent*, and they don't think it's God they should fear when they fall under his gaze.

He's a good kid, though—all four of them are.

My brother, Finnigan, the pretty boy who has been turning heads with his baby blues and curly blond locks, long before he started filling those shoulders and pecs with muscle.

Maddox Severin, who has never looked his age, towers over all of us. His wide, muscled frame growing month by month, nurtured by his hunger for grueling workouts and fighting. He's the one who trains all our men and we've had to build him a gym so he can focus his brute force there, not on our guys.

Then there's Carter Pierce, the man with peculiar dark blue and hazel eyes, that are as beautiful as they are empty. He's always prim and proper, with his white shirts, sleeves rolled up to his elbows, tweed waistcoats, and impeccable slicked-back hair and undercut. He doesn't really look like he's from this time. He's quite something—

different. A man of few words and the ones he sometimes chooses make me wonder about the skeletons in his closet. Or maybe severed heads in the fridge. Yet he's the one I gravitate toward the most, and even after all these years, I still don't understand why.

We started this organization more or less together, even though Carter and Finn were away at university for a portion of it. It worked to our benefit. All the connections they sought there have proved fruitful, while Vin, Madds, and I built the bases here.

"There he goes again. He's gone."

"Fuck you!" I spit at Madds, who kicks my seat from behind.

"Wouldn't mind being lost in that blue-eyed little thing either," Finn teases.

"Gray..." I whisper. But it comes out more like a grunt. A visceral need to smack my brother's head against the dashboard arises, and I can't make sense of it. Even aware that the asshole is just messing with me.

"What did you say?"

"Nothing."

The engine roars to life, covering the rest of the bullshit coming out of their mouths. But it does nothing against my intrusive thoughts about the woman who almost took my damn breath away. I don't even dare ask myself if they all noticed it. I already know they did.

Fuck!

I put my foot down, the streetlights of Queenscove blurring as I drive through the night, knowing full well I'm stupidly attracting the attention of both the residents and the tourists of this seaside city. The majority of them are currently out on the streets since it's Saturday night.

Does it really matter, when we have most of the police in our pocket anyway? They won't stop us.

With my fingers tightening around the steering wheel, my mind drifts to those prominent cheeks, her round eyes, silky brown hair, square, yet delicate jaw... that high cupid's bow that begs to be licked.

Jesus Christ, what is wrong with me?

More importantly, what the hell is going on with her? Who is she and what is she doing here? A woman like her, so delicate and soft, doesn't belong in this cruel world— our world. It's too harsh for her, but I have to admit... she stands out beautifully.

That wicked gaze she left me with haunts my mind, a touch of darkness weaving through her soul, and I want to reach in and grab it by the throat. Squeeze it just enough that my dick wakes up at the slight tremor of fear that will no doubt shake her flesh.

Annika

DID I THINK the man I saw in a photo weeks ago was going to be like *that* in real life?

No.

Did I think my skin would hold a constant stream of goosebumps during the entirety of our meeting, like I was being shocked the whole time?

No.

Did I think the man I've been obsessing over would fixate on me to the point I kept forgetting there were other people in the room?

No. But he did.

I was in a state of disbelief, of unrelenting tension, and something else... something that was making me both want to run and never leave his scrutinizing gaze.

I'm not sure what I expected from this meeting. I know what I hoped for but was certain wasn't going to happen. Men don't notice me, not when my best friend and business partner is around. With her golden hair always neat and sleek, her light brown eyes enhanced by perfect make-up, her professional clothes clinging to every delicate curve. She's full of color, brightness, and confidence, and I'm the one who blends into the background—one with the shadows at times.

This time, though, it wasn't like that. Even when he addressed her, Ronan Hennessey was looking at me. And no matter how much I prepared myself, I still had no idea what to do with myself.

I would feel guilty for not paying full attention to the business deal we were making, but my part in this usually finishes before this type of meeting takes place. It's normal for me to be tucked away in a corner, only intervening if someone asks specifics about the paintings. Hanna, or Erika, as the men we just met know her as, is the brains behind it all. I, Annika, not Ingrid, as I told them, craves the adrenaline of this business, but not the leadership of it. So I keep to myself, observing everything, supporting her. This time around, it was different.

After their organization won the black-market auction we launched for the long-lost Dubois painting—The Lady in White—Hanna began her usual research into the buyers. It was then that the photo of Ronan Hennessey fell in my lap, and I had trouble forming words. My skin was damp in a second, my breathing went wild, and my lower belly was doing strange somersaults. Never in my twenty-three years have I had a reaction like this to a man. Let alone just a photo of one. Unbeknownst to her, I started forming my own plan.

My usual shyness went out the damn window in that meeting. I still can't believe how I talked back to him. Hanna couldn't either. She asked me afterwards what had gotten into me, but I couldn't respond. Not yet.

Before I met him, I had so many questions about the wide-shouldered man with eyes as blue as the clear summer sky. Was he a hard man? Were his good looks deceiving? Like a carnivorous plant, attracting insects with its pretty flowers and sweet nectar? Was he a horrible man? A rapist? A murderer?

Now, after I met him, I've answered none of the above, but have so many more questions.

I know nothing beyond how strong his jaw is, how soft his slicked back dirty-blond hair looks, and how contrasting the kindness of his eyes is to his overall image. That's what trapped me, just like those carnivorous plants—his eyes.

Before the meeting, I started forming a plan, knowing full well I never had to put it in motion. Not until I met him, until I got a sense for him in real life. See if his voice stirred the same feeling in me as his looks did. Find out if his eyes were deceiving or if he really did have some kindness in him. Men who ran entire mafias, who bought black-market paintings worth millions on the dark web, who dealt in God knows what else, rarely were.

After the meeting, my decision was made. The way he spoke of my eyes cemented my plan. That and how he spit back at me about my sharp tongue, sending a shock all through my body, settling deep in my belly, and refusing to let go. I'm constantly squeezing my thighs together, failing to release whatever hold he has on me, and I would curse myself for being so damn weak. I would, but I won't. This is exactly what I want. What I need... What I crave.

I want to fuel this obsession.

Nurture it into a new life.

Because I knew from the way he watched me, like he wanted to devour me whole, that he would be my end and my new beginning.

CHAPTER 2
Annika

"ARE YOU READY?" Hanna asks, smiling at me before she climbs into the back seat of the car.

One of our security guys holds the door open so I can follow.

"I am."

I'm lying.

I know what her question means—are you ready to close the last deal of our career and retire to the dream houses we bought in Falk Isle?

I'm not.

I've lived more in the four years since starting this business than most people live in a lifetime. I've met some of the sweetest people and others who make my skin crawl to this day. I've had more identities than I have surviving family members. I've lived in more cities than I have fingers on both hands. And yet I'm not done.

She clasps my hand and squeezes it reassuringly.

"You're fidgeting. It's going to be fine, Anni. It's no different than all the other jobs."

I pull my hand out of her hold when I feel it getting clammy, wiping it on my dress before I grab onto the collar of it and make some room for air to go through.

"It's hot in here. Why didn't we cool the car before we left? The painting is going to melt."

"It's insulated and protected. It will be fine," she says, squeezing my hand again.

I won't.

Before every meeting, I ask myself, sometimes Hanna too, the same sort of questions. Will they know? Did I make a mistake? Did I miss something? It's funny how the same questions give me anxiety, only I'm looking for different answers now. I'll get them soon enough, if my plan goes well.

I slam back into the seat, catching the gaze of the driver in the rear-view mirror. He averts it quickly, but I don't miss the slight uneasiness.

"Is there something going on with..." I subtly point to him as I whisper to Hanna.

She's smirking. "I think you're a myth to them. They didn't have much proof of your existence until recently."

"What are you talking about?"

"We've had this team for months now, and up until two days ago, none have seen you properly. I think they've seen your shadow around the house, the blur of you as you quickly emerged for snacks before running back to your studio. But nothing more."

"Oh…"

I turn back in my seat and catch a glimpse of both the driver and the passenger trying to steal looks. It dawns on me that I don't even know their names. I'm awful. They'll think I don't care, that I'm some bitch who thinks nothing of them. But that's not the case at all. I just… disappear.

"Don't worry. I've explained to them that when you work, you retreat in your own little world, like a parallel dimension where you can live in the strokes of your paintings. They knew they wouldn't really get to see you, but they had to keep you safe wherever you were hiding. I think they're just getting their fill of your beautiful face while they have you."

I can't help but roll my eyes.

"Sure. Stop talking like I'm some fair maiden living in a tower with princes lining up to catch a glimpse."

"You may as well be."

I scoff, ending that subject then and there. I'm a weird recluse, not some freaking fair maiden.

The period buildings of Queenscove's old center make an appearance outside the car windows, distracting me. They're imposing in their beauty, not their size, the ocean acting as their background on the left side.

We've been here for a little longer than we usually settle in one place. Although we've been fairly hidden, since this last deal has taken so much longer to complete. But I would be lying if I didn't admit that I've stalled slightly too. One day, after I was cooped up in my studio for just over four weeks, frustrations running high, anxiety beginning to cripple me, I needed air. I had to get away from that space, the house. It happens rarely, but this particular job has been different. It's the end of our journey, and there's something about this Laurent Dubois painting that gave me so much trouble.

Maybe it's the meaning of it.

Either way, that night I ran out of my studio, out of the house, and lost myself in Queenscove's streets. Before I knew it, I was here, in the old center, and the ocean at the end of all these streets made me fall in love hard. There's something about this city that speaks to a different side of me than the one who wants to live in a cottage, in a small fishing village.

So, I stalled. Just a little bit.

"We're here." Hanna startles me out of my thoughts.

The car stops and out her window, the private back entrance of the Rosenberg Hotel greets us. It's been one day, twenty-three hours, and thirty-five minutes since I laid eyes on Ronan Hennessey for the first time. In person.

My heartbeats seem to echo in my chest, like the cavity is entirely hollow, this anticipation excruciating. I almost jump when one of the guys opens my car door.

"Here we go." I whisper to myself.

It will be the last deal we strike together... and the first I strike on my own.

Ronan

IT'S JUST LIKE any other business meeting—we meet, we see the asset, we pay, we shake hands, and we leave.

But this is not like any other business meeting at all... is it?

This one is with *her*.

It's been forty-eight fucking hours of those blue-gray eyes haunting every single moment of my day, and every second of my nights. She creeped into my thoughts at the most inconvenient of times, distracting me, keeping me awake, filling my dreams. Last night I could barely sleep because I knew those eyes would be staring at me today. Reinforcing their hold, along with the spell she must have put on me.

Even now, as I sit at this table in one of Rosenberg's private dining rooms, her eyes cloud my mind. Enticing, entirely too fucking mesmerizing.

And suddenly, they're real. Staring right at me.

"Gentlemen. Good evening."

I rise from the chair at the same time as the guys, and inhale so fucking deep, I think my lungs will rip at the seams. I need all the oxygen I can muster to get through being in this small room with her. But a faint wildflower scent fills me, and all that air gets knocked right out of me. *Shit.* My cock twitches—I don't think it got the memo that this is a business meeting. Who can blame it? She looks like a siren, that black dress hugging her perky tits and small waist before falling off her delicate hips, revealing nothing more than her slender arms and perfect legs below the knees.

We all greet them, shaking hands over the table. When I touch *hers*, she pulls away so damn fast, you'd think I burned her. But she's the one who seared my skin.

"Please. Have a seat," Carter says, pointing to the chairs on the other side of the table.

Another deep breath fills my lungs and I steady myself. I need to be present this time around. I can't have a repeat of the first meeting.

Only, my eyes betray me, and when I catch her gaze already on me, it feels stolen. She turns immediately, running over all the faces in the room, and it's not hard to notice that she's forcing her composure. I cock my head just as her eyes land back on mine, grinning just enough that it throws her off her game and her alabaster cheeks flush pink.

Either she's just as affected by me as I am by her, or... it's the meeting making her uneasy. Which is another reason why I need to focus.

"Gentlemen, I hope you understand that Ingrid and I don't want to linger too long, so if you don't mind, we would like to go straight to business." Erika, the prim and polished one my brother wouldn't shut up about yesterday, speaks.

But that's not what I want; I want this meeting to last as long as it takes me to get my fill of Ingrid.

"Just a moment," I say, lifting a finger.

She frowns, but a knock sounds at the door.

"Come in."

The women and their security stiffen, but Finn lets them know the waiter is here. We quickly order our drinks and refuse food, anxious to get to the important part of the evening.

"Apologies. You see that horizontal thin strip of glass about a third way up the common wall with the corridor?" Finn explains. "It was Rosenberg's delicate way of ensuring you can see if someone's coming so you can halt the conversation."

"This place was built with a purpose, I see," Erika says, brightening a shade as she looks at my brother.

I turn to him, and the man is the same. What the fuck is it with these women? We spoke three words, yet somehow, we seem wrapped around their little fingers.

"I suggest we wait until the waiter returns with the drinks before you show us the painting. In the meantime, we wouldn't mind learning more of its provenance, especially since it has been lost for... almost a hundred years now, is it?"

I try to distract them from each other.

"Over." Ingrid speaks just above a whisper, and her voice sends a rush of shivers through my chest.

I'm back in that meadow again.

"*Over* a hundred years," she clarifies more boldly.

I nod and rest my elbows on the table, clutching my hands together, a grin slowly pulling at my lips.

"So how did you come across it after it's been lost for *over* a hundred years?"

"I'm afraid the story is as anticlimactic as we've shared before. It was found hidden in an attic," Erika replies instead.

"Just like that, The Lady in White, the long-lost Dubois, forgotten in an attic." I direct my response to Erika, but my eyes never leave the steel-eyed witch.

"It was my attic. Well, my grandfather's, actually." Ingrid speaks, that revelation making me straighten my back.

But her partner seems to have followed too. Once again, I think the woman is doing something out of character.

Is this an insight into her life? Why did she willingly share it? Is she trying to make the information more believable? Because, to be honest, the fact that it is a piece of her makes it all that more unbelievable since she's sharing it with us, of all people.

"My great-grandfather worked at Venator Castle. He was there in 1931 when the fire broke out, and he was so deeply attached to the painting, that he had to rescue it before the flames took it. According to my grandfather, The Lady in White was the spitting image of my great-grandmother. She was already dead. She died in childbirth and was the absolute love of great-grandpa's life. He refused to take another woman after her, and the only photo he had of her was misplaced. He was left with only The Lady in White. So, the official story was that it was charred in the fire."

Fuck...

She's not lying. I have no idea how I can tell, but she's not. Maybe it's the slight sparkle in her eyes or her flushed cheeks, but the woman before me has just bared a part of herself.

For what purpose?

I look at the guys and they all match my stare, even the stern Vin and the emotionless Carter—her story is true.

The waiter knocks before entering with our drinks, holding us all in a strangely uncomfortable silence, more questions lingering in the air. I'm not sure what it was about that story, but it held emotions, and this transaction has suddenly become more personal.

Or more dangerous.

"Please," I say, gesturing to the painting as soon as the waiter closes the door behind him.

Erika rises and gently unwraps it, the tension sizzling in the windowless room, and as soon as the last of the covering comes off, I suck in a breath.

It's her.

Spitting goddamn image of the woman sitting across from me. Sure, her lips are thinner, her nose just a bit larger, her hair more on the blond side than Ingrid's, but... the resemblance is there.

Am I imagining it? I turn to my right and catch Vin's eyes going between Ingrid and the woman in the painting at rapid speed. No, I'm not imagining it.

Carter rises at the same time as Anthony and Jonathan, the appraisers we brought with us, and they circle the piece of art like hawks.

Technically, Jonathan is far from an appraiser, but the man was born, raised, and bred in galleries, auctions, and museums. It's his love for art that made him dive into the stealing and selling of it too. Even though now he's moved up and he runs a criminal organization which facilitates smuggling and other endeavors. But art is how he met his partner in both crime and life, Anthony. He's the appraiser. That was his job when they met. He investigated the authenticity of paintings and sculptures. From what we've heard from Carter, who put us in contact with Jonathan—his father's best friend—Anthony almost called the police on him when he realized he was authenticating a stolen painting. They've been together ever since. Quite romantic, really.

In our underworld, not many stories have happy beginnings. Or ends, for that matter.

"Fascinating," Anthony mutters to himself.

They pull out a series of rare old photographs which were digitized and blown up, to attempt to compare the two. They are the same age as Ingrid's great-grandfather, so they work more as general guidelines, unfortunately. But even in that poor quality, you can see the tinge of a resemblance with the woman before us.

The final confirmation of authenticity will be in the chemical analysis. And it better check out, because the only way we can order that whole lot of tests, is by buying the piece.

We're hoping Anthony and Jonathan's eyes can spot any inconsistencies, if there are any.

"And you mentioned some restoration has happened?"

"Yes. Unfortunately, there was some smoke damage, so it has been cleaned, and some small areas restored," Ingrid replies to Anthony.

He nods, returning to his inspection while Jonathan steps back, looking intently at the work of art, his gaze flashing to Ingrid every few minutes.

This lasts for the better part of an hour. The two men even step out twice to discuss in private, and when they return for the second time, even though Jonathan seems more reserved, they declare their satisfaction. Much to the pleasure of my partners, Madds doing a very bad job at hiding his restlessness.

I can't blame him, especially since the conversation was strained. Finn couldn't take his eyes off Erika, and Ingrid and I appeared to be looking anywhere but at each other. It didn't ease the tension, though, constantly being drawn to the woman before me.

"Well, gentlemen, it was a pleasure doing business with you." Erika firmly shakes our hands after the money transfer is confirmed, lingering a moment longer on Finn. Ingrid, steps back, nodding her goodbye. She's either eager to leave this room or is avoiding touching us. Or me.

At this point, I'm eager to get the fuck out of here too, my body so tightly wound, my back damp from the strangeness of this interaction. I haven't touched a cigarette since I was in school, but I'll be damned if I wouldn't smoke a whole pack of them right now.

Nah, I need to hit the gym. Maybe jump into the ring with Madds. Either way, I need to blow off some steam as soon as possible. Beat the image of Ingrid out of my damn mind and erase her brief touch from my body.

It's not like I'm ever going to see her again anyway.

Then why is that thought making me even more antsy?

CHAPTER 3
Ronan

"SO DID IT check out?"

My brother enters the office of our latest business venture. A legal one this time—Midnight, our speakeasy. Carter and I were looking through some new membership applications who have gone through our vetting, since the clientèle has to be very carefully chosen. It was his idea to open something like this. A place inspired by the roaring twenties, private, comfortable, an interesting space for all sorts of people to meet, whether for business or pleasure.

It's also the safest place for the painting until we wash our hands of it and make a small fortune too.

"It did," I say, my brows furrowing. "Why exactly do you look disappointed?"

"What? No, I'm glad. I'm happy... so happy," he trails off.

"For fuck's sake, man. Don't tell me; you wanted to see Erika again."

His eyes widen for a moment—I fucking caught the bastard.

"You know you could just ask her out, right? You don't need an excuse like a fake painting to see her again."

"Nah, man, you're so off. I'm not interested."

If only I hadn't known him since he was born. I roll my eyes and turn to one of the documents Carter pushes my way.

"So, it's all good, we can move forward with this deal?" he continues.

"Yeah, we can. There was a little bit of doubt with one of the colors, apparently. Back in those days, they used plants and natural sources or substances to obtain them. One of the shades of blue posed some uncertainty, but not enough to warrant it being fake. The margin of error is way beyond that," Carter explains.

"Right, right..." Finn drifts off again before he finally walks out, a bit deflated.

He's going to drive me mad until he meets this woman again. I've never seen him like this. It's been over a week, and every time we're outside, or in a bar, or restaurant, or goddamn anywhere, for that matter, he's on edge. Constantly looking around, just in case he sees her again.

But... fuck, I've been looking right along with him.

Maybe because of the masked sinfulness in Ingrid's gaze, or the softness of her. Of the way she looks, like she belongs in those times when this painting was done, draped in fine silks, with a crown of flowers on her head.

"Do you guys need me tonight?"

Madds all but bursts through the office door.

"Christ, man, one of these days we'll fucking shoot you by accident if you keep barging in like you're about to kill us all."

He scrunches his eyebrows like he has no clue what I'm referring to.

"So, do you?" he asks again.

"I don't think so. Why? What the hell did you do?" I walk around the desk and take a better look at him—red cheek, faint bruise under his left eye, his knuckles banged up.

The man simply shrugs.

"Just blew off some steam."

"I hope you kept it under wraps."

I'm getting a headache.

"Umm... yeah. Sure."

He straightens, and I can't help but laugh. Our friendly giant isn't even trying to hide the fact that he's lying.

"It was for a good cause. I was helping a lady in need," he explains.

"You know... ladies?"

"I know one for sure."

I want to ask more, so much more, but his grip on the door handle and frame threatens to break them both if he doesn't leave.

"I swear, we might as well build a damn bare-knuckle boxing establishment in our basement. At least you can make some money out of all this pent-up energy of yours."

He cocks his head, scrunching his eyebrows like he's genuinely considering the idea.

"I mean..." I hear Carter behind me, and I turn my head to him as he crosses his arms. "It could certainly be interesting. We've been trying to find a better solution for the money laundering side of things."

I can see the wheels turning in his head, but Madds pulls me back to him.

"Sounds good to me. I'm gonna go now. Call me if you need me."

Where the fuck is he running to?

"Just... take it easy," I tell him, knowing full well that is not what he's going to do.

I want to touch the painting and feel Ingrid's skin against mine. That one searing touch when we shook hands was nowhere near enough. Never in my fucking life have I been so wrapped up in a woman. Yet so reluctant to seek her.

What am I afraid of?

"She's perfect, isn't she?" Carter asks, appearing next to me.

"She is..."

"She would look quite perfect out in the bar if we didn't have to sell her."

Sell her?!

Fucking hell, he's talking about the painting... of course. I rub my temples and sit in the leather chair behind the desk, clearly needing some space from the image of *her*.

She is spellbinding, and the sooner I get rid of that steely gaze following me around this room, the sooner I can go back to business as usual.

Wait... I quickly go back to the canvas, leaning over to take a closer look at her eyes. The painting itself is only about twenty inches in height and fifteen in width, but it's not a close-up portrait. It's the full image of her sitting in a chair. So even though the details are quite clear, like her facial features, the texture of the various fabrics and surfaces, the scale of the woman itself is quite small.

A tiny detail like her eyes could be missed, especially when there aren't many records of it.

I might be mistaken. I may be remembering this wrong... but if I'm right, we're fucked. Erika and Ingrid even more so.

"Carter, I seem to remember there is an old tale about Venator. It briefly mentions Lady Bournwell. Can you please do some research, find it, and call me as soon as you do," I tell him as I quickly walk around the desk, grabbing my phone and shooting a quick text before I grab my car keys too.

"Will do. What are you seeing, Ronan?"

"I'm not sure, but if I'm right..."

"Yeah, I'm still here. Why?" Finn startles us when he slams through the door, in response to my text.

"I think you might get your wish and see your darling Erika once more. But I'm not sure either of you will enjoy this meeting."

I can't pinpoint the look in his eyes—confusion, excitement, anger? Either way, I have a hunch that it matches mine.

"Ronan," Carter warns. "What are you seeing?"

I turn to The Lady in White aka Lady Bournwell, making sure once again that my eyes aren't playing tricks on me. They're not.

"The color of her eyes..."

Annika

MY DAMP SKIN burns under his palm as he drags his hand down over my breast, without pausing to give it the attention it needs. Only a gentle squeeze, not enough before he moves down my middle, pushing his front against my back, steadying me with his firm touch on my lower belly. My body melts against him when he reaches my wet pussy, sliding a finger between my folds, spreading that wetness over my clit. Knees threatening to buckle, I don't have time to steady myself before I'm bent over the table in front of me and he's down on his knees behind me. I grab onto the edge of the wood, just as he spreads my legs and grabs my ass cheeks, opening me up to him. I'm shaking for different reasons now. When he blows against my center, my whole body shudders and the dirty sound that escapes my parted lips makes him growl. I know it's coming, his tongue is so close to my clit, I can almost feel it, and...

"Anni..."

"Ronan..." I moan.

"Anni!"

Huh?

"Babe, wake up. We have to go soon."

My eyes snap open, and I look around me like the house is on fire. But it's only Hanna here, watching me with a strangely suggestive look. Heat grows in my cheeks, but I turn and quickly jump out of bed, heading toward the bathroom.

"So... did you sleep well?"

"Yes, fine," I mumble before shutting the bathroom door behind me.

"Just fine. Interesting." I hear her muffled chuckling.

Fuck's sake.

Was I moaning in my sleep? Oh God, this is mortifying.

Bracing myself against the sink, I'm met with the most serene face in the mirror. I'm not sure who that woman is, but she doesn't quite look like me. The gray-blue eyes resemble a gemstone instead of the usual muted steel. She's... glowing.

"It must be the humidity." I roll my eyes at myself and turn the faucet on cold, before splashing enough water on my face to erase the lingering touches from that dream.

By the time I'm done, I know it's not enough. It's changed nothing, because every time I close my eyes, I can see his hand on my breast, sliding down my body, even the shock of the moment I'm slammed against the wood, bent over the table.

"Shower. I just need a shower. A cold one."

I quickly turn it on, undressing as fast as I can, and jump straight in. Instant goosebumps rush over me, the water becomes like ice against my hot skin and, unfortunately those chills have the opposite effect on my pussy. It constricts so tightly around nothing but the memory of those fingers sliding between my folds, frustrated that I woke up before it got further.

"Focus, Annika. Focus!"

But how can I when this fantasy is fueled by adrenaline of my own creation?

Is he going to find me? Find us?

I need to get away from Hanna. She shouldn't be involved in any of this. She's going to kill me when she finds out what I've done. She's going to ask me why and I have no concise answer.

* * *

Leaning against the open front door, I watch as the last of our belongings are loaded into the moving truck. My paintings are there, most of my supplies, some of Hanna's favorite pieces of furniture, irreplaceable antiques, most sourced through questionable means. Only a select few are there, and they're all going into storage for now, before they'll be loaded in a container and shipped home.

Home.

What a strange word... after all these years of being nomads, of being different people, we will finally have everything we worked for.

Then why do I feel so utterly incomplete?

The doors to the truck close with a loud, metallic bang, then the movers walk over to Hanna, and I watch them have a brief discussion. One of them looks besotted as he listens to her speak, the other glances my way, nodding once. That's it. No one ever lingers, no one ever watches me with that yearning look, with hunger.

Except...

No. Not now. You need to focus!

But then again, there is a reason why I'm going off plan, and he has far too much to do with it all.

"It's strange, isn't it?"

Hanna startles me. When did she finish talking with the movers? When did she walk next to me? I swear, I'm losing it.

"What is?"

The two guys wave at us before they climb into their truck. I wave back, then turn my attention to her.

"This... it's over. Everything in the house is gone. The charity called to say thank you, by the way. The rest of our prized possessions are on their way to our forever homes. I don't know, this whole adventure we've been on for the last few years is finally done and somehow it feels..."

"Bittersweet." I fill the pause.

She nods, her gaze on the truck disappearing behind the hedgerow at the edge of the property.

"Most people could only dream of retiring before they hit thirty... or forty, or fifty, for that matter. And we now have that," she says, turning to me with a sheepish smile on her red lips. "The adventure is over."

"And you're okay with that. Right?" I question, lightly narrowing my eyes.

She nods again, pausing a bit longer than necessary.

"Hanna, are you alright?"

"I am, yes, sorry. It's just strange. All these business deals, the risks, the rush... I'm so used to them. Don't get me wrong, I'm looking forward to the cocktails on the beach, the nights swimming in the ocean or my pool, the books, all the projects I have planned. I was even thinking of opening a charity of my own, doing something more with all this money. But it will just be a bit of an adjustment, I guess."

Only, I'm not ready to adjust. She seems to be. Which is why what I'm about to tell her might fuck with all that peace.

I sigh and take a seat on the first step.

"I'm looking forward to all of that too, but... not just yet."

She climbs down the few stairs until she stands in front of me, her eyes wide, expectant.

"What do you mean, Annika?"

Shit, she only ever calls me by my full first name when she's serious. I rub my hands over my face, thankful to be make-up free right now.

"I... shit, I don't know how to tell you this."

"You better try. Fast."

"Before I say anything, I just want you to know that I did this for me and me alone. I don't want this to mess with you, your dream, the peace and quiet in your new life. I would actually prefer you to be as far away as possible, because I need you safe. I'm only telling you this because you deserve to know."

"Anni, you're freaking me out. What the hell is going on?!" she snaps, crossing her arms and tightening them around herself.

"I'm not ready to be done."

I let that sink in. I could have sworn I saw a glimmer of understanding in her eyes.

"I'm not talking about the business. I'm done with the deals, forging, etc. That chapter is very much closed. But... it's the thrill I'm not done with. I guess... shit, I don't know. I don't know why, I can't explain it. I'm fooling myself by justifying it with the fact that I was cooped up in the studio for a lot of this time and I somehow didn't get my fill. But I'm only using that excuse because I can't explain it otherwise."

She narrows her eyes, clearly trying hard to be patient with me.

"I made a mistake, Hanna. An intentional one. The painting we sold to R... The Lady in White—I gave her my eyes."

"You did what?!" she shouts, hands going to her hips as her mouth falls open.

"Slightly. It's not obvious. It's not at all common knowledge what color her eyes were, and due to the size of the painting and the size of her head, it's not easy to tell, unless the person who looks at it knows..."

"The color of yours. Oh my God! You did it for..."

"Myself, Hanna!" I interrupt, my tone growing higher. "I did it for myself. I'm ready to give them the money back. I put it aside specifically for this, but I need... fuck! It's hard to explain, okay? I can't even fully explain it to myself."

"Don't lie to me. This is about Ronan."

"The craving was there before he showed up in the picture. But I don't think I would have acted on it and set the plan in motion if it wasn't for Ronan," I admit.

"Annika, what the fuck!? They're gonna fucking kill you! What were you thinking?! You want the thrill of the chase?! Where? To your death?! Because this is where it's headed! Jesus Christ, they're a goddamn crime syndicate, for God's sakes! What are you gonna do when he finds out?! Seriously, what are you going to do? Run, let him chase you for bit, let him catch you? Then tell him it's okay, you'll give them the money back, and expect him to be like... *yeah, sure Annika, you fucked us over, but now all is well, and we'll fuck and live happily ever after.* Goddamn it!" She whips around, stomping away toward the corner of the house.

I get up to go after her, but she spins around, pointing at me.

"No! You better not follow me."

Shit.

I stop, frozen in place like a puppy who just got scolded, because I know this mood, that look from her eyes—I need to let her go process.

* * *

Forty-something minutes have passed and I'm navigating nervously through my phone, scrolling aimlessly from clip to clip on the addictive app I'd discovered a few months ago. Numerous funny dog videos later, and people lip-syncing, and I can't take it anymore. The tension is too much. Even the cool AC of the car is not doing anything to soothe me.

When I look around, I finally see Hanna coming from the house, somehow more relaxed. I climb out of the SUV and walk over to meet her.

"I want in."

I stop dead in my tracks, taken aback by the confidence of the words she just spoke before she even reached me.

"No. This has nothing to do with you, and I don't need you to babysit me. You're not responsible for me." I'm quite aggravated by this sudden change.

"I'm not gonna lie and tell you that there isn't a part of me that wants in because I'm scared something will happen to you. You're my best friend; I will not say you're like my sister, because if I ever had one, I probably would have hated her, but you're my family, and I cannot fuck off to my dream island home and sit there, worrying about you. But... I get it, Anni. One last adventure, and what better people to choose to chase you, than the Hennessey's."

I can't process her words. I refuse to. I shake my head until she stops talking, because this is not how this is supposed to go.

"This is my plan, my idea, my infatuation, the risk *I* am taking. I cannot drag you into this. God forbid anything happens, it will be on me, my fault. I can't let you join me."

"It may have been your idea, but you're not forcing me to join."

"But if it wasn't for me, this insane scenario wouldn't have even existed. You wouldn't have had any danger to put yourself in. Shit... I should have just told you I'm going on holiday alone," I grumble, running my hands through my hair as I begin pacing around the brick driveway.

"Oh yeah, because lying to me is a much better idea. I get it, Anni, I do, but I'm a consenting adult. I can choose for myself if I wish to put myself in danger or not, and if I didn't want to do this. If I thought it was truly a horrid idea, then not only would I not choose to join you, but I would convince you not to do it either."

Taking a breath, I pause and weigh her words. She cocks her head, crossing her arms, knowing full well I'm just about to come to the same conclusion as her; if she wanted to convince me not to go through with this plan, I would be in the car on our way to Falk Isle right now. She could sell ice to an Eskimo, as cliche as it sounds. She's the best salesperson I know, and convincing me to drop this plan would be child's play.

Damn it.

"I need it too, honey." She comes to me and gently grabs my shoulders before pulling me into a warm hug.

When she releases me, everything about her has softened, but her eyes sparkle in that same way they do before we're about to strike a new deal and meet our next clients.

"I've been preparing myself for this for a while, psyching myself up, planning. You've been thinking about it for half an hour," I tell her in a gentle tone.

"The adventures we've had in the last few years have come with a different kind of pressure. It was thrilling, no denying that, but this is... unlike it. It's personal.

Exhilarating in a whole new way I cannot possibly pass on."

I know what she means. There's a heat growing inside my chest the closer I'm getting to the moment it will truly happen. I want to scream at the top of my lungs, scream with joy in anticipation of the little chase I planned and the unknown it will bring.

"Okay, but, Hanna, I'm not messing around with your safety. You have to be really, really sure. It could go terribly wrong."

"It could. But so could everything else. Everything about this life could go terribly wrong at every single moment and turn. And just like you... I need this. I feel like I'm not done."

"If you're sure..."

She might be able to convince me to go her way, but there's no way I'm changing her mind when she's set on something. And who am I to tell her it's wrong when she's doing it for the same sort of reasons I am.

"I'm sure. Now, walk me through the plan."

CHAPTER 4
Ronan

WE BURST INTO their house like we thought they'd actually still be in here. Rushing through its empty corridors like we didn't already know it would be devoid of furniture, no speckle of dust, no life. I bet my left arm that if we check every inch of this villa, even the fingerprints will be wiped clean. They're gone. Fled to yet another city, dumped yet another identity. We knew it was unlikely that Ingrid Thorp and Erika Brand were their real names, but Carter confirmed it today. No trace of their real ones yet, though.

But the villa they called home during their stay in Queenscove is not entirely empty. Even in my wildest dreams, I couldn't have fathomed finding *this*.

She's right here, steel eyes sparkling through the brush strokes painted on this canvas, innocence staring back at me as Vin re-reads the handwritten text we found on the back of it.

By the old cottage, deep into the woods,
Where the water runs warm from the hills above,
One night a year they all gather,
Filling the forest with their songs and laughter.

I'm joining them just this once,
Hiding amongst their sways and their songs.
I will give back all that you seek,
I only wish to know if your cravings run just as deep.

A taunt. That's exactly what this is—a taunt, sitting neatly on a wooden pedestal in the middle of this large room.

It took my fucking breath away when we opened the double doors and found it.

There is no Lady in White here, though. This is Ingrid. Her nose, her defined jawline, her high cheeks, perfectly supple lips. But it's her eyes that draw you in, because beyond all that innocence, something new looks back at you from the canvas's surface—need. A challenge.

I can't make sense of this. She's painted in the same style, in clothes from the same era, she's just closer in the frame. Close enough to see every beauty mark, the faint freckles that dust her nose, yet these brush strokes look like they were painted centuries ago.

It might as well have been done by Dubois himself.

How the...

"Fuck...?" I trail off as the puzzle pieces don't fall, but crash into place. One by one, they shake my very core, and I don't know if I should be angry or impressed.

"What?" Vin questions, raising an eyebrow.

"This, it's a self-portrait. They're not just selling forged paintings."

I look to Finn, who's now standing beside me, and I can see the exact moment realization strikes. They're making them. *She* is making them. I just fucking know it!

She paints.

I knew she was fucking special, but this is way beyond anything I imagined. And the surprises seem to keep coming. I can't wait to tell Anthony that the painting he appraised and concluded it's the real deal, not only is fake, but it was painted by the woman who stood right before him the whole time he was analyzing it.

What now, though? My partners expect me to shove this information away and focus on business, on... payback. How can I when my need for this woman has just reached different heights? I have to know so much more about her. Discover her. Her name. Find out what else she can do with her delicate, talented hands and her beautiful brain.

I can't take my eyes off of her. I'm drawn in like a moth to a flame, and even though I know I'm going to burn, I can't choose to stop flying. This is how I know she's a witch. Otherwise, I can't explain why I have it in my mind that if I touch her painted cheek, I will feel the softness of her skin under my fingertips instead of the surface of the canvas. I'm almost certain that if I get close enough, I'll even smell her perfume.

Her natural one, seeped in wildflowers and rain.

There's no denying this—I'm fucked. Slowly and painfully, I'm being ripped apart, split in two; one side has to fulfill a duty, treat them... her, like any other person we've done business with. The other side, though, it needs to chase her, take this challenge, and find out just where she'll lead me. It's aimed at me, there's no denying that.

She quite literally propped herself on a pedestal for me.

"I'm slightly confused. They're mocking us, but why like this? Why a portrait of herself? I don't get it," Vin says, crossing his arms over his chest.

"I think I do. If I'm right, it has nothing to do with *us*," I say, raising my gaze for a moment, enough to see him cocking his head and an eyebrow.

I thought it was a mistake at first, those blue-gray eyes replacing The Lady in White. It was all deliberate. Perfectly planned. If not for me, then for whom?

There's a tint of jealousy springing up inside of me. It's fueled by the knowledge that there's no way she painted this self-portrait so quickly... since the moment we met until now. No way.

Maybe, maybe it wasn't for me after all.

When I realized the painting they sold to us was forged, it wasn't the prospect of getting back what we are owed that thrilled me. No. It was seeing her again. An excuse for more time. I know I'm supposed to get some sort of revenge for her deceit, but the only punishment I can think of executing will make her beg for more.

Somewhere not that deep inside, I have already decided—*she's mine*. At least until this chase is over.

"Wait. Can you read that again?" Finn asks.

"*By the old cottage, deep into the woods, where the water runs warm from the hills above, one night a year they…*"

"I know what it means! Fuck, we all do!"

Vin looks at him like he's lost the plot.

"Midsummer night!" I continue, the ball dropping.

"The Falls!" he hollers.

The younger residents of Queenscove have a party once a year in the woods, next to a natural pool fed by a waterfall. It's a keg party, but amongst the ancient trees that surround the clearing, dancing under the fairy-lights they drape in their branches, it feels different. I haven't been in a few years.

"When is it?" I ask, sounding much too eager.

"Tomorrow," Vin replies.

When I look at him, I'm met with a grave expression.

"We'll get the money back." I straighten myself, wiping whatever trace of enthusiasm off my face.

"If they were men, would we spare them with just a *refund*? What about the damage to the reputation we're so carefully trying to curate for our organization?"

I fucking hate when Vin is right, but goddamn it, this is not about him. I'm frustrated, confused, fucking excited. Not pursuing this causes a sensation of dread to seep inside of me and I can't allow it. But I'm not against Vin or the others. The little witch dared to cross us, fool us, steal from us.

Right now, I both want to make her pay for her deceit, and punish her for her wickedness.

Which one will I enjoy more?

Annika

I'M ON MY third beer, and even though I know I should stop, keep a level head, I can't help myself. I'm guided by the sound of the waterfall blending in with the music, by the smell of the trees, of the warm water where some people swim, the twinkling lights draped in the trees. I haven't danced like this in so long. To be fair, I've *never* danced like this, pirouetting around the trees, while others use them as their little corners, to laugh, talk, get more… intimate.

Mixed with the anxious anticipation, the atmosphere is electric.

Hanna's a few yards away from me, lost in dance like I've never seen her lost before.

She looks relaxed, so welcomed, considering how she's always had to be the serious one. Always level-headed, since she's the reason why the business worked flawlessly all these years. We've had breaks between jobs, but her part never truly stopped. She had to be on the ball and constantly aware of what was going on before and after a business deal. Seeing her like this, carefree, is quite a wonderful sight.

Smiling, I move with the music, turning my back on her as I take another swig of my drink. But I almost choke on it when prickles rush down my back. I whip around to the sight of none other than Finnigan Hennessey startling Hanna as he wraps his arms around her and pulls her back to his front.

They got our message.

A smile creeps on her lips, but it falls before it settles, her eyes widening instead as she looks past me.

This is it. This is the moment.

The prickles have found their way back up my spine, converging on the nape of my neck, wrapping around my throat like ribbons. They tighten, seeping down my chest, over my breasts... down over my abdomen. Right where an arm suddenly circles me, holding me in place as another comes around my arm and chest.

It's... different.

Hanna attempts to step my way, eyes wide with concern, but Finnigan keeps her in place.

I swallow an invisible lump lodged in my throat and reluctantly look up behind me. The eyes that stare down into mine freeze me in place—Carter Pierce, one of Ronan's partners.

But the prickles that mark my skin aren't for him. They're still here... like the predator still lurks.

Carter turns me around, sliding his hand on my lower back, the other gripping my free hand.

"Don't spill, please." He signals to the cup I'm holding.

His politeness is sincere, but chilling.

He leads me into a slow dance around the trees, taking control with such security. Not once have we caught our feet on a branch or a root, yet his eyes have never left mine.

"You got the message," I dare say, but speaking to him gives me the impression that I should ask for permission first.

"*We* did, yes. It wasn't meant for all of us, though."

His palm on my lower back presses just a bit harder, but he doesn't pull me closer. He keeps this interaction strangely appropriate.

"Did you all come?" I finally ask in a shaky voice.

He nods. "I found you first."

There it is, a grin pulling at his lips and, my God, I want to scream and run. I'm suddenly a fucking rabbit circled by a wolf pack foaming at the mouth, only it's just one of them. Only Carter.

"Please, I..."

"Don't beg. Just dance."

I don't even want to protest. I can't explain it. His will is somehow my command

and self-preservation tells me I have to follow.

Hanna's back in my line of sight as Carter spins us around gently. That expression still haunts her features and Finnigan notices. He pulls her, slightly forcefully, into a dance, but once he leans over, whispering something into her ear, she calms, giving me a reassuring smile that makes me slightly confused. But it works, it calms me too.

Until I look back up into Carter's cold gaze.

"Will you hurt me?"

It's then that I see through a small crack, beyond this shell.

"Only if you ask nicely."

I accidentally step on him, caught off guard by the answer that makes me blush instantly, and I know he's being sincere again. Too sincere, my mind jumping to all sorts of ideas. But he doesn't dwell.

"I looked into you. So many identities, so many successful jobs, no hiccups. All these risks and never any issues, as far as I found. Why this, why now?"

"What do you mean?"

His only response to that is a *don't insult me* kind of expression.

"I saw the way you looked at him." He pauses, his gaze flickering somewhere behind me. I try to follow it, but he continues. "The way he looked at you too, *Annika Backstrom*."

He knows my name.

"So, you found out our real identities."

"I did."

"Well, I guess the cat's out of the bag, then."

"No, not really. I only peeked into it. Nothing's out yet."

Wait.

"So, you're telling me that Ronan doesn't...?" I'm shell-shocked.

"No, he doesn't. I didn't want to take that pleasure away from you."

"Oh..." How interesting.

He grabs the cup from my hand and sets it on a small table, then pulls me into him, guiding me into a dance that's definitely more intimate than I'm comfortable.

"You're playing a game." He delicately grips my hand, spinning me, before he pulls me back into his body. "I like games." He spins me once more, but this time he stops me with my back to his front, his hand on my middle as he sways us slowly. "Let's hope he likes them too."

It's then that I see him, maybe seven or eight feet away, leaning against a tree, his arms crossed, his expression dangerously close to anger. That one single look makes me question this whole plan, my infatuation with him. The worst thing is that it fuels it too.

Carter brushes the hair off one of my shoulders, exposing my neck, and leans in to whisper in my ear. At that same time, Ronan pushes away from the tree, his gaze murderous, explosive. It's impossible, but I swear that his heavy steps are sending vibrations into the ground, right into my chest, gripping my lungs and squeezing all the air out of them.

"I'm only here to prove a point. He's all yours now," Carter whispers. Then he's gone.

But Ronan's pace never slows, and I take quick steps backwards as he closes in. My back hits the harsh bark of a tree at the same time the man himself reaches me, caging me in as his hands slam on either side of my head.

The strained rise and fall of his chest sends a hot breeze coasting against my own. No part of him is touching me, yet every bit of my skin responds all the same.

"The moment I first laid eyes on you, I knew you were a witch. But I didn't quite know the magnitude of it. You're the one who's been putting spells on all these people... for so many years. Bewitching us with your brush strokes that cover all sorts of lies."

I've heard that warm voice in my dreams every night for almost two weeks now. Sometimes I hear it when I'm awake too. It reaches a dangerous level in its haunting, and it's breaching a boundary too close to obsession.

"The spell wore off now, little witch, and all that's left is you, me, and The Lady... with steely eyes. Or should I say, ladies."

That boundary is turning to smoke with each word he speaks in that menacing voice, with its slight gravel laced with fury. It fuels my self-destructive need that has gained a new life in the last few weeks. It craved a challenge, and the challenge is right here in front of me, stealing my air and giving me pure fire in return.

"It warms me, knowing that you remembered the color of my eyes... and recognized it. How delightful, Mr. Hennessey." I say with a smirk, yet I'm surprised at my boldness.

"That sharp tongue of yours begs for punishment yet again."

I stop breathing at that moment. Blinking too. But I manage to keep my back straight, my gaze on his as I retort.

"Maybe yours deserves a taste of it too."

I don't miss how his eyes flicker to my lips. How his breathing is so much heavier. How he's so much closer now. Is he aware?

"Carter's working on finding all there is to know about yours and your partner's business. Learning all about the different names, cities, all those lost paintings suddenly uncovered, and a hell of a lot of money you made."

He's talking slow, emphasizing his words in a way that makes me wonder what else he can do with that slithering tongue. I can barely focus on what he's actually saying.

"And they all have one rather important thing in common—not one of them was discovered as a fake. Not a single person was able to identify any inconsistencies, not even in the chemical analysis. You've never. Ever. Made a mistake, little witch."

"Surprised?" I ask, cocking an eyebrow as I straighten my posture, pushing away from the tree, just about touching him.

He doesn't play, though. One hand goes straight to my chest, pressed right at the base of my throat as he shoves me back against the rough bark, taking my breath away with a slight ache.

"I am. Because we both know this was no mistake. Why?"

Jesus Christ.

His searing touch spreads fire over every inch of my skin, settling deep between my legs, forcing them to press together for some sort of relief.

"I'll answer. If you do something for me."

"More than let you live for deceiving us? Stealing from us?"

I smile, and I don't know why, but his hard gaze falters for a moment.

"Smaller scale than that."

He watches me for a few moments, his gaze caressing my jaw, my cheeks, studying every bit of my face as his hand moves up around my throat. He doesn't squeeze, though, just holds it there in this possessive grip, my pulse bouncing off his skin.

I take the silence as my cue to go on.

"Dance with me, Ronan Hennessey."

CHAPTER 5

Ronan

DANCE?

Her small hands reach for my waist, her touch startling me even over this t-shirt, and they move up until they wrap around the sides of my neck.

She holds me there and, for some reason, I let her. I'm afraid to move. I can't explain it. It's like I've just met a bear on a walk and I have to stay completely still so I don't get eaten alive. And at the same time, I know that if I take just one step, if I let go of her throat and grip her waist instead, my reality will change. I will no longer be skirting on the edge between business and pleasure... the line will be gone completely, and the purpose will change.

Was it ever about business?

My life will change too.

I keep that hold on her throat, squeezing slightly, enjoying how her lips part, feeling her life pulsate against my palm. I think that maybe if I squeeze just a little harder, she'll give up.

Only the little witch slides those hands until she grips my short hair between her long fingers, pulling just enough that an image flashes through my mind. Not a memory—*a fantasy*. Her soft skin beneath me, damp with sweat as I drive my cock into her, her legs around my waist, those fingers tight in my hair, holding on. It's a goddamn beautiful image and I want to turn it from fantasy to premonition.

My dick seems to want the same thing as it grows stiffer than it should at a public party. Even here, in the shadows of these trees.

Moving my grip to the nape of her neck, I pull her to me with one hand on the middle of her back.

She's got me so deep under her spell, breaking my reality and replacing it with illusions I crave to materialize.

"One dance," I say as I look down at her. She's so fucking close, I struggle to keep my half-hard cock away from her.

Only, she shakes her head slowly.

"Two dances," I try again.

The softest of smiles pulls at her lips before she shakes her head again. I spin her around in a pirouette, watching that smile turn from shock into gentle laughter, her hair a flowing veil as it whips around her face. If her voice sounds like birdsong, her laughter is a whole flock making up their own melody.

"Three is my limit, little witch. Besides, I'm not here to dance. I'm here to get what we are owed. Including your punishment."

Her cheeks flush the brightest red, her lips part in shock, and her eyes... they're showing her wickedness in such bright shades. Clearly, we're not thinking of the same type of punishment, but when she pulls a bit of her bottom lip between her teeth, I forget what punishment I had in mind.

I'm trying to change the mood, to stop from losing myself into the night with her. What the hell does she want from me? Why did she bring me here?

She circles one arm around my neck and pulls herself up until her lips hover too close to my ear.

"I can fix The Lady's eyes and you can still sell it as the original. No one will ever know."

I shake my head as she comes back to face me. Closer than she was before.

"We're not in the business of selling fakes."

"Only contraband and stolen antiquities, then?" she taunts, cocking her head, but the smile never leaves her lips.

"Is that what you think we do?"

"Amongst other things. Is my painting not good enough for you? You'll make millions on it. So many more than the ones you gave us."

I narrow my eyes and grip her hand, pushing her into another pirouette, before I slam her body in mine, taking her breath away and enjoying it.

"There's no guarantee that whoever buys it won't find out. Besides, I would rather have the money back, for the inconvenience. For the deceit. For dragging us here in your little game."

I lean in closer and closer as I say those words, almost brushing her lips before I move to her ear.

I'm so tempted to get a taste... just a small one.

But as the song ends, I completely let go of her and take a step back, putting much needed distance between us.

She looks momentarily lost at the move, and I can't ignore how that innocence seems to settle back on her features, in her body language. I think the alcohol is fueling her courage, and she might need more to hold on to this audacious façade. She's so fucking delicate, I want to scoop her up in my arms and wrap her in silks and soft furs, keep her on a pedestal and feed her grapes.

God-fucking-damnit!

I need to step away. I'll tell Carter to take over and get our money back, but knowing the bastard, he'll probably tie her to a chair and torture her until she returns it with interest.

I whip around and walk away.

Two... four... six steps...

I try not to look back to check if she's still there, watching me, or maybe following. But I fail... and what I see when I turn, stops me dead in my tracks. She's walking around the left-hand side of the large, natural pool, casually stripping her top off.

"What the actual fuck?"

All these people, all these fucking men around, and she's taking her top off! I can already see a couple of guys sizing her up as she bends over to slide her shorts down her legs and pull off her Converse.

Only when I've crossed half the distance do I realize I've started heading her way.

I'm not sure what annoys me more, the fact that she's so careless in front of other men when she's all alone, or the fact that all those assholes are fucking drooling over her sweet little body in that skimpy swimsuit. In her retro-style bikini she's covered more than others, but I don't give a fuck.

She doesn't even look my way. The damn woman already knew I was going to return. That in itself gets me even more annoyed, but this time at myself.

How can I not be predictable when she just added fuel to the fire of the already enticing game she's playing. She looks devastatingly breathtaking as she walks up a high boulder, the waterfall acting like her background in this cinematic image.

She dives in just as I get there, barely making a splash before she emerges a few yards away. And I'm just standing here, like an idiot, unable to peel my eyes away.

Fuck!

Her gaze falls on me as she smooths her wet hair back, and I'm trying very hard to find reasons not to jump in with her. Vin will fucking kill me. We're here for a reason—business, or better yet, payback. They crossed us, and they have to suffer the consequence.

But they're women, Ronan... we don't fucking hurt women.

No, that we don't. Plus, in that little riddle she so carefully crafted for me on the back of her painting, she already said she's returning the money. This... all of this is not about that—it's about cravings, desires, deep needs we both seem to want to settle.

I managed to peel my eyes away from her and catch a glimpse of Finn. The man is completely lost in Erika, dancing like they're the only people in this forest. He's given up the whole purpose of this, if he even took it seriously in the first instance. My bet is on *no*. In a way, he's a better man than I am. He knew what he wanted and went straight for it, no beating around the bush.

Suddenly, I'm distracted.

"I'm definitely tapping that tonight."

"Fuck you, man. You only like blondes anyway. This one's mine. She has my name written all over that sweet ass."

I'm not sure how many shades of red exist, but I know for a fact that I'm seeing all of them right now. I turn to find somewhere to my left the same assholes that were watching her before she dove in.

"One more word about *my* woman and I'll slice off your tongue and shove it down *his* throat."

"Who the fuck do you—" he spits out, a smug look on his face.

His wide-eyed friend interrupts him, whispering something in his ear. The next moment, the color drains from his face at the same time his shoulders tense and he averts his gaze from me.

I don't have time for this.

"You have five seconds to apologize and fuck off out of here. Three... Four..."

"I'm sorry, Mr. Hennessey. I—It won't ha—happen again."

I've never seen anyone walk that fast. They didn't even pick up their clothes.

A sharp pain draws my attention to my palm, and I realize I've been squeezing my fist hard enough that I left red marks with my short nails.

If I wasn't sure what I wanted before, this whole interaction pretty much sums it up. I can't deny myself. I won't. I want to play her game. I want to sink into this spell of hers.

I realize that, in this moment, I'm able to predict my own future. When I look back at her, this will be it. I'll be lost. Maybe for a night, maybe for two, maybe a month, or forever. I'll be lost in her, and climbing back out of whatever abyss I'll be caught in will be close to impossible.

It can change my life. Scar me permanently...

So, I turn and meet her gaze, falling straight into the void, as I lose my clothes down to my boxer briefs, and dive into the chilly water.

When I emerge close to her, she's almost expressionless. There's a completely different intensity in those eyes and it creeps up my spine. Like she knows something I don't, in on some sort of secret about my life that only she can reveal.

"What did you think, little witch? That you can tease me? Make me chase you around our city? Get me to play your games, just so you can expose your pretty ass and tits in front of all these men, showing them what's so... clearly... *mine?*"

Her eyes widen, lips parting as she focuses on me, my words crashing down on her harder than this waterfall that drowns out the party raging beyond the pool. I grab Ingrid's hand, pulling her with me as I begin swimming toward the waterfall without waiting for her reaction or response. She struggles to break free, screaming in vain, so I pull her in front of me so fast, she swallows water, and it shuts her up. I keep swimming forward with her facing me, the sound of the falls deafening as the spray becomes much thicker.

"Hold your breath!" I yell.

"What?"

She barely has a moment to take a gulp of air, before I dive underwater, pushing us through the weight of the falls smashing us.

When we come up for air, we're on the other side, the thundering of the waterfall softening in this narrow cavern. She barely takes a shallow breath and she's yelling at me, brushing her hair away from her face. But once she's finally wiped her eyes, she stops mid protest, looking around us in awe.

I pull her up a step naturally formed in the rock, beyond it creating a calm pool the size of a large jacuzzi tub, where the water reaches the middle of my thighs. She follows blindly.

"Oh my God..." her whisper echoes softly.

The waterfall still splashes us, but I press us against the eroded rock, as far as we can go. We're utterly isolated here. Alone in this atmosphere broken out of fairytales, moss, and low plants clinging against the rock.

"I believe I promised you punishment. This feels like the perfect place to start," I tell her.

Disbelief laced with uneasiness falls on her features and she turns around, pretending to admire the space.

Oh, so that's how it is.

Grabbing her shoulders, I whip her around, and press her back against the hard, rock wall.

"I've done my part. I came here, played your game, danced with you, now it's your turn. You have a debt to pay, little witch."

Her eyes widen as I strengthen my hold on her. She looks between us, her body stiffening as she weighs the implications of my words, twisting them in her mind.

"L—Like, now?!"

"Now, later, tomorrow, many days after. You crossed us, cheated us, and stole from us. Did you think you would get away with a dance?"

"I have your money," she says, her voice losing its courage.

"And we have a reputation that won't be built on leniency."

Her lips part, but she's stunned into silence.

"You wanted to be in control, paint me to your liking, and wield my shadows. But our world is built on the shadows of yours, and no amount of color will pull it out of darkness. You need to learn that these things do not go unpunished."

Fear falls over her gaze, but her expression transitions seamlessly to brazenness.

"Teach me, then."

It takes me a couple of seconds for my brain to fall back into its place. *What did she just say?*

Instinctively my hand goes straight to her throat, squeezing lightly until her pulse vibrates against my skin, and with parted lips and doe eyes, she awaits her punishment.

I should... I really should make her pay. But I knew from the moment I saw her face painted so beautifully on that canvas that I was lying to myself—it was never going to happen. Not in the way men like us are expected to do it. Our mafia will not be built on her shadow, there are plenty of others out there who will be part of the ground we step on.

"What's your real name, little witch?"

"Annika." She doesn't even hesitate.

"Annika..." I drag the sound through my throat and fuck me if it doesn't belong.

Leaning in, I brace my forearm on the rock wall.

"Tell me why."

My hand on her throat is just a touch now, brushing my thumb against her pulse as I cock my head and wait for her words to come.

"Umm... why what?"

She swallows, slow and hard, her pulse quickening as I drag my palm up her throat.

"Why—" Pressing my thumb against her jaw, I turn her head to the left—"did you decide to"—I lean in, dragging my nose up the length of her throat, drawing in her scent—"play this game with me?"

A shudder shakes her flesh as my breath caresses the sensitive skin under her ear.

"Because... uhm..."

Her chest rises and falls in rapid successions, pressing against me.

"Because why, little witch?" I punctuate the question with my teeth around her lobe, and she swallows a whimper that puts a smile on my face.

"Because I haven't been able..." She pauses as I flick my tongue over the bite, then swipe up the contour of her ear. "To stop thinking about you."

Me neither, but I'm more interested in her side of things now. "That's all it took? A meeting with me and..."

"No."

Her hand presses on my waist, holding me in place, as she takes a slow breath in.

"It was more. We look into all our potential clients, Ronan."

Goddamn my name on her lips when she's so breathless. It's not fair that it sounds enthralling, like goddamn black magic. I pull away just barely, and when I turn her head to face me, our breaths turn into one.

"So, you looked into me."

"Yes. Well, Hanna did... or Erika, as you know her. I saw your photo."

She's covered in goosebumps, beautifully flushed, and I'm not sure she's conscious of the slight roll of her hips into me. So, I press myself into her in return, reveling in that sweet moment she realizes, her lips parting with a gasp. My hard fucking cock might have something to do with that too.

I grip her jaw and can't help myself from dragging my index over that soft lip, and dipping in her mouth for one delicious moment that makes her pause.

"Go on," I coax her.

"This was our last business deal. We were supposed to leave it all behind after this. But I just... I could not pry you out of my mind. I needed more." She takes a deep breath as I brush my thumb on her lower lip, before dragging my hand down her throat, my hand now a pretty necklace as it presses against the base of it, on her chest.

"What did you need more of?"

"I can't explain it. I knew something was missing, but only after I saw your photo did I understand. I needed a... particular thrill."

"A thrill?!" I push on her chest, pressing her harder against the wet rock, slightly offended. "Is that what I am, then? One last adventure before you retire?"

I don't miss the slight hurt in her eyes, but fuck it, I'm no one's plaything. She wraps her hands around my arm, pulling me to her.

"You were a feeling, Ronan. I knew nothing of you, couldn't assume anything, including if it would be returned. I just... craved. Until I met you. Then it became impossible to stop fant—thinking of you."

Fantasizing?

I can't help the slight grin pulling at my lips, nor the sudden roll in my hips, grinding against her.

"I know I sound like a crazy stalker. I just can't help—"

"You've haunted me since the moment I laid eyes on you," I interrupt her, and she sucks in a breath.

"Have I?"

"Every day. Even when I thought I should kill you for how you crossed us." I drag my hand down her chest, between her breasts, across her stomach until I grip her hip harshly. "Even when I dream. Especially when I dream."

Are these confessions too much? Too soon? Somehow, it seems bad that it doesn't feel soon at all, but just right.

"It's only fair. You've been taking over my dreams too." She smiles and goddamn her lips and those wicked eyes.

Her hips move in an enticing, slow grind against mine, but her eyes are so focused on me, I don't think she knows how fucking crazy she's making me right now. My cock is bursting to feel her properly, my hands itch to stroke her soft breasts, her ass, and fuck me if I don't want to fall on my knees right here, right now, so I can taste her little pussy too. She's maddening and she's not even trying.

"Tell me, little witch..." My thumb circles that soft skin around her hip bone. "Through all those fantasies, did you make yourself come thinking of me?"

Her eyes widen, slight shock filling them as she pulls the side of her bottom lip between her teeth, her smile turning sinful. "I couldn't."

"Was I not enough? Was the thought of my tongue on your skin not enough to get you off?" I dip into that sensitive spot where her neck meets her ear and swipe it with my tongue. "Or my hands stroking every inch of you?"

She shakes her head, rubbing her cheek against mine.

"I refused to give myself that—an orgasm to a fantasy of you."

I almost freeze, but I meet her gaze, so close, our lips almost touch. Almost.

"Why, Annika?"

"I felt like... like I was stealing it away from you. The real you. This first orgasm had to be yours. It *has* to be yours."

Sweet Mary mother of God.

The world stops spinning, time on pause. I can't even hear the waterfall anymore. Life seems to have ceased. Apart from ours. Just as our lips gravitate closer, with no space left for even a breath, annoying fucking screeches split our silence and the whole moment crashes around us.

I exhale as I pull back, turning to the people who just passed through the waterfall—one girl, two guys.

The spell is broken.

"Oooh, looks like we have a party on our hands! Who's this little lady?" A lanky, smug looking asshole smirks toward Annika, and I feel her wince under my tightening grip. "She looks positively delicious, perfect for a sandwich. Willing to share?"

The dead man wiggles his fucking eyebrows at me, and it takes but a second for my hand to wrap around his throat, slamming his back against the wall, his fingers clawing on my arm. Someone gasps behind me, then I feel a hand on my back, but this is not the fucking time.

"I usually enjoy teaching dickheads like you a lesson," I seethe. "But you wiped off the line when you crossed it, and I need to redraw it in your goddamn blood."

He's writhing against the cave wall, smashing his hand onto my arm, trying to pull it off as he repeatedly attempts to gasp for air but fails. He sounds like a dying cat, and I squeeze his throat harder to silence him. Turning purple, his eyes bulge as more hands slam against my back, and an arm wraps around my throat, trying to pull me off of him. I throw my head back and a sharp pain splits up the nape of my neck as a screeching woman shouts abuse at me.

"Shut the fuck up!" I yell and whip my gaze to the side, my eyes landing on the woman who freezes in place, next to an idiot who's holding onto his bleeding nose.

"Ro—Ronan?"

A sweet, meek voice pulls my attention, and I look to my right where Annika stands, wide-eyed, hands pressed against her chest. Fear is painted in her eyes, but more vivid than that is something else—realization. This is her first-hand experience of what she's gotten herself into.

When the man suddenly gasps against my hand, I throw him into the other two, watching them fall like dominos.

"Next time, you're all fucking dead," I grunt.

"You asshole! Wait until I tell my fucking father! You'll be in jail before the end of the fucking week!" the one who's supposed to be dead yells between gasps.

"Good. Go tell him. Tell him that Ronan Hennessey strangled you for propositioning *his woman* in front of him."

He scrunches his eyebrows, calculating my words like there's a familiarity to them. I don't wait for the ball to drop, but I hear their whispers after I turn around.

I ignore Annika's stunned expression, grab her hand, and pull her away with me, disappearing through the thick curtain of water, back into the real world.

CHAPTER 6
Annika

HE PULLS ME through the violent spray threatening to catch me in its underwater whirlpool. My hand is still in his as he guides me away from the waterfall, and with the other one, I'm frantically pushing off the hair clinging to my face. The world seems to explode around us all at once. Music and laughter, incessant background noise mixing with the cascade, and it's almost too much, too soon.

I turn my gaze to the falls, even as Ronan still moves us away from it. I want back... back in that moment where he kept me on the precipice of pleasure and longing. His touch on my skin, the electric bursts rushing from head to toe, his breath against my pulse, those hungry eyes on me.

Then the fury came, the violence, and I should be terrified. It should make me scream and run. But it was the protective look in his eyes that keeps me here.

I'm screwed.

Is he what I expected?

No.

He is more, so much more. He's the promise of everything I fantasized about and everything a man like him would never give a woman like me. I'm not falling, I can't fall. I'm leaving soon.

But he called me *his woman*.

No! Goddamn it, Annika! It was the heat of the moment and he was just proving a point. Focus!

"Ronan, stop." I pull my hand from his and break free.

He turns to me, the look in his eyes filled with a desperation that takes me aback. It's... feral. Raw. Angry.

"I'm not using you." I have no idea why I just said that. I could smack myself right now.

He cocks his head as he treads water, his gaze unchanged.

"Then what are you doing?"

"It's already set. Your money will be returned tonight. If it's not already in your account."

He scoffs and shakes his head.

"So that's it? You had your little fun. You brought me here so you can see how I fit against you, and now you quite literally paid me for it?"

"What?! No!" I almost shout, in shock at the sudden switch in him.

"Then what do you want, Annika? You said you came after me because you crave more. What do you crave, little witch? It's not just my hands on you, my tongue on your skin, my thick cock inside that tight little pussy. It's not just that orgasm you saved for me."

The water I'm submerged in has nothing to do with the sleekness between my folds or the shudder that turns the fabric of my bra into sandpaper against my peaked nipples. I shake myself mentally, because the answer to his question seems harder to put together than I thought.

"You felt like... you would notice me in the background, see me in the shadows. You felt like, if I ran, you would actually chase me."

I drop my gaze, shaking my head.

Pathetic—this is how it feels—fucking pathetic. A ball of self-pity and insecurities thrown in this goddamn pond for a man I've known for a couple of weeks and seen three times. I have no idea what the hell is going on with me, how a simple image of him on a screen sent me down this rabbit hole of cravings and potential destruction. Hanna was right. All of this is a stupid fantasy that could go sideways.

I don't know this man. He could be anything... he could be all kinds of wrong.

A shudder explodes up my spine, prickles spreading all over my skin when I look back up at him. Because his gaze spells words I couldn't possibly say out loud. *Desire* wouldn't be a good enough word. *Craving* is not quite right. But there's a blaze spreading in the blue of his irises, and it envelops me in its heat.

"It would be impossible not to see you in the shadows. You don't blend, Annika, you fucking shine."

Ronan

I MAY BE going insane, but fuck if I care right now.

A piece of her looks broken, and I yearn to mend it. She thinks she's invisible. Jesus, she doesn't notice all the people who can't take their eyes off of her.

Maybe she only notices the right ones.

I'm swimming closer, pulled toward that abyss filled with nothing but her, enjoying the way her features brighten as my words sink in. The silence between us is intense, begging for no interruption, nothing but exchanged gazes. It makes me want to sink into that abyss all on my own.

So, I do.

I let the water swallow me, pushing through the sting in my eyes so I can see as

I grip her waist and pull her down with me. She fights me for a few moments before I stop her right in front of me, and by God... she's a nymph, dangerously beautiful with her soft hair flowing around her.

I grab the back of her head, wrap my arm around her middle, and press her against me as the water seems to be pulling us deeper. All of a sudden, she seems to awaken from the spell, looking around her frantically and pushing against my shoulders, panic for air starting to settle in.

I should go back up, I know that. But that's not why I'm here with her, and that's not what I'm about to do.

My lips meet hers, and I kiss her almost desperately, forcing her to me as the pressure of the water threatens to pull us apart. I sink into the softness of her lips, demanding more, pushing my way into her sweet mouth, and taking my fill of her. Nothing could have stopped this kiss after that broken moment behind the waterfall.

She writhes against me, both in attempts to break up to the surface for air, and to get closer to me. She slams her fist against my shoulder, but to no avail. And there's one moment, one sweet fucking moment, when the tension in her muscles gives in. Submitting to the fear, the adrenaline, to my tongue fighting her own, to my touch too, and I grin against her as I blow air into her mouth through the kiss.

She stills, eyes widening as she realizes what I teased. There's no hesitation when she grabs the sides of my head and kisses me like her life depends on it. Ironically, it does.

But her famine is not just for air. She swipes her tongue through my mouth, tasting me as wildly as I was tasting her. Then she sucks against me like she's trying to pull the air right out of my lungs. I give her nothing. Only a grin.

She stuns me, though, wrapping her legs around my middle, catching me in a strong grip and jerking me once, like she wants to force the air out of me.

The effort is useless, but I commend it with a smirk as I press my hand harder against her head and decide to reward her. I slowly blow air into her mouth, and she sucks it in greedily. When my lungs empty... all that's left is us, our kiss. Slow now, dragged out, our tongues drawing lazy circles around one another. Even here she tastes of honey and dreams, wrapped into everything that's good in this world. Like she was made just for me. So, I savor her some more, until I think she forgot she was drowning just seconds ago, forgot she's underwater, because she's confused when we break the surface and the world screams to life around us.

"You son of a bitch!" Slamming her fist against me, she gasps for air. "You could have killed me!" she yells, the sharp sound almost unnatural coming from her. The noise of the waterfall drowns it, and others can't hear her panic... or anger.

I catch her wrist as she attempts to slap me, but let the other one land against my cheek, just so I can grab the back of her head and crash my lips to hers all over again. She squeals against my mouth, but she can't hide the lust that shudders through her when I bite her bottom lip.

"I could have, yes," I say as I break the kiss.

Her expression falls. Reality gently settling in.

"No. You wouldn't do that."

"Why are you so convinced?"

She stills, slowly sinking. I pull her close, her ear near my lips.

"You said you craved more. I'm giving you... *more*," I whisper.

Pulling away enough that she can look at me, her eyes flash somewhere behind me for a split second. A peculiar smile tugs at her lips, but it vanishes as fast as it appeared.

"How much more can you give?"

That wickedness is back in her eyes, and it sends a quake straight through me. I didn't realize I released her wrists, not until she lets herself sink and disappears underwater.

I shake my head, and the spell of her gaze along with it, letting out a short cackle, then I follow her beneath the surface.

I can only see a few feet in front of me, if that, but she's not here.

What the fuck?

How is that even possible? I whip around, trying to distinguish something through this darkness, but it's futile. Did she sink too far? I let myself go, swimming farther, but the pool is not actually that deep. Where the hell is she?

I rise back to the surface, frantically searching for a trace of her, before I take a deep breath, ready to dive back under. But the witch is perfectly fucking fine. The water runs over her smooth skin as she walks out of the pool, right next to the boulder from where she dove in. I was right, she is a nymph, because how the hell did she swim so fast? She grabs her clothes and pulls her shoes on in a hurry, before joining her friend who's waiting for her.

This is not fucking happening! Goddamn this woman!

I'm already swimming toward the shore, but she's at the edge of the forest already. Then the little witch stops, turns to me, and even from this distance, I can't miss the paradox of a smile she throws at me—both devilish and timid—before she disappears into the darkness of the trees.

I'm out, pulling my clothes on as quickly as I can, uncomfortable with how they stick to my damp skin, then look around for my brother. I finally see him coming back from the opposite direction the girls ran to and meet him halfway.

"They're gone."

"What?!" he questions, frowning.

"Just now. They grabbed their stuff and disappeared into the forest. Where's Carter?"

"He left not long after you found Ingrid."

"Annika," I correct him.

He raises his eyebrows and laughs.

"What did we get ourselves into?"

I rake a hand through my wet hair, sighing.

"Fuck if I know. But let's face it, it's all because of me and... *her*."

"Yeah, we're just willing collateral damage," he says, laughing again, completely unbothered. "Come on, show me where they went."

* * *

"What the hell just happened, brother?"

After they sped away from the parking lot from the edge of the forest, we just about managed to catch up with them.

Far too late though.

We didn't stand a chance.

Now, we're on the floating dock, watching them wave dramatically at us from the boat that speeds away. They had everything ready for their theatrical exit. There's no time for us to prep our boat. They'll be out of sigh before we finish.

"They played us, that's what happened," I say, wiping a hand over my face.

"Nah, we're players too. This is just our official invitation." Finn turns his back on the calm sea, tapping my shoulder as he walks away with a great big smile on his face. "Let the games begin, brother."

I'm powered by adrenaline, desire, and frustration, but they seem to go hand in hand. Somehow fueling each other and putting more kindling to this obsession that grows for this woman.

Maybe it's that pure, naive look that makes me so damn hard, or maybe it's the fact that underneath it all, there's probably not an ounce of innocence about her. She's a witch in disguise, stirring a potion that drags me closer and closer to her. But her potion smells of wildflowers in bloom and she might as well douse me in it because I'm coming for her.

Wherever the woman is, she's already mine.

But I'll play her game. Relinquish the control. Because she's been doing a damn good job so far with the rules.

* * *

"You guys are fucked, aren't you?" Madds smirks.

He cocks his head as I take a seat on the couch across from him and Vin. We've gathered in Midnight, as we always seem to do since we opened this place. I look up at my brother and he just shrugs, turning to head to the bar.

"Don't answer that," Madds continues, shaking his head as he leans back. "I'm not gonna sit here and tell you that you shouldn't. You're big boys, you know yourselves you shouldn't. But... the dick wants what the dick wants, and sometimes the heart agrees with it too."

"Damn, you're a veritable poet, man." Finn places a drink in front of me before he takes a seat on the free armchair to my right. "Realistically, it's not common knowledge who they chose to strike the deal with. The people who would try undermining us theoretically don't know, and even if the information would get out, it's information we can control. How much damage can it really do to our reputation?"

"Just get our money back and we'll be good," Vin grumbles, shaking his head in some sort of acceptance. But I can see the shadow of a smirk there.

"We will. As of now, we're the only ones who know the painting isn't real, so it's all under wraps."

"Actually..." Carter walks into the barroom from the corridor that leads to the office. "Our money has been returned, and that second part isn't entirely true."

She really did send the money back. I didn't fully believe her when she said it, yet now this seems like some sort of test. Technically, I got what I was chasing her for. *Technically.*

"Explain," Vin says, cocking his head, and my shoulders suddenly tense up.

"I kept an ear out since we found out the painting was a fake. Someone's been knocking on some doors for information, very low key around the underground art world. I did a bit of digging and one very angry man who bought a disturbingly expensive painting from two women, found out a couple of months ago that a fake had been sitting behind his alarmed glass display in his mansion."

My chest tightens, and Finn is suddenly still. So damn still, I'm afraid he'll shatter if I touch him. I have no idea what's going through his head. I don't even know what's going through mine. Varying emotions that amount to one that dominates them all—confusion.

I'm fucking confused. Am I scared this man will go after her? Am I scared she'll get hurt or killed? Am I reserved because I just met the woman mere weeks ago and caring about her fate is fucking ridiculous?

Bewilderment... this is exactly what clouds my mind.

If she was any other woman, she would be long gone from my radar. I wouldn't care. I would barely remember her name.

"Fuck," I sigh, shaking my head at myself—she's not any other woman. This one I like. Really fucking like. Like I'm goddamn hypnotized. "Who is he, and does he know who he's looking for? I wonder if the girls know."

"There're feelers out there, placed by people who work for him. However, he seems to have deep pockets. I have my men working on identity. For now, it might be okay. They seem to be based far away in the northeast."

"We can handle deep pockets. Hanna mentioned that she keeps an eye on the people they sold to, so they might know," Finn says as he rises.

"We can," Carter agrees, nodding calmly, "but just because I haven't found his name, it doesn't mean he's a nobody. It means the exact opposite; he's a somebody big enough that his identity is effortlessly hidden, and anyone but him does the work."

"See what else you can find," Finn adds.

"Carter..." My voice seems to simmer angrily. "Did you find them? They didn't disappear into thin air. It's been three days. Where are they?"

He raises one eyebrow at me, and I swear I can see my maddened expression reflecting in his own. I want to rein it in, but I can't seem to manage. It's all too much. Stealing my oxygen and weighing me down. I need to get the fuck out of here.

I need air.

I need to think.

Shit.

I step around the coffee table, ready to jump over the damn thing, and head toward the door.

"I did find them."

His words stop me dead in my tracks. I don't turn to face him.

"Bovely Island."

CHAPTER 7
Ronan

WE'RE SNEAKING THROUGH the ferns, making our way up on the slight slope of the small laurel forest, the last of the sunshine lighting our way. We strayed from the path when we heard something that sounded a lot like a voice out in the distance, as we headed up to the villa that sits at the top of this hill.

There's little chance that Annika and Hanna didn't see the speedboat Finn and I came in. Despite the dark clouds that followed us here and whatever violence was brewing at sea, the position of the house gives you quite an advantage. Which means that we definitely didn't imagine the voices we heard—it's them.

Out of all the islands in this archipelago, they chose Bovely, the smallest one. Fifteen minutes is all it takes to walk from one end to the other. It's privately owned, with just one house, and a clear neon sign pointed at our targets, just for us.

I've never been here, but our parents were invited a few times. Back when old man Bovely still had his stamina and health, he used to throw some fancy, weekend-long parties. He can't come here anymore, even if it's only thirty-forty minutes away by speedboat, but he lends it over to his closest friends whenever they want an escape. I doubt there're many of them left, though. Once you become old and frail, people seem to abandon you. You become too easy to forget. It begs the question—how did Annika and her friend manage to get their slender fingers on it? I'll add it to the list of things I want to find out about the witch.

It gets my blood boiling, knowing this foolish woman not only challenged me, but she fucking lured me, a damn stranger to her, to a private, isolated island, where she's utterly defenseless. Fortunately, it's also what gets me both intrigued and painfully hard.

Not far ahead, rustling of leaves catches my attention, my adrenaline spiking almost instantly, and I signal the direction to Finn, who's about six feet away.

The wind picks up, and the whole forest becomes alive in seconds. It's the strangest thing, like the trees begin to sing, covering our steps as we hurry cautiously.

The sun must have hidden behind some clouds because it's much darker here now. Even more of an advantage for us. It's exhilarating. Stalking through the shadows, hoping I'll catch her at a vulnerable moment, then... pounce.

And just like that, I catch a glimpse of them, scurrying around the trees, peeking around themselves... looking for us, and it puts a great big grin on my face. Finn's too. He's not even paying attention to me anymore. He's found his target, and he's going for it. The whole ride here, he wouldn't shut up about Hanna, how amazing she was, how smart, all the things he wanted to do to her. I shut my ears at that part—no brother should hear about the places the other's tongue wants to reach.

I share the sentiment, but I don't need to share the mental image.

It's only been three days, but seeing her again does something peculiar to my insides. For the first time in my life, I have to wonder... is this what everyone means by *butterflies?*

"It's gonna hammer down in a minute!" one of them, maybe Hanna, shouts over the loud wind in an urgent tone.

Raindrops have started to fall, no trace of the warm light from the setting sun anymore, the forest much darker than it should be at this time of day. Its song much more violent.

They pick up the pace, but we're right there with them, and I'm focused on the woman who clouds my judgment with the need for her. Her brown hair, black in this lack of light, flowing as she begins to run. She's practically goddamn floating. This is one of those moments that would be shown in slow motion in movies... it feels like it is.

They stop, catching their breath, and carefully look around before they exchange a knowing gaze, probably realizing that all this rustling of leaves might not be just from the wind. Finn and I made sure to hide, stalking behind trees and dense bushes, getting closer and closer to the creatures who lured us here.

Suddenly, lightning bathes the forest in an eerie light, just as the first thunder of this brewing storm cracks, and my witch jumps into a sprint with a loud yelp.

I don't hesitate. I run after her, the adrenaline and excitement pulling at my lips, the roaring anticipation of getting my hands on her, something I've never experienced. My cock is already hard—too hard—rubbing uncomfortably against my jeans. I want her more than I've ever wanted any other woman. Every other desire I've had before her pales in comparison. I almost regret not taking her behind that waterfall. Almost.

The smell of her skin, the taste of her, the way she fit against me, it was so goddamn intoxicating. I was close... but I couldn't. Even without the interruption, I didn't want to take it further in that place. I fooled myself by reasoning that teasing her was my retaliation for pulling me into her game, but in reality, I wanted more for her. She deserves better than a quick fuck.

But after three nights of dreams haunted by her, as I watch her sweet body move through this thickening rain, I don't think I can give her better. I don't think I can wait. I can't fucking help myself. I need her.

My flesh feels wrong without her body wrapped around me, my fucking lungs won't stop heaving unless she's swallowing my breaths, and my heart won't stop racing unless she's there to soothe it. I almost hate myself for these thoughts... they taste slightly bitter, like weakness. But maybe it's because she's not officially mine yet.

Then, it's time to make her.

Lightning splashes our whole world in shades of blue, and she turns her head right at that moment, stumbling as she sees me running not that far behind her. She yelps as I grin, and I could have sworn I caught a glimpse of a smile before she turned back around, quickening her steps.

I could try so much harder, run so much faster. I could catch her in the next few seconds. But why spoil the fun? Especially seeing how hard she's pushing herself, knowing full well goosebumps mar her skin because of me. Even better, knowing that she still hasn't touched her pussy, made herself come without me.

I can guarantee she's getting slicker by the second between those sweet thighs. It's not even wishful thinking. It's a fact.

And I'm about to prove it.

"Such an easy game you're playing, little witch?" I shout.

We must be nearing the house now, but as I finish that taunt, the damn woman takes a sharp right through some tall ferns and bushes, and I lose her. Clearly, this is not all she has. This rain is falling harder now, and as I stop to wipe it from my eyes, I listen to the forest. Listen for her.

I think she stopped too.

Walking slowly in the direction she disappeared in, I use the wind to cover my movements. I catch a glimpse of her signaling something to her friend still in the distance, as she moves fluidly from the shadow of a tall bush to hide behind a large tree.

Then I'm there, on the other side of that tree, and before I can do anything, I see Finn stalk behind Hanna, suddenly wrapping a hand around her middle while covering her face and pulling her back behind some tall foliage, the wind drowning her muffled yelp.

"Hanna?" Annika calls for her friend, forgetting about her cover, and turns to find her gone. "Hanna?!" Her breathing picks up, forcing herself to control the panic. "This is not funny! Hanna!"

She's distracted, and just like that, I round the tree and I'm right behind her. She's dripping wet from the rain, as am I, yet the heat of her body warms me, even though we're not touching. Her muscles still all at once, her shoulders frozen in place. The tension is palpable. I could do it. Take her right here, right now.

I could flip her around and sink into her against this tree. I could do so much more.

But I like this game.

"Run," I growl in her ear.

"Aaah!" she yelps and sprints away, not even daring to look back.

I take off after her, a great big fucking grin making my cheeks hurt, reveling in her quick step, her nerves, her growing sense of dread as she stumbles, caught by various roots and plants.

Even if it's already raining, somehow I can sense the moment the skies break open all at once, and the water that falls on us is so dense, I can barely see a few yards in front of me and the ground becomes a slippery mess. It makes this hunt even more rousing.

"You wanted a chase, Annika! But you don't seem to be running fast enough! Almost like you don't want it as bad as I thought you did."

I let the words drift through the trees, and they seem to fuel her as she picks up the pace.

It's no use. I'm determined. More than that, this is making me ravenous. I'm right behind her now, just as thunder shatters the atmosphere once more. She yelps and stumbles, and I watch her dive forward, almost in slow motion. I'm not sure how I got here, but I'm suddenly next to her, throwing myself as far forward as I can to catch her and break her fall.

She screams as she lands on top of me, but we roll on the ground, caking ourselves in mud and broken leaves, as I hold her to me. Beneath me, she's caged in, breathing frantically.

The predator caught the prey. And my, my, what delicious prey.

Before she can even think of running, I grab her arms, stretching them above her head, and grip her wrists in one hand, pinning her down. Her gaze fixes on me, her chest pushing against me with every ragged breath, but when her lips part, I'm done. Mine crash against hers, kissing like the world is about to end with this raging storm and this is the last chance I'll ever get to taste her. She moans into my mouth, her body softening beneath me, her hips pushing up into me, before she wraps one leg around my waist and holds me against her. Her tongue in my mouth is frantic, licking every bit of me she can reach, and I realize how much I'm loving her game. I'd play it every day for the rest of my life if the chase would end with a moment like this one, nestled between her legs, with her sweet tongue in my mouth, desperate to have me.

We're sinking into the wet ground, the storm turning from bad to worse, but I can't possibly stop. I won't. Only for a moment do I break the kiss to admire her. Wet, muddy, red cheeks—she's a goddamn vision. She's a deity dropped on this ruthless earth just for me to taste, to worship, to own. She's fucking mine. There's no other option. No way out.

Not for her, and definitely not for me.

"Are you hurt?" It dawns on me that we rolled a few times.

She shakes her head as she bites her lip, and my eyes almost roll in the back of my head as she grinds her hips against my hard on.

"Goddamn witch, you'll be the death of me."

My lips find hers again, this kiss turning into a violent affair, the waves of rain our melody, and the trees thrashing in the wind our song.

I'm leaning on my forearm next to her head, running my other hand all over her body, no regard to the mud as I reach underneath her top, straight for those pretty tits of hers. She feels so fucking good in my hand, her hard nipples screaming for attention, and I couldn't possibly deny them. I squeeze lightly, enough that she whimpers into my mouth, pushing her hips into me with another needy grind, begging for more.

So, I do, I give her more, pressing my dick against the warmth of her center, cursing every single layer of clothes covering us right now. But I keep going, dry humping her into the mud, kneading her tits, and biting her lips and tongue until we're a fucking mess of greed and lust.

I can't wait anymore. I probably should. I should stop. Take her to the house and sink into the heat of her properly, in a soft bed, beneath clean linens like she fucking deserves.

"I'm sorry...." I plead against her lips as I rise on my knees. Dragging my palms down her inner thighs, I grip the thin fabric of her leggings, pausing for a moment. Waiting for a reaction, a plea to stop. But her pretty face is caught somewhere between shock and desire, lips forming a perfect O as she stares between her legs. I pull sharply, splitting her leggings at the seams so I can get exactly what I ache for.

Jesus Christ, she's not wearing panties.

It's a fucking sign, and by God, what a pretty sign it is.

I fumble with my jeans, almost ripping them open, desperate to sink into that beautiful cunt of hers, and by the time my cock is aligned with her slit, I'm caging her in once more, and she wraps her arms around me.

Enticing whimpers fill my ears as I push in between her sleek lips, my thick cock strangled by the tightening pulses. It's a cruel form of torture, because I'm not sure how I'm supposed to last beyond three pumps when she feels so flawless wrapped around me. I have to. I have to stretch this insane sensation for as long as I can, just as I'm stretching her right now, pressing farther until I meet the end of her. We're both panting. Her eyes sparkle, looking at me like I splattered the sky with stars myself. I hold that gaze as I slide back, then immediately pound into her, watching those steel irises explode as her whimpers turn into sharp, echoing moans.

So, I do it again, slowly sliding out, before slamming back in, just to savor that explosion in her eyes again, the pleasure rippling through her features, her brows pulling together, her cheeks flushed as she bites her bottom lip.

We're soaking wet. The rain is so heavy, we might as well be fucking underwater. But I couldn't care less. This is exhilarating! I just cage her in, shielding her as much as I can from the onslaught of the downpour. Then I dive in, pressing my lips to hers as I fall into a delirious rhythm, fucking her frantically until I swear we've made a little nest within the soaked soil.

She mewls into my mouth, forcing me to swallow my own name as it spills off her lips, and it makes me buck my hips harder into her, grinding after each thrust so I can rub against her clit, reveling in how her pussy clenches when I do.

"You're perfect, little witch, and you're mine. You're fucking mine!" I all but roar.

She moans louder, the sweetest of smiles painted in lust, the perfect answer to my confession.

I pick up the pace until I can't tell if she's crying or moaning, and just when I think I can't possibly hold back anymore, her soaked cunt clutches my shaft, rippling as she screams. My name falling in waves of euphoria off her lips does something to me. Maybe even more than the tremble of her whole body with the violent orgasm that triggers mine in a split fucking second. I roar as I come inside of her so fucking hard, she spasms with each burst that fills her.

My brain is in pieces; I'm not quite sure what the hell just happened. All I know is that it's never been like this for me. I've never screamed my release. Or felt this animalistic need to take... I'm not even sure I've sated it yet.

"Ronan..."

"Yes, baby."

"I... wow..."

I smile, dropping small kisses all over her face.

"I know," I tell her.

"I feel like I need to thank you."

"I think I'm supposed to do the thanking, little witch. And the apologizing."

I slowly pull out of her, do up my jeans and rise, before I pull her up to her feet.

"You already said you were sorry, before..." she says with a confused smile, "but I'm not sure why."

"Because I couldn't wait. I didn't give you something better, softer, at least in a house."

She laughs, that damn birdsong filling my ears again.

"You gave me exactly what I wanted. Everything I needed."

Those words would get me hard again if I wasn't still halfway there. But suddenly it dawns on me what an idiot I've just been.

"Oh, Annika. Shit, I... fuck! In the heat of the moment, I completely forgot about a condom. I promise I'm clean, but... I'm so sorry."

She raises her eyebrows with a thoughtful look.

"I forgot too. Don't worry, I have an IUD, and considering I haven't had sex in over eight months, I'm clean too."

She laughs, but in typical man style, all I focus on is that she hasn't touched a man in that long. It strangely makes me feel good that I was the one to break her dry spell. Like she chose me specifically. How peculiar.

"But now that you said that... umm... your c—you are dripping down my legs. And this storm is getting a bit scary now."

It's my turn to laugh, but knowing that my cum is rubbing between her thighs makes me want to do some dirty things that might delay us even further.

But we're *actually* dirty, our clothes caked in mud.

"Let's go to the house."

She takes the lead, and we walk through the thick storm, and I can't help but wonder what's happening with my small boat right now. I can hear the waves from here, even though we're almost in the middle of the island. I didn't even think to have a look at the weather forecast. It might have been a mistake, but I guess we'll find out.

When the house comes into view between the trees, I thank the gods, because I've been walking behind this woman, watching her ass cheeks peek from between the rip in her leggings, and I need to be close to her. I want to wash myself and touch every single bit of her body, stroke, and lick, I want it all.

We burst through the door, shutting it behind us as the rain threatens to soak the inside. I don't know where my brother and Hanna are. They might already be inside, so we need to hurry before they see Annika with her ripped clothes.

"Bathroom." I can't seem to form any other words.

I follow as she leads me through the house, and I'm learning what tunnel vision is, because I could be anywhere right now, in a crowd, in a damn dungeon, literally anywhere, and I wouldn't even notice.

All I see is her.

When the resemblance of a shower enclosure blurs behind her, I reach for the door I just passed through and slam it behind me. I don't wait. I lean in slightly, wrapping an arm under her ass, lifting her to me as she wraps her legs around me, and presses her lips to mine.

I walk in the shower, blindly reaching for something to turn on the water. When I finally find it, the first spray comes out cold, but it doesn't deter us. We only break the kiss when our muddy, soaked clothes are too much of a barrier, and we all but rip them off each other. Then we wash the mud off our bodies with such speed, you'd think we were about to win a damn prize.

I guess we are.

"I played your game, little witch," I say, pausing as I take a hard, deep breath. "Now it's your turn to play mine."

She smiles at me, but the sheepish expression turns wicked as she drops to her knees before me, and I don't have time to process before her hand is at the base of my cock and the tip of me hits the back of her throat. I'm seeing stars and almost choke on my own spit.

"Fuck... Annika."

Who am I kidding? This is still her game. And I don't think I'll ever stop playing it.

She sucks me slow and deep, her small hand following her lips as her tongue licks the underside of my cock. I'm going to burst right here. It's torture. Slow, grueling, delicious torture, and I would take it to the very end if I didn't want to be deep inside of her.

I grab her under the arms and haul her up, my cock falling with a sloppy pop from between her lips. Gripping her head in my hands, I kiss her so fucking roughly her teeth split my lip. But fuck if I care. My goal is clear—sink inside her cunt until she screams my name again and wipes the memory of all other women from my mind.

Spinning her around, I bend her over, and hold her in place with a hand on the middle of her arched back. I can't help but pump my shaft a few times at the view of her eagerly awaiting my cock, as she braces her hands against the wall.

Her cunt is far too inviting to keep her waiting.

I press between her folds, parting her as I rub over her slit, reveling in the shudder that shakes her body. She pulses around me, and I take it as my cue, wrapping my hand around her hip, fingers digging into her flesh, and push through her tightening walls.

Dear God, how am I going to last when she does this to me?

I slam home with one hard thrust, and she yelps, almost slipping against the wet shower wall.

"I dreamed of this. Your little cunt wrapped around my cock, your steel eyes filled with need... I thought I knew what to expect. Turns out, I'm a clueless bastard and thank the gods I am."

This is different from what happened in the forest. The hunger is still here, but I'm fucking feasting on her now, sinking into her cunt like it's Nirvana itself and I'm building my own home inside of it.

"Ronan..." She rolls my name off her tongue like a lustful prayer, threatening to make me come dangerously fast.

Then I wrap one hand around her neck, holding her in place as my thrusts threaten to topple her, and with the other, I reach around her middle, until her clit is beneath the tips of my fingers. The moment I roll them over her swollen bundle, her legs begin to shake, her cunt pulses around me, and her walls milk me thoroughly from the inside out.

"Ro—Ronan... I—I'm coming!" she cries so sweetly as she shatters around me. But it breaks me too. Making me come like never before.

Christ, what have I done?

Her spell is complete.

There will be no one else.

CHAPTER 8
Annika

WE EMERGED FROM the shower much later. I didn't want to leave. It felt like a sanctuary, sheltering us in a bubble of sex and desperation. Such sweet desperation. Keeping our hands off each other to wash ourselves was torture. The shower gel pouring too slow, the mud not washing off fast enough, and I couldn't wait any longer to get my hands on him and mouth around his cock. After he fucked me so damn well, we still weren't fully sated, and my hair was taking too long to wash. So he dropped to his knees, stopping my efforts, threw my leg over his shoulder, and ate my pussy like it was the richest feast after being starved. He made me come so intensely, I couldn't hold myself up and slid against the wet wall until my ass hit the floor. But he saw me there, all shattered and powerless and he pulled me under him, my leg still hooked over his shoulder, and slid inside me until I was utterly full. Begging for more was futile. He fucked me as the shower rained over us, caging me in with his ridiculous body, muscles flexing above me, sinew making him look like a raging beast, and all I could do was moan and smile.

I couldn't stop smiling...

I still can't. And it's been three days.

Three days of fucking, although one of those times I could have almost described it as *making love*. Three days of his hands constantly on me. Three days wrapped up in a cocoon, prisoners of this seemingly never-ending storm. I would thank the gods for the opportunity, but this was supposed to be one night. Would we have been the same if we weren't stuck here together? Would the hunger be the same? Would this need to constantly touch each other still be here?

The weather has been merciless, the pouring rain an understatement to what has been bashing against our windows. The sea is a torment, ruthless waves smashing against this small island with such force, there have been a couple of times when Ronan has had to hold me, soothe me when my anxiety got a bit out of hand at the thought of this storm worsening. But waking up because of shattering thunder has been strangely comforting, because even in his sleep, this man wrapped an arm around me and pulled me to him, sheltering me in his comfort.

Our life inside this house is like a strange fairytale. Such a brutal contrast to the harsh tempest fracturing the world outside. We're trapped in our bubble of decadence, watching it like a movie through our windows.

I've only been out of the bedroom two or three times since he arrived. We've barely seen Finnigan and Hanna, especially since they're on the other side of the villa. Which in hindsight is a good thing, because I've passed way too close to their side of the house when they were in the middle of some... interesting action... and distance is exactly what we need in those situations.

When I did have a bit of alone time with Hanna, she looked happy in a satisfied, content kind of way. I've never seen her like this. Disheveled, beautifully broken. I wonder if I look the same. I feel it.

"Tell me then, was it your dad who inspired you to paint?" Ronan walks into the bedroom with a tray of finger foods for us. I'm starving.

I grab a cherry tomato and a piece of mozzarella, stuffing them in my mouth before I answer. Mmm... Thank God we stocked up the kitchen before this storm hit.

"Yeah." I give a partial answer with my mouth full.

"I'm not sure you look quite that happy when I make you come."

I stuff a piece of bread in my mouth too.

"It's not your fault. Nothing will ever compare to food."

This time he laughs, and it makes me pause. He's a beautiful man, but when his eyes crinkle from laughter and smile lines crease his cheeks, he's godlike.

"Go on, tell me," he pushes.

"Both my parents are artists." I take little bites of the delicious food, so I can still talk. "My mother is a free soul. Always painting these extravagant modern pieces that most people don't quite understand. My father is the lover of the ancients, the classics, the renaissance... everything that stopped being painted two hundred years ago. He dedicated his life to restoring art, traveling the world, and sometimes taking us with him. I learned everything from him."

"Is he as successful as you are?"

I give him a knowing look.

"Definitely not in the same way. As far as I am aware, my father doesn't forge famous and lost paintings for a living."

"You certainly do have quite a talent. You fooled so many appraisers, so many people..." he trails off with a look on his face that looks a lot like pride. "I'm not sure I've ever heard of anyone like you. You're a genius with a paintbrush, little witch."

My cheeks burn, and I bow my head, stuffing another cherry tomato in my mouth to keep from saying something stupid. I appreciate compliments, but there is something about them that makes me want to run and hide while shouting *thank you, but I don't deserve it, or maybe just a little bit*. I wish my mind would make sense.

"Out of curiosity, was it true? The story you told us about the *original* Lady in White painting."

"That great-grandpa took it?"

He nods.

"Yup. All true. Only it wasn't exactly saved. About a third of it was burnt. I have it in storage, which is why I was so sure I could forge this one with minimal risk. I studied it thoroughly over the years and there was never a risk of anyone finding the original."

"It's ironic that this is the one you decided to screw up intentionally." He smiles, shaking his head.

"None of this situation has made any logical sense to me." I admit.

"Weren't you worried that your dad would find out that this painting was on the market?"

"No. He doesn't know about the painting. Grandpa told me that my dad's a bit too honorable and would end up returning it if he knew. Why he thought I wouldn't do the same... I don't know. Plus, black-markets are not my dad's playground."

"Your grandpa must have seen something in you. Where are your parents now?" he asks.

"West Coast. In a small fishing village, living in this crazy split-personality cottage, that literally looks like they built it at the same time, but separately. Half the house is all mom, colors splashed everywhere, almost psychedelic with a touch of bohemian, while the other half is neat, in elegant, neutral colors and fine antiques. Somehow, it works... just like them."

He laughs lightly, the way that emotion once again pulls at his lips and crinkles his eyes, making me melt. I've seen plenty of beautiful men before, but none hold a torch to Ronan. He wears his looks with such nonchalance, like he's barely aware of how stunningly attractive he is, yet he's utterly comfortable in his own skin.

"With their combined lifestyles, it sounds like it could get intense between them," he jokes.

"It does. They've been together for almost thirty years, so they're used to each other. But it also means that they love getting on each other's nerves. They're a weirdly beautiful couple," I say, rolling my eyes at the memory of their house and life together. But I catch a tinge of longing in Ronan's eyes. For a moment there he loses himself.

"What do your parents think you do for work? Especially with all this traveling?"

"The same thing as dad—restoration—which is great since it's normal to travel a lot in this job. However, I told them I work for private collections, so they can never to see my work out there. Unlike my dad's work, which is public since he works on monuments, churches, and other public buildings."

"That's quite interesting, straightforward, since you didn't have to put too much effort into the cover."

He has this sparkle in his eyes that looks a lot like respect.

"Considering that neither he nor your mom know of your job," he continues, "do they actually know how talented you are? Or the fact that you probably surpassed your father's skills?"

I shrug, swallowing another bit of food.

"I never thought about that, to be honest. Proving myself to them was never really on my mind, and they were quite relaxed in their parenting. They didn't make my talent a competition. And in terms of my dad, I would never say I surpassed him. Our talents have just been specialized differently. He restores, and I like recreating. I've been doing it since I was young enough to hold a paintbrush."

"What made you start?" he asks as he grabs another piece of salami, pushing my way the mozzarella he can see I'm obsessing over.

"Emotions. I looked at a painting, and I could see the expression of the subject. Even in those posed portraits, you could see how they clutched the fingers, the tension in the shoulders, or the love in the eyes. But recreating it... it makes me experience it myself. The first time I did it well, I cried. I was painting loss, a mother holding her dead son draped limply in her arms, as she stared at the sky, begging God for a miracle. When I look at a painting, I can admire how it depicts the emotions we're all supposed to see, but when I paint it myself, I can feel them."

"Damn... that's not what I was expecting, if I was expecting anything at all."

"I'm sorry. I know it sounds a bit... crazy." Can I hide under the covers now?

I keep wondering when this man is going to realize his mistake and run far away from me.

"It sounds beautiful." He pulls the tray away, setting it on the nightstand, before crawling on top of me, pushing my legs apart with his and nestling between them, as he swipes the stray strands of hair from my face. "And there's nothing wrong with a little crazy."

"Hey!"

I smack his shoulder, but he catches my wrist, pinning it above my head, a grave, mildly amused rumble vibrating through his chest.

"Careful, little witch, or I might punish you for that."

"Promises, promises."

Ronan

I REACH OVER next to me before I even open my eyes, frowning when I fail to find what I need—Annika. Blinking a few times, I attempt to focus on the world around me and the empty bed. I lift my head and look toward the en-suite bathroom, but the door is open, light off. She's not there.

My head sinks back into the pillow and I rub my eyes in an attempt to wake up quicker. We went to sleep so late last night, and we didn't even end in sex. We were talking for hours. About life, her wants, needs, dreams, and everything in between. It was surreal. Like I was living in some chick flick movie where they played a montage as the couple kept shifting in bed in all sorts of awkward positions while telling stories and laughing. This wasn't a movie, though; this was real life... my life. This woman has turned me upside down. If this isn't black magic, I don't know what is.

I throw off the covers, looking for my phone to check the time, since this damn storm is keeping us in a constant state of darkness and we never know if it's morning or afternoon. I track it down—seven twenty-three a.m. Damn, she got up early.

I'm about to head out the door when it dawns on me that I'm stark-fucking-naked, and I'm sure if Hanna is out there, she would prefer not to see quite this much of me. I washed my boxers last night and my jeans a couple of nights ago, since the very few things we brought with us we stupidly left on the boat. We're not even sure if it's still there on the shore, let alone our clothes. I go to the bathroom, thankful when I find my clothes dry on the heated towel rail, then I quickly wash my face and brush my teeth.

Now it's time to find my woman.

When I enter the living area, it's quiet, the sounds of the storm playing on repeat in the background, bashing at the windows in hectic waves. It seems to be easing down, but not enough that we could leave this house. Let alone this island. But fuck if I care that I'm stuck here. If I left, I wouldn't be able to enjoy this incredible view— Annika sitting at the round breakfast table in the bay window, chair turned toward the ocean, a small canvas in front of her, lost in her brush strokes as she paints, completely oblivious to my presence. Her hair is wrapped in a loose bun at the crown of her head, messy strands fallen around her slender neck and soft face, and I'm not sure if I want to make myself known. There's something about this image, the serenity of her against the tumultuous storm in the background. There's so much perfection in this paradox.

I lean against the kitchen island, arms crossed over my chest, watching her delicate fingers swirl a brush in a small color palette, before moving it with ease on the canvas that's no longer white.

I want this—her—for more than just now. I want her when the storm is over. I want her back in Queenscove. I want her for as long as she'll want me. Only, I fear I'll keep her even after that.

My bare feet start moving before I made the decision, and her shoulders jerk ever so slightly when she realizes she's no longer alone.

"Morning, baby."

My voice comes out croakier than it should, my throat dry. Dehydration or thirst for her... not sure which. The bare skin of her neck and shoulders comes alive with goosebumps.

"Morning, baby." She matches my words with sweetness in her voice I want to taste.

I lean in, wrapping my arm around her chest, careful not to disturb her right arm that she paints with, and kiss the nape of her neck, before moving to that sweet spot where it meets the shoulder. She sinks into me, but doesn't stop painting. So I sneak a peek at the canvas. It's almost the complete opposite of her other works I have seen so far. She showed me quite a few photos on her phone, and this is nothing like them. The strokes are rough, almost chaotic, yet there's a hidden order in all that chaos, because I can see it as clear as it looks out the window... the storm.

She painted it all; the waves, the thrashing trees, the broken skies, and the rush of the rain.

Only the feeling it gives me is not of turmoil, but of calm. A strange sense of elation. It feels as ethereal as what her and I are experiencing inside this house, even if the strokes depict the anarchy outside of it.

"It's beautiful, Annika."

"Thank you. I wanted to capture this moment... and maybe someday, if I want to remember what it was like, I can feel it all over again."

I don't realize I'm squeezing her until she stops painting. I'm jealous. I wish I could do that, find a way to experience something all over again, almost like it's the first time.

I release her and rise, standing behind her.

"You'll have to tell me what it's like."

She tips her head back, and I lean in, pressing a kiss to her forehead. But when I rise again, she looks back at me with wide eyes.

"What?"

"You're saying it like you—like you're going to be next to me years from now," she says on a shaky breath that both confuses me and makes me fear its implications.

"Annika, I—"

"Morning!" Hanna's voice interrupts me, and I'm slightly annoyed. But at the same time, a little thankful.

We haven't known each other for that long. I have no idea if what I'm feeling is the result of our forced proximity, cooped up in this—granted, large—villa, or if it's all real. There's this sense inside me like I want her for the rest of my life, but is it real? What about her, does she share the sentiment? Can she trust it? Or is she going through the same erratic trains of thought as I am?

"Morning." I turn to Hanna, swallowing my worries for now.

She's wearing what is clearly my brother's t-shirt, and he shows up right behind her, in nothing but his joggers. Thank God I take care of myself and have a fairly fit body, because otherwise I would have quite a complex next to him looking like a damn surfer-boy with his sun-kissed, toned form, and wild blond curls. I am a little jealous that Annika is witnessing this.

I look down and catch her gaze on him, lingering after she says good morning, before she turns her attention back to the painting. Okay, maybe I'm a bit more than a little jealous.

Hanna takes a seat on the other side of the table, and I join Finn in the kitchen, fiddling with a pot of coffee as he pulls some ingredients out of the fridge.

"This storm better be easing soon, because we're quite low on food. These are the last ones." He places a half empty carton of eggs on the gray granite countertop.

"I'll just have some granola and yogurt. There's still plenty of that," I say.

"Actually, I could go for some of that as well," Annika says without turning her head from the canvas, and Hanna signals that she would like that too.

"Three to one, I guess. Enjoy your eggs." I turn to Finn, and he seems pleased. He's always been well taken care of, not that he doesn't know the value of money, but he's never really been in a situation where food was running low and there was no indication of when the next meal would be.

I hope he will never be.

I take bowls, yogurt, and granola to the table, while Finn makes an omelet for himself, and brings the coffee over.

"Any news on when this storm is supposed to finish?" Hanna asks.

"Why? Are you in a hurry to run away from me, darling?" Finn slides in the seat next to her, pinching her chin and pulling her to him.

"Yup."

He laughs, and she playfully rolls her eyes. I'm not sure what to make of this, but my brother's eyes are awfully sparkly.

"Forecast said that it should have eased off today. Obviously, that's not the case.

So hopefully in max two or three days, it will be over. We'll have to check if our boat is still whole, but honestly, I doubt it."

"I'm not gonna cry about it," Finn adds. "It was a fairly cheap speedboat."

"You'll give us a ride back to Queenscove, right?" I nudge Annika, and she smiles.

"Can I think about it?"

"No."

She laughs and shakes her head.

"Ours—well, our rental, is in the boathouse. So hopefully there's no damage," Hanna says.

"One of the other guys will come and get us if not. No worries there," Finn reassures them.

"You're coming with us after the storm anyway," I add, watching as Annika turns to face me with a lifted brow.

"Are we now?" She asks in a high tone, dropping her canvas and paintbrush on the table.

"Well, you're no longer in your house, you're running out of supplies here, and I... umm... I want you there."

"You don't sound very convincing, brother."

I feel the need to eradicate that amusement with a punch. Maybe a kick in the teeth to wipe that pretty smile off his face.

"Fuck you!"

"We can temporarily rent our own place," Annika says, laughing at us.

"Waste of money. Especially since you've had to refund us for that painting," I joke.

"Funny. But I have plenty left." She smirks.

Does she not want to spend more time with me? I can't figure out if she thinks she's imposing, or we really aren't on the same wavelength.

"We'll talk about it later."

Even if this discussion affects her friend, this is between Annika and me. There's this feral need I'm having an inner fight with, one that wants to throw her over my shoulder, haul her ass into my penthouse, and keep her there. But at the same time I have to remind myself I'm not a caveman, and I have to let this be her choice. None of those sides are winning right now, so I would rather wait to have this talk when it's just us two.

"Anni, your painting is gorgeous! So different." Hanna finally looks at her friend's work of art.

"Yeah, real different, actually. At least from the one you left for my brother," Finn adds, winking at her.

I really will punch him.

"I've been meaning to ask actually" Finn continues. "Did you just randomly haul around a self-portrait of yourself, or did you paint it in that short week?"

"I started it a while ago, but never felt the need to finish it. It felt a bit narcissistic to randomly have a portrait of myself in my house. This... situation..." she says as her haze flickers to me, "gave me the incentive to finish it."

"How convenient." My brother snickers, and I feel the need to move on. Talking about me or us feels oddly uncomfortable.

"How did you end up doing what you do?" I finally begin eating my yogurt, waiting for one of them to start.

"Well, we're done now. Your job was the last one. Although considering Annika's change of plans, the previous one was technically the last one." Hanna speaks first. "Starting it just kind of happened. It was one of those crazy ideas, like when you get drunk with your friends, and you start saying that you should all open a bar or something. It was kind of like that. I was watching Hanna in her restoration classes, and I was joking that she would be an amazing forger."

"I think we can relate, since we did exactly that—opened a bar with our friends." Finn laughs.

"You have a bar?" Annika turns to me, and I realize that all this time, we've been talking about us and her, not much about me. She's far more intriguing to talk about, though.

"You didn't pay full attention to the background check I showed you, Anni, did you?" Hanna crosses her arms over her chest, leaning back into her chair as she watches her friend with a quirked eyebrow.

"Umm... yes, sure I did. I guess I forgot."

"Or I made the mistake of showing you a photo of Ronan before I showed you all the important bits."

Well, damn if I don't feel good knowing that I was such a distraction for her.

"We both went to the Hardwin Institute of Art. She was a year older than me, but I don't know, we just clicked. I was in Restoration, and she was in Art History," Annika tries changing the subject.

"Yeah, Carter uncovered as much." I nod.

"I guess we just saw potential in one another. A different purpose than all the future starving artists channeling their inner DaVinci around us."

"It's quite a leap, though, isn't it? The life of a painter to a life of crime?" I ask. It's not necessarily that, but the fact that Annika's personality is a contrast to this type of life.

"It was a leap, but I gladly made it. I don't know how to explain it. I didn't know back then either. There was this need inside of me that kept screaming for more. I was the shy one, not because I don't have courage, but because the opportunities around me didn't seem to fit what I truly wanted. The moment I was presented with the prospect of forging a painting for our first deal, I ate up that adrenaline like it was my first meal after starvation."

"You were restless," Hanna says, nodding. "For days at the time, you weren't sleeping. All you wanted to do was paint."

"I really was. I've always been introverted, never put myself in any uncomfortable or simply different situations. The idea that I had to stand quietly during a shady business deal, watch someone analyze my painting, then get away with the con, gave me a sensation like no other. Obviously bypassing the whole starving artist phase of my career was a bonus too," Annika says with a giggle, and it pulls a strange reaction out of me. An endearing smile... and isn't that just a little bit too close for comfort.

"You craved the thrill..." I comment, remembering our conversation from the waterfall.

"I did. It felt like a different persona. I craved to bring her forth—me... you know what I mean. It was like sliding over a mask over my usual shyness."

Seeing her blush, I tug her to me, and she nestles into my side. As she melts into my comfort, I drop a quick kiss to her forehead. I'm just glad that whole journey brought her to me.

Only this seems to be a slippery slope. I keep sliding down further and the rabbit hole is in my sight. I'm losing myself and it's only been a few days. Well... technically, it's been a few days trapped in the same house, in the same bedroom with her. But she's been haunting my dreams and crawling under my skin since the moment I laid eyes on her.

Being in this house, unable to even go out for a walk, completely glued to one another, is both incredible and terrifying.

Is this real? This weird warmth spreading like liquid fire between my ribs, pulsing with every beat of my heart whenever she simply smiles at me? Or the ache that makes my hands tingle whenever she's out of reach?

I want her more than I've wanted anything in my whole goddamn life. Even when she's right next to me, she's not close enough. I ache with the need to crawl under her skin, feel her every moment of every day. Have her steel gaze on me, enjoy that wicked smile. I want my cock inside of her at all times, her tongue in my mouth, her soft hands caressing my skin. She redefines addiction and it fucking scares me.

Four days brought me to this point. God knows what will happen to me by the time this storm ends.

CHAPTER 9
Annika

AFTER A WHOLE week trapped in the storm, the background noise of the seaside city of Queenscove is like a sweet lullaby. We arrived yesterday afternoon on the boat Hanna and I rented, which luckily survived the storm. Ronan's speedboat didn't. It was shattered, laying all sad a bit too far from the shore.

The island seemed to be in fairly good condition, and we left a lot of our stuff there since, technically, our visit to the city is only temporary. I tell myself that I plan on staying just a bit longer than needed to refill our supplies, only to appease Ronan. I'm kidding myself. I know it's not true. I want more time with him, but there's this nagging voice in my head reminding me this is temporary—I'm leaving soon.

Although as I watch Ronan shift all the clothes in his walk-in wardrobe to make room for mine, then empty two drawers, I have a feeling he has something different in mind.

"I don't need that much space, Ronan. I barely have any clothes with me. A drawer will be fine."

But the man simply turns his head, gives me a smile that appeases my obvious delusion, and carries on with his task. He finishes and comes to me, sliding his hands over my hips until they settle on my ass and pulls me to him.

"Are you sure you're okay with me being out all day? I feel bad. It's your first proper day here, with me, and I get pulled away for business. I just... I need to catch up with the guys, and we have some meetings I can't miss."

"It's okay, Ronan, I survived just fine without you, you know."

In reality, I'm not so sure I'm okay with it. Not because I want him with me, but because staying with him in his lavish penthouse, sleeping in his bedroom while he goes to work, seems far too close to real life. Our island bubble burst; we're no longer trapped in this fever dream. This is real life... and he's welcomed me right into it.

I know I signed up for this thing with Ronan but, honestly, I didn't think past the chase, past the adventure, past the thrill of it all. It never crossed my mind that this could be more than sex.

But here I am, standing in this ravishing man's walk-in closet, my smell all over his sheets, the painting of myself that I left for him leaned against the wall of his bedroom, and my future doesn't seem to be in my hands anymore.

"You're doing that thing where you get lost in your thoughts," he says, bringing me back to the now.

I scrunch my eyebrows. *Thing?*

"What thing?!"

"You look right through me, narrowing your eyes like you're calculating the world's most difficult physics formula."

"Oh."

He cocks his head, and I can tell he wants to ask more. Obviously, he's noticed this expression on me before, and I wonder if I do it every time I think about the future. Is that what he wants to ask me?

"So you'll be gone all day?"

He pulls his lower lip between his teeth, sighing almost silently before he finally answers.

"I'll pick you up at seven. We have a reservation."

"Oh, that sounds nice. Restaurant?"

"Yeah, nice one, up on the hill."

"Sounds like it will be our first date." I feel the heat in my cheeks. Why, though? We've already slept together—many, many times.

"We could do a movie too, if you want to keep it classic." He laughs, his features brightening up all at once as he gazes at me from under his low eyebrows, the uptilt toward the temples giving him a mischievous quality. Even with the slight crook of his otherwise straight nose, the godlike beauty of this man makes me weak in the knees.

"Next time." I wrap my hands around his neck, pulling him down to me and pressing a long, soft kiss to his full lips.

We sink into ourselves, deep enough that his hands are now kneading my ass, rolling my cheeks and making me a whole mess between my thighs. His brother's voice startles us into reality, calling him. Ronan swears against my lips, nibbling at my lips as I start laughing.

His erection is now blatantly visible against the dark blue suit trousers, and he gives me a menacing look when I shrug and start backing away into the bedroom.

"Work is calling, baby," I tease.

"I might let it *ring* a little longer."

He's about to pounce on me, when a knock sounds on the door and Finn's voice comes through.

"*Did you hear me? We got to go, Carter just called.*"

"Coming! Give me a minute!" he shouts back.

He's readjusting his cock, and I didn't realize I was licking my lips until his eyes turned hungry on them.

"Okay. So, I'm going to go to the bathroom, because at this rate, you will never leave this bedroom," I say, going to him to press a quick peck on his cheek before I scurry away. "See you at seven."

I shut the door behind me, locking it before I flatten my back to it, exhaling so loudly I'm sure he heard me from the other side.

What did I get myself into?

* * *

Hanna looks at me with an inquisitive gaze as she holds the straw of her cocktail between her slender fingers.

It's already our fourth day here and we're still nowhere close to doing what we came here for—restocking our supplies for Bovely Island. We've been out on a couple of dates, a few times with the rest of the guys too, and today, Hanna and I have been exploring more of Queenscove. Still, neither of us has mentioned even once anything about when our time here will end.

We've done a great job of avoiding our reality.

After stopping at the penthouse to change into something a bit more stylish, we decided to go to an outdoor cocktail lounge, close to the beach so we can enjoy the salty breeze of the early evening. Being here outside the context of work is different. With no security with us either. Our guys are gone; we relieved them of their duties when we decided we were going to do this crazy thing... taunt the men of a damn criminal organization.

"You're different, you know," my best friend says, a strange smile on her lips.

"What are you talking about?"

"You look more... settled within yourself. Like your skin fits you better now."

What a strange thing to say.

All I can do is narrow my eyes as I try to understand her words.

She shakes her head and grins.

"I'm excited for Midnight tonight. I've never been to a speakeasy before," she says, her tone turning giddy.

"It will be interesting."

"You seem unsure."

"I guess I am. All the places we've been to with them, apart from the penthouse, have been either chosen by us or have been in public. We've never actually been in their world. This will be different. It will be our first real taste of the men we've been living with for almost two weeks now."

"Anni, it's just a bar," she shakes her head, smirking. "What do you think they'll have there? Thugs and guns everywhere, shady business deals in every corner, piles of cash on every table?"

I smack her forearm and cross my arms.

"Hanna, you know exactly what I mean. Everything we've been experiencing so far was skirting at the edge of it all."

"Well, you better get ready to dive in, because Finn just texted me that they're outside."

I take a deep breath, then down the rest of my Espresso Martini.

"Let's go, then."

I rise, heading through the indoor area of the lounge, Hanna in tow, already catching a glimpse of my man leaning against his sleek black Mercedes, strong arms crossed over his suit-covered chest, watching me from beyond the glass doors.

Jesus fuck, he's sexy.

I don't miss the two women who slowed down right in front of me as they were walking on the sidewalk, their eyes fixed on Ronan, their short, tight dresses suddenly riding just a bit higher. But the man cocks his head to look right past them, a wicked smile on his lips as he extends his hand to me. Only I seem to notice how the women look at me in mild shock, flip their hair over their shoulders, and quicken their steps.

"Hello, stranger."

Placing my hand in his, I let him pull me against him, his other hand sinking into my hair, crushing me onto his lips, devouring me like he's been hungry all day.

When we break apart, I look over to my right, to where Finn opens the door to his own car for Hanna, and I can't help but catch a glimpse of the two women who passed by. They look positively sour, as they quickly turn back around and keep walking.

It feels good, being the woman others envy. I've never experienced this before.

"What are you snickering about?"

Was I?

"Oh, nothing."

"Shall we go, then?"

I nod as we pull away from each other, and once again he opens the door for me. He's been doing this every time we go somewhere—always opening the door for me. I can't help but wonder if this is a honeymoon phase thing, or if it's simply Ronan.

He slides in the driver's seat, turning on the purring engine of his car, then pulls onto the street after Finn.

"How come you didn't come with only one car?" I ask him.

"We weren't together. I had a meeting, and he was closing a deal out of town."

"Out of town?"

"Yeah, Levane, a city about an hour and a half away. He only just came back now, so we ended up synchronizing."

"I'm still not fully sure I understand how your organization operates."

I look at him, trying to see in his expression if by any chance I crossed a line by asking.

"What do you want to know?" He reaches over, wrapping his large palm around my leg, giving it a slight squeeze.

Focus, Annika, focus.

But his fingers tickling my inner thigh in his possessive hold are replacing all my thoughts with filthy fantasies.

It's just a hand, Annika. Pull yourself together, for God's sake.

Tell that to my pussy. She didn't get the message.

"Little witch?" He glances over when I don't respond, trying to keep his eyes on the road.

"So, it's you, Finnigan, Vincent, Carter, and Maddox, but who's the actual leader?"

"None of us. That was the whole point when this all came together. We didn't exactly plan it this way, but it was a natural progression. Obviously they're five-six years younger than me, so we didn't start at the same time, but we lead together. Each with our own set of skills."

"Were you the first?"

"Kind of, but not in the way you think. I decided not to go to university, and I went into the family business instead. Not because I wanted to follow in my parents' footsteps, but because I wanted to learn. Then a few years ago, I took over a strip club that sort of landed in their laps when they purchased a building here in the city. I pitched an idea, asked for a small investment from them with a promise of a return with interest. Not that they needed the money, but it was for my ego. I transformed it into a luxury gentlemen's club that turned very profitable, from more points of view than one."

He pauses for a moment as he takes a turn away from the main boulevard we were on.

"More points of view?" I ask, curiosity spiking.

"First, I started getting into the black market, using every bit of profit from the club, after paying back my parents, and with time, we were dealing in more and more expensive pieces. Finn and the guys were always around. I'm not sure how they found each other, but I swear menace attracts menace, because they compliment each other so fucking well. Finn wanted in before he was even eighteen. I refused, but he didn't give a shit. I wanted something better, legal, for his future, but I couldn't get rid of him. The compromise was that he had to at least try and go to university. So he followed Carter there. Madds and Vin stayed here. Two businesses evolved from the club—an escort service, that's run by an associate, and information. Vincent was most attracted to the former. Anyway, it all went from there, and here we are, still early in the journey, but fuck, we've been through some shit."

"I didn't know you owned an escort service."

We're driving behind a building, still close to the city center, and we seem to be slowing down in a parking lot that doesn't really look like anything special.

"Some cards we keep very close to our chests and the escort service is one of them. Nobody knows it's ours. We try to keep it way in the background, because the escort service is a front. They're all basically trained to extract information. People get stupid and reckless when they see a pretty thing or they're horny. So we take advantage of that. Whoever sees us with one of the girls and recognizes her, they just think we hired them for the night just as they do."

"What do you do with all that information?"

He presses on the breaks as he swiftly pulls into a space, his eyes fixed on me, the look in them darker than I've known it.

"We use it."

This is where the insight ends—on a chilling note that leaves me with even more questions. Only, I think I should stay ignorant to the answers, because I have a suspicion this is where the violent side of their business begins.

He gives my thigh another squeeze, then captures my chin between his thumb and index fingers, then pulls me to him until his lips meet mine. He kisses me breathless, and before he lets me go, he swipes his tongue over my top lip, like he's getting one more taste. I'm not sure what this man does to me, but I would spread myself open on a platter for him so he can keep going.

He slides out of the car, walks over to my side, and helps me out of my seat, guiding me toward a metal door that looks like the entrance to the building's boiler room, not a fancy bar. Another car pulls into the parking lot and Finn and Hanna come out, heading our way with great big smiles on their faces. She looks so damn happy.

"I was expecting one of those tiny sliding doors and a thug looking through it," I tell Ronan.

He laughs and scans a card against a panel I didn't notice, then presses his finger to it.

"This is the back entrance."

"So you have that at the front?!"

"Something like that."

I follow him through a corridor, then another, then through a door to what feels like another world. Slow, deep music fills the space that smells of wood, leather, and expensive cigars. There's a decadence to this place I've never experienced anywhere else. The wallpapered and wood-paneled walls are covered in paintings and vintage decor, dim lamps strategically placed in the space, lighting it in just the right way, hiding some of the faces who are filling the seats. I love that the wooden tables are not all the same. There's a mixture of coffee, dining, and bar height tables, and every chair and sofa is mismatched, adorned in expensive, dark-colored leathers.

But the bar is a work of art and it draws my attention instantly. It's pulled right out of the twenties with its wood, marble, and gold accents. Right behind it, in the center of the wall, there is a gold décor piece made entirely of thin metal strips. Lines that form a starburst, surround the shape of an eye, all inside a circle. It's very stylized, in the nineteen-twenties elegance—apart from the eyeball itself. It looks so incredibly real, you would swear it's watching, following you around the room. It's beauty is slightly unsettling.

Everything in here seems to be left over from the art deco era and it got infused with southern blues vibes.

"I think I'm in love..." I almost whisper, marveling at the beauty of it.

"Thank you."

Carter shows up out of nowhere, giving a courtesy nod, his features as straight as ever, but I swear I can see a trace of a smile on those lips.

"The speakeasy was Carter's idea, same as the decor," Ronan explains.

I can see why. The man looks like he belongs here, with his slicked back hair and undercut, shirt with sleeves rolled up to his elbows, and tailored suit trousers and waistcoat.

"It really is beautiful. It's nice to see you again, Carter." I think I'm lying. I'm not sure, though. It's not like I dislike him, but I'm slightly terrified of him.

We follow him to the back of the locale to a more private area, dodging the curious looks some of the patrons give us—or me. Talking of terrifying, Vincent Sinclair is right there, sitting next to Maddox at a dining table. He's dressed in all black from shoes to shirt, matching his hair and eyes, and a chill runs down my spine at the sight. I have no idea what to make of him. I can't hold his gaze for too long. If Carter's is empty, devoid of humanity, Vincent's is filled with promises of peril. I don't think he trusts me either.

I did steal his money—albeit I did return it, but still.

I take a seat next to Hanna as Maddox pushes toward me a matte black menu with foiled gold accents. The attention to detail in this place tickles all my artistic senses.

We fall into chatter, talking amongst ourselves as the guys seem to have been getting more comfortable having us around, since we returned from the island. I've been more intrigued by Ronan; observing him in this environment has given me a different perspective on him. His shoulders are more pulled back, his head held a little higher, his features more stern. Even now, in what's supposed to be a familiar and comfortable environment for him, he doesn't carry himself the same as he does with me in private, or how he did on the island. I like this side of him. I like both, but seeing him so stern and serious, goddamnit if I don't lo—like him even more.

Christ.

"Excuse me," he says, kissing my forehead before he rises, disappearing behind me.

Maybe five minutes pass, and Hanna interrupts our conversation, leaning in.

"Jesus, who are those two talking to your man?"

I turn my head to the bar, trying to be as discreet as possible, but failing miserably when my eyes land on two of the most beautiful women I've ever seen. Both of them are tall, gorgeous, and elegant. They're a true vision. Ronan is in a fairly intense discussion with the older one of the two, a stunning redhead with a short bob haircut, while the other has turned her attention to the bartender.

"I don't know," I finally respond to her.

I wish I did though, because there's this burning sensation in my chest, and god dammit if it doesn't feel dangerously close to jealousy. But my insecurities are the ones that are more prevalent right now—I look nothing like her. I'm close to asking myself—and him—what the fuck I'm doing here.

He looks so comfortable and familiar with her. She belongs. In this world, in this space, next to him. I don't.

When she turns her head, her gaze lands directly on me, like she knows my thoughts are of her. Her expression is blank, utterly unreadable, but in such a natural way that it's chilling. It doesn't falter when she sees me watching her, unable to stop. With a woman as beautiful as her, I expect the air of superiority, but it never comes.

She briefly brings her attention back to Ronan, nodding her head once, before they both turn and start walking. In this direction. *My* direction.

I'm slightly nauseous. I can't explain why. Maybe because this could have just been a beautiful dream, and I'm about to find out he has a wife at home who's about to kick my ass out of his life. She has that look about her that tells me she might not be above slitting my throat here, in the middle of this bar.

Finn catches my attention as he slides next to Hanna and says something that seems to go right past my ears.

Ronan and the mystery woman, who looks even more stunning up close, are right in front of us now. They look so comfortable together. Like they've been around each other for years.

"Ekaterina, this is Annika. My girlfriend."

My... what now?!

She extends her hand to me, a prim, elegant smile pulling very gently at the corners of her lips. I push the chair back and rise, capturing her hand and giving it a gentle shake.

"It's a pleasure to meet you, Annika. I've heard quite a bit about you."

The expression in her eyes is warm in such a strange, rigid way. I would have thought she mocks, but no... she looks at Ronan in the same way.

"Oh... it's nice to meet you too."

"Ekaterina is our associate. If you remember our conversation from the car."

It takes me a minute, but eventually, the wheels click into place.

"Associate, yes. Sorry, Ronan didn't mention your name then." Or the fact that their associate who runs the escort service is a woman.

I guess it makes sense. But there's still a tinge of jealousy pulling at my heartstrings. She just smiles, shaking Hanna's hand now as Finn introduces them.

A conversation starts, but I'm not talking. I hear none of it. Ronan doesn't speak either. His head cocked, a questioning gaze aimed right at me. He holds it, yet neither of us speaks. It's intense, growing its own heartbeat I can hear inside of me. Thumping from his blue eyes to mine, grazing my skin with goosebumps from the inside out, my nipples turning to sharp points, my belly fluttering, my core clenching on itself.

A flush heats my cheeks when he leans in, his lips against my ear, the heat of his breath traveling into my soul.

"I've never found jealousy enticing until it painted your blue-gray eyes in such vivid strokes. It makes my cock twitch to sink so deep into your cunt, I'll fuck all the threads of doubt out of you."

My lips part, eyes widening, as he pulls away and straightens, his composure unbroken, completely nonchalant like he didn't just fill my mind with filth and my pussy with desire.

"Annika, do you want another one?"

I'm startled back into this world when Hanna touches my shoulder.

"Sorry?"

"Another drink?" she asks again.

I turn to find a server smiling at me.

"Actually, just water for me. With a couple of slices of lemon, please."

He nods and walks away. Between the two of us, Hanna is the cocktail drinker. I'll have one once in a while if it's a nice place that does special ones. Other than that I don't bother.

"I hope you all have a good evening. I'm going to go back to my meeting," Ekaterina says, nodding to all of us.

We all sit back down after saying goodbye to her.

"So, do they even know about this bar?" Hanna directs the question at Finn, but lifts a curious eyebrow at me like I'm supposed to know what the hell she's talking about. My mind is still reeling from Ronan's words.

"Who?" I ask.

"Finn and Ronan's parents."

Oh. We haven't actually spoken about them. Only mentioned in passing.

"No. We stay out of their businesses, and they stay out of ours," Finn answers.

I turn to Ronan. "Do they know what you do?"

He takes a sip of the amber drink the server just brought over, and his expression turns serious. More so than I've ever seen before in his features.

"They have some knowledge, but in our business, the less they know, the better for all of us. That way, no one can be accused of anything, be implicated, or held accountable."

"Well, if that's not cryptic, I'm not sure what is," I say, eyebrows furrowing.

"Let's just say our parents have never been your typical involved parents. We grew up with a bunch of nannies, chefs, and drivers while our parents skirted at the edge of the law and every tax paradise out there, adding more and more buildings and businesses to their portfolio."

"It sounds... cold." I can't imagine living like that, being cared for by strangers, without my parents' warmth or love. Yet there isn't even a trace of sadness or longing in his eyes when he talks of these things... it's all he knows.

"It was, in most ways. Their involvement was different. They always made sure we had access to every opportunity. They provided, and took care of us, even disciplined us, but... parenting wasn't quite their thing," Ronan tells us.

"No, we didn't learn many things from them," Finnigan continues. "Except that when it comes to business, turn a blind eye, unless it concerns you. Catherine and Christian Hennessey are quite the pair. To this day, I'm not convinced they actually love us."

"They do. In their own, detached way," Ronan states, unconvinced.

"If you say so. I think that if you died, they would just send me a condolences card." Finnigan says with a laugh, and my curiosity spikes further.

"Where are they?" I ask.

"Not quite sure. They decided to retire early, selling most of their businesses and holding on mainly to the passive ones, like real estate. They've been traveling ever since. Last I talked to them, they were on a yacht somewhere on the North Coast." Ronan shrugs.

"Sounds like a pretty good life."

I'm not sure what else I can say. I never gave kids a serious thought, but birthing two just to have nothing to do with them at all from birth to... well, now, is a bit odd. Cruel even.

He smiles and wraps his hand around my thigh under the table, his fingers running higher and higher, my pulse too.

"I think it sounds like we need to stop talking about our parents and head home," he says with a smile and a quirked eyebrow.

Home.

Only, I'm not so sure it's mine.

CHAPTER 10
Annika

I WAKE UP submerged in a sheer darkness, slithers of sunlight breaking through the cracks of the blinds that haven't been rolled down all the way. His scent surrounds every fiber of my being, the same as it has for days now. No. More than that. Has it been more than a week since we've been here? It feels like it.

Actually, it feels more like a lifetime.

The moment he came to the island feels far enough away in my past that a future with him is becoming more vivid. It's not that far at all... a few weeks. But it hasn't stopped him from crawling beneath every fiber of my being, clutching onto each delicate thread that forms me, and making it part of him.

It's fucking terrifying.

He's turning my world upside down, and I have nothing to hold on to. Except for him.

How could I have something to clutch when I've been a nomad for years? I have my family... somewhere on this continent. But my only rock, the only constant in my life, is spinning right along with me. She's currently sleeping on the other side of this penthouse, with the brother of the one currently sliding his hand over my bare belly, pulling me into him.

The softness of his skin against my back sends shivers straight into my skull, ridding all those thoughts that made me doubt, made me question us. Everything about him feels like it belongs with me. Even with the mind of an artist, I'm still seeking the logic in what's happening. Only, I can't find it. It makes no sense.

Maybe I am a witch, like he keeps telling me.

Maybe this is a spell I put on both of us, not just him.

Maybe it's the black magic making us lose ourselves to each other.

Maybe I want to be blind to it, because usually if it's too good to be true... *it's too good.*

"Mmm..." I hum as I press myself against his bare chest.

His hand slides up from my belly, between my breasts, until it reaches the base of my throat, settling there. It puts a pressure on my airways that grows from the inside out, in my lips, my flushed cheeks, and right under my tired eyes as my pulse seems to slow.

"Good morning," I whisper on a raspy breath.

"There's no such thing as a bad one waking up next to you." He says it like he's admitting that to himself, not me.

Holy hell!

His voice in the morning is like raw honey laced with hunger. The vibrations of it run through me like the links of zipper, splitting me apart. He's my undoing.

"If there will ever be, please keep holding me like this, but squeeze my throat harder."

He growls in my ear, and I'm suddenly rolled onto my belly as he straddles me, his cock slapping against my bare ass, sending a shudder straight to my core.

"I promise." His breath tickles my ear as he drops on his forearm next to me.

A warm hand palms my ass cheeks, kneading and spreading them open as it dives down, reaches my folds and parts them with skillful digits that make my hips shoot up. He drives inside of me without warning, his cock twitching against my back, and I get wet so damn fast, I'm convinced the man found an "ON" button inside of me.

"Always so damn ready for me, my fingers, for my cock..."

I'm starting to think he could just snap his fingers and I would be an instant, soaking mess.

All I can seem to do is moan, drawn out, soft... as I sink into the warmth of him, into his slow, deep thrusts. *This* is fucking magic.

He pulls those digits out of me, and I expect his cock to replace them. Instead, he brushes them on my lips, the smell of my pussy oddly arousing. Sliding them into my mouth, he presses on my tongue...

And a very annoying sound pulls us out of this spell. His phone rings on the nightstand, but he ignores it until it stops. Only, it starts again immediately after, and he sighs as he stretches to grab it without getting off me.

"This better be good."

His muscles tense against me, most definitely not in a good way.

There's too much silence. He's listening too intently.

"Where is he?"

He slowly shifts off me, and I roll over to see him. With every second, the frown lines on his forehead deepen. His eyes flash to me, but avert quickly enough that something strange grows in the pit of my stomach.

"How much time do we have?"

I can't put my finger on it, but it reminds me that the man next to me is not just any man—he's part of an underworld I know almost nothing about.

"Ten. Yes. Bye."

He turns completely, throwing his legs off the bed, rising into a sitting position, and sighs heavily as he runs his fingers through his soft blond hair. I want to ask, but I'm not sure where we stand when it comes to his business, talking about it. I don't want to intrude or be nosy. More importantly, do I want to know?

"We have to talk." He turns to me, his gaze not just serious, but it looks somewhere close to being unhinged, cutting off my thoughts.

That answers it—I want to know.

"What happened?"

"Let's get dressed. We need to get Finn and Hanna."

"Ronan, what the hell is going on? Why do we need them?!"

I crawl next to him, sitting on my knees on the bed, not just suspicious, but uneasy down to the bones. This is about me. Hanna as well? He captures my chin between his thumb and index, pulling my lips to his, dropping a quick, but deep kiss.

"Get dressed." He orders me before he rises and disappears in his closet. Moments later, he has sweatpants on, hanging low on his hips, the elastic of his boxers showing just above, then he slides a white t-shirt on.

"Now, Annika. I'm gonna go get them and bring them to the kitchen. Wait there."

I take a deep breath in, and it seems to get lodged in my lungs until the bedroom door shuts behind him.

"What the hell is happening?"

I make quick work of pulling some leggings and a t-shirt on and all but run to the living area.

Faint voices sound on the other side of the penthouse, the whole place split in two with the living area in the middle, Ronan's side to the right and Finnigan's to the left.

They own the whole building—well, technically, his parents do, but my understanding is that this particular building has been transferred to the brothers. It's a skyscraper reminiscent of the golden age but modernized.

I busy myself with the espresso machine and begin making some coffee, instead of spiraling into my own thoughts.

Before I turn, I already know Ronan came into the kitchen. He's quick, sidling up next to me, one hand around my waist, sorting his own coffee with the other one. He kisses my forehead without a word, giving me a bit of reassurance.

He guides me to the dining table and sits next to me just as Hanna and Finnigan appear, dressed comfortably, but sleepy and confused. At least Hanna is. Finnigan seems to carry the same sort of hard expression as his brother. It looks even more strange on the man who seems to be eternally happy and easygoing.

The morning sun streams through the huge floor-to-ceiling windows, a contrast to the silent, yet heavy atmosphere. Dread has closed in around me, my chest tight as Ronan sets his forearms on the table, clutching his hands together.

"What's happened?" Hanna speaks first.

It's almost like I'm back in our business meetings, craving to blend in with background. It's not an option now, though, with Ronan's eyes fixed on me.

"You said once that you keep tabs on the people who have bought paintings from you," Finnigan responds, his serious tone making me even more nervous.

"I do... yes."

"Have you heard anything?"

The moment the question lands, Hanna's expression is a mixture of annoyance, dread, and shock. She only manages to shake her head... but we both already know what's coming.

"We're not the only ones who found out about the forged paintings." His words clutch my lungs and rip them straight out of my chest.

I'm frozen, unable to look Hanna in the eyes anymore.

What have I done?

Ronan

"WHAT DO YOU mean? Have you told someone?" Hanna finally manages to ask, disbelief in her tone.

Finn repeats what Carter told us before we went to the island. That someone powerful is looking for two women who match their descriptions, regarding an art deal struck some time ago.

"That can't be... I would have heard something."

Hanna's eyes become slightly vacant, searching deep into her memories.

"It's my fault. I've done something... I've screwed it up," Annika says, wrapping her arms around herself, her gaze fixed on the dining table, as she gently shakes her head.

An urgent knock on the door interrupts us, and Finn rushes to answer it as we all turn to see who's arrived. Vin, Carter and Madds walk through, keeping the pleasantries brief as they sit around the table. Carter is opening the laptop he brought with him, his fingers sliding fast over the keyboard.

"It's not you." Hanna rubs Annika's back, trying to soothe her shaking as I squeeze her thigh. "I should have heard something. I didn't look hard enough."

I wish I could say their enemy and his team are so good at what they do, that they made sure she wouldn't find out they're looking for them. But the guys and I talked about this... whoever these people are, they're not hiding. Even if they've kept their enquiries within a tight circle, the message is clear—*I'm coming for you.*

"No," Annika continues. "I should have been more careful. I must have..." she trails off, that soft bottom lip trembling slightly, and there's this deep-seated need inside of me to wrap her in my arms, comfort her. But unfortunately... there's more.

"Please stop. We always knew this was a risk. We both understood this right from the start. Even if we weren't fully ready, we knew there was a big chance someone could find out at any point in the transaction or after it." Hanna grabs her friend by the shoulders, forcing her to look at her.

"But that doesn't change—"

"It does, Annika! This is not on you!" Hanna raises her voice, but pain still settles in her friend's features.

"It really isn't on you." Carter's calm tone forces a tense silence in the room, all eyes snapping to him. He stops typing, lacing his fingers together as he settles his forearms on the table and turns to the girls. "There was no mistake in the painting. That's not how he found out it is a fake."

"How then?" Hanna asks.

"The original was found."

"Jesus Christ," Annika mutters under her breath. "Which one?"

"The Punishment of Innocents by—"

"Gravano!" Annika's chair grunts painfully as she abruptly pushes back, the look in her eyes one of utter terror that I can't fucking bear to witness.

"Little—" I go to touch her, but she's breaking away.

"You're wrong. You're wrong!" She raises her voice in panic. "It's not possible. If it was, the art world would have gone mad over this. It's a Gravano, for fuck's sake! No, you're fucking lying!" She's almost shouting now, pleading with Carter to reveal the lie, the mistake, anything but let this be the truth. The color has drained from her face, building inside of me a rage I never thought I could feel.

"What the fuck did he do to you, Annika?!" I seethe, already plotting the death of a man I don't even know by name.

She ignores me. Hanna turns to her, and I notice now that she doesn't look better at all.

"We'll b—be okay. You'll see. We'll be fine."

What's even more unsettling is the fact that, for the first time since meeting her, I can see that Hanna doesn't believe a single word she speaks, her usual confidence gone. Annika glances at her, almost wide-eyed—she doesn't believe her either.

"Annika," I warn, "fucking tell me. Did he touch you?!"

She finally turns to me and shakes her head.

Fuck. Me. I let out a loud breath and turn to Carter.

"Who?"

"Roberto Bartiste. He works in shipment far from here, right on the East Coast. But from what I gather, he's been expanding his business. He has power, taking over more and more territory."

"Shipment. Drugs?"

"Amongst other things, drugs. But that's not his main business and not the one he appears to be expanding. It's—"

"People," Annika finishes for him. "He is a human trafficker. Something he is... highly passionate about."

I grip the leg of her chair and attempt to pull it to me, but she plants her feet on the ground, pushing back and standing.

"We have to go. Run," she says with urgency, turning to her friend.

But her words are ringing in my ears. *Run.* Away from me.

"No."

She whips her head to face me as I utter that word, a fear in her expression that I'm not sure I can soothe.

"Sit down, Annika." I grab her wrist, and she stills.

"You don't understand. If this is true, if Bartiste is coming for us, we can't just stay here."

I shake my head as she tries to rip her wrist out of my hold. I pull her until she's standing right next to me, my arm wrapped around her hips, holding her tight.

"Annika..." I both warn and comfort her, meeting the challenge in her steel-blue eyes. The submission prevails, her gaze drops, and she leans into me slightly, before sliding back down on the chair.

"What do you know? Why hasn't the world found out about the real painting being found?" Hanna asks.

"Bartiste is keeping the information under wraps. He's on a mission, and part of that might be to protect his reputation," Vincent answers, speaking for the first time since he walked in.

"Mission?"

"To find you. He wants you to pay, and I don't think it's money he wants."

Annika trembles at his words, and once again I wonder who the hell this man is.

"Your multiple identities probably slowed him down. The Lady in White going out for auction might have been his last lead," Carter continues. "I'm not sure what resources he has to find you, but all I've seen so far suggests he has very deep pockets. He's close. Too close."

"Oh, he has plenty of resources." Hanna sighs, and Annika just retires within herself, her gaze almost vacant.

"Does he know they're here?" Finn asks.

"Put it this way, he's left the East Coast, heading south."

"Fuck... Okay. Can he be bought?"

"We can try, but I guarantee that money's not going to stir this guy. Men like him go to extremes when their ego is played with. Pride and reputation sit above all else," Vincent chimes in.

"We have to run," Annika insists.

"No!" My voice comes out as a growl this time. This idea she keeps pushing irritates me now.

"You don't understand, Ronan, this man... he can't find us," Hanna tries to reason with me, her wide eyes pleading.

"How exactly did you get into business with him? I thought you vetted everyone beforehand," I ask her, yet my eyes stay on Annika, who looks paler by the second.

"Our contact was an art dealer. Not uncommon. Trying to figure out who the buyer was turned no results, but their client list looked fairly safe. We agreed to keep working with them, and everything went smoothly, as it usually did, until the day we closed. Buyers always left these things to their dealers... but *he* came. It was too late for us to back out once we realized who he was." She pauses, taking a deep breath and rubbing her eyes. "He took a liking to us. Annika, in particular. This man... he speaks in constant threats, and the one he gave Annika, concerning the authenticity of the painting, was bad. Sexual trafficking bad."

Before Hanna speaks the last word, Annika pushes her chair back violently, ripping away from me, her hand on her mouth as she sprints away into the corridor. I'm already on my feet, but Hanna stops me and follows her.

"We have to help them," Finn says, palpable fear shining in his eyes as he looks at me.

"How deep are you both invested in... them?" Vincent asks, leaning back in his chair, arms crossed over his chest.

I don't miss how Carter cocks an eyebrow at the question, like it's a stupid thing to ask since the obvious is staring us straight in the face.

A part of me is in disbelief at how fast this woman crawled under my skin. It's almost hard to admit it to myself, like it's some sort of weakness. It's been a few weeks, but somehow it feels like eons.

"Deep," I answer in unison with my brother.

"It's a big risk. This could make or break us."

"It better fucking make us. If anything's going to be our mark on the underworld of this city, breaking a man like him will be it. I don't give a shit about a lot of things. I'll deal, blackmail, steal, con, and kill, but human trafficking?! If there is anything our organization has to take a stance against on our goddamn turf, and hopefully beyond, this is it."

"Agreed." Maddox finally speaks, nodding as he looks to Vincent.

"We're moving in different circles right now. Lower risk. We have power, but this will change our reputation," I continue.

"We have to be careful, brother. We are doing this for them, not for our syndicate's benefit. Hanna and Annika are the priority."

Finn looks more concerned than I've ever seen him.

"*We*"—I point between the two of us—"are doing this for them. Our brothers might need more motivation."

"We should be motivation enough," he says with a chilling glare, yet it turns pleading when he turns to them.

I get it, but I think somewhere in my brain, there's a bit of a disconnect between keeping Annika safe and not getting my *brothers* killed for my own selfish reasons.

"We would never leave you in a situation like this." Maddox's expression darkens.

"I'm going to keep Brendan, Tina, and Jian on his tail. We can use CCTV and traffic cams to track him and at least know when he's in town." Carter turns his laptop screen toward us to show what he has so far.

"We'll have men tail him the moment he gets in. I'll keep an eye out and get my hands on one of his guys. That will help us to find out their plan," Vin continues.

"You might not need to. If you can get me one of their phones, I can try to sneak my way through their network. I might find out more that way," Carter adds.

"Can't we do both?" I ask.

There's a pause, and I can almost hear the wheels spinning in their brains.

"Yes, we can." Carter confirms with a nod. "But what about the girls? Is it wise for them to be here while all this goes down?"

I look at my brother, the question lingering between us. I know what I want to do, but I also know what's safer.

"They should stay with us." He speaks first, saying exactly the thing I want, but hearing it confirms my fears.

"I don't think that's the best idea." I counter. If only there was more confidence in my tone of voice.

"But it is."

We all turn at the sound of Hanna's voice, as she and Annika walk back in. They've gained a bit of color back in their complexion, but not near enough for me to stop worrying about my little witch.

"We have to go. This is on us. Our mistake. Our problem. We're not bringing this on you."

"What the fuck, Hanna?" Finn rasps. "Just like that, you want to fucking leave me?"

She shakes her head and smiles, but it doesn't quite reach her eyes. I extend my arm, willing Annika to come to me, and like in a trance, she complies in a heartbeat, sitting back down.

"Of course I don't want to leave you," Hanna replies to my brother. "But I also don't want you to take the fall for us. I can't have any of you hurt."

I pull Annika's chair as close as I can, and she settles into my side, her small hand on my thigh, and I can't help but cover it with mine. Just as I want to cover her, wrap myself around her, and keep her safe forever.

"We can't force you into this, into our mistake." She sighs. "We know Bartiste. It could turn so, so ugly. We cannot be the reason why something happens to you."

"While I appreciate the sentiment, little witch, I'm helping you. Whether you like it or not."

"*We* are helping them," Finn rasps.

"He's right," Maddox says. "We are helping you."

Silence descends upon the room. Annika looks around to all of us with red, tired eyes, worry painted far too vividly within them.

"Thank you. Really, thank you."

"We're still leaving, though," Hanna says. "Anni and I talked about this already. I think we should go back to Bovely Island."

It's not the worst idea. Vin nods, Madds cocks his head, pondering, and Carter's stance is unchanged.

"We'll send as many men as we can spare with them for protection. Bartiste obviously caught a trail to them into Queenscove, but there's a smaller chance for him to be aware of that island. We'll go to old man Bovely, explain to him how important it is to keep his mouth shut, and maybe even take him into hiding to be safe."

"This is absurd!" Finn rages. "How the fuck will they be safe if we're not there to protect them?! It's madness!"

"We have to go..." Annika says to me and me alone. Like she knows that I understand somehow.

"I don't want you to."

"We won't be that far, only Bovely. We can't be in your way. I'll never forgive myself if something happens just because I dragged you into this."

"Annika, baby, you may be a witch, but even you don't have that sort of power over me, the ability to drag me into something I don't feel like doing."

"You gotta be kidding, Ronan!" Finn turns to me now. "Fuck!"

"I'm considering it because there is a big chance Bartiste is unaware of the island. No matter what, we'll go head-to-head with this guy, and we don't know what to expect from him. Not now anyway."

"What if he finds them and we're nowhere near there?!"

"How is it different with him sending his men here while we're out there fighting?"

He's stunned into silence finally, pondering my words. I know why he's arguing, I want to argue with myself on this too, but... fuck, I don't know.

"Finn, listen, I'm not saying that this is the best solution. I want them close too, but what if Bartiste comes with more firepower than we can handle? Or more men? We don't know this guy. The only advantage we have over him is the fact that we know our territory and he doesn't. At least... as far as we're aware."

My brother is stretching this silence for an uncomfortable amount of time. Enough for Madds to get restless, the tapping of his foot making a hollow noise on the wooden floor, while doubt starts to creep in the quiet threads of my mind.

"What if—what if he finds them, and we're not there to save them? I just can't stop thinking about that possibility. Fuck, Ronan!" He gets up and starts pacing around the table.

Annika still looks a little pale, further making me question my point of view on the matter. I need to be with her. How can I abandon her when this whole thing just makes her sick?

I pull her harder into my side, pressing my lips to the top of her head.

"I'm okay. Just a bit queasy," she whispers my unspoken concern.

"Your brother's right, Finn," Hanna answers instead. "If we're here, you'll worry about us more than the task at hand. Your mind won't be in the right place. Obviously, neither of these two situations are ideal, but considering that we got ourselves in this mess, I would rather stay out of your way. We'll be okay." She cups his jaw, soothing him just as he's about to argue some more.

"Baby..."

"It's gonna be okay," she insists, and he slowly seems to accept our fate.

We exchange looks, then we all turn to Vin, Carter, and Madds for their confirmation as well.

"We've already started the work," Carter says with nonchalance. Like it was the most obvious and logical thing in the world to do.

"I have men on standby. As soon as Carter gives me a name and a person, we'll bring them in and find out as much as we can. He's convinced there's a scout in the city already."

Did these three come here out of damn courtesy? Because they seem to have anticipated the outcome.

"If there is, shouldn't we find him before Bartiste arrives?" Finn asks.

"Yes, but we don't know who to look for. We're keeping an ear out for people asking questions, but I'm not putting my hopes on finding this person," Vin answers.

"We must lay low. You'll make a list." I turn to Annika. "Everything you need for the island. We'll send someone to buy it all, then you'll go. You might even have to split, just in case there is a scout here for you. Maybe even disguise yourselves." This sounds surreal.

I harshly swipe my hand over my face, wishing I could fucking wipe away this whole goddamn day. This whole problem. I have this gut feeling that it will turn ugly and it's eating me inside. But I have to get over it, all that matters is keeping Annika safe.

"Sounds like a plan. Thank you," she says, smiling at me, and I swear I already feel a bit better. "To all of you, thank you."

Carter nods, then stands, the other two frowning.

"This needs to happen fast. I'll be back tonight to finalize the plan."

He shuts his laptop, and walks away, toward the front door. Vin and Madds get the message and follow him.

I'm not sure how much time we have, but I plan to spend all of it with her. I don't linger. I need to get the fuck out of here, away from my brother's scrutinizing gaze. Grabbing Annika, I head straight to my side of the penthouse and into our bedroom.

"Are you okay?" I ask, shutting the door behind me.

"I'm fine. I just got nauseous. The thought of that man... he gives me the creeps in the worst way possible. I think I just got overwhelmed for a moment. This is not how I expected this day to go."

I narrow my eyes, watching how she drops her gaze to the side, rubbing her arm.

"Are you sure you're okay?" I ask, since that doesn't sound like it's the entire truth. But then again, even Hanna looked a bit sickly at the sound of his name.

She nods, meeting my gaze as she sits at the edge of the bed.

"I think my *profession* has given me this badass image. You know by now that it's not me. Blending into the background is my thing, observing and staying out of trouble. I wasn't naive; I prepared myself for some form of danger. I weighed the risks, and of course, some situations were unavoidable over the years."

The thought of her being in danger riles up a feral instinct inside of me that begs to find every single fucking soul on this Earth who wronged her, whoever put my little witch in harm's way, and rip them to pieces.

"But this—Bartiste—is different. When he looked at me, there was no humanity in his eyes. It's like he saw potential, a price tag on a precious stone that he could cut and shape into the exact gem he needs to fulfill his fucked-up purpose. Use it, chip it away bit by bit, until there's nothing but dust left behind, and the world forgets there was anything precious occupying that space to begin with."

A pressure grows in my head, my bottom lip pierced from biting it too hard, and my jaw hurts from the constant flexing.

"Hanna said he threatened you. What did he say?"

This is going to get me even angrier, but... I have to know.

"It's been over a year; I don't fully remember. He didn't threaten me with death, but one of the things I do remember him saying was that if he ever found out that there was something wrong with the painting, he'll hunt me down, and make me pay in flesh and blood, before he'll sell me to people who will do much more to me than get their dicks wet with my cunt."

My blood is no longer boiling—it turns cold. I have a feeling that the type of human trafficking this man enables is not the virgin auction type of affair.

"Listen to me." I close the space between us, dropping to my knees in front of her, cupping her jaw in my hands. "You don't have to worry about him. He won't get his hands on you. He won't even get to lay his eyes on you. Do you understand me?"

"You can't promise me that. No one can..."

She looks at me with doe eyes, innocent and scared, and it fucking kills me not being able to turn my words into a promise. I want to give her the world, the whole goddamn thing. Just wrap it up in a pretty bow and place it at her feet for her to do whatever she pleases with it.

But I'm terrified this enemy will be too much.

"I'll do everything I can to keep you safe. You know that."

She nods, but she still seems reserved.

"I know you will, but I'm scared."

"You'll be—"

"No, you don't understand," she interrupts. "Not for myself. For you. All of this, the danger you're putting yourself in, your brother... the rest of your friends, it's because of me and Hanna. If anything happens to any of you, it will be all my fault. I cannot bear the idea that you are putting yourself on the line for me."

"We're big boys, darling Annika. The only choices we make are the ones we deem right," I say, gripping her jaw and holding her attention to me.

She tries to shake her head, but my hold tightens.

"I'm just a random woman..."

"That's where you're wrong, little witch. You're the right woman."

Her lips part on a muted gasp, her eyes widening, fixing on me, and I think she's stopped breathing. I'm trying hard not to close the distance between us; I don't want to be an asshole after the fucking news we just threw at her. But she has this pleading look in her eyes that I ache to soothe.

I pull her to me, pressing my lips to her delicate ones, but a switch flips, and she pushes against me until my ass is on my heels and she's straddling me. Her nails dig into my sides, almost clawing at my t-shirt, trying to force it off my body.

"Annika..."

"I just want to forget... just for a moment. Please, Ronan, make me forget."

I can't deny her. I let go, raising my arms and giving her access, and before I can do the same to her, she's already stripping her top, exposing those luscious tits. I sink between them, kissing my way to her perky nipples, her back arching, head falling back as a shudder shakes her flesh, her skin bursting in goosebumps.

"Fuck me, Ronan..." The breathy whisper is a command I'm following before my brain acknowledges the movement.

Her back hits the bed at the same time my sweatpants drop to the floor. I pull her leggings off, happy to see she didn't even bother with underwear today.

The witch reaches for me, spreading her legs in a spellbinding invite, exposing that pretty pussy as I stroke my shaft. I could come on the spot when she reaches down, splitting her lips apart with two fingers. But a devious grin pulls at my lips, and I reach over, flipping her onto her front before I grab her hips and jerk her up, that soft ass in the air as she yelps. She's glistening already, her slit so goddamn inviting, it takes too much effort not to sink my cock inside her.

But I want a taste first.

I drop onto an elbow, splitting her slowly with my tongue, from her clit, up to that tight asshole, enjoying how every muscle in her body seems to quiver all at once. I do that enough times that she begins begging me in hushed tones, her face buried in the pillow that she fists in her small hands. I sink my tongue into her sweet pussy, lapping her in the same rhythm as her increasing moans, and when I press two fingers against her clit, she screams into the pillow.

"Fuck! So close... so close. Don't stop! Please!"

A few more seconds of this assault, and when I pull away completely, she turns feral, her head whipping back, reaching over to force me back between her legs.

"If only you were the one making the rules here," I say with a grin.

"Ronan, what the fuck!"

I laugh as I flip her on her back once more. Wrapping my hand around her frail neck, I sink two fingers into that tight cunt, smirking as she gasps and grabs my forearm with both hands. I finger-fuck her slow and hard, with every other thrust rubbing that bundle of nerves with teasing movements, as her heels dig into the bed, her whole lower body rolling on a frantic rhythm.

I feel the spasms in the walls of her pussy before her legs begin to shake. She squeezes her eyes shut, but I tighten my grip on her throat.

"Eyes on me, little witch."

When they flash open, she goddamn glows. Pleasure ripples through her and my hand on her throat is the only thing keeping her from screaming this house down. She's fucking mesmerizing and I can't wait anymore.

I line up my cock with her twitching pussy, and push through those spasms, through her nails clawing at my back, through her breathy curses, until I reach the end of her and almost come on contact.

But before the last ripple of her orgasm ends, I pull out until she grips only the head, and slam back in on a thrust that makes her slide up the bed. A pleasure-filled grin paints her lips as she props her hands against the headboard, and it's my cue. I do it again, pulling almost all the way out before I slam back in. Over and over, as she cries out with each thrust, that smirk fueling me to keep it there, to see her come while smiling at me, because it might just be the most stunning thing in this cruel world.

I'm falling over the edge, the euphoria taking over all the nerve endings in my body, so I reach between us, finding her clit, because I refuse to come before her. Two fingers against that nub of flesh, rubbing in small circles, just how she showed me she likes it, and it's all it takes. Stars explode behind my eyes when her walls clamp down on me. Spasming, she drives me mad, her moans turning to music to my ears, and I spill inside of her on a low grunt. It goes on and on, and I can't fucking stop it.

All because of her... everything about this woman makes me come in my pants like a damn teenager.

I crash on top of her, trying to prop myself on my elbows so I don't crush her, but the woman pulls me tight.

"I like..." she pauses, panting like she ran a marathon as she comes down from that high. "I like your weight on me. It's satisfying."

I give her a little bit of it, pressing her into the mattress until I can tell it's too much, and I hold back, brushing the loose strands of hair from her face.

"I need to know that this is real."

I have no idea where that came from. The blood hasn't returned to my fucking brain.

"Your cock is still buried inside of me, Ronan."

She has an amused look on her face, and it calms me a bit. I shrug because I have no fucking clue what else to say. I would slap myself if I wasn't lying on top of her.

"I didn't know it could be... I thought you would just be an adventure, something I never had and desperately needed. I guess I was more right than I planned. You are exactly what I need... This is real, Ronan. As real as you want it to be."

I think I want it forever...

CHAPTER 11
Annika

I HELD IN a nagging nausea all day. I held it in while I got dressed and packed my small bag. I held it while the guys were running over the next steps. I even held it in when Carter told us Bartiste was in the neighboring city.

They had the suspicion that he knew we were in the area, but not Queenscove specifically. This was our opportunity to go.

I swallowed through that bile as Ronan held me like he really didn't want to let me go. Like in this short amount of time he's actually attached himself to me. Has he really? I've been telling myself that this was nothing more than a summer adventure, but with the way my soul has been feeling... like it would get ripped out of my body if he wasn't part of my life, I'm pretty sure I'm fooling myself. He held my head in his big hands, whispering promises of safety and happiness, before kissing me like he was going to war. I suppose in a way, he is...

Then we were picked up by one of his men in an inconspicuous car, and we got on a boat.

There, I couldn't hold the nausea in anymore. I was sick until my throat was burning and my stomach screamed in pain. I've never had motion sickness, but if it was going to happen, it makes sense it was today.

Now, as I sit back at the round table overlooking the sea through the bay window of Bovely Island's villa, I wonder if it was all a dream. Ronan and I here was like living in a bubble of discovery, laughter, and lust. I thought it felt like a dream, but I was wrong. Queenscove was the real dream, because it's there I got a taste of what life would be like by his side. Actual life, in the real world, not isolated here.

It all happened so fast. Yesterday, I woke up in a dream. Today, it marked the beginning of a nightmare. Now... it feels like I'm trapped in an omen.

"They'll be okay," Hanna assures me as she places a steaming cup of chamomile tea in front of me.

I try to smile at her, but I'm not entirely sure if my lips moved. Her expression is so gentle, though, and I appreciate how she's trying to be comforting. Even as I see the worry in her own eyes. She's my voice of reason, my rock, why I'm not a total recluse, the one who has fed my happiness in these last few years. She always buries her own worries to settle mine.

"Are *you* okay?" I take her hand and squeeze it.

She opens her mouth, but pauses, before letting out a heavy breath.

"Yeah. I'm fine."

"It's okay not to be okay. You can let go for once..."

Tears slowly pool in her eyes, yet she doesn't say a word. Her eyes redden, her jaw gently trembles, and she shakes her head, letting those tears fall down her cheeks.

"It's all my fault," she finally whispers.

"Don't be ridiculous." My sadness is forgotten when I see the guilt splashed all over her face.

"I should have known; I should have kept better tabs on Bartiste. That way, we could have had an escape plan formed and we would have been long gone. Safe." More tears fall, her voice cracking.

Technically, that's true. She takes it upon herself to keep tabs on everyone, and find out if they discover that the paintings we sold to them are fakes, but...

"We both know that if a man like Bartiste wants to find us, it happens sooner or later. Him discovering the real painting was a chance in a damn million. But whether you would have found this out or not doesn't change the fact that the asshole would have still hunted us down."

"We would have been better prepared..." she tries to argue.

"To run. From one hiding place to another, constantly looking over our shoulders. Now we have an entire mafia helping us."

She takes a deep breath in, wiping her eyes as she exhales and gathers herself. Slowly, the normal Hanna falls back into place.

"You're right," she says, nodding. "But I still fear that nothing can protect us from Bartiste."

I fear she may be right.

Ronan

I'M NOT ENTIRELY sure what I expected when I looked at the footage our hacker team recorded of Bartiste. This wasn't quite it, though.

Maybe I envisioned a suited businessman who made you stumble on your own feet whenever he showed up in your path, dripping with power and respect.

What I saw on that screen was nothing like that. He's the definition of average—medium-short haircut with a receding hairline, oval head, not much of a defined jaw on him, crooked nose. His choice of clothes made him look like he was going to his job as a mid-level manager at some finance company, not on a manhunt for two women who cheated him out of millions.

The motherfucker would blend in anywhere.

And he's currently blending here, in Queenscove. He arrived the evening after Annika and Hanna left for the island, and we couldn't waste any time. We're still trying to figure out how the fuck he knew to come here. But Carter's been bumping into some invisible walls, more proof that Bartiste has some smart people on his team.

We're trained to expect the worst, but we've been thriving on owning and juggling information, and this particular one has eluded us.

Carter's little birds have been doing a good job of keeping track of him and his men throughout the city. We know where he's staying, who he's met so far, and most importantly, where he is right at this moment—Rosenberg. In the same goddamn private room we met Annika and Hanna in when we bought the painting.

Two cars with our men pull in behind us as we park at the back, where the private entrance to Rosenberg is. Eight men exit the cars, the drivers staying put, and two others stay outside in case anyone plans to sneak up on us.

"I think they're announcing our arrival." Finn jerks his head in the direction of one of the two men posted by the entrance. He's looking right at us, tilting his head as he speaks, far too obvious that he's talking in an earpiece.

"Good," Vin says with a deep rumble.

The man thrives on pulling metaphorical teeth, harnessing secrets and confessions from his victims, sometimes without lifting a finger. But other times, you see it in the dark slits of his narrowing eyes, he wants to lift more than just a finger. He craves the violence that our life choices can deliver. A man like Bartiste can awaken a monster in everyone who has basic morals. But it's even worse when the morals are ingrained in a world of possibilities, where death is never out of the question.

"This entrance is closed." One of the men standing by the door raises his hand to stop us, while the other looks us up and down.

"Take a picture, sweetheart. It will last longer." Madds steps up, looking down at him, dead in the eyes, with a challenge.

"This entrance is never closed for us. Step away. *Please*." I feign politeness.

"It is today."

"Move."

My ears vibrate when Finn speaks, his voice rough with anger, fear, and anxiousness that seem to be rising every day he's without Hanna. I, on the other hand, have spent every second of waiting time in the fighting ring under the speakeasy with Madds, my dark blue suit covering bruises that calm my unease toward this situation every time I touch them.

"I don't have time for this." Vin steps forward, getting right in the man's face. "Your friend over there is going to open the door for us and bow as we walk past."

"Step—"

But Vin interrupts him and tilts his head with a devious grin on his lips. The unmistakable sound of a gun cocking pulls the man's attention down to his crotch.

"Door, please." Vin jerks the gun, and the man sucks in a breath. He attempts to protest, but something in the way Vin tilts his head and looks at him makes him pause.

"O-open it," he tells the other one.

His *friend* follows the order, holding the door open for us.

"If any of you dare to even look at us the wrong way, I'll pry your eyes out with my fingers and feed them to each other."

On that disturbing image Vin leaves us with, we all pass through the door, walking straight to the room where we know their boss is. Two other men stand by the door.

"Gentlemen. A word with your boss, if we may." Finn approaches, but one of the gorillas standing there scoffs without even looking at him.

We surround the men, staring them down until one of them rolls his eyes and enters the room, leaving us there to wait. When the door opens again, he moves out of the way to let us pass. I nod to two of our men and they remain outside. The door closes behind us, and we're met with a twelve-seater table, but only two of the chairs are empty.

"Let me guess, you're here to piss on the walls and let me know it's your turf."

I raise my eyebrows and turn toward the owner of that voice—Roberto Bartiste himself. I get it now. As average looking as he is, there is nothing average about that filthy look in his eyes, the weirdly curved shape of his lips, and those inward tilted teeth exposed to us as he blows out the smoke of his harsh cigar.

"We have toilets in this part of the country, and the only thing that wets our walls is the blood of the people who think they can piss on them." I take a step forward, looking at the man who sits at the end of the table. "What's your business here?"

He glares at me, like I disrespected him in his house. But this is *my* goddamn house.

"I don't see how that's any of your business, boy."

Boy... I force myself not to grit my teeth or pull my gun out and sink a bullet between his eyes right here. The only thing stopping me is how outnumbered we are in this small room. We have to play our cards right.

"You're on our territory, old man," I bite out at his reference of me, enjoying the twitch of his mouth, "and nothing moves around here without us. Now, I will ask one last time, what's your goddamn business here?"

He leans back in his chair, taking another puff of his cigar.

"No business. Just pleasure," he says, a sleazy grin pulling at his lips.

His attention is suddenly shifted next to me, his expression faltering for a mere second, enough for me to know there's something in Vin's eyes that makes him uncomfortable. I let it sink in for a moment longer.

"There's no pleasure for you in Queenscove, Bartiste," I all but growl. "We know what you do, what you deal in. There's no place for you here at all."

His whole expression mutates. If I thought the man's aura was doused in filth, it's goddamn dripping off him now.

"You have the pleasure of knowing my name, but I don't know yours."

He takes another puff of that cigar, filling the room with its sickly scent.

"You can pretend all you want that you don't know who we are. Just like we're pretending we don't know why you're actually in Queenscove." Finn speaks, and for a moment, I want to punch him.

We needed to hold on to some advantage. But I'm itching as well to lay all the cards on the table and get this over and done with.

"Name your price," he continues.

Surprise flashes in Bartiste's features, quickly morphing into a widening grin.

"They got you boys too, didn't they? Little whores. It was only a matter of time until some suckers fell for their charms and did their dirty work."

Finn seethes, ready to pounce at the man, and I take a deep, painful breath.

"Watch your fucking mouth," I warn. This asshole thrives on weakness, and I'll fucking die before I show him any.

"The only way I'm leaving this place is with those bitches gagged and bound in the back of my car."

I shake my head once, pushing back at the rage filling my veins with every second that passes and every word Bartiste spits our way.

"That's not an option."

"You know the rules of the game—stay in our way and you die."

I cackle at Bartiste's threat because I can't quite believe the disrespect and audacity.

"There's no game here, old man. This is a goddamn jungle, and the rules are clear. You don't eat on our territory, you don't touch what's ours, and if you don't leave empty-handed, you don't leave at all." This time around, no self-restraint in the world would have kept me from growling at the man, watching as the veins in his temples swell by the second.

"I think—"

"The money you lost on the deal will be returned to you," I interrupt. "We'll add ten percent on top for the trouble. But only if you leave in the next twenty-four hours."

"I'm not open for negotiations," he seethes and as the look in his eyes darkens, I wonder if we're actually going to leave this room alive.

"We are. You get what you're owed, and everyone's happy," Finn says.

"That's not how it works in my world." Bartiste rises, stubbing out his cigar on the plate in front of him. All his men tense at the same time.

"You're in our world now." Vin speaks with a voice so cold the temperature in the room seems to drop.

"We're not negotiating for women, Bartiste. We're negotiating for the terms of your departure," I continue.

"Expect a call tomorrow," Finn finishes.

"Fine. But only if *you*"—he points his stubby finger at me—"are the one to make it."

And with that, we turn around and leave the room, our men ensuring our backs are covered all the way through the corridor and out of the back door.

Maybe there's a chance he'll take the deal.

When we reach the car, we all seem to breathe a little easier.

"We have to go and protect the girls. This deal isn't going to work." Finn breaks the tense silence.

I shake my head and rub a hand over my face, scraping the five o'clock shadow I didn't have time to shave.

"It's not a good idea," Carter replies before I get to shoot down that idea.

It fucking breaks me. I want to see her, hold her, kiss her. Worship the fucking ground she walks on. Choosing the right thing is getting harder and harder, because every step of the damn way, I'm questioning my decisions. The analytical side of my brain is slowly being drowned by fear.

"They need more protection!" Finn argues. "You've seen that motherfucker! He made even my skin crawl, for fuck's sake!"

"He knows who we are, what we look like. We have to assume he knows more about us than we think. We cannot be the ones to go, we can't risk it. We'll be followed."

"But you agree they need more protection?"

Finn lays back in the backseat.

"Definitely," I say with a nod, looking out at the moonlit streets of Queenscove as we pull out into the calm traffic.

"I'll send another team."

Even though we can barely spare a few. We're not deep enough in this business to have armies... and we're going to need all the men we can get for whatever Bartiste could have in store for us.

"Not on our boat, though," I continue. "Carter, talk to Jonathan and ask him if he can lend us one. Finn, choose the men you want to send over, but make sure you give them specific instructions and explain how detrimental it is to take precautions. They cannot be seen or followed. And tomorrow... we find out what kind of man Bartiste really is."

But Carter ends the exchange on a chilling, ominous note.

"I think we're going to war."

Annika

HE'S SO GODDAMN beautiful. My heart hurts as I stare at Ronan in this video call. I don't know how I got here from lusting over a guy I saw in a photo, to begging him to come to me and not risk his life trying to get me out of the shit I caused. I miss his touch, crave his rumbling whispers in my ear, his possessive grip on me when he sleeps.

"I can't bear the risk you're taking for me. Please send someone else. Or just... run. Come to me."

I can see the fall of his chest as he exhales, the expression on his face holding a hint of pity.

"It's too late, my little witch. He wants me there, and if there's any chance he'll be willing to make a deal with us, I can't risk pissing him off by not being there."

"What if he says no?"

I dread the answer or the prospect that question poses.

"We'll kill him."

Such a short, matter-of-fact answer. I was always running around dangerous circles, but never have I been posed face to face with the prospect of a man being killed for me without a second thought or a shift in expression. This man right here would do it without even flinching. He would kill for me. I should tell him it's wrong. Murder is wrong. But I can't even convince myself that it is.

"Just like that," I reply.

"I wanted to do it the moment I entered that room. I understood the fear in your voice as soon as I laid eyes on him. But we were outnumbered… it was risky.”

“Not to mention, you were in a busy restaurant?!” I point out the obvious.

“Yeah, not gonna lie, if we weren’t outnumbered, I would have done it anyway. Public place or not. The room was private enough.”

“You would have gone to jail.” I shake my head.

“But you would have been safe.”

I swallow the knot that’s suddenly formed in my throat as I take in those words. They’re heavy. The implication is so much more than I expected.

“I would have waited for you,” I all but whisper.

“You would have had no choice.”

A cheeky grin pulls at his lips and suddenly that heaviness migrates somewhere deep in my belly, and I miss him for a whole other reason now.

“Being away from me might do you some good,” I say, matching his expression.

“I doubt it. I’ll come in ten seconds flat when I finally get my hands on you.”

“It’s only been a few days, Ronan.” I playfully roll my eyes.

“Like your panties aren’t wet right now, and you haven’t even started properly imagining how hard I’ll fuck you when I see you again.”

I bite my lip as an image begins forming in my head, and I’m just about to respond, when a door opens behind him, and someone stands in the frame.

“For fuck’s sake,” he mutters as he turns around, rolling his eyes.

“Something’s happening.” I hear someone speak.

“I’ll be right there.”

When he turns back to me, the look in his eyes tears that muscle that sits in my chest.

“I think I have to tell you something.” My voice cracks.

“No, baby girl. Tell me when you see me.”

He shakes his head and bites his lip, his nervousness reinforcing my uneasiness.

“I just—”

“Annika,” he warns. “Don’t look at me with those pretty eyes of yours like it’s the last time. I’ll get you out of this. I promise.”

I’m struggling to hold back my tears. I want to be strong. I want to be like Hanna, ready to fucking take on anything and everything, doused in main character energy. But I have no superpowers, no hidden talents to magically make everything better.

“Are the guys we sent, okay?” He quickly changes the subject.

“They are. A few of them are patrolling the island, and six, I think, are in the house.”

“Good. Stay with them at all times.”

“I will.” I sigh. I would rather him be with me than risking his life out there. Nothing about me is worth all this trouble.

“I’ll see you soon, little witch.”

He smiles as I say my goodbye, and when the screen goes black, I feel like my whole world goes right along with it.

CHAPTER 12
Ronan

THE PRIVATE CLIFF-SIDE terrace of Coveview Estate has enviable views of Queenscove shores, the marina, and on a really clear day, some of the islands off the coast. However, I'm not entirely sure why Bartiste chose this place to meet us this morning.

I step onto the flagstone floor, joined by my brother, Maddox, Vincent, and eight of our men. We're stretched thin. I wish we were more established than this so that we could afford an entire fucking army. But good help is hard to find. At least we have enough men to watch the girls and some to lurk around in the shadows of the estate. Carter is with the hacker team, just in case.

"I take it you have my answer," I say, nodding to the man as he turns away from the view.

"You're quite the morning person, aren't you?" he deflects. "Seven in the morning is definitely not the time I was expecting you to call at."

"You're an experienced businessman. I presumed you made your decision long before that. Was I wrong?"

He's brought just as many people as us. I don't feel outnumbered anymore if this deal goes south. But I would lie if I said at least two of these motherfuckers didn't scare me. More scarred than Maddox, and just as tall and broad.

"I have. But that doesn't mean that I appreciate being rushed."

That sleazy grin makes another appearance on Bartiste's face, and goddamnit if I don't want to wipe it off with a bullet. But I don't know the man, what contingencies he has in place. As much as I want to kill him right now, I can't until I make sure there's no ace up his sleeve.

"I see no point in wasting each other's time. We both know what we want, so we might as well get it over with," I say.

He takes a few aimless steps, hands clutched behind his back, as his gaze moves between us.

"You're still quite young. There's so much more to learn about this work of ours. How to handle business. What things to let go. What matters and what doesn't."

I sigh as I urge my patience to hold on, because all I want is a goddamn answer. The pulse begins to hammer in my temples.

"Some very important rules are," he continues, like he's checking off a list, "to always take back what you're owed, never give anyone a second chance, and keep your word. You see, I may not have many morals, if any, but I will always make good by my promises. No matter what they are, or who I made them to. Why is it important to be strict about these rules, you may ask?"

No one did. But I'm starting to hear the pulse in my ears now. He makes me more nervous by the second.

"Because there is one thing the underworld values over everything else—reputation. You should know this. And you should also know that money is only a printed piece of paper that anyone can make. I don't give two shits about theirs or yours."

My fists are itching to flex, fingers needing to feel the trigger of my gun, because I don't like this one bit. It's creeping up my spine—a sense of terror that's settling deep in my chest. Suddenly, regret replaces it.

I should be with Annika.

This was a fucking mistake.

"Money means nothing when reputation is at stake," Bartiste continues, and I'm so tense, I could snap in half. "I'm keeping my promise to those whores of yours. I'm going to take them, put them to some hard, grueling tests to see what they're made of. I'll do that shy bitch myself, just like I promised. And then we'll use them the best way we know how. Hard—until their cunts wither and nothing will be left of them. But that shy one might go up for auction. She has what it takes, that innocent look about her. Well... we'll see once I'm done with her."

Darkness descends upon me. Visions of this slimy creature putting his hands on *my* woman. His guts on the floor in front of me. His head mounted as a trophy in my office. He will never. Ever. Get to even look in her goddamn direction!

I suddenly realize that my gun is aimed straight at Bartiste.

"Cheeky. You sneaked that piece in. You better put it down, boy," he warns.

There was a *no gun* rule. We all checked each other before we entered, but I know how to hide mine.

"That's not how it works, old man. You can't come on our turf, threaten our women, and make the rules. No matter what happened in the past, we approached you, gentlemen to gentlemen. Proposed a fucking. Generous. Solution." Each word I speak comes out more seething than the last, my throat straining as I struggle not to rage at him. "So, considering the circumstances, if I were you, I'd count myself lucky I'm not chewing on a bullet right now. This gun stays up until you agree to the offer, then fuck off from the South Coast. If you do not agree, none of you motherfuckers leave."

The tension in the air isn't cleared up by the contrasting gentle sea breeze sweeping the terrace. The complete opposite happens. I don't even dare to turn and look at my brothers, at our men. I know they're ready to fight, even if some of them might think I'm fucking stupid right now for being so goddamn emotional and reckless.

But was there another choice? No fucking way. Not when this pitiful excuse of a man speaks that way about them. About *her*. Annika.

My fucking Annika!

Goosebumps snake around my neck, along with the need to crack it, just as the expression in Bartiste's eyes shifts. They look exactly the same, it makes no sense, but something in them is almost unnoticeably different and my gut tells me to press the trigger. He knows something we don't.

This is bad. This is really bad.

It lasts a moment more before the unnoticeable becomes very much noticeable, cracking into a grin just as he turns his head slowly toward the sea. He doesn't seem to give two shits about the gun aimed perfectly at his chest.

I don't have time to wonder why he turned his attention. A blast splits the eerie silence, breaking my attention from the man. First instinct is to check if I have to take cover. But it sounded like it came from afar. Second instinct is to look in the same direction as Bartiste. But I only dare to peek for a split second—*the marina*. I keep my eyes on him with a sinking feeling in my gut, but I swallow the bile and stay silent. My phone vibrates in my pocket, and I hear the same distinctive noise from the guys around me.

"You should check that," Bartiste says as he turns his attention back to me and nods with that slimy grin.

I quickly pull out the phone and a message from Carter lights up the screen.

Our boat was blown up in the marina. Something's not right.

"All it took is one of your men. The right one. He broke so easily. Turns out, there's some pretty islands around here."

Fuck this shit!

I shoot my gun at Bartiste, but some asshole jumps and takes the bullet for him as he hurries away. Then it happens all at once. His men crowd us. Knives out. A cacophony of grunts and roars sounds as we jump straight into action. More men show up out of nowhere to pull him away. I hear Maddox's distinctive raging growls somewhere around me. Something hard and sharp slams against my right cheek as I'm distracted trying to aim for that slimy motherfucker again. I manage to shoot three more rounds in between punches. Screams sound, but I don't know where they're coming from. Did I hit him?

There're two on me now and no sign of their boss. Instinct kicks in and I pistol-whip one straight in the cheek, the distinct crack of bones fueling me. But I get tackled and, in this madness, I can't even tell how many are on me. I struggle against them, punching and shoving into them, yet I can't seem to get unstuck. Annika's beautiful face flashes for a moment before my eyes. A deep roar shakes everything around us, and I manage to break free and get back on my feet. *Was that me?* The predicament sinks into the depths of my goddamn soul and when another man tries to come at me, I fall into a frenzy, punching him in the ribs in rapid succession, backing him up until he's bent over backwards against the stonewall of the terrace, choking on his own goddamn blood.

Another man grabs me from behind, and I shift against him, but not quick enough to avoid the blade that sinks in my back all the way in. Before I can even think to move away, another guy approaches from my left and something slams hard against my cheek turning my world upside down. The impact echoes inside my skull, creating a strange sort of hollowness.

I don't hear a crack, though. And the knife's still in.

Good. At least I'm not bleeding out.

Yet I wish it would hurt. I wish adrenaline wouldn't fuel me because I fucking deserve the pain.

Annika's sweet voice echoes in my mind. Begging me to come to her and not do this. Run away, hide from the man who is now so much closer to her.

Because of me.

I failed.

I snap my head back, feeling the crunch of bones as it connects with the asshole's nose, then I elbow him hard enough that he releases me. I dodge the next punch from the guy to my left, charging into him until we crash into a hard wall.

Only it's not a wall at all—it's Madds.

He stands behind the motherfucker, bloody and bruised, like a berserker in battle. Looking down in disgust at the man trapped between us, one second his hands are on the sides of his head, the next one his head is facing the opposite direction on a chilling crack that creeps up my spine. The guy crumples to the ground just as I realize the commotion has subsided.

Looking around, the last of Bartiste's men go down at the hands of ours. It's a goddamn bloodbath.

"The girls," Finn heaves, as blood rushes from the split skin on his lip and brow arch.

"Call the clean-up crew now!" Madds orders our men.

Finn comes to me and checks the knife stuck in my back. It's in my right side, close to my waist. I think it missed everything vital. With a nod, he plants a hand on my shoulder, and fire splits my flesh as he pulls the blade out. I don't dwell. There's no time. Quickly ripping my suit jacket off, I tie it around my waist, putting as much pressure there as I can. The blade is thin, so I don't think it did much damage.

"I'm going to go sort out this situation with management. Make sure it's under wraps. You guys go!" Vincent orders us.

I don't need to hear more. I run down the terrace steps, thankful I don't have to go through the main grounds or the reception area of the estate, and head straight to the back parking lot. I really hope our damn car is okay; otherwise, we're fucked. I hear others running behind me, but I don't care who came. I just know I need to get there.

When the car comes into view, I turn on the keyless ignition, sighing with relief when there's no bang. Madds drops to the ground and looks for any surprises underneath it. Ben, one of our guys, pops the hood and does the same.

All clear.

By the time I'm in the passenger seat, my phone is in my hand, finger just about to swipe on Annika's number, but her name lights up on the screen before I get the chance.

"Are you okay?!" I almost shout.

"Someone's here, Ronan! Two boats came." Her voice is shaky, quiet.

"When?"

"They docked some time ago, maybe ten minutes. We were outside, we thought it was you guys…" She's heaving like she's been running a marathon, and I don't know if it's from fear, anxiety, or if she's actually been running. "We wanted to go meet you…"

"Baby, where are you?!"

"Then we heard shots fired. We ran back…"

"Where are our men? Is there someone with you?" I rasp.

"Louis and Dan were out with us. Another one remained at the house. But… Ronan, I can't hear anymore gunfire."

Shit.

Either our men eliminated the threat, or… the chilling alternative I can't bear to think of.

"We're coming, baby, we're on our way."

"You're on a boat? I don't hear a boat. Where—" Her voice breaks with hope. "Where are you?"

"Tell me you're hiding right now."

"Ronan!" she warns, but it comes out more as begging.

"We're not on a boat, but we're on the way."

All the rage I felt earlier has now seeped into a fear so deep, the knife wound in my side is a tickle compared to the pain this terror brings.

"Please hurry." She sounds so goddamn pure, so soft and breakable.

And I'm failing her.

"We're in that hidden room that leads from the library to the dining room. Louis and Dan are with us. I think there're two more in the house. Maybe. I'm not sure."

She's not alone. Good.

"Hide anyway, even if it's under a goddamn desk, just hide, okay? I'll be there before you know it, baby." But I'm struggling to believe my own words.

Our tires screech on the asphalt as Ben speeds down the serpentines of the hill. I can't believe Bartiste pulled a stunt like this in the middle of the goddamn day.

"What if… what if you won't?" she whispers.

"Goddamnit, hurry the fuck up, Ben!" I yell so loud, my throat hurts and the man flinches.

I can't. I can't answer her. I can't allow myself to think this could happen.

I have no idea how it came to this. How my life turned upside down on its axis in such a way that it only makes sense with her in it. I rolled my eyes at people claiming love at first sight, or merely a few dates before they claimed mad love. It made no sense at all. Until it did.

"Baby, I…"

"Ronan…" she interrupts on a shaky whisper. "I'm late. I think I'm pregnant."

CHAPTER 13
Ronan

I THINK I'M pregnant... I think... I'm pregnant.

The echo of each word falls with each thump of my heart. My mind is devoid of anything else, and the haunting sounds trap me inside of it. I can't escape. It goes on, and on... and on.

Ronan...?

"Ronan?" Her sheepish voice manages to catch my attention. Barely.

Then the car swerves as Ben takes the last sharp turn down the hill and onto one of Queenscove's main streets, pulling me fully back into the now.

"I'm sorry, I didn't mean to... uhm... I just thought you should know."

Oh hell, there's a whole fucking criminal organization knocking at her door, and she thinks I might have a problem with what she told me? God, I'm a fucking idiot.

"My little witch, we'll have all the time in the world to talk about anything and everything. For now, I want you to stay safe and hidden until I get there." My words come out with such conviction, I think I manage to fool even myself.

"I don't know if I can do that," she says in a shaky voice.

"Do they know where you are?"

"I don't think so. No one's attempted to get in yet."

"That's good. Stay low to the ground. Away from any window and have as much furniture as possible around you. Okay?"

"Okay."

I can tell how hard she's trying to show that she's strong, even in a whisper.

"You're going to be okay, baby." I wish I could turn this into a promise. "I know I fucked up. I should have been there, and I'll spend the rest of my goddamn life making it up to you."

"All of it?"

"I would spend more if I could."

A low chuckle coming from her breaks my fucking heart. What if... What if this is the last time I hear that sound from her? The last time I hear her voice. The last time I make her smile.

Suddenly, I hear a commotion in the background and a yelp from her, but she quickly muffles it.

"They're here..." she whispers, and I think I stop breathing.

"Stay quiet, baby girl, stay quiet. They might not know you're there yet."

"Ronan, I'm scared."

"Just focus on me. On us. On the whole life that we have left to live together now that we found each other. We can do anything we want."

"Like what?" I can barely hear her, she's whispering so low.

"First, I'll take you to Venator Castle, walk into the footsteps of your great-grandfather, since I hold the man responsible for meeting you. Without him and this painting... who knows how long I would have been wandering this continent looking for you."

The commotion sounds even louder now, strong bangs frightening her, her breathing staggered, jumpy with every hit.

"A—And then?"

"Then we can go up north, beyond the hills of Venator, up in the mountains. Rent a cabin in the middle of the forest... chase you amongst the pine trees while you let out that songbird of a laugh of yours, before I eventually catch you and..."

I twitch, almost jumping in my seat when I hear a heavy bang and Annika's muffled cry. They know they're in there. They're gonna get in. I can barely fucking breathe.

"Then we can go to the West Coast," I continue, attempting to distract her, keep her calm. "Travel the length of it and hit every remote beach we can find, every hidden lagoon, and waterfall. We can spend every minute of every day swimming and floating around, as the sunshine, then the moonlight hits our skin."

"You would do all of this, with me?"

"Not would, but will. The first time I laid eyes on you, I was sure you were the end of everything I've known up to that point. You're my wicked beginning, the start of a life I never knew I needed. If I can figure out a way to find you even after we perish of old age, I will."

She's about to speak, but gunfire and a sharp scream interrupt her.

"Hanna!!!" Finn shouts from the backseat. He's on the phone too.

"They're shooting through the wall," Annika sobs.

"Ben, for the love of all the fucking gods, drive faster!" I turn to the man, seething through gritted teeth. If he can find a goddamn way to fly, I need him to do it right now!

"They stopped. I heard shouting behind the wall."

But heavy, loud bangs replace them. I can hear them disturbingly clear even through the phone.

"Bartiste doesn't want to kill you. They wouldn't want to risk shooting you and Hanna by accident."

"You saw him..."

"Don't think about him right now."

"Where are you, Ronan?" Her voice breaks in such a tragic way

"On my way, I promise, I'll be there in a bit."

"You're lying to me..."

I am...

"I wasn't lying about everything I want to do with you. I want to see this continent with you, discover its hidden gems, discover all of yours too."

"I haven't had enough time with you. I need more."

"You'll have more."

"I'm falling for you, Ronan."

"I fell the moment I came for you and all I found was the painting of yourself you left for me."

"Nooo!!!" Her scream is followed by a thundering crash and someone else's cries in the background.

"Get away, you asshole!" I hear Hanna.

Finn yells behind me, begging her to hide.

The distinctive sound of breaking wood makes Annika yelp. Thuds and violent noises make me dizzy, the pulse in my temples sending me into a silent frenzy.

I'm not there, goddamnit! I'm not there... She's alone because of me! In danger because of me!

"Annika, baby, please just hide. Stay low. Please..."

"They're inside, Ronan! Ben and Louis are trying to—"

"I want you to listen to me. No matter what happens, I'm coming for you. No matter where you are or where you will be, I'm coming for you."

Her staggered voice turns to whimpers, and through tears, the rage comes through. That unmistakable fury that only comes out when you're backed up into a corner and there is no escape in sight. And she lets it all out on an ear-piercing howl.

"Annika!"

"Ronan, please..."

Gunfire interrupts her and more screams fill my ears, seeping fear into my gut.

"They're dead... Nooo! Let her go! Goddamnit, let her gooo!"

With a loud crash, the line goes dead. Finn hollers in the back of the car, but a sort of shocked numbness fills my veins. Disbelief... utter and total disbelief.

This—no, this didn't happen. What have I done?

A thundering roar rattles the windows of the car, blind rage replaces the numbness, and I don't realize I've been banging my fist on the dashboard until pain slices through my hand, a deep dent left in its wake.

What the fuck have I done?!

* * *

Jonathan, *The Ghost,* lent us his boat and even at full speed, we knew there was no chance. It was too late. When my feet touched the sands of Bovely Island's shore, I ran inland through the trees of the small woodland, plagued with memories of the last time I did that... *chasing Annika.*

I was holding on for dear life to my self-control as we were spotting our men, lying lifeless under the shadows of the trees. As much as I was running after Annika, I couldn't help being pained by the heaviness of having to break the news of their death to whatever families they had left.

The torment grew every time I had to get close enough to make sure none of them was... her.

Then we got to the house, heart in my throat as I walked through, witnessing the destruction. Pain splattered in shades of crimson on the walls, through the shards of broken furniture, the bullet holes. I knew in my gut that what I was looking for wasn't there... I knew she wouldn't have magically fought the beasts that came for her. It was then that I acknowledged hope for what it truly is—the cruelest form of torture.

As I walked through the broken wall of the hidden room, the absence of her body was the only saving grace.

"I know who we need to go after." Carter rushes through the door, in the empty main room of Midnight, pulling me out of the painful flashback.

He's been in the office, checking in with his team, while the rest of us have been devising a plan out here. Far too many hours have passed since we returned, since they were taken. Finn gets off his chair, anxiously waiting for Carter to approach and continue. I down my drink and lean forward, bracing my forearms on my knees, nervously rubbing my thumb over the palm of my hand.

"There." He pops the laptop he was carrying on the table and points to a spot on a map.

"That's fucking hours away. Is that where they're keeping them?" Finn asks.

"No. That's where Nathan Hayes is. I've been trying long before we even met Bartiste to find this man."

"And we fucking care, why?" I ask with an unintended bite.

"As much as he is the boss, he would be nothing without Nathan. He's the little mole working in the background, orchestrating the whole operation, and I finally fucking found him!"

There's a sparkle in Carter's eyes. This is a vengeful victory for him. He pops a grainy photo of the man on the screen.

"He wasn't with Bartiste either time we met him," Vincent points out.

"No. He's highly important to Bartiste. He would crash and burn without him. So he keeps him out of harm's way, hidden."

"Then, we go get him."

"No."

We all stop and look at Carter, pulling our brows together almost in unison. He straightens, sliding his hands in his pockets.

"It's almost six hours away, too much can happen by the time we get there."

"Okay, what now?" I ask him.

"Don't you see where he is? Venator, specifically Alnit Hill territory..."

"Oh."

"I think it's time to reconnect with your cousin."

"I think you're right." I nod.

"You're talking about Buchanan?" Finn steps forward, frowning at me.

"He runs Alnit. We would be stupid not to ask for his assistance."

"Make the call," Carter growls, his gaze darkening with bloodthirst vividly painted in his blueish-hazel eyes.

"We barely know the man, brother. Why would he help us?" Finn asks.

"Because this is not about us, this is about our women. Sloan would never say no to that."

Annika

I THOUGHT I knew what fear was. How it shattered your will and stinted any self-preservation instincts.

I thought I felt it when those men quite literally burst through the door and killed the ones who were protecting us.

That wasn't it.

I thought I finally felt the worst of it when we struggled and tried to fight our way out of the boat that was ripping us away from our life. Then that first punch hit my ribs, before it landed in my temple and knocked me out.

I thought it couldn't get any worse than the moment I woke up in pitch-black darkness, willing my eyes to adjust, but to no avail. My head was pounding, every bit of my body shivered, but I managed to find Hanna as she was waking up, probably with the same concussion I had.

But that wasn't it either.

Real fear is staring into the eyes of death and knowing that it's not coming just yet. It's the constant expectation. The road leading to it. Torturous, grueling, painful. It's not knowing when it will all finally end, and you will be taken away.

The anticipation of death—this is real fear.

"I wonder what I can fit in this tight cunt of yours?" Bartiste grips me harshly in his hand, squeezing the part of me that was only meant for one man.

But I can't seem to react. Numbness fills every vein. There's nothing I can do to stop him. Not when I'm hung by my tied wrists on a meat hook fixed in the ceiling, painfully naked.

"I still haven't decided how I'm gonna take my payment. Which bodes well for you, since I haven't ripped you to pieces. *Yet.* Lucky bitch."

He's annoyed with his own decision, and lashes out at me, pulling his fist back. I start crying out before it even connects with my middle. Through the pain that brings violent nausea, I breathe a sigh of relief because he hit me in the stomach, not the belly. There's little to no chance that we will escape this, but if we do, and if I'm really pregnant... I can't let him take it away from me.

"Too bad you don't care as much about her friend," a pitiful excuse of a man says with a sleazy chuckle from his spot in the corner of the room. He pushes his heavy boot on the back of Hanna's limp body, welts and cuts marring her once perfect skin.

A shudder rips through me, and I want to cry when Bartiste grips my core tighter with a sordid grin on his face before he slaps me harshly.

I would beg for my life, for Hanna's life, I would beg him to stop hurting us, to stop touching us, to kill us, to take our money, to do anything other than what he's been doing for however long he's had us. But we've already done all that. All that and more. He doesn't care about anything else but our slow punishment.

Grueling, never-ending punishment. All I can do is cry, hiss, and yell. Nothing more, nothing less... and even that's getting old.

"Maybe I should start treating you the same. Shove my hard dick in that little slit of yours, and pull you apart as you bleed for me. But your greedy cunt might like it and we don't want that. Do we?"

Bile rises in my throat, and I swallow when it threatens to reach the surface. His hand slides farther back and that vile grin spreads. "But this tight asshole is guaranteed to rip and bleed."

An unfamiliar chill rushes through my body as his finger pushes against that ring of muscle and suddenly my knee connects with a soft part of him. The movement happens before my brain registers it, or the potential consequences. But somehow, I found that power in some newfound anger-fueled adrenaline.

"You bitch!" He grabs onto his middle, right above his dick I'm sorry I missed, and his other hand connects with my face so hard, I'm swinging as I dangle from the ceiling.

When he comes back into view, he hits me a second time, the whiplash so harsh I'm amazed my neck didn't snap.

The third time, the world goes black.

* * *

No matter what happens, I'm coming for you... I'm coming for you... I'm coming...

That eerie voice echoes, and I wake up with a start. For a moment, for one excruciating moment, I thought it was real. But once more, only darkness fills my vision, no Ronan, no light, no hope.

Only a dream... a cruel memory.

"Are you okay?" Hanna's strained voice sounds in the darkness.

She's lying next to me. Shivering. But it's not cold here.

"Yeah..." I lie.

I rise into a sitting position, resting my back against the concrete wall, then I grab onto her and pull her to me until her head rests on my lap. We're both naked, but it stopped mattering a while ago. She wraps an arm around me and pulls the rest of her body until she's nestled against mine, her shivering subsiding.

"They're coming for us," I tell her as I stroke her hair.

I don't fully believe they'll actually find us, but I want to give her something. She needs hope. These people have ripped the fight out of her after the second time they took her away and brought her back beaten, bleeding, and... broken. There was nothing we could do to stop the bleeding. It flowed freely between her legs until it eventually ended.

The guilt riddling me is indescribable. It should be me. I begged them not to take her. It earned me a brutal slap that sent me straight onto the floor. Still, they haven't done that to me, haven't raped me. Only her. Making me watch my best friend go through this, planting this seed in my mind and soul, is a whole other form of torture.

It's a while until she talks again.

"If they don't come in time..."

"They'll be here soon," I interrupt.

"You never were a good liar."

For the first time since I've been here, I almost smile. She's right.

"I'm sorry."

"For what? Your lie? I get it. There's no light at the end of this tunnel, so we might as well make ourselves feel better." She speaks those words so slowly, no energy left in her.

"No. For what they did to you, Hanna. You... and not me."

She stiffens against me, but soon begins to soften. Relaxed or defeated?

"I'm not sorry. I love you, Anni. Don't think for a second that I have some fucked-up feeling of anger that they haven't touched you too—in that way." She adds that at the end, knowing that they've touched me plenty.

But her words don't soothe the guilt; they give me a sense of relief for a whole other reason. One I haven't shared with her yet.

"I love you too."

If we really aren't getting out of here, I might never get the opportunity to share this. "I have to tell you something."

"What is it?" she asks when the silence stretches too long.

"I think I may be pregnant."

"What?!" Old Hanna rises to the surface for a few moments, her voice close to the normal pitch it had before we were brought to this place.

She gets up to sit next to me, which is pointless since it's pitch-black in here and we can't see each other.

"I'm not a hundred percent sure, since I obviously didn't have a test handy, but I missed my period."

"And you've been nauseous and sick recently. I thought it was this whole situation."

"It's probably part of it. But I'm sore, my breasts feel different, and they ache, my nipples extra sensitive. I don't know. Maybe I'm imagining it."

"But if you're not..."

"Yeah."

"Fuck."

"Yeah..."

"This is not a great advertisement for the brand that made your IUD. How do you feel about it?"

"I don't know. I didn't exactly have time to adjust to the idea. With everything that's been happening, I lost track of time. But it's been in the back of my mind for a few days, when I realized that I should have had my period by now."

"Wow... I wonder what Ronan would think about this. And Finn..." Her voice trails of with longing as she talks about the man she's been falling for. "He would be an uncle. And I'm Auntie Hanna. Huh. I love the sound of that."

For a moment, it seems that she's drifting into a dream... an illusion of what our lives could be. And probably never will.

"I told him. Before the assholes broke in when I was on the phone with him. I couldn't... I couldn't disappear without telling him. It felt wrong for him to never know it if I die. Maybe it was selfish of me too. Maybe out of desperation, I thought that the revelation might make him search harder..." God, this is terrible to admit.

"You thought you weren't enough?!"

"I don't know."

"You're blind if you haven't seen how that man looks at you, Anni."

"Like Finnigan looks at you?"

I smile, even if she can't see it in this darkness. She sighs, and I wish I could soothe her. But here... nothing can.

"I miss him," she continues. "He crawled under my skin so deep... He's younger than me too. I have no idea how I've allowed this."

"Allow? Nothing allows Finnigan Hennessey anything. The moment he laid eyes on you, you had no way out."

"I really didn't. He's honest. Wears his heart on his sleeve. So open to show it all to me, his heart, his soul, his dirty as fuck mind. It's refreshing meeting a man like that."

Those beautiful thoughts end in a muffled cry. I know what she's thinking—she'll never see him again. I know because that's exactly what I'm thinking about Ronan. My parents too... they'll never know what happened to me if I die.

I don't doubt that Ronan's searching tirelessly for us. I truly do not doubt it. They put their asses on the line for us. But that doesn't mean they'll find us.

Roberto Bartiste is a resourceful man. Cunning. And vengeful.

He's doing everything in his power to keep us.

Keep me.

CHAPTER 14
Ronan

"YOU'RE SURE HE'S coming?"

Finn is getting on my nerves, asking this exact goddamn question for the third time now. Second time since we arrived at our meeting location, midway between our cities—about three hours away from Queenscove.

I'm struggling to keep it together. I haven't slept in two days, since Annika was taken away from me. Yet somehow it feels like it's been longer. Much, much longer.

I never knew love could be like this. So ruthless and all-consuming. Giving you the very essence of your existence, only to feel like your soul is ripped away from your very being when they're not around.

"How do you know we can trust him?"

"I swear to God, Finn, ask me one more time and I'm gonna put you into a grave myself." I turn to him, my lips in a tight line, glaring as I flex my fists.

"Well, fuck you too! Like this whole thing is easy! What kind of cold bastard are you?! I can't fucking breathe, Ronan! I can't breathe knowing she's out there. That these motherfuckers put their hands on her! Knowing I can't get to her fast enough! I can't risk it, not on some guy who's supposed to be family, who I've only met a handful of times and don't know if I can trust!"

I wipe a hand over my face, tightening it around my jaw like I can physically rub away the weight of it all. The weight of my brother's pain... my own.

"So ex-fucking-cuse me for asking a million times! We can't all be cool and collected like golden boy Ronan!"

"You're crossing a line, Finnigan," I seethe.

"Guys, this is not the time," Madds tries to interrupt.

"Stay the fuck out of this!" I turn and shoot him a look that makes him raise his palms at me in defense, before backing away and joining the others by the car.

Then I spin back to my brother. "You think I'm cool and collected? You think I'm not in pain?" My tone lowers the angrier I get. "That I can close my eyes and suppress her helpless cries, ignore how they get louder with each echo inside my head? You think I can allow myself to breathe, knowing I'm the only thing that can get her and our baby out?!"

"W—what?"

Finn's eyes bulge, and I'm confused for a second, before I realize what I said.

"Is Annika..."

"Fuck!" I grab onto the sides of my hair, pulling hard enough that the pain reminds me I need to chill the fuck out and stay rational.

Anger will fuel me, but I can't allow it to turn reckless. I let out a long, strained breath before I turn back to him.

"Yeah, I think, I don't know. Before it all went south on the phone, she said she thinks she's pregnant. She obviously didn't have tests to take on the island... It doesn't matter. Even if there's the smallest chance, I can't ignore it."

"Why didn't you tell me?"

I don't know... denial?

"I needed to stay focused. If it's true, more than two lives depend on me. I can't fuck this up. Thinking about it too much distracts me."

Finn's finally speechless. There's something in his eyes that resembles pity, and I would erase that expression off his face with a punch if I didn't see headlights approaching from the distance. Blood pressure rises in my veins at the prospect of what's to come.

Three SUVs stop before us. Passenger doors open and a bunch of men with fierce, hard features, climb out. But it's the one with the thick, short beard, disheveled black hair, and vivid green eyes who we're interested in. Sloan Buchanan steps out and wastes no time as he walks straight to us.

He's different from the last time I saw him. It's been less than a year, yet he seems older, tougher, wiser somehow. Being both a young single father of a teenager and the head of a crime syndicate has taken a toll on him. Yet the man looks fitter than ever. Sharp. His strong shoulders pulled back, head held high, chest pumped, he walks like each step shakes the earth around him. But there's a softness flickering in his eyes at the sight of us.

"Sloan," I say with a nod and extend my hand, but the man takes it in his and pulls me into a quick hug with a strong pat on my back.

He does the same to Finn, who looks more uncomfortable with it, but doesn't pull away.

"Ronan, Finnigan, I must say, I'm not happy to see you under these circumstances."

He doesn't beat around the bush, snapping his fingers twice, and two men open the back door of the car Sloan drove in. They pull a bound man out of it, dragging him right to our feet. A gift wrapped so nicely for us.

"You rode with him," Finn states, narrowing his eyes on our cousin.

"I wasn't going to let him out of my sight." He says it like the alternative is absolutely ridiculous.

My brother is more than satisfied with that answer. I catch a glimpse of Carter who came up beside me, and even through his cold demeanor, I can still catch a glimpse of respect for Sloan. Respect for understanding the importance of this and making it his personal mission.

"Thank you. Did he by any chance spare us the time and say anything to you?"

Sloan looks down at the sack of meat that stares at us with hate and masked fear.

"We tried. But our mission was to get to you as fast as we could. We didn't want to waste any time."

"I appreciate that."

"We put feelers out, talked to some people to keep an ear out in case his boss is hiding in Venator. It's not easy, with Onasis and Santo so overprotective of their territory."

Venator is an old city built on three perfectly aligned hills, but they all almost work as individual territories, and these three crime families run each of them.

"But at least the youngest of the former can understand reason. To an extent," Sloan continues.

"Pandora?"

I turn to Carter, confused by his question.

"You know her?" our cousin asks.

"University. She was quiet."

That's all he offers. Quiet, in Carter's book, is a good thing. He likes quiet.

Sloan nods in understanding. "Do you need more men for the rescue? My team and I are more than willing to stay. I can call over more."

I turn to Vin and Madds, who are both a few steps behind, watching us. Vin approaches first.

"It would be much appreciated, thank you. We lost too many of our men."

"This is Vincent Sinclair, and Maddox Severin."

Sloan nods and shakes their hands firmly, but pauses on the former, cocking his head.

"The Serpent," Sloan acknowledges in a low tone.

I nod, trying to ignore how far his reputation has traveled, then turn to the last of us. "And this is Carter Pierce."

My cousin acknowledges him, but neither of them says anything.

"What about the other one, boss?" one of his men asks.

I lift an eyebrow at our cousin.

"Hayes wasn't alone, and we didn't want to separate the couple." He pushes the man with his foot, rolling him a little closer our way, just as the other guy is dragged out of the car.

"Couple?" Finn asks.

"That one's cock was buried deep into Hayes's ass when we busted in. Not sure if he's important to him, but thought we would bring him anyway."

"He's important."

Carter steps a foot closer, cocking his head as he observes. He has this look in his eyes—annoyance. "He covers their tracks. Blocking my search almost every step of the way. He works hand in hand with Hayes."

"Well, well. How lucky for us."

The expression on the man's face as he stands, all bound gagged, is smug, but none of us could miss the fear in his eyes. As much as he wants to hide it.

Sloan turns slightly toward his car. "Now, should we get to it?"

* * *

Carter found us a cozy little place in this area. In the middle of nowhere. Abandoned. Perfect for the job. And *my oh my* what a job this is.

We're usually patient men when it comes to extracting information.

Normally, it would be Vincent doing the delicate work. His form of torture is almost free of violence. Sometimes he simply stares at a person for long enough and they spill their deepest, darkest secrets. But most times, he uses carefully curated information he has on them to torture them with visions of the future, with endless possibilities of their life burning to the ground, while all they can do is watch and suffer. Information is power and Vincent *The Serpent* Sinclair knows how to wield it.

But this situation calls for physical torture. Plus, Nathan Hayes is mine. As much as my brother wanted to sink his claws into him, he's fucking *mine*.

Finn got his friend, the one currently kneeling between us, who I'm holding by the hair so he can focus on my brother. We've been hoping that smashing this one's face in will make Hayes talk, but maybe they're not as close as we thought, since he hasn't spoken a damn word. Maybe only a fuckbuddy, then.

"Fucking talk, you goddamn piece of shit!" Finn rages, thick veins marring his temples, eyes red as he lands another punch on the side of his head.

He didn't even wait for the answer. He knows it's not coming. We all do now. Finn lands one more hit on his cheek, brutal enough that when his head snaps to the side, blood splatters even on me, and I'm left with a chunk of hair in my hand. I'm certain there's skin attached to it too.

Not that it matters much. The guy's not going to care either. We all heard the crack of his bones—once when Finn's punch landed, and the second when his head hit the concrete floor.

If he's not dead now, he will be in a minute.

I didn't beat the guy, yet I still seem to be panting heavily. I can taste the blood in the air.

But I don't linger. I grab the metal chair we found in this abandoned place, a shriek of metal on concrete echoing in this desolate space as I drag it in front of Hayes. He's tied to another one of these chairs, not gagged, though. Yet he has not spilled a word. He flinched. Whimpered once. But he stood his ground. Metaphorically, of course.

That ends now, along with my patience.

"Not sure which one was more heartless, you or us? You're just as guilty for what happened," I say, pointing to the man currently bleeding on the floor. "You could have stopped it, Nathan."

For a moment, I search his eyes for remorse, an inkling that he's ready to talk. He's looking everywhere except at me or his friend, his mouth sealed shut. Finn breathes heavily behind me, ready to split this guy's skull open so he can get the information out of there himself.

"Where the fuck are they?" I seethe.

"Who?" He speaks for the first time, and the goddamn audacity makes my ears ring. My restraint is officially gone.

I slam a blade right above his knee, the vibration of the crunch to the bone tickling my palm. But his pain filled cries are annoying me with their delay.

"Focus." I slap him against the jaw. "Right here, goddamnit. Or I'll slice through your kneecap and rip it right out. Where the fuck are *our* women?"

He yells as spit falls from his lips, pain clouding his mind.

"I said focus!" Rage spills from my lips as I twist the knife, the grind of it against the bone jittery in my hand.

"Stop! Stop! Stop!!!" he finally cries.

I do it, giving him a chance to speak. He takes a deep, shaky breath as he fights through the pain.

"Burfield, in the industrial area at the..." He lets out another cry, and it earns him another smack across the face to keep him focused. "...the old pipe factory. He takes them to warehouses and..."

He trails off, and Finn loses his patience, stepping right behind the man, and bending his head back until his breaths are strained. He points a knife right at his eye, bare millimeters away from his pupil, and the madness I see in him is as disturbing as it's excruciating.

"And what?!" I shout, tilting the knife under his bone.

The man is almost choking on his own saliva as he hollers in pain, his throat stretched so far back that his Adam's apple looks like it's about to pierce through his skin.

"He gets them assessed, prepared..."

Finn doesn't even flinch as he slowly sinks that knife down. It slides into his eye like butter. Even through the excruciating screams, he pushes the thin blade until all I can see is the hilt. Screams turn to whimpers. The shaking dies down. Then the man dies too.

Good. I didn't want to hear anymore, didn't need the mental image of his implication.

"Burfield..." I whisper on an exhausted exhale.

I'm tired, so goddamn tired. It's not because of the sleepless nights, the fights, or the stress—it's the fucking fear. So far, it's both fueled and drained me, but more recently, it seems to be draining me more.

I pull the knife out of the man's leg, but Finn leaves his stuck in his skull. When I turn around, Carter's looking right at me, an unbothered calmness in his eyes. I used to wait, expecting some sort of change in his demeanor, but I no longer expect any of this to affect him. He's like a statue as he stands by the wall.

I wonder if one day I'll find out what shakes this motherfucker.

Maddox is untroubled too, but not in the same lack of soul or empathy kind of way. He's seen and inflicted enough pain in and outside of the fighting ring that he's grown accustomed to the violence. But at least he flinches from time to time. He reacts.

Not Carter, though. The most he'll do is cock his head, and I'm convinced he does it so he can examine the destruction from a different angle.

Suddenly, he moves, walking to the guy lying on the floor. He stops a few feet away, observes him for a moment, and I don't know if it's the exhaustion in me or if the guy moved, but in one fluid motion, Carter pulls his gun, aims, and shoots. Brain matter paints the floor, yet he fires one more time. Then he spins around and heads toward the exit, calling for us.

"Time to go."

* * *

I think I'm pregnant... pregnant...
I'm falling for you...
Ronan...

I jump in the seat, turning to the space to my right. *Shit, I fell asleep.*

"You okay?" Carter asks, narrowing his eyes from his spot in the backseat next to me.

I nod and turn my attention out the window. Her words still echo in my head like it wasn't a dream. A goddamn nightmare! I shouldn't have fallen asleep, for fuck's sake.

"Was I out for long?" I ask Carter, who's still watching me.

"Not long enough. Are you up for this?"

"Are you doubting my abilities?!"

"You're capable and motivated. I don't doubt that. But you're running on no sleep."

"Aren't we all?"

"Not like you. Or Finn. We're forty-five minutes away. You can still sleep for half an hour more."

"I'm fine. I need to be alert, not groggy."

I'm lying, I could sleep for a year. My body is already shaky, struggling to regulate its temperature. It needs rest. But I can't bear hearing her voice in my dreams anymore... that haunting echo. It's tearing whatever's left of my heart and destroying my focus.

Carter nods, but the bastard knows me all too well. Out of all the guys, with my brother's exception, I'm closest to him. Finn and he are the same age, both twenty-one, but you couldn't guess it from looking at him. He gives off the most confusing aura; it's like that *old soul* expression bled out of him and shows on the surface.

He's *different*. Lacking empathy, but not emotions. I've seen him experience annoyance, slight rage, even joy, in small amounts. Yet, everything else that makes us human, Carter learned. He copied. He adapted. Highly intelligent, logical, most likely a genius by normal standards. Which is why his age, or most of anything about him, is hard to pinpoint. I'd say he's a chameleon, but in reality... I think he's wearing a mask. Showing people exactly what they should see.

Sometimes I wonder if he's doing it with us too.

I trust him with my life and, logically, I know that he would never fuck us over. But he's the kind of man who's only guided by practicality and reason. If he stops seeing it in us, will he leave us too?

His eyes narrow on me for a split moment. At times, I wonder if he can read minds too. I swear he knows I'm thinking of him now.

I turn my attention back out the window. It's a new moon tonight, and we're in the middle of nowhere. There're no streetlights, and too late for traffic, so we're immersed in darkness.

"I know you're staring at me, asshole," I spit at him without turning. "Do you have something to say?"

"Do you?" He doesn't waste a breath and takes me by surprise with the question.

"No."

My lungs begin to burn, and when I feel free of his gaze, I finally breathe again.

After too many moments of silence, we start running through the plan we fleshed out before we set off. We've done all the remote research we could have possibly done in the limited time we had. Our strategy is challenging, and once we get there, we might have to adapt. I pray the location won't raise too many unanticipated issues.

I wish we could fucking fly there. It's only fifteen minutes away now, but I swear the closer I get to her, the farther it becomes.

What if this doesn't work?

Will I fail again?

CHAPTER 15
Annika

"PLEASE... PLEASE, DON'T do this..."

I have no soul left in my voice. The hoarseness taking over from too much crying and pleading Bartiste to stop.

"You're truly boring me now. I would say I'm losing interest, but in truth... you haven't begged for your *own* life yet."

How could I? It's Hanna lying on the floor, on her belly, being ripped apart by the brute thrusting into her. Her eyes are closed now; I'm not even sure if she's still conscious.

I'm praying she isn't.

It's a different type of torture, letting me witness all the horrible things he's been doing to her.

This is what I want to do to you, sweet Annika. He told me that as he swiped the tip of his knife down from the base of her throat, long past her belly button, leaving a thin trail of blood behind. He said it again as he ordered one of his men to spin her around to face me, bent her over in front of me, and ripped into her from behind. Even after she closed her eyes, he threatened to slice her throat in front of me if I closed mine, if I stopped watching. One of his men has a rough rope around my throat, holding me tight in this chair, even though I'm not tied to anything.

He's been using Hanna like a voodoo doll. Hurting her where he wants to hurt me. And goddamnit, I can almost feel it all...

Only, this torture is different. The guilt is ripping me apart, and I've begged and begged to take me instead, to let her go. To no avail. Even Hanna has screamed at them not to touch me.

I have no one to pray to anymore, no one to sacrifice my soul to so I can save her...

"You've begged repeatedly to stop. You've been annoyingly selfless and attempted to sacrifice yourself for your best friend's life. But... it's not quite enough," he continues, as he moves a bit sluggishly.

He's been limping since he brought us here. I don't know why. I tried kicking him in the leg to use it against him, but I didn't manage.

"Just... let her go. Give her, safe and sound, back to Hennessey, and then you'll just have me. I'll have myself to beg for."

He's slowly swiping his thumb over the blade he holds, the madman actually cutting himself, cocking his head as his blood mixes with Hanna's on the metal. For a few moments I start to believe he's pondering the option. There's no time to acknowledge the shift in him.

"How about we do something else instead."

Fire slices through my thigh, jostling me up in the chair I'm forced to sit in, the rope tightening suddenly around my throat. Bartiste's blade sticks out from my leg and tears fall from my eyes. No whimpers, though, no sound leaves my gaping mouth. I'm too stunned by the agony.

"I should have shot you there, just like your fucking piece of shit of a boyfriend did to me."

That's why he's limping.

"If I leave this in, you'll live. But if I pull it out, my men will be annoyed at the mess they'll have to clean up after you bleed out on our floor." He huffs, but even in this state, I can't miss the sparkle in his eyes as he orders. "Beg me."

Somehow, I manage to take a breath, not a full one, but enough.

"Beg for what? You'll kill me anyway. I told you..." I take a deep breath to push through the pain. "Let her go. Alive. Then it will only be me to inflict your pain on."

"I'm already inflicting pain on you. And you know I'm not referring to the knife fit so snug in your meat."

Meat. This is what we are to him—meat.

"There's no point to this..."

"Oh, but there is—my pleasure. After the humiliation of cheating me, I'm taking my revenge."

"Haven't you taken enough?"

"You haven't begged yet." He's getting angrier.

"I've begged plenty, goddamnit!"

"Not for your own motherfucking life!"

The burning brightens, as in two swift movements, he pulls the blade out and slams it into my other thigh with such force the hilt bruises me. This time, the adrenaline escapes me, tears fill my bulging eyes, blinding pain fills all my senses, and I shriek so loud that Hanna startles awake.

The broken look in her eyes distracts me, if only for a few moments.

"It's okay... it's okay," I try to soothe her through gritted teeth.

But the guy brutalizing her seems to get a new lease of life, a horrifying grin on his face, just as tears well in Hanna's eyes.

"Anni..." she whimpers.

"I'm so sorry..."

But she doesn't respond to that, her eyes terrifyingly stuck on my body, to the knife in my thigh.

Can she even feel what's being done to her anymore?

Tears fall freely down my cheeks, my soul in pieces at her plight. I've begged so much for them to take me instead; I'm out of options. I've never felt so powerless... useless. I just want her pain to stop.

Please, make it stop.

"Is that all you want? For me to beg for my life?" I ask, turning my attention back to Bartiste, forcing myself to ignore the pain in my thighs.

But Bartiste's attention has shifted. It's still on me, but as I look between him and Hanna, I realize they're fixed on the same spot—Hanna with horrible fear in her eyes, and Bartiste with newfound power. It hits me then... my hands sit possessively over my belly. Even as I'm bleeding out of one leg, and with a knife in the other, I'm covering my belly.

I can't let go. Not as sickening goosebumps spread all over my skin from the hungry look in his eyes. It's a different type of hunger than I've ever seen before. It's foaming at the mouth and demanding payment in pain and suffering. It's stripping me bare and waiting patiently, because it knows... My time to beg starts now.

"Anni..." Hanna whimpers.

Bartiste slowly wraps his hand around the handle of the knife, with each finger tightening around it the blade widening the hole in my leg and I have to bite my lip so as not to scream again.

"Could it be?" he almost whispers.

"Kill me. If I start begging, nothing will change. My fate is sealed."

"*When*. When you start begging."

He slides the knife out as I seethe through gritted teeth.

"And *when* you kill me, your plan will have the same effect on me. It's a waste of our time... just do it now." I sound brave, but my insides are shaking.

"Who said that my plan is to kill you?"

He's speaking in the same chilling tone he used when we first met him, and he gave his promises of what would happen to me if we crossed him. I refuse to focus on it because I know I haven't found out yet the true extent of his wrath.

"Don't you get it? I'm using you to my benefit. At this moment, the benefit is my pleasure. Once I'm bored, and I expect it will happen soon, you will be my payment for the trouble you've caused. Now, I haven't decided how many dicks you'll have to take for the debt to be repaid. It could be a few hundred, or... maybe you'll fetch a good price at auction."

A shudder rips through my whole body, but I only seem to feel it in the stab wounds in my thighs. The prickles pure torture in that bloody mess.

"Which brings me to the second part of my pleasure. Considering how protective you appear to be of your belly, you might actually fetch a pretty damn good price. They love the pregnant ones at these events. They especially love those spawns that come out of you. The things they do to those babies, tsk tsk tsk."

Nausea hits me so fast and hard, there's nothing I can do to stop the wave that rushes through me. I vomit on the floor, narrowly missing my legs and his shoes, my stomach spasming even after there's nothing left. There wasn't much in there to begin with, since we haven't exactly been fed three meals a day.

"I'll die before anyone can get their hands on this baby!" I hiss, spitting right in front of his feet, the thoughts he just planted in my brain so vile, I would rather kill myself than let this baby be born in this world.

The asshole laughs. He fucking laughs and more damn tears stream from my eyes, but I'm not even sure why anymore. Too many reasons are thrown at me.

"Wishful thinking, pretty bitch. I think it's time to assess that snatch of yours and see for myself just how much you could fetch at auction. Although... a hole is just a hole, doubt yours will be any different."

No, no, no!

Bartiste steps forward, reaching behind me, and suddenly I'm yanked up, the rope around my throat tightening as I'm forced to my feet. Blinding pain rips through my stab wounds, but the shriek that shreds my lungs is caught in my throat, right behind the rough rope I'm hanging from when my muscles refuse to work and my legs buckle.

I desperately reach up, trying to grab onto the rope to hoist myself, and I'm met with the asshole's harsh grin.

"I don't want you on your knees just yet."

He yanks me up with such force, I have no choice than to rise and grab onto his forearm to keep from falling. There's no option to debate the pain I'm in, not with the cold blade he suddenly pressed onto my cheek. I find whole new ways to fight through it as it tears through my muscles.

"If you cut me," I mutter slowly, "you'll fetch nothing for me."

He cocks his head, then yanks the rope another fraction of an inch, and I immediately feel the nick of the knife on my skin.

He doesn't give a shit.

"You've seen too many movies, little girl. This is no luxury virgin auction where you end up in some millionaire's mansion. This is the type of auction where only people with very particular tastes attend. There's a world of possibilities for someone in your condition. Their imaginations will run wild, and you'll be lucky if by the time they're done with that progeny of yours, you'll still have all your limbs left, or organs, for that matter. They can't even make horror movies about the people who buy your kind of meat."

My eyes burn with every word he speaks, and I realize that anything... absolutely anything is better than what he just described. Death before it all is an absolute gift I'm ready to receive.

My knees give out, my arms drop, but he still holds me firm by the rope circled around my throat. Only, it's not a rope anymore—it's a noose.

"You're so fucking stupid. You think I'll allow you to die like this and escape your destiny?" I spit at him, but cough frantically when he yanks me up even harder.

It lasts a second more, roughly swallowed when his dirty hand cups the bare center of me, his grip unrelenting.

"Like I said, it's time to assess your snatch," he says as he slides a finger through my slit, and I manage to cry out in anticipation.

"Leave her... the fuck... alone." Hanna's raspy voice sounds from the floor behind Bartiste, almost startling us, but more importantly, distracting him.

She swings backward with vigor I haven't seen in her since we were brought here, the crack of bone resonating through the concrete room as she connects with the man behind her. The rope loosens and I reach for Bartiste's knife, but the asshole turns as

I'm about to grab it. All of a sudden, he shouts indecipherable profanity as he looks down, where Hanna claws at his legs, pulling and making him lose his balance.

"You fucking bitch!" He spins, dragging me with him, and in one swift move, he kicks her straight in the belly.

But time slows after this. A sick goddamn joke the universe is playing on us... because my world crumbles as I watch him bend over and slam his knife into her middle.

Twice.

He tugs me back as I scramble to get to her, but the air feels like molasses, slowing my movements as a harrowing shriek bursts my eardrums.

The scene plays in slow motion, a movie I can't wrap my head around, because there's no way anything I'm seeing is real. It must be a nightmare. It has to be. Just like I've had every day since I've been here. That must be it—a nightmare.

"Shut up!" someone yells, just as a deep slam in my ribs takes my breath away, the noose falling limp around my neck.

It's not a nightmare.

"Hanna!" I cry out.

Something scratches my leg as it pulls on me, but I don't care, I'm almost next to her, witnessing the pain slowly dissolve from her eyes.

"Hanna! Please, please, honey, please stay with me!"

There's a commotion around me, urgent exchanges between men, but I can't focus on them. All I see is her.

Metal on metal screeches, then a different light streams in, giving me a better view of the pool of blood gathering underneath the woman who has given me life over the last six years. I don't turn, though. I refuse to break eye contact.

I finally reach her, roll her onto her back, and press my arms on the bloody mess on her stomach. Breaking eye contact for a moment, I look around the room in a panic, searching for something to wrap around her, to apply pressure. A screeching metallic sound splits the air once more, the dim light all that remains in the space. That, Hanna's staggered breaths, and my whimpers. Nothing else.

We're alone.

"Please, hold on! You're so strong. Between us, you've always been the strongest. A goddamn force to be reckoned with!" I sob as I take in her paling face.

"Anni..." she whispers, grabbing onto my forearm with a shaking hand. Her whole body is trembling.

"No! Don't you dare show weakness now. If anyone can do this, if anyone can survive this, it's you!"

"I love you, Anni. So much..."

Blood begins to spill out of her mouth, a trickle at first, then more with each breath. I lean over and lift her head so she doesn't choke, while trying to apply pressure to her stomach with my other arm.

"Hanna, please, please don't leave me." Pushing through the sting in my eyes, my tears fall onto her body, mixing with her blood.

Yelling and frantic thuds distract me, a whirlwind of crashes and noises coming from beyond this door. *Fighting?* Gunfire sounds a second later, jolting me, confirming.

The blood rushes back into me with a welcomed force. *Is it them? Ronan?!*

"We're in here!!!" I scream repeatedly with newfound power, holding Hanna to me. "They're coming for us. Hang on, just a little longer, honey. I'm begging you, just a little longer."

But she's not shaking anymore. She's still, apart from her chest that moves with slow breaths, too much time between each one. And she's smiling.

"Please, please don't leave me."

"We had some fun…" She quirks her lips.

"We'll have some more. Me, you, whoever's growing inside my belly. You can't leave me. I can't do this without you."

She takes a staggered breath, choking silently on the blood that fills her mouth.

"You're so mu—much stronger than you think. And… you'll never be alone again. You'll have everything… you've ever wished for."

"Please, not without you. Please… I love you."

She's too goddamn calm!

"We're in here!" I yell even harder this time, the commotion closer to us now.

"I love you… You better tell your baby all about me."

"Goddamnit, Hanna! Fight! You have to fight! You have to tell them yourself!"

"Tell Finn… tell him I want him to forgive himself. And you… too."

Her breaths are not breaths anymore. Only a wheezing noise that doesn't pass through her throat.

"Hanna?" *No, no, no.* "Hanna?!" There's no light in her eyes… "Hanna!!!"

A desperate cry splinters the air, just as light fills the room. Moments later, warmth envelops me, my throat raw, but I can't stop the onslaught of wails. My lungs are constricted by the grip around me, but I can't stop crying, bellowing, and begging the gods to bring her back. That warmth holds me tighter, wrapping me in a protective shield as all I can do is break.

Someone falls on the other side of her, gripping her beautiful face, swiping the stray hairs back.

Finnigan…

I'm struggling to see, my vision blurry, like I'm underwater with no goggles. Even so, it's impossible not to recognize it in him—agony. It's filling me too right now, the type that burrows inside of you and demands a home. It marks you. Taking away something precious, irreplaceable.

He gathers her in his arms, holding her bloody, broken body to his chest, speaking to her in loving, begging tones.

But she doesn't hear him.

She'll never hear him again.

She'll never hear me… see me… give me her sassy looks with her perfectly trimmed cocked eyebrows. She'll never light up a room again.

She'll never be…

I can't pry my eyes off her, afraid she'll disappear for the final time. I can't… I sit there on the cold floor, crying as Ronan kisses my forehead and whispers things to me that I can't understand. He might as well speak a different language, all of them could. He rips his t-shirt and ties scraps around my bleeding thighs, then wraps me in his jacket. There's silence in my eardrums, my throat sore and scratchy, my eyes dull and burning from all the tears.

I think they ask me questions. Or maybe Ronan does. But speaking just seems... wrong. Blasphemous. Why do we deserve to have a voice when hers was so brutally taken away in an instant?

I'm lifted off the ground completely, watching as Finnigan does the same to the only friend who has ever meant anything to me.

I'm forced to break eye contact as I'm carried out the door. When the smell of rusty metal combines with wet grass, I finally turn to Ronan. I thought there was nothing left of me to break, but his gaze proves me wrong. More of me shatters at the conflict marring his eyes. Gratitude tears him apart, the rips filling to the brim with agonizing guilt.

The same one that begins to drown me.

It's all my fault...

Every broken piece of me sinks with the excruciating weight of this shame.

I'm still here. *We* are here. My body is warm. Alive. Cradled in his arms. We have a chance, a future together. And Hanna has nothing...

How are we supposed to carry on in this unfair universe? How am I supposed to bring a child into this world when my first memories of them in my belly are filled with violence and grief?

"I'm sorry," Ronan whispers.

Me too.

I can't seem to say it, though.

Our lives are forever changed. In such cruel, contradictory ways.

I drop my head to his shoulder and let myself get carried away to wherever this pain can fester in peace.

CHAPTER 16
Ronan

I'M THE BIG brother. I'm supposed to fix this. I'm supposed to do something, anything, to make this better. No. Better sounds wrong.

It's been four days since our world crumbled. Annika hasn't left our bedroom, has barely spoken, barely eaten.

Katya and I started making arrangements. We've tried to track down Hanna's family, but it turns out that Annika is all she had. There are some distant relatives out there, but none who were part of her life—she was adopted. I had no idea...

How could I? I never even fucking bothered to ask her about her life. I don't even know if Finn was aware; I couldn't ask him.

He can't even bear to look at me.

Guilt eats at me every time I head toward my side of the penthouse to check on Annika. I know what he's thinking, and it's impossible to ignore. When I enter our bedroom, where she lies under the covers, silent, her soft breaths the only sound in the room, her empty, broken gaze tells me that she's thinking the exact same thing too.

Such a cruel twist of fate.

She's been borderline catatonic since she woke up in the hospital after the brief surgery on her sliced thigh muscles. I haven't pushed. I've just taken care of her in silence, giving her what little comfort I have to offer.

I had to fight the hospital staff to tell me of her condition, since I'm not family. Apart from the two stab wounds, she has a broken rib, bruising, and a few cuts. They haven't said if she was sexually assaulted. I don't have the heart to ask her yet. She's broken, no matter what her body shows.

Then there's the thick bruise around her neck... I've built so many scenarios in my head around it and each is worse than the last. I know it's from a rope. I pulled it off of her when I found her in that concrete box, whaling as she held the lifeless body of her best friend. Did they hang her? Was she dying when I burst through that goddamn door? What the fuck was happening in there?! If I would have been a few minutes late... would I be organizing two funerals right now?

That mark around her throat is a constant reminder of how badly I fucked up. I'm a failure... and I don't think there's anything I can do to fix this for her and my brother.

Finn is barely recognizable and he's not transitioning through the stages of grief. I thought he was about to... but then we got Hanna's autopsy report. We saw her body, we thought we knew what to expect written on those papers. We were wrong. Parts of it made bile rise to my throat. We're no angels; we've done some terrible shit in this *career* of ours, but I could never justify this kind of mindless, pointless torture and sexual assault on a person. I tried to keep the report away from Finn. I didn't want him to see what they did to her, but he forced it from me.

I guess he had a right to know, but I would have done anything to protect him from another wave of pain. It piled up on top of everything else that burdens him, like the sense of failure we both share. He read that report with a straight face, but his staggered breathing betrayed that composure. I thought he would break, lash out, but he said nothing. Did nothing. Finn swallowed every devastating feeling, absorbed it all within himself, then he left. I didn't see him until the next day. I have no idea where he went and, even if I asked, he wouldn't have told me anyway.

He'll never look at me the same again.

Not when I have Annika back.

I'm supposed to grieve too. But... she's here. My Annika is still here. The happiness I feel is overwhelming. And sickening.

I still hear that harrowing bellow when I drift off. It shook the basement of that house, where we found them. It made me sick to my stomach, and I almost blacked out as I killed the rest of the men that stood in my way. When we finally burst in, in that dim light, I couldn't tell who was lying on the floor and who was crying over who.

There is no way I'll ever forget how my heart sank. It was at that moment I realized just how much I love her. Just how much my soul depends on her.

Funny... what love does to a person. It alters our chemistry, making us dependent on them like it's the oxygen in the air and we would never be able to breathe without them ever again. Annika is my oxygen, running through my veins, and keeping my heart beating.

When I realized it was Hanna lying there... unmoving, through relief and guilt, I wondered if my brother felt the same about her as I do about Annika.

I never asked... Talking about our feelings in such detail has never been a thing of ours.

Probably because neither of us has ever felt *this*.

Death is not new to us, not in our profession. But violent deaths of the people we love... those we're not familiar with.

I'm standing midway between the door and the bed, hoping for a sparkle from her eyes that seems to look right through me. A hint of recognition. Something... anything.

Nothing comes.

So I do what I've been doing every day since I brought her home—I wash her, help her to the bathroom, re-dress her wounds, brush her hair, and try to feed her, then slide into bed next to her, drifting in a restless sleep. She functions, she walks, she sits, she does everything she's supposed to, but she's just existing here... going through the motions.

I don't push. As much as I crave her comfort... she's the most important thing right now. I'll be here for her, for as long as she needs me.

* * *

I open the door to our bedroom with one hand, carrying a tray in the other, with tea and buttered toast lathered in her favorite plum jam, but I'm stopped dead in my tracks. For the first time since I brought her here six days ago... she turns to me.

It startles me and I stand, dumbfounded, marveling at the beauty of this sight. She's actually looking at me, not through... and she's stunning. Even with pain-stricken eyes, she's everything.

I kneel next to the bed, not even realizing I've put the tray down somewhere, pulling her small hand in a tight grip and holding it to my lips.

She rolls over fully, moving intentionally for the first time since she's been here, and she grabs onto me, pulling me up. I have no idea what's happening, but I let her take me with her as she scoots back in the bed, making me crawl under the covers, and when she doesn't stop me, I scoop her in my arms, enveloping her in my body as she rests her cheek against my chest.

I could fucking scream right now. Her warmth seeps under my skin and suddenly I can breathe again.

My t-shirt dampens, her tears soaking it as soft cries gently vibrate against me. They come in almost silent waves, her arms gathered to her chest, trapped between us, and I could get on my knees and thank the gods for this. Instead, I tighten my hold, pressing soft kisses to the top of her head as I gently rub her back and let her weep.

I don't think she's cried since I brought her here. Maybe when she was alone, but never in my presence. Most definitely not in my arms. I've touched her to clean her, dress her wounds, but she hasn't sought my touch. Maybe it's shallow, or selfish, but it terrified me; the fact that this loss would have such an impact that she might have never allowed herself to carry on... with me. With *us*.

Through the partially open blinds, the sun streams in, shifting slowly as we lie here, entangled in comfort we so desperately need.

"She was being raped, yet she was trying to save... me. I don't know how to live with that. She was murdered because of me."

"No... Annika, she was murdered because a psychopath made the decision to kill her."

"You weren't there... if she hadn't tried to pull him off me, she wouldn't have made him angry, and he wouldn't have stabbed her. You came mere minutes later... we would have both been saved." She pauses, sobbing softly and catching her breath. "I can't stop blaming myself for her death."

"You're not alone, baby. I feel that guilt too. If I made a different decision, if I listened to my gut..."

Fuck!

"Ronan... I'm scared."

I pull away, enough to look into her eyes.

"Little witch, I'm never, ever, letting you out of my sight. I'll protect you with all I have."

"No... I'm scared because I don't know how to be happy without her."

The sadness in her eyes as she speaks those words is heartbreaking. She's lost, and I can't even claim to know how to help her.

"It will take time. It's too soon to think of that now. Eventually, a little voice will pop up inside your head that will sound like her, and she'll bully you into getting your shit together."

"She was very bossy."

I scoff. "In the best ways, really."

"She could have ruled the world," she trails off.

"She would have made a great aunt."

That statement brings a whole other wave of sadness, and I regret saying it. I don't need to add more pain.

"This is really happening..." She touches her belly, and I dare cover her hand with mine.

"It is, little witch."

The hospital did a blood test before the surgery and a scan when she woke up. She's early on, but she's definitely pregnant. With my child. *Mine.*

I thought this moment would scare me. That it would bring unknown anxiety and doubts about my future. None of that happened. Instead, I felt enormous relief when the doctor told us everything looked good and was developing as expected.

There are no doubts, but the opposite actually. It took no time at all to make a decision about my future— *our* future.

Now I just have to wait for the right time, to see how she feels about it.

Annika

CHIRPING WOKE ME up. Loud. Sharp somehow. Demanding. Breaking through the brain fog that has plagued me for days. I lift my head from the dense pillow and blink the sleep away, but I can't see anything. The blind is down and it's dark in here.

Dark.

Too dark.

A sickening feeling fills my throat, and my body starts to shake from the inside out. It settles in my chest with such terror, I'm somehow choking. I'm suddenly cold, shivers coating my skin, my muscles frozen in place, as panic sets in.

I will my lungs to pump, do something, anything, but my chest only spasms, tiny bursts of air barely passing through my nose. My vision blurs.

Then a scent penetrates the rising blood pressure. It's rich, deep, and comforting. It smells of cedar and jasmine. *It smells of Ronan.* And it breaks through the barrier, my lungs filling with the relief he brings.

You're in his bed.

My fingers twitch against the soft touch of the comforter, pushing me to further focus, rationalize the shadows around me.

It's a different kind of darkness.

But it's darkness nonetheless. A surge of fear-fueled adrenaline passes through my muscles, and I jump out of bed, almost ripping the cord of the blinds as I roll them up. Bright sunshine penetrates Ronan's bedroom, making me take a few steps back while covering my face with my forearm. I'm panting as the sunshine heats my cold skin, making the shivers subside.

Shit.

The last thing I need is an aversion to darkness.

"Aaah, Christ!"

I bend over, gently pressing my palms over the bandaged stab wounds in my thighs, realizing I jumped out of bed far too quick. My muscles will take time to recover, and sprinting like that is not freaking helping. But feeling something, anything, is better than this numbing heartbreak. And I feel a lot... ribs hurt, my lungs seem to ache, my shoulders, neck and back. None compares to my heart.

Nausea hits me like a ton of bricks, and I rush to the bathroom through the pain in my thighs. I drop to my knees, hugging the toilet, and emptying my stomach. There's not much food in there, enough to keep this nugget in my belly growing, but that's it. I haven't had much of an appetite. Luckily, I haven't had too much morning sickness either. Hopefully, this is not the start of it.

That sharp chirping distracts me again. It's not birdsong, it's more like... a call. A long, demanding noise.

Is it coming from inside the penthouse?

I brush my teeth, then go to the bedroom door, opening it for the first time since Ronan brought me back. I wince as I get the first peek through the corridor that leads to the open living area. There is so much sunshine there, it sparkles against the space, and suddenly I hate everything about being here. It's... beautiful. Cheerful.

Nothing deserves to be beautiful right now. Not for a long time.

It's the silence that keeps me from slamming that door closed and crawling back into bed. Silence, apart from that damn bird.

Am I alone?

I've heard voices before. The guys always seem to come here now, probably for their business meetings, since Ronan has been reluctant to leave. Even Ekaterina was here, the only one, apart from a doctor and Ronan, who had stepped into the bedroom. She helped him, helped me.

But I don't think anyone's here, not even Ronan.

I haven't had the power to move, to breathe too hard, to do anything but lie in bed, sleep, or occasionally deal with morning sickness in the en-suite bathroom. I can't find the will to pretend I can carry on. But that's not the only reason I've stayed in Ronan's bedroom. He shares this penthouse with his brother. Finnigan—the man who lost her too.

I'm terrified of facing him. I know he wasn't with her for that long, but if their connection was anything like what mine is with Ronan... fuck.

Does he blame me as much as I blame myself?

I take a tentative step forward. Then another. And by the third one, I still can't hear any sound. So, I go on until I'm in the living area, the floor-to-ceiling windows to my right letting far too much sunshine through those sheer white curtains. But one of the doors that leads out to the terrace is open, one of the curtains dancing slowly in the breeze. The salty scent of the ocean drifts through, and I take a deep breath.

That chirping calls to me again, urging me to move farther. My instinct tugs at me to go back, pull the blinds down, and crawl under the covers until this reality dissipates, because it's all too much. Against my better judgment, I step into the doorway of the terrace, and the view knocks me out. It's offensive... with its calm ocean, blue sky dusted with fluffy clouds, and the source of the incessant chirping darting around—two swifts flying happily.

The birds soar right in front of the terrace in a crazy dance around each other, chirping away like a bickering couple. Then they disappear to the right, yet their peeping remains. I follow the sound, and when I find the source, I'm met with more pain—they have a nest in the corner of the terrace, right under the awning of the roof. I can hear more of them, not as loud... baby swifts.

One of them flies around again, the ocean view its backdrop, before it lands on the railing, only a few feet before me.

When have I stepped out onto the terrace?

The bird cocks its head from one side to the other repeatedly, watching me. I've never been so close to a bird. Especially a swift. They're always on the move, flying so fast, their movements sharp and controlled, so gorgeous with that forked tail and graceful wings. They remind me of Hanna. Elegant, slim, energetic, intelligent.

Slowly, I lift my hand in its direction, then take another step forward. I don't know why. I just do. Then another step. Then another. Then stop, dropping my arm.

I'm fooling myself.

Just like Hanna, this bird will fly away too soon. I'll never touch it... ever. The only difference is that I'll hear that bird sing, but I'll never hear Hanna's voice ever again. I'll see that bird in its flight, moving with such grace in the sky, but I'll never see Hanna move with that grace ever again.

As expected, the bird darts away, but stains my view with its flight, before the other one joins in once more. Queenscove buzzes below. So alive, oblivious to this loss that stopped my world in its tracks.

It's beautiful. Idyllic. That type of view that puts a smile on your face, and makes your day better, makes you happy. It's horrible. The world doesn't deserve to be happy when she's not here to experience it. I don't deserve to be happy when I didn't do everything in my power to save her.

She did everything in hers to save me.

Everything.

She gave her life to protect me.

And soon... soon, she'll be just a pile of ashes.

The breeze hits my face, chilling the tears that fell against my cheeks, and I don't dare wonder if they'll ever stop. I deserve this—the pain. I deserve to have this guilt eat away at my soul until I'm like her... dead. I deserve so much worse than this.

The tears fall faster, whimpers being carried away by the breeze. They're mine.

That contradiction hits me like a brick, the weight of it pushing me to my knees as sobs fall in harsh waves. Because I know that in however many months, I will have at least one reason to be happy. There will be a light in my life that will pull me out of this state, maybe even before the baby growing inside my belly will be born. I know that eventually excitement will fill me. The anticipation of a new soul born out of love in a world that rips it away in an agonizing heartbeat.

I'll be happy... I'll be fucking happy, and nothing feels more horrible, more terrifying than that in this moment. How can I allow myself to be happy when she cannot even *be*?!

Sobs turn to wails, covering the birdsong of the swifts as I sit on my heels, hands braced on the tiled floor, and every tear that falls on the skin of my bare thighs feels like tar.

Someday, when this baby is born, I will have to be strong, for Hanna... She'll want me to be strong and smiling. But today is not that day and it won't be for a while. Even when it comes, it won't erase the guilt that tarnishes my soul.

I don't know how long I sit here crying. This reality hurts... this world that keeps spinning like she wasn't taken away just days ago. It makes no sense.

The breeze sweeps against the back of my neck, but this one feels different... chilling. I whip my head around, and I'm met with cold blue eyes staring at me from the doorway—*Finnigan*.

There's something indescribable passing through his gaze. He's completely still; he doesn't frown, doesn't curl his lips, doesn't even seem to breathe. His eyes fixed on me make mine burn. My soul urges me to run, suddenly in the sight of a predator, but my heart... it shatters all over again. It recognizes the anguish gazing back at me.

I earned the malice he wants to inflict on me. Judging from his expression, death would be it. Only, there's a smugness in those eyes, the message loud and clear— gracing me with the pain of this life will hurt so much more than the ease of death.

Not one muscle moves. Not even in his tightly clenched jaw. He looks at me like I'm wasting the air that fills my lungs. Then he turns and leaves.

"I'm... sorry." I finally whisper.

CHAPTER 17
Ronan

BEING AWAY FROM her makes my muscles twitch and I'm fucking struggling to breathe. It's excruciating. I crave to be around her, even if she has been distant lately, colder than the night she hugged me and fell asleep against my chest. It doesn't matter—being in the same space as her is enough. I hate that I had to leave the apartment. It was way too soon.

My stress levels are through the roof, even knowing that the penthouse has become a fortress with all the security stationed not only at the door, but all through the building and its entrance. She had security the day she was taken. What good did that do? It meant nothing against Bartiste's men, his firepower. Lesson fucking learned.

However... Finn is on his way to the penthouse now, and I wish the thought would calm my nerves. The opposite is happening.

I had no choice but to be here. I insisted on it and Finn drew the short end of the stick. We all feared he would kill before extracting information. He's not rational enough right now for this. I'm not sure I am either, but I've been cooped up in the penthouse for so long now, fantasizing about all the horrible ways I want to exact my revenge, that I'm fucking famished for it. But I refuse to be irrational. Not when the man who did this to our women escaped and it's imperative to find him.

"I don't know where he is."

The voice of the men tied to the metal chair bounces off the walls of the concrete room, as he stares up at Vin standing before him. He cocks his head, the act so slow, the guy blinks rapidly, erratically, the growing discomfort palpable.

"I'm... I'm serious," the asshole stutters.

Vin straightens, and the man's eyes flicker to the small knife he is lazily rolling between his fingers, his other hand casually sitting in the pocket of his black trousers.

"Fuck, man! I get it, he took your women, but I had nothing to do with it! I'm not in Bartiste's inner circle. I have no idea where he's gone!"

"I didn't ask," Vin finally replies.

"Then what the fuck do you want from me?"

"To tell me where you think he is."

"Is he for real?" He turns to look at Madds toward the left corner of the room, before his gaze drifts to me, his attitude growing cocky. "I just told you I don't know where he is, man."

The shriek is the first thing we hear, before we even register the swift, fluid movement with which Vincent threw the knife. It pierced the man's inner thigh.

"You seem to have an attention issue. I asked you where you *think* Bartiste is, not if you know his location. Now..." Vin leans in, just enough that he grips the end of the knife handle with the tips of his thumb and middle finger. "You have until I completely pull out this blade from your thigh to answer me with enough detail that Maddox here can imagine every single street, door, and window, so he can fucking paint it afterward. He's not good at painting, you see, so you have to make sure you're very accurate. If you give us everything I want, I'll stick the knife back in and you won't bleed out on our new floor."

"Fuck you!" he spits, but Vincent dips to the left quick enough that it misses him.

His answer is the slow, harrowing pull of the knife as the asshole seethes through clenched teeth.

"It has a very short blade, as you saw, and right now it's the only thing blocking the flow of blood in your femoral artery."

"Like you won't kill me anyway."

"I'm a man of my word. If I tell you I'll stick this knife back in and won't kill you, I mean it. Now... you don't have long. Spill. Oh... sorry, no pun intended." He puts the man in a daze, constantly switching his attention from his words to the blade slowly sliding out from his flesh.

It confuses him, and he *spills*, telling us the details of the two locations he's heard Bartiste talk about. The motherfucker escaped. He was shot—twice, yet he still fucking escaped. He might be dead, but we don't want to take the chance. We need to make sure.

When we're satisfied with the amount of information he offers, I take a few steps forward as Vin slides the knife back in, then steps back. The man lets out a strained sigh, relieved as he looks down at his leg. He might be lying to us, but the information was too specific, and it's better than nothing. Hope shines in his eyes when he meets mine, ready to be released and make good on Vin's word. He wasn't lying. He is indeed a man of his word, and if he says he won't kill him—he won't.

I made no such promise.

The last expression in his eyes before my bullet pierces his lung is of confusion. It paused on his features for a couple of seconds before he realized his blood was replacing the oxygen needed to breathe.

"You said..." he gurgled as blood rose and spilled from his mouth.

"*I* didn't say anything."

His eyes widen and pain fills them with such speed, the realization that he's facing a slow, painful death hitting him far too early. He will suffer. Yet not nearly as much as he deserves.

I don't care if he wasn't one of the culprits who hurt Annika, or Hanna. They all deserve to burn. I would have strung him by his toes to the fucking ceiling if I wasn't on a mission to find the man who needs to pay in blood, flesh, and bones for touching what's mine. He will die.

I turn and look toward Vin, but he speaks before I get to.

"Go. I'll tell Carter."

I nod, head to the door, but stop after I pull it open.

"I have this gut feeling we won't find him," I tell him without looking his way, my lungs heaving with anger and exhaustion.

"In my experience, pieces of shit like him always pay the price of their sins. Eventually, he'll make a mistake and crawl out of his hole, and we'll be there when he does." He's talking about his father.

"At least you sent yours to the hole yourself. You got that satisfaction," I push back.

"One day, he'll come out. Vile men like him can't fathom bowing down, and it's always their downfall."

For both our sakes, I hope that's true.

"I can't wait as long as you're willing to." I sigh.

"And if you don't have a choice?"

I step into the dark corridor, letting the heavy door slam behind me, refusing to think of that possibility. There's this gnawing pressure building in my head with every step I take. I fucked up... I fucking fucked up! And Bartiste is still out there.

I wipe a hand over my face, trying to pry Vin's words out of my head. *I need the fucking choice!*

He's been through a lot. The only one of us who didn't come from money. He came from poverty, emotional, and physical abuse. I don't know if it shaped him differently, or if he was always this way, but Vincent Sinclair does not need anything to make people crawl to his feet. He can turn over his pockets and let dust fall from them, and people will still spill all their secrets.

Maybe it's his charm too. Maybe it's the deadly look in his eyes.

Or maybe it's the effect of that one singular moment when he brought his father to the brink of death and kept him there until he agreed to fuck off out of our city. Either way, no one's been missing the man. Especially not Vincent's mom.

I hope I get to witness Bartiste's downfall soon, even though it might not make a difference to the idea that formed in my head, the thoughts surrounding it getting louder every day.

That's not what I want for Bartiste, though. There will be no mercy for the man who dared take Annika away from me and kill my brother's woman. He will not be chased away. No, he will be hunted down and gutted like the scum he is.

Annika

I CAN'T EXPLAIN why, but the moment the bedroom door opened behind me, I pretended to be asleep. I didn't need to turn around to know it was Ronan, even in this room laced with his scent, I could recognize how much stronger it becomes with his presence. It was him. And I just lay here, hugging the comforter to my chest, my back to the door, and my eyes closed.

I stayed like that while he paused next to the bed, listening to his strained breaths like the weight of the world sat on his shoulders. I laid here while he stroked my hair, before he gently lifted the comforter from my legs to check on my bandages, as he's done multiple times a day since he brought me here. I even stayed like this while he went to the bathroom and took a shower.

I didn't even move when I heard a loud thud that rattled the shared bathroom wall and the hiss that followed. I stayed like that as he crawled into bed with me, keeping his distance, yet... extending a touch to me, a gentle one between my shoulder blades. No, he wasn't–isn't keeping his distance—he's giving me space. The two are worlds apart.

But everything feels wrong now and I'm not sure how to make it right.

I can feel the heaviness that weighs down the mattress right along with him as he returns from his shower, the anger, the frustration, the burden of everything else. I want to turn around, soothe him, tell him it will all get better. But I can't move... I can't lie to him.

Eventually, I fall asleep for real, but even in that slumber, I can feel him—I'm safe.

* * *

I woke up with a start. Multiple voices sounding past the bedroom door, and this goddamn room is dark again. I take a deep breath, praying his scent will ground me yet again. Only I seem to have gotten used to it now. It's not as strong anymore... and it smells like me too. *Like us.*

Jumping out of bed quickly, I'm careful not to force my muscles, and pull the blinds open. I head toward the door and listen, breathing easier when I recognize the voices. There're three of them. One of them is Ronan, one is probably Finn, but I'm not entirely sure who the third is.

I turn around, slowly walking back to the large window, taking in yet another marvelous view of Queenscove and the sea beyond. But today... today I don't seem to hate it as much as I did yesterday.

I can't avoid the world any longer. I can't avoid the arrangements that have to be made for Hanna either. Although Ronan did dare to ask me some very general questions about her, like her favorite color, music, and her favorite flower. He stopped when my voice began to tremble, on the verge of sobbing.

After brushing my teeth, I pull one of Ronan's shirts on. It's long enough that it covers my ass, but doesn't quite reach the middle of my thighs. It doesn't matter; since those days with Bartiste, my nakedness hasn't felt important.

The voices are louder when I walk into the corridor and near the living area, but when I step into view, the room goes silent. There're more than three people here— Ronan, Finnigan, Vincent, and Ekaterina. All sitting or standing around the kitchen island.

It seems like I interrupted a discussion I'm not supposed to be privy to. But it's not that, is it? I'm the elephant in the room. The woman who got kidnapped along with her best friend, but only she came back.

Ronan rushes to me before I even finish that thought. He wants to comfort me so badly, but I attempt to step around him and toward the fridge.

"Sit down. I'll get you what you need."

"It's okay, I can do it."

"Annika," he warns. "Sit down. Tell me what you want to eat, and I'll do it for you."

I drag my eyes up and look at him briefly before turning my head toward the empty seat. It's between Ekaterina and Vincent. That means I will be facing Finnigan... fuck.

It's okay, I don't have to look at anyone.

I comply and go to sit, mumbling something about wanting fried eggs, bacon, and maple syrup. The reality is that I would also want some French toast, a whole bucket of syrup, maybe some pancakes too, and some hash browns. This pregnancy is starting to mess with my appetite.

I suck in a wince as I attempt to lift myself onto the stool, and before I know it, Ronan is there, hands around my waist, lifting me up and setting me down gently. I didn't expect it... my gaze flashes to Finnigan involuntarily, and I catch him glaring at me. Ekaterina clears her throat, and he suddenly looks away.

I'm still not sure how I feel about her. She's done nothing to me. On the contrary, she's been helping Ronan and I, but I can't figure her out. She gives off a chilling vibe, guarded, like she takes years to warm up to someone, and trust is a privilege she doesn't give freely.

She's in her element amongst these guys, though, comfortable, at ease. I just feel... out of place.

The reason why sits across from me.

A generic conversation begins, but I'm so unfocused, I don't register a thing about what they're saying. They could be speaking to me, but my attention is glued to the man currently pottering around the kitchen, cooking me breakfast. I try really hard not to meet Finnigan's eyes, even as they seem to challenge me. The heat of his gaze is so different to Ronan's. There's no comfort in that warmth; it burns me in the worst kind of way.

Not long after, a plate with two fried eggs and many more slices of streaky bacon is set before me, and I drench it in maple syrup before I begin eating. Finnigan keeps watching me, and once in a while, Ekaterina clears her throat again, making the burn on my skin ease. I don't know how to change this, how to make it better.

Annika.

Hmm?

"Annika?"

I twitch, pulled back into the room, when I realize Ekaterina is trying to get my attention.

"Yes?"

"When you have a minute, would you mind if we have a word?"

Her expression is a shred gentler than usual, but I'm still taken aback by the request. I don't remember ever speaking with her in private.

"Um, sure. Whenever you want."

She spots my apprehension and confusion and continues.

"It's about the ceremony. We just want to make sure we're doing everything right."

About the... what?

"Ceremony?"

"Funeral."

I flinch at Finnigan's cold voice. That one word knocks at an imaginary door inside of me, which holds the raw emotions I'm trying to keep at bay.

"O—Of course." I push the plate away, my appetite gone. "Do you want to go now?"

She nods and slides off the barstool, offering me a hand to help me. If this numbness wasn't so deeply etched inside of me, I would be real sick of being treated like an invalid... but I couldn't give less fucks about it.

"Where do you think you're going?" Ekaterina asks, and I turn to find her looking at Finnigan, who's following us.

"She was mine. I get to be part of this," he warns.

"I don't deny that, but you already know what's happening. Annika should be the one to have the final say in everything and let us know if we're missing anything.

"It's okay..." I say gingerly, trying to diffuse the growing tension.

Ekaterina straightens, her stance shifting in this commanding way that reminds me so much of Hanna.

"No. Finnigan, if we need you, we'll let you know. Annika was—"

"There when my Hanna drew her last breath?! The reason why she—"

"Careful, brother! You're crossing a line!"

Ronan's at his side now, Carter on the other. Veins bulge in Finnigan's temples.

"What?! You know it, I know it, everyone motherfucking knows it! She fucking died because of you!" He throws his arm out, pointing at me with such anger and disgust, I actually take a step back.

Tears well behind my eyes, heat flashes through me, and it sears through numbness that has plagued me. It turns to fire, walls crumbling at my feet, and before I know it, I've stepped toward him, heaving as I watch Ronan put his hand up to keep me away. But I don't give a shit.

"Fuck you, asshole!" He doesn't have time to react before my hand slaps him across the cheek, snapping his head to the side, but the guys pull him back. "Fuck you! You think I don't fucking blame myself every single goddamn day?! She died in my arms! She died in my fucking arms! I lost her! She was everything to me, the goddamn soul in my body! I am nothing, fucking nothing without that insane aura she projected!"

Carter and Ronan are holding him as he pulls to move closer to me, struggling in their grip.

"Let me go, asshole!" he spits, giving his brother a warning look. "Don't think for a second that I will ever stop blaming you for holding us from going with them on that goddamn island."

I can see Ronan wants to respond, but... he doesn't seem to have a comeback for that.

"I lost her too!" Finn rasps. "She was mine. She was the present and the future and you fucking sent her way back to the past! Yet everyone is treating me like goddamn nothing!" He turns back to me and bellows, "You let her fucking die!"

"I did nothing! I couldn't do anything! They made me fucking watch, Finnigan! I begged until I lost my voice! She bled on my flesh, she bled with your goddamn name on her lips, and there was nothing I could do to stop the hurt, to stop her from leaving me! Your blame on me pales in comparison! I don't need you to tell me she's fucking gone because of me!" I close the distance between us, my hand flexing, ready to hit him again. "Because I already know that!"

He holds still, defiantly, his eyes on mine. No, not defiantly... but painfully. Harrowing, devastating pain. He's waiting for his punishment. So, I do the one thing I don't want to do, but need to. Because he's the only one who has lost her almost as much as I did.

I wrap my arms around his waist and bury my face in his chest, putting all my emotions in my grip, all the grief, the anger, the sadness. I don't know when the tears started falling, but they're soaking his t-shirt, and his hard body softens. As my grip loosens, and I'm about to pull away, his arms wrap around me, keeping me close, his hot breath hitting the top of my head.

"I should have never left that island," he whispers to me alone.

This is not just about my guilt. I hold him tighter again as I feel his staggered breaths against me. I want to tell him to let go, but I have a feeling he's closing off that part of himself that accepts these kinds of emotions. I know in my gut this will be the first and last moment Finnigan Hennessey opens himself to me.

Nobody speaks a word until we pull away. We both take a step back, looking at each other with different eyes, yet we both know that the blame and the guilt will be with us for a long time. If not forever.

CHAPTER 18
Annika

I'M NOT SURE there are accurate words for my state of mind since Hanna's death. I laid in bed, but my body was on the concrete floor... next to her. My mind was not here, not in Ronan's bed, not in this penthouse, not in Queenscove. I wasn't here. I was there with her... holding her hand as she shifted further and further into the darkness. Only, that darkness wasn't the absence of light, it was my mind. It was a thick, unforgiving smoke that wouldn't dissipate. It flooded my lungs, and took everything that didn't seem to matter anymore, choking it until it almost died.

There was so much of it, and I didn't want to break through. I deserved it. I needed it to make sure the pain of everything would always be fresh, burn my lungs, and rip me apart from the inside.

Until one day, broken blue eyes penetrated the smoke. I saw them before, a slightly brighter shadow in the smog, but that day they looked... defeated. The light was dim, so dim I wasn't sure if they were simply moving further away. They weren't. The light was dying. I couldn't let something else die because of me... I deserved the agony, the punishment. I deserve it and more. But those blue eyes were paying for my sins, and I couldn't allow it.

So, he became clearer as he knelt next to the bed that felt less like a concrete floor. And when I touched his hand and pulled him to me, such an odd thing happened... those eyes slowly filled with saturation. The more I touched him, the more vivid they became, breaking through the smog, making me crave more of their light.

That was the first day I saw, truly saw with a clearer mind, the weight of me. I wasn't nothing... I was someone to this beautiful person who had scoured this continent to save me. Ronan saved me. I was worth something. In the midst of that smoke, it wasn't what I wanted, because I knew I didn't deserve even an ounce of what he was offering. I wanted to let him go. As horrifying as the impact of his absence would be on my heart, I wanted better for him. But when the color was coming back in his eyes, when I saw the brightness returning, I knew I could do no such thing. He was mine... and I couldn't be the reason something else died. Even if this was a feeling, not a person.

It took little time for him to break further through the barrier of my mind and, slowly, I was seeing just how much everyone, not just him, was doing for me. Memories of the last few days flooded, snippets of conversations, of worry, sadness, and anger. All of them, even Vincent and Carter, were involved. These people, who I was a stranger to mere weeks ago, cared in their own way.

Now, as I watch Ekaterina summarize the decisions we just made during our discussion, I understand it even more. We came into the bedroom after what happened with Finnigan, and had an uncomfortable conversation that needed to happen. But now, Hanna's simple, yet beautiful, ceremony is fully planned out, mainly because most of it was done before I even got involved. Ekaterina is so much different than I thought. Behind that stern, poised exterior, there's a kindness she offers selflessly. She has her own, fairly internalized way of expressing it, and I'm grateful I got to feel it. She even helped me send the rest of Hanna's things to storage, where we shipped everything when we emptied the house we rented here.

But it is done now... Hanna's ceremony is all set. Small, intimate, since she didn't have any close friends, and definitely no family. It's been just us, like sisters, for the best part of six years. Making lasting connections through all the traveling and the shady deals was never an option for us. We had each other.

She adored the sea, which is why our *retirement* homes were on a quiet island, which held only a couple of towns and villages. The houses are close to the sea, with uninterrupted views, and a private beach. So, we're going to hold the ceremony on the edge of a small cliff, above a private cove, then we can scatter her ashes over the rippling waves.

I take a deep breath, urging some composure. I can't pretend this is easy, it's nowhere near that... yet, strangely enough, the outburst Finnigan and I had helped somehow. He and I will never be close, I know that, but I think we helped let out some plaguing demons today. I know that the darkness that had me trapped is dissipating. I hope his will too someday.

"Ekaterina?" I stop before we leave the bedroom and turn to her.

"Please, just call me Katya. I like my full name, but it is a bit of a mouthful."

"Oh, okay, Katya, it is. I know *this* is not in your job description, so I just want to say thank you. For taking the time to take this on while I was..." I trail off because I have no idea what I want to say. Injured? Grieving? Numb?

She shakes her head gently, her sandy blond braid falling off her shoulder and down her back.

"I've seen enough loss to know that help is usually never requested, but always needed. There's plenty of men in your life now, but if you need a woman... I'm here."

She doesn't reach for me, but her words are like a warm hug. She may look like a hard woman with her stern features, but she's oddly comforting, even from the distance. Maybe that's why the girls who have been working for her and the guys are so keen.

We walk out of the room, heading back to the living area, when I hear an exchange that makes no sense.

"Did Carter find any trace that Bartiste was there recently?"

I stop in the middle of the room, looking at the men who sit around the sofa, staring at a laptop screen, speaking of things that... shouldn't be.

"Did you... did you just say, Bartiste is..." The vase sitting on the table I'm leaning against is rattling on the wood, and my legs seem oddly soft.

Finnigan and Vincent turn to Ronan, while he looks at me with wide eyes.

"Does she not know?!" Katya exclaims, a comforting hand coming to rest on my back.

"What the hell is going on? Is Bartiste still alive?!" I can't seem to control the tone of my voice.

Ronan rises from the sofa, and when he takes a step in my direction, I step backward. I can see the deep fall of his chest as he exhales, weighing his words. But I can already tell there isn't any sort of remorse in his eyes.

"None of you get to judge me, and you"—he nods to me—"you don't get to be mad at this. There wasn't a right time to tell you that the man who did this to you, to Hanna, escaped."

"No, you don't get to decide that, Ronan. It's not your call when is or isn't the right time to tell me something like this."

"That's where you're mistaken, little witch."

I flinch at that term of endearment thrown so casually in a room full of people, Finnigan's gaze burning a damn hole through me at the sound of it.

But Ronan doesn't care as he continues. "After everything you've been through, your healing was the most important thing to me. So yes, I decided that after my mistake, after what Bartiste did to you, to Hanna, after your surgery, through this loss, the last thing you needed was to know the motherfucker was alive. You don't get to be mad at that."

I'm speechless, mouth gaping, shocked at the audacity of this man.

"I had a right to know!" I seethe.

"And now you do. At the right time."

He takes another step, and I have the urge to slap him.

"Right time? I walked into this conversation. If I didn't, when would you have told me?"

"At. The right. Time."

I don't know when he closed the distance between us, but he's too close, brushing his hand up my arm, then my shoulder, and just as he's about to touch my cheek, my eyes flicker to his brother, to the anger and flickering sadness in his eyes. I step out of his orbit, turning on my heel and heading straight to the bathroom.

I attempt to slam the door, but a thud sounds behind me instead. The bastard's scent hits me before the door bangs against the frame and the lock clicks. I turn, ready to kick Ronan out of here, but before I can say a word, he rushes to me, forcing me to step backwards until my shoulders hit the bathroom cabinet. He towers over me, his energy different than before, the gentleness he has been treating me with since bringing me here, long gone.

There's a simmering rage behind the blue of his eyes, like a ruthless storm in the middle of an ocean and I'm about to be caught by one of the waves.

"I can't read your mind, Annika. You're pulling away from me, and I'm trying very,

very hard to give you space. But I can only give you so much before I fear you're going to pull away completely."

Fuck.

"I just..."

"Don't say this is about grief."

"It is!"

"Do you not want me anymore?" I can practically taste the fear in his angry voice.

"This is not about you, dammit!"

"Is it not? It's me who you're pulling away from. It's my touch you've been avoiding or rejecting, when I've only ever wanted to comfort you. I'm not imagining this, little witch."

"I need time."

He inhales deeply, pulling his lips into his mouth, but his eyes hold an intensity I want to dive into head on. He's so... everything. He's fucking everything. All kinds of wrong when the world has fallen off its axis because Ronan Hennessey's *comforting* touch is not what I'm supposed to be thinking of right now. Especially since his thoughts are innocent... mine aren't.

"I'm okay with that, as long as you'll still be here when that time's up. But I need to know if it's more than grief that made you shrug away from my touch out there." He points toward the door.

"Are you kidding me?! Is this what this is about? Me rejecting you in front of your *friends*?! What is this, high school?! Get out of my way, please." But there's no politeness in the tone.

His gaze darkens, head tipping down to me so slowly I can practically taste his annoyance.

"You could do it in front of the goddamn king, little witch, I don't give a fuck. I only pointed it out because it was the last time you did it. Now, tell me what's going on," he seethes, but I'm already pissed off.

"No. Get out of my way." I'm deflecting, and I can't seem to stop myself.

But the bastard is like a wall in front of me, refusing to move an inch and I can't bear to have this conversation right now. I slam my hands against his middle in an attempt to shift him away, and the man winces, his body folding ever-so slightly. *What the fuck?* I'm not that strong. I lift my hands to touch him again, but he covers his middle with his forearm before I can reach.

I look up at him, brows furrowed, but not in anger, then pull his arm away and lift his shirt.

"Ronan! Oh my God, you're hurt!" I grab his biceps, turning him around until his back hits the bathroom cabinet, switching places, then touch the mean stitching on the side of his abdomen, not far from his waist.

"What happened? Who did this?! When did this happen?"

It looks similar to the ones marring my thighs. So very similar. I lift his shirt higher and frantically begin to check every inch of his torso, panicking that there might be more. There are bruises, so many bruises, at various degrees of healing, some darker than they should be, some already in the faint yellow stage.

"Have you been hurt this whole time?! Goddamnit, tell me what happened!"

But the man stands there, pulling his lips between his teeth, and I could have sworn I caught a glimpse of amusement in his eyes. They're... warmer now.

"Answer me!"

And he does... but it's not the reply I was expecting.

He grabs my head in his hands and presses his lips to mine with such fierceness, I grab onto his forearm to steady myself. He kisses me like he's been thirsty for decades and I'm the only lagoon in the middle of a desert. My legs turn to mush and those stab wounds have nothing to do with it. Core tightening, my already sensitive nipples hurt against the graze of the bra.

Fuck... I didn't realize how much I missed this. His lips on mine, his touch, him. All of him.

I let him in, and he doesn't hesitate as he slides his tongue into my mouth, exploring every inch of me with a subdued hunger. There's more of him to give, but it's not that kind of kiss. This kiss is filled with longing... the soul demanding the connection, not the body.

His hand threads into my hair, pulling my head back to deepen the kiss, only I wince into his mouth, and it all stops in a heartbeat.

"Fuck! I'm sorry." He brushes that hand against my head, soothing it immediately.

"It's okay. It's gone. It's just a bit sensitive."

He brushes a palm over his face, and it's like he takes off a mask. The look in his eyes, the color under them, the curl in his lips, they all change into something I want to nurture and nurse back to health. It's pain, fear, and something... something that looks back at me every time I look in a mirror—guilt.

I caress his cheek, wishing I could wipe it all away and make it better. But it doesn't go anywhere.

"Baby," he sighs. "I have to ask. I'm so sorry, I just, I want to try to understand, and learn how to... how to help. Did they *touch* you?"

I'm not sure what I was expecting, but it wasn't this question.

"You don't know?" I'm a tad confused, and he shakes his head. "I thought they would have said something at the hospital when they did the checkup."

"No. It felt... private. Invasive in a way. I asked about everything else, but unless there was something medically necessary, I thought you would tell me when you felt like it. And I stand by that. If you don't want to talk about it now, I'll be here when you do."

"They didn't rape me, Ronan."

The way his chest collapses is like the weight of the whole Earth rolled off of him.

"But... they've touched me enough to leave a mark."

Telling him that might have been a bit of a mistake. If I ever wondered if fury has a face, I don't need to anymore. It's here in front of me, staring into my soul.

"I'm going to hang him by his fucking dick," he seethes between gritted teeth.

"You're going after him?"

"Will we ever have peace if I don't?"

I don't know. But... do I want him to leave me all over again? I don't know that either. The idea of Bartiste being out there scares the shit out of me. However, being away from Ronan again scares me so much more. Not because of me being taken, but because I cannot possibly lose him too. I can't bear that. I already can't bear the way Finnigan looks at me.

"Can't the others go?"

"They can, but that son-of-a-bitch touched you, Annika. What he did to both you and Hanna... he's not getting away from that. If Finnigan doesn't get to him first, I'm gutting him from dick to throat."

"No..." I whisper.

"No?! You're the sweetest person I know, Annika, but even you couldn't possibly tell me that the asshole doesn't deserve it." His brows furrow as he cocks his head.

I rub my eyes, pressing my hands a bit too hard, attempting to erase the conflicting feelings.

"Fuck, Ronan, I'm not saying I don't want him to die a horrible death. I would gut him myself for what he did to Hanna if I had the stomach for it. But... I just can't be away from you again," I finally confess.

His eyes soften, but the expression doesn't last.

"I don't either. I can't take any more guilt. I fucked up, I fucked up so bad. Finn was right, we should have stayed with you. And those days while Bartiste had you... I thought I knew what pain was. I was so wrong. I was so wrong, little witch. It's why I can't let him get away with this."

"Long and hard, I thought about that moment when Hanna told you two that you should go. She and I spoke about it too... while we were *in there*. You didn't see his men on the island, Ronan. They were on a mission, and you and Finnigan wouldn't have stood in their way. You would have died, and there wouldn't have been anyone to save... me."

I almost said *us* for a moment there.

"Maybe you're right. But it doesn't change the fact that he might still be out there, and he doesn't deserve to be."

"Wait. Might?" I ask, confused.

"He didn't escape unscathed. He was shot several times, but we couldn't find him in the vicinity of the building or surrounding area. So we're going on the assumption that he's still alive, but we have no idea where he could be."

"Then, you're not going anywhere for now." I sigh, relieved.

"I was going to go to one of his locations to see if there's any trace of him there. Sloane's territory is close to one of his other locations, and he said no one has been there."

"Wait, who's Sloane?"

"Oh, he's our cousin. He runs an... organization, up in Venator, and he helped us with the rescue and all."

"He was there when..."

"Yes."

"I'm sorry, I don't remember. I don't remember anything from Hanna's death until the drive here from the hospital." I've been trying, but I really can't recall a thing. Maybe it was the anesthesia, or, yeah, I actually don't know.

"I didn't expect you to. It's not like we had time for introductions. He's helping us with Bartiste now, since our numbers are down, but I—"

"I want him dead, Ronan," I interrupt. "But I want you here with me more."

Ronan

WELL, FUCK. WHAT am I *supposed to say to that? No, I want to kill the motherfucker who wronged you more?*

The look in her eyes breaks me apart. She begged me once before to come with her... I didn't. Look where it led us. The choice is clear because it isn't even a choice—I'm staying here with her.

But the guys and I, we better start recruiting soon, because I need more people to make sure there're enough eyes on the motherfucker.

I wrap my hands around Annika's waist and hold her there, at enough distance that I can still look at her beautiful face without her craning her neck up to look at me.

"You haven't told me why you're pulling away from me," I deflect.

"Are you staying?"

I pull her to me, kissing her plush lips that seem to taste of peaches. Sweet, soft peaches.

"I'm not letting you out of my sight," I finally reply.

She sighs, an invisible weight coming off her as her body relaxes, and she looks somewhere beyond me.

"It's Finnigan. He looks at me like he's about to wrap a noose around my neck and throw me over the terrace railing. And I can't blame him one bit."

"If you want me to talk to him..."

"No. He's hurting. If anyone understands, it's me. He resents me... and not because he blames me for her death. The displays of us, our love... I feel like I'm rubbing it in his face."

"*We*, little witch, *we*. You are not alone in this." I thought I was paying attention to them. I've been focused on their individual healing, on our interactions. My brain acknowledged but skimmed over my brother's reactions at the sight of Annika, the mention of her name. And us.

"I know, but you're not the one he's livid at," she almost whispers, looking up at me with sad eyes.

"Yeah, I am. He blames me for not staying on the island. But I understand. We'll keep it lighter around him."

"Thank you."

Her small hands slide around my waist until she pulls her whole body against mine. I'm not the first Hennessey she's hugged today, but the first one needed it so much more than me.

I sink into this, into her, reveling in the feel of her, how perfectly she fits wrapped around me. I'm not a believer in fate, but fuck me if she didn't make me one. Even through these horrid circumstances, I found her, and I just can't be mad about that.

I don't want to break this moment, but since she seems to be feeling a bit better, I wonder if she's up for something different.

"Baby, do you, by any chance, fancy a change of scenery? A breath of fresh air?"

Leaning back slightly, she looks up at me, arms still linked around my neck.

"Umm... I don't know if it's a good idea. I don't really want to see anyone."

"No. I was thinking we could go to the waterfall." Her brows furrow, but I see a little sparkle in her eyes.

"What, in the forest? Where we went to that party."

"The very one. It's usually quiet there, especially during the week."

She ponders the proposition, chewing on her lip as the cogs spin.

"I'm not sure if I'm up for it today. After Finnigan and... Bartiste. And honestly, I could use a bath. I'm sick of just washing myself with a cloth. The doctor said I could take a bath starting today."

I don't know if she can see the slight defeat on my face because she quickly follows up. "How about tomorrow?"

I'm beaming from the inside out. I don't want to get too excited, but... I'm proud. She's making some progress, letting herself heal slowly.

"Sounds good. Tomorrow then. Now, let's go say goodbye to everyone and go get you in a bath."

I begin to pull away when she forces me back to her.

"Not so fast. You still haven't told me why you're stitched up!"

I almost forgot about that. How rude of me, considering it's the discovery of that stab wound that flipped her attitude just minutes ago, from anger and rejection to full-blown concern, all the above dissipating in a matter of seconds. I couldn't suppress my grin when I realized that she definitely did not stop loving me.

I tell her a shortened version of the events leading up to her kidnapping and I'm sickly enjoying the worry and shock on her face. She's constantly asking me if I'm okay, if it still hurts, how I feel, and so on, like she's not sporting worse wounds in her thighs at the very moment. She worries about me, completely forgetting her own condition. If that's not good mother material, I'm not sure what is.

When we finally leave the bathroom, I catch a glimpse of Finn retiring to his side of the penthouse, and the rest of the space seems silent.

Good, we're alone.

"Bath now?" she asks with a ginger expression.

"Bath now."

But I'm looking forward to tomorrow.

CHAPTER 19
Annika

THE SCENT OF the forest, the wildflowers toward the end of their bloom, and the wet ground around the waterfall are a treat to the senses. Last time I was here, on a midsummer night, Hanna and I were playing what seemed like a dangerous game. If only we would have known what was coming... I guess it's better we didn't. We were so free, so happy. It's August now, yet that night seems like it happened much longer ago, in a different life.

Yet Ronan's touch on me, his lips on mine for the first time, they linger. I can't help but fall into that memory. I had a lot of liquid courage, but it wasn't just the alcohol that took me out of my shell, it was the man holding my hand right now. I looked at him and something in me stirred, a sort of animalistic hunger that demanded him. And I let it consume me. I don't think that hunger is gone, just dormant somehow.

We walk around to the right edge of the pool, and he pulls me on top of this large, flat rock.

"We'll sit here for a bit, yeah?"

I nod and lean over to get my shoes off, but his hand on my shoulder stops me. I turn to him, confused, but then he drops on one knee in front of me, picks up my foot, and begins untying my shoelaces. Looking at him in awe, I steady myself on his shoulders.

He's on his freaking knee helping me out of my shoes!

I'm not sure if it's showing on my face, but internally I'm squeaking.

He removes my Converse, giving my bare foot a quick swipe of his thumb, sending a shudder through me. I think I might ask him for a foot massage at some point. He's good with his fingers, so he'll be amazing at that too. He does the same to the other foot, then he rises, and helps me sit on the edge of the rock, my feet submerged in the slightly chilly water.

God, it feels good.

He takes off his own sneakers, rolling up the legs of his sweatpants, his toned, defined calves distracting me before he sits next to me.

We say nothing for a while, enjoying the day, the sounds of the forest, the scent of everything, the sun on our skin. There's something to be said about the ability to sit in silence next to someone and to be so utterly comfortable.

The sun has been high in the sky for some time, the rays making the pool sparkle. It all looks so incredibly different in the light of the day than it looked that night in the middle of that party. It's peaceful, idyllic.

"I wish I could have stopped her from trying to save me that day... One more minute, and your intrusion would have turned Bartiste away from us. Just one more..."

Ronan looks down at me, some stray strands of hair falling over his forehead making his handsome features look more boyish.

"My mother didn't teach me many things herself, but one lesson will always stay with me. As much as I'm not a believer in the mysticism of life, this I tend to believe—if it's meant to be, it's going to be."

"Isn't that usually applied to good things? Lovers reunited and all that?" I ask.

"That's not how she spoke of it. We use it for these hopeful contexts, like when we're trying to make ourselves feel better about a love lost, but like anything else in this world, there is a balance. Tragedies are also meant to be, and when death calls... it's unavoidable. This was her lesson when my grandfather died in an accident. It taught me that hindsight is the death of peace of mind."

I turn my attention back to the waterfall, letting out a heavy breath.

"Your mother chose a harsh lesson."

"She did. We all wish we had done things differently. We regret and are riddled with guilt. But hindsight... it's a whole other type of haunting."

"For a man who doesn't quite believe in the more mystical side of life, or death, for that matter, you sure do have a way with words."

He chuckles low in his chest, and I find him staring straight at me with a slight grin on his lips.

I'm not sure if I'll ever get used to how beautiful this man is. That defined jaw of his, those high cheekbones, and deep blue eyes, are a hypnotizing combination. They stir something low in my belly and make me squeeze my thighs together.

Yet we haven't touched each other since my return. It's not that the attraction isn't there, but... any type of joy feels wrong right now. Out of place. Disrespectful.

"It won't always be like this," he tells me.

"Logically, I know that this will get better. But I can't help but wonder if it will get worse again."

"What do you mean?"

"My world was dangerous, Ronan, but the one you and your organization are part of is so much more than that. I just don't know if I'm ready to take on all this tragedy." I place my hand over my belly, rubbing gently, and his eyes drop there, before turning his gaze toward the waterfall.

I see the irony in my words, considering it wasn't his world that took Hanna away... it was mine. But the connection is there—I know it, and he knows it too.

He's thoughtful in a different way. There's a heaviness weighing him down and I'm not sure how to make it better. What I'm saying is harsh, but I don't want to hide anything from him. Not when it's not just about us.

"The whole world is dangerous, Annika. I don't think there is any way for any of us to escape that." He turns to me, then covers my hand with his, putting a protective pressure on my belly. "But I'll do anything in my power to shield you from it."

The promise is in his eyes, not only in his words. There's a peculiar clarity staring back at me, and I need to be *in* on the secret it holds.

"I made promises to you, and I intend to keep each and every one of them," he says to me.

"Promises? When?"

"On the phone, before Bartiste's men..."

"Oh."

Venator... the mountains... the West Coast, traveling through this whole continent. It feels like eons ago, yet still not far enough.

"You weren't just distracting me."

"Not only, no. I've never thought of doing anything like that, not until you." The blue of his eyes gleams with his words. "I want every experience I can get with you. I want to see you paint in every corner of this country. I want to swim with freaking dolphins. Take all the baby classes. I want... everything. With you."

"You do?"

"I want our great-grandkids to talk about our love the way you talk about the love between your great-grandparents. Only I'll do everything I can to keep you alive until old age takes us both."

I laugh and I swear it sounds foreign. He notices too, that gleam in his eyes growing brighter.

"You have zero control over my death. But... I think I want all of that too."

He doesn't question my choice of words. Maybe deeper inside of me, I don't just think I want it—I know. He probably knows that as well.

"We'll have more photos of each other, though," he says with a smile.

"Yeah, we definitely will. Too bad my grandpa lost great-grandma's locket... I would have had one."

"Locket? Oh, wait. When we met to buy the painting, you said the only photo of her was lost. Was that it?"

He remembers! Oh my God... It was such a small detail. I can't believe he was paying attention to that.

"Y-Yes. She had a beautiful, oval silver locket, not expensive, but special, nonetheless. Inside, there was a photo of great-grandma and great-grandpa. I saw it once when I was very little, and grandpa showed it to me and told me it will be mine one day. He moved houses not long after, and years later, after he died, we realized it was missing. No one really thought about it for years, until we started going through some old boxes. The assumption is that it was probably lost when he moved. Or maybe it got sold. Anyway, it's lost now."

"I'm sorry." He places his hand over mine on the rock and gives it a quick squeeze. "I don't know, important things have a way of coming back to you. Who knows."

I giggle at his optimism.

"Now that would truly be a miracle."

He pauses on me for a moment, a smile I didn't realize I missed so much etched on his features, refusing to let go. It makes me fall deeper into this sensation. We're both smiling... in what seems like forever. It feels like a stolen bit of time we need to protect so it isn't taken away from us.

"Come on, let's go for a dip."

My first instinct is to refuse him. My mouth is open, about to spill the words, when a shrieking birdsong distracts me. Two swifts engaged in an enticing dance as they fly above the pool, before soaring high and beyond the waterfall.

Such a beautiful moment. And it might be my last one here.

"Okay. Just a little dip."

Ronan helps me up, and we walk off the rock and to the edge of the water.

"Little witch, you don't have to go all the way. Keep your underwear on, your bra... I want you to be comfortable."

I stop moving, realizing I'm about to unclasp my bra with no regard whatsoever to my nakedness. I seem to be forgetting that I'm no longer trapped in that basement... with no care about my modesty.

Looking down my body, at the ground where my summer dress lies crumpled on top of the pile of his clothes, I don't know how to proceed. I'm... stuck. What do *I* want? How do *I* feel about it?

Ronan narrows his eyebrows, clearly noticing the shift in me at the inner-turmoil, and he circles his arms around me, pulling me into his strong, bare chest. *Home.* He feels like home, his skin against mine, his heat warming me, his breath brushing against the top of my head, the pressure of his possessive hold. I'm here... I made it.

I make the decision, drop my hands, and leave my bra on, sinking into his hold.

We saw our baby today, heard the thumping of their little heart, and I let myself fall into the fantasy of having a family with the man who looked at the monitor like it was a miracle captured on screen for the first time. I knew then that I couldn't let myself go... couldn't sink into this sadness and loss of control. No matter how much guilt I feel for having to move forward—I must do it. Hanna would understand. She didn't have one selfish bone in her body, especially when it came to me. She helped me so much over the years to build me up. She took me under her wing when she noticed the will, the need for more in me, for the darker side of the world, for the dangers lurking in the underbelly of society. I wanted a taste, and she gave it to me. Even when she saw I was finally interested in a man for more than a fling, she put a pause on all our plans to get me what I wanted. It was usually easy for her, but not for me. She pushed me, but on my own terms. She would be fucking pissed if she saw me right now, pulling back on everything we both worked for.

It's why I know now, there is no other choice. I will be strong enough to stand on my own, no matter what Ronan decides. I can do this. All of it.

I snake my arms around his middle, running my hands over his slightly damp back, so warm from the sun hitting his soft skin, enjoying how the muscles beneath harden one by one. When he loosens one arm and its heat runs up my skin until it reaches the back of my neck, I look up and I'm met with conflict in his eyes. Such damn gorgeous eyes, a complex blue that sometimes makes you feel like you're lost in the sky in a wingless flight, and other times ruthless waves catching you in the middle of the sea.

I'm distracted once more as his cock hardens between us, and I don't miss the slight guilt in his eyes when it presses against me. He wants me. He's never once even implied anything sexual. He's kept his distance, never pushed more than comfort on me. I don't like that he feels guilty for a natural reaction, the same kind I'm having right now.

I sink into the growing possessiveness of his hand tightening around the back of my neck as he leans in. When his lips finally touch mine, I can't control the soft moan erupting from me just as he can't control the low rumble vibrating in his chest. We kiss under the summer sun and the sound of birdsong and falling water until we're breathless. We kiss until the world looks just a little bit different when I open my eyes. Nothing has changed in it, only my outlook on it, on us, on my future.

"Come." He drops his arms, running his hand down from my shoulder until it forces me to let go of him and snake my fingers between his.

He pulls me into the water, and I jump with a shriek—it's definitely colder than I expected.

"Oh, Ronan, this is... no!"

He lets out a bark of laughter that takes me aback. The asshole is laughing at me!

"You'll be fine, come on. I promise it will get warmer. Our skin is just heated from the sun."

"It's not like I remember it..." I trail off.

He stops for a moment, knowing full well I'm referring to the night that changed my life. Maybe his too.

"Even if this pool was minus ten degrees that night, it would have still felt like molten lava with you in it."

Holly hell.

My mouth falls open slightly, and he's stuck there for a moment, watching me with a hunger I know he's pushing himself hard to suppress.

Suddenly, the water is not that bad.

We swim for a while, letting the water take away some of the tension from our muscles. I spend most of the time floating on my back, letting the sun warm my body. It's so soothing, my ears beneath the surface, listening to the rush of the waterfall. It's not close to us, this pool is big enough that its waves are light here. But underwater, it's like a different world. One that calms and heals. An odd type of therapy.

I've always known I wanted to live next to water. It's why Hanna and I bought our houses pretty much on the beach, on Falk Isle. I want to do exactly this as much as possible. But... with all that's happening, this baby growing inside of me, everything's muddled in my brain. It's too early for a decision, but even so, is Queenscove the right place for this?

I drop my feet and rise, treading water, the sounds of the forest replacing the loud underwater void, and find Ronan leaning against a large rock, watching me. His strong, long arms are spread wide on either side of him as he braces them against the rock, his head tilted slightly, his gaze filled with need he quickly shadows when he catches my eyes.

"I'm sorry, I kind of lost myself."

He shakes his head, but says nothing in response. I can't take my eyes off of his, the intensity of his stare reaching for me like tentacles through the water, wrapping around me, all of me, snaking through my blood and gripping my flesh from the inside out. My parted lips are suddenly dry, my mouth parched, my soul on fire.

Yet neither of us moves.

My breaths quicken, but treading water has nothing to do with that effort.

I'm not sure I've seen this greedy look in his eyes before. This desire demands more than my body. No, it wants all of me. It wants my soul, my heart, it wants to steal it all and never let go. Ever.

I wouldn't hesitate to give it all to him.

Not when that gaze makes me feel like there could be a harem of attractive women around us, and he wouldn't notice any of them. That need is for me and me alone.

And to think we were almost broken apart. After Hanna was murdered... I was next. There was no doubt about that.

I swipe my hands through the water, moving toward him, when he suddenly breaks the intense silence.

"I think we should go back."

His words startle me. Did I mistake the look in his eyes? The... intention? He swims to shore, and I catch a glimpse of his wet boxers—I most definitely was not mistaken. His erection can barely be contained. Turning his back to me quickly, he sheds the underwear, giving me the most delicious view I could have ever asked for of his taught round ass, before pulling his sweatpants on.

I can't imagine that feels pleasant. His skin is still wet. Why is he in such a hurry?

"Come, little witch." He turns to me, hand outstretched in my direction, as beads of water slide over the ridges of his muscles, over his torso carved of stone, the contour of his shaft far too defined behind the light fabric of his sweatpants.

Parched...

So I go to him, leaving the sanctuary of the water, and place my hand in his. I don't even attempt to mask the way I'm looking at him. He's goddamn magnificent.

We didn't come prepared, no towels, nothing to dry ourselves with. Luckily, my dress is fairly casual and loose, but I'm still not looking forward to it clinging to my wet body. Only, I don't have a choice and Ronan helps me pull it down over my head, before guiding me to turn, so he can zip the back. He does it fast, too fast, and there's a pang of disappointment in my chest. Then he guides me to turn back around, his hands lingering on my waist, slowly sliding down my hips, and I think there are fireworks going off in my belly. I didn't realize how much I missed his touch, this type of comfort, not the innocent kind, until today.

But that damn worry and guilt flashes in his eyes all over again, and he stops, taking a step back.

Guilt...

For one moment, one beautiful moment in this stunning place, I forgot about those teeth embedded in me.

I thank him anyway.

"For what?" he asks.

"Bringing me here. It helped. I needed it." A little too much.

"Yeah... me too. Come on, little witch, let's get some food, then you have to rest.

It's a big day tomorrow."

Just on cue, my stomach makes an embarrassing rumble that earns me a chuckle from Ronan. This pregnancy makes this hunger pop in out of nowhere. I could just see food and suddenly I'm hungry. Even if I just ate. But it seems to fade when I focus on what Ronan said after... tomorrow. It's a big day indeed. The day of all the goodbyes I'm not ready for, of the pain, the finality of it all.

I'm supposed to be strong for her. Watch that casket disappear in the room beyond the curtains, where her body will enter the cruel flames of the furnace that will render her to dust.

My amazing Hanna... she will be nothing but ashes.

Ronan

IT WAS TOO beautiful of a day for such sorrow. There was nothing I could have done to soothe the pain in either Annika or my brother. They kept their distance from each other the whole day. In the morning, during the ceremony, they sat at opposite ends. They did the same at the restaurant we went to after. They barely even looked at each other when Hanna's ashes were delivered to us and handed to Annika.

Not now, though. At the edge of this small cliff, with the soft breeze brushing against our skin warmed by the afternoon sun in an offensively pleasant way, Finn stands next to Annika. I'm on the other side, Maddox, Vincent, and Carter are right behind us, and some of our men behind them.

Annika hands Finn the container that holds her best friend, signaling for him to wait a moment as she reaches into the pocket of her black blazer. Her body's turned toward my brother and I have no idea what she's holding, but he looks down for a moment, then his gaze quickly jumps to hers. Eyes wide, conflict and pain furrowing his eyebrows, then his shoulders slump and he unscrews the lid. Annika reaches in and I have this urge to step around and see what the hell she's doing.

Instead, I turn to Katya, and she seems to be in on it. There's no shift whatsoever in her compassionate expression as she watches them. I reluctantly stay in my place, watching Annika as she removes her hand, fiddles with something and then reaches in the container yet again. She hands Katya what appears to be a little funnel and a scoop, and I finally catch a glimpse of two small, intricately decorated silver vials, before she slides one in Finn's breast pocket, then in hers.

She looks up at my brother, and they share something unspoken for a few long moments, before he nods. She takes the urn from him, then turns to the glistening calm water before us, and kneels on the ground.

In the faintest of whispers, she says... "I love you," then begins slowly tipping Hanna's ashes, watching the breeze take them away and spread them over the sea. Finn kneels next to her, covering her hands with his when her own begin to shake, and they do it together.

I'm here for comfort, her rock and shoulder to cry on, but this moment... this moment is not mine. It's hers—theirs.

So I watch as the last of the ashes spill, then nod to the men behind us, who turn and walk back down the hill, to the cars. Madds, Vin, and Carter begin to walk away, but stop a few paces from us, giving us space. Katya approaches Finn, while I help Annika close the, now empty, urn and help her up.

Before we move away from the cliff, Annika grabs my hand pulling me to her. I wrap her in my arms as she buries her head in my chest, but she doesn't cry. Her hold tightens around me as she breathes slow and deep through the ache in her heart.

Such a terrible, early end to such an amazing journey. Is this to be all of our ends? Too soon to fully leave? Violent and cruel? Is this what I have to look forward to?

A few months ago, I wouldn't have blinked an eye at it. It always crossed my mind, but it meant nothing. Now, with this delicate, stunning woman wrapped around my body, my baby growing in her belly, I can't even fathom it.

This will not be our end.

Yet I'm not sure my brothers will understand.

CHAPTER 20
Ronan

"FUCKING HELL," I mutter to myself when the first image I see walking down the stairs is Finn getting voluntarily pummeled by Madds in the ring.

I step through the main room of the space that is going to become what Maddox now calls *The Fightclub*. I argued that maybe it requires a classier name, but the reality of it is that it's exactly that—a fight club. It will be savage, bare-knuckle, real, nothing like typical boxing rings with rules that protect the fighters. It will be what Maddox has been craving, a place where the need for pain finds its home. Whether you need to feel it or inflict it.

As I watch Finn now, I'm not sure on what side of that pain my brother found himself in. He's been spending a lot of time here since it started to look like something.

The Fightclub is close to being ready, but not quite there yet as some renovations are still ongoing. On top of that, we're setting up the basis for our money laundering side of things. Fighting is all well and good, but the real money will be in the exchanges, the bets, and it has to work seamlessly.

Madds lands another punch in Finn's gut, and steps back when he falls to the ground, bracing himself on his hands and one knee. He taps once, then twice on the ring floor, and Maddox pulls him up.

In the last month since the funeral, things have started to fall back into some semblance of normal, although my brother appears to have found a new one. All his free time, as little as there is of it, since we've been working hard to consolidate our organization, is spent letting out steam in this ring, or... in bars. He hasn't brought a woman home, but we keep an eye on our own... and our own is out with a different woman almost every night. Sometimes more than one. I'm not asking him about it. He'll just yell at me that I'm not his father. He's done that since we were much younger and our parents were away, as always.

God knows our father had a very interesting lifestyle himself. Always fucking around, never the same woman, no issue whatsoever in having them throw themselves at his feet, considering his looks and bank account. Then our mother came along and, all of a sudden, he forgot other women existed. He and Uncle Preston told us the stories on a drunken night years ago. I can't help but wonder if Finn takes after him? Or was Hanna that woman?

Fuck, he's only twenty-one. There's so much life before him. There has to be more. I take a deep breath and push all those thoughts away.

"Are you guys gonna clean up? The newbies have joined us upstairs," I ask.

"Fucking hell, you're light on your feet." Finn startles slightly. "What time is it?"

"Just passed eight-thirty. Midnight is getting busy tonight."

"Nice! Yeah, give us a few minutes. We'll be right up."

I nod and walk back upstairs and through the corridor that connects to the back entrance to our establishments. I take the door that leads to the back rooms of our speakeasy and debate if I should head to the office to take care of some business or go to the bar.

It's been a hard month. Constantly working, not only here, but home too, making sure our organization is back on stronger feet than before. We lost a lot of men, at least one stream of income, but our reputation seems to be growing by the day. What we did to Bartiste is spoken about in hushed tones through the underground of ours and neighboring cities. I guess taking most of his army down with the few men we had made an impression. At the time, we didn't give a shit; we didn't really see that because the purpose was almost blinding us. If only we had some confirmation of Bartiste's life status...

Fuck it, I deserve a few drinks.

I take the door to the bar and suck in a deep breath as the scents that feel more like home than that penthouse, assault me. Wood, musk, worn leather, basking in the low, warm lights hidden all around the space, in the nooks and crannies, bathing this space in a mysterious aura. The music is a bit louder at this time, deep, southern blues covers the nefarious conversations the patrons are engaged in as they sit in the deep leather chairs, sipping their intricate smoky cocktails or the expensive liquor. This is not the place for just anyone—this is for people like us. Hidden in plain sight and accessible only by memberships or passwords.

This night is one of many to come when we welcome new men within our ranks. These ones in particular came from our cousin, Sloan. He's been really good to us, asking some of his men if they would like to join our ranks. Some of them were happy to climb down the hills of Venator and come to the coast. We couldn't refuse the offer, not when these were men with experience, years under their belt spent in the underbelly of our worlds, reliable, and more importantly, trustworthy.

They took over one of the more private corners of the bar area, happily mingling with some of our men who joined us tonight. I signal to the bartender my order— he already knows my preference; bourbon, on whiskey stones to keep it cool, but not watered down—and join the guys.

It's going well. We discuss, we plan, we share ideas, we talk about life, and drink until I'm feeling a little bit too warm inside. Finn has already bonded with a couple of guys, and they laugh loudly in their corner, talking about God knows what.

Carter observes everyone from a small round table next to us, sipping his absinthe. He joins in the conversation a few times, but the man mainly keeps quiet, as always, taking note of each and every little thing happening around him. Sometimes I wonder how that brain of his works. Does he see numbers that he calculates to figure out what to make of the world and people around him, or is it colors?

Madds sits next to Vin, acting polite to everyone, but that mountain of a man always has an expression that tells you that he might crush you under his brutal grip if you look at him a little bit funny. It's not always intentional, it's just how his features align, with his strong jaw, slightly crooked nose, and low eyebrows that shadow his eyes. The scars marking his skin don't help his brutal aura. Yet sometimes I wonder if he's the softest of all of us. He has a heart under all the muscles, and it seems to beat a bit too hard. Although, much like Carter, he keeps quiet unless he's truly interested in the subject.

Vin's wearing his all-black suit and shirt, as usual, his wide shoulders and lean frame resting against the back of the sofa, as he taps a finger to his glass and explains something to some of our men. He carries himself with such a natural imposing allure, he gets attention without demanding it.

The pits of his eyes flash to me, as if reading my mind and knowing I was thinking of him, and I raise my glass, cocking an eyebrow. He nods and does the same, without interrupting the conversation he was having.

"I've been a bit homesick after moving to Queenscove… but damn, I think I'm about to be cured." One of our new men, Stefan, speaks, both eyebrows raised as he looks somewhere behind me.

"Christ, one more drink, and I'll lay myself at their feet. Especially the shorter one on the left. Fuck me, she looks like she belongs in the old-world atmosphere of this place," Otto, next to him, continues, his eyes glued to the same spot.

Old world? My back warms with something that snakes all over my spine, and when I turn, I'm met with the unmistakable curve of Annika's ass leaning over the bar to speak to the bartender. She's dressed in a form-fitting little number that seems to shine with every movement. A dark sage green satin hugs her body, barely touching the middle of her thighs, and when she turns, I'm fucking parched as I witness the soft curve of her breasts peeking between the plunging neckline.

Suddenly, I want to fucking punch these two, slam their heads together, then throw their limp bodies into all the other men in this place who seem to be sneaking looks in her direction. A few women too. She's here with Katya and Ashley, one of her girls, all dressed to impress, but still tasteful.

"Do you think I have a chance?" Otto asks the other one.

"All you can do is try, brother."

I swear I'm going to pummel him through the goddamn table.

He doesn't know her, Ronan.

It doesn't matter. She's fucking mine either way. Even if he learns the hard way. I'm about to turn back to him and smash my glass on his head, when Annika's steel eyes find mine, distracting me and changing my whole purpose. I think she can tell, because her whole body shifts. I could have sworn I saw her nipples perking up through the thin fabric.

Fuck me.

She looks at me like she's ready to devour me.

It's been so long since I felt her around my cock. I've kept my distance. Tried to be respectful and kind to her situation, to what she's been through, and her best friend's death. But this... her lean, soft legs in those heels are going to drive me fucking crazy.

Does she know what she's doing? Is this fucking intentional?

"Okay, I'm going in." I hear Otto behind me.

But I swing my arm back, pushing my glass into his chest until he takes it, confused, along with the fucking message to stay put.

This one's mine.

I stalk toward her, my steps heavy on the floor, reveling in how her legs seem to squeeze together as she watches me, hands wrapped around that glass as she sucks the orange liquid between her soft lips. By the time I reach her, I'm almost fully hard, my cock strained against my trousers, but she still holds that straw between her lips, doe eyes staring up at me with the same innocence that pulled me to her in the first place. It takes but a moment, and her wickedness takes over, my little witch beaming as she releases the straw and gently places her glass on the bar.

"What do you think you're doing here?" I'm fucking pissed she left the apartment without me, but she's a goddamn vision.

"The bed got cold. All these evenings, plotting to take over the world..."

I lean back a fraction, dragging my gaze down her body, then back up into those steel eyes.

"And you thought it would be smart to come here, amongst all these men, dressed like... you want to be undressed." I'm fucking thirsty. If Midnight wasn't full, I would throw her over the bar and lick her cunt until she quenched this unbearable feeling.

"I just"—she drags her bottom lip into her mouth, unsure of her words—"wanted to make sure you still want to be the one to warm my bed."

What the fuck?

I lean over her, but don't touch her. Close enough that I can smell the orange juice on her lips, feel the heat of her skin, the desire coursing through her pulse. She thinks she can come here dressed like she wants to be fucked, with ridiculous notions that I might not want to warm her bed.

"Little witch, I want to set it on fire."

At those words, her eyes seem to sparkle, before she closes them for a moment as she slowly fills her lungs with air. Her breath brushes against me, the air far too hot, my cock far too hard, her body a glowing vision of need.

"I wasn't sure. After all this time..."

"Don't confuse my patience and respect for lack of hunger. I can barely contain myself, Annika. You look insatiable right now, but you could be wearing a goddamn potato sack and I would still want to rip every inch of it off your body and bury myself in that tight cunt of yours."

She gasps, a cute little gasp that quickens her breaths, her breasts twitching in a way that drives me even more mad. The pregnancy has started to fill her body in all the right ways, and I'm not sure she fully understands how fucking gorgeous she looks in her evolving form.

"You even got our new men mad with lust. They had their eyes on you from the moment you stepped foot in here. One of them almost came here, to this bar, to try to take what's *mine*." A low rumble that sounds more like a growl escapes my throat.

"Yours..." she says on a breathy voice.

"I should introduce you. After all, they need to know who you are and who you belong to."

She doesn't question my words.

"And after that?"

"After that, you can show me exactly how much you and your greedy pussy need me."

She swallows roughly, her skin bursting with goosebumps as a shudder passes through her, and I back up slightly. She breaks eye contact, gets her drink, throws away the straw, and downs half of it, before turning back.

"Okay, let's go. Now."

I can't help the grin. I like the bossy side of her, the needy one.

When I look back in the corner where I left our men, the same two are still stealing glances, while others have joined. Some aren't looking in our direction, but a bit beyond us—Ekaterina and Ashley.

"Katya," I get her attention, "shall I introduce you two?"

She nods, picks up her clear drink that I can guarantee is vodka, and we all walk together toward our men. The two I left there straighten in an instant.

"Gentlemen, may I introduce you to Ashley"—I point to the blonde woman—"one of our valuable employees. She and her colleagues are to be protected and kept an eye on at all times. But Ekaterina"—I glance at the redhead woman who looks like she could eat them all whole—"is the one who will give you all the information you need to know about that side of the business. It operates a bit differently. She's very protective of her girls, and she'll cut you just as easily as she would cut a stranger. What she says goes. Understood?" More men gather before us, and they all nod almost in unison.

Otto and Stefan can barely contain their gaze from flickering to the women standing to my right.

"And finally, this is Annika Backstrom, future Mrs. Hennessey, and mother to my unborn child."

I almost laugh when their faces drop, a sickly color taking over their features.

"Mr—" One begins to speak.

"Now, we're going to leave, but I'll see you boys tomorrow," I interrupt.

"Yes, sir, of course."

I spin on my heel, grabbing Annika's hand and pulling her with me as we head toward the back.

"Oh my God, Ronan, that was harsh. The poor men were mortified." But the sweet tone of her voice is betrayed by the deep flush in her cheeks and sparkle in her eyes.

"Let them be. They have to learn how to speak around people they're just getting to know. Information is becoming our main business, and they have to know how to control it." I push through the back door, thankful the dimly lit corridor is quiet. "Now, where were we?"

Annika

HE PULLS ME through the door and pushes me against the wall, slamming his hand somewhere above me as he leans in so close, my breath catches in my chest.

"Annika..." There's a warning in the rumble of his voice. "Are you sure about this? Because I swear to God, baby, I'm fucking ravenous, and I don't think I can be what you need."

"What do you think I need? Or shall I say, what the *future Mrs. Hennessey* needs?" That introduction made my heart skip a beat. He presented me like a mafia-fucking-queen.

"You need slow, soft, and careful. Since..."

I'm shaking my head before he can finish. "No. That's not what I need, Ronan. I need to *feel*. I need you to remind me of the taste of life, of pleasure and pain, the taste of you."

He grins, a delicious, dark grin that drives me to lick my lips. My tongue doesn't reach the other side of my mouth before his hand is diving under my dress, finding the center of me with a groan.

"Tsk, tsk, tsk, you came here with no panties covering this pussy. *My* pussy." He cups me, two fingers parting my lips, before plunging inside of me, dragging the sweetest of moans up my throat. "So fucking wet and ready, aren't you?"

"Yes..."

How I missed this. I thought memories of the last time I was touched like this, without the pleasure of it all, would cripple me. But they're barely an afterthought. I'll have to thank him later for giving me space... somehow, he knew what I needed better than I did.

He pulls out just enough that when he thrusts back in, it makes me lift on my heels and I have to grab onto his shoulders.

"Such a greedy little cunt, trying to suck me inside of you."

He leans over, the filthy words brushing against my ear, sending shudders all through me as he thrusts inside over and over again, my walls tightening around him.

"But I'm fucking parched, little witch. I need more than this."

Before I take the next breath, he pulls his fingers out of me, drops on one knee, throws my leg over his shoulder, and shoves his face between my legs, dragging the flat of his tongue from the back to the front, sucking my clit as I cry out.

"Ronan! Fuck, someone could come here at any moment!" I shriek, my eyes wide, looking toward the door to my right, but my mind's trapped between my legs, at the quivering mess he's making of me.

He ignores me and doesn't waste any time, his tongue inside of me, lapping at the sensitive flesh like a starved animal. It draws maddening circles against my walls before coming out and teasing my clit. Then relishes every bit of flesh around my pussy, before diving back in. He's ruthless! I'm not even sure if he's doing it for my pleasure or his, as he eats me out like his goddamn life depends on it.

He pulls away for a moment, and I yelp when he slaps my pussy, my mouth gaping at the gesture. Even if my core shakes with pleasure.

"Eyes on me, little witch."

I do as told, and he swallows me whole once more.

But I hear faint voices beyond this damn door... footsteps...

"Fuck. Ronan, there's someone..."

But he doesn't let me go, he doesn't move, he forces my gaze on his as he sucks on my clit, rolling it with his tongue.

"Please..."

What am I begging for?

"You taste so fucking good. Oh... how I missed you."

I'm right there, on the cusp of the most intense orgasm of my life, but he keeps me there... lapping at me until my knee almost gives out.

"Ronan... please!" I beg, the footsteps beyond the door louder, closer.

"What do you want, baby girl?"

"T—to come. Please, make me come!" I plead.

Just like that, fingers replace his tongue, thrusting inside of me as his mouth comes down on my clit, and the whole goddamn world explodes inside of me. My body shudders, and I'm biting on my forearm to keep from screaming so we're not heard, but almost failing as wave after wave consumes me from head to toe. Letting a whimper escape, I'm not sure when his fingers left me and his tongue came back, licking every bit of wetness brought by the orgasm that still has me trembling.

The man is already on his feet, but I can barely hold myself up. I'm giggling as he pulls me after him, out through the back door of the building, and into the private parking lot at the back.

Only it's not that private anymore.

A man we seem to have startled with our presence jumps back away from the door, a screwdriver in one hand and a gun in the other, aimed straight at us. The metal door slams behind me, jolting both me and Ronan.

"Ro—Ronan?"

He steps in front of me, shielding me from the gun. I would run back inside, but it's a secure door, and I can't access the lock.

"Put your fucking gun down." Ronan's tone is frighteningly calm.

"Just the man I was looking for. Well, one of them anyway." The guy says, his tone a mixture of cockiness and anxiousness. We definitely took him by surprise.

"I recognize you. You were there when Bartiste blew up my boat and went after my woman. You ran with him, like a fucking coward."

"I was also there when he shoved his fingers in her cunt."

A distressing laugh charges the atmosphere and a chill runs all through my body. Bile rises, burning its way up to the back of my throat, and I heave instantly.

Ronan reaches behind, finds me, and presses me against his body in a comforting hold, at the same time he pulls a gun out from somewhere under his suit jacket.

"You had a chance to survive this. At least for the next day or two, while we tortured you for information. But you just pulled the rug from under your own feet with that little piece of information. Now... you have to make a decision. You either tell me where the fuck Bartiste is now, or I'll make sure you live for a whole fucking week while Carter carves you like a goddamn Thanksgiving turkey."

"What?" The man sounds confused.

"Where the fuck is Bartiste?!" It's a menacing growl that vibrates through his whole body, malice dripping off his tongue.

A gun cocks, and I flinch.

"You—wait. You don't have him?"

Ronan leans his head ever-so slightly, and I know what's going through his mind. It's going through mine as well.

"You came here because you thought we have him. So you have no clue where he is or if he's alive, then," he states as a matter of fact.

"Fuck..." That's the last thing the man speaks before a shot splits the night, and I yelp as I grab onto Ronan's jacket. A loud thump sounds next, and I peek to see the man crumbled onto the concrete.

Very much dead.

I step around Ronan and catch a glimpse of the man's face. He looks familiar, but not memorable. If he was there, I don't remember when or why. He's definitely memorable now with that bullet hole in the middle of his forehead.

"Are you okay?" Ronan spins me around to look at him, gripping my face in his hands.

Nodding, I narrow my eyes on his expression. I can't pinpoint it, but his breathing quickens, brows furrowing, and I'm not sure if he's gonna settle on anger or worry.

He releases me quickly, urging me to climb into his car, while he pulls out his phone and makes a call. Moments later, all the guys rush out the back door. They talk for a few minutes before he leaves them and slides into the driver's seat, slamming the door with unneeded force behind him.

"We're leaving?" I ask.

"Yes."

"What about the body?"

"They'll handle it. Buckle your seatbelt, Annika."

Annika... when does he ever call me by my name? What a clusterfuck this night has turned into.

And isn't it all freaking levels of wrong that I'm still turned on...

* * *

"You just saw me kill a man. A man who was there for the whole trauma you experienced," he says as he captures my wrists in his when I try to get closer to him, in the elevator on the way up to his penthouse.

"And now he's dead. Gone."

He was quiet, tense, throughout the whole car ride back to the building. And yes, I did just witness him kill a man, but... something snapped within me when I watched someone murder my best friend. After that... everything pales in comparison.

"I'm not putting you through this right now. You need to rest."

"No! Ronan... please. I want—I *need* to replace all these shitty things happening in my life with good ones."

"You literally want me to fuck the memories out of your mind," he says, staring at me in disbelief. Though there's a tinge of amusement in his eyes.

The elevator dings, doors opening far too slowly, and he rushes through the penthouse, as I almost run after him.

"Yes! That's right! I know who you are, Ronan! I see you. You protect me, take care of me, keep me safe in a fluffy bubble, and now... I need you to fuck me."

He stops dead in his tracks in the middle of the bedroom, and it halts me in place. His shoulders roll back slowly, his hands curling into tight fists, but other than that, he somehow looks bigger. Stronger.

"Get down on your knees," he says as the bedroom door slams shut behind me.

I don't hesitate. Right there, in the middle of the room, I kneel and watch him with hungry eyes as he walks toward me.

"Good girl." He grips my chin between his thumb and finger, a wicked quirk on his lips only adding to the spell those words put on my pussy. "I'm going to ask you once, are you sure you don't want slow and careful?"

I nod.

"I need you to say it."

"I don't want slow and careful. Make me feel everything, Ronan Hennessey."

Darkness passes through his eyes, and it turns to a shudder when it reaches my flesh.

"Undress."

I rip the garment over my head, and he growls at the sight of me.

"I can't believe you fucking walked out this door with nothing more than that thin slip of a dress on."

He looks furious and, for a moment, I regret that stupid decision. But he doesn't waste another breath as he takes off his belt, unzips his trousers, and pulls his cock out of his boxers.

My throat suddenly feels utterly empty at the sight of him. So damn thick and beautiful, veins adorn his smooth shaft, the head glistening with exactly what I need.

I lean over, mouth open, about to taste it, when suddenly my head is yanked back by the hair, but I'm too stunned to react. I gaze up at him and I'm met with nothing but mischief in those blues that appear black in this dim lighting.

He wraps his hand around his length, running it up and down as he looks at my mouth.

"Tongue out."

I comply, and he comes closer, but not close enough. I try to inch forward, but his grip on my hair holds me in place, and I cry out. Not in pain, but need, and he smiles at the sound of it, a crooked, devious, and delicious smile that makes me squeeze my legs together.

"Hungry, little witch?" He snickers. "Is this what you want? You want my cock in your mouth?"

"Yesss..." I hiss.

"Well, I want it down your throat." And in one thrust, he shoves it past any barrier that stood in his way, making me gag violently.

"Swallow me," he orders.

Tears fill my eyes, struggling through the gagging, the splutter, the noises far too embarrassing, and I'm afraid I'm going to throw up. But his eyes tell me that he doesn't give a shit.

"Relax." He pets my head. "Swallow slowly."

And I do, swallowing the depravity, filling myself with wanton need and the feral look in his eyes that shows a sinful kind of pride.

Just before I think I can't take the lack of air any longer, he pulls out enough to fill my mouth, then pushes down my throat again, saliva spilling from my lips onto my chest. Holding me steady with his hand on the back of my head, he begins a brutal thrusting.

It feels so dirty, so very different from the Ronan I've experienced so far. Sure, he's fucked my mouth before, but it was softer in a way, leaving me time to accommodate. Not now. Not even a little bit. I'm falling down a rabbit hole of pleasure and he's giving it to me, my throat already sore, but between my legs, I'm a sleek mess.

He fucks my mouth through violent gags, smeared tears, and spit falling constantly from my lips, grunting his ruthless pleasure as I moan my divine pain. And the only thing I regret is that he's still wearing clothes while I'm stark naked. I can't see the ripple of his muscles, his exquisite body as I give him exactly what he wants.

"Jesus Christ, woman. I could fuck this pretty mouth of yours for hours. But it's not where I want to come."

He pulls out from between my lips, steadying me as I gag and splutter, then lifts my head and smiles at me.

"So fucking pretty."

I must have mascara running down my face, saliva falling off my chin, but he doesn't seem to care. He lifts me from under my arms and pushes me face first on the bed.

"Ass up."

Once again, I do as told, and he quickly slides a pillow under my hips. There's no warning after that, his fingers suddenly thrust inside of me, in and out, something between a moan and a sob spilling from my aching throat as I grip the sheets tightly. I hear rustling of clothes behind me, but I have no desire to look and interrupt the pleasure he quite literally stirs inside of me as he swirls his fingers around, before pulling out.

"I'm gonna apologize now, because this is gonna be fast. I've been on the verge for so long... But I'll make it up to you."

"Just fuck me, please! I need you!"

The bed dips on either side of me as he straddles my thighs and the thick head of his cock rubs against my core until it finds my entrance, and in one long thrust, he drives home. I could come right here, right now. The fullness of him is something I almost forgot. There is no more space, nothing as my walls constrict around him.

"Christ... you're exquisite."

Every inch of my skin bursts into tiny electric shocks, and I'm certain I'm melting into the damn bed. His hand slamming next to me startles me, the other tangling in my hair, pulling my head back until our cheeks touch and I'm forced onto my forearms. He drags his tongue over my skin as his slight movements become torturous inside of me.

"You think I can't feel how you're squeezing my cock? Urging me? This is on my terms, little witch, not yours. Your spells have no power here."

"Oh no?" I slam back, my ass meeting his hips, forcing a groan from the man who dominates every part of me.

So I do it again for good measure, but he growls, releasing my hair and shoving me down. He shifts until he's basically sitting on my thighs, his hands painfully gripping my cheeks and spreading them apart as he slams inside of me with such delightful force, I'm seeing stars.

Each thrust is harder, deeper, each one making me cry out louder, my fingers cramping as I grip the sheets. He rises, and with one hand, he grips my hip and flips me over, and as he rips through me once more, with my ass elevated on the pillow, this time I'm sure... he's reached the end of me. Touching a part of me that makes goosebumps explode over my flesh, shudders rippling through my body until they caress my pussy, my nipples aching.

He snakes his arms under my knees, bringing them up as he falls on top of me and the angle makes my eyes bulge, a few tears sliding from my lashes as he moves in a wild rhythm that crumbles all my walls.

"Don't you fucking dare come, Annika."

What?!

"I can't control it!" I mewl. Does he not know? I can't control this, just like I couldn't control my infatuation for him when I'd only seen him in a picture.

"No!"

"Please, let me..." I'm begging because I know it's coming.

"Not until I tell you," he growls, only that tone is doing things to my body.

"Ronan..."

"Not-fucking-yet, Annika!"

But he keeps thrusting inside of me like I have fucking magical powers. For a moment, I truly think I do, because there's something electric brewing inside of me, rippling beneath my flesh, holding on for dear life.

"Now! Come for me, little witch!"

I hastily reach between us, but I barely touch my clit before those walls shatter and trembling pleasure floods me. Then he does too, filling my pussy as he comes with such force, his jerks send me deeper into this world where nothing but blinding pleasure exists. It carries me through endless shock waves that threaten to render my body completely useless.

When the spasms subside, he begins pulling out of me, but I cry out.

"No." I need him in there... I don't know why, I just need to feel him.

He frowns for a moment before he lets my legs fall around him. Leaning in, he then rolls us over until I'm laid on top of him, my head on his chest, legs on either side of him, and his cock nestled exactly where it belongs.

I fall asleep with his hands stroking my back, my body satisfyingly spent, and my heart full.

CHAPTER 21
Ronan

"WELL, IT'S PRETTY damn impressive." I look around the newly renovated space, the fight club looking both rough and somehow luxurious. The ring is in the middle of the vast room with a low ceiling, a few rows of seats surround it on two sides, while the other two have a few small round tables, reminiscent of the speakeasy upstairs.

It lacks decor on its black walls and the only lights in the room are directed toward the ring, everything else bathed in darkness. The lack of windows enhances the privacy of the space, even if it's not really that small. The stairs that lead up to the bar and office are now separated by a wall, and without the right fingerprint you cannot get through the door. On the opposite side, there's a door leading to a couple of locker rooms, toilets, and a gym that looks more like a space where you can take sledgehammers to an old car.

The money laundering business is all set up as well. The club renovations finished a couple of weeks ago, but we gave ourselves more time to make sure the covert side of things will work exactly as it should. It's the start of November now, and it's finally opening night.

"It's perfect." Madds takes one last look around the empty club that's about to fill soon.

We've invited a select few, but word has spread, and even the dark elite of Queenscove wants a piece of the action. There's something about a brutal fight that brings people together.

"I'm still surprised that you don't want to be the first one to fight." I say as I catch a flickering look from Vin. I could have sworn there was a hint of worry in there.

"For a good show I would have to hold back. And I'm not in the mood for that." Madds says flatly.

One could think he's smug, but we've seen him fight—both in the ring and with enemies—he's unforgiving. The act of fighting in itself is not what he's after, but the release it provides, and he doesn't tend to stop until he gets what he needs. Sometimes the brink of death is where he finds it.

But the man is well over six foot, packed with muscles, not really lean, more of a beast with human eyes, yet scarily agile. This makes him a threat to any adversaries and, unfortunately, it rarely takes much effort or time for him to put someone down.

"Yeah, I guess it's wise to let someone else go first."

At least the fights can last longer.

"It's going to be a good show." Vin quirks his lips.

"And we're gonna need that. Two of Katya's girls are bringing their *dates* here tonight. We want them entertained and loose-lipped. One of them is Jonah Holt, and as a favor to The Ghost, we have to get some info out of him," Finn chimes in.

Good. The girls are experts at gathering the precious information we want, leverage to hold on people or to sell, perfect material for negotiation, and maybe a bit of light blackmail. Or heavy ones. Men turn into idiots when they're boozed up or horny, and Katya's training and skill in recruiting is proving invaluable to our operation. Especially since no one knows that the escort service has any business affiliation with us. In Queenscove's hungry eyes, it's only an elite escort service catering to the rich and famous. Definitely not what it actually is.

"What about you?" I turn to Finn.

"What about me?"

"Are you bringing... a date?"

He narrows his eyes before lifting an eyebrow.

"So what if I am? Do you have a problem with that?!"

"It's the excess I have a problem with."

I barely hold myself from rolling my eyes, and Finn scoffs, shaking his head.

"If I wanna fuck a different girl every day of the week, it has nothing to do with you, brother. Mind your own damn business."

"You can do whatever you want with your sex life, I just... you seem to be going down the deep end."

The man turns to me and steps so close, his body almost touches mine, a dark look on his face.

"Like I said, mind your own goddamn business." He holds that stare for a moment longer, then turns and heads to the back rooms.

He's giving me a fucking headache. Madds shrugs and leaves too, although he's probably going to go deal with club business.

"Sometimes I wonder if he would go back to being the Finn I know if we would actually find Bartiste." I say, without turning to Vin.

"I think we've all learned by now that vengeance doesn't change the past. And considering that the guy you killed behind Midnight worked for Bartiste and was looking for him as well, it's safe to say you may never find out if he'll go back to who he was before."

"Shit..."

"He'll be fine, Ronan," Vin says.

"Will he be? Because he's skipped all fucking stages of grief after anger and dove headfirst into pussy. I can't keep track anymore, but every time I see him out, he has a different woman on his arm. I don't even know where he finds them."

"Maybe it's just how he copes."

"Or how he buries his feelings," I say, rubbing my temple.

"There's nothing you can do either way. He's a big boy, he's gonna deal with heartbreak in his own way... He'll learn eventually."

I turn my head, looking into Vin's black gaze.

"Did you learn?"

Those dark pits seem to swallow me as his eyes narrow into slits, The Serpent everyone else knows suddenly making an appearance before me.

"You thought Madds was the only one who knows about your girl?" I ask when he doesn't respond, pushing away the uneasy feeling that gaze fills me with.

"She's in the past," he warns, his tone of voice a low rumble.

"Funny. Could have sworn I caught a glimpse of fiery red hair in some surveillance photos on your phone screen the other day."

Oh, fuck. The look in his eyes turns murderous. Yet I can't seem to stop myself.

"Only... you broke your own heart, didn't you? It wasn't Morri—"

"Careful now," he interrupts. "I'm not your brother, Ronan, and I'll have no issues slitting your throat so you can keep *her* name off your lips."

In the past, my ass.

I put my hands up in surrender, but he doesn't miss the slight quirk of my lips.

"Come on. Let's go upstairs and finalize tonight's preparations."

He holds that gaze on me even after I've turned around to head for the door. I can feel it on the back of my neck. It brings a full-blown smile to my face because I seem to have found the one thing that makes The Serpent twitch—his own *Eve.*

* * *

Today marks one of the last steps in our organization's legacy. The space is booming with cheers and laughter, the ring is splattered with enough blood to paint a whole wall, and the money is rolling in better than we expected. The Fightclub will be a success; there's no doubt about that anymore. Which means that I can move to the next phase of my plan without a guilty conscience. Well... at least with less of one.

When the last patrons finally left, I didn't waste any time. The guys knew I wanted to leave as soon as possible. They urged me to, even as the fights were still happening, but I needed to convince myself. To make sure everything went okay, that it was a triumph.

For almost eleven at night, there was an annoyingly high amount of traffic on the streets of Queenscove, and it made the drive more aggravating than it should have been. But as I step through the door of my penthouse and catch a glimpse of silky light brown hair flowing gently in the breeze, all that annoyance dissipates.

She stands on the terrace, leaning against the railing as she looks toward the sea, the moon lighting a trail across the soft waves. The doors are open, and the sheer curtains flow inside the space on the same rhythm as her hair. Even now, three or so months later, I still can't believe how close I came to losing her. How lucky I am that I get to watch her like this... peaceful, healthy.

I don't know when I started walking again, but I've passed the threshold onto the terrace, and Annika slowly tilts her head to the side. An invitation.

Two more steps, and I've closed the distance between us, slid my arms around her middle, and buried my face in the crook of her neck, inhaling her intoxicating scent. She leans into my hold, laying her forearms on mine.

"So... how did it go?" she asks hesitantly.

"Better than I thought. It's all going to be okay," I say between kisses I dot along her neck.

Her body relaxes against mine, like this whole time I was away, she's been in a constant state of tension. Maybe she was. I think I was too. I slide one hand down, stopping on her belly, where a bump has appeared. She hasn't popped yet, but the slight curve of that belly is unmistakable.

"Let's go to bed," I say, reluctantly pulling away from her neck.

"Can we sit here for a bit? Please?"

I'm not sure why she's asking for my permission.

I pull her with me as I head to one of the outdoor armchairs, sit down, and guide her on my lap. We're still facing the view, the calmness of the sea and quietness of the late hour almost hypnotizing. Although she's the one truly hypnotizing here, because it's her I can't tear my eyes off.

She turns to me when my gaze burns her skin, and I don't get to take the next breath before she captures my face in her soft palms and presses her lips against mine.

I never really enjoyed kissing that much before her. It was always a means to an end, and if I could avoid it, I usually did. But with Annika, it's addictive, her supple lips, the way she nibbles on mine, before she takes me like she wants to eat me alive.

I could kiss her forever.

I could kiss her for the rest of our lives.

"Annika..." I say against her lips.

"Mmm?" She doesn't break the kiss.

"Marry me."

Annika

DID HE JUST ask me to...?

I freeze against his mouth, wide-eyed, as I slowly pull away and break the kiss.

No... he didn't actually ask me.

His blue eyes sparkle with something like hope in the light of this bright moon.

"Are you asking me, or...?"

"I don't think I can give you the choice. I want to marry you, Annika."

"What if I don't want to marry you?"

Something dark flashes in his gaze.

"Don't you?"

"I need to know why."

He narrows his eyes, yet he appears confused.

"Do you want to marry me because I'm pregnant?" I add hesitantly.

The slight quirk on his lips throws me off. I'm uneasy in a strange kind of way.

"Yes and no," he says, and I'm not sure how I'm supposed to feel about that.

"What does that even mean? And why the hell are you smiling?" I try to pull away from him, but he holds me so tight, my efforts are futile.

"Yes, because I thought the sense of a traditional family was lost on me. I thought I had that modern way of thinking, where families didn't have to be connected by a piece of paper to be just that. But it turns out, I'm more traditional than I thought. By law, our child will have my name, even if double barreled, but I want you to have it too."

I ponder his words, trying to figure out if I agree.

"And no," he continues, "because the idea of marrying you, of making you mine in the most official way I can think of, does something extraordinary to my fucking soul. Don't distract yourself with futile insecurities about your pregnancy, because it doesn't change the fact that you want me as much as I want you." He captures my chin between his fingers, the touch endearing, possessive... loving, "I wanna be yours, Annika."

My lips part in surprise because I'm not sure if I should react to his presumptuousness or the way he called me out on my feelings. Our story started with obsession—mine—after barely seeing him in a photo. Truth is... I'm pretty sure I want him more than he'll ever want me. I want his blue eyes on me, his hands touching every part of me, his lips on my skin sending shivers to my core, and his filthy words in my ears jolting my damn soul. I want to consume him. Every loving caress, every sweet declaration, every little thing he does to take care of me, they all add onto the need, the pure hunger I have for this man.

A wicked grin pulls at my eyes, and then he mirrors it, before he speaks again.

"Marry me, Annika."

CHAPTER 22
Annika

THIS LAST MONTH since Ronan proposed to me, or... told me to marry him, a fact that made my mom giggle when I told her, has been an absolute whirlwind. Not just because we decided to get married in only a month, but because I had to navigate the treacherous waters that is my former job, Ronan's job, a kidnapping, death, pregnancy, and engagement in the context of my oblivious parents.

They are normal people—well, most might not call my mom normal—but in comparison to the general society, they are. Organized crime, forgeries, dealings on the dark web, kidnapping in a human trafficking ring, and the brutal death of my best friend, are things they only ever read about on the internet or listened about in a true crime podcast. Which meant I had to make sure they didn't hear any of this from us. I did, however, have to offer some sort of explanation regarding my best-friend's death, and a horrible car accident was the most pertinent, realistic option.

They were upset I didn't tell them, because they would have come to the funeral, but they seemed to accept my explanation about being in such shock and upset that I struggled to even plan the thing. In reality, the aftermath of Bartiste's disappearance was still being sorted through, and there was no way I was going to risk exposing them to that.

Nonetheless, my surprise engagement when they weren't even aware of my relationship, was met with mixed feelings. Quite literally. Because my free-spirited mother went mad with joy, singing and jumping around the house on the videocall, while my father looked at me with a scowl bunching his bushy eyebrows, before proceeding to grill me about him and us.

I anticipated this. What he didn't know was that I wrote down potential questions and answers and had them in front of me the whole time. Ronan couldn't stop laughing when he saw me taking notes, telling me he couldn't believe I needed a cheat-sheet to talk to my parents. He quickly shut up and asked for a copy when I reminded him that he has parents too, and he might not want to tell them the real circumstances of our love story. Which meant that our stories had to match.

His parents are not totally oblivious, though. They don't have clean hands, that's for sure, but they deal more in real estate and dicey deals. Or used to, anyway. Either way, they are not in the know about all their kids' activities, which is a choice they made and one that Ronan and Finnigan pushed on them, just for security reasons. So, the cheat-sheet will be very useful for him too.

My father seemed content with my answers, and considering the look on his chubby face right now, as he stands in the doorway of the bedroom, seeing me for the first time in my wedding dress, I would say he's definitely warming up to my situation. He had a long talk with Ronan too, after arriving at the penthouse, and he seemed happy afterwards.

"Oh, Anni." He takes a step in, looking me up and down with such emotion, he's making me emotional too. "You're beautiful. You always are, but... it's the happiness in your eyes that's making you even more beautiful now."

"Thank you, Pappa." I get up from the chair and walk straight into his arms. His hugs always felt like more, like a protective, love-filled cocoon, and as a child, I used to force him to hug me until I fell asleep.

He kisses the top of my head and tightens his hold one last time.

"I don't want to ruin your makeup or your hair," he tells me as he pulls away.

"Don't worry."

I wipe my ring fingers under my eyes, turning back to look in the mirror. I haven't smudged the light mascara. The delicate, simple makeup is very much in place, and the tiny flowers weaved through the loose fishtail braid Katya did for me are still there.

"You look perfect."

I turn back around, smiling at him. I don't know if I do, but I love this dress. It's perfect for our beach ceremony. I'm grateful we live in a subtropical climate, because otherwise I couldn't wear this dress in December. It's long enough that it touches the tops of my wedge sandals, but not too long that I'll drag it through the sand. It's light and flowy, the A-line skirt topped with a few layers of soft tulle, giving it a delicate quality. It will flow beautifully in the sea breeze. I hook my fingers under the thin straps, making sure they're in the right place, drag my fingers over the delicate sparkles lining the top of the bodice, checking that the deep V-neck isn't slipping around, and take one long, deep breath.

If Hanna was here, she would be running around like a busy bee, making sure everything is perfect, in the right place. She would insist on checking my dress herself, retouching my makeup every five minutes. She would be a whirlwind.

Her absence is the reason why I didn't assign the role of maid of honor. It's also why Katya tried hard to refuse the bridesmaid role... knowing full well she would be the only one. She only accepted because she insisted on helping me with the wedding, so she was already doing the *job*. The woman has been everything I never asked for. Whatever free time she had, she used to help me. Granted, we're keeping our wedding very simple and small, so not that many preparations were needed anyway.

Hanna would have insisted on organizing a grand, luxurious affair. Totally out of my comfort zone, as opposed to this twenty-three-person wedding. Which also includes Ronan's parents, who surprised us with their arrival. Although *surprise* is not what I would call Ronan and Finnigan's reactions when they appeared at our door—

utter shock was more like it.

"Oooh, my little jellybean, you look incredible!" Mamma suddenly appears and all but runs to me, tears already in her eyes. "Look at you, I just... I can't believe you're going to be a wife. And a mother!" She's fully crying now.

She's been doing this since her arrival, two days ago. I love her, but my pregnancy hormones are barely contained.

"I'm sorry, I'm sorry. I'm a mess." She turns and heads to the vanity, pulling a few tissues out of the box and dabbing her eyes. "Thank God for waterproof mascara. Okay. I'm okay."

Pappa and I look at each other, and a moment later, we burst into laughter. Mamma has this talent of starting a full-blown emotional breakdown and ending it herself within a span of twenty seconds. It's a whole journey, predictable and unpredictable at the same time. It's been worse since I told them I'm also pregnant. The knowledge that she's going to be a grandma has broken through the front she was trying to keep together. I guess it's better than Ronan's mother, who simply said, *"How lovely. Congratulations to you both."* And that was that.

"I don't mean to interrupt." Katya appears in the doorway. "Mr. and Mrs. Backstrom, I believe it's time."

She smiles as she looks at me from head to toe.

"Please—Andrea and Alexander. No need for the formalities," Pappa tells her.

"You heard the woman," I say, trying to usher them out.

"Just one more thing." My father stops us, pulling a velvet box the size of his palm, out of his jacket pocket. "Ronan asked me to give you this before you go out—a gift."

"Oh..." I reach out, catching their knowing looks. Even Katya seems to know what I'm about to see. It's most definitely jewelry and she probably helped him pick it.

Only the smile fades from my face the moment I pop the lid open. I must have blinked ten times before I could even understand what I was looking at.

"This can't..."

"I know," Pappa says, clearly emotional.

"Great-grandma's locket..." I whisper.

"He found it... I don't know how. I can't even imagine the things he must have done in the last three weeks to dig that out."

I run my hand over the delicate flower reliefs that decorate the locket, then pull the necklace out, as Mamma takes the box away.

"But I thought it disappeared when you cleared granddad's house." I latch my nails in the middle seam, and when it pops open, I can't help but gasp.

There they are... in weathered black and white, my great-grandparents, looking at me with their soft, young features.

"You really do look like her." Mamma smiles.

"I don't understand how their photos are still in here." I'm lost, completely lost. I cannot believe Ronan found this... for me. I can't even fathom where he started, let alone how he found it.

For me...

Tears fill my eyes, and I don't even hesitate as I unclasp the expensive diamond necklace that hangs around my neck, replacing it with the locket.

I press it against my skin and, suddenly, I can't bear to be in this villa anymore. My dad will have to hold me from running down that damn aisle, because I need to go marry Ronan Hennessey.

* * *

It was a miracle I didn't cry for the entire ceremony. Pregnancy hormones were running wild, and the vision of my hot as hell man in that light blue linen suit, waiting for me under that flower arch, made me all kinds of emotional. The walk down the aisle felt like the longest of my life as the world blurred around me to the point that I saw no one but him. The closer I got, the more vivid the wild gaze in his eyes was. I could tell—he wanted to run toward me just as much as I wanted to run toward him.

But that's not what got me emotional. It was how his lips parted the moment I stepped into view. He looked at me like I hung the sun and lit up the moon myself. I didn't miss how he was trying really hard to be tough as he watched me walk to him. In the end, he lost that battle, and I caught him quickly wiping his cheeks the moment I reached him.

I never thought that anyone, let alone Ronan, would have this reaction to me.

There's a different look in his eyes right now, as he watches me from across the room, neither of us paying attention to the people currently talking to us. He glares at me, the hairs on the back of my neck rising, a shiver running down my spine until it wraps around me and makes me squeeze my thighs together.

The corner of his lips quirks, and I'm not sure how, but he seems to know the effect he's having on me.

It's been like this since the moment the wedding reception started. We're in Midnight; I insisted on doing it here, rather than at some typical wedding venue. I wanted it to feel more like home, like us. I asked Finnigan, Vincent, Carter, and Maddox myself, since ultimately, it's their secret locale, and I wouldn't entertain the idea without their approval, but they had no argument since, apart from our parents, everyone in our small party has been here before.

But now, as I catch Ronan's hungry gaze again, the walls seem to be closing in on me. This space is too small, the people around us are a sea of shadows and his bright blue eyes shine amidst them. A trickle of sweat runs down my back, and I constantly feel the need to touch the base of my throat, pressing a bit harder every time to steady myself.

"You still haven't told me, honey, did you plan a honeymoon?" ... "Anni?"

"Huh? Oh, so sorry." The noise of the room explodes in my ears all of a sudden and I turn to find my mom giving me a knowing look. Thank God Pappa isn't here to see me all flustered. "What did you ask, sorry?"

"Honeymoon. Have you planned one?"

"Oh, umm... yes, in a way."

"What does that mean?"

I can't tell her, though. We haven't told anyone, but they'll all find out soon enough.

"We're just not calling it a honeymoon, but yes, we planned something."

She nods, but frowns, and just as she's about to say something else, Pappa shows up, pulling me into a side hug and kissing the top of my head.

"It's a very interesting business that your *husband* and his friends have here. I heard they're involved in other endeavors as well, but it seems the subject has been changed every time I tried to ask what they are."

Oh, Christ.

"It's no time for talking about work." I laugh, trying to push the nervousness down. "I'm sure everyone just wants to unwind and have fun."

I look up at him, and he smiles, seemingly satisfied with my explanation.

Our conversation continues on a safe path, Mamma and Pappa reminiscing about their own wedding, and the moment they begin talking about their honeymoon, I force myself to space out. These people have never been shy enough around me when it comes to the love they share. And while I'm happy for them, I would rather keep all those images out of my head.

An unfamiliar southern tune fills the room as I drag my gaze over the people dancing in the small space we cleared up as a dance floor, and I sense a pull toward a spot at the end of the bar. Ronan's eyes are on me. Darker somehow as he sips the amber liquid from his glass. Maddox and Finnigan are talking around him, and even as he responds, his gaze doesn't shift. Not even for a split second.

A drop of that amber seems to slide down his bottom lip, and when he catches it with his top lip, dragging it slowly, I'm suddenly parched. I swallow the knot that's formed in my throat, but it does nothing to the heat growing in my core.

Our wedding night, our own celebration of our marriage, can't possibly come sooner. Even as we tried to steal some kisses, we still got pulled in some form of cheers, a dance, a drink, a conversation. I need him. I need to feel his hands against my skin, his lips... fuck, this night seems to be never-ending. Only as I look at the time on my phone, I realize it has barely begun. Even if we already had our first dance, and we cut the cake early because my cravings were adamant I needed it then and there, we haven't even been here for two hours.

But now I want him more than cake.

I pull my bottom lip between my teeth as I watch him take another long sip from his glass, and the man cocks his head at me, a wicked grin tugging at his lips.

"We're gonna go get a drink. Do you want something, Anni?"

They're genuinely going to think I'm crazy for constantly spacing out of their conversation with me. But it's better than them knowing I'm just becoming a puddle at the sight of my new husband's feral stare.

"I'm okay. Thank you, Mamma."

They step away, walking toward the bar, at the opposite end from Ronan, and another presence replaces them at my side. I really want a break from people now, but when I look to my left, Carter's chilling gaze is on me.

"Are you enjoying yourself?" I ask, slightly uncomfortable.

"I am, thank you."

"I haven't seen you dance or..."

"I haven't found a partner," he says, smiling politely. "But, if you do me the honor,

I would happily steal a dance from the bride."

He extends his hand, waiting for mine, and I look at it for a second too long before I finally accept. I didn't even realize what song was playing until he pulled me onto the makeshift dance floor—it's a slow one. He keeps a polite, comfortable distance between us as he sways us around, holding my hand up in his, the other gently laid on my ribs, just above my waist.

I'm not sure what it is about Carter. He's the most gentlemanly out of all of them, cold, calculated, a bit of a recluse, and I admire his ability to simply walk out of a conversation without remorse when he's no longer interested. But there's this look in his eyes, like everyone around him is simply prey he hasn't chosen to devour yet. It's uneasy, but at the same time, it gives me a privileged feeling because I haven't been chosen—he likes me.

"Could I ask you something?"

He nods.

"Are you actually enjoying yourself tonight?"

He spins me gently, his eyes fixed on me, no expression or emotion in them—yet they're not entirely blank.

"I am, yes."

"It took you a while to respond."

"There's a fine line between enjoying and tolerating. Sometimes I have to think back and figure out which one it is," he tells me with utmost sincerity.

"Doesn't that mean you're at the cusp of toleration?" I ask.

"Close."

"Why?"

He actually narrows his eyes on me for a split second, but they seem to brighten up afterwards.

"If you're wondering if it has to do with the company—it doesn't."

I smile, and he does too. There's a sharp, brutal beauty about this man, and I can't help but wonder what type of person he'll end up with. If any.

"The type of entertainment I enjoy is slightly different from this. But I like this atmosphere, surrounded by people I'm familiar with. Minus your parents, although they seem nice." He turns his head, catching a glimpse of my mother, hands in the air, dancing to a different song in her head. "Although your mother seems... interesting."

I giggle and swallow it when he turns his attention back to me. "Yes, Mamma is quite a character."

He gives me a polite smile, and I know instantly that this thread of conversation is over.

"How are *you* doing?"

He's not asking me about the wedding, the look in his strange blue eyes that seep into hazel is too intense for that.

"Better. Thank you for asking."

"But you're not comfortable here."

"Comfortable?" I cock my head.

"With the unknown about Bartiste. With everything that happened."

If he wasn't leading this dance, I think my feet would stop moving involuntarily.

"Is it bittersweet," he continues, turning his gaze to the room, "knowing that this will be the last—"

"Excuse me," Ronan interrupts, just as my heart falls to my damn feet.

"Of course." Carter stops moving, his gaze back on me, but his unfinished words linger between us as he lets go and steps back. "Thank you for the dance, Mrs. Hennessey."

I take a deep breath, forcing a smile. "My pleasure."

Ronan pulls me against him, my hand in his, while his other presses on my lower back. There is no way I could miss his hard cock against my belly. How the hell has he been walking around with that thing on display?

"Ronan…"

"I think it's time to go," he interrupts, towering over me.

His face is so close to mine, his hot breath tickling my bare skin, and my lips go dry in an instant at his expression.

"We're in the middle of our—"

"Since the moment we stepped into this place, I was forced to watch you from a distance. Every time I tried touching you, you were just out of reach. Every time I tried to feel your lips against mine, someone pulled us apart. Constantly teased by these pretty pink lips I want to see swollen around my cock, that deep, teasing cleavage that I want to rip apart so I can feast my fucking eyes on your perfect tits. I can't stand it anymore, we're going. Now."

The man all but growls at me, his tone of voice low, gravelly, demanding, and my panties are unbelievably soaked by the time he's done talking.

"It would be rude, wouldn't it, to leave now?" I quickly glance around me, various people watching us as we dance to the slow tune, oblivious to our conversation.

"Now, little witch. Or I swear I'll bend you over right here and fuck you where all can see."

I gasp, and he doesn't waste a breath, grabbing my hand and pulling me behind him as he walks toward the back.

We pass through the back door, but this time around, he doesn't stop in the corridor, like he did last time. Instead, he rushes me into the office, slams the door behind me, and turns the lock.

"I can't wait," he grunts.

I'm dripping wet, my delicate lingerie an assault against my skin, and the last damn thing I want to do is wait. He's on me before I can tell him that I can't either. His lips crash onto mine, his hands hastily lifting the layers of the dress until, finally, I can feel his touch against my skin and my ass hits the edge of the desk. I didn't even realize we were walking.

"Fuck," he growls on my lips as his fingers finally touch the wet mess of my panties.

He doesn't waste a moment, as he pulls them aside and fills me with his fingers as I bite onto his lip to keep the desperate moan as quiet as possible. But he pumps inside of me with desperation, dragging soft mewls of ecstasy from my lips instead, and when the pad of his hand begins rubbing against my clit, I'm beginning to see goddamn stars.

"Nooo!" I cry when he pulls out, just as a surge of pleasure was gathering in my lower belly.

"Shh."

I can't believe it, he freaking shushed me!

In one swift move, he spins me around, folds me over the desk, and throws the skirt of my dress up until my ass is exposed.

"You better hold on."

I yelp when the lace scrapes against my skin, the ripping of fabric. But all air is lost from my lungs when the head of his cock touches my entrance, and in one long, harsh stroke, he drives inside of me.

I grasp the edge of the desk in front of me, as Ronan grips my ass cheeks and fucks me with such fierceness, I'm sinking into the ecstasy of the moment. There's no speed in this assault, but a sheer force that drives me deeper into his oblivion, one hard thrust at a time.

"I couldn't fucking wait anymore, little witch." *Thrust.* "Couldn't wait to bend you over and feel this sweet cunt"—*thrust*—"wrapped around me." *Thrust.* "Begging me for every"—*thrust*—"thick"—*thrust*—"hard"—*thrust*—"inch of my cock."

"Ahh... goddamnit, Ronan..."

"Tell me what you want."

"I... please..."

"Tell me what you want!"

"Come! I want to come!"

My head is yanked back by my braid in a rough pull, and his hot breath brushes my ear as whispers, "Beg me, baby."

The shudder that shakes my body takes control, my nerve endings flying high.

"Please, Ronan, please make me come," I mewl with desperation.

I'm lying here, desperate, hopeful, waiting patiently for the powerful thrusts that will send me to that magical place I've begged him to send me to. But emptiness meets me instead. Cold emptiness as he pulls his cock out of me.

It only lasts a moment. His mouth covers my pussy, his tongue running over every bit of me, licking, pressing, sucking at me until I'm biting onto my arm to keep myself from screaming. I'm almost there, so close but not close enough, as I'm rolling my hips against his face, and when he suddenly pushes his fingers inside of me, curling them to reach that one spot that only he seems to know where it is, my legs shake and spasm, and I whimper through the waves of the orgasm taking over.

Ronan is on his feet in the next second, and I'm still riding through the shocks of pleasure when his cock fills me again. He uses my crying, shaking body as he gets himself off, and I'm not sure I've ever felt so thoroughly satisfied, so full, so fucking happy.

This is my future.

This man who goes down on his knees to give me what I want. This man who runs headfirst into danger to save me. This man who will give everything up... for us. He's my future.

He falls over me with the last threads of his release jerking inside of me, as he peppers kisses on the bare skin of my back.

"Don't move," he says as he pulls out and moves away.

But I don't think I could have, even if he told me to do it. A moment later, he returns, and a warm, wet cloth is on me as he gently wipes my skin clean.

"I don't think I'll ever stop finding this a little embarrassing."

"What? Me cleaning you?" he asks, surprised.

"Yes... it's like... trickling out of me. Sometimes for ages."

He just laughs and heat flushes my cheeks. I'm about to protest, when he continues.

"I could lick you clean if you want."

I think I forget how to breathe. I think even my heart stops. No. *I know* my heart stops. And another trickle flows out when the walls of my pussy tighten at the thought of him... licking me clean of his cum.

Fuck. Me.

He chuckles behind me, amused at my reaction, and my cheeks are flaming when I finally peel myself off the desk and get up to face him.

"Some other time, then."

When he smirks, I think my heart skips a beat this time. I swear this muscle inside my chest can't catch a break around this man.

My husband.

"Come on, Mrs. Hennessey. Let's make up some excuse and go home." He takes my hand in his and leads us out of the office, but I stop him before we go through the door.

"Ronan, I think Carter knows."

CHAPTER 23
Ronan

ALL MY WORK, the efforts, the planning from the last three-four mont since Annika and I talked after our trip to the waterfall, have come to this. Our wedding was only two days ago, but this moment will undoubtedly bring ruin and anger... and also happiness. Happiness for us two. I would hope for the others as well, but I doubt it.

"We already know you're pregnant, so why are we all *gathered* here?" Finn looks around from his spot, standing behind the sofa. Everyone's here—Vincent, Carter, Maddox, and Katya. All waiting for us to speak.

There's no reason to drag this out.

"Annika and I... we're leaving." Silence descends.

Finn's mouth falls open in a mixture of shock and disgust, Vin raises an eyebrow, cocking his head slightly, Madds scrunches his eyebrows, a tinge of anger settling in those creases, Katya is unreadable, and Carter... looks exactly as he did when he walked in. There's no change in his expression.

The bastard does know.

"You're not leaving, brother. You're running," Finn seethes, his fingers digging into the upholstery of the couch.

"If I was running, I would have been gone months ago. I'm not running. I'm making a decision for the future of my wife, my family."

He scoffs, stalking around the furniture and stopping a few feet away from me.

"Family?! She's taking you away from us!" He angrily points at Annika, and I'm going to chop that finger off if he doesn't calculate his next words. "From me! I... we are your goddamn family, Ronan!"

"Watch your words, brother! You know her well enough by now, or at least you fucking should, to be aware that she is not the type of person you accuse her of. Annika is the love of my fucking life and she's carrying my unborn baby, your niece or nephew. I will protect them and make sure they are comfortable until I take my last goddamn breath. Maybe even after."

"She's ripping you away from your life!" he shouts, and I swear he hasn't heard a word I've said.

Annika's hand wraps around my bicep, but I'm not sure if it's because she wants to hold me back in case I jump him or because she needs the support.

"No, Finn. I decided this. I proposed this. I planned every single fucking detail of this. Me, brother, not her! I've been through fucking hell when she was taken. Out of all the people in this room, *you* should be the one to understand why I cannot risk that kind of danger again. I have to do this for them, for us, for me... and don't think for a fucking second that this was an easy decision."

The veins in his temples and throat are bulging, and I'm not entirely sure if he's going to blow. I can't quite blame him. But he takes a deep breath, and it's then I see what that anger shields—pain.

I look at him, remembering the little bundle Mom and Dad put in my lap when Grandpa brought me to the hospital where she gave birth. He was swaddled tightly in a soft fabric, and I saw the ringlets of wild gold peeking out before I focused on his mushy baby face. He opened his eyes, and huge blue irises stared at me with a kind of recognition only blood can understand. I fell for him at that moment. He was mine before he was my parents'. I was barely six, but it didn't make a difference. He was mine to love and protect.

The only thing he needs protection from now is me. He's broken... and I'm not going to be here to fix him. He thinks it doesn't hurt. But explaining my pain to him is futile. It won't change a goddamn thing. I don't want to lose him, but he's pushing me away and I don't know how to make it better. All these months, I wracked my brain trying to think of a solution for this situation... I found none.

"When?" Vin asks, suddenly pushing air back into the room.

"Today."

Annika did say she feels terrible to do this a few weeks before Christmas, but I'm looking forward to our first tradition together.

"You mean now." He gives me that look that tells me he needs the real answer, and I sigh.

"Not right now... but I guess it depends on how this conversation goes."

Finn scoffs again, turns and goes back to stand behind the sofa. It fucking hurts, seeing that look in his eyes.

"One day, you will understand, little brother."

The day will come when his heart heals. It's Vin who speaks when it's clear Finn is done talking.

"You're leaving everything behind, this syndicate, all you've built..."

"Is all yours now." I finish his sentence.

"That's why you didn't leave earlier," Carter states, matter of fact. "The business."

"Not just, but you knew that already, didn't you? I needed time for myself, time with you... and yes, I needed to make sure I left when I was no longer needed."

"You'll always be needed." Madds rises from the armchair, his anger seemingly gone as he approaches me. He wraps his large hands around my shoulders and looks down at me with a tinge of questioning, but he shakes it away and pulls me into a hug. "You'll be missed, *brother.*"

I smile, and it finally hits me... I'm leaving. We're leaving... These are our goodbyes.

It's not like it took me by surprise—we planned this—but there was no way to plan for the feelings that would come.

"You'll be missed too, Anni." Maddox turns to her and pulls her small body and growing belly into him. "That little one too."

"Please visit. You'll have to meet him or her. You just have to," she begs, sadness in her eyes.

"We will," he agrees, but I'm not sure how true that is.

He tightens his hold around her one more time, then steps away.

Carter comes before me.

"I'm not going to pretend that I understand this... love, this need that all but plagues you, but I understand the need to protect your own, to create a different, better environment for them."

"One day, your world will turn upside down, and you'll flip right around with it. You'll understand then, you'll see that it's actually the right way around."

A crooked smile pulls at the corner of his lips, a rare sight. It's even rarer for it to touch his eyes too.

"That sort of thing happens in fantasy only, Hennessey. I'll see you soon."

I nod and shake his hand. This one is not much of a hugger, and I respect that, but he still holds my hand in his for a bit longer than necessary. I'm not sure how Carter and I got close. Maybe because we're almost complete opposites, maybe because we balanced each other. Maybe because I see a bit of me in him. Somewhere deep in there.

He moves to Annika, and she looks at him, a bit unsure.

"It was... bittersweet," she says, but I have no idea what she's talking about. Carter nods—he seems to know.

"I'm glad you stayed as long as you did," he tells her.

"How long have you known we were planning to leave?"

"Five weeks and three days."

That's specific.

"Five weeks?!"

Finn makes all our heads turn. He mutters something under his breath and shakes his head.

"It was not my secret to tell. I saw no benefit in it. It would not have changed the outcome."

"At least I would have known," Finn seethes.

"I needed time with you, brother..." I tell him, and his stern look pierces me.

He knows as well as I do that he would have been too angry or stopped talking to me. I wanted this period of time to be... normal.

Vin steps in front of me, gives my shoulder a squeeze, and shakes my hand. "We could have protected you here. She would have been safe. Plenty of people have a family in this underworld."

"I don't doubt that, but this is my responsibility, not yours. I know there are other solutions, but... sometimes these things, love and the mind, they defy logic."

"I like logic."

I tighten the handshake and pull him to me, whispering in his ear.

"Someday, that girl with hair made of fire will come back into your life, and all logic will disappear."

His fingers dig into my shoulder bone, and when he relaxes, and I pull away, the black of his eyes is an entire abyss. There's nothing there but darkness, no hope, no shining light... but there's a slither of red that cuts through.

Katya follows. I brought her into this when she was running a tiny business all on her own. I offered her protection, a home, and it feels like I'm abandoning a child, even if she is older than me.

"Take care of him," I whisper as I pull her into a hug.

She pulls away slightly and looks at me.

"You should have told me, Ronan. I had a right to know. I could have..."

"Done nothing to change my mind."

She puffs and shakes her head. "I know. But this feels so extreme."

"It feels right to me. We'll be on an island, a house on the beach... a tiny town. Paradise."

"So that's it, then. Just like that... it feels more like abandonment."

"Only if you stop talking to me." I kiss her cheek, and she smiles.

"We'll see, I guess. Take care of her, and I want photos and updates."

"Done."

She goes to Annika, and they hug for a while, talking to each other and making promises I'm not sure they'll be able to keep.

"Finn..." I turn to him, but he's unmoving. It fucking breaks my heart. "I'm not removing myself from your life, just from the business, from *this* life."

"Sure, Ronan. My words don't have any pull on you anymore, so I'll keep them to myself."

"It doesn't have to be this way."

"But it is. You chose this."

"Even if I'm not here, this"—I point to everyone—"will always be our own sanctum. I'm not choosing to leave you, I'm choosing to go away with her. It's different. I fucking love you, and I love her and the life growing inside of her. My blood... *our* blood, Finn."

"No, brother. This"—Finn points a circle between everyone but Annika and I—"is *The Sanctum.* You are choosing to leave it, run without even attempting to find what you or Annika need, here. You are leaving... us."

He means him–that I'm leaving him. He thinks it doesn't fucking hurt, that it's easy to go after all we've been through—what he's been through. Although the constant stream of women warming his bed makes me believe he's doing much better than I think. Annika, though, she can't heal here, and I cannot leave her; it would hurt so much more. It's a different kind of love, the kind that will leave you lifeless if it's ripped away, and one day... he will understand. Because I have a feeling that Hanna was not his end game.

"You can't return. If you leave, that's it."

There's such coldness in his words, they don't sound like they came from the same kid who used to follow me around like a lost puppy after he learned how to walk. It cuts deep, too deep. Even though the plan is to stay away for a long while, just in case Bartiste is still alive, to avoid revealing our location, knowing my own brother is basically exiling me is a whole different kind of pain.

"You don't mean that."

"If you're out, you're out." He speaks with such indifference, I wonder if he ripped some pages out of Vin's book, or even Carter's.

"I love you, brother," I say in a calmer tone, sadness so goddamn clear in it.

But he says nothing. A few seconds pass, and he turns and heads to the front door.

"Finnigan!" Annika calls after him, and he stops but doesn't turn. "I am so sorry. I never intended any of this. I hope... please, remove me from your life, but not him, not your brother."

He lingers for a moment, then rips the door open and disappears through, letting it slam behind him, the impact of it like an earthquake aftershock.

He's my baby brother and I have no clue how to fix this.

One by one, everyone else leaves the penthouse and Annika and I are left licking our wounds. Yet with all this sadness, there is so much light, so much to look forward to. This world... it never was really mine. It was always meant to be theirs—Vincent's, Finnigan's, Carter's, and Maddox's.

I wrap my arms around Annika and revel in how she buries her face in my chest, the feel of her against my body, faint heartbeats against my flesh, little kicks in the belly pressed against me, her warmth. This is my world—she is it.

"I think it's time to go, little witch. Away to our own sanctuary."

But too many moments pass, and she seems to be holding me tighter.

"I fear that you will end up resenting me, that you will regret leaving everything behind, regret being with me," she almost whispers.

"*You* are the only one I would ever regret leaving behind. I choose you because I cannot make sense of this world without you in it." I tilt her head, forcing her steel eyes on me. "You are not regret, Annika. You are the guiding light in a sea of it, and I'll always make sure that brightness never fades."

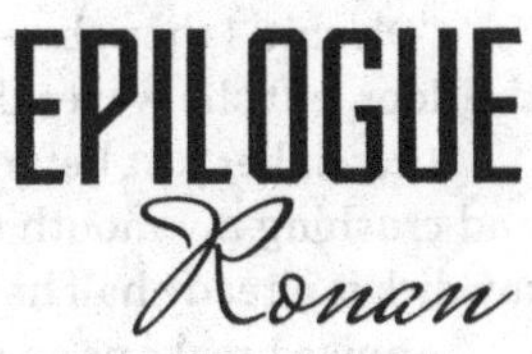

EPILOGUE
Ronan

Nine months later

LILAC FILLS MY senses when I open the door to Annika's studio. She has at least a dozen clusters of candles of that scent dotted around the bright space. When she first started burning the candles, I argued that open flames around all this paint, paper, and canvases might not be the best idea. Especially since she started painting again, she's been losing herself to it, totally oblivious to her surroundings. Her solution was to fill the space with enough of them that she could smell it even if she only burns one. I laughed, but the sparkles in her eyes made me drop it immediately.

She's in that state now... lost in the brush strokes as she swipes the wide brush over the canvas. She's turned the easel away from the door, because she hates it when anyone looks at her paintings before she's ready, so I don't know what she's painting over there. But I know for a fact that the canvas on that easel is the same one she placed there at least a month ago. She's been spending a long time on it, and even if I'm curious, I don't want to pry.

"Little witch, it's time to go soon."

She jumps, and the most stunning of smiles crinkles the corners of her eyes when she sees me.

Jesus, she's the most incredible thing in this world, and she fucking belongs in this room filled with works of art. She even dared to fall back into copying the works of the greats... just for our eyes this time. Even so, she's still the most beautiful work of art in this space... in any space.

I take a step into the room, needing to feel her in my arms, like I haven't had her already this morning, waking her up with my tongue between her sweet thighs.

"No. Stop right there!"

"But I—"

"No, mister. It's almost finished, but not quite yet."

I shake my head, but I stop where I am, smiling.

"Then you better move that sweet ass quicker, because we're gonna be late."

She's flushed now, the color on her cheeks prettier than any of the ones in her palette. She starts washing her paintbrushes, cleaning with delicate movements, her eyes flickering at me from under her thick eyebrows.

"Is Aaro still sleeping?"

"Yeah, he's out. He'll probably wake up after we leave, but Rosa arrived a couple of hours ago."

"A couple? My God, I've lost track of time. Wait, when do we have to leave?"

"Fifteen minutes."

"Oh shit! I thought—" She throws the paintbrushes down, a couple scattering on the floor, but she waves them off and darts toward the door.

I catch her just before she's about to rush past me, pressing her against my body and crushing my mouth to hers. She falls into the kiss, moaning into my mouth, and my dick is already half hard. *Shit... we'll never leave this house.*

Annika breaks us apart and gently swats my arms away.

"I have to clean up and change. Come on, baby, let me go."

"Mmm.... Fine," I concede, place a kiss on her forehead, and release her.

She's so quick nowadays, since she's been losing the baby weight. Lucky for me, it's been a slow and steady process, because I'm kind of missing that thick softness, sinking into her, kneading her flesh... her full hips. I've been enjoying her changing body, constantly finding something new to love about her.

I shake my head and pull at the fabric that now grinds tightly against my cock, readjusting and muttering to myself.

"Jesus Christ... that woman's gonna be the death of me."

I'm about to turn around and leave, but I spot the brushes she dropped on the floor, and I go to at least pick them up and place them on the table for her.

I tried, I really tried not to look to my left, to the canvas she's been working on for so long. But the vivid shades of lilac caught my attention, and I couldn't stop myself.

"Hanna..." I whisper as I look at the woman who's been gone out of my wife's life for far too long now. It was a year and two months ago. She's smiling, dressed in a lilac garment that wraps like a thin veil around her form, looking down at the chubbiest, cutest baby cradled in her arms. My baby... our boy. I could recognize him anywhere. The painting is not finished, but fuck me... the emotion in it is more vivid than the colors that form this image, because its beauty lies well behind this canvas.

It's perfect...

"Baby?" she calls for me from somewhere in the house. I drop the paintbrushes before she can come and catch me snooping.

Closing the door behind me, I walk through the bright corridor that holds a wall of windows overlooking our wild garden, and head toward the entryway. When I get upstairs, I find her rushing from one side of the bedroom to the other, one shoe in hand, one on her foot, her sundress unzipped at the back, ponytail whipping around in a whirlwind.

"Baby girl, easy... we'll get there in time."

"Yes, yes. I couldn't find the other shoe, but I got it now."

I can't help it, and I start laughing when she holds the sandal up, victorious.

"Zip me up, please." She turns around, bending over and sliding the shoe on, but she's flustered in her rush.

"Come here." I pull her up, then spin her around, and drop to one knee.

She calms instantly when my hands are on her leg, and I pull her foot up to rest on my bent knee, then slowly close the strap around her ankle. I can't help but linger, my hands trailing up her leg, past her knee, a shiver running through me as goosebumps cover the skin I'm touching.

"Ronan..." She speaks with an enticing, breathy voice that makes me want to flip her over and fuck her right now.

I look up just as she visibly swallows, and she's about to say something, when we hear footsteps out in the corridor. Considering I left the bedroom door open, it would be wise for our son's lovely nanny not to catch us fucking on the bedroom floor.

"Are you in here, Mrs. Hennessey?"

I drop my wife's foot and reluctantly rise, adjusting my erection before I turn.

"Yes, Rosa."

The middle-aged woman appears in the doorway, her plump cheeks flushed from the heat. She's our son's nanny, but she loves baking, so she's been in the kitchen for the last hour, filling the house with a sweet aroma that makes my mouth water.

"Can you please call me Annika? You've been with us for months now, Rosa."

I know she's not going to do it. Her expression already says it all. The woman is old school, and if she won't call her Mrs. Hennessey, she'll probably end up calling her Mrs. Annika instead. Which is funny, because she's been acting more like a mother with us, always making sure we're fed and happy. I reckon she would either be best friends or mortal enemies with Mamaw June, Vin's mother. They're quite alike.

I walk behind Annika and zip up her dress before dropping a kiss on her shoulder.

"You're gonna be late, you two, go on."

"Yes, all done here. I'll go check on Aaro one more time."

I follow her out of the room, thanking Rosa on the way, and enter the nursery, where our son is sleeping in his cot. It's dark here, with the exception of the faint lights projected on the ceiling, of constellations and galaxies.

Aaro lies in his bed, sleeping soundly, and probably dreaming, considering how he moves his little, chubby fingers.

"I can't believe he's almost six months old. Am I going to blink and he'll be on his first day of school?" she whispers.

"Time's our worst enemy... but we're gonna make the most of it."

I reach over, rolling one of his blond curls in my fingers. It's bittersweet, how much he looks like him... even if he inherited my hair color, a darker shade of blond, those are my brother's curls.

Annika sighs next to me, and I pull her to my side.

"Do you think Finnigan will ever get to meet him?"

I swear this woman can read my mind.

"I hope so... at the moment, I can't even get him to meet me."

About three months ago, we went back to Queenscove for a visit. We kept a low profile and stayed at my parents' house, since they came home for a couple of days and wanted to meet their grandson. Everyone else came to see us. Everyone... except Finn.

He was *busy*.

I wanted to hunt him down and put some sense into him, but I've been told by more than one person to let him be. Death and loss change a person... and, unfortunately, I'm guilty of the former. I did this to him... I can't force him back to me.

"How long can he really hold on to the anger?"

"He's always been stubborn, so probably for a long time, but this is more than anger—it's betrayal. He'll probably hold on to that for much longer."

"I just... I want Aaro to have an uncle."

"I guess time will tell, baby girl."

I kiss the top of her head and pull her with me as I walk out of the nursery. We say goodbye to Rosa, then Adam and Taylor, the men we hired as security who actually live with us. Ten minutes later, we're driving down the narrow roads of our small town on Falk Isle. A slow song fills the car as the night slowly descends.

"Our life now is such a contrast to how it was. I was a nomad, and you were one of the leaders of a criminal organization–The Sanctum, as they now call it. Do you miss it?" she asks me, her hand on my thigh as I make my way through town.

"Sometimes. The art and contraband deals I started the business with weren't really about the money. It brought us a pretty penny, but I wouldn't have kept at it if it wasn't for the excitement, the adrenaline. But even surrounded by all those people, people I loved and cared for, it was... lonely. What about you, do you miss it?"

I place my hand over hers.

"Same. I miss it sometimes for the same reasons. The thrill of a new business deal was quite something. I would never go back, though. I'm sure I can find another way to get that... excitement."

I glance at her, and her cheeky smile makes me want to stop the car in the middle of the road and make her show me exactly what type of excitement she's thinking about.

"Eyes on the road, mister."

But my dick wants something else entirely.

"I wonder if the guys will hate me forever for taking you out of the business." She changes the subject.

"They don't hate you, Annika."

"One certainly does," she mutters.

"Don't worry, they'll understand. Maybe not right now, but they will when love eventually hits them out of nowhere, just like it hit me."

She chuckles, and it fills my chest with warmth.

"Who do you think will be next?"

"I don't know. They're not ready yet, that's for sure. Power and money are their priority," I reply.

"It won't be Finn, that's for sure."

"No..."

She's not referring just to what happened to Hanna, but to the new habits he's been developing. My brother, with his tall, fit build, blond curls, and baby blues, has always been popular, with girls in school and women after. Only, now he's been fully embracing those opportunities.

"Carter?" She asks.

"Only if he finds the spawn of Satan..."

"Or the complete opposite?" Annika says, giggling. "Maddox?"

"Possible, but I think it might be Vin."

"The Serpent, of all people?!"

I nod. "He was in love once, not that long ago. He thinks he hides it well, but he's been keeping tabs on her. Not stalking, but once in a while, he makes sure... she's okay."

"And no one else knows?"

"Maddox does. The others weren't even here when Vin was with her."

"Oh... Did he keep her away from them?"

"Not really. I think they knew of her, but Finn and Carter were away at university when Vin got with her, and it was... intense. He was possessive, protective, and she was almost forbidden. She comes from a different world than the one he is from—the high society of Queenscove. It looked like he tried hard to stay away from her at first. Once they started, he was reluctant to flaunt her, not only because of her family, but because she was his weakness, and he didn't want that to put her in danger."

"What happened?"

"I'm not sure. He just broke up with her one day, out of nowhere. The guys were still at university, so I doubt they even knew about them. Madds seems to have been sworn to secrecy for some reason. Either way, I have a feeling we haven't seen the last of Morrigan O'Rourke."

* * *

We're about forty minutes into the movie playing on the big screen of the outdoor cinema. I know because I've been looking at the time every five-fucking-minutes. Not because I'm not enjoying watching Casablanca, but because I've had a constant semi since I went to get her from the studio.

I can't seem to calm myself.

"Fun fact, I chose my last identity because of her," Annika whispers. "I was in love with the old movies when I was a kid, and Ingrid Bergman was stunning. I wanted to be like her."

When I finally think I'm over it, her melodic giggle fills me, and my cock responds all over again. Then she gives me those pretty steel-blue eyes, looking more steel than blue in this light, and I can't help but imagine them painted with ecstasy.

What is wrong with me today?!

The movie moves into a flashback of Rick and Ilsa riding happily on the streets of Paris, their connection suddenly explained, when Annika whispers she's just going to the ladies' room, before she gives me a quick peck on the cheek.

She rises from the blanket and moves carefully around the ones of the other people watching the movie, heading to the edge of the clearing of the small forest. I watch her as she disappears through the door of the bathroom set up at the far end of the area, luckily not that far away, as we didn't want to be in the middle of the crowd. But Bergman and Bogart distract me when the man himself speaks one of the most iconic lines in cinematic history.

I've seen this movie before, but Annika was so excited when she heard that not only was there an outdoor cinema in our small town, but it was playing Casablanca today as well, that I knew I had no choice but to watch it all over again. If only just to see the giddiness in her eyes.

The flashback scene ends, but my wife is not back yet.

I turn and look toward the bathrooms—no movement, no sign of her. As I drag my gaze over the area, I spot her, walking alongside the edge of the forest. She stops halfway, turning to me when she sees me watching her.

Just like that, my world flips on its axis all over again when the woman gives me her most wicked smile, and there's no denying my cock anymore. Then her dress becomes a fluttering whirlwind as she whips around and disappears through the trees.

You wanted excitement, little witch... let's see how much of it you can take.

Annika

I THOUGHT I would hide behind a tree and wait to make sure he saw me, that he was on my trail. But I seem to have underestimated the man who is stalking toward me with a fierce gaze promising something so wicked, my feet burn with the need to run.

So I do.

I take off through the forest, the soft ground kind to my feet as I jump over small obstacles made of branches and rocks.

Humphrey Bogart's voice is a faint echo, the trees far enough apart that the light of the film flashes between them, and my feet seem to be moving in a strange slow motion. Goosebumps scatter over my skin, Ronan's feral gaze burning my flesh, my pussy slick with his silent promises as my thighs rub together.

Each heavy thump of his footsteps sends shivers up my spine, wrapping around my neck, tightening like his hand is there instead.

"Is this what you want, little witch? For me to chase you? Fuck that little cunt of yours and make you come with my name on your lips?" His tone is lower, harsher, a surreal echo through the woods. "Well, you better fucking work for it, because you don't seem to want it hard enough."

His voice is suddenly closer, the rustling of leaves and thumping of footsteps nearer, and with a yelp, I pick up the pace, a surge of adrenaline rippling through me.

I change direction, falling into the darkness of a thicket of trees, and I catch my breath in their shelter. He stops too, but not near me.

He doesn't see me.

"Come out, come out wherever you are..." he taunts, walking in my direction, as he looks all around.

A smile pulls at my lips—I can play with him. Only, that thought is squashed in an instant when he sprints right toward me, and leaps between the trees. I yelp and dart out of the way, but one arm wraps around my middle, pulling me into his body.

Grabbing his forearm, I push it away, squirming and kicking. He pulls me harder, my back against him, so I dig my heels into the ground and push back. But he's a mountain, barely moving at all. When he chuckles at my feeble attempt, I give it one last shove. He loses his footing slightly, enough that his grip loosens just enough. I screech and take off into a sprint in the opposite direction, a raging roar splitting the soundwaves, making my wetness drip down my thighs.

The light of the film is brighter, but I can't tell if I'm running toward the clearing where the cinema is, or alongside it. I can't focus on it when this adrenaline burns so sweet.

"You're gonna fucking pay for that, witch!" His grunts send shivers through my body because, yes, please...

"Make me!" I shout.

I turn my head to the side, trying to catch a glimpse behind me as I skip over the fallen branches, and see the man himself, so much closer than I thought he was.

Instinctively, I shriek, a strange sort of fear infused exhilaration breaking apart inside of me. When my foot catches onto something, I snap my head back to look in front of me and manage to fix my balance, the much brighter lights of the movie helping me find my feet.

Only, it lasts but a moment, before I'm slammed forward, all the air whooshing out of me as his hard body crashes me against the harsh bark of a tree. His hand protects my head, before it tangles in my hair, yanking it back. I shriek as if the man behind me is not my husband. But logic works differently in moments like this because my pussy wants something else entirely.

"You thought you fooled me," he growls, and I'm about to snap back when his hand rushes down between my ass cheeks, pushing my panties to the side, and his fingers rip through me. I scream as my back arches, involuntarily pushing into him. He thrusts his fingers into my pussy, slow and hard, my core tightening around him.

"Is that what you want? My fingers spreading this wet cunt?"

He yanks my head back harder when I don't respond, but my mouth seems full of moans, devoid of words.

"Aaah!" I yelp as he tugs me hard against him and away from the tree.

"Careful, baby girl," he whispers against my ear, "someone might hear you."

My eyes flick toward the lights, realizing I ran almost to the edge of the clearing. The voices and music of Casablanca are all that covers my shrieks because there aren't many trees between us and the first people laid in the blankets in the clearing.

"Ronan, I—"

But before I can continue, he covers my mouth.

"Don't you fucking dare," he warns.

I squirm in his grip, pushing away, but failing miserably and falling on the ground. I rush to push myself up, and yelp when his hand wraps around my ankle, yanking me back a few feet. Reaching forward, I try to grab onto something, my dress riding up, exposing my whole lower half.

"We're too close. Someone will see us, someone..."

His hand smacks my ass, the burn reaching my pussy, quieting me with a shudder.

"Stop pretending this doesn't make you wet." He slams down onto his elbow next to my face, his other hand pulling at my panties until they rip, then his fingers find my pussy once again, sinking inside as my whole body lurches forward.

He's right... it does make me wet.

He rolls those digits inside of me, rubbing against everything that makes my body sing. But the song is not loud enough, I need more.

"Look at them, laying quietly on their picnic blankets, sipping their wine, oblivious to the strong pulses of your walls around my fingers, begging for more."

My gaze snaps up and I see them all. A surreal, calm image as the man who lays on top of me thrusts in and out of me harshly, spreading his fingers as he pulls out, rolling them over and over, hitting that spot that makes me see stars, but not lingering long enough to make them explode behind my eyes.

A heat takes over my body, one that begs to fucking burst into flames, but he doesn't add the goddamn fuel. I want it, I need it...

"Please..." My inner thoughts break out, my voice surprisingly pained.

But he keeps teasing that spot, a ghost of a touch hitting my clit, making my back arch, my hips pushing against him, begging.

"I want... please, Ronan... I need..." I mewl, unable to form the sentence.

"I know *exactly* what you need," he growls, and before my next inhale, his cock impales me in one deep stroke. I cry out in both pleasure and pain, watching, horrified, when one of the people on the blankets turns their head.

Ronan doesn't stop, fiercely slamming inside of me, the slapping of our skin barely masked by the sounds of the music, the buckle of his belt scratching me, but it feels so goddamn good. He wraps his arm around my hip until his fingers reach that nub of flesh, and when he presses two against the top of it and rolls them in small, fast circles... those stars finally explode.

My toes curl, my body shakes, all my nerve endings sing all at once, and I swear I'm seeing all the fucking colors of the rainbow as I bite into Ronan's forearm to keep from screaming. He really did know exactly what I needed.

I think I'm done, but Ronan is harsher than before, fucking me like a wild beast, pressing me harder into the forest floor. His fingers rub against my clit again, but my orgasm has barely dissipated.

"Oh God, baby..." I moan, silently pleading for him to stop because I'm too sensitive. Far too sensitive. But his thrusts are relentless, and his digits drive me to the point of insanity.

"Come for me *again!*" he orders.

"I can't..." I cry out, writhing against his body that uses mine like I'm his to do as he pleases.

Oh, but I am... fuck, he can do anything... everything. He smacks my clit with his fingers, and I throw my head back as I'm starting to see those stars again. Catching my hair, he pulls my head down and presses the side of my face on the ground, leaning in.

"Annika..." he groans. "I said come for me!"

He presses onto my clit and, *my God,* can I?!

"I can't..." But I think I'm lying.

He pinches it before he rubs in a motion that makes my body shake uncontrollably, my pussy clamping down on his cock, feeling him fill me so utterly well, rubbing against that spot that makes my eyes roll into the back of my head. All of a sudden, all those stars explode into goddamn galaxies and I'm coming with such force, I have tears in my eyes. And even through my cries and his grunts as he spills inside of me, I couldn't care less if anyone sees us here, between the trees, getting fucked by this beautiful man on the dirty ground.

"Jesus Christ…" I pant. "That was insane."

"I had fantasies like this." He catches his breath as he slowly pulls out of me. "But who would have thought that the little shy, delicate girl would be the one to fulfill them."

"Yeah… I wouldn't have thought that in a million years. I guess… you bring it out of me."

"Good." He kisses my cheek and rolls me over, lifting me until I'm on his lap and he's wrapped around me in a comforting hold. I sink into him, my head snuggled under his chin, listening to his quick pulse. I'm still panting, but he strokes my hair, and everything seems to calm.

"Life is funny that way. I never wanted it all, but somehow, I seem to have got it."

"All?" he asks.

"The amazing husband, love, a baby, beautiful house, comfortable life, incredible sex-life… I don't think I deserve any of this," I confess.

"Sometimes I look at you and us and I think I'm gonna blink and you'll go away. Like it was a beautiful dream, because this sort of happiness feels impossible."

It's strange how we seem to share our fears. I smile, pulling away slightly so I can look at him and wrap my arms around his neck.

"Well, darling husband, here's to an impossible life together."

Then I press my lips to his and we sink into the forest floor once more, embracing all that we thought could never be.

THE END

BONUS EPILOGUE
Annika

Eight years later

DARKNESS DROWNS ME. *Total and utter darkness. Whimpers shred the heavy silence, but they're not mine. A woman's... scared, but brave, suffering, but defiant. When recognition hits, those whimpers shred through my heart too. They grow louder, pain dripping like poison from every note, calling for me. It knows I'm here. Knows I'm listening. The whimpers turn to wails of agony, and it dawns on me—it knows I can't find it. I can't save her. It's a derision.*

This is my torture.

I wake up with a start, panting heavily as I push up to sit in the soft bed, drenched in sweat.

"Hanna..." I murmur.

Almost eight years have passed since her death. Eight years filled with joy, sorrow, incredible milestones, and more love than I ever thought I could feel or give. Eight years of life, but her death has haunted more dreams than I could count.

Her memory has survived, both the incredible times and the excruciating ones. Years of therapy have not erased my guilt. I'm not sure I've even tried to help myself. It's my burden to bear. But not one that has kept me from moving on with my life, with Ronan and Aaro. Hanna wouldn't allow such a thing to happen anyway.

I take one more deep breath, then turn to look beside me on the bed.

"Where is he?"

Climbing out, I revel in the feel of the tiled, cold floor beneath my feet as I walk out of the bedroom and into the hallway, stopping to listen for a sound.

Nothing.

I head for Aaro's room, opening the door slowly, and peek through, forcing back a cackle when I notice him. He's right at the edge of his double bed, one arm and leg hanging off the side. All that space and this kid still favors the edge, looking like he's always ready to leap out and jump into a sprint, prepared for the next adventure. Even as a toddler, when he was too young for a bed, he would slide his chubby arm and leg through the wooden spindles of his cot, sleeping in the exact same position. Such a little weirdo.

Closing the door, I move forward down the moonlit corridor, passing through the empty kitchen, then the living room. Still... nothing.

He's in the office.

I sigh, unmoving from my spot in front of the floor-to-ceiling windows, looking at the waves beyond the beach our villa sits on, nestled between palms, ferns, and perfumed hydrangeas, weighing my next move.

Should I go?

There's a nagging voice living beyond my consciousness, creeping in closer and closer to the front of my mind over the last few weeks. It scares me. It came around at the same time my dreams of the past, or nightmares, have become frequent once again. Just as Ronan has started closing the door to his office, disappearing more often.

I know this man maybe better than I know myself. I've noticed the change in him. He's getting lost in his thoughts, a hint of unease shadowing his blue eyes. Yet he hasn't shared anything with me. That fleeting expression is also the reason why I haven't asked him about it, confirmed I'm not imagining it. That expression hasn't been painted on his face in years... about seven or eight of them.

That nagging voice speaks to me... words that I have heard, but never listened to.

While you're dreaming of the past, darling Annika, your husband spies on the future.

I gather my wits and will my feet to move toward that room. A deep breath fills my lungs as I wrap my hand around the handle of the office door.

Darkness.

"What the..."

I swallow the worry, pushing away those vexing thoughts, all the doubt. I'm imagining it. Planting stupid seeds in my own brain. Nothing's happening. He's not looking into anything.

A shuffle somewhere behind startles me. I whip around, facing the door to my art studio—it's cracked open, a faint light streaming through.

Stepping forward slowly, I press my palm to the warm wood, pushing hesitantly, and I finally find him.

"What are you doing, baby?" I ask.

Ronan startles, slowly dropping the stack of paintings leaning against each other by the wall, turning and walking over to me.

"Nothing. Sorry. I couldn't sleep, and I wandered in here, looking at your paintings."

That unease is back in his gaze. No, I'm convinced I'm not imagining anything. I know something is happening, just as I know with absolute certainty what painting he was just looking at. I painted it the day happy memories with Hanna started breaking through the tragic ones. She would have loved my son, so I had this vision swirling through my imagination, and I had to capture it. Her serene expression, the look in her eyes as she watched him, his contempt as he was held by her. I've looked at this painting countless times, but I don't think Ronan's ever looked at it once after that one time I showed it to him.

"Are you okay?" I narrow my eyes on him, but he tilts his head and mirrors my stare.

"Are you? You're flushed."

"I'm fine, just... a dream."

But the look in his eyes, and the cocked eyebrow, calls me on my bullshit. He knows I'm twisting the truth.

"Come." He captures my hand in his, turning off the electric candle he had on, and walks me out of the studio.

He doesn't push. We both know what torment my nightmares hold, so no explanation is needed. But even he's noticed their increased frequency. He leads me back to our bedroom, but doesn't stop there. Instead, we pass through, into our bathroom, where he turns on the night light, before he shuts the door. The space is bathed in a dim, dark green hue, the combination with the multitude of plants and green tiles making me feel like I'm in the middle of the rainforest on a full moon.

Facing me, he gently forces me to step backward until my back hits the countertop of the sink cabinet. There's an intensity radiating from within him, in his flexed muscles, his tensed, strong jaw, but this low lighting hides whatever secret lies in his eyes.

Almost.

Because slowly but surely, hunger begins to shine in them. If this was seven or eight years ago, I would argue that he's trying to distract me from asking questions. But after all this time, our souls speak to each other with such ease; I know this is his way of relieving certain tensions. How he sorts through some thoughts. He needs the connection—our connection—so he can find the answer, the solution he's looking for.

I have no doubt that whatever has been plaguing him will be revealed soon.

His hands go to the hem of my tank top, and I lift my arms as he pulls it off me, cupping my breast before the fabric even hits the floor. His thumb brushes my perked nipple at the same time his other hand goes to the back of my head and his lips crash down onto mine.

For a moment, a long, excruciating moment, he doesn't move. He inhales slowly, dragging the air that surrounds me like he's breathing in the very essence of me—of us. Only when my hands touch the soft skin of his hips does he seem to awaken. And with feverish urgency, he licks me, pushing his tongue into my mouth, kissing me like my lips begged for punishment. I cry against his when he pinches my nipple, and his hips press into mine in response, a shudder passing through my body at the feel of his hardening cock.

"What do you need, baby?" I ask him between nips and licks.

"You..." Pulling me hard against him, he breaks the kiss completely, teeth going straight for my neck, as he nudges my legs open with his knee. "I need you."

My head falls back, mewling in aching greed when he bites my skin at the same time his fingers reach for my core, pressing against my entrance, not bothering to push away the panties currently covering me. The scrape of the fabric soaked in my arousal feels oddly satisfying. He does it again, pushing harder, rougher, his breaths quickening with his desire, and his patience suddenly falters. He grips the garment, ripping it with one harsh tug, and before the yelp from the burn of the fabric escapes my throat, he covers my mouth with his hand, silencing me. His gaze bores into mine, and I get one moment, one silent moment before two fingers plunge inside of me, and my knees buckle at the crude contact.

Ronan presses me back against the counter, steadying me as he finger fucks me to the edge of surrender.

But I'm not giving in.

Through the goosebumps pebbling my skin, the electric fire raging in my belly, the stars beginning to dance in my vision, I refuse to give in.

"Come for me, Annika," he orders in a breathy, gruff tone.

His hand on my mouth muffles my refusal. But he retaliates, his thumb swiping that traitorous bundle of nerves. My whole body shakes, nirvana gazing at me from beyond the edge of the cliff I'm on. I close my eyes, refusing to fall into it.

"Little witch, I said. Come. For. Me!" There's no softness in his voice, only unequivocal demand.

I shake my head at the same time the pad of his palm rubs harshly against my clit in that precise way he knows makes me crumble to my knees, and I cry out in reckless abandon. My pussy spasms around his fingers, body shaking so hard that he releases my mouth and circles his arm around me, holding me. Protecting me.

He pushes me over the edge of that cliff. And I gladly fall. But he's always there to catch me. Always.

In moments like this, I know what he wants, what he needs—my fight and my surrender. He wants to work for it... and I try not to give in too quickly. Only, he takes advantage of his intimate knowledge of my body and mind, playing me like a violin, and it's hard not to be grateful for how well he knows my songs.

Four breaths, that's all I manage to inhale before he leans over slightly, wrapping his arm around my ass, and lifts me to him, carrying me into the shower.

Two more breaths I inhale before the spray crashes down on us, cold water first, before the warm spray pulls me back into this divine reality.

One last breath, and I'm flipped around, arms braced against the floor-to-ceiling window overlooking the sea, and his cock rips through me from behind until there's nothing left but us. No air, no space, just us. I'm so full, so goddamn full, his cock stretching my walls with such intensity, even my legs refuse to move to adjust to a more comfortable position. It doesn't matter, in three more thrusts I'll forget even my name, let alone if my legs are comfortable. He settles into a brutal rhythm, skin slapping against skin, hands wrapped around my hips, fingers digging harshly into my flesh as he pulls me to meet each plunge.

He's using me, my body. Using me like a puppet for the release he needs, his mind coiling within itself as he starts a new song of grunts and heaving breaths, joined by my own moans and breathy mewls.

My head is yanked back, and his lips meet my ear at the same time his fingers find that bundle of nerves between my legs once again, rubbing it in the cruelest of rhythms.

"You're mine, now and forever. All. Fucking. Mine." His assault on my sensitive clit quickens, erratic but intentional movements taking me back to that precipice in seconds. "And I am yours."

I cry out his name. Over and over, it spills from my lips like he's the demon I've been begging to summon for a lifetime. And he finally came.

But so did I. Then his cum floods me, hot bursts intensifying my orgasm, and once again... I find myself held by him, one arm circling my middle as I barely brace myself against the glass, but he doesn't mind.

Eventually, I feel the spray of the shower again, even though we never turned it off. I can hear the sound of it, our staggered breaths, even our heartbeats. Mine, for sure. My gaze focuses, the stars disappearing, but all I have before me is the sea, the moon reflecting into it like it belongs so very well in its embrace.

While Ronan insisted on having this dim, green night light, I insisted on a floor-to-ceiling window right in the shower. Both elements fit so well together.

"Fuck, you are perfect," he speaks against my wet hair.

"And here I thought that after all these years you'd discover the rouse. There's no perfection here, my dear husband."

"Shush." He snickers.

He's back. He feels lighter. While I'm glad I helped, sooner or later, I need to find out what's happening.

"Wash me." I turn around in his hold, narrowing my eyes on him.

"Yes, ma'am." He cocks an eyebrow, grabbing the shower gel, and proceeds to wash me with bare hands until every inch of me is clean, the sweat of the nightmare completely gone.

"Go." He nods toward the bedroom. "I'll come in a moment."

My lip quirks as I step out of the shower and quickly wipe myself. When I begin to move away, that voice bred by instinct nags me again. So I turn back to him.

"Will you tell me then? Will you tell me what's going on?"

No words leave his mouth, but his eyes widen, a tinge of fear rippling through them. One nod, that's all he gives me. One brief nod.

* * *

"Mamma..."

Mmm?

"Mamma... Wake up. Pappa said he'll eat your pancakes if you don't hurry."

I open my eyes to a mass of curly, blonde hair in my line of sight, bright blue eyes staring at me with far too much mischief sparkling in them.

"Is that what Daddy said, or... is it you who's about to eat my pancakes?" I ask Aaro, watching as he curls his lips, trying to hide his deception.

"Ummm... no. Pappa. Not me. Definitely not me."

"Well, okay then. Pappa can eat my pancakes."

"What?! No! They're mi—" he squeals, quickly straightening his little face when he realizes he screwed up.

"You sneaky little man!" I grab him in one swift move, lifting and throwing him on the bed beside me, and we fall into a tickling war that fills the whole house with shouts and laughter.

I finally stop when tears fill his eyes and he starts begging me to stop.

"How many have you had?" I ask him.

"Two," he almost shouts, shoving two fingers too close to my face.

I don't say anything, I only cock my head, catching the twitch in his eyes. If I'm not careful, this little man will grow up just like his father... or uncle.

"Umm... fine, three," he finally admits, his shoulders slumping.

"Are you still hungry, or are you just hunting for the maple syrup?"

"No, I really am hungry." He rubs his belly and throws in some puppy eyes that melt me every single damn time.

"Okay, Aaro. Let me get dressed and I'll come out. You can have another pancake."

"Aaaah!" He starts jumping on the bed a couple of times before he leaps down on the floor and sprints right out of our bedroom.

I hear him shouting from the other side of the house, *"thank you, Mamma,"* and I can't help but laugh. That kid is such a handful. He's too smart for his own good, but he's already getting a bit cocky. He has that Hennessey blood, and I can't help but wonder if he'll have the same sense of business someday. The chances are a bit too high.

Scrambling out of bed, I grab a pair of shorts and my favorite oversized Guns N' Roses t-shirt that's holding on by a thread, and splash some water on my face before I head to the kitchen. I shot myself in the foot last night, falling asleep before Ronan even finished his shower. Waking up in the middle of the night left me quite tired anyway, but sex with him always exhausts me. Today is the day, though. I'm not falling asleep until he tells me what the hell is going on.

"Morning, baby girl," he says without turning his attention from the pan he's currently washing.

I walk over to him, wrapping my arms around his waist, and press my cheek to his strong back, inhaling his scent. "Morning."

"Did you promise him another pancake?"

"Yeah, why?"

"I wasn't sure if he was messing with me."

I giggle, loosening my grip as he twists and grabs the sides of my face, willing my lips to his.

"I'm sorry I fell asleep last night," I say once he releases me.

"It's okay. It was far too late anyway."

"I want to talk, though."

He nods, that damn worry peering once again from under his low eyebrows.

"Can I have my pancake now?" Aaro shows up in the kitchen, panting from his excitement.

Half an hour later, we're on the patio, watching the almost still sea, the sun making the sand sparkle as Aaro works on his newest sandcastle. Although *fortress* is more accurate. He started it four days ago, and he's not even remotely close to finishing it.

"He asked me about his uncle yesterday," Ronan says.

"His actual uncle?" I snap my head to his, brows furrowed. We call all of them—Carter, Vincent, and Maddox—his uncles, and Katya his aunt. But... it's Finnigan he's referring to now.

He nods, but he keeps looking toward Aaro. "He heard me talking to Katya over the phone. His name was mentioned."

"What did he ask?"

"Why his uncle doesn't like him." Ronan sighs, and I swear I felt the crack in my heart.

"Fuck..." I whisper. "He's older now. He picks up on and begins to understand emotions. There's no escape, not like when he was little. I wonder if actually meeting him would change his mind."

Ronan turns to me, a tinge of yearning in his expression. I know he misses his brother. They used to be almost inseparable until Hanna was murdered... until we left. Now, they're pretty much strangers. Finnigan refuses to talk to him, to have any sort of relationship with him. But, strangely enough, every year on Aaro's birthday, he sends him a card and a gift. I'm convinced it's Katya doing it in his name, but Ronan has hope.

"How's Katya then?"

He sighs, wiping a hand over his face.

"She's good. Business is better than ever. They're really thriving over there," he says, clearly avoiding what he really wants to tell me.

I know they're thriving. Word about The Sanctum, the criminal organization controlling Queenscove and far beyond, has spread like wildfire. The underworld is no longer the only place their name is spoken. They're still a mystery to the world, their work and actions mere rumors, but their social standing is high. High enough that even politicians do their bidding. Vincent always insisted that information is power. I guess they leaned hard into that. At least that's what I've been hearing.

"But...?" I finally ask when he looks like he's not going to continue.

"Something is stirring. They've already had some trouble there. It's sorted it now, but something bigger might be coming." He sighs before continuing. "I've been keeping an eye on Queenscove over the years. Outside of whatever information Katya or Carter have been giving me."

Years...

I still, eyes wide as I try to wrap my head around it. I want to be annoyed at him for hiding this from me. But who am I kidding? I had a gut feeling, but I just didn't want to chase it. It makes sense... I get it. We left fairly suddenly, so I cannot expect him not to want to be in the know. He's a protector; this wouldn't stop with his departure.

But... years? Shit.

"What have you found out?"

"A connection. Something Finn, Madds, Vincent, and even Carter, might not know about yet."

"Big?" I ask.

"Yes."

"How big?"

"Enough that this has to be a face-to-face conversation," he says, certainty settling in his tone of voice.

I shake my head and open my mouth to speak, but he interrupts me.

"They're my family, Annika. I have to tell them, even if Finn won't want my help."

"No. They're *our* family. Aaro's family."

"What are you saying, little witch?" A sparkle splits the shadows that have been marring his eyes. This is how I know this is the right decision. Dangerous, but right. A temporary arrangement.

"*We* are going back to Queenscove."

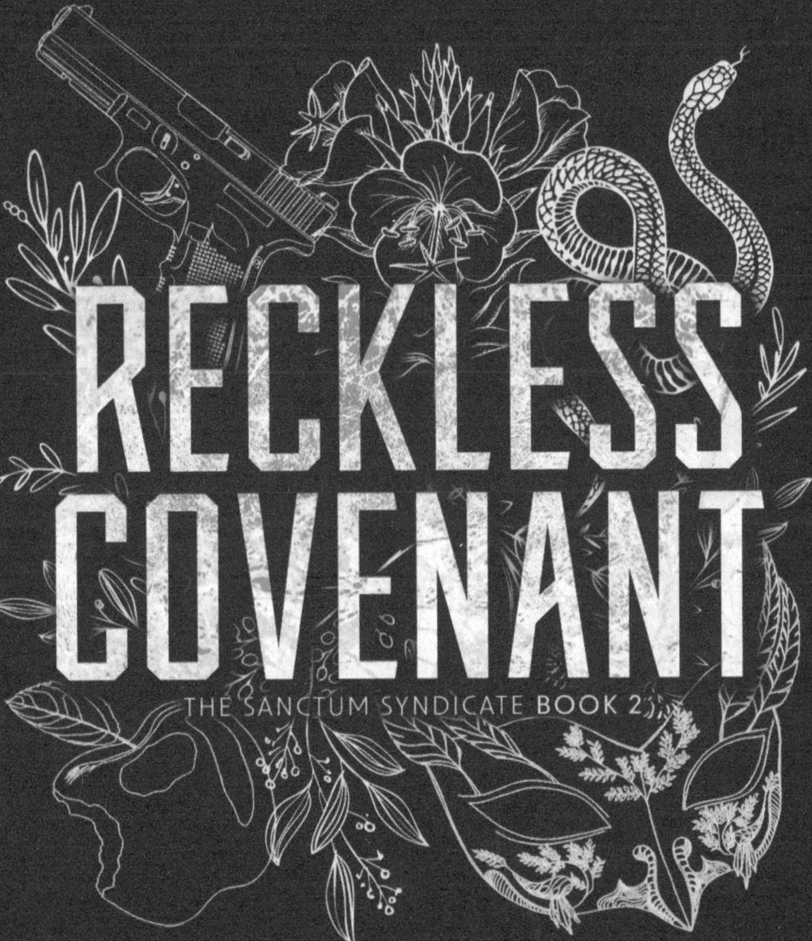

RECKLESS COVENANT

THE SANCTUM SYNDICATE BOOK 2

LILITH ROMAN

BLURB

In another life, I used to love him. Now, I just need him.
But will he break me all over again?
For years, I made sure to keep the handsome, black-eyed devil out of my life. I never expected to be the one to pull him back in.
What choice do I have when my own family betrays me?
I was building a life for myself, and now I'm trapped. But I refuse to run. I don't want to hide. And I certainly will not submit.
The only way to escape with my life is to threaten theirs. Only one man is powerful enough to help me—Vincent "The Serpent" Sinclair. My ex-boyfriend. My first love. And one of the leaders of his ruthless underworld.
So we make a pact for my salvation, only he doesn't tell me what he wants in return.
I may have sold my soul to the devil, but will he keep my heart too?

CONTENT WARNING

This is a work of fiction and should be taken as such. It contains dark themes and sensitive content including graphic violence, murder, emotional and physical abuse, gun violence, BDSM inspired scenes, cheating (not between MCs), fat phobia/body shaming, gaslighting, forced marriage (not MCs), female oppression, and mentions of sex trafficking of both adults and children. There is no cheating and it has a HEA. If you are easily offended or triggered by any of this content, please do not read this book. Your mental health matters.

PLAYLIST

Broken Bones – KALEO
The Devil is a Gentleman – Merci Raines
Devils Got You Beat – Blues Saraceno
The Wicked – Blues Saraceno
Forgiveness Don't Grow on Trees – Bad Flamingo
Sinners and Saints – Andrea Wasse
Ain't No Devil – Andrea Wasse
The Hearse – Matt Maeson
Devil With Angel Eyes – Royal Bliss
Window – Bonefield
The Devil Never Sleeps – Blues Saraceno, Nine One One
God Damn Better – The Dirty Diary
I Know His Blood – Vienna Ditto
Graves – Whiskey Shivers
Mausoleum – Rafferty
Shake off Your Flesh – The Huntress and Holder of Hands
Blood Moon – Yoav
Devil Devil – MILCK
Every Breath You Take – Chase Holfelder
Murky – Saint Mesa
Bad Things – Jace Everett
God Be You – Nostalghia
The Killer – Kevin Costner & Modern West, Jaida Dreyer
Devil Like You – Gareth Dunlop
Swamp Hymns – Osi And The Jupiter
Mount Everest – Labrinth
Love Is a Bitch – Two Feet
Twisted – Two Feet
Down So Low – Royal Deluxe
Been a Bad Woman – Black Casino and the Ghost

Eight years earlier

THE UNMISTAKABLE CRACK of bones twists the sound waves, and my muscles, too, as I wince at the sharp vibration tainting the air.

Madds and I watch as the guy grabs onto his jaw on a pain-filled bellow, but the enraged curses the redhead spits at him almost shadow it. His screams fuel her. Her eyes fill with a familiar madness, yet… it's much richer than the reflection gazing back at me in the mirror. She's a fucking tornado of punches, slaps, and kicks as her small body shoves him in a frenzied attack.

She's goddamn mesmerizing—Morrigan O'Rourke—the girl with forest eyes and hair kissed by fire.

Even Madds gawks with starry eyes at the angry woman, wrapped in a tornado of wild curls.

And this bastard never admires anything.

But when she throws herself on top of the kid, her knee digging into his stomach as she leans onto the forearm she's locked against his throat, it's time to stop her.

I step forward, sliding my hands under her armpits to pull her off the guy who's at the brink of tears, his nose a bleeding mess. Only, the girl pushes me back with more force than should reside in her slim frame. She's on fire, and I might just let myself get burnt.

I signal Madds to replace me so I can *tend* to the guy bleeding on the ground, and he grabs Morrigan just as she pulls back her elbow, ready to land another fist in the asshole's face. She's yanked back, kicking her legs, screeching in frustration at the restriction, but Madds, with his tall, broad, and strong body, doesn't flinch. He lifts her effortlessly, her back to his front, an arm wrapped around her as she thrashes, willing him to let her go.

He doesn't. Even looks a little bored as he allows her to get it all out, while I press my boot on the stomach of the mangled piece of crap lying on the ground, pushing him back down.

"I'm gonna fucking ruin y'all! Send your asses to jail, fucking white trash!" He spits blood onto the ground, and splatters hit my shoes, the words slurred through the pain in his jaw as he pushes his broken body to get up.

My foot lands on his throat a moment later, and when his gaze meets mine, he falters, eyes growing wider as his body stills and tenses. There's fear in those dilating pupils, and I peek at my reflection in the car window to find what terrifies him so—it's all me. My eyes drip with the sort of malice that could make angels fall, villains rise, and summon armies.

Our army has been assembling for only a little while, and he's exactly the type of person who would be a target in our criminal endeavors. Only this pathetic pussy right here poses no advantage to our less than charitable cause. His dad though, yes... we could entice him with a deal he definitely can't refuse since he holds some information we could exploit. Maybe his kid is not useless after all.

"I wonder what your daddy would think if we threatened to expose his only son, the future of the Bray name, the heir of his business... as a rapist." I press a little harder on his trachea as those words spill calmly off my tongue, and when his hands grab onto my leg, I increase the pressure. "Get your filthy hands off me," I bite out in a low, guttural voice.

Only a gurgling sound comes out when his mouth moves, and he quickly taps his palm on the ground.

"Give him a chance, Vincent," Madds says, laughing behind me, the girl's screeches now having quieted.

I shrug and take my foot off his throat, his following coughs growing boring real fast.

"Spit it the fuck out!" I rasp, enjoying the wince that crumples his face.

"I didn't ra—" he all but whispers as he rolls onto his front, pushing his no doubt aching body onto all fours so he can get up.

"Speak up, motherfucker!"

"I didn't rape her." He spits blood again, rising and sitting on his heels.

"Who the fuck do you think you're playing?! I got one word for you: Rose."

The seconds stretch as his shoulders tense, and he slowly turns his head toward me.

"She couldn't go to the police," I carry on, my eyes searing into his. "There wouldn't be enough evidence for them, but there's more than enough for her father and us, motherfucker. We were already coming for you, but catching you on Lover's Lane with your tiny dick in your hand, as you're about to force yourself on another girl who's clearly refusing you, is some sort of cruel luck. At least we caught you before you ruined another—"

But I don't get a chance to finish.

"I'm not goddamn ruined, asshole!" The girl sneers at me. Her attitude pulls at my lips, but I don't turn for her to see it.

"She—she asked for—" Bray begins to speak.

"I'll kill you, motherfucker! I'll chop off your dick and shove it up your ass, you goddamn son of a bitch!" Morrigan shrieks with a sharp, angry voice, and I resist the urge to cup my own dick at the disturbing thought.

I have no idea how, but she slips out of Madds' hold, and rushes to the guy. landing a fierce kick to his chest. He drops onto his back with a harsh thud, and a mere second later, a pain-filled bellow fills Lover's Lane as she thrusts another strong kick between his legs. The poor bastard curls into a fetal position, crying in curses and threats that will never come true.

Reaching over, I grab onto her waist, attempting to pull her back. But in the next moment, the shock of an impact knocks me back a step, my ear ringing as I realize she smashed her elbow into the side of my face.

"Jesus fuck!" I rasp, ready to haul her ass over my shoulder and end this.

But when I catch her eyes, I'm trapped.

The fury looks too fucking pretty in those greens devoid of remorse. She delivers one more punch in the guy's ribs, her gaze on me the entire time. And something far more shattering hits me. Only it doesn't land on my flesh, nor in my bones, but within my fucking heart and soul, and I know... I'm ruined.

CHAPTER 1
Morrigan

Present Day

I FELT THE air shift before my eyes caught on to the silent disturbance. The skin of my back prickled with an uncomfortable chill, even in this sticky humidity.

Now, it spreads up my spine, onto my shoulders, and grips my neck, forcing my body to turn. One by one, the surrounding people change their tune, either to silence or whispers, just as my gaze reluctantly lands on them.

It's almost impossible to think of the four men as individuals. They unintentionally carry themselves as one entity. Yet the shift in the air would make one feel they are a legion, commanding the attention of all who are around. They are not from the same family, but somehow cut from the same cloth, moving in unison like they share blood, muscles, bones, and DNA. Their arms sway in unison, their feet gliding in a matching beat on the moonlit asphalt, and fuck me if it doesn't feel like time slows down. If only to allow everyone to take in the creatures who bend the air into compliance.

Only, they aren't creatures at all... just four people forming one important faction—The Sanctum. The anomaly of the underworlds, four men ruling as one—Carter Pierce, Finnigan Hennessey, Maddox Severin, and Vincent '*The Serpent*' Sinclair.

Even thinking of that last name on the list leaves an awful taste on my tongue. It fills me with distaste and loathing for the man.

Queenscove, our southern, seaside city filled with period buildings and very few skyscrapers, is not the place where everyone knows everyone. Unless you're part of the fairly extensive high society of this wealthy place. Yet wherever *they* make an appearance, the world stands still. Only, it's not fear you're feeling, it's power. Fear is simply a byproduct. It stems from the rumors swerving about them and their Syndicate—violence, black-market deals, sex, secrets, murders—and no matter which you've heard, they amount to one thing and one thing only: *danger*.

No one knows how many of these rumors are true. None have been denied, or addressed, for that matter, and their presence alone is enough to make you believe all of them and more.

It annoys me that Queenscove feels safer because they're here.

I knew them once. Well, I knew two of them, one... far too intimately. But I remember all of them when they were young, still in school. I was a starry-eyed kid, four grades lower than them, but even then, they were a force of fucking nature. Even through the shivers they gave you, you still craved to throw yourself in the middle of their storm.

Their affairs aren't common knowledge, but my family's position in this society poses some advantages for me. Although nowadays I would rather not be part of this family at all, it does mean that I end up hearing all sorts of interesting things. I've built up all this information, piece by piece, and amongst other things, I know that their most profitable business is secrets. They harness them, keep them safe until the time comes, and they have to use them to their advantage. Whether for new business deals or to manipulate other people. The wheel is constantly spinning.

Information is power and power is worth more than money.

The Serpent should know.

He's the only one of The Sanctum who didn't come from money. Instead, he built his reputation on pure talent. One he wields dangerously well. People say all he needs is his piercing gaze to gather all the information he requires from someone. Although, I'm pretty sure he doesn't shy away from physical torture. His intensity is brutal, and using it to manipulate his *victims* is what earned him his reputation. Both between the criminal world and the aristocracy.

He doesn't need *old money*. His pockets could be as empty as they were ten years ago, but the world would still bow at his feet. He *is* power.

The black-eyed devil himself—my ex-boyfriend.

And my first love.

The scar running across my palm itches at the sight of him.

Suddenly, I'm painfully aware of the man sitting next to me right now. He would probably kill for The Serpent's skill. And this is not a thought I would have had about him six months ago... but things change. So many things have changed.

The four men walk on the sidewalk, calm and determined, passing by the old-time cinema, a quirky flower shop, then one of the city's fanciest restaurants, before shifting directions to a dark and narrow side street. Hushed rumors have spread through the high society of Queenscove about a speakeasy they own, nestled in plain sight, somewhere in the middle of the city. Maybe that's where they're headed now. I have a vague idea of where it could be, a radius more than anything, but neither me nor my family have been invited. Although, those who have been, cannot speak of it. So who knows.

I would be lying if I said I wasn't intrigued. That I wouldn't want a taste, a little peek.

The first man dips into the shadows of the street, then the second one, and after the third man follows, their black suit covered bodies absorbed by the darkness, The Serpent takes one more step and stops.

I swear time slows down just for him, his body turning ever so slightly, his eyes closed as he moves to look over his shoulder. Then they open... not wide, but the slits of a snake who found its next meal—and that's exactly what I am.

What happens when you gaze upon the devil... and he catches you?

When his eyes land on yours and he marks you as a target?

What happens when the devil doesn't look like a devil at all?

Dozens of people sit at the tables of this street-side bar terrace, yet his gaze landed straight on mine. I'm forced to take in his strong, almost square jaw that's dusted with thick hair, those full lips, and straight, wide nose. He's kept his black hair short on the sides, but the top is a few inches long, messily swept back, and I hate how good he looks.

Saliva pools in my mouth, but swallowing means moving, and somehow moving seems to be the wrong action right now. He's fixed on me. Unnaturally still. But the shadows of the street swallow him, as if the darkness is part of him, a coat he wears so well.

Whispers break out in unison on the terrace and the back of my neck heats up— they're talking about me. No one missed their presence on the street, so hiding this silent, yet powerful exchange is impossible.

Moments pass, the night breeze unhelpful as my eyes begin to burn with the need to blink. Only I have a fucking point to prove. I am not submitting to him. I will not break eye contact first.

"Darling?"

Shut the fuck up, Ryan.

"Morrigan?!" His tone switches to commanding.

The Serpent's gaze suddenly darkens even more. I'm not sure how I know this, but I'm convinced no one else notices the subtle shift, the gentle scowl forming between his eyebrows. I'm also sure it's not meant for me either, but for...

A hand waves in front of my eyes, breaking the connection.

Goddamnit, Ryan!

When that palm vacates my line of sight, The Serpent is gone, the side street empty.

Turning to Ryan, the ruckus of the terrace patrons fills the night again. Stealing a glance around myself, it's impossible to miss how they watch me from the corners of their eyes, even if their conversations are not about me.

"Yes, Ryan." My eyes land on him before I fully face him, and I'm met with his pursed lips, flared nostrils, and scrunched eyebrows.

There isn't much more I can take from my relationship with him, even though I do kind of care about him. A year ago, I would have said with certainty that I loved him. Now, as the veil has been pulled away further, I'm convinced that love is far too strong of a word for what we have... *had*.

I've been ready to leave for a while. Ever since it all started to change. When *he* started to change.

However, our families seem just as involved in our relationship as we are. Actually... more than I am. Leaving him seems like breaking a treaty between two nations. As I've been distancing myself, they seem to insist harder on meeting, pushing us together, forcing us to dinners and events. Every encounter breaks the confidence I've been trying to build. And it's just as difficult for me to break away from my own family.

"What the hell was that?!" he presses, struggling to control the distaste in his tone.

"I don't know," I say, shrugging.

I'm not fully lying. I don't know what it was from The Serpent's point of view, but I do know what it was from mine—hate. Luckily, this city is big enough that I managed to avoid him almost unintentionally over the years. We've rarely crossed paths, and I like it this way. Months must have passed since the last time I saw him...

God, I'm fucking fooling myself.

It's been exactly five months, three weeks, and two days—my mother's 50th fucking birthday. The elite were invited. The Sanctum, too. I was sure my parents did it as a power move, either to display some sort of fake alliance or because they were begging for a business deal.

Five fucking months and that night still haunts me.

If only it was the only one that did...

I focus on Ryan's murky brown eyes, like a marsh, with hints of green. They used to be kind of pretty, but now all I can think of is a swamp when I look into them. Nothing special sparks in them anymore.

"He was just staring at you," he speaks again, his tone grating.

Blinking, I turn my gaze back toward the dark side street.

Yes, he was.

"Answer me, goddamnit." He lowers his tone, but almost hisses at me.

"You didn't ask a question."

He huffs so loudly I catch the people at the next table over briefly turning their attention to us.

"Don't act like I don't know your past, Morrigan."

"My past?! What are you talking about, Ryan?" I ask, baffled by his insinuation. He knows about The Serpent and I, since we were all in the same school at one time, but he also knows how long ago it was.

"Don't play stupid, you know very well what I'm talking about. I know you saw him at your parents' party, too. If anything is going on, I swear..."

"Did you want me to keep my eyes closed throughout the entire night so The Serpent wouldn't grace my line of sight?" My sarcastic tone is louder, and I don't miss the bulging of his eyes as he subtly glances around us.

It seems to shut him up, and he shifts his attention elsewhere.

The Sanctum is fearless, seemingly indestructible, and that whole invitation must mean that my father is doing business with them, or maybe attempting to. For five months, I've been trying to figure out what's happening with my family. They are dysfunctional in their normal state, but things have been changing. It feels different. Like we're sitting at the edge of a cliff, and any moment now, a storm will tip us over.

I wish I wouldn't think about it as *us*. I wish I wouldn't be involved in whatever the fuck it is, but I seem to be pulled into it, if their recent cushy attitude toward Ryan is anything to go by. But if this is a game of chess, I'm no Queen in it. Not even a Knight— I'm a pawn. Not that I was ever anything more to my parents, my father specifically. I was never as important as my older brother, Cillian. He is the future of this family, the one to take over whatever businesses father has, and the O'Rourke name further. Carry it deeper into our fucked-up family history. Even our ancestors were crazy sons of bitches. Some were worse than others. Cruel, despicable, lacking remorse, even slave owners a few centuries ago.

I'm not implying I'm a saint. I know where my soul belongs. But it doesn't mean my place is with them. My brand of sin is different from theirs, and as long as I continue to be careful, they won't know I'm trying to get away from all of them until it's too late to stop me.

It's funny how Ryan used to be my escape from them. Not anymore. Not since he realized he couldn't quite tame me, and his views started aligning with his father's... and my father's. My boyfriend's exertion of control these days runs deeper than I would care to admit. His time will come, and just like my family, he will pay, too.

If only I would actually get my fucking balls back.

"I think I'm ready to go home now," I say.

"Alone?!"

I mentally roll my eyes. *As if I'm ever alone.* There are constant eyes on me, especially as of late. Since Ryan's father passed away, he is slowly taking over the crooked family business and accepting his place as the head of it. Something is brewing, but no matter how hard I try, I can't find out what it is. All I know is that our families, before the passing of Jonah Holt, were working on something, a business deal. An alliance. Why or for what, I have no clue. But it feels like the terms have changed now that he's not here anymore.

"Alone, yes. I have things to do."

"Things?" He spits the word out like the lack of respect he has toward my work isn't already blatantly obvious.

Just because my branding and design work takes place exclusively online, it doesn't mean it's not work. I majored in graphic design and took my talent to a pretty damn profitable business, banking at least a couple of grand per project. I'm quick though, and I've been pushing myself hard enough that I can take quite a few per month. But Ryan does not know that.

I get up before he can say anything else, then dip down and give him a peck on the lips. I know he won't let me leave without the mimicked affection. But he catches my upper arm just as I'm almost standing and pulls me back down, his lips crashing onto mine in a much deeper kiss.

It's a sort of claim on me, for everyone around us to see.

After The Serpent's earlier display, such a rare sight, I'm sure he feels the need to piss all over me. Mark his territory and make sure everyone knows who I belong to.

I allow the kiss mostly because I have no other choice. But it's for my own survival. I have to play nice.

Hopefully not for long.

CHAPTER 2
Morrigan

I SLIDE INTO my car, eager to start the AC and escape the humidity, shutting the door as the engine roars to life. The busy street drowns the noise of it, but it's not like people didn't already turn their heads as I sat inside. They look at this car and instantly think it's either my boyfriend's or my daddy's. I fucking hate that they're not entirely wrong.

As I was finishing university last year, my parents suddenly decided moving about in taxis wasn't safe for their daughter anymore. They insisted they buy me a car, no matter my protests. I didn't want to be tied to their money, but the only way to escape their flashy choice, which would have ensured I would flaunt their wealth around the city, was to concede. After some negotiation, I managed to sway them from the same mid-life crisis red Ferrari my father has, toward this black beauty, a Dodge Challenger GT.

I love this car, but it's a constant reminder of their control over me. I fucking pray for the day I can just drop the keys on their table and buy my own. The day I'll be able to afford to move out and escape their damn clutches. Ryan's too.

Going to university was the loophole in that control. Their desire to raise good *stock* meant that they could do little to protest my desire to attend university over 400 miles away, up north, well past the hills of Venator. I even stretched the time with a master's degree too. They attempted to protest, but that was a prestigious university, and they could do little to justify why they didn't want me so far away.

Early on, I started seeing that my family's values and their views of women, of me, are much different from modern society standards. I had to plan my way out. That temporary freedom allowed me to have a job without them knowing. Along with most of the allowance I've been saving since I was fifteen, that plan for the future was becoming clearer.

But now, all those savings are tied up in my first business venture in which I'm a silent partner. There's no way I can let my family, or anyone else, know that I'm involved. Not just yet. Lulu and I worked too hard for it.

I pull away from the curb just as my dashboard flashes with a phone call, Lulu's name popping on the screen. Turning the volume down, I press a button to answer.

"Give me a sec, let me put an earbud in. I'm in the car."

I fiddle with it and switch the connection on my phone as I stop at the traffic lights. These days, I'm careful we're not overheard, especially when it's about business.

"You good?" I hear her sweet, soft voice come through the other line.

It's deceiving. The woman may sound sweet, but she's vicious. Calm, but vicious.

"Yeah, all good. I was just thinking of you. What's up?"

"I'm just having a little trouble making a decision, and I wanted to ask if you can come in and help me out." I hear her long nails tap one by one on a solid surface. She sounds impatient.

"Sure, give me ten, or actually, fifteen minutes. I need to—"

"I know," she interrupts.

She knows my life all too well, including the regression of my relationship. I need to lose my tail, if there is one, since I told Ryan I'm going home. My friendship with her isn't a secret, and neither is her location, but I would rather have a head start anyway.

The four-story period building looms, the beautiful details of the century-old façade hiding many secrets beyond it. On the top floor, Lulu lives with Luke, her boyfriend, the two floors below are unused, and on the ground floor, she opened a quirky little café, which brings her a constant stream of income.

I look around before I leave the car, a habit that has become second nature now—I wasn't followed. Before walking into the café, I glance briefly at the windows of the floor under Lulu's apartment, the one she insisted I should have. I didn't want to bring my fucked-up life so close to her, but Lulu's love is the only unconditional one I know, and in the end, I accepted her offer.

This place was an inheritance from her late grandmother, who had it from her own mother, and it's been rotting since the 50s, stuck in time. Lulu took it upon herself to restore it to its former glory. Renovations started quite a while back with work on the structure and roof, then part of the ground floor for the café and lobby, alongside her apartment on the top floor. But when our business idea fully formed, all the financial efforts shifted, and the work on what's supposed to be my apartment halted before they properly began. It doesn't even have a floor right now, just bare beams that used to hold the rotting parquet floor.

"Hey, sugar!" I greet the bartender as I enter the ground floor café.

He nods and smiles as I pass by the bar he's currently wiping. It's placed by the entrance, at the front of the narrow space, giving the patrons quite a lot of privacy from the people passing by on the street, since the tables are located beyond it, toward the back. The space is much longer than it is wide, but people seem to enjoy the coziness.

The rest of the ground floor and the extensive basement area are being turned into something much, much more interesting. I can't help but grin to myself as I walk past the tables, toward the back door.

This location is perfect for our business, because even if someone was following me, going to see my best friend at her café or her place is nothing unusual.

After punching in a code, I step into the well-lit short corridor surveyed by two cameras, arriving at two other doors, both leading to two secure foyers. One leads to the front of the building for the apartment access, and the other, where I'm currently inputting the code on the keypad to get through, leads to the back of the building. To our new business venture—our fetish club.

As I pass through the door, my steps falter. The lobby wasn't finished the last time I was here. I turn my head in awe, admiring the black 3D diamond pattern covering most of the walls, bathed in a decadent, gold glow reflecting off some of the facets.

It's fucking beautiful!

To my left, black double doors, sculpted with an art-deco pattern, open up to the entrance hallway that leads to the private parking and courtyard at the back of the building, while to my right sits what will be a staffed wardrobe.

And right before me, stretching the entire length of the space, sits *la pièce de résistance*—the black marble and dark wood, semi-circle shaped reception desk with the most stunning backdrop I've ever seen. Although the backdrop itself, the wall, is the main event.

I step closer, in awe of the beauty our artist created on the black velvet covered wall, interrupted by two entryways, five feet away on either side of the reception desk. Bas-reliefs of naked bodies protrude out of the flat surface, the gold light absorbed by their sinful positions.

On the left-hand side, on his hands and knees, there is a bas-relief of a man with a leash clearly wrapped around his neck, held by a woman standing on the inside of the reception desk, her legs spread in an imposing stance.

On the right-hand side sits a woman, ass on her heels, palms on her thighs, a rope around her throat, held by a man standing on the inside of the desk.

And between these two scenes, centered on the wall behind the reception, is my favorite—a beast of a man standing sideways, tall and strong, the gold light bouncing off his sculpted muscles. He has one hand wrapped in the hair of the sinful, naked woman before him, bending her neck uncomfortably, while his other hand is lost in the relief, right where their hips join.

They are beautifully and flawlessly sculpted behind the soft fabric, enchanting and strangely hypnotic.

I pass through the left entryway into a wide corridor. There are a couple of sitting areas here, doors to the powder and dressing rooms sitting on the opposite side, but my attention is caught somewhere else. On the other side of the reception, against the same wall, right above the stairs that lead down into our club, one word is written in large, brushed-gold letters, telling you exactly what awaits you while you're down there—METAMORPHOSIS.

It shines discreetly against the black velvet, and its meaning is as much tied to our own evolution as it is to the experience of the people who will join us here.

With each step down the stairs illuminated by gold spotlights as a sultry rebel Blues song touches my ears, my soul feels freer. The irony of finding my freedom underground doesn't escape me.

The moment the block heels of my knee-high boots hit the floor and my eyes sweep over the space before me, I clutch the handrail so hard my bones ache.

"It's ready," I whisper to myself.

"Tadaaaa!" Lulu cheers, startling me as she jumps from behind the bar.

It sits against the right wall, fairly close to the stairs, because we wanted to give people this proximity, as some could be overwhelmed when they first step into the fetish club. Even in normal clubs, most people run to the bar first. It's a comfort thing.

"I can't believe it's finished..." I whisper in disbelief.

Her icy blonde ponytail whips around as she dips behind the black marble-topped bar, and the music quiets. I walk toward her, but my eyes are gazing anywhere but in her direction, mesmerized by the reality of this finished space. I'm in awe, speechless at how insane the finished product looks. I mean, I'd seen it only a week ago, and it wasn't far from this stage, yet I can't help my shock. The implication of it being finished hits harder, more than the look of it.

"Is it really finished?" I ask in disbelief, whipping my head to Lulu, my excitement seeping through.

"It is! I was dying to tell you we would be done today, but I wanted to surprise you! It's fucking beautiful, isn't it?" She clenches her fists to her chest, an emotional look in her eyes as she glances around.

I rest my back against the bar, facing the expansive space filled with a combination of booths, sofas, and normal tables, with enough room between them for dancing. And in the center of it all stands a large, circular stage with two stripper poles. As much as it is a fetish club, everyone loves watching a woman with good dancing skills. I'm excited and apprehensive at the same time. Lulu insisted we install them, and I know it's because she's trying to tempt me. I love pole dancing. Back in university, I visited the local studio several times a week, but she knows how hard I shy away from being seen doing it. I reckon this is her way of kicking my confidence into gear.

Either way, the stripping, the dancing, it will provide amazing background entertainment when the stage isn't being used for its main purpose—shows. Our inspiration comes from the club in Rosston, where we went to university. When we visited it, experienced couples or groups booked the stage for various activities, either actual play or instructional sessions. I'm excited to see this place in action.

"I can't believe we're three weeks ahead of schedule," I say, pushing away from the bar and walking around the counter.

My gaze lands on the bottle and glasses stashed behind it. The bar isn't stocked yet, but we kept Bourbon here for tough times. There's just under a third left... There have been quite a few tough times so far.

I pour two fingers worth into each glass, and hand one over to Lulu, clinking with her.

"Congratulations, Miss Dietrich."

"Congratulations to you too, Miss O'Rourke."

I take a large sip, then head toward the opposite side of the room from the stairs, where a wide corridor splits the wall in two. But it's not just a normal corridor. On either side of it, large windows cover the whole length of the walls, peering into each of the six playrooms. They're special double windows that allow the people inside the rooms to decide if they wish to see the crowd watching them, or if they want to turn it into a mirror. Only on their side, though. Some people love the intrigue of being watched, but don't enjoy seeing the people watching them. And finally, if they don't want to be watched at all, one button pulls down a blind, and they have private playtime instead.

I drag my free hand over the dark wood paneling covering the wall, admiring the equipment sitting behind the windows—benches, St. Andrew's crosses, toys, crops, tables, and just simple chairs. The main reason this place has cost us pretty much all our savings is because we made sure all the equipment is of excellent quality, and comfortable, a lot of it handmade by a great local carpenter and tanner we found.

One of the things the club in Rosston was lacking was quality equipment. We're new to the business world, and we wanted everything about this club to scream excellence and taste. The last thing we need is to give someone an excuse to tell us we're not serious about this venture, especially since our market research showed us there's enough elite in this city seeking this kind of place somewhere else.

More intriguing was the fact that, after making all these items for us, the man who crafted all these pieces, decided he will be our first member. Still subject to vetting and interview, but he was pretty much our test subject, and we're very happy that he passed.

"We're keeping the same opening date, right?" I ask Lulu.

We reach the end of the corridor, which opens into a small hallway, to the right heading toward the bathrooms, a security desk, and the fire exit, and toward the left, where we're heading right now, is our office and private bathroom. Lulu walks in, sits behind the desk, legs crossed on top of it as she leans back in the chair.

"I think it's a clever idea," she answers.

I follow suit, sinking into the sofa and propping my legs up on the coffee table.

"It gives us time to reach our member goal, but we could potentially hold a pre-opening party for the ones who have signed up so far," I say to her. "There's enough there for a solid event, and I'm almost done with their background checks. Interviews will follow soon. We should invite some people to play and put up a show to create an unforgettable atmosphere. Then we offer an incentive at the party for the current members, if they recommend another potential patron."

"Those are some great ideas! I'll ask Rose and Jasmine if they are available to entertain earlier than planned. And I'll invite some experienced people from the club in Rosston, to set the tone." The excitement is pretty damn clear in her voice.

"Are you gonna play?" I ask, watching as she downs the rest of her drink.

If she wants to, people won't recognize her anyway. We want to give members the comfort of feeling free, without others knowing who they are, or seeing that they are in the presence of someone they know personally. Of course, it's impossible to promise true anonymity since it depends more on them than us, especially when tattoos or distinct marks are involved, but the least we can do for them, and our staff as well, is to make masks mandatory; simple carnival style, or on the tasteful horror side, it doesn't matter to us.

"I'm sure Luke would enjoy that, but no. Not now. The party and the opening are too important. I'll have enough on my plate, and I have to stay focused. I can't get involved as well."

"Yeah, you're right," I agree.

I pop my glass on the coffee table and lie all the way down on the sofa. Damn, this thing is comfortable. I would rather sleep here than go to my parents'.

Lulu actually met Luke in the fetish club up in Rosston, and they clicked from the start. After university, he pretty much followed her here, not that it was a big move, as his hometown is about 200 miles up north, close to Venator. However, who wouldn't want to be here on this Topaz coast, close to the light blue waters and white sands it got its name from. The subtropical climate is such a welcomed medium, especially when it comes to the mild winters and breezy summers. Although we still have the humidity.

This place attracts a healthy number of tourists, but our mayor has limited the number of hotels that can be built, by local ordinance, to avoid ruining the landscape and infrastructure. Every single local agreed. That number was reached a few years ago, so even as a tourist town, it's fairly exclusive. And not many people move in, since most don't want to leave, and the real estate is through-the-roof expensive.

Queenscove is a corner of paradise.

These were some of the main reasons why I knew I had to bite down on my pride and accept my best friend's offer. It wasn't only that, though, but the simple fact that I didn't want to take advantage of her. Although she would smack me if I ever said this to her face. In the end, getting this apartment from her is a godsend... for the sheer amount of money I'm saving, and the time. She's freeing me from my family's control, Ryan's too. I would thank Lulu's grandmother, if I could speak to dead people, for leaving this building to her, along with some money to help with renovations.

The rest of the Dietrich family got an equal share of the inheritance, some property too, but none as large as this. Or as dilapidated, for that matter. It's like her grandmother knew that Lulu was the right person to take proper care of this beautiful old building. Long before our time, it was a small hotel, which Lulu's great-great-grandmother owned, only she decided she would make each floor its own apartment instead.

"You alright?" She pulls me out of my thoughts. "You want to crash at mine?"

"Nah, you and Luke need your space. Besides... I don't wanna give my parents, or Ryan, any other reason to be suspicious of me." I get up and down the rest of the drink. I really want more, but I have to drive back.

"There's always space for you, Morri. But... I understand."

I know she does, but Luke is kind of weird about his privacy. He was the same in university when he came to our apartment. I like him, but there is something about him that makes me feel like I'm in the way. Not just my presence, but me as a person.

"Thanks, honey."

"Did you find out anything else?" She settles back into the chair, the expression on her face suddenly serious.

"Let's not do this. We need to enjoy this huge victory. Our club is ready... *fuck*! It's incredible! My family and darling boyfriend can wait for another time."

I don't miss the silent sigh as her chest slowly deflates.

"Come on. I want to show you something else." She rises and strides out of the office without waiting for me to agree. All I can do is scramble to rush after her.

What the fuck?!

I follow her through the corridor, then the club, up the stairs, passing through the reception, and back into the small corridor I came through from the café. But she takes the door leading to the foyer for the apartments.

"Babe, I don't want to disturb Luke... Maybe he's—"

"We're not going there." She shuts me up.

Following her into the elevator, I watch as she presses the *No. 2* button—the floor of my future apartment. I turn my head to her, confusion straining my features, but I'm met with an impassive expression. The woman's poker face has always been far too good. But I know her better than anyone. Even Luke. I can see the tinge of mischief in those golden eyes.

When the elevator stops and the doors part, she flips the switch of a faint, dangling light, and my mouth falls open instantly. I cover the sharp gasp that escapes my throat with shaking hands, unable to fully comprehend what I'm seeing.

"You... how? Where did you... Fuck..."

She laughs as she excitedly grabs my wrist and yanks me inside, onto the dirty, bare concrete floor.

"I made some calculations some time ago and realized I have some spare money to start the renovations slowly. Build some bones."

Lulu is smart with her money. She gives herself a salary from the café downstairs, and the rest comes from dividends from various investments, at her father's advice. But she no longer has expendable funds to waste on this slow-return investment. Renovating the actual building, the structure, the plumbing, electrics, and other bare minimum, is done at her expense. This was her decision. When she invited me to move into this apartment, we agreed, at my insistence, that everything from flooring to furniture will be paid for by me. However, since our priorities changed to the club, we halted everything to do with this apartment, or the one beneath it, and redirected all our funds to the business. The arrangement was that a percentage from the club profit will go into this apartment.

Only, it seems the vixen was cunning and already found money. I'm not entirely sure what's stopping me from screaming in joy and jumping all over this damn place. Maybe the pure shock. Or maybe the memories of the rotten, broken floor we deemed a hazard after Lulu's foot went through it when we were surveying the space. It's all gone now. Brand-new bare concrete sits under our feet, fully ready for flooring.

"Fucking hell... Oh, my God!" It's all I can express right now, and the wide smile on her face makes me wanna goddamn kiss her!

The walls are cleaned and scrapped back to the brick, and the mold which riddled every surface is gone. Even the wood frames for the walls are built, electric cables already weaving through some of them.

Fuck, this is amazing!

"The electrics will be done in about a week, maximum two, and the walls will be rebuilt after. It will take a bit of time. We'll see what position we are in by then." She walks straight ahead toward the tall windows on the opposite side of the room, the soft moonlight shining through them, filling the space with a deep blue shade.

I suddenly have the urge to steal some money, just so I can get this place done quicker and move in.

"Wouldn't you want this space when it's ready?" I ask, watching her as she stands by one of the windows, looking between the two rows of buildings toward the sea, only a five, maybe ten-minute walk away.

"Nah..." She turns to me. "I love the apartment above. I built it exactly as I wanted it. What's the point in copying and pasting it here, since I wouldn't change a thing about it."

I shrug. She's right.

"This is amazing, Lu! It speeds up this process so much!" My process. My chase for independence.

She nods and pulls me into a brief hug. She knows my situation all too well. If I wish to get out of my parents' control, simply moving out and renting an apartment won't do it. They have enough influence to tell most landlords in this city to fuck off and refuse me. Only they cannot treat Lulu as any other landlord.

No one tells a Dietrich what to do.

Her family might not be part of The Sanctum, or live in Queenscove, for that matter, but they have old ties to this place. Not to mention, a fierce reputation that still bears a heavy weight within the high society and politics here.

When I returned from university, my family insisted I live with them. It was either that or live with Ryan. But he wasn't even on my short list of choices. Unfortunately, they noticed. I was naive thinking they were taking me in out of the goodness of their hearts.

No matter. I'm a step closer to freedom now.

CHAPTER 3
Vincent

"WHERE IS HE?!" my voice booms, bouncing off the concrete of the basement surrounding us. "Where the fuck is he?!"

"Boseman?"

"Don't fucking play with me, Finn!" I rasp, pointing at the blue-eyed pretty boy as I stop and turn. "I will not fucking hesitate!"

I haven't been this angry, this out of control, in a long, long time, and he can certainly see it.

"Jesus, man... calm down," he says, narrowing his brows as he rubs the back of his neck, under those messy, blonde curls.

"I swear to God, Hennessey!"

I can feel that vein pulsing in my temple, my throat strained with pain as I grit my teeth. I'm being unfair. It's not his fault, nor his responsibility—that falls on all of us.

"I don't know, Vin." Crossing his arms, he surveys me.

I sigh as I go deeper through the concrete corridor of the basement. Although, it was built more like a nuclear bunker, since the thickness of the walls and the depth of the space is necessary to ensure no noise escapes to the surface. The light reflects off the satin-finish walls, every step taking me closer to the son of a bitch who will pay for this. I even have a hole already dug up for the motherfucker.

He's not leaving this place, but parts of him will.

That thought brings me a bit of peace and a muscle twitches in the corner of my mouth. I don't feel anything in particular during the killing process. I do enjoy unloading the weight off my shoulders on someone's internal organs, but it's only a tool taking me to that decadent ecstasy—death. There's something about that finality, that brief flash when the pain seeps out of their eyes and serenity replaces it, before they're gone. When their light goes out, mine shines brighter.

"Serpent..." the piece of shit hisses through bloody teeth the moment I open the heavy metal door to the room that has probably seen more death than the cemetery downtown.

He is not the same piece of shit I wanted to see here. But he's connected enough that he could be useful, I guess. He's on the other side of the room, opposite the only door into this concrete box, tied to a metal chair bolted to the floor. Carter and Madds stand next to the only other piece of furniture in this space, a metal table holding a few... instruments.

"Mr. Crowley, pleasure to see you." I peel off my suit jacket and hang it on the hook on the door, pulling on a disposable plastic coverall to protect my clothes and shoes.

We keep a healthy stash here, since we went through a period of time where we were constantly burning clothes. The amount we were spending on new ones was getting ridiculous. Full body coveralls are a godsend.

I zip up the suit as I move toward Crowley, his eyes growing bigger with each of my determined steps. He knows what all this means, this preparation, the simmering anger bleeding out of my eyes. And when my foot hits the ground in front of him, my fist connects with his cheek hard enough his head snaps to the side with a crack, and blood sprays out of his mouth.

Carter sneers, and when I turn to him, he's looking from his shoes to me, and then to our prisoner, annoyance and slight disgust shimmering in his eyes. I look down and notice the speckles of red.

"They're new. Fucking. Shoes!" Each of his words are punctuated by a booming step as he walks toward us and lands another punch to the other side of Crowley's face.

"Happy?" I ask, cocking an eyebrow.

"Quite, yes." Carter turns and goes back next to Madds, looking with distaste toward his fancy shoes.

He's gonna burn them later, yet he still pulls a handkerchief out of his waistcoat pocket and wipes them. With slicked-back hair and an undercut, dressed in the style of another era in his brogues, waistcoats, and breast pocket handkerchiefs, he looks like a gangster. He even has a pocket watch. But the son of a bitch pulls it all off effortlessly.

"You can kill me now. I have nothing to say to you." Crowley draws my attention back to him, before he spits blood on me.

I can't help the rumble vibrating from my chest through my throat, coming out in a menacing laugh. Violence is never my first method of extracting information, but there's something about today that makes me want to draw blood. Lots of it.

"I'm not entirely sure why you believe that the moment you die is a decision you make. No, Mr. Crowley, we have exactly"—I lift my left hand to look at the simple Vacheron watch wrapped around my wrist—"thirty-four minutes until I have to get ready to go out to dinner. So, ten, maybe fifteen minutes, seems like a good amount of time for you to share where the fuck Boseman is. I seem to remember a deal we made when a certain transgression of yours was suddenly forgotten by the police. You have not delivered on your end of that."

Crossing my arms, I take one more deep breath as I cock my head and regard the asshole before me. That jab to his cheek helped me release some of this fucking tension. It's easy to see why Maddox likes to go in the ring of our place, *The Fightclub*, so much. It's exactly what the name says—our fight club. And we all frequent it to some degree, either in private or public matches.

Crowley squirms in his seat, pupils dilating as he forces himself to hold eye contact. It's quite interesting how silence sometimes seems to be enough to get people to talk. That constant, unbroken eye contact turns their blood cold as they squirm in their seats, their throats bobbing as they swallow invisible lumps. The anticipation of pain is sometimes torture enough, and they think they can avoid the physical one by spilling their secrets.

It's more time-consuming, for sure, but oddly satisfying.

I don't think this particular man is going to last too long. My frustrations are still simmering under my skin, and today doesn't feel like the day I can be patient. I inhale loud enough that he flinches, eyes flickering from side to side, fighting the urge to submit to that voice in his head screaming at him to choose self-preservation.

Nothing like Miss O'Rourke yesterday— there was no such urge in her searing gaze.

Morrigan...

I narrow my eyes as that intrusive thought of the fiery redhead penetrates my mind. She needs to get the fuck out. This is not the time! But her intensity lingers and that need to draw blood comes back with a vengeance. So I slam my fist into Crowley's gut with such force, my fist aches. It helps, seeming to push her image further back into my mind.

"Joanne. Fifteen Harrigan Road," I spit at Crowley. "She's home right now, cooking dinner. I believe it was beef roast, your favorite."

He flinches, his pupils dilating for a split second as he regards my words about his wife. I don't linger for the rest of his reaction. Walking to the table, I run my fingers over the few, but effective items we hold here—the disposal instruments, some chains, a couple of pliers, a cleaver, then right at the end, two knives, one serrated and one smooth. I pick the smooth one and head back to the man, eyes on his tied wrists, palms up.

"Normally, I would take my time, but like I said, I don't have that luxury today. Are you going to speak?" I ask as I clasp his left hand in a cruel handshake.

There's no surprise when three seconds pass and he hasn't answered. So I bring the blade to the outside of his wrist and sink it into his skin. His eyes bulge, blood vessels exploding over the whites as he barely holds in a scream and grips me hard. At first, anyway. But as I slice deeper, sliding the knife to the other side of his wrist, splitting open veins and tendons, his fingers lose strength and give out. His tongue too, wailing through gritted teeth like the bitch he is, blood and saliva sputtering.

When I repeat the process on the other wrist, all bets are off, and his teeth are no longer clenched as his bellows fill the room. This is not the first time I've done this particular cut, and I really do enjoy its effects. These men do so much with their hands, from killing, to striking their wives, stealing money, and shaking on deals. But once these tendons are split, the loss of control, of power, brings a cruel type of joy to me. Plus, the cut serves like a nice guide for later on when we have to remove the hands completely to get rid of the fingerprints.

"I guess the thought of us killing your wife doesn't move you," I say with a smirk. "Figures."

"Fuck you!" he seethes, splatters of red staining my plastic suit.

Okay then.

His breaths stagger as he pushes through pain and blood loss, but I carry on. One by one, I slice the skin between each of his fingers, and when he finally starts pleading for me to stop, I use that desperation as motivation to keep going.

All the people who end up in this chair reach this moment—the first pleas when they finally give in, ready to spill their secrets. They all seem to have the same false belief that their life is in their hands, that they make the decisions here. Even if they think they're ready to talk, it only matters if we're ready to listen.

I'm not ready. It's too early. Not enough agony has seeped into his bones. I've seen plenty of others like him who still backed up at this point and stopped talking again.

When I'm done with his hands and raise my gaze to his, his mouth is tightly closed, fury and fear staining his eyes, blood vessels broken as red spreads through the white.

"Scott is there, too." His son's name lands like a final blow, eyes bulging as he regards me. But it might be because of the blade I brought to the corner of his mouth.

I'm gonna make the words spill, whether he likes it or not. He pointlessly tightens his lips, but the tip of the sharp knife slides through his flesh with such ease, the tears pool in his eyes before I hear the broken cry he swallows. Slowly, I slice through his cheek as tears mix with the crimson flowing to the tune of his muffled screams, until he stares at me with a brand-new half smile. It looks gruesome, more like something Carter would do, but I guess it's good to mix it up sometimes.

Crowley leans his head against his shoulder, forcing his mouth to stay closed, his light blue shirt turning purple fast. But his whimpers begin to bore me.

"Please... please, just... leave my son alone." Defeated sobs scrape my ears as he finally speaks.

I cross my arms and sigh, my patience already dangerously thin. Now that his son is the one being threatened, he's ready to talk. I'm not surprised. From what I heard, he would throw his wife to the wolves for a good glass of whiskey. Not that there's anything wrong with the poor woman. He's a misogynistic, abusive piece of shit, and apparently his ways have been brushing off onto his son, too.

"I lied," he continues as he spits the blood that's pooling into his mouth. "I don't know where Boseman is. I thought I could find out before you came to collect. I just wanted to get out."

I can barely understand what he's saying, the words not forming fully since his lips don't properly connect anymore. But I guess that's my fault.

"Get out? This is not the first time we've done *business* together, Crowley. Did you fucking forget who you're dealing with? Who. We. Are?!" Rage rattles through each word that breaks out of my throat. "We are The *fucking* Sanctum!"

I smash my fist so hard into his broken cheek, the slice rips even more, and I could have sworn I felt teeth dislodge under my knuckles.

"Do you think that if it was easy to find this motherfucker, we would have had any need for you?"

His cries bounce off the concrete walls, and somewhere deep in my soul, I do feel a little bit of pity for him. But he deceived us, wasted our time, and unfortunately for him, it negates that tinge of pity.

"Holt," he groans.

My eyes flicker to Carter and Madds, whose attention snap back to us.

"Holt is dead," I hear Finn say somewhere behind me.

"Mhm... son."

"You're saying his son knows where Boseman is?" I take a step back from the puddle forming at his feet. The guy's bleeding all over the fucking place.

"Maybe. There was a party... few months ago. I was behind him when he was talking... on the phone. He spoke the name..." He spits another mouthful of blood onto the floor, pulling in pain-filled breaths. "I asked him about it... He pretended not to know what I was talking about. He was lying."

"And Holt is now going into business with Liam O'Rourke too," I say, mostly to myself as I try to piece two and two together.

Motherfucking O'Rourke!

These sons of bitches are playing mafia now. If O'Rourke is knowingly going into business with Boseman, then I'll take it as a personal attack. But if Ryan is at it alone, then there might be a chance for the old man. We need to find out more.

Turning around, I stalk toward the door where Finn still stands. I shed the coveralls, throw them into the bin by the door, and grab my jacket from the hook.

I glance at my watch, then at the heaving man.

"Thank you, Mr. Crowley. You've been helpful, but it should never have reached this point. I'm afraid I will not have the pleasure of taking your life today, as I have my dinner to prepare for. Good evening."

I nod, and his eyes go wide, brightening at my words. They fill with hope, even as the blood dripping out of his wrists drains him of life.

Turning to Finn, I meet his inquisitive gaze. I know what he wants to ask, but he's saving it for later. I'm violent, yet it rarely takes over like this. Carter is the carver, not me. Instead, he takes a deep breath, and I can see the question leaving his eyes. Then a wicked smile pulls at my lips, and his gaze fills with a menace that takes me aback sometimes. I almost chuckle—menace looks good on his pretty boy face. It turns his soft, bright blue eyes into ice.

Opening the door, I look at Crowley over my shoulder.

"Mr. Hennessey is going to finish carving that smile. I hear you put one of ours and Ekaterina's girls into hospital, then claimed 'the whore deserved it.' Our girls are anything but whores, Mr. Crowley, and Finnigan here sure does hate it when they're called that."

The hope falls from his face, his mangled mouth parting, either from surprise that the escort he hired actually works for us, or that he's not leaving this room alive. I nod to Carter and Madds before I walk out the door, letting it fall closed behind me, drowning out a scream so excruciating, it makes my muscles tingle.

"We all pay for our sins eventually..." I whisper to myself as I walk back the way I came.

Morrigan

"YOU ALWAYS WERE a dirty liar. I can never believe a word you tell me." Ryan's tone is grave, fixing me with a disgusted stare as he sips his white wine.

He lets that silence linger long enough that it allows too many scenarios to run through my head, since nowadays almost everything I tell him is a lie meant to protect myself. But I grab my glass of dry red and sip as I force myself to hold his gaze.

"Please, do tell me what you believe I lied about." My snippy attitude hides my dishonesty, but as much as I practiced it, I'm still anxious.

I wish I could say it's only because I'm weary that he could find out about Metamorphosis. But that's not the only reason. His behavior toward me has changed so much, that even his compliments are laced with poison. He threatens my freedom and safety more frequently, even though he's never touched me beyond gripping my arm too hard or pushing me. His favorite form of abuse is the emotional kind. I guess I should be grateful that he insists on teaching me that physical violence is not always more effective than psychological.

"Spoken like someone who has a bit too much to hide."

"Or someone who can't keep up with your ridiculous mood swings," I counter.

"I'm not enjoying this attitude of yours."

"Really?! Funny, considering that my attitude was far more over the top when we met, when we fucking fell in love!"

"Keep your goddamn voice down." His voice lowers to a chilling whisper, his furious gaze freezing my muscles in place.

"This has gone too far, Ryan. I can't—"

"I said—" His hand wraps around my thigh, fingers digging hard enough into my muscles that I lurch over, swallowing my gasp. "Lower. Your. Voice."

I don't know what happened, when I slipped so far under his control. I've been focused on my parents for so many years, constantly seeking an escape from them, that I didn't notice when my escape turned into a new prison. I glazed over so many comments he made and let them turn into contactless blows. He made me lose my confidence, but it's my fault too. I let him. Not sure how, or when, but I did.

Sighing, he joins his hands, and I try to think of the last time he didn't look at me like that, cold, detached, like he's looking at an object he covets, not a girlfriend he should love. We became a couple just over two years ago, after knowing each other since school, but he was a different man. For ages, I beat myself up for missing the red flags—I didn't, though. He simply hid them too well. The worst thing is that I still hold hope for the man he used to be. For my sake more than his, because I refuse to believe I was this fucking blind to who he really is, this goddamn stupid.

"Jesus, you think you're such a smart fucking bitch." He shakes his head, a worrying grin grazing his lips. "I think it's time to tighten that leash."

Excuse me?!

"You're out of line, Ryan. Have you no shame anymore? No care in the world that you're speaking to me like this in a damn public place?" I look around the fancy space, the most expensive restaurant in the city, and I'm not sure why he brought us here if his plan was to make a scene.

But then again, nowadays, he rarely misses an opportunity to *put me in my place* publicly, even if it is only calling me a derogatory term or stating some sort of failure he believes I have achieved. Like the clothes I wear... they never fit me well, always showing my fat belly... my thick thighs... my big ass.

"You didn't go home yesterday, after you left." He ignores my words.

"So?"

"Don't fucking play with me," he seethes. "You see too much of that... *Lulu.* When you tell me you're going home, you're going straight-goddamn-home."

The fucking audacity of this man!

"Jesus Christ, Ryan, what happened to you? Do you fucking hear yourself? The bullshit leaving your mouth?!"

I keep telling myself that his behavior changed when his father died a few months ago. It's not true, though. It started long before that. But since his dad's passing, the escalation has been distinguishable, far too blunt. Like a noose that loosened all of a sudden. He didn't turn into this abusive piece of shit—he's always been one.

"You have such a filthy, spoiled mouth! For once, act like a damn woman, and have some class!"

"You don't get to tell me how to talk, Ryan." I lean in a little closer, my heart thumping violently in my chest, hands shaking as I force myself not to make a scene. "You don't get to tell me what to do, who to see, or how to act. You don't *fucking* own me."

But the asshole laughs. He actually laughs and it takes me aback.

"I've owned you since that night in the woods, all those years ago."

My heart beats faster at his words. That night is part of the reason why I'm still here with him. He knows too much...

"You're mine, darling. Always have been. Even your parents agree now." He continues, a seedy grin pulling at his lips as he grabs my wrist under the table in a bruising grip. "And friends? You don't need any. You have me."

"You're delusional! I'm going." I attempt to pull my hand away, but he crushes it in his, my fingers twitching from the pain that makes me buckle over the table, my mouth open in a silent gasp.

"There's nowhere for you to go, Morrigan. Your future is decided. You'll learn that pretty soon."

"Fuck you," I spit through clenched teeth.

What the hell is he talking about? Learn what? Those are not just words thrown at me for the sake of it. His smirk tells me that much.

"I plan to."

My eyes go wide for a split second. I've done a decent job at avoiding sex with him over the last couple of months. Except for one occasion... But I'm not sure for how long I can keep avoiding it before it's going to get violent. I'm not a fearful woman, but there's something about him that fucking scares me.

The grip on my wrist tightens even more, and this time, I can't hold the wince as I feel a pop in my bones. I open my mouth to rasp at him—

"Good evening. How *nice* to see you here."

That fucking voice. That low, slithering voice making people bow their heads in fear and submission, I would recognize anywhere. It awakens a fire Ryan has been slowly extinguishing over time, filling me with a need to draw blood—his.

That thought makes a part of me heat and throb. A part I wish would mind its own fucking business.

Ryan releases my wrist, and I resist the urge to rub it, as I hold it in my lap, leaning back in the chair as if I can get away from him.

"Hello. Nice to see you too." Ryan shakes his hand, and I can't help but notice the veins under The Serpent's skin, menacing, like his grip could shatter bones.

I wonder if he could shatter my boyfriend's bones...

The Serpent turns briefly toward me and nods once.

A second and a half, that's all the attention I get, apparently. Christ, what do I have to do around here to be seen as more than just a piece of fucking furniture?

"Are we going to see you next week?" Ryan continues.

"Yes, we're looking forward to it. This time of year can get a little... dull." The Serpent's eyes flash to me for another moment. Not to my eyes, but under the table, where my hand rests on my aching wrist.

I don't dare look down at it, but something cruel seems to simmer in the black pits of his eyes.

"I couldn't agree more. This one is definitely going to be entertaining. Talk of the season, for sure." Ryan's expression is peculiar as he speaks those words, his teeth gleaming with a disturbing sense of pride. "And with the demand of the business, I could definitely use the entertainment."

The fact that I have no clue what they're talking about makes me uneasy. I don't have a good feeling about this.

"Business takeover is going well, I gather? My condolences for your father." The Serpent's politeness is borderline deranged, yet so natural.

It makes it worse. Not that I expect him to be some rude thug lashing out at people, but his interaction is so proper, it makes one question his reputation as a terrifying organized crime boss. Or one of them. He and his friends all seem to be in charge of their mafia empire.

"Very well. The changes I'm making are quite... fruitful," Ryan answers.

Since no one's paying attention to me, all I can do is listen to them, feigning boredom as I study my nails. I wasn't aware that these two knew anything of each other's businesses. It shouldn't surprise me though, the black-eyed snake somehow knows everything that moves through Queenscove. Even through the cryptic conversation they're having now, I can tell he knows a lot about Ryan's, or better yet, his late father's business. And here I am, completely clueless about my boyfriend's party, where even The Serpent is invited.

I look up at him, wondering why even after all this time it's still hard—no, uncomfortable—to look at him. He's always been stupidly handsome, but goddamnit, the years have been good to him.

Everything about this man is laced in obsidian, from his eyes to his hair, the thick stubble covering his jaw, and even his clothes. He wears a black tie over a shirt of the same color, and the dark jacket is fitted ridiculously well over his wide, round shoulders of his six-foot-something frame. I hate that I can note the trace of his pecs under the soft fibers of his shirt.

I snap out of it, pulling my gaze away since I have no fucking business noticing the lines of this asshole's sculpted body. Only, my eyes stop on his square jaw, drawing along the sharp line of it, and up his soft, thick lips that seem tense. Then over his mostly straight nose, apart from a slight bump on one side of the bridge, and on those thick lashes that would make any woman jealous.

I'm ready to scream at myself to wake the fuck up, but there's no need. Not when I focus on his eyes and remember how they looked at me when he broke my young heart and shattered my entire world.

I can't deny The Serpent is attractive, but he better screw off and be attractive somewhere else, because I have a damn date to escape from. And my resentment for him is not improving my damn mood.

"Sounds good to me," Ryan says.

Wait. What sounds good? I should have been listening.

"I will see you then. Enjoy the rest of the evening." The Serpent ends the conversation, then turns to me, nodding yet again.

Only this time, he lingers for a moment longer on my hands. When his eyes draw back to mine, the gaze in those dark pits is... grave.

Does he know?

The Serpent's interruption wasn't on purpose. Right? No, it couldn't have been. A mere coincidence.

Is it also a coincidence that in the last seven or eight years, we've only ever interacted three or four times? One of those times was this year. Yet we've just met twice in two fucking days.

"What was that about?" I turn to Ryan.

"Nothing you need to know of yet."

Somewhere at the backend of his words, I find a bit more strength to fight with the man.

"Why do you do this? What happened to you to have changed you so much? This shift... You were never this person, never talked to me this way."

His expression is one of exasperation, as if I'm a problem and he's brainstorming a solution. Does he even care anymore? Only, a deviant grin spreads over his lips, a mad look in his eyes.

"I did not change." Four words, only four words he speaks, and they're enough to shake my soul. They imply too much, they change my view of him, our relationship, our past, they change everything.

Even my future.

CHAPTER 4
Vincent

"TELL ME AGAIN why we're here?" Finn asks. He's standing beside me, along with Carter and Madds, in the grand doorway of the Rosenberg Hotel ballroom.

The aroma of fresh flowers and vanilla assaults me as I lazily drag my eyes over Queenscove's elite. The way they're not so inconspicuously stealing glances at us whilst forcing themselves to carry on their conversations is almost comical.

I push down a sigh as I prepare myself to lie.

"You know why, Finn. We need to find out what Ryan Holt knows about Boseman."

"If we're to believe Crowley's confession."

I turn at his words, catching as he wiggles one eyebrow at a beautiful bleach blonde woman passing by, her arm hooked around the elbow of a man three times her age. Her eyes sparkle at the sight of our very own surfer boy, bright, blue eyes, and shoulder length, curly hair wild against the contrasting tailored suit.

"That's why we have to get close. Since Liam O'Rourke invited us here and, according to Carter's sources, he's going into some sort of business with Holt, then this is our best way in."

Finn, or the others, for that matter, doesn't need to know the real reason I personally wanted to come. Yes, the O'Rourke and Holt part was true, but I could have arranged that any other time. I wanted to be here so I could see *her*.

I want her to look into my fucking eyes with the bright green of hers when she shares with the world why we were all invited here today.

But... that brightness was dangerously dull when I saw her last.

Truth is, I'm not sure what I'm hoping to achieve by coming here. The sadist in me needs to burn this place to the ground as punishment for the celebration that's to come. But it's the masochist side that decided to be here, to witness this—them. I broke my own fucking heart once; I wonder if I'm going to burn the leftover shards today.

I thought I had time to get to her... I really thought I had more time.

"Can't we just tie them to a chair and extract it the old-fashioned way?" Madds grunts, the slight amusement in his tone pulling me out of my self-destructive thoughts.

I don't need to look to know that amusement hasn't registered in his deep, amber gaze. Very few things make the man laugh, or smile even. Most happen within our inner circle, but outside of it... I don't think I've ever seen him smile at anyone else. Not for a long time anyway.

"I second that," Carter follows.

I catch a glimpse of the man, and his hazel eyes, bleeding into blue, are utterly impassive. He's serious. But then again, this man never, ever, says anything he doesn't mean. That is, if he says anything at all. I've known him for about twelve years, since we were around sixteen years old, yet I'm still not sure if his lack of a filter is intentional or a sign of something that would require a diagnosis.

"We all know the answer to that," I say to them.

I would love to. Eventually we will, because O'Rourke, that goddamn son of a bitch, deserves my fucking fury tenfold. And Ryan Holt... I'm starting to believe he may deserve it just as much.

I take a step in, and don't miss the collective twitch in the crowd's flesh. Like a pack of gazelles noticing the rustling in the bushes and the sparkling gaze of the lions peeking through.

"So we're socializing," Finn says with a sigh.

"Yes. O'Rourke is desperate to get into business with us, and by association, Holt is, too. If we play our cards right, we'll find out not only what we need to know about Boseman, but why they're so desperate too. Our business is based on a wealth of information that we accumulate and wield to our benefit or our allies'. But right under our noses, something is happening that we're not privy to, and that just won't do."

As we walk through the middle of the crowded space, people don't fail to make room, most of them averting their gazes, and I see O'Rourke and his wife noticing us.

No daughter...

I wouldn't be surprised if she's somewhere in the back, tending to the pristine look she's adopted in recent years. She used to have this untamed aura about her, red curls flowed freely, makeup free fresh face, freckles on full display. Now, she's different, her hair slick, no stray strand, no loose thread on her expensive clothes, makeup always perfect. It feels—it looks forced on her. She's clearly changed, adapting to fit into this society she was fighting so hard to reject all those years ago. There's a tinge of disappointment in the back of my mind.

I would much prefer to see her disheveled, with runny makeup, wild hair... tangled limbs between my sheets.

Fuck.

Clearly, I'm not quite that bothered about her new look. My cock certainly isn't.

"I'm struggling to figure out what the connection between Holt and Boseman is. How would they know each other, or *of* each other?" Finn asks, pulling my thoughts from that dangerous direction.

"Well, that's why we're here. This whole thing gives me a really bad vibe, and we need to get our foot in it. These sons of bitches can't move without us knowing about it," I say to him, just before we reach O'Rourke and his wife.

"Gentlemen, thank you so much for joining us!" His enthusiasm appears to be genuine, and I resist the urge to cock an eyebrow.

If I didn't know any better, I would say he forgot our past, what he did. Or maybe he thinks I forgot. No, he's just feigning ignorance since he now has something to gain from me, from us. No one forgets something like that.

I think the party we were invited to about five months ago was to test the waters, observe my reaction to him. Now he's diving all the way in.

One by one, he shakes our hands, pulling Finn's attention from yet another blonde in a skimpy skirt. We all nod to Mrs. O'Rourke, a woman in her early fifties, wearing a form-fitted dark blue dress that's just... too much. Too sparkly, too overfilled with lace details, too flashy and most likely an intentional choice. They're the type of people who have this burning need to stand out at all times.

What definitely stands out is the look O'Rourke gives her every time she touches that high neckline. It could do with a little tugging down to give her some room to breathe, but he doesn't seem to approve.

"Thank you for inviting us, and congratulations to you both." Fuck, bile rises in my throat with those words. It hurts my vocal cords to say them, but I had to. He has to believe I have no emotional connection to that past.

Mrs. O'Rourke looks slightly flustered as her gaze flickers to her husband, unsure of her next move.

"Thank you. Sheila will take you to your table," he says with a nod, the movement staggered. "I do hope we can have a... drink together later. Enjoy your evening, gentlemen."

I nod in return and follow the woman.

The tables are all round, ranging in size from four to eight seats, and luckily, we are led to one which sits four. *Good, it will be just us.* I watch Mrs. O'Rourke as she moves away, and I can't help but wonder what that woman's life is like at home. She has this smug, proud aura about her, ready to flaunt her wealth and status, but when her husband looks at her, she's like a soldier—still, waiting for the next order.

Gripping the wooden frame of the chair, I start pulling it away, but freeze. I see her red, silky hair first, flowing in large waves around her alabaster skin, bouncing with each slow step. The tips of the strands touch the V-neckline that plunges low between her breasts, the black satin dress held only by two thin straps, covering just enough that you want to beg for more. The smooth fabric of the knee-length dress clings to her full curves without being tight, and in proper Morrigan fashion, instead of the pumps the women around us wear, the high slit reveals the end of thigh-high leather boots.

Never in my life have I noticed all these details in the way a woman dresses. Yet I always do with her. And I was right. There's no hair out of place—pristine.

Someone intentionally clears their throat, and as I turn, Maddox follows my previous line of sight, eyes widening and stilling. He takes one more moment before he turns and takes a seat. Finn, though, he has a stupid grin plastered all over his face, and Carter just... watches me. The scrutiny is uncomfortable. I might have a talent for making people talk, but I swear Carter just reads your fucking mind.

"She's off limits, man. Especially now," Finn whispers as we all take our seats.

There are no limits when it comes to Morrigan O'Rourke.

I swipe my gaze back to the redhead, her steps light as she heads toward her parents, arm curled around Holt's, her green eyes stern. Only, the look in them shifts in an instant the moment they fall on me, her surprise evident before irritation replaces it. It brings me joy, seeing that flustered side of her, her control stripped, even if for a moment. I hold that gaze because it's a challenge. She would rip her eyes out before she would submit to me. And doesn't that sound fucking fun.

Her nostrils flare when she approaches her parents and has no choice but to look away. A tinge of a grin pulls at my lips at the slight victory.

"Jesus, she looked like she could gut you right here, right now," Finn says with a smirk.

"Knowing her, she probably would," Madds continues as he snatches the Bourbon bottle from the waiter after he fills his glass. I want to fucking punch him for what he just said.

"Sorry, but how well do you guys know her, exactly?" Finn slides his empty glass toward Madds, who regards me from under his eyebrows.

He is the only one who knows exactly who Morrigan was to me back then. Carter and Finn were at university, one buried in computers, the other probably in pussy. Madds and I were still here, putting the bases down for what was going to become our empire, along with the man Finn doesn't allow us to speak of. They knew of her because it was impossible not to, but not of how deeply her and I were involved. If they did, they have never mentioned it to me.

It ended before they came home, before it could become more. So I never told them everything. It was better that way.

"*Knew* her," Madds corrects his previous words. "She was hard not to notice. A firecracker. We watched her beat the shit out of this guy once. She broke his jaw... put him in the hospital."

What the fuck has gotten into him?!

In all these years, he's barely acknowledged her existence or uttered two sentences about her. All of a sudden, he's in her presence for more than ten seconds and he speaks of the past with such ease that I want to shove that whole Bourbon bottle down his throat to shut him up. I know why, though, don't I? Morrigan O'Rourke had an impact on Madds even back then, when she was barely sixteen. He never said a word, but it was hard to miss it when this man never warmed up to anyone but us. I know he's been keeping his mouth shut out of respect.

"*Watched* her? You didn't intervene?" Finn asks.

Carter stays silent. He's paying attention though, far too closely for my liking, his head cocked as he files in every single word for future use. Or research.

"I didn't need to. She was doing fine on her own," Madds says with a shrug.

"That's not what I... fucking hell, man."

Finn's laugh turns some heads, even above the music that seems to be getting louder. Although people haven't exactly stopped stealing glances at us. Private events are not our scene, but O'Rourke wants to make a statement with our presence. We're letting them have their moment until we get what we need.

* * *

My sweet tooth led me to the dessert table stacked with multi-level ornate cake stands, filled with macarons, meringues, fruit next to a decadent chocolate fountain, and dozens of different mini cakes in all the colors of the fucking rainbow. Now I understand why the crowd gathered around it the whole evening.

Just as the person who stands next to me begins to move away, I lean over and reach for a mini chocolate éclair, when my hand bumps into another, sending the tips of their fingers straight into the chocolate stream of the fountain.

"Fucking hell!" She curses loud enough that the person standing between us is gone in a split second.

I swallow my apology, when I realize before I even look up who that voice belongs to—Morrigan.

"You!" she seethes when her eyes land on me.

"Hello." I allow a moment to take her in, her enchanting eyes gleaming with fury, the slight flush on her high cheekbones, and the freckles barely visible under the makeup. All framed by her smooth, brick-red waves falling over her bare shoulders, grazing the smooth skin of her chest.

I prefer the natural, wild curls on her.

"I don't get it. What the fuck are my parents playing at? Why are you here? All of you?"

That's one way of saying hello back... I guess.

She notices the chocolate dripping from her fingers onto the white tablecloth, and the vixen does the goddamn unthinkable. One by one, she slides those digits into her mouth, and I freeze. There's no sexual intention in the gesture, but time slows down, nonetheless. I'm mesmerized. Utterly fucking mesmerized as I follow those lush lips sucking every drop of chocolate, leaving a faint red lipstick ring on them.

This woman... this goddamn woman.

The blood flow shifts from my brain to my cock, and I yank her fingers to me, hand wrapped tight around her slim wrist, stopping it inches from my face. She parts her lips to spit her protest, but her jaw locks as her eyes fix onto mine. I don't know if hunger gazes back at her, or pure fury that she did this in public, for others to see the magic, too.

I have to force myself not to drag her away, and make her do all that again, just for me. Instead, I break eye contact, still feeling her thunderous gaze on me as I grab a bunch of napkins from the stack farther down the table and push them in her trapped hand. I really don't want to, but I release her wrist before I do anything stupid, like clean her fingers with my own fucking tongue.

She snatches her hand away like she's disgusted by the contact, watching me without blinking, her lips parted with unspoken words that I know she would much rather shout at me. Yet to my surprise, she stays silent.

There's nothing left on her fingers beyond the red trace of her lipstick, but she uses the napkins to wipe anyway, looking at me as if she's about to stab me with a dessert knife. Better than a serrated steak one, I guess.

"You're welcome," I scold, as she shoots me the most defiant gaze she can muster.

"I'm serious, Serpent. What the hell are my parents involved in? Or getting involved in?" She forces her tone to stay low. "It has to be fucking atrocious if it's with you."

She throws my nickname around with such distaste. Even so, it comes out with a tantalizing hiss that I would very much like to hear again. She really doesn't like us. Well... me. But she's not exactly an angel, not with goddamn Ryan-fucking-Holt on her arm. Not with the man who now controls half the docks, his late father's business. From the sounds of it, his trafficking business has been growing since his death. She doesn't have a moral leg to stand on when she's involved with him.

I casually reach over to one of the cake stands and grab a mini-éclair. Shoving it in my mouth, I lean back against the table, and turn to the crowd dancing to some pop song I don't recognize.

"Atrocious... okay."

"You're not answering my goddamn questions!" Her words pour like lava, burning their way through the loud music, and drawing my eyes back to those emeralds of hers.

"Nothing you need to concern yourself with."

There's an intentional bite in my tone, and judging by the fury searing through her gaze, she clearly didn't like it. But I did. She's beautiful on a normal day, but she's fucking gorgeous when she's in flames.

"*Concern* myself? Motherfucker! Am I just a fucking doorknob to you people? Grab me and turn me in whatever direction is beneficial to you! Like"—she leans in ever so slightly, her tone lowering almost to a whisper—"I don't know the rules of the *fight club*, the right way to do *laundry*, the fastest way to *take one's breath away*, or the best route when *escorting* someone?"

She raises one eyebrow, her eyes shining with mischief. She's clearly pleased with herself. She listed almost all our businesses—the fight club, the money laundering, the killings, but the one that bewilders me is... the escort service. As far as we know, nobody is aware of it. How the fuck did Morrigan find out? She doesn't even have access to our bar.

The trail leading to us is so thin, it's almost nonexistent. And that's because we don't directly run it, Ekaterina—Katya—does. It all started with her, and we decided that it needs to stay that way. Our secret weapon. Whenever we meet, she comes to Midnight, our speakeasy. And when we join her or one of the girls in public, to the prying eyes who recognize them, it looks like we hired them. Just as they do.

"I will take your silence as shock and pat myself on the back for a job well done." Her tone is far too smug for my liking.

She leans back against the table, facing the crowd as a song fades out and comes to an end. I can't stop looking at the smirk pulling at her pretty red lips.

"Still as reckless as ever, aren't you?" I ask, following her gaze to the dance floor.

Before she can bite back, her family and boyfriend pull her attention as they step in front of the stage, waiting for everyone to go silent. I turn back to Morrigan, watching as she stiffens at the sight. So I take the opportunity and strike again.

"You think you're so much better than me, than us? I've seen you get high on X. I fucking rescued you when some shithead was forcing himself on you. Then I watched you shatter his jaw with an utter lack of remorse, and you weren't even legal yet. Fuck knows what else you've done since. Especially considering your *association* with Holt." I spit out that last sentence and her grin falls. Did the mention of her boyfriend wipe it off, or the memories from our past?

"Ladies and gentlemen!" Liam O'Rourke's voice booms through the ballroom, and the party goes quiet.

"Get off your fucking moral high horse, baby," I carry on, "because you missed a few entries in that list you're so proud of putting together."

"We are sorry to interrupt your dancing," her father continues, *"but we're quite excited to share the reason for this party, so we can start celebrating properly."*

Her shoulders suddenly tense, and she crosses her arms against her middle, like she's holding herself together. But I immediately find out why.

"Welcome, everyone! It's so good to have you all here for this special occasion." Holt's voice replaces her father's but pauses for effect.

I quickly fill that silence, leaning in sideways, our shoulders barely touching as I whisper, "If tonight goes well, soon enough you'll find out what else we do, since it will be your family business too... *Mrs. Holt.*"

I straighten just as she whips her head around in a flurry of red waves, and her eyes land on me like a sledgehammer. Disgust and fury bleed out of her gaze as her brows furrow, looking as if I insulted her. But none of those emotions have time to settle in her features as Holt continues.

"I am pleased to announce that Morrigan O'Rourke and I are getting married!"

When chaos erupts around us, the crowd bursting into cheers and applause, a shattering fear cracks her eyes. Time seems to have stopped for her. But suddenly, she's blinking way too fast, vivid shock pulling her apart.

What the fuck?

Slowly, she turns as people gather around us, and we're split apart when one by one, they pull her into congratulatory embraces. She hasn't opened her mouth once, hasn't said a word or made any sound. I'm not sure if her soul left her body or imploded into itself, but fear and anger still glaze over her eyes and I know one thing for certain— this wasn't the shock of the happy news revealed too early out of excitement.

Her eyes find me through the crowd and the desperation in them hits me like goddamn lightning.

She didn't know.

CHAPTER 5
Morrigan

A LUMP FORMS in my throat. It grows bigger and bigger with every *"congratulations"* I hear from the faceless people who hug me, or squeeze my shoulders, or kiss my cheeks. I don't know where The Serpent went, but I find myself overcome with the need to disappear along with him.

He knew. He fucking knew before I did.

I'm a pawn in a game I'm not privy to. What are they doing to me? Why?

My family. My fucking family planned this! They all fucking sold me. Passed me on like some piece of goddamn meat. Did they also tell The Sanctum, or have they found out all on their own?

And Ryan... goddamn motherfucking Ryan!

He thinks he can just force me to marry him? Is this the nail in the coffin? The apex of all his lovely treatment?

It's his ultimate display of control over me.

My mind is reeling with too many questions. I feel fucking dizzy. But my imagination is running wild with the despicable things I would love to do to him. It's useless, though, because my body won't budge. I can't seem to make a move. Any move.

Goddamnit! Do something, you stupid woman!

I'm not even sure if my emotions are masked or if they're plastered all over my face. There's an impossibly big lump stuck in my throat, right at the base of my tongue, and breathing becomes difficult. My body begins to tremble as I force myself to look around for an escape, something, anything, to pull me out of this fucking nightmare. But a new song starts, covering the ruckus of debilitating congratulatory chatter, and it makes me pause as the title of the song and its first four words seep into the room.

Every breath you take...

It's a cover, not the original, but the disturbing meaning is unchanged. I catch Ryan's eyes through the crowd, a special evil residing in them as he walks toward me.

The next verse of the iconic song gains new meaning in my soul. He chose this specifically.

He takes a few more steps and my heart beats so hard it shakes my flesh. I'm frantic on the inside, searching for something that could indicate I'm not awake right now. It's only a nightmare... this is not my life. It cannot be.

I look away from him, hoping to catch a glimpse of Lulu, or anyone to fucking ground me right now before I implode.

But the song continues with every step he makes toward me, the words resonating in such a way, like he's speaking them himself. It's a dedication, giving me an ominous glimpse into my future.

The crowd parts, all the ones who were congratulating me moving out of the way, clutching their hands against their chests, sweet emotions plastered over their faces for us—the happy couple.

I want to vomit. But even my stomach refuses to shift.

What is wrong with me?

The chorus ends with that sinister verse that cripples me further, because I know... *he›ll be watching me too.*

Then he's here, crowding my personal space in such a silent assault, only I seem to notice it. His hands slide around my waist, like bruising tentacles constricting my insides as he pulls me toward the center of the ballroom. Bile burns its way up my throat as his lips press onto mine. They feel like the slimy underside of a slug. Have they always felt this way?

No.

Every single muscle in my body is tense to the point of pain, and all I can manage are shallow breaths that barely brush my lungs. He ends the kiss and captures my hand in his before I can step away. Pulling me into his body, he leads me into a dance on the rest of the disturbingly suggestive song.

"You belong to me..." Ryan whispers into my ear, at the same time as the song.

He holds my palm in a bone crushing grip, his hand on my waist unnecessarily firm, and I silently pray.

No—I beg, beg my goddamn soul to come back into my body, because this is not me. Whatever weak version of myself moves on this dancefloor is fucking pathetic, and I'm trapped inside of it. I'm banging my fists against the mental walls, but I can't seem to burst through.

The real me would have this hand wrapped around his throat, not his shoulder. Squeezing until his eyes would pop out of the sockets, and he would choke on his Adam's apple.

Instead, the pathetic me follows his fucking lead.

I used to have some love for the famous song The Police graced us with, no matter how creepy I find it. It›s all gone now.

I can't look at him as he spins me around and around. My gaze drifts over his shoulder, seeking something to ground my soul. Anything could work, an object, a face, a piece of goddamn food, it doesn't matter. I just need to focus and remember how to breathe again.

Through the blurred faces, I finally see her—Lulu. She clutches Luke's bicep, completely still, looking at me with a shock that does nothing to settle me. It makes me even more uneasy, my breath staggering dangerously, because her expression is a mirror of mine.

But as Ryan spins me farther, a black shadow with a sharp, beautiful face breaks through the sea of blurred ones. It's still, fixed on me unlike anyone else from this room, because this one sees *me*. Not us, not this deception, but me.

He draws me in, commanding my attention with that dark, almost hypnotic gaze he's so well known for—The Serpent.

Dark pits of tar make me sink deeper and deeper, and pull me into the denseness of them, putting a deeply satisfying pressure on my soul. My throat softens, and the lump shrinks slightly. I come out of that hypnosis and actually look at him—there's no joy, no pity, no excitement, no shock in his expression. Only a calm severity, that somehow cheers me on. It's a silent urge to focus, driving me toward the right path as my muscles slowly relax, and that lump in my throat shrinks enough that I can control my breathing again.

I don't know how or why, but it worked. His presence... worked. And I hate myself for it. I hate him even more.

Soon, I'll have to have a little chat with The Serpent.

I take one deep breath and start to feel like myself.

"What the fuck did you do, Ryan?" I pull my head back, facing him.

"You think I didn't know you've been planning to break up with me?" he says.

I attempt to pull away, but he presses his palm on the small of my back and tugs me hard against him as the rhythm of the song increases.

"You're not going anywhere," Ryan continues. "You. Belong. To me." He finishes that sentence with a crooked quirk of his lips, his muddy eyes rabid with victory.

"You think that I'll go through with this farce, just because you made a fucking scene and put me in this situation?! You think I'll marry you against my will?! What the hell makes you think I will hesitate to leave you the moment this dance is over?" The son of a bitch knew exactly what he was doing; he knew how much it would fucking hurt my soul not to be able lash out and rip his goddamn throat out. So he did it in front of half the fucking city, at a party that he apparently planned with *my* parents.

There's a strange sort of madness in his eyes. It's been infusing his features for a little while now and I'm not sure what to make of it. I don't know how to handle it or how to make it fucking go away. Because it's true lunacy, seeping in his words and actions, making him do stupid shit like announcing a fucking fictional engagement that will never take place.

"Try," he seethes.

Too many promises and threats lie in that one word, and I know for a fact that the man I knew is gone. I see no traces of him in the eyes staring back at me. This man right here would throw me to the fucking alligators in the delta at the edge of the city without thinking twice about it.

He spins me with a little bit more force than necessary, but at this point, more couples have joined us on the dance floor and the move goes unnoticed. I think. I'm not sure, because my spine tingles with that feeling you get when someone's watching you.

"You see your parents dancing next to the Chief of Police?"

I follow his gaze, but when I don't respond, he squeezes my hand until I wince.

"Yes," I spit.

"They signed you off to me." Those words carry an amusement that I want to fucking strangle out of him. "They're not going to support you if you do something stupid. Not when you are a price they paid."

I turn my head to him fast enough that my hair whips around me, wrapping around my throat, and slowly falls against my chest as my gaze settles on him.

"I'm not goddamn currency, Ryan! You've gone insane!"

"Maybe. But I'm not about to reject the insanity when the prospect of it is so entertaining. And you have to understand something. You're mine, Morrigan. I fought hard to make you mine, to make you love me when I loved you for so long. And I'll have you forever."

"This is not love! This is madness, pure fucking madness! I'm a possession to you, not a partner, not a girlfriend. I am nothing to you, and I cannot figure out why the hell you want me. Why would you want a woman who doesn't love you anymore?" My tone grows just a little bit louder.

"Shh..." he whispers in mockery, puckering his lips. "Why do I want you? Because your freedom becomes mine, and isn't that just a lovely, lovely thing to own. Freedom is all we are. It holds our wants and needs, our soul, our mind... our personality. It holds it all, like a little crystal ball, so full of wonder... so easy to shatter."

He bursts into maniacal laughter, and the couples around us mistake it for joy as they smile sweetly. Ryan's gone. He's completely fucking insane.

"You can't have me. I'm not yours. I haven't been for a long time. And you know it." My voice cracks a bit.

"I worked too hard not to have you, Morrigan. Breaking up is not an option. You're either mine forever, or no one else can have you. There's simply no other way."

"I will not marry you. This will not happen." I shake my head and fail to hold his gaze as an unfamiliar sting grazes my eyes.

"Oh, but it will, because if you don't"—he turns toward my family, waving at them, watching as they respond with polite, devious smiles. Then he spins us and waves at my brother dancing with some girl, who responds with a nod—"they all die."

And just like that, the song ends.

The dance ends.

My freedom ends with it...

Vincent

THE GUYS AND I walk around the dance floor of the ballroom, toward the corridor where O'Rourke waits for us a moment longer before he disappears through. He signaled to us after most of the guests finished congratulating him for marrying off his daughter. Funny, the things people celebrate nowadays.

I catch Morrigan's eyes following me as she stands beside her future husband, accepting even more congratulations from people ecstatic for her tragedy.

"Something's off, isn't it?" Madds questions on a low tone, and I find him watching the same person I am.

Both Finn and Carter, who walk in front of us, turn their heads to confirm what we're referring to, then hum their approval in unison.

"She didn't know," I tell them, but look at Madds most of all.

He had a soft spot for her back then. Because of all I know of him, I couldn't feel the jealousy I was supposed to. She was mine, yes, but he's my best friend. I trust him more than anyone else. Not so deep down, I was happy to know he cared for someone who wasn't us. And I carried a tinge of pain that he liked her, but she wasn't his. I think she cared for him too. There was always a spark in his amber eyes when he looked at her, and a strange curiosity in hers. He and I never talked about it, especially after Morrigan and I ended. So I don't actually know if he liked or just wanted her.

As Madd's looks at her now, under his olive skin around his temples and forehead, the veins bulge, looking like they could burst any second. His buzzcut does nothing to hide them. It's the most anger he tends to show outside the fighting ring. He's fighting to control it now.

"What the hell do you mean? She didn't know about the party or—?"

"The engagement., I interrupt and answer his question.

"And we're just supposed to let this go."

Carter clears his throat, stopping the argument. We're walking through the corridor now, and even whispers might carry over.

"We need to see what her father wants," I whisper to Madds.

Outside the ring, he's always been calm in fights. But as years have passed, his composure has turned eerie. Even as he smashes someone's face in with his fists alone, he's calculated. He simmers that anger, debating the most efficient move, and I've seen many adversaries backing out before the first punch was thrown. Only because of his grim expression and throbbing veins. It helps that, at six-foot-seven, he looks down at pretty much everyone around him. He's stacked with muscles like a fucking bull and has a menacing scar going down from the middle of his forehead across to the outside of his cheekbone.

His only response is a guttural grunt as he looks over to the end of the corridor, where Liam waits with his son.

"Gentlemen, please, have a seat." O'Rourke leads us into a private lounge room that has its own bar, and we take a seat on the ornate sofa and armchair.

Only Madds chooses to stand. He usually does.

"I'm not sure if you've been introduced to my son, Cillian," he continues, nodding to the redhead.

I know who he is. His dad should know this too, since he's just one year younger than us and we went to the same goddamn school. The old man is pretending the past no longer happened.

I suppress an exasperated sigh, noting the sibling resemblance to Morrigan. Only Cillian's eyes are darker, and his wiry beard and ginger hair trapped in a messy bun at the back of his head is more muted in tone than hers.

"Cillian, this is Vincent Sinclair, Finnigan Hennessey, Maddox Severin, and Carter Pierce."

We all nod, but Finn speaks.

"We've met. I had the pleasure of breaking his nose with my knee."

Liam quirks an eyebrow, and a hint of that protective father figure peeks through. Cillian keeps a straight face, the flare of his nostrils the only hint of a reaction. But a smirk flashes in his eyes as he heads over behind the stocked bar.

"After I dislocated your shoulder in that legendary tackle," he says as he grabs a bottle of Bourbon.

"Fair." Finn smiles now. He has a talent in diffusing tension. But he's equally talented at building it, even in the most inappropriate of moments.

Cillian lifts the bottle to us, a silent question, but we all refuse the drink. Suddenly, the wooden door opens loudly and Holt walks in, his stride too proud for my liking. He lets it close slowly behind him as his gaze drags over us, one by one. Maddox stills. Not even his chest moves with his breaths. If he attacks, I won't stop him.

I expect Holt to linger on me, but he doesn't. He's oblivious to my desire to cave his face in right now. I saw the way he acted with his *fiancée* in that restaurant. It was enough to tell me exactly the kind of man he is. And the announcement tonight... that just tipped the fucking scale.

O'Rourke starts the unnecessary introductions yet again, and a generic conversation follows. I'm listening but paying no attention. Let the others carry this shit. I'm focusing on not killing this motherfucker for touching her.

I have no right to be protective of her. She's not mine. She would cut me if I tried to help now. But I would happily bleed for her, because she was mine once. I've been telling myself that what we had wasn't mature enough, an infatuation, a crazy obsession. It wasn't deep enough to warrant the pain that lingered for so long after. I kept repeating that she was too young for what we had to be that real. I've started using these words as a mantra, hoping that someday they will sink in.

Around eight years have passed—they still haven't.

It's why I'm here.

I found out of the engagement, and I needed to see the look in her eyes as she told the world she's going to marry Ryan Holt, breed his filthy empire. I needed to see if the memories of us stained her gaze as she spoke those words.

What I got instead is both better and worse. Hate, fury, fear, and... hope.

It was disturbing to see the petrified look in her eyes as he led her onto the dance floor. She's fierce, reckless to a fault, and strong, but I've never seen true fear in her eyes until today. Even through her hate for me, she fixed onto my gaze, desperate for a lifeline. So I pinned her there and willed her to hold on to me through this invisible connection we seemed to share. She needed it, and it worked. It was like she took some sort of fucking life force from me, but it didn't feel like a loss. It somehow belonged to her already.

That's what gave me hope.

Madds' boots scrape the old wooden floor as he moves to stand behind me, and Holt's gaze lingers on him. I'm not going to look up to figure out why, but I can't help but wonder if those throbbing veins are still there.

"Congratulations on your... engagement." Finn's tone holds his usual charm, but I know even without looking, that the blue of his eyes has turned to ice.

"Thank you. We're looking forward to having a wedding as soon as possible," he says as he sits in the last empty armchair across from me.

We...

None of us say any more on that subject.

"Look, gentlemen, I'm going to go straight to business. I am looking to branch out my import business, and Mr. Holt and I are joining forces. However, we find that we need more... room to grow." Liam O'Rourke starts the conversation we're here for.

Okay, so he's not skirting the edge of the law anymore. He wants to dive straight to the other side—smuggling.

"Only, the one person that has the ability to give me more room at the seaside is... a ghost. All I have is a name, no face, no contact, and it's not enough to get in touch with the man."

The Ghost—Jonathan Rees. He controls the other half of the docks that Ryan doesn't have access to. Indeed, he is an enigma. To others, not us.

"We would also like to make a deal on transport, as we heard he holds the rails as well. It would be long-term business. Profitable for all parts," Holt adds, too much ego in the tone as he swipes his gaze over us.

The cargo trains are controlled by The Ghost as well. That means these two are looking to expand beyond Queenscove. Why?

"What's the load?" I ask.

"That's none of your business, *snake*," Holt all but spits at me, and in unison all three of us rise.

Madds is behind him in three steps, and I in front of him in two, my hand at his throat. The air in the room shifts, the lights appear dimmer, and the asshole's body twitches, as he forces himself to stand straight. He can't move, not with the *beast* behind him and a venomous *snake* in front of him.

"You're a motherfucking cub in this jungle, Holt. You haven't learned the rules, haven't lived here long enough, and definitely haven't earned your fucking place." I wouldn't usually get quite this heated, but it's a combination of what happened out in the ballroom and the motherfucker's insolence. "I don't fucking tolerate insults."

"Ryan, shit... gentlemen, my apologies," O'Rourke says, but I don't turn.

I'm not sure where Holt found his balls, but he better shove them back in their hiding spot before we rip them off and stuff them up his fucking ass.

"Maybe this was premature," Carter says in an even, almost bored tone of voice.

"It is definitely premature for Ryan to speak before thinking." O'Rourke's tone is cold and stern as he tries to coax us into staying.

"No," Carter interrupts. "Maybe this meeting was premature."

I step back, looking at the old man. Holt may hold a dirtier business than him, putting him in our field, but he's never controlled any of that shit until now. O'Rourke, though, skirted the law for long enough to know how the game is played. The only reason he hasn't jumped fully to our side until now is because he's been aware of how to play the system to his favor. His mafia is a different brand from ours, but it's still mafia. He's a businessman through and through and knows all too well how to play his cards right.

From the corner of my eye, I can see Madds grab Holt's shoulder hard enough that he winces, but this time around, he keeps his mouth shut. *Snake* is not far away from *Serpent*, but one is a derogatory term and the other a title.

I am no snake. I have never deceived, never cheated in the life games we play. People fear us because they know exactly who we are and what we are capable of. We make sure they're aware that The Sanctum doesn't give second chances, especially not when we are disrespected. O'Rourke is well aware. Which is why the lack of repercussions will mean something to him. He'll see it as a favor. Usually, there are three options: they repent, they die, or they simply cease to exist in our line of sight. In this particular situation, dying is not yet an option, as we need something from them, from Holt.

As Finn and Carter step closer toward the door, ready to leave, we hear a grunt. Turning, I find Cillian looking straight at his future brother-in-law, a scowl deepening every wrinkle of his freckled forehead. There's something about the man, a brand of madness I've only ever recognized in his sister, shimmers in his eyes. Not as bright, though. But I've had the pleasure of seeing what she's capable of.

"I spoke without thinking." Holt finally opens his mouth. I can see how much it hurts him to submit. I revel in it. We all do. "I apologize."

I turn straight to O'Rourke.

"You need to make a deal for access to the docks and the lines. What are you moving, when do you want to start, how often, and how many? No one will even acknowledge a meeting without knowing the reason for it. Not that I can guarantee a meeting, or that I can reach him."

I can reach him.

"Rounds and dust. In about three months. The pattern will change—between one and two weeks. Two to four containers at a time to start off with. We just need to make sure we spread them thinly first. Test the territory," Liam responds without hesitation, and I make a mental note.

"We'll be in touch." I nod, before I turn and head toward the door behind the others.

"Wait. You haven't named your price."

I turn just enough that I can see him when I look over my shoulder. "I'll tell you the terms of the pact once I am assured I can grant your request. Have a nice evening." I walk away, the door slamming on its own behind me.

I don't miss O'Rourke's booming voice through the thin walls.

"Boy, you will learn your goddamn lesson too soon, and it will be too harsh if this is how you think business is done! We need them if you want this business deal to work! You have no leg to stand on! Your business may be old, but you're goddamn new, and you suddenly think you're the big kahuna? Sit back in your place and learn how it's done!"

"*Old man...*" Holt says something else, but he's not loud enough for any of us to hear. Safe to say, from the way Cillian just rasped his name, it wasn't good.

We walk away, back into the ballroom, where the lights have dimmed, turning into a nice party. We absorb the gazes everyone gives us as we head toward the exit, willing one in particular to hit my skin.

It doesn't.
She's not here anymore.
Good.

CHAPTER 6
Morrigan

THE SOFT LIGHT reflects off the leather that barely covers my body and the five chains wrapped over it. I've been staring at myself in the mirror for too long now, but here, in Lulu's apartment, dressed this way, surrounded by the smell of jasmine that always seems to gravitate around Lulu herself, I feel more like myself than I have in months. Disregarding the couple of weeks since... *the announcement.*

That's how we refer to it now, Lulu and I—"*the announcement.*" Impersonal. Cold. It allows me to detach from it, like it has nothing to do with me.

I check the wig again, making sure it's unmovable, the bobby pins tight. I chose to cover my easily recognizable ginger with sleek black. It's such a contrast against my pale, freckly skin, not that it will matter much in the gold light of the club. I love black. It gives me back the confidence I seem to have lost in the last few months. Plus, blondes are more memorable, and since I'm a silent partner, I'm trying to blend in with the other employees.

I slide my fingers over the leather bodysuit that's technically a bra and panties connected together. In the middle of my torso, there's a three-inch gold ring, to which thin strips are attached, two pairs spread over and under my breasts, and four more are connected to the hem of the panties portion of the garment. From the same ring, five gold chains spread in almost the same way, two over the strips on top of my breasts, two others wrap around my waist, and one—the riskiest of them all—runs straight between my legs, up the seam of my ass, until it connects with the waist chains. I've paired the bodysuit with thigh-high velvet boots that make me feel less naked, and covered myself with a soft, see-through, long lapel jacket that has a subtle gold sheen that catches the light.

"Going to the toilet is gonna be a bitch in that thing." Lulu walks in, but my jaw drops at her sight.

"Fucking hell, woman!" I exclaim, unable to stop myself. It takes a bit too much effort to reassure myself that I'm straight.

She wears a floor-length leather skirt that would be tight if not for the two slits on the front of each leg, running right up to the velvet waistband that cinches her waist. A velvet bra barely covers the rest of her, the straps meeting at the back of her neck, and the bottom band wraps behind her back before coming around to the front, where it's tied into a cute bow. It's simple, but damn... every man in that club will want to see what's behind those slits that make her legs look like they go on for miles.

"You look incredible, Lu!"

"You too, love. Look at you... those straps. You're gonna fucking kill it tonight." She comes next to me, and we both turn to the full-length mirror, admiring our work.

"I'm nervous," I confess.

"Because of the opening night party, or the dance?" She tucks her icy blonde hair behind her ears.

"Both." I exhale as I pick up the mask from the side table next to the mirror.

"Yeah..." Lulu says, nodding before she picks up hers, and we help each other strap them on.

We chose venetian inspired masks, with black and gold details, from the same collection. It's not as if we wouldn't recognize each other in the club, but it made us feel better that, even though I will be pretending to be a random member of staff, we're actually on the same level. My mask comes to a point at the tip of my nose and, from its lowest point between my eyebrows, it curves upwards above each one, to a sharp point in my hairline. Lu's is the opposite, curving down her cheeks and raising into one sharp point just above the middle of her forehead, close to the hairline.

They fit.

We fit.

She smiles at me, and I feel like I'm swallowing my heart. This is it. Months of work have come down to this moment.

"I think it's time to go."

* * *

My heels fall heavy on the hard floor as I step slowly between the small crowds, observing them as they stand in front of the wall-to-wall windows. They're so deeply enthralled by the couples enjoying themselves in the playrooms, that no one is talking to each other.

Some sway to the lascivious music, some couples rub on each other, and some are simply lost. Lost in the images they witness behind the glass. In the way the flesh trembles and the skin reddens when the leather paddle connects. In the way the arm muscles tighten as they pull on the straps of the St. Andrews cross. In the way her eyes roll to the back of her head as the orgasm shakes her body. The way his cock spasms at the pull of his balls when his mistress denies his own. Each and every spectator is either lost in themselves or the beautiful acts they're watching. And two of the rooms are occupied by guests, not the people we specifically invited to spice up the atmosphere. *That* is a success.

I step into the main club, the bar to my left surprisingly not as busy as the rest of the floor. I was expecting people to huddle there; however, everyone seems to be relaxed.

Some of them captivated by the show the couple we met in Rosston is putting on up on the main stage. Others are joined in intimate dances between the busy tables. And at the back of the space, opposite the bar, the tables we intentionally submerged in shadows appear to be fully occupied. Most likely with people enjoying more private exhibitions.

The whole atmosphere is loose, comfortable, and enticing—so much better than we hoped this night would be.

"I can't believe how incredible this is!" Lulu appears from behind some people she was engaging with, and grabs my hand, pulling me toward the bar. She leans in with a great big smile on her face. "Everyone came! I checked with the door a few times, and every single member who signed up was scanned in!"

Fuck!

"E—everyone?"

I didn't think *he* would. Vincent, *The Serpent*, Sinclair—his name showed up in the membership applications and I had half a mind to reject it. I really fucking wanted to. But I didn't want to cause any issues for Lulu, since no one knows of my involvement in the club, and technically, she has no reason to reject him. I don't have one either, no real one beyond the flashes of memories from eons ago. I was so young, and he was building an empire with his friends... then one day, he was gone. And I... I changed my life forever.

I turn my head slightly, and swipe my eyes over the crowds, in the hopes that I'll manage to figure out which one he is.

"Morri?! Are you okay?"

"Yes, sorry, I was just—" I quickly take a deep breath. "It's incredible! Such a fucking success, and people are engaging too! Two of the playrooms are occupied by actual members!" I grab her forearms, shaking her lightly with girlish enthusiasm.

"No way! I have to go watch," she squeals.

We worked hard on this club, and we have so much to be proud of. This party, the atmosphere... it's perfect. Fuck it, it's beyond perfect.

"Jaz told me that she and Richie are coming back!" she all but yells at me.

"But they live so far away."

"They don't care. They said this doesn't compare with the club back home. The equipment, the quality, the intimate décor, it's all better. I'm not complaining. They put on such an amazing show, I mean... look at them." She points to the stage, where Jaz weeps from pain and ecstasy as Richie canes her red ass, finger-fucking her between hits. "And they're perfect for BDSM education as well. We would be lucky to have them."

"Yeah, I wonder how we can convince them to move here," I say, laughing as I watch the middle-aged couple absolutely killing it on stage.

We met at the club in Rosston and fell in love with them, their interactions, their connection. It was incredible to see how in tune they were. There was no need for words, because he could read into the tenseness of her muscles, or the pitch of her voice, even the look in her eyes. He could tell when something was wrong. Like when Jaz was completely caught in the play, exhausted, slightly delirious from too much pleasure and a little too much pain, and her safe word, the same one she's had for years, completely skipped her mind. But Richie took a few seconds to realize something was not right, and stopped immediately, swooping her in his arms and dropping to the floor. She was curled up between his legs as he cradled and whispered sweet nothings into her ear, until she came out of it.

The whole crowd watched in silence, taking in that image filled with love, the understanding, the bond. That night, we were all proven just how much we had to learn.

It was them who encouraged us to build Metamorphosis when we told them about our idea. It didn't come from our passion to practice, but a different kind of desire. We want to offer people a safe, comfortable, and high-quality space. Along with the freedom they don't have in their real lives. Freedom to indulge, to push their limits, freedom to remove their everyday masks, put on the right ones, and unleash who and what they truly are.

There's nothing more important than freedom. Soon, I'll have mine.

"I have to go up there in a bit," I say, nodding toward the stage.

"How do you feel?"

"Anxious, but a good kind of anxious. Do you think they will be disappointed that I won't actually strip?" I tuck the hair of the wig behind my right ear, and signal to Rachel, one of the bartenders.

She knows who I am, but not that I'm her boss too. Everyone is on a need-to-know basis, so I'm simply Lulu's friend. She grabs a bottle of tequila and a bowl of lemon wedges on her way to us, then fills two shot glasses, before she pulls a saltshaker out from behind the bar.

I'm about to open my mouth to speak, to thank her, when my skin begins to tingle. Soft goose bumps burst between my shoulder blades, riding up to the back of my neck. They wrap around toward the right, until they sizzle behind my ear, where cold air brushes my skin.

It's him. He's here. I just know it.

I want to turn, but my head is suddenly filled with voices screaming at me not to move, to stay put, and not meet the devil's eyes. Yet, self-preservation has no place under my masochistic skin.

So I turn, chin held high, and swipe my gaze slowly over the crowd. But no one stands out.

"Do you think he'll be watching you?" Lulu leans in, pushing a shot glass to me.

How did she know I was thinking of him?

"He won't know it's me. But, you said all members came, so..." I trail off.

The idea that The Serpent's watching me fills me with anger. It brings back more memories than I'm comfortable with. He used to watch me dance. Long ago, in a different life. I would rather pull out his black eyes than see him watching me as if he forgot who I was, who he was... what *we* were.

Only, he hasn't forgotten everything. As he reminded me before *the announcement*, he remembers very well how I smashed Johnny Bray's jaw. Until then, and at my mother's birthday party from a few months back, I didn't even think he still remembered my last name. I guess I was wrong.

I'm not in love with him or some shit. He just brings out parts of me that have no business being on the surface. I have enough reasons to be angry, without him adding onto it.

"In all fairness, he could just be in one of the rooms already." Lulu taps me on the shoulder in reassurance.

I don't care.

I don't care if he's in the playrooms, or at the bar, or dancing, or right in front of the stage, watching Jaz and Richie's show end.

Even though I can't get his onyx gaze out of my head, the one that pinned me within its darkness as Ryan led me in that uncomfortable dance.

Even though it was enough to pull me out from the shock and momentary terror.

Even though it was him who calmed me down with nothing but his eyes...

No, I don't care!

I lick the skin between my index finger and thumb, sprinkle salt, swipe my tongue over it, and down the shot after cheering with Lulu. Rachel returns, tequila bottle clutched as she pours another one, and I drink it without bothering with the salt. Hell, I didn't even bother with the lemon after the first shot. I tap my glass on the bar before she moves away, and she pours a third as Lulu watches me with interest. I know that under that mask, there's a quirked eyebrow.

"Just... don't fall off the fucking stage." She pushes the shot glass away from me, then downs hers before gripping a lemon wedge with her teeth. "Are you ready?" she asks after she swallows the zesty juice.

I nod, then drag my hands all over my wig and outfit, making sure all is in place. Lulu weaves through the excited crowd, before she jumps on stage. She's been up there a few times already, first to welcome the members and start the party, and a few times after that to introduce the dancers, or various guests, like Jaz and Richie.

The lights dim and two assistants jump in to clean, as Lulu thanks the couple and the crowd bursts into cheers. They loved them. I'm a bit anxious to follow after them.

"Up next, we have something a bit more casual. Another person from university, actually." She presents me to the crowd, and I have to laugh at my cover. "Someone who discovered pole dancing whilst there. I know, our expensive education has certainly taught us some useful skills, right?"

The crowd laughs, and I can't help but admire how nonchalant she is in front of an audience.

"She's a good girl," Lulu continues. "You won't get to see the goods, but she has the body of a goddess and she'll make you wish you are that pole. So please... enjoy the show."

As I walk toward the stage, the light dims more, hiding me in a welcoming darkness. My inhibitions slowly dissipate with each step that gets me closer, and Lulu gives my hand a reassuring squeeze when I pass by her. When my foot hits the first step up to the stage, *"God Be You"* by Nostalghia pours from the speakers, filling the atmosphere and my veins. My muscles respond to the slow, sultry beat, tingles spreading under my skin as I step onto the stage. They're good tingles. Like the ones you get before your first kiss with someone new, or the first touch in just the right place, or the anticipation of a cock slamming into you that first time.

The red spotlight hits only one pole, and as I force the rest of my nerves away, I dare a look toward the crowd, breathing out in surprise—I can't see anyone. The whole place is bathed in darkness, apart for the faint light under the shelves at the back of the bar, and the fire exit signs. It's almost like I'm alone. I sway my hips to the rhythm of the music, undulating as I slowly step toward the pole, and run my hands from my throat, and down my breasts. When I reach my waist, I untie the see-through jacket and let it drop to the floor, my leather strapped body on full display. I still don't have full confidence in my soft body, my plump belly, or my full thighs, but this has always helped me.

I'm a couple of steps away from the pole, and I throw my body into a handstand right next to it, swinging my legs around the metal on a collective gasp from the hidden crowd. But I don't get up right away... no. Grasping the pole behind me, I let it spin as I tighten the tops of my thighs around it, legs falling almost parallel to the ground, and roll my ass against the metal. At this point, I forget there's a crowd. The music floods me, and the ecstasy takes over, filling me with lust. As I raise my upper body and grip the pole, I open my legs as wide as they allow.

I release the blocks in my mind, dancing against the metal bar, rubbing, splitting, dropping to the floor in moves that I would make for a lover only. Intense tingles touch my skin, almost like a sharp gaze that wants more than just to look. So I move for whoever that person is. I touch myself for them, roll my hips for them, lick my lips and suck my fingers for them. I hook one foot at the bottom of the pole and the other above my head for them, then open my legs in splits that make my muscles ache and tendons burn. And goddamnit, it's so fucking satisfying.

Before the song ends, I'm almost at the top, with my hands above my head. My breasts are squeezed together with the pole between them, and I bring my legs up, heels under my ass as my thighs grip the metal. Then I let go, sliding down fast, and on that last note my kneeling body hits the floor, legs open wide toward the shadowed crowd, palms on my thighs.

For a long moment, there's nothing but silence. Then the club bursts into cheers and applause, so loud the next song is completely covered by their enthusiasm. I can't help but blush. I've only ever done this a few times. Yes, I go to a pole dancing club, since I don't have one in my home. But actually dancing on stage, I've only ever done three times. That first time doesn't count, as I would rather not remember it. I laugh at myself as I rise to my feet, my muscles aching as the hired dancers come back to the stage to keep the atmosphere going in the background.

"You smashed it! You fucking smashed it! To the point that a few couples had to retire into the playrooms and the back tables, you were so fucking hot!" Lulu pulls me into a big hug as I step off the stairs.

When the lights come back on to a dim level, I notice all the heads that turn to me as we walk back to the bar—men and women. Yet when I reach our earlier spot and grab the shot that Rachel already poured for me, I feel that cold breath again, those tingles wrapping around my throat in such a possessive way that it makes me want to drop my head back, lean into it, and let it choke me. As invisible as it is.

I swipe my gaze around the crowd yet again, and just as before, not one person stands out, but there are definitely more eyes on me now.

Yet this feeling, it becomes as uneasy as it is intriguing.

CHAPTER 7

Vincent

"ARE YOU SURE he's coming today?" Finn asks as he sits next to me on the leather sofa.

"A password was requested, and Carter spoke with him. So, yes, he's coming." I pull out the little glass of Absinthe that I've been patiently waiting to be ready, the sugar now dissolved, and take that first satisfying sip that burns straight down my throat.

We're at Midnight, the speakeasy we own in the center of the city. It's a useful business when you want to have control over the patrons of your bar, and over information too. It was Carter's idea. His whole aura seems to belong in the golden age, and he designed this whole space himself. The barroom is bathed in low lights, leather and wood furnish the space, and most of the antiques, paintings, and décor pieces were sourced through one of our first businesses, years ago. Expensive and rare drinks fill the bar shelves, and signature cocktails, that even Madds touches once in a while, are made by our bartenders.

But this Absinthe is Carter's fault. He got me hooked on it. I didn't know how to drink it properly until we opened this place and Carter found the right bartender to show me.

I take another sip and let it warm me all the way through. I know Jonathan Rees is coming, yet I'm still impatient. It's been a long time since I felt this way, but I want to close this deal with O'Rourke, so I can get my hands on Holt, and ultimately on Boseman.

I must say, I do admire Rees, how he managed to maintain his privacy all these years. He lives up to his nickname—The Ghost. The man has a peculiar way of doing business. Very few people outside his faction know who he is or what he looks like. He rules with an iron fist, and he's nothing most would expect. We've known him for years, mostly because of Carter, as he was his dad's best friend, but we don't normally do business with him. We collaborate sometimes and help each other out, but other than that, he's just a friend and frequent customer of our speakeasy.

"Even I'm not sure if he's going to be down for this deal." Carter comes from the bar, dropping into the wingback armchair to my left.

"He will. The speculations around why O'Rourke and Holt want to get in on his territory are enough to convince him, even without the information we offered."

"The money they're offering will help sway him too." Finn smirks.

"Yes, how lucky of Holt to marry O'Rourke's daughter, and get into business with him just at the right time." It takes effort not to roll my eyes or react in a way that tells the guys that I'm affected by this for a whole other reason.

But what Carter and his hacker team found was most enlightening. Turns out that old man Holt wasn't that smart with money, and his son needs this, or he and his wretched mother will lose everything.

"Money won't sway him. Jonathan doesn't care about money if the business is not the right fit," Carter counters.

"Will he do it for us then?" I ask, but Carter's gaze snaps to the entrance.

I turn to find Jonathan and Anthony, his husband, walking in, gazing inconspicuously around the locale, as they make their way toward an empty table.

We don't pounce on them right away. It's not how this works.

"So how was the other night? You tried the new fetish club in town, didn't you? Was it worth it?" Carter asks.

"I signed up," Finn replies. "Five people already recommended it or invited me, and only three of them are women. That told me enough."

"Yeah, that you're a manwhore no matter the gender."

But Finn winks at Carter. "I know you're jealous, baby, but it's okay, you can join too."

I turn to him, catching the devious smirk as he shakes his head at Finn's confidence. I don't doubt that if Finn would try a little harder, he could probably get any of us in bed. The man is too pretty for his own good.

"The official opening is in a few days. I think you should join, try it out," I agree. "It was much better than I expected. The owner did a pretty fucking good job. Even if you just go to enjoy the shows, it's still worth it."

"Who did you say the owner is?" Finn asks.

"You should really pay more attention to this shit, man. Especially considering the family she comes from," I answer. "Loreley Dietrich is the owner."

"Or Lulu. She's O'Rourke's best friend." Madds shows up out of nowhere, dropping his bulky frame on the sofa next to me, and I notice the scraped, bruised hands right away. He fought bare-knuckled again.

"Liam's?!" Finn gasps.

"Morrigan, you idiot."

"Oh. Yeah, I remember Loreley from the party. She was holding on to this guy for dear life. I think she was just as shocked as Morrigan about the news," Finn says, relaxing back in his seat as Madds hums his distaste for that entire situation.

"I think it's time." Carter nods toward Jonathan, and we watch as the bartender leaves their table after delivering their drinks.

I get up, grabbing my drink, and walk toward the man who can make or break our whole plan.

Morrigan

I BURST THROUGH the front door of the house that hasn't felt like home since a month ago, when my parents all but sold me off to the highest fucking bidder. And my mother, my goddamn mother, should have known better, because she's one of two people I told that I wanted to break it off for real with Ryan. One of two people I had the guts to admit why to. Now I understand why she was insistent on me holding off.

"I didn't love your father when I married him. Our parents worked in the same business, and back then... this is how you strengthened your legacy. By uniting two fronts, two strong families. I learned to love him. I would never take it back."

Fucking liar. She gave me that speech the last time I talked to her about this. I wasn't even the one to open the subject, she did. Now I'm convinced she discussed it with my father, and he told her to have this conversation.

"Have you lost your goddamn mind?" I storm through the house, straight to the living room, where I know she sits reading her magazine, as she always does at this time. "You're seriously going ahead with this charade? I just got a fucking call about a cake tasting."

"Language!" My mother barely raises her head from the magazine, her eyes flashing to me briefly before they return to whatever bullshit she's reading.

"Don't you dare! I will not bend to your will like I'm still that kid who took your word as law, and thought she wanted the same things as you, just because that's what you told her. I'm not marrying him! I'm not as stupid as you to ruin my life."

I'm fucking seething. When that bakery called me, I was in disbelief. I thought they had the wrong number. They had to fucking convince me that it was the right one, and it took everything in me not smash my phone, or everything else around me. But I was in the office at the Metamorphosis, and I worked too hard on that place to destroy it.

My mother watches me, her eyes colder than usual, emotionless in a way that makes me wonder if she's always seen me as their puppet. Has my only purpose here been for their strings to have limbs to attach to? I refuse to let them think they're my puppet masters. She cocks her head ever so slightly, her gaze deepening with the movement, and my spine urges my body to straighten.

"Are you done?" That eerie calmness transfers to her tone as well.

I wish her words would surprise me. Yet they only disappoint.

"For some strange, unknown to me, and useless reason," my father's deep, threatening voice booms behind me, and I stiffen, "you seem to believe that you have a choice."

I watch my mother's reaction to the man behind me, and one thing becomes clear—I'm not the only puppet here. I don't turn to him.

I'm completely still as I stand in the middle of the large living room of our—*their* house. They insisted so much on me coming back here after university. I foolishly thought it was their subtle love or some newfound protective parental instinct, and that's why they wanted to help me out, while I saved my own money to buy a place. But it was just as I always feared... all about control. Now they're refusing to let me move, unless it's to Ryan's house.

What a fucking idiot I was. Probably still am.

I'm not sure if I feel betrayed, disappointed, or just broken.

My father appears to my right, walking toward the gaudy, floral sofa where my mother sits, without sparing me a glance.

"I'm not your slave, of course I have a choice." My tone grows urgent, but I don't yell, don't raise my voice too high, which is a feat in and of itself since I can feel that all too familiar simmer under my skin.

My father sits down on the sofa, and I swear the grandfather clock at the end of the hallway has slowed down its ticking for effect.

"Mmm... true. You're not a slave, and you do have a choice. Many, actually." He speaks in a low, calm tone, and I'm about to don a victorious smile when he carries on. "You have the choice between Coveview Estate or Ruthford Hotel for the reception. You have your choice of lavish wedding dresses, flowers, jewelry, and decorations. You have plenty of choices for your inevitable wedding to Ryan Holt." He leans forward, as if he wants to make sure I hear him, his eyes darkening at the movement.

"No!" My self-control is but a memory now as my tone heightens.

"You have a duty toward this family!" My father's voice follows mine, an octave higher, and I have the urge to step back.

"Marrying a man I don't even want to be with is not a fucking duty! What Cillian is doing, training to take over your business, *that's* fucking duty! This is a forced union. A marriage of convenience, and it's not *my* goddamn convenience!"

"Not yours? So all we ever gave you, all we've provided, the troubles we got you out of, were not for your convenience? Or our protection, the university, the money, the car, the roof over your head, were not either? What about the simple fact that you never had or have to work a day in your life, even though you keep fucking insisting on it?"

Now I do step back, just as he stands from the sofa. I've played this game before with him, and I know exactly what's coming. It's in these moments that the fiery attitude I'm known for sizzles out and bleeds into him. My body shuts down from years of this... this displaced dominance, the emotional distress that a father should never cause. As my eyes flicker to my mother, I can see that she knows what's coming as well.

"I didn't realize there were conditions attached to parenting. I didn't know there was a price to pay for being born, being your daughter!" I keep talking because I have nothing more to lose.

His brows furrow, but the deranged smirk on his lips screams *peril* as he rushes toward me, his steps falling heavy on the parquet floor. I back up quickly, and the moment my shoulder blades hit the wall, his heavy hand slams against the left side of my face. My head whips to the side in a flash of pain, and the metallic taste of blood flows over my tongue.

"There's always a price to pay, girl! Just be thankful that you at least like Ryan."

"I don't," I say quietly, licking the cut on my inner cheek, resisting the urge to rub my hot skin, or my aching jaw. But I've shown enough weakness to this man, and I'm not about to fuel his abusive ego further.

I catch my mother's eyes as she turns toward the window, a flicker of sadness in them. But it's gone as fast as it appeared. *She's fucking useless.*

"You will marry him, you will have his children, and you will do your duty to this family." He steps back, but I refuse to bow to him, so I step forward.

"Why? Why are you so desperate to unite our families? Or whatever is left of his."

"You always ask too many questions that don't concern you. Those are answers you couldn't begin to understand." He looks bored under his bushy eyebrows.

I smirk. I don't plan to entertain this misogynistic pissing game of his. "So that's how it is. Fine. But if you care about me at all, don't send me to the man who wants to break me."

Blinking slowly, he reveals the terrible truth through his gaze. He doesn't even bother to hide it.

"I'm nothing to you..." I whisper, moving a little closer. "I'm a tool, the right kind of currency for you to pave your way down the fucking lawless rabbit hole you're digging... I'm nothing."

He doesn't speak, just shifts a little closer.

"Did you ever care? Was I ever anything else but a trade commodity?" My voice cracks, disappointment, fear, rage, all mixing together.

He blinks slowly like he can't wait for me to shut up and bend to his will. I can't take it anymore, and I slam the side of my fist against his chest.

"You fucking bastard! I'm your fucking daughter, goddamnit! Your fucking daughter, and you're selling me without a fucking second thought!" I'm screaming now, a guttural sound that scrapes my throat. "You can take back all your shit! You can take my goddamn diploma, my clothes, my room, take it all! You're stealing my fucking life away! Well, take back the price I paid and just leave me alone!"

I don't see the next move coming. The moment his palm slams across the side of my face again, I'm thrown straight to the ground, my ribs hitting the side of an end-table, and all air leaves my lungs on a hitched breath.

I swallow the sharp pain, because I refuse to show him any more weakness.

"You're not going anywhere. You're not giving anything back. It will simply go to waste, so it might as well stay with you. And you're not getting out of this. This is your forever."

I get up on a strained exhale, then push the ache away, and without blinking, I slap my father so hard across his cheek, his glasses fly off.

"You're no fucking father, not to me anyway. Not anymore."

I catch that stunned, furious look in his eyes for a moment. But I don't give him the chance to abuse me even more, and I turn on my heel and storm out.

When I rip open the front door, I almost run straight into my brother.

"Christ! What are you—?" He stops, narrowing his eyes and cocking his head as he takes me in.

"Welcome home, Cillian." My tone seeps sarcasm as I take him in. We look so similar; it fucking hurts to know that we share blood, yet we are so different.

"Morri, what happened?" He reaches over, his fingers just about touching the strands of hair partially covering my cheek.

"Don't. Just fucking don't!" I swipe his hands away. "Unless the next words out of your mouth are '*Morrigan, I'm your brother, I care about you, and I will help you get out of this bullshit,*' don't speak to me."

"I can't—"

"Yeah, I fucking thought so. And to think you're taking over this fucking circus when the old man croaks. Nice to know you'll carry on his legacy. Just do me a favor. Don't ever fucking have kids."

I push him aside and storm past, skipping down the front steps, then stop at the bottom, turning to him.

"I thought more of you, brother. So much more..."

CHAPTER 8
Morrigan

I DRIVE LIKE a madwoman, swerving through the easing traffic, dinnertime clearing the roads enough that I can overtake both on the left and the right as an angry song from a random playlist on my phone reverberates through my speakers. I weave around the cars that honk, a blur of lights around me, my mind too far gone. Heaving breaths make my throat sore as I blink through the tears of frustration threatening to cloud my vision.

More honking sounds around me as tires screech on the asphalt, and the sun is now a trace of decadent lavender in the sky, the clouds in angry shades of burnt orange. The streets are clearer, and the roads bumpier. I avoid potholes rather than cars, the edge of the city much bumpier than the rest. But I don't care, I just... drive.

The playlist changes. A harsh voice singing the moody, modern blues soothes my ears. My soul is in flames, my heart broken, and my mind... my mind struggles to find reasons why I should hold back anymore.

Why... why in God's name am I holding back? How the hell have I become so conditioned? The transition has been so smooth, I completely missed their manipulations. This includes Ryan too. This is not me. This isn't fucking me!

No one but Lulu cares. No one! My goddamn fucking parents care only as far as my auction value. If I wouldn't have met Ryan, if my father wouldn't have had dealings, or attempts at, with his family, who would I have belonged to now? Who would he have given me to? Sold me to?

"Aaah!" My screams get louder as my foot pushes deeper onto the gas pedal, the engine roaring just as viciously as I am. But it's more than that—I'm fucking hurt!

Suddenly, the music stops, and my phone rings, pulling me out of my rage. As I finally acknowledge my surroundings beyond driving on autopilot, I realize the sun's traces are almost gone from the sky. Shit, I must have been driving for at least an hour. The phone keeps ringing and Ryan's name flashes on the car's middle console display.

I would let it ring out, but I'm a sucker for pain.

"Yes," I finally answer.

"Why the fuck aren't you answering your texts?!" Jesus, he sounds furious.

"Why are you calling me?"

"Excuse me?! You're my future wife, my *fiancée*!" Fucking hell, that last word doesn't spill off his tongue. No, it scrapes its way from his throat and spits out at me like a medieval weapon only designed for torture. "I don't need to justify my call. Where are you?!"

"Out."

"Where?"

"Driving."

"Get the fuck home, right now," he seethes.

"No."

"You fucking bitch, I said get home now, or I swear to God…"

"What? What are you going to do, Ryan?"

"Do not test me. I don't have time for this. Move your goddamn ass home, to my house, right now."

"Your house is not my home. And you… *you* don't fucking own me."

But what follows chills my bones. A maniacal laugh, one so familiar it even makes me picture the look in his eyes when those sounds work their way up from deep within his chest. The mania is most visible in these moments, and no matter how clear the vision of him is, I'm glad I'm not there.

"Oh, silly woman, it is your home, not your house, of course. There will be nothing in your name. I'll make sure the prenup is solid. But more importantly, I *do* own you. All that you are belongs to me, and once we are married, I will have so much more." His laugh booms through my car, and I swear I can hear unspoken words, secrets… He's plotting something. "There's no escape for you."

"Fuck you!" I spit.

Only, he continues like he didn't hear me. "I am trying to be a bit more courteous by keeping the leash loose while I'm busy reorganizing the business. But make no mistake, if you push me, I'll lock you in a spare room. Push me even harder, and I'll be the only person you will ever see, and my only use for you will be for that tight hole of yours. But careful, there's better pussy than yours out there, prettier women, skinnier, more attractive. I might just use that leash like a noose if you don't behave."

The men in my life only know betrayal. Cunning, double-faced cunts, showing their true faces today. His words cut in strange ways, different from my father's, and just as the road before me sinks into darkness, my soul does, too. I can see the color of it now—fury.

I can't describe its shade, but this is what it is.

Fury.

"You seem so sure that this plan of yours will work. Father too. You confuse confidence for brains. This alliance is between you and him, not me. I shook no hand, signed no contract. I'm not yours. I'm not anyone's. Strap your leash on someone else, because I'm not your fucking bitch."

My headlights light up the road out of town, the dense forest surrounding me as Ryan's unhinged laugh vibrates through my speakers, and suddenly his tone turns grave.

"You're so brave over the phone. But we both know you crumble in front of me. It took a while to break you, but I think I'm there. Just in time."

A shiver runs up my spine. Months of little digs that turned into more than that. I can't even describe how it happened, but it did. Always putting me down, criticizing, humiliating me, pressuring me... controlling me.

"Tell me. Which version of yourself will you be when my gun is aimed at your father's head?"

The shadows of the forest seem to come down at me, swallowing the glow of the headlights.

"How about when your mother looks down that barrel?"

Shit! He was fucking serious when he said, *"If you don't, they all die."*

"What about your brother? Will you be as brave? Or will you crumble at my feet and beg me to let them live?"

I slam my finger on the mute button and violently pound my hand against the steering wheel, the car swerving dangerously on every curse I spit out.

"Son of a fucking bitch! He's blackmailing me with my family's lives?!" Another series of screams make my throat raw, but I unmute the phone before he starts believing I caved.

"They sold me off to you. What makes you think I fucking give a shit about them?" I finally reply to him.

"Because you might fool everyone else with that harsh exterior of yours, but you don't fool me. You still believe they'll come around."

I truly don't.

"And..." he continues, "you wouldn't want your brother to die, would you?"

I lied. Secretly, I do think he will come around. He's my brother...

"Go ahead! We both know your threats of violence and death are as empty as your fucking skull. You won't touch them. Not now, not until you've set up whatever goddamn business you have with them. We both know you can't do shit alone." I finish in a low tone, and the grunt I hear on the other side is answer enough.

So I hang up, floor the gas once more, and the music returns to full blast as my pulse speeds on anxious beats.

"Fuck!"

I can feel the rush of blood in my veins, the pressure in my temples rising, my breathing staggered, my grip painful on the steering wheel.

"Goddamnit!"

I think... *shit*... I slow down the car and spot a forest road to the right, so I take the turn, the car making cruel noises on the uneven terrain. I press one hand on my chest, the pressure painful in my lungs, air not quite filling them.

Fucking hell, is this a panic attack? I push through that uneasiness, and drop the beam of my headlights, the adrenaline rising when the visibility dissipates.

I drive deeper into the woods, my headlights the only light here, as a slow, modern Blues song begins to blare through the speakers. Those heavy, sultry notes... they do something to me. They reach somewhere deep under my skin, brushing softly over my muscles, and they begin to relax.

My tires skid on the gravelly road as I follow the turns through the forest, and I know I'm gonna get lost. But fuck if I care. I don't just need to be lost, I need to lose myself.

My body begins to rock in the car seat, fingers tapping nervously on the steering wheel, and I'm running out of fucking air.

"I need to get out!"

I need ground under my feet. My brain feels like it's on fire.

I slam my foot on the brake, tightening my grip on the wheel to keep it from skidding as it comes to a halting stop. Before me, in the glare of the headlights, surrounded by grass and wildflowers, lies an eerie crossroads.

Right here, in the middle of the forest, where I decided to stop, two roads cross, with four directions to choose from.

Before my mind can sink further into the panic of my hypothetical road ahead, I turn the music as loud as it'll go, rip open the door, and rush out to the middle of this crossroads. The wave of panic slams into me from the inside out, and I fall to my knees, banging my fist into the ground on a painful bellow. It bleeds from the pits of my lungs, shrieking until my throat burns, until the desperation that taints it eases.

They betrayed me... they all betrayed me.

I take a deep breath that finally fills my lungs enough that it cools the burn in my brain, and slow drum beats fill my ears as they echo through the forest around me. The song coming from my car lulls my nerves, guiding my body to stand. My feet respond too, my hips following as the music carries me... it always does. I don't know the moment my whole body listened to the song, but I'm dancing like there is nothing but me in this entire world. Mad southern sounds guide me as I sway and spin, arms up in the air, t-shirt riding up as my hips roll on every beat, and the panic dissipates with every movement.

The damp smell of moss and wildflowers comforts my senses as a breeze makes its way through the branches of the trees. Their leaves rustle on the bass of the song, and I'm dancing along with them. With the hypnotizing, sweet scents of the forest, with the breeze that wraps around my bare stomach guiding me, the softness of the soil beneath my feet, my mind loses itself in the heathen beats echoing around me. But the only heathen here is me. Wild and... free.

Here... I am free.

But am I alone?

Vincent

IT WAS THE bass of the music vibrating through the trees that called to me. But her scream, the pain and desperation... that's what summoned me. The last thing I expected to see when I found the source was the blur of red hair whipping around as she moved freely to the dark music, the dipped headlights bathing her in a strange light.

Morrigan O'Rourke.

Those wild locks I would recognize anywhere, but I certainly didn't expect to see them on my run tonight.

I stand in the shadow of the trees, hidden from the headlights. Even if she looks in this direction, she cannot see me. And I don't want her to.

She sways her hips, then rolls her whole body to a low bass, moving on light steps as she spins over and over in a hypnotic dance. I stalk through the shadows until I'm almost behind the car, my eyes glued to her luscious body swaying, every movement an exquisite shock to my cock.

But I force myself to focus on the recklessness of this woman. Christ, anyone coming from behind those headlights is invisible to her. They could attack her. What the fuck is she thinking?!

But my mind is drawn back to that scream... *She's not thinking of that. She doesn't care.*

Something happened.

I move behind the trees again and stop when her fingers run through her hair. She's pulling it up, exposing the soft flesh of her belly when her T-shirt rides up, and when her body undulates on the notes of the song, all the blood vanishes from my brain.

I can't help myself from moving forward. She lures me in. My steps crunch on the gravel as I come out into the light and slowly walk in a wide circle around her, close to the line of trees.

With my next move, as the song quiets, her muscles tense all at once, and her eyes dart open, straight onto mine. I expect to see panic or fear in them, but I feel more like prey than the predator, with the fury so vividly painted on her features.

"Serpent..." she hisses, her shoulders falling when she realizes it's me. The fury stays put.

Interesting.

I continue walking around her, taking slow steps as she turns my way, keeping me in her line of sight. No words are exchanged. Not yet. She drags her gaze over me, head to toe, assessing my state, but she's blinded once I'm in front of the car. I stand between the headlights, and the stubborn woman still forces herself to look in my direction. As with wild animals, dropping one's gaze means submission. And that just won't do for Morrigan O'Rourke. I can't help but grin, because the fire in her eyes burns just as bright as her hair right now.

There's something bugging me, though. She's stubborn as a mule, strong and feisty to the point of self-destruction, yet she's submitting to this arrangement her father made with her.

It doesn't fit. There's a story here, and I need to hear it.

A dark and moody guitar fills the forest in slow tones as I step toward her.

"What happened?" Finally, I speak, and she flinches.

"Don't pretend to give a shit. It doesn't look good on you," she spits fire at me.

"Why are you here?" I ignore her faint insult.

"It's none of your fucking business, Serpent!" She crosses her arms, tight against her chest. "We both know you don't concern yourself with feelings, so don't pretend to give a shit now. Now, go! Leave me... alone."

Damn, I'm a fool thinking that she has moved on from the shit I had to pull all those years ago. Judging by the look in her eyes, even if twenty went by, her disdain toward me would be just as vivid.

I hurt her...

"What did he do?" I can't lie and say her situation doesn't bother me. It does. A lot.

I don't miss the hitch in her shoulders.

"Who?" She feigns ignorance.

Stopping a few feet away from her, I cock my head and watch. I won't entertain that question with a response.

"Why do you wanna know? Seriously, what's it to you?"

I have no answer for her. I barely have one for myself.

She sighs, long and loud, exasperation in her tone, but her eyes tell a much more painful story as she concedes. "I can't get out of it..."

"Why? What's holding you?"

"I can achieve many things on my own, but this..." She shakes her head, and for a moment, she looks away in the distance, taking a deep breath before continuing. "It's bigger than I am, and I don't know how big. I'm some sort of card in an unknown game, and I don't know how many players are involved. I need an ally at the table."

I nod. She's caught in the middle of the game I've already started inserting myself into. I suspect somehow this was meant to be. But there's a tinge of shame in those green eyes that look as black as mine in the night.

"You want to get away from Holt."

"Obviously! Don't you play games with me too. You were there, Serpent. You know very well what you saw." She sighs again, trying to rein in her anger. "I have for a while now."

Oh. Interesting.

I shove my hands into my pockets, narrowing my eyes on her. As I cock my head, the light that pours from behind me hits her pale face. Only, it's not as pale as it should be... not with the angry reddening on the side of it. The other side doesn't look intact either now that I'm seeing it more clearly.

"He hit you." My hands come out of my pockets, rolling into tight fists as I fight to hold in a growl.

She shakes her head, her expression honest.

"My father. Ryan is more creative with his pain." That fire in her eyes falters for a second.

Motherfucking O'Rourke!

"I'm gonna fucking—"

She puts her hand up, goddamn silencing me. "I don't need you to be my knight in shining-fucking-armor."

Reckless to the fucking bone. But I'm drawn back to her words about Holt.

"You don't need to be so stubborn. I'm just trying to..." I pause for a moment. I don't want to fuck this up. "What does Holt do to you?"

"Stop! I don't want you to pretend to care."

Fuck! That asshole is abusive, and I'm supposed to just... leave it.

"What *do* you want?" I ask through gritted teeth.

She debates telling me for a moment too long.

"I want to be free. Free of him. Of them. I can't marry him."

"Run, then." I know it's a useless thing to say the moment I open my month.

"Never!" she seethes. "That son of a bitch took one thing too many away from me. He doesn't get to chase me away from my home. Away from my damn future! He has to pay. I *will* make him pay!" She spits every single word, hate vibrating in her throat.

"How?"

She stands there, cocking her head and watching me intensely for a moment longer than I'm comfortable.

"You." She drags out those letters, like a spell she's mouthing under the light of the moon.

And I'm thoroughly enthralled, taking a step closer.

They say the serpent tricked Eve out of Eden, tempted her with promises of power and desire. I think he was merely answering her call, an obscured need to escape the oppression of the man who didn't want her to have a stray thought beyond servitude. Eve craved more. She had an appetite for the wicked. She wanted to be free, so the serpent freed her.

As I look into Morrigan's eyes, I recognize it—I may be wicked, but she's just like Eve... a heathen in disguise.

I can't help the slight quirk in the corner of my lips.

"You want to make a deal with me. Just like that."

I know she hates me. She doesn't hide the feeling, so this is utterly disturbing. Even through that disdain, she looks at me with apprehension, as if she's about to sign off her soul. I suppose she's about to do just that. A deal with me is always an exchange, never free.

"Yes. I can do it... but not alone. I—I need help." Those words pour like lava straight from the depths of her soul, and they pain her.

I step even closer, offering my open hand to her. Her brows furrow as she looks between it and my eyes, but then caves with a small sigh. The moment her soft skin touches mine, prickles trigger memories and sensations that I pushed back deep into my soul, ensuring prying them out would be near impossible. But I don't think it was the touch that made it happen—it's her acceptance.

She's giving herself to me... the Eve to my Serpent.

I tighten my grip on her right hand, lifting it above her head as I guide her in three slow pirouettes on the dark, southern tune, then pull her against me. Her free hand braces on my chest, holding me at a distance, and mine is on the small of her back. But I don't allow her a moment to rethink the stance. Instead, I follow the music, and lead her in a languid dance on its notes.

After all, a pact with the devil requires a seal, but I have a feeling she'll stab me with a rock if I try to kiss her.

I bring my thumb down to her pulse, watching as her eyes turn black, her pupils dilating to the max at the delicate gesture. But as I slowly drag it up her palm, she flinches slightly when I reach a thin strip of skin that seems rougher than the rest—*a scar*. The question is on the tip of my tongue, but something in her gaze gives me pause.

I'll ask later.

She's antsy, waiting for a response as she pretends she doesn't enjoy the feel of me against her. The hand holding me away has softened. Not her eyes, though. They're burning my soul. I made my decision before she even told me her desire. There's no way I'm refusing the opportunity to insert myself into her life at her request. But I'm enjoying this moment, her skin electric against mine. Only, it triggers more old memories—her lips on mine, mine on her bare skin, her screams of pleasure, her cries, my moans, her gaze on me hypnotizing as she unraveled... and so many more. I hope this is happening to her too, because it's a whole other brand of torture.

"I will help you."

I spin her in another pirouette, before I bring her back into my body.

"What am I trading for this dangerous pact?" she asks.

"What are you willing to give?" I'm testing her. She may be making a deal with the devil, but by God, I'll take as little as possible just to make sure this pact will be sealed. But what I want... that's a whole other thing.

She drops her gaze and turns her head to the side.

"I—"

"You," I interrupt.

Her gaze whips back to me. She tenses, and I can see in the flicker of her gaze the hope that more will follow that one single word... a complete sentence, maybe. She'll be waiting for something that will never come.

Her steps don't falter, though. They follow my lead to the music.

"Give me your trust and patience... for now. Before I can get rid of Holt, I need something from him. I will give you what you want, you have my word."

She narrows her eyes, lips parting, but I interrupt and dip her, leaning over, with my lips next to her ear and my breath brushing against it.

"For now..." she whispers back. "What about later? After you got what you wanted and made me wait."

I straighten, pulling her with me as I hold her cunning, green gaze. So many things I want from her, but none I'm willing to take unless they're willingly offered. I need her to give herself to me.

"Deal," she says with a shake of her head aimed at herself, interrupting her own doubts.

Fuck. No one in their right mind would make a deal with me without knowing the terms. If I'm her only choice at survival, it says more than it should.

"You need to know that what I want from Holt might not be owned by him alone. Your father is involved now." The flesh between my eyebrows tenses as I await some sort of surprised reaction, only she doesn't move a muscle. I suspect by the end of it all, Holt will not be the only one paying, and she doesn't seem to mind.

"You may be The Serpent, but my choice is between losing everything to them, or losing something to you." She's desperate, agreeing on incomplete conditions.

Nodding once, I reluctantly pull my hand away from the small of her back, and spin her one last time, her feet kicking stones through the crossroads. When she stops, her palm is in mine, my index finger on her quickening pulse, and I keep my gaze on hers as I lightly press my lips on the top of her hand. A faint vibration passes through her tense flesh, and it goes straight through mine, warming me with her fire.

"It's a deal... Little Eve." I flash a faint, wicked grin as she narrows her eyes, and I don't miss the goose bumps that flare on her skin. But I let go of her anyway.

If I'm The Serpent, then this covenant is the forbidden fruit, and this forest is our Eden.

I take one last look at the fire in her eyes, then skip back into a jog, leaving her behind as I continue my trail through the dark forest.

Morrigan-fucking-O'Rourke just made a deal with The Serpent at some crossroads in the middle of the forest.

How fucking poetic.

This must be my lucky day.

CHAPTER 9
Morrigan

"JESUS, YOU SCARED me, woman. I don't think I'll ever get used to you wearing that wig." Lulu sits back in the desk chair, a little rattled from my sudden presence in the office, as I pull off the mask. "I thought you couldn't come tonight."

"I managed to escape another grueling, show-off dinner. He got a call. I'm telling you, it's harder and harder to get away from him." I crash onto the sofa, resisting the urge to rub a hand over my freshly made-up face.

I didn't need to draw the inky cat eye on my lid, or roll the mascara over my eyelashes, but sometimes the makeup serves as a switch to a different version of myself. A better one at times. Not the one that seems to have lost all levels of courage, or self-respect, in Ryan's presence.

"Did he do something?" Lulu leans over the desk, narrowing her eyes.

"Not really. At this point, I'm sure he has a mistress. Wait. Is it a mistress if I'm thankful for it?"

"Probably not." She leans back into the chair. "So he didn't..."

"Not more than the usual slimy touches, grabbing my ass, my jaw..." There's more, but I don't burden her with the rest.

Luckily, he seems to take out any sexual tension he may hold on someone else. It doesn't make me feel less like a victim, though. And I hate this so fucking much... the idea of being a victim, because a little voice in my head tells me I'm not worthy of the title.

I have to hold on. I know The Serpent is on it, even though I haven't seen the bastard since the crossroads. But I have to trust him. I know this game is too complex for the results to be immediate. As much as I would love for him to just shoot Ryan and throw him in the middle of the ocean, we have to be smart about this.

"I just..." Lulu huffs. "I don't know how you do it, Morri. I don't get it. How can you take it? You're not yourself with him, at least I don't recognize you. Do you? You are a fucking force of nature, yet next to him, you're barely a broken leaf carried around by a breeze. How is he doing it?"

Fuck... I wish I could explain in a way that doesn't make me sound as if I'm wallowing in self-pity. Sometimes I can't make sense of it either. His words cut. The threats, the degradation, unworthiness... constant waves of it. Like I'm floating in the middle of the sea and his rough waters bash me, over and over, with no time to breathe. I can't explain, can't make sense of it.

I do have one suspicion, though. A secret I've been holding for years, one that only Ryan is privy to. He hasn't held it against me outright, but I still feel like that's what's happening. I don't think Lulu will look at me the same way when she finds out about it... what I've done. Her, The Sanctum, this club, are the only things keeping me afloat. Everything else is just internal pain that causes a numbness I cannot shake.

"I don't want you involved, Lu. The less you know, the better. I love you too much to bring you in the middle of this. But it's being handled."

"By The Sanctum." She crosses her arms over her deep cleavage. She wears a tank top made of thin chain-link, and I can't tell if there's anything underneath covering her boobs.

"By The Sanctum," I confirm.

"You made a fucking deal with the devil, Morri, and I fear you've sold your soul to him. Yet another man taking something from you. The Serpent, The Sanctum, they don't give anything away for free."

I laugh, because this is just fitting. "We've come full circle—this isn't the first time he took something from me, and he was the first ever to do so."

"You're right. You were such different people back then that I forget it happened. It's quite interesting how he suddenly appeared back into your life... when you needed him most."

Funny... yeah. I've been thinking the same thing. The timing is impeccable.

"I'm not gonna complain, he's useful now. Just... please, as I said before, do not whisper a word of this to Luke. No one can know of my involvement with *him*. It could ruin everything."

Lulu nods, bracing herself against the desk. "You have my word." She rises and I notice the chain-link is actually a dress, the hem right under her ass.

"Jesus, doesn't your ass hurt when you sit?"

"Not gonna lie, it wasn't meant for sitting. Wanna get a drink? Watch a show?" she asks as she winces, offering me her hand.

"Yes to both."

"Let me see you!" She steps back, running her gaze over the see-through circle dress that covers a lingerie set made more of straps than fabric. The panties rise in a V to my waist while the biggest piece of fabric of the bra covers only my nipples. "Morri, you look like you want to play tonight!"

I'm quite exposed, I know... fairly unusual for me. Plus, I never wear dresses this short, or this transparent.

"Nah, you know me, I love watching much, much more," I say with a wink, watching her checks flush. "If I ever find the right person, maybe I will test out the equipment, but the chances are slim to none. Either way, this club is not for me, it's for them."

"Fair enough. Come on, let's find something good to drink, and something better to drool over."

* * *

We've spent some time observing the patrons, taking care of some business, watching the girls dance, and two couples engage up on the stage. I can't suppress the unbelievable pride I feel when I see how comfortable and at ease our members are. This is why I worked my ass off with countless sleepless nights doing my freelance design work, after the part-time job, and university courses. This is why I want to fight back, not run. Metamorphosis is my future—our future—and he doesn't get to take it away from me.

A crowd gathered by one of the playroom windows catches my attention, as a moody song fills the air, sending a shiver down my spine. I signal Lulu toward the playrooms, making our way through the crowd, and the sight greeting us behind that window forces me to steady myself against the bottom of the window frame.

Fuck...

I feel Lulu's gaze on me, the same stunned expression most likely plastered over her face as well, but I can't look away.

A dark green mask covers the eyes of the woman hanging from the ceiling hook, by the restraint that ties her hands together. Her legs are spread wide, heeled feet barely touching the ground as she stands over a triangle-frame bench that's maybe a couple of inches in width at the top. These are used for a specific type of pussy teasing, but they usually have a narrower piece laid on top, which has been removed this time. Instead, between the black-haired women's spread legs, sits a dildo. A very thick, violent looking, monster-type dildo that's definitely inspired by hentai porn or monster romance novels, and the tip of it is buried inside of her.

Behind her, one of the hottest men I've ever seen paddles her ass in controlled hits. The man wears a disheveled white shirt, a few buttons opened at the top and at the bottom, tattoos running up to his neck peeking through, and black slacks. He looks like he swims every single fucking day, his shoulders wide, his body taught without being bulky, and he wears a black mask with glossy thin patterns on it. His tattoos would make him recognizable, but if he's willing to show them here, I have a feeling it's not something he does often.

They look so in sync, her trembles anticipating the hits, eyes sodden with ecstasy, and his attention on her is mesmerizing. I'm not sure if they chose to see the crowd on the other side of the window, or if it's their reflection staring back at them. But her eyes are aimed low, probably at the reflection of the girth she squeezes her dripping wet pussy around, and I think I can guess it's the mirror.

When the paddle slaps against her skin once more, we can hear the impact through the microphone they turned on inside. His technique is impeccable—he hits hard but pulls back at the same moment it makes contact, so not to push her over, slapping, rather than hitting. I can actually see the flesh of her perfectly shaved pussy squeezing around the thick toy. I can see the moment it just about pushes her over the edge as she struggles through that pleasure and pain.

"Remember, do not dare come." We just about hear his deep voice through the microphone, mixing with the music of the club.

"Ye—yes, Sir." Her flexed thighs tremble, and I realize she's keeping herself from impaling her pussy, not because she fears the monster-dildo, but because she'll come if she does.

A strange energy surrounds me suddenly. Tiny prickles cover my back, pouring in wave after wave over my skin, and I roll my neck, absorbing it into my body. There's a lot of people around me, so the breath that touches the top of my shoulder as my hair falls to the side doesn't surprise me.

Yet it does entice me.

He hits her again, and again... tears fall from under her mask as she bites her lips, and my pussy tightens on a long shiver as my fingers dig into the window frame. Again, the slap of the wood on skin makes her grip the rope above her head, and the muscles of her arms flex hard when she struggles to pull herself up. As her legs tremble, my pussy clenches.

The man moves to her side, his back to us as he brings the paddle down on her breasts, and her mouth falls open on a silent scream just as she comes down farther onto the dildo. Female voices gasp somewhere behind me, and I whip my head around out of instinct. It causes me to lose my balance and sends me straight into the man standing behind me. My shoulders press against his chest and my ass right onto his obviously hard cock. I gasp, catching a glimpse of him as his gaze falls on my profile, and he wraps his hand around my upper arm to steady me. The contact is fucking electric. Lightning searing through flesh and muscle, and a deep, primal craving grows within me, fed by the image of the couple behind the glass.

But he steadies me, gently pushing me away, and I can no longer feel his chest, nor his cock. Yet, his hand is still wrapped around my bicep, and I don't dare turn to look up at his mask-covered face. I don't want to. Instead, I turn my attention back to the playroom.

When the paddle reaches the skin of her ass again, the stranger squeezes my arm ever so slightly, and the woman drops her head to the side, her eyes rolling to the back of her head for a split second before they come back. There's a lost look in them, filled with pleasure and pain, an ecstasy she's lost control of, now held by her lover. He ghosts his palm over her cheek, his thumb swiping over her lips, almost like he's discreetly checking on her, before it drops to her throat and grips possessively.

"Look at me," he orders.

And she does. In an instant. The look in her eyes is still lost, but he assesses her, rubs his thumb over her pulse, then dips in and touches his lips to her cheek. She smiles, her lips slightly parted, and just like that, his hand goes to one breast, squeezing her nipple before the paddle hits her clit on a sharp note.

I can't help it, a moan escapes my lips as my muscles tense, and I'm suddenly more aware of the stranger's grip on me. Or maybe he just squeezed harder, I can't tell.

Someone touches my hand and when I look over to my right, Lulu signals me to Luke, who now stands next to her—I forgot she was here. She points in the direction of the office, asking me if I'm okay here, and doesn't leave until I smile and nod. Then I'm left on my own, and a couple takes her place, embracing as they watch the scene unfold before them.

But I'm not alone, am I? As that paddle makes contact with one of her breasts, I feel *his* breath on my shoulder, and I can't help but roll my neck as goose bumps snake over my skin.

My gaze follows the man as he walks behind her, his eyes on the mirror, watching her, but God... it feels as if he's watching all of us. He reaches in front of her, sliding his fingers through the wetness she drips onto the dildo, before he pulls away, and his hand disappears between them. Her mouth falls open on a hitched breath, eyes wide as her body stills, and suddenly I realize where those fingers disappeared, and I can't help but gasp softly.

I don't notice the stranger's front against my back until his hand grips my hip, steadying me once more as my body leans into him. His grasp is tight, yet I have a feeling that if I decide to move away, he will let me go. But I'm not going anywhere. I'm too enthralled in the way the man before me denies the woman's orgasm. In the way she skirts just on the edge of it and pushes herself to live in that permanent state of torturous ecstasy, without the knowledge of when the denial will end. She cries, she screams, she moans... and I moan right along with her.

The man who holds me pushes a little closer against me, and only now do I realize the slight reluctance he held in his body until this moment. The purpose of his grip on my arm wasn't just to steady me, but to keep me away too.

Not anymore.

With each thrust of the man's fingers in her ass, my body jolts with ecstasy and the stranger's fingers flex on my hip. I fail to control myself any longer, and my head falls against his shoulder. But when his hand glides onto the curve of my ass, my body thrums with such sweet anticipation. The man slaps the paddle against her flesh, finger-fucking her as my stranger's hand reaches under my short dress and grips my ass cheek with a firmness that makes me quiver.

I don't stop him.

I don't want to.

I don't even want to look at him.

I'm curious, but why break this spell?

I've never done this before. I engaged in some closed curtain play back in Rosston, but here, where so many people know me, it's different. Especially since I might be doing this with someone who might not be a stranger at all. The masks hold an eerie power in a moment like this.

He could be a friend.

Or an enemy.

He could be anyone.

My knees almost give out at the excitement of those thoughts.

His hand continues this gentle kneading of my ass on the same rhythm of the couple playing behind the glass, and I want to cry and beg him to do more, when his fingers snake closer between my cheeks. The adrenaline rises through my lungs when he dips lower, touching the sensitive skin beneath my ass cheeks, and brushes slowly toward my center.

It happens fast and in slow motion altogether—the paddle swats over her pussy on a strained moan, and my stranger's fingers dip between my legs, slide under my panties, and push inside of me on a brutal thrust. Too late I swallow down a scream as he presses his free hand on my chest to hold me against him. But I can't swallow the moan that sneaked its way out of me. I can only brace myself against the window frame as he continues to thrust in and out on the same rhythm as the man before us. They're looking into the mirror, as we watch them, and it's all kinds of incredible. I feel an achy stretch when he pushes in another digit, just as the rhythm picks up. He's harsher now, and my knees grow weaker with each assault, his hand on my chest feeling like fire on my flesh. I fix my gaze on the couple, only to brace myself and not fall to my damn knees.

I have a burning need to push onto his fingers, onto him, ride him. I—I want...

"More..." I whisper on a ragged moan.

Just when I think he did not hear me, my pussy stretches with the push of another finger, my lips curling inward as I bite back a screech.

It's so much... fuck... too much!

But it isn't at all. It's fucking perfect.

He holds me tighter as my legs shake, the tips of my fingers pained as my grip on the window frame tightens, and my body is dying to do anything but stand right now. Only, he thrusts harder, making me jolt with every brutal movement, and I'm floating on the precipice of a cliff... just there... at the edge. My whole entire being craves to dive into the abyss, into the unknown, into the filthy promise of ecstasy.

"Touch yourself." A whisper brushes against my ear, so soft I'm not even sure if it came from him or from the inside of my mind.

I comply either way, without even bothering to gaze around and check if anyone is watching. I slide my hand over the front of my dress, lifting the hem enough that I can reach inside my panties, and go straight to that swollen bundle of nerves that aches for attention.

The moment the pads of my fingers touch that sensitive flesh, it spreads a current through every single part of my body, every muscle shaking at the contact, and I'm sure that any moment now I'm going to implode.

Suddenly, the man before me throws the paddle on the floor, pulls his cock out of his pants, and at the same time he presses his fingers onto her clit, he thrusts into her ass on her wanton moans. He whispers something into her ear, and she smiles through messy tears, sliding farther down onto the dildo on a crazed cry. My stranger finger-fucks me harder, faster, spreading those three fingers and rubbing against parts of me I had no fucking clue existed. I watch as she looks into the mirror, right in my direction, and comes so fucking hard and fast everything shakes—her body, the bench, the toy, his own body too... And so do I.

I come on the stranger's fingers, on trembling legs and swallowed moans, as he drags them slowly through my orgasm, and for a moment there, I could have sworn I hear him moan, too.

I'm lost... my eyes closed as I lean against the stranger, and his hand on my chest glides just under my throat, holding me still when his fingers leave my drenched pussy. I feel that loss much deeper than I should, deep enough that my soul wants it all over again. It needs it. The release, this reality that should be mine in its entirety, not whatever the fuck I'm living outside of this club. This... this was incredible. Exactly what I needed without even asking for it.

I open my eyes to see the woman before me being released from the man's tight hold, and I don't even know when she left the narrow bench. Or when she ended up in his arms, smiling. Another minute passes and he walks her to the door and opens it for her. As they pass through, I still when his eyes land straight on me and the man I'm leaning against. I could be mistaken, but even behind that mask, they sparkle and hold my gaze.

My eyes flicker between the room and him, but then I catch the woman's gaze behind her simple pink mask—she's looking straight at me too.

Wait...

He nods, and she smiles.

Jesus fuck!

Was the mirror off? Were they watching me—us—all along?

Heat rushes to my cheeks at the knowledge that I engaged in some sort of fetish without intention. Yes, the people around us could have been watching us too, but this feels different. The couple watched me as he held me, as he finger-fucked me, as I rubbed my clit right in front of them, staring at them. Her and I... we came while looking into each other's eyes, and there's something so dirty and satisfying about that.

I slowly turn around and the stranger releases me. He moves away just as I catch a glimpse of his black mask, thin green accents decorating it, but I lose him through the darkness.

Holy fuck.

Watching a show behind this glass will never be the same.

CHAPTER 10
Vincent

THE BUSY RESTAURANT is filled with a constant stream of noise—music, chatter, clinking of plates and cutlery. Some days, I enjoy this switch from the ever-calm atmosphere of Midnight.

"Evening." Carter pulls a chair, distracted for a second by the waiter carrying a couple of plates of what smells like a very delicious steak. He sits across from me, taking off his sunglasses, and revealing tired eyes.

"Have fun last night?" I smirk, knowing full well the extents of his activities.

A shallow grin quirks his lips.

"Quite, yes. What about you?" He rests his elbows on the table, intertwining his fingers as he leans in.

"It was certainly interesting." I grab the bottle of wine and fill our glasses.

Before I continue, I catch movement in the corner of my eye.

"—maybe it's time to collect." Finn's voice reaches me before I turn in his direction. He takes a seat next to Carter, and Madds shows up beside me a second later.

"Collect what?" I ask.

Finn leans in. "You made a deal with the O'Rourke girl. You didn't consult with us, and we're supposed to save her? We're supposed to get involved between O'Rourke, Holt, The Ghost, and who knows who the fuck else, so she doesn't get married to that asshole? Why? And more importantly... for what?" he rants almost in a whisper.

"Christ, you can hold a grudge. It's been a month. Get over it already," Madds says, rolling his eyes as he signals the waiter.

"No. Because I want to know exactly how this will affect us, our business... our lives. Especially since you bargained for nothing."

Oh, I bargained for something alright, only it's not for The Sanctum's benefit.

"I admit it, this one was more for me than us."

But I remember a time, long ago, when The Sanctum put everything on hold for Finn and his brother. The purpose was the same—women. I can't remind him of that, though, not when his happy ending was ripped away, and he refuses to even speak of or acknowledge Ronan's existence.

"Our deals are usually much more calculated than this," Finn continues.

"You're right," I say, turning to Carter.

He's the calculated one, the one who coordinates and plans. With his hacker team, he has a huge advantage over us all, but even without, he's a goddamn wealth of knowledge. I know without asking that the man started writing the formula on the board long before I made the deal with Morrigan, because he doesn't shift unless he knows at least the next three moves. Being calculated is a deep-set need, not just a desire, for him.

"That's why we need to shake hands with Holt and O'Rourke on this business," I continue.

"What? That makes no sense. I'm talking about one problem, and your answer is introducing another one." Finn leans back in his chair, dragging a hand over his face.

"It's the only thing that makes sense." Carter shrugs as his gaze roves between all of us, like that conclusion is the most logical one in the world and he doesn't understand why no one else sees it. "There's a reason O'Rourke was so keen to hand over his daughter to his new business partner. This arrangement is new. It wasn't part of the one he was making with Holt Sr., and we need to find out why. The logical explanation is that Holt has something O'Rourke really wants, or maybe their deal is much more ambitious and needed further payment."

He picks up his glass and takes a polite sip as he glances around the busy restaurant floor.

Finn huffs from his chair, shaking his head. "I hate it when you make so much fucking sense."

"I know." There's no smugness in Carter's eyes. Only logical self-awareness. "They've arrived, by the way."

I hum my acknowledgment. I caught a glimpse of Liam O'Rourke taking a seat on the other side of the restaurant.

"O'Rourke is the type of man who loves the limelight. And he certainly enjoys people knowing that he's associated with us in some way. So I thought we would shake on the deal in public. Give his ego a boost. It will bring him closer to us, and we need him fucking close. What do you all think?"

They all nod without hesitation.

This is how it works with us, how it's always been. We pick a direction together, we move together, and we lead together. We learned young that we move on the same tune, and we were smart enough to understand that the song shouldn't be disrupted. We don't always agree, we challenge each other, and debate the best course of action, but in the end, we make all decisions together.

Except with her... but then again, Morrigan O'Rourke is not a business deal.

"Hello, gentlemen."

"Jasmine, Roxanne. Glad you could join us. Please, sit." Finn points to the empty chair next to me, then makes Carter scoot so Roxanne can sit next to him.

"How are you, darling?" I smile at Jasmine and kiss her cheek.

I don't miss the stolen glances from most of the men from the restaurant, and some of the women. This is the exact reason why we brought them here. Both brunette, with shiny, wavy hair framing their slim and chiseled cheeks and plump lips, both leaving enough to the imagination in their tight, yet fairly conservative dresses.

"Very well, thank you. Am I your date for the evening?" she asks politely.

"You are." I nod as she gives me her sexiest smile. She plays her role well.

We asked Katya to send two girls, because our plan is to get involved with Holt and O'Rourke from all fronts. We have our team of hackers, our vault of secrets, but most men forget themselves around the right women. And we have the right women right here.

"And whose attention am I catching?" She throws an electric gaze around all the tables.

"You'll see soon."

"Perfect." She holds her glass and settles into her role as I pour her some wine.

Our game isn't prostitution, but an escort service with a set of skills specific to us. Our business deals in information—and so do they. They're high end, intelligent, strong, and their beauty distracts all who can afford to hire them. Katya is incredible at finding and recruiting people with the right skills and desires. She runs, trains, and takes care of them, but technically, Finn is the one in control of that part of the business. Just as Carter has the hackers and Madds, the fight club.

However, even Finn doesn't stand in Katya's path. She's the only one who knows exactly what should go into the training and how to take care of the escorts. She's been doing it for so many years, before we took her under our wing. The older Hennessey brother, who was part of our syndicate before we even called ourselves The Sanctum, met Katya when she was running this service on her own. It wasn't at this scale. She needed help to do exactly what she wanted. So we absorbed her business into our world, adapted it to fit our *mission*, and helped her make it better. But it's her advice we take when we make any decisions regarding the escort service. Her background is unlike ours, brutal in a specific way, as she was trained as an asset to her country. Her knowledge has been invaluable to our operation and the girls interested in it.

They're not like normal escorts, with one simple goal in mind and a clear path to get there. These women crave a level of control that they can only obtain through the risks they take and the power they wield. They're here to get under people's skin and extract just the right information. Their beauty and brains work in tandem, proving to be an irresistible weapon.

Katya, or Miss Ekaterina, as they call her, knows exactly how to harness these talents.

I catch Finn's eyes flickering to me, some distaste lingering. I'm not sure if this is personal, or if he's projecting. Only one other time did women get involved in our business, and it didn't end well for him.

"I want to make something clear about Morrigan O'Rourke—this was not *our* deal." I look at Finn in particular. "It was mine. But as it happens, she's one of the cards in a game we're interested in learning, and she may be useful."

Finn narrows his eyes on me, takes one deep breath, and nods on an exhale. He seems to accept the predicament.

But it's Carter who pulls my attention with a sly smile in his eyes. "She's here too."

My gaze whips to their table in a heartbeat, fully struggling to be inconspicuous in front of the others. Only, I forget all about that when I meet the surprised gaze of one impossibly beautiful redhead.

I didn't know she'd be here.

She struggles to be inconspicuous too. Especially when I feel a slender arm wrap around mine, and some words I can't focus on are whispered in my ear. Morrigan's eyes darken, and she frowns as she scrutinizes the woman next to me.

Am I seeing what I think I'm seeing?

My line of sight is quickly cut off. "What may I get you this evening? Would you like to start with an appetizer?"

I mentally curse the waiter, and we order quickly, adding another bottle of wine to the bill.

"I thought you guys wouldn't touch alcohol after last night."

I turn to Madds at his words, a grin on his lips aimed at Carter and me.

"It's not that kind of club. There are much better ways to quench your thirst there," I say, winking at Carter, who smirks at me.

"Yes, much more satisfying."

"You should come next time, Madds. Even just for a drink."

"I don't think it's my scene." He turns his attention back to the O'Rourke table on the far side of the restaurant, dismissing the whole thing.

"I think it's exactly the scene you need once in a while. Your only hobby these days is fighting in that ring... you need some diversity," Finn chimes in.

"I'm sure there's a particular blonde who wouldn't mind visiting Metamorphosis with you." Roxanne winks as she lazily brushes her long fingernails over Finn's bicep, clearly referring to one of the girls who has a thing for him.

"Should we go give Liam the news?" Madds halts the entire conversation, clearly done with the fetish club subject.

"No, not yet," Carter responds.

When I look back at the table, O'Rourke's gaze is on me, a different brand of surprise in his eyes. I lift my glass, nodding to him, and he returns the gesture. Holt turns to me too, but I ignore him on principle.

"He knows we're here. He either comes to us himself, or waits for our convenience," I tell them.

He better wait, because I see a flicker of a red dress on my Eve, and I would very much like to see up close how it looks on her pale skin. I want to find out if it matches her hair, if it brings out her eyes.

But most of all, I left her in the dark since we made the pact, and I want to see if she's squirming.

* * *

As we walk across the restaurant, the people who know who we are can't help but steal glances. Men straighten and nod their hellos to us, while women can't bat their eyelids any faster. We attract their attention in a whole other way.

I glance at Carter, who walks next to me, and find it fascinating how oblivious he is to their attention. He seems like it anyway. He has a unique vibe—well-groomed and put together with his undercut, slicked-back hair, and expensive waistcoats, but his gaze is so sharp it feels like it slices you from the inside out. Yet as terrified as women are of his predatory vibe, they're attracted to him at an almost hypnotic level. But the man has a special kind of tunnel vision, because the moment someone truly catches his eye, he is so hyper-focused, he becomes relentless.

We stop at one of the tables, where an acquaintance greets us, and Carter speaks to him as his wife's eyes flicker to our table, where Finn and Madds still sit.

Finn is quite different from Carter; from any of us, really. He would bury himself in pussy if he could. He's rarely seen multiple times with the same woman, and he makes sure his arrangements are so strict, he doesn't even allow them to pine for him. Seven years ago, he was willing to lose everything to fight for the right woman, but that Finn died with her. Now, I think he relies on tourists to get a good fuck, because there's no way he hasn't gone through every pussy in this city by now. And I'm pretty sure Katya forbade him from using the women employed by our escort service, because I know for a fact he hasn't fucked any of them.

Then there's our resident beast—Madds. He's had women over the years, flings mostly, but no long relationships. None seemed to keep him interested. He comes across as broody and hard to get, which obviously makes women pile up to him. Add on his huge, intimidating frame, scarred face, and... *big hands*, and you've got yourself an irresistible concoction. He's selective, though, and never dives in.

We leave the couple behind and continue on our way to the O'Rourke table, my fingers tingling with anticipation. They're sitting at a corner booth table, the daughter and wife with their backs to us, Holt and Cillian O'Rourke on the opposite side, while the head of the family took his rightful place at the head of the table on the sofa.

The neat waves of red hair fall over the back of her chair, and almost like she feels us coming, she turns to look over her shoulder, but stalls at the last moment. She's still for a second longer, before she turns back, just as we stop behind her chair.

"Good evening. Pleasure to see you here," I greet them, swiping our gazes over everyone at the table.

I can't miss how her shoulders tense at my voice, yet she makes no attempt to turn to greet me, let alone look at me. Though, when Carter speaks, she leans back slightly so she can see him. That heats my blood a little more than I'm comfortable with.

"How are you all this evening?" His charm rubs off on Sheila O'Rourke in an instant, her smile shy as she greets us.

He's a man of few words, yet he likes these interactions. They give him a level of control he feeds off of.

"Gentlemen. It's been a while." There's a tinge of entitlement in O'Rourke's voice.

We made him wait, and apparently, he's been sweating for some news. He knew what he wanted required patience and planning. Yet he still couldn't control his impatient nature. The Ghost told us he's been trying to find other ways to get to him, which he, of course, ignored. But that was one of the reasons we decided to let him wait longer than necessary. This is on our terms, not his, and he needs to understand who is in control.

"It has indeed. Work has been keeping us quite busy," Carter says, giving him an insinuating smile. "Some deals are more time-consuming, and we tend to retire until we are satisfied they are successful."

At that, Morrigan turns to look up at me for a couple of seconds, her gaze leveled, but her thoughts are clear in her eyes. I slide my hand on the back of the chair, under her hair, enjoying the way her muscles flex as she pulls her shoulders back gently. The table is oblivious since Carter and I flank her, and all eyes are on him as he continues the conversation. I, however, tune out, my gaze lazily moving between them, wherever I see lips moving, but my focus is solely on the woman before me.

She smells of the evening primrose that grows around my property—sweet, yet when the rain hits, a woodsy, spicy aroma envelops you. She smells as if she laid there in the rays of the setting sun during a wild summer storm, and I find myself craving to be right there with her. It's strange, but this scent awakens a recent memory I can't pinpoint. I can almost taste it, feel the pressure of it in my chest, and damn... it tastes good.

My thumb moves from the backrest of the chair, brushing over the skin of her back that suddenly loses its softness, bursting in goose bumps. She's tense, yet utterly and completely nonchalant, like nothing's happening. Like the devil isn't on her shoulder. Like The Serpent isn't brushing against her skin, enticing her with his touch.

The conversation Carter carries lives somewhere in the back of my mind, because the main sound that fills my ears is one that I can't actually hear. It's what I imagine the slow brush of my skin against hers sounds like. Back and forth... a soft abrasion, as I think of her lying on her stomach in my bed, my head on her shoulder, as I drag a finger across her spine. A minute passes, maybe two, maybe more, and the goose bumps and tenseness in her flesh have been replaced by smooth skin and enticing heat, as she all but leans into my touch.

I've been watching the men in the meantime. O'Rourke is nodding excessively, and Cillian's narrowed eyes are turning over each of Carter's words in his head, repeatedly, checking for traps or dishonesty. When I get to Holt, he's staring right at me.

I've met enough arrogant assholes to recognize the ones who try to hide it, hell, I'm probably one. Yet this motherfucker before me... his arrogance borderlines so hard on stupidity that I'm not entirely sure if it's already crossed the line. He's slumped, head leaned back, watching me with such boredom in his eyes. He's truly delusional, thinking that he's better than everyone here, and the sheer disrespect breeds this urge in me to pull out my gun and shoot him straight in the gut.

It gives me yet another reason to wonder what the hell Morrigan saw in him? I'm baffled, but then again, I wasn't there for their beginning. Maybe whatever she saw disappeared in the meantime. I've certainly heard that story before. And it hits close to home.

I need to find out why she hasn't left him yet.

Looking at Carter, I catch his gaze flicker down to the back of the chair, his expression utterly unchanged. He doesn't give anything away, but the way his pupils shrunk told me he knows exactly where my fingers lie.

"Yes," he says, answering the most important question of the night. "As expected, some negotiations will be in order, however the terms have been agreed."

"We are ready to move to the next phase," I say, dragging my stern gaze over all the men, as a grin forms on each of their faces. Satisfied. *Good*.

"We should return to our table. Our guests are waiting for us." Carter follows, an inuendo in his voice as he shakes hands with the man.

Morrigan snaps her head to me. Her eyes bore holes when they latch onto mine, but she returns it to her plate a moment later. The bastard mentioned *our guests* on purpose. But she reacted. How very interesting.

"It was *very* good seeing you. Enjoy the rest of your evening," the oldest O'Rourke says with a great big fucking smile, as I slowly slide my hand off of his daughter's skin.

I immediately miss the feel of it on the tips of my fingers. So I move away before they extend their hands to shake mine too. I can't have their touch taint the memory of her on me.

Do her family, or her fiancé, consider this behavior of hers normal? Or is her distaste giving us away? I wonder so many things about her. I wonder how she normally behaves with them. How she would be with me if I invited her to dinner. I wonder if it was her choice to wear that sleek red dress tonight. I wonder what she ate. Are garlic fries and a simple burger with far too many layers of pickles still her favorite foods?

I wonder how she's changed in all these years.

CHAPTER 11
Morrigan

WAS I HOLDING my breath the whole time?

My lungs spasm, burning as I force my breathing to stay even when air finally fills my lungs. But that burn only reminds me of what I'm missing. That touch ghosting over my skin... *left, right, left, right,* moving like a pendulum, yet painfully slow. It was hypnotic, willing me to keep a straight face before my family. Ryan especially.

Torture—it's the only way I can describe his searing fingers—torture. Because I never thought I would refer to his touch as that.

Ever again.

It came out of nowhere, disrupting my balance and perfectly crafted stoicism. It felt as if it was the first time... all over again.

"So we're in." The enthusiasm in Ryan's voice makes me want to roll my eyes.

"Yes, we are. We'll set up a meeting and discuss all the details. The wait was worth it." Father's voice sounds somewhere in the background, my mind distracted by the strange prickle running under my skin.

"Especially since none of the other sources amounted to anything. It was all wasted money. Fucking crooks."

I swallow a large gulp of wine as I listen to my *fiancé*. I knew The Serpent and his Sanctum made a deal with them, but he's already delivering. What about me? Every day that passes brings me closer to being permanently trapped with Ryan. Bile rises in my chest as I look at him, slowly burning its way up my throat, and I swallow it down with the rest of the wine. I could down three more and it still wouldn't help.

"Excuse me." Placing the glass on the table, I rise.

"Where are you going?"

You have to be kidding me.

I stare at him, with every intention of not answering. But I cave... "Ladies' room." I always fucking cave. Fucking asshole.

"Don't be long."

"I will be as long as I need to be." Before he can spout anymore bullshit at me, I turn, catching my dear brother's gaze.

He and I were never that close. Our four-year age gap separated us, and he never really took it upon himself to find out who his sister was. I tried, but he probably just saw me as his annoying little sister. I was a kid when he was in high school, then when I got older, he went to university. By the time he finished, it was my time to go away, and we never really synced. Holidays were not enough to maintain a close relationship. Yet, deep down, I hoped that he wasn't cut from the same cloth as my father. I thought he would defend me.

I was wrong.

I head straight to the bathroom as the words he spoke to me a couple of weeks back, run through my mind. *"We all have our roles to play, this one is yours. And I know you're strong enough to do it."*

Bastard!

I shouldn't have any need to be strong enough to do this! This *role* should not exist, dammit! I shouldn't have to make a deal with The Serpent to save myself! There should not have been a need for any of this! Family, fucking family should be on my side, not... a stranger.

But he's not really a stranger, is he? His touch lingers on my back. It tickles me still, making this whole night, this situation, just a smidge easier to handle. But it fills my head with memories of him naked in bed beside me, running his fingers over my bare back, as we lie spent.

As I hurry to the bathroom, the loud clicking of my high heels is absorbed by the music and background noise, and I'm visibly heaving now. I step behind the wall that conceals the corridor to the bathrooms, and suddenly the air turns cold, and I can't breathe anymore. From the other end of the corridor, The Serpent narrows his black eyes on me.

My steps falter only for a second before I carry on. And so does he.

I'm not sure if time slows down or we do, the milliseconds stretching between the moment my foot leaves the ground and the next one finds it again. My gaze is on that bathroom door, walking on the left as a lump forms in my throat, one I need to swallow badly. The fabric of the flowy knee-length dress brushes against my skin, spreading goose bumps all over, my nipples all of a sudden pained by the bra grazing against them.

My palms dampen as he gets closer, and when his body slowly passes by mine, the breeze his movement creates, makes my hair and dress flow and graze against my skin. But that's not what makes my whole body shiver... but the ghost of a touch as the backs of our hands brush against each other.

One simple touch. One of many more before it. Yet somehow... the sizzling energy of it makes it feel new.

I can finally breathe. The pressure in my chest eases, and I pat myself on the back for resisting the urge to look back before I stepped into the bathroom. I check all three stalls are empty, and finally manage to swallow that lump in my throat as I brace myself against the cold porcelain sink. But my lungs fill with the excessively perfumed air that somehow reminds me of Ryan and his house, and anger fills my veins. I wish this anger would be more prominent in his presence.

I drag my gaze over my reflection, sighing at its pathetic look.

Who am I with him?

How deep has he crawled under my skin? Bit by bit, he's ripped out pieces of me, then replaced the voids with this unsettling cowardice. No one, absolutely no one, makes me feel so unbelievably meek. The only comfort I have is that I'm only this way with him. As my eyelids begin to burn, the person looking back at me in the mirror becomes even more unrecognizable.

"Who are you?" I whisper at her.

"Vincent Sinclair."

I flinch as those words taint the air around me. Then I inhale deeply, letting them taint me as well.

My fingers ache, my grip brutal against the porcelain, and the burn in my eyes is gone. At the sight of him, those feelings from mere moments ago, dissipate, and the woman in the mirror looks more familiar. Her shoulders are pulled back, her chin higher, and the green in her eyes shines with a feral darkness. That darkness smiles back at me.

Now her, I recognize.

"You're risking an awful lot, *Serpent.*"

The man appears in the mirror in his expensive all-black outfit that fits him so well, tight against his pecs and strong shoulders. I bet it's tight against his nice ass too.

Christ, get a fucking grip, Morrigan.

But he doesn't answer. A ghost of a smirk brushes his cheeks, and I use that cockiness to fuel the anger I carry for this man.

"Someone could walk in. It could be my mother," I continue.

I don't know when this man noticed me again. Was it at my mother's party all those months ago? Was it on the street when I was with Ryan at that outdoor bar? At my surprise engagement? When did the devil's eyes become so focused on me?

He takes one step forward, and I cock my head at his reflection, noting the all too familiar shift in the air. I force myself to resist that dark gaze in the slits of his eyes, the one that penetrates deep, and makes most either freeze or tremble at the power he emanates. Only, that's not what I feel right now, but... the ghost of our touch out in the corridor. I feel his fingers brushing against my back as I sat at the table. I feel his lips against my ear as he whispered to me in the woods.

He steps behind me, invading my space, his front against my back, barely touching. Deep notes of bergamot and cedar cover the gaudy bathroom perfume, pulling me into a place I desperately wish to escape to. *The forest...*

His eyes trail over my features, following my pulse down my throat, to that soft spot between the neck and shoulder, and as my flesh explodes in an exhilarating shiver, I close my eyes, letting my head fall to the side.

I'm drowning in his proximity, and the moment warm air blows against my shoulder, my eyes dart open, and I straighten, the spell evident.

Fuck, what is this man doing to me?!

"I'm serious, dammit! What are you doing in here?!"

Suddenly, he swipes to the side the hair that lays against my neck, the tips of it tickling my skin and sending another betraying shiver down my spine.

"Stop it!" I turn on my heels and slap his hand away. "I don't know what you think you're doing, but I'm not it. This"—I point swiftly between us, finishing with my palm pressed hard against his chest, trying to push him away—"is a business transaction. If you think I'm giving myself in exchange for your help, you're sorely mistaken. I would rather die by my own hands than get trapped by another man again."

"Die by your own hands? Seems a bit radical," he says, pushing against my hand.

"Did you just confirm that you want *me* in exchange?" He better choose his next words carefully, or I swear to God...

I bring the other hand to his chest as well and shove him away. I'm heaving as I watch him take no more than two steps back, effortlessly, as if he allowed me to push him, my force barely affecting him.

"What makes you think that you would feel trapped with me? Is that how you feel with me now?" He cocks an eyebrow. The way that gaze molds his handsome features is fucking panty-melting, and I'm even more furious. More at myself than him, at my inability to suppress my attraction to him. But his non-answer unsettles me.

"This wheel doesn't go around, *Serpent*. It's broken. It cannot roll on the road that damaged it the first time around."

There's a flicker in his eyes, that charm cracking for a moment. I know he remembers our end, but I don't know if it affects him in any way.

"Broken wheels can be fixed, *Little Eve,* especially when there was no intention behind the damage." He takes a step closer, and I flinch on a hitched breath.

What the fuck is he talking about?

"No intention? You're taking this metaphor too far and you don't seem to understand the message—I. Don't. Want. You." I straighten my back, crossing my arms over my chest.

But as he takes another step, the fabric of his suit brushes against the hairs that stand on my arms, and I have to tighten them just a bit more. Just to hold myself together, and not make a liar out of myself.

"You only want my help." He pushes his hands in his pockets, cocking his head as he looks down at me.

He's a head taller, maybe a bit more. But I give him my best disdainful look from under my lashes and refuse to bend my head to look at him.

"I *need* your help." There's a difference.

He nods slowly as he straightens, and his hands leave his pockets. Then he moves and I stiffen. His chest presses against my crossed arms, pushing my body back as he leans forward and braces his palms on the marble on either side of me.

I'm out of air.

Entirely out of it, and a strange sizzle infiltrates my airways instead. It bends my will and turns my mind into this creature that I secretly wish to be. Because this creature craves him. Not just body, but soul and mind. The man before me bathes in this mysterious obscurity which my soul wants to touch... a delicious abyss it wants to be part of. It got a taste of it once.

As his head dips down, mine turns to the side, and his breath coasts over my shoulder. It's velvet against my skin. Soft and heavy. Warm. Too warm.

Until it's more than that.

Skin brushes against mine, and my chest rises on a long, heavy inhale. The air is not the only thing sizzling anymore—my whole body is too. His parted lips drag slowly along my shoulder, sensual and enthralling, catching me somewhere between intrigue and protest. He reaches that sensitive spot at the base of my neck, and when his tongue touches it, I cannot hide my sharp gasp.

I should push him away again. Tell him to stop. I know for a fact that he would. But my protests are trapped in the same throat his tongue drags over. My breasts are pained under the pressure of my arms, and I cannot resist the urge to tighten my thighs together, reveling in the faint burst of pleasure. When he reaches my ear, catching the soft lobe between his tongue and teeth, my body shudders on a slow exhale, the treachery seeping deeper into my flesh.

Then, he moves away.

He fucking moves away. Leaves me cold, breathless and... furious.

"And you don't *want* me." His tongue slithers slowly over each of those words.

Son of a bitch!

No! I fucking don't. He simply caught me off-guard.

"I *want* you to honor the pact. Help me get the fuck out of this situation."

He nods once in agreement, but the smirk is not yet wiped off his face, his arrogant ass infuriating me.

"Okay, so now that's fucking settled, what's the plan? I see you're keen to shake with my father and *fiancé*"—I don't miss the slight scrunch of his nose at my last word—"but not me."

"I thought we already shook."

"Technically, yet it's been a month and I'm still planning a fucking wedding!" My tone rises, and he takes a lazy look at the door.

"Careful..." he says on a low tone.

He returns his gaze to me, and I catch that subtle way in which he bites his lip, sending another shiver straight down to my fucking pussy.

"Serpent—"

"I told you I needed Holt and your father first. I'll send you a text in the next few days with a time and a place. We'll talk then."

With those words, he slips out the door, and I realize he doesn't have my number. I'm left with less knowledge than when I first came in here, if that's even possible.

But I have something else—hope.

Even with the memories of when I first lost it, sparking through my mind.

* * *

8 years ago

The moment I opened my eyes this morning the air felt different. Heavy. The pressure in the atmosphere is too high. Not even the sun's out today. It's the gloomiest of days, the clouds converging above our city like it's protecting us from the fucking joy in the world.

It's one of those days when the universe knows your fate, and it doesn't want to give you hope that it might be a good day. It's setting the scene for whatever demise awaits.

Could I avoid it?

No.

Because it will come tomorrow instead. Or the day after that. Or the one after. It will find me, eventually.

My movements are sluggish all through the morning, dragging out the moment I have to leave the house and face whatever pivotal moment awaits.

A knock sounds at the door when I'm finally dressed and ready for school.

"Yes?"

It cracks open, and Alex, my father's trusty driver, peeks through.

"Morning, Miss O'Rourke." I roll my eyes at the formality. The man has known me since I was ten. "We'll be late if we don't go now."

I sigh and grab my school bag, swinging it over my shoulder. One more year, and I'm fucking done with this damn school.

Following Alex through the house as we walk toward the garage, the pressure, the anticipation seems to settle somewhere in my stomach. It sits a bit too heavy in there. It makes me think of Cillian.

There's nothing wrong with Alex, but I miss doing this with my brother. Even though I'm not that sure he liked it as much. It's all we had, though, because Cillian and I have never really been close. I don't think either of us tried hard enough. Our four-year age gap contributed to that too. We were always out of sync.

Since he left for university, it got worse. I see him for the holidays and rare weekends. But even then, Father kidnaps him. He's going to be the heir to the O'Rourke Empire... whatever the fuck that means. He's being groomed for a takeover decades away, and he and I barely have a relationship. I would say it's because of it, but it's our own fault too.

So I cling to the memories of the drives to school. We used to bond then. I asked him about his plans, and he always deflected by asking about my bullies. Being ginger, with unruly curls, and a fat ass hasn't earned me any favors in school.

It doesn't matter now.

Since Cillian left, the bullying pretty much stopped. Not because he did anything about it, but because I did. Maybe being stuck with my controlling parents has something to do with it. Day by day, they add more kindling to the fiery beast growing inside of me.

I like to blame pent-up anger and frustration, but it's all me. A need for violence grows inside of me day by day, and sometimes it truly scares me. But I love it too, because those bitches who used to make my life hell, now run for their fucking lives. I caught their leader in the showers at the end of gym class and smashed her face against the tiles, breaking both her nose and her brow bone. Then I told her nicely that if she even dares to breathe in my direction ever again, I'll come into her room at night and kill her in her sleep. She seemed to believe me. Especially after I made her best friends pay too.

It's not the only reason I like this anger, though. Love it even. It brought me to him.

Vincent Sinclair, my boyfriend. He got his eyes on me during one of my rage episodes. He stopped me from going too far and killing the guy who intended to rape me. We've been together since, and he's the one who helped me manage this anger. He knew how it felt and spent years learning to control his.

But even thoughts of the man I love haven't helped me get through today's school day. Hour after uneventful hour passed, class after boring class, and nothing happened. Apart from the increasing weight in the pit of my stomach. It felt like the silence before the storm, and I kept looking out the window of each classroom I was in, half expecting to see someone there... watching me.

Then school ended, and still... nothing.

That weight shifted to my chest, even heavier than before, as I walked the twenty minutes to my contemporary dance class, in the old center of Queenscove. I kept looking behind me, wondering if someone was following me, or watching me. The hairs stood up on every inch of my body, but there was no one there.

The anxiety riddled me all through that class. The anticipation for whatever disaster the universe had in store for me, sat in my chest the whole way through.

Then it ended, and still... nothing. Fucking. Happened.

And Vincent didn't come to meet me either.

Our relationship is frowned upon. Being with someone four years older, who deals in some very questionable criminal activities, is not everyone's ideal. Naturally, this means my parents fucking hate him. So we pick moments like this to see each other without issues.

Meeting after my dance class has turned into a fairly regular thing. Sometimes he comes and watches me. Technically, no one is supposed to be there, but everyone, including our instructor, drools over the black-eyed devil. They definitely don't mind swaying their asses in front of him.

I do.

He's fucking mine.

But the whole time he's there, always leaning against a wall with his arms crossed, he's watching me. Sometimes I even forget it's a class and there are other people there... I dance for him.

He didn't text to tell me if he was coming today, but I guess I hoped that he was going to surprise me. Help me ease this goddamn tension, and break whatever spell the universe has me under.

I even went to the beach, to the spot we sometimes go to after dance. I waited there until the sun was catching fire at the horizon. But there was no sign of him.

That heaviness was sliding up from my stomach, lodging at the base of my throat, and I couldn't fucking take it anymore.

I took a taxi home, and I swear the clouds followed me there.

Not even a shower helped ease the invisible tension.

I felt like I was going goddamn crazy.

So I came to my only other happy place inside this house—the library. My parents don't ever come here unless they're organizing a party and want to brag about all the first editions they own, and never read. Not that they admit that to anyone. The huge room is on the opposite side of the mansion from the living rooms and kitchen, and because it's easily accessible from outside, this is where Vincent and I spend quite a bit of time. I feel like an idiot for having to sneak my adult boyfriend into my house. To say that I feel unworthy of him is an understatement.

Only, the man doesn't give a shit. At all.

When I walked in, the room was dark and silent. But I couldn't bear to deal with this tension in my bedroom. So I grabbed the horror novel I started a few days ago, snuggled on the sofa, and tried to get lost in the story.

But I drifted off with the image of Vincent in my mind, dreaming of our future. A life I never thought I would ever have, with a man I didn't dare think would love me.

When I wake up suddenly, startled by a creepy dream, I'm not sure how much time has passed. I'm completely submerged in darkness. But the moonlight streaming through the windows confirms I'm definitely not alone.

"Hi." His husky whisper is a caress over all my senses.

Vincent.

I swallow down the panic, only to find that the heaviness that has plagued me all day, is still fucking there.

Goddamnit! What is that?

"Vincent. What's happening? What time is it?" I ask.

"Late."

What the hell?

"Baby, wh—"

"Morrigan, we need to talk."

It's happening. His words work like a switch, sending that weight lodged in my throat, straight to my head. My temples throb with fear and bubbling anger.

"We need to talk, or... we need to talk?" I ask.

I'm fooling myself by pretending my question is necessary.

Now, I realize that I've expected this conversation since we had our first proper kiss. Even after we had sex for the first time—well, my first time. I've been expecting it for weeks, months. For the whole time we've been together. Everyone's jealousy over me, and my own fucking insecurities, fueled this belief that I'm somehow unworthy.

But this beautiful, sinful, incredible man fed my confidence. He treats me like the most precious thing in the world, even as he scares the shit out of other people. So, I relaxed, truly believing that he wants to be with me.

I dropped my goddamn guard, and I shouldn't have.

Because my heart doesn't know what to do right now. Pressure grows somewhere behind my ears, a ringing splits through them, and I brace myself for what I know is coming.

"I'm sorry, but—"

"Turn on the lights," I interrupt, my tone grave.

"What?"

"Turn on the fucking lights, Vincent. Do not dare do this without looking into my eyes." Heat sears the back of them as he stalks to the other side of the room and flicks the switch on.

The image of the man hits me like a punch in the gut. He's on his way to turning into a dark god. His eyes are the purest of obsidians, his chiseled jaw seems to get stronger month by month, and his body is turning into a work of fucking art.

He sighs as he takes me in. Only, he doesn't seem to be able to look at me for long. Either he's a coward, or he can't fucking bear it.

I rise from the sofa and move around the coffee table, standing a few feet away from him. I'm trembling, though. He hasn't said much, yet my soul is slowly pulling away from my body. He's my first love… he is everything. He is more than I thought he could be.

Everyone told me that what I'm feeling is just young love. The first obsession all people go through. And we feel like it's the end of the world when we eventually break up. Because no one ever stays with their first love.

But Vincent… his darkness speaks to mine. They have their own language and I stupidly thought we were different.

"Don't be a coward now, Vincent," I seethe at him.

His gaze shoots to mine and his viciousness shines. But something so much more dangerous flickers there… agony. It disappears before it can take form, and it makes me falter.

"I'm sorry, Morrigan, but I can't see you anymore."

"You fucking asshole!" I snap at him. "Why?"

"We just… can't be together anymore. Our worlds are too far apart from each other."

"Bullshit! You know as well as I do that's not true!" I shout at him, not caring who the fuck hears me in this house. Although everyone's probably asleep by now.

"It is. You don't see it now, but you will someday. When you'll be—"

"Don't you fucking dare say it."

"—older."

I shake my head, the tears that burned behind my eyes now falling over my cheeks. He knows how insecure I used to be about our age difference. The gap is small, but I felt like he would find nothing in common with me. He never gave a shit, though. He always said that I was his forbidden fruit and fit so very well in his Eden.

"You bastard," I whisper through the tears.

"I'm involved in things you shouldn't be close to. Our business is taking a shape someone like you shouldn't be aware of. And you need to finish school and go to university. Build something for yourself."

"Who are you?!" I see him speaking, but I swear those words make no sense coming from his mouth. "Because the Vincent I know would tear the fucking world apart to make room for me."

He drops his head, and the breath he inhales is so long and deep, he suddenly looks taller.

"There are many things you don't know, Morrigan. And it's better that you never will." He looks at me with a coldness I've only ever seen directed at other people. It takes me aback.

"Did y—did you ever actually love me?" My voice breaks, but the crack in my heart is harsher.

His gaze pins me with such intensity, I want to cry out.

"It's over."

Those words threaten to swipe the legs from under me, but I stay completely still, clenching my fists at my sides.

I can't find the words. And I can't seem to take my eyes off of him either.

I'm memorizing every line of his face, every strand of hair, every flicker of his eyes, imprinting them into my memory.

"You promised me the world," I cry out.

"This is the only way I can give it to you."

Jesus Christ, I never thought that imaginary pain could rip through me with such malice. My breath is stolen from me at the same time as whatever pumped lifeforce inside my chest bursts open, bleeding its feelings through my being.

"I love you..." I whisper, but it comes out as pleading.

For a moment, he parts his lips, and I think he's gonna say it back. But he closes his mouth and turns, his side to me.

"Goodbye, Morrigan."

Something cracks inside of me, fury and pain mix together, and I realize it's a whole other beast that's finding a home in my soul. Only he could breed that. No one else has this kind of power over me.

"I fucking hate you!" I shout after him. "I fucking hate you, Vincent Sinclair! I never asked for anything from you, but you insisted on giving it all. You gave me fucking hope, now you're ripping it away, and stealing my fucking heart too. I hate you."

He takes the slowest and deepest of breaths as he looks into my eyes, then he leaves for the last time.

* * *

Present

Throughout my life I learned that pain takes many shapes, but that was my first taste of the type of pain that shapes a person. Because it sticks to your being and grows into a beast that's almost impossible to control. Even if one day you manage to rip it out, its claw marks will remain.

CHAPTER 12
Vincent

THE UNEASINESS IN her green eyes is the first thing I notice as I rush out of the office at the sound of Madds' booming, urgent voice. I'm certain there's a quicker way for my brain to process what I'm seeing, only I haven't found it yet.

Morrigan is standing in the main area of Midnight—our *secret* bar. Fortunately, it's currently closed, but this is still confusing me.

With determined steps, I walk toward them, the look in Madds' eyes feral, but it's something more than anger that I see in them, and it concerns me.

"What the fuck?!" Finn rasps as he steps out behind me. "What the hell is she doing here?"

"Careful, brother..." I warn, and I swear I hear him hissing.

Carter rises from the sofa before we get to them, his eyes narrowed ever so slightly on us. There's barely any emotion on his features, but those tensed shoulders as he watches Madds and my Eve are hard to miss.

My... Eve.

When the fuck did that happen?!

The way she shadows that uneasiness from her bones with that cocky attitude that has gotten her into a fair amount of trouble in the past is fascinating. She's breathless though, cheeks flushed. Has she been running?

"What's going on?" My tone is low as I look between them.

"Tell him." Madds nods to her.

"My father... I don't know what it means." She swallows, catching her breath. "I don't have your number. It took me too long to find you."

"I found her rushing through the alleys, trying to find the entrance," Madds explains.

Carter suddenly appears with a glass of water for her. She downs half of it and carries on.

"I don't know what it means. I overheard a phone conversation. Maybe it was with Ryan, I don't know. He was angry. He said... umm... *He needs to be put back in his place! He's going after some bitch, Ekaterina or something."* At that last word, we exchange serious looks, and Finn pulls out his phone immediately.

"What else did he say?!" His finger hovers over the phone screen, eyes wide and lips tense.

"He said…"—she rubs her temples, squeezing her eyes shut for a few moments—*"I don't know who she is, but he thinks she's important to Sinclair, so he wants to mess with him."* For a split second, she fixes on me. *"Boseman will fucking ruin everything! He's your guy, rein him in."*

"Shit," Madds mutters.

"Fucking Boseman… Find Katya!" I almost rasp at Finn, who already has the phone to his ear. "Carter, we need to make sure they're all accounted for, and okay."

"We have to be inconspicuous," Madds interrupts. "We start rushing around now and we'll draw the wrong kind of attention to us, to the girls. At this moment, Boseman, O'Rourke, and Holt think Katya is your woman. We cannot let them know who she truly is to us, and how we're involved."

I sigh and nod. Carter agrees too, and Finn paces like a cornered animal, phone to his ear as he curses under his breath. Morrigan, though, she's breathing easier and quietly observes us all.

"Katya! Fuck, baby, where are you?!" Finn finally gets an answer on the other line. "Fine, I won't call you baby. Where the fuck are you?! … Okay, check in with all the girls, please. When you're done, call me. Lock your doors and windows, grab a gun, and wait for one of us. Okay? … I don't know yet. But… Yeah. Okay. See you soon." He hangs up and rushes to us. "She's home. She's fine. I'm going to—"

"No. Madds has a point. We'll attract attention if we start running around town now."

He stops, narrowing his dark blond eyebrows, the wheels spinning in his head as his gaze goes from confusion to understanding, and he nervously runs his fingers through his wavy hair.

"It should be you," Madds says to me. "If Boseman thinks you two are together, it won't look unnatural. Go. Bring her here. Take an unusual route, and make sure you're not followed."

"Okay." I turn on my heel and rush back into the direction of the office, but her voice suddenly makes me halt.

"Who is Ekaterina—to you all, I mean?"

We go silent. I look over my shoulder, catching the forest-green that looks back at me, strands of red caught on her freckled cheek.

"And… Boseman?" she adds.

I inhale one deep breath, the tension and urgency ripping at me, but she gives me the smallest of nods in understanding. With that, I turn on my heels and run to the hallway that leads to the back entrance.

"Maddox, stay with her!" I yell before disappearing through.

The sunset burns in shades of lavender, the humidity high in the air, and I inhale the warmth that lingers.

She came to warn us… even when she didn't know who against.

Morrigan

IF I WASN'T already clued in that they own this place, by the rumors and the fact that they're in here while it's closed, the scents of bergamot and cedar, lavender and... something else, something decadent, would definitely clue me in. This whole place smells like *him*. And the others too, but I can distinguish his scent the best.

The atmosphere is tense, but quiet, and since I'm not sure what to do after Maddox urges me to sit, I just swipe my gaze around. It looks like a giant, dark and decadent living room. I would imagine the Gryffindor common room looks something like this, which is surprising, since a serpent owns the place. Everything in here is made out of stained wood and vintage leather, from the mismatched chairs, sofas, and armchairs, to the coffee and dining tables. Even the low ceilings are split by rough wood beams. But the vintage, almost art-deco style bar, with the overly thick marble top and brass pump handles ties everything together. Right behind it, in the center of the wall, there is a gold décor piece made entirely of thin metal strips. Lines that form a starburst surround the shape of an eye, all inside a circle. It's stylized, in the same art-deco style, apart from the eye itself—that looks real. Too real. I swear it's looking at me.

I suddenly feel watched. Carter Pierce leans in, placing a glass of something in front of me on the coffee table, only my stern gaze is fixed on him. I may be coming from a point of assertion of my strength, but I'm also enthralled by the man. Everything about the way he looks and moves belongs perfectly in this space. Almost as if it's his world, and his world alone.

"Lavender Martini Vermouth, with a kick. It will calm your nerves," he says in a monotone, gravelly voice.

"My nerves are fine, thank you." I hold his strange gaze, a deeply saturated blue seeping into hazel, shadowed by thick long lashes.

But he holds mine too. It's a fight for power here, only I can't read the man. He's still, in an eerie kind of way. Different from The Serpent. Almost as if emotions are useless in his world... *Almost.*

"If you say so," he finally answers.

Just like this bar, the man has an old-world look about him, with his square, chiseled features, wearing suit trousers, a white textured shirt, and waistcoat. He nods, a slight quirk in his full lips, and I follow it up over the defined hollows of his cheeks, and strong, high cheekbones, to his effortlessly neat undercut, the longer hair on the top of his head slicked-back. It's those hollowed, high cheekbones that give me a dejá vu feeling, though.

Carter takes a seat on the sofa, next to a gorgeous specimen of a man—Finnigan Hennessey. Every girl I knew in school had a crush on him. Hell, every teacher too. He probably fucked half of them as well. He has this surfer-boy look about him, with slightly wild wavy, blond hair, and shoulders that could easily carry you if he threw you over them. He's a pretty boy through and through, but I bet he can throw a deadly punch.

"You came to tell us. I'm surprised," he states, one eyebrow cocked above his beautiful bright blue eyes, his lips straight.

"Was I supposed to keep the information to myself?" I finally look down at my drink, the violet concoction served in a martini glass, with a sugary rim, looking so appetizing. I take a sip and hum in approval as the sweet, boozy lavender hits my tongue. "Damn..."

"You're welcome." Carter watches me, a smirk shining only in his eyes.

"You owe us nothing." Finn ignores him.

He doesn't like me at all. Unless he's this bitchy and blunt with everyone he knows. Somehow, I doubt it. He strikes me like the kind of man who doesn't bother to put a filter on between what he thinks and says. I have a feeling Carter is very similar, although more calculated.

I can't help but sigh and roll my eyes. "You've been cooped up in this world of secrets, sins, and chaos, for long enough that you don't seem to recognize human decency anymore, do you? I'm sure The Serpent told you by now about our little deal. You think I can sit around and watch your world burn to the ground, when I was offered help to keep mine standing?"

Silence falls upon the room, the only sound is that of drinks being sipped.

"I recognize it just fine." He pauses, letting out a deep sigh. "Thank you."

Well, fuck.

"So who is Ekaterina to you?" I ask again, but once again, all they do is exchange looks. "Okay, who is Boseman, then?" Once more... nothing. "Oh, for fuck's sake, come on! She's part of the escort service, isn't she?" I rasp as I rise and look between the three men.

There's yet another round of exchanged looks, and considering their expressions, I wonder if The Serpent told them I know of the escort service.

"You think you're the only ones holding your secrets in your world, but—"

The memory hits me like a ton of bricks, and I fall back into the armchair, eyes wide, mouth open.

"Morrigan?" Maddox's heavy footsteps move toward me. "What is it?"

"I was wrong..."

"About what?! Morri, talk to me!" The warmth of his large hand wraps around my entire bicep.

"My brother. Fucking hell, how could I forget this? How did it skip my mind?!" I sigh, bracing my elbows over my knees, mumbling under my breath. "He's not on his side."

"You have to talk to us. What about Cillian?" Finn leans in.

I focus back on the room, the men's gazes impatient.

"A few months ago, maybe five or so, my mother asked me to take something to my brother's house. When I got there, he wasn't inside, but out in the pool. As I was walking through, I ran into his open laptop. He never leaves that thing unattended, but he wasn't expecting me, so he had no reason to put it away. Anyway, I managed to read quite a bit before I went to him, and it was all about you—The Sanctum. A roadmap of your businesses and connections. One of them was the escort service, and only now did I make the connection. How could I forget this?! Ekaterina's name was there—dead center. Only hers. She runs it, doesn't she?"

"Yes," Maddox responds.

"Might as well just give her our laptop passwords." Finn sighs, annoyed.

"No, you don't understand." I shake my head. "My brother knows who Ekaterina is to you all. This was months ago, yet my father had no idea over the phone today. None at all."

Then it clicks, for all of them.

"He's not on his side," Maddox says, sitting down.

"Then whose?" Finn asks.

Cillian's words run through my head again. *"We all have our roles to play, this one is yours. And I know you're strong enough to do it."*

"Hopefully mine."

CHAPTER 13
Morrigan

"DARLING, THERE YOU are." I'm frozen, squeezing the cold metal of the door handle, as my heart tries to weigh the consequences of my next move.

Darling. To many, it's a term of endearment. Once, it was one for me too. Not anymore, not coming from this man standing in the middle of my parents' foyer, head cocked as his muddy eyes study me.

"I've come to take you *home.*"

My body hasn't moved, but a burst of current splits me in a shudder at his words. I should have stayed with The Sanctum. I should have waited for The Serpent to return after he called Finn to tell us Ekaterina, or Katya, was safe, but I couldn't stay too long. I couldn't risk these people knowing I have any dealings with their underworld.

"I am home." The words crack as they tumble off my tongue.

"Don't be silly, darling. We're getting married. It's time you come and live with me."

I still haven't moved, my entire brain activity focused on how to get out of this. It's been a month and a half or so since the announcement, and I managed to avoid his advances. Only I suspect it wasn't due to my own efforts. With his attention pulled on establishing the new business, he's just been giving me slack. Now, as that shudder lingers, my knees slightly weaker, I'm not sure how to keep him away.

"No." I don't think I can convince anyone with that whisper. I'm definitely not convincing myself.

"What did you say?" He turns his head, ear toward me, one brow cocked.

"N—No." It comes out louder this time, and he draws back.

He takes one determined step in my direction, and I still on a hitched breath.

"What are you doing standing there with the door open? I'm trying to keep the humidity out and this house cool!" I have never been more thankful for my mother's annoyingly high-pitched scolding voice.

I take the opportunity, shut the door, and step quickly toward the stairs, keeping to the edge of the foyer, away from Ryan.

"Morrigan." My foot pauses just above the first step, fingers digging into the warm wood of the ornate balustrade. "Look at me."

Taking a deep breath, blinking slowly as the air fills my lungs, I turn around and hold his stern gaze.

"This—"

"No!" I interrupt, my mother looking positively shocked at my daring attitude, and I do feel just a little bit sick. Not because of the attitude, that in and of itself is probably my most defining trait, but because I know... he'll use it against me. "You cannot have any more say in what I do with my own life, Ryan Holt. I was yours once... once. Not anymore."

"So you think you can stay here?" That voice sends chills down my spine, as the man who owns it appears in the foyer. "You have a duty to your husband."

I roll my eyes, digging myself a deeper hole. "He's not my husband."

"Yet," Ryan punctuates. "I packed a bag. You're coming with me tonight. You can return tomorrow, if you wish."

Wait, what? This is not how it works.

"You're coming for dinner tomorrow anyway." My father fiddles with a letter opener, ripping open an envelope he carries. Who gets letters anymore?

"Of course. Not sure if Morrigan's going to be doing much eating, though." Ryan runs his eyes slowly over my body, an eyebrow raised, lips pursed, and my throat fills with bile. If my appetite wasn't lost the moment I saw him here, it's lost now. He walks next to the staircase and picks up a weekender bag I didn't notice before. "Shall we, *darling?*"

My parents' gazes on me are enough to drag me down the steps, as Ryan extends his hand to me. What choice do I have? There is no escape for me here, not amongst them. Cillian's words echo through my mind as Ryan's eyes flare at me— *"You're strong enough..."*

Am I?

Everything that I am feels trapped in a tsunami, splashing violently around my axis, but when Ryan is around me... it dissipates, and breaks to the ground in an anti-climactic wave.

And I succumb.

* * *

"I've been busy and made your illusion of freedom too real. We'll have to remedy that, won't we? No Holt woman gets so much unsupervised freedom."

Those words have been playing like a broken record in my mind since we came back to the beach mansion that has been in his family for at least three generations. He forced me into his car, since mine offers a freedom he apparently doesn't agree with anymore, for the most part. He said that the freedom he allows is an illusion, but I'm beginning to think that what we once were was also one.

"I have a surprise for you." His grin curves his top lip in a way that makes him look... sleazy.

Has his lip always done that? Am I just noticing this? Or is it another aspect of his new personality that even Jekyll and Hyde would be envious of? *A surprise?* Nah... this version of Ryan doesn't prepare surprises, not good ones anyway.

"Thanks, but I'm good." If he's waiting for my enthusiastic response, he's going to wait forever.

I turn and begin to walk toward the library, the only place in this house that gives me a semblance of comfort. I'm not a huge reader, not of the books that lie on those shelves, but neither he nor his father ever spent time in that space. It's not tainted; it doesn't feel as if it belongs to them.

"It's in *our* bedroom," he says with such giddiness in his voice, it makes me uneasy.

I've barely made it five steps. I don't turn, though.

"Come," he insists.

I take a deep breath and move forward on a shaky step.

"NOW!" His voice changes its tune, booming through the grand space.

"Ryan, Morrigan, you've returned." I'm startled by the sound of his mother's voice and turn to find her walking toward us from the living room. "Have you eaten? Should I get Pierre to prepare something for you?"

"Hello, Mrs. Holt." She hates being called by her first name, and even as a widow, when she should be called Ms., not Mrs. She still rejects it.

At least she's always hated me calling her by her first name. Although I think she just hates me... period.

"No, I've eaten and"—he swipes his eyes over me once more, lingering on my belly, as he does all too often—"Morrigan's not hungry. Dismiss the chef. You can go too."

Her gaze widens as she takes in those words, before she looks between him, the top of the stairs, and me. There's a peculiar, all-knowing look in her eyes.

"Very well. Have a... good evening." The woman actually hesitates to move away.

What the fuck is going on?

Involuntarily, I look at the top of the stairs as well, hoping that there's some sort of indication of the *surprise* that made even Mrs. Holt wary. Suddenly, I feel the need to make some excuse and bring her back. She's a good buffer. Only, she seems to be just another pawn in her son's life since her husband's death. I wonder if she inherited anything from him. If she did, I wouldn't put it against Ryan to take it away from her.

I know it's not going to work, but I begin walking away again.

"Morrigan, this will be much easier for you if you just listen to me." His tone lowers, deepening, and shakes my insides.

Sighing, I turn and walk up the stairs, then toward his bedroom at the end of the hall. At the thought of what could possibly await on the other side, I grip the door handle much harder than necessary, the metal digging into my palm.

You can do this. Soon, you'll be out of this.

I take a deep breath, attempting to force away a lump that made its way into my throat.

You'll be okay. Just... just relax. Even if he does anything... you've done it before, it will be quick.

"Open!" His rasp startles me.

So I do. I push that door open, ready to face the reality of my situation, the one I've been trying very hard to avoid for over a month. But the image before me stuns me in a completely unusual way. I'm confused, irritated, shocked, and slightly relieved, all bundled into one emotion I cannot name.

"What the fuck is this?" Against the left wall, on top of a white fur throw that covers the whole of his super king-size bed, lies a naked woman—spread eagle.

"This" —he pushes me into the middle of the room to face the bed, then walks toward it, his eyes meeting hers as she smirks and licks her lips—"is Jasmine."

She's the woman who was sitting next to The Serpent at the restaurant a few days ago. The one attached to him, who he kissed on the cheek.

She's one of the escorts!

I thought she was, well, his date. No, she was fucking bait! Now I get why Ryan was so transfixed in the direction of their table. I know for a fact that Cillian hasn't shared his knowledge on the escort service, so Ryan has no clue that she works for The Sanctum. This is all about pissing on The Serpent's territory, because he saw that's the woman he chose for himself. I used to be his woman too. Why the sudden vendetta?

He stops near the bed, and she swings her legs over the edge, then slides off it until she's on her knees, her ass on her heels and hands on his belt.

"What the actual hell, Ryan? You talk to me of marriage and then—" My body's suddenly awoken from the shock, and I rush to the door, ripping it open.

"If you dare step out of this room, I'll fucking cut your head off and deliver it to Loreley myself. Then I'll fucking cut hers off too."

Shit.

"Shut that door."

I turn to him and do as told, giving him the best disgusted look I can muster. The blonde kneeling in front of him is not phased one bit. She continues her task as she looks up at him, unbuttoning his slacks, and her hand goes straight to his cotton-covered dick, rubbing slowly up and down.

"Jasmine here is going to do for me what you refuse to."

I can't help but roll my eyes, even through the bitterness of what he's doing, what's about to happen. "Well, shucks. Am I supposed to be sad about—"

"Until we're married," he cuts me off. "Until those hips get smaller and that belly flatter, and I can stand to look at you naked again. Maybe the wedding preparations have stressed you out a bit too much, and you've been raiding the junk drawer. Because you seem to have added more pounds on top of the existing extra ones. Until you lose them, you will sit here and watch."

Jasmine has his dick out and in her mouth by the time he finishes that sentence.

This whole scene is surreal. His words, his disgust, mine, this... cheating. Fuck. Is it cheating? I don't even...

I blink more times than I should, forcing away those hot tears threatening to sear their way out. It's impossible to settle on one feeling. Too many run through me, and my chest burns as I swallow each and every tear away. I'm not even sure why I'm shedding them. I don't love him anymore...

I *don't* love him anymore.

I don't love him!

Then why the fuck does it hurt? Why does it feel like he's ripping apart even more than he already has? Why does it feel exactly like it's not supposed to?

Because I cared about him. I thought he cared about me too.

"You're sick," I manage to whisper in a shaky voice.

"Maybe. But you're going to stand there and be sick with me." He grins, grabbing the woman's hair and gagging her violently with his dick.

I turn my head toward the window, wondering what the fuck my life has come to, why am I here, why does it hurt, when will it stop. They all seem like rhetorical questions.

"Don't you fucking dare take your eyes off. Look at me now!" he rasps as I hear the woman gag yet again.

I do as he says, all thoughts slowly dissipating... One by one, they leave me... until my features are void of feeling, until my muscles are limp, until I'm but an empty shell.

Or so I wish to be.

I want to be void of any emotion I've ever had for this man. I'm not sure where it hurts. Is it my soul, or my ego? A bit of it is in my heart. I just never thought that his disrespect for me would reach such lows.

Yet, the man threatened to kill my whole family and my best friend if I even dared to leave him. Why am I shocked by what lies before me? Quite literally, as Ryan pulled her up by the hair and laid her on the bed. He flips her over, pulling her ass up, then fists her blonde locks while throwing me the sleaziest smile he can muster. Then he impales her on a savage move, and her scream makes me cringe. I can't even tell if it's in pleasure or actual pain.

He does it over, and over, and over again... his eyes on me the whole time, guiding her by the hair so she can look at me too. I'm forcing myself to control the bile in my throat.

I've watched plenty of people have sex in the club in Rosston, and I fucking own one now, yet this... this is different. It's malice; revenge; evil. This is a man I've been with for two years. I've cared about him, and we've known each other from school. But he's also the man who, at this very moment, carries in his gaze the promise that he will do to me exactly what he's doing to her.

Only I will not be willing, and he will not care.

This helps, though. I should thank him for this moment. It pushes me over the edge, killing off that part of me that still believed there was hope for the old him to return. That this period was only some sort of temporary madness, driven by the stress over the death of his father and the business takeover.

It's not. It's pure madness.

The man before me doesn't deserve any emotions from me, not even disgust. And I suddenly realize that even most of my reactions to his abusive behavior were tied to my lingering emotions, that lingering hope.

So I carry on as he orders—I watch him.

I watch him fuck the woman's brains out. Watch as he grins at me. How she moans her pleasure, or her fake one. I watch it all because he's making every decision I will have to make from this moment on so much easier. Every thrust, every sound as their skin slaps together, every grunt, every way in which he squeezes her flesh, kills another part of the person I am around him. My family, too.

So I smile at him.

He's just decided his own fate, and he doesn't even know he did.

CHAPTER 14
Morrigan

MAYBE I'M ALREADY dead, because this definitely feels like some sort of hell.

"It's so exciting, isn't it, Morrigan?"

My mother's friend shrieks as she sits on the other side of the dining table, trying to smile, but failing miserably. Whoever the fuck injected that Botox into her face should have their license revoked. It looks revolting.

I open my mouth to respond, but my mother cuts me off.

"Oh yes, so very exciting! Organizing the wedding is a dream."

The woman blinks once at me before turning to my mother. I can't be bothered to be affected in any way, so I just stick my fork in another tomato and shove it into my mouth, chewing through her next question.

"So have you made any arrangements? Did you set a date?"

I chew the rest of that tomato, and again, I'm just about to speak, when Ryan's voice booms next to me.

"We've made plenty of arrangements, and we did actually set a date as well. We are very excited."

They're really scared I'll open my mouth and out them, aren't they? He grabs my thigh under the table, squeezing hard enough that my back straightens and my body twitches. I slap my hand over his, pulling at one of his fingers to try to get him off.

"But then again, there is no—" I begin.

"Point in waiting."

The motherfucker interrupts me again!

"We want to do it as soon as we can. We're just waiting for me to settle into the business." His fingers tighten so harshly, I'm struggling not to hunch over at the pain.

His gaze on me is a masked threat invented just for my benefit. It doesn't move me one bit. A heavy indifference has made a home in me since last night, and I'm basking in its chill. He doesn't like it though, and his bruising grip tightens suddenly, but I only allow a heartbeat to pass and I dig my fingernails into his skin with such force, dragging them down excruciatingly slow. His eyes bulge, pupils dilate, and he scrunches his nose, snapping his hand away.

I'm gonna pay for that. But at least I have the satisfaction.

"I agree," my mother continues. "There is no reason for a couple in love to wait too long to get married. Especially when you've known each other since school, and it's not like you have to wait to save money or anything."

I turn my gaze to the woman, an incredulous smile creeping on my lips. She's trying too hard with her deception. Does she think the people around us are blind? Fuck, maybe they are.

"I'm afraid I'm going to have to excuse myself." Ryan peeks at his phone screen, his brows furrowing slightly, before putting it back on the table, screen down. "I'm putting out fires everywhere nowadays." He laughs at the guests, his gaze fixing longer on my parents.

"It's to be expected. Picking up a new business, it takes a while to adjust and work out all its kinks." My father takes a sip of his red wine as he places his knife and fork on his plate, next to the half-eaten steak. "I'll walk you out."

"Thank you, Liam, but that won't be necessary. My fiancée will walk me out. Sheila, this was delicious. So sorry I couldn't stay any longer. Everyone"—he turns to the rest of the guests—"it was a pleasure."

His politeness just about turns my stomach over, but everyone else at the table swallows the bullshit, smiling and extending their well wishes. Goddamn idiots, all of them, with two notable exceptions—The Serpent and Maddox. They sit on the far right next to my father, and they nod at Ryan in such a slight way, you could blink and miss it.

"Morrigan." He's already pulling my chair back with me in it, forcing me to drop my cutlery onto the plate with a loud rattle.

I would very much like to make a scene right now. Only, after last night, I have little energy, and I would prefer using it to plan my next move.

I follow him out of the room, the rest of the guests continuing their meal and chatter as we head to the foyer. I stop a few steps away from the door.

"Walk me to my car," he says as he opens the door, without even turning to me.

I roll my eyes and follow him out the door, and luckily his BMW is parked just to the right of it, on the circular drive. He opens the driver door, but doesn't get in—instead, he comes out with a large brown envelope that he hands to me.

"I would advise you don't open it around your parents, or anyone else, for that matter."

"What is this?" I reluctantly reach over. It's on the heavier side, but I can tell there's paper inside.

"I figured that threatening your family's or friend's life might not be enough motivation for you to stop your refusal to marry me. So I'm threatening yours as well."

What the hell?!

I don't have time to react, too consumed by his words, when he grabs the back of my head and pulls me to him. His slimy lips press onto mine, and my attempts to push him away are in vain.

There was a time when kissing him was pleasurable. It feels as if eons have passed. The memories don't feel like they belong to me anymore.

"By the way, they're not the originals. You can stay at your parents tonight, if you need time to process," he says, with a grin that lingers in my memory minutes after he climbs in his car and drives off.

I'm itching to open it. I would do it right now, but they expect me to go back to the table. If I don't go, my mother is bound to come after me, and if Ryan *advises* me to be alone when I open it, then I can't risk her presence.

No one really notices when I walk back into the dining room, all caught up in conversation. Except for two penetrating pairs of eyes. They didn't miss the envelope I put away on my lap. I manage to finish dinner with minimal conversation, and even The Serpent and Maddox attempted polite exchanges. Enough not to seem rude, but not enough that it would allude to our current proximity. After all, both my parents are fully aware that we knew each other, long ago.

Now that dinner is over, my parents are inviting the guests to the formal living room on the other side of the house for drinks. And I take the cue to excuse myself.

"What's that?" My mother's voice stops me in my tracks, and I think the hand clutching the envelope is beginning to sweat.

"Something... for the wedding," I improvise. "I just want to go look it over. I'll be back in a while."

"Oh, I should look too if it's about the wedding."

Fuck!

"This is a bit more private—some honeymoon arrangements."

Fire and ice hit my back at the same time, yet somehow, they both burn. I know in my gut whose gaze is doing that to me.

I move away before more questions are thrown my way, and the moment I'm out of sight, I all but run upstairs, heading to my room. My whole body feels hot, and there's a lump in my chest urging me to scream, just to release this tension that has sat there for the last wretched hour.

Bursting through the door, I go to the bed, turn on the lamp closest to me, and throw the envelope onto it. It lands with a thud, threatening me somehow. It's staring at me, that rough, brown paper hiding something he said endangers my life too. I know it's not possible for it to be what I think. I fucking know it. Yet this man managed to flip a switch on the person he used to be, so he makes me believe in the impossible.

I rake my fingers through my loose hair and finally rip the envelope open. Large photos fall onto the bed, and my heartbeat thuds in my ears. It takes but a second to recognize what I'm looking at, another second for my breath to hitch painfully in my lungs, and another one for the shock to reach my heart. My hand is against it, pressing on my chest, yet no beat vibrates through it.

"Son of a bitch..." I say on a pained exhale.

A slight creak makes me jump and turn to the door. The tall, strong body that fills the doorway looks oh-so stern in his all-black ensemble. His darkness arrives with a rise in the pressure of the air, and as he steps into my space, that pressure becomes almost unbearable. Yet strangely satisfying in a peculiar way. The type that quickens your heartbeat, that makes you forget to breathe, and makes your knees weak.

I don't move the moment he steps farther in and keep my back to the photos I try to conceal. His eyes still flicker to the bed, but they don't linger. Instead, he prolongs the torture as he looks around the room, his whole body tense as he takes in the parts of me that exist here, clearly curious by the insight. He pauses on certain things, only I don't care enough in this moment to figure out which, or what it could mean. This room has evolved with me over the years. There are no traces left of the teenager I used to be, the one he used to know.

That teenager died young.

And those photos laid on my bed show the reason why.

When he finally turns to me, in this room that holds secret memories we share, his dark gaze is savage. He looks at me as if I'm both good and evil, Heaven and Hell, love and malice, like I'm... everything. And my heart suddenly thunders in my chest, its beats shaking me to my core.

He closes the distance between us and grips my chin between two fingers, cocking his head as he holds me still.

"Private honeymoon arrangements?" he asks in his signature calm voice that chills bones. But what shocks me is that he does not hide the blatant jealousy.

I don't have the courage to speak, though, not when it means those fingers will leave my skin. Not when the alternative is for him to see how Ryan has just complicated things.

But he narrows his eyes and cocks his head, his gaze flickering to the bed. I sigh as he lets go and steps to my side, and I wish I could stop him from picking up the photos.

"What is this?" His tone changes its tune.

He leans over, assessing each image as I run my fingers through my hair, grabbing two handfuls, feeding the sting on my scalp as I tighten my grip.

"That's you." He pins me with a stern gaze and throws the evidence onto the bed. "These were taken years ago. Who took them? And who the fuck is the person you're burying?!"

* * *

One by one, the photos from the night I killed a man imprint in my memory. This outside perspective is so different from mine. It's not as if I needed to be reminded I did it, as it's not something one forgets. But I never truly regretted doing it, so I rarely ever think of it. And that's what brings me true guilt.

"Tell me!" He raises his voice as high as he can in this room, but I hesitate.

Not because I'm afraid to admit what he can clearly see already, but because of how that story, what I've done, could affect him. Or maybe it won't affect him at all, maybe he won't give a shit about me, and that scares me more.

My lips part, but I'm interrupted by that slight creak in the floor again, and we both turn, shielding the evidence. My heart falls back in its place when I see Maddox entering and quickly shutting the door.

"What?!" He looks between us as he steps closer. "What the hell is thi—" he cuts off as recognition hits him, and his wide eyes snap to me. "What the fuck, Morri?! Is this who I think it is?"

The Serpent turns to me, and my eyes flash from one man to the other, both waiting for different explanations.

"Yes." I sigh.

"We don't have much time. You need to tell me what the fuck is going on." The black-eyed devil tenses his shoulders as he regards me.

I pick up one of the photos and stare at it. I'm in the middle of the forest, a flashlight lighting me and the patch of ground before me as I dig the hole, the body of a man laid next to it. Even in this grainy image, you can tell there's no life in that body. Only Ryan could have taken this, and the more I look at it, I realize that I know exactly when. All this time, all these years, this son of a bitch had leverage on me. All these fucking years!

"That's Johnny Bray, isn't it?" Maddox asks.

"Wait, is that the guy we caught almost..." The Serpent navigates around that particular piece of memory. "The one whose jaw you broke?"

"Yes."

"When was this taken? For fuck's sake, just tell us already! Stop prolonging this."

"There's a goddamn reason for that! It was taken not long after we... after you left." After *he broke up with me* out of the blue. "When he noticed you weren't around anymore, and I was no longer under your protection, he decided to get his revenge for that night I broke his jaw."

Maddox quickly grabs one of the photos, bringing it closer to his eyes. "Is this your blood? Ripped clothes... Morrigan, what the hell happened?!" He slams his large hand on the bed, on top of the photo, his tone threatening.

Even if he is built like a beast, the scariest one of them all, who much prefers hurting a man than showing feelings, I know he cares. In a ruthless, rough around the edges, kind of way, he cares.

"In a way, I was lucky, because he came after me alone. Maybe he didn't have the courage to tell any of his friends that it was a girl who broke his face that night." I lean over and gather all the photos back in the envelope. "I still remember the sick grin on his face when he told me that you're not there to save me again."

"Not that you needed much saving." Maddox becomes slightly uncomfortable with my insinuation of what they saved me from that night, but the darkness in The Serpent's eyes never shifts.

It may have looked to them like I didn't need saving, but it didn't feel the same to me. I was unhinged, definitely not in control, and only control can give you the confidence to win something like that. I had none of it, I was just... manic.

"Ryan used to be like a puppy after I became single, always following me, always around. Now I wonder if any of that was a normal crush, or if it was just a growing, unnatural obsession. It turns out that he was around that night as well. At least that's my conclusion, because there's no way anyone else would have found us there. And I'm sure Ryan wasn't expecting what he saw when he did."

"What *did* he find?" The Serpent speaks in a different tone now, lower, rougher, each word spilled slowly, punctuated, my skin responding with goose bumps before my brain even registers the need for a reply.

"Johnny knocked me out and put me in his car. I woke up in the forest, not far from Brook Lane, as he was trying to rip my clothes off."

I hear the growl coming from Maddox before my eyes land on his fury. But it's the darkness, the possessiveness in The Serpent's eyes that pulls my attention.

"He didn't intend to finish what he started. Believe me," I continue. "He wanted to beat the shit out of me, humiliate me, and leave me for dead, naked, for the animals to find me. When I woke up and pushed him off, he got two more kicks in my stomach before I managed to grab onto his leg and get him on the ground. I was terrified, heartbroken, and angry. I got onto my feet and took it all out on him. I guess Ryan saw his car at the side of the road and came into the forest. Maybe he thought he was coming to my rescue, but I wasn't the one in need of it."

I pause for a moment, catching my breath.

"I fell into a frenzy. I saw red and no other colors. He screamed, Ryan did, when he saw me bashing Johnny's head in with a thick tree branch. I couldn't stop myself. I'm not even sure I thought of stopping at all. I broke it on his mangled skull, then I picked up a rock, kneeled next to him and kept going until there was nothing there to recognize."

"Jesus," Vincent whispers.

But I don't know what to make of that reaction. He stands there, his eyes just a tad wider than normal, enough for that to be a complete shift in his demeanor.

It's strange, but I always think about Johnny Bray as my first kill, and this haunts me more than the memory of his cracking skull. I haven't killed since. He's my one and only, yet my brain seems to have already calculated the risks, considering my nature. Maybe it's just a matter of time. I wish that fact would actually scare me.

"Ryan helped me. He left to get shovels and some clothes, and I stayed in the forest. He helped me bury him. He helped me move his car, then took me home. I thought it was done. To this day, we never spoke of it ever again." I look at the envelope clutched in my small hands. "Now I understand why."

"So he's the one that took the photos," Maddox states.

"Definitely. I remember there was a point when he said he was going to the car to pick up something, since we had some fingerprints to wipe off Bray's skin. I was in the middle of digging. I didn't think anything of it, he was so helpful. I was broken, exhausted, and that's most likely when he took the photos."

I turn toward the window, watching the clouds move slowly in the night sky, at the same speed as the breeze that moves the branches of the walnut tree hovering from the right-hand side of the window.

"The world moved on from Johnny Bray. He was so problematic, even his dad thought he ran away. No one even questioned the fact that he disappeared suddenly. More girls were coming out, accusing him of rape or sexual assault. Everyone just thought he ran away to escape a trial. I moved on too. Never did I think that it would come back to bite me in the ass this way."

"We need to get all the copies." Maddox speaks as he walks to the door, his ear close to it as he listens for movement. He opens it and peeks through, then walks out without another word.

We should go too. We can't risk my parents even thinking we're friendly any time but in their presence.

"We'll never get the copies. He's not going to tell us anything, you know that." I turn off the lamp and walk toward the door.

I stop when his arm wraps around my waist from behind, and the other pulls the envelope from my hand. My body hums in awareness, tense as I force myself not to sink into him. The corridor is lit, but here, in my childhood bedroom, we're bathed in the shadows. The same shadows that adore The Serpent so much.

"We'll get all the copies." His breath brushes that sensitive spot under my ear. "Then we'll get him, Little Eve. Then your parents. We'll get them all, pull them into our hell and burn them in your heathen fire. They'll all pay for their sins."

Each and every syllable slithers around his tongue, dripping from it onto my skin, as he whispers into my ear. Then he kisses the edge of it, sending electric shocks through my whole body with that soft touch of his lips. When he releases me from his hold, my legs almost give out. Almost. I'm convinced. I'm not sure if it's his confidence, the tone of his voice, or his soft touch, but I believe him.

So I walk into the light, carrying his darkness on my skin.

CHAPTER 15
Vincent

THE SCENT OF her room brought back memories I didn't think affected me anymore. It was another life, when my future looked different, fuller—because it still had her in it. But it was ripped away from me by the man I just cut a deal with—her goddamn father.

My fury toward him never went away, but being there enveloped in our past, it brought back *that* fury. What I felt all those years before, and I wanted to rip into him with all I had. Rip him away from life itself.

I couldn't do it then, but I can now.

Before I do, I will make sure to tell him why—*my* reason, not the new one his daughter gave me.

Morrigan... fuck, she felt like a dream. Her soft red curls brushing against me, the curves that turned the girl she used to be into this goddess, and her scent called to me like I was finally in the presence of what my soul has been searching for, missing all along. Every fiber of my being was screaming at me to fucking take her, then and there, rip her clothes off and fuck her in her parents' house, for all to hear. Wicked, lovely things went through my mind, and my cock was hard through the whole goddamn car ride.

I followed her Dodge as she drove to her friend's building. For her safety, but my curiosity too. I need to know if Holt put a tail on her. If we're going to keep meeting, and we certainly will, I need to know if I have to give her instructions, how to take precautions. But as I got there, my curiosity was fed in a completely different way.

I walk into Midnight and spot Madds at our usual table.

"Why didn't you tell me that her best friend lives in the same building where Metamorphosis is?" I ask as I reach him.

"I thought Carter would have told you when you went there with him. He did the research before you guys signed up."

There're already quite a few people here, yet a bit less than usual at this time. Saturdays tend to be busy nights for Midnight. Everyone needs to let off some steam, only I have a feeling even more are going to go to Metamorphosis for that purpose. Carter arrives just as I settle onto the sofa, nodding his hello to us.

"Hell, maybe he did. I followed her last night, after we left her parents' dinner."

"Morrigan? You... followed... her?" Carter raises an eyebrow at me.

"Jesus Christ, get over yourself. I wanted to see if Ryan tracks her. It's to our benefit after all."

He says nothing, but he's clearly not convinced in the slightest.

"It's Loreley's club and building. What's so unusual about her living there too?" Maddox shrugs.

True, there isn't anything unusual about it. I just wonder if whenever she goes to visit her friend, she maybe... visits the club too. It's her best friend after all, right? Is she even into that world? I asked myself these questions before, but this was before I realized that the image I had of this Morrigan was pretty much a façade built by her parents. I thought the women I knew was gone, and I didn't ponder the possibility that she could be frequenting Metamorphosis herself. Now, it's a whole other situation. She could have been there, the few times I've gone, and the idea that she could be *playing* with other men brings an unpleasant heat to my chest and a tension in my temples.

Goddamnit!

I have to constantly remind myself that Morrigan-fucking-O'Rourke is not mine.

But if I imagine her any longer strapped to a St. Andrew's cross while some random guy does filthy things to her, I'm definitely gonna make her.

I haven't caught sight of her signature red locks there, though. Maybe it's not her scene after all.

"I think I'm going to go out tonight," I say to no one in particular. Clearly, my curiosity cannot be contained.

There's a faint twitch between Carter's eyebrows, but he doesn't question me. He only nods, but I don't miss that sneaky sparkle in his eyes.

"I'm waiting for Katya. I need to catch up with her, then I'm going to go look into those photos," he says, signaling one of the waitresses, letting her know we're ready to get some drinks. They know not to disturb us until we ask.

"I'm going downstairs."

We both turn to Madds. If he goes downstairs to The Fightclub when there isn't a scheduled match, something has to be wrong. I suspect it has something to do with the story Morrigan told us.

When he says those three words, there's usually one of two looks in his eyes—the fairly placid one that says he's just supervising, or the one that hides the feral beast scratching its way to the surface. It's the beast we see now, not yet at the surface, and he needs to let it out, de-stress.

"Okay," I say, lingering on his features a little longer. I can't get a read on him, and it's really pissing me off.

Sometimes it's better for one of us to be there, just in case he goes too far. And he has gone too far, a few times.

"Stop fucking looking at me like that," he spits at me. "Call Finn if you want. He can *supervise* me." He leaves the table, his heavy footsteps shaking the floor on the way to the back rooms.

"What is going on with him?" Carter asks, but the waitress interrupts us, and we send her on her way with our order.

"I think it's guilt." I suspect it is because it's been fucking plaguing me since I left the dinner. "Morrigan and him always had this... connection. What she revealed tonight stirred him." Not that he would ever admit it.

"But you and Morrigan had a *connection*," he says, narrowing his eyes on me.

"It was more like a wild beast recognizing its kind and latching onto it." But her and I... we're a different kind of beast altogether. I don't tell Carter that, though.

"And you're okay with it?"

I sigh before I answer, because I'm not sure how I feel about it. Even then, it didn't really bother me the way it should have. And it's only because it's Madds. If it was anyone else, I would rip their fucking heads off for looking at her the wrong way.

"Is it strange if I didn't feel that raw jealousy when it came to him? Don't get me wrong, I feel some, but not the way I should."

"It's not strange at all. Your brain is trying to think of it through the window of societal norms, but you need to accept your own. You and Madds have known each other before any of us, you've pulled each other from bad situations..."

I've sacrificed too. But I don't tell him that.

"I'm no gonna pretend to understand relationships or emotions. But what you have is selfless, unconditional."

"It is. I would do anything for him. Any you as well, obviously, but Madds... I don't think he thinks he deserves anything good. He doesn't latch onto anything, ever. Only us. I didn't want to take her away from him."

"And now? What if he still wants her?"

"He's attracted to her, and I know he cared about her. Considering tonight, he still does. But no, he would never want to *be* with her. Not even if I was dead. Morrigan was never meant to be his, and he knows it."

He nods, then leans back into his seat.

"Why are you going to Metamorphosis, Vincent?" The man rarely calls me by my whole name.

The waitress sets our drink order on the table with a soft smile, not lingering once the last glass touches the surface.

"We both know why, Carter. Is there any chance she wouldn't support for best friend?"

"Maybe she's not into the scene."

"Maybe. But I don't play, yet I still go for the atmosphere."

He quirks an eyebrow. "If you don't, then wh—"

"Don't even say it. That was... an anomaly." It really was. "I was thinking that even at the pre-opening party, I saw no one with her recognizable red hair. Did you?"

"I can't say I have, no," he answers, a smirk pulling at his lips.

I nod, pondering the situation. "I don't know, something's just eating at me. I wonder if there's more to it all."

"Well, I hope you enjoy your journey finding that out," he says with a suggestive look in his eyes, and I can't help but laugh.

"I'm sure I will."

* * *

The gold details shine in the darkness of the club. Metamorphosis was most definitely built with both style and comfort in mind, and as I sit on the upholstered barstool, sipping a glass of quality Bourbon, I have to give an extra point for that comfort. I didn't think I would enjoy it much. I joined more because The Sanctum has to ensure it has a foot through every door in this city. But the anonymity is refreshing. Exhilarating even.

The music, the atmosphere, the people... it's immersive.

The song changes, but it's the rise in volume that stops me mid sip, and when the lights dim to the cusp of darkness, it pulls my attention away from the bar. The moment I turn in my chair, a wild scent envelops me. It's fresh, reminding me of a flower I can't place. So different from the smells dominating this space. It submerges me into a visceral memory, and like a warm summer breeze, it passes by me. A woman. Our eyes meet for a brief moment, before she disappears through the crowd. It was too dark to see more than the faint shine of her eyes behind the mask, but her scent lingers, and I don't want to exhale just yet. I don't want to let it go.

I recognize that mask, though.

Suddenly, she appears on the stage, the only light in the space aimed at her, but not blinding, just bright enough that it's like an aura around her body. She wears a long skirt that looks more like multiple wide ribbons tied around her waistband, her luscious legs with thighs that beg for teeth marks, peeking through the high slits. The song intensifies just as she sprints the small distance from the steps to the pole, and jumps onto it, clutching the metal between her hands and bent legs. The long skirt flows as she throws her head back, eyes closed, spinning around to an ethereal tune. She's pulled everyone's attention without even an announcement. All eyes are on the mesmerizing woman who I have seen dance once before.

The one I couldn't take my eyes from since the first time I stepped in here.

The same one who I finger-fucked as we watched Carter in one of the playrooms.

I recognize the mask, the hair, but most of all... I recognize her scent.

Her shiny, black hair flows in waves as she pole dances, switching positions slowly, following each note of the song. She's treating the pole as her partner, each movement a testament to her passion for dancing, evidence of her sensuality. She moves like she's all alone in this club, and considering the darkness around her, she probably feels as though she is.

I'm caught in this spell, and I feel guilty. Have I ever had this sentiment? I'm enthralled by this woman, while actively pursuing another—the one and only.

She lets go of the pole, filling the stage with an elegant, contemporary routine, but it's the borrowed ballet movements that make me drop down from my seat in an instant. The moment she flies into the air, doing the splits mid-leap, I head straight toward the stage, my heartbeat thumping in my ears.

"It's called a Grand Jeté, not jumping splits, Vincent."

I can practically hear her voice in my head, correcting me like she did years ago. She was behind the school. I came to find some asshole and teach him a lesson about the bullshit laced drugs he was selling, and instead I caught her dancing. It was the first time I allowed myself to talk to her. I asked her why she wasn't in the dance studio, and she angrily muttered something under her breath about size as she rubbed her hands on her thighs, but never answered me.

I catch glimpses of her as I walk between the people gathered to watch the routine, and by the time I reach the steps, she's back on the pole. Before I get the chance to linger on her swaying curves, the beat drops... and so does she. She slides down the pole until her ass hits the floor at the same time the bass vibrates through my feet and straight to my damn cock. The pole is snug between her breasts as she holds on to it with her arms stretched high above her head, and her legs spread wide, the crowd getting a clear view of her red-fucking-lingerie.

This stirs a jealousy within me I should have no business feeling. Yet that's not the dominant emotion, because it stirs pride, too.

Cheers and claps burst in unison around us as she rises to her feet, her lips curving into a shy smile as she bows her head gently. My God, I just want to grab her and tell her just how fucking amazing she is, how talented, how gorgeous. Jesus Christ, am I really this soppy and soft? I want to roll my eyes at myself, but as the light returns to its usual dimness, she runs off the stage, and I refrain from the gesture. Her steps falter the moment she takes the first step down and notices me at the bottom.

Does she recognize me from the other night? She wasn't exactly facing me, so I would be surprised.

The closer she gets, the better I see behind the shadow of her mask, and her forest-green eyes are so much clearer.

The Eve to my Serpent.

My Eve.

She cocks her head as she stops right before me, and her gaze pins mine. I feel like I'm under some sort of scrutiny, and I wish I could see her expression. But in a split second, the mood changes, and her hands shoot to the collar of my black shirt, pulling open the buttons with clumsy urgency.

Fuck. I don't need to see her expression—she knows. But I let her get her confirmation.

Morrigan pulls away one side of the fabric and brushes her soft fingers against the scar she left there, on my left peck, a few months before. Her eyes shoot back to mine, and I'm not entirely sure what I see there—anger, shock, annoyance... relief?

I think the music stopped playing because all I can hear are her heavy breaths. They echo somehow. Her chest rises and falls slowly, her nostrils flare, and I feel like I'm waiting for her to strike.

When she removes her hands, I button my shirt back up, never leaving her gaze. I'm thankful for the masks concealing our identities, because half of bloody Queenscove is in attendance and we can't be seen together. More so, they can't see me—The Serpent—left speechless by the youngest O'Rourke.

I am, though. I'm fucking speechless. What am I supposed to say to the woman I thought I last touched years ago, only it turns out it was much more recent than that? In public, of all places.

Yet, my pull to the creature behind the mask finally makes sense.

All of a sudden, she moves away, shaking her head as she steps around me, and the music and background noise seem to explode. Sighing, I follow her, touching the spot over my shirt that's a constant reminder of her.

The night she gave me this scar was when I realized she hasn't let go of the past. Until that moment, I thought she had, but I was stupid to believe that. After all, I left her out of the blue with someone else's lie on my lips as the only explanation.

I knew why I went to her mother's party that night, but her anger, her passion, confirmed without a shadow of a doubt the reason why I was there—I want her back.

But does she want me?

Morrigan

Six months earlier

"WHAT IS—ARE THEY doing here?!"

Cillian follows my line of sight to where my mother and father are greeting our new guests. I can't fucking believe my eyes—it's The-motherfucking-Sanctum. Of all the people I expected to see at my mother's birthday party, a crime syndicate wasn't it. But more importantly... Vincent The Serpent Sinclair, my goddamn ex-boyfriend. They don't show their faces unless they're coming to collect, or—

"Please tell me this isn't what I think it is." I turn to my brother, forcing down the rising anger.

"Depends on what you think it is."

"Goddamnit, Cillian. Just tell me what the fuck is happening."

"What are you mad about, Morri? Them or... *him*?" he asks, taking a sip of the amber liquid swirling in his glass.

"Are you going to answer my question?"

"They were invited by our parents."

Jesus Christ, this was intentional. I turn and catch the smug looks on my mother's and father's faces as they absorb the gazes their other guests give them. This was some sort of power play on their part, using The Sanctum for a new ploy. But my father's business is legit, as far as I know. Although saying that, I barely know anything. I kept an ear in since I was a teenager, since my darling father is a misogynistic piece of shit who doesn't want to think of women as intelligent creatures. There was no way I could learn everything, though.

"Are they going into business together?"

Silence.

I turn to my brother, and he's pursing his lips, avoiding my gaze.

"It's either that, or our father fucked up so badly, that The Sanctum had to come and fucking collect at Mother's birthday party." Is it bad that I wish it would be the second option?

It's bad, I know, but Father and I never got along. How could we? He always hated me not just for the shit I used to get into, the fights, the mildly illegal crap, but because I have a backbone. He cannot stand women who dare to stand up to him. And I've been doing it since I was only a girl. Safe to say, he never shied away from corporal punishment; he has a mean palm, and an even meaner backhand.

When I look back toward them, my lungs drain of air in an instant, and painful prickles spread through my whole chest, up my throat, down my arms, and straight through my belly, until I'm utterly pinned in place.

He's looking straight at me.

The Serpent's black pits are wholly focused on me, and I'm taken aback by the feel of that gaping hole inside of me. I rarely notice the jagged edges of it anymore. Time hasn't healed my wounds, but I sure as fuck have gotten used to them enough that I made myself skirt around the hollowness until it felt normal. But now, looking at the man who burned that part of me to a crisp, I'm painfully aware of it.

Yet nothing hurts more than the realization that his simple presence in my space and his eyes on me, are already smoothing the edges of that wound. No! No fucking way am I allowing any of this shit!

"Where do you think you're going?" Cillian's hand wraps around my wrist, stopping me dead in my tracks.

"To find out what the fuck he's doing here, and then kick him out of my goddamn house!"

"Your house?"

If looks could truly pierce, my brother would be a dead man right about now.

"You're just like him, you know."

"Who? The Serpent?!" He's taken aback, but he's wrong.

"Father. Just let me know when you start hitting the women in your life too. At least I can warn them before they get too close."

I didn't think they would, but those words hit hard enough that his eyes bulge, he lets go of me, and if I wouldn't know any better, I would think he looks utterly insulted. Shocked, too.

Good.

But this small fit of temper didn't help the bubbling anger at the sight of the man who broke my heart and disappeared from my life without a goddamn care in the world. Just like all the other men in my life. I thought that after all these years I would have let it go, that the pain, disappointment, and embarrassment would have fizzled out. That's what's supposed to happen after a breakup. You move the fuck on.

I did. But it seems that my wretched heart didn't.

The fact that we've never actually been together in a private space since then doesn't help. I know I've been avoiding him, but I think he's been avoiding me too. I've seen him in passing, at a distance, but very few times over the years. We've never spoken, never been in the same space. As far as I know, we've had no contact at all. Maybe it's the lack of closure that's making me so fucking furious, or maybe it's just his godlike handsome face that feels so goddamn right in my eyesight that drives this rage.

I started walking before I even realized, my heels digging almost painfully into the floor, and The Serpent simply... turns and moves away. He fucking moves away!

The fucking nerve!

He comes into my house, and he doesn't even give me the courtesy of a *hello*?!

I could scream right now. Oh, this man drives me crazy!

"Darling, have you said hello to all our guests?" My mother's voice comes from somewhere to my right, and I have to take a deep breath before I open my mouth.

"They are your guests, Mother."

"You live in this house too. You are also a hostess, and you should act like one. Please control your antics tonight. This is an exquisite evening with important guests, and your father will not be happy if you make a bad impression."

Nope, I can't do this. I'll lash out at her.

"Sure, *Mother*." I practically spit that word at her before moving away.

It takes only a few seconds to catch my father's gaze as I walk through the busy living room. There's no malice in his eyes, but his gaze just screams *I'm watching you.*

When I reach the dining room, the lush dessert table catches my eye and I head straight for it. Chocolate will solve everything. I don't smoke or do any kind of drugs, although I'm seriously regretting that right now, so chocolate is my only guilty pleasure that makes me feel better. Alcohol helps too, but I can't risk getting even slightly tipsy here.

I grab a small knife, and I'm just about to sink it into an éclair and split it in half, when Ryan's voice grits my ears.

"Are you sure you want to eat that?"

Motherfucker.

I can't catch a break today.

"I am, yes," I answer as I turn back to the chocolaty goodness.

"I'm not. All that sugar settles in all the wrong places."

I lift my eyes from the table and inhale slow and deep as I turn my attention to my boyfriend. How dare he make me feel like shit about what I eat or how I look.

"You have no right, R—"

"Sorry, darling, our fathers are signaling me over. Lay off the sweets, okay?" he interrupts me without even thinking about it, kisses my cheek, and disappears.

You have to be kidding me.

I'm moving again, heading straight to the kitchen, but there are waiters and all sorts of people trotting about, and my head is spinning. I can't be around them. Around anyone. I turn to the corridor that leads to the small library that's bound to be empty. The moment I walk into the empty space, my lungs finally fill with air. Pointlessly, because I start panting with the pent-up anger and my eyes begin to burn. Only, whatever tears sit at the back of them are not of weakness. No... it's goddamn frustration.

"Good evening."

The world stops in an instant.

"Serpent." I turn, seething already at the audacity of this man. "You're not welcome here. Leave."

"I was invited."

"Not by me. Not here." I don't move, but I don't think I could even if I wanted to. There's no air in this room. No space for me to move where his energy wouldn't reach me. I'm afraid it's gonna pull me in if I get too close. It's been fucking years, but—no! Get a fucking grip, Morrigan.

"Are you planning on doing something about it?" he asks, nodding to my right hand.

I'm confused, but when I look down, I realize I'm still holding the knife I was about to use on the éclair.

"Tempt me, and I will," I answer, looking back at him and pinning those black eyes with my own.

Green against black, alone in this dusty space, untouched by the wretched people of this house. He and I used to come here and do despicable things on that sofa whilst my parents weren't home. Sometimes even when they were. It was practical, since this ground floor window leads to a secluded area of the garden through which he could easily sneak without anyone catching him.

He takes a step toward me, and my breath catches. I need a distraction.

"Why are you here?" I ask.

"I wanted to say hello."

"But you completely ignored me when you entered my house."

"You seemed to be in the middle of a conversation with your brother. I didn't want to be rude and interrupt."

I narrow my eyes on him. He's different from the man I used to know, still himself, but... more chiseled, distinguished in a ruthless kind of way. I know his reputation, as it's hard to miss. I know the rumors too, but the man before me is a whole other kind of dangerous. He's calculated, and I can tell he's been honing his talents.

"Why are you here, Serpent?" I ask again, my tone grittier. I can't fucking take everyone's attitude toward me anymore.

He cocks his head. "I was invited by your parents."

"Why? Just fucking answer me, or I swear to God..." I trail off because I don't actually know what I would do.

He takes one more step toward me, and this time around, I match it. We're a step away from each other now.

"You're overthinking this. I did not come here with an agenda. Your parents invited us, all of us, to your mother's birthday party, and we came. If you want to know why we were invited, I'm afraid you're going to have to ask your parents."

"I'm asking you. Stop acting like you're not The-fucking-Serpent and don't know everything that moves in this world. Give me some goddamn respect!" Christ, I can't seem to ease the tension building in my temples.

"You're angry," he states the obvious like it's some goddamn revelation.

"I'm furious! You have no right to be here. All these years, all these fucking years, and you show up at my house, in league with... *them*?!" I'm bleeding my emotions in this godforsaken room, and I hate myself for it, but most of all... I hate him.

"We're not in business with the—"

"Stop fucking talking if all you're going to say are lies. Just like before. You're lying to me about the future just like you did back then. I'm not an idiot, and you should know that better than *them*. Do not pretend this is not the beginning of some arrangement," I seethe and shake my head, tightening my fists, the metal handle of the knife hot in my palm. "Out of all the people in Queenscove, you couldn't find anyone else to do business with? Anyone at all?"

He moves closer, a mere foot away from me, and my eyes widen, burning yet again as I watch the tinge of familiarity in his expression. It fucking breaks my soul.

Then he reaches for me, wrapping his hands gently around my biceps, attempting to close the leftover distance between us. I'm suddenly so hot I can't bear the tightness of my own skin, my teeth are painfully clenched, and the pressure in my temples is close to agony.

"Don't you fucking dare act like I mean something. Get the fuck away from me!" I almost screech at him, but I couldn't control the coming frenzy even if I tried. I see red in all its shade spectrum, as I slam the knife straight into his chest.

I'm heaving loudly, suddenly feeling a bit better, especially at the sight of the surprise in his onyx gaze. But it lasts only a moment, because it transitions into a grin. The sick bastard is grinning at me! My ears are buzzing. I don't even look down as I pull the blade out of his flesh, step around him, and walk straight out of this goddamn room.

I was hoping the air would be lighter in this corridor, but it does nothing to erase his fucking smile from my mind. I hear footsteps. Moving quickly, I head straight to the powder room at the end of the corridor. The moment I step in and slam the door behind me, pain shoots through my hand.

The dessert knife hits the porcelain sink with a loud clatter, and blood follows, staining the white in bright crimson. I didn't realize that when I stabbed The Serpent, the knife slid in my hand and sliced my skin.

"Shit."

It's not deep, just like I'm pretty sure the wound I left on him isn't either, otherwise the motherfucker wouldn't be grinning. But I hate the fact that the wound I left on him, left one on me, too.

Yet another thing to remind me of the first man to ever break my heart.

CHAPTER 16

Morrigan

Present Day

VINCENT-MOTHERFUCKING-SINCLAIR!

Son of a bitch! I'm heaving as I make my way through the crowd, wishing I would be back in the middle of that forest. Because God-fucking-damnit, the rage is blinding. The scar on my palm itches, but right now I would happily risk re-opening it, just so I can stab this motherfucker again!

Did he know?

Did The Serpent fucking know that the woman he touched in the middle of my goddamn club was me?!

Wait...

My steps falter, and I slow down just as I reach the stairs that lead up to the reception.

Does he know it's my club, too?

I feel a grip around my wrist, but carry on up the stairs, shaking it off violently. He must be following, but rage makes its way through my bones. It's a beast I can't always control, but I can't let it take over, not right now. I cannot make a scene here.

So I keep going up the stairs, through the reception, where there're still people walking about, then I unlock the door that takes me away from it all. Only, I'm not the one pushing open the door. Bergamot and cedar fill my nose and almost cloud my senses as his hand lands right next to my head, and he does it for me.

"Miss M?"

We both stop at the sound of that voice, and I turn slowly toward the receptionist.

"Everything... okay?"

A few more people turn their heads in our direction. She's aware of who I am and has seen me walk through here before, but never this angry, and definitely not with a man in tow.

I take a quiet, deep breath that was definitely a mistake, since all I can smell is him now, and answer her.

"All good, honey. See you soon."

She nods, returning to the customers talking to her, and I push through the door he kept ajar as that rage seeps back in.

"You!" I seethe as I whip around, pointing at him the moment the door closes behind us. I have no idea what else I want to say to him, but I'm only seeing shades of red.

Gritting my teeth, I turn back around, heading to the door that leads to the lobby, and punch in another code. I push it open myself when it unlocks, but this time around, I stop him as he tries to walk through with me.

"Did you know?!" I have one hand on the edge of the door, the other on the frame, blocking his access. "No, fuck, scratch that. I don't wanna know!"

"Know what, Little Eve?" I catch his grin, shadowed by the mask he wears, the low, even tone of his voice making me even angrier.

"Don't play with me, Serpent."

He places his palm on the door and pushes, only I hold it tighter.

"No, you're not coming through here. This is where this ends."

"Where *what* exactly ends?" Stepping forward, barely a foot away, he looks down at me.

"You knew, you fucking bastard. You knew!" The sentence finishes on a dragged-out scream, and I release the door frame, swinging my palm at his handsome face. But he catches my wrist. So I swing the other one too, and the bastard has both in his grip now.

I barely register when he pushes me into the room, turns me, and cages me against the wall. But I flinch when the door shuts next to us.

Our heaving breaths feed off of each other, our bodies too close as my chest brushes against him with every rise and fall. He has me pinned with both wrists above my head, held with just one large hand, and his whole front is now against mine, his free hand gripping my hip.

"I will ask one final time." He's speaking firmly, but I can't meet his gaze. "Where. *What*. Ends?"

I swing my leg up, ready to knee him where it hurts the most, but he fucking predicts that too. The bastard pushes my leg to the side with his, his thigh now firmly pressed between my legs, and I'm cursing myself for allowing myself to be this exposed. *Fuck.*

"Little Eve, do not make me ask again." His tone is lower, menacing, gravelly in a way it's never been like before.

Ever.

It's not a voice I recognize on him, and my body shudders from my throat, down my chest, through my hardening nipples, and my belly. But it doesn't stop there. It goes straight to the one spot I really hoped would not react to him anymore, then finally reaches my toes.

I swear he feels it, because his thigh presses onto my center, and I have to bite my inner cheek to keep from letting him know just what that does to me.

"This. Where this ends," I spit, looking down between us. "You knew it was me, you son of a bitch, in the club when you—It. Ends Now." I push out those last three words, because I somehow feel betrayed. He took advantage of me!

Didn't he...?

"This." He copies me, his eyes dragging down to the point where we are joined, where he can feel my hardened peaks against him. "I wasn't aware it even begun. I did *not* know it was you when I played with your tight cunt as Carter and his partner watched."

My mouth falls open, stretching wide while my eyes threaten to pop out of their sockets.

"Carter! Wha—Carter?! Are you shitting me?!" Sweet Jesus. "That was him?! Oh my God. Get the fuck off me!"

Only, I'm pushing against a brick wall.

"Listen to me. I didn't know it was you who put a fucking spell on me with those sinful hips. I. Did. Not. Know," he says as he cocks his head.

His eyes are dark pits under his mask, his look utterly devilish since no light shines there. All that looks back is sincerity, and I have to avert my gaze. I just can't trust in it, not now when my body seems to listen to him more than me.

"I don't believe you!" I snap.

"It's the truth. Want to hear another one?"

My eyebrows furrow, but I stay silent.

"When I left you wet and satisfied in front of that window, I was fucking starving. I was dying to know what you tasted like. But you were a stranger... I couldn't put a stranger's cum in my mouth. There was something about you though, your soft body against mine, those lush hips, your scent that I haven't been able to forget."

A wicked grin paints his lips as he speaks those words, and with each one, my breathing quickens, already knowing how it will end.

"So I did it. I tasted you. I brought those fingers to my lips, sinking them beyond... and allowed myself one taste. Just one. Little. Taste."

I steal a glance in his direction and catch him as he licks his lips. I find myself licking mine at the same time. My mouth waters at the thought of the mighty Serpent sucking my cum from his fingers. His eyes flicker between us at the same moment a shiver runs through my breasts, and my perked nipples press a little harder into him. He did not miss that.

"I almost came back to you after that one taste. I wanted more. You felt different and familiar all at the same time. You tasted like I needed all of you. So I walked away."

Why?

Slowly, he leans in, our gazes fixed on each other's, as the air feels heavier with each breath. Wickedness shines in his eyes, and he shifts his thigh against my pussy, rubbing down just enough.

Lord have mercy!

If I can feel my wetness against the thin slip of my underwear, he can definitely feel it too. He better not mistake it for neediness.

I most certainly am not needy for him. I make sure to hold my defiant gaze, but he shifts once again against me, and the moment our noses touch and his grip loosens, I quickly rip my wrists away and push him off me.

Too goddamn close.

I rush to the stairs that lead up to the apartments, because there's no way I'm waiting for the elevator. Taking two at a time, I dash past the first floor, up the next flight, stealing a glance behind me... I can't see him. I keep going, reaching what will be my apartment, and punch in the code for the door, thankful I don't have to fiddle with keys, since it's easier this way with the contractors going in and out. Walking into the darkness, I push the door closed with both hands... but at the last damn moment, a shiny black shoe wedges in, and the door bursts open, throwing me back a few steps.

"I don't want you." The words fall too fast off my tongue.

Too fast for even me to believe them. Because here, in what will be my home, dressed in his signature all-black that hugs every inch of his lean body, he looks exactly like what I want.

Slowly, I step backwards, but he follows.

"You don't want my hands on you," he all but growls at me, taking another step. "My palms on your soft breasts."

Another one.

"My fingers stretching your pussy."

Another...

"My tongue sucking at your clit."

One more.

"My cock pressing inside of you."

I think I'm swallowing stones and breathing in water. It all feels too hard.

"No." My denial comes out harsh.

He's right in front of me.

"No..." he taunts.

He reaches up, and as his fingers touch my forehead, I'm afraid to move. Not fearful of him, but of what I might do as the image of him balls deep inside of me haunts my way too vivid imagination.

"You look good in black, sweet Eve, but stunning in red." He runs those fingers through the hair of my wig, and I hope he leaves it in place, because I'm not ready to be myself in front of him just yet.

He reaches to the back and tugs once, but it's my mask falling, not the wig. It hangs by its ribbon in his hand, and he holds it there as he reaches over and pulls his own mask off.

We're on even ground—Eve and The Serpent.

I blink once... twice... then push a hand on his chest once more, holding him enough away that I can catch every flicker in his eyes. Only, I think I'm actually holding myself from sinking into the enticing abyss of them.

"You didn't know it was me." I'm somehow calmer now, and I'll know if he lies.

"I didn't know it was you, in *your* club." No shift, no dilating of the pupils, no hitch in his breath, no change.

I believe him. I've seen the look of a lie in his eyes before. Even if he's gotten better at it, I think I would still be able to see a flicker of it.

Wait.

"*My* club?" I repeat, an eyebrow raised as I steady my pulse.

He only nods.

"It's not—"

"It is," he interrupts, cocking his head, his eyes boring into me once again.

Is it hotter in here? It feels hotter. I feel hotter. No, no, control yourself, breathe, for the love of God, breathe.

"No." My voice is a little firmer, but not enough to convince him.

Fuck... I need to practice this. I can't be caught this way by my family, or by Ryan. Only, The Serpent is neither of them, is he? He never was. My subconscious knows my dirty secrets are safe with him, but I have to push back anyway. I think of the risks, of what I could lose, and of what Lulu has built.

"It's not my club." I'm firmer this time.

"Only The Sanctum will know, no one else."

I think I lost this battle before it began. There's no point. He's on a mission now and he'll find out anyway.

"Listen to me, Serpent! Does anyone else know? Anyone but you or your precious Sanctum?!" I grip his shirt, holding him tight.

"No one else. Not even The Sanctum yet," he says with devious grin pulling at his lips. "I didn't know for sure until now."

"You tricked me," I all but whisper.

"I simply chased a hunch."

My grip tightens, and I pull him to me as panic and fury simmer inside my chest. "You better not be lying. If this information gets to my family, or anyone else, for that matter, from yours or The Sanctum's mouth, I will fucking kill you myself. I may not be the strongest, the most terrifying, or fucking brightest, but I swear it—I'll kill you all."

He nods. That's it. Just a simple nod of acknowledgment. Is he laughing internally at my threat? As long as he keeps this promise, he can laugh all he wants.

"How did you figure it out?" I ask.

"I've connected the dots. But your eyes don't believe your lies, Little Eve. You'll have to get better at that." He grips the side of my throat, his thumb swiping over my bottom lip, and I swear he does it so he can feel my quickening pulse beneath his palm.

"I'm not your Eve." I find my balance and step back.

"Are you not? Is a forest so different from a garden? Did you not seek an escape, or make a deal with the *devil*? Granted, I didn't offer you an apple, but we still shook on it and sealed the deal."

"We shook, yes, but I don't remember sealing anything." I'm playing with fire, because we all know the legends of how demons seal deals at the crossroads.

"Then I believe it's time."

It happens too fast—one short step, and he's against me, grabbing the back of my head. The moment our lips touch, a dam opens, and desire floods through me in waves. Everything I've suppressed when I thought of him over the years, everything I've pushed away since he came back into my life, it all bursts through and I almost scream. His soft lips press harder against mine, bruising and demanding, and I let go of the grip on his shirt. Not for long though, because a frenzy takes over, and I grab onto anything.... Everything; the back of his neck, threading into his hair, his strong shoulders. And in all of this, he demands entry into my mouth, trying to break through that resistance.

I thought the devil seals the deal with a kiss. But this Serpent demands more. So much more.

And tonight, I'm going to give him everything.

Fuck denial.

Fuck Ryan.

Fuck my life.

Fuck it all.

I'm taking that fucking apple and giving in to sin in my own Eden.

Our steps fall backward until the back of my knees hit a ledge, but my shoulder takes another second to find a surface to lean against, and this one is cold, the thud unlike a wall. Our teeth clash as we fight each other in a game of dominance and lust, tongues swiping our words away, and our hands sink too hard into our flesh. But it feels divine.

When I open my eyes, he looks clearer, brighter, an electric blue shining through the black of his eyes. I turn my head, breaking the kiss to find that I'm pressed against the window, but I only catch a glimpse of the street below before his hand wraps around my jaw, and turns me to him.

We pant in unison, his dark eyes feral with a matching need, before his lips slam down on mine again, and his tongue pushes through, finally exploring every bit of my soft mouth. He reaches to my shoulder, his fingers wrapping around the straps of my top and bra, and doesn't hesitate as he pulls down, letting the brisk air caress my bare breast. Not for long, because his hand covers it in an instant, and at the feel of his skin against my pebbled nipple, a moan vibrates against his tongue—mine.

But he swallows it whole. Just as the next one. And the next one after that.

I swear he pinches harder, just so he can feed on my cries. He plays with me in a way that drives me mad. With lust. With need. Mad with the unknown of what's to come beyond tonight.

Letting go of my jaw, he exposes me fully, my lace bra now uncomfortably tight under my breasts. But I draw on that discomfort, delighting in it as he bites my bottom lip and pinches my other nipple.

Releasing my mouth, he pushes me down, and my ass hits the low windowsill. The man stands before me like a dark god, not the devil himself, and the blue hues of the moonlight hit him in such an ethereal way, I allow myself a moment to take him in.

"I didn't think you could get more beautiful than you were then." His words echo hauntingly through the baren space. "I was wrong."

I don't have time to react as he reaches over, pinches my chin between his thumb and index fingers, and looks down at me with a need that all but bleeds out of his eyes.

I'm a second away from acting on what I think he's insinuating, when the man himself drops to his knees between my legs. I gasp and steady myself, gripping the edge of the wood when he pushes my thighs apart. He runs his hands over my skin, and inches closer to where they join, his gaze on mine the whole fucking time. I could come just like this, from this tension, from this fervor dripping from him through me. He dips down on my breasts, his tongue flicking my nipples before he goes all in, sucking, licking... worshiping. It's the only way I can describe it—worshiping.

He looks up at me and tiny prickles slither onto my cheeks, at the same time his hands reach the very top of my thighs and his thumbs touch the seams of my panties.

"Oh, beautiful Eve… Pleasure looks so fucking stunning in your eyes."

I smile, because this is so goddamn perfect, it hurts my soul.

"And you, Serpent, look so fucking pretty kneeling at my feet."

I'm definitely playing with fire. And from the flicker in his eyes, I know I'm gonna get burnt. Though I have a feeling I'm going to enjoy the heat of it.

The man smirks, his lips parted, the crinkles at the corners of his eyes deepening as his tongue sweeps over the side of his top lip. But the moment the dimples appear on his cheeks, I'm done for.

They're my fucking weakness when it comes to this man. It twists his already handsome face into something that was made just for me, perfectly to my taste. Like I gave some god a sketch and they made *him* for me.

I used to swipe my tongue over those dimples, force a smile on his lips just so they would appear for me.

He pulls back enough that he can get a better look at me, and quickly finds the small buckle that holds my skirt up. With one tug, he unravels it. Lingerie covers me and I expect him to rip it apart instantly, to get to his prize. Instead, he looks at me like I'm the most carefully wrapped present, and he's gonna take his time unwrapping it. He presses two fingers onto the dead center of me, dragging them up over the soaked fabric, and I clamp my mouth shut when I realize I was just about to beg him to tear them the hell off.

"The day you stabbed me almost in the heart, I wanted to throw you over that reading chair, and do exactly this to you."

He's not looking for an answer from me. It's a game of show and tell, as he leans in and swipes his tongue over the whole lace-covered center of me. I moan through the sweet pressure, letting my eyes drift closed and head fall back, as he grips the inside of my thighs, and the tips of his fingers dig into my flesh.

"You smell so fucking good…" he hums his approval.

"Good enough to eat, I hope."

Vincent

THE DIM MOONLIGHT hits her from the side, the cheeky grin that pulls at the corners of her mouth beautifully lit.

Definitely good enough to eat, lick, suck, stretch, and fuck. More than good enough for it all.

"Don't move." I pull out the knife I hid in the small holster above my ankle, and look up at her, before pressing the blunt edge on the inside of her thigh.

Her mouth falls open on a hitched breath, echoing softly through whatever space we're in right now, but she does as told. I drag that knife up her thigh until I reach the lace that covers what I crave the most right now. More than I should. I slide the tip under the fabric and drag it along, until it falls apart, careful not to nick her soft flesh.

Jesus fuck, she's gorgeous.

I can't help myself from making her squirm just a bit. I blow on that pretty pink cunt that glistens in the faint light, watching it tighten as goose bumps spread over her thighs, but her moan makes my dick hurt, constricted under too many layers.

Pressing two fingers on her center, I drag them down as she holds her herself from bucking forward, and I open up those pretty lips for me. Damn, I forgot how pretty her pussy is. It really does beg for some teasing. So I flip over the knife and press the slim handle onto her clit, the foreign object making her jump ever so slightly. But I rub it over the bundle of nerves, and her gaze darts straight onto it when I tease her entrance. Her lips are parted, and she squirms, pressing herself onto the handle on the faintest of gasps.

"Goddamnit, Serpent, just... fuck me!"

Her impatience makes me laugh.

"Don't worry, sweetheart. I will." But I pull the knife away, holstering it while I revel in the utter disappointment on her features.

"Please..." Christ, her begging voice would put me to my knees if I wasn't already here.

Without notice, I push two fingers inside her wet cunt, and her ass jolts off the windowsill, but I press my mouth onto her clit, holding her down.

This is my goddamn prize—her taste on my tongue, her pleasure seeping into me.

I slide in and out slowly, as I suck and bite that bundle of nerves that triggers the softest of mewls from her pretty lips. She squirms so much, I have to hold her down with my other hand wrapped around her hip.

"Oh God, please... Vi—"

I almost stall when I hear the start of my actual name on her lips, but she stops herself from that vulnerable moment, and on a tortured moan, she grips my hair, holding me tight as she starts grinding into me. I up my rhythm, and her walls tighten around my fingers, her cries growing louder, and the grip on my head stronger.

Fuck, she's going to break me. Maybe in a good way, maybe in the worst kinds of ways. But I'm not going anywhere. The moment our lives reconnected, I knew she would be it.

It was reckless of her to make a pact with me, because there is no escape, not after the events of our past, and certainly not after today.

This covenant is forever—her soul is mine.

My tongue flicks her clit over and over, my lips pressing, rolling, sucking, as I pump those two digits harder inside of her, over and over and over. My forearm muscles tighten, a slight burn spreading through from the assault, but her cries intensify, and I'm loving every moment of it. As her walls grip me in bursts of contractions, and her legs gently begin to shake, I know—

"I'm coming..." she whispers through hard pants. "I'm coming! Hoooly fuck!" Her legs convulse, her pussy gripping me even tighter, and I slow my rhythm, dragging her through the pleasure riddling her body.

"There's nothing holy about this, Little Eve," I say as I get up, and lift her from under the armpits.

I don't give her time to come down from the high of her orgasm, and I flip her trembling body around.

"No, there isn't, is there?" The glass steams with her whisper as she steadies herself against the window frame, arching her back as I grip her hip.

It's such a pretty sight, her hair wild down her back, her ass perched out for me, with the view of the moonlit sea as a backdrop.

I release myself from my trousers and boxers in record time, and grip my dick painfully hard, willing it to calm as her delicious taste lingers on my tongue. I need to last more than ten fucking seconds, but as I watch her now, still catching her breath from the orgasm, with her lush hips, full ass, and that soft skin... I realize I might not last at all.

Fuck!

I fumble quickly with the condom I pulled out of my pocket, and give my dick a final squeeze, the pain doing a good job at keeping me sane. Then I drag the glistening tip down between her ass cheeks, and her head falls back the moment it reaches her pussy.

I can't hold myself back, give her time to adjust. I'm dying to be inside of her.

Wrapping a hand around her throat, the other around her hip, I slam into her in one long stroke, and the sharp cry that echoes through the dark space is enough to make me come right now.

"Holy fuck!"

"I thought there was nothing holy about this." She laughs.

"This is as fucking close to it as I'll ever get." I pull out and slam right back into her.

The window rattles, the slapping of our skin a cheer, pushing us further and further into this depravity.

"More..." she moans.

And I give her exactly that, slamming into her with a force that I'm afraid might break that window. So I pull her up, wrapping my hands around her, and carry on with the assault we both so desperately need. It goes past the moment of craving. Past the moment of mindless lust. I'm not even sure if it was ever only that.

She moans her protest as I pull out of her and turns around with fury painted brightly in her eyes. But I grab her face, pressing a bruising kiss on her lips as I push her against the wall next to the window. Then I lean over, hook her knee on my arm, teasing her as I rub the tip of my cock along her wet pussy. I insist just a bit longer on that swollen clit, as her nails rake over the skin of my back and waist.

"Don't fucking play with me, Serpent. Fuck me or get down on your knees, either way... make me come!"

"Oh, you've got a filthy mouth on you, Little Eve. Is this what you want?" I slam into her, balls deep, and her body hits the wall with a loud thud, knocking the air out of her. I slide out slowly, and her pussy drives me crazy as it grips every single inch of me. "Or this?" As I thrust harder, she yelps with a smirk on her lips.

"More!"

With one arm hooked under her knee, holding her beautifully spread for me, and the other braced on the wall next to her head, I give her exactly what she wants. I fuck her weeping pussy with harsh thrusts, her body definitely bruising as it slams into the wall, and her sharp fingernails sink hard enough into my skin that she must be drawing blood.

"Is this what you want?"

She only pants in response, a divine smile pulling at her lips.

Far too many times in the last few months, I imagined her wrapped around my cock. I've dreamt of it too since our little dance in the forest. Having her here, now, feels like a damn dream.

"Your cunt weeps for me, sweet Eve. Tell me how you want to be fucked."

A shudder rips through her and her gaze pins me with such wanton need, fire shines through the green.

"Harder! Find the end of me, Serpent!"

And I do. I spread her leg so far back, she cries at the stretch, but when I drive into her, I'm fully fucking sheathed. She yells, either in pleasure or pain, or maybe both, but her core spasms around me, threatening to milk me dry as I repeat the motion, and I take it as my cue. Pressing my fingers onto her clit, I barely rub twice, and she explodes around me, pulling me into the deep and I shatter right along with her.

I rest my forehead onto hers as her whole body spasms, and she swallows her moans as she wraps both arms around my neck, holding herself together. My knees begin to shake, this pleasure too much. Everything is too much.

She moans filthy words against my mouth, one more intelligible than the former, and I could have sworn that one of them was my name... not Serpent. My actual name.

Gods, I wish she would say it. The hate I bred in her is keeping it off her lips.

We crash onto the floor together, her arms still around my neck as she straddles me, panting. She's slightly reluctant, but her body finally relaxes, and her head falls on my chest, as I wrap my arms around her. There's a voice in the back of my mind that wills me to tighten my hold, like she's about to wake up, realize what she's just done, and bolt. But I push it in the background, and instead enjoy what I have, drawing lazy circles on her back as we come down to earth.

I cannot think of a time when sex was like this, when I needed a minute, not to catch my breath, but to reel my mind back in, too.

Was it ever?

CHAPTER 17
Morrigan

"I HAVE TO go," I whisper.

"No." That's all Vincent says—short, firm, no breath wasted.

"I've disappeared for too long." I push myself up, clumsily getting to my feet, and pull on my bra and top.

I have no idea how to feel about this. It was the most mind-blowing sex I've ever had, and I can't believe I lost myself this way. Huge fucking mistake though. His touch will linger on my skin for too long, and the last thing I need is to crave this wicked man.

Using the moonlight, I find my skirt, and when I pick it up and wrap it around my waist, I realize how pointless this is. This thing is made of just eight or ten wide ribbons of fabric, hanging from what could only be described as a belt, and my panties are hanging from my hips, split where I need them most.

Fuck.

Time to improvise. I grab the two ribbons at the front, pass them between my legs and loop them around the waistband at the back, before coming back to the front for a second layer of covering. It will have to do, so hopefully it holds on.

"Do they miss you that much downstairs? I don't think you can dance in that anymore."

When I look back up at The Serpent, I find him watching me with a slightly impressed expression, as he points at my makeshift underwear. He pauses for a moment longer before he zips up his trousers and covers the scar I gave him as he buttons up his shirt.

"I'm not dancing anymore. Not tonight," I answer, but my gaze fixes on his chest.

God, I was so angry that day. My family and Ryan had already made me feel like shit, and then he appeared. It was the first time I'd seen him in years, and his voice, his scent, his eyes, everything about him made me furious. His sheer presence in my space was an insult. But the worst thing was that it didn't feel any different from all those years before—it felt as if he belonged right there, next to me. And that enraged me further. Ultimately, it was the reason why I stabbed him. He was getting too close, and

I was terrified of how good that comfort could feel.

"How badly did I hurt you?" I ask, nodding to his chest, as I rub a thumb over my own scar.

"It only went in about an inch and a half. Could have been worse."

"I'll keep it in mind for next time." I feel bad, but I don't want to develop compassion for the man. No matter how well he just fucked me.

"It's cute of you to think that it will happen again," he says, cocking an eyebrow in that effortlessly arrogant way that makes me want to ask him to fuck me all over again. "Why are you in such a rush to leave?"

I try to look around for our masks, but this darkness is too thick. I know there's a switch next to the unfinished kitchen cabinets, so I fumble my way over.

"It's not the club I've disappeared for too long from." I flip the switch and the open space fills with a soft light, both of us blinking a few times to adjust to it.

"Then who?"

Suddenly, the door flies open.

"Mooorri!" Lulu bursts through, panic in her voice.

She stops, panting as she looks between me and The Serpent, confusion slowly narrowing her eyes. But she shakes her head and points to the window.

"He's here."

"No, no, no. Fuck!" I flip that switch back off, then rush to the window, slowly peeking down, trying to confirm the bad news. "I have to go!"

"What the fuck is going on?!" The Serpent's voice booms through the open space.

"It's Ryan, he's downstairs. Security alerted me that there's someone in front of the building, trying to get inside the lobby of the apartments." Lulu's still trying to catch her breath, and I know she probably didn't even wait for the elevator, she just ran up. "Wait. What are *you* doing here? Morri, what is *he* doing here?"

She turns to me, the light of the moon shining on her, bright enough that I can't miss that scolding gaze.

"Just... sealing a deal," he answers for me, and I can read the smirk in his voice even if I can't see it. "Why is Holt here?"

"Because I'm not supposed to be. I have to go."

I see our masks on the floor and pick them both up, handing one to him and mine to Lulu. I quickly unwrap my wig, flipping my hair over a few times and handing that to her too.

"I need a long dress, something I can quickly throw over this. All my clothes are in the club."

"Come to my place. Quick!" She runs to the door, ripping it open, and it's then that I hear the loud bangs, rattling the metal of the lobby doors, way down on the ground floor.

"Listen to me, goddamnit!" The Serpent yells, his hand wrapping around my upper arm, turning me around to face him. "I can protect you. You don't need to go."

I shake my head, tears burning their way through my lids, and emotions I've never shown to Vincent slowly seep through. I'm terrified. Fucking terrified that right now I risk exposing our hard work to the man I want to rip out of this world. He's threatening everything I am—my family, my brother, my best friend, my goddamn freedom. And

I've disappeared for too long. I knew it was a mistake coming to the club tonight. I should have gone anywhere else. But then again, he probably would have searched here first anyway.

"He can't know. Listen to me, he can't know." My tone is urgent, and frantic, and his usual dark slits widen for a moment. "You're the last hope I have to take them all down. I won't risk you. You're my secret weapon, and it's too soon to draw you out."

I pull myself out of his grip and rush to the door, pulling it open.

"Come on." I keep my tone low as I turn to him. With a deep sigh, he finally hurries to me and follows up the stairs.

We reach Lulu's floor at the same time she comes out the door, a casual, long black dress in tow. I quickly pull it on and look between them.

"I'm going to try to talk to him. He knows that sometimes I spend the night here, so this shouldn't be any different. Obviously, he will protest, but he usually gives up. He claimed I still get some freedom until the knot is tied, so I'm gonna try to reason." I give Lulu a quick peck on the cheek, then look one last time at Vincent. The fury painted so vividly on his features takes me aback, but I can't stay and ask if it's directed at me or Ryan, so I quickly rush down the stairs instead.

There was no way I was going to tell either of them, but a sickness has filled my insides, like never before. Ryan has never done this, and I have a feeling there will be no reasoning with him this time, no matter how hard I try.

But what choice do I have?

Vincent

"COME WITH ME." Loreley grabs my wrist, displaying no sense of self-preservation, no worry that she's bossing the fucking Serpent around. What is it with these two women? Have they no fear?

The moment we're inside her apartment, I pull my hand from her grip, and she stops, turning to me. Now, in this closed space, all alone, judging by the look in her eyes, she finally realizes who stands before her. I don't miss the slight shiver running down her body.

"I know who you are." She tightens her shoulders. "I also know who to come to if anything happens to her, because you two made a deal, and I know the terms." She stands tall, unmoving, holding her ground.

"You know everything?"

She narrows her eyes but stays silent. Does she know about my past with Morrigan? Or about the guy she murdered? About the leverage Holt has against her?

My bet is she knows what she needs to.

"Come." She finally speaks and runs toward the window.

The lights are off, so we're slightly protected from whoever looks up from below. But the image before me breaks a part of me I didn't know existed until now, and I grab onto those pieces, holding them tight because I need to put them back together eventually.

I'm losing her...

My hands tighten into fists, nostrils flaring with a painful tension that rips through my chest, as I watch Morrigan. She's fighting off two guys as they grab each of her arms at Holt's orders. The moment Loreley cracks the window slightly, Morrigan's scream splits me in half, and my short nails dig into my palms painfully.

"Let me gooo! Dammit, Ryan, let me go, you're better than this. Just—"

Holt takes one step, just one step toward her, and she freezes. The woefully defeated, submissive look in her eyes, pushes me over the fucking edge. It brings back memories I've buried. Memories of a woman broken at the hands of a controlling, abusive man. But there's no way I'll let this situation get as far as I allowed it with my mom.

Ryan Holt is as good as dead. Just as my goddamn sperm donor will eventually be. Morrigan's, too.

His death sentence was signed already, but this might just warrant a more special execution.

A feral growl fills my ears, and when Loreley's head whips in my direction, I realize it was mine. But I'm already on the move. Only a few more steps, and I'll be out the door, ready to fucking end this right here, right now.

"No! Vincent, stop! She's right. You can't do anything now." There's such desperation in Loreley's voice. It cracks with a similar pain to the one ripping me apart at this moment. Its familiarity makes me stop.

She whirls around me, gripping my arms, her golden eyes pleading, as unshed tears pool there. That's her best friend out there and we share this pain. Her throat bobs, once... twice, and she swallows her breaths, as a tear falls onto her cheek. Then another, and another.

With no notice whatsoever from my brain, I shake off her hands and pull her in, wrapping my arms around her. Then she breaks. She cries into my chest, quiet whimpers of fear as I hold her. I'm tense, fully out of my comfort zone, but Loreley is all alone in this, and I cannot just stand here and watch her break down.

"He will pay for this," I whisper.

She pulls away, her lips parting to speak, but a commotion distracts us, and we rush to the cracked window. One of the guys is on his knees, clutching his crotch, and the other one holds both Morrigan's hands behind her back. In the next moment, Holt's hand slams against her cheek so hard, the guy behind has to hold her up.

I see fucking red, visions of crimson rivers of their blood filling these motherfucking streets, and I know one thing for sure—that's not my imagination, it's the fucking future.

"You'll never see that Dietrich bitch ever again. You'll never step foot here, or anywhere else, for that matter, unless you're with me. I hope you enjoyed yourself tonight, because it was last of your freedom," Holt spits at her before shoving her in the back of the SUV. *"Oh, and by the way, I moved the wedding date."* He slams the door closed on her screams, and we hide as he turns to look up.

I have to get her back.

"She'll be okay. She'll be okay. My girl is strong. She'll be okay." Loreley repeats those words like a mantra.

She will be okay, right?

Tires screech on the asphalt, and we both peek out the window—they're gone. She's gone. And this complicates things.

"What are we going to do?" Loreley asks.

"*We* are not going to do anything. You will carry on as per usual, take care of your club, and whatever else you do. If you need any help with that in *her* absence, you let me know."

"No offense. Morri might be desperate enough to make a deal with you, but I would rather not." Her chin raises and her gaze is a far cry from moments ago when she was sobbing into my chest.

Like a switch, she flipped it and whoever she was a minute ago is buried deep. If it's even buried at all. It might just be gone. It's peculiar, but her sweet voice doesn't quite match that stern look in her eyes.

"I'm not making a deal with you. I'm offering support." I take a step forward. Not toward her, but to the door.

"Yeah. You seem to be a very... supportive man. I didn't peg you as the type to hold a crying woman as you did."

I turn my head to her, the muscles of my face slowly relaxing in their usual state that makes people around me uncomfortable, fearful.

"I've never claimed to be heartless, Miss Dietrich." I move away, toward the exit, and stop before I'm out. "But I would still appreciate it if you kept that information to yourself."

"Sure. We wouldn't want people to know that The Serpent has a soft side." There's a hint of sarcasm in her voice.

"Not when his enemies could rip away the reason why he does."

On the slight hitch in her breath, I walk out.

CHAPTER 18
Morrigan

THAT VEIL OF hate has fallen thick over me, over us, over everything we were, are, and never will be.

Who imagines a relationship ending in a forced beginning? No one. Not even me, knowing I live in this world where the barrier between good and evil is drawn with chalk.

"You brought this on yourself," Ryan rasps.

I've never seen him this angry, never felt the sting of his palm on my face until today, and I think that shocked me most of all. The fury in his eyes rendered me speechless when we were out on the street, because it's not a usual emotion for him. Not with me anyway.

"I didn't do anything!" My pitch heightens as I clutch the sides of my face, fear and anger mixing in a concoction that has the stupidest effect on me. I'm erratic and frozen at the same time and my brain can't fucking decide on the next move.

"Oh, of course you did, darling. You made me go out on the streets looking for your trampy ass! Then you made a show out of it all where anyone could have seen." He moves toward me, and I shuffle backwards on the bed in an instant.

But something marvelous happens—a victorious smirk creeps through his eyes, pulling at the corners of his lips, and it fuels me with such disdain. He does not get to win over me. He may have kidnapped me, but he does not get to hold the power. That smirk brings back the threads of what makes me... *me*, and the apprehension I felt toward him just seconds before, begins to dissipate. It's not completely gone, and it will not be until I'll be the one holding the power. But this is a goddamn start.

So I hang on to that feeling and make a silent promise to the man who's trying to break me—*you will pay for this, Ryan Holt. I'll make sure you suffer before you take your last breath.*

"*My* trampy ass?! You screwed a woman in front of me to prove some sort of point that only made sense to you! You've gone mad. You lost yourself in this dark world, in the money it can bring and the power you will never, ever obtain. You delusional motherfucker!" My tone grows stronger with each sentence, and it only triggers him more.

"I didn't lose myself, Morrigan, on the contrary, I found myself. I goddamn found myself, who I'm meant to be, and it took me long enough to get here. Too long did I have to kiss my dear father's ass, until he was finally out of the equation, and yours, too. But you're not going anywhere. You always thought you were so much better than me, up there on your high horse with your rich, clueless family who bailed you out of all the fucking bullshit you've caused. And they don't even know the full extent of it yet. Like how you killed a man before you were even eighteen years old." His arms are all over the place, waving in the air to match his tone and the wild gaze.

It engages my fight-or-flight response. The former much more.

"And even without that knowledge, they still fucking hate you. Enough to sell you to me without a second thought."

His maniacal laugh echoes off the walls, the creases in his skin bizarre in the dim light of the only lit lamp in the room.

"I didn't ask you to kiss my ass, Ryan. I didn't fucking ask you for anything," I argue.

"But I wanted you. Needed you! For so long, I waited in the background for you to notice me. Even in those teenage years in school, when you had eyes for anyone but me. Then I waited for you through goddamn university, and I finally got you. I fucked and ruined you, and I want more!" Madness shines in his eyes with those last words. "I want everything you are and everything you have! I want to destroy every fucking piece of you until all you'll be is a shadow under my control."

The veins in his temple and the ones in his throat are bulging, the pulse raging high as his eyes grow so wide, they look feral. A cold shiver runs through me, and I don't know where to go from here. I'm shocked, confused, and definitely creeped out. I can't make sense of him.

"Why? Why are you so intent on destroying me?" It comes out barely louder than a whisper.

"Because you said no."

I'm stunned into silence, but I'm more confused than shocked.

"Are you jo—"

"You ignored me for so long, and when I asked you out, you said no. I loved you, and you said no. I worshiped you, and you said no! I always knew that we were perfect for each other, and you still fucking said no. You are my first love, Morrigan!" He's strangely emotional, but it comes out as manic. Yet he still continues. "You only noticed me when the time came for me to help you bury a goddamn body. It felt like betrayal. But betrayal tastes fucking bitter and you filled me with it."

"Jesus, Ryan, what are you talking about? How did I betray you?"

"Don't patronize me!" His sudden rage makes me flinch. Then he takes a deep breath and continues like nothing happened. "You only had eyes for the *snake*. Only for him... Then that night, you gave me exactly what I needed to make sure you will have no escape from me—you gave me leverage."

"We were fucking teenagers! You cannot be serious. You're doing this because of something that happened over six years ago? You have some sort of sick vendetta, even though we did end up together?" He's insane, Jesus Christ, he's insane. I—I don't know how to deal with this. "This makes no sense, Ryan. You keep blaming this on me, but *you* ruined us."

"We may have been young, but were we not human? We were. And I loved you and you went to someone else. Either way, after that night, I knew I needed to wait for all the pieces to fall into place—my father, the business, then you. I watched my father take too little risks, make too many mistakes over the years, and I knew I could do so much better than him. I could bring this business to a greatness that would control this whole fucking city and everything around it!" He raises his arms to the sides, palms up, like he's presenting his victory to me. A megalomaniac in action... "And you fit perfectly in my new world, only your place is no longer on the throne, my love, it's on your knees in front of mine."

I suppress the retching, but it's hard-fucking-work. He walks around the bed, and I stiffen as he leans over, swiping the backs of his fingers against my cheek. One by one, each of my muscles flinches in awareness as it prepares my body to flee.

"I loved you. You know I did, and you shit on everything anyway," I say, holding his gaze.

"Until you didn't and planned to leave me. I couldn't allow that." He leans in closer, planting his hands on the bed, and just as he's about to climb up, a ringing blares through the room, making him pause.

He waits, enough to inhale and exhale his irritation, before he rises and pulls the phone from his front pocket.

He frowns at the name on the screen and answers. "What? ... When?"

I try to listen, hoping I can pick up something from the other line.

"And they want to throw in another dozen? ... Okay, we need the space... In the—" He catches himself, turning to me just before he reveals something I most certainly shouldn't know. "Yeah, I'll come now." He grins at me and hangs up.

Walking around the bed, he stops in the middle of the room. "This is yours." He gestures around the space. "You will not leave unless I allow you to. You will be out for meals downstairs and nothing more. You have essentials here, and if anything else is needed... well, you can try asking my mother. You will stay in here until I can trust you with me in my bedroom. It will not change your condition, but you will be allowed more freedom in this house."

It's a whirlwind. I'm pulled in directions I cannot even think of anymore. What's up, what's down, what the hell is going on? This night that started so beautifully crashed and burned in an unexpected way. All I anticipated was a heated reaction, not a kidnapping.

Ryan rips open the door, and before he disappears through it, he turns his head slightly.

"And by the way, there is no question that I will obtain the power I deserve. I will rip it right out of the clutches of the *sanctity* that rules this city."

And with that last spit off his tongue, he slams the door behind him, the pictures rattling on the walls in his wake.

The last thing I hear is the click of the locks.

Vincent

I SHOULDN'T BE in this state. Her absence should not make me feel like a savage, ready to burn down his fucking castle to claim her back. But it does. Goddamnit, it does, and I can't figure out when I fell. When the shadow of my obsession for her shifted forward. The one that always cast its darkness in a deep corner of my soul, noticeable even amidst the crepuscule that already resides there.

She's always been there. Always.

My little obsession.

The one I was forced to let go of too many years ago.

In the meantime, I had to move on. I convinced myself that she was too young for this life anyway, even though it was bullshit. The preconceptions that come with certain ages barely applied to her, and when they did, they gave her a sort of naivety that made her even more desirable. She was eager, headstrong in all the right and wrong ways, but perfect to mold with the right qualities. Not that she needed much molding. Morrigan O'Rourke has always been a force to be reckoned with, but I wanted to be the one to teach her about the afflictions of this world and show her how to corrupt them so they bend at your will. And goddamnit, she had will. Her fire was ravenous even then, and so dangerous, it took me too long to stop worrying that she'd end up in fucking jail, or... dead.

Eventually, I had no choice. And I managed to convince myself that, without me, she would stay out of this world, my world, and she'd be safer.

I still kept my eyes on her. I couldn't help myself. Not in a stalkerish way, but once in a while, I would *check in* and see what she was up to. She still got into fights. I would have thought that by now she would have actually taken some lessons, but no. Her bar fights are sloppy, violent, and brash, but she enters this state of delirium that fills her with adrenaline and she's unstoppable then. Last fight I saw her in was maybe a year ago, in Levane, the next town over. She was with Loreley in this dive of a bar that's stupidly popular, and some guy couldn't take no for an answer and crossed the line. She didn't know I was there too. It was pure coincidence, and I was fully out of her sight, but ready to jump and rip that asshole's head off. I didn't need to—she broke his nose with the peanut bowl from the bar, then absolutely destroyed two barstools on his body. The sight was utterly divine. It took two people to get her off him, and a fight almost broke out in the whole bar. She left before she found out I was there.

Yet here we are... magnets that finally turned the right way around and got pulled back together.

"You look rough." Finn's voice sounds somewhere next to me.

I sigh and look up. Bright blue eyes grin at me, only, the moment they actually catch my gaze, they darken.

"What's wrong?!"

You can always tell when Finn gets serious, because that pretty boy face suddenly becomes sharper, and his lean, wide shoulders pull back and seem to widen. His whole stance shifts, making you feel like you're in the savannah, out in the open, and a cheetah has its eyes on you. You want to run, and even if you do, you know there's no way you're going to be fast enough.

I open my mouth to speak as Madds walks in. "You know, one of these days, I'm going to walk into this bar and your faces are not going to look the way they do now. What the fuck happened now?"

I swipe a palm over my face, then settle my elbows on my knees, clutching my hands together.

"Holt took Morrigan O'Rourke."

"Wait, what do you mean he *took* her? I thought they live together, future wife and all." Finn sits in the opposite armchair, confused, and I narrow my eyes on him, slits warning him off.

"They don't. Since the engagement, he and her family have forced her to stay with him, but whenever her parents aren't paying attention, she stays at their house. Fucking gems they are." Madds crosses his arms, looking a little uneasy.

"I don't get it. Why doesn't she just run away?" Finn asks.

Madds and I exchange looks, a silent conversation taking place. It's not our secret to tell, but then again, it's the one we need to, if the whole Sanctum is going to help her. Even if the deal was made just with me, I need my brothers in this. I can't fucking risk her.

"Because Holt helped her bury a dead man and is now blackmailing her." We all turn at the same time, watching Carter walk quickly toward us.

"What the fu—How the hell did you know?"

I agree with Madds. What is going on here?

"We're in. I finally got into Holt's personal computer, but I have limited access. He's either not great with technology, or he's paranoid. So he doesn't back up into clouds or online servers. I only have access when it's actually turned on. Tina and Jian traced it and got in about an hour ago. We didn't have much time before we got disconnected, and only managed to copy about twenty percent of his drives. But one of the folders we copied"—Carter turns his gaze to me—"is a photo album of a younger Morrigan O'Rourke, digging a hole in the ground and looking over a dead body."

"Is there any way to find out where else he holds this information? If he copied it on an external hard drive?" I ask.

"Wait, you know of this?" Finn leans over, looking between us.

"We found out the other day, pretty much at the same time as her. She had no idea the bastard took photos and had them this whole time," Madds responds.

"Wait, I understand why Vin would know, but why do *you* know?!"

"Because Holt decided to reveal this to her when we were at the dinner party the other day, the one O'Rourke invited us to. Before he left, he gave her an envelope of photos and we walked in on her after she opened it," I explain, and he rubs his jaw as he listens.

"I have a feeling I already know the answer to this, but what the heck? Who killed the guy she was burying?" Finn continues the line of questioning.

"She did, and it was my fault."

The room goes silent at those last words. Madds is the only one who knows the whole story. Almost the whole thing.

Jesus, I don't want to be a soppy prick and bare my fucking heart and soul out to them. This is not who we are, no matter how tight our bond is. *Shit.* But they have to know something; they need some context.

"Fucking hell." I swipe a hand over my face, sighing. "Look, you already know Morrigan and I were together. A long time ago, when you and Carter were in university. And... yeah, shit happened. We were at that point when all of this"—I point around us—"was starting, when we were making our first deals and establishing ourselves. And it ended."

"You're skipping a few parts of that story, brother..." Madds' tone is lower, pinning me with his deep amber eyes from under his eyebrows.

Fuck, I know I'm skipping over a few parts!

I'm skipping over the fact that I noticed her years before we got together. I'm skipping over the way her green eyes stood out in school, no matter the crowds of girls who swooned over us.

I'm skipping over the fact that through those crowds, hers was the only face I saw. I noticed her when no one else seemed to, and I couldn't believe that wild red hair framing that freckled pale skin could ever be overlooked.

I'm skipping over how I broke up a fight one day between her and some kid who was bullying her, and she was winning. I stood there and admired the fire in her for a while, before I stopped her from making a big mistake. I'm skipping over how I pulled her away and dragged her behind the maintenance building to calm her rage.

I'm skipping over how I felt when her heaving breaths were turning to something else other than rage and I had to step away from her. Over how she ran to me after I turned to leave, jumped into my arms, and pressed her soft lips to mine. I'm definitely skipping over how pure and wild it felt. And over how she smirked at me and ran back to class, but not before telling me...

"I saved that one for you. My first one."

Her first goddamn kiss.

I'm skipping over how she left me speechless and confused. How I finished school and moved on. How I found her again a couple of years later, beating up the guy who was forcing himself on her. I'm skipping over how important she became in a stupidly short amount of time. How deep she crawled under my skin, seeped into my blood, and filled every part of my heart.

I'm skipping over how I got to ask her...

"Did you save this first for me as well?" As I looked down at where we were almost joined.

And she did. It meant more than I ever thought something like that would. Because it was her. Because everything she was, her mind, her soul, her heart, fit with mine like perfect puzzle pieces, and it made no sense how it was possible.

I'm skipping over all of this and more.

"Madds and I saved her from the guy we told you about a while back, the one whose jaw she broke. And we got together not long after, for a few months." I hold myself straight, pulling that shield up, strapping on the armor that contains The

Serpent they all know. It's not a mask, this is all me, but that armor protects and conceals those vulnerable parts of me, the softer sides that enjoy their privacy. "When we broke up, that same guy came for her, because he knew she was no longer under my protection. He knew I was out of her life and was all alone." I briefly repeat the story Morrigan shared with us.

Finn has a sympathetic look in his eyes, whilst Carter... well, emotions aren't his strong suit, so that analytical look in his doesn't quite surprise me.

"Why did you break up?" Carter asks, cocking his head subtly.

"It doesn't matter now." My eyes flicker to Madds for a split second. "What matters is that Morrigan O'Rourke cannot leave. Holt threatened to kill her parents, her brother, and when she seemed not to care that much about that, he threatened her with jail. And there's no way she would get out on self-defense, not after hiding it and burying the guy. He threatened Loreley too... and she cares more about her than she does her own freedom. She's stuck, hence—"

"Why she asked you for help," Carter says as a matter of fact.

"Yes, well, she asked for my help when it wasn't even quite this bad. I think she still had some hope then. But I've seen how Holt treated her. He kidnapped her from the sidewalk, threatened, and slapped her. And there's one more thing that has to stay between us only. She'll fucking kill me if it gets out."

They all nod in unison.

"Metamorphosis is hers too. She's a silent partner."

"Why silent? I mean, it wouldn't be unusual for two friends to go into business together. Look at us."

"Yeah, Finn, but none of us have abusive families and partners who want to destroy us."

Carter clears his throat in an all-knowing way, but I interrupt him.

"You know what I mean."

"Knowing her, she's doing it for Loreley more than for herself. Holt, even her family, would use the club against her," Madds says, nodding in understanding.

"What would they do if they found out we're backing them?"

Finn's words lay heavy in the air and grins form on all of our lips.

"As much as I will love seeing that, we have to hold off until the time is right. No one can know. No one."

CHAPTER 19
Vincent

"HELLO, MY DARLINGS," Jonathan, *The Ghost*, greets us.

He's a lean man, well into his fifties, very well-dressed in his tweed suit that Carter is currently admiring. Both men have style, but Jonathan definitely has an edge, and always wears some sort of flashy accessory. A little something to give him that touch of extravagance, whilst remaining tasteful. This time around, a filigree gold brooch shines on his lapel.

"Jonathan," Carter says with a nod.

He's the one who built this connection between the man and The Sanctum. When they were younger, Jonathan was Carter's father's best friend, but their relationship slowed down because of his mother. She was overbearing in a special kind of way. Life and Jonathan's business got in the way after that, and they didn't properly reconnect before his death. A year or so later, Carter's friendship with the man started, just before he left for university, and although we don't appeal to him too much in business, he is a very useful ally.

We all came here, at Jonathan's urgent request, and we're anxious to find out what the hell is going on. He's never *ordered* us to hurry up, ever before.

"Come, come. Follow me."

He leads us quickly inside a warehouse, and we're eagle-eyed as we pass large industrial shelves filled with packed boxes of all shapes, sizes, and materials. Some more heavy duty than others. But we don't stop at any of them, instead we go straight to the other end of it, where two of Jonathan's men stand by a sliding door that's probably about nine foot high and just as wide.

He stops and turns to us.

"This is one thing I won't work with, and I'm convinced you won't agree with it either."

His men slide open the large door, and we're looking right at the back of a container, its doors cracked. Since it opens inside the warehouse, it's a clever way of checking the contents without having outside eyes on you. But when he opens up the container, we're all stuck for words.

The stench is horrendous. The image even worse.

Girls and boys are huddled together, all in a horrible state. They're dirty, scared, or just catatonic. None of them dare say a word to us or even make eye contact. They're completely still, clearly afraid that the wrong move would be fatal. Some of them look drugged out of their mind.

"How long have they been in there?!" Finn reacts first.

When I turn to him, I can't pinpoint his expression—his lips are parted, he's blinking rapidly, but he quickly shakes himself, taking a deep breath before looking away.

"The container has been traveling for three days. We fed them and gave them water when we found them. That was about an hour or so ago, and we haven't logged the receipt of the container yet. But I will have to soon."

"Are you telling me that this is O'Rourke's container?" I take one more step forward, swiping my eyes over the delicate faces that don't dare look at me. They're probably between ten and sixteen, at most.

"And Holt's," Jonathan confirms.

"But the deal was for ammunition and goddamn cocaine!" When I turn to Madds, he's barely containing himself.

The man is a beast. He looks like one. He sounds like one, but he doesn't act like one unless he's in the ring of The Fightclub or he has a good fucking reason to waste his energy on killing a man. None of that applies to crimes against children, though, especially sexual crimes. The people involved in something like this are at the top of his 'no questions asked murder.'

"That was indeed the deal. I'm supposed to be discreet too. But one of my guys heard crying when we pulled the container off the ship and set it in the docking area. I won't condone this, Vincent." He turns to me, a stern gravity in his eyes.

"I agree. It needs to stop now." Madds steps forward and walks inside the container. Some of the kids cower instantly, trying to make themselves invisible, and it's fucking hard to watch.

It's just as hard to say the next words out loud.

"We can't stop it now."

Everyone freezes. When their predatory gazes turn to me, various levels of outrage and fury meet mine, but I continue before they start protesting.

"If we do, all hell breaks loose, the deal is off, we become enemies, and all of them"—I point to the poor souls in the container—"along with the ones before and the ones after, will be lost. They'll find another way, probably a better one, and this operation will continue behind our backs. What we need is to find out more without Holt and O'Rourke knowing, then end them and their entire operation."

"That's complete fucking madness!" Madds' voice booms through the small space of the container and some of the kids start crying. But he sighs, swiping a hand over his buzzcut, and I know he sees the reasoning too.

"Are you fucking saying that we're supposed to close these doors and let them go, wherever the fuck those assholes are taking them?!" The anger and pain in Finn's voice is unmistakable.

If anyone is going to be sensitive about this, it's definitely him. He's the only one here who has lost someone to this *trade*, and he's never spoken a word about it since. Not to me anyway.

"We don't have a choice. They can't know we're aware of this. This is the quickest way to find out where they're taking them, because this operation might be bigger than this one container. The hydra has many heads, and we need to cut the root and find all of them." As harsh as I sound, as horrible as this solution is, I know I'm making sense. From the looks I'm getting, it's clear that the wheels are spinning in their brains right now. "Saving just them will not save all the others. If there are any others."

"We need someone on the inside. But none of Katya's employees would fit in, none of them look remotely young enough." Carter cocks his head, swiping his gaze through the faces in the container.

"Jesus Christ." I hear Finn somewhere next to me, as he starts pacing around. I understand he's uncomfortable with this, but it's the quickest choice we have right now.

"I'll—I'll do it." We all turn at the same time a girl, one of the older ones in there, gets up on very shaky legs, and tries to walk from the back of the container.

Madds rushes to her, reaching over to help, but she pulls back quickly. No one speaks, so we don't freak her out more than she already is. Eventually, after a brief pause gazing into his eyes, she gently places her small hand in Madds' large one and walks forward. I don't miss the way every single soul in that container turns as she walks past. They quite literally look up to her. If she's the eldest, she probably protected them in there or before they were put in.

She steps out into the brighter light of the warehouse, and now we can see she's older than the others in there. She's maybe five-foot-three and slim, too slim, and she looks exhausted. One of Jonathan's men rushes away and quickly returns with a chair.

"I'll do it. If there's more"—she looks back toward the inside of the container—"I want to find them. But it has to happen fast. I can't risk them getting... I can't." She sighs, unable to finish that sentence.

"I know. I understand." I try to be comforting, but I don't think my current stern attitude works for her. I'm blinded by the disgust I have toward this entire situation. I turn to Jonathan. "How much time do we have until you have to let them know the container arrived?"

"An hour, tops."

"Okay. We need a tracker." I look at Carter who nods and wastes no time, rushing through the warehouse. Seconds later, we hear the car leaving. "We're going to put a tracker on you. It's going to be small. You might have to swallow it or—"

"It's okay. I'll do whatever it takes. Slice me open and put it under my skin, I don't care. Just... help them."

Not us, not me—*them*.

"What's your name?" I ask her.

"Evelyn." Her voice is calm, not defeated, but composed, as if she's been trying to hold herself together through all of this.

"How old are you?" Finn steps forward, the look in his eyes hard to pinpoint. Somewhere between anger, shock, and heartbreaking sadness.

"Seventeen..." She turns her head toward the container. "My sister is seven."

"Fucking hell," he mutters to himself, swiping a hand over his face.

Everyone in this room right now is broken in some way. I drag my gaze over all their faces, and even the two men I don't know, Jonathan's men, look as if they could cry and kill at the same time. We all may be criminals, but this is not our kind of crime.

"We'll get you all out. That's a promise. But you all have to be strong. I just don't know what will happen as soon as you'll arrive wherever they're taking you." I wish I didn't have to say those words, but I can't promise her she'll be fully safe.

I attempt to comfort her again though and place my hand on her shoulder.

She flinches but doesn't move away. Her eyes narrow on mine for a moment before she nods. Maybe she sees my promise in them. Or maybe the violence I plan to unleash on the people who did this to them. She looks up at Madds, and even as he stands beside her, she seems comfortable with that.

"Will they—will they get to the children?" She lowers her tone to a whisper.

Her big eyes, a thick, dark ring surrounding a bright gray seeping into amber, fix on me, begging for an answer I don't have.

"I really hope not, but I don't want to lie to you."

Tears slowly fill her eyes, but she doesn't cry, doesn't even whimper. She lets them pool in her lids until there's no more space and they trail down her dirty cheeks, before she finally wipes them with the back of her hand.

"I understand." She turns to the others again, and nods once. A gentle reassurance she doesn't really believe in.

"Where did they take you from?" Madds asks her.

"Various places. We're not all from the same city... They just brought us all to the same place. My sister and I, they took us when I was picking her up from school after work."

"What about your parents? They must be looking for you two," he continues.

She shakes her head. "They, um—It's only us two." She pauses and inhales deeply, wiping more tears before they find her cheeks. "I can't fail her."

"You won't. We'll get you out before anything happens," Finn promises as he approaches and squats down at a safe distance, his gaze leveled with hers.

But he shouldn't promise that at all. As much as I want to guarantee it, I can't. None of us can. We'll do our fucking best, though. But judging by the look in Finn's eyes as he fixes on Evelyn in a peculiar way, our best will not be enough. He'll make it his fucking mission to save her and everyone else in there before anything bad happens. He looks at her like he's making a silent oath.

Gods know what will happen to him if he won't be able to deliver.

Not long passes and Carter returns with a small tracker, small enough that he managed to put it in a pill cartridge. I'm not gonna lie, the advances of technology are rather scary.

"It won't dissolve; it's specially made. But it will pass through. Keep it in your mouth for as long as you can. Swallow it only if they try to check your mouth, okay?" Carter explains, handing her the pill.

"We should go," I say, swiping my gaze over everyone here.

Finn's gaze is fixed on Evelyn as Madds helps her up, and back into the space that's probably going to become her nightmare. She stops and turns before the container doors close.

"When it's done, I can't have the police knowing of me and my sister. It's only us, and they'll split us up. I'll lose her to the system."

Madds nods in acknowledgement. Considering what we're about to do, the police will be the last people to hear of this. Their idea of justice doesn't quite align with ours.

Terrified eyes look upon us as we're forced to shut the container doors. But I can guarantee that each and every one of the men standing here today are making silent vows and murderous promises for all those children.

"Carter?" I turn to him.

"It's already tracking. I texted Brendan and he confirmed. He's staying on it and following the girl's signal."

"We're going to get a team ready to follow, but do you all want to be involved as well?" I ask them.

"Yes," Finn answers without wasting a breath.

"We'll go change quickly in the Fightclub. Have a team on alert close by, ready to follow as they leave."

"We can't go in all guns blazing," Carter follows up. "We'll do recon to make sure we cut their communication and any surveillance they have, then take out everyone. We can't risk them, or Holt and O'Rourke, knowing we're coming or are involved in any way."

"I'll talk to Katya to look into a safe space to hide and take care of the children. I'll ask some of the girls for help as well. But we don't really know what number to prepare for."

"It's not going to matter. They'll just be happy to be somewhere safe," I continue, turning to Jonathan. "Are you staying for the pickup?"

"No. The less I have to deal with this, the better. I have eyes on them though, constantly. But I'm happy to get my men involved, if you need extra power."

We assembled an entire army as the years have passed; however, it will be wise not to use too many of them for this operation. So I confirm to The Ghost that his help would be much appreciated.

Apart from Jonathan's guys who stay to coordinate the pickup, we all rush out of the space and straight to our cars. Carter opens a line with his hackers, shoving a small pod in his ear to listen to the running commentary, in case it all starts moving before we get to The Fightclub.

"Follow us," I tell Jonathan. "We'll meet at Midnight and figure it all out. Actually, meet us in the club, through the back entrance. It's closed tonight."

It sits deep underneath our bar, with its entrance at the back of the building, and a private one for us through Midnight. Besides an outlet this city definitely needs, we use The Fightclub to move money illicitly obtained or made. Madds is the one in charge of the fighting and Carter of the operation.

The fighting happening there is not pretty, clean boxing. Most of the time, it's some form of MMA or bare-knuckle boxing. There are very few rules, and most of the time, it's a fucking massacre. Some people barely make it out alive. It's their choice to fight, though, and some people pay to be in that ring. But we're just as selective with our fighters and clientele, as we are with the ones in Midnight.

It's Monday, one of four times a week it's closed, so we'll have privacy. Plus, we have a change of clothes there, ones appropriate for what we're about to do.

This is going to be brutal, and I can't help but think of Morrigan. I'm convinced she doesn't know of this human trafficking operation, and I wonder what she'll think of her family and fiancé when she finds out.

No matter how strong she is, I was already worried about her. We've had zero contact since she was taken. But if her future husband is involved in something like this, then how exactly is she being treated? Is she okay?

What the hell is Ryan Holt doing to her right now?

CHAPTER 20

Morrigan

THREE DAYS HAVE passed, and for three days, one thing hasn't left my mind: The Serpent.

I cling to memories of him because they seem to be the only thing keeping me sane in this surreal confinement. They bring me a strange sort of hope, and at the same time, anger. We made a pact that he would be the one to help me get out of this bullshit. But these new memories of him, of his touch as he dances me through the forest, of him fucking me against the window he didn't know belongs to me, all of these are infiltrated by that heartbroken teenager he left behind.

I'm not that girl anymore, but I fear he might just be the same man he was then.

The silverware clacks loudly on the fine china, pulling me into the grueling present, and the overly decorated formal dining room of the Holt's house.

My prison.

Although it's harsh calling it a prison since the actual conditions aren't fully lacking. I'm simply trapped in here.

Bringing my attention back to the sparsely filled plate, I move some bland steamed broccoli around. Nothing about this dish is appetizing enough to force my empty stomach to accept the nutrients. I'm not entirely sure if I ate today. I think I did. Maybe? The last three days have been a strange blur. A nightmare I've been witnessing through someone else's consciousness. I did try tonight, but when I took a few bites, bile rose up my throat.

I look up at the row of windows opposite me, seeking comfort in the burnt orange and deep teal shades of the sunset reflecting on the calm sea. Flashbacks from a few weeks ago spring to mind, when once again, Ryan and I fought, and I ran out onto the beach. Not for theatrics, but for escape. Anger, that fickle bitch, seared my insides, but in his presence, it disappointedly sizzled out before it reached the surface. Again.

I remember the feel of the wet sand under my feet as the soft waves danced over it. It usually calmed me. Not that day. Too much pain, fury, and frustration piled up. They riddled my body. Like a virus, they tainted my blood, sickening and debilitating.

Then I turned to the beach mansion that was to be my home after the wedding, and a vision flashed, my imagination running rampant. Flames exploded through each and every window, spreading, hugging every wall, every bit of the structure, and a smile crept onto my lips. Relief grew in my chest. And so much goddamn joy flooded me that I couldn't help but be wary of it.

It made my darkness shine and sparkle.

When I blinked, it was all gone. The perfect white mansion was unscathed, and that dread seeped in once again. Sometimes, when I close my eyes, I can still see those flames. They're my happy, yet fake memory, but it gives me hope nonetheless.

It's within that memory that The Serpent snakes through. I see his eyes carrying the same look he had when we were in my apartment and I told him I had to leave. There were promises and desires in his gaze that I wanted to ignore, because my fucking heart was beginning to betray me.

Or maybe I'm fooling myself with the desires of that teenager from long ago. The one who dreamed outside of her bounds, foolishly infatuated with the sinful and dangerous older guy she couldn't have. The one she had crushed on for years, and hoped would fall madly in love with her.

It was a sick love powered by a misfit soul and young lust. But a darkness crept through my veins, growing with me, and it found The Serpent before that was even his nickname. It recognized the kindred soul, and latched onto it, refusing to believe that it could never be.

Then suddenly... it was. He noticed me, too.

I couldn't believe it was happening, just as none of the popular girls from school could either. They all lusted for him too, and they always fucking hated me. Only, by the time I got used to the idea that he chose me, that he was mine, it was too late. He was gone, and I was left behind, foolishly in love.

It ruined me.

Will he ruin me again, or will he be my salvation?

Somewhere in the distance, a rough sound scratches my ears. Only it's not in the distance at all... it's Ryan clearing his throat. I don't bother turning to look at him. I may feel ill, I may feel weak, but that asshole can go fuck himself with barbed wire.

I look down at my plate once again, moving slices of steamed carrot around since that broccoli definitely got enough exercise.

"You better finish your food. You're not getting anything else."

Even his voice sounds wrong. Everything about him is just... wrong. I close my eyes and take a deep breath before I turn to meet his gaze. But those muddy irises hold a pleased, secretive grin. What the hell does he have in store for me now?

"We have to make sure you fit into the wedding dress I chose for you," he continues. "Otherwise, we might have to hire another person just to stuff you and the fat on your hips into it instead."

I ignore the shaming comments. I'm used to them by now. God forbid I ever eat a square of chocolate in front of him. The comments about my *fat* body never stop. He started with one every few months, simple remarks about me that I was able to overlook. Then they became more and more frequent, until they were happening every day, and the delivery was no longer simple.

At this point, I have no idea if what I see in the mirror is his vision of me or my own.

I see softness, I see love handles, I see jiggle when I jump, I see a big ass that's not quite round, a soft pouch on my belly. I see so much that never mattered to me before. But I pass over those words, because they're not new.

However, his confidence in his plans I cannot ignore.

I believe there is nothing more dangerous than a powerful man riddled by delusions of grandeur that have seeped too deep into his brain. He's truly convinced that I will allow this wedding to go ahead, and that this insane plan of his will have the end he envisions. This controlling behavior is being taken to a whole other level and the man he used to be has been completely replaced by the one next to me. One I hardly recognize.

"You can't keep me locked in your house forever. Whatever plan you have is going to fizzle out eventually. And when it does…" I trail off, that darkness that lives inside of me getting a bit denser. Subdued fury has made a home there, and for these last three days, I've worked so fucking hard to be rational, when all I've wanted to do is slit his throat, cut his head off, and shove it on a spike on his front lawn.

That's another aspect of my imagination that puts a smile on my face.

"*Our*, not mine—*our* house." A tinge of exasperation touches the tone of his voice, and I can't help but roll my eyes.

The next second, a feral sound leaves his chest, a strange sort of growl, and I stiffen in my chair.

"You're such an ungrateful little bitch, aren't you? Your eyes will end up getting stuck to the back of your head if you don't cut this bullshit. There's only so much patience one can have." The flare of his nostrils and the look in his beaded eyes make me swallow my disgust.

"Language, Ryan," his mother calmly scolds.

I turn to her at the other end of the table, watching as she slides another piece of chicken into her mouth. *Language*. That's what she's worried about. Not the fact that her son has kidnapped a woman, the same one he is forcing to marry him, whilst bringing whores into her home. Fucking language.

I stop myself just as my eyes begin their all too familiar roll. God-fucking-damnit, I hate the control he has on me.

"I'll speak exactly how I please in *my* house, Mother," he spits as he cuts into that piece of meat as though it wronged him.

We're in *his* house now, I keep forgetting that little bit of information. In *his* lavish dining room, having dinner with his mother for the third night in a row. The mother he allows to still live in *his* house. It hasn't belonged to his mother since the moment the dirt covered his father's body.

I hold my fingers crossed that he'll get pulled away with business and leave me alone. Maybe tonight I'll manage to finally sleep.

The bags under my eyes seem to get heavier, and I swear I can feel them without touching them. My eyelids are dying to fall closed and it's barely seven o'clock. But I can't let this fatigue get me. Not until I'm sure he'll be out for the night.

I've been lucky the first two nights. He left just after dinner, on both occasions.

Two veins bulged dangerously in his temples as he took the phone call that pulled him away yesterday, and the sinew in his throat seemed to pulse. I've seen him angry before, but this was different. It had nothing to do with me, but his business. Something went terribly wrong, and I almost smiled when he grabbed me and shoved me into my bedroom without a word. But I didn't know when he was going to be back and if he would focus all that fury on me.

Somewhere deep inside, I thought that whatever happened was some sort of distraction to get me out of here.

But no one came.

I never laid on the bed though, even as sleep threatened to take me. I couldn't allow that vulnerability.

The second night was the same. But my eyes betrayed me for a few minutes, and I woke up just as my back hit the soft mattress. It was at that moment, when I shot up straight to my feet, that I realized just what this man does to me. What he's made of me and what he took away.

When that night passed and no one came for me, I understood that I could not wait for anyone to save me. I will always have to rely on myself. That was the only way to regain my strength in front of this man.

"I think everyone will have an early night tonight." Ryan looks straight into my eyes. "All of us."

"Fine by me." I place the cutlery on the plate and get up with a screech of the chair on the wood floor, his mother hissing at the sound. "Goodnight."

Just as I thought I was off the hook, the motherfucker speaks.

"I'll see you in a minute."

Something in the depths of my soul stiffens.

No fucking way.

* * *

The moment I'm out of view, I'm sprinting up the stairs, and burst through the door to my bedroom on a strained breath, leaning against it as I shut it behind me.

"Fuck."

I'm gasping, but I don't linger. Walking to the other side of the dresser that sits against the wall, I dig my feet into the ground and push the piece of furniture toward the door.

Only, a soft knock interrupts me before it opens without warning.

I stiffen as my fucking heart gets lodged in my throat.

"I don't have much time."

It's not Ryan, but his mother. Though, I don't feel any relief, just a different type of tension.

"He just took a call," she continues.

I haven't moved yet. In this house, I always expect traps, and Mrs. Holt is never a good sign of anything. But the woman holds a tray with a small porcelain cup of steaming water, a tea bag, and teaspoon on the side. She hands them to me, and I frown, my mind racing. Reluctantly, I take the tray and set it on the bed.

"I need more than tea, Mrs. Holt." I hold her gaze in a tight grip. I don't want her to look away, I don't want her shrugging or brushing me off. "I need to get away from your fucking son. The man you raised into the savage he is." I nod suggestively toward the stairs.

She blinks rapidly, taking in the insult and my crude words, and tries to look away. But submitting to another woman doesn't quite seem her nature.

"I—I didn't do this."

"Yeah," I scoff. "Just as my parents didn't raise me as cattle to take to the market and sell to the highest bidder. Pathetic. But then again, I guess they had no say in how my personality turned out. Your son, though, he's fucking certifiable."

Shaking her head, she finally breaks eye contact, and her eyebrows strain with a frown. She mumbles something under her breath, and the woman I usually see at the other end of the dining room table flickers away.

"I don't know how... I don't know what happened to him." She sighs.

There's a tinge of defeat in her eyes. I'm not sure if it concerns her failed son, or her inability to stay strong in front of me.

Has she been holding on to hope? Is she finally allowing herself to see the truth?

Sounds like me, not long ago.

"There's something wrong with him. I can't stop him." Her voice lowers, head shaking with exasperation.

"Oh, fucking hell. No shit! What tipped you off?" My tone rises with every word and the woman steps forward, eyes wide.

"Please," she whispers. "He's only downstairs."

"Then tell me why you're here, and what your son really wants from me."

I don't give a flying fuck about her regrets. This woman has never shown me an ounce of kindness in all the years since I've known her.

"I'm not sure."

"You're a bad liar." I step closer, getting right into her space, bringing us eye to eye. "What does your son want from me? I know his desire to take me as a wife has nothing to do with matters of the heart."

She turns her head, listening for any movement or voices coming from downstairs.

"Some time ago, before my husband died, I found some files. Printed. I'm increasingly convinced that they did not belong to my husband," she whispers hesitantly, still listening beyond the walls of this room. "I couldn't look in great detail, but some of the files were quite complex in nature and others were documents."

"Okay, so how does this pertain to me?" I frown, crossing my arms.

"Because they all bore your family name. All your names— yours, your brother's, your mother's, your father's. They were all there, on bank statements, business documents, assets, contracts, deeds, birth and marriage certificates. Everything."

That is fucking weird, and really concerning.

"And you think Ryan was gathering all that information about us?"

She nods, her attention half on me, half out the open door.

"What use could he have with that?" I understand the business documents. If I were to involve myself in a significant business deal with someone new, I would probably check them out as well. But birth certificates?

"I don't know, but it was strange. All those documents in one place?"

"Like he's counting assets," I mumble.

"And how to get to them," she says slowly, fixing me with her gaze.

Son of a bitch!

"Why should I believe any of this, Mrs. Holt?" Her name drips from my tongue like tar.

She frowns. "I never liked you, Miss O'Rourke."

"My point exactly. Then why are you doing this?" I want to spit more comebacks at this woman, but her answer comes too quick.

"Because I was wrong."

My turn to frown.

"About you," she continues. "I was wrong about you. You saw the change in my son long before any of us did. I caught it far too late. And now, only blood binds my son and I, and it's not thick enough anymore."

"I don't think you understand what you're saying," I say, narrowing my eyes on her in disbelief.

"He needs to be stopped." She turns toward the open door. "Whoever that person is downstairs, it's not him. That's not my son."

"There might be only one way to stop him." Softness touches my voice this time around.

This whole interaction feels surreal. Only, the moment her eyes catch mine again, a different type of pain lives there.

"I think he killed my husband."

My mouth drops open at the same time as my arms fall to my sides. But suddenly, the heavy steps from downstairs become a tad louder, and she walks out the door without another word or glance. I'm left wondering what the fuck alternate reality I've just fallen into.

Utterly surreal.

I shake my head and rush to close the door behind her, then turn my attention back to the large chest of drawers. The damn thing is heavy, but I plant my feet on the floor, and with a deep screech, it finally moves. It only reaches the middle of the door, when a disturbing laugh echoes in the corridor behind it.

"Shit."

"You fool yourself thinking that a piece of furniture will keep me away from you. If I want you, I will get you!" The door flies open, hitting the corner of the dresser that partially blocks it, and Ryan slips through.

I manage two steps before my back hits the wall, and his hand wraps around my throat, while the other one grips my hip.

"There is no escape from me. There will never be any escape for you. No matter where you go, no matter where you run, I will fucking hunt you down. Those photos of you burying the man you killed will haunt you. The video I took as you stood and looked at his corpse, with no remorse in your eyes, will fucking haunt you. I can destroy you. And that alone strips you of that freedom."

The back of my tongue feels too big for my mouth as his grip tightens, and that hand on my hip suddenly hits bare skin, sliding upwards under my shirt. I'm not sure how many muscles one has in their torso, but all of mine tighten to the point my lungs refuse to take in any air. I claw at his hand, pulling it away from my skin with as much force as I can muster, but he goes back in, straight up to my bra covered breast, gripping it. A pained, strained scream escapes my throat, taking with it the last of the air I had in my lungs, and I can't force him off now... not when he holds me that way.

"This is mine too."

The elastic of my bra scrapes my ribs as he grips the cup and yanks it down, then presses his hand over my bare breast. My brain is telling me to launch at him. To kick him in the balls. To do anything but stand here in his grip and allow him to touch me this way. But my body isn't cooperating. I can't fucking explain it. It's like in the nightmares I have once in a while, where I'm getting attacked and I try to scream, but no words come out. Not because I'm mute, but because I'm frozen. There's a disconnect between my brain and my nerves and it happens when those muddy eyes pin me the way they're doing now.

"It took a while to break you. But look at you now... it was fucking worth it," he says with a wide grin pulling at the corners of his mouth as he leans forward.

His lips are almost on mine, and something inside of me breaks. The idea of him touching me like that is so utterly repulsive that my knee suddenly connects with his groin before I've even finished thinking about doing it.

Only it wasn't hard enough to get him off me.

As he pulls back and that frenzied gaze hits me, I understand it was definitely hard enough to piss him off.

"Sir." A knock on the cracked open door interrupts us. "Your guest has arrived. Shall I bring her up?"

"Fucking lucky you are," he whispers to me. "Yes, Gordon, take her to my room."

"Will do, sir."

"Would you like to meet this one too? Maybe you should. It will teach you a thing or two for when you're going to do your wifely duty."

"Fuck you." I'm seething. I swear it comes and goes at all the wrong moments. Never when I truly need it.

"Oh, you will. Not now, though." He releases me and steps back, looking me up and down. The corner of his lips curve downwards, and he cocks one eyebrow. It's a look that makes me want to cover myself in baggy clothes and run.

He turns, walking back to the door, and pushes the chest of drawers back in its place.

"Stop moving my furniture around."

When he pulls open the door, a tall, slim woman stops before it, with hair so dark it looks like a starless sky, and eyes a gray so bright, as the stars that fell off it. I'm surprised she's not afraid to make any movement in that dress. I would certainly be scared it would snap, but then again, it's short enough that it doesn't constrict her legs in any way. The deep red suits her, though.

"Hello, Raven," Ryan greets her.

She catches my gaze for only a split second, but when she turns to him, the most lascivious smile I've seen on a woman paints her lips. My eyebrows furrow, wondering whether her presence here is free of charge or not. But when Ryan's foot leaves my doorway, I don't linger on that thought and slam the door behind him.

Moments later, the lock clicks from the outside.

I cherish that lock.

Too bad I'm not the one with the key.

CHAPTER 21
Morrigan

THE DISTINCTIVE TURN of the doorknob wakes me up. Not a hard turn, not loud, only a faint click. I snap into a sitting position, the sheets gritty against my clenched fists, and wait. My breath hitches when a soft knock sounds on the door. Just one. The next moment, a small white paper slides on the floor, stopping at the edge of the rug the bed sits on.

My eyes flicker between it and the door, my broken mind waiting for the trap to come. Like the monster is under the bed and the moment my feet touch the ground, he'll grab them.

Nothing comes, only a barely audible sound of a door closing.

Maybe a minute passes and muffled voices come through from the other side of the wall, where Ryan's bedroom is. The tone of that voice makes my stomach tighten with disgust. I know what's coming. I heard it before I fell asleep, but at least the asshole didn't make me watch him having sex again.

I slowly step out of bed, trying not to make a sound, and grab the paper. It's kind of heavy, and it's not a piece of paper at all, but an envelope. I discard its contents onto the bed, and the moment I see it, my gaze snaps back to the door. A fucking key!

Who...?

There are only a few people in this house at one time: two guards, Gordon, who's more of a coordinator, Ryan, and his mother. None of them would have done this for me, not even his mother, even after our earlier conversation. When I pick it up, I find that it's smoother than a normal key, and lighter, like it's made of some sort of plastic. There's only one person who could have supplied this—Raven.

As I rub the key between my fingers, my gaze drifts out the window, to the dark clouds approaching fast, swallowing the puffy white ones until nothing is left of them.

Raven! Son of a bitch.

It hits fast and hard, and somewhere in my chest, my heart rushes, beating a million miles per minute the moment I realize what's happening. It all clicks into place, just as I know this key will click easily in that door, even without trying it. The Serpent is certainly sneaky, and I'm starting to understand that the women The Sanctum employs in their escort service have an even more important skill set than *escorting*.

I quickly change the blouse I fell asleep in and pull a comfortable T-shirt over my head. I have no sneakers here, no comfortable shoes whatsoever, so barefoot it is.

The noises from behind the wall become strained. Moans, slapping of skin, and others I would rather ignore. But they increase in intensity, and it's the perfect cover up.

I head to the door to try the key, grabbing the cold doorknob and twisting as gently as I can, yet it still makes a pretty loud noise for the quiet night. It makes sense why Raven didn't unlock it for me. Instead, she orchestrated the opportunity for me to open it myself without that asshole hearing. I wait for any sound in response from the other side, but I don't think any of the guards are up here. Ryan doesn't exactly run this house like a fortress, and tonight he might regret that. The key slides in with an ease that makes me wanna jump in excitement, and the moment I turn it and the lock clicks, thunder rattles the windows.

I can't help but smile. It's like the gods are rooting for me. There's something about a summer storm that brings promises of delicious chaos and new beginnings. Fuck knows I need them both.

As I slowly open the door, the noises from next door are louder and I have to swallow down the only visceral sensation this man instills in me now—*sickness*. I must focus. The corridor seems empty, so I slip out, and close the door behind me. But I won't lock it. I can't have him know I had a key. He can go ahead and think I learned how to pick locks or something.

The foyer is underneath me, and from there, a grand staircase leads to a landing about halfway up, then splits into two smaller staircases that take a U-turn on either side, against the walls. I step closer to the handrail, looking down the main steps, which are dimly brightened by the moonlight from the landing windows. There's no one there. And I can't hear anything beyond the moans coming from Ryan's room at the end of the corridor, and the roaring thunder closing in.

I have to take a chance.

Turning to one of the staircases, I step down as carefully as I can, my attention on the ground floor that starts to peek through. There's no movement, but my heart beats like I'm running a marathon, muscles tensed to the cusp of pain.

I reach the landing and stand flush against the wall, trying to hide from the moonlight as I look for movement, the ground floor much more visible now. I can only see the left-hand side of the foyer, and as I lean in, I catch a shadow disappearing toward the right. Somewhere in the distance, a doorknob clicks... then nothing. It might be the bathroom, since there's one around there, close to the kitchen.

I swallow my worries and rush down the steps, struggling to contain the elation the prospect of freedom brings. I can fucking taste it as my feet hit the marble floor. The front door is so goddamn clear in my sight, even with all the lights turned off.

Suddenly, a doorknob clicks again, and my head snaps toward the noise. But I only get to see a shadow, before a hand covers my mouth, and a huge arm encircles me. It traps both of mine against the sides of my body, then slams me against his front. I'm about to kick and scream, but he pulls me under the staircase before I get the chance, right in the sheltering shadows of the far back wall.

Fight-or-flight clouds my logic as I struggle against the man, but he presses his hand harder on my face, gripping my jaw, and holding me tight. The moment I feel his breath on the top of my ear, followed by the brush of his lips, something visceral erupts deep inside. That gesture throws me back in time, to a dingy bar at the edge of the city. I was drunk, careless, surrounded by questionable people with bad intentions, and dressed in ripped shorts that barely covered my ass and a flimsy T-shirt knotted under my breasts.

When the wrong people noticed me, he came out of nowhere, and wrapped his arm around my waist. Before I could protest, he pulled me against his front, and brushed his lips on the top of my ear, whispering...

"Reckless little Morri."

I knew that voice, I knew that smell, but that touch was new. I never felt it in that intimate way before.

Because I belonged to someone else.

Not anymore. Vincent left me a broken mess, made me into a killer, and my carelessness turned dangerous. That same carelessness brought me here, all alone, for his friend to find me.

Maddox.

Another soft blow of air coasts against my ear, down the side of my throat. My body relaxes, coming off that flight response, but the man doesn't let me go. His grip only loosens slightly, enough that it allows my arms to bend, and I wrap my hands on his bare forearm he holds against my chest. My breathing doesn't steady, though. Memories of that night run rampant through my nerves—the dirty dancing, the sexual tension, the knowledge that he was taking care of me. No one took care of me anymore, not since Vincent. It made me wonder if he sent him, but I was so far gone, I didn't allow myself to dwell on the thought.

We didn't do anything more than dance, albeit in a very sexual kind of way. He has too much respect for Vincent, and as much as I wanted to get revenge, I was far too in love with the man then. We didn't even kiss, yet later on, I definitely regretted that decision. Even now I wish we would have. I wish we would've fucked. I wish I got my revenge. And I wish I got this angst toward Maddox out of my system.

I wonder what he's thinking of as he holds me to him. How did he know I would recognize him?

Steps sounding on the hard floor remind me of where I am. From within the shadows, I watch one of the guards pass through the foyer, toward the other side of the house. He's out of sight, but Maddox doesn't move, and I attempt to pull on him so we can leave already. But another set of steps comes from that direction, entering the foyer—the second guard.

Fuck.

I'm holding my breath, wary that he could hear even that, but the noises coming from upstairs of my *future husband* fucking Raven into oblivion, rip through the house. I can't help but feel for his mother. She's hearing all this shit, the disrespect. Music suddenly mixes with that bile-rising noise pollution, and I can see the guard looking up to the second floor.

"Jesus Christ." He shakes his head and disappears somewhere in front of the staircase, where we can't see him.

All we can do is wait calmly.

Only, my calmness breaks and shatters the moment the darkness opposite us... moves. My feet dig into the floor, and I push against Maddox, as a shadow flows like smoke in our direction. But I seem to be the only panicked one.

Notes of bergamot and rich decadence slither through my senses when I take another slow breath, and as that darkness nears and the scent becomes denser, cedar mixes in the fragrance, and my heart stops.

Vincent.

The entire house is dipped in darkness, yet his black eyes shine, thriving in the shadows he seems to belong in.

Another step and he's right in front of me, his body so close, yet not touching mine. I release one hand from Maddox's forearms and reach for him, fingers gripping the edge of a smooth, dense material.

You came for me, I want to say to him.

He doesn't move, though. Doesn't let himself be pulled in, and keeps his shoulders straight, locked firm in an imposing stance. Maddox slowly drops his hand from my mouth, brushes it over my shoulder, grazing my waist, and pauses for a moment before it rests on my hip. Those memories of him rip through me once more, and even after all this time, that Bluesy dirty song we slow danced to that night floods my mind, making me squeeze his forearm involuntarily. I wonder if he still remembers it.

The Serpent reaches for me, and places his palm over my chest, right under my throat, as the steps of the guard sound yet again. Only, they don't leave the room. They pace through it, and that all too familiar frenzy begins to simmer inside of me. Adrenaline, fear, and desire mix into one, but a need for destruction takes over—I want to burn this whole goddamn house to the ground, with everyone but us and Raven in it. The guard sounds like he's getting closer, spiking my pulse with every step, and as The Serpent presses his fingers on the base of my throat, and drags them up until he holds me with his whole hand, I realize I would like to be the one to burn first.

In an entirely different way.

His grip is firm, possessive, and so goddamn satisfying that I instantly sink backwards. Right into Maddox's body. My head falls against his chest, and he instantly tenses. I can feel the flex of his muscles, and the soft hitch in his breath, but he doesn't move. And The Serpent doesn't pull me away. He grips my jaw, then slides that hand over my cheek, dragging his thumb over my lower lip, and Maddox's fingers dig harder into my hip. Goose bumps burst over my skin, and in these moments, I forget where I am.

The guard's steps get closer, my body becomes suddenly aware. Too fucking aware—my nipples peak against Maddox's forearm, and I know he felt them. Because his grip tightens on me, and with it, my gaze drifts into his. And right in that moment, when he looks down at me, The Serpent's thumb dips into my mouth, pressing on my tongue, almost like he's opening me up for his best friend. Against the top of my ass, I feel a distinctive twitch, just as the man before me presses his body onto mine, trapping me. His darkness dips slowly over me, his breath touching my lips as his thumb slides out gently. He's so close to me now. I swallow the heaviness that sits in my chest, and can almost taste his lips on mine, just as Maddox's hand slides from my hip over my lower belly.

Then movement in the corner of my eyes pulls my attention away, and brief, silent chaos erupts. The Serpent aims his free hand where my eyes drifted, and a muffled *pop* startles me. He shifts in a split second and catches the man in his arms before he falls to the floor, then pulls him into the shadow. A moment passes and the second guard steps back into the foyer, looking around for the disturbance. The Serpent moves out of the shadow with such fluid elegance, one that has no business being there, as he aims his gun at the man, and pulls the trigger before he can even open his mouth. He dips in, catching him before he hits the ground, and lowers him slowly.

This is our opportunity.

Maddox releases me, but I linger a moment longer against him, my eyes on The Serpent who's turned toward us. Only a moment. Just as tense. Just as suffocating. But this suffocation is welcome. Craved. Needed.

They came for me.

Vincent breaks the tension, and turns, moving away down the same corridor the last guard came from, and we follow.

"Shit." I couldn't stop that sharp whisper before it came out.

Both the men stop to look at me as I lift my foot off the ground, shaking the warm wetness from it as I realize what it is.

"Are you barefoot?" Maddox whispers, and I nod.

Before I can protest, he reaches down, and slides one arm against my back, then the other under my knees, lifting me to his chest. The Serpent doesn't move. His eyes turn to slits, narrowing on the man who holds me, and his shoulders seem stiffer than usual. I swear I feel that possessiveness in my bones as that gaze splits me. I bet Maddox can feel it too.

"We have to go," I whisper through gritted teeth.

The dark slits turn to me for a moment, before he shifts on his heels, and starts running through the corridors, as thunder fills the night. Holding on to Maddox, I will my gaze to stay away from his, the intimacy of the moment we shared seconds before, leaving a lingering tension behind. I can feel it in the way he holds me, almost avoiding squeezing me too tight, or to touch me in the wrong place. Yet the rigidity in his thick muscles is unmissable.

We turn on the corridor, through some smaller service rooms, and when The Serpent opens the last door, the whole sky explodes in electric white. Lightning zips through the night sky, and the magnitude of it falters our steps. But we don't linger when the thunder splits the silence in its roaring boom, or when the rain suddenly crashes down on us, heavy and dense.

We're slipping between the house and some thick bushes, then stop right in front of the boundary wall of the property.

"What are we doing here?" I turn to Maddox.

He nods toward the wall, confused. "Escaping."

Of course. What did I expect? For them to have driven on the driveway?!

The Serpent jumps, grips the top of the wall, and leaps in another impressively fluid movement, disappearing beyond it. Maddox then puts me down, grips my hips, and lifts me until I can reach the wall and climb over it.

When my feet touch the ground on the other side, and I turn, Vincent is right here, in my space, and he's looking straight at me. The possessiveness in his eyes is as clear as the lighting that splits this sky, and I can't stop myself. I simply can't do it. I don't want to.

He fucking came for me.

I rise on my tiptoes, grab his face in my hands, and when my lips crash onto his, my world turns upside down. It feels right. As if it actually turned the right way around. His intoxicating scent smells like home. So I kiss him again. And again. A second later, his arms take hold of me, and like a fucking python, they wrap and tighten around my body, taking my breath away.

He might as well keep it, because I think it's always belonged to him.

"Come on." Maddox pulls us from our spell.

I didn't even hear him jump over the wall. It's such a surreal night. Everything is happening so fast. Almost like we're in a movie. Only, I keep blinking and I'm in a different scene before I can settle in the previous one. We reach a car, and I quickly climb into the back seat.

"Fuck!" The occupied driver's seat startles me.

"Good evening." Carter nods at me.

"You scared the hell out of me," I say, panting.

"Are you okay?" The Serpent climbs in after me and finally speaks.

"Yes."

"Holt didn't—you're sure?" He's asking specific questions, without being specific at all.

"I'm okay. Is Raven yours?" I ask, looking between the men, Maddox now in the passenger seat.

"All ours. She did good, no?" Carter turns to me.

"Very good. Thank you," I say with a gentle smile on my lips aimed at each of them. They nod in acknowledgement, but none of them return the smile or say anything else, so I continue. "His mother came to me. She confirmed something I suspected. There's more to this arrangement than the sheer desire to marry me. Some time ago, she found paperwork. A lot of it. All about my family and I."

"What kind?" Carter asks, his empty eyes in the central mirror glancing back at me.

"Every single kind you can think of. Including birth and marriage certificates. Banks. Deeds. Business statements. Everything about each and every one of us. One might think there are ulterior motives for a future spouse to hold so much information on their betrothed's family. Honestly, I wouldn't mind getting my hands on it all."

"And we believe this woman?" Maddox asks.

"I've never cared enough to put stock in her words, but she is very rude in her sincerity. I doubt she would ever bother to be anything but honest. This time around, though, there was genuine fear in her bones. It was palpable. Before she had to run away from me, because Ryan was coming, she said something else." I take one deep breath, those words carrying consequences, and potentially changing the whole game.

"She suspects Ryan killed his father."

A synchronized sigh fills the car. One by one, the men turn, backs sinking into their seats as Carter starts the engine.

"I want to go back," Maddox says quickly. "I want to find that paperwork."

"It's too risky. This is just my ego talking. None of it will help us in any way," I tell him, shaking my head as nerves flood me.

"We don't know. It might. And this storm is the perfect cover to roam through his house. We still have a little while before Raven is done with him," The Serpent counters, pulling my attention to him. "Madds, go. But if the music stops, get the fuck out of there."

Carter kills the engine as Maddox nods and slides out of the car. The guys seem to believe we're hidden well enough here, so all we can do now is sit and wait for him to return. In their presence, the air seems to be a little lighter, easier to breathe in, and my muscles are suddenly feeling the tension of the last few days. So I sink into the seat, praying to the gods that this night will finish well.

I cannot help but feel as though these men are risking too much for me.

Am I really worth it?

CHAPTER 22
Vincent

WATCHING THE FIRE of her hair on my black sheets, her freckled, soft skin tangled in them, and the peaceful rise and fall of her chest as she sleeps, brings me a strange satisfaction. A calmness in my soul I haven't experienced in years.

She hugs the pillow under her head, and this peculiar sense of belonging takes over. I've been watching her for the last hour. When the sun was rising, the rays touched her, and made her hair look like she was on fire. The red shades of the sunrise matched hers. I've been lying here almost motionless. Afraid that if I wake her, the spell will be broken and my Eve will disappear.

A soft moan escapes her lips, and she blinks slowly.

"Mmm..." she hums, rubbing her cheek against the soft fabric as she slowly opens her eyes.

She smiles at first, as she pushes her nose into the pillow and inhales. Then her gaze widens, and a slight shock appears there when she realizes where she is.

"Good morning, Little Eve."

She lifts her head suddenly, quickly looking around us, and takes in the unfamiliar space, before she turns back to me.

"You're in my house." I attempt to calm her.

And I don't miss how her gaze softens for that split second before she catches herself.

"Um... how did I get here?"

"You fell asleep in the car. I brought you here, where you're safe."

"Okay. But how? I don't remember a thing," she asks, her gaze mixed with worry, confusion, but also a comfort she tries to hide.

"That's because you didn't wake up through it. Madds picked you up from the car, and even as he passed you to me, you were dead asleep. You just *nestled* into my shoulder, and I brought you in."

She looks at me in disbelief, blinking rapidly, before she slowly drops her head back onto the pillow.

"You could have taken me to Lulu's," she all but whispers.

"No."

"You're not making the same mistake as Ryan, are you, Serpent? Bringing me here and not letting me go?" She narrows her eyes on me.

"I want to keep you safe, that's all. And Loreley's would be a far too obvious place for you to escape to."

"Son of a bitch! He'll fucking hurt Lulu. He hates her! I have to go," she rasps as she throws the sheets aside and sits up, just about to jump out of bed.

Before she can make the next move, I catch her and slam her back onto the bed. "She's safe, she's okay. We sent people to keep an eye on her. Nothing will happen to her."

"No, no, I don't—"

"I give you my word," I say, my voice stern but gentle.

My arm is wrapped around her ribs, pinning her to the bed, and her body softens. Only, that look in her eyes I darkens with a chilling edge.

"I've had your word before, Serpent," she says ever so slowly, her eyes searching mine with a flicker of resentment. "And in the end, it meant nothing."

Morrigan pushes against the arm I've draped over her, but I don't waver. Instead, I slide one leg over both of hers and hold her in place. I had to let her go once, and there's no way I'm doing it again. Not until she has all the information to make her own choice.

"It meant everything, and that's why it hurt the way it did." I finally speak through her attempts to push me away.

Her body's strong, yet not strong enough for my will. And at this point, when it comes to her, my will is unmoving.

"That's why it hurt *me*," she spits.

"It hurt me too, Morrigan!"

At the sound of her name falling from my tongue, she falters, and her brows furrow, her expression strained with broken emotions.

We call each other made-up names. We call each other everything but who we are, because our names on our lips carry the weight of a love that never was. They carry promises and shattered dreams, and they sound too much like hope.

And the hardest fucking thing in this world is allowing hope to brush your soul.

Yet here I am.

"Then... then why did you do it?" Her voice breaks for a moment, and for some reason, it makes me feel better.

"Because I had to. I had no choice."

How many times over the years have I imagined this exact moment?

How many times have I wished to find her, trap her beneath me, and tell her everything?

How many times have I almost risked it all and drove to her university?

How many times have I been forced to give up on her, on us?

Too many. Far too many.

"Had to? *Had* to?!" The fire returns in her eyes with the raised tone of her voice.

With all her strength, she shoves me enough that she slips out of bed. There's so much rage in her eyes that it reminds me of the night Maddox and I found her at Lover's Lane.

The night I knew she was mine.

I jump after her and close the distance between us.

"You *had* to leave me?!" She slams her hands against my bare chest, pushing me away.

The woman is relentless. She tries to slap me, and I block her hand.

"You *had* to tell me that you didn't love me anymore?!" She pushes me once more. "You didn't fucking love me!"

Her rage is filled with anguish, but I need her to shut the fuck up. I grab her and throw her on the bed before she even realizes what's happening.

"I never. Fucking. Stopped!"

She stills, and props on her elbows, frowning. Her lips part, but she's finally speechless, and I feel some relief. I know what I *had* to do to distance myself from her. I know how much it fucking hurt. Because no matter how brief it was, how inexperienced, or how young we were, we recognized that our souls lived in the same shadows and found their matching darkness.

"Your father forced me. He blackmailed me," I finally admit for the first time ever. To anyone.

I remember it like it was yesterday. No matter how hard I tried to forget the day I was forced to break up with her, it's imprinted in my goddamn mind.

* * *

8 years ago

"You can't make me do this." We've been going back and forth for fifteen minutes, but it feels like hours.

"I can. I'm her father, and you—" He looks at me like I'm the purest of filth. The definition of it. "You have no business in her life. This proves it." He shakes the folder in front of me.

"I'm not fucking leaving her! She's the—"

"Silence!" Liam O'Rourke's voice booms at a level I've never heard it before. "Is she worth your boy going to jail?"

I open my mouth to speak, but no words come out. None fill my mind either. Yes, and no?

"You can't fucking make me choose," I seethe.

"I'm not making you choose, boy. I'm telling you that you have to break up with her, make her hate you, and convince her that there is no chance for you two to ever be together again. Otherwise, Maddox Severin is going to be arrested for murder. Tomorrow. This is not a choice. It's this, or I'm going to ruin his goddamn life. Yours too."

"You'll pay for this." The threat vibrates through my chest.

But the asshole smirks.

"Sure. How are you gonna make me pay?" Again, the man looks me up and down like I'm shit on his shoe. "You are no one. You're nothing."

"You don't know me, old man." I snatch the folder that contains the evidence against Maddox out of his hand and turn to leave. But I stop before the open door and look at him over my shoulder. "One day, she'll find out about this, and the Morrigan you fear, will come for you. But when she does, I'll be right there, her own fucking weapon to take you down. You will pay for this, O'Rourke."

I let the door slam behind me as I walk out of his office and go to find my future ex-girlfriend. My first love.

And I fear she'll be the last.

I watched her as much as I could all through the day. I went straight to her school, but I wasn't going to break up with her there. I simply stood under the thick clouds that seemed to get more ominous by the hour and watched from under the bandstand. She couldn't see me from her classroom windows even if she tried. But I was there. When I wasn't watching the windows and main door to try to get a peek at her, I was flipping through the goddamn folder. Over and over again.

Then I followed her to her dance class. God, she was fucking stunning. The way she moved, how she glided, the way her hips swayed, and her arms undulated on the slow rhythm of the music, broke me every single time. She's exquisite.

She's fucking mine.

Only she won't be mine for long... will she?

I'm so damn proud of her regardless. She never said the words to me, but I know she got kicked out from ballet because she didn't fit their shitty body standards. I knew how much she loved dancing, so I found this class for her, and she fucking blossomed. It's the only time her eyes sparkle almost the same as they do when they land on me. And I'm about to extinguish that light. Even as I stood like a creep across the street from the building, where the class was held, I tried my fucking hardest to find a solution to get Maddox out of the issue and keep her too.

When I saw Morrigan's beautifully sad face as she came out of the class, looking around the street like she was waiting for something, I was close to running after her to confess the whole affair.

I stopped myself, though. She can never know that her father is holding Maddox, the man she's grown so attached to, against us. She would never put his freedom before us, just like I wouldn't. And telling her gives us too much strength. We would fail at staying away from each other, and Maddox would still end up in jail. Her father was fucking right; there is no choice. I can't put on her this shattering guilt and conflict that's ripping through me. She can't have a choice.

Instead, I followed her to the beach, watching as she sat on the same large driftwood we went for each time we came here together. Again, she kept looking around, but she couldn't see me in the shadows. When I realized that it was me she was looking for, waiting for me... I almost called Ronan, Finn's brother, to see if he could help me with this fucking situation. But I couldn't risk this information reaching Maddox. He would hate himself, and then he would sacrifice himself for her. For us. No one could help me. Our organization is not strong enough yet to take down O'Rourke.

But how was I supposed to do this? To break her? Break myself? How am I supposed to learn to live without her fucking smile, and forest-green eyes, when I barely just adjusted to the idea that she's truly mine?

Fucking mine!

The sting in my palms from my nails digging into it was nothing, and I needed more. I needed punishment, even though this is no one's fucking fault. I can't blame Maddox either. The guy he killed actually died a week later from complications, and it wasn't an instant death. But the injuries were caused by him. I wasn't with him. He lost control and he still hasn't told me why. All I know is that the man he killed was his uncle, his mother's brother. I know enough about Maddox, his family, and his past, to trust that the beating was justified. It's not even recent. It happened about a year ago, so how the fuck it just came to light now, I have no idea.

After more than half an hour of sitting on the beach, waiting in vain, even though I was right there, she left. I caught the worry in her features, the sadness, and if I didn't know any better, I would have thought she knew what was coming. And it was coming.

I got in the car and followed the taxi that took her home. Then I waited outside their huge property to make sure she got in. Only, I waited much longer than that... There was a speech inside my head that I kept repeating, over and over again, like there was any chance what I was about to do would get easier. Then I went through the speech I'm preparing for Maddox, because he knows what Morrigan is to me, and I know what she is to him.

The sun has long set now, and I can't put it off any longer. If she's truly been waiting for me to appear all day, then there's only one place she will be right now—the library.

I don't bother hiding my presence. Her asshole of a father is probably home, but I couldn't give a shit. Normally, I would leave the car here, outside the boundary, and walk through the shadows of the garden to the other side of the house. Where the library is. Then I would sneak in through the window or one of the side doors. Not tonight. She won't see me coming since the driveway is on the other side of the library.

I park the car and walk straight through the front door. It takes only a few seconds, and the angry presence of Liam O'Rourke casts its shadow on mine. He knows why I'm here. He's not gonna kick me out now. It doesn't stop the anger in his eyes, though. I take a deep breath, letting my disdain roll off me and straight into him, then turn to head to where I know Morrigan is.

There's no noise beyond the door, and when I finally open it, all the lights are off. It's complete silence. But she's here.

I step in farther and gently close the door behind me, before I walk to stand next to the dark fireplace. She's right here, lying on the sofa, sleeping all curled up with her hands clutched against her chest. The moon shines on her, and she looks so fucking peaceful, I don't want to ruin it just yet. So I stand here, blending in the shadows, watching the beautiful creature before me, and go through the whole predicament all over again. Just in case there is anything I missed, any chance that all our hearts could be saved.

Truth is, I can't wake her up because I need this. I need to take her in. Map out every line of her body, every curve, the softness of her skin, and the way her curls fall around her face. I need her for a little longer.

Maybe an hour passes, and I still haven't found any solution. When Morrigan wakes up with a start, the decision is made for me.

She looks at me like I hung the fucking stars in the sky, then lit up the moon, and for the first time ever, I'm going to lie to her.

* * *

Present

The pain that followed, I still carry on my soul. There are many scars there, but this one is the deepest. The only one that will never be mended. Even if I have her back now.

"He—wait. What?" Morrigan slides up in bed, almost in a sitting position.

"You know very well how much the man didn't want me with you back then. It turns out that a cop friend of his found something. A mistake. The one and only that caught the eyes of the law, back when we weren't The Sanctum. Your father gave me a choice—either break up with you, or Madds goes to jail for the rest of his life."

Her eyes go wide at those words, and she clutches the sheets by her sides.

"Countless times, I thought of telling you about this," I continue, taking a breath, "but I knew that there was no way we would be able to stay away from each other. We would have fucked up. We would have ruined it all. Ruined Madds' life."

"Our love in exchange for his freedom..." She pulls her knees to her chest, and wraps her arms around them, as she turns her gaze toward the window.

A charged silence settles. Questions linger in the atmosphere, and for the first time in a very long time, I can't anticipate what happens next. Her lips are parted as she swallows dry sobs, gasping softly for air, and her knuckles turn white from the tight grip around her legs.

She climbs out of bed once more, but this time, there's no rage. She holds her stomach as she takes tentative steps closer to the window, her breathing quickening. Running my fingers through my hair nervously, I have to force myself not to go to her. Not to pull her into my arms. Not to guide her in the direction I want her in.

Fuck!

I can't force her to believe me, and to accept this. But goddamnit, how much I want to. I want to grab her delicate jaw in my large palm, wrap her fiery hair around my fist, and bend her into understanding. Force her to accept everything I tell her with no questions asked.

Make her fucking want me.

Make her love me.

Make her fuck me and never leave.

But I'm no different from Holt if I do any of that.

Morrigan O'Rourke is mine. She always was. I spent all these years building an empire with a lost empress, and now she's back.

The smart thing to do is to keep a safe distance, so she can take her throne by her own choice.

"Why now?" Her voice is smaller. "Why did you come back now?"

"The evidence is gone. The cop is under our control now. Madds is safe."

"And my father? After all of this? All he's done to Maddox, to us, you decide to go into business with him?"

"I told you, Holt has something I want, and him and your father are a package deal. But your father's time will come, and he will suffer the consequences of his actions. There was never any question about that. I've envisioned the moment too many times over the years. Even if you and I weren't here right now, he would have still paid. If not for us, for Maddox."

"When did the evidence go away?"

I sigh. "About six or seven months ago."

In the reflection, I can see her eyes widening. She turns and looks over her shoulder for a few moments, before returning her gaze to the window.

"Six, seven months," she whispers.

"Mhm," I hum.

"My mother's party."

Slowly, I close the distance between us, and stand just behind her. I tower over her, but not by too much. Enough to see over her head, and watch our reflections in the window, through the dense forest and cloudless sky.

"There were rumors about what your father and Holt had planned. Rumors that they were sniffing around the docks. However, what they wanted couldn't be done without the right connections. And The Sanctum has those connections. All we had to do was plant the seeds, and all of a sudden, all was forgotten by your dear father. Then we were invited to your mother's birthday party."

"Was it intentional? Your timing, I mean," she asks, narrowing her eyes.

"Yes." I don't miss a beat. "It took me too long. The longest it has ever taken me to do a job. I didn't care that you were spoken for. I needed to be around you. To see if there was still something there. And there was."

She shakes her head but doesn't turn. "I stabbed you. How would you possibly believe there was?"

"Little Eve, I knew I had a chance the moment you pierced my chest. It was that look in your eyes, not of remorse, but passion so dark I could see your hurt. And your love too. You wanted to sink that blade deeper, but you knew you would feel that pain as well."

She rubs her right palm as I listen to her soft breathing. My fate is in those delicate hands of hers, and my blood pressure spikes. It's all come to this moment, and I can't bear the wait. The unknown.

"So what?" She finally speaks again. "If Ryan and I were in a different situation, you would have broken us up?"

"I would be a liar if I said that I wouldn't have tried. I knew you were mine. I would have done my fucking best to make sure you knew that too. But, no. I wouldn't have broken you up unless that was what you wanted. I've hurt you enough."

"You broke me. You hold a power over me that I cannot understand. And I fucking hate it. I hate how deep you can reach inside my soul. How many layers you can peel away and leave me but a shadow. I hate how long it took me to feel that I'm alive again. I hate that I could never truly love again after you."

She whips around, pins me with her gaze, and suddenly I feel as though I'm smaller. Weaker.

"I still hate you, because you're the only one who saw exactly who I was, and you pushed me further into that darkness. Then you left. And there was no one else like you."

"I never left." I'm finding it increasingly more difficult to stay leveled as I watch her spiral.

Tears fill her eyes, the green in her irises so fucking vivid it's like I'm lost in the forest outside of my window on a rainy afternoon.

"I had no choice, Morrigan. But I never actually left. I kept tabs on you as much as I could without arising suspicion. I knew how your life was going. How much smarter you were becoming. And how strong too. Through gritted teeth and a broken heart, I was forced to watch you meet others. And eventually, Holt. But I wanted to kill them all."

I fucking wanted to rip them apart into tiny little pieces, then drop them on her doorstep to show her what happens to the men who touch her without my permission. I wanted to fuck her in a sea of their broken limbs and desecrate their goddamn remains with our ecstasy.

I still do. Only, Holt can fucking die whilst watching as she rides me on his future motherfucking grave.

CHAPTER 23

Morrigan

I DELIBERATELY HOLD my breath and force myself not to blink through the tears I cannot seem to stop from flowing. Just in case I miss a clue, any sign that he's lying to me.

Goddamnit... there's none. But he's The Serpent. Cunning in more ways than most would know or would recognize. What the hell makes me think that I would recognize betrayal on his features?

I give in and blink, pushing a steady stream of tears down my cheeks. My chest shakes, my hands are painful from the tenseness in my fists, and a deep pressure fills my head. Along with my own voice of reason.

You know you would have no trouble recognizing his deceit. You saw it the night he left you. You knew he was lying.

I fucking did. I did!

I don't know if he allowed me to see it, but deep down, I knew he was lying to me. I just didn't know about what. And my insecurities stopped me from accepting that what I was seeing was true. I had no trouble believing that he didn't actually love me.

My fucking Serpent.

All this time, I've hated him. I killed because of how broken I was. I did so many stupid things. I almost did his friend too—Maddox. I always had a soft spot for that brutal man. That gentle beast who kept an eye on me. And the reason Vincent and I never were. Although he cannot be blamed for it.

No one can, apart from my father. I would have done exactly the same thing Vincent did if I was in his position.

"So much time lost," I whisper, unable to drop my gaze from those dark pits of his eyes.

"Yet no love was lost," he whispers back on a long breath.

There's a warmth in his voice that makes a home inside my chest, and instant goosebump flare over my skin. I shake my head gently as my bottom lip quivers, and he cocks his head slightly. Reaching over, he brushes his thumb over my tears, then swipes his tongue over it.

Then he dips in, and I'm expecting a kiss to my lips, but he presses it to my cheek instead. He kisses away the tears that fell there, and microscopic currents burst beneath my skin. Like tiny electric shocks in the shape of his kisses, and he follows the trail down my face. When he reaches my jaw, a ticklish sensation explodes through me, and my body shudders, my hands grabbing onto his naked waist instinctively.

I could have sworn I heard a low moan somewhere deep in his chest at the same time I felt his muscles tense. He doesn't stop, though. He slides one hand into my hair, bending my head back, and continues to follow those stray tears. Right under my jaw, down my neck, until there's nothing left.

My fingers tighten against his flesh, but I only meet hard muscle there. Very little softness. Fuck, he didn't look like this all those years ago, with these defined muscles and wide shoulders. Now he's the kind of man you expect to do at least fifty laps a day in the Olympic pool. My hands itch to explore, but I'm more intrigued by his own exploration.

I close my eyes as his grip on my hair tightens, pulling on it harder as he grabs my ass with his free hand. A tortured moan fills the room as he presses my hips into his. Mine or his, I'm not even sure. But then his tongue swipes over my clavicle, up my neck, and down again, sinking his teeth where it meets the shoulder, and a sharp pain pushes me into him.

"Vincent..." I mewl softly, and every single muscle in his body tenses.

Mine do too. I haven't called him that in years.

"Again," he groans his order to me.

"What?" I open my eyes lazily, and the look that meets me is feral.

Feral in a way that instantly hardens my nipples, painful against even the loose fabric draped against them.

"Say. It. Again."

Oh... A smirk creeps onto my lips.

"Vincent..."

I have no idea how or when it happens. It's all a blur of movement as he all but roars as he grips my ass, lifts me to him, and slams me onto the soft bed. Climbing over me, he traps my wrists in his grip high above my head, pressing them harshly into the mattress. His other hand cups my jaw, and his index finger dips ever so slightly into my mouth, pulling my bottom lip down.

"Fuck... *Morrigan*." My name slips off his lips like honey. "It's kind of poetic—the sound of my name on your lips, and the sound of yours on mine. Isn't it? Yet it in a fucked up kind of way, you're still my Eve, and I'm still the Serpent who lured you into sin."

"The original sin. Only I was always a sinner. You were just the devil who embraced me." I smile, grinding my hips up to meet his.

He drags his hand down my throat, to the neckline of my T-shirt, and in one brisk move, he rips it. I hold in a cry as the fabric grits my skin, but the leftover burn feels strangely good. Reaching the hem of my bra, he pulls it down, exposing my breast, and the moment the colder air brushes my nipple, I can't help but moan.

"Always a heathen." He dips down, capturing that peak between his teeth, then sucks it to the point that pain seeps through, and my back arches just as he releases. "You carry a darkness that somehow found mine through the shadows. And it never let me go."

"No love lost," I whisper, my gaze fixed on his with an intensity I feel in my temples. "None. Your darkness lives in my soul. If you take it out, I won't be whole."

"I want to trust every word you say to me. I want to believe it all, and deep down, I know I do. But there is a part of me that has fought this bond for all these years. It's been trained to protect me, and it currently lives in disbelief. Almost as that teenager from long ago. The one who couldn't believe that you would look at me, that *you* would love me."

He shakes his head slightly, swallowing, before he speaks.

"Trust is earned and I'm going to take my time earning yours." He pauses, letting those words sink in. "But I saw you, Morrigan."

He drags a finger over my breast, down my abdomen, and dips down over my belly. I fight to focus on his words, rather than that electrifying sensation he leaves behind, but he's excruciatingly sensual.

"I saw you long before you think I did," he continues. "Only, I fought you, and our connection. I fought the prospect of what we could be, because I didn't believe in it. I didn't want to, not after seeing what love does to people. But you, goddamnit, you wrapped so fucking tight around me, I couldn't shake you off even if I wanted to. My soul was yours, long before you became mine."

I don't have the right response for this confession. My soul feels like it's been thrown into a grinder, and my heart is close to bursting out of my fucking chest.

"Oh, Mr. Sinclair, you definitely know the right words to get into a lady's panties." This moment feels too heavy with confessions, with these matters of the heart. I'm not used to it.

He narrows his eyes for a moment, and I swear he can read my mind.

"I'm already in your panties, Miss O'Rourke."

He mirrors my grin at the same moment his hand dips down and he grips my pussy, before he pushes two fingers inside. I'm not even sure when he unbuttoned my jeans.

"Jesus... fuck!" I moan, my back arching once again, and my core grinds on his hand involuntarily.

"It's the devil fucking you now, baby." He pulls that finger out, then adds one more, slowly pumping in and out.

"Vincent, oh God... please!"

I can't explain it. I've had men finger me before, and I've done it myself plenty of times. Yet him, the way he spreads them, the way he curls them, the way he pumps in hard, and drags out slowly. Christ, it makes me melt.

"What the hell, Serpent!"

The asshole pulls out, completely.

"Oh, I'm Serpent again, then?" There's a cheekiness in his eyes that drives me crazy.

He lets go of me, and pulls my jeans down, leaving me covered only by a bra and a ripped T-shirt. But he solves that fast, ripping the rest of the fabric, before he undoes the bra and peels it off. I prop myself on my elbows to see him standing at the foot of the bed, staring at me. With one eyebrow raised, he looks famished as his eyes drag up and down my body.

Shit... I don't have the confidence for this.

"Vincent, I—" I'm just about to reach for the sheet and pull it over myself.

"You're so goddamn perfect."

I'm not, but the hungry look in his eyes comforts me. My muscles relax a little, and I smirk as my plump flesh flares with goose bumps. He doesn't peel his eyes off me as he drops his pajama bottoms straight down to the floor. Even though I've had him inside of me, the sight of him naked, in all his glory, standing before me, feels forbidden.

He›s a work of fucking art.

I want to run my tongue all over him. Over his wide pecks, his defined abs trailing into that sinful V of muscles, even over his long, lean legs. But his cock... Christ almighty, his damn cock, with those soft veins, and the glistening, thick head. If you could ever call a cock beautiful, this would be it.

I finally drag my gaze back up, and when I reach his eyes, his head is tilted, a knowing grin pulling at his lips.

"You seem to like what you see too."

"Couldn›t say for certain." I feign ignorance. "At this distance, it's a bit blurry. I can't quite tell."

The laugh that follows, loud and deep, shaking his whole body as he presses a hand over his belly, spreads a sort of warmth through me that I haven't felt in a while—happiness.

He steps right to the edge of the bed, and I quickly flip over. I'm not fucking around. My face is up close and personal with that beautiful cock, and I don't drag it out. No... I wrap my hand around his length, and swallow him in one go, until he hits the back of my throat.

"Fucking hell, woman!" His legs shake, hands grabbing onto my hair, and I can't help but feel a little pride.

Meeting his gaze, I slowly slide my lips back to the tip of him, and his eyes widen on me as his mouth falls open slightly. His chest rises and falls with staggered breaths, and I dip back in, sucking him until I'm choking. But I don't waver. I drag my tongue over his cock as he hits the back of my throat again and again, letting spit fall down my chin, and I cup his balls, holding them tight to his body. Every choking sound I make, he matches with a groan, and as his grip on me tightens, he begins to thrust. His ragged breaths coax me on, and I would smile if I could.

Fuck, there's nothing quite like subduing a man like this. Only, I've never really had a man so eager to fall at my feet, and this one looks as if he might.

All of a sudden, he pulls me back by the hair, forcing me to get up on my knees as my saliva falls onto my breasts.

"I—I can't. Fuck! I may be The Serpent, but you're a goddamn devil woman with that tongue of yours," he rasps, gripping my waist, and in one swift move, he lifts me and throws me on my back.

Grabbing my legs, he pulls me to him until my ass is at the edge of the bed, and he sinks to his knees between my spread thighs.

"Vincent, just—just fuck me. Please."

All I want right now, all I need, is to feel the stretch of his cock inside me.

"If my dick goes anywhere near you right now, I'm gonna come. And it's too fucking early for that." He doesn't waste another moment. His head disappears between my legs, then his tongue swipes right over the seam of me, and when it dips inside my pussy, I fall back on a sharp moan.

"That's it, my darling Eve."

I'm thrashing all over the place as his tongue assaults me, and he rubs my clit with such erratic precision, I'm fucking jealous he learned these skills on someone else. He pushes his hand on my belly to stop me from squirming but doesn't stop.

Then he switches. His fingers fucking me methodically, rubbing that delicious spot inside of me as he gently presses on my belly, and I'm sure I'm going to fucking implode. When he adds another finger, the stretch is so fucking delicious, my cries are bouncing off the walls. It's a satisfying fullness that makes me crawl backwards in bed and drives me to beg the devil for more.

"Goddamnit, Serpent! Fuck me."

But he doesn't listen. Instead, he presses his tongue hard onto my clit, before sucking it slowly, and my hips are only held down by the fingers he hooks inside of me. The rhythm rises higher, the strokes reach deeper, and the thrusts are harsher.

It hits out of nowhere. It rips through my belly like liquid fire, my core spasming uncontrollably, and my whole body follows. The orgasm takes control of me, and it explodes on such a high, my vision goes white and my ears ring. I'm blind to the image of him crawling on top of me; deaf to the sound that makes my throat raw the moment his cock impales me; speechless to the mixture of sensations and emotions I feel when he thrusts into me as I'm still riding my release.

It's painful and ecstatic all at the same time, and all I can do is ride it along. I'm a slave to him, and it feels amazing.

"Vincent..." I moan as I plant my feet onto the bed, knees bent, and push my hips into him.

"Fucking hell, Morrigan!"

His cock reaches deeper, stretching my pussy just at the edge of stinging, and when I lift my hands above my head, he takes the cue and traps my wrists. Bracing himself on his other hand, he pistons into me with a raw force that brings me right to the fucking edge again.

I have no idea how much time passes. I'm fully lost in the strength of his body pressing against mine. His rhythm shifts, his hips grinding against mine, and he withdraws slowly before he drives back in with force. I look down to watch where we're joined, and the image is enough to make me come again. I'm panting harder, losing myself in that delicious image, and my mind goes blank. There are no thoughts there, no worries, no... nothing. Only this moment. Only his body on top of mine, our skins touching, his cock inside of me. There's only he and I. Only us.

And just like that, with one more thrust, my pussy pulses violently, sucking him in as another orgasm destroys my body. He swears under his breath as he drops onto his forearms, caging me in, and I force myself to hold that pitch black gaze, but I'm shaking with pleasure and my eyes drift closed. A guttural grunt vibrates from his chest and onto my lips as he presses them to mine, just as his cock begins to jerk inside of me. His release is just as violent, and the most satisfied of grins pulls at my lips.

So much warmth spreads inside of me, his cum filling me to the point that I'm sure it's starting to spill out around his cock now. Implications of us fucking raw snake through my mind. I'm not worrying, though. With any other man, I would have had a problem, but not with Vincent. A man like him keeps himself healthy. But it's not that knowledge that eases my mind, it's the fact that I seem to trust he wouldn't put me in a nasty situation.

"This," he pants, "is… fuck. This was—" He swipes a hand over his face, clearly unable to form even the shortest of sentences.

I can't help it. I laugh, instantly feeling the need to run to the toilet as his cum starts dripping out of me. But his cock feels far too good where it is.

"You're gonna push me out, woman." He looks down between us. "Shit. I'm sorry, I got carried away."

"It's okay. We're safe, and I'm okay. Clean."

He shakes his head. "I'm never this stupid, but Christ, fucking you bare is just—"

"I know." I really do.

He dips in, pressing his lips onto mine, and this kiss has a touch of sentiment to it. It's different. Deeper, even though it's soft in its delivery. I grab his head in my hands and hold him here, hold him tight, because there's no way I'm letting him go. Not again.

Not *ever* again.

CHAPTER 24
Morrigan

THE SUN STREAMS through the large window, its rays warming us, and the only thing I can see is the tops of the trees. I have no idea where I am, where his house is, and I thought I would be much more concerned about that. Maybe I'm being stupid. Or maybe for the first time in a long time, I'm allowing myself to just *be*.

His fingers run lazy circles on my hip, goose bumps spreading from that caress over the rest of me, and I nestle closer into his side. My head rests on that soft spot at the edge of his chest, as I drape one leg over his, and my palm enjoys the slow beat of his heart.

Everything right here is a contrast from my life beyond this house, this sanctuary. The madness, the chaos, the pain, and the deceit all live somewhere far beyond these walls.

Here, we are different. Not because we're acting, but because here we can be ourselves.

He can be the man who softens when his eyes land on me, the one who cleans me up with a warm, wet washcloth after he fucks me into oblivion. The man who cuddles me when I'm spent.

And I... I can finally allow myself to feel hope. Hope for the little things. Like talking about my day, what I've done at the club, the things I'm proud of in my old and new career. Hope that I won't be looked at and immediately criticized for my looks or lack of. Hope that I can finally be by Vincent's side, that I can support him as he does me, and that I can live the life I deserve.

Here, I can hope for freedom.

"I'm not sure why your organization is called The Sanctum, but this place, this moment, this feels like a sanctuary."

"It wasn't intentional." He shifts a little, sinking deeper into the pillow. "Before we were four, we used to be five."

"I have a feeling I know who you're talking about."

"Finn has a brother—Ronan. A while back, after you and I broke up, something happened, and he decided to leave. On the day he left, he said that, no matter what, this is our sanctum. Finn didn't exactly agree; they parted on bad terms, but he did say that we—the four of us—are The Sanctum. It stuck after that," he explains, but I don't miss how his gaze drifts. There is definitely more to that story, but I'll ask another day.

"It's quite interesting. Pretty original way of naming a crime syndicate," I say, laughing.

"Well, to be fair, even though that was technically the official moment, there was something else that sort of lead to it," Vincent continues. "When we were kids, Madds and I found this beat-up old tree house in this forest. We used to sneak up at night, or when things got bad, and we hid there. It was our sanctuary, our safe space. Carter and Finn followed shortly after. Ronan too, but he was older than us, and he had his own stuff going on. We had our backs always, and we were each other's sanctuary too."

Fuck. There's beauty in that sadness, I suppose.

"When things got bad?" I pry, hoping for more insight.

"Mhm. My father was a mean motherfucker. I didn't care about how he treated me, but my mother... she went through a world of sorrow because of that son of a bitch. He was physical, but not extreme; however, there are other ways to abuse a person, and he mastered them all. She had no life, she wasn't allowed one. She had no money, no friends, no job, and no self-esteem left. Toward their end, she had very little will."

I stiffen, because all of that sounds like the journey I'm on, and it hurts me, knowing that this man watched his mother go through that. And now, when he came back into my life, he found me in a similar predicament.

"I'm sorry... I didn't know about him. He wasn't around when we were together."

"No. I chased him away a couple of years before. I grew, matured, got some balls, and the slithering devil in me grew as well."

"It's been a while... have you seen him since? Do you know where he is?"

"I have not seen him, and no, I don't know where he is. I kept tabs on him, but he went under the radar a while back. I do think he believes I grew complacent, and I will have to get rid of him for good."

Does he mean—? "Kill him."

"Yes. Leaving him alive the first time around was a mistake I regret to this day."

I nod against him. It should bother me, this blunt confession, yet I feel nothing. There's no denying I feel slightly disgusted with myself because of it. I don't know if it's not affecting me because of my growing hate for my own parents, or Vincent's nonchalant attitude about murder is rubbing off on me.

"Your mom was a sweetheart when I met her, and so strong-willed. If you wouldn't have told me, I would have never noticed in her the effects of years of abuse."

"She recovered very fast. She only took it all before in order to protect me. Nowadays, she has no problem bossing around four grown-ass men, our security, and some of our scariest men. In reality, we're all a little scared of her. It's fucked up." The way he speaks those words is endearing. There's happiness for his mother, but pride also.

"What about the others? What bad things were they sheltering from?" I pry once again.

"They have their own stories, but they're not mine to tell. Finn and Ronan were the only ones to have remotely normal parents. Absent, but normal."

I nod in understanding. Although I know a bit of Maddox's story. A bit, and yet it's still hard to stomach.

My eyes bulge, and I suck in a breath, but quickly recover, before Vincent can notice the shift. Maddox... fuck! The scene from last night springs to mind, and I have no idea what to make of it now. No. No, I can't think of that now.

But the questions spring in my mind anyway— Why did Vincent watch as his best friend held me, then pressed me into him himself?

A shudder curls around my spine, and I have to strain to keep it away from shooting to my core.

"Eventually, we will have to go out there and face the world," I whisper, pressing my palm a little harder onto his chest.

I let the beat of his heart pulse through my flesh and push those thoughts away.

"Eventually," he repeats.

I look up at him, and his eyes are closed, the sunlight making The Serpent look quite angelic. Black stubble covers his jaw, fading as it reaches his cheeks, his hair is wild around his face, and his thick black lashes give him a tinge of innocence. He's a beautiful man, handsome in a way that makes you feel a little small when you're around him. But here, wrapped in my limbs, calm and serene, he looks like a completely different man—*my* man. I feel strangely possessive of this side of him. I don't want anyone else to see it.

"Where are we, Vincent?" I ask him.

He doesn't open his eyes, but a glorious smirk crinkles the skin around them. Fuck me if happiness doesn't look breathtaking on this man. And I'm the one who made it happen. *I put that smile on his lips.*

"Home."

I need more than just this one word. On its own, it can mean too many different things. It can mean just that, or it could be an implication of a future I stopped envisioning long ago. A future I craved and cried for. One I gave up on when the pain became too much.

"Your home?" l ask, because l can't allow my mind to spiral.

Opening his eyes, he turns his head to look down at me before he answers. "Just... home."

He holds me in his dark gaze reminiscent of the moonless sky, yet there's a glimmer of stars in them, and it looks a lot like longing. He wraps his hand around my hip, giving it a quick squeeze before he reaches for my cheek, and rubs his thumb gently on my skin.

"It can be whatever you want it to be. It can be yours too," he adds.

I'm searching for the right words that would fit this situation, but I'm not sure if I can find them.

"I don't know what to say, Vincent."

"You don't have to say anything now."

"I do. Because it sounds as if just like that, we're together." It's not that I don't like the idea, it's just... sudden. "No questions asked."

"I can think of a question to ask you."

My heart stops, and it wants to beg him to keep talking. Not my brain, though. No, my head wants to sit back and process.

"But yes, Morrigan, just like that. You can hate me all you want, but your eyes don't lie," he continues, to my relief. "Now, a month from now, or a year... no matter how long we wait, we will always end up right here. So, it might as well be now."

Well, fuck. It's hard to argue with logic. It's not really that easy.

"Is that what you really want? For me to be here and live with you?" I ask, narrowing my eyes. The idea feels insane, after all this time.

"I've lived too long without you, my sweet Eve. Having you in my bed when I go to sleep at night would be a privilege I've stopped dreaming of. But it is a privilege nonetheless, so I'll settle with simply knowing you're mine. The rest can follow when you're ready."

I'm listening to his words, but it's not where my focus is. I'm looking for a change in his tone, a hitch in his breath, or pupils dilating. A sign to identify not only a lie, but any insecurity. There's none.

None at all.

I keep waiting, but it doesn't seem to be coming. How have I reached this point? Mere days ago, my life was a stark contrast to this moment. Is it real?

"The night Ryan took me to his house—"

"When we fucked against the window." He grins at me, and I playfully slap his chest.

"Yes." I smirk. "We were in my future apartment."

"Oh, I didn't realize. Loreley owns the building, right?"

"Yes, she lives on the top floor with Luke. She insisted I take the apartment under hers. Plus, since we own the club together, the proximity is useful. However, beyond all that, I like it."

"I don't remember it being finished."

"No. We stalled when we got the idea for Metamorphosis and redirected the funds. Work has only just restarted," I explain.

"But you will move in there once it is done."

"Once I'm out of my predicament and the apartment is livable, yes. It's beautiful. I can see the sea from there. I love its old charm and character, and it's in an excellent location." I don't take my eyes off of him because I need to see how he truly feels about this.

"Definitely a great location. Not that far from Midnight," he says as he lifts an eyebrow.

"Your speakeasy?"

"Yes."

"What does it have to do with it?" I'm a bit anxious. I haven't gotten the reaction I was hoping from him, and I don't want yet another man who wants to control me.

"I don't have to drive far after a long day, when I'll need your comfort. Or your touch. Or the taste of your pretty cunt on my tongue."

My eyes bulge and heat flushes my cheeks.

"I fully see the appeal. It will give you the independence you haven't had before, and you deserve to experience it all," he says in a more serious tone, his eyes softening.

There it is.

That's what I need from him. Not that words are enough when actions are the ones that matter, but he's not exactly known for deceiving people. On the contrary, he is painfully honest.

"Yes," I agree, smiling back as I turn toward the window, and nestle deeper into him. Damn, this man is so good to cuddle.

I've seen him kill a man in cold blood without blinking, yet here he is... cuddling me.

A small flock of birds suddenly flies away from the trees, pulling my attention to the window.

But really, where exactly are we?

I know there's pretty much just trees on this side of the house, but what about on the other sides? I reluctantly pull away from him and climb out, walking to the window.

It's only when I reach it that I notice I'm completely and utterly naked. It takes me a few more seconds to realize I'm not uncomfortable. I could never do this around Ryan. He would condemn me since I'm too plump for his standards, but now... I'm smiling. The man watching from the bed gives me a confidence I've been losing. I know if I turn, he'll be looking at me with hunger in his eyes.

As much as I know I shouldn't need a man's appreciation of my looks to give me confidence, it fucking helps after being put down for months.

"Are we at the edge of the forest?" I ask, noticing movement through the trees. Wait— "Is that a deer?!"

"Probably. There're quite a few around. Sometimes I see this stag, and its antlers are something out of a storybook. But no, we're not at the edge of the forest." His voice grows closer, until his warmth brushes against my skin. "We're pretty much in the middle of it."

I look up and over my shoulder in a bit of disbelief. The man looks like he belongs in the penthouse of the Rimbauer, the poshest apartment building in Queenscove. Yet he is here...

The forest stretches for miles. It's the only one at the edge of the city; I just never realized someone lived in it. I've walked through its trails many times, yet never even seen glimpses of a house.

Suddenly, a loud gurgle vibrates through my stomach, and I press my hand to it. When did I last eat a full meal? Being in Ryan's house made me feel sick enough that I haven't been able to eat properly.

"I think that's our cue to go downstairs." He rubs his hands on my upper arms and turns away from me.

I pull my gaze from the forest and swing around, stopping dead in my tracks when I catch how, one by one, his muscles ripple. With each step, his legs tense, his ass a fucking sight for sore eyes, and his back... *damn*, his back. He walks toward the dressing room, and I finally move when he disappears inside, the mirage over.

"T-shirt or button-up?" he asks, as I finally follow him in.

"I'm going to live my cliché and choose the button-up, please."

I don't miss the slight grin in his eyes. Am I missing something? Was there a wrong answer?

He hands me a black one that I pull on as I walk over to my discarded jeans and panties, but I only put the panties on.

"I would argue that there's no need for them, but... who knows." I hear him behind me.

"Who knows? What do you mean?" I turn to him, watching as he pulls on a black T-shirt over his black joggers, while heading out of the room.

As we walk down the floating wood staircase, I wonder how the hell this man carried me up these stairs last night. Opposite the stairs on the ground floor sits a beautifully carved wooden double door. I briefly glance to the left, noting the huge wood dining table sitting in front of the large windows at the front of the house, and when we turn to the right, I note the kitchen. It's furnished with dark, rough wood and black stone worktops, and an oversized island in the middle.

But when I fully turn toward the back of the house, I stop dead in my tracks. Windows cover the whole length of it, only interrupted once every ten feet or so by thick wood pillars the same shade as the kitchen. It feels like I'm outside. And that view...

"Fuck..." That's all I seem to be able to express.

My mouth drops, too caught up in this view. A large deck sits right outside the windows, with a dining and sitting area, all overlooking the dense, vast forest. Nothing else. Only green, vibrant forest.

"It's beautiful, isn't it?" he asks.

It's more than that. I understand now why he's here. The atmosphere is broken out of a fucking dream, with the soft sway of the leaf covered trees, the pale blue of the sky, and the peacefulness.

It really could be... *home.*

CHAPTER 25
Vincent

MORRIGAN WAS STILL by the window, looking at the view, when I left the bedroom. I do that sometimes too, especially when it rains. Living in the middle of a forest has its disadvantages too but being surrounded by that view beats all of them.

I turn on the espresso machine before I head to the fridge and pull out some breakfast ingredients. When I turn around, she's standing before the island, her head cocked, eyes fixed on me.

"What?" I stop in my tracks.

"You look... very domesticated. Unusual."

She takes a seat at the island, resting her forearms on it, still very focused on me.

"Unusual?" I drop everything on the worktop, bringing over some eggs, veg, and some utensils and bowls. "Did you think I would be surrounded by servants?"

She pulls her shoulders back, her eyes widening slightly. "Maybe a cook? Or a maid?"

"Is it still called a maid?"

"You're right. A butler would be more fitting for you." Her condescending tone makes me frown, but when I see the tinge of amusement in her eyes, I want to smack her ass with this butter knife.

"A butler, really? Nah, no butler here. Sorry to disappoint. We do have assistants, and yes, I do get meals made for me sometimes, but I don't have a live-in chef. Don't get me wrong, I like having staff deal with a lot of the mundane shit I don't have time for, but I didn't grow up with a silver spoon in my mouth. Doing things for myself keeps me grounded, and I don't like people constantly running around my house, except for the guards roaming the grounds. I enjoy the privacy, and there's something about being surrounded by this luscious green oasis that brings me so much comfort."

"Sorry, I didn't mean to imply anything. But I'll be honest, in recent years, I've developed a pretty specific image of you. I guess it all looks different from the outside." She's not shying away from the underlying insult.

"Yeah, well... I've developed a certain idea about you too. I agree, everything looks different from the outside." It wasn't long ago that I thought she turned into the stuck-up version her parents always wanted her to be.

"You're *The Serpent*. It's hard to imagine you in a home like this one, cozy and beautiful, while cooking breakfast. Shit, I have a warped perspective on everything, to be honest. I've been surrounded by the wrong people," she says, sighing as she intertwines her fingers, rubbing them nervously.

"There's no denying that. But things will change. Soon. Very soon."

God, her smile is infectious.

"So... it's only you here. All the time?" she asks, raising an eyebrow.

"Cheeky, Little Eve. Why don't you just ask the questions you want answers to?"

"Maybe it's not my place to be that direct. I'm trying to give you a chance to refuse to acknowledge the question, I guess." She grabs a small bowl, cracks a few eggs in, and begins whisking them.

"If you're asking me about women, then no. I do not bring women here."

I can't help but smirk when I catch her expression at my answer.

"Not here. Okay."

"You know, jealousy looks good on you."

She shoots me a look that tells me she might beat me with that whisk, but hell, I'm going to keep going because I know everything she does to me will feel good.

"No women here, don't worry. I mean, apart from my mamaw and my ex." I say that last word with a shrug, like it's no big deal. But I almost burst into laughter when Morrigan violently whisks some egg out of the bowl.

"You son of a bitch, you're doing this on purpose."

I smirk as I continue. "Am I? Huh. Either way, other than them, only the guys and the security team come by now."

"Who's your ex?" She doesn't waste a breath.

"She doesn't live around here. Don't worry, you won't run into her."

"Did you break up on... good terms?"

"Yes. She's also married now, and we were only together for about eight months or so."

I feel bad using that word—*only*—because Morrigan and I weren't together for too long either. But Belle certainly didn't feel like her. I got over Belle in days. I never got over Morrigan.

I turn to the coffee machine and fill two cups.

"Cream and two sugars?" I ask over my shoulder.

"Umm... no sugar is fine."

Her tone sounds off. I whip around and narrow my eyes on her. "You don't like it with sugar anymore?" I'm skeptical.

"I—I do. It's just better for me without." She's fidgeting, chewing on her bottom lip as her hand presses against her stomach.

What the fuck is going on?

I drop two sugars in her coffee and round the island, straight to her. The moment I'm in her space, I rotate her stool, and spread her naked thighs, stepping between them. Then I slide my hands under my shirt that looks so fucking good on her, sinking my palms and fingers into her soft sides, right below the waist.

"I don't know what you see in the mirror, Morrigan, but what I see is fucking stunning. No matter how much sugar you have, that will not change."

She braces her delicate hands on my forearms, and before she can chew on that lip again, I catch it in a breathless kiss that makes me dizzy. When I'm done with her, she sucks in a deep breath, and I could have sworn her green eyes brightened. She doesn't say anything, though, only a smile moves her lips, and it's enough for me.

I head straight to the stove and begin frying some maple-cured smoked bacon that Mamaw always makes sure she brings to me from her favorite butcher. It smells divine, and judging from the twinkle in Morrigan's eyes, and the growling in her stomach, she's going to enjoy it too.

"How is your mom? June, right?" she asks.

I stop with the kitchen tongs in midair and turn my head to her. "Yes. You remember."

"Of course. I know I only met her a few times, but that type of kindness stays with you. She lives in town, East Side, right?"

She's not wrong. Mamaw is a sweet woman, too sweet sometimes, and she paid for it in the past. But the life she's led has slowly toughened her up. The guys are all a little terrified of her, and she has them wrapped around her little finger. Maddox considers her his mother too, and she's never called him anything but *son*.

"Not for a while. On this land, there used to be two dilapidated cabins, which I tore down. There was a big one here, where I built this house, and a second hunting cabin about two miles south, where I built hers. I like keeping her close to me. Safe," I explain.

"That's nice. I know you haven't had an easy life, but you have a loving family— your mom, The Sanctum. It's precious, you know."

There's a sadness in her eyes that I wish I would be able to wipe away. I wish I could make things better for her, give her a new life, and new memories.

I wish I could give it all to her.

I hope I will.

* * *

"Could we eat outside, please?" There's another twinkle in her eyes as she points toward the deck, and I wonder if this is normal. For little things like this to pierce my darkness with her rays of light. Because if that's the case, I'll feed that twinkle so it becomes a permanent sparkle.

I don't answer, I just grab the plates and head toward the back door, explaining to her how to unlock and open it. The air is crisp when we settle at the dewy dining table, but neither of us mind. It's refreshing. Not many words are exchanged, both content to simply be in each other's presence, the silence anything but awkward as we eat. Her eyes wander to the forest around us, to the birds that fly from tree to tree, to where the leaves rustle.

But my gaze stays right on her.

I'm happy observing her, every shift in her movements, her curious gaze when she notices something else to look at, the plumpness in her cheeks when she smiles, and the soft wrinkles in her features. I take it all in. Everything. Even the way she delicately slides the food off the fork with her plush lips, the way stray strands of her brick-red hair gently flow around her face in the forest breeze, and the barely audible moan deep in her throat when she bites another piece of bacon.

I'm mesmerized, trapped in this surreal image before me. Morrigan—my Eve, sitting on my deck, eating my food, and finally enjoying my company.

"I'm not letting you go, Morrigan."

Her head whips to me, hair whirling over her face, and she quickly swipes it away, revealing the slight shock, laced with fear, in her eyes.

"I don't mean out of this house," I correct myself. "I mean you... us. You're mine. I don't fucking care how condescending and possessive that sounds. I genuinely don't give a shit. I will fight for you. I will fight to get you back. Unless you tell me right here, right now, that it will never be what I want it to be."

I drop the knife and fork and stare at her, feeling the strain between my eyebrows, and the shadows deepening over my eyes.

"What do you want it to be?" she asks with a slight scowl.

"Forever." I don't hesitate.

She nods slowly, pursing her lips, and the lack of a response brings a whole other level of anxiety rushing through me. One that I don't remember ever feeling. But I've thought of this moment before. The moment I reveal why I had to break up with her, that I never stopped wanting her, and what I want us to be. I've been perfectly aware that she could just reject me. Yet now, as I'm faced with the prospect, I realize that I haven't prepared myself as well as I should have.

Was I too smug about it?

My heart thumps louder in my ears, and a slight ringing starts to sound amongst her silence.

"I can practically taste your nervousness, Serpent," she says slowly, as her gaze darkens.

As I take in the image of her against the background, it hits me all at once—the color of her eyes is the same as the forest that surrounds us. Is that why I find so much comfort living between these trees?

"I think you're imagining things, baby." I straighten slowly.

"Am I?" She drops her cutlery on the plate, pushing her chair back with a loud grind, and stalks toward me.

She brushes her hand over my bare chest, and I know my heartbeat will betray me. Only, she doesn't linger. Instead, she continues her exploration down my abdomen, reaching over my cock that's been half hard since she slid my shirt over her naked body, and my toes curl when she gives it a squeeze. Even through the fabric of my joggers, it feels fucking good.

But she doesn't stop there. She tightens her grip once more, before she rubs her palm over the growing length of my shaft, then throws her leg over the chair, straddling me.

Her knees are resting over the armrests, her legs dangling over the sides as her ass sits far too comfortably in my lap. The minx doesn't waste a moment, and her hips begin this ruthless grind against my cock, just as her hand presses right over my heart.

Like she wants to feel the beats of it beneath her flesh, the effect she has on me.

"You're doing a good job at distracting me," I say, as I dig my heels into the floor and push, sliding my chair back enough that it gives her space to move.

My God, the smile she gives me is so fucking stunning. She reaches between us, sliding her hand under the hem of my joggers, and presses her palm on my cock before wrapping it around, dragging it slowly to the tip of me. *Fuck,* I have to keep my eyes from rolling to the back of my head as she pumps two more times, the feel of her is almost too much to handle. I'm at the precipice of slamming her on the fucking table and driving into her, but it appears she's the one who wants to do the fucking now. And who the hell am I to say no to that.

"You're gonna fucking kill me, aren't you?" I ask as she shoves my joggers down, freeing me from them.

"You'll die a happy man then, no?"

She grins as she presses my cock to her lace covered pussy, the grit of the fabric and the wetness of her so fucking enticing as she moves up and down.

"I don't know. Will I?" I say, cocking an eyebrow, and she licks the corner of her lips, challenging.

She releases me, and my dick slaps against my abdomen. She presses her pussy to it, rolling her hips as she grabs onto my neck, and her back arches as she drops her head back, closing her eyes.

There's no shame, no inhibition, no restraint as she gets herself off on me, and Christ if that's not enough to push me over the edge. She's using me for her own pleasure, and I'm a willing participant at the cusp of begging her for more.

I don't. Instead I dig my fingers into her waist, and push her harder against me, helping her grind until her moans echo through the forest. Until I know the security detail that patrols my land can hear every note of it.

Just as her legs begin to shake, when I can feel the pulse of her cunt against me, she reaches between us, and in one swift motion, pulls her panties to the side, rises, and impales herself on me.

"Jesus fuck!" I can't help the rasp that leaves me. It's almost covered by the pleasure filled cry coming from her.

I think I will die a happy man.

One stroke and I'm balls deep as she unravels around me, shaking and strangling my dick. Goddamnit, it's a view to behold.

"You're so fucking beautiful, all broken like that on my cock."

When her pussy relaxes, she moves again, rolling her hips slowly, and rising until just the tip of me is inside of her. Fuck, it's a different type of pleasure. Euphoric, almost.

I slide my hands under the shirt, one on her hip, the other on her breasts, and my head drops back, eyes closed as I savor the feel of her wrapped around my cock. She moves nice and slow, and I revel in every drop of ecstasy connecting us in this moment.

"You're so damn handsome, all enthralled like that inside my cunt..." She moans those delicious words, and my cock jerks inside of her, making her gasp and twitch.

I smirk as her rhythm quickens, and when I open my eyes, the intensity of her gaze on me makes me flex harder. It draws out a violent cry from her lips, one that echoes a few times before the forest swallows it. I release her breast and clasp her throat in my hand, pulling her to me just as I push my ass up, my cock reaching much deeper inside of her at the same moment I press my lips to hers and she screams into my mouth.

"Fuck me, darling Eve, take everything," I coax her on.

The rhythm takes another turn, as she slams onto me, and I push up into her.

"Make me come, goddamnit!" she almost yells the command at me, and I can't help but grin at my vixen.

I release her waist and reach between us, pressing two fingers on her clit, rubbing circles on it. I watch her lips part, her moans increase, and my fucking balls can't take it anymore. Wrapped tight around my cock, milking me hard, I try to pull myself together and hold on, but goddamnit, it's too much.

I come so hard my balls hurt, my cock jerks, my abs tighten, and I fucking roar the moment she screams and shakes, coming with the same rhythm. I release her throat and she wraps her arms around me, holding on for dear life as she presses her head in the crook of my neck and I hug her to my chest.

Minutes... so many fucking minutes it takes just for her pussy to stop twitching around me, and I can feel my cum slowly seeping out. She couldn't care less.

Finally, she pulls away, just enough so she can see me, and she smiles—a glorious fucking smile that could move mountains and tame monsters.

There's a sweet innocence to it that I've never seen in her before.

I want to keep it, preserve it until death comes and we get to continue our dance in the great beyond.

Morrigan

THE HUMIDITY OF our southern city somehow feels fresh against my skin here in the middle of the forest. We're in the same spot. I'm draped over him, and he holds me in his arms, one hand threaded through my hair in a tight grip. Yet, I finally feel like I can breathe. The air is lighter than it ever has been. I'm out in the open, yet I'm safe.

"I have men out here, baby. Men that might have just watched you ride me. They most definitely heard us." He talks softly in my ear, his words wicked.

"Do you think we gave them a good show? Or should we try again for good measure?"

The rumble that shakes his chest as he forces himself not to laugh is endearing.

"I'm sorry, I keep forgetting you own a sex club now."

I pull away enough to see his handsome face. "Sir, please. I own a *fetish* club. While sex might be happening, not everyone comes there for it. They come to satisfy needs beyond it." I dip in slowly, my gaze switching to his lips. "Cravings." I touch mine to his, brushing left to right. "Fulfill fantasies." Then I press closer, sinking my fingers through his hair, his stubble a delicious scrape against my face.

"My apologies, Miss." He speaks between kisses. "And do you fulfill any of your fantasies there?"

"I certainly fulfilled one a few weeks ago. One I never knew I had. Being fingered by a stranger while watching another woman being fucked by a dildo and a man was definitely a highlight."

His grip in my hair tightens and he pulls down, deepening the kiss as he leans slightly over me.

"Mmm…" he hums against me. "How peculiar. I had a similar experience. I don't know how I had so much chemistry with that woman, you know…" He's dripping in sarcasm. "Why I wanted to taste her so badly, or why I wanted to press her against that window and fuck her while everyone watched."

"Is that your fantasy, Serpent? Fuck me as everyone watches?" I lick his lips and pull on his hair just as he does the same to me.

"Oh, my Little Eve, I have many fantasies I wish to fulfill with you. And I have a feeling there's one in particular that we share." He jerks my head back and when I feel his lips on my throat, a shudder shakes me. "What fantasy fills that pretty little head of yours?" He licks me from the base of my neck to just under my ear.

"There are many," I say on a shaky breath.

"I bet there are. Tell me the biggest one. The riskiest one. The most forbidden one of them all."

"I don't know…" I'm lying. I definitely know.

"What makes that tight cunt of yours wet when you're alone at night?" He traps my earlobe between his teeth, biting just hard enough that my nipples perk up.

Oh, fuck.

"Dirty… filthy things," I answer.

"Filthy," he whispers against my throat, dragging his teeth down. "Who's doing these filthy things to you?"

"You," I moan as the scrape of his teeth gets me fucking hot all over again, his cock half hard under me again.

"And what am I doing to you, baby?"

"Vincent, please—"

"Am I finger-fucking that pretty cunt?" That crude word sends a tingle straight to it. It works magic every single time.

"No."

"Am I licking it?" he asks.

"No."

"Am I fucking it, Morrigan?"

"N—no."

His palm reaches my center, cupping me in an almost bruising grip.

"Oh, you filthy little thing." I can practically taste the smirk in his words. "Is it your ass I'm stretching with my cock?"

He squeezes my pussy harder, and I mewl, "Yesss."

"That sounds positively divine, but definitely not like the riskiest, most forbidden fantasy."

Shit. Please… don't ask…

"Are we alone?"

What?

"Yes."

"Are you sure about that?" His finger rips through my pussy, sinking so deep inside of me, my body jerks up. But his hand in my hair holds me down.

"Fuck!"

He adds another as the heel of his palm rubs against my overly sensitive clit.

"Your cunt betrays you, beautiful. With my cock in your ass, it's lonely in your delicious fantasy. Isn't it?" He pumps in and out, and I swear he can drag the truth out of me through my goddamn pussy.

"It is," I finally admit.

"Are we lying in bed, or are we... in the shadows of stairs?" The rhythm quickens, his thrusts harsher, and my brain shuts down as my body goes almost limp. *Wait, stairs?!*

"Vincent, I—"

"Focus on the fantasy." He rolls those fingers over that treacherous spot inside of me, hypnotizing me. "Who else is in it when you fuck this pretty cunt of yours alone at night? Who else do you imagine?"

"I can't. Please, don't—"

"You can. Say it, baby." He slams hard into me, his thumb now on my aching clit, and I think I'm losing my mind.

"Maddox!" I cry as a shudder rips through me.

I'm losing my mind. Did I just admit to him I fantasize about his best friend?! I don't have another second to dwell on it, as he adds one more finger, stretching me just a little wider, and I yelp.

"Your pussy would have to take more than just three fingers to accommodate him, filthy Little Eve." He bites into the side of my neck, his words sinking in at the same time. "He's a mean motherfucker. He would stretch that pussy so hard, but I would be right there with him."

"Vincent—"

"Yes, right here." He pulls his fingers just enough to reposition himself, and suddenly I can feel one pushing against that tight back hole. It's so wet from my pussy and his cum that was still inside of me, that it slides right in, and I don't bother to hold in the lust-filled moan that tears from my throat. "I would fuck this tight little ass of yours, as he would pump into your pussy, and goddamnit... wouldn't that be fucking beautiful?"

I must be dreaming.

He rolls those fingers with such skill that I've fallen backwards, my shoulders against the table, and his words... they fill me with the image of the man before me sharing me with the beast I've always craved. Just once would be enough to sate my hunger. Vincent taking my ass... Maddox owning my greedy pussy.

The orgasm hits with that image front and center, clawing its way through me so violently, Vincent has to hold me so I don't fall off of his lap. It feels... it feels dirty. This climax shouldn't be this strong. I shouldn't like this fantasy quite this much.

I'm wrapped in his arms and I'm not entirely sure when he pulled me there, but he holds me tight, lazily running his fingers through my hair. I shift slightly and kiss his lips, lingering for a moment longer.

"Did you always know?" My voice is soft as I ask, and I have to force myself to look him in the eyes.

He nods.

"Not always, but I saw the curiosity in your eyes even back then. I can always recognize lust in your eyes. I've always known you like him, just as he likes you."

"Vincent, it's not like that. No, not like you."

"I know, don't worry," he assures, a soft smile on his lips.

"How do you know? How does this not make you jealous, or possessive, or upset?"

"Oh, I'm possessive over you, don't you fucking think otherwise. I would happily cut the hand off any man who touches you. Which makes this whole predicament you're in very hard for me. But with Madds, it's different."

"How?" I ask, my question coming out shakily.

"There's something about the way he looks at you that gives me this sense of pride. Like... he appreciates this amazing thing I get to have to myself, and I want to show you off. But beyond that, I trust him with my whole life, and I know that no matter what, he would respect any boundary I would set. And you, no matter how much you hated me, it was never me you wanted to destroy, so I trust you too."

He pauses, his eyes scrutinizing as he watches for my reactions for a moment longer, before continuing.

"He cares about you. He sees something in you he relates to, and I know in my gut, he's not a threat to your heart. Maybe it's the reason why I'm not jealous of him."

I'm not entirely sure how to respond to all of this, but all I can think is that this man never ceases to amaze me. This kind of freedom is so fucking refreshing.

CHAPTER 26
Morrigan

I MANAGED TO get Vincent off me in the shower and proved that I could wash myself on my own, although he insisted he could do it so much better. He's somewhere in the bedroom as I dry myself, but all of a sudden, I hear a door close downstairs.

"Vin, sugar, are you in?"

My head whips to the bathroom door, heart lodging in my throat, and *"sugar"* opens the door, looking at me with interest.

"Is that your mom?!" I ask frantically.

"It is."

"This feels like an ambush," I whisper. "Did you know she was coming?!"

"No idea. But sometimes she comes to bring dinner, because... well, she's a southern mother." He shrugs. "Your jeans are on the bed, along with your T-shirt, but you're welcome to keep my shirt on. It looks good on you." Those dimples make an appearance on his cheeks.

I just about melt, forgetting his mother is downstairs in an instant.

I quickly wipe the rest of my body, run back through the dressing room and to the bed, pulling on the jeans and his shirt as fast as I can. I tuck it in so it's not too obvious, then try to tame my frizzy curls.

Oh fuck, no matter what, I still look like I just came out of his shower.

"Here goes nothing."

As I walk down the stairs, I can hear them talking in the kitchen, and my heart won't slow its thumping.

"Just reheat it and it will be good as new," she instructs him.

I finally see them, and the sight is such a contrast to The Serpent's image to the outside world. I can't quite fathom it's true. She's a short woman, a few inches shorter than me, with curly black hair, just like Vincent's. Only hers is dusted with grays, caught in a loose bun at the nape of her neck. She looks unnaturally sweet next to this man, in her flowery knee-length dress draping over her full hips, while... pinching her son's cheek.

When she turns and her gaze lands on me, she scrunches her eyebrows, takes a step forward, and cocks her head.

"Mamaw, this is—"

"Morrigan?! Morrigan O'Rourke, as I live and breathe!"

Ummm...

"Come here, sugar, let me look at you!"

"Hello, Ms. Sinclair." I walk quickly to the woman who holds her arms open to me, too shocked to say more than that.

"Oh please, call me Mamaw June. Everyone does." She grabs me by the shoulders, holding me at an arm's length, her smile so bright it could turn a sinner into a saint. "You're even more beautiful than I remember."

"I'm just surprised you remember me."

"No one forgets a girl like you, honey. Truth be told, I've been wondering for years when you would be back." She draws me into her arms before I can gasp at her words and squeezes me tight. It's warm. It smells of peach pie and a summer garden.

She smells of love.

I hug her back, and only after she releases me do I remember her son is in here too. When I look at him, I can't quite pin the look in his eyes. Somewhere between surprise and disbelief.

"Come, eat, you look a bit too skinny," she says, pulling me along with her, toward the island.

I burst into a full belly laugh, all too aware of my soft, plump body. She ignores me, pulling out a casserole that makes my stomach grumble with its smell alone, along with a basket of biscuits.

"I guess we're eating." Vincent sits next to me and takes a plate his mother sets on the island.

"We might have to go for a walk after this, because I can't help myself." I'm not shy with the serving size, as it truly does smell incredible. I grab a couple of biscuits too. "Damn, they're still warm," I whisper to myself.

"There's pecan pie too." Mamaw June points to a dish in the far corner of the kitchen.

"Two walks," I mutter to the man, ignoring his snickering.

"I'm gonna get out of your way, because I had no idea he had a guest, but you have to come for tea soon!" She steps over and gives me one more warm hug, and my God, this woman feels so... homey.

I almost forgot how sweet she is. I guess growing up with parents like mine, you forget how they're actually supposed to act.

"Thank you for the food! It smells so delicious!"

"My pleasure, honey. Take care of yourselves." She walks out the door after kissing her son on the cheek, and I grab a spoonful of whatever she cooked, moaning like I just got fucked all over again.

I turn to Vincent, my cheeks full, chewing excitedly, but stop when I note his glaring eyes.

"What?" I mumble.

He shakes his head, biting his lip as those dimples threaten to grace his cheeks, then turns back to his own plate.

Screw him, this food is more important right now.

And pecan pie!

* * *

Now that I spoke with Lulu, and made sure she's good and safe, my head feels lighter. No matter Vincent's words, I needed to hear her for myself. She agreed that a couple of days in hiding might not be the worst idea. And she has his number if she needs to reach me.

"When are you going to tell me what the plan is?" I slide my feet into a pair of flip-flops that Vincent's mom left in his mudroom, then follow him out the door.

Definitely inappropriate footwear for a forest walk, but I don't have anything else, and it's far too hot and sticky anyway. We walk down the deck steps, through his back garden, toward a path I can see through the trees.

The sun begins to set just as we enter the forest. I'm using this walk as a way to get some distance and clear my head. Even though I'm still with Vincent, I needed to be away from that house. I feared we would never stop fucking. As much as I enjoyed every second of it, I need to enjoy him beyond the feel of his cock filling me.

"A lot has happened, so now is probably the right time," he answers me.

"I hope nothing has changed about my plan for Ryan. At this point, I don't even fucking care if my father goes down with him."

He steals glances at me as we stroll side by side, and he seems to be tense.

"I'm not going to lie, Morrigan, that's where this is headed."

My steps falter for a moment at his words, but I keep going as he takes in a deep, heavy breath. It's giving me anxiety to see how he has to prepare himself for the words he's about to speak.

Then he starts.

An hour must have passed, and I haven't said a word. Just nodded, gasped from time to time, and even stopped dead in my tracks, shaking my head.

He eased me in, explaining why he couldn't take out Ryan when we first made our deal, as they need him for his connection with another man—Boseman. Then he told me all about that bastard, their past, and more importantly, how he's currently messing with the present. He's been trying to threaten The Sanctum's business, carrying minor attacks on them, and even on Mamaw June, but failing at all of them, luckily. It doesn't make them any less frustrating and dangerous. Vincent said Boseman's like a shadow, but I think he's just a coward. As much as I hate that Ryan has not been dealt with yet, I understand the importance of finding Boseman and getting rid of him.

This is where the easing in ended. Because Vincent followed with details about my father and Ryan's new drug and ammunition trafficking business, about the docks, and the expansion through the country.

My father is dealing with drugs... and I realized I had no idea who that man is. Or Ryan, for that matter.

Over time, I made a point to keep tabs on what my father was doing for work. More out of stubbornness, because that man's opinion of women is that we're not worth much more than cattle. The only difference would be that he expects women to always be made-up and dressed to a certain standard, since he cares so fucking much about image. But since women have no place in business, and couldn't possibly understand it, both my mother and I were always kept in the dark. So I found my own way in. Something never really felt right with him and his organization. I knew he skirted at the edge of the law, but I couldn't see beyond that. And when I went to university, I couldn't keep a proper foot in, and I had no way of knowing if the man crossed the line into crime or if he was already there this whole time.

Is that really who he is? A man building his own organized crime empire?

Or is he just adding onto it?

It's not the crime itself that bothers me, it's his self-righteous, duplicitous ways.

But then the story got worse, crossing the line of insanity when Vincent told me my father and Ryan traffic much more than drugs and ammunition. My stomach almost turned inside out as I heard about the container, about the children, about all the others they found after.

We walked in silence for a bit because I needed to come to terms with *what* my father and Ryan truly are, before hearing more of the story. I thought I was done being shocked. God-fucking-damnit, I was wrong.

I've been mulling over Vincent's words for a while, not even knowing where he's leading me through this forest. I've spiraled and come back, then spiraled again, wondering if I'm making a mistake. If my trust in him is blind. Because… Liam O'Rourke raised me and my brother. He's my goddamn father!

I finally take a deep breath, closing my eyes until my lungs are full, then release it and open them on the man walking beside me. As hard as it is to believe it, he has no reason to lie to me in such a brutal way about my father. The trust I have in him is not blind. As horrifying as it all is, it's the truth.

"Okay." I finally speak.

"I know it's so much to take in."

"Yeah—yeah, it is. But I need to hear it all. I don't want to allow myself to doubt anything. I need the whole truth about who my father and Ryan really are."

Vincent looks slightly apprehensive but continues anyway.

"After we closed the container and left, readying to follow it, we thought it would stay fairly local. Instead, we found out why the freight trains were imperative in their business deal with us and The Ghost. It's an easy way to traffic people, as you do not have to worry about transferring them between transport methods, or about being seen. With the trains, you just load the container on, and it's all done. We ended up following them about fifty miles east, to what seemed to be a sorting hub."

"What do you mean by sorting hub?" I ask.

"Basically, a human warehouse, where they assess the *merchandise*. They evaluate them, check their condition, what type of work they would be fit for, if they should go on the streets, or private buyers, or auctions—"

"Jesus Christ, okay, and what happened after?" I'm going to fucking throw up if I hear more about the ways my father planned to abuse these children.

"We waited for all our reinforcements to arrive, scouted the place, and attacked. It was fucking hard. We lost a few men, luckily not too many, but we saved so many souls. So many fucking children."

His eyes glaze over, and he looks pained. Like what he found that day scarred him.

"What happened with all of them?" I ask.

"We've kept everything under wraps and dealt with it ourselves. The police couldn't be involved, or any other agencies. And Holt and O'Rourke—I mean Liam," he corrects himself, using my father's first name instead of the godforsaken family name we share, "can't know it was us who rescued all those people and fucked over their business. We intend to keep it that way until we can lay our cards on the table all at once. So we've been taking care of the children and finding their families ourselves. Katya has been working nonstop with Carter's team of hackers and got home almost all the kids. Only a few remain, placed with a great foster family, and we paid everyone off to keep it under lock and key." "What about the girl who took the tracker and helped you?"

"She decided to stay a while longer in Queenscove, until she can get back on her feet. She's not eighteen yet, and needs to stay away from CPS' radar, otherwise they're gonna take her little sister away from her. She's safe. Traumatized, but safe."

I cannot even imagine what she went through. The fear, not just for herself, but her little sister too. The trauma of having to willingly go in that *sorting hub* after she could have been saved. I'm really hoping nothing happened to her there, before the guys rescued her.

"I'm fucking afraid to ask this, but... here goes nothing. How many did you find there?"

"One hundred and twenty-three." He doesn't waste a fucking breath, and I swallow mine.

I stop dead in my tracks, my hand on my stomach as I process that number. Bile burns its way up my throat, and no matter how much I swallow, it keeps coming back with the image of faceless children popping in my mind.

One hundred and twenty-three.

It doesn't even sound like a real number.

"But I thought they only just started this operation." My voice trembles.

"A few of them were Holt's doing before he joined forces with your father and struck the deal with The Ghost. Not many, though."

The path we're on in the forest is wide enough that the moonlight hits us here, highlighting the disdain in Vincent's eyes. Visceral disgust shines there, and his features are heavy with everything he's been through since I've been taken to Holt's house. When I think of The Sanctum, I think *crime empire*, not covert rescue operation of trafficked children. Seeing the impact of this on a man, who kills without blinking, is almost confusing. It pains me that I held on to the preconceived ideas about this man. About all of them. They may be criminals, but my father and my future ex are the scum of the fucking earth.

And one thing's for sure—the conflicted feelings I had about making them pay are well and truly gone. Vengeance will be so much sweeter now.

We walk in silence for a while, and I allow the darkness that lives in my soul to feed on the horrors my vivid imagination is conjuring. It's fuel for whatever revenge will soon come.

When the moon glows brighter, and the forest thickens around us, the dust seems to have settled and my head is clearer, my soul calmer.

"What happens now?" I break that silence.

"You can imagine that messing with their human trafficking business had quite an impact on them. So we decided to make them feel even shittier and hit two of their warehouses too. We burned them to the ground and took away all the ammunition. Now, we're making sure they have no idea it's us, then we're going to take advantage of their state. Holt is frantic. It's a massive financial loss, and they're also losing trust with their *clients*. He's bound to make a mistake, and it's the perfect time for me to find out what his deal with Boseman is, and where I can find the motherfucker."

I realize something, and I turn to him, grabbing his hand. "You kept Ryan away from me. Every night I was there, he got pulled away on some phone calls that made him rage and leave the house. He never got the opportunity to do anything to me because he kept having to leave. Indirectly, you saved me from him."

I'm fully focused on him as we keep walking through the darkness. The fact that he and The Sanctum are the reason for my safety in there, even unintentionally, makes me feel something indescribable.

"It didn't feel like that from our side. Madds was worried that Holt was going to lash out at you, make you his outlet for the anger we were causing him."

We stop in a clearing, my feet sore, since we've been walking for quite a while. But the smells of the forest, the crisp night, the starry sky... they make up for it.

"What about you?" I turn to him, our fronts brushing against each other, and I have to crane my neck to look into his eyes.

"Morrigan, when I look at you, I see something that most don't. I see exactly what you saw all those years ago in me, and I in you—a darkness that matches mine. I see strength, fury, and resilience. When you were taken, I was terrified, and fucking riddled with guilt for what that asshole could be doing to you. It would have been all my fault. But this bond we seem to have clawed at me, and I had to trust that you could take care of yourself. Not because I was trying to make myself feel better, but because of who you are. You always fight back with everything you have."

He sighs, shaking his head as he continues, "You say that we saved you from him, but in reality, there's a reason why Holt hasn't forced himself on you all these months. This man has seen what you are capable of, and the only way to get to you was to wear you down. But even after all this time, he's unsure if he's managed to. It's why he's been putting it off. I've had the pleasure of killing a few men who thought they could just take what they wanted no matter how loud the word 'no' was shouted, and none of them were willing to put it off and wait as long as Holt has."

Fuck. I didn't expect this, his reaction, the pain, or his faith in me.

I grab his face, pulling him to me and out of that daze, and crush my lips onto his with such force, it hurts.

Because it hurts our souls, too.

It hurts to know what could have been and how much he would have hated himself for it.

It hurts to know this man is exactly what my soul needs—not the one to save me, but the one to help me save myself.

It hurts... seeing how much we have lost, but it's such a good hurt, knowing that we have found our way back to each other now.

Vincent wraps me in his arms, deepening the kiss, and I can feel its magic in my fucking soul, my heart aching for this to never end. But a gust of wind pulls us from the spell, bringing with it a humid scent that usually means rain in these parts. We both look up, but luckily, the skies look fairly clear. Then I skate my eyes around us, releasing him when I realize where we stand.

"The crossroads!"

"Little Eve, are you telling me that you really didn't know where you came that night? Where you were?" A smirk pulls at his lips.

I shake my head, inhaling that scent of wildflowers. "I had no clue. I went off a side road, ended up in the forest, and just drove."

"I was convinced that you came here specifically to find me."

"And this is part of your land?" I ask.

"Yes. You missed the private road and property sign that night."

"So you really were just out for a run. Shit. Here I was thinking you were some creepy guy stalking through the forest."

"Well, just because it's my forest, it doesn't mean I'm not." He shrugs, and I feel a rumble of laughter growing in my chest.

"It may sound crazy, but it feels like it was meant to be." I almost laugh at the ridiculousness of my own words.

"It is crazy, but I thought about that too, and I think I agree—it was meant to be."

"You know, I'm still not sure what the price was for the deal I made with you."

"You," he answers too quickly, reminding me of how he uttered the same thing that night. "You willingly gave yourself to me at these very crossroads, Morrigan. You knew it too, it's why you never really questioned me or insisted on the terms. You gave me a bit of your soul"—he grips my waist and pulls me into his hard body—"and little by little, you willingly offered more, until you became mine. Such a beautiful, beautiful gift..." he murmurs, trailing off.

"My soul is mine, sir, thank you very much." I lift my nose and quirk my eyebrows as I regard him, palms pressed on his chest.

"Oh, baby, it's so very sweet that you believe that."

The grin he gives me, with those devious dimples, is devastating. Truly and utterly devastating.

He presses his lips onto mine, his arms wrapping me in a possessive hold, and I fear that my soul has been his long before we struck a deal for it.

CHAPTER 27
Vincent

SHE TAPS HER fingers, one by one, on the marble top of the coffee table, making me a bit uneasy.

"And you're sure this plan will work?" Morrigan asks me for the second time now.

I've shared with her all the details of the plan we've set up. She knows everything The Sanctum does, even if I had to work harder to convince Finn that she needs to know. He has a bit of a stick up the ass when it comes to her, but I'm not fully convinced if it's Morrigan he's not warmed up to, or the idea of her—what she represents.

However, the plan she's asking me about now, is one I've only shared with her—a backup plan. An insane, batshit crazy backup plan, and judging by the look in her eyes, she thinks so, too.

"We've considered as many risks as we could think of. We have all these bastards in a tight grip, but if something goes wrong, then this it's the best solution we have to protect you," I confirm again, staying as calm as possible, as I know that what I'm suggesting is not a simple matter.

"Sorry, I don—I don't mean to sound like I don't trust in your judgement. I just don't want them to slip through the cracks. They have to pay. It's not only about me anymore." She sits back on the sofa, head falling against the edge as she rubs her palms over her beautiful face.

Oh, her worries are not the same as mine. I'm more concerned about the impact it has on her, but she's thinking about all those bastards and our payback.

"They won't. The Sanctum is bigger than they think. It's bigger than you think as well. There is no chance for them now. You will certainly not marry that goddamn piece of shit, and all the children they have wronged will be avenged. You have my word on that."

She seems satisfied with the reassurance, but I can still see the turmoil in her eyes. "Make the arrangements, then."

"It's all been arranged, baby. One text to confirm your approval, and we're ready."

"Then I believe it's time for us to leave our sanctuary, Mr. Sinclair."

Indeed, it is. I nod once, rising from the armchair, and offer my hand to her. She takes it with a smile on her face, and goddamnit, her acceptance of me, our bond, was worth the fucking wait.

* * *

The evening offers the cover we need, and by the time the wheels of my Camaro hit the asphalt of Queenscove's downtown, it's just past nine. We're heading straight to Midnight to meet the others, along with Loreley. Morrigan demanded to see her as soon as possible.

No one can see my Little Eve through the tinted windows of the car. She's safe here. But I do worry that someone might spot us walking into Midnight. As secret as that bar is, The Sanctum is not the only one in this city with access to information. Our only advantage is the fact that as far as we know, neither O'Rourke nor Holt know that Morrigan has any involvement with us. It's never safe to assume.

The chirping sound of my phone disturbs her focus. She seemed to be trapped deep in thought, and I would very much like to find out what pulled her away like that. Instead of asking, I pick up my phone from the center console, but the number on the screen gives me an unsettling feeling.

I think she catches on to it, looking at me with a cocked eyebrow as I slide my finger on the screen.

"Everything o—" But I'm interrupted by angry and terrified cries. "What the fuck happened?!"

"Vincent?!" Morrigan's eyes are wide as she clutches my thigh. Something in that gaze tells me she already knows who's distressed on the other end of the line.

"We're on our way! Stay away from it!" Fuck, fuck.... *Fuck!*

"What happened, Vincent?! Was that Lulu?!" She turns in her chair, but I ignore her, pressing my foot on the gas as I weave through traffic, ignoring the honking, and flying through too many red lights.

"Put your seatbelt on!" I rasp to cover the sound of the angry engine, as I whip my forearm over her chest, and press her back into the seat.

"Goddamnit, Serpent! What the fuck happened to Lulu?!"

Oh, reckless Morrigan has come to play. I can feel her fire touching me, her rage growing with every second that passes. It fucking terrifies me right now, because we were doing so well... so goddamn well.

"Fuck." She's gonna hate me.

"We've passed Midnight," she breathes out, as she looks back to the turn we were supposed to make. My tires screech on the asphalt when I take the next turn, and she instantly whips her head back at me, recognizing the direction. "The apartments... the club."

I sigh, exhaling a breath that strains my throat, as I pull onto the street that takes us closer to what she just recognized.

"The club is burning," I tell her, dejected.

A gasp, that's the only sound that comes out of her mouth. Nothing more. And her usual searing gaze turns cold.

I stop the car and look at her, only I'm met with her profile, too stern and sharp, her chest rising and falling in panting breaths she's struggling to control. I'm used to her lashing out, screaming, raging, beating the shit out of people, but this... this is fucking terrifying, because it's a stage I've never seen her in.

The fire truck lights shine from the back of the building, where the parking lot for the club is. But I pulled in at the side of the building, since I don't want to risk being seen at the front, or at the club's entrance. The moment the car doors open, we can smell it. Burnt wood and leather fills the air, but there are no flames out here. Maybe it's a good sign.

We disappear in the shadows, quickly slipping through a side entrance that's fairly concealed, and once that door opens, the thick, choking smoke hits us first. Then the heat comes.

"Morrigan, you can't go in there!" I grab her forearm, pulling her back to me.

But the woman shakes herself so hard, she escapes my grip, giving me a look of hurt that hits my soul.

"Don't fucking touch me!" she yells, then runs through the corridor.

I realize we walked in through the fire exit, ironically, and I follow her down some steps, and through a corridor. At the end of it, I find the playrooms that luckily look intact.

"Nooo!" Morrigan's cry splits the air, shattering some part of me that's too connected with her. She's fucking heartbroken.

And I can see why. The flames have taken over the entire bar area, along with the storeroom in the back of it, and most of the stage. The seating area that surrounds it was also in flames at some point. Only black, scorched wood and melted leather remains there.

"Ma'am, you have to leave right now!" A fireman pops out of the gap in the flames and grabs her upper arm just as I get to her. The moment he sees me, he freezes for a split second. "Please, it's not safe."

Other firefighters are battling the flames that engulf the bar area, the heat so strong, it scorches my airways. But Morrigan is just frozen in place, watching the disaster before her in utter disbelief. I shake her, but she pushes back at me, angrily.

"For fuck's sake, woman! This is not the time nor the place." I'm not fucking playing anymore. "And Lulu is not here! We need to get the fuck out now!"

Holding on to her upper arm, I force her to me, following the suited man toward the stairs that lead to the front entrance. I'm definitely bruising her flesh right now, but I don't give a shit, and even through her protests and screams, I keep pulling her after me. I only care about getting her to safety.

We reach the foyer, but the smoke is still so damn thick, I can't see anything. There's no one but firemen moving up and down the steps.

"They're in there." One of them points toward the service door that leads to the corridor Morrigan took me through before.

She tugs away from me, and rushes for the door, punching some keys on the number pad. But the electrics must be screwed because nothing happens, and she bangs her fists onto the door, screaming at it like it could magically open.

And it fucking does.

One of my men opens it reluctantly, and his shoulders relax when he sees me, nodding as he steps to the side to let us in.

"It's open." He points to another door, and I don't have time to ask him any questions as Morrigan sprints to it and rips it open.

Fucking hell, this woman would jump headfirst into any fucking situation. I don't know what the hell awaits after that door, and she has no regard for her damn life. I follow her and end up in a small café, catching the moment Morrigan screams for Lulu, who's sitting at one of the tables.

"Are you okay?!" She holds her friend's face in her hands, forcing it in every direction so she can examine her. Then she continues patting her body, searching for any sign of injury.

"Morri! I'm okay!" Loreley rasps.

She grabs onto her, her boyfriend reluctantly leaning in his chair, far away from them. Only when his eyes land on me, they widen for a moment too long.

Suddenly, Maddox and two of my men walk through the same door we came from and it's my turn to contain my surprise.

"What happened, Loreley?" I ask, stepping closer as I clasp Morrigan's shoulder. Only she shrugs it off, throwing me a look that very clearly spells *fuck off*.

"Ryan happened. We saw his men on the cameras. He watched as they ran out after setting the place on fire, then the motherfucker had the audacity to smile at the camera." The disdain in her voice matches exactly what I'm feeling.

"Lulu, I'm so sorry. I'm so fucking sorry. I should have never kept you anywhere near me! This is all my fault. Goddamnit, it's all my fault!" Morrigan's voice breaks into painful sobs.

But her friend shakes her head, wrapping her arms around her. I step away, leaving them to comfort each other, since Morrigan fucking hates me right now. I turn my attention to my best friend instead.

"Why are *you* here, brother?" I whisper to him.

His lips part for a split second, his amber eyes darkening as they flicker toward the women.

"The men called me," he answers.

Right, and you came for... the men.

I hold his gaze for a moment longer, before returning my attention to the girls.

"It's all my fault, all my fucking baggage, and I knew it was going to crash onto you to someday. I'll make up for it all. I'll pay you back and help you rebuild, then I'll be fucking gone. I'll leave, because you don't deserve this." Morrigan's pain roughens her voice, tears streaming down her freckled cheeks, and I can't stand her dejection. I want to wrap her in my arms and help her through this.

"Don't be fucking stupid," Loreley rasps, rising to her feet. "You didn't do this. That motherfucker who's forcing you to marry him did. And if you don't make him pay"—her golden eyes turn to me—"I sure fucking will."

Her eyes flicker to Maddox, brows narrowing for two seconds before returning her attention to Morrigan.

I have a feeling that if I don't do as she pretty much just ordered, she'll make me pay too.

Loreley's family name carries weight too, even if she's not participating in the family business. Her father rarely gets involved in shit around here. His business lies elsewhere, and his money as well. Usually, if he does poke his nose around Queenscove, it means something is very, very wrong. And Mr. Dietrich is one of our prized allies outside of our city.

"Goddamnit, Lulu! This, all of this, is on me! If I didn't let that asshole control me the way he has, and turn into this goddamn monster in front of my eyes, none of this would have happened. You don't fucking deserve this."

Then the woman turns to me, and I'm taken aback the moment her palm whips my head so viciously to the side, my neck aches. My ego snaps into place just as she's about to do it once more, but I catch her wrist in mine, pinning her in place.

"You!" she seethes with palpable fury and something else.

Something that pulls at my fucking soul—disgust. She slams her fist against my chest when I don't let go of her, but then continues anyway.

"You fucking promised me she was safe! You looked me in the eyes and told me she was taken care of, that you had people protecting her, and I had no reason at all to worry. You fucking promised me." Her voice booms through the barroom.

"Morri, it's not his fault." Loreley grips her shoulder to no avail.

"It is! You fucking promised, and I was stupid enough to trust you. Goddamnit, Serpent, she could have been there. Lulu could have been downstairs! She could have fucking died!" She spits the words at me like I'm made of fire, and she needs to put me out.

As hurt as I am by her distrust, and all this anger focused seemingly just on me, it comes from a place of fear. Nothing I could say right now will make any of this better for her. She tries to strike me again, but I grip both her wrists, holding them to my chest as she works through her loud, heaving breaths. Tears spill over her plump cheeks, and her green eyes glow more vivid than ever. They seem to emphasize the pain she's feeling. And all I can do is hold her through it.

This is not the time to rationalize with her. It's not what she needs. What will help her, what has always helped her, is to let those demons out. Fight it out. Shout it out. Just... let it out. All she can see right now is what could have been, how her best friend could have ended.

Although, something's nagging at me.

Loreley was here all day, up until the moment one of our guys took her to Midnight.

Almost immediately after, the fire happened.

Did Holt know Loreley wasn't in the club?

CHAPTER 28
Morrigan

MY RAGE HAS subsided, if only for a few moments, enough to hear what the firemen who came into the café, have to say.

"It's all extinguished. But I hope you know insurance might not cover the damage. It was no accident, I'm afraid, but I believe you are already aware."

Lulu nods, gripping my hand.

"It didn't all burn out," he continues, and we let out a joint relieved sigh.

"There's plenty of damage, but some areas were untouched, thankfully. It looks like you have some floor fire barriers and most of them did their job. Please be careful going down there. The stairs are safe, but I cannot guarantee the whole ceiling or the floors are. Okay?"

"We have some hardhats upstairs, from the apartment renovation. I can bring them," Luke states, and Lulu nods to him.

He joined us a few minutes ago, and no one missed how his steps faltered the moment he saw who else was here with us—Vincent and Maddox. He didn't know that the security guys who have been keeping an eye on Lulu were The Sanctum's. We decided that it would be best to say it's her dad's, as we still don't want anyone else to know of my association with them.

"However," the fireman continues, "the car from the parking lot... I'm afraid that one is totaled."

"What car?" My voice raises an octave, and my eyes bulge as I take in the look of pity on Lulu's face.

"Your car, Morri... I'm sorry."

Only hours ago, I was in relishing pure and total bliss, isolated from the world, from the reality of my situation, and it's hard not to think that this is some sort of punishment. I was finally living something I stopped dreaming about long ago. We were making plans, setting up contingencies, we were discussing my freedom and the rest of our lives. But as I look into those black eyes now, all I feel is fury. The type that will not push me to attack but walk away disappointed... and never come back.

Shit. I fucking loved that car.

But after the things Vincent told me about my father, it feels like it was bought with blood money. Being burnt to a crisp and removed out of my possession might just add to the clean slate I need.

The firemen leave, and we're left all alone to deal with our pain and anger.

"He probably thought that you came here after you escaped," Vincent says. "Your car at the back confirmed it to him. Do you have any idea what he knew about the club?"

My lips tighten into a thin line at The Serpent's question.

"Morri?" Maddox asks, a slight warning in his voice.

Fuck's sake!

"Whilst I was with him, he's never mentioned it," I answer with a scowl. "Anyone who wanted to know the information could easily find out it's Lulu's. It's a legal establishment, after all. However, when it comes to my involvement, only *you* knew." I narrow my eyes on The Serpent, my brain fighting to believe anything else but the obvious conclusion.

He doesn't miss the accusation, and I don't miss the hurt that suddenly appears in his eyes. It has to be him. Or one of The Sanctum. There's no one else.

"Don't insult me." Each word lands with a harsh bite, and with his gaze trained on me, a freezing cold seeps into my bones.

Right now, that's exactly what I wish to do—fucking insult him.

"Come on!" Lulu rasps, pulling my hand. "Let's see the damage."

"Let me go get some helmets." Luke steps away, but she stops him.

"Fuck the helmets. Get them later. I need you there with me," Loreley pleads, and he looks at her, then at the door, lingering for a moment. He nervously fiddles with his fingers, as he turns back and comes to us. I can't blame him for being worried about safety.

"Here, I got some flashlights from the storeroom." Beau, one of our security guys, hands them to some of us, and carries on walking at the front.

"He was here," Lulu leans in and whispers to me as we walk back into the foyer. "They followed him, and waited until he went to the bathroom." We walk down the steps of the club, the smoke almost cleared now. "Then they trapped him in there. Literally trapped him. He could have fucking died, burning to death in a goddamn toilet, Morri. This was not The Sanctum's mistake, nor your fault."

Shit, I can't blame the poor guy. I could blame The Sanctum for not having more men in the club, but then again, their priority was Lulu. They had her all protected. I guess it was fucking lucky she was already out of here, by the time Ryan came to burn the place down.

Lucky.

I stopped believing in luck a while back. I guess there's still something to it.

As we reach the bottom of the stairs, the smell of wet ash, scorched wood, and burnt leather, seems to stick to the inside of my nostrils. In the eerie glow of the flashlights, the image before us is dire. With each step farther in, Lulu exhales small gasps, or clutches her belly, cheeks, or chest, and holds back little sobs.

I already saw the untouched playrooms, and as she notices them too, a wave of relief washes over her. The windows and walls are black from smoke, but that whole area is still standing, and it gives me a slither of hope.

But no matter what... we're closed for business. And fuck knows how I'm going to get the money to rebuild and start over. The bar was a fucking work of art, the furniture was custom made, and the stage was perfection. This was the only public place where I felt truly and utterly comfortable pole dancing, and that bastard took it away from me. I didn't think I could hate him more. I was wrong.

I take a few more steps into the space, trying to find anything salvageable. But it looks like every single table and chair has to be thrown away, the floors need replacing, and—

"Watch out!" Arms wrap around my waist and chest from behind, and I'm whipped backwards just as one of the large light fixtures crashes in the spot where I stood a second before.

Even through the stench of wet ash, I can still scent the bergamot wrapped around The Serpent. I can also feel the strong rise and fall of his chest against my back, and I would shrug him off if he wasn't holding me so tight.

He may have just saved me, but it doesn't negate the promise he almost failed to keep. Or the fact that he may be the reason this happened in the first place. I put more force into my movements, and shake away from his grip, reaching for Lulu.

"We'll be okay. We'll rebuild. We'll come back stronger than before. I'm so sorry... So sorry." I don't know what else to say to make this better.

I rub her arm, looking up at her sweet smile. Even through all of this, she's still smiling at me. I don't fucking deserve it.

"You've lost the club too, not just me. Fucking Holt took it away from us. This is not your fault, Morri."

I hear a hitched breath from the other side, where Luke stands with his arm tight around her waist. Only, I could have sworn it sounded more like a scoff. When I lean in ever so slightly to look at him, he quickly averts his gaze.

How fucking bizarre.

Lulu didn't seem to notice it.

But I catch Maddox's gaze, and it's narrowed in on the guy, sizing him up.

"What are *they* doing here?" Luke's not bothering to hide his distaste as he whispers to Lulu, pointing his head at Vincent, Maddox, and his men.

"We're here because we are in business with Mr. O'Rourke and Mr. Holt. And we"—Maddox steps up closer to us, the red glare from the emergency lighting making him look more menacing than usual—"always keep an eye on the people we associate with."

"And you just... happened to be in the area?" Luke asks, sarcasm dripping from his tone.

"You don't seem to be fully aware of who we are. But I assure you, we are *everywhere*." Maddox glares at him, and I swear I've never seen him react like this.

"Luke, for God's sake, stop it. If it wasn't for them noticing the smoke, this whole place, this whole building, would have been up in flames. Morri and I would have lost everything." Lulu tries to put down the subject, well aware that Luke shouldn't find out about my connection with The Sanctum, or the fact that the security following Lulu is not her dad's.

Luke scoffs, rolling his eyes. "I'll go see if the firemen are still outside and find out what the next step is, since it's obviously an accident." He says it with clear disgust in voice.

Lulu may not be blaming me, but Luke definitely is.

"Alright." She nods reluctantly and pulls away from us, walking over to the burnt-out bar as he leaves.

Maddox's gaze follows him without bothering to hide the fact. He really doesn't like him.

The moment Luke reaches the top of the stairs, Vincent nods at one of his men and he leaves quickly, following him. All of a sudden, he wants to make sure everyone's safe now. I shake my head, rolling my eyes, but manage to suppress a huff.

"I'm not sure what to do here..." Lulu says, pulling my attention back to her.

"We'll figure it out. We'll talk to the insurance company and convince them to cover us." I move around the broken light fixture, my feet slushing in the wetness left after the firemen put out the fire.

"I'm not sure about that," Vincent chimes in. "Even though it wasn't your doing, considering it was criminal, the insurance company will launch a full-on investigation with the police. It could be a long time until this is sorted, as they need to prove it wasn't one of you who did it."

"Fuck." I swipe a palm over my face, wondering how I'm going to make this work. "That will open a whole can of worms. And delay things."

I spent pretty much every penny I had on this. Nowadays, I'm not exactly making money, since I've been unable to work. I'm fucked. And she's fucked too, just because of me.

For the first time today, Lulu cries.

Not hard, not loud, but a few whimpers escape and tears fall. She wipes them quickly, like she has no right to break down.

I don't remember the last time I saw her cry. Have I ever? She's the strongest, toughest person I know, and her emotions are always in check. Always. Even if she gets mad, she's cold as fucking ice. I feel even more horrible now.

"I'm sure we can find a way, honey. We'll find an investor. The club proved how profitable it can be in the small amount of time it was open. Everything will be okay, Lu, I promise you."

Most of her inheritance went into restructuring the building, renovating her apartment, starting the renovations on mine, and Metamorphosis. It was too early to get any profit from the investment. Whatever money she has left, or profit from the small café at the front, is not going to reach very far into renovating this place.

I wrap my arm around her shoulder and pull her to me, powerless to make her feel better.

Silence falls upon the charred remnants of the main room of the club. Apart from her soft whimpers.

"The Sanctum will invest," Maddox's rough voice booms through the dark space, and my gaze instantly darts between him and Vincent.

I can tell Vincent is taken by surprise by the statement, but he composes himself quickly enough, watching his friend.

"We'll front you the money and assist you in the renovations to ensure everything is done properly and in a timely manner, so you can reopen quickly," Maddox continues.

"Don't be mad!" Lulu exclaims. "You're asking us to be in business with The Sanctum?! No. This is Morrigan's and my business, no one else's. Not even Luke is involved in this."

"We don't want to be partners. Return the investment when the money comes in and you are able to do so, and we'll be out of your hair. No commission, no partnership." Maddox is now a few steps away, his eyes fixed on Lulu, not on us. Just her.

"So you can come and claim some sort of interest on me? I know how you lot work, racketeering and all that shit. Nah, I'd rather step on my pride and ask my father." Jesus, she's feisty, but in front of Maddox? That's a bit risky.

My whole body freezes the moment I hear a smirk from Vincent's direction. I look at him, and he bites his lips, trying to keep serious, but his eyes fail him. *He's fucking laughing!*

"Doll, you don't seem like the type of woman who believes rumors that fly around. We don't deal with racketeering," Maddox counters, a smirk on his lips too.

Even through the red emergency light, I swear I can see Lulu's cheeks flushing. And it doesn't look like embarrassment. But then she hisses, actually hisses at the man.

"I am not. Your. *Doll!*"

Maddox smiles, then turns his gaze to me.

"What do you think, Morri?"

"Lulu and I will discuss it and we'll let you know. Thank you for the offer, Maddox. Should we get out of here before the ceiling collapses on us?"

"We should," Vincent speaks. "We'll leave the detail. They'll stick to staying out of sight, but we cannot risk Holt or O'Rourke finding out we're... too close."

"We have to meet Holt anyway." Maddox follows. "I believe he may have what we're looking for now, and it's time to pay up on our investment."

"Perfect timing. We have to see if he says anything about this." Vincent points around, stopping at me.

"What if he knows about us?" I ask. "Or what if he has surveillance to see if I was going to return here? It could have all just been a ploy to draw me out. What if he sees you guys leave, or—"

Fuck! I was expecting some things to go wrong. But this? This was definitely not on that list.

"We'll keep to the story we told Loreley's boyfriend. After all, we did not get where we are today without knowing all that moves around the people we associate with. Your father knows this by now," he answers with a sigh. "I'll leave the way I came. I'll talk to you later." When he steps closer, I know he can see my apprehension.

I hold his gaze, wishing he would just go, because my mind is a mangled mess, and I'm not sure if he's the right one to trust right now.

"Morrigan, he will pay for this. They will *all* pay for this. Of that, I can assure you."

"Will you pay for this too?" The words spill off my tongue before I can stop them, and the hurt slashing through his dark eyes tears my heart in two.

He shakes his head, then twists on his heel, walking away. Maddox follows him, and even he looks hurt by my words.

Did I really get this wrong?

No one else knows. There is no other explanation.

"We need a drink." Lulu takes my hand and pulls me away from the chaos surrounding us.

I guess we'll deal with the cleanup later.

CHAPTER 29
Vincent

"SO, WHY DID you say you were so adamant on finding this Boseman character?" Holt asks after we go through brief pleasantries.

We met in a parking lot downtown, a random spot that's actually not random at all. It's one of our many public spots under surveillance.

"We didn't." Finn squashes his curiosity then and there.

"Right." He warily looks between all of us. "Well, if you're looking for him, then I'm just glad I didn't end up getting into business with the man."

"What did he offer?" I ask.

Holt looks at me for a moment too long. Just when I think he won't answer, he opens his mouth.

"Too many terms and conditions. We didn't like either."

I nod. I would say that it sounds like him, but in truth, I have no goddamn clue what he sounds like now. The man I remember wouldn't have a leg to stand on in front of the elite of this city. Not to mention, me or The Sanctum. He's changed. Still stupid, as always, since he's gone after my family, my Sanctum, and my goddamn fucking territory. But he's definitely changed. Otherwise, he wouldn't have had business connections with the likes of Holt and O'Rourke.

But his balls are growing bigger than his brain is, our little spies talking of takeover and infiltration into business he has no place in. But *he wants* a place. So we need to find him and eliminate him before his claws dig too deep and leave a mark.

"Do you have something for us?" Carter asks, ending the pleasantries. I welcome his lack of patience, as we need to move this along.

"The bastard was hard to find." Holt nods, grabbing an envelope one of his men gives him, then he hands it over to me.

I pull it open, inspecting its contents: an address and a name—*Jackson Davenport*. I raise an eyebrow at Holt.

"That's the name he's living under." He preempts my question.

"Interesting choice," I say, cocking an eyebrow.

It's hard to keep from rolling my eyes. Jackson fucking Davenport?! Good ol' Lester Boseman chose a pretty fancy name there, and it matches none of the man he actually is. Carter reads the name and looks at me with a stern expression, before he slides the envelope in his inner pocket.

"Posh, I know. I guess it bodes well if you want to go into business with the right crowd. Some years ago, *my own pops* pulled the same stunt. He needed a pseudonym for a certain shell corporation and gave himself a high society name to fit in with the investors he was chasing," Holt says with a scoff as he slides his hands in his pockets. "Turns out, most people don't give a shit what name you go by."

His own pops...

Fucking bingo! My mind goes into overdrive at Holt's story and choice of words. But I keep my face straight, resisting the urge to look at the others.

This changes everything. I can't wait to find out if the others caught onto it.

"Names don't cover sins," I respond, feeling the spark that threatens to reach my eyes. Adrenaline, or enthusiasm, I don't know what it is, but I need to get the hell out of here now. "Pleasure doing business with you." I end the conversation.

"Have a good night." He nods, his eyes swiping over us all.

We turn on our heels and head to our cars. Madds came in his, Finn and Carter together, and I'm alone in mine. But we're not going to the same place, and I need to talk to them about this meeting, and Holt's slip up.

Madds is about to go pick up two lovely women and bring them to the man waiting patiently in the basement of our safe-house, and we're all dying to hear what the hell he has to say to them.

Only, the women have no idea what's coming, and their reactions will definitely determine if the plan Morrigan and I discussed earlier is still going to happen.

As it stands... I doubt it will. She seems convinced that I told Holt about her involvement in the club, and it fucking hurts. Does she really think that I would double cross her like that? That I would cheat her in this way with the man I'm trying to save her from?

Fuck.

Can I blame her?

When your parents pretty much end up selling you off to the man you're trying to escape, just to enable some fucked-up business transaction, trusting others is difficult. Especially the man who left you all those years before without another word.

"Finally!" I rasp, as all their cars start moving.

We weave into traffic, heading toward the safe house, while Madds rushes in the opposite direction.

It's been quiet on our front recently. There haven't been any other attacks or attempts, but I'm still anxious about Madds being followed. Especially after he picks up Loreley and Morrigan.

But the blood buzzes through my veins, and I'm fucking ecstatic at the turn this night took.

* * *

"You better have a good fucking explanation for why we were practically dragged here by this neanderthal, Serpent!" It's Loreley's melodic voice that splits our ears, and Maddox rolls his eyes.

Her and Morrigan are at the entrance into this concrete corridor, and the echo of her words is shattering. Both Finn and I cringe slightly at the sound, as we stand at this other end, waiting for them to come.

She walks with such determination in her step, making her look as imposing as us. A businesswoman. Fearless.

Morrigan, on the other hand, has such a straight, controlled expression, the fury in her green eyes fucking shines. She's fixed on me, and I'm not even sure she blinks as she walks over. Her face is frozen, no scowl, no crinkle, no twitch moves her skin. But my gaze drags down the length of her and notices her hands rolling into fists, over and over. I've seen fury in her before, but when she's controlled like this, I'm not sure what she's capable of.

"You cannot demand us to just do whatever the hell you want, got it? Luke is gonna be worried." Loreley keeps shouting as they near us.

"Oh, I very much doubt that." Finn smirks next to me.

"What?!" She quickens her step. "What the fuck did you do to him?! Is this your goddamn ploy? Your way of convincing us to take your money and bring us into some shady fucking business?!"

Madds slips by Morrigan and catches Loreley by the upper arms just as she's about to lunge at Finn.

"I swear to God, you brute, if you don't let me go right now, I'll chop your dick off!" She shakes her body as she tries to get a good look at the man who's a head taller than her, and I have to give it to her... she has balls.

The scar that sweeps down from his forehead to his cheek, just about missing his eye, gives his powerful and grave look a menacing touch. Not that he needs it. His six-foot-seven frame, wide and packed with fighting muscles, is enough to make people twitch. He scares the living daylights out of most people just by leaning his head in the right direction. Yet Loreley doesn't seem to flinch around him.

"Luke is here," Finn says, his hand pausing on the door handle. "But he has nothing to do with our proposal for Metamorphosis. On the contrary..." he trails off dramatically and slowly opens the door.

"The contrary?" Morrigan finally speaks.

She's been quiet up until now. I was expecting her to lash out already. I guess her recklessness chooses its battles after all.

"Luke!" Loreley screams as she rushes past us.

"What the fuck did you do, Serpent?" Morrigan's voice is almost a growl as she whispers to me.

She stops only for a moment, not meeting my eyes. Her lips settle in a straight line and her eyebrows furrow. Her expression is caught somewhere between anger, and what I'm quite convinced is apprehension. And that particular sentiment is definitely not directed at me.

Without lingering, she steps into the room, taking in the image before her— bleeding out of his nose, with a swollen eye, and split browbone, Luke is tied to a chair in the middle of the sterile room. Two of our men keep watch, including Beau, who was at the club with us.

Carter quietly lingers, leaning against the wall, arms crossed over his broad chest, but he looks positively bored. I know why. Luke cracked too early. He was no fun for The Carver.

"Baby, untie me! Get me out of here!" the asshole pleads with his girl.

"What did they do to you?" Loreley frantically touches his body, assessing the damage.

"This is all your fault, bitch!" he spits at Morrigan who just walked into the room. "You fucking ruined everything for my Lulu!"

Morrigan doesn't respond, but I don't miss the flinch of the muscles in her back.

"How about we tell these lovely ladies what you so graciously told us after only two punches. What do you say? Or better yet, let's start with the phone call you made when you were *'going to talk to the firemen'* when Sinclair and Severin were at the club with you all." Finn walks around to the table and grabs Luke's phone.

"Baby, don't listen to them. They're all lies. They're trying to fool you, turn you against me, and get in the middle of us!" he almost begins to beg, a pathetic sort of desperation clear in his eyes.

Does he really think his girlfriend is stupid?

"Let him the hell out of these ties!" She swings around, heaving as she looks at Finn.

"Give us a moment, and then you can decide for yourself what you want to do." Finn brings the phone and stands next to the chair.

"Start explaining. I'm losing my damn patience here." Morrigan is behind her friend, a shield protecting her from us.

"When darling Luke over here went upstairs to supposedly talk to the firemen, he actually went to make a phone call," he responds, a wicked smile pulling at his lips, but it's doused in cunning satisfaction.

"You probably remember that we sent one of our men to go after him." I take over, stepping around into their view.

"I do." She nods. "For his protection." But I can see she doesn't believe her words.

"For confirmation," I clarify, and she scowls. "When we left you, we found him restrained by two of our men. He was trying hard to get away, spouting all sorts of bullshit. But the one who followed him confirmed my suspicion. He caught him on a call, about to throw *you*"—I point to Morrigan—"under the bus."

"What?" she asks, brows furrowed, interrupting me.

"Beau, could you please share with the ladies what you overheard?" I turn to the man standing tall against the wall.

He takes one step forward. "His exact words over the phone, were: '*Morrigan is out of hiding. She came back, but she's not al—*'" He pauses and steps back.

"Beau's timing was fucking impeccable. He took Luke's phone away just as he was about to reveal our dirty little secret." I try to not be too condescending, because I don't want to throw in her face that she was wrong about me. As much as I want to, I'm revealing a harsh betrayal, and it probably lands with a healthy dose of heartache.

"Surely you don't expect me to have blind faith in your man's words. Or yours."

That last one was a hard dig at me. "This means nothing." Morrigan keeps her tone level now. But I can see the wheels are spinning in that pretty head of hers.

"Finn, give Morrigan the phone," I instruct him.

She takes it, confused.

"Check the number. Call it if you wish."

She waves in front of Luke's face to unlock it, then checks the call list. Her eyes go wide instantly, shooting straight to Loreley. She's frozen. Her lips part, but I can see the conflict riddling her body, faced with the task of telling her best friend that her longtime boyfriend betrayed her. She has to break the news that she's about to lose who she loves, the one she shares her life with, her house, her bed.

"Morri?" Loreley's voice is meek, begging almost, pleading that the reality she sees plastered all over her best friend's expression is not the same one we presented to her.

She pulls the phone out of her hands and looks for herself.

"The timestamp fits. Morri, whose number is this?" She pauses, waiting on a bated breath. "Answer me!" she rasps when the response doesn't come.

"It's Ryan's number..." It's almost as if she's afraid to speak the words that spell betrayal.

The soft, broken threads on Loreley's pale features morph until they settle on one vicious emotion, as she turns to face her boyfriend. Her cheeks are flushed, a deep crease gathers her eyebrows, her golden eyes seem to glow, and her lips are pursed tightly. I'm surprised she's not snarling. And with that phone in hand, she pulls back then smashes her man right across the jaw, whipping his head to the side with enough force that we hear the crack of the phone screen.

Morrigan goes to pull her away, but I grab her hand and shake my head at her. We'll stop her if it goes too far, but for now... Loreley needs this. She looks at me, emotions clear in her eyes, but it's not the time or place to talk about this. Sure, I would like an apology for her belief that I would betray her in such a way, but then again, the man Loreley has been living with for quite some time has done exactly that. The ball most definitely isn't in our court tonight.

"Why? You goddamn son of a bitch! You motherfucker!" She doesn't wait for a response.

The crack of Luke's nose echoes through the concrete room, as Loreley smashes her fist right in the middle of his face.

"Answer me!" she seethes but doesn't give him the chance to respond.

She goes again, sinking her fist into his stomach as he spits blood on his T-shirt.

"For you! For us. Because I love you! I want it to be the two of us, as we're meant to be!" he shouts as his bloody nose drips into his mouth.

"What?" she yells, but we're all confused at this point.

"I wanted that bitch out of our lives!" he spits, turning toward Morrigan. "I fucking hated you since the moment we met. I knew you would get in my way. Too many fucking opinions, too much advice, too much influence you have on Loreley. We would have been more if it wasn't for you, always in the fucking way, always around. And now in business together, living under my goddamn roof, spending our money! I couldn't have you live a floor below, no fucking way could I allow that."

"*My* roof! *My* goddamn money! Not yours, *mine*!" Loreley pulls his attention back to her. "You're telling me you did this because you were jealous of my relationship with my friend?"

"I loathe her! She's a horrible influence. Always pulling you down, into her fucking drama, her issues. And now she's dragging you into a crime syndicate, of all things?! I wanted to make it look like you lost everything because of her. I wanted you to see the same thing I do when I look at her and drop her. Send her fucking packing! Away from us! Away from you. You don't need friends! You have me! You don't need anyone else to get in our way! I want it to be us two, just us, forever!!!"

At this point, we're all a bit flabbergasted, watching the ramblings of this man who has a few too many control issues, and they're not even the good ones. Fair enough, I would be wary of who Morrigan associates with, but this is weird.

"That's it. You wanted to have me to yourself. Forever," Loreley states with the same disbelief we're feeling. "You wanted Morrigan out of my life, *our* life. And your solution was to tell the man forcing her to marry him, the one who abuses her, the one who fucking kidnapped her in front of my eyes, that she's in business with me, so he can hurt her? Then you wanted to ruin things further by telling him that she's involved with the only people who can help her out of it. Do you forget what family I come from, you motherfucker?" She's eerily calm as she basically spells out this explanation for him.

Luke's gaze becomes clearer as his eyes widen, the realization that he fucked up only now dawning on him. Yet, he still seems to have some hope in there as he begins to plead with her again.

He doesn't get the chance.

Loreley falls into a frenzy of punches, slaps, and kicks, probably hurting herself more than him. And just as I'm about to jump in, Madds closes the distance between them, wraps his arms around her, and pulls her away, even as she kicks and screams.

"What do you want me to do with him, doll?" he quietly asks Loreley.

"Oh, I know what I would do to him." Finn pulls out a gun and sticks the end of the barrel to Luke's temple.

The man freezes in place, his mangled eyes barely opening, and his gaping, bloody mouth showing one missing tooth. He's not from our world—Loreley's, too—so he doesn't fully grasp our ways. I'm sure he's never even seen a gun before, let alone felt the cold metal of the barrel against his skin.

"No!" she shouts. "I want him to pay, but no death. Please, no death."

"Thank you, my love, then—"

"How dare you call me that?! You will go as far away as possible from me, from us, from any family I have on this continent." She reaches for Morri's hand, and she quickly grabs it. "You will never contact me, never fucking think of me, never dare step foot, even in the neighboring towns! If you do, The Sanctum will be the least of your problems. You will disappear from my life, unless you wish to disappear altogether." And with that, she turns on her heel and leaves the room, taking Morrigan out of my grasp with her.

Finn, Carter, and Madds follow the girls, but I stay behind to talk to Beau and our other guy standing guard.

"Do not let him go until we tell you. Set up a schedule to watch him. Don't break him. When our plan has ended, throw his ass as far away from this town as possible. Got it?" They all nod, and I walk out after the others.

He's a liability, and we can't risk him going to Holt or O'Rourke before we get to them ourselves. And goddamnit, my hands are itching to get to Holt. The gun strapped against my ribs hums, begging me to go and blow his fucking brains out right now.

Only, I can't. He's my only way in with Boseman. Because if the address he gave me for him is a trap, which I suspect it is, I have to keep him alive until he gives me what I want. Although I think I may have to fight with Morrigan over who gets to end Holt.

A smirk pulls at my lips, because it sounds like the good kind of fight.

Morrigan

WE'RE IN A small room at the end of that barren corridor, my arm wrapped around Lulu's shoulder as I watch the man who I thought betrayed me, walk in. I was pretty much convinced it was him. The tiny part of me that thought he wouldn't do this to me, was mainly made of hope, not conviction.

I went to the worst-case scenario in two seconds flat, and as his obsidian eyes fall on me, I'm not sure how to apologize.

I realize that it's not because I can't find the right words, but because I fear that it will not be the only time something like this will happen and I will automatically throw the blame on him because of past events.

Do I not trust him?

Do I not believe in him?

Because if that's the case, maybe our involvement should end the moment the pact is fulfilled.

"Morrigan." He speaks first, but pauses, that deep voice penetrating my soul, sending a shiver to pass through me.

There's a warmth in him that seems to show only for me. One that exists beyond those straight lips and grave gaze. He didn't lash out. He didn't even get angry as I accused him of betraying me to the one man I hate most in this world. He simply waited until he could rectify the situation.

Just like he did for the last eight years—he waited until his friend was safe and the time was right.

We stare at each other, both of us unable to find the right words. I should apologize, but I can't seem to do it.

I snap out of it, because this moment is not about us. I need to be there for my best friend.

"I think Lulu and I need to go." I finally speak. She's my priority right now.

"Will I see you the day after tomorrow?" I can just about hear a hint of uncertainty in Vincent's voice. Or is it concern?

It does something to me.

"Yes," I answer.

That one single word seems to trigger a sparkle in the depths of his gaze. And that does even more to me. It means that I have the same impact on him, as he does on me.

Our secret plan will go ahead, and I have more to say to him, but not now. I need to clear my head, and make sure this is not the biggest fucking mistake of my life, made out of pure desperation.

"Eleven," I add, then turn to Maddox. "Will you pick us up about half an hour before, please?"

"As soon as I find out what you're talking about, sure."

Oh, they will. All of them will, soon enough. And I reckon they're all going to call us crazy, with Lulu in the lead.

*   *   *

We're nestled on Lulu's comfy sofa, in what has suddenly become only *her* apartment, sipping some hot chamomile tea. It calms the nerves, as her grandma taught her. Maybe it's an old wives' tale, but it does feel like it's working.

"Lu, I'm not even sure what to say. However much you're going to try to convince me, I will still feel responsible."

"Why?" She scrunches her eyebrows at me. "Look, the man is clearly insane. I just…" She huffs and rolls her eyes. "There were red flags, I'm not gonna lie. But I ignored them because it was never something too crazy, too deep, or too concerning."

"I can't believe he hated me that much." I never thought anyone could. I've never done anything to him.

"Did you ever see anything that could indicate… this?" she asks.

"Well, sort of. I knew he didn't like me pretty much from the start. But it wasn't me he needed to like, it was you. So I just got over the weird things he sometimes did or said. However, I've never seen anything to indicate this level of madness."

"It's funny, isn't it?" she says with a smirk, and it's the first hint of a smile I've seen on her face since the club caught on fire. "We both ended up with such insane men, obsessive, completely off their rockers."

I chuckle at the realization.

"I always knew we had similar taste in men, but this is a bit over the top."

My snickers turn into a full belly laugh. I wonder how fucking deranged I look right now. Lu joins in, and we laugh our asses off at the terrible situation we've gotten ourselves into. How the fuck did it happen? One crazier than the other, and here I thought getting involved with The Sanctum was the worst thing I could do.

How fucking wrong I was.

And how right it feels to be involved with them. One, in particular.

"How do you really feel?" I ask her once we calm down.

"I'm not sure. I think if it was a normal breakup, or at least a normal betrayal, I would have a harder time. But this… it's so fucking surreal that I'm struggling to focus on my broken heart. I'm mostly angry." She finishes her tea and sets the mug on the table. "It was getting rocky with him, you know? It wasn't the same for me… He was becoming a bit too possessive, a bit too controlling. I don't know if it was because of the club, but he always wanted to have eyes on me, see where I was, who I was with. And that spark just wasn't there anymore."

"I think that, in your subconscious, you did add two and two together, all those red flags. I'm pissed off it reached this point where he had to burn down our club to fuel his delusion. But I'm glad you're rid of him," I rationalize her train of thought.

I don't want her to slip into a spiral. She's strong, but her heart is precious. I'm relieved he's not in her life anymore. I never liked the guy. Not just for her, I just never liked him and his vibes.

She pulls the throw from the back of the sofa and drapes it over herself, turning her attention to me.

"What about you, canoodling with a mafia boss?" She winks at me, and I can feel a blush creeping over my cheeks.

"He's not a *mafia* boss. Also, he's not really the boss at all. The Sanctum functions differently from what I've seen—they rule together."

"Honey, you can call it whatever you want, mafia, a syndicate, organized crime. It all amounts to the same underworld," she says with a shake of her head and a roll of her eyes.

"You should know," I counter.

Her gaze darkens, and she stills for only a moment. The name Dietrich is spoken in hushed tones in some parts of this country, and no matter how much she was allowed to do her own thing, Lulu is very much aware of her family's *heritage*.

"Don't make me tap into my roots and smack you, woman!"

"Fine, fine!" I say, suppressing a laugh. "I'm actually worried I fucked it all up... I thought it was him. I feel like shit, but at the same time, I don't know if I trust him."

"He didn't seem upset in the least when we left." She shrugs. "I think you're scared. You know very well how I feel... or felt, about The Sanctum. But even I have to admit that they've done all they could to be there for you. For us."

"I wish he would just yell at me so we can get it over with."

"Vincent Sinclair does not seem like the type to yell at a woman. Let alone you."

I rub my hands over my face, pressing a bit too harshly, like I could wipe all this anxiety and doubt away. But Lulu is right. Vincent is not the type of guy to yell at me. Not in a situation like this anyway.

Maybe I can get him to punish me in some other way.

I'm blushing just thinking about it, but I do feel like I need to get it out of my system. Admitting I was wrong and apologizing would be the ideal way, but not the easiest one.

"And what's the deal with the offer *that guy* made?" she starts saying, but trails off.

I cock an eyebrow when she pauses for too long. She knows his name, but I think she prefers to call him a brute instead.

"I think the name you're looking for is Maddox."

"Yeah, whatever. What was that all about?" she asks with such annoyance in her golden eyes.

"He wants to help. Madds is a pretty good guy."

"He's a brute, Morri."

I blush, because that doesn't put me off at all. On the contrary.

"What the fuck was that?" she rasps, shocked.

"What?" I'm confused.

"Did you...? Wait, are you fucking blushing? You like him!" She's squealing now.

"They're all hot, Lulu. Don't fucking pretend they aren't."

"We're not talking about *they*, we're talking about *him*. The guy I believe is your man's best friend." She's smiling, but still pretty shocked.

But something else catches my attention: *your man*. I never thought of Vincent as *my man*. It has a fucking delicious ring to it.

"Can we please not talk about this?" I argue.

"Oh, damn, what would The Serpent think?" she taunts me.

I blush so red now, I can feel the heat spreading throughout my body, and her face falls in an instant. Christ, this woman knows me all too well.

"Drop it, Loreley."

She's even more shocked at the sound of her full first name on my lips.

"Fine." But she's scowling dramatically. "What was Vincent saying about the day after tomorrow, by the way?"

"About that..."

My back straightens as I brace myself for her reaction to the sound of the plan The Serpent and I have devised. But I'm going to ease her in and start with some spicy details about what happened at his house. That will butter her up.

* * *

"Vincent just asked me if I would like to go have dinner with him. At his place." I set my phone on the island, looking at Lulu for some guidance.

"Someone's impatient." She flashes her eyebrows suggestively. "You gonna go?"

We woke up this morning feeling a bit lighter. We talked, we planned, we talked some more. It's been a pretty damn good day so far.

It's been a long time since I've been able to spend time with her, without Luke. And last night she reacted surprisingly well to the plan Vincent and I devised. At least after the initial shock. She was, probably still is, apprehensive about it, but she said that she can see that this is the best safety net for me. It felt like a boulder was lifted off my chest. I needed that. Not her approval, necessarily, but she's my Lu, and I needed to see the look on her face to know I'm not fucking over my life.

She reacted even better to the dirty little tidbits I shared, like the mind-blowing sex and his skilled fingers.

"I don't want to leave you," I say to her.

"Oh please. I'll be fine. Someone from The Sanctum is probably lurking in the shadows, watching over me. And to be honest... I wouldn't mind some alone time. I have to get used to it anyway."

"Are you gonna break while I'm gone? Will I come back and find you crying in that big bathtub of yours?"

"Yeah, tears of joy!" She raises her eyebrow in that *obvious* way. "Nah, seriously now, you know me. I might cry to get this frustration out, but to be honest, I'm more susceptible to going back to Luke and killing the motherfucker. Now that the shock has passed, the Dietrich part of me is fighting to come to the surface."

I was a little surprised that she stopped Finn from taking it too far down in the basement. I guess she has some sort of moral compass. Unlike me.

"Go. Seriously. Enjoy that hunky man of yours, and I'm gonna enjoy a bottle of wine on my own."

"Okay. I will. I'll let him know to send someone for me. I love you, you know."

"I know. After all, what's not to love."

"Epitome of modesty," I say with an eyeroll and a laugh.

She hugs me and smacks my ass as I walk toward their—*her* bedroom. I have no clothes here, so finding something to fit me from her closet might be a bit of a challenge. Where she has lean, beautifully sculpted legs, I have thick thighs and round hips. And my boobs would be a bit too strained in her tops. So I need to dig deep for a loose dress.

I'm anxious about this *date*. Vincent's invitation felt charged. Like he was holding himself back from sharing something important. But I could have sworn there was excitement in his voice.

He said he has something for me.

A present?

I don't want anything from him. I don't need anything from him.

But he told me that I definitely want this.

CHAPTER 30

Morrigan

WHEN I ARRIVED at Vincent's house earlier, I almost skipped on my way up the steps. But I was so fucking apprehensive as well.

Only, the man welcomed me with a cheeky smile on his full lips. No sign of upset, or anger in his obsidian eyes. Though he is The Serpent, expecting him to not know how to mask his emotions is truly ridiculous.

"Did you enjoy your dinner?" he asks, as I dab my napkin around my mouth, careful not to smudge whatever's left of the deep red lipstick I'm wearing.

"Delicious. And highly intriguing, which is why I have trouble believing you prepared it," I answer him, with a playful smirk lifting my lips.

The appetizer was oysters, and they were such a tasty surprise. Then, what seemed to be an intricate pasta dish, that left me utterly confused with its shrimp and smoked pancetta combination. I have no idea what to make of it, but I really wanted seconds.

"You were there when I finished making it," he said, laughing at me.

I don't miss the way his gaze darkens. He looks ready to flip me over his knee and spank me into obedience.

"Hey, I only saw you stirring a pot. I don't know how those ingredients got in there."

He rolls his eyes, and I have to bite my lips. He's been the perfect gentleman, but the night is young, and I'm hoping he'll turn into a deviant once dinner ends.

We're sitting on opposite sides of the dining table, unable to touch, and barely reaching to cheer our wineglasses.

My skin itches for him.

It's been goddamn hard.

Even harder finding the right time to apologize for doubting him.

"Vincent... about what happened." I can't wait any longer.

The man places his napkin on the table, and settles back into his chair, one eyebrow cocked. He knows what's coming.

He's expecting.

Almost demanding it.

"I was wrong. About thinking that you were the one who betrayed me... I was wrong." I exhale with enough force that his napkin flutters slightly. "I'm not gonna lie, it was a peculiar instinct, an involuntary reaction driven by the past. You dropped me... just like that. My brain is now fully aware of the reason why you had to, but my heart is taking a little while to catch up. Because, no matter what... it still broke me. And after all of that, all I had was my family and their *endearing* qualities that are bound to leave scars when it comes to trust. Then, it was all topped by Ryan..." Shit. I'm less coherent than I thought I would be. "I know, I know you're not any of them. I know... Fuck! Look, Vincent, I'm... I'm so sorry."

He straightens, dropping his elbows on the table, and laces his fingers. Only, I can't read his expression. I feel as though I'm looking at The Serpent now, not Vincent.

"I really am sorry. I didn't want to believe it, but I hope I can make it up to you," I continue when he doesn't say anything, my heart speeding up as I wait not so patiently.

Suddenly, a wicked smile tugs at his lips, and he quickly glances at the time on his wristwatch.

"I think you can make it up to me."

He pushes his chair back, rising elegantly, then rounds the table, and stops behind me. I have no idea what's happening, but the moment his hand touches my almost bare shoulder, swiping to the front of my throat, I don't fucking care. That touch is electric, and it's doing something to me I can't quite explain. It's hypnotic and so utterly soothing. He applies a little pressure, tipping my head back, then the man dips in and kisses me on a ragged inhale, turning me into a puddle.

"Come, Little Eve." He offers me his hand, and I take it willingly, following him toward the stairs.

He guides me up and turns me as we head to the bedroom I'm comfortably familiar with now. But he stops me in the open doorway and turns to me.

"I want to see the heathen in you tonight."

I almost freeze at his words, but the sharp rise and fall of my chest betrays the stillness.

"I can be a heathen for you, Serpent."

I can almost feel the grin on his lips, as they touch my shoulder. And I let my head fall back against him, as I absorb the shivers he spreads all over my flesh.

"And I want you to trust me," he adds.

When he stops me just as I begin turning to him, I see a strip of black before the light goes out. He covers my eyes with the softest of materials, a thick sort of silk that molds against my face and takes away one of my senses.

"Trust me." His whisper brings another wave of goose bumps as his breath caresses the nape of my neck.

He stops me once again from turning, and I drop my hands from the blindfold. I'm both intrigued and a bit frightened.

"Is there any point in asking what you plan on doing to me?" I question as he gently pushes me into his bedroom.

"*With* you, Morrigan. What I plan to do *with* you. I may have taken your sight, but you will be a willing participant."

I may be scared, but it doesn't trump the excitement of the unknown. Unless he's planning to slit my throat here, I think it's safe to say that he's forgiven me for not trusting him.

His hand runs over the middle of my back, and I hear the delicate zipper of the dress as he drags it down, then swipes the straps off my shoulders. He tugs it down over my breasts, then over the full hips it pauses on, and eventually it falls to the floor.

Then there's nothing. Only dragged-out moments of silence.

I can't even hear his breathing.

My arms are suddenly too heavy at my sides, and I fist my hands, resisting the urge to lift them to cover myself.

"I'll never tire of looking at you." His hoarse voice just about startles me. "I almost don't want to do it for too long because I still want to discover new things about you later."

"Vincent—" His admission sends a sensation through me that has little to do with lust and more to do with that muscle that hurries its beat inside my chest.

"Take your panties off," he interrupts.

Inhaling slowly, I hook my thumbs on the waistband, then pull down as slow as I possibly can, bending over at the hips as I step out of them and rise. His heavy breaths follow the rhythm of my heartbeat, and fuck if they don't sound like music to my ears.

His footsteps approach, and I feel the vibrations in the hardwood floor as he circles me. I'm not sure I've ever felt so exposed. I could be in a room full of people, and I would have no clue. The air is heavier to breathe in, and my spine tingles in such a brutal way, like a predator is just at the precipice of devouring.

A hand on the middle of my back startles me ever so slightly, then pushes me gently until my legs hit the upholstered bed.

"Climb up. On your forearms and knees," he orders.

Again, I do as I'm told, and when I reach the position, my back rolls with the thrill of the exposure. With my ass up in the air, every part of me is on full display, my bare pussy the main event. My ass too.

"So *fucking* beautiful, Morrigan."

He's behind me, not touching, but somehow his energy is there. His eyes are traveling down my body, and my back arches in anticipation.

When his finger swipes through the seam of my pussy, I feel how dripping wet I am for him. Digging my hands into the sheets, I fist the fabric, readying myself, because I know so much more is coming.

Then, in one long stroke, he pushes two fingers into me and the mewls spilling from my lips are almost embarrassing. He's determined and goes in straight for the kill, assaulting that treacherous spot that makes my legs shake. He curls those digits until the sounds coming from my drenched pussy turn into the backup melody to my moans. When he pushes one more inside me, I throw my head back, the slight stretch so goddamn exhilarating, sending another shiver through my whole body. The sensitive buds of my nipples revel in the soft scrape of the lace of my bra, adding to the sensations.

But the bastard pulls out of me without warning, and I fucking curse myself for whimpering at the loss.

Only, my protests stop the moment the bed dips and his wet tongue swipes through me. And by God, this man could make me come just with a flick of his tongue. He licks me, sucks me, eats me fucking whole, and I just want to lie down on a fucking platter for him.

He swipes from my pussy to my ass, sending yet another shudder through my body, that tight hole tensing even more at the feel of him there.

"This will be mine tonight, Little Eve. I'm gonna fuck you until you scream, and when you do, I'll fuck you even harder."

At that declaration, my pussy clenches around nothing but air, and I can feel it... the wetness slowly dripping down my thighs.

"Look at you, so fucking ready, aren't you?"

Then he leaves me. But I don't move.

I hear some shuffling behind me, and the distinctive sound of a metal clasp, then nothing.

"But for now, I'll have your cunt."

His hand grips my ass cheek, fingers bruising my flesh, as the thick head of his cock presses against my entrance. Just like that... on one long, deliciously painful thrust, he drives home, and my head whips back on a vicious cry.

"You were made for me, Morrigan. You are the Eve to my Serpent." He withdraws until just the tip of him remains. "And even your sweet pussy agrees with me, trying to suck me back in."

He's right. My muscles tighten around the head of his cook, and I revel in the groan that shakes his chest.

"Fuck me, Serpent. Fuck me until I'll forget my own name!" I beg, but it sounds more like an order.

"You better fucking remember mine," he all but growls, as he fists my hair, and slams into me with too much force. Yet somehow not enough.

He goes at me like a wild animal, and I need it. I need to feel him everywhere. I need to hurt. I need to cry. I need everything! His brutal thrusts make me lose my balance, and I collapse onto the bed, although it feels more like my muscles are dissolving into it. But his arm rounds my belly, and jerks me up, forcing me back into position. He fucks me like he can't get deep enough, yet I know he's reached the end. He insists, though, as his other hand roves my body and he grounds his hips into my ass, using my hair for leverage. I want exactly what he's searching for—more.

I need more.

More of us.

More of him.

There's so much pleasure zapping through my body, that my brain is caught in a storm of ecstasy. And with each rough thrust, his cock massaging my overstimulated walls, my consciousness becomes trapped there.

All I feel is him, and I want—

"More!" I demand on a hoarse breath.

"Hold the fuck on then."

My whole body shudders at his crude order, but I fist the sheets, bracing myself just in time. He withdraws until the very tip of him remains, and when his hips slam against my ass, my head is jerked back by my hair. My scalp burns at the same time my pussy does, but one is pain, the other is pure euphoria.

"Yes... yes... yes..." I whisper like a mantra, thanking the goddamn gods for the divine pleasure rocking through me.

I'm not even sure if I'm close to an orgasm, but I truly hope I'm not, because there's no fucking way I want this to stop.

Gripping my chin, he dips his thumb into my mouth, and I suck on it, rolling my tongue around, before he pulls it out. As his rhythm slows, I flinch when he pushes that digit against my ass. He gives me time to adjust, until the discomfort, the tension, turns arousing.

He keeps fucking me, moving in and out of my ass, and when he releases my hair and brings his other thumb to my mouth, I know what's coming.

"That's it... you look so damn pretty with my fingers stretching this tight hole." He has both in there, pulling in opposite directions, sliding in and out.

Not sure if I feel pretty, but I sure do feel goddamn incredible.

I hear the sound before I feel his spit hit my ass, and then he pulls his thumbs out, rubbing it there. The pressure comes with more force now, definitely more than just two thumbs, spreading as they draw out.

He's getting me ready.

That thrill sends heat into my pussy.

My moans are getting hungrier and hungrier, demanding more, because having him fill me this way is a whole different type of pleasure. I bring my fingers to my clit, pressing against it as he drives into me, and mere seconds pass before I'm screaming like a little whore. I'm coming on his cock, strangling the damn thing with all I have, and relishing the delicious feel of his fingers in my ass.

I fall onto the bed as he pulls out of me, but he barely gives me any time to breathe before he climbs behind me.

"Come to me." He pulls me onto his body, my back to his front, and drags his hands all over my flesh. He's kneading and rubbing as I relax deeper into him. "I'm nowhere near done with you," he whispers.

My eyes would dart open, but I'm blindfolded and it makes no difference.

"Get on your knees, Morrigan. Straddle me."

"You're gonna kill me tonight, aren't you?" I say through a strained laugh.

"Hopefully not. I have more planned for you."

For me.

I want to ask what, but I'm interrupted by the sound of something squirting.

"Is that...?"

It is.

I can hear it as he rubs it on his cock, and then the cold feel of that lube covers my asshole, and I flinch. But he doesn't stop, and I relax as he dips inside of me again, slipping easily now.

Damn, that feels so good.

Only, I know what's coming, and I can't help being apprehensive about his thick cock going inside my ass. Intrigued, too.

I don't have time to linger on that thought, though. He pulls his fingers out and grips my waist, guiding me to rise right where he wants me. Where I crave to be too.

I've been fucked there before, but not with this much attention. And definitely not in this position. Because, when he releases my waist, and I feel the tip of him against my ass, I realize I'm the one in control here. Yes, he can manhandle me in the best of ways, but I can take my time to adjust. To feel good. As I press down, there's a different type of pleasure that stems from this. The lube makes it slightly easier, and I'm probably not halfway in when I realize the ache is one I crave more of. So I press down, taking more inches of him, savoring the curses that come from the man beneath me.

"It's too much..." I moan.

"Oh, you can take it," he coaxes me on.

"I didn't say I couldn't," I say with a smirk he can't see, then he groans when I push down hard, and my ass hits his hips.

I'm so fucking full. Deliciously so.

When his cock twitches inside of me, I brace myself on his legs, and begin to ride him slowly. I'm probably moving excruciatingly slow, but I don't care—this pleasure is all mine, and I'm gonna fuck him exactly the way I need to.

I can hear every groan, every breathy curse, and I wish I could see the look in his eyes right now.

"Oh, Little Eve, you ride so very well. You're so goddamn beautiful on my cock," he praises me, and I swear it's like pushed a button.

My ass slams onto his hips, my rhythm quickening, and he lets me do it a few more times, before his hands go to my hips, slowing me down. Then he circles my waist, gently guiding me backward, and I pull my legs from under me, planting my feet on either side of his thighs. I don't bother bracing my elbows on the bed, because Vincent wraps an arm just under my breasts trapping me against his front, as his other hand grips my hip. Slowly, we find a new rhythm, as he pushes up and into me, and I roll and grind back into him. The angle hits a whole other part of me, my pussy now missing the feel of his cock, but getting a slight taste of it, as it rubs on the other side of its wall.

"Do you trust me?" he asks, startling me from this reverie.

His tone is sultry, but firm. I feel all too aware all of a sudden. My skin sizzles, and my nipples perk up under the lace of my bra.

"Y—yes."

"I would never do anything you don't want to. You know that." His tone softens just enough to comfort me.

"I do."

"Trust me to give you what you want. What you need." He pauses for a moment. "What you desire."

Those words dip into recent memories, and I'm about to ask if he's being serious, when I hear footsteps on the wooden floor. I stiffen, but Vincent doesn't. He carries on fucking my ass, and it suddenly hurts.

"Relax, Morrigan."

I trust him, right? I do... he wouldn't do anything I don't want, and he would stop if I asked him to.

Not only are we not alone in the room, but I know without a shadow of a doubt that we never were. Not this evening. Not when I stepped foot in Vincent's bedroom. I didn't feel it before; I was too wrapped up in him, but I know it now.

My ass grinds into his hips ever so slightly, the realization taking over in a scary yet thrilling way.

But then the bed dips, and now I know we're not alone here either.

I lift one leg, instinctively trying to close them, but Vincent widens his, blocking me. The instinct to cover myself, like the soft pouch of my belly, is strong.

"Trust me," he whispers, tightening his hold on my ribcage.

I'm not sure how his words work so easily, how they affect me, but they sink in immediately. And as they do, that second person comes so close I can feel their body heat. When a calloused hand presses against the base of my throat, it startles me, pulling a gasp from my chest.

But that touch... that scent... I recognize them.

"She's beautiful, isn't she?" Vincent asks.

"Goddamn gorgeous."

Maddox.

It's fucking Maddox!

Between my spread legs.

With his hand on my throat.

Looking at my dripping pussy.

While Vincent fucks me in the ass.

I swallow my moans, because I fear that the wrong sound will ruin this moment. No. It won't. There's no denying where this is headed.

Maddox drags that hand from my throat and down between my breasts without touching them. He's slow, taking his time exploring me, and when it reaches just above my pussy, he stops.

"This is the moment when you tell me to fuck off. And I'll go," he says to me, a grit in his voice lighting me up inside. Not Vincent. Just me.

My lips part ever so slightly, pausing at the range of thoughts flying through my head. My mind is muddled by the cock that's making me feel too good, by the fantasies that live in my thoughts, and the cravings I've always had for Maddox—my man's best friend. But there's also the fear of having two at the same time, the implications of it, and the impact it could have on us.

But then it all goes back to Vincent and my trust in him. This is not a decision he made on a whim. He thought this through, including the possible repercussions. He's thought it through so I don't have to.

I can't do it. I can't say no. I can't tell Maddox to go away.

I want this so fucking much. More so because Vincent wants it, too.

"Stay," I whisper, and Maddox doesn't spare a second.

Just like that, his thick fingers slip inside my pussy, and on a loud moan, my head falls back against Vincent's shoulder. I have no idea how close these two men really are, but the barrier between my ass and my cunt is thin as fuck, and those fingers are definitely rubbing against my man's length.

A shudder rips through me, and I whimper just at the mental image of it. Holy hotness, I would love for someone to film that close up, just so I can play it on repeat every time I want to get off when alone.

They sync their rhythm, and I'm not entirely sure how I'm supposed to stay sane as Maddox spreads those digits every time he almost pulls out. But then a third one pushes in, and I'm lost.

I know for sure his fingers are thicker than Vincent's, because a wicked sting lays in their wake as he stretches me. I'm so lost in the feeling, that it takes me a moment to realize that I'm rolling my hips onto them, just as much as they're pushing into me.

Fuck.

Those digits leave me on a low groan and all movement stops. Vincent holds me, adjusting me slightly, and a moment later, what presses against my entrance is much, much thicker.

Maddox's cock is just about to impale me, and it feels bigger than anything that has ever been inside me.

I have flashback of Vincent and I on his patio, his fingers spreading me open, whispering to me that *I have to take more than just three fingers to accommodate him.* I mean, I believe him, but this is not what I expected.

He slowly pushes inside, and the burn begins, the stretch already too much. Yet, I want more. I want it all, no matter the sting, because even without Vincent telling me, I know this will never happen again. I don't think I want it to either. So I will take my fucking fill now.

It's surreal, though... I can't believe this is happening.

"Take it off," I rasp without thinking, and both men stop moving in an in instant.

"Take what off?" Vincent asks, confused.

"The blindfold."

I feel the brush of the fabric against my face, and when I open my eyes, blinking a couple of times to adjust, he's there—Maddox. His intense honey eyes are on me, guiding his impossibly large, condom-covered cock inside of me. He's fucking beautiful. A beast of a man, with this bulging, stacked muscles, and handsome, scarred face.

A small grin tugs at the corner of my lips. It mirrors in his eyes, yet the man still looks feral.

And I'm a little scared. But a whole lot of desperate for more.

"Lift your legs." His words come across more as growls, and I do as told.

I go to brace myself on my elbows, but Vincent presses his hand on my chest, whispering in my ear to let them do the work. Then he captures my breast in his hand, distracting me with his touch as Maddox wraps a hand against my hip, and the other around my thigh, pulling it close to his torso.

I don't even bother to understand where all our legs go, but mine seem to be on top of theirs as I lay between them.

Then Maddox pushes that scary cock of his deeper inside of me and I'm not entirely sure if I begin to disassociate, but the fullness... fucking hell, the fullness! The stretch... it's a bundle of pain, pleasure, sweet torment, and ecstasy all at once.

Then he's all in, and I'm sure he's rearranged an organ or two on his way there. The sensation of both of them inside of me is nothing like what I expected. I can feel them against each other, but I can't quite understand how.

The moment Maddox begins to move, I don't care how.

"Jesus Christ..." I moan and he takes that as his cue.

They both do. They move almost at the same time, and my mouth falls open as the strain and bliss spread like lightning through my body.

Maddox tightens his hold on my leg as his thrusts quicken, out of sync with Vincent, their pace primal. I'm both limp and frantic—my legs have stopped functioning, but my hands are wildly clawing and grabbing at everything in their reach. Vincent's pinching my nipple between his fingers, holding my throat in his other hand, as he whispers beautiful, sinful things into my ear.

"You're such a good girl, Little Eve. You're taking us so fucking well."

"She's a goddamn dream, brother," Maddox adds, and I whimper through a shudder, as a weird kind of pride warms me.

"Is this everything you ever fantasized about?" Vincent asks, panting with his wild thrusts.

"Yes," Maddox and I answer at the same time, and our gazes shoot to each other's. Our grins are mirrored, and it feels both sweet and crazy at the same time.

"Good." Vincent's voice turns gravelly, filled with a lust that drips off his tongue and straight into my bloodstream.

The feel of them almost rubbing against each other inside of me is such an unexpected turn-on. And so fucking hot, especially knowing that these two are straight. But obviously completely unbothered by their proximity or contact.

They thrust harder into me. One grunts, the other one growls, and I'm just the little toy between them, taking everything they've got. And by God, they have a lot to give.

"I would have never thought..." The man above me speaks through heaving breaths, but never finishes.

"Me neither," I moan.

I drop my head against Vincent's shoulder, turning my head to look at him. His wicked grin tugs at one corner of his lips, and I reach back to grab his head, and pull him into a bruising kiss. This seems to coax them both on, and they drive harder into me until I almost scream into Vincent's mouth. But the man dips his tongue in and feeds on each sharp note.

I want this moment to last for days, the euphoria of it, but those electric threads begin to pull at me from both ends. They're wrapping around my core, around my ass, and I break the kiss, my eyes fixed on Maddox. He knows immediately what he needs to do.

His shoulders, arm, and chest flex dangerously as he braces himself on one hand on the bed, reaching with the other between us. The moment his roughened fingers begin rubbing against my clit, I shoot up, propping myself up on my forearms, and closer to the man before me. His head drops, our foreheads almost touching, and our gazes so fucking transfixed, I'm mesmerized. The magnitude of this moment is too much.

Too fucking much!

"Oh my God!"

My cries fill the room as my whole body begins to shake. My pussy and ass convulse violently around the men who stretch me, and I grind my hips against both of them on a frantic, demanding rhythm. Their groans and growls follow my cries, and as Vincent pulls me down against his front, he replaces Maddox's fingers on my clit, his touch slow as he guides me through the orgasm. The other man wraps his hand around my thigh in a bruising grip, pulling me harshly to him. It feels like they're using me for their pleasure, while bleeding me dry.

It feels godlike. Utterly divine in its depravity.

They both begin to twitch as they sink deep inside of me. I don't know who comes first, but the feel of those jerks against one another while I'm riding this incredible high, can't be matched by fantasies. I revel in each and every one of them, concentrating on every single pulse, every sensation, every breath, every groan and grunt.

I focus on them all, because I know this will never happen again.

I don't think I would even want it to.

It's perfect in each and every fucking way already.

"Thank you... thank you..." I whisper, heaving.

When I finally open my eyes, the men begin to pull out of me, and I don't think I've ever felt this empty. Physically. I look between them curiously, still in a haze, and I'm met with mirrored smiles on their lips. I can't help but laugh.

What the hell just happened?!

CHAPTER 31
Morrigan

THE ATMOSPHERE TODAY has been peculiar. And not because it was awkward, or bad in any way, but because it wasn't any of those things. It was… normal. Light. Almost perfect.

Vincent's plan has been set into motion, and somehow the entire day flowed like a strange, beautiful dream.

I'm now sitting at Lulu's kitchen island, looking out the window at the sea through the row of beautiful period buildings, and I wonder when the next step will be. Ryan is bound to make his move, and since we returned from Vincent's house, we've been on edge.

My *darling fiancé* hasn't made an attempt to contact me. He is still, as far as we know, unaware of my connection to The Sanctum, but he knows I'm here, at Lulu's. I insisted for her to stay away. Stay at Vincent's place, or anywhere else with The Sanctum until it's all finished. But in true Lulu fashion, she refuses to cower away from the conflict, and wants to be in the middle of it all. She's not fooling me, though; I know she wants it because I'm here, too.

I love her, but sometimes she's just as careless as I am. Only, in different ways.

It's the middle of the afternoon, and I'm not sure if it's in my mind, but the world seems to have gone silent. It's eerie and slightly disturbing.

The sudden vibrations of my phone on the marble countertop startle both Lulu and me.

"Christ on a cracker." Lulu rubs her forehead as I shake my head at her.

I think she feels this strange tension in the air, too.

"Yes?" I answer.

"I'm going to Midnight soon. I can send someone to pick you up if it would make you feel safer. The guys are already there." Vincent's voice eases me.

"It's not a good idea. If he's going to make a move, the last place I should be at is Midnight…" I trail off, stating the obvious. He knows this, but he wants me near him. I do too.

He sighs on the other line. "I know. But it doesn't mean that I can easily wrap my head around putting you in harm's way intentionally. I feel like you're the bait and this is a huge mistake."

"Serpent, it's unlike you to be... shall I say, insecure?"

"Never!" he scoffs. "Maybe... Fuck." He pauses long enough that it brings a giddy smile to my lips. "I just got you back, Morrigan. If something happens, if I lose you—"

"Got me back? I don't think we established anything, dear sir. You're getting a bit ahead of yourself there," I say sarcastically, and can't help but laugh. As much as I know I'm full of shit.

"You're mine, Morrigan O'Rourke. Whether you're ready to accept it or not. Your soul knows it's mine. Your heart has always been mine. And eventually... your beautiful brain will allow you to realize it too. No matter what, you will still end up next to me, with your hand on the scar you left above my heart, and your lips on mine. Maybe then you'll also recognize that I've always been yours too."

"It's not in my nature to easily accept my fate, but I think I've al—"

A loud bang interrupts me, and I whip around, looking for the source, but I'm only met with Lulu's confused gaze on the other side of the kitchen island. Then I realize it was coming from the other line.

It was loud.

"Vincent?" My voice trembles, but no answer comes. "Vincent!" I shout it this time, dread filling my stomach. "Goddamnit, answer me!"

Another blast echoes through the already loud commotion I hear on the phone, and my shouts turn relentless. I'm fucking pleading for a reply. For any noise.

Something that sounds like him.

"Goddamnit, Serpent! Say something!"

But the line goes dead. The silence deafening.

Eerie.

I knew something was wrong.

Panic rushes through my blood. It touches my bones and seeps into my marrow, until every part of me is filled with a destructive range of emotions.

And when regret joins in... I break. Never have I felt the paralyzing fear that splits me now.

"I just got you back..." His words ring in my ear.

I call him over and over again, yet it goes straight to voicemail every single time.

"I just got you back..."

Now I'm shouting at my phone from the depths of my lungs as I wait for Maddox to answer the fucking call. And as I hear a sound that's just a bit different than the normal ringing, I just start talking.

"Something's wrong! Go to Vincent! There were two blasts! I couldn't hear him anymore! Go the fuck now!" I shout my pleading orders without even knowing if somebody's listening.

"I just got you back..."

"Morrigan, what are you talking about?!" His deep, gravelly voice just doesn't seem urgent enough.

"Goddamnit, Maddox! I was on the phone with Vincent! It went dead!"

This time, he doesn't linger. He starts shouting at the group, ordering around whoever else is there with them. Then chaos erupts on his side of the call as they all sound like they spring into action.

"We'll send someone for you."

"I'm okay! Just go to him! Grab everyone, dammit!"

Madds hangs up, and I pace through the open-plan space, back and forth, threading my fingers through my hair as I force myself to cope with this helplessness. Even Lulu has no words for this. She stares at me with a worried gaze, but I can't fucking bear it.

The possibility shining in those golden eyes cripples me.

What if...

No, no, no. He's fine. He is fine!

He's The—*motherfucking*—Serpent. He is fine!

No one can touch him.

But what if...

No!

The internal battle pulls at me, tugging in different directions, and I wanna fucking scream.

Tears fall from my eyes as I chase away those devastating thoughts. I realize that my fear of losing him, when I didn't even acknowledge that I am his in this call, trumps the question I haven't answered to myself about trusting him. It fucking squashes it to the ground. Because I can build that fucking trust. I can kill my insecurities and find out who *this* man is. Not the one I knew so long ago.

But my heart? My heart already bleeds for him with the most decadent, unhealthy kind of love. I'm his, no matter what.

I am his and he is mine.

And I didn't get to tell him that...

* * *

Too much time passes, yet I know it's not a lot at all. Not even enough for the guys to drive from Midnight to Vincent's house in the woods.

It still feels like too long.

I've kept calling, but that goddamn voicemail was the only sound at the other end, gritty and irritating. It took everything in me not to smash this phone on the ground.

"It will be okay. You'll see, everything will be okay."

I shake my head at Lulu's words, wiping the tears off my cheeks and eyes.

"Fuck... Luke was right. You should not be friends with me. I should be thousands of miles away from you, on the other side of the damn globe, because you do not deserve this. Look at me! I'm a fuckling mess. And you're getting dragged into this bullshit. Fuck, if Ryan hurts you because of me..."

I trail off, slapping my palms against the windowsill, somehow searching for an answer in the faint shades of burnt orange that start appearing in the sky. All that fear, panic, and anger mix into this explosive feeling, that seems to be denied a proper release.

"What will you do?"

My soul leaves my body as the sound of that voice slices through my eardrums. A shiver shakes my flesh as I turn around slowly, like I'm afraid I'm going to spook him, and he'll make the wrong move if I turn too fast.

There he is—Ryan Holt. In the middle of Lulu's apartment, with one arm wrapped around her from behind, the other holding a knife to her throat. Three of his men stand tall and firm behind him.

"Let her go," I demand of him.

I'm trapped. We're trapped. The detail The Sanctum had on us probably went to find Vincent.

"Where would the fun in that be?" he taunts me, the grin lifting the corners of his lips and eyes truly disturbing.

"Drop the knife, Ryan."

I heard somewhere that attackers respond favorably when you use their names. It reaches them at a deeper level for some reason, like you're reminding them of their humanity. That they're still a person.

"But it would sink so beautifully into her soft skin." His smile turns grim, his expression like puppy eyes on a rabid dog.

"And if it does, you will never have me. I'll remove myself from this plane, if one hair on her head is disturbed. Let. Her. Go." I squeeze my fists as I will myself to keep my tone even. For Lulu's sake.

He narrows his eyes ever so slightly as his features become more serious.

"If anyone gets the privilege of removing you from this earth, dear fiancée, it is me, and me alone."

"Try me." My foot lands on the floor with a determined, loud thud as I step toward him.

I may have become a different person recently, obedient and low-key afraid of this man who threatens to kill my best friend. But the thought of Lulu being involved has brought a whole other type of courage to rise within me. Even if my insides are shaking.

It's strange how one person could have this invisible hold on you. It's as if my soul knows the consequences of his madness, and it wrapped a rope around itself, just so he can't do it himself. Only that rope is loosening, slowly turning into a noose, and I will not stand for that. Not anymore.

Cocking his head slightly, he regards me with a bit more seriousness. He begins pulling the knife away, but just at the last moment, Lulu hisses, and a red line appears in the trail of the blade. The motherfucker cut her!

"Oh, I'm sorry. Did I nick you?" He feigns distress, but that mad smirk lives happily on his face.

He pushes Lulu away, and I catch her, checking her throat. It's a cut, but it's shallow.

"I'm so sorry..." I plead to her.

"Come! I spared her life, now come. Before I change my mind." Ryan reaches for me, waiting impatiently.

"Don't, Morri. Please, don't," Lulu begs, holding my wrist as I move toward the man that is to be my husband. The one who only plans to keep me until my family fortune is his.

"I have to. I can risk myself, but not you, Lulu. Never you."

I'm yanked away while Lulu's screams echo through the space, mixing in my mind with the blasts I heard on Vincent's call. I wonder if any other devastating sounds will be added to the pile by the end of today.

A day that started in such a surprisingly wonderful way, when in the middle of the forest, Vincent and I made our pact. All after an absolutely insane night with him and his best friend.

It's all fading into nothingness now.

* * *

I sat in the backseat of Ryan's Mercedes, unable to control the tears that fell freely from my eyes. Vincent's last words on the phone ran on a loop in my head, until my chest hurt too much to contain myself. I've clutched my hands together so tight, my nails drew blood from my palm, and my shoulders cramped from the tenseness. On the inside, though, I feel empty. Numb. Broken.

I had him. For a moment, a split moment in time, I had him. Vincent was mine. He came back to me. Even when I didn't want him, he came back to me.

There's an aching pressure in my chest, causing tears to fall in waves. But they all stem from frustration. I'm mad. I'm fucking livid at the man who's about to marry me.

Or so he thinks.

I'll fight him to the end of the fucking days. I'll kill him in his sleep. I don't even care if I make him suffer or not, I just want him dead.

Vincent was supposed to be here... to help me. I have no clue where he is. Or if he's still alive.

The stone walls of the back room of the church absorb my heaving breaths. My pain and fury taint this space that should be filled with happy memories, with a sorrow that only seems to grow heavier.

I opened a dam, and I cannot seem to stop it.

"She is my sister! You will let me in now, or I'll make sure that old mausoleum at the back will have a new inhabitant!" Cillian's voice sounds from the other side of the thick wooden door, which separates this room from the corridor leading to the main hall of the old church.

The wood creaks as one of the doors flies open, and I quickly swipe a sleeve over my eyes, rising from the chair to go to the window.

I don't think my brother has seen me cry since I was seven. I fractured my wrist punching one of my father's friends who told me that, since I'm a girl, I should smile more, otherwise boys won't like me. I've rarely heard Cillian laugh the way he did that day. Not at me, or at me being hurt, but at my reaction. There was pride in that laugh, and it was the only thing that encouraged me to be brave in the emergency room. My parents didn't come. They had company. Our housekeeper was sent with us instead.

I don't know what happened to Cillian and me. To him.

"How are you, Morri?" I don't quite recognize the tone of his voice.

There's a level of care in there that I'm not sure if I should take as manipulation.

"Peachy, brother."

I don't turn as I hear him walk away from me. What is he doing?

I peek to my right and he's inside the small bathroom at the end of the room, signaling for me to come in. Narrowing my eyes on him, I finally make a move, watching me rolling his. When I walk in, he turns on the tap to the max, and comes closer. Not touching, though. My brother never really touches anyone, for that matter.

"He has not been found at the house," he whispers, and my eyes widen, my heart beginning to race.

"What? What the hell are you talking about?" I almost rasp at him.

"I've spoken with his friend," he cuts me off, whispering again and gesturing for me to do the same. "I gave him an address for the man who is responsible. He might be there."

Vincent. He's definitely talking about Vincent and Maddox. I clutch the shirt over my heart, somehow more at ease than I was thirty seconds ago. If he wasn't at the house, maybe... *fuck*... maybe he's not gone. However—

"Why are you telling *me* this, brother?"

He blinks, once... twice... three times, then sighs. Hidden pain flashes in those light green eyes.

"Because I had a feeling that when I abandoned you, you found help elsewhere. But I got confirmation when the friend contacted me to deliver this message to you."

I felt utterly betrayed by my brother. No matter our distance, we had only each other, and then it was only me. He has barely been present in this affair. Never really lent a hand apart from some fleeting words of encouragement. And suddenly, he's helping The Sanctum. This feels wrong. But I recognize it's because of my issues with him.

"You really aren't aligned with them"—I nod toward the door—"are you?!"

He shakes his head once, his eyes fixed on mine.

"I was never given any reasons not to trust Dad. Not until the last year or so." He seems to drift to a dark place in his mind. "I slowly realized that even though he's been grooming me his whole life to take over the business when he's dead, things have shifted. I thought I was imagining it, but slowly I could see myself being kept at arm's length—*need to know basis* only. I get half-truths and incomplete information. So I started gathering my own."

Shit.

"I—I think I saw some of it, when I came over a few months ago. Your laptop was open."

He nods and continues. "I know you did. I have cameras at my place, Morri."

"Why didn't you say anything to me?"

"It was too early. I needed more. What you saw was recon. I couldn't get you involved and risk your life. If I wasn't able to find the information I needed about our father and his new business, I was going to look for outside help. In the end, I realized I had to keep quiet, because it felt off. Like we are only one head of the hydra, and I was the only man who could gain this one's trust. Plus, my *army* is not big enough to take Ryan, and to ensure that Dad doesn't find someone else to continue the same sickening business. But I had enough, so I reached out to one of your *associates*."

"Did you? When?" Vincent didn't tell me any of this.

"A few days ago, after some of Dad's and Ryan's affairs started crumbling. Literally. The business was getting hit left and right, and I was fucking ecstatic. The plan was to come and break you out after talking to *them*, only to find that somebody beat me to it. I met with them, and I was told they were waiting for the last of the group to discuss. Only he was... unavailable." There's a tinge of a smile at the corner of his mouth as he says that lost word, and I could have sworn I felt the rush of a blush on my cheeks.

"You wanted to save me."

"Too late, it seems. And you had to rely on someone else..."

An uncomfortable silence falls between us. I cannot blame him, yet he is not without fault either.

"Why didn't you run away?" He finally breaks that silence.

"Like you, brother, the man controls too much. He held too many things against me. Including you."

"Me?" he asks, confused.

I nod, continuing. "If I was to run, hide, or even kill myself, he threatened to murder you all. This includes Mother, Father, and Lulu, of course. As you can imagine, at this point, I would erase Father from this earth myself, and I couldn't give two shits about Mother. But you and Lulu? I couldn't risk you. Even if I hated your guts."

Pain flashes in his eyes, his skin a shade paler as he takes in my confession. He failed me, and it's painted so vividly on his face.

"I'm sorry," he finally whispers. "I can't believe I... we are the reason you're caught in this bullshit. My God, Morrigan, you could have saved yourself. You should have said something, and we would have found a solution."

I smirk and shake my head. "I tried speaking with Father once, and all I got was two hard slaps across the face. Plus, it wasn't only the threat to your life that held me here. First of all, I refuse to run. I would rather fucking die than give Ryan the satisfaction of breaking me. Second of all, he holds something on me. Something that could land me in jail for a very, very long time."

Cillian furrows his eyebrows.

"Do I dare ask?"

"If I ever end up getting out of this situation"—I wave around me—"maybe I'll tell you. Although, the fewer people who know, the better. However, what are you going to do now that you know all of this?"

"The problem is that the most recent events have pulled all resources away to find the missing *man*. I'm unsure when my backup returns. But rest assured, sister, one way or another, you will escape this."

Suddenly, a hard knock sounds on the door and my body goes stiff. But Cillian runs out of the bathroom to check it out.

It's rather surreal. I feel like I got my brother back, only to find out that he didn't really go anywhere. We were just absolute shit at communicating with each other, until it was too late.

Mrs. Holt appears in the door frame, sighing with such sadness in her eyes, and I can't help but match it.

"I thought you got out..." she whispers, walking toward me, and stops a foot away. "I was told to come help you get ready for the ceremony."

Those words seem to hurt her. I've never seen Mrs. Holt quite like this, but I guess once you crack the door open, letting some feelings out, it's hard to close it.

"I thought so too."

My mind drifts to the night I escaped. Or better yet, when I was helped to escape. Maddox and Vincent under the stairs come into my mind, yet it's only Vincent that I see vividly.

And I may never get to see him again.

CHAPTER 32
Morrigan

THE WOMAN GLARING back at me in the mirror, covered in the hideous, sparkly, princess style wedding dress, looks nothing like me. It should be someone else's reflection. She's living a nightmare. Her green irises shine too bright from dried tears, her eyes so red and swollen that even the rushed bridal makeup doesn't succeed to mask it.

Mrs. Holt left my wavy red hair loose, only pulling together two thick strands from my temples. She braided them at the back of my head, and fixed a long, thin veil into it with a sparkly comb.

The hair is the only thing I like about this image.

"You look beautiful," she says to me, her tone sincere.

I look at her reflection as she stands behind me, but I have no words for her. We haven't spoken since the moment she walked into this room. Nothing would have been appropriate for the situation, the atmosphere too tense and somber.

I still have trouble believing this is the same woman I met years ago. It seems like whoever she used to be has slowly died, as the belief that her son killed her husband has strengthened.

I want to answer her and be polite. The words don't come, and neither does the will to find them.

The whole time I spent with her in here, getting ready for this ridiculous affair, I've dissociated deeply. I'm caught somewhere in the recent memories made at Vincent's house. I'm in his bed, between his sheets, then in his shower, and finally in the forest. Where it all began for the last time.

A tear forms and falls too fast for me to blink it away, and I watch in the mirror as it pulls with it some of the makeup that covers my face. I don't bother fixing it. Mrs. Holt doesn't either. She simply puts her head down and turns away.

This day would have gone to plan if Vincent wasn't missing... or potentially dead. Not anymore. There's no one else to save me now.

Technically the backup plan is still in place even without him, but there's no guarantee.

Even the anger has abandoned me, and all that's left behind is hollowness. Only, it can't truly be called hollow if anguish and grief reside there.

I hold on to some twisted hope that the pact we made must be fulfilled. Like a thread of fate wrapped around us the moment we sealed that deal, and it won't allow him not to keep his word to me.

He cannot break the covenant.

He cannot...

I feel like I should be distressed, more emotional, cry in anguish or rage, but nothing comes. I wrap one arm around my middle, looking down as I wait for my end. Metaphorically, of course. It's the end of my life as I know it. Of my family ties and my friendship. Of my business too. Well, it will be Lulu's business.

The only thing I can do is focus on myself. I cannot allow myself to break. Even if Vincent will not be here to save me, if he will never return... I cannot break. Eventually, I will save myself. When I've devised a plan that won't land me dead or in jail, I will find my freedom.

A knock on the door startles me, but I only lift my head to look out the window at the burnished sky bathing the world in shades of fire.

Too bad it's not all up in flames.

"It's about to start," Mrs. Holt announces.

The end of my life—that was the knock that signaled it. The emotions I was willing into myself seconds before, seem to rush into me all at once. Anger, fear, and even hopelessness filling every vein and nerve with their dangerous concoction. It spikes my adrenaline. I straighten, turning to Mrs. Holt, who now stands closer to the door.

Yet, I can't seem to be able to move. My feet are glued to the floor.

"We must go," she pleads, more with her eyes than her voice.

But I can't. I can't go. Not to him, not ever. I shake my head as the knock on the door turns to slight bangs.

"Go away!" I finally shout, but I can't fully recognize that voice.

The knock is harsher, rattling the hinges and shaking the door, and even as I watch it, I still flinch at the sight.

When the door opens with a loud bang, swinging so far, it hits the wall, Mrs. Holt almost falls to the floor as she jumps out of the way. The guard standing in the door frame holds an arrogant look in his eyes. I recognize him—he was there the night Ryan kidnapped me in front of Lulu's building. He held me as his boss hit me in the middle of the street. *Son of a fucking bitch.*

"It's time. Mr. Holt is waiting." There's exasperation in his tone, and I can't imagine why. It's not him waiting at the damn altar.

"No." I stand firm, looking him straight in the eyes.

"There is no time. Move. Now!" He stalks closer, and he's only a couple of steps away when my ass hits the desk.

I brace myself on it, and he sighs, coming straight into my face. He rolls his eyes as he grips my left arm, yanking me away. Only, I grab onto the desk, plant my feet onto the floor, and pull back as hard as I can.

"Fuck off, you asshole!" I shout.

Gripping the wood harder, I reach farther back as I force myself out of his hold. But my hand slides through a stack of papers, and I'm just about to lose my grip, when something smooth and cold grazes my hand. I grab onto the thin, long metal, and with the adrenaline growing a little higher, I stomp my heel onto his foot, and watch as he stumbles back, just about yelping in pain.

"You fucking bitch!" he rasps as he regains his balance.

He doesn't waste a breath, reaching for my throat with his large hand, but I knock it off before it touches me. I'm not fast enough to catch the other one, though. He wraps it around my windpipe, holding tight as he steps back and pulls me toward him. I push onto his chest, trying to force him away, but the fucking wall of a man doesn't move. Even banging my fists against his body doesn't make him flinch.

"Stop fucking fighting," he tries to order me. But I don't listen to men like him.

Loosening his grip, he uses it to guide me toward the door, and through the dark corridor that takes us to the main room of the church. As I look for the light at the end of this tunnel, I swear it seems to lengthen before my eyes. Three words echo repeatedly into my mind as a slight dizziness clouds it—*dead man walking*.

This is the path to my electric chair. My noose. My damn lethal injection.

And I'm not. Fucking. Ready.

As the man who holds me in his grip is about to force me through that corridor, fire fills my veins, and I strengthen my hold around the metal object clasped in my hand. Just as I swing my arm up, hoping it has a sharp fucking end, I jam it straight into the side of his throat. He gasps like a fish out of the water as he releases me, the shock so beautifully clear on his face.

The moment I pull away from him, I take that metal with me, sliding it out of his flesh.

And crimson becomes my new favorite color.

It sprays like a goddamn garden hose out of his throat, on the sweet notes of Mrs. Holt's screams. It splashes all over my hair, my face, my chest, and as the man collapses onto his knees, it paints a morbidly beautiful, abstract painting all over my pristine white dress.

It's finally beautiful. I'm a crimson princess, and it feels like it was meant to be. It almost matches my hair color.

When he falls flat onto the floor, gasping one last time for air, I take a step back away from his body and realize... I'm smiling.

The pool of blood beneath him is not large. Most of it is soaked into the many layers of my dress, and I wonder... should this bother me? Should I be disgusted? Run and hide and freak out that I just killed *another* man?

Maybe it should.

Yet as I step over his body, watching the door at the end of the corridor swing open and two more men walk through, I realize I feel nothing for him. No guilt. No disgust. No fear. That numbness inside of me, the one filled with anguish and grief, revels in the ruthless, careless rage that took over. It feeds on it. Because feeling even the most damaging of emotions is better than feeling nothing at all.

Tucking what appears to be a letter opener somewhere in the folds of my dress, I walk straight toward the men who entered the corridor. I'm completely unfazed by their presence. Somewhere in this rage, I found the courage to take this whole thing head on. I have nothing else to lose.

Nothing at all.

They might see that in my eyes, too. Or maybe it's the blood on my dress, or the splatters staining my freshly made-up face, that makes them pause and look at me with apprehension. They even make room, pressing against the walls as I stride between them, and to the room where the man I loathe waits at the altar.

I bask in the drama, pulling open that door into the small foyer where my father gasps loudly as he waits to walk me down the aisle. My main instinct is to continue my path, but the heathen in me wants to give him a moment to take me in. He drags his eyes over my bloody form, and by the time they return to my face, my smile is fucking menacing.

He's stunned, and I take that as my cue to join my goddamn fiancé at the end of that aisle. I confidently move past my father, glancing at every single person who just stood up and turned to me in the pews of the church. Watching the smiles fall off their faces the moment they see me is a beautiful thing to behold. And I hold each and every one of their gazes as I make my way down that aisle, convinced that I'm leaving splatters of blood over the stone floor behind me.

There aren't many people here anyway. My mother, my brother, and maybe a dozen others I don't recognize. I doubt they're friends, maybe guards, maybe associates. Truth is, I don't care. The chief of police could be here, and I wouldn't give a shit.

The man of the hour stands at the altar, trying but failing to contain his astounded expression. It quickly morphs into displeasure. The priest, a step behind him, is completely pale as he takes me in, and I kind of feel for the man. I know him. He's a good man, and he was definitely forced into this situation. Just as I was. Only, he doesn't look like he just slaughtered something—I do. Yet again, that thought widens the smile that pulls at my lips.

My steps don't falter when I reach Ryan. I stand right next to him, my eyes fixed on the priest, who seems to flinch at this contact, and forces his gaze back to the bible he holds. But I don't miss how his eyes flicker on various bloody spots on my dress.

"What the fuck happened?" I hear Ryan's gritty voice next to me, and with a serene feeling settling deep in my chest, I turn my head to him.

"The man you sent after me... he spilled." I should get an award for how eerily calm my voice is.

I shrug, then turn my attention back to the priest, who closes his mouth just as I look at him. His eyes are wide enough that I'm sure it hurts.

"You killed him?" Ryan doesn't sound happy with my reply.

"Oh no. He died all on his own." I pause for a few seconds, then turn completely toward him. "Is there a problem?" I grab onto the sides of my dress, lifting it ever so slightly, and look down at it. "I think this looks rather pretty, better than it did when I first put it on."

My theatrics are fueled further as I begin to twirl on the gasps coming from the pews. When I stop, facing Ryan once more, he takes a step back with a disgusted look on his face. Two bright red spots stain his white shirt, just under the collar.

"Stop it!" he rasps between gritted teeth.

My grin falls, and I cock my head, utterly focused on him. His eyebrows flinch, narrowing at me, but what they leave in their wake is not rage. Not even annoyance. It's apprehension.

"Wait a damn second, *fiancé*." I spit that word at him with utter revulsion in my tone. "Did you think that I would make this easy for you? You goddamn gaslighting, abusive piece of shit. You and my degenerate father are both delusional if you think that I will allow you to use me for your benefit. You thought you could kidnap me—twice—then burn my fucking house and business down, even put my best friend in danger, and I would just roll over? Ask for more?"

He tries to speak, but I raise my hand, shushing him, and when my father attempts to protest, I talk over him.

"I am done, *darling fiancé*. You've put me down long enough, and the funny thing is... when one realizes that there's nothing left to lose, all bets are off." I take a small step toward him, feeling the growing insanity seeping out of my gaze. "And they are definitely off. You better pray that this arrangement won't take. You may abuse me, you may beat me, and you may rape me. But I will make sure that you will fear going to sleep each and every single fucking night for the rest of your life. This is my vow to you."

All of a sudden, the heavy double doors of the church burst open, pulling our attention. Bright light floods the space, and a man is violently thrown in, sliding halfway down the aisle.

But then I get to witness the most beautiful sight. One that makes me want to jump in joy.

They're like warriors returning from battle—dirty, bloody, muscles rippling with heaving breaths. Their steps are thunderous and confident as they follow the blood trail of the stranger who curls into himself, moaning in pain on the stone floor.

They command the room into stunned silence. Some of the witnesses drop their gazes to the floor, wishing they would be invisible right about now, as the group stops in the middle of the aisle. Right where the broken man is lying. And their attention is right on us.

They look vicious. Yet there's an eerie calmness in their bones, in their muscles, in their stances. Like their assurance was profoundly boosted by whatever trials they've just faced.

Then there's *him*. The man whose terrifying gaze is solely on me. He has no business looking that fucking hot covered in bruises and blood.

And I greet him with a calm, sweet smile on my lips.

"Hi."

CHAPTER 33
Vincent

"HI," I GREET her back, and her smile spreads impossibly wide. It's almost sinister, but it looks stunning on her. She doesn't even notice the scowl on Holt's face at our interaction.

Something swells in my chest at the thought that I put that happiness on her beautiful face. I would crumble to the fucking ground and kiss her feet if that son of a bitch wasn't standing next to her right now. If none of them were standing around us right now.

When I walked in, and my gaze fell on the bloody princess standing in front of that altar, the shade of red I saw before my eyes was more visceral than the one staining her skin and dress. In that moment, all I wanted was to put a bullet in every single person who simply stood here, watching her agony.

My fucking Eve...

He hurt her. They all fucking hurt her, and I was ready to burn them all.

Until I got a better look. A bright sparkle filled the green of her eyes, and it dawns on me that the blood splattered over her freckled skin, looks goddamn gorgeous on her. It belongs in her chaos. That smile, the way she stands, strong and proud, painted in crimson, told me all I need to know—the blood isn't hers. She was simply the cause of it.

My crazy, beautiful Eve isn't hurt.

And she's looking at me like I hung the fucking moon.

The whole room goes silent, apart from the moans coming from the waste of space lying on the floor before us, as he tries to get up on his feet. My gaze moves to Holt, and I cock my head, waiting for him to understand who he's looking at.

"What is the meaning of this?!" It's O'Rourke who gets up first, feigning some sort of confusion at the situation.

I force my attention to the old man.

"We were hurt we were not invited to this... happy affair. So we decided to invite ourselves. With the help of Holt's friend over here." I hear Finn behind me.

"What are you talking about? Who is that man?" O'Rourke continues.

"Oh, my apologies. The bruises on his face might confuse you. Although I believe you've never actually met my guest, not in his current identity as Jackson Davenport," I answer him, watching the confusion muddle his features. "Although I doubt that in his real identity you ever got to know him. He used to run in very different circles than you. However, I guess introductions are in order. Liam O'Rourke, meet Lester Boseman. Your business partner, and Ryan Holt's best man. We thought you might need him at the wedding, so we graciously brought him to you."

I don't miss the way Ryan fidgets slightly, and if I were him, knowing what he knows, I would too.

"You might be confused, Mr. O'Rourke. You thought you were Holt's partner, and I hate to be the bearer of bad news, but you're just the bank account. Nothing more, nothing less," I continue, then kick Boseman so he can slide farther onto the floor, and I can get closer to the altar. But I also do it because I really fucking enjoy hearing him moan in pain.

"I don't know what you think you know, Serpent, but you need to leave right now. This is a private family event, and business will be discussed another time." Holt's tactful approach puts a tinge of a smile on my face.

Interesting. Is he trying to diffuse the tension and avoid the crash and burn of his whole plan, with pleasantries?

"Who said anything about business? I enjoy a good event, a good party, and I would very much like to bear witness to the fall of the O'Rourke family. Or the attempt at it anyway." I swipe my gaze over the people sitting in the pew to my right, pausing a little longer on Cillian, the man to whom, apparently, I owe a debt now.

"What are you talking about? The O'Rourke's will never fall!" the head of the family rages at me.

"Holt, care to explain your cunning plan to your business partner? Or shall I do it for you, starting with him?" I grab Boseman by the hair and lift the lump of meat enough so he can look in the direction of the family.

"You need to get out of here, right now, Serpent!" Holt seethes. "Take them out! Now!" He waves at three of his men, ordering them in our direction, and they comply.

One by one, they rush around the pews, down the aisle, and toward us.

And one by one, they fall to the ground on the distinctive silencer pop of Carter's gun and the yelps of the women present.

I cock my head at the man holding *my* woman by the arm. "You must have more than that up your sleeve. Right? Or was all your security based solely on Boseman's people? Your daddy really left you high and dry, didn't he?" I say, holding in a laugh. "In hindsight, mine wasn't much better. I do regret not stomping on the back of his head when I made him bite that curb, before I chased him out of town."

His eyes twitch. He wants to look away, look down to the man writhing on the ground before me, but he can't. I have a gift, part of the reason why people fear me so. I can hold them here, dangerously enthralled in my gaze, until I know their bones shake. Until what I have to say is etched in them.

"You're going to go to jail! All of you! I'm calling the police, right now!" O'Rourke's wife shouts, interrupting me with her fear and desperation.

I ignore the woman and continue, my gaze on Holt. "When we last met and you fulfilled your end of our deal, you slipped up. I haven't figured out if it was intentional or by mistake, but it's irrelevant now anyway. In case you're lost, I'm speaking of the comparison you made to your *own pops*."

Holt shifts his weight from one leg to the other, blinking a couple of times more than he usually does in these few seconds.

"With those two words, you gave away your actual level of knowledge regarding Boseman, and your closeness to him. You knew who he was to me all along. This raised some interesting questions, simple ones like *how* and *why*? In the end, it made me realize that your bullshit about it taking months to track him down and give me the info I needed from you, was just that—bullshit. Because you knew all along not only who he was, but where he was, and exactly what he was doing."

I kick Boseman once more when he looks like he might succeed in rising on his feet. He crumbles back onto the ground as I continue, wielding the silence of all the others in the room.

"You tried to play The Sanctum. Play me. Motherfucker, you thought we wouldn't find out he's been your partner long before O'Rourke joined the game?! Overconfidence doesn't suit you at all. You can't just slap some shiny new gloves on, then walk into the ring, and think you can box."

"Jesus, how do you have time to make this stuff up? You have an overactive imagination," Holt says, laughing a proper belly laugh. This seems like a glimpse into the gaslighting behavior Morrigan told me about.

"Imagination? Am I imagining what's happening at this moment in this church? Am I imagining your empty bank accounts that only see action when Boseman transfers his dirty money into them? Or the debt collectors threatening to break your bones? We both know I'm not. Just like I'm not imagining the containers of children we opened in the docks. Or the houses and warehouses you filled with them." I pause for a moment, watching as that information sinks in, and he realizes who's been causing all this mayhem for them.

"It was you!" He points at me, venom dripping out of his mouth, his eyes bulging, and his veins threaten to burst in his temples.

Mrs. O'Rourke pauses with her phone in hand, her gaze flickering between Holt and her husband, the shock vivid on her face. *I guess she didn't know.*

"It was us, yes. And since I did not imagine any of that, I know for a fact that I also didn't imagine the fact that you're the one who brought back Boseman into your lives. Although I'm not yet certain who gifted him this newfound power."

It makes no sense to me. Boseman didn't have power. Yes, he was working his way through some seedy circles, but he's always been a lowlife. Somewhere, between his sudden departure and now, he made some new friends. I'm convinced of that, because there's no way I'm going to believe that he can raise an army or build an empire.

"You lost us tens of millions!" Ryan pulls me from my train of thought.

"Hundreds, I believe," I say with a smirk. "It's your own fault. You could have stuck to guns and drugs, rather than branch out to children."

"Is that it? That was the reason why you decided to ruin everything for us?"

"No. I had something much bigger to gain," I confirm, my gaze flickering to the crimson princess standing next to him.

The one I would do this for all over again.

"But let's not digress. This is your moment, mine will come a little later. You see, Mr. O'Rourke," I continue, turning my attention to the old man, "Holt killed his father. I'm sure you had your suspicions about Jonah's untimely demise, but I can confirm it for you. Our source tells us that he despised his father's control over him, his business style, and the fact that he wasn't allowed to be as involved as he wanted to be. Once he was out of the way, he was ready to take over his mighty empire. Only to discover his daddy not only left him penniless, but in a mountain of questionable debt too."

The wheels seem to be turning in O'Rourke's head. He doesn't attempt to speak over me anymore, and his wife is trying to make sense of it all, pausing her efforts to call the authorities.

"Holt is your fifty-fifty business partner in name only. Your actual financial partner, and the man who's been pulling the reins, is him." I lift Boseman by the head a little higher, enjoying the hiss of pain.

"You're wrong." O'Rourke finally speaks, and I let him this time. "I already know they work together, but his role is very, very small. A source of information only."

"Oh, you poor bastard. Maybe Holt is better at manipulation than I thought he was. I wonder, whose idea was it to traffic more than ammunition and drugs?" I ask him.

His nostrils flare as he snatches the phone out of his wife's hand and turns his attention to Holt.

"You better tell me right now if that's true, boy."

"He's just trying to fuck up the rest of our plans. Just as he's been doing all along. You know very well who Boseman is—my associate. Like you said, a source of information. Everything else has nothing to do with you." Holt is shaking slightly as he tries to control his anger. Or his madness. They both peek through, though.

"Is he, really? Because he seems to know an awful lot about our business, and the way you're sweating right now doesn't give me much fucking confidence." O'Rourke grips the back of the pew in front of him, the wood creaking under his hands. "Are you broke?"

Holt takes a deep breath, and I think he's just about to blow, but he sighs instead. Not defeated but exasperated. He rolls his eyes, and there's a finality in his expression that makes me wonder if we can move to the next part of our day already.

"Goddamnit, Lester. You were supposed to kill him." Holt finally cracks, turning to the man bleeding on the floor. A crazed look grows in his eyes, at the same pace as his rage. "You've been obsessed with the idea of destroying The Serpent. You even put your—our—whole operation in danger for your obsession with him. After he got us our deal with The Ghost, you had the green light. And you fucked it all up."

He's seething, his face red as he looks at the man, waiting for an explanation. A gurgled noise comes, nothing more.

"Fucking answer me, old man!" he shouts, and Boseman frantically shakes his head, blood splattering onto the stone floor.

"He can't," I answer instead. "He lost his talking privileges. Along with his tongue. He's here for dramatic effect, to be honest."

Someone gasps in the *audience*, and I continue, suppressing a grin.

"His mistake, and yours too, was assuming I was the same boy who chased him away ten or so years ago. As you know by now, Mr. O'Rourke," I say, directing my attention to him, "Lester Boseman is my sperm donor. Since he and my mother never married, and he never claimed me as his own until long after the birth certificate was issued, she was free to give me her family name. A fact that, as you can imagine, I'm very thankful for."

I look down at my father, pulling him back by the hair, until he can look into my eyes.

"But I'm done with you now," I tell the man who I should have killed long ago.

I pull him up by the collar, and bring him to his knees, his back to me as he faces the altar and our audience. No one makes a sound, no one protests, or at least I can't hear them. All I hear are his heaving breaths echoing through the space. I grab his head with both hands, and in one harsh move, I twist so far to the right, the blood-curdling crack replaces the echo of his breath. I let go, and he falls to the floor with a loud thump.

Finally.

An eerie, calm silence descends in my mind. Like a door I closed on a chaos I could never truly escape.

I'm definitely not the boy I used to be. That boy knew what had to be done, but he didn't have it in him to do it. Not because death was a stranger to him, but because he thought it was the right thing to do. He still had a heart and didn't see the truth in the darkness. That boy is gone. The only remnants of him are reflected in the forest-green eyes of my Little Eve. I will always have a heart for her. It's hers and hers alone.

"What did you do?!" Holt rages.

He takes two steps forward, dragging Morrigan with him, and gapes at the lifeless body of the man who was helping him build an empire and get his fortune back.

"Patricide is your thing, you should understand why I had to do it. Especially since you already planned for another father to drop at your hands." I step over the corpse, stopping next to the pew before the one Liam O'Rourke sits in, and give him a suggestive, fleeting look.

"None of this concerned you! None of it! I fulfilled my end of the bargain and gave him to you. No matter who Boseman is—was—to you or me, it was done. You had no right to ruin my goddamn wedding, or my business for that matter. None of it concerned you anymore! Now get the fuck out, and clean up your goddamn mess! Your business with Liam and I is done, so you have no reason to be here," Holt shouts at me.

He's crazed, his behavior turning erratic now that he's backed into a corner. It's fairly understandable since he can't see the whole board, and there's a whole game being played on the rest of it.

It's time for the final move.

"Who said I was here for either of you?"

CHAPTER 34
Morrigan

ME. THE SERPENT is here for me!

My heart swells. Not only because he's alive, or that he came for me, but because he finally got his closure. His deadbeat father lies dead on the aisle, and I can't help the smile spreading over my lips, or the shiver running down my spine.

I feel like that teenager from years ago. The one who turned into a puddle and got butterflies in her stomach when Vincent Sinclair swiped a lock of hair from her cheek and tucked it behind her ear, before he even spoke two words to her. I want to run to him, jump into his arms, and claim him in the middle of this goddamn church. He locks his eyes with mine, and I swear he looks as if he wants to do the exact same thing with me.

I'm enjoying this show, though. All these revelations, the confessions, it feels like watching a fucked-up reality show on TV. Only, I'm in the center of the action.

Might as well add some fuel to the fire.

"Tsk, tsk, tsk, how the tables have turned."

"Keep your mouth shut, bitch." Holt jerks me, his grip on my forearm tightening. I ignore him.

"One deadbeat dad down. One to go." I grin at my father, looking him dead in the eyes as everyone's attention turns to me.

"One to go?" he says, scoffing at me. "So what, you're gonna get rid of me now? Are you gonna do it?"

He's laughing out loud, mocking me without even considering that it could be true. I could do it. But he loves putting me down. I'm not touched by his behavior anymore, nor the fact that he's doing it with an audience now.

"You stupid, ignorant man. You're convinced you're the most intelligent person in every room, yet you let yourself be played by the sociopath you're forcing me to marry. You're his damn piggybank! Our whole family is!"

Ryan forces me in front of him, violently attempting to cover my mouth, but I manage to push him away and continue.

"You stooped so fucking low for him. I mean, you were already scum in my eyes, but now you're child trafficking scum!"

With every word, my voice rises to a loud, gravelly note, and I bite Ryan's hand away when he tries to cover my mouth again. He grips my throat instead, holding me tight enough that he can keep me from moving away from him.

I don't miss Vincent's eyes moving between his hand and face with such a vicious look in them, even I'm fucking shaking.

"You ungrateful little bitch!" My father pushes my mother out of the way, trying to get out of the pews and come at me, but stops before he even makes a step.

"I think not." Only three little words my brother speaks as he presses a gun against the back of father's head.

"Cillian? What are you doing, son?" Father's voice shakes ever so slightly.

He doesn't reply right away. He looks between Vincent and I, giving us time to protest, then cocks the gun when neither of us says a thing, and Father flinches against the slight vibration.

"You're asking Morrigan to be grateful to you? For what? Selling her to a man who plans to wipe your entire family off the face of the fucking earth? Starting with you? It feels a tad idiotic. Don't you think?"

Father's nostrils flare at those words. I wonder how it feels to be betrayed by your own daughter, son, and business partner. All in one blessed day. He has no one else to trust. Yes, he has his wife, but she doesn't mean anything to him. She's not a bargaining chip or a business deal.

"You've done some really terrible things, Father," Cillian continues, "and I'm tempted to let Ryan put the beginning of his plan in action, just so it saves me from doing it."

"Cillian!" Mother gasps and covers her mouth. But our father stays silent.

"It's true, you know," I continue and can't help but smile, "the business partner you're selling me to plans to kill you, your son, then mother. In that specific order. This to ensure the whole inheritance goes to me. Once all the assets and businesses are secured, he plans on killing me too, so he can gain everything we ever had, and finally have the fortune his father lost."

"That's enough!" Ryan roars. "Stop getting your nose in business you don't understand. Fucking paranoid woman..."

He wraps his hand tighter around my throat, and I catch Vincent take a short step forward. But I quirk my lip at him. I want to be here next to Ryan, because when the time comes, when the ball drops... the motherfucker is mine.

"Is it all true?" After an awkward pause, my father asks Ryan. "Was that your end goal? To kill me for my money?"

"Isn't it obvious?! They're working with each other, inventing insane scenarios so they can get Morrigan out of this wedding. We made a deal. Your daughter is mine, and our business is ours. It can't be undone. Not now, not when my other business partner is... out." He pauses, and his tone changes. It's maniacal. "Not when I know what I know about you, and your involvements in such... heinous activities."

The motherfucker actually snickers as he speaks those last two words.

"You son of a bitch!" my father snaps. Truly snaps. He rages at Ryan whose hand is now tightening a bit too hard around my throat. "I'm fucking saving you from bankruptcy. I let you into my house, gave you my fucking daughter, and blackmail is my thanks?! You ungrateful, entitled little shit, I'm going to end you!"

"Oh no, Father. *You* don't get to end him. Nor do you get to judge him, not after all you've done." I ignore his comment about *giving me* away.

He stops his rant and looks at me like I have the audacity to talk.

"And you do? Your dear father might not know what you've done, but don't ever forget that I do." Ryan pulls me by the throat and brings me to his right side, turning me so I can look at him as he tries to scare me.

"You dare threaten me too? Don't worry, *darling*, after tonight, none of it will matter," I say with a smirk, not even feeling when he squeezes me a little tighter as he grits his exposed teeth. "I may be a sinner, and I will pay someday. But today is all about you and Father. It's judgement day."

"I've been lenient with you," Ryan says, scoffing at me. "I've given you freedom and allowed you more than I should have. You're taking advantage of my kindness, and I'm losing my goddamn patience. We're getting this pitiful excuse of a wedding done. Now!"

He rolls his eyes at me, the exasperated expression appearing more desperate than he thinks.

"I believe the word you're looking for, Ryan, is deranged. More and more, I'm convinced that you've always been *this*," I say with clear disgust dripping off my tongue, "but it was your father who was unwittingly keeping you in line. Forcing down this side of you."

"You b—"

"There will be no other vows tonight, apart from this one," I interrupt him. "I vow that your soul will leave this church today, independently of your body. Because that lump of meat is going in the graveyard at the back. It's my vow to you too... Father." I slide my gaze to the man who stands between the pews.

My brother is behind him, but the gun is no longer aimed at his head. It's in his hand still, though.

Ryan tries to pull me to him yet again, heaving as he grabs me with the other hand, but he stops the moment Vincent's voice fills the church with menace that could freeze blood right in the veins.

"I wouldn't do that if I was you."

God, that man's voice penetrates so fucking deep beneath my flesh, I'm convinced he's the devil, because he's touching my soul. The husky tone is like the smoothest of caresses against it, teasing and alluring.

Fuck.

I look toward the man I love and still when I see all of The Sanctum, including some of their guys in the back, with guns aimed right at us. Ryan tenses for a moment too, and when he tries to step behind me, the cocking of Vincent's gun echoes gently through the stone-walled church, making him rethink the move.

"I should have sent Severin to jail all those years ago. And you too, Serpent. Then maybe I wouldn't have had to deal with this goddamn charade now!" my father rasps.

Maddox steps right next to Vincent at the sound of his last name. His eyes are dead set on his friend, the questions so vivid in them. Yet he doesn't say a thing.

I'm angry for him. He has no clue why my father looks at Vincent with such certainty. And now was not the right time to find out about this.

My blood rushes through my veins, my pulse thrums somewhere behind my ears, and my fingers and palms itch in that particular way they do when they feel the need to smash someone's face in. Memories flash in the back of my mind, from those moments in time when I was a girl in love. All that anger, the confusion, the regret... the goddamn heartbreak, they all flood me at once. Then there's Vincent. He's gone years of living with this knowledge. Without us.

"There are many sins for which you will pay tonight, Father. Taking Vincent away from me by blackmailing him is one of them."

I can almost feel the frenzy in the strain of my eyes. I'm done with this. I'm done with the fucking chatter. I'm done with my father, with Ryan. I'm done with it all.

"Wait. How the hell does she know that I threatened to send Severin to jail? I know for a fact she wasn't aware then." My father turns to Vincent, and I love the grin that quirks his devious lips.

"Because I told her." He looks at Ryan and that grin has a destructive confidence in it. "When we helped her escape your house, and brought her into mine, where we stayed... for days." He finishes that sentence in an almost lewd tone.

"Yo—you and The Serpent?!" Ryan hisses at me, and I can't help the beautifully wide smile that forms on my face. "That's it! I'm fucking done with this insolence! Father, get us fucking married, right now!"

He tries to turn me toward the priest, who seems to have taken a few steps back from the altar, keeping his distance.

"No!" I hear my brother shout in the next moment.

"Don't worry, Cillian," Vincent speaks, calm and collected. "He can't marry them, not legally anyway."

"What the hell do you mean?" My father takes a step forward past my mother, just as my brother aims his gun back at his head.

Vincent throws a devastating smile at me.

"She's already married," he says, the room falling silent. "To me."

The collective gasps are positively exhilarating. They're not of congratulatory joy. They are pure, delicious shock.

"As of this morning, Vincent, *The Serpent,* Sinclair is my husband." I let that sink in for a moment. I'm a sucker for that dramatic effect. "It was a beautiful ceremony. After all your effort, Father, after all you've done, we still ended up together. You blackmailed him away from me, forced him to leave me to protect our friend, and then"—I laugh— "all these years later, it was you who brought us back together. I guess in a cynical kind of way, we have you to thank for it."

"You whore!" Ryan rasps and raises his hand at me.

I cock my head. "You're sure you want to hit The Serpent's *wife*?" I ask, just as he's about to swing at me.

"Fuck, that sounds good." My husband's husky voice fills me with a bit too much delight.

Ryan rethinks the move but gives me a look that used to infuse me with terror.

It doesn't work now. I don't know if it's because I've been gaining back the confidence I thought I lost, or if it's because Vincent is here with me and I finally have hope. Now I just use Ryan's gaze as kindling on my fire, and I want to make him burn.

"I'm a whore? Says the man who forced me to watch as he fucked another woman." I don't miss the outraged gasp from one of the women in this room. "Spare me the righteous bullshit. This was our backup plan. If something went wrong and he was unable to get to me before you said *I do,* at least on paper it wouldn't be legal. Your whole plan, your only plan, is ruined."

"You're a disgrace to this family!" my mother shouts from the pews, as my father suddenly charges out.

He stops in the middle of the aisle and looks straight at me.

"I knew you were a lost cause. Always so rebellious, always so disrespectful, but I never thought you would do something like this behind mine and your mother's backs. You ruined everything, as you've done since the moment you were born."

My father perches himself on that high horse and it almost makes me laugh. But when he reaches inside his coat and aims his hand right at me, I realize I'm staring at the barrel of a gun. Maybe a second passes, and two consecutive pops split my eardrums, the sound bouncing off the walls of the church, and blood splatters all over me. It adds to the carnage already painting my skin and dress.

The first pop knocked his hand away and the gun fell. The second one was the fatal blow. I catch the moment of disbelief in his gaping eyes. That very moment just before the light goes out, when realization strikes. Then he's gone.

He crumbles onto his knees, then falls face down onto the floor, on a loud crack as his head makes contact with the stone.

A blood-curdling shriek makes me roll my head in discomfort, as my mother launches herself on top of my father's lifeless body. The man who oppressed her for so long is gone, and all she sees is loss, not freedom. *Jesus.* How fucking pathetic.

As her screams still fill me with exasperation, she reaches somewhere under my father's body, and when she pulls her hand out, that gun is yet again aimed right at me. My muscles stiffen.

I expected this from Father, but not from her. Not my own mother.

When another pop makes my body flinch, the bottom of my dress gets splattered with yet another shade of red. Then my mother falls face first over her husband.

Somewhere in the backs of my eyes, I can feel a subtle burn as I watch her body go limp. Did I have hope? Did I think that without my father, she would be a different woman? The one she suppressed during the years she spent under his iron fist... maybe.

Did I think that she would finally... love me?

I did.

She was my mother.

My gaze flickers to my brother, whose gun is no longer aimed at anyone. He looks up at me, and we stare at each other for a few moments. It hurts.

It hurts that it had to come to this. That we were nothing to the people who birthed us. It hurts that nothing could be done to save any of them. That they didn't love us as normal parents do, even though, somewhere deep down, we still had hope.

I realize that I have no idea who shot either of them. Was it my brother? Was it

Vincent?

The idea that my brother was forced to shoot either of his parents fills my stomach with sickness. No matter how horrible these two people were, no matter if they deserved it, killing a parent carries a different weight on your soul.

Do I want to know?

Does it matter?

It does. I will have to find out, because if it was my brother, I refuse to let him carry this weight on his own. I bear the responsibility too, even if I didn't pull the trigger.

I see movement in the corner of my eye, and I realize there is only one man left in this massacre. Slowly turning, I swipe my gaze from my parents' dead bodies to the man I blame for most of this. Then I take a small step toward him.

"What now, *darling*? Your plan is ruined. You have no money, no life, no one who cares. You'll lose your house, your cars, racketeers are on your tail. You're done." I get closer, but this time, he takes the same step back. "Almost done."

"I'm going to make you pay for this." He grabs my arm, his fingers digging hard into my bicep. "You'll pay for destroying my life. You've been the poison in my blood since the first moment I laid eyes o—"

Before he finishes the sentence, I pull out the letter opener, and with a hard swing upwards, I sink it under his chin. In between those muscles that fill the hollow space inside his mandible, where it connects with the throat. His mouth falls open with shock, and I can see the sharp metal inside it. It pierced his tongue, hitting the roof of his mouth, and blood pours out of it with a speed I didn't quite expect.

For those few moments, the horror keeping him from reacting to the pain is utterly satisfying. I was expecting screams, begging, swearing, lunging at me, but for those few moments, it's silent.

Then chaos descends as he hauls me to him, his hand still gripping my upper arm, and I pull the metal out of his mouth before he manages to. When his hand reaches for the letter opener, I knee the bastard in the balls. The moment he instinctively bends over, I grab him by the bow tie, hold him tight, and sink the motherfucking metal straight into his left ear as hard and fast as I can.

The screams that follow are so visceral, I would feel sorry for him if this wasn't exactly what the asshole deserves.

Only, he doesn't fucking die!

My breathing quickens, my whole body taken over by a raging heat that feels a lot like desperation, and I lunge back at the metal. I push his hands away as he tries to pull it out, so I can pry it out myself and shove it in all over again.

He needs to fucking die already!

But an arm wraps around me, pulling me back against a warm body that smells of enticing bergamot, and he holds me so tight. In such comfort. My lungs seem to slow down their effort, smothering whatever fire started inside of me. Then another arm extends on the other side of me. At the end of it a gun is aimed at Ryan, writhing in pain in front of us.

My fidgeting stops.

The end is in sight.

I sigh and sink back into the man who keeps me safe.

"End it." Two words I whisper, and the pop of the silenced gun sounds like sharp metal on metal, sinking through molasses.

Just like that... it's all over.

He falls at our feet, limp. Blood puddles underneath his head, spreading farther and farther.

I hear voices around me. Orders and instructions. There's movement too. Only, I'm stuck here, watching him, unable to pry my eyes away.

Just in case... Just in case he somehow gets up.

Just in case I'm imagining it. Dreaming it. Hallucinating...

Just in case it isn't over.

"Come on, Little Eve. Let's go."

"What if—?"

"It's over. He's gone. They all are. Just as I promised you." Vincent pulls me away gently, and my body complies.

Yet even as I move, my eyes are still stuck on the limp man. Blackness fills my vision, blocking my view of him, then two warm hands grip the sides of my face and guide my head up. The most beautiful, dark and vicious black eyes meet me, carrying more emotion than I thought possible.

"It's all done, Morrigan. All done." He crushes his lips to mine, hard and possessive, holding me there for a moment longer than needed.

When he breaks away, leaving me panting for air, there is something in his eyes I cannot quite place.

Is it relief?

Or is it worry?

CHAPTER 35
Vincent

FOR THE FIRST time in weeks... months... maybe even years, I wake up and the world isn't spinning aimlessly. The dust has settled. The woman who's haunted my dreams for far too long is wrapped tight in my arms.

I brought her to my home last night. Mamaw June was in the house, riddled with worry. Maddox called to tell her I'm alive as soon as he and the guys found me. But she didn't see me for herself until I came home.

She stopped in front of me, red eyes still wet with tears, and couldn't bring herself to come too close. Instead, she took Morrigan by the shoulders, looked her over, and pulled her to her chest. She hugged her so tight, until my Little Eve broke down. They stood there as she finished crying, and I felt completely helpless. In awe too. I'm used to reckless Morrigan. I'm used to her anger, her violence, her outbursts, and her sass. But seeing this vulnerability, after the actual victory showed her in such a different light, it's a different type of strength.

Mamaw June made sure we ate, then in her true fashion, quite literally sent us to shower and to bed before she left. Like we were nothing but children, not two grown-ass adults who pretty much came from battle. Morrigan still had blood on her face, even though we tried to wash it off in the back room of the church, as our clean up team were working their magic on the church. Carter and the guys were handling the leftover people. Luckily, most of them were useless security.

We left everything in order for Father Brown, but nothing can scrub those memories from his mind. Safe to say, I don't think we're ever going to be welcome in church.

As Mamaw was leaving my house, she stopped and turned in the doorway, both pain and relief shining in her eyes. In that moment, I actually felt sorry for the life I pulled her into.

"I can't ask you to stop this, to choose a different path anymore. This is it for you, I understand that, but I want you to know I'm proud of you. I'm sorry you had to do it, but I am proud of you."

I was expecting the first part of that speech, but not the second.

"You did all of this for her. You did it for her life, for love, you did it to save her. But I know you did it for me too. You used that darkness that dominates you for selfless reasons. I hear how people speak of you in this city. They say you're evil. You're not. You never were. You're simply strong enough to make the hard choices."

Then she finally hugged me. She wrapped her arms tight around me, my aching muscles hurting, but I couldn't tell her that. She thought I was dead.

Just as Morrigan did.

When I went upstairs, I found *my wife* standing in front of the shower, still dressed, just looking at it. At that point, I don't think it had hit her yet that it was over. Truly over. That she is free.

She's been living behind a wall for the last year, at least. She's thrown behind it all the shit her family put her through, then her boyfriend. Even in university, she pretended that all was well, and that a different life wasn't actually waiting for her when she returned home. As she stood before that shower, for the first time ever, she was truly free. And I don't think she knew what to do with herself.

So I took over for her.

I undressed her whilst she watched me, her eyes never leaving me. Then I undressed myself as the room was steaming up and pulled her with me under the spray. I washed her body, cleansed the blood off her, and then her beautiful red curls. There was nothing sexual about it; I just needed to care for her. Then I washed myself, and just as I was about to get us out, she wrapped her arms around my waist, stopping me. She pressed her head against my chest, and... held me.

Nothing more. Nothing less. She just held me.

I thought that it was only her who needed this intimacy, this comfort. As she squeezed just a little bit tighter, the memories of the day started flooding me. One by one, they poured in—the attack inside my house, the gunfire, being struck unconscious and taken to Boseman's safe-house. Yes, I got out, but not unscathed. I'm a bit broken and bruised. I'm pretty sure I have a few fractured ribs, but I got out.

Because all I could think of when I was tied to that fucking chair was Morrigan. I didn't wait for all those years just so it could end in a few hours.

Then there's church. My fucking father is finally dead. Her family, too, and Holt. Motherfucking Holt is dead. All of this didn't just end for her. This was the end of a large chapter of my life as well.

This wasn't just her revenge, it was mine too.

So we just held each other under the warm spray of the shower, waiting as it washed away some of our sins, and some of our sorrows. I think it worked. We fell asleep instantly after we got out. Both naked, skin still damp, glistening in the moonlight streaming through the floor-to-ceiling windows.

Now, as I watch the sun streaming in, it really does feel as though it's the first day of the rest of my life. As cliché as it sounds.

And I can't fucking wait to start living it.

Hopefully, with this vixen by my side.

"Mmm..." she moans softly, rubbing her cheek on that soft spot between my chest and shoulder.

When she opens her eyes and finds me looking straight at her, she stops mid inhale.

The seconds that pass feel more like time itself stands still.

Desperation seems to fill her all of a sudden, and she grabs me by the hair, tugging at me to meet her lips. She crushes them harshly to mine, until they ache against my teeth, but I don't stop her. She only releases me for a split second to take a breath, before she dives back in, and kisses me hard and fast, frantically pulling at my hair. My scalp aches, yet I can't help but smile through these urgent kisses.

When she finally releases me, I realize she's smiling.

My Little Eve.

"It's over, isn't it?" Hope shines so fucking bright in her eyes, the grin is more vivid than ever.

"It is. You're free to do, well, everything."

I rub a thumb over her smile, because I forgot how beautiful the genuine one looks on her. When I run my fingers through her red locks, she hums softly and pulls herself to my lips again.

"Can I start by doing you?" she whispers against me.

The laughter that bursts out of me gains me a hard slap on my chest.

"Maybe not, then." She tries to pull away from me, but in one swift move, I yank her whole body on top of mine.

She scrambles to prop herself up and straddle me but tries to push away.

"Oh no, don't you dare. You already offered. You can't take it back," I tease.

"Watch me," she bites back, pursing her lips.

"Indeed, I will, Morrigan. I'm going to watch you... as you take me."

I take her by the throat and pull her to me and shut her up with a deep kiss. I force my tongue into her mouth, battling her own, before she finally melts. Her small hands grip my throat, tightening, taking my breath away as her hips grind onto mine, her pussy getting wetter against my growing erection.

Grabbing one ass cheek, I press her harder against me as I push my hips up and swallow the sharp moan that drips out of her. *Fuck...* she sounds so goddamn beautiful when she's filled with ecstasy.

I slide my hand between her ass cheeks, past her ass, and straight to her tight, wet cunt. When I slip two fingers inside of her, her back arches and she breaks our kiss as she whips her head back on a loud moan. Her lush tits push right into my face, and I don't miss the opportunity to swipe my tongue over her sensitive nipple.

"So goddamn beautiful."

I lick my lips, watching as she rolls her hips against mine like she's on that stage in Metamorphosis. My cock swells between us at the stunning sight. And when her eyes drop down to mine, the flames of fucking Hell itself stare back at me.

"Fuck me, Serpent."

That smile spells menace, and the Morrigan I know, the one she never lets out for long enough, comes to play.

I pull my fingers out of her, grip my cock, and guide the head to the wet center of her. The tip of it is barely in, when in one long stroke, she drops down the length of me. Balls fucking deep.

"Goddamnit!" I release her throat and grab her ass as my own back arches.

I push myself so fucking deep inside of her, I think I saw Hell, Heaven, and goddamn fucking Valhalla, all rolled into one.

She doesn't waste time. I'm holding on for dear life so I don't come right here, right now, and she just fucks me with no care in the world. She rises, then slams down onto me with such harsh movements, I swear I can feel the end of her on the tip of my dick. But she's lost in the pleasure, probably a bit of pain, too, and all I can do is hold on to her hips. She leans back, propping herself on my thighs, and lets her head fall back, her long hair tickling the skin of my legs. Then she fucks me so roughly, the only way I can describe it is her using me to get off.

I'm her goddamn toy right now.

She uses me for her own pleasure, rolling her hips in all and every direction it suits her, and I'm just enjoying the fucking ride.

And what a ride it is.

Her moans fill my bedroom. A sinful song along with the slapping of our skin. Her cunt is so damn tight around me, especially when she does that wicked thing where she squeezes as she lifts herself up, and my tip is the only part of me inside of her.

My fingers bruise her hips, but as my grip tightens, her movements are more vicious. Her moans are louder, her cunt tighter. The pain seems to fuel her.

As her heaving breaths show exhaustion, I reach over and grab a fistful of hair, then pull her to my chest. I grip her ass cheek in one hand, and brutally thrust up into her. She screams against my skin and sinks her teeth into my shoulder.

"Fuck, Little Eve!" I growl, fucking her through the pain in my flesh.

"More," she moans as she drags her tongue over the edge of my ear.

So I give her more. Not fast, but hard, long strokes as I piston into her, pulling her head back. Swiping my tongue over her exposed throat, I release her ass and slide my free hand between us. The moment I reach that sensitive skin that covers her clit and press hard on her, she shakes. Not in an orgasm, but with the realization that she's so terribly close.

And so am I.

My balls draw up. The only thing keeping me from spilling inside of her is the fact that I have to get her there first.

I rub two fingers against her clit in fast, small circles, enjoying the way she squeezes her eyes shut, and bites her lip as she swallows a long cry. When her legs begin to tremble and her pussy spasms around me, I'm at my wit's fucking end.

She falls on top of me, crying out in ecstasy against my chest, and my cum spills into her in strong bursts that seem to be sucked out of me by her weeping pussy.

"I could never tire of this," I whisper because I can't possibly find my voice right now.

"Never..." she pants.

Our loud, heaving breaths work in unison as we come down from this high. Even though I know we need to move at some point to clean ourselves up, I could just lie like this forever. With her soft body on top of mine, skin against skin, our hearts beating too fast, too hard, too loud... *fuck*.

This is it for me, isn't it?

Morrigan

"WHAT NOW, VINCENT?"

We cleaned up, and despite his protests, I covered myself with one of his T-shirts. Now we lie in bed again, yet it feels like a strange limbo.

We're married. I'm married... Only, it's not quite a real marriage, is it?

"Now, I think we should go get some food," he replies, and I narrow my eyes.

"That's not what I meant," I say, shaking my head. "I know it was your idea for us to marry, as a precaution in case something happened and ruined our plan. But... you're free to get out of this arrangement now."

He regards me for a few moments, and his lack of blinking is rather disturbing. I feel like I'm under scrutiny as he quite visibly gathers his thoughts. I could have sworn a tinge of regret flashed over his expression. But I blinked and it was gone. Did I imagine it?

He was forced into this, just as I was. Only I don't—

"We can get an annulment," he interrupts my thoughts. "I told you, Morrigan, you're free now. Free to make your own choices, build your own path outside anyone's control, and I will not stop you."

"Really? You wouldn't stop me or protest if I told you right now that I want an annulment? You wouldn't be angry, or hurt, or upset?" I'm struggling to rein back my disappointment in his response. "It wouldn't affect you in the slightest?"

"I wouldn't stop you. Wouldn't be angry or hurt. And if I would be upset, I definitely wouldn't tell you. Us getting married was about your protection. Just another union forced on yourself because of circumstance. There's too much fire in you, and it was never given enough oxygen to burn at its true potential. I definitely will not be the one to hold you back, if that's what you wish."

He sighs, shaking his head, and the expression in his eyes shifts all at once. A veil falls, uncovering truths, desires, and fears.

"But I can't lie and say I wouldn't be affected. I want you, Morrigan. I want you by my side now and for the rest of time. I want a life with you. You're the Eve to my Serpent. Everything I forced myself not to dream of all those years ago. That's what I want. I want to be the first thing you see in the morning and the last thing you see at night. I want you in every way possible."

He swipes a hand over his face, and yet again, he sighs, then continues.

"I just... I want you so much it fucking hurts. But this is not about what I want, it's about you. I will never be the same as the men we killed for your freedom. No matter how much I would love to tie you to my bed and never ever let you go, I will never do that unless it's your wish."

My lips part in shock. He looks at me like we're two universes that have finally collided after a millennia of trying to find each other. Lovers who had to travel through time until they found the right one where they're supposed to be together.

There isn't just love in those eyes. There is an obsession that eats at him, because he has to subdue it like a caged beast. And I cannot do anything but admire how much he forces that just for me. To give me space, to let me grow and be whoever I need to be. He holds back out of fucking respect, and there's no way I would need anything more than that from the man I love.

"However"—he stops my train of thought yet again—"don't mistake my respect for lack of passion. Because I will do everything in my power to make you mine. I will go through what we've been through all over again if I have to. Because we belong together, and I know you know it. You are meant to be my wife and I your husband, and I will wait for you to discover yourself. But make no mistake, Morrigan, my ring will still end up on your finger. No matter how much you will delay it... you are *mine*, and I am yours."

I cock my head slightly, lifting one eyebrow as I look at the man who was always meant to be mine.

I'm not sure if he caught on to the slight insecurity in his speech, no matter how confident he is. There is a tinge of fear in it that I will reject him, that I will ask for that annulment.

One corner of my lips quirks up, and he narrows his eyes in slight confusion, like a man feeling mocked. I can't help but release the smile I've held back, because he is so fucking right—I am his.

We're restarting our journey somewhere in the middle, but it's exactly where I need to be.

"You are mine, Vincent."

His features morph altogether in that utterly devastating smile.

"Till death do us part?" he asks.

"Till death do us part."

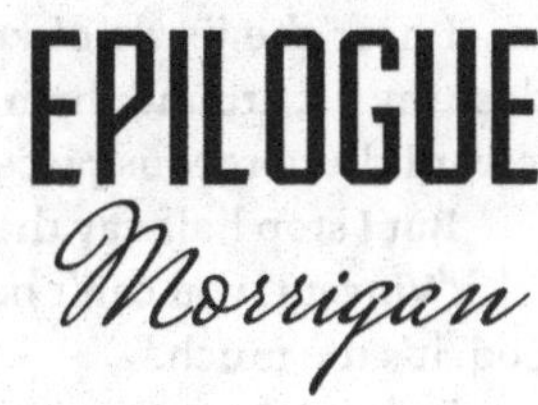

EPILOGUE

Morrigan

Three months later

"KEEP THEM CLOSED."

"Last time you restricted my sight, you and your best f—"

"I'm not about to fuck you in this parking lot, Morrigan," Vincent interrupts, a sweet bite in his tone as he leads me through the back door of Midnight.

"Oh."

"Don't sound so disappointed." I can practically hear the roll of his eyes.

I snicker under my breath as I let him guide me. I love teasing him, and the night when I was sandwiched between him and Maddox is a prime little weapon. He enjoys it, though. It gets him so fucking hard, and the funny thing is, that it's also the tinge of jealousy that gets him there. It's a strange type of masochism, and he enjoys the fuck out of it.

As much as I think Maddox is hot as hell, he and I got it out of our systems. Now, we're just close, and I would kill for that man. As I know he would do for me.

"Okay, you can look now."

I drop my hands and I'm just as confused as I'm faced with... surprise, surprise... the parking lot. Vincent's Mercedes sits a few spaces to my right, and there are a few more ridiculously expensive cars dotted around. Midnight patrons, of course. But the most ridiculous of them all is the one I'm about to drool over, if I don't avert my eyes soon.

"I don't get it." I turn to him, cocking an eyebrow.

"Happy Birthday, wife," he says with a sly grin, pointing to the opposite side of us.

No.

Uh-uh. No way.

It takes me five more seconds to actually turn my head in the direction of his index finger. Mainly because I refuse to believe he's pointing at the dark green beauty my mouth waters for.

But he is.

"Th—the Pontiac?!" I didn't expect my question to come out as a squeal, but there we go.

I whip back around to him, my hair a whirlwind as I stare into the obsidian of his eyes and wait for confirmation. He nods once, and my mouth falls open as I turn back to the vintage beauty.

It sits so fucking proud, surrounded by the modern cars that can't possibly outshine it. A dark jewel-like green, the 1967 Pontiac GTO Judge, shimmers with its pearl paintjob.

I hear the jingle of keys, but I can't peel my eyes off the lines of this car. I just close my fist around them when Vincent presses them into my palm, then walk slowly toward the gorgeous piece of machinery.

But I stop halfway there, jolting out from the mirage.

"Vincent, you can't be serious. You did not just buy me a car for my birthday. My God, it's too much."

"I didn't buy you *a* car. I bought you *the* car."

Of course I know what he means. *The* car. The car I had a poster of in my bedroom when I was a teen. The one I still catch my breath over every time it appears on TV or on very, very rare occasions, in town. It's been my dream car for as long as I can remember.

"I know what you're going to say."

But I say it anyway. "I wanted to buy it for myself. I *needed* to do it."

This car was supposed to be my reward to myself, bought out of the profit I was going to make from Metamorphosis, my baby. My hard fucking work.

I feel slightly robbed by the pride I would have felt.

"Like I said, I know. You've been dealt too many bad hands, Morrigan—your parents, Holt, all their deaths, the fire at the club, your apartment renovation, and then all the unpredictable costs that came with the repairs. I wanted to show you how fucking incredible you are. I wanted to reward you now. You've been putting every penny into the club and your apartment, and I want—scratch that—I need, I need to help."

Even though we are legally married, I've been adamant that we were going to take the time to actually build a relationship. I've been dying to rush into it, my soul has been screaming for it, but I've been shutting it down every step of the way. My mind needs to get up to speed with my heart. It's not just about letting myself process what's happened in the last year, but also to accept that Vincent is really not going anywhere this time around. Adding onto that the damage control from the shit Ryan put me through.

It's been about three months since his fortunate demise, even though it feels like an eternity, and I've been doing well at building myself and our business up. No matter how rich Vincent is, and how many of these Pontiacs he can afford, I wanted to buy it for myself to prove that I can, to have something of my own. Something that doesn't feel like a handout.

Holding on to my apartment, finishing the renovations, and making it into my home, was part of that too. Vincent almost insisted on this particular side of our deal. He couldn't give a shit about money, but having my own space, finding my independence, again, had to happen. It was my right of passage.

I think it was one for him too. He needed the reassurance that without our pact, without living in the same house non-stop, I would still want to be with him. It's confirmation that I wasn't conditioned by circumstance.

I wasn't.

"I'm sorry I robbed you of the satisfaction," he adds when I don't continue. "But this is for me too. You've worked so fucking hard in the last three months. I need to make your life easier."

"I don't know what to say," I finally admit. I'm slowly learning how much Vincent likes to take care of the people he loves, and I can't shoot him down.

"Say thank you, then take me for a ride, Morrigan."

I grin and look down at the keys in my hand.

"That, I can certainly do." I throw my arms around his neck, press my body into him as his hands grip my hips, and crush my lips against his. I make sure to leave him breathless when I break the kiss to speak again. "Thank you, husband."

* * *

I spent about fifteen minutes just admiring everything about this car, before I even turned the engine on. I was edging myself, because I knew the moment it purred to life it would fucking vibrate straight through my pussy.

And Jesus Christ, it did.

The roaring of the engine was not just music to my ears, it sang to my soul, too. We drove for about forty-five minutes before Vincent told me we should head home, to my apartment. I asked why the rush, and he shrugged and said Lulu was waiting for me, since it's my birthday and all.

Only, this man suddenly found the dark green leather of the car door very interesting, and was not looking for a second at me. Something smelled fishy, and it wasn't from the ocean breeze coming through the open windows. But I did as he suggested and headed to the apartment. Although keeping the little smile off my lips was a feat.

"One of these days I'm gonna have to fuck you here."

I stop dead in my tracks at his words, almost missing the step, as we walk up to my apartment.

"Here?" I point at the step. "Why?"

He shakes his head, his eyes fixed on my ass. "You have no clue what you do to me, do you? The way those hips sway, that ass right in my face as you walk up, drives me fucking crazy."

He grinds his teeth and suddenly slaps my right ass cheek, making me yelp and climb up another step.

"So what? You'll just bend me over—"

"On all fours, baby. I will shove my face between your cheeks first, eat your pussy until you fill this stairwell with screams of my name, then I'll fuck you until Loreley will definitely want to move."

The sound that escapes my mouth, heats my cheeks, and makes me feel goddamn sixteen again, because I just fucking giggled. I... Morrigan Sinclair... giggled. It's not even the dirtiest thing this man has ever told me. It's not even that dirty. But the fact that he can barely restrain himself, keep his hands off of me, and be around me without fucking me after watching me... walk up some stairs, is a beautiful thing.

I hope this never stops.

I hope he'll be desperate for me and my body until we grow old and wrinkly.

He slaps my ass again and urges me up the stairs before he really does fuck me here, and by the time I get to my apartment door, my thighs rubbing together have not done me any favors. At all. I really need him to fuck me right now, but I have a feeling whatever he's been avoiding revealing to me about tonight, will stand in my way.

I open the door and the shouting makes me flinch, even as I kind of expected it.

"Surpriiise!"

I touch my chest, mouth gaping as I look over the people gathered in the large central open space of my home, and heat fills me. It has nothing to do with Vincent, but... all these people here. All the ones I love more than my life, the ones I would die for, and the ones I would kill for.

"Happy Birthday!" They carry on the unsynchronized cheers.

"Thank you so much!"

Who would have thought that this would be mine, this family of mismatched people who actually give a shit about me. It's the family I never had, and they give me more love and attention than the one I lost.

Not Cillian, though. I didn't lose him, but the opposite. I feel like I gained a brother even though he was already mine. But now he's ever present. Week by week, our relationship grows and it's shocking how much of a different man he is outside of our father's shadow. Turns out he was planning his exit for quite some time, but he didn't have the resources yet. He was gathering them, and apparently, even The Sanctum was included in his plans. What happened with me just sped things up. I also found out that he did fire one of the shots that killed one of our parents. He didn't say which one, though, and I didn't press.

He's the first one who rushes to me. He wraps his arms around my waist and lifts me to him before he spins us around a few times.

"Happy Birthday, Morri." He gives me a bruising kiss on the cheek.

"Thank you, Cillian." When he puts me down, I pull him to me again, burying my head in his chest.

I missed him. I missed this. Even though we never really had... this. I still missed out on it and having him in my life now is the best fucking thing in the world.

"Morri!" Lulu squeals, pulling me away and into her arms. "Tell me, are you surprised?"

"So surprised."

"You bitch!" She slaps my shoulder. "You knew, didn't you? Did Vincent spill? Or did that brute?" Her eyes flicker somewhere behind me, and I know exactly who she's scowling at.

"None of them did." I laugh. "I just had a feeling."

"You and your feelings..." She sighs, shaking her head.

"If it makes you feel any better, I only suspected it on the car ride here."

"Okay, yeah," she says, nodding as the brightest of smiles spreads over her face. "That does make me feel better."

After a few minutes with her, I spent a healthy amount of time saying hello to every single person here. Katya shocked me by wearing flat shoes for the first time in her life. That woman seems to permanently live in high heels, and she finally looks more casual.

Raven came too, the black-haired, stunning woman who helped get me out of Ryan's villa all those months ago. I would turn lesbian for that woman. She's sharp and cunning, but so sweet, and we've gotten quite close. Lulu adores her too, even though she was slightly jealous at first.

Maddox, of course, pulled me into a tight hug that made Vincent raise an amused eyebrow, and it was even more amusing to watch Lulu's reaction to him. I'm convinced those two are going to kill each other.

Rachel, one of our bartenders from Metamorphosis, is here too. She's been so good at helping us coordinate the renovation of the club after the fire. We hit a few snags, especially since we had to do some work on the structure, which was definitely unexpected. Even though we were paying all our staff during the process, with no expectation to work since there was no work, she insisted. She's fantastic, and sweet as anything. Becoming a friend was so easy with her.

Beau, one of The Sanctum's guys joined us too. We've clicked in Midnight, and it's been entertaining watching the man attempt to court Tina, one of Carter's hackers, who is here too. I say *court* because it's literally what happened. The man, as handsome as he is, hasn't ever had to try too hard with women. But Tina is a bit of a recluse who couldn't care less about men, and she ignored him for a month before the guy started shoving flowers in her face to get her attention. Carter hasn't been too pleased with the distraction one of his key team members has been facing, but I told him to sit back and enjoy the show instead of moaning about it.

Interestingly, he has. He's not watching them now, though. He's been quiet for a while. I mean, he is usually quiet, it's his nature, but he seems a bit lost in thought. It worries me slightly, but Vincent assured me it's all good. There's nothing going on, no major threats, or anything. I've even noticed it on Katya too. They both seem to focus harder on us, although they seem to watch Finn more than anyone.

And that's exactly where Carter's gaze is now—on Finn, who's currently looking at me with his flirty blue eyes.

"I have a confession to make," he says, looking down at me.

"Go on..."

"I didn't like you at first."

I press my hand to my heart, letting my mouth drop. "Oh my! I had no idea!"

He rolls his eyes and flashes me his charming smile. "Alright, alright. Christ, you wouldn't win any acting prizes."

"Fuck you, Finnigan."

"You wish."

"Do not let Vincent hear that. He'll fucking scalp you," I say, laughing, but my lips quickly straighten. "What did you have against me?"

He takes a deep breath before answering. "Everything. I don't think it was you, specifically. Although I was quite skeptical. I didn't like what you represented... to Vincent."

"I'm not taking him away from you, Finnigan." I reach over and rub his arm, soothing.

"No. I think that's when those feeling started going away. When I realized you weren't going to change a thing. Well, obviously, some things have changed."

"They will, of course. For all of you, eventually," I say to him.

"Nah, not for me, darlin'. I'm happy as I am."

"Fucking everything in sight and never getting attached to anyone?" I push.

"I have standards, Morrigan. I don't fuck *everything*."

"You're avoiding the attachment thing, though," I say, cocking an eyebrow.

I know he is. He doesn't need to confirm it. He's a proper playboy; he defines the fucking thing. I'm not judging, but this man deserves so much better. He's selfless, even if he hates admitting it. But I guess not everyone is built for relationships.

"Avoiding would entail a prospect. I simply make sure there is no prospect. Ever."

"Whatever works for you, buddy." I smirk, and he draws me into a hug.

"Happy Birthday, Morrigan."

I smile at him just as my gaze gets pulled to the front door.

"Evie!" I exclaim and wave.

"Who?" Finn asks, his eyes narrowing.

"Evelyn Shaw. You know her, the girl you rescued."

But his eyes widen slightly the moment I finish speaking her full name and he turns slowly in her direction. I open my mouth to ask him why he's looking at her like that but shut it the moment the scowl hits his gaze.

What the fuck?

"What exactly is she doing here?" he asks.

"She's my friend. She also lives in the apartment underneath with her little sister, and works downstairs?" And from the looks of the huge box Maddox is relieving her of, she brought the birthday cake. She bakes a mean fucking cake.

"In Metamorphosis?!" His wild, surfer boy hair whips around him as he turns to me.

"No. In the café. Finn, what—"

"What do you mean she lives here?! Since when?"

"About a month ago. We took her in, to help her out while she's saving some money." I'm so confused. "How do you not know this?"

Granted, after the rescue operation, it wasn't his job to keep track of everyone. They have people who kept on eye on all the children. But I'm surprised Vincent didn't tell him. Or Maddox, who actually helped her move in.

"I guess... I tuned out." The scowl goes back on his face as Evelyn walks in our direction.

She's a natural blonde, with smooth, wheat-colored hair that grazes her waist, slightly taller than me, and with a thin frame that reminds me of a ballerina. Her big, hazel eyes sparkle against her medium-toned olive skin. She and Maddox could easily look like siblings with their almost matching skin tone. Her stride is confident, her hugely oversized cardigan, draped over faux leather leggings and band T-shirt, adding onto her attitude. She looks like a delicate rocker chick, dressed in all-black, with a clear edge and she wears it all so fucking well.

"Morrigan! Happy Birthday! Sorry, I'm late, I was adding the finishing touches." She pulls me into a quick hug.

"We barely just started. Thank you so much for coming. You remember Finnigan Hennessey?" I grab his forearm to pull him a little closer, but he doesn't budge.

"Hi." She doesn't even turn her head to him, just shoots him a quick, barely polite glance.

"Hello." He seems to do the bloody same, then turns on his heel and leaves.

What the hell is happening here? What am I missing?

"Are you guys okay?" I ask.

"I barely know him."

That doesn't answer my question.

"How's your birthday party going? Did they actually manage to surprise you?" She changes the subject quickly.

"No," I say, laughing. "But to be fair, I didn't catch on to something until I was on the way here. So that's definitely a success."

"I told Loreley this would happen." She smiles at me, her gaze drifting over everyone drinking and laughing. "You have a good bunch here, you know."

"I love Vincent to the ends of the Earth, but having this... you guys around me, is so fucking precious."

Evie nods but doesn't add onto it. There's a slight sadness in her eyes.

"Where's Maya?" I ask.

"Downstairs, with Mamaw June. She offered to babysit so I could come here."

"Oh, yes, of course. She mentioned something about being busy tonight and that's why she insisted on seeing us in the morning, to give me my present." I can't help but laugh to myself, as the puzzle pieces fall into place. "She's a good egg."

"She reminds me of my mum." Evelyn's gaze turns back to me, and there's both sadness and a bit of hope in there. "Maya has fallen in love with her. I swear these days she wants to spend more time with her than me."

"It's not the worst thing in the world, you know. You've given a lot of yourself away. This is an opportunity to take it back, live a little. Don't get me wrong, the responsibility is still there, but... you're not alone anymore."

She turned eighteen two months ago, but her adulthood started long before. She never got to be a proper teen, not even a big sister. She was basically a mother in the shittiest of situations.

"Easier said than done, right?"

I nod, but Maddox pulls my attention.

"Is he asking for me, or you?"

"Me." Evelyn waves to him. "Probably something to do with the cake." See you in a bit.

She leaves, and I look around the room, catching sight of Finn, who follows her with his gaze, but pulls away quickly, shaking his head to himself. I pop my drink down and turn, heading to the corridor leading to my bedroom. I don't bother turning on the lights as I walk straight through and to my bathroom. I use the toilet, wash my hands, and I'm barely out the door and into the bedroom, when the scent of bergamot and cedar fills my senses.

I don't have time to react before my hands are trapped behind my back and I'm slammed forward, against the wall, Vincent's warm hand over my mouth.

"You've turned me into a weak man, Morrigan *Sinclair*." He pronounces our last name like it holds much more power now that we share it. "I cannot stand being in a room with you and not touching you. Your absence burns my fucking skin," he seethes into my left ear, but only his breath touches my skin.

I mumble into his hand, trying to bite back at him, but he doesn't even attempt to remove it.

"Then there's this ass, your fucking legs, and your filthy mouth. Jesus fuck, woman, all I want to do nowadays is sink my cock into every hole you have for me, or slide it between your tits, mark your body as mine. Every second. Of every. Fucking. Day."

I moan against his palm, but this time, there are no words trying to breach the barrier. My ass responds, though, pushing back into him, and feeling his thick cock right away.

"You want it?" he asks.

I shake my head, and on a hitched breath, he bites down on my earlobe. It sends shock waves of pain straight into my core and the whimper that comes out in response, was spoken by my body, not me.

"Too. Fucking. Bad."

When his hand releases my wrists, he rushes straight to the button and zipper of my jeans, pulling at them with harsh tugs. Yet, he's got them open and the waistband pushed down against my thighs in mere seconds.

His fingers rush to my core from behind, and of course, I'm still fucking wet since we climbed those damn stairs. He plunges inside of me harshly, and I moan with need into his palm. I know it's gonna tip him over the edge before the sound finished leaving my throat.

I'm right.

He pulls me against his body, his hands staying in place, and bends me over the dresser. Three pumps of his fingers later, I hear his zipper through the cloud of pleasure swirling through my mind, and the tip of his cock prods my entrance. I smile against his palm, but it falters too goddamn quick when I realize the bedroom door is open. Anyone could come by at any second.

That thought has only a second to linger in my brain before his cock thrusts into me with such force, the dresser moves a little, and I have to bite down a cry.

His moves are torturous inside of me. His cock twitches, and instead of fucking me harshly, Vincent grinds his hips against my ass, rubbing his cock inside of me, against all the nerves that drive me insane.

I can't even protest, with his hand still covering my mouth. I don't even dare, considering the door he fucking left open. Anyone could hear us. And the motherfucker chooses this moment to pull out and slam into me. Thank fuck for his palm covering my cry. I tell myself it's enough to keep it from leaving this room. But I'm not so sure.

When my knees begin to shake from his cock's delicious assault on my weeping core, I'm biting down on my lip to keep the moans in.

"What would you do, Little Eve?" His husky voice sends more shivers down to my core. Like I needed any more. "What would you do if someone showed up in that doorway right now?"

A whimper I didn't manage to swallow slips out.

"Would you make me stop?" he asks.

Thrust.

"Would you push me away?"

Thrust.

"Would you look them in the eyes as you come all over my fucking cock?"

Thrust.

I'm off. Before I even register what's happened, my core spasms around his length, and my knees give out. I'm digging my fingers into the wood of the dresser, holding on for dear life as my body shakes. I'm not falling. I'm completely pinned in place as Vincent's thrusts quicken. With one rough buck of his hips, the lowest of growls rumbles in his throat, and he spills inside of me. His cock jerks repeatedly, and it teases my easing orgasm, pushing it just a little bit further.

When he finally releases my mouth, I'm panting like I ran a damn marathon.

"You're such a dirty little thing, aren't you?" he whispers softly, running his hand over my back as I come down from the ecstasy.

"I wasn't the one putting those filthy scenarios in my head, dear sir."

"It's you who puts them there. It's not fair not to share them."

Well, fuck.

He helps me up and guides me to the bathroom. He proceeds to clean me up, like he does almost every single time we fuck, and I'm sinking in this ritual of ours more and more. My eyes are closed as I lean into his soothing touch, enjoying our intimacy.

When he's done, he pulls my jeans up properly, and fastens them, before running a hand through my loose curls, guiding my gaze into his.

"Will I ever tire, Morrigan?"

"Tire of...?"

"Your evening primrose scent. The softness of your skin. Your green gaze into mine. The tight grip of your pussy and the way you unravel around me. Or the feel of you against me. All of you. Every second of every fucking day. And the nights when you seek me in your sleep, even if you're just hugging one arm, you seek me. When you don't... I do."

He takes a deep breath in, the intensity in his black eyes adding onto the sting in mine.

"Will I ever tire?" he asks again.

"You already know the answer."

He smirks, pressing a soft kiss to my lips.

"I'll always crave more," he admits.

"It's only fair, Mr. Sinclair. We're equals, after all."

"Indeed, we are, Mrs. Sinclair. Indeed, we are."

BONUS SCENE

Alternate POV Chapter 21

Vincent

WALKING QUIETLY THROUGH the shadows isn't how I wanted to come into Holt's house. I wanted violent chaos. Guns blazing. Bodies falling. But the circumstance demands discretion, and for Morrigan, I'll be obedient.

I *must* get her back.

Three days. That's how long Holt has kept her captive here.

Three days of mind-bending fear and uncertainty clawing at me.

Three fucking days of unfathomable rage.

All I could do is trust that my wild, beautiful Morrigan would stand her ground. She may not know it yet, but she is mine. She always has been. I know she's strong. Formidable, even. But when someone claws beneath the surface, strips away defenses, your self-esteem, and shreds the soul, even the strongest of people become meek. Morrigan has learned too well how to wear a brave face.

I fucking hate that she had to.

Logically, I know her choices were her own. She had control over her life. But when it comes to her, logic doesn't prevail—I'm responsible. It began the moment I had to leave her. If I'd been stronger then, if The Sanctum had been what it is now, I could've eliminated the man standing in our way. Her slow demise would've never happened.

And she would have hated you for it.

Well, there's that.

Ahead of me, Maddox moves with practiced stealth, his heavy footfalls tempered as he leads the way through the dark corridor toward the main foyer of Holt's house. We slipped in through a back door, taking out one guard on the way. Two more patrol inside, and one just disappeared down the opposite hallway. At best, we have a minute before he returns.

Maddox signals it's time to bolt, and we dart through the corridor, slipping into the shadows beneath the grand staircase. The sound of a door shutting nearby sends a jolt through me. A lock clicks. My grip tightens on the gun in my hand. If the floor plans are accurate, the sound came from either the utility room or the bathroom. My bet's on the latter. That buys us time.

"Should we wait for him to come out, or head upstairs now?" Maddox whispers.

I barely have time to consider before he gestures sharply, calling for silence. Above us, footsteps come carefully down the stairs.

Could it be her?

My pulse hammers as I back up, sinking deeper into the shadows, fists clenching and unclenching with bitter anticipation. Maddox moves to the edge of the staircase, his gaze locked upward, while I linger in the shadows, waiting. Wanting. Hoping.

Then the faint click of a doorknob nearby jolts me. Maddox pounces forward, a split moment before he returns to the shadows. But he's not alone.

Morrigan—*my* Morrigan is pressed against him, immobilized. One of his arms pins both of hers to her sides while his hand clamps over her mouth. He holds there, on the opposite side from me, as she struggles, her body twisting against his. Maddox holds firm, lowering them both deeper into the shadows.

Lightning flashes through the windows, bathing the space in electric blue, and the thunder that rattles the windows just moments later, matches Morrigan's wild energy.

Then she stills.

Maddox has pressed her harder against himself. He slides his large hand to her jaw, silencing her further. He dips down, brushing his lips against the tip of her ear, more gentleness in the gesture than I thought him capable.

Heat rises in my chest as I watch. Lightning throws a bright slither over them—a flicker of recognition softens her fierce resistance. Maddox drops his hand like he feels her soften. Her lips part, body relaxing as she reaches for him, wrapping her delicate hands around his flexed forearm that holds her tight against him.

How does she know it's him? His scent? His touch?

Tension ripples through my back, muscles coiling as I watch them. Something must have happened to call for this recognition.

She wants him. Maddox wants her, too. But he would have never crossed that invisible line drawn in brotherhood and deep trust. Not when he's always known where my heart draws blood from. Where it pumps. And where it will always beat.

Not in my chest, but in hers.

Always hers.

Because it hasn't belonged to me in so many years.

My heart only beats for her.

But there's no denying their attraction. Nor the tearing possession it rises within me. Jealousy flares, raw and primal, but not born of malice. It's laced with something deeper.

Ardor.

A toe-curling pulse at the tip of my cock thrums with one dark, beautifully-jarring thought—I have full and utter control over their desires for each other. With my permission, they could explore their attraction.

Even if Morrigan is more than entitled to throw a massive 'fuck you' in my face and do what she wants with him, I know she wouldn't. She cares enough not to force him to ruin mine and his friendship. Because she knows it's more than that. No matter the

DNA, he and I are brothers. She would never jeopardize that. So, I do—I control their desires. Their outcome.

My length throbs and hardens, urging me further on this enticing train of thought. An image sears into my mind—Morrigan's naked body arching. Wet and wanting. Maddox watching as I fuck her sweet cunt. Running his hand down her body as she writhes between us. Her whimpers as we both press into her, together, riding on waves of unfathomable pleasure.

Steps echo nearby, pulling me from the exquisite vision. Morrigan tenses, trying to free herself as another guard passes. Maddox's hold tightens, keeping her safe. And I want to be there too, part of their intimate moment. Sharing their rushing pulse as they allow themselves this indulging, innocent touch.

I step out of the shadows, letting the light catch me. A grin tugs at my lips as Morrigan freezes, her body rigid as her gaze locks on mine. I can feel Maddox's gaze trained on me as he calms her nerves when I stop barely two paces away. On a sharp inhale, her eyes turn to shining stars in the comforting darkness, flashes of lightning bathing her in a decadent glow as recognition washes over her. So, I step deeper into their space, until I'm close enough for the intoxicating scent that is utterly her, to invade my senses.

Morrigan's hand shoots out, gripping my lapel as though anchoring herself.

I don't let her pull me closer. Not yet. I savor this moment, studying her, reading every flicker of emotion across her face. Take in her reactions in this intense situation. Under the roof of the man who forced her into an undesirable engagement, then kidnapped her. While his guards patrol around us. Standing between the man who holds an ounce of her wanton desire, and the one who is her forever.

Maddox's hand grazes down her shoulder, brushing over her waist, before he rests it on her hip. Her breath catches, and not because of the thunder rattling the windows. Or why she holds it in as if the only way out would be through a needy moan that could give our position away. I want to feel it. Feel how it coils beneath her flesh.

I reach out, pressing my palm to the delicate curve of the base of her throat. Her pulse flutters beneath my touch, wild and erratic.

The guard returns in the foyer, pacing through without leaving, and Morrigan's heartbeats speed up. I drag my hand up her throat, tightening my fingers around the delicate shape of it, indulging in the marvelous speed of her pulse. She's thriving in this slither of madness, reveling in my possessive touch as she sinks backward, head falling against Maddox's shoulder. But her gaze stays fixed on me.

Gods, she's a thing of fucking beauty. Born of fire and reckless abandon. So perfectly mine.

Releasing her throat, I reach for the softness of her cheek, and as I brush the tip of my thumb over her plump lips, feeling them part beneath my touch, she finally exhales. Slow and heavy. A tremble gently shaking her flesh, chest rising and falling on strained breaths.

Lightning flashes. The guard's steps close in. Thunder roars over the music still filtering through from upstairs. Maddox tightens his hold around her, gaze falling onto her. Goosebumps bloom beneath my touch. On a whisper of a moan her eyes drift up, into his, and I dip my thumb between her soft lips, pressing deeper into her warmth.

Her body shifts nervously, and I press mine into hers, pinning her between my brother and me.

I want to capture those sultry lips between mine, bite and suck until I can imprint her taste in my memory for the rest of my days. I want to fuck her sweet, tight cunt right here, in her *betrothed's* house, until she's addicted to the feel of my cock. I want to make her scream. Moan and cry. And come so fucking hard, the gods above would know her pleasure.

Somewhere in the middle of that fantasy I've dipped down, enough for her breath to warm my lips, reveling in the torturing intimacy of this stolen moment. Steps around us intensify. I slide my thumb from between her lips as she lets out a wanton breath, and I tighten my grip around the gun. I press her harder into Maddox, my cock pulsing against her belly.

Movement darkens the corner of my vision. I aim my gun before my eyes drift to the target, and on a muffled pop, the guard crumbles.

I catch his body before it hits the floor, dragging him into the shadows just as another emerges. He doesn't even have time to call out before my bullet lodges firmly inside his skull. I catch him too, lowering him to the ground to avoid our *gracious host* hearing us.

Morrigan's gaze finds me in the darkness. The storm rages outside, lightning illuminating her face. Thunder roars as the tension between us crackles like a live wire.

But I force myself to look away. Not because I want to. Because I have to.

But even as I do that, my gaze meets Morrigan's. As lightning flashes through the high windows, the intensity between us sizzles through the air. Tension roars like the thunder that follows, and I have to force myself to turn and head for the exit. Because I certainly don't want to break this moment willingly.

* * *

"Is she okay?" Maddox asks as he climbs onto the passenger seat of the car. He insisted on going back into Holt's house after Morrigan shared what she learned about the documents Holt apparently holds on her and her family.

"I think so," I look down at Morrigan's sleeping form curled up on the back seat, head resting peacefully in my lap, "I'm not sure how much she slept while in that house. She was running on adrenaline, but it took only a few minutes, and she crashed."

"That's not all it took," Carter mutters in a low, suggestive tone from the driver's seat.

His usually empty gaze holds a tinge of brazen suggestiveness. I cock an eyebrow, challenging him as I look at this reflection in the rearview mirror.

Maddox stares between us, but shakes his head, rolling his eyes, "I got these." He changes the subject, dumping a stack of papers on the center console.

Carter itches to get his hands on them and investigate further. I can see it in the way his lips tense, and beneath his cheeks he seems to hollow further. But he has to drive us out of here. We know that these documents are likely printouts of digital files, but before he or his team hack into Holt's system, this will give us the opportunity to see what the asshole holds on the O'Rourke's. Maybe a sign as to why as well.

I want to reach out and look too, but as Carter speeds away from the property, driving in darkness before he hits the main road and turns on the headlights, I'm more focused on holding onto Morrigan. She grabs my thigh as the car swerves through the streets of Queenscove, and shifts on the seat, tugging herself closer and closer to me. Crawling higher onto my lap.

Even in her sleep she seeks comfort. *She seeks me.*

Behind my ribs, that blood-pumping muscle swells, giving me a hope I haven't allowed myself to feel all these goddamn years living without her.

Carter drives us fast through the city. It doesn't take long for him to reach the edge of it, then the road through the forest that leads to my house, and eventually the front of my house where he parks.

"You got her?" Maddox asks as he passes her to me after he picks her passed out body from the backseat.

"Yeah."

"Call tomorrow. The surveillance team is on their way to Holt's house, and all the rest are on high alert in case of retaliation." Carter says.

"Tell Finnigan to keep an eye on Raven. We need to make sure she's okay and gets out safely."

"He knows."

I know he knows, but sometimes our escorts take risks that could lead to painful, deadly consequences, and we have to do everything in our power to protect them. It was that worry talking, not me.

The guys leave after I enter the house, and cradled in my arms, Morrigan nestles her head deeper into the crook of my neck.

Jesus, she's completely out. She barely even stirred when Maddox lifted her out of the car. I don't need further confirmation she didn't get a wink of sleep the nights she spent at Holt's. My blood boils thinking of how stressed out and unsafe she must have felt. Constantly on alert in case he came. In case he—*no!* She already confirmed he didn't touch her. But I bet he fucking tried. I bet he fucking wanted to. And that thought alone is enough for me to launch a murderous campaign against the asshole.

I lay Morrigan in my bed, fire-red hair like sunburst against my pillow, and stand by her. Watching her sink into the mattress, settling into the comfort of it all, before she takes one deep breath in. A soft moan follows, stirring too many feelings inside me.

She likes it here. In my bed. In my safe space. Surrounded by my scent.

There's something inherently primal about this and I know for a fact... It's where Morrigan belongs.

With me.

Until one of us draws our last breath.

Even after.

"Sleep tight, little Eve. This is only our beginning."

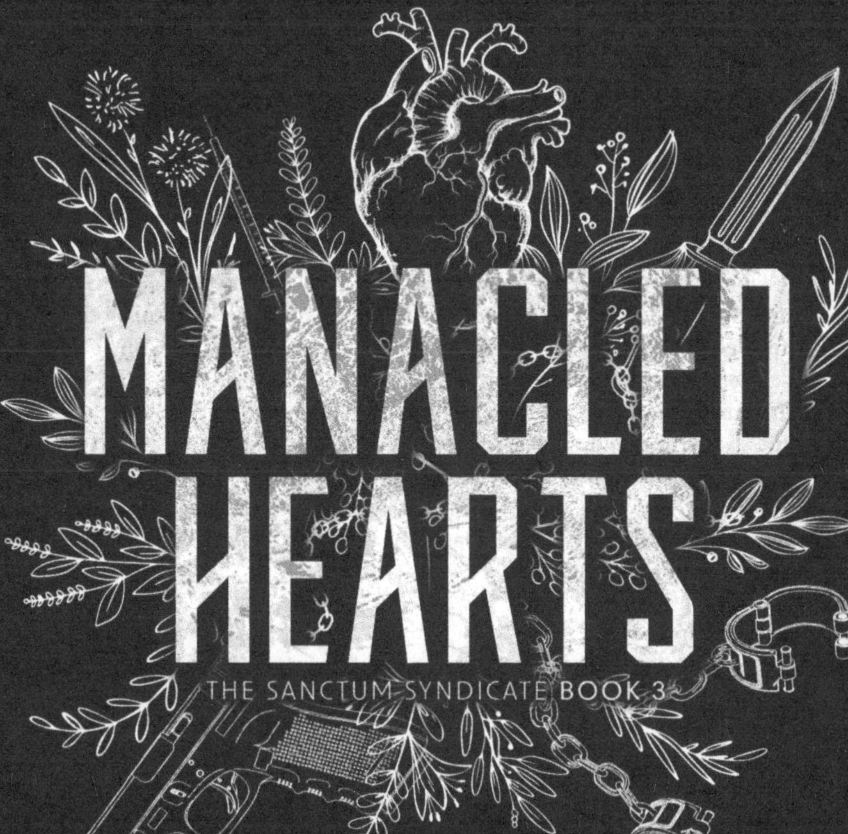

MANACLED HEARTS

THE SANCTUM SYNDICATE BOOK 3

LILITH ROMAN

BLURB

I found salvation in his underworld.
But he looks at me like I'm his damnation.
Alone and homeless after my family was torn apart, my only goal was to protect my little sister. I failed. Being kidnapped and trafficked across the country shattered the life I was still piecing back together.

The Sanctum saved us. Provided refuge. A temporary haven within their criminal empire. While our enemies still lurk, plotting and hunting, the jagged scars I gained to protect Maya cannot heal.

Still, The Sanctum's resident playboy treats me with dismay. Finnigan Hennessey hides behind possessive, infuriating arrogance, yet his broken soul calls out to mine. He's determined to deny the tempting, forbidden heat between us, but I don't care about the eleven years separating us.

Finn is everything I should hate. After all, his world destroyed mine. But not all villains are the same shade, and in my quest for revenge, my hidden colors are surfacing.

I'm not the innocent victim he thinks I am, and he's not the heartless jerk I took him to be.

Will he forever deny our magnetic attraction? Or will he break my soul long before our enemies even get the chance?

CONTENT WARNING

This is a work of fiction and should be taken as such. This is a work of fiction and should be taken as such. It contains dark themes and sensitive content including graphic violence, knife and gun violence, sexual assault, rape, memories of forced drug use, memory loss, PTSD, murder, and sex trafficking of both adults and children. There is no cheating and it has a HEA. If you are easily offended or triggered by any of this content, please do not read this book. Your mental health matters.

PLAYLIST

Dirge - Death in Vegas
Your Hands - GRAE
Daylight - David Kushner
Chokehold - Sleep Token
Alkaline - Sleep Token
Burning Sea - Daniel Spaleniak, Tomasz Mrénca
Iron Sky - Paolo Nutini
Left Me for Dead - Rob Dougan
Daddy - Ramsey
Running Up That Hill - Placebo
For You — HIM
Vermilion, Pt.2 - Slipknot
Lullaby - Low
In Bad Dreams - Crippled Black Phoenix
Shadows of My Name - Emma Ruth Rundle
Marked for Death - Emma Ruth Rundle
This Will Make You Love Again - IAMX
Dead Flowers for Her - Skywatchers
Shadows & Light - Saudade, Chelsea Wolfe, Chino Moreno
Depraved - Mammals
Cities - Toby May, Two Feet
The Kill - Thirty Seconds to Mars
Be My Man - Nostalghia
Unfurl - Katatonia
It Will All Make Sense in the Morning - Halou
Bitches Brew - † † † (Crosses)
16 Psyche - Chelsea Wolfe
The Space in Between - How To Destroy Angels
Secrets - Omido, Ordell, Rick Jansen
Phantom - Kaphy, BLVKES
Good Looking - Suki Waterhouse
Like U - Rosenfeld
Looking for the Summer - Chris Rea

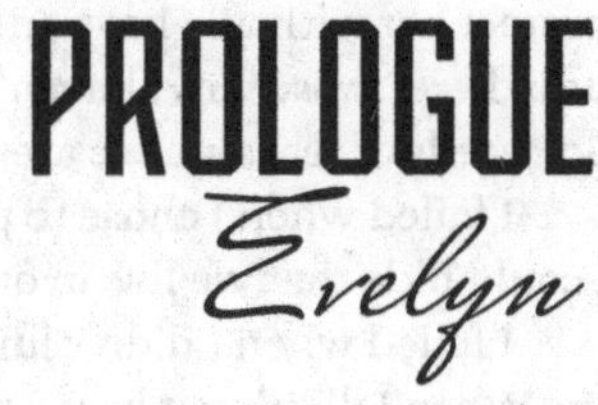

PROLOGUE
Evelyn

One month earlier

THE SCREECH OF the container door plays on a disturbing loop in my head. Hours must have passed since the last time I heard it, closing with a shattering bang that held a finality to it. The loop is never-ending, an excruciating background noise to the whimpers and cries currently reverberating against these walls.

It took me a while, but I finally understood why it plagues me so. My subconscious is demanding retribution for my failure to save Maya from the bastards who took us. Who locked us in this godforsaken place, along with so many others like her.

I had one job—protect my little sister.

I failed.

Miserably.

As if becoming homeless, unexpected orphans, and evading CPS wasn't enough, now we're kidnapped. Stuck in this hot, metal box with thirty other children, suffocating in the smell of urine and God knows what else.

Only, I'm the odd one out. I'm not a child.

I'm just shy of turning eighteen, still a minor in the eyes of some laws, but my childhood ended with our mom's sudden death. Overnight, I became my sister's guardian, and without siblings, grandparents or other family, we had no one else in the world on our side. Almost two years have passed since she became my whole life.

Sometimes it's like I'm trapped in a Lemony Snicket novel. Event after unfortunate event seems to have taken a horrible hold of us, and the passing of years did nothing to improve our situation.

It didn't start with Mom, though.

In reality, it all started with the events that took Dad from us.

The container jolts. Terrified cries erupt from the children, serving as a reminder that the unlucky events haven't ceased.

"Hold on to each other. It's all going to be over soon." I try to soothe them with empty promises.

Still, the cries never stop. Like the little light that used to shine in their souls, they quiet down to fear-stricken murmurs.

Tightening my hold around my sister, I whisper words of reassurance to her. She wasn't one of the kids who screamed. Maybe that's why I'm holding her harder. I'm hoping her silence stems from my comfort, but the alternative plays in my mind. Is she in some sort of catatonic state from the trauma?

I yearn for a sliver of light in here. At least then she could look into my eyes with her pretty green ones and see the promises in them. I will never fail her again. I will protect her with all I have and make sure she will be safe. Since they took us and locked us in here, those vows haven't touched my lips. I'm afraid I won't be able to keep them. So, words of reassurance are all I can provide. I'm a coward. A failure.

I failed when I chose to park on the dark side too far away from the school—all so I could hide that we live in our car.

I failed when I didn't immediately notice the men following us, after I picked her up. When I didn't get her to the car in time.

I failed when they yanked me by my hair, struck me in the ribs, then pushed me away from her. When she screamed my name with such terror in her sweet little voice, it clawed into my soul. I jumped on the man who grabbed her, erratically punching him in the face, aiming at his eyes until he finally dropped Maya.

Then I failed to hold on to her. They ripped her out of my weak arms, punching me hard enough in the gut that I almost threw up before my head even hit the ground. But I got up and ran after them like the pain didn't exist, following my sister's muffled cries deeper into the darkness of the alley. I ran even as the worn soles of my shoes gave out and the rocks gouged my socked feet.

When I saw my sister being shoved in the back of the black van, I pushed my way in without thinking. I couldn't get her out. Instead, the men spit their curses at my hysterics and decided it was safer to take me, too.

Since then, there have been no opportunities to attempt an escape, but I refuse to accept that none will come. There is no other choice. No more room for failure.

With guilt fogging my mind, my exhaustion takes me before I can stop it, and I drift into a restless sleep.

I drift in and out, frequently woken up by the metal screeching or the kids. Even when I manage some sleep, I'm woken up by the children. Some require calming, the really young ones need help to relieve themselves, and I need to make sure they all eat the cheap bread that's provided. Before closing the doors, the bastards who took us threw in sealed bags of sandwich bread and bottles of water. I tested them on myself before I let any of the kids touch them, and I was fine.

I'm not sure how much time has passed since we've been here. The absence of light creates deceit, but I think at least two days have gone by. Although, my measuring system may be flawed. I can't truly trust my stomach since it's used to such little food, but I've been keeping track of Maya's hunger. So far, she's asked for food, albeit reluctantly, six times. I can't fully trust this method. It's not like we've been sleeping well. We drift in and out, caught in a daze that sometimes gets interrupted by the movements of the container.

I'm convinced we're on water, but I've been praying to all the gods I know that we're not leaving the country. It covers a vast continent, so maybe we're going to a different side of it. The alternative is dire. Even *when* we escape, it will add many more challenges. Requesting asylum with a child who isn't in my custody will be a sure way of losing Maya to the system. But at least she'll be out of here.

More time passes by, more meals for Maya, more screams, more cries, more begging for mamas and papas, more drifting in and out of sleep.

Until the jolts come.

I urge the kids to huddle together and protect each other while I keep Maya curled under my arm and the other kids hold on to us. My sister is the happiest, most easygoing and trusting kid, and the fact that she's been so quiet is unbearable. I've talked to her and soothed her the best I could, but even now, as the container jolts in all directions, she barely whimpers.

The exhaustion is almost debilitating, but when the container stops moving and thrashing us around, adrenaline kicks in, pumping new energy back into me. Not the good kind of energy. No, the kind of jittery energy that makes me shake with the fearful anticipation of what's coming next. I hope that when the time comes, I'll find the physical strength to do what I need to protect her.

Muffled words sound outside these metal walls, and the cries of the kids grow.

"Shh..." I attempt to calm them. Only some of them listen.

The side of the container rattles, and my sister finally makes a sound, yelping as her small body flinches.

When the noises intensify, I squeeze her tighter. "I'll keep you safe, Maya."

The metal box jolts again, and it feels like we're being lifted. Controlling my fear is proving so much harder than I thought it would be. When my sister groans, I realize I've been squeezing her a bit too tight.

My thoughts stray to this unbearable helplessness, to our dad, and to the fact that no one will search for us. Maybe Maya's school will contact the police when they discover that the address they have for her is fake. That could be our shot at having someone to look for us, but the people who took us are highly professional, so I doubt there's even the slightest trail.

We're screwed.

I don't realize the container has stopped moving until the door cracks open, and the screeching pierces through my eardrums. All at once the kids throw themselves back against the walls.

Squeezing Maya to me, I brace myself for the worst.

* * *

From the moment those doors opened to what seems like a vast warehouse, everything has been happening so fast, and I'm struggling to wrap my mind around things. Initially, I thought we reached our destination, but the shock and disbelief in the expressions of the men looking back at us made it clear these were not the same ones who took us. Those types of emotions cannot be faked, not by men who look as hard as them.

Slowly, pity bled through their gazes.

I counted eight people walking around, running their hands nervously through their hair, talking heatedly. Though a few of them seemed to only stand silent and take orders. Some were dressed for combat—boots, cargo pants, casual T-shirts—but others gave me grave vibes in their black, tailored suits. One in particular seemed to be in charge, and the man stood out in his three-piece suit, ordering the others around to do things for us.

They gave us food, more water, and asked the kids if they were hurt.

But they didn't let us out.

Instead, they left the doors cracked open so we could get some air and light.

I tried to peek around for an escape route, but I'm too deep into this space. Even so, running while herding thirty kids will be impossible. All I could do was sit, wait, and listen.

Now, something is changing.

More footsteps approach, and with them, another spike of adrenaline surges through my veins. Though it prickles up my spine more like fear.

"This is one thing I won't work with, and I'm convinced you won't agree with it either."

The container opens fully again, and I grab onto my sister, trying to peek from the darkness—four new men stand in front of us. Their features are grim, but there's something about the look in their eyes that doesn't just remind me of anger. It's something more.

Darker.

My gaze flickers to the wavy-haired blonde one who asked a question I didn't hear, and I can't tear my eyes away. I can't see his from here, but that expression... It's different from the others.

Parts of their conversation breaks through the haze. It sounds like this container belongs to someone they made some sort of business deal with, only, they weren't supposed to be transporting people.

The moment I hear someone say that they have to close it back up, heat fills my chest. I want to scream, I want to shout at them and beg them to reconsider. But the words don't come. My mouth falls open, yet the sounds don't even reach my throat. I manage to rise and lean toward the men and their plan to seal our fate.

The discussion turns heated, kids begin crying, covering their ears as they likely struggle to understand what they're hearing. I barely can.

"That's complete fucking madness!" someone shouts.

I think it was the man who towers over all the others. He looks ready to pounce and fight them all, angrily swiping a hand over his buzz-cut hair.

I agree, it *is* complete madness! My sister and all these kids need to be saved. They have to save us. They have to let us go. I want to shout at them, demand they free us. But the blonde one speaks again, and my thoughts pause all at once when his voice breaks through my own raging thoughts.

"Are you fucking saying that we're supposed to close these doors and let them go wherever the fuck those assholes are taking them?!" He shouts those words with so much rage woven through each syllable, that I almost miss the emotion at the base of it—*pain*.

There's something deep within his chiseled features, behind those golden curls, which hold a particular type of pain. I can't take my eyes off of him, and he looks like he can't bear to look at us. Maybe he's disgusted. I wouldn't blame him. However, his outrage is unmissable.

"We don't have a choice," the man with black hair, who is dressed from head to toe in the same color, says. "They can't know we're aware of this. This is the quickest way to find out where they're taking them, because this operation might be bigger than this one container. The hydra has many heads, and we need to cut the root and find all of them. Saving just them will not save all the others. If there are any others."

Oh my god, there could be more kids?

I've been so wrapped up in our circumstances—our fate. I didn't even think about the possibility that there are more. That we may not be the first *shipment*. How many more could there be? Before us... after us? How many children are missing their parents, their grandparents, their siblings? Children stolen from their beautiful lives, maybe even unfortunate ones, now made so much worse.

"We need someone on the inside. But none of Katya's employees would fit in. None of them look remotely young enough," someone else says.

My mind reels with images of what those men are doing to these pure souls. Countless missing posters holding the faces of the kids surrounding me flash behind my eyes. Some of them aren't even in school yet, young enough that it wasn't long since they stopped wearing diapers. There are others like them taken by the same scumbags. They're abusing them... raping them.

Oh, my god.

Tears well in my eyes.

They're raping them!

A visceral shake erupts from deep within my bones, and I squeeze Maya closer. God, why does she have to hear this? Why do all the other children have to hear this conversation? But there could be many more like them who are actually experiencing all these horrific things.

I could do it. Right? I could be their person on the inside.

No, no, no! What if something happens to Maya? Or to me, and I'm unable to protect her? I can't do this. I have nothing to offer them.

But they're sending us anyway. Whether I volunteer myself or not, they said they need to make sure there aren't others, and I'll end up in the same place. At least this way, not only do we have a better shot at being rescued, potentially not being hunted down again, but more kids might be saved.

Bending down slightly, I whisper to my sister, "I think I'm going to help them."

"But it sounds dangerous," she whispers back.

"I'm going to be fine, sweet girl."

It's not technically a lie.

"Is it true? Are there others?" she asks, her voice shaky.

"Maybe..."

I feel the bobbing of her head against me, and I have to let go of her, because my trembling seems to increase as the decision sinks in. Two deep breaths don't seem to help. The third one doesn't even reach too deep. But this is the only way... the only control I have over this situation.

"I'll—I'll do it," I say out loud before I can talk myself out of it.

I struggle up to my feet, urging Maya to stay where she is. The tall man with a buzz-cut rushes to me as I force my weak legs to move forward. He's moving too fast, his eyes fierce as he reaches for me, and I scurry back.

The whole space falls silent—both the container and the men watching us. My gaze drifts over each of them, but no one says a word.

I've already made a horribly poor choice this week by parking in that alley. Am I about to make yet another one by offering myself up and trusting them? It could be a stupid move, but the anger and disgust at our situation bleeding out of their gazes, gives me confidence.

They will rescue us, even if it's not happening right now.

It's a choice I will likely regret, because they can't guarantee our safety once we're out of their hands. And something about these men screams of a world I loathe, illegitimate business affairs, and danger. Yet, between the two evils currently in my life, they might be the better one.

One deep breath later, I reach over to the man who, in this confined space, looks like an absolute beast, and he takes my hand, leading me out of the metal box. There's no missing the wet spots my broken shoes leave on the floor. I would crawl into a hole if I could.

Will they know what that is? What I'm leaving behind?

It's silly to ponder, but surrounded by all these well-dressed, clean men, I experience an incredibly overwhelming sense of inferiority.

Someone brings a chair, and I'm urged to take a seat. I stifle a groan when I settle on the basic wooden structure that shouldn't feel like anything special, but after sitting on the floor of a shipping container for God knows how long, this is heaven.

"I'll do it. If there's more," I glance toward the inside of the container, "I want to find them. But it has to happen fast. I can't risk them getting... I can't." I sigh, forcing the images of what could be done to them out of my mind.

"I know. I understand," the one dressed in all black answers.

When I look at him, I swear my soul stalls. He has black eyes, too, like a dark devil. He stands here, and the anger simmering just beneath the surface is all kinds of wrong. Disturbing.

He says something about a tracker and my gaze wanders to another man I only catch a glimpse of before he turns on his heels and rushes toward a door.

"We're going to put a tracker on you. It's going to be small. You might have to swallow it or—" The black-eyed man stops short, as if he's thinking.

"It's okay. I'll do whatever it takes. Slice me open and put it under my skin. I don't care. Just... help them."

Guilt has a louder voice than my logic, and I think it's why I'm so driven to sacrifice myself now. Closing my eyes, I take a deep, centering breath, but I startle when someone asks my name.

"Evelyn," I answer, though it comes out more like a whisper.

My gaze wanders around the space but settles on the blonde man with sun-kissed curls, and I have to swallow one too many times as his broken, blue gaze pins me in place.

"How old are you?" he asks.

I wasn't mistaken before—sadness definitely hides behind his anger.

"Seventeen." I turn toward the container. "My sister is seven." This is not a piece of information I thought I would share, but it might work as motivation for them. Appeal to their compassionate side—if they have one.

"Fucking hell." His voice lowers with a different type of fury. An uncontrollable one. Maybe I was successful.

"We'll get you all out. That's a promise. But you have to be strong. I just don't know what will happen as soon as you'll arrive wherever they're taking you," the black-eyed one says. He's convincing in his uncomfortably honest tone.

I flinch when he reaches over and attempts to soothe me, his hand touching my shoulder. I'm not sure why, but my gaze shifts to the buzz-cut man who stands firm next to me. Maybe I'm going crazy, but for some reason, I think I'm looking for reassurance from him. How bizarre.

Yet, I get exactly that. His eyes reveal the gentlest, most tragic gaze. He's built like a beast, but all I see is compassion and warmth in his gaze.

"Will they—will they get to the children?" I all but whisper. I don't want the kids to hear me.

"I really hope not, but I don't want to lie to you."

It was a stupid question I can't believe I asked. They're not psychic. How are they supposed to know?

"I understand."

"Where did they take you from?" the one standing beside me asks.

"Various places. We're not all from the same city... They just brought us all to the same place. My sister and I, they took us when I was picking her up from school after work."

"What about your parents? They must be looking for you."

I hesitate. We need to be saved, but we can't be sent back to Fleeton. Not until I figure it all out. Will they hand us over to CPS? I'm over-thinking this. I need to take it one step at a time.

"They, um—It's only us two." I stop to wipe from my cheeks tears I didn't realize were falling. "I can't fail her."

"You won't. We'll get you out before anything happens," the blonde one promises, and once again, I'm fully trapped in his gaze.

It's so different from everyone else's in this room. Emotional and tragic. Why is he reacting so differently than the others, even though they all look cut from the same cloth?

Something inside of me, a stray piece of my soul, wants to reach out and find out why. It's a visceral need, inappropriate too, but it demands his comfort. To give and receive.

Jesus, this is—it's wrong. I'm... wrong.

The men talk between themselves now, and I quietly ask the one beside me where we are.

"Queenscove," he answers.

"On the South coast?" I'm filled with a bit more hope.

"Yes."

Thank God! We're still in the country. Just... around twelve hundred miles away.

The man who left earlier returns, walking toward me with determined steps.

I sense the blonde man's gaze, like the brush of heat over my skin. Even as everyone in this room have their eyes on me, only his touch me. It burns. It stings. It almost hurts. Although, that hurt might be self-inflicted by my shame at the pleasure of the heat.

"This is the tracker." I'm handed a pill. *This* is a tracker? "It won't dissolve, it's specially made. But it will pass through. Keep it in your mouth for as long as you can. Swallow it only if they try to check your mouth, okay?"

I nod, looking at the pill in disbelief before sliding it between my cheek and molars.

The man next to me helps me up and guides me back into the metal box that threatens to be my demise. I won't let it, though. I refuse to have anything happen to my sister—to any of these kids.

The metal doors grind my eardrums as they screech behind me, and I flinch, memories of the first time I heard them scaring the soul out of me. But it's different now. These men are trying to save us. They might be seeking their own goals, but a lot of effort seems to be put into us. So, I decide to entrust them with something else.

I stop and turn just before the door swallows the light.

"When it's done," the door stops and the men watch me and wait, "I can't have the police knowing of me and my sister. It's only us, and they'll split us up. I'll lose her to the system."

The buzz-cut beast nods, the promise vivid in his eyes.

Then, the world turns dark.

The fear returns with a vengeance, but at least now I have something else to balance it—hope.

If only it lasts.

Half an hour passes by. The doors open again, and dread fills me with such force, bile rises up my throat. Especially when my eyes land on the man who took us. He stands next to a new guy who points at me as we're urged out of the container and into the back of a truck.

The new guy watches me with far too much interest for my liking, but I get it—I wasn't supposed to be here. I'm too old.

Which means that they might try to get rid of me. I'm no use to them.

The insoluble tracker-pill sits against my cheek, and it grounds me peculiarly. It's a reminder that I have to stay strong for Maya. And for the other kids.

The urge to grab my sister and run is so strong, my legs shake and fingers twitch. But we're pushed and forced to move faster, and the truck door closes behind us before the urge settles.

I can't even process how much time passes until the drive ends. I've spent it all going through likely scenarios in my head, whilst holding onto Maya for dear life. She's still quiet. In a way, I'm happy. Maybe she's dissociated somehow.

What should I do?

How do I protect her?

I just have to stall. I have to keep an eye on her. Just until the men who own this tracker come for us.

And they will come.

They will come on time.

The curly-haired blonde one promised.

"Take them all to the assessment room!" a man shouts over the voices of crying children as we're *herded* out of the truck and into what looks like an abandoned factory.

I stumble but catch myself just as the same man who was watching me before, turns to look at me. He was the one shouting. He leans in toward the guy beside him and whispers something into his ear, his eyes never leaving mine.

I don't feel good about this. At all.

Driven by instinct, I swallow the tracker pill I was holding in my mouth.

"Evie?" Maya's voice startles me. "Evie, what's happ—"

"Not you." A hand wraps painfully around my bicep, hauling me away with enough force that I lose my feet.

"No! Let me go!" I shout, thrashing to break free as another guy grabs Maya from behind.

All the kids turn, and at the sight, a cacophony of fear fills the space. They cry and yell, some of them shout in pain when the men who watch them hit them to silence, and tears of frustration and fear blur my vision.

I fight the one who holds me, kicking and punching in a whirl of untrained moves that don't take me anywhere. But I do it anyway, aiming for low spots, for his belly and groin, anything that could make him lose his grip.

With the loudest of thuds, my ear rings. It takes a second to register the pain that comes with it.

"Shut the fuck up!" someone shouts, but the threat sounds muffled.

"Let me go! I need to be there with them! With—"

"No. You're coming with me. I need to find out what you're worth."

I turn my gaze to the man who spoke those heavy words. It's him... the one who seems to run things. The one who watched me.

"Although," he continues, "I might keep you all to myself, regardless."

My lungs heave with quickening breaths, and the visceral scream that breaks out of me is followed by furious thrashes in an attempt to escape once more. But he grabs me by the hair, my messy ponytail so tight in his hand, my skull burns.

It takes but two seconds more, then pain shoots on the right side of my skull, and my world falls into darkness.

CHAPTER 1

Finnigan

THE FLOWERS WEIGH strangely heavy in my hand. As heavy as the uncertainty weighing me down.

What the hell am I doing coming here with flowers?

I already knocked, damn it. Footsteps approach behind the door—it's too late to throw them away.

The lock clicks and Katya greets me, but she's not alone. A little figure squeezes between her and the edge of the door, looking at me with green doe eyes.

The sister.

"Hennessey. Come on in," Katya greets, dressed much more casually than her usual pantsuits. "Maya, go on, let him in."

"Who are you?" she asks before she dares to move.

"I'm Finnigan."

The little girl narrows her eyes on me, scrutinizing my presence, though it comes across as more cute than menacing.

Her eyes seem to sparkle when they notice the flowers. She's around seven years old, if I remember correctly, yet she seems untouched by the events that almost took her on an unthinkable path.

"Are those for me?" she asks.

"Maya," Katya warns.

"Yes, sugar." She gives me a way out, and I'm gladly taking it, leaning in and handing her the bouquet.

"Lilacs!" she exclaims, looking back at me in awe. "My favorites! How did you know?"

I realize that I'm fidgeting with my fingers, and I shove my hands in my pockets to stop myself. I'm not used to interacting with such small humans, even if I do have a nephew roughly her age. Granted, I've never met him. But Maya's smile is infectious, and one pulls at my lips too.

"Lucky guess," I answer.

"Thank you!" She jumps in excitement and disappears inside.

Katya shakes her head, gesturing me in, her expression as composed as ever. I don't miss the amusement in her dark eyes, though.

"How is *she*?" I ask.

"Not as well as she tries to make it up to be." She knows I'm not referring to the tiny human.

We walk into her kitchen, and I prop my elbows on the central island, looking into the open-plan living area. Katya fills a vase with water and takes it over to the coffee table. Maya carefully places each flower stem in, looking at the scented greenery like they're the greatest gift.

"Were those for Evelyn?" Katya asks when she returns next to me, watching me intently.

"No."

The answer comes too quick and one of her perfectly plucked eyebrows quirks. But she doesn't press. She knows better than to do it.

"Where is she?" I ask.

"In the bedroom."

"She trusts you with her sister?" I ask.

"No. She doesn't trust anyone. Though I think she acknowledges I'm not a threat. But whatever they did to her in there is still coming out of her system. She drifts in and out, no matter how much she fights it." Katya sighs, crossing her arms against her chest, and looks over to the little girl. "And she really is a fighter, Finnigan."

I have limited information about the girl beyond her name—Evelyn Shaw—but based on what I've witnessed, I am convinced that she is a fighter. She didn't hesitate to throw herself in the deep end in order to save all the children. One hundred and twenty-three souls are alive because of her sacrifice.

"Can I see her?" I ask before I can stop myself.

"Why?" Katya narrows her eyes on me.

Why, indeed. What am I looking to achieve?

"If she's up for it, I have some questions."

"She's already been asked questions by the others, Finnigan."

"We have more."

No, we don't.

She sighs and points to the corridor leading to the bedrooms. Only, we're both taken by surprise when we turn that way. Me more than Katya.

Evelyn stands at the entrance to that hall, holding her sister against her front, arms slid protectively over her chest. Her fierce gaze lingers on me. She's watching me closely, not like prey, but equally ready to flee at the first sight of danger.

She hasn't blinked yet.

Neither have I.

There's an internal struggle happening, bleeding through her distant gaze. She's tired. Still alert, but on the edge of disorientation.

No words leave her full, berry-colored lips, but she looks weary. Almost scared.

"It's okay, Evelyn. He just came to check on you and Maya," Katya says, breaking the silence.

"I'm sorry to wake you," I say to her, forcing my voice to steady so I don't make her more uncomfortable than she already is.

Only... I can't break eye contact. I try, but the little voice in my head tells me she might never look me in the eye again if I do. For some reason, that bothers me.

"Did something happen?" Evelyn asks.

Christ, her voice is so soft. The tonality like cashmere, brushing dangerously pleasant against my ears. Her gaze is more focused—but luckily still fixed on me.

"Nothing happened. I wanted to see how yo—*both* of you are doing." I think I forgot how words work.

She notices, and I swear she looks a shade brighter.

There's no denying she just woke up. Her wheat-colored hair is messy and wrapped in a bun above her head. Stray strands fall around her delicate, slightly gaunt features. She looks sun-kissed with her medium-toned olive skin. It makes her eyes pop—golden sun-burst seeping into ash, followed by a thick, dark ring.

She is...

She's quite something.

I shake the thought away before it has a chance to linger. This is far beyond dangerous territory. It doesn't just touch on the forbidden, it's smack bang in the middle of it.

"He brought me flowers!" Maya exclaims, pointing enthusiastically at the bouquet on the coffee table and pulling all of us out of this tension.

Her sister isn't impressed. On the contrary—There's suspicion in her eyes.

"We're okay," she adds. "Ekaterina has been good to us."

We're the reason why Katya has been good to them, we arranged it all, and made sure they were taken care of and provided for.

But I say nothing to her.

"If you're here to find out how long we'll be staying, we will leave as soon as we are able to. I just need to—"

"I'm not here to make you leave," I interrupt. "Stay as long as you want. We can find you a place of your own when you feel safer—"

"No. We'll be fine. Thanks." She cuts me off before I can continue.

Her gaze finds other interests, like the top of her sister's head, or the floor. It flickers from her feet to me. Almost like she's stealing looks.

A discomfort seems to settle in her.

Considering what she's been through, I can't blame her. Though, she hasn't shared much about that. Only details about the kids, what she saw and heard, but nothing about herself. She brushed all those questions off like they were irrelevant. Maddox was the one who found her that night, and in the chaos of the rescue, I didn't lay eyes on her. He said if she has anything to share, she will, but we won't force it out of her.

"It's no bother at all. We're more than willing to help."

"We don't need any more help from people li—We're fine." Her tone is firmer, with an edge of disdain, and her eyes don't meet mine anymore. I don't fail to see the aversion in her expression, though.

Well, what the fuck was that?

To say I'm a little confused is an understatement. Seconds ago, she was watching me like a hawk. I could have sworn her cheeks even flushed.

I take a step around the kitchen island, and she tightens her hold around her sister as her eyes shoot to mine, but it's for a few moments and she averts them again.

Those moments were enough to send all the wrong sensations through me.

"Right. Well, if you need anything..." I take a couple of steps away. "I have to go."

I rush to the door and grip the handle.

"I thought you had questions," Katya says behind me.

"Later. I realized I have a previous *engagement*."

"Date?" Katya raises her voice after me.

"Yeah, a date." It's a lie, but right now, I think it's exactly what I need. A woman to take my mind off of... everything.

I'm out in a split second, snapping the door shut behind me, and I exhale so loudly, one would think I held my breath the entire time I was in there.

What happened in that apartment?

And do I actually want the answer to that question?

Evelyn

I STOOD PINNED in place in Ekaterina's living room for far too long after the blonde man—the man I now know as Finnigan—left. Only when Maya began to forcefully wiggle out of my grip did I snap out of the daze I was trapped in, and I realized I was still watching the hallway leading to the front door.

Why?

He looked like he couldn't bear to be here anymore. To see my pitiful self. Like my presence was a stain on his pristine image. He walked out of here so fast.

Then why is his image still lingering in my mind?

Because it never left.

Not since the first moment I saw the cracks in his blue eyes. They stayed with me after the container doors closed for the last time. His image was burned into my retinas as my kidnapper separated me from the children. And it turned sour when his promise was broken... when the man with the lisp asked the others to pin me down so he could find a good vein. Even as I stared at my attacker, Finnigan's face appeared like a mirage before my eyes, their faces blending together.

We'll get you out before anything happens...

His words lost all their meaning then, as my reality began to break after the needle left my arm, and I was flipped to my front. His was the last face I saw when I closed my eyes as my pants were being yanked down. When my ass cheeks were being pulled open and spit hit the tight spot between them.

His beautiful blue eyes were watching in my mind as tears spilled from mine, and searing pain ripped my scalp and body before the colorful, confusing darkness took me away.

That's why I can't move. Because seeing him again feels like he's still watching me as he repeats his broken promise to me. Over and over again. Through the haze of my attack... he's there.

"Evelyn? I think you should come sit and eat something." Ekaterina's voice is soft as she gently attempts to grab my attention.

The frown pulling at her arched eyebrows doesn't match the tone, though. She's worried.

I'm not even sure how long we've been staying here with her. Two, three days? No, it can't be. It's been longer than that. Maybe a week. The drugs, whatever those men filled my veins with, should be gone by now. Then why am I still so hazy? So broken? So... thirsty?

Sweat drips down my spine, my hands turn clammy, my muscles heat beneath my skin, and my blood vessels... they scream at me.

They scream for that sickly rush. The disgusting pleasure it brought with it. For the haze that pulled me from reality, into a place far, far away, where my body wasn't mine.

Where I was... not in pain.

"Evelyn?" Ekaterina's voice is louder, and I flinch.

My whole back is wet now. My temples too. Air spasms in my chest.

"I'm sorry. I just need a minute."

I stumble backwards and turn to rush through the short corridor. I reach the bathroom just as the bile sears my throat, and my knees hit the cold tiles.

I retch repeatedly, but there's nothing to throw up. Only this foamy thing that burns too much.

Delicate hands pull my hair away from the toilet, and the blood freezes in my veins. I want to scream, but bile comes out instead, and a fierce tremor takes over my body. I manage to swat the hands away from my hair, and I fall on my ass, scrambling backward until my back hits the wall.

I know it's Ekaterina. I am aware that it's her squatting before me. Yet my brain, my heart, my lungs aren't acknowledging it.

Her gaze softens—I'm not sure what she thinks she knows about my reaction, but she understands. Her eyes shift down, and I realize I've gathered all my hair to the side and I'm holding onto it like it's made of threads of pure gold.

She doesn't linger. Instead, she moves to wet a washcloth and approaches me slowly.

I let her.

She wipes my face gently and hands me something. When I look down, she holds a silk scrunchy. Funny how a silly hair tie has so much power in this moment.

I take it and wrap my hair into a low bun. It's quick and messy, but it doesn't matter. It's out of the way and I'm... safe.

"Come. Let's have some food. You need some meat on those bones."

I smile at her. The idea of being able to eat enough to put meat on my bones is enticing, and I'm definitely going to take her up on it. Lord knows this privilege won't last. I need to make sure Maya experiences it all before we have to move on.

"Thank you, Ekaterina." I take her hand and rise, my body feeling more like it's mine again. The shivers haven't left me though.

"Please, call me Katya."

Katya. Like Finnigan called her.

What does she call him, I wonder?

Boss? Friend? Business partner? Lover?

That last one sounds wrong. And I truly hate myself for even thinking it does.

I follow the stunning redhead through her apartment, back into the living area where Maya quietly sits and watches an oldie cartoon on TV. She seems oblivious to it all. To our situation. To my failures.

"We can't stay here," I say as I take a seat at the kitchen island, suppressing a wince when I put my weight on my bottom. At this point I'm not sure if it still hurts or if it's the memory of my assault that does.

"Of course you can."

"No. You have your own life, and my sister and I need to get on with ours."

Katya quirks an eyebrow.

"It's not my place to question this, but I have to. What life is that, Evelyn?"

I'm both surprised and insulted. I'm aware I'm doing a shitty job at caring for my sister, but this doesn't mean I'm incompetent. We *do* have a life.

"You're right—it's not your place."

She doesn't react. Either she expected my reaction, or she simply doesn't care. She's not taking me seriously.

There's no way I'm going to show my weakness to this woman, to anyone for that matter, but... lord, she is right. What life? My sister cannot return to her old school. They probably already reported her as missing. The police would arrive as soon as she stepped over the threshold. She'd be taken away from me.

Katya is oblivious to my erratic and panicked train of thought as she slides over a deep plate with a soup that doesn't smell like any soup I've ever had.

I can't even bring myself to lift the spoon.

What will I do? I'll be eighteen soon. I'm not sure what date it is, but it must be a few weeks away. They can't take Maya from me then, I'll be a legal adult.

Yes. That's it. We can return to our home.

Home?

We have no home. My car has probably been towed by now. Social Services wouldn't allow Maya to stay with a homeless person. What if the men who took us come looking for us?

"Eat, Evelyn."

I attempt to shake all those thoughts away.

"But Maya."

"She's eaten already. Two bowls."

I shouldn't take her word for it. I should ask my sister myself. But this woman has done nothing but take care of us, of her, since she took us in.

Focusing on picking up the spoon, I take a whiff of the strange soup, and maybe it's the heat, or the blend of flavors, but it seems to calm my mind. It smells delicious.

"What is it?" I ask, dipping my spoon in.

"Borscht. It's like a sour soup. I made a leaner one, so as not to overload your stomach."

Do I truly look so malnourished? I don't remember the last time I looked at myself in a mirror from the bust down, when I wasn't drowning in my old, tattered clothes.

"Borscht," I repeat in a whisper.

The first sip of the *borscht* warms my whole soul in one swallow, and nothing can stop the moan vibrating in my chest. Either I'm really hungry, or this is one of the best dishes I've ever had. There are egg noodles in here, some finely sliced veg, potatoes, and delicious herbs that make me want to moan some more.

I dig in so hard, I don't even notice a shadow has fallen close to me until I've swallowed the last of the sour soup. It takes a lot of force not to fall off my chair when I turn toward the gigantic man standing at the end of the island—Maddox.

"Sorry, I didn't mean to—" He lifts a hand to excuse himself.

My memories of the night are fuzzy at best, but his strong, scared face floats there. He rescued me that night. Or he was one of the ones who did; I'm not sure if he was alone.

The day after, I woke up and screamed the house down for my sister. I still remember the terror in her eyes. Not because she was in danger, but because my screams scared her. She was... fine. Sleeping soundly on the sofa next to my bed, her head on the lap of this bear of a man.

He didn't quite know what to do with me apart from... being there. Quiet. Trying to make himself as nonthreatening as possible. After I calmed down slightly, he brought a doctor in. A female one, thankfully, and she checked us both over. I don't remember much of that interaction, apart from that fact that I didn't consent to more than a general checkup. He waited patiently outside until we were done, then came back in and asked me a bunch of questions about everything that happened.

There's something about his presence, about the way he looks at me and Maya. It seems very similar to the way I see my sister. There's comfort in that gaze, but I have questions, too. It's not my place, though.

"Sorry, I'm just a bit..."

"No need to explain. A few days have gone by, and I thought I would check up on you. See if you need anything," he says, pulling out a chair and taking a seat.

He's so tall, the bar stool looks like a normal chair for him.

"You too?" Katya asks.

He cocks his head and looks between us.

"Finnigan was here. Not even half an hour ago." She answers the unasked question.

He nods but doesn't add to that. For some reason, he doesn't seem that surprised, like it makes sense to him. To Katya too.

"How are you doing?" He turns to me.

"We're okay. Maya seems to be doing good, thanks to Eka—Katya," I say, quirking a lip at her. "It's strange, like she almost forgot what happened to her."

"What about you?" he asks again, and I'm a bit confused by the question. I just answered it.

"Like I said, we're okay."

For some reason that answer doesn't satisfy him, and a brief glance is exchanged with the redhead.

"Did you find them?" I ask, changing the subject.

"Not yet. Their operation is big. Established. You're safe, though. Do not worry about that, okay?" He says it with such conviction, I almost believe him.

I'm not sure what safety is anymore. The feeling of it is foreign now. I nod and push the empty bowl away from me, thanking Katya, before I step off the stool and walk toward my sister. She snuggles into me, laughing at whatever *Scooby Doo* has been doing. She's barely spoken about what happened to us, and this truly worries me. Is this how her trauma manifests? Did she compartmentalize in such a deep way that she has no idea what happened?

Maybe...

I sigh because the thought is ridiculous, considering my situation.

Maybe she needs a therapist.

I try not to laugh at myself. What am I gonna do? Get my ass to the doctor and tell her that my sister and I are homeless, that we got kidnapped by a human trafficking ring, rescued by something that looks a lot like a crime syndicate, and now I'm worried my sister has repressed trauma? I'm sure the therapist will just be like *okay, let's crack on then,* and they're not going to call CPS and the police.

But I have to do something. She needs to have the best care. I can't fail her again, especially not when it comes to her mental health.

The last thing I want to do is ask these people for help. They took us in, but I do not want them to give me much more than this. Not when it might come at a cost I cannot pay.

I know nothing of this organization. They're probably just as bad as the people who took us in the first place.

No, not as bad.

Otherwise, I wouldn't be sleeping in the most comfortable bed in the world every night.

There has to be another way to get Maya into therapy. I will make it happen somehow. Maybe some homeschooling too; I don't want her schoolwork to suffer.

But I cannot accept more help. I refuse to sell my soul to them. I need to find a way out of this limbo. Regain some strength and then... get a job, I guess.

That thought makes me even more uncomfortable because it implies some sort of permanence here, in Queenscove. And that just can't be.

I cannot stay. *We* cannot stay.

We have something to return to back in Fleeton.

CHAPTER 2
Evelyn

TWO MEN STAND before Katya and me in her kitchen. Ice fills my chest, spreading over my lungs as far too many scenarios go through my head as I stare at the bald men. The instinct to run, find my sister, and hide with her, is straining my muscles.

But it's Katya's nonchalant presence keeping me in place as two pairs of brown eyes watch us with straight faces.

They look so similar.

"Evelyn, this is Brinn"—she points at the shorter, stockier man—"and this is Jay, his brother." She nods toward the taller, leaner one, with softer features.

Ah, that makes sense.

Yet my nerves haven't calmed. Fisting my hands, I try to hide my apprehension, but I don't think it's working.

"They look out for me," Katya continues. "They're usually either here, the apartment next door, or walking about the building. They've been staying out of sight while you two got more used to your environment, but it's about time you met since you'll see more of them."

My chest staggers with heavy, strained breaths. Having these strangers around me is not my idea of security. Logically, I know that Katya's ease around them should help me calm down, but... they are still men.

Visions of the man with a lisp snap into my mind, and a shudder ripples through my spine at the lingering disgust.

"It's okay, they're here for my security, and now for yours and Maya's, too," Katya says quickly, noticing the sudden shake in my bones.

I don't think my sister and I are in enough danger to require *security*. What worries me more is the fact that I seem to have stumbled into a world where these people deem it normal to have their own security... just lingering about.

I shake my head. "Thank you, but we don't ne—"

"There are others that will come and go as well," she interrupts. "They will always report to Brinn or Jay, whichever one of them is here. They both have instructions to introduce you or make you aware of their presence until you remember who is who. Okay?"

Her words caught a stern tone toward the end, leaving no room to argue. I debate it for a few seconds, but in the end I nod. I understand that Katya and the others live a vastly different life than me, even compared to when my parents were still around, but on the clock security who have their own apartment next door?

Who is Katya? Who are all these people?

And why are we being given this privilege?

"If I'm not here and you feel unsafe, call for them." She shows me a shiny phone and places it on the island counter. "This is yours. The red app on the first screen is a direct signal to them. If you want to go out and neither me nor one of the guys are around, use Jay or Brinn. They can drive you around, show you shops, cafés, the beach—anywhere you want, so you can get accustomed to Queenscove."

I scowl, finding this situation rather ridiculous. First of all, we're a bunch of nobodies. Two homeless, pretty much orphaned girls who got stupidly unlucky. Having a security escort is preposterous. On the other hand, I also want to burst out laughing at her mention of shops and cafés. Like I have money or can afford to be shopping around. I'm uncomfortable lounging in Katya's clothes, but even if I had money to spare, it would still be spent making sure Maya has everything she needs. I don't actually remember the last time I bought clothes for myself. And every time these people offered to do it for me, I refused.

I've taken too much from Katya already. I can't accept this too. Hand-me-downs are fine for now. Not for Maya, though. She got some new clothes from her.

"I appreciate it, but they should stay focused on you. We don't need any *security*." That word tastes wrong on my tongue.

"Evelyn, they are focused on me. And you and Maya are here, so they are focused on you too. You have everything you need in this apartment, but we both know that you will burst out of your skin soon, being cooped up for so long. It's not my place, but you've been through hell all on your own. This way, you won't be alone as you see the city and get used to it. You'll be safe."

But being alone is exactly what I want. She's both right and wrong about the whole bursting out of my skin business, but it's not a matter of the future. I'm already there. The shivers, the cold sweats, the gnawing somewhere in the hollow of my chest is screaming at me. I want to go out. I want to be alone. I want to search the seedy streets of Queenscove to find something. I don't know what it is, but my veins are begging for it either way. I'm afraid I may be willing to risk too much to find it.

Sinking my teeth into my tongue, I try to push the perilous thought away. But it's been with me since I woke up from the daze. When I forced down the groans that came with each movement that made my body burn with pain. When I wondered who pulled my clothes back up? Who cleaned me, wiped the blood from between my legs? *Was* there any blood?

A few more memories came back to me, though they feel like disjointed nightmares, not things I experienced. Just over a week has passed, and I'm done remembering. I don't want the memories to come back. I can't... I can't have them back.

I want oblivion.

"Hi, I'm Maya." My sister jumps out of nowhere, startling me.

A drop of sweat trickles down my spine, and I'm itching to jump into a shower. A cold one.

"Hi," the men say in unison. "It's nice to meet you, Maya."

Looking at my little sister, I realize that it would be stupid of me to fight this and refuse the privilege. It's not about me. I wasn't able to protect her, so why risk not having the extra hand that is so much more capable than mine?

"It's my turn today," Jay says, "but we wanted to drop by together to introduce ourselves. Get acquainted."

"I have to leave for the day. I have quite a bit of work to do. But I will be back tonight," Katya says, turning to grab her expensive looking bag off the bar stool. "I don't think I'll be here in time for dinner, but there is food in the fridge and the boys know the good take outs in the area as well."

"Thank you," I say, already knowing we will be eating whatever is available here.

I feel sorry about this. She hasn't left this apartment since we came here. Not while I was awake, anyway. We've kept her away from her work, from whatever responsibilities she holds. I should ask her what she does for a living.

She's only around mid-thirties, and this apartment cannot be cheap. Even if she rents. And the way she's dressed—a tailored dark green pantsuit hugs her slender, tall body, and shiny high heels that must cost more than all the clothes I've ever worn are wrapped around her feet. She's important, and I kept her from whatever fuels her lifestyle.

"We appreciate this... Brinn, Jay," I say, finally addressing the men. "Thank you, Katya."

Brinn nods and follows her out.

"I'll be outside if you need me," Jay says with an almost cold, impersonal expression in his features.

I want to ask him what he means by that. Where outside? Literally standing in the corridor? Will he stand or sit? I feel bad, but I don't know the man, so I don't ask a thing. He leaves a moment later, and for the first time since we were taken, Maya and I are alone. Not just that, we're in a *home*. Albeit a neatly manicured one, but a home, nonetheless. No car. No shoddy motel. No... danger.

Looking around, it takes but a second to realize that I have no idea what to do with myself.

"Do you think Katya will mind if I take out one of her books?" Maya pulls my attention, standing in front of a narrow bookcase.

I head her way and glance at some of the titles—classics. Foreign titles, too. Kafka, Dostoevsky, Orwell.

"I'm afraid none of these books are for your age, honey."

The complexities of the works are unsurprising for a woman like Katya. There is warmth in her, but it's hidden under cold, hard layers only she can peel. She's done it for me—briefly. She does it for Maya more.

Everyone does it for my sister, though. She bears our mother's soft eyes, but not her personality. None of ours, actually. Maya's a social extrovert in a family of introverts, and not only that, but people naturally gravitate toward her. Then she pries them open and doesn't even acknowledge *no* as a valid answer. Or one that exists. She understands limits, but I swear she can see right through a person and notice that the limits they set are not the ones they truly want. So, she feigns ignorance and pushes on. She's going to be a force to be reckoned with when she grows up.

I spot something familiar on the bookshelf. A book that looks out of place amongst the others, not because of the subject matter, but because of how cracked the spine is—*Twenty Thousand Leagues under the Sea*, by Jules Verne. I reach for it and carefully slide it out.

"This one, Maya. I think you'll like Captain Nemo's adventure." I flip briefly through its pages to make sure it's still in good condition, then hand it over to her.

She reaches over, eyes sparkling with excitement, and turns it carefully in her little palms like it's some sort of treasure. In two seconds flat she's throwing herself on the sofa, the world around her lost. I won't get a word out of her until dinner. But I can't help but smile at her joy. Yet the muscles in my cheeks seem strained at the movement. Like they haven't done such an exercise in so long.

***

Lights flicker from an overhead bulb. Two men speak around me—it's him, the one who took me. The one who...

"You're my glory hole now," he speaks into my ear, his pronounced lisp sending tiny splatters of spittle along with the words.

I say nothing. I can't. My tongue is numb and heavy in my mouth. It's not clear if those words were actually spoken, or I imagined them. They float in my world of colors like they were thrown into the universe, and I happen to encounter them here.

Something sharp breaks through my skin, and an uncomfortable heat fills my body. Even after the weight of the man with the lisp leaves my back, the heaviness lingers. I want to reach for that sensation, wrap it in a soft cocoon, and nurture it back to something beautiful.

I can't get to it, though. In this kaleidoscope of colors, that one is a void, and I can't latch onto it.

"I think I'll ask the boss to keep you. All to myself." His voice echoes.

My mind reels. It doesn't feel like it's mine. My veins carry a fire in them, a comfortable one that tickles all my nerves, sending enough pleasure through the fibers, and the void seems to be pushed farther in the background.

I don't understand what's happening. It's heaven and hell, beauty and sickness all at once.

A new person appears in my line of sight. Older, walking with a limp, and ordering everyone around.

"Vassallo," I hear someone say. What a strange name.

I try to focus on their conversation, but the words don't register.

They're looking at me now. The voices grow louder.

"Why is she still alive?" the limping man asks, sending a deep shiver down my spine. "She's too old."

Too old? Oh yes, they're talking about me. They were only interested in kids. Like my sister.

My sister! Where is she?

My brain begins to register who it belongs to, but those signals don't reach my limbs. They refuse the connection with their nerves, but I need to find Maya.

Tar has my arms trapped, but a cold thread zaps through one of them. It moves, but I'm not sure I'm the one controlling it. It doesn't feel like it.

None of this feels like me.

I can't tell if my body is mine anymore. There is no longer a sense of being connected.

But when the limping older man presses his thick boot against my shoulder and rolls me over ever so slightly, I know that I don't want to be me right now. Not when evil pours out of his gaze and spills onto me with such disdain, I don't understand.

A scream driven by nothing but fear lodges in my throat. Something hot trickles at the corner of my eye. The younger of the two men drops on one knee next to me, leans in slightly, and reaches over. Stings rip my scalp as my head is yanked up by the hair, and a seedy grin contorts his face as he stares at me.

"I want to keep her," he says to the older man standing next to him, his gaze fixed on me.

Then Vassallo cocks his head, and with one simple grin, he chills my bones.

"You might have to share this one."

The scream bursts out of me at the same time my limbs are released, and my whole upper body shoots up. Only, I'm no longer in that warehouse, but sitting on a soft bed, surrounded by ridiculously fluffy pillows.

"Evie?"

I follow my sister's voice, turning to my right, and lit up by the faint moonlight is her pretty face, marred by worry and slight fear.

"I'm so sorry, honey. It was just a bad dream. I'm sorry." I lean over to kiss her soft forehead, then lie down next to her and scoop her in my arms.

"But you—you were crying and saying some things."

The sleep leaves me in an instant and my eyes widen with the impact of her words. I'm scared to ask what I was saying.

"I'm sorry I woke you. It was just a nightmare. Everything's okay."

Only, it's not.

I can't do this to her—bleed my trauma onto her innocent soul. And the talking? It simply won't do. I have to find a solution for this. A different arrangement. If we continue sharing a room and the nightmares carry on, it could traumatize her. Especially if I talk in my sleep about things that should never reach her innocent ears.

"What did I say?" I risk it because I have to know how grave it is or could be.

Maya hesitates for a moment. "You were mumbling about keeping something, then you kept asking for me. Where I was, I think."

"I'm sorry, honey. Go on, go back to sleep."

A soft knock sounds at the door.

"Yes?" I answer, but I can't hide the apprehension in my tone.

It opens slightly and Katya peeks through, light streaming in with her. Brinn stands behind her, his expression stern.

"Are you okay?" she asks.

"Yes, sorry, just a bad dream. I'm sorry I woke you."

"No need to apologize. Do you need anything?"

"I'm okay. Thank you... I'm sor—"

She raises a palm to stop me. "I'm here if you need... anything."

There's an implication there. An invitation to be comforted, to talk if I need to. I'm grateful but talking is the last thing I wish to do. Talking means rehashing, and all I want to do is forget.

Not that I remember that much anyway.

I nod and she leaves, closing the door and returning us into darkness.

One thing I'm grateful for is that our experience didn't take away from me the comfort of the shadows and replace it with fear. Whether dimly moonlit or pitch black, the absence of light brings me a sense of calm and security. It's ironic, I know.

Why do I feel guilty that those horrible people didn't take this away from me?

It shouldn't be like this. Right? Other vic—No!

I will not say that word.

I am not *that*.

Stroking Maya's hair, I urge her to fall back asleep, only I notice that the faint light I was seeing wasn't moonlight at all. The sun rises slowly, and I urge myself to fall back asleep, even if just for another hour or so.

Only, my mind wanders. It wanders back to the man who came here with flowers he never gave me and left with ire in his eyes.

He confused me, and I've been trying to understand what happened for the last two days. He was eager, then a switch flipped, and he couldn't distance himself fast enough.

But unfortunately, that's not all... my mind wanders to the brightness of his blue eyes, his messy, blonde curls, and to his high, defined cheekbones.

It's all flavors of wrong.

Yet, I'm curious of the taste of them all.

CHAPTER 3
Evelyn

KATYA WAS RIGHT—I'M bursting out of my skin in this apartment. I have more space here than in our old house. Much more than my car or the shoddy motel rooms. Still, I'm beginning to feel claustrophobic.

There's an ache beneath my skin, an itch I can't scratch, and thirst that I fail to quench no matter how I occupy my time. Maybe getting out of here is the solution. I have to.

I need to.

Jay is here today. We're alone again as Katya had to go to work sometime around nine this morning, and I still didn't ask about her job. The opportunity came, but I chickened out. Even confined to this apartment, it's not hard to piece things together and understand the type of world I stumbled into. And I fear I might judge her when she reveals it. I don't want to resent her for being part of what's clearly an organization dealing in less than legal endeavors. Even if she's been helping us selflessly.

At least, I think it is selfless. Nothing has been asked of me—of us—so far.

If I'm right about her and their world, it might be better for mine and my sister's safety to remain oblivious.

I shake my head before dropping it in my hands and rub my face as I brace my elbows against my knees.

That's not me, though. No matter what the truth is, I've never been, nor will I ever be, a foolish, oblivious person. I can't live in the belly of the beast without knowing its breed. I need to find out what I have gotten us into, and how to leave.

I jump when a knock sounds at the door, but it opens before I can react. Jay walks in, followed by a tall, dark shadow.

"Maddox," I say on a sharp exhale, my back relaxing the moment the man comes into view.

He nods his hello, looking awkward as he walks into the apartment and shoves his hands in his pockets. I'm not sure if he's uncomfortable being here, or in those jeans that seem a little too stiff on him. Are they new?

"Is everything okay?" I ask when he doesn't say anything.

This might be the best opportunity for me to get answers to all those questions I've been having. Although, I've noticed that he's quite guarded and doesn't like to speak much. It's not like I can ask anyone else, besides Katya. I don't know the others.

Yes, you do—the golden-haired man who slipped into your dream once you fell back asleep last night.

I shut down that ridiculous train of thought before it has time to settle.

"Everything's fine. Just wanted to see how you're doing," Maddox finally answers, and I'm so freaking thankful he did, because my mind needs to stay occupied. And distracted.

Definitely distracted.

"Actually, I remembered something, a name." I pause, but Maddox doesn't say a thing, just waits. "Vassallo. That *guy* with a lisp called him boss."

Maddox nods and pulls out his phone that looks comical in his huge hands.

"Katya mentioned you haven't left the apartment yet," he says as he slides the phone back in his pocket.

"Not yet, no. We just"—*we don't have money to go anywhere*—"didn't know where to go."

Maddox tilts his head, fixing me with his gaze.

"I thought Katya told you to use Jay or Brinn. They know Queenscove like the back of their hands, they can show you everything. You must need something. Clothes or... whatever cosmetics you women use."

Women. The choice to use that word instead of *girl* feels good enough that I'm tempted to confess why I haven't been doing any of the above. I despise being called a *girl*.

"She did, but I didn't want to bother anyone."

I don't realize I'm chewing on my lip until a coppery taste touches my tongue.

"You're not bothering anyone. No matter. Incidentally, I came here to take you and your sister out."

Did he really? Or does he know how pathetic I am? Who am I kidding, of course he does. Where would I have money from?

He's perfectly aware.

My lips part, but I'm unsure of the answer I want to give him.

"Can we go for ice cream, please?" Maya rushes into the room, skipping the entire way to Maddox and me with a great big grin on her face.

I need to have a talk with her. She's too... open. Too eager. Too trusting with these people she's barely just met. It scares me.

"Of course. If your sister agrees, we can," Maddox answers.

"I can't, umm... I don't—"

"It would be my treat," he interrupts, his gaze flickering to mine for a moment. It's stern enough to show he knows exactly what I'm thinking and that I can't argue with him.

"Can we, Evie? Please, can we?" Maya tugs at my sleeve.

"Yes." I cave, knowing full well there's no getting out of this. "Go brush your hair and put your shoes on."

"Yaaay!" She jumps and sprints out of the living area before I speak the entire sentence.

There was no way I was going to say no. Not because I can't deny her, but because

I need to see if this outing will scratch this incessant itch and ease the ache beneath my flesh. I'm praying even to the gods I don't believe in that it will work.

I know what would, but I'm afraid to do to myself what was done to me.

Twenty minutes later, Maya, Maddox, and I are walking through the clean, bright streets of Queenscove. Katya's apartment overlooks a large natural park, and I didn't realize how close she actually is to the center of the city.

Or town?

I'm not entirely sure what this place is. I think it's big, yet there are no modern skyscrapers or cold architecture made of nothing but metal and glass. There's not enough concrete to make it feel like a metropolis. The building Katya lives in is one of the tallest, and I only counted seven stories.

The streets are lined with period buildings, grass and flower bed verges, and mature palms amongst beautiful birches. And the smell... It's intoxicating. Honey and sea. Sweet and salty weaving through the humidity that's just at the edge of too much.

Maddox insisted on walking. Now I understand why. We're quite close to everything. Dozens of both luxurious and charming storefronts, cafés and cocktail bars with tables outside, and people walking about everywhere. Yet, they all have a strange calmness in their step. Like they have no care in the world, no worries, nowhere to rush off to.

They seem happy.

Such a contrast to the place I call home. Fleeton always looks gray, like a cloud covers it permanently. The streets are nowhere near this clean, there's barely any patches of grass, let alone trees. And the only people who smile are the ones who can afford to.

Maddox leads us to the right onto a cobblestoned side street, and my breath catches at the view at the end of it—the ocean. Sun sizzles the calm surface and that ache that has settled beneath my skin quiets.

Beautiful.

I had no idea it was going to be like this. I barely register Maya's excitement as she pulls at my hand.

We near the beach, catching a glimpse of people sunbathing on the soft sand as Maddox leads us to a charming, small building right at the edge of it. Big, bold letters signal that we're about to have *Ice Cream and Coffee*, and the corner of my lips twitch at the sight of this place. It's simple. No pompous luxury or fancy branding. Stepping inside is like stepping back in the 1960s. An old-time, classic ice cream parlor with all its signs of aging.

But the decor blurs behind the patron's reactions to us. There are probably a dozen people in here, half of them got a glimpse and averted their gazes in an instant, the tenseness evident in their shoulders. The other half are staring with a fervent mixture of sentiments etched on their faces. Everything from fear, to awe, and lust.

None are directed at my sister and me. They look at Maddox like they want to flee, yet I get the feeling that they're deepest desire is to throw themselves at his feet.

Who did I come here with?

I narrow my eyes on the man who walks a step in front of me completely ignoring everyone around him, apart from the old shopkeeper who gives him a warm smile. He nods as he leads us out on the other side of the establishment and onto a small wooden deck set on the beach.

I want to ask what's happening, but more sets of eyes fall on us. This time around they notice me too and stare in confusion. I don't blame them. I feel utterly out of place in my too-big worn out jeans and ripped Converse—I didn't want to wear Katya's hand-me-downs out, so I'm dressed in the same clothes I was kidnapped in. Albeit washed way too many times to drown some of those memories. Maddox is wearing jeans too, but not only are they perfectly fitted on him, they look brand new.

Yes, clothes haven't been my priority in the last couple of years, yet I've never felt so inadequate.

"Sit, Evelyn."

I rip my gaze off my poor shoes and let go of Maya's hand. She already took a seat and is dangling her legs excitedly as she reaches for the menu. I awkwardly sit, my gaze drifting to the eyes fixed on us.

"You get used to it," Maddox mutters.

He shifts enough to swipe his gaze over the curious ones, and in unison, they all go back to their drinks.

"Why are they staring at us?"

He turns, sighing, and looks over to the soft waves of the calm sea. "Nothing better to do," he grumbles.

No other explanation then. Maybe I should push and ask about them.

"I appreciate all Katya and you have done for us. Offering us a temporary place to stay and feeding us. I just..." The words fail me. Courage too. I'll sound ungrateful, not just nosy.

"No worries. You've been through enough, you deserve it. Plus, your... situation." He skirts around that particular area, pushing a menu toward me.

"I'm okay. I don't need anything." I slide it away without opening it.

"Nobody needs our gelato, little lady." The man from the counter startles me as he shows up at my side, a notepad in hand. "Everyone wants it, though. All you need is a taste, and you'll be hooked."

His smile is infectious, a single gold tooth gleaming in the sunlight as he scribbles something on the paper.

"Usual for me, Genaro," Maddox says, pushing the menu my way yet again.

His gaze tells me he's not going to take my crap. He's onto me, and I hate it. It's not only embarrassing, but down right humiliating not having money of my own to buy my sister an ice cream. Having strangers do these things for us is uncomfortable. Wrong, even.

"Can I have the salted caramel millionaire's Sunday, please? And lemonade?" my sister orders, grinning from ear to ear, oblivious to my struggle.

Christ, she's glowing. Thriving, even, here in Queenscove, with Maddox's attention and Katya's books. I'm heartbroken that I haven't been able to put a smile like that on her face in... actually, I don't know in how long.

Have I ever?

"And you, gorgeous?" Genaro turns his attention back to me.

"Oh, I'm sorry, I didn't read the menu. Um—"

"Tell you what, I'll surprise you." He interrupts, and the prospect seems to excite him. Like I gave him an interesting challenge. Although, technically he gave it to himself. "What don't you like?"

"Mint. I hate mint."

"Finally! I swear everyone loves mint, and I can't stand it. They all ask for it when they come into my shop, but I refuse to make it. Even the smell puts me off. You're my kind of gal!" He squeezes my shoulder and shakes me a little.

The old man is filled with such energy, for a few moments I forget that I was feeling miserable.

"I'll trust you then," I say, giving him a gentle smile, and he seems to brighten even more. "And a cappuccino, please?" My gaze moves to Maddox involuntarily, seeking some sort of approval.

He doesn't react, he only listens.

"Coming right up." Genaro leaves and I'm left with Maddox's gaze on me.

"What?" I ask.

He shakes his head once.

"Evelyn?" Maya pulls my attention. "Can I go there until the ice cream comes?" She points to a half built sandcastle at the edge of the wood decking, a small plastic bucket and little tools forgotten next to it.

"Sure. But you can't move any further than that without me." She's only a few feet away, yet here, out in the open, it makes me tense.

When they took her from me, I was still holding onto her. Nothing could stop them now. Well, this giant of a man could.

"Take Jay shopping this afternoon, or tomorrow," Maddox says out of the blue, his palm sliding on the table toward me. When he lifts it, a shiny black card remains.

"No." I almost rasp, offended by the piece of plastic.

"You need clothes. Something of your own. Maya—"

"We're fine." I push the card back to him.

"Are you?" the question is rhetorical. "You're in limbo, and refusing to leave this state is pointless. You have to get comfortable, and I know Katya's clothes don't fit you properly. Plus, wearing the same clothes as *that* night," he nods toward my outfit, "is probably not doing you any good."

"My clothes are none of your concern. We. Are. Fine."

My tone seems to attract some looks around us, and I lower it immediately. Not because of the attention, but because I'm too embarrassed for people to hear we're arguing over my crappy clothes.

"And it's not forever," I add, "I'm looking to get a job, then we will go back to our home."

He raises an eyebrow at that last word.

"Home, Evelyn?"

"Do not dare—"

"You are stubborn. We both know you need this." Once again, he slides the card my way. "Why are you refusing the help?"

"Why are you giving it?"

My question lands with a thud, and he narrows his eyes on me.

"Because it's the right thing to do."

"Forgive me, Maddox, but you and your... friends... don't seem like the type of people to help someone off the street for free. Not only that but let them into your homes. Why us?"

"You didn't come off the street, *Evelyn*." He emphasizes my name with a hint of condescension.

"It's not good enough. For days I've been trying to wrap my head around what we've been offered. Yes, I did tell you my sister and I can't go back to Fleeton yet, but I was expecting to be put up in a motel. Not in Katya's home. And judging from what I've seen so far, her work gravitates around yours. This is... it's too much." I breathe in deeply and prop my forearms on the glass table. "Why me, Maddox?"

"Like I said, it's the right thing to do."

Once again, I inhale deeply, focusing on that breath rather than the growing tension in my temples.

"What did you do for the other kids? Did you place them with people that work for you?" I ask, pushing the subject.

"Most are back with their families, but they have gone under the radar for their protection. Others have been placed in... a home, let's say, as we track down their families."

Wait, they actually care?

"Any of them with you guys? Anyone but us?" I press.

He doesn't answer right away. I already know what he's going to say.

"No."

There it is.

"It makes no sense to me, Maddox. Why are you and Katya doing this? Why us?"

"We don't want anything from you, if that's what you're trying to ask," he answers, yet I'm not freaking satisfied with it.

I don't think he's hiding something important from me. More like he would rather keep the reason to himself. Is it more personal? Surely, it's not because he likes me or something. That would be ridiculous.

"You don't like me, do you?" I slap my hand over my mouth the moment the sentence spills out.

The man's eyes bulge, and I swear he slid his chair back a few inches.

"No!" he answers quickly. "Christ, Evie, it's not like that. Not with me. I mean I do like you, but definitely not like that."

Thank God. I think I kind of like him too. As a friend, a protector, and without a doubt in no other way.

Wait, did he say *not with me*? God, none of my business.

"You helped us. If it wasn't for you and your... sacrifice." His words trigger the itch in my veins and flashbacks threaten to sneak through. "We wouldn't have saved all those kids. A hotel was out of the question."

Okay, when he puts it that way, it kind of makes sense. It doesn't mean it's easier to accept, but it does make sense.

"Fine. But tell me one more thing..."

He cocks his head, waiting.

"Who are you people?"

CHAPTER 4
Finnigan

I SPRING FROM one foot to the other, jumping back before Madd's jab connects to my ribs.

"You're too slow, Hennessey."

"Fuck you, Severin. I dodged it, didn't I?" I spit back.

Only, he wasn't wrong. I'm distracted.

He shakes his head and in two steps I barely acknowledge, he's facing my side and punches me straight in the middle of my back. I land chest first on the rope of the ring, my breath snapped out of my lungs. The asshole doesn't even bother to rub it in—he proved his point.

"I saw her yesterday," he says as I push away, back into position.

"*Her* who?" The question doesn't come out as nonchalant as I hoped.

"Evelyn Shaw."

I miss his jaw when I take a swing, distracted by those two words. He whips around like he's not just shy of seven feet tall and built like a mountain, and I turn, narrowing my eyes on him.

"What you do on your own time, Severin, is not my concern."

How was she doing? I don't dare ask out loud, pushing the curiosity away.

"I took her and her sister out for ice cream," he continues, disregarding my words.

I swing at him again, catching his jaw, but not hard enough to make him shut up about her.

Was she happy to go, or did she fight you?

"Ice cream? Really? What the hell is your goal there?" I ask.

What flavor did she get?

"You tell me," he counters, swinging his leg in a turning kick that catches me in the hip.

"I'm minding my own business. You should too." I haven't seen the girl since I went to Katya's a few days ago.

He scoffs and I spurt toward him, side-kicking him in the stomach before swinging for his jaw again. But my fist doesn't connect. He swats my hand away, kicks my feet from under me, and slams me back against the floor.

"And what is your business, Hennessey? Does it have to do with the shiny black card Katya gave me this morning?" He presses his forearm into my chest, his amber gaze pinning me in place.

My eyes widen, and I lift my leg, attempting to push him off. Why did Katya give my goddamn bank card to him? She was supposed to use it on Evelyn herself.

"Or maybe it has to do with the two people who were told to keep an eye on her, help her, follow her around, even if they are assigned to Katya and the building?" he continues, pressing just a bit harder into my chest before he snaps back and rises.

He offers me his hand to help me up, but the pulse in my temples rages. I grab his hand and use all my force to swing my legs around, hook them around his ankles and pull him down, throwing him over my head. The floor of the ring shakes like a goddamn earthquake, but I'm even more furious when I rise and find Madds snickering to himself as he lies there.

I draw a deep breath, trying to steady myself, because he's reading too much into this. There is no ulterior motive. "I was simply trying to help Katya, since she took on this situation, and it's unfair to leave her on her own. We need her to be focused on the escort service."

"Situation..." he repeats as he rises back to his full height. "So, are you going to go see the *situation* again?"

Yes.

"No. I have no reason to," I answer.

"She's a smart woman, you know," he says, and I lunge at him just to shut him the fuck up.

I don't want to hear any more about the silver and gold eyes that have haunted me since the moment she came out of that godforsaken container. I don't want to be reminded of the glow of her olive skin. Her wheat-colored hair that grazes her too-slim waist. Nor of the look of disdain she shot me the last time I saw her.

The girl can't occupy any space in my mind.

I'm a sick bastard for allowing any of these thoughts.

"She's been taking care of her sister for the best part of two years." Madds deflects my attack, but I block his back.

Why has she been doing this?

"Working to support her through school, while dodging the authorities. She's resourceful. She fooled the system."

Then she got herself kidnapped by the scum of the fucking earth. The same type of bastards who took—no!

"She asked about us," Madds continues, distracting me from that dangerous train of thought.

"What did she ask?" I stop, scowling at him.

"Who we are. *What* we are." He throws a combination of jabs and crosses that I just about manage to block.

Why the hell would Evelyn ask these things? She doesn't need to know who we are, and she doesn't need to know what we do.

"And you didn't find that strange, Severin?"

"No."

Fucking idiot!

"What did you tell her?"

I swing a few punches at him, barely managing to catch him with an uppercut. He's fast. And good. Too good. It's why he's the one in charge of training our men. But our sessions are not about beating the shit out of each other. Over the last eight years or so I discovered that this is my way of coping. It's masochism in its purest form. And fuck knows I need the punishment.

"I kept it vague," he answers, "Told her we're businessmen. We have a few ventures around town."

It's not a lie. We do. We have this space here—The Fightclub—which is exactly what it says on the tin. Only, we organize high-stake matches with a select audience, bare knuckle boxing, and some brutal sessions that end close to death. Over the years, a few have ended up that way. Maddox is the one who handles all the affairs here. He's also the reigning champion.

This place is also a front for money laundering. But that's the back of house business. Carter Pierce, our resident, brutal genius started that hustle, but I took over a few years back. I don't regret not finishing university, but for years I felt like I couldn't match the talents of the rest of the Sanctum. However, it turns out I have a knack for numbers and strategies.

Above this expansive basement we have our speakeasy, Midnight, which is our most legit business. It's another one of Carter's ideas, and his true baby. It only caters to a select clientele, and even those on our list need to request a password for every visit in order to enter. No one can simply show up, and it's not open to the public.

However, our primary business, for years now, has been gaining and using information. And no one is better at extracting it than Vincent *The Serpent* Sinclair. We make it our business to know as much as possible about everything moving in our city and beyond, and we control it all, too. Some call it blackmail, we call it good business. Information is power, and in our underworld, we are kings. Even normal folk whisper about us, but in their ears, our ventures are mere rumors. Legends. They fear us, yet respect us. Likely scared that we know their biggest secrets.

We do.

This side of our business is where Katya and her girls are involved. The escort service is a front, and the women working for us have bigger goals and stunning skills much more important than accompanying someone to a restaurant or fucking them. They know how to get information out of people, they know how to steal it, too, and they're highly trained. Katya oversees them all, and I'm also involved there, supporting her.

I'm glad Madds had the sense not to get into all these details with Evelyn.

"She was fine with that vague answer?"

"No," Madds answers.

I stiffen, exasperated that I keep having to pry the answers out of him. "And?"

"She's not an idiot, Hennessey, she knows we're not legit. Especially considering how we found her, and then... rescued her. Though, I'm not sure she remembers anything of her rescue."

"But that doesn't mean we have to give her a goddamn introduction course to our business," I snap.

"I didn't. But I had to give her something since it was impossible to hide how everyone was looking at me. I told her our organization is called The Sanctum, and our business means people know us around town." Madds drops his arms to his sides, his head cocked. "Why are you so tightly wound when it involves her?"

"What the hell are you talking about?" I am not tightly wound. He's being fucking ridiculous. "She's an outsider, Severin. I don't want her living at Katya's biting us in the ass. She's a stranger."

The man grunts, and I scowl.

"Whatever makes you feel better, man. Don't fucking expect her to stay blind to our world, not when she's living in it now."

"Not for long," I mutter.

"What's that supposed to mean?"

"Did she say when she plans on leaving?" I deflect.

"And go where? Who's gonna protect her since we're still finding the rest of the trafficking ring? And where is she getting money from? Not to mention that we already know she can't go back until she becomes her sister's legal guardian."

A man can dream.

"I'll give her money."

"Yeah." He scoffs like it's the most idiotic thing I could have said. "Good luck with that."

What's that supposed to mean?

"She did ask something else."

I already know I'm going to regret his next words. Though, what bothers me more is her features materializing in my mind the more we talk about her. I'm about to beg him to slam his fist into my temple, in the off-chance it will make them disappear.

"Spit it out already," I rasp.

"Why are we helping them. Why her."

My scowl softens, my stomach drops. I wipe a gloved hand over my face and wonder just how fucked I am.

Yeah... good question—why her?

"I gave her my answer," Madds continues. "Someday maybe you'll give her yours."

I right hook him in the cheek before his last word finishes its short echo.

Evelyn

I DON'T RECOGNIZE the person looking back at me from this gold framed bathroom mirror. She doesn't belong in this beautiful, expensive room. Even if her wheat-colored hair matches the theme of this apartment she's been living in for a few weeks now.

I rake my fingers through my long strands, hating how even my own touch makes me feel so vulnerable. I used to love my hair. My only pride, even when my fading body stopped feeling like mine as my meals became more scattered. The sweet memories of my mother brushing it when I was a child are now tainted.

We have to go back. There's no way we can stay here amongst these strangers. Maddox told me what they allegedly do—businessmen. I scoff at the thought. Sure… because businessmen rescue little girls from containers. Organize operations to destroy sex trafficking rings. And have 24/7 security.

They may be businessmen, but they are definitely on the wrong side of the law.

Just as the men who took us.

Burning flares over my scalp, and I find myself clutching my hair, pulling at it. There's a few too many hairs tangled between my fingers when I release it, and bile rises in the back of my throat. *Even by my own hands I can't handle it…*

God, I need to pull myself together.

It's too early for me to leave. I need money. A bit of time. And a plan on becoming Maya's legal guardian. When we're returning to Fleeton, it will be in a place of our own, not on the streets again.

Which means I need a job.

I flinch when a knock sounds at the door, startling me out of my thoughts.

"It's me," Katya says. "I wanted to let you know I'm home and that we've been invited somewhere."

"I'll be out in a second."

Invited somewhere?

I rush to wash my hands, running them through my hair to fix the mess I made, and walk out. Katya's in her bedroom, door open as she takes off her blouse.

I whip around, cringing. "I'm so sorry."

"It's okay, don't worry. I'm only changing."

I've never been part of a family or group of friends where undressing in front of each other was normal. Nudity has always been something rather private in my life. I always found it peculiar when girls from school casually mentioned going into their bathrooms when their moms took a bath or something.

When I turn, I find her pulling on a T-shirt and switching her skirt to a pair of loose jeans. I can deal with that, but something about nudity makes me feel like they're going to think I'm gawking at all their private parts.

"Where were you invited?"

"Not just me, all three of us," she answers.

"I don't understand."

"One of the guys is having a little get-together at his house. Just our… *group*."

Did she want to say *The Sanctum*? Maddox said that's how they're known in Queenscove. Like that isn't another indication that they are more than just a *business*.

"They suggested it would be good for you and Maya to join," Katya says. "Socialize in a comfortable, safe environment."

"Who's *they*?"

"Maddox and the others." I hate that I was hoping she would name a certain blue-eyed, striking man. "He lives in a secluded house in the middle of Queen's Woods. It's safe and private. I'm not forcing you, but Maddox and I think it would be nice for you to meet a few more people."

My gut tightens with unease, but intrigue too. Diving deeper into their world is something I really want to avoid, especially when it's in their home. But this might be the only opportunity I have to see just how safe Maya and I are. I don't trust them, even with Katya I have reservations, and I need to find out if I'm making the right choice by staying here, or if we should take our chances out there on our own.

"I promise, you'll be perfectly safe. Brinn is driving us, and he's staying too. So, if at any point you are uncomfortable, he will bring you right back."

That doesn't sound too bad.

"I guess it would be okay."

"Great. Now, I stopped by a shop and got you and Maya some new clothes since I heard you're choosing to be stubborn." She walks out before I have a chance to voice my protest.

I follow and find her pulling some garments from an expensive-looking bag. "Nothing crazy, a few T-shirts, some joggers, leggings, underwear, sports bras, and jeans. Basic colors. I have the receipt if the sizes are too big." She forces the clothes into my hands. "Now, go try them on and pick something comfy to wear. We're leaving in twenty minutes."

I want to protest yet again, but it's beginning to sound not only repetitive, but silly. Are new clothes really so bad? I'm not signing my soul away or anything. I can force myself to accept them and repay them when I can to make sure there are no strings attached.

"Oh, um okay. I'll go get Maya."

"Don't worry, I'll sort her out."

"Katya." My voice holds too much urgency, and she whips around instantly. "Can I see what you bought for her?"

The brief confusion softens, and she nods, pulling out more clothes than she bought for me. It pulls at my heartstrings just a bit seeing this, and I'm thankful she's not insulted by my need to be aware of what she got for Maya. There are leggings, T-shirts, underwear, a couple of skirts and dresses in an array of colors. I can't help the meek smile, and she takes it as a seal of approval and walks back out.

I'm stuck in place, watching the door and debating if I should go be with Maya while she picks clothes... when she gets dressed. I have no reason not to trust Katya, but getting used to letting someone else alone in a room with her has been more difficult than I thought it would be. I'm not sure if I'll ever get used to it, but I know deep down I hope I will. Having constant eyes on my sister will be impossible, especially if I get a job.

I'll try harder tomorrow, but for now, I leave the door cracked so I can hear her voice in the other room as she squeals and giggles.

Ten minutes later, dressed in a simple, black T-shirt, mom-style jeans rolled up at the bottom, and brand-new Converse, I'm back at staring in the gold-rimmed mirror, debating using some of Katya's make up. It's been so long since I've used any. Before our life went to shit, I was just starting to dabble in it, and I knew exactly the style I loved. Dark, moody, edgy, just like the rock music my dad was playing when he tinkered in the garage. I was terrible at it though; no one taught me how to draw a proper wing with the liquid eye liner. At the end of most of my experiments and practice runs, I looked like a panda. By the time I started getting better at makeup, I couldn't afford it anymore.

Maybe I should just settle for some concealer today. Cover the dark circles.

Katya's reflection pops up in the mirror as she stands in the open doorway. "Do you need any help?"

"I'm not sure. I don't think I want to wear any makeup, but..." I trail off because I don't actually know where I'm going with this.

"There's more stuff in that drawer." She points to the right, in the tall, corner cabinet.

"Thank you." I cast a quick glance, but stay in place.

"You're beautiful no matter what, Evelyn. And where we're going you don't need to worry about make up. Only if you want to make yourself feel better."

I didn't realize I was tense, but with her words, my spine relaxes instantly. She puts a smile on my lips, too.

Yes, makeup does make me feel better.

I pick up the concealer and dab a bit under my eyes. It's a bit too light for my complexion, but it will do. I decide to add some mascara, the silver and gold of my eyes popping when my dark blonde lashes turn black, and finish with a little peach blush.

"Here." Katya hands me a lipstick. "It's new. Sheer and natural."

It's a pinkish-peachy color that instantly puts me off. But Katya's nodding to me to use it, so I reluctantly open it and swipe it over my lips.

"Oh, it's sheer." This is more a balm than lipstick. "Thank you."

I love a bold lip, but I don't feel bold at all right now. This is perfect.

"Don't mention it. All done?"

I nod, glancing in the mirror one final time, before I walk out to find Maya in the living room, twirling in her new dress.

"She chose it herself," Katya says, "I suggested some leggings and a blouse, but she saw the dress and I think I stopped existing for her after that."

I smirk, knowing full well that girl adores dresses. As girly as possible, too. She's not that fussed about colors, although she seems to love this dusty-pink. This one is casual, long enough to cover her knees and slightly pinched at the waist. When I shift my gaze lower, I realize Katya bought us matching Converse, and Maya is wearing hers, too. This might be the cutest thing.

She's adorable.

"Come on, little girl, let's go." I grab her hand and follow Brinn and Katya out the door.

* * *

When Katya mentioned woods, this stunning house was not what I expected to find in the middle of it. Dark wood and enormous windows blend seamlessly between the trees of the forest. But that's not what's been making me gawk like an idiot—it's the people. The atmosphere.

"Welcome! Come in, come in." A stunning woman with wild, red curls waves us inside.

The enticing smells of grilled meat and something deliciously sweet make my mouth water, but the laughter from the background distracts me. This house is *alive*.

"Hello!" my sister says with a teeth-showing grin, but she doesn't leave my hold.

"Hi! You must be Maya," the redhead says. "I'm Morrigan. You can call me Morri."

"Hello, Morri!" My sister waves with enthusiasm, a great big smile on her face.

She switches her attention to me, and her red-lipped smile and striking green eyes pull me in. "And you must be Evelyn."

Christ, she's gorgeous.

"I am. Hi. Thank you for inviting us."

"Well, I heard the trip to Genaro's went well, so I thought we could take it a step further."

"It did. His ice cream was delicious," I say with a smile.

Morrigan shakes her head and pats her full hips. "And utterly addictive."

"Good," a deep voice sounds behind her as a tall, broad man approaches, wrapping her in his arms. "I should ask him for a daily supply."

He gives her a sweet, yet suggestive smile before turning his attention to Maya and me.

"Hi Evelyn. Maya." He nods at us, but that smile is already gone. "I see you met my wife."

He's not rude, though. It's like his smiles are only reserved for her.

I know him—he's Vincent, the owner of this house. He helped rescue us, Maya specifically. When Maddox returned the next day to ask me some questions about the warehouse, Vincent came too, and I was instantly apprehensive. The man looked cut from stone. Stern and hard with his pitch-black eyes.

"Thank you for inviting us," I tell him.

"No need to thank me."

I doubt that. We're in their home. Their actual home. I really don't think any outsiders ever step foot in here, and I'm definitely one.

We're led into the open space kitchen and living area, and there's a view to die for at the back of the house. Floor-to-ceiling windows overlook a cozy deck, and the forest surrounds the whole thing. It's so beautiful, I want to scream. If it weren't for the people sitting on the outdoor sofas and chairs, talking and laughing, there would probably be no sound out there beyond the rustling of leaves and bird song.

"Hello there!" A sweet voice pulls my attention to the kitchen, and an older woman with an apron dusted with flower, comes toward us. "Come in, come in. Food will be ready in a bit, the boys are grilling out there too, but come get a drink. I'm Mamaw June."

Okay, this is getting more surreal by the second. "Hi, nice to meet you." I stumble over those words as my brain struggles to compute what I'm seeing. "This is Maya, and I'm Evelyn."

"I heard, yes. I'm so happy to finally meet you both." She grabs my hand in hers, her warm smile bringing a uniquely warm sensation. What is that?

"She's my mother-in-law," Morrigan says as she heads over to the kitchen island and grabs a wooden spoon to mix something in a large bowl, and Mamaw June joins her.

"Come, I'll get you both something to drink." Vincent signals us to follow toward a bar area that's next to the kitchen.

My mind is spinning, and I follow him without question, stealing another glance outside. It takes a ridiculous amount of effort not to trip over my own feet at the sight—Finnigan Hennessey is staring right at me. Only, unlike everyone else here, he does not smile. That sharp gaze does something to me. Good or bad, I don't know. I haven't figured that part out yet.

"We have everything. Juice, fizzy drinks, lots of alcohol."

"Do you have apple juice?" Maya asks, pulling her hand from mine.

I rip my gaze from the blonde man and place my hand on my sister's shoulder, turning to Vincent.

"I do. Evelyn, what would you like?"

"I'm not sure. Um... beer?"

He raises an eyebrow but straightens it immediately.

"Do you like Corona?"

Did I think he was going to question my age?

"I do, thank you," I answer.

He pulls one out of a glass door fridge, pops the cap, and points to a glass and lime, but I shake my head to both.

"Feel free to come here and grab whatever you want. Including the stronger stuff."

Ah, that's why he raised his brow. He was surprised I didn't go for spirits.

"Come, meet the others." I hear Morrigan before she appears next to me.

We walk out onto the patio, and I stiffen when all focus turns to us. They're not scrutinizing, but all this attention is daunting.

"You already know them." Vincent waves a hand toward Maddox, Finnigan, and a man who's name I didn't catch that day in the container. He brought me the tracker. "And this is Cillian, Morrigan's brother." He points to a bearded, redheaded man who belongs on a magazine cover. "That's Tina and Beau."

Two people sharing an armchair nod and smile—definitely a couple.

"And this is Raven." Morrigan points at one of the most beautiful, black-haired women I've ever seen in my life. "And my lovely Loreley. Or Lulu."

I was wrong, Loreley might be the most beautiful, with her long, icy blonde hair and golden eyes. Jesus, they're all beautiful. Not even a normal amount of beautiful, crazy stunning and handsome. Maddox's jagged scar sweeping from his forehead down his cheek just adds to the charm. Even dressed in joggers, leggings, and casual T-shirts, they could just jump on the catwalk right now and no one would bat an eyelid.

"It's nice to meet you," Maya says, leaning into me a bit more.

I stifle a laugh. Wow, she finally found her shyness.

CHAPTER 5
Evelyn

THERE WAS NO way I wouldn't doubt if it would be appropriate for Maya to be in this environment, but my worries have been squashed. Everyone so far has been... oddly perfect. No one is bothered by Maya's presence, even as I thought a kid might become annoying. She's making sure to pull everyone up if they swear in front of her, which has made most of them laugh and comply with her demands. Some of the guys retired inside or walked farther away whenever it looked like a conversation was turning a bit too serious.

The whole evening is... strange.

Not bad. Definitely not bad.

It's homey.

Such a contrast to what I thought this experience would be. Mamaw June is infectious in her attitude. These brutal men are menacing even when they smile, yet they'd probably kneel at her feet. They might even be a little afraid of her.

Their whole dynamic is peculiar. I didn't ask, but it looks like they've known each other for a long time. It sounds like Mamaw June helped raise at least one more of these guys besides her own son. And she's so warm.

She's the only thing that made me sad this evening. I saw it in Maya's eyes too. Passing memories from our once happy life... the woman who gave us more love than we could ever ask for. Something about Vincent's mother reminds us of ours.

Even that sadness brings a strange sense of comfort.

One thing has distracted me from it this evening—the icy stares of the blue-eyed man sitting across from me. Though, I think his stare only flickered into ice when mine landed on his.

I'm lounging in a comfy outdoor armchair, watching the sun bleed in dark shades of orange just above the tree line, and wonder if I'm getting too comfortable. Not in this chair, not with their support, but with them. With who they are. So far this evening I've heard things in passing—something about a fight, meeting a hotelier who has some interesting information for the guys, and there was something about money. But

I must have heard that one wrong because the number mentioned didn't sound real with all those zeros at the end.

"You need to put some meat on your bones, little lady. It will help with the chills."

I shudder as Morrigan drops a soft throw on my lap. Some meat on my bones would be great indeed, but it hasn't been in the cards for me. I did, however, notice a slight difference since staying at Katya's. Folding my legs under me, I wrap the blanket around my shoulders. It smells divine, like pine needles and sugar.

"How are you doing?" she asks as she sits on her husband's lap at the dining table to my left.

"We're doing well, thanks to Katya. And all of you." I haven't been told who's actually contributing to helping us, yet one can assume. "But my sister and I will have to move on soon; we can't take advantage of your hospitality for so long."

A brief, throaty sound pulls my attention to the armchair across from me. Finnigan has a bottle of Corona stuck to his lips, and his eyes fixed on me. Did he just mockingly clear his throat?

What is his problem?

I've been trying to ignore him all evening, but this time I hold his gaze, challenging him.

"Don't worry," I hear Maddox say, but don't turn to him. "All in good time. There's no reason to rush this. No one is kicking you out."

Finnigan raises an eyebrow, and I narrow both of mine. I bet he wants to kick me out. I just can't quite figure out why.

"You're uncomfortable with us."

I turn without sparing a breath, the gorgeous, blonde woman with mile-high legs pulling my attention to her. The others look like they want to argue with her for her daring, yet they bite their tongues. Finnigan rests the bottle on his knee and straightens.

What am I supposed to say? It wasn't a question, and it's not an untrue statement.

This evening has been peculiarly comfortable. The complete opposite of what I was expecting from, what I'm further inclined to believe is, a criminal organization. This is what I'm uncomfortable with. It took me by surprise.

"It's okay," Loreley says, continuing without my answer. "We're a bit desensitized to it all. But I want you to understand that no one here is going to put a mask on for your sake."

Excuse me, what? My eyebrows shoot up, but I refrain from saying anything.

"Lulu!" Morrigan says with slight shock in her tone.

"What I mean to say, Evelyn, is that what you've seen so far is exactly who we are. We're not putting a pretty face on just for you, and we don't have any pretenses for this evening. I understand how you came to be here with us, and I just want to make sure you know that you're not being deceived into seeing something we want you to believe."

"You're telling me that you really are this... *family*." The word tastes strange on my tongue.

"The guys are a family. I'm Morri's friend, and my involvement in this little group of theirs has been reluctant at best."

I don't miss the scoff from Maddox. Loreley doesn't either and shoots him a piercing gaze with eyes that almost match his in color.

"But I didn't want you to think that anyone was putting on a show for you. Maybe you'll find some comfort in that."

Oddly, I do.

I nod, but my gaze drifts toward the inside of the house, to Mamaw June and Maya fiddling with something on the kitchen island. My sister has a great big smile on her face, and Vincent's mom is beaming, fully focused on her, clearly enjoying the young company. Even if I know Maya has been happy and content all evening, what bothers me is the fact that I felt in my gut that we've been safe all this time. I wasn't uneasy, I wasn't on edge, and after an hour or so, I stopped looking over to her every minute to make sure she was okay.

I relaxed. And I'm terrified of this feeling. Truly and utterly terrified.

Back in Fleeton, when those scum tried to take her away from me, I was relaxed as well. I was comfortable in our situation, and it caused our downfall.

I cannot be guilty of that all over again.

Yet... Maya looks so happy. I haven't seen her like this in so long. No matter how hard I tried to protect her, to shelter her, we were still living in motels or our car. I could never offer her... this.

There's no way I can wipe that happiness off of her sweet soul. Not yet anyway.

I have to do better for her.

"Evelyn?"

I turn at the sound of my name, but I don't know who spoke it.

My gaze involuntarily falls on the wavy-haired blonde man who seems to glow in these burnt orange hues of the sun. The dying light sharpens his almost square jaw, the wide bridge of his nose, and perfectly sculpted cupid's bow. I hate the ethereal light Finnigan's painted in. Especially as he sits in that armchair like it's his throne, one leg crossed over the knee of the other, back straight, and head cocked, slightly leaned back. He could make any chair look like his own, personal throne.

Christ, Evelyn, get it together.

I turn to Loreley with an apologetic smile. "Sorry, I got distracted by Maya. Yes, I understand where you're coming from, and I appreciate it."

"Just don't expect us to suddenly start sharing all our fucking secrets." Finnigan snarls, addressing me directly for the first time tonight. The unnecessary harshness startles me.

"Finn!" Morri snaps.

I don't dignify him with a response, turning to Vincent and the others instead.

"Do you have any news on the two men who seemed to lead that operation when you found me?" I ignore Finnigan altogether, asking a question that defies his whole speech about their secrets. Though, this shouldn't really be a secret. Not from me.

I swear I practically hear him sneer at me, and I bite the inside of my cheek to keep the grin off my face.

"Not yet," The man whose name I was reminded earlier is Carter replies. "There's little to go on, but we will. Let us know if you remember anything else."

"I will."

It was a true stroke of luck that the men who... did things to me, Frankie B, as I recalled his name, and the one they called Vassallo, left before The Sanctum arrived. From the snippets I caught through the haze, they were meeting someone. They weren't tipped off; they simply left for their meeting probably mere minutes before. Though I was so out of it, minutes or hours felt the same to me.

It was pure, dumb luck.

"Have you? Remembered anything else, I mean," Morrigan asks.

Very little, and nothing I wish to share with the group. There are still wide gaps in my memory, and considering the little I do remember, I'm thankful for those holes.

"Nothing relevant that could trace to them."

"Everything is relevant, Evelyn. Not to this, but to you... your healing. If you ever need to talk..."

"I'm okay. Thank you."

She nods but clearly doesn't believe me.

"Just know you're safe here. We didn't leave a trail, so it's unlikely anyone's going to come knocking on our door. Or yours," Maddox says.

His rough features, devoid of a smile, are comforting.

They all fall into comfortable chatter, and I catch brief mentions about a club Morrigan and Loreley apparently own. Something about renovations after a fire, playrooms, and... a stage?

I haven't asked what exactly this club is, but my curiosity is piqued. I've never actually experienced any clubs to be fair, no matter what type theirs is, it's going to be a novelty for me.

A few minutes later, I walk back into the house to check on my sister. She's getting tired, but she's engrossed in a fairytale Vincent's mom is reciting. Maya doesn't care much that I'm here, too engrossed in the storytelling, and I step away to the bathroom at the opposite end of the house.

I spend a minute longer here than I need to, enjoying the silence on this side of the house. I'm not used to being surrounded by so many people, so many conversations. It's overwhelming at times.

Turning the light off, I take a deep breath in the comfort of the darkness and walk out onto the short corridor that leads back into the living room. Only, without light, I smash straight into a hard chest, failing to see that I'm not alone.

"I'm so sorry." I pull away, but someone grips my shoulders, holding me in place.

"It's my fault."

Finnigan.

I can't help the gasp, drawing in the scent of sea salt and something... sweet and rich, like dark chocolate. *Sweet Mary Mother of God.* It's intoxicating. I can almost taste him.

"I want to apologize." His words startle me.

"For?"

"I was rude... out there," he answers.

I stay silent because I have nothing to add. He was, indeed, rude.

"You're not saying anything?"

"No. You said you want to apologize. I didn't want to interrupt you." I shrug in his grip.

"I just did." His scowl taints even his tone.

"You didn't. You said you *want* to apologize. You didn't actually do it."

The harsh exhale brushes against my forehead and the hands that still hold me tighten against my shoulders. "I'm sorry."

"What do you have against me?" the question drops from my mouth before I have a chance to stop it.

"I don't have anything against you."

"Don't lie. You'll have something else to apologize for again."

Maybe my eyes haven't adjusted fully to the low light, and I imagined the corner of his lips quirking.

"I think you should go back to the patio, Evelyn." God... the way he says my name. He adds an old world twang to it, like a strange caress.

I don't move. I can't.

"You're the one holding me here," I say.

He doesn't let go.

Silence falls. More dark chocolate whirls around me. A peculiar electric quiver brushes over my spine, wrapping around my neck and my belly simultaneously, and I think I moved closer to him. Or did I lean in? I don't know, but my front turns warmer. My mouth drier. The air weighs heavy between us. Even if the hairs on my arms stand up.

"Finnigan..." I whisper.

His hands fall like his name on my lips burned him, and he steps around me, stopping shoulder to shoulder, albeit his is quite a bit higher.

"Go, Evelyn."

I sigh, disappointed, but with what... I'm not sure.

Finnigan

I TRULY AM an idiot.

Why did I follow her here?

What did I hope to achieve?

All I got is confirmation that I'm a sick fuck.

I hoped that when it was just us two, when she was that close to me, when I could touch her, that I would see I've been imagining everything. Over-thinking the horrible thoughts I've been having about her.

There are many reasons why someone like me should not dare even think of someone like her, but to add our age difference on top of it all... it's disgusting.

What the fuck is wrong with me?

I was wrong. I was so goddamn wrong. What I felt was worse than what I imagined. Even my name on her lips sounded a thousand times better than in my dreams.

I slam my hands on the vanity, barely able to gaze at myself in the mirror.

How could I? I fucked my way through every pussy in Queenscove. I'm all kinds of disgusting and dirty. But having Evelyn Shaw haunt me, is even fucking worse.

Turning the faucet on, I let it run cold for a minute before I splash some of the water on my face.

Okay. I can do this. I can stop.

There are ways to distract myself.

After all, she's just a random girl we're helping. I've had more women than I can count, and I barely remember their names or faces. Yet I've had them in so many memorable ways.

I've only ever looked at Evelyn. She's not going to linger in my mind for long.

That's it. I'll focus only on helping her. She did say she doesn't want to impose for too long. I'll give her an incentive to leave quicker than planned.

She's not going to refuse me. Not if she was serious about what she said.

I'll offer her more if that will help convince her. I'll fucking give her everything to get her out of Queenscove. Out of my goddamn sight.

I take a few extra minutes in the bathroom, and when I finally walk out, self-assured and with a brand new plan, I find the house completely empty. Shifting my gaze past the floor to ceiling windows, I notice Mamaw June outside, but there's no little human with her. And no Evelyn either.

They left.

That's what you wanted, you asshole. You wanted her gone.

Yeah... I did.

Movement stirs from the patio, and I curse the disappointment when Carter walks in, stepping toward me.

"What?" I ask when he doesn't say anything.

His silence pisses me off sometimes.

"I'm asking The Ghost to come to Midnight tomorrow. I need to find out if he's heard anything after that whole unsavory business with O'Rourke, Holt, and Boseman. Enough time has passed, and things might start to stir again."

"Sounds good," I agree.

Jonathan Reese, aka The Ghost, controls half of the docks and a very lucrative on-ground transport route. A few months ago, Liam O'Rourke, Morrigan's father, and Holt, her ex-boyfriend, went into business together. They needed what only Jonathan could offer, and that's where we came in. The man is a recluse, doesn't do business with just anyone, and we put them in contact. For our own benefit, of course. Morrigan's hand in marriage was also sold in this partnership between father and boyfriend. She's Vincent's first love, and The Serpent wanted her back. A lot of shit went down there. Plus, the containers they needed to shift were supposed to carry ammo and drugs. Some did, but then the children came... and along with them, Evelyn.

In their quest for power, the two men along with Boseman, thought they had what it takes to take down The Sanctum. It was rather funny. They didn't even make a fucking dent. However, considering what Evelyn shared with us, we've concluded that the operation the trio started was part of a much larger partnership. They weren't doing it alone.

"I think you should get in contact with someone else. Just in case word has spread,"

Carter says.

"Who?"

"Your cousin."

I grit my teeth at the mention. My distant cousin is not the reason why, but the old memories I sometimes associate with him. Haunting memories...

"You think word of this has reached Venator?" I ask, disbelief clear in my tone.

"I think we must be smart and use all of our resources. Sloan Buchanan is a good, reliable resource that we can trust."

"It's not the only source we have in Venator. You know that woman from school. What was her name? Pandora?"

"It's not the same thing," Carter replies. "With Pandora, it's an exchange, and I have no desire to trade anything. Talk to Sloan."

Sighing, I roll my eyes and walk toward the patio door. "Fine."

I have nothing against Buchanan. Carter's right, we can trust him with our lives. Eight years ago, he helped us come out of a small war. Only, I came home with a dead body in my arms instead of a future. It's why mentions of him, or anything to do with that time, makes me irrationally angry.

It's not like I haven't kept in touch with my cousin. But I try not to overdo it. The man's empire in the city of three hills where he rules one of them, has grown stronger than ever. More dangerous than ever. It's the rumors of the brewing conflicts with the other two hills that make me reluctant to get too involved with him. We have enough on our plates in Queenscove and beyond, we don't have time for someone else's battles.

However, there's nothing I hate more than scumbags who traffic humans. The proximity of these ones to Queenscove disgusts me. So, if there's even the smallest chance Sloan heard something, I'll talk to him.

I say my goodbyes to everyone and get in my car. I've only had two Corona's. The moment I heard Evelyn was invited, I knew I couldn't drink more in case I needed to escape.

But now... I could smash a whole ass bottle of vodka on my own. I'm gonna drop the car off at home, then go to a bar to do just that.

Any bar... as long as there are women there who can make me forget.

CHAPTER 6
Evelyn

THE NIGHTMARES CAME back in full force, and I wake up with a chilling shudder. Cold sweats shatter my body, the dreams and memories mixing into a debilitating concoction, venom seeping beneath my skin.

A feverish itch blooms, turning relentless through my flesh. I scratch at my forearms, determined to bleed the poison out of my skin. Tears I didn't realize I was shedding blur my vision and the pain... the pain becomes unbearable.

I thought it was hidden, but it's not—it's entombed. Burrowing deeper and deeper, sinking its claws so it can find a permanent home in the fabrics of my being. I can't reach; I can't rip it out.

So, I dig my fingernails deeper, breaking the skin on a tearful wince, hoping I can bleed it out. Only, it itches more. It hurts more.

I need more!

Tears of frustration stain my cheeks, and I swallow in a bellow at the shame plaguing me. Only one thing will fulfill this need, scratch the relentless itch and dilute these nightmares. And I cry harder because that one thing I crave is exactly what those bastards injected me with.

But... it kind of helped then. Maybe now, it could keep the nightmares out of my living world.

Maybe it will help.

Make me forget.

The shame. The feel of him. The loss of control. The disappointment I am. How I failed her.

I have to forget. Even if for a few hours. I want to be back in that place where my body isn't mine, where I am... free.

Reality sets in, and the inner pain quiets in favor of the outside one, and in the faint morning light, I see what I've done.

"Oh my god."

I jump to my feet, realizing that I fell asleep on the sofa, and run to the bathroom.

My inner forearms are scratched badly enough that I'm bleeding, stinging when I run them under the cold water.

At least I wasn't in bed with Maya.

My muscles still when I catch the first glimpse of myself in the mirror. I look exactly like I feel—a failure. Maya's smile and laughter filters through my mind, emotions I didn't give her, but these people we now live with. I'm not taking care of her—they are. I have done nothing to contribute to her happiness.

Did I really deserve to leave that warehouse alive? Is there a point for my presence here?

Looking down at my forearms, blood seeps out of the jagged scratches; their ugliness sure does fit on my skin. I shake my head on a sharp exhale and start rummaging through the cupboards for some gauze or anything to cover the evidence of my nightmares. Or better yet, of that searing need begging from inside my veins. I find a small basket stocked up with all sorts of first aid stuff and skip the antiseptic and whatever else I should do to tend to my skin, going straight for the roll of gauze. I make quick work of wrapping it around my forearms and hurry to go throw a long-sleeve on before Maya and Katya wake up and see me.

Living here for free makes me feel like a leech, so I've been trying to pull my weight as much as I can. Washing, cleaning, cooking, whatever needs doing, even if Katya keeps telling me off. Now, I'm about to pull some oats out of the cupboard for some oatmeal, but my phone pings on the counter. I twitch at the unfamiliar noise.

"What the...? Who has this number?"

Reluctant, I grab it and a new text flashes on the screen.

> Hey! It's Loreley. Katya gave me your number. Morri and I are going out for breakfast. Come join us. Pick you up in fifteen?

I look around the quiet space, bewildered as I scratch the back of my head.

This is wrong, I can't just leave my sister here... alone. Since we've been brought here, I've always been around, even passed out in the other room, I was around. No, I can't go. I have to be here with Maya.

But the pacing continues. As does the scratching.

What if I go, though? Is this something I can do? Just... go out for breakfast? On my own, without Maya?

God, this is strange.

I'm on my eighth tour around the kitchen island, and the idea sounds better and better with each one.

"You okay?"

"Ah!" I jump, pressing a palm to my heaving chest.

"Sorry, sorry." Katya puts her hands up in apology.

"My fault, I was distracted."

"Did something happen?"

"No, it's just..." I sigh, realizing I'm worrying her with my reaction. "Loreley texted me. I guess you gave her the number. She invited me for breakfast."

"Go," she says before I even finished the last syllable.

"I can't just—Maya is—"

"She's fine. I'll stay with her here. I have nothing planned today anyway." She cuts me off.

"Katya, I know I shouldn't have any reasons to be uncomfortable with this, any rational ones anyway, but... Look, after everything her and I have been through, the only time we've spent apart in the last two years was when she went to school and when we got separated in that container. That's it. Leaving her..."

"I understand. I'm not going to force trust on you. I can't do that. But sometimes you have to listen to your gut. If yours tells you to keep your guard up around us, around me, then fair enough. Just make sure that's the reason you're doing it. All I can tell you is that none of us are here to hurt you."

I know. Rationally I know all they've done has been more than generous. Selfless too. Maybe they're keeping me around in the hopes that I'll remember something useful about the men who took us, which is fair enough. But if that was the only reason, we wouldn't be sleeping in Katya's soft bed and expensive sheets every night.

I have to try this. Let go, if only for a bit.

Perhaps later on I will be able to go out on my own and seek something more.

It's my birthday today, after all.

I look at the phone and my fingers fly over the letters.

I'll be downstairs. Thank you.

* * *

"This one would work so well on you." Loreley holds up against my front a blouse with a deep V neckline. It's in a goldish color that would, indeed, look great with my skin tone.

Morrigan cocks her head as she looks in our direction, but she seems more focused on my face rather than the blouse.

"I don't think it's a winner, Lu," she says.

"Why not? It looks lovely." Loreley pauses and looks up from the blouse to me. "Oh, my bad, I think you're right."

I stifle a laugh because the interaction between these two has been both hilarious and sweet all morning. They fit together like they share DNA, not just a close friendship.

They took me out for breakfast at the cutest café in the center of Queenscove. A narrow little building nestled in-between two large, elegant facades, and it didn't really look like much. Only, as we passed through the small, cozy space, I quickly found that the attraction of the place wasn't inside, but at the back. We passed through the back door and found ourselves in a stunning enclosed courtyard where every inch of the walls were covered in trailing plants and two large trees shaded the space.

Maybe I was imagining it, but that café, the atmosphere, really helped me be more comfortable with the situation. The fact that Katya has been sending me photos of her and Maya might have also had something to do with it.

We had a surprisingly enjoyable time. They didn't push me to talk but involved me in every conversation. They didn't ask intrusive questions or urged me to open up about what happened to Maya and me. They did ask a bit about my family and how we ended up on the streets, however they were fine when I decided to keep it vague, and simply tell them that we were staying with our mom, and she died.

Telling them the whole story would pose too many questions and reveal more than I'm comfortable with right now. My aversion to what and who they are as well.

Either way, they didn't push, even as they could clearly tell there was more to everything, and I appreciated that.

Afterward, they dragged me around town, showing me all sorts of interesting places, including a quirky little bookstore that seemed to have been there for at least a hundred years. I went inside to find a couple of books for Maya, and that's when I caught sight of that shiny little black bank card again. Same one that Maddox tried to give me, only now it was in Morrigan's hand as she paid for the books.

She gave me a look that told me not to dare protest, and I kept my mouth shut. I think that if I do decide to buy anything from the department store we're currently in, I'll see that card again.

Will she try to slip it in my pocket when we leave?

Will I protest?

Loreley puts the blouse back on its rack and turns, stopping to look at me. "This is not you, is it?"

"What do you mean?"

"All of this"—she waves around the clothing racks and shelves—"is not your style, is it?"

I don't want to sound ungrateful. I can't afford to be picky. "I'm not really fussy. I'm okay with what I have."

"That was not the question, Evie."

Evie... that sounded rather sweet.

Morrigan hooks her arm around mine and gently drags me away from the pastel-themed shelves.

"Come on, dare to dream a little. If you could have anything, what would it be?" she asks.

If I could have anything, I would buy it for Maya. Not me. There's no guarantee for how long I would have *everything*, because just like our mom, it could be taken away in the blink of an eye.

"Anything." Loreley joins in and grabs my other arm.

I sigh, finding that there's no escaping this. Yet, I don't actually want to. Maybe I could dream a little.

"Black," I say.

"Black?" Morrigan asks.

"And really dark greens, teal, and purple."

"Oh." Her eyes sparkle.

"Fishnets and platform Doc Martens."

"Hmm." Loreley says with a cheeky smile, and I swear I can hear cogs spinning in that beautiful head of hers.

"Leather, velvet, and oversized sweaters."

"Now we're talking." Morrigan tightens her hold.

"We can definitely do leather." Loreley joins in, that cheeky grin turning down-right devious.

"You should see our collection. Though it's probably a different vibe," Morrigan says, laughing.

"I've never actually worn anything like that. Never had the opportunity, but it's the style I've always admired. Dark, rock on the side of gothic, moody," I explain.

"I love that. I can honestly see it on you," Loreley says.

"I think we should," Morrigan adds. "Come on, I know where to take you."

"Honestly, you don't have to. I can't buy anything anyway, but I also don't need to, it's all good. Really," I argue, tugging them back uselessly.

"It's only a few doors down from here, and you don't have to buy anything," she continues as we exit the department store and turn right. "And if it's money you're worrying about—don't. Seriously, you have to stop that. None of us are going to allow you to struggle or feel bad because you can't buy your sister two books or some clothes for yourself. I get it, it feels like shit, but it's not your fault you were kidnapped, or that you're like two thousand miles away from home, or that you can't pull money out of your ass. You're here because The Sanctum wants to help you, just like they helped all the others."

"Hey," Loreley argues.

"I know, I know, you're not part of The Sanctum. That's not the point here. The point is that we are the ones offering to help you, you are not taking advantage of us. Okay?" Morrigan finishes just as we turn another right into a side street with smaller, quainter shops.

"I appreciate it. I really do."

I'm prepared to argue against it again, but I realize that it just means that I will be having the same debate later. I know what's stopping me, and it's not just my ego, but the provenance of this money I'm being offered and the fact that I'm still not convinced that it comes with no strings attached.

"I'm used to taking care of my sister and I on my own. This is difficult to adjust to. Harder to accept."

"We can start small, right about now." Morrigan halts us in front of a small storefront, black baroque style woodwork framing the window and the glass-paneled door.

The window display looks like it might just be the store of my dreams. Platform boots, combat boots, lace-ups, leather skirts and thick, dark lace and velvet, cozy knitted sweaters, and some sexier things I would never dare to buy. Maybe.

Damn...

They don't have to drag me into this one, I walk in willingly.

"I understand it's hard. Lulu had to beg me to accept the apartment she gave me in her building when I had no money of my own to move out of my parents' house, after university," Morrigan says.

Loreley has an entire apartment building? If she's not part of The Sanctum, what exactly does she do for work?

"I thought you live with Vincent in the woods."

"Our situation is a little different. Our marriage is quite new and let's just say it was not planned. But the apartment happened before this, and it's still mine." She starts looking through the clothing racks, pulling a myriad of items out as we move through the store and showing them to me for approval.

"Sorry, I didn't mean to pry," I apologize.

"No, don't worry. It's no secret. But I just wanted to tell you that in a small way, since our situations are different, I do understand that accepting help is hard on the soul. God knows I had to make a deal with the devil just to justify accepting help."

Loreley snickers at that, and I narrow my brows.

"She's referring to her *hubby*. He's The Serpent... and he calls her his *Little Eve*. Get it?" the blonde woman shakes her head in mock disapproval. "They did make an actual deal... crossroads and all."

Well, someday I will pry a little more to find out the whole intriguing story.

"I want to do this for myself," I say.

"You will. But you can't expect it to happen right away. You have some serious healing to do." Morrigan hands me the clothes I nodded to in approval. "Try them on."

"I'm not buying all of these." I hold the items like they burn me.

"You don't have to. Just try them on. At least now you know where the store is," she says, shrugging.

Before I close the dressing room door, I turn to her and Lulu. "It's not stubbornness, by the way. Getting back on my feet is more about Maya and my responsibilities back in Fleeton than it is for myself. I will search for a job and start saving as soon as I figure out the logistics about my sister."

I close the changing room door before either of them can continue this conversation. There's no debating this plan. Pulling my clothes off, I'm happy when I notice the gauze is still neatly in place and there's no blood seeping through from the shallow wounds. The first thing I try on is a pair of tight black jeans and a thin, oversized knitted sweater.

"Childcare for Maya can be arranged." Morrigan raises her voice behind the door and says, "I believe that a certain mother of the group would be happy to help. But you can also enroll her in school here."

I know she's referring to Mamaw June and I don't disagree.

"I want to enroll her, but I can't." I crack the door and peek through so I can whisper, "She was enrolled in Fleeton under a slight misspelled name. Intentionally, of course. But that doesn't mean that CPS, and probably the police if the school alerted them of a missing child, couldn't make the connection. More importantly, I don't have custody of her yet, and I won't risk going on the radar until then."

"I think all that can be sorted. I'm sure The Sanctum has some *resources* at their disposal," Loreley says in a lowered tone.

I'm not sure what she means by that, and as intriguing as it sounds, accepting more help from them is off the table. At least until I'm convinced it doesn't come at a cost. No matter what, it has to start with custody, and I can't even begin to fathom how incredibly difficult that will be.

"A job can be arranged too. I could always use the extra help," Loreley adds.

"Maddox and Finnigan will kill us if we bring her in Metamorphosis," Morrigan counters, as I close the door back up, to try on more clothes.

I scowl at the sound of that. What does Finnigan have to do with this decision? I can do whatever I want to do. But, what's Metamorphosis and why shouldn't I be there?

"Christ, babe, no. I meant the café," Loreley says, laughing.

"Aaah. Okay, yeah, that makes more sense."

"That's kind of you, but it's okay. I'm sure I will find something," I say.

"It's up to you. The offer is there."

Loreley basically offered me a job. Just like that. Though accepting it wouldn't be any different from taking their money.

Or maybe I'm overthinking this too. After all, Loreley isn't part of The Sanctum, is she?

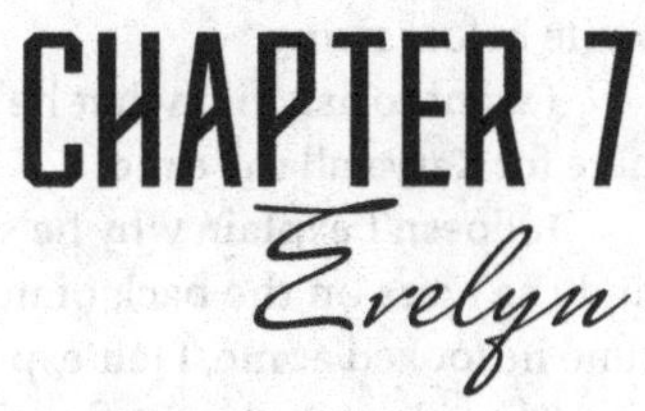

IT'S LUNCHTIME WHEN I get back to Katya's place with three large bags and a shiny new black card that Morrigan threw in one of them. She gave me a warning glare that told me she was gonna bite me if I dared return it, then said it's not hers, anyway. I haven't touched it. It's Maddox's for sure. It looks exactly the same as the one he tried to give me at the ice cream place.

Jay helps me with the bags as I walk in, opening the door for me, but I stagger when the living room comes into view. It's not Katya I find sitting on the couch with Maya.

What the hell is Finnigan doing here with my sister?

My steps toward them quicken, but falter when I see Katya in the kitchen, calm as she potters about. Feigning a relaxed wave to her takes effort, but it's the strained smile she puts on in response that confuses me. I don't stop to ask her about it, because I'm curious about the intense conversation my seven-year-old sister is engaged in with a man twenty years her senior. The back of the sofa faces me, and they don't appear to see me coming.

"Evie told me that some of the other books are for older kids, but I still want to read them." I hear Maya's little voice.

"I may be in favor of breaking the rules once in a while, but she's right with this one, sugar. I read them when I was older than you." His gaze drifts to me. He knew I was here all along.

I'm sorry, what? Finnigan Hennessey is talking books with my sister?

My sister turns too and jumps and squeaks when she sees me, rushing toward me with yet another great big smile on her face that I didn't put there.

"You're not going to believe it, Evie! Finnigan likes Jules Verne, too. We've been talking about the one I'm reading now, and he said there's another one I will love when I finish this one—*Treasure Island*. Can you get it for me, Evie? Please? It has pirates!"

My eyes widen, lips parting as I creep back to the entryway on uneasy steps, pulling out of one of the bags I came with exactly that—Treasure Island—a secondhand copy I bought from that little bookstore.

I'm still wrapped tight in disbelief as I return to her and hand her the paperback. Her eyes bulge when the title sinks in, then with an ear-piercing shriek, she throws her arms around me. It only lasts a second before she whips around and jumps back on the sofa, showing the man who looks like he just came from a beach photo shoot. He looks just as stunned as I am.

"Look, look!" She jumps on the sofa next to him. "It's the same one. It's like you talked!"

He only manages a nod before he straightens his surprise and gives her a quick smile before rising.

I want to ask him what he's doing here, but it's not my house. He probably comes here for Katya all the time.

It doesn't explain why he's watching me like that, though. His focus heats my skin and the hairs on the back of my neck rise. It was the same at Vincent's house—every time he looked at me, I felt exposed down to my soul.

Tiny electric shocks flourish down my back, wrapping around my waist, and I move before they can reach the area that threatens deeply inappropriate thoughts.

"Could we talk for a moment?"

His voice stops me dead in my tracks. On a slow inhale, I turn, breathing in through the tightness gripping my chest. Katya walks over, a cold annoyance in her gaze directed straight at him. She obviously knows what this is about, and I'm not loving her expression.

"Evelyn, you—" she begins.

"Katya," Finnigan warns, and her nostrils flare in response.

She wants to but doesn't argue. I cross my arms against my chest, tightening them ever so slightly, as I cock my head.

"Maya, could you come with me for a moment?" Katya shifts toward my sister, and a moment later they are both out of the room.

This is only the second time Finnigan and I have been alone, and the first one did not go well at all. I suspect this one won't be any different.

"You can't tell me to leave again." I begin because I can't stand this silence, not when that prickle is back on my spine, "I live here. You'll have to be the one to go."

He drops his gaze for a second and my heart follows the moment realization strikes. That's exactly what he's about to do. I take a step back, eyes widening as I force my composure.

"I'm going to give you money so you can go back home. I know this is the only reason you're not going back yet, and I want to make it happen. I will provide transport or a car, a place to stay when you get there, and enough money for you and your sister to be comfortable for a long while."

Excuse me?

"You're messing with me, right?" My arms drop, fists tightening as I force my anger into them rather than my tone.

"I'm happy to do it this week. I have a number in mind, you tell me if it's enough or if this is gonna cost more."

"Cost?" I choke on the word. "You're actually being serious?"

This is not help, this is borderline bribery. The fact that my voice stayed at an almost calm level is nothing short of a miracle.

"Yes, I am." His tone is cool, so matter-of-fact something tightens in my chest in response. "You need money to leave, and I have money to make it happen."

Taking an involuntary step toward him as heat fills my chest, I let his words sink in along with their implication. Conflict flickered in his eyes for a split second, but I don't care to unpack that right now. We're two steps away from each other, too close, yet not close enough for me to slap him. And God, how my palm twitches to slap his handsome face.

"How dare you?!" The disdain bleeds through my voice, but I'm keeping my tone low since Maya's in the other room.

"Excuse me?" he says with a scowl.

"You heard me. How dare you pay me off to leave Queenscove? Do you really think I'm that type of person?"

"It's not any different from us helping to return all those kids to their parents or to whomever they were taken from." He shrugs, the gesture irritating me further.

"Is that what you tell yourself to justify this? It definitely doesn't have anything to do with the other night?" I take another step toward him, flexing my hands at my sides as the itch intensifies.

The man sneers. "I don't know what you're talking about."

The conflict is way clearer in his eyes now. The ire too.

"Prove it, then. Because I've been trying to make sense of your attitude toward me, Finnigan."

His eyes flicker at the sound of his name and nostrils flare.

"From the first moment I saw you, when you found me in that container, you looked at me like I broke something of yours I didn't know existed. And you had such... revulsion for me. I understood it then—I'm a poor, dirty, uneducated homeless girl who screwed up and got herself in trouble. But you still have not stopped watching me. You're doing a better job at hiding the revulsion, but now it's like you're demanding I fix whatever you think it is I broke." Where did I get the guts to call this man out on his attitude?

This is going to bite me right in the ass, judging by his darkening expression.

"You're crossing a line, girl." His tone turns to a low rumble, and my palm whips against his cheek on a loud crack.

"Do not call me *girl*!"

I freeze, eyes widening as if what I did only just sinks in. His eyes widen in shock, his lips are pursed in annoyance, but the man is too stunned to speak. Or act.

Nope, I was wrong. So, so wrong. On rushed steps, my back is pressed against the wall, the hand I slapped him with pinned by the wrist above my head, as his other slams against the wall next my head. I'm caged in. His chest rises and falls on strained, heavy breaths that sizzle against my skin. He's so... so close, yet his hand around my wrist is the only part of him touching me.

I have to crane my neck to look him in the eyes, but the intensity in them presses against my soul. My breath is trapped somewhere in my lungs as I await the impending punishment. All the courage I had a moment ago has stalled, simmering beyond this painful anticipation.

But something else seeps in through it all. Through the closeness of our bodies, in the heat radiating between us, amongst the heavy breaths and the touch of his powerful grip, invisible threads sizzle. They start over my lips, sliding down and wrapping around my throat, turning to goosebumps as they fall over my chest. They graze my breasts before they drop to my belly and my gaze widens on a slight gasp when I realize I can't stop where the sizzling sensation is heading to.

This is so wrong. The man just insulted me down to my bones, and yet my body has no reservations. I expected punishment, but he looks at me like he's the one being punished. I may be seeing things, but I swear he looks just as I feel—charged with a heated tension we can't control.

"Evelyn," he whispers my name like it's too heavy on his tongue. "I need you to go."

"Why?" It comes out like something between a breath and a whimper.

"Leave Queenscove." He ignores my question.

"No."

"Goddamn it, woman!" His hand flexes around my wrist and my free hand shoots up before me instinctively.

His muscles tense when I grab onto his side yet he doesn't let go. Doesn't even move an inch. But his bright blue eyes darken, and a few curly strands I itch to wrap around my finger fall around his face as he leans in further.

Christ, no man should ever be allowed to look this good.

"You can't do it, can you?" I whisper, my gaze straining to stay on his eyes and not move further down. "You can't prove that you're not chasing me away because of the other night. What are you afraid of, Finnigan? Why do you want to get rid of me so badly?"

"You're reading too much into it."

"Am I reading too much into this too?" I look between us, at the closeness of our bodies, before returning to his azure eyes.

His nostrils flare again, and his gaze drops to my lips for a heavy moment before it comes back to my eyes. A raging fire burns through the blue.

"Yes. You're just a—"

"Don't you dare say it again." I seethe. God, the way I despise being called a girl.

"Too young. Far, far too young."

"For what?" I challenge.

He sighs, too many seconds passing without an answer.

"Stop being fucking stubborn. I'm offering you money with no strings attached. An easy way out," he deflects again, but this time I'm absolutely done with it.

"No strings attached?" I scoff. "I don't believe that for a second. Your kind doesn't operate like that, and we both know it. There's always a price to pay with the *mafia*,"—I throw the word to see how it lands, if he's going to deny it—"and I've had enough taken away by your world. I will never, ever accept your blood money."

That, he did not like.

He releases me in a split second and takes a step back.

"Blood money?" he says, raising his voice. "We saved you, Evelyn. When the hell did you get up on your high horse and forget about that fact? This fucking *blood money* made it possible!"

He doesn't deny the name I called them by. Anger seeps through my veins like liquid fire, throbbing in my temples.

No. I refuse to entertain this. I had no choice in any of this. His world took everything from mine. Even if he didn't wield the hand who did it.

"I'm not taking your money, and I refuse to be chased away. You know very well why I can't return to Fleeton yet. But don't worry, I will gladly leave *you* and this place once I earn my way back."

"Looking forward to it!" he spits back with a sneer.

And with those harsh words, he spins on his heels and walks out.

CHAPTER 8
Finnigan

"TWO OF THE same?" the bartender asks.

"Yes!" I raise my voice over the loud music.

"The fact that you called me was a shock, but this mood you're in tonight is an even better surprise, baby!" Clara, the blonde I probably made a mistake inviting out again tonight, says in my ear.

The need to wipe her breath off of it gnaws at me, but I refrain, turning to her with a reluctant, cold smile. This might not have been a good idea, and it's gonna bite me in the ass, because I rarely invite a girl out more than twice. It creates an expectation I'm never going to meet. I refuse to. Relationships are not my thing. Dating is not my thing. Fucking is. And I make it clear to all the women I do it with.

But this is the third time I asked Clara out, and she's perfectly aware it's out of character. I know I have a reputation. Even if I'm not the only bachelor in The Sanctum, I'm the only one who sees women on a regular and fairly public basis. I think I inadvertently made it into a challenge for women to try to get me past that second interaction. Many have tried, but I shot them down without remorse.

I'm not a dick, at least I don't think I come across as that, but I have my boundaries and I make sure whoever I go out with is perfectly aware of them too.

Clara, here, might be getting the wrong impression, and it's my own fucking fault. However, after the day I had, after that stubborn gir—*woman*—decided to screw over my plan of getting rid of her, I had to get out, wipe my memory of her, and replace her with someone else. I was livid and impatient. There was no time to find someone else, and I picked the first woman I knew is everything Evelyn Shaw isn't.

Though, I must admit I felt something strangely close to pride at her attitude toward me. Weeks prior, she could hardly make eye contact with others.

The four vodka sours, six Jager shots, and loud music help ease the worries about Clara.

What they don't do is drown Evelyn out.

When I look at Clara's brown eyes, I see bright gray seeping into gold. When I look at her dark brown hair, I see blonde like wheat on a cloudy day. When I look at Clara's voluptuous body, I see slender. And instead of her porcelain skin, I see soft, olive tones, sun-kissed even if Queenscove's sun hasn't touched her.

Another shot, along with a fifth vodka sour is slid in front of me, and Clara's wide smile fills my vision.

"Here, baby!" she shouts, handing me the drinks.

That pet name rakes through my eardrums.

I take the shot, cheer quickly, and down it in the hopes that the spirit will make it sound better.

It doesn't.

"Another one!" I holler at the bartender who just turned away from us.

He narrows his eyes on me for a moment, but when I cock my head and give him a look Carter would be proud of, he quickly straightens and jumps into gear without question.

"You're on a mission tonight. Bad day?"

"I just want to have some fun," I answer.

"That's what I like to hear. Let's dance!"

I glance between her and the dance floor, debating it. I would normally say yes, but tonight I need at least one more drink in me.

"Later."

"No problem, *baby*, we could just sit here and..." she trails off and so does her hand, sliding up my thigh as her eyes spell something even more suggestive.

Another shot appears in front of me, and I down it before she can say something else, then step off the bar stool, grabbing her hand. I guide her to the dance floor in the middle of this bar that's both seedy and kind of nice at the same time and pull her to me once we're in the middle of all the bodies swaying on a hip-hop song I don't recognize.

Clara wraps her whole body around mine, clutching my nape and pressing her breasts against my chest, her hips against my own, rubbing against my cock. It responds to the friction, but in this hypnotic flickering low light, her face morphs into the one I'm fighting to fucking forget. The whole reason I'm drinking my weight in alcohol and rubbing against a woman I don't actually want.

I flip Clara around, her back against my front, shutting down the image of the forbidden woman.

It works.

Gripping her hips as she rolls them against me, we sway to the rhythm of the music, and I fall deeper into the alcohol haze. *Christ, I really overdid it.* My feet move on their own accord, my body weightless, yet something is off. Closing my eyes, I tighten my grip like it could push Clara deeper into my mind, and I run through the filthy things I'll do to her once we're out of here. Only, I'm finding myself forcing my way through those thoughts, because somehow... not sure how... each and every one of them feels wrong.

This whole situation is—the body in my arms, the sensation against me—it's all wrong. Even her scent.

Until it's not...

Drawing in a deep, hypnotizing breath, spicy ginger sneaks through my senses.

It's on the verge of faint, catching my attention without overpowering. A moment later the sweet smell of rich brown sugar hits me with mind-bending force and my steps falter.

I'm at a precipice, but I can't quite make the leap to rationalize, or accept its implication. It's delicious, decadent, and disturbingly familiar.

My eyes pop open when I pinpoint the familiarity of the combination, and who it belongs to.

Goddamn it! She was finally out of my mind.

Okay, not completely out, but I was so fucking close.

Someone bumps into my back, probably another dancer.

"Sorry, man." A deep voice follows, teetering on slurring. "How about I get you a drink, baby?" I know that's not aimed at me.

I lazily turn my head—the man who spoke wasn't the one who bumped into me, and *her* fucking scent wasn't in my head. Our eyes meet, hers as glassy as mine probably are, and the shock at my sight quickly gets replaced by anger.

"A drink sounds great!" she raises her voice over the music and walks away, some random guy on her tail.

What the actual fuck just happened?

Evelyn-motherfucking-Shaw is in this bar right now.

With a random guy hitting on her.

Drunk.

Oh, hell no!

"Come on, baby, come back to me." Clara's voice is just another thing about her that's wrong.

I turn my gaze from the spot where Evelyn stood, back to the dark-haired woman. Two options run in a loop through my dizzy head: put Clara in a taxi and send her away... or do that to Evelyn and go home with Clara.

Fuck!

"What is it, baby?" she asks.

Did I say that out loud?

She wraps her arms around my neck, running her fingers through my hair, and I have an urge to shove her as far away as possible. What is happening with me?

"Let's get another drink," I tell her, prying her hands off my neck.

"Um, yeah, sure... okay." She doesn't sound all that sure.

I force my gaze on our seats, refusing to stray and search for Evelyn. I don't understand what she's doing here. She's not even old enough to be in this bar, goddamn it!

On clenched teeth I take a deep inhale, trying to rationalize it. Nah, I must be overthinking. She must be with Morrigan, Lulu, or Katya.

She's fine.

I reach the bar, my untouched vodka sour waiting patiently. I throw back half of it, then sit.

She's fine.

But I'm not. My only choice is to use Clara as goddamn bleach and drown myself in her to forget about the woman who threatens the wall I built in the last eight years. All the work I've done to be able to survive as I have, is now at risk. My goddamn integrity too since she's... fuck! Way too young!

I turn to the right, and just on cue, Clare steps between my legs, wrapping an arm around my back, the other palm laid over my chest. She leans in, her hot breath on my ear, before she wraps her lips around my lobe.

"Maybe we should head to my place before the alcohol does more damage. It would be such a shame not to... consummate this night," she whispers sensually in my ear.

I'm just about to open my mouth to answer when I catch sight of something that boils the blood from my veins in one second flat—Evelyn dancing far too close for comfort with that same douche. He's behind her, his hands on her hips, and looking down at her like he wants way more than a dance.

Then I notice she's dressed differently. All black. Tight high-waisted jeans, intentionally ripped in too many places showing far too much skin, combat boots, a loose leather crop top that doesn't touch her waist, and a thin, oversized cardigan that's fallen off one shoulder, exposing her soft skin and thin straps of her top. She looks... at home.

She looks goddamn perfect.

I'm fucked.

But so is the guy currently lowering his hands dangerously.

"Excuse me."

I calmly push Clara back before I get off the stool, and head straight to the wretched woman and the asshole who plans to fuck her.

"You!" I point at him as I near. "Leave," I order him.

"Get your own, man. This one's mine," he says with amusement in his tone, not sparing me a glance.

"*This?*" I sneer. She's not a fucking object. And she's definitely not his.

He also doesn't sound like he's drunk, which pisses me off further because now I know he plans on taking advantage of Evelyn. I step as close as I can get, caging her between us, and I wrap my hand around the guy's throat without hesitation. Evelyn gasps but doesn't move. He lets go of her and goes to grab onto my arm, but his eyes land on mine before his touch does, and I don't miss the moment recognition hits through the haze of the dim lights.

"My bad. She's all yours." He quickly throws his hands up in surrender, but with his throat in my hand, he can't move.

I give it one last squeeze before I let go, but don't step away from her.

She turns toward the asshole. "Hey, no. You don't have to go. I am *not* his!" Evelyn argues, but her words come together a little slow.

"Um, yes, I really do. So... yeah, thanks for a good night. Bye." And with that, he disappears into the crowd.

I sense eyes on us from the other patrons, but I couldn't give a shit about the attention we're attracting.

"You need to go home," I say to her, but it comes out like an order.

She narrows her eyes, slowly cocking her head, and uneasiness scrapes its way up my spine. It leaves goosebumps in its wake. I feel horribly seen. Logic whispers to me that I'm imagining it, but the way her gaze seeps into my veins makes me wonder if she's discovering all my secrets right about now.

My fear eases when her gaze softens, but dread replaces it when she slowly, so fucking slowly, bites one side of her luscious bottom lip. I'm transfixed. It's impossible to rip my gaze away.

Then the woman does the unthinkable—she laughs.

She motherfucking laughs!

And it sounds ridiculously good. Dangerously so.

Brown sugar and ginger intensifies through my senses, contributing to the haze that already took over my brain. Only, now I'm drunk on her.

I'm sick... so goddamn sick.

"I was dancing. You interrupted me," she complains, yet her eyes spell mischief in multiple languages.

I was expecting more protest, fighting back, but it's clear as day—she really is drunk. How did they serve her here? The legal age is eighteen.

"Who are you here with? Katya? Morrigan?" I ask.

She shakes her head slowly and smiles. "I am all on my own. Can you believe it? On my own." She's giddy as she says those words, oddly proud too.

There aren't enough curses and swear words in the English language for me to express how I feel about this piece of information.

"What the hell were you thinking?" I swipe a hand over my face at the stupidity of what she's done. After all that happened to her, being alone is the last thing she should do.

She shrugs and starts looking around, seemingly uninterested in the direction of this conversation.

"I was thinking that I deserve this... especially today."

"You need to go home, where you are safe, and sleep it off," I tell her, my tone grave.

She laughs again and moves along to the music. To my dismay, a slow, R&B tune fills the barroom, and her hips sway torturously from side to side. We're lost in the crowd as more people join on the dance floor, and in a strange paradox, it's turning more intimate. Like we're alone.

"You, mister, need to go back to your girlfriend," she says.

"She's not my girlfriend."

She purses her lips, but then shrugs and straightens.

"Home. Now!" I insist.

"You don't get to tell me what to do, Finnigan Hennessey. Remember?" She pokes me in the middle of the chest as her steps falter, and I quickly grab her bicep to steady her.

She takes it as a cue and wraps her hand around my nape, gripping my side with the other, so warm on my ribs. She starts moving against me without warning, swaying her whole body as she pulls me to follow her rhythm.

All night I felt wrong with Clara around me. But now, with Evelyn's body lined against mine, her scent wrapped around every inch of me, her incredible eyes holding mine in their invisible tether, it feels disturbingly right.

I can't tell if it's the alcohol guiding my feet or my will, but they move with her. As if hypnotized, they follow her flow, our eyes locked onto each other as we lose ourselves in a world that's only ours. It feels both right and wrong. It's perfect and forbidden. It's meant to be and doomed to fail.

This makes no sense.

She makes no sense.

But us... we make all the sense in the world.

It's been too many years, and not one woman has managed to stick to me. But Evelyn has crawled right under my skin, and she's slowly bleeding her soul into my veins. My muscles tense when her warm touch leaves slithering electric current in its wake as she draws down to my clenched fist. I didn't register the ache from the strain until she guided me to relax my hand, then pulled it to her waist.

My touch meets bare skin, the softness so electrifying that it seems as if she's the one caressing me. I can't help but squeeze her delicate flesh. Just once. That's all I allow myself.

But the minx pulls herself closer, pressing against me and making me far too aware of the hard on that I'm failing to control. She's not acknowledging it, and I'm not sure if I'm relieved or slightly disappointed. Before I can think better of it, I reach up and brush the back of my fingers against her cheek, down the soft line of her jaw, and under her delicate chin, guiding it up. Liquid gold sparkles where it meets the gray in her mesmerizing irises, and I don't know if it's her gaze or the touch, but whatever it is ignites a heat that floods my chest like it's seeping out of my very soul. And there's nothing foreign about it. It's a slotted piece of a puzzle I decided long ago I will not try to solve. It's been begging to be let out, to slot into place in the fabric of my being and wrap around the one thing inside my chest I have to protect.

Keeping it at bay has been easy. Until now. After all these years, all it took was one look at *her*.

My fingers trace her bare flesh mindlessly and my feet are still guided by her. I should stop this. It's not right, none of this is right. This must be a sickness.

She's too young, she's not for me. I've never done anything this stupid in my entire life. I'm better than this, and she deserves to find someone better than me.

A man she can trust. A man who can take care of her. Who can protect her. Who *deserves* her.

I am not that man now, nor will I ever be.

Before I can change my mind, I grab her hand, spin on my heels and move away from the dance floor, pulling her with me. She follows willingly as we head toward the exit.

"Wait!" She tugs at my hand. "My bag."

"Where is it?" I stop and turn to her.

She points toward the bar, and I gesture to her to take the lead. There's a joyful sprint in her step. It's new, and it looks peculiar. Not wrong. Not right either. Just... out of character.

You don't know her character, asshole.

When we reach the bar, she gets the attention of the bartender who nods before turning and heading out of sight.

"Oh, my drink!" she exclaims and reaches over to a glass of some pink liquid.

She grabs it quickly, and in a split second, I smack my hand over it, pushing it back on the bar top.

"What the hell do you think you're doing?!" I raise my tone, unapologetically.

"It's—um... my drink."

"That you left unattended for God knows for how fucking long. Literally anyone could have spiked it. Do you understand how much danger you could be in? Jesus Christ, Evelyn! Anyone could take advantage of you!"

She opens her mouth probably to protest, but I can see the exact moment she acknowledges my words, and as her gaze softens, I feel a tinge of guilt at my outburst.

"I didn't think. I've never... this is my first time." Her brows draw together as her eyes lower.

"No, you didn't think. Wait. First time out?"

She nods.

"Well, you shouldn't have been. I should kick the bartender's teeth in for even serving you."

She frowns for a few moments, and then her expression shifts to a realization she doesn't share with me. Just on cue the bartender shows up, sliding a small bag toward her. Before I can grab the guy by the collar, she swipes the bag from him and pushes me away from the bar until we're too far away for me to do anything.

"Where are you going to take me?" she asks, an expectant expression on her face, but her hand doesn't leave my chest.

"I'm putting you in a car and sending you home."

"What? You're joking, right? After all of... that?!" She gestures wildly to the dance floor.

The glassiness over her eyes seems to dissipate, replaced by pure annoyance.

"Goddamn it, you're doing it again. There's nothing here, there can't be anything between us. Do you understand? You're fucking jail-bait, Evelyn!"

She throws her head back, laughing hard enough that she attracts attention.

"That's what bothers you? My age? You can stop feeling so guilty because I'm officially eighteen today. Well, according to that clock on the wall it's past midnight, so technically it happened yesterday."

Oh, fuck...

My mind is spinning with the flurry of thoughts assaulting me. Too many voices argue inside my head, throwing arguments that shouldn't matter right now. I strain to focus and the first emotion I grasp is sadness. This creature has had so much taken away from her, and now this pivotal moment in her life might have passed without proper celebration. We should have known. We should have tried to make her feel special.

Am I overthinking it? She was out with Morri and Lulu today, after all. She probably celebrated.

Then why didn't Katya mention anything? I shake the subject away and grasp one other voice screaming inside my mind. It's the loudest one and the one I want to squash the most—*she's legal now.* I would punch myself in the face if there weren't so many people around me, because that thought eases the sickening guilt. It shouldn't.

It will not, because her age makes no difference at all. One year added onto it is still too many away from mine. This is still wrong.

But it could feel so fucking right.

Goddamn it, no!

"It's your birthday? Did anyone know?" I strain to pull myself out of the cesspit of dangerous thoughts.

"Nope. But don't change the subject. There's nothing stopping you now," she says, a smug expression on her pretty face.

I shake my head and snort. "It doesn't change anything."

Before she can further protest, and before I can convince myself that it does, indeed, change something, I grab her hand and pull her toward the exit. This time she does fight me, but I don't give her any leeway as we pass through the door and into the crisp night air.

"Are you serious right now?" Even now, in her drunken state, she still doesn't yell.

Her tone is filled with annoyance and a hint of embarrassment, but no raised voice. I ignore her as I catch sight of one of my guys who's my designated driver tonight and gesture him over.

"Are you even listening to me?" She pulls on me to grab my attention.

The hurt in her eyes takes me aback, but I can't fucking falter.

"Listen to me, Evelyn. You and I are never going to happen. I don't do relationships, and I certainly don't do quick fucks with *girls* like you."

Her nostrils flare at my choice of words and tears pool in her eyes, but there's much more fury than upset shining in her gaze. She's livid. The rejection seeps through her just as fast as the regret does through me. But it had to be done.

My driver pulls the car next to us, and I yank the back door open. When my eyes drift back to her, the drunk Evelyn is gone. The one I see now could cut me into a million pieces and not even bother burying me. Her back is straight, her gaze stern, and I almost... almost cave and go back on my words. Even if they are for her own protection.

I can't stand the way she looks at me. Fear seeps down to my bones, the kind I never wanted to suffer. Because now, I'm scared she'll never again look at me like she did mere moments ago.

What have I done?

CHAPTER 9
Evelyn

I WAKE UP with wrongness in my veins.

It burns all the way up my throat, and the flood of emotions and pain from all those weeks ago when I was taken, fills me with a raging vengeance. I flip the cover off my body and run to the bathroom, sliding to my knees and hugging the toilet.

Not much comes out as I wretch—apart from the alcohol I drank last night that burns all through my throat. Though I'm surprised I didn't just absorb it all into my system, because it certainly appears that way.

Only, that's not what's making me sick right now. This sickness is different, raw and needy, emptying my veins and leaving me desperate. The itch beneath my skin, the need in my blood vessels, the craving for escape, is back. I should be used to it by now. It comes every morning, and even as it eases through the day, it returns at night. It haunts my dreams and calls for me in my nightmares.

I want to rationalize it, I try to anyway, but I haven't managed yet. I can't wrap my head around the fact that I was only drugged on one occasion. Yes, it was multiple times in a short amount of time, but that was it—one night. I can't justify why this need is chasing me still... it was just one time. It's a terrifying desire to poison my blood, and I'm not sure for how long I can resist this call.

I don't know if I want to anymore.

Images from last night flash through my treacherous memory, and I slide all the way down to the floor, my back hitting the cold tiles as the blue-eyed bane appears in my mind.

"God, what have I done?"

I completely threw myself at him, stupidly thinking he was dragging me out of the bar with such possessiveness because he wanted me. All day at Vincent's house he pushed me away, until we were alone, and suddenly, he seemed lost. It twisted my perception of us.

"You and I are never going to happen."

The stare he pinned me with was just as cold as those words. Then he threw the final blow.

"I don't do relationships, and I certainly don't do quick fucks with girls like you."

How could I have been so stupid as to think that this man wanted something to do with me? He's right—I read far too much into it.

Didn't I...?

I must have imagined the conflict that tightened his eyebrows and darkened his gaze as he threw his rejection in my face. More than once.

I probably read too much in his possessiveness last night, when he found me dancing with that guy who touched me a bit too insistently. Though, even as I protested, I was secretly thankful he got rid of him in that over-the-top display of power.

No, I didn't read too much into that.

This man holds a power over me I don't understand. He stirs something that has been growing deep within the fabric of my soul for a long time. A longing for selfishness and hedonism. A heated look, a lingering touch, even his harsh rejection makes that unfulfilled creature inside of me think it could reach the surface and be free. But it can't.

Especially as I'm slowly seeing the staggering truth—I didn't imagine the way he touched me, how he fought to hold himself back, or his stare as we lost ourselves to the rhythm of the music.

It was real. All of it was real.

"And I was an idiot to think that it could mean something." I slam my palm against the tile, and a knock on the door sends a tremor through me.

Christ.

"Evie, are you in there?"

"Yes, Maya." I jump to my feet, and I catch myself on the door frame as dizziness sweeps through me.

I swallow, forcing back the nausea, and open the door.

"Oh, you look bad. You got so much beauty sleep today, you should be all perfect and glowing," she says, giggling with that cheeky amusement.

"Beauty sleep?" I ask, ignoring the childish insult she doesn't notice.

"Yes. I asked Katya why you weren't having lunch with us, and she said you were having your beauty sleep. I didn't know what that meant, so she said that it's so it helps you be healthy, beautiful, and glowing."

Glowing? I snort, knowing full well sweat is the only thing that could make me glow right now. It sounds like Katya got uncomfortable and had no idea what to say to her. Wait, lunch? What time is it?

"I'm sorry I didn't wake up, sweet girl. I was very tired."

"That's okay. Katya said to tell you that Mamaw June is coming over later to see me, if that's okay with you. So... you can continue that beauty sleep."

At this point I would like it to turn into a coma. No sleep is going to help with what I'm feeling.

"Are you comfortable with her, Maya? Is this something you want to do?"

"Yes. Mamaw June tells me stories, all sorts of fairy tales and legends. And her food is delicious. She said she's gonna teach me to make crêpes. You know, like the ones you used to make all the time. And the cakes too. And—"

"Okay," I interrupt her before she walks further down memory lane and pushes me deeper in this despicable feeling that's making me sick right now. Though, I don't understand how she could possibly remember me baking; she was so young. "If you want to spend time with her, as long as you are comfortable, I'm okay with it. But you tell me if this changes. Yes?"

"I promise."

"Good. Now, let me brush my teeth."

She turns on her heels, skipping out of view, and I close the door, locking it behind me. All I can do right now is allow her to spend time with people who can offer her what I can't. A life, food on the table, safety. People who bring happiness in her life. Who enriches it in some way and puts a smile on her face and laughter in her voice.

I can't offer her any of that.

I haven't been able to in so long. She deserves better, so much better, and all these people... Katya, June, the bloody Sanctum, are giving her just that.

Once again, I slide down until my ass hits the cold tiles, and gather my knees to my chest, clutching my temples in my palms. I know what I need—a plan. A job, money, a roof over our heads, and... to go back to Fleeton.

The idea of returning to that wretched place turns the itch under my skin into molten lava, searing me from the inside out. It's my home. I was born there. Lived there my whole life. Everything left of me, of us, is there. But the pain and sorrow have replaced the good memories I have of that city.

Whether I like it or not, we have to go back. There's no other choice. No matter how much it will hurt to return to the place that took so much away from me—I must.

That thought brings another wave of nausea, and only when the pain becomes too much do I realize I'm digging my nails so hard in my skin, I'm piercing it.

I just need a little help. Just this once. A little help to quiet the rush of dread, to find a happy place, to escape, even if just for a few hours, or minutes. Only once, so after I can come back to the real world ready to tackle it, to make a plan that gives my sister the best life, maybe build one for myself too. A little escape, that's all I need.

I wasn't dancing with that guy last night by pure chance. I chose him because I caught him wiping a certain white powder off his nose and knew he could help. He didn't have what I'm looking for, but told me about someone who sells all sorts of substances and where to go to find him. I saved the information on my phone. It would be so easy. *It will be.* I have no idea how much it costs, but there's enough on Finnigan's card to take out at an ATM along the way. Yeah... Finnigan's card.

I found out that tidbit of information in the bar last night. Because it was either Maddox or Morrigan who used it for me, I didn't pay attention to the name written in gold. I just assumed it belonged to Maddox and didn't bother to look. When I tapped it on the card machine, the name caught my eyes and I swear I bought more alcohol just to spite the man.

Buying something harder than alcohol to quench this need is fitting, after all... he's the one who turned me into this. With his empty promise of saving me before something happened to me. Him who makes me think I could feel alive. Who rejects the possibility of us.

"Oh my god, what am I doing?"

My sister's laugh sounds farther away on the other side of this door, and it wakes me up from this self-destructive trance.

I can't do this to myself, chase the need for this high, I have to be strong for her. If not for me, definitely for her.

I peel myself off the floor and jump straight into the shower, washing off the stickiness from my skin, the stench of alcohol, and hopefully this disgusting craving with it, too.

* * *

For two hours I sat in an armchair listening to or watching Maya smile, laugh, and overall, fully enjoy her time with Mamaw June. Two hours of stories, of June teaching her how to beat eggs, how to mix in flour so it doesn't clump, two hours of twitching. On my part. My legs have been so jittery, I had to gather them both under me on the seat, because both my sister and Mamaw June started looking at me a little funny.

I thought staying here with them would help take my mind off of things. But it did nothing. I'm still a failure. The man with the lisp and his touch on me still haunt. And Finnigan's blue eyes are still here... rejection shining like a lighthouse in the recesses of my mind.

And after the sun went down, night began to fall, and I was feeling even worse, I left. Not before I put Maya to bed and kissed her goodnight. Not before I told her just how much I love her. But before I told her more... like how I wish I didn't fail her, that I didn't bring us to this point where strangers are taking better care of her than I ever could, how I wished she wasn't exposed to the ugly things she still doesn't talk about.

I left before I spilled it all into a confession her little ears didn't deserve to be burdened with. The buzzing in my ears and the sharp prickle in my veins got worse as I told Katya I was going for a walk. She was apprehensive, but I assured her I'll stay close; I just needed to be alone and clear my head. She told me I have to take someone with me, otherwise Finnigan or Maddox are going to kill her, and I mumbled something that sounded like approval before walking out. It was hard to sneak by the security they have in this building, and I thought I was successful until I got downstairs. I lied through my teeth when the guy downstairs asked me if I was going out alone. I told him Maddox was waiting for me outside. He wanted to check himself, but I told him we're in a rush and walked out before he could argue, and disappeared around the corner out of view.

My lies will probably bite me in the ass later, but I can't worry about that now. It's been about twenty minutes and no one has tried to find me, so I must be good. The ride I booked dropped me off a couple of streets away from my destination, since I thought it would be weird to show up right on the dealer's doorstep. Now, I'm walking wherever the navigation app on my phone tells me to. It's following the directions the guy from the bar gave me. I still don't remember his name. I'm not even sure I asked, or if he even offered it to me. Did I tell him mine? Christ, last night was a mess.

However,... tonight will be an even bigger one.

I take another left out onto a main street, crossing toward a road that takes me further toward the edge of Queenscove. It doesn't look quite as elegant as the main street. Not bad, just not as well maintained. There are a few bars dotted around, and what look like tourists walking about the street making a mess of themselves, clearly drunk on this Saturday night.

Maybe I should abandon this *mission* and take the safer way out. Alcohol will be safer. More controlled. Less, much less damaging.

Only, alcohol won't take me to that place where happiness comes in waves of purity and filth. Where it hurts and exhilarates at the same time. Where I forget how to feel and just... exist. Not live—exist. I don't want to live right now.

I turn onto a darker side street, a little quieter too, and the app says I'll be there in one minute. My nerves quiver with anxiety as I near the destination, and I mentally go through each step of my plan to settle them. I already stopped at an ATM and took out enough money to be able to afford a motel for the night. Considering my last experience, I'll probably wake up in a few hours. Though, if I dose wrong I might not wake up. It wouldn't be much of a loss... not when Maya is so well taken care of.

"This is it," I whisper to myself when the app signals I reached my destination.

I look around at the mundane-looking street like I was expecting a giant neon sign saying 'Drugs Here' with an arrow pointing at some guy. But there's nothing out of the ordinary here. A few townhouses, a couple of shops that are closed now, a tattoo shop that still seems to have some people inside, and a bar.

"What the hell am I looking for?"

"Me."

I whip around so fast, I stagger, and five feet away from me stands the guy from last night. At least I think it's him. My memory's a little hazy, but he looks familiar enough.

"You came," he says when he sees I wasn't going to initiate.

"Was I supposed to?" I'm confused.

"After last night's conversation I had a feeling you would show up. You looked a little... impatient."

Sounds about right. Though, his presence fills me with a different anxiety. It's the reality check I needed, but it's not sinking in the way it should, shadowed by the need inside my veins screaming over the recklessness of my predicament.

He grins, obviously reading me like an open book, and takes a step closer.

"You're going to go in that bar over there"—he points to the only establishment of its kind on this street—"you're going to ask for Carl and say a redheaded chick is looking for him outside, then you're gonna walk out. After a guy walks out, follow him. He usually picks an alleyway or something. Got it?"

I don't move a muscle.

"I'm not coming with you." He turns his head toward a storefront a few buildings back. "I own that barber shop, and I was cleaning up when I saw you walk by. My kid's in there waiting for me."

"Okay," I finally say. Kid or not, I just want to get away from him and be on my way. "Did you tell *Carl* I was coming?"

"No. But he's used to strangers asking for his... merchandise."

I nod and take a step backward. "Right. Thanks."

"Sure."

I turn before he can say anything more and speed my pace as I head to the bar. One deep breath later, I stop staring at the door handle and walk inside. A few people turn to look at me, but there's a game on TV they're more interested in. I wait far too long for the bartender to be free, even though probably not even half a minute has passed.

"What can I get you?"

I repeat in my head the words I was told to say, making sure I don't mess it up somehow. I'm sure the *code*, if I can call it that, only works if it's said in the right order.

"Umm... Is Carl around? A redheaded chick is looking for him outside."

The bartender cocks his head, scrutinizing me for a few too many stressful moments, allowing me too much time to remember what a ridiculously reckless situation this is.

Finally, he nods. "I'll let him know."

With a brief thanks, I turn on my heels, wiping my now sweaty palms against my jeans as I walk out of the bar. I stand awkwardly a few steps away from the door, questioning my life choices, when the same door opens, and a man comes out. He barely even glances at me as he turns right and walks away, and I'm debating if this is the right guy that I'm supposed to follow. I look back into the bar, but everything looks normal. No other people are walking about. I turn to the man walking away and he doesn't stop or turn to give me a sign.

I run a hand through my hair, gripping tighter the further back I reach, and just as I'm about to give myself a bald spot, the man turns toward an alley and for a brief, charged moment, he looks at me with a knowing look.

That's him.

All my anxiety toward this situation seeps somewhere in the back of my mind where ignorance sits as well, and I finally follow him.

"What do you need?" he asks the moment I'm a few paces away from him in the alley.

He's maybe mid-forties, with a receding hairline and the most inconspicuous outfit ever. He looks so normal, I wonder why I expected him to scream *drug dealer*.

"I'm not quite sure. I think—"

"You came seriously unprepared, didn't you?" he interrupts. "Look, I'm not some mall shop where you can just browse for hours. What are you looking to achieve?" He raises his eyebrows in a slight exasperation.

"Escape," I say before he barely finished the sentence.

"You want... the hard stuff?" He's rather reluctant.

"Yes."

"Vein, smoke, or nose?"

"Vein," I answer.

He cocks his head yet again and for a few moments, I really thought he was going to tell me off and send me on my way.

"Oh, screw it. Who am I to judge? H, right?" he asks for confirmation.

According to my research, the effects of heroin—H—are the closest to what I experienced when Frankie B injected me.

"Yes," I answer.

"I'll give you enough to make you escape, but not enough to go for good." I should admire his business skills. He's trying to keep his clients alive.

"Okay.

"Sixty, please."

I scramble to get the money out of my pocket and clumsily pull out three bills. I hand them over to him at the same time he pulls out a couple of little baggies from his pocket.

The air shifts behind me just as the tips of my fingers touch the clear plastic.

"What the fuck do you think you're doing?!"

The blood freezes in my veins all at once at the sound of *that* voice.

Shit, I'm screwed.

CHAPTER 10
Evelyn

I THINK I turned to stone, because even my lungs have stopped working. I'm not even sure my heart is beating anymore.

"Answer the fucking question."

A shiver explodes beneath my sternum, and it shakes me out of my stupor as I fully register just who stands behind me.

The dealer's hand snaps back into his pocket and something past apprehension strains his features as he takes in Finnigan.

"Move along, man," the dealer answers, yet it seems like the wrong thing for him to say.

A shadow looms over me, and that shiver that was running rabid through my nerves, now reaches my feet. I start to move when his stern voice stops me dead in my tracks.

"I'm not talking to you, asshole," Finnigan warns as he steps to my right. "You're not doing what I think you are. Right, Evelyn? You're not buying drugs, because that would be fucking ridiculous. Even stupid."

"Did you follow me here? That's seriously screwed up, Finnigan. Am I under surveillance?"

Or is he *stalking* me? How long has this been going?

"Answer me." His tone lowers just as his head does, the blue of his eyes turning to ice, "Are you buying drugs?"

"It's none of your business," I answer, but my voice comes out much shakier than it sounded in my head.

"Everything to do with you is my goddamn business!" he roars, and I flinch.

It's not the tone drawing the reaction, but the underlying implication of his words. In the slight widening of his eyes that lasted less than a blink I can see that his words surprise him too.

From my periphery I notice the dealer attempts a step away from us.

"I didn't say you could leave, motherfucker." In one swift move, Finnigan's arm is extended and at the end of it, right in my eyesight, a gun with a silencer attached is aimed at the man.

I take a step back, but don't dare another when those icy eyes pin me in place. This is a different Finnigan Hennessey than the one who brought me flowers. Different from the one who pinned me against the wall after I slapped him. This Finnigan is made of malice and rage. Even with the soft curls of his hair brushing over his ears, his preppy, pretty boy look has dissipated into an abyss brimming with dangerous power.

Yet, this display is not what shocks me the most—the tingles blooming out of nowhere deep into my lower belly do. They're running wild, chasing a thrill straight to parts of my body that should not react to this aggression. But they do... and I'm forced even stiller, because there is no way I will cross my arms over my breasts or move my legs closer together. I fear I'll give myself away. Though I fear rubbing against those sensitive parts more.

"What did she buy from you?" Finnigan asks the dealer.

"Like the lady said, it's none of your business," he answers.

My breath hitches a moment after the snapping cock of the gun, and the guy's hands shoot up in surrender.

"Heroin."

"Are you fucking kidding me, Evelyn?! Heroin?! Is this it? You're a junkie?" He's truly appalled. And most of all, furious.

Though, it's the look in his eyes that affects me more than his words or tone. It squeezes at my heart because the disappointment is painfully vivid.

"Stop it. No, I am not." There must be another explanation for why my body bellows for it. "You don't understand. You will never understand what it all feels like."

"Make me." He utters those two words like he asked me for a glass of water, not to share my entire story and how I ended up here.

"Excuse me? Yesterday you tried to pay me off to leave. Hours later you shipped me off back to your friend's home because you wanted nothing to do with me. Now all of a sudden you want to pretend that you wish to understand me?" I scoff as I shake my head. "Seriously, go away, and leave the man alone."

The itch beneath my skin grows, and on instinct, I go to scratch my forearms but wince when at the first run on it, Finnigan notices. I drop my hands in the calmest way possible, hoping he doesn't want to investigate the reaction.

"Last night has *nothing* to do with this. You expect me to stand by, watch you destroy yourself for a cheap thrill? Damn it, Evelyn. I thought you were way smarter than this. This is..." But he only shakes his head, emphasizing his disappointment. Then he focuses on the man whose arms are still in the air. "You're seriously protecting the guy who was contributing to your self-destruction?"

I shake my head, scoffing. "A thrill? I may have kept you all at arm's length, but you don't need to get too close to know *thrills* are not what I want in life. You're perched too high on your gilded throne, and you're failing to see what the world looks like for the rest of us. I may be wrong, but if I'm not, then you're a hypocrite. Here's a hard lesson for you: when the horrors of this world put their hands on you, they sear through your flesh until they reach your very soul and brandish you. But that mark never scars, it sizzles. Constantly. An ember that catches fire once in a while and brings you down to your knees all over again. I'm not chasing a thrill, Finnigan. I'm chasing anything else but... this."

I'm heaving when the words finally die on my tongue, and though he only glances at me as he keeps an eye on the drug dealer who looks more horrified by the second. I can still see the shift in his expression. I can't make sense of the feelings breaking through his icy gaze. There's hatred, pain, too, and I wonder if he also bears a sizzling scar that never heals.

"Evelyn," he begins through gritted teeth, "you need to get in the fucking car."

"No. What I do is none of your business, you yourself set that boundary. If anyone's going to leave, it's you."

"So you can continue the *transaction?*" He doesn't disguise the disgust in his tone.

"If I want to do drugs, Finnigan, it's nothing to do with you. Go home and leave us to it," I yell and it actually startles him. At this point, I don't want to continue the transaction anyway, and I'm pretty sure I can pay this dealer all the money in the world, and he won't sell to me, but I'm standing up for the bloody principle of it.

"Oh, is that how it is?! Okay."

Finnigan whips his head back at the dealer and the gun jerks before me with a muffled pop. The noises that follow are ones I'm not sure I understand—a short gasp, a strange thump, a soft crack, a gargle. I follow the direction the gun is pointed at, but there's nothing there. The man is no longer in its aim.

I gasp when I look at the ground, covering my mouth with my hands as my vision remains stuck to the small hole in his forehead and the blood that starts to pool underneath his head.

"There. No drugs for you tonight." he says calmly as he turns his attention back to me.

"Yo—you..." But the words get stuck somewhere in my throat.

"I solved a problem, yes."

There's a dead man here... at our feet. There's panic skirting at the edge of my senses, but outrage is what comes forth instead.

"You're insane. A murderer."

He cocks an eyebrow, looking increasingly bored at my words, slightly confused as to why I'm pointing out the obvious.

"This means nothing to you..." I add.

"It does, but not in the way you think. I refuse to have any remorse for taking his miserable life. Men like him shouldn't be tainting our city."

"Men like him? You just put a bullet in his skull, what makes you so much better than him? Is your perception of the world so twisted?" I lose my cool because for the life of me I can't understand why he thinks what he's doing is better.

"Did I say I'm better? What I do, what *we* do, is fucking different! There are rules, limits that we draw, and they aren't made of chalk or smoke. They are clear as fucking day. Like... human trafficking, in case you forgot, Evie darling."

Oh, he's using that?! No, he's not winning this. But it looks like tonight I'm not winning anything either. Though, the itch I came here to scratch seems to have eased with our heated interaction, and that is downright terrible. He cannot be the one this craving depends on.

"There must be many others in this city. I will find someone else," I blurt out, like that's what matters right now. Christ, I'm an idiot.

"Go ahead, sugar, I dare you. Find ten. Find a hundred. Do me a fucking favor so I can get to them all and clean these streets of filth."

"You wouldn't," I say in disbelief.

"Try me. Fucking try me. I will kill each and every one of them until there are none left for you to seek." There's a feral look in his icy eyes as he speaks those words, two menacing veins pulsing in his temples, and I swear he got taller... wider, all of a sudden. Not that he doesn't tower over me already.

"Christ, Finnigan! You don't want anything to do with me, you made that abundantly clear. Why can't you apply that to this too?"

"I didn't save you out of that container so you can disgrace yourself like this. You fought for your sister! For what?! So you can stick a motherfucking needle in your arm and abandon her? Just so you can feel something other than pain?"

"You don't know anything," I shake my head, holding back a sob as the pain strips me bare. "You don't know what your world did to mine. Even if you did, I doubt you would understand."

He frowns, but I rip my gaze away from his because I can't stand the scrutiny anymore. He looks at me like I'm a circus animal. With disappointment and anger, intrigue and pity, and I can't take it anymore. But when my eyes land on the dead man on the ground once more, I whip around and walk away before I take the blame for his death too.

Silly girl, you are already to blame. It is your fault... whether you run away from the thought or not. You may not have pulled the trigger, but it was your finger on it.

I make it a few steps before my wrist is caught in a strong grip and I'm halted.

"Where do you think you're going?"

"Home. Let go of me." I try to wrench my hand out of his just as his other hand grips my waist and pulls me toward him.

"Get in the car, Evelyn." He points toward the black, boxy SUV a few feet away.

"I'm not going anywhere with you."

"Why? Do you still think it's a good idea to walk alone, in the dark, in an unfamiliar neighborhood? You really have no self-preservation instincts?"

"Why do you care?" I whip around stepping right in his face.

His chest rises and falls with deep, controlled breaths that look too slow to be calm. No words come, but his gaze on me is so intense, focused to the point that it seems to burrow into me. It digs further and further until I'm afraid it's going to find a home inside of me. My eyes widen and my chest bursts in uncomfortable prickles.

"Fine." I roll my eyes and turn toward his car when no answer comes.

Ever the gentleman, he opens the door for me, and before we leave, he pulls his phone out, typing furiously as his gaze snaps between me and his screen.

"Feels like an inappropriate time to text your *girlfriends*," I snap, crossing my arms against my chest, hating the tinge of jealousy that slipped through.

Finnigan cocks an eyebrow and I expect a pinch of amusement at the corner of his lips, but it never comes. I can't tell if I was right or just very wrong.

"Clean-up crew," he mutters under his breath.

I'm confused for a brief moment until my gaze drifts to the dark alley where the dealers body lays in the shadows.

"Oh." I leave it at that since I have no idea what else to add. I don't feel bad for assuming it was one of his women.

My phone vibrates in my pocket, and I jerk at the sensation, pulling it out in confusion. *Maddox Severin* lights up the screen, and I stare at it until Finnigan huffs next to me. I shoot him an angry look as I swipe over the screen and answer.

"Are you safe?!"

Maddox sounds anxious. Almost breathless.

"Umm yes."

"Then what the hell are you doing on Lloyd's Street?"

"Wait, you know where I am too? Are you guys tracking me?" I turn to Finnigan, but he just cocks an eyebrow like I just asked a ridiculous question.

"Yes. Katya called to tell us she was worried and found out you didn't take security with you, just left alone. You could still be in danger, Evelyn." His tone is right on the cusp of guttural, his protective instinct bleeding through. *"Why are you there?"*

"It's my own business," I answer with a clear edge to my voice.

"To buy fucking heroin!" Finnigan raises his voice over me, and I shoot him a piercing look, seething. "What? Embarrassed?" he taunts.

"I did not just fucking hear that," Maddox seethes.

"I'm done with this conversation. Thanks for the worry. Finnigan is taking me home." I end the call before the man who's making me feel two inches tall can show anymore disappointment in what I was about to do. I can't stand it.

This car feels too small, even if it's one of the biggest SUVs I've seen, I'm too close to him and the air is too heavy. I pull at the collar of my T-shirt, I fiddle with the sleeves, I do anything and everything to calm me down, but it doesn't work.

I'm heaving. "Can we go already?"

"Once the crew arrives. A few more minutes."

I run my fingers through the length of my hair, urging time to pass by faster.

"What the fuck is that?" Finnigan exclaims, and I quickly swipe my gaze out the windows, looking for whatever triggered him.

But tightness bounds my wrist, and he extends my arm toward him. My blood turns cold and before I turn to look, I know exactly where I'll find his gaze. He lifts the sleeve of my cardigan, looking at the gauze wrapped around my forearm and no matter how hard I try to wrench it out of his grip, it's futile.

"It's just one more thing that's none of your business," I snap at him.

"Did someone hurt you, Evelyn?" His eyes shine and darken all at once, malice seeping through. He looks too affected by the thought that someone might have.

"No one hurt me."

"Please tell me you're not—"

"No." I cut off his train of thought, knowing where it was going.

I managed to rip my wrist out of his grip, but in the process, he reached over and grabbed the other one, exposing yet another gauze. His gaze shoots to mine and pierces right through my very soul, demanding and ruthless.

"For fuck's sake, Evelyn. Explain what's happening."

"Stop it. Let go of me. I told you it's none of your business." I pull the sleeves down, fisting them in my palm, and wrap my arms around my middle, turning to the side window.

I watch as a van drives down the street toward us, but stops in front of the alley, blocking the access and our view. Finnigan starts our car at the same moment, flashes his headlights twice and drives off.

Freaking finally!

"I need to know you're okay. Safe... even from yourself." He drops his tone, pulling a sense of calmness in it.

My chest rises with a deep, strained breath, and I drop my head against the headrest on a long exhale.

"Sometimes the nightmares seep into reality and it's hard to tell the difference." I let the answer flow out of me without turning, without offering further explanation.

He can do with this what he wishes, because I'm never going to say more of it. But Finnigan doesn't ask anything else. Silence falls inside the car, and he takes me on one of the most uncomfortable rides of my entire life. Our tension is a palpable, living thing mixing together.

But underneath it all, not as deep as I would like it, there's something else. A sizzling sensation made of heat and unquenchable thirst.

Even as the car slides to a stop in front of Katya's building, my breaths aren't lighter. The tension still there.

"Remember, Evelyn"—Finnigan says as I open the door, and step out—"find another and I'll fucking kill them too."

His words crash straight in my gut. He knows what he's doing, that I'll be reluctant to try again in case he speaks the truth, and I'll end up with more blood on my hands. Even if I'm not the one pulling the trigger.

"I'll kill them all before you ever get your chance to poison your soul," he adds as I whip around, slamming the door behind me.

Jokes on him... the poison is already in. Though, I'm not sure why the state of my soul is on his mind.

* * *

This time around I actually woke up in the morning. Not that I slept much after the events of last night.

As much as I hate to admit it, my interaction with Finnigan did something to me I didn't expect. It calmed the itch, and I think I hate him more for it.

What bothers me more, though, is the fact that I am not more affected by the murder I witnessed. Until I drifted off to sleep, I replayed it in my head. I woke up expecting to be completely torn up, traumatized. None of that happened.

You know why, Evelyn, but admitting it means swallowing your pride and accepting more than you're ready to.

That incessant voice speaks in my head yet again. The dark side of my consciousness.

You don't care...

I care. I do!

You didn't care back then either...

I'm losing my damn mind!

I pull a cardigan over the tank top and jeans, and walk out of the bedroom, straight to where Maya is sitting at the dining room table, eating her breakfast.

I need coffee. I need to get out.

"Maya, want to go for a walk?" I ask her as she pushes the empty bowl away from her.

"Umm... yeah, sure. Can we go to the park?"

"We can. Are you okay? You don't seem that keen," I ask.

She nods. "It's just that... not sleeping in the same bed has been strange," she says in her sweet little voice, and it pulls at my heartstrings.

My lovely, sweet girl. I thought she would enjoy having a bed all to herself, finally. Although that's not the reason why I did it. I'm terrified that I'll become even more vocal during my nightmares, and she'll hear something she shouldn't. I don't want to traumatize her, especially if I say something about what happened to me after we were separated in that warehouse. So, I make it up like I'm going to bed later, wait until she falls asleep, and then settle for the night on the sofa. It's safer.

"Don't worry, you'll get used to it. But I can keep you company until you fall asleep, how about that?"

"Yes, please!" Her eyes light up and that little bit of happiness I gave her warms me.

I did that. I put that smile on her face. There may be some hope for me after all.

"Katya came last night when you were gone. I like her. She came and kissed my forehead, Evie. Can you believe that?!"

I almost can't, no. Yet, from the way she looked at me when I came back last night, I can understand it. She stood in the middle of the open space living area, arms crossed tight against her chest, and no word at all fell out of her mouth. Her stern eyes and tightly pursed lips were making me feel horrible enough, even a bit afraid, but the disappointment was the one tearing through my soul. Yet another person I disappointed, all in one night.

"That was very nice of her. Now, go on, get your shoes on and we'll leave," I urge my sister.

She climbs off the chair and rushes to the hallway as I follow, pulling my own shoes on. When Jay shows up in the corridor outside the apartment, he insists on coming with us. I assure him we're only going to the park next door, but he's having none of it. Only after I text Maddox and tell him I'm going out with Maya, alone, does he finally relent. I'm not a prisoner. I know they're doing this for my safety, I'm sort of happy someone cares, but it's annoying, nonetheless.

"Oh, wait." Maya tugs her hand out of mine as we walk through the ground floor lobby of the apartment building toward the exit. "Need to retie my laces."

I turn to her but pull my phone out to look on the maps for a coffee stand in the park. I'm engrossed in the search, when the elevator dings and only moments later a chill runs down my spine.

"Finnigan!" Maya calls out excitedly, and I swear, the blood freezes in my veins.

I turn, ready to berate the man for daring to follow me yet again, but what I find instead leaves me speechless, mouth slightly agape. The doors of the private elevator I've never been on close behind him, and attached to him is a gorgeous, tall, platinum-haired woman with enviable curves she sways as she walks in my direction. No, not my direction, the exit.

The woman is all over him. He doesn't react to her touch, his gaze fixed on me, but he doesn't push her away either. I'm nervously scratching the edge of the phone case, acknowledging silently that it's ten in the morning. There's only one reason why he would be leaving her place at this time in the morning—he's sleeping with her.

Here... in the same damn building I live in.

The nerve! Did he pick her up in front of the building or something after he dropped me off? Did he already know her? Couldn't he have picked a woman who doesn't live *here*?!

And this is a completely different woman than the one he was with at the bar. Fleeting comments I caught from his friends cross my mind, like the one that Finnigan doesn't settle, always a different woman. The man is a playboy. According to Maddox he's making his way through all of Queenscove and its tourists.

But he could do that anywhere but here.

That pang of irrational jealousy pulls at me again, and I curse it back down. I have no claim on this man, he doesn't owe me anything, and he certainly wants nothing to do with me. If we don't count the following. And wanting to keep me safe. And the heated dance in the bar.

Something brushes against the edges of that wretched muscle pumping blood in my chest, but I refuse to acknowledge what blooms at the touch.

"Good morning, Evelyn," he says calmly, yet his gaze flickers away from me.

Is that discomfort? No, it can't be.

"Here, Finnigan? Really?" The words spill before I can stop them, but the man infuriates me. "You couldn't go do *this* at your place?" I wanted to say *her*, not *this*.

Lifting an eyebrow, he cocks his head and amusement replaces the slight confusion. "This *is* my place. This entire building, actually, and I live in the penthouse."

Excuse me, what?! I finally know how it feels for your soul to leave your body—this is it. Mortification isn't quite a strong enough word to describe the horrifying embarrassment, shock, and emptiness plaguing me. He owns the building I currently live in. He lives here. This whole time.

I don't understand how this has never come up before. All this security makes much more sense.

"Right." That's all I manage to say.

It doesn't erase the amused expression pulling at all the painfully handsome lines of his face. The chances I will bump into him now that I go out of the house more, just like this, with another model-looking *date* on his arm, late at night or too early in the morning, will grow exponentially.

That's the cherry on top, because his presence alone is enough to drive my anxiety off the wall. He lives here... in the same building as me, and I'm somehow supposed to find the strength and peace of mind to sleep soundly at night with the knowledge he's just above me. Doing *things*.

The thought makes me mildly nauseous.

No. I can't do it. I won't.

"Maya, come on. We're going."

She looks between us, her little brows scrunching as she tries to understand what's happening, but fails. She's still staring as she moves to grab my open hand.

I don't even say goodbye as I walk out in the mildly humid, warm air of Queenscove and breathe in the slight salty scent.

"The park is that way." Maya pulls on me, trying to sway me in the opposite direction.

"Change of plans, honey. We're going to go see Loreley."

"What for?"

"I think it's time we move out of Katya's and into our own place."

CHAPTER 11
Finnigan

YOU DON'T KNOW what your world did to mine.

Evelyn's soft voice wraps around the threads of my mind for the hundredth time.

After a few days of wondering what had been done to her, I went to barge into Katya's and demand she tell me what she knows. I managed to turn around just in time. A little horrible voice in my head had to repeat to me over and over that Evelyn Shaw was trouble, and getting close, knowing more about her, will destroy me.

All over again.

I barely stopped myself when, after over a week of being haunted by those words, I wanted to call Carter and ask him to find out every single aspect of her life. It was a horrible invasion of privacy and trust, but I couldn't bear those words anymore. Everything in me was demanding to know what she meant. That horrible voice I know to be mine, raged at me to back away from her. Far, far away, where the feelings taking root inside of me could rot and die before the tendrils could reach too deep. I stopped myself, nonetheless.

Weeks have passed now, and I'm just as clueless about the meaning of those words as I was when she all but spit them in my face. I haven't laid eyes on Evelyn in just as much time.

Their meaning is a mystery, but they offend me too. What did she mean about *my world?* What did I, or us, ever do to her? We saved her, damn it! We helped her. Offered her shelter, food, money, even a one-way ticket back to where she came from.

Yet, as the tip of the stiletto knife draws the slowest drop of blood from under the chin of the long-haired bastard currently strapped to a chair before me, and his condescending beady eyes attempt to stare me down, I understand Evelyn's words just a little more.

My world is this one. Where men like him roam the streets freely, kill families, rape little children, sell boys and girls, and use people like they're worth less than cattle. *My world* ripped her and her little sister out of theirs and tried to take their innocence away.

Though, I can't help but be angry and downright offended that she thinks I fit in the same category as him. What she thinks of me shouldn't affect me like this, and I hate her because it does. I hate myself more for allowing it.

There's no worth in me for a woman like her. *My world* will ruin her... I'll find her naked body, broken gruesomely, dead in a pool of her own blood, before I can reach her. I won't save her. I will only damn her. Just like I did *Hanna*.

There is no other outcome.

It doesn't matter that Roberto Bartiste was the one who wielded the blade that cut the soul out of her; I might as well have handed it to him.

My brother, Ronan, and Vincent are idiots for bringing women they love into this world. My brother left for this reason, but I don't think he can ever be truly out. *Crime* is not our job, this is not a goddamn profession. It's a force that lives in our blood and the fibers that form our being, programming our brain from its early development. Eventually, this life will find my brother, his wife, their son, and drag them back into it. For their sake, I hope they can skirt at the edge of it rather than submerge themselves back in its enticing clutches.

Because it is enticing. I could never live a different life devoid of this power, adrenaline, and blood. This is where I belong, and no woman should be here with me.

"Who is your boss?" I ask the man tied to the chair in the middle of the warehouse we found him in.

I don't wait for words to fall out of his mouth and sink the tip of the knife deeper into the hollow part under his chin. If I go deep enough, I'll impale the tendons first, then his tongue.

Not yet though, I need to know who he works for. All we have are two untraceable names that are leading us in circles. And the only men who could have given us the information are dead—Morrigan's father, Liam O'Rourke, her ex, Ryan Holt, and Vincent's father, Lester Boseman. Now we know they were just a connection to the docks of Queenscove and the trading routes, and the operation is bigger, run by a whole other organization.

Right now, we're almost two hundred miles away from Queenscove, on the tip Dietrich, Loreley's father gave us. We're finally face to face with someone higher up in the organization we're trying to find. Higher, but not fucking high enough.

"You're pathetic. All of you," the guy says, laughing maniacally like he has a leg to stand on. "You came all this way, and you don't even know who you're looking for. Who are you people?"

I ignore the question about who we are. It's not like he'll be alive long enough for the answer to matter.

"You think that we would have found you if we didn't know something? We need *real* names!" I say, watching his blood drip down the shiny silver, quicker after I push the blade deeper holding the back of his head steady at the same time.

A mangled cry escapes his exposed throat and satisfaction blooms. No words do, though.

Carter stands behind the man, and need sparks in his hazel eyes as he looks down at him. He's *The Carver* after all, a nickname he has thoroughly earned in the last two, three years. Carving is not my thing, but torturing for information, pouring emotions into an instrument that draws blood, I do thoroughly enjoy sometimes. But Carter... he needs this. I'm not sure if blood is what he sees when he peels the skin off his victims. I don't think it's emotions he draws on either. It always looks more like punishment. Of his victims or him, I don't know.

Carter is twitching now as I interrogate this man, but this one is mine.

"Give me a name. You think that there's no point in talking since we're gonna kill you anyway, right?" I wait and he just stares at me, afraid to breathe so my knife doesn't sink deeper in his flesh. "But keep in mind that you're not alone in this world. You seem to have made some commendable efforts to hide your family, but..."

His eyes widen with fear as I pause for a reaction, and what I'm seeing is what I need.

"It wasn't enough to hide them from us," I continue.

"Your wife is pretty..." Vincent appears on my right, phone in hand, showing our prisoner a photo of his betrothed in front of their lavish house in a secure, gated community.

"How did you get in?" The man dares to speak and hisses in pain as the knife sinks a little deeper with the movement of his jaw.

"You can get in anywhere as long as you know the right information about the right people. Everyone has a weak spot to exploit, and information is always the key," I explain.

"For example," Vincent continues, "I know that this photo of your wife will make you twitch, but it's the next one that will loosen your tongue and make you spill your secrets."

He swipes once on the screen and the man all but jumps off the chair when he sees his dear mother on it. I pull the knife down to avoid this idiot slicing his own throat on it.

Finding out he's a mama's boy was easy, finding out that the sick bastard has had an inappropriate relationship with her for years was a bit harder. But we did. Anyone who *loves* their mother that much will sacrifice their wife for her.

"Leave her the fuck alone! Where is she?!" he bellows.

"Give. Me. A. Name!" I scream right in his face, and his ass hits the chair with a thud.

"I don't know it!" he cries.

He actually fucking cries, and I exchange looks with Carter and Vincent. Carter looks bored and Vincent shrugs.

"He told us to call him Vassallo, but only some of us know it's not his real name. None of us know what it is though. The only one who might, is Frankie B," he says.

Frankie B. What a stupid fucking name.

But we already know these names, we need the real fucking ones. However, it is interesting to find out that not only do people in their organization not know Vassallo's real name, but most don't even know it isn't. So, we'll need to go straight to the top.

"Who is the guy for the organization?" I ask.

"He comes across like an idiot, but he's Vassallo's right-hand man. Young, half his age maybe. He's not the sharpest tool in the shed, but even that blunt edge could do some damage."

I know for a fact it does. Evelyn's memory from that night is patchy, she has more gaps than information. When Maddox found her, he said she was out of her fucking mind, in a trance from how heavily she was drugged. She refused to tell us if she remembers what happened to her after she was separated from her sister. I noticed a few winces, some straining when she moved or sat down, so I know the motherfucker hurt her, she doesn't need to spell it out for me. I'll crucify Frankie either way, slice him from throat to dick, and deliver his guts to her.

I owe her that much.

Goddammit... why is this just dawning on me? Was she seeking drugs that night because she's starting to remember more?

I take one deep breath, looking at the man panicking before me, and wonder if there's any more I can get out of him.

"Where is their headquarters?" I ask.

"Not with the rest of us. There are multiple centers of operations. He visits, but he has his Sergeants who handle each one. Vassallo prefers to meet in random locations for briefings, missions, and others. He only comes when an important shipment arrives. I don't know where the other centers are, he keeps his operation fragmented so if something happens, we don't all go down. My center is in Eastling, North of the city in an old asylum. It's big, but I don't even know if it's the biggest one. Now, is my mother going to be okay?"

The man spilled the information like it was nothing, all loyalties and fears gone when it came to his dear mother.

"Vassallo only comes when big shipments arrive?" I ask.

"He used to, but rumor has it one of them got raided a month or so ago by someone, and if they would have come half an hour earlier or something, they would have found him there. He hasn't intercepted shipments since," he answers.

"The only chance is to catch him if he meets with his Sergeants or visits a center?" Vincent asks.

"Most likely. What about my mother?!" he asks impatiently.

"Give me the name of the Sergeants." I ignore his plea.

"Is my mother safe?" he rages, fear reddening his eyes.

"The names, motherfucker!" I slam my knife right under his balls, scratching his suite trousers, his mouth gaping as he attempts to move backward in the chair. Carter is truly bored now, and he already walks toward the exit. Vincent moves away, ready to follow.

"We don't have knowledge of the others." He shakes as I push the blade up just enough to make him sweat, and breathes out loudly when I decide to retreat and pack it in my rib holster. "Mine, the one who's supposed to come here today to make sure this warehouse is ready for the next shipment, is called Leopold Gr—"

The word sticks in his throat as his head whips backward with a bullet lodged in the middle of his forehead. I jump to the left, ducking and rolling onto the dirty, concrete floor, just as gunfire and grunts erupt all at once.

We weren't stupid enough to come here alone. A whole team is outside, and from the sounds of it, they're all fighting. I catch a faint flashing light at the other end of the warehouse, between some old, rusty equipment forgotten here, and I draw my gun as I duck behind a concrete column. I'm strung so goddamn tight, a buzzing grows in my ears, and my hands twitch to squeeze the trigger and release this pressure.

A moment later a bullet lodges itself at the edge of the pillar, and I lower myself, taking aim toward its source. Three more shots, a loud thud, and the gunshots aimed at me stop.

"I think it was a stray. Clear!" I hear Vin somewhere behind me.

He was caught close to the exit, but ducked behind some rusty machinery. That was quick. Yet, the pressure in my head hasn't eased, and the buzzing is still there.

Slowly, the commotion dies down outside, and we move toward the exit. The door creaks open, and both Vin and I take aim. Carter steps through, a thick streak of blood running from the base of his throat, down to his crotch, stray splatters everywhere.

"Yours?" I ask quickly.

"No." He turns and exits, leaving Vin and I with no further explanation.

"Okay, I guess." I gesture at The Serpent to walk out, and I follow.

"I'll call the clean-up crew," one of our men say.

And boy are we gonna need them. In this thirty-second massacre, at least twenty bodies dropped. I spot a couple more around the corner as we head to our car, and one more in the bushes. I'll have to give Madds a pat on the back, because he's damn good at training our men.

"I need a driver, the rest of you stay here and wait for the clean-up crew. Leave the bodies where they are, but hide and guard the outside perimeter in case more come," Vincent orders our men.

"I'm staying. I think a shipment is coming. If it is, I want to coordinate the rescue." Carter steps away from us.

"Okay. What's the plan if it is?" I ask.

"Kill all the bad guys, clean it up, and give an anonymous tip to the local police to deal with the shipment. They'll interview the victims, and I'll get all the info from their system after," he answers.

I nod, liking the idea. As much as it would be nice of us to deal with this *shipment*, we don't have the capacity to accommodate more people. The last rescue operation was so complex mainly because we had to figure out who all those kids belonged to. It was fucking expensive to protect their families after we returned them, and it ate a lot of our time, leaving us uncomfortably vulnerable. We really weren't, but it felt like it.

"Let's go then." I gesture to Vin, turning and heading toward our car.

I climb in the back seat, rubbing a hand over my face and wondering just how I'm gonna burn out through this gnawing pressure that's making me twitch. My usual method, getting pinned under a woman bouncing away on my cock, isn't going to work. It hasn't worked for weeks... no matter how much I tried. I'm not even excited over a blow job anymore. When lips wrapped around me, it was like slugs sliming their way up my length.

Twice I managed to fuck to completion... and both times I left their place like I was being chased away. I couldn't bear looking them in the eyes and holding a conversation, not when they were a cheap version of the one woman who haunts my dreams and fills every conscious thought when I'm awake.

"Take me home," I say to the driver who climbs in after Vin.

Though I plan on going a few floors below mine.

Maybe this time she'll actually be there.

CHAPTER 12
Finnigan

"YOU'RE NOT HERE for me," Katya states bluntly when I show up in her apartment.

I narrow my eyes on Katya, that gnawing pressure turning hot at her knowing gaze. I don't need her to tell me why I'm here, and I certainly don't want her to act like she knows me so fucking well that she can predict what I'm thinking.

It's my own fault for allowing it. No matter if she's basically family.

"Evelyn doesn't live here anymore." She continues.

That much I gathered, but I can no longer track her phone, so I couldn't be sure. I know Carter can track her in a different way, easily, but I couldn't fucking ask without arousing suspicion or a long line of questioning. Despite this, more than once I had to stop myself from asking him or Maddox about her. Maddox, especially, since I know he's been training her. At what times, I have no idea, because no matter when I go to the Fightclub, I never cross paths with her.

"I'm here to talk about a mission." I say, crossing my arms against my chest.

It's difficult, but I ignore her cocked eyebrow and suggestive look. It's even harder to keep my eyes from wandering about the space in search of *her*.

"And the *mission needs* to be executed tonight?"

"No."

"Then why did you drag me out of bed?" She crosses her arms over her chest, dressed in her silk pajamas.

"We need to try a different angle." I ignore her question. "We found out that their operation is fractured intentionally, so the different centers don't know where the others are or who works there. It's why no matter who we find, we can't get any fucking useful information out of them. The guy from tonight said their center is North of Eastling, just a bit further West than we were, in an old asylum."

She narrows her brows, pursing her lips like she always does when she's mulling over the information.

"And?"

"Think of who you know out West, around Eastling, if you have any connections there. Someone over there would have heard something. These people aren't fucking perfect. Just like the ones in Queenscove, they'll talk when they think no one important is listening. I want to avoid sending girls, but if you sniff something that tells you we should, then go for it. And here, focus on people who knew O'Rourke and Holt, not necessarily professionally, with some sort of connection out West."

Thank fuck for thinking on my feet, because leaving Katya's apartment without saying anything, after her implication about Evelyn, would have proved her right.

Is Evelyn here, though? I pace casually, my gaze sweeping around the spots she might appear from. Like the door leading to the pantry, where I once found her checking out some small jars of colorful sprinkles, before she put them down as if I caught her doing something she shouldn't have. Or out on the terrace, where I saw her several times from outside, quietly watching the world beyond her with heartbreaking hope in her eyes. Like the world could be hers... in another time, another life, breeding a disturbing need inside of me to prove to her it could happen in this one. Or maybe she'll come out from the corridor that led to the room that was briefly hers.

"Yeah, I know a couple in the general area. One is luxury, the other more... common. I might have to go, but I'll put feelers out first. How many girls do you want me to send out in Queenscove?" Katya's voice pulls me back in the moment.

I can't think of the girl who's now technically a woman. The issue of her legality doesn't change how screwed up this is for me to think of how she felt against me when we danced.

What the fuck am I doing here?

"Maximum five, we don't want to attract attention when they all start sniffing around about the same subject," I answer Katya, continuing to pace, my steps heavier now, following my increasing pulse.

"I'll do three and start tomorrow."

We'll soon have to stop calling them *our girls*, because we've recruited a few men too recently, since some targets swing that way and we had a gap in our service. But the men aren't fully trained yet and we value safety and skill above all else. Katya's been hard at work, as always, coordinating, training, and everything in-between. Though Raven has taken on part of the responsibilities too since she's our most skilled employee in that department.

This is not your run-of-the-mill luxury escort service. Their training is not only about sex, but spying and extracting information. They are taught various methods of manipulation, but they also handle the installation of trackers and listening devices. Most of them started off as escorts and wanted more, or even attempted more on their own as they had better skills and inclinations. Some don't even get to the sex part since they deal in particular kinks and sexual desires. They are all brilliant at what they do. We also train them hard in self-defense and combat, though they are never alone at a job. But the brilliant part about all of this is that no one outside of our organization knows the escort service is ours.

We only interact with Katya publicly if she has an employee with her and it looks like we're assessing or hiring, but even that happens very, very rarely. Our interactions are always in private to ensure that whoever hires the girls doesn't suspect that whatever information they spill gets to us. Some of these pompous cunts treat them like the help, and it doesn't cross their minds that they pose a threat.

It's done now, Katya has all the information she needs, and I have mine—she's not here. And I can't be in here anymore either, in this space that was never Evelyn's, yet she haunts incessantly. Even if it's my memories and wishful thinking doing the haunting. I say goodbye and head out the door, but before it closes, I hear Katya's voice behind me.

"She doesn't live here anymore, Finnigan. I don't know what happened between you two, but she told me not to tell you where she went. If you asked."

I slam my hand against the door, stopping it before it shuts. "I didn't fucking ask."

"And I didn't tell you. When you go looking for her, keep in mind that sometimes, in order to escape the past, you have to let yourself experience the future. You don't have to let what Bartiste did to you take everything away."

Why the hell does she think I'm going after Evelyn?

"You're crossing a line, Ekaterina. Don't fucking dare analyze me or assume what I want." My tone is low, but hard enough that the security guy closest to the apartment stiffens.

I turn once again and leave.

"You deserve it, Finnigan! It's time!"

The door slams over Katya's raised voice, and I stifle a laugh. She has no idea what the fuck she's talking about.

Deserve...

No, I don't. And I won't fool myself into thinking there's a goddamn chance.

Evelyn

"WHY ARE YOU here?"

The words don't linger in the air. This room gives off the impression of a padded box with large, period windows and classy decor. The words melt when they touch the wallpapered walls. It's my fourth session here and every time I hold back from appeasing my curiosity about this structure.

"Evelyn, why are you here?"

Same thing—the sounds dissipate in the softest way.

The Dr. clears her throat in that polite gesture women of her caliber tend to make. My vision focuses on her once again just as she tilts her head and narrows her eyes for only a split second. The analysis has begun.

Who am I kidding? It began the moment I walked through that solid, paneled wooden door.

"Is this room soundproof?" I finally ask that burning question I've kept in since the first time I stepped foot in here.

Or am I just stalling?

She straightens her head, and her eyes soften.

"It is. I believe in my patient's privacy."

"It's quite extreme, don't you think? Are we expecting people on the other side of this wall to press their drinking glasses against it to hear the confessions of depressed housewives and men who fantasize about their mommies?"

Her gaze narrows on me once more, only, this time it doesn't shift back. Either she's finally losing her patience with me, or my words gave her new and brighter ideas for the next lines of questioning.

"Wait. You are," I continue, slightly shocked. "This is not just for privacy, is it?"

She draws in a deep breath and relaxes back into her thickly padded, high-back armchair.

"It is, Evelyn. For protection as well."

"Victims…"

"And criminals," she adds. "I take private patients, referrals from hospitals, and also from the police. I work as a forensic psychologist too, which means that I took precautions to keep these conversations as private as possible, before court appearances."

She's honest. Interesting.

"What most surprises me is that people actually end up in court in this city."

She leans forward in the dark brown armchair. "What do you mean?"

She places the tip of her shiny black pen against the paper notebook she holds on the armrest, ready to add to what is probably her conclusion of me. It's distracting, and it takes me a few seconds longer than necessary to answer.

"Look around you; crime is everywhere. Walking on the same streets, eating in the same restaurants, waiting in the same lines as everyone else before they return to their underworld." I scoff. "Underworld… Like it's not all out in the open. Yet, no one seems to care around here."

"Is this *underworld* the reason why you are here?" the Dr. asks.

Nothing makes me angrier than the answer to this question. It's a battle between good and evil—not just in my brain, but my morals too. My heart screams at me every day to deal with it, but the rest of me can't obey. Not when the flashbacks come… when the ghosts of my scars remind me that they're still there even if they no longer mark the skin of my forearms, and the ridiculous need to poison my veins flares up.

"Yes," I answer, but even I don't miss the slight tremble in my voice.

"Yes?"

"Umm… no." I look down to my tightly clenched hands, then back up at her, hating how little self-control I have over my feelings and body language.

"No. Okay." She cocks her eyebrow, and I itch to push it back down with the tip of my finger.

"Look, it's complicated."

"How?" the Dr. asks.

My gaze fixes on hers and she holds it. Doesn't blink, doesn't move. I'm not even sure she's breathing. She's like a soft, dark-skinned statue, glowing in the sunlight streaming through the window.

"Why is it complicated, Evelyn? Were they the ones who hurt you?"

I sigh and turn my attention to the view, the thick, sharp leaves of an old palm tree just about touching the glass with every breeze. Every time it gets real close and I think it's going to make contact, I open my mouth to answer her question. But it never does, so I don't either.

"It's funny, isn't it? How this concept gets ingrained in us as children—good and evil—like it could ever be so black and white. Like good doesn't depend on evil for the universe to consider it good, and evil doesn't depend on it to become despicable. In reality, there's no such thing." I turn back to her. "Is there, Dr. Moss?"

"It is one way of looking at it all," she answers, seemingly accepting the slight change in the subject.

"It's all gray. We're all morally corrupt in some way. Most of us are willing to do the unimaginable for the ones we love, but the ones more inclined are willing to do it just because. Evil isn't just evil." A soft thud pulls my attention to the window—the palm leaf. It's time to answer the previous question then. "Evil has many shades, and I was both hurt and saved by it."

"Which one makes you angrier?" she asks. "The evil who hurt you, or the one who saved you?"

My lips part as that question takes me aback.

Both... right?

"Or is it you who actually makes you angry? Do you belong on the same color spectrum, Evelyn?"

My gaze whips to hers, eyes wide as the words crash into my bones. It doesn't take me more than a couple of seconds to realize that the question was rhetorical in her eyes. She only asked it so I can answer it for myself. So I can admit it to myself.

"*They* make me angry. The ones who hurt me, who took me away from my home, and the one who promised to save me before it was too late, yet failed." This is the only thing I'm admitting today.

I don't share a color palette with *them*.

I definitely do not, no matter my vicious crimson dreams, once the nightmares end.

* * *

I left Dr. Moss's office with a new need inside of me. One that took me straight to Maddox and The Fightclub. He brought me here a few weeks ago, after I had a particularly bad reaction to a man walking behind us on the street. It wasn't exactly a panic attack, but I freaked out.

It reinforced how powerless I truly feel. The vulnerability was slowly killing me, and Madds acknowledged that I needed to gain control. Not back, but more than I had before. Because mine and my sister's kidnapping happened while I was technically in control.

I wasn't.

I glance down at my strapped hands for a moment, rejoicing in the ache in my knuckles. After that therapy session, I needed a different type of treatment for that frustration.

"Duck," Maddox orders, and I follow, narrowly avoiding his heavy fist. "Sidestep left. Good. Now right, duck, and jab to the sternum."

He grunts slightly, as I follow each of his commands and strike him as ordered. Only, he doesn't stop there. He ducks quicker than a man his size should, and swipes at my feet. He manages to catch one, but I jump before he can catch the other.

"Good. And after a move like this, your opponent might have their guard down while they get their balance back or rise to their feet. So, you strike the vulnerable spot closest to you. Throat, nose, in the hollow spot under the sternum, or anything else close to you," he instructs.

He's already up but, for some reason, I decide to strike anyway. I lunge, but my back hits the springy floor before my fist hits him.

"Wrong timing, Evie," he scolds and reaches over to help me up.

"I know, I just..." I trail off, thankful that the Fightclub is almost empty tonight, save for three guys sparing in the ring.

"Burning anger?" Madds asks.

I pause for a moment on my way up, wondering just how transparent I am. Because neither the therapist, nor him, have had any trouble reading me today.

He doesn't press when I don't answer right away, instead turns to put away the equipment we used in my training. I'm not sure what he thinks of my progress, but I believe it's been going quite well. I feel it in my muscles, my reflexes, and in my confidence too. I'm weary about it too, because confidence can be deceiving, and I don't want to get too cocky. That will definitely get me hurt. I can't deny the increased strength though. And not only the physical one.

"There's nothing wrong about it," Madds says from somewhere behind me, and I stop mid unwrapping my hands.

"About what?"

"Burning anger, frustration, or... other emotions." His last two words are loaded, but I don't dare pry.

Maddox is an interesting character. Usually quiet. The type of person who can happily sit in a comfortable silence and doesn't feel the need to talk just for the sake of it. He's been better since we got closer, not that we've had any deep conversations, but I swear sometimes I see these sparks. Like he wants to ask a slightly more personal question or give an insight that allows a tinge of vulnerability, but then he stops himself, using words like *other emotions*.

Sometimes I even think that it's the right time to push, ask about the scars I've seen etched into his skin when he was training shirtless. So many of them. Long, short, thin, thick, round... most of them over his torso. Apart from the one sweeping from the middle of his forehead down to his cheek, luckily missing his amber eye.

I never ask though. Just as he doesn't ask me. If I'm not ready, I can't expect him to be. His mostly silent support is enough, and he's given so much of it. Even Maya is slowly starting to see him as a big brother. It scares me, this platonic emotional attachment to him, to Lulu, Morri, June... it's growing roots that will bleed when finally cut. And they'll have to be cut, because my sister and I will have to go back to Fleeton.

I realize I haven't moved, midway through unwrapping my hand, the answer to his statement resting at the border of my mind.

"Is that why you fight?" all those thoughts about never prying, and here I am… crossing that invisible threshold.

He doesn't answer for a long while, and I wonder if he's still there.

"Sometimes. More so in the past. Nowadays things are somehow calmer."

I turn around to face him, as it seems the polite thing to do when the man answered my first remotely personal question.

"Baby girl, here you are!" Lulu's melodic voice fills the expansive space of The Fightclub, but it's followed by a peculiar grunt from the giant before me.

I fight a curious frown as I take in his expression. The calmness he spoke of has evaporated.

"Lulu, what are you doing here?" I ask.

"And how did you get in?" Maddox's voice is an octave or two lower, a deep frown thickening the scar on his face.

The woman raises an almost frustrated eyebrow, giving him a quick once over pausing for only a moment. A very curious moment. But she quickly turns her attention to me.

"Your security knows me, obviously," she answers, but her gaze is on me.

"Knowing you and being authorized to waltz in here are not the same thing."

Wow! There's nothing calm about the man now. I've never seen him like this. As a matter of fact, I've never seen Lulu like this either.

"Train them better, then," she bites back.

Maddox grunts and turns to leave.

"You're coming tomorrow, yes?" she shouts after him, but all she gets in response is a louder grunt. I don't realize my eyebrows are raised in shocked surprise until Lulu gives me a stern look, and I quickly straighten.

"Do you need to change out of your training clothes?" she asks.

"Umm, maybe. Why?"

"I've been trying to find you. Did you forget you asked me to take you with me to the supermarket, to get the red paint thing?"

"Red food coloring, crap. Yes. I'm sorry. I just… time got away from me," I apologize, quickly running to my bag.

I desperately need the food coloring for Morrigan's birthday cake.

"It's fine. I know you had a therapy session today. I figured you would be here afterward."

I exhale sharply, frustration seeping through my tone. "Am I really that obvious?"

"What do you mean?" she asks as I whip around, clutching my bag to my chest.

"My therapist, Maddox, you… all of you seem to read me like a book. My thoughts, my emotions, my—hell, everything."

She chews on her lips for a few moments, weighing her next words.

"The therapist is trained to read you, honey. But us… we tend to recognize our *symptoms* in others."

Oh.

That stops me dead in my tracks.

"I didn't—"

"Don't get me wrong, I'm not saying any of us went through the same thing as you did, but perhaps experienced the same or similar emotions. Some had it easier, some so much worse. Recognition comes from experience."

"I'm not sure I like the sound of that, of Maddox and… you, recognizing from experience."

"I'm just good at observing your behavioral patterns whenever you go to a session."

Which means Maddox has the experience.

"I'll give you that." I shake my head, wondering if I should try harder in the future to mask my emotions. And patterns.

"When's Maya next in with Dr. Moss?" she asks.

"Tomorrow."

"I presume before the party?" Lulu asks.

"Yes, at one o'clock. I spoke with Mamaw June, and she's coming over after we return. She'll watch her for the evening."

"Sounds good. You deserve to let your hair down a little."

I'm not sure if Morrigan's surprise birthday party will be the best place for me to let my hair down. Not with the knowledge that I may be seeing a certain blue-eyed man.

Every time I walk in here I wonder if he's going to be around. Even if I go to Morrigan's apartment, I still wonder if he's going to drop by without warning. But it's been weeks now without setting eyes on him. Weeks since I found out I was living in his building while he screwed other women there.

The way I feel in my skin now… it might as well have been years.

And I still don't know if I'm ready to see Finnigan.

CHAPTER 13
Finnigan

I'M STILL PISSED. Though the chill, fluttering inside my chest is different from any anger I've experienced in the past. I get it—it's Morrigan's surprise birthday party, and it's for family and close friends only, but I'm desperate for the distraction tonight. One girl is all I asked for, a date to hold my attention.

Though, it seems I may be in luck. I've been here, at Morrigan's apartment, for about an hour now. We've already surprised the birthday girl, though her reaction to our enthusiastic screams showed a tinge of knowledge. And I have been watching her accept wishes and hugs from everyone.

Cillian, her red-haired pain in the ass of a brother, wrapped her in his arms and spun her a few times, and put quite a smile on her face. The man is actually quite decent, but I just like to give him a hard time. He helped us save his sister a few months ago from a really shitty situation.

A bunch of our people are here too, Katya, Raven, Beau, and Tina, since Morrigan has become friends with them. Her bartender from Metamorphosis is here as well. And of course, Maddox and Carter. But no Evelyn... thank fuck.

Though Carter has been watching me peculiarly since I got here. The man is peculiar all around, so it shouldn't flag as strange, yet there's something in his weird hazel eyes. I can't put my finger on it, but it's like he knows something I don't, and it's making me uneasy as fuck.

Come to think of it, Katya has been giving me some strange looks tonight, too. I want to ask about it, but I'm more focused on the fact that the wheat-haired woman is absent. Maybe she's gone. I want to smile about it, I want to rejoice, but... for some reason that thought fills me with something that doesn't evoke relief. The chill in my chest seems more like icicles stabbing into me. I think I need to cut this party short. I'm nearing Morrigan when Lulu sweeps in and wraps her into a tight hug.

She has been running around like crazy to make sure the party is perfectly planned for her best friend. Though, I've gotten to know Morrigan pretty well in the last few months, and I'm certain she won't care if all this turns into a clusterfuck. She only cares that we're together. That's something that surprised me about her. My expectations were set a few years back by my brother and his wife, and I waited for the moment Morrigan took Vincent away from our Sanctum. Only, the opposite happened with the wild redheaded vixen. She fits right in. Lulu too, even as she rejects it.

The two women burst out laughing and as I approach, I catch snippets of their conversation.

"You knew, didn't you? Did Vincent spill? Or did that brute?" Lulu's smile falls ever so slightly as she looks beyond Morrigan, straight at Madds.

And he scowls right back at her.

I have a sound theory about these two, but I've been told by Vincent to keep it to myself if I don't want the wrath of both Dietrich and Severin upon me. Loreley's family is old money crime syndicate. The Dietrich mafia legacy is one built on blood, bullets, and a fortune bigger than my family's. Even though Lulu pulled out of the family business, her blood is theirs, and I see that ruthless spark in her eyes. I won't dare step on her toes.

I wait patiently until the two women finish talking, then swoop in. I don't want to prolong this night more than necessary. Evelyn might have left town, but why risk it if she didn't?

"I have a confession to make," I say to the woman.

"Go on..." She eyes me wearily.

"I didn't like you at first."

She dramatically presses her hand to her heart as her mouth drops. "Oh my! I had no idea!"

I can't help but roll my eyes at the theatrics, but the need to smile prevails. She's taking it much better than I thought she would.

"Alright, alright. Christ, you wouldn't win any acting prizes," I tease.

"Fuck you, Finnigan."

"You wish." I flash her another wicked smile.

"Do not let Vincent hear that. He'll fucking scalp you," she jokes, yet there's truth in that. "What did you have against me?"

Here goes nothing. "Everything. I don't think it was you, specifically. Although I was quite skeptical. I didn't like what you represented... to Vincent."

"I'm not taking him away from you, Finnigan." She reaches over and rubs my arm.

My breath hitches at the unexpected, soothing gesture, but her words are heavy enough to make me think she knows exactly what, or better yet, who she is talking about.

"No. I think that's when those feelings started going away. When I realized you weren't going to change a thing. Well, obviously, some things have changed."

"They will, of course. For all of you, eventually," she says.

"Nah, not for me, darlin'. I'm happy as I am."

"Fucking everything in sight and never getting attached to anyone?" she insists.

"I have standards, Morrigan. I don't fuck *everything*."

"You're avoiding the attachment thing, though," she cocks her head slightly, her green eyes fixed on me.

I swear she stole the look out of Vincent's book, because I think she's peering straight into my goddamn soul.

"Avoiding would entail a prospect. I simply make sure there is no prospect. Ever."

"Whatever works for you, buddy." She flashes a smirk, and I decide to shut her up, pulling her into a hug.

"Happy Birthday, Morrigan."

She finally accepts my explanation and smiles warmly. It broadens into an excited one as her gaze flashes past me, and the next word that comes out of her mouth makes the hairs on the back of my neck stand still.

"Evie!" she exclaims before pulling out of my arms and waving.

"Who?" My god, could I have asked a more stupid question?

"Evelyn Shaw. You know her, the girl you rescued."

Yeah, unfortunately I know exactly who she is. As I slowly turn around, trying to think through the booming pulse getting louder in my head, I vaguely hear Morrigan mumble something about me seeing Evie at her house a few months back. I don't bother acknowledging the comment, my temples starting to throb as a scowl settles deep between my brows. It dawns on me that Evelyn hasn't talked about me to Morrigan, since she thinks she has to explain to me who she is. Katya clearly hasn't said what Evelyn asked of her, not to tell me where she lives now. How very interesting. And somehow fucking annoying too.

"What exactly is she doing here?" I didn't even bother covering my disdain at her presence.

Though shock weaved through it too. Not the bad kind, unfortunately. Those icicles stabbing through my chest have turned into something else, hot and sharp, and yet so soothing, it feels dangerously close to excitement. I can't help but look over my shoulder.

Christ, she's stunning.

She's walking over, looking like a different woman. Her features are somehow more settled, fuller, still skinny, yet no longer gaunt, and more mature than last time I saw her. Only weeks have passed, and though it's still Evelyn, she somehow looks different. Comfortable. There's a confidence in her step that was not there before, and in those 'fuck me' leather leggings, she could be walking all over me, and I'd fucking thank her.

I'm so screwed.

"She's my friend. She also lives in the apartment underneath with her little sister, and works downstairs."

"In Metamorphosis?!" I whip around so fast, I have to brush away the hair from my eyes.

"No. In the café. Finn, what—"

"What do you mean she lives here? Since when?"

This is where she went after she left Katya's? Not out of town? Goddamn it, I have so many questions, but judging from the look in Morrigan's eyes, I'm already arousing suspicion.

"About a month ago. We took her in to help her out while she's saving some money. How do you not know this?"

Yup—suspicion. I'm part of The Sanctum. If Evelyn and her sister were offered a home in the same building as Vincent's wife, I should have technically been aware. Maddox should have said something. Though, Carter is the one I'm most disappointed in. He knows everything that moves, and yet this particular piece of information didn't slip his tight lips.

You didn't ask, you asshole.

"I guess... I tuned out," I finally answer, avoiding the curious look in her eyes.

"Morrigan! Happy Birthday! Sorry, I'm late, I was adding the finishing touches," Evelyn exclaims enthusiastically as she pulls the birthday girl into a tight hug.

My feet turn to lead and pin me in place. Though I'm not sure I would move even if I could. Her perfume whips by me, and once again I'm being buried in her wicked world filled with forbidden temptation. I'm back in the bar on her birthday, swaying against her body, my hand on her bare waist, hers on me, and all the thoughts I've been burying deep since the last time I saw her, hit me like a ton of bricks.

Fuck. If just her scent does this to me, what will her touch do?

I can't take my eyes off of her. Her soft, olive skin seems to glow in this light, and I curse that oversized cardigan for covering so much of her. I curse the T-shirt she's wearing even more, because she would look so much fucking better if she were wearing mine.

Oh my god, stop it!

"You remember Finnigan Hennessey?"

My gaze whips to Morrigan when I hear my name.

"Hi," Evelyn says with such bite in that word, the teeth scrape against a part of my soul I thought didn't exist anymore.

I'm confused. My breathing turns to short heaves, my heart begins to pound erratically in my chest. What is happening?

"Hello," I manage to say before prying my feet away from this spot I've been stuck in, and get the fuck away from this witch.

I don't dare turn to check their reactions—or their possible shock at my strange one. All I know is that I need to be as far away as possible from Evelyn. My steps follow every second beat of my heart, the heaviness of them seemingly crushing any intention I had but a second ago.

I stop at the far wall by the kitchen counter and look toward the door that could take me to my freedom. Away from the woman who wrapped a goddamn noose around the hollowness left in my soul years ago. Yet, I don't move any farther. I can't.

Turning around slowly, I catch the exact moment she shifts away from Morrigan and heads toward Maddox who carries a huge, tall box. Probably a present. As if she can sense my eyes on her, she turns and hers land straight on mine. They don't stop on any other person, or object—but straight on me. I would fall on my ass if this counter wasn't holding me steady, because what I see in her gaze is made of pure silver flames, cold and searing at the same time—a challenge.

Yup... I'm fucked.

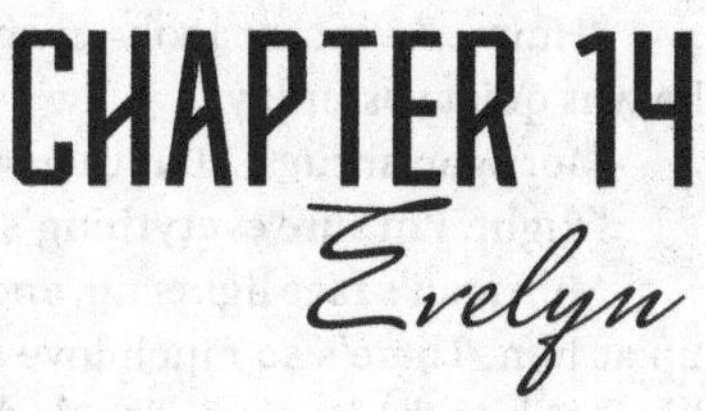

CHAPTER 14
Evelyn

"YOU ARE GOING to be the death of my hips. And belly. And... mmm damn." Morrigan groans as she takes another bite of the coffee and walnut cake I finished baking with Mamaw June. She loved the birthday cake I made for her a few days ago, so I'm not surprised.

"I'm not complaining." Vincent walks into the kitchen, giving his wife a once over, and pausing suggestively over her ass.

"You know I'm here, right?" his mom asks rhetorically, even as her focus is on the dishes she's currently washing.

"We need to find her a man to focus on so she can stop judging us," he whispers to Morrigan, and I choke on the sip of iced tea.

"For god's sake, I'm too old for that."

"Old?!" her daughter-in-law exclaims. "You're not even sixty yet. I'm sure we can find you a good man to keep you busy."

"I have Maya keeping me exactly as busy as I want to be. And she's more worth it than any man. No offense, son." June shrugs at Vincent currently scowling at her.

But his gaze softens when he turns to his wife, as if he's reminded of why there's truth in his mother's words.

"Aren't you supposed to be leaving in a few minutes?" Morrigan asks her husband.

"Change of plans. They're coming here." Vincent presses a quick kiss on her lips, but my mind is spiraling.

They? Who's they? Carter, Maddox... Finnigan?!

The echo of his name inside my mind awakens the visceral urge that's been making a home inside of me. A beast growing hungrier each day, but it's a picky bitch. I've already decided that my life will not stop just because of what happened to me. I may not give into the hunger wholly, but I need something to sustain me. The problem is, I can only bear the thought of one person feeding it. But he sees me as unripe, forbidden fruit.

My thighs squeeze together at the thought of making him change his mind, and I have a ridiculous need to go check my new hair in the mirror. I've seen the women he takes out... none of them look like me.

"I have no idea, but he did sound... strange." Vincent's words pull me back into the room, and I'm kicking myself for missing part of the conversation.

"Somehow, I'm not surprised. Did you notice something three days ago?" Morrigan asks.

"When? The day before your birthday?"

"Yeah. Because at the party I noticed he was a bit different. I don't know, I just noticed some passing looks."

"Hmm..." Vincent looks away, pondering the question. "No, I don't think so. But he was quiet yesterday."

Morrigan shrugs. "But then again, none of this is out of character for him, right?"

"Right. I'm sure everything's fine, and even if it isn't, I'll handle it."

Morrigan's face lights up, and she wraps her arms around Vincent's waist, looking up at him. There's so much love in her gaze, it almost hurts. Yet, it's the adoration in his that hits the hardest. The dark pits of his eyes sparkle with the stars she put there. He may have hung the moon for her, but she filled the sky with stars for him. In the last six weeks or so, I've been spending enough time with Morrigan to grow to understand that my view of her world—*their world*—was very inaccurate.

I was in Morrigan's apartment once when her husband returned from a *job*. Only, the person who passed through the door wasn't Vincent, but The Serpent. There was a look in his eyes that could stop the flow of my blood, cold and vengeful, ready to rip the world apart so he could punish whoever filled him with that simmering rage. But then his pitch black eyes landed on Morrigan... and his gaze flipped, but did not change. Now he looked at her like he would rip the world apart at her signal, only because she desired it.

Their paradox is what made me question my judgment. My preconceptions.

I've known evil. Felt it on my skin. But them... they're a whole other brand. I understand this world much better now. It's not black and white as I thought. Not all villains are the same shade, and these... they scare me.

Downright terrify me at times. Because more and more they make me feel like I belong.

And the more I think of the man who took me, the one who haunts my nightmares and ruins my dreams, the more I start to believe that I do belong with The Sanctum. Because the things I would like to do to Frankie certainly do not fit in the brand of person I thought I was. It's all a moot point, because I can't stay in Queenscove, not when I have a responsibility in Fleeton.

"Evie..." My sister comes in from the patio.

I know that voice. It's her *I'm gonna play cute and put on a sweet voice so I can get something I'm not supposed to have* voice.

"Yes, Maya?" I turn to her, crossing my arms over my chest, ready to be stern, but I burst out laughing instead when I see her sweet little face. "Did you just smash your face into that cake and forget about the spoon?"

Her eyes go wide, and she quickly goes to both lick and wipe the cream and crumbs stuck to her face. She did something similar with her own birthday cake a few weeks back, when she turned eight.

"Maybe?" she says innocently. "Look, it was delicious."

"And let me guess, you want another piece."

Her little dimples make an appearance as she looks between me and Mamaw June in the hopes that at least one of us will say yes. I can't help it, the happiness I put on her face makes me give in. I'm already turning to the cake platter when she continues.

"It's been so long since you baked. I don't know if you'll stop again, so I have to take advantage."

I cut a small piece, pop it on her plate, and she all but runs back on the patio. Like I'll take it back from her if she doesn't move fast enough.

"What did she mean by that?" Morrigan asks.

"I protected her as much as I could, so it seems she believes that I chose to stop baking."

"And that's not the case?"

"My car or the motels we managed to stay in didn't exactly offer the facilities. And the few times we managed to underhandedly rent studios with kitchens, my priorities didn't allow it."

Morrigan nods at my explanation.

But it's not the whole truth, is it?

I sigh at that voice inside my head. It *is* the truth. There were other priorities. More important things to spend our money on than this *hobby*.

Though, I did miss the chemistry of it all. The anticipation of the oven timer going off after experimenting with new flavor combinations or recipes, the excitement of that first taste, and then there's the decorating part of it. That is my true ecstasy. Before I was taken, I kept a tattered old notebook where I drew—in pencil—all the designs I hoped one day I would get to do. It was the only thing I owned that I cared about. It's gone now. I thought I forgot those designs, but just like the baking techniques, they're all coming back to me like I've been doing it all this time. After moving out of Katya's and into Loreley's downstairs apartment, I fell right back into it. Well, not straight away, because I pushed back at first. Harder than I probably needed to. I had a point to prove, though I already forgot what it was. And I'm not fond of the reasoning my therapist suggested.

I'm not saying she's wrong, or right, I'm just not fond of it. I still don't have an answer to her question, and I'm unsure why it stumped me so hard.

Do you think you matter, Evelyn?

"You could make money out of this." Morrigan catches my attention again, punctuating that sentence with a deep moan as she takes another bite of cake.

I could.

"Sure." I laugh awkwardly instead.

The monitor next to the TV signals that the motion sensors have detected movement on the long drive to Vincent's forest house.

"It looks like Madds," he says as he watches the car drive down.

"Hide the cake!" Morrigan yelps and jumps off the bar stool.

We all burst into laughter, and I can't resist imagining that if I were ever to do this for money, she would be my most loyal customer.

Stop wasting your time on silly dreams, Evelyn.
I sigh internally, wondering if my therapist was right.

Finnigan

"HE REALLY DIDN'T say anything to you?" I ask Madds for the second time since we got into his car.

"He didn't. But I think he found something big."

It better be. Too much time has passed since we've been trying to find Vassallo. It's never taken us this long to track down a person or group and it's getting downright embarrassing. I can't keep track anymore of all the people we blackmailed, tortured, or killed for this goddamn information. It kills me that this asshole, whoever the fuck he is, bested us. Not only when we rescued the children, though, according to Evelyn, it was dumb luck that they left just before we arrived, but he's besting us now too.

Carter is even more frustrated. Even if Vin tried to calm him by reasoning that we have absolutely nothing to go on, apart from an alias, he was not satisfied. The man allows only success in his portfolio, and this frustration is bringing The Carver out... and he demands satisfaction in pounds of flesh.

The motherfucker is scary. But fuck me if he's not effective. And it sounds like the blood paid off because he's finally got something.

"He's not here yet," Madds says when we pull into Vin's driveway.

I push the car door open and draw in a deep breath that makes me feel more at home than my penthouse. Damp moss, faint sea salt, and tree bark drown me, but there's a tension in the air I can't quite put my finger on.

Foreboding.

It prickles my skin and turns my head, watching for something, anything, to come out of the shadows of the forest trees.

But nothing does. It's just us here.

"Coming?" Maddox calls for me, a few steps in front.

"Yeah..." I trail off, following him to the front door, just as he pushes it open.

The smell hits me so hard, I stop dead in my tracks.

"Oh wow!" I can practically hear the drool pooling in Madds' mouth.

Can I blame him? Food is nothing more than sustenance to me, no matter what it tastes like, it's all the same to me, because it serves only one purpose. But this smell... Christ, what is that?

We advance and head straight to the kitchen, the aroma drawing us in like hypnosis, and we're powerless to its charms.

"Hey guys!" Morrigan spins in the barstool to face us.

We both wave, but Madds goes straight for the cake sitting on the kitchen island. *What is that flavor?* It smells divine.

Divine?

What the fuck is wrong with me?

It's just cake.

Mamaw June comes out of the pantry, and my fellow giant only has time for another quick wave before he cuts a piece of the dessert, slaps it on his plate, and digs in. The moan that follows raises some brows in the room and a chuckle from Morrigan.

"I can die happy now," Madds mumbles through bites.

"Eat like that and you'll definitely die."

"Shut up, prude. Go back to your plain oatmeal like a damn heathen. Who eats plain oatmeal?" He shakes his head.

"It's just food. It does the job it was meant for." I shrug.

Yet, I can't take my eyes off that cake. It looks so good, but the smell it infused this house with is downright decadent.

I'm exaggerating. It's just cake. It will taste like cake. Nothing special.

Okay, maybe just one bite?

"Go on, Finnigan. I know you're not a sweet person, but it won't hurt to try it," Morrigan coaxes me.

"Fine." I pretend to agree reluctantly, because honestly, when I actually see the cake up close, I couldn't stop myself even if I tried.

Mamaw June cuts a slice and slides it over on the kitchen island. I take a seat and dig the dessert spoon into the sponge, bringing it to my mouth still thinking it likely smells better than it tastes. But the moment it touches my tongue, I'm seeing fucking stars. Walnut, coffee, and something I can't quite pinpoint fills my mouth with something so akin to ecstasy, I burst into goosebumps.

Jesus Christ, this is incredible. The soft and light coffee cream, the walnut sponge, the crunchiness of the actual walnuts... it's unreal.

Is rum the mystery flavor?

I take three more bites, one bigger than the last, and confirm in triumph. *Definitely rum.*

"I have never, ever, seen you enjoy dessert quite this way." I hear Morrigan's remark next to me, just as I swallow another bite and repress an embarrassing moan.

"Mamaw June." I look up at the woman across the island, wiping the top. "You have outdone yourself. I've never eaten anything as good as this cake."

The woman laughs and shakes her head. "I can't take the credit, son, it's all Evie."

I must have been chewing too loudly and not heard right, because I think the woman said *Evie* baked this cake.

But then she turns her attention to her left, somewhere beyond me, with an all-knowing look in her eyes.

No, this is not happening.

"Hey Evelyn," Madds greets her.

I'm too stunned to move. Or chew. The only shift in me is the blood rushing in all the wrong places, like my damn head because I'm getting a headache. But then there's my chest, and the sudden hollowness in my stomach... the anticipation, the curiosity.

The cake seems to melt in my mouth, and the spoon clanks on the porcelain plate as I drop it.

Finally, when eyes burn into me from all directions, I turn my head, and I instantly wish I didn't. It shouldn't, but the vision before me fills me with such visceral emotions, I swear the seat shakes beneath me.

Who am I kidding?! I'm the one shaking, and the chair is holding on for dear fucking life, because I have no idea how to physically react to what I'm seeing.

Plum-colored hair, shining a deep red where the sun rays hit it, barely grazes that treacherous spot where the neck meets the shoulder. High-waisted, black, flared jeans hug gentle curves I never noticed on her, cinching a narrow waist I could wrap my hands around, with an oversized distressed T-shirt tucked in, but ripped in a V-neck shape to reveal just enough cleavage to make me wanna rip it further. Then there's the makeup—black winged eyeliner that makes her gray and gold eyes shine like fucking stars even on the day sky, sculpted brows, and the same color lipstick on her lips as her hair.

I can't look away. I can't stop taking in the details of the woman standing before me. She's... different. Yet she looks more like herself than ever. Gone is the natural wheat-colored blonde, gone is the long hair she frequently wore tucked away, gone is the innocence she exhumed.

Now, Evelyn looks... dangerous.

Unlike any woman I ever looked at before, yet I can't seem to stop.

Her olive skin shines in the contrast with the purple that, on her, looks like it belongs. Like she should have been born with the unnatural color. And that bob-length haircut, parted in the middle and framing her delicate features, is not anything I would have imagined her with.

Stunning.

And I get angrier. More at myself than her, because she looks like the dessert I want to taste, the flavor I want to discover, one layer at a time, until I get to know all her notes.

She watches me with a mixture of curiosity and embarrassment, and the sudden flush in her cheeks fills me with a warm, thrilling emotion.

I open my mouth to speak, to say something, anything. Either about the cake she apparently baked like she's been doing this her whole life, or maybe about her new look. Does she look stronger? I swear there's more meat on her bones, more muscle too. But the sound of the front door distracts me before any sound spills from my lips.

As I turn and my eyes land on it, I wish I wouldn't have turned at all. Or came here. My lungs strain with the pain of a suppressed gasp at the sight of him, but that ache goes way beyond the physical, through my very soul, and stabs me straight in the fucking heart.

"Hello, little brother."

CHAPTER 15
Finnigan

I BLINK ONCE, twice, but the third time it's clear that the image before me isn't going away.

He's here.

No—they are.

Annika, an older but somehow more beautiful version of her, walks in holding the little hand of a child hiding somewhere behind his *father*. Christ, that word tastes bitter even when it doesn't touch my tongue.

"Hello, Finnigan," my *darling* brother's wife greets me, and her tone throws me far in the past, because she sounds just as shy as she was eight years ago. "Aaro, come here." She looks down at her son—my nephew—and the little boy finally steps out from his father's shadow.

I hear a small gasp somewhere behind me, and as my eyes find the little boy's, I share the sentiment in its entirety. I know that kids often take traits from their uncles or aunts, but this is too much. That head of wild, sun-kissed curls is mine, not my brother's, and that bright-blue of his eyes is much more like mine than Ronan's.

I wonder if it kills him, looking at his son every day and constantly being reminded of me. Of what he left behind. Who he abandoned.

"Hello." Aaro's little voice comes out. There's a forced confidence in it, yet it compels me, nevertheless.

"Hi," I answer. To him only, not my brother, nor his wife.

"Are you Uncle Finn?"

I swallow a lump caught in my throat, because the anger that's seeping through me, searing one vein at a time, is forced to hold back. This kid hasn't done anything to me. But his father's eyes burn through me, and my god do I wanna pummel him back through that goddamn door.

"I suppose I am, yes," I answer reluctantly.

I'm an uncle.

I knew the theory of it all, I knew I was an uncle. After all, Annika's pregnancy was one of two driving forces in my brother's decision to quit this life and leave. But I was never faced with the prospect of it. Never faced with my... nephew. The moment Ronan left us—left *me*—he was all but dead to me. Eight years have passed, and still I haven't spoken a word to him. Yet here I am, talking to his son... my blood.

"You don't seem too happy about it," the boy states bluntly, in such a matter-of-fact, casual way, that I twitch in my chair, close to losing my balance, and I swear I hear someone snort to my left.

When I turn my head in that direction, Evelyn's lips are curled inward and she averts her eyes instantly.

"Aaro!" Annika warns her son. "Sorry, Finnigan. He is... umm... very straightforward."

I turn back to face them but realize that none of the words I have for them are good. What the actual fuck are they doing here of all places? Then I see Carter stand to their left—he brought them here. Is this why he called the meeting?

My fists clench repeatedly, pushing back a need to drive them into something, anything, until it crumbles beneath them. My temples pulse violently, and my lungs sting at the brink of heaving. I can't fucking do this, not with them here.

"Annika..." It's not a greeting, but a request, and she catches onto it right away.

"Aaro, didn't you say you needed the bathroom?"

"I'll take you there." Mamaw June passes by me and ushers them out of earshot.

I turn to Evelyn who's firmly planted in place, but I really need her to get out of here. As far away as fucking possible, because I can tell by that look in her eyes that she knows she's getting an insight into me. And she's staying for it. But this is not fucking happening. I'm barely containing these wretched emotions, but I force them down because I can't give them the satisfaction. I refuse to let my brother see how he affects me, and I most certainly can't let the purple-haired vixen any closer. She cannot know me any better. Not now. Not when she looks like she found sin and decided to douse herself in it, pulling me to the brink of deviancy.

Morrigan still sits next to me, watching this interaction, or lack thereof, with a mixture of apprehension and curiosity.

"You must be Morrigan," my brother says, and when I hear his footsteps, my head whips to him.

He stops halfway between us, his gaze flashing to my angry one, and the redhead jumps off the stool to go greet him, reading the room.

"I am, yes. Hi..."

"Ronan. I'm Finnigan's older brother."

I scoff. Yes, technically it's true, but blood is the only thing tying us together. That doesn't make him a brother, just a fucking sibling.

"Yes, I've heard. Welcome back," Morrigan greets him.

"Thanks. Sorry I didn't get a chance to introduce you to my wife, Annika and our son."

"It's okay." She takes a look around the room then meets my brother's eyes once more. "I think I'll go find them and introduce myself."

He nods and Morrigan moves past him.

"Evelyn, how about you introduce yourself too," I say, turning my head slightly in her direction, my gaze still pinned on my brother.

I don't hear any movement or agreement and when I finally meet her eyes, I swear the silver in them turned to steel, like she's forging a dagger she's about to stab me with. She holds my stare with such intensity, it weighs down in the pit of my stomach. There's a challenge in there I crave to unpack, but shouldn't.

"Hi, Ronan," she says at the same time she breaks my gaze and turns to my brother. "I'm Evelyn. Excuse me, I'm gonna go check on my sister."

She whirls around and walks out the patio shutting the door behind her before my brother can reply. The annoyance in her step is unmissable, though.

"So, she's—"

"Morrigan's friend," I interrupt Ronan before he dares to insinuate anything.

He doesn't respond to that, but his cocked eyebrow spells too many words I want to shove down his throat.

"Why did you bring them here?" I ask the burning question lingering like ash in the air.

Only, I direct it at Carter, not my brother. He cocks his head and waits a few seconds before he finally decides he's replying.

"There was no other way. Something changed, and it was with Ronan's help that I uncovered it all."

"Excuse me? Are you telling me that you're involving him in *our* business? He's an outsider!" I snap, dropping to my feet off the chair.

"Easy, brother."

"You shut the fuck up! I told you if you leave, you're out. You gave up the right to be my goddamn brother eight years ago." My tone lowers, my voice vibrating through my chest.

Christ, I thought those memories were forgotten. Seeing him now, his sleek blonde hair a shade or two darker than mine, his deeper blues, and features that resemble mine so much, that night comes back to me like a goddamn truck slamming through my chest. That phone call in the car as we were rushing to save Annika and Hanna before they were taken, the moment we reached the empty island and witnessed the aftermath of their abduction, all these moments crash down on me like no time has passed at all. And the blood... so much blood. The anger finally breaks the surface too.

"I came because—"

"You made your goddamn choice!" my voice cracks to the precipice of shouting, interrupting him. "You decided to leave us. And you agreed that you can't. Fucking. Come back. Now Carter tells me that he's involving you in *our* business? Our motherfucking Sanctum? No. Either you leave or I do."

The man only sighs, standing here in all his glory, his stance rigid and proud, but his eyes... his eyes are the ones threatening to break me. There's pity, sadness, and regret all balled into one in there, and I fucking hate each one of those sentiments.

"Fine. I'll go."

But I only manage two steps.

"No." Carter stops me. "We have work to do."

"You don't understand, Pierce. You're different and I get it, but—"

"I don't have to," he interrupts. "This is important. Ronan is here for a reason.

He's—*your* family, too. I'm gonna go set up in the office. Follow me." Carter whirls around and heads toward the room in question, leaving me all riled up.

"I'll come with you," my brother says, his tone wearier this time.

"I need air." I turn and walk toward the terrace, and rush over the threshold, shutting the door behind me.

"Who exactly do you dare think you are?" There's a chilling quality to her voice, her tone filled with an eerie calmness, but I can practically taste the anger beneath it.

"Excuse me?" I turn to face the purple-haired woman, realizing the grave mistake I made.

I knew she was out here. Why the hell didn't I go literally anywhere else in this huge house?

"I must have done something wrong if I gave you the impression that you can boss me around as you see fit. And in front of other people, nonetheless. How dare you?" There it is again, that low, calm tone.

Somehow it fills me with even more frustration, fueling the unnatural anger my brother's arrival instilled in me.

And the dam cracks.

"This is none of your business, goddamn it! All of this!" I wave my hands around. "This is not your world, and whatever the fuck just happened in there has nothing to do with you! You are not part of it!"

She all but sneers at me, her eyes darkening with the type of malice I never thought could mar her features.

"You have no idea what I'm part of. You're not here to witness it. You haven't been for a while. You made it very clear that I have no place in your life, not to mention the impression you have of me—"

"Impression? How would you know what I think of you?" I ask, seeping anger through the seams.

She wouldn't talk to me like this if she knew exactly what I thought of her. If she knew how she filled my dreams. What nightmares she bred. If she found out how depraved my mind truly is. The things I want to do to her, force on her, take from her. And the things I'd beg her to do to me.

She wouldn't talk to me like this if she truly knew my sickness.

"Because you told me." She seethes, the only break in her calm tone of voice. "You thought you could pay me off to get me out of here. You thought I would take it, just like that. You think I'm some worthless homeless woman, who can be bought. Though, that's not exactly what you were doing, was it? You were buying yourself distance— escape."

She pauses, not for effect, but to give me a chance to intervene. Only, I'm stuck. Not stunned, but actually stuck on her words. *Escape.*

No. I was buying *her* escape from Queenscove. A chance to go back to where she was taken from, and I can't believe she's still pissy about that. Then again, it wasn't quite the best idea on my part, and I knew the moment I left the apartment that day. I knew Vassallo and his men were still out there and even though we have no confirmation of this, he could be looking for her. Plus, she doesn't have custody of Maya yet, so of course it was a bad fucking idea for me to tell her to go back to Fleeton.

But I couldn't think straight. I never can when it comes to her.

"You're a coward, Finnigan Hennessey. A coward. You can't face what's staring you right in the face. Because you fear it."

"Yeah? And what exactly is staring me right in the fucking face, Evelyn?" In two strides I'm right in front of her, our bodies close to touching, her neck craned to look up at me.

Up close like this there's no missing it—the fire might be absent from her voice, but it burns feverishly in the gold of her eyes.

"Go on," I coax her. "What's stari—"

"Me."

The bluntness of her answer jolts something inside my chest. It spreads a chill through my body, and my skin sizzles, finally realizing just how close it is to the woman who makes my soul burn. Only, I want to feel the sting, the ache, the pain... the pleasure. I can't move.

Christ, there are so many appropriate and smart things I want to say to her right now. But what comes out of my mouth is neither appropriate, nor smart. It's retaliation in its most immature form, and I can't stop myself.

"Is that why you got a makeover? To grab my attention? Trying to turn dark and mysterious, dressing skimpy and tight? Is that how it works? You learn to do make up and get dolled up? You're eighteen now and you're coming out to play, trying to attract all this attention of men to you?"

Her mouth falls open wider and wider with every idiotic sentence that falls out of mine.

She takes a long, deep breath. "This is how you're fighting this fear? By trying to hurt me?"

"I have no fear!"

"Yet you still hurt me."

"Goddamn it, woman! What do you want from me?"

"For you to admit it." She moves closer, our fronts touching now, our breaths feeding off each other. "Admit that you don't see me as a girl at all. You're hiding. Fighting it." Her delicate hands go to rest on my chest, and her touch turns to electric fire, and I crave to douse myself in that feeling.

"Evelyn," I warn.

"You wanted more when you touched me, pressed me against you and danced with me. Admit it, Finnigan. It was not enough. We both know it. It's been months now."

Her scent of ginger and brown sugar wraps around me like the finest, lightest of silks, yet there's an odd heaviness in it, pulling me down to her. A peculiar spell I'm trapped in. I did, I wanted more. More than she could give, and definitely more than I should take.

"Admit that you wanted your hands to go lower, to press harder, to sink further. Admit you like the feel of me, the thought that when I do all those things to myself, it's you I'm thinking of."

She's hypnotizing me, and I can't help being pulled deep into those words, imagining every move she speaks of. This is so goddamn wrong, it almost feels right.

"Stay away, Evelyn. Do not dare cross this line," I warn with venom in my voice. "Even by yourself, do not fucking think of me when you..."

She raises an eyebrow at that addition.

"Tell me, then." Her chest rises and falls on erratic breaths, yet she again reins in her anger, and I'm kind of disappointed. "Tell me you don't want me, and I'll never speak a word of it ever again. Like it never happened."

I have to squash this.

"I'm going to say it one last time—do not cross the line. You're leaning too hard into this rebellious, childish phase that you girls go through. But I'm not your target!"

"You—"

"We're done here." And on that note, I turn and walk away.

The door doesn't move after I walk through and close it behind me. She's not following. What a great mood to go into this fucked up meeting with.

I didn't tell her though. I couldn't tell her I don't want her.

That was close. Too close. I wanted, no, I *needed* to touch her. To feel her. But there is a line, and I have to be on the other side of it.

"Finally."

I give Maddox a grave look in response to his exasperation, as I step into Vin's office and close the door behind me.

"Let's start," Carter orders, turning to the two large screens on the wall behind the desk.

"Not yet," I interrupt, ignoring The Carver's sigh.

"Why come now after all these years?" I turn to my brother who was already watching me. "And for how long?"

He exhales a heavy sigh, and replies, "It's not permanent. But in order to protect my family, while doing what we will need to do, this was the best place for us."

"Protect them... what are you talking about? There is no *we*, Ronan. Why are you here?"

"Because, brother, I'm not the only one who came back."

What?

A picture pops up on the screens, and all at once my heart stops, blood stills, and air leaves my lungs.

It's not possible.

My past is staring me right in the face, brought back to the present in what looks like a very recent photo, and it crashes down on me with enough force that the assault of memories breaks me.

Roberto-motherfucking-Bartiste was supposed to be fucking dead!

A shocked, delicate gasp pulls me back. I whip around at the same time everyone turns to find Evelyn standing in the doorway. Her eyes are wide, not with shock, but terror, her lips parted in a silent cry that seems to split open a dead part of my soul, and the revelation hits me at the same time she utters the name.

"Vassallo."

CHAPTER 16
Evelyn

THOUSANDS OF NEEDLES pierce my body all at once. Each and every one of them is a figment of my imagination, bred of fear and grueling nightmares. They hurt, nonetheless. They paralyze me anyway.

Though, my muscles ache like I'm shaking.

Maybe I am... I don't know.

The world around me disappears. All but the face of the man who was pleased to see that I wasn't broken beyond use, and joined my destruction. Because he wanted a piece of me too.

This memory was vague until now, lost in the drug haze they put me through. I remember him, his limp as he walked closer to where I laid flat on my stomach, his fat hand squeezing my jaw as he lifted my head to inspect me, and now... his weight on top of me.

I had a feeling, but I hoped the memories of him wouldn't come. Vassallo, the one whose face faded from my nightmares. He was lost in the darkness I was taken in. But now, in the brightness of this room... I see nothing else but him.

He's staring at me.

Frozen eyes bore into me, gouging to the surface more of the pain buried beneath the drug-induced memory loss.

My ears pick up on activity around me, but the stinging in my veins and the incessant buzzing in my head mixed with Vassallo's voice, pull me further away from reality and throw me in a pit filled with all I've been avoiding. No, that's the wrong way of putting this, because I haven't been avoiding what happened to me. I came to terms with it. But only because I could barely rember it.

What I have been avoiding is remembering.

A frigid ghostly touch grips my nape, my spine tingles with beads of sweat running down it, and my hands hurt, like caught in a crushing vice.

Burning sears my muscles, the pain contracting them around my bones and crushing me from the inside out. Only, the pain holds direction, like he's yanking on them, controlling the fibers and forcing them to bind me until I can't escape. Until I return to that dark room where he will come for me again. The other one, Frankie B, too. The one who vowed to keep me.

No, no, no!

They can't have me! They can't!

Warm, comfortable pressure tightens around my upper arm, but soft velvet engulfs my cheek.

"Evelyn! Evelyn, please!"

With a painful jolt in my soul, I'm wrenched back to reality. My hand flies to my chest when the shock of the agony growing there hits me. I'm heaving, hard, and aches burst all over my body. Turning my palm over, I find indentations from my fingernails. They pierced the skin well enough that blood trickles out. I hiss when it hits me that the pain in my other hand comes from the doorknob I've been squeezing so tight, it imprinted on my palm.

"That's it, come back, Evelyn. You're okay."

That voice... that touch... the odd softness.

As if only now I realize he's here, my gaze shoots up, and I'm met with piercing, bright-blue eyes the color of the sunlit sky on the coolest of summer days. His soft touch stroking against my cheek is warm, comforting. For a moment, one cruel moment, I lose myself in that blue, flying through the atmosphere he always pulls me in. And this time, he allows me to.

The ache in my muscles melts away, my lungs find a focus, a calmer rhythm within the chaos, and Vassallo is no longer in my line of sight. Finnigan is.

"Good. That's it. You're here, safe, with me." He clears his throat. "With *us*."

My gaze drifts away and, holy mother, mortification hits me like a ton of bricks.

"I am so sorry, I didn't realize you were all in here. I thought this was—I don't—I'm sorry. I'm going to—"

"Evelyn," Finnigan interrupts my erratic speech, as he drops his hand from my cheek.

Without his touch, I'm exposed. Like the contact shielded me from the outside world.

"You didn't know we were here," Maddox says, and I realize he's standing right next to Finnigan.

Was he always there? All the eyes in the room are aimed at me, each in various states of either concern or curiosity.

"Are you okay?" Finnigan asks.

"Yes. Sorry, I was just coming to..." *Shout at you,* I want to say, but it feels inappropriate now. I thought he was going to be alone, I think. I don't know. I was so angry, I didn't think straight.

"Seriously, don't worry. I think we can all agree the timing was... perfect."

Maddox turns away. "Did you know that Vassallo is Bartiste? That he's the one O'Rourke, Holt, and Boseman worked with?"

"No." *Carter.*

His tone is sharper than I've ever heard him. Not that Carter tends to speak too much. I rarely ever see the man, to be fair, but now he sounds downright annoyed.

"So, this meeting was to tell us that Roberto Bartiste is back, but you had no clue—"

"No," Carter interrupts Maddox, the bluntness chilling.

"Evelyn, I know this is tough, but we need to talk about what happened when you were taken. Knowing who Vassallo is changes everything." Maddox turns to me.

I open my mouth to speak, but I'm lost for words.

"No!" Finnigan answers for me. "Look at her, she's shaking like a leaf after seeing that bastard's face on the screen. We can't put her through that!"

"There may not be any other choice." Carter argues the logic. "It's been eight years, and we all thought he was dead. Not only he fucking isn't, but he's been trying to get back into Queenscove right under our noses."

"You think I don't fucking know that?!" The bite in Finnigan's voice pales against the emotions bleeding through the cracks in what I'm starting to believe is a carefully constructed mask.

Because what I see now on his cruelly beautiful face is the same thing I saw the moment I came out of that container months ago—anguish. He's broken...

Just like I am.

Only now I realize that the eyes in this room are no longer aimed at me, but at him. And they hold a hesitant, all knowing expression that makes no sense to me. I can also tell it's making Finnigan uncomfortable. *Why?* Who is Vassallo? Or, what did they call him, Bartiste? Who is he to them? Who is he to Finnigan?

His brother's expression is the worst of them all. It may be that he hasn't been part of this world for a while from what I can tell, but he doesn't mask his feelings like the others. Or at all. His eyes are strained with sadness and something that looks a lot like shame.

"Who is he?" I blurt out and want to slap my hand over my mouth instantly.

The attention returns to me, but no one says a word.

"An old enemy," Finnigan finally replies.

"And a new one?" I ask.

His gaze fixes on mine, the intensity of it pins me in place and stuns my breath. For some reason I start counting the unspoken moments. I reach to five when the charge in the air seems to ease, and the clarity in his eyes takes me aback.

"Yes."

One word was enough to turn my world on its axis.

One word that seems to carry a weight I'm not prepared for. Because his answer had nothing to do with the fact that Carter announced this man's return into their lives. He is a new enemy for a whole new reason... a whole new crime. And this one is against me.

"Come, let's go somewhere quiet." Finnigan's hand wrapped around my upper arm attempts to guide me away.

"Finn, man, I think it would be better for me—"

"No." He cuts Maddox off without sparing him a glance.

"I just think we're closer, and you..." Maddox trails off while everyone else stays deathly silent.

"*I* will be the one to talk to Evelyn." Finnigan's hand tightens around my arm, and

I don't get a chance to argue as he guides me out of the room.

Why is he insisting for him to be the one to speak to me? Or better yet, why isn't he allowing anyone else to? I have so many freaking questions.

There's a peculiar possessiveness in his words, his eyes, even his touch, and I can't fully make sense of it. I'm not even sure if it's about me, or their past.

What happened to Finnigan Hennessey?

Finnigan

THE PRESSURE RIPPING through my chest bleeds doom into my soul. If that makes any fucking sense at all. It hurts like it, it terrifies me. Something snapped the moment her gasp split the horrifying scream that filled my head when that photo appeared on the screen. It tore through this old wound, and when she spoke that alias with such horror in her voice, a new wound marked my soul.

But purpose followed it.

Certainty.

"You were rude to Maddox," I hear her say as I all but drag her behind me, and the visceral possessiveness I have over this woman right now, makes those words land heavier than they should.

"He'll survive," I spit out.

"He just wants to protect me," Evelyn insists.

I want to answer, *I'll be the one to protect you. No one else gets the privilege,* but the words don't form. They could, but I don't allow them. It's the least good sense I can have when I've been acting like a goddamn caveman since I saw motherfucking Roberto Bartiste on that screen.

Alive and well. Sipping on a goddamn espresso on the terrace of a coffee shop.

He took her...

I guide Evelyn into a guest bedroom, shutting the door behind me. I hoped I could breathe easier in here, but the air is just as heavy. And I'm staring at the reason why.

Christ, she's beautiful.

She's standing three paces away, watching me with pain stricken doe eyes, and I'm trapped within that thick dark ring surrounding the bright gray that seeps into gold. I could stare at her eyes for the rest of my life, they're that unique and mesmerizing.

We don't speak a word. Both breathing harshly, trying to find a centering point that could bring us down from the shock we just experienced. For different reasons, one more tragic than the other. Yet, as I sink further in her broken gaze, I know my pain doesn't compare. All I have is old loss, but Evelyn... she has fresh wounds, unhealed and seeping their tragedy like a dark shadow looming over her.

I know she hasn't attempted to drown her pain in drugs again. I told Maddox to ensure there are eyes on her. I couldn't do it myself. I couldn't let myself be in her proximity or know where she was... it was too hard. Too tempting.

That resistance broke into a million pieces the moment I realized that Bartiste is the man responsible for her abduction. The possessiveness I feel over her tears through my restraints as I'm finally realizing that the asshole could've taken her from me before I even made her mine.

He can't have her.

Not her as well.

I won't allow it.

I can't fail her too.

"I'm sorry," I blurt out.

Confusion breaks through the pain in her eyes, and she cocks her head as she attempts to understand what I'm apologizing for.

"Okay... why did you insist that you would be the one to speak with me?"

Oh. That's not why I was apologizing, but it's a good enough reason. The dam may have broken but admitting it to her is a whole different thing. Admitting it to myself out loud is even harder.

"Sit down. Please," I add that final word after a brief pause, trying to deter from the blatant order.

She narrows her eyes for a split moment, then shakes her head ever so slightly, before she looks around herself, and walks to the edge of the bed, but doesn't sit.

"You're wasting your time if you want to talk about *that* night. I have no more useful info to give you," she says before I can ask the question.

"Knowing what we know now, any detail, even the ones you already told us, might mean something else entirely. We know Bartiste. Or at least we knew him... we're looking at what happened to you, to the children, with fresh eyes now."

She sighs, averting her eyes. I can tell her mind is wandering, falling into a memory she doesn't want to be in. I fucking hate myself for pushing her in it, but if anyone's going to do it, it has to be me. I hope Madds isn't going to ask me for justification as to why exactly that is. The only answer I have is not one I want to share with him, or the others. Not yet anyway. I must be the one to comfort her, to protect her... to take on her pain.

"Will you tell me?" She lets the incomplete question flow in the heavy atmosphere before she turns her attention to me. "Will you tell me what he did to you?"

Three rapid blinks it took to fully register what she's asking. Why does it sound like she knows something already?

"Did that bastard, Severin, fucking tell you?" I snap, unable to rein in my temper. The anxiety and adrenaline are a nasty combination.

She frowns and her lips part for a moment before she presses them into a hard line, debating something. Maybe a lie. Maybe a secret.

"He didn't."

I'm not sure I believe her.

"What do you know?"

"That he's the reason why you've learned that pain deals more damage on the inside than out. There's a reason why they say eyes are the mirror to the soul... yours have that broken quality I'm all too familiar with."

I say nothing to that. There are no words that could deter her from this conclusion.

There's no hiding. No point in it.

"Will you tell me?" she asks again, her voice softer.

I flinch when she takes a step my way.

We're in here because I wanted to soothe her, protect her, and get her to talk to me about what happened to her. She flipped the coin, and I'm dreading this side of it.

It's not how this is supposed to go.

"Perhaps someday," I finally answer, though I don't understand why I'm giving her hope.

She stops moving, cocking her head and pulling my gaze to hers.

"You want me to talk, Finnigan." She speaks my name like an ethereal chant. "You want me to be vulnerable. Meet me on even ground then."

I take one slow, deep breath, and I don't release it until it tightens my lungs and pressure grows in my temples. Evelyn doesn't push. She waits patiently for me to reach the decision she desires.

She's not giving me a choice.

"Eight years ago, Bartiste came here chasing people who conned him in a black-market deal. Annika, my brother's wife, was involved. A lot happened, it was violent, and Bartiste kidnapped her moments after she told my brother she was pregnant. We tried really fucking hard, but we couldn't get to the—*her* in time." I correct myself before I get too vulnerable with the plum-haired woman. "He had her for a few days, tortured her, and we couldn't find him. When we finally did, a whole-ass battle erupted. We know Bartiste was shot. More than once. But in the whole commotion and after all was said and done, we couldn't find him. We assumed one of his men took his body, because the last we saw of him he was all but crawling. Even his men came to us days later, thinking we had him, and months after we were still finding men who used to work for him who swore they thought he was dead. After Ronan got Annika back, he decided to leave The Sanctum, Queenscove, and start a new *crime-free* life somewhere else."

There, I said it. Kind of.

Evelyn narrows her eyes on me.

"That's terrible." She offers, but there's uncertainty in her tone. "And you were so broken up about your brother's wife being taken?"

Wait, I don't think that came out the way I thought it did.

"The whole situation was intense. We were almost too late," I add.

She's not convinced, her darkening eyes tell me as much. But she takes a deep breath, her shoulders drop, and I think she relents.

"I've already told you all I remember that's relevant to you," Evelyn says.

"You can't make that decision. We don't see things the same way, and every detail could help us."

She turns away, shaking her head slowly, and even though she tries to hide them, I can see the emotions she blinks away. They're raw, and the brutality of them awakens something in me I thought died with Hanna all those years ago.

"I'm sorry."

She whips her head around at my quiet words. Her eyes are narrowed, the question lingering without spoken words.

"For doing this. For asking this of you. I know reliving this must be... hard," I clarify.

"It's fine." But her tone says otherwise. She sits at the edge of the bed, and I join her.

"Have you started remembering more?"

She hesitates and I already don't like this. "Bits and pieces. Nothing that could help you."

"Walk me through it from the beginning," I insist.

"Nothing has changed about when they took us. They were swift, violent, and they only wanted my sister. They grabbed me by the hair and hindered me useless. I fought them as much as I could and jumped in the nondescript van myself. Only, I failed to get us out. I failed to save her. All they said were curses that they couldn't get rid of me and deemed it safer to take me with them. I didn't even really see their faces. I didn't get the chance to."

"Did you notice anything about the van? Like a smell? Or the way it looked on the inside? Did it feel new or well used? How did it sound?"

My questions took her by surprise. Because she squints and her gaze drifts somewhere in the distance as she ponders.

"Actually, it was pretty quiet. It didn't have the new car smell, but there were some scratches and dents inside, like it transported things in the past. It was used, but barely. There were some food wrappers around, actually."

"So, it's possible it wasn't a rental. What color?"

"Black."

"Did you hear any names? Did they talk at all?" I ask.

"Barely. We were maybe an hour away from the docks, and all they mentioned was that taking me too would cause some trouble. After that we were sedated, and I woke up in the darkness of the container."

They didn't even speak of directions to the docks, so they are familiar with the city and the area in general. We already know they took a few children from Fleeton and neighboring ones, but not needing even one direction is a bit peculiar.

"Nothing else happened during the time we traveled. Then we met you, and half an hour after all that, I met *him*."

"Him?" I ask.

"Frankie B, the one who..." she trails off, swallowing nervously. "The one who separated me from my sister."

There's so much more to this that she's not sharing.

"He seemed in charge. He was young, not as young as me, but not as old as you. He instructed for everyone to be taken to an assessment room... everyone but me. I don't know," she trails off, and I notice a slight tremor in her flesh, "I don't know what they did there. My sister has not given many details."

"What about you? What happened after they separated you?" I ask knowing full well I only have part of the story. I wasn't the one to find her—Maddox was. The bastard is just as quiet as she is, keeps so much to himself.

She gives up looking into my eyes but finds a spot somewhere on the wall, and she's focused on it like it's about to morph into something else.

"The kids' cries still echo in my mind some nights. The fear in their screams when

I was grabbed and taken away is alive inside of me. But they hit some of them to silence them, and that... I don't think I'll recover from my failure to protect them."

"It's not your failure, Evelyn."

"I begged to let me go with them, with my sister," she continues, ignoring my words, "but Frankie said I needed to go with him. To find out what I'm worth."

My pulse shudders beneath my skin, and I'm not sure I manage to control my features. Because those words fill me with such rage, I don't know if I should blame that asshole or myself.

"What else did he say?" I ask through gritted teeth. I'm failing to control my reaction.

"Umm... that he might keep me to himself."

Motherfucker!

Evelyn is not his to keep! She is goddamn mi—

"Then he grabbed me by the hair, someone hit me, maybe it was him, and I passed out." She takes a breath that was meant to be deep, but staggers its way down her lungs instead. "After that it's fuzzy. They drugged me, but this time it wasn't a sedative. I've never done drugs before, but I know now it was heroin."

And here I basically accused her of being a junky when I caught her buying drugs.

"I was put in a cold room alone, without any children. There was just this flickering, faint overhead bulb there that went out frequently. That's where Vassallo came and questioned Frankie as to why I was still alive, because I was too old. He told him he wanted to keep me, and I took the fact that they didn't share any incriminating information around me as a good sign... Perhaps I was naive, but you don't usually censor yourself if you plan to kill the person who hears you."

I don't think it would have mattered, but I don't tell her that.

"Do you remember why they drugged you?"

Now her gaze shoots straight to mine, her brows furrowing in both annoyance and confusion.

"You already know why," she spits back at me.

My brows draw together, tension pulling at my temples along with the confusion.

"I don't..." I shake my head, forced ignorance burning through my chest.

Her features morph to fury, eyes turn glassy as she frowns. But the truth stares me right in the face, it spills from her eyes in wordless whispers, telling me what I've been refusing to accept since the moment Maddox found her.

No... fuck! No, they didn't! Did they...?

"Evelyn..."

"Don't make me say it, Finnigan. You already know why."

"I don't. I wasn't there," I say quickly, the strain too noticeable in my voice.

Her eyes widen, and she flinches back. "But Maddox said—"

"I was part of the rescue mission, but I was with some of the kids... Maddox alone found you."

"And he didn't tell you?"

"Evelyn!" I raise my voice involuntarily, raking a hand through my hair as I force down my own anguish. "What happened?"

Small tears pool in her eyes, and a shuddering crack inside my chest sends shockwaves through my soul. Before I realize what I'm doing, I'm on one knee in front of her, my hands covering hers as she clutches the bedspread. She doesn't pull away, not that it would matter. I wouldn't let her.

"What did he do to you?" I whisper, unable to ignore the reality any longer. If she's suffering, then I should be too.

"They pinned me down, on my front..." She pauses as a light tear grazes down her cheek, and the pain exploding inside my chest makes my ears ring. "I was a virgin before *them*."

They hurt my Evelyn. They took her fucking innocence away!

I don't need to hear more. The echo of unspoken words carry enough pain for me to taste it for myself.

Bartiste fucking touched her. And Maddox didn't tell me!

"Evelyn, I'm so, so—"

"Don't." She stops me. "I don't need your pity."

"It's not pity, I'm just sorry that—"

"You broke your word?" She interrupts me again. "That your failure got me in that situation? Is that what you're sorry for? I sacrificed myself and you, Finnigan, you failed me."

I all but fall on my ass. I... I didn't... she's right.

"You promised me. You promised you would get me out before anything happened to me. You failed." On those last words, she pushes me back and gets off the bed, leaving me on one knee, mouth agape and a big fucking hole in my soul. She didn't even yell. Her tone held a calm disappointment in it.

I wish she would have yelled.

She's right. I failed her.

"Evelyn, stop!" I jump to my feet and slam shut the door she was just opening.

Her back is to my front, her scent filling me with more heat, more guilt, more longing. *I failed her.*

"We'll find them. I promise you on everything I am, we will find them, and I will kill them. I will kill them all for what they did to you." My tone lowers with each of those words because this promise is thick, heavy, and unbreakable.

I will not fail her again.

There will be blood, and I will bring her their heads.

"Forgive me if I have trouble trusting in your promise," she spits as she turns, pressing a hand on my chest to push me away.

I let her, and just as she opens her mouth again, a ringing stops her. She's so pissed, she doesn't even look at the screen as she pulls the phone out and answers it.

"Yes?" she rasps.

But a moment later she lets out a hiss as she briefly glances at the screen, then at me. I skip around, placing myself between her and the door before she can seek her escape, and I Christ almighty, if eyes could shoot daggers, I would be dead on the floor.

"No, it's fine. Did something happen?" she asks on the phone. "Really? For how long?" Her gaze turns to earth-moving sparkles.

Happiness shines in her eyes and she turns to the door, but when she sees I'm not moving, she rushes to the opposite end of the room, standing by the window. She wants to hide something, though it feels more like a secret she's been holding for a long time. The happiness shining in her eyes plagues my soul more than the secret, and it feels a lot like wretched jealousy.

Yet another emotion I didn't think I could feel anymore.

"Oh, yes! Yes, please!" Her enthusiasm brightens her voice, and I find myself stepping toward that light.

Then the next two words stop me dead in my tracks.

"Hi, Daddy."

CHAPTER 17
Evelyn

I WAS DESPERATE to leave this room, to keep this private, but I don't have time to fight Finnigan. Not when my father is experiencing a rare moment of lucidity.

"Hi, Daddy." I barely suppress the emotions shaking my voice.

"Hi, my sweet Evie." His voice turns my legs to jelly, and I feel around me until I find the edge of the bed again.

"I miss you, Daddy. So much."

"Come see me. It's been so long…"

It has. Months. Maya and I used to go see him every week. More often if the nurses told us over the phone that he was having a good week, when he was actually remembering us. We tried to avoid the weeks when he remembered that the love of his life, our mom, is dead. I wanted to be there to hold him through it, even if he didn't know who I was, but I couldn't put Maya through it.

She didn't understand why Daddy was angry, why he didn't know who she was. Especially since his Alzheimer's has been getting progressively worse in the last year. I had to protect her, no matter how much it hurt not to be able to see my only living parent.

"I can't right now, but I promise I'll come soon."

"Why not, sweet Evie? Today feels perfect. The sun seems to be shining for the first time in weeks. Maybe longer." He trails off and I wander with him, my gaze going out the window, toward the back of the house where Maya is playing outside with her new friend—Aaro.

"Maya and I had to leave town for a bit, Daddy. But we're doing well."

"Why? Where are you?"

"On the South coast. We're safe, I promise. We're staying with—" I turn my head until Finnigan hits my line of sight, and my breath hitches when I catch the unfamiliar worry in his eyes. "Friends. We're safe. Maya's happy." I turn back to look out the window at my sister playing with the curly-haired little boy.

"Is she? You're so good with her, she's so lucky to have you. I'm so sorry I'm not there to take care of you... I'm so sorry, my sweet Evie."

I choke up, swallowing unshed tears. He hasn't been this lucid in so long, and I'm not there to experience it in person. To hug him. Hold him. For him to hold me. Like he used to. Rubbing a big hand down my hair, kissing the top of my head. He made me feel so safe. Even as his memories of me were drifting away.

"You're the best dad ever, you're always with us. No matter the distance."

"Oh, I love you, honey."

"Love you too, Daddy."

"But, why are you there, sweet Evie? It's thousands of miles away."

"I found better work here with the help of friends, and a good school for Maya." Technically the first part is true—my job at Lulu's Café is great, and higher paid for sure.

I hate lying to my father, even if he's likely to forget this conversation by the end of the week. Maybe even the day. It feels disrespectful.

"Okay honey. I trust you. If you thought that was the best for your sister and you. When are you coming back?"

"We'll come home soon, Daddy."

At those words I hear shuffling behind me, and I tense.

"Once we finish here, we'll be back, and we'll come straight to see you."

"I can't wait. It's been too long."

I don't miss the change in his voice. I've heard it enough to recognize it and I wonder if I have any time left.

"Do you want to speak to Maya?" I ask, a hint of hope lifting my tone.

"Yes. But, umm... can I, can I talk to your mom first?"

Sometimes I think there aren't any pieces left of my heart to break. Yet, every time he says something like this, his words find a stray shard big enough to shatter.

He's going away again...

"She's not here, Daddy."

"Where is she?" there's a slight tremble in his voice.

"She's... out." I can't do it. I've broken his heart so many times now, I must have reached a hundred.

"Oh..."

"Is nurse Jackie taking good care of you?" I attempt to distract him.

"She cheats at chess."

I burst out in a short laugh, because only he could have said something so random.

"Let me talk to her, I'll give her a piece of my mind."

"You can try, but she won't admit it. Call me soon, sweet Evie, yes?"

"Of course, Daddy. We'll speak soon. I love you, and Maya loves you so much."

"Um... Maya... oh yes. I love you too."

He's losing her again.

"Thank you, Jackie. I appreciate the call." I tell the woman when her voice comes back on the other line.

"Always, sweetheart. I waited to make sure he was truly there. Did he speak with Maya?" she asks.

"No. He asked about Mom."

"I heard. Don't worry. He's in good hands."

"I know. Thank you, Jackie."

"Are you safe? Last time we talked you said you're down South."

"Yes, I'm safe. I have a good job now, nice place to stay, I'll be back soon," I answer her.

"Okay honey, you take good care of the little firecracker, okay?"

I'm reluctant to say goodbye to the woman, knowing that I will have to turn around and face the man who has listened to this entire conversation. At least my side of it. But I do. I say goodbye and hang up, though the sadness doesn't leave me as I watch my sister out there, oblivious to the fact that I had two good minutes with our father, and she missed out on this sense of utter joy.

Only, that's not quite the case for her. I shake my head as I drop the phone on the bed.

My sister doesn't perceive our father in the same way that I do. She was too young to form the same attachment as me, the same relationship. He's been in the care home for half her short life. She's always been excited to see him, she loves him, but she's young... she thankfully doesn't hurt like I do.

It's probably why he forgets her quicker than he forgets me.

It hurts so much when he forgets. When his safety is ripped away from me.

I can't help the tears pooling in my eyes now, nor the one sliding down my cheeks, mourning the father I used to have.

"Does anyone else know?" I flinch at Finnigan's soft voice, clutching the bedspread in my fists.

"Only Lulu," I whisper.

"Why didn't you tell us? We can help him... you." His steps are closing in.

Do I have the heart to tell him I did this to protect my father from them?

"I don't need it. He's perfect where he is. It's a specialized home for people with dementia. They have all the facilities, and great staff," I answer.

"But they don't have you..." Finnigan trails off and the kindness in his words takes my breath away. "I'm sorry I stopped you from leaving the room, then. Maya didn't get to talk to him."

I sigh because I wish I could blame him, but in truth, it was too late.

"It's okay. She wouldn't have managed to. He was already slipping away. It's probably better this way."

His shadow looms over me for a moment before the bed dips, my body involuntarily leaning toward him, and I quickly gather my hands in my lap. I don't turn, don't pay him any attention as my focus stays on my sister beyond the window.

"Why didn't you tell us about him? We thought you were homeless because he... passed away."

I take in a shallow breath and realize I don't have the energy to invent a different reason that might not hurt his feelings.

"Because I didn't know anything about you. All of you. Not that I know that much now." I rub my thumbs nervously on my lap. "There was no reason to trust you, and I will protect my family at all costs. I could never risk him being used in any way because of my screw up."

A slow, deep inhale coming from him tenses me up. I wait for the retaliation, for the snappy remark.

"Okay, fair."

My brows pull together, but I hold myself from turning to him.

"Has your opinion of us changed?" he asks.

"Yes," I answer without hesitation, surprising myself.

I know my instincts spoke before me because it's true. They treat my sister and I with nothing but kindness. From shelter, to food, to a decent job, and... friendship. As terrifying as that is, since I cannot stay in this city, they give me friendship. Unconditionally.

"For the better?" he asks.

"You're not what I expected. All of you, I mean." I quickly correct myself. "People whisper about you in town, about the *ruthless* Sanctum, the crime, the sex, the power. They fear you. I'm not saying you're not to be feared, you probably are, but what I've seen so far... it's exponentially different from their perception of you."

The exhale I hear coming from him warms me. There's relief in that whiff of air, and a tinge of hope blossoms beneath my flesh.

"Tell me about your parents." He speaks those words in such a calm, soothing tone, I feel compelled to share.

"They were normal people. Not rich, not poor, normal jobs. We lived in one of those suburban neighborhoods that's almost in the countryside, with plenty of space between houses. It was just the four of us. My mother came from the foster system and didn't know her parents, my father's mom died when I was two, and my grandpa when I was six. No siblings on either side, no great aunts or uncles. It was just us... we were happy." I inhale slowly, defeated. "Until we weren't."

I watch as Maya comes back into the garden, shyly handing Aaro a little plate with a piece of my cake. They both blush and there's something so endearing about this sweet moment.

Finn doesn't say a word. He's perfectly still in my periphery, patiently waiting on me to spill my story. Maybe there's hope yet for whatever this is between us. Though he seems reluctant to even admit it.

"About five years ago, our lives changed. Dad started having strange symptoms that didn't quite add up. At first, they kind of ignored them and passed them off as stress. But then the forgetfulness came, and from then on, he deteriorated. He has early-onset Alzheimer's, and it's aggressive enough that the decision was made for him to go to a care home that specializes in dementia. He insisted himself on one of his good days. Mom fought him so hard, I thought she would win. She didn't, Dad wouldn't let her."

I remember that period like it was yesterday. There was no yelling, no actual fighting, but begging. So much begging from both sides.

"Dad couldn't work anymore, of course, and mom not only had to work harder, but take care of a three-year-old, a thirteen-year-old, and my father. It got to the point where she couldn't leave him alone with us. I had to go find him after school on more than one occasion, because he got lost in the neighborhood. Once he almost burnt down the kitchen. Dad couldn't do this to mom, he loved her and us too much to make us suffer. So he went to the home. A good one."

"Evelyn... I'm so sorry." The sincerity in his tone splits open a little part of me I haven't been allowing to get too close.

"It's okay. I got used to it."

"But who's paying for him now? Who has been paying since you've been on your own?"

"Their savings. Mom put it in a sort of trust and a direct debit runs out of there monthly. She wanted to make sure that money is secure. But... it's running out. No one could have anticipated she—" I have to take a deep breath, swallowing through the emotions the memory of her brings. "That she wouldn't be here now."

"What happened?" Finnigan asks.

"Dad was already in the care home by this point. For quite some time. Mom went to the grocery store, came out to head to her car and... got caught in the middle of a gang war. She was shot in the parking lot. Police called her collateral damage, wrong place at the wrong time and all that. She stood no chance and died on scene."

I think we both stopped breathing, because you could hear a needle drop in this heavy silence.

"Some time ago you told me something—*you don't know what your world did to mine*—is this what you meant?"

I flinch at Finnigan's question. How does he even remember that? I blamed him and his world, and it's hard not to feel a little guilty about it now. A little right, too.

"It's easy to put all crime in one pot. Gangs are still criminal organizations, seeing the commonalities isn't that hard." I answer sincerely. Then there's what happened after... what their world turned me into, but I barely admit that to myself, so I'm not going to tell him. "And after all that, Maya and I fell into the clutches of another side of this dangerous world."

"I understand. I'm sorry about your mom, Evie." He moves on from the subject. Though, he doesn't deny it.

"Thank you. It's been long enough that I've gotten used to the entire situation."

"You shouldn't have to get used to something like this. You're supposed to have support, people around you to help you through it all. How did you end up on the streets?"

"We had nowhere to go." I shrug. "We couldn't stay home, not as two minors. The only solution was placement, but in different foster families. And under no circumstances was I going to allow Maya to be separated from me."

"How did you escape the system?"

"I never went in it," I answer bluntly. "After the police came to the door to tell us about mom, I gathered everything I could hold in two backpacks, and ran. I knew what the system meant, and I wasn't going to allow it to swallow us whole. I was inspired enough to grab all photos of us as well, though they're all lost now. I wanted the memories, but it was mainly for Maya's benefit. I knew the police would put our faces on the side of a milk carton, especially Maya since she was so young. She's probably on the *missing children* list with no photo, just a name and birthplace."

"How did you manage to get her enrolled in school?"

"Fake documents and a person pretending to be our mom. It helped that Maya was never in school before, it was her first year. And we changed her name from Shaw to Shawn. Thought it would be easy to brush it off as a typo whenever I did manage to get custody and enroll her properly under her real name."

"Jesus…" He sighs, rubbing a hand over his face. He takes a deep breath, and I know he's pondering his next question. I bet he has a lot of them. "I just don't understand how you managed all of this on your own. This… fuck, it's so much, Evelyn. You were what, sixteen? Christ."

"I didn't have a choice. It was between this or losing my sister in the system. Imagine if she ended up in a closed adoption or something. It was not an option in my book. Though, I do wonder sometimes"—more often than I want to admit—"if Maya would have had a better life. If she would have found an amazing family. One who didn't live in shady motels or in their car. Who didn't get kidnapped in a trafficking ring."

Warmth and softness wrap around both my hands on my lap and I'm speechless when I look down—his large hand holds mine. Squeezing. Soothing. Comforting.

"You made the best choice."

I have no idea what to say to that, because his touch is a welcome distraction from all the sorrow I shared. His hand over both of mine drives me down a path of forbidden touch and untapped desire. If only he would move it higher, run it all up my arm, drag this electric current over my shoulders, my throat, my cheek… down my back, over my ass, and—

"How were you able to visit your dad?" He interrupts my dangerous thoughts. "Didn't the staff report you?"

"No. I knew one of the nurses. She wanted to call CPS at first, but I convinced her eventually. When her boyfriend was away on business, she used to take us in for the night. She's the one who called—Jackie. The rest of the staff I came in contact with didn't really ask, but Jackie told them we were in foster care. No one has time to question that." I'm still looking at our hands. "Where are your parents?" I ask.

"This month, on a yacht somewhere off the East coast. I think. They travel a lot." He shrugs.

How peculiar. He's not even bothered by it. His thumb has started moving, rubbing slowly, mindlessly over my knuckles, distracting me.

"You're not close?"

"As close as I can be to two parents who filled their time with work their whole life, and when they retired, they left."

"I'm sorry. That must be rough."

"Not at all," he says, his thumb still stroking over my hand. "It's what I've always known from them. I did have Mamaw June though."

"Vincent's mom, really? How long have you all known each other?" I didn't expect that. I thought they were close because they were business partners.

"Since we were kids. We were in school together. Madds and Vin were already friends, then we came along not long after. June was like a surrogate mother for all of us. She always had enough love in her for all of us."

God, I want to hug him. I may not have my parents anymore, or at least my mom, but the memories I have of them… of my mom teaching me to bake cookies, making pink meringues with my dad, our little adventures through the woods collecting pinecones, or at the beach gathering all the pretty pebbles, and so many more. I would be lost without those memories. Especially now that our photos no longer exist. Well, technically they do, in my old car that's probably in a dump somewhere.

"Mamaw June truly is incredible."

"She's good with Maya," he agrees.

"She's good with me too," I admit.

At my words he tightens his hold around my hands. This means something to both of us. A strange common ground born out of two different situations, different needs, different wants.

"With everything you went through, you fucking prevailed. Look at you now. You're surrounded by people who care."

"Do you?" I turn, my gaze pinned onto the azure of his. "Do you care about me, Finnigan?"

He flinches, his lips parting, but only unspoken words pass through that slight gap.

Damn it! We've opened up. I've opened up! I thought this was going somewhere, that he was finally going to acknowledge... this. Whatever this is. I'm such a fool.

"I'm not good for you, Evelyn. This"—he points between us, releasing my hands,— "can't go anywhere. We can't cross this line."

"Jesus, Finnigan. You're the one with the chalk in hand drawing lines only you care about." I rise, clenching my fists, trying to rein in my anger, but for the first time in a long time, I fail. "Just... just *fucking* stop it!"

CHAPTER 18
Finnigan

I'M FLABBERGASTED. EVELYN Shaw not only got angry, which is something she hasn't done even when I was pissing the hell out of her, but she raised her voice. And she swore. She actually swore.

She's the calmest person I've ever met. I don't know if it's because she's been putting up a front for Maya, or she just got used to it for her benefit, but seeing her like this... close to disheveled, wakes up a primal urge within me.

"You and your goddamn line! I'm done with this." She turns on her heels and storms out of the room, leaving me all alone with her words lingering in the air.

This is for the best. She has to be done with this. As I rake my fingers through my already messy hair, I can't help but wonder if I'm done with this at all.

I'm not. Not even fucking close.

On the contrary. Knowing that Bartiste was responsible for her kidnapping as well, changed the game for me. I refuse to let that asshole take another person from me. Evelyn might not be mine the way Hanna was, but she is... something else.

Don't make me say it, Finnigan... Her words echo through my thoughts. The bastard touched her. He raped her. He raped my Evelyn when he didn't even have the right to fucking gaze upon her.

Did I just call her...? Yeah, I did—I called her *my Evelyn.* Christ, I'm so screwed. It's not even the first time I thought of her as mine, yet I tell her she can't cross the line. Hypocrisy looks like shit on me.

But she really is something else, something to cherish. To admire. I know she's been going to therapy, Katya mentioned it, but living every day with all that sorrow and pain is unfathomable. Her life is a series of tragic events, and no sane person would have come out on the other side the way she did. She's a force of nature.

Evelyn appears in my line of sight out in the garden, squatting to speak with Aaro. My nephew. I might just have to punch Carter in the face for doing this to me.

A knock startles me and I turn to the door.

"Can we talk?"

No.

I'm not prepared for this. I doubt I ever will be.

Ronan takes my silence as a *yes* and walks toward me, taking a seat where Evelyn sat before him.

"I didn't want to blindside you. I told Carter and Katya, and they convinced me to keep quiet."

"I'm sorry, Katya knows too?" My brows pull together, a tension drawing a headache through my temples.

"I brought her in the business. Her and I never stopped being friends."

"But we did." I end that sentence for him.

"That was not my choice, brother."

I can't help but scoff, keeping my gaze toward the garden, on her. "It was. You left."

"But you banished me."

"I was in pain, goddamn it! I was fucking broken, and you abandoned me!" I slam my hands on the bed, turning to him. "What did you expect me to do? I never loved before, Ronan. I didn't know how it felt to have it be ripped away from you... in such a literal sense of the word. I needed you!"

"I know... I'm sorry. You know this. I just couldn't keep Annika and Aaro in that situation. I couldn't keep myself. I know I was selfish, believe me, it fucking hurt me too, but I couldn't see any other choice."

I say nothing because he's not wrong, and goddamn it, I hate that.

"You had The Sanctum, Annika had no one who could understand. Her best friend was brutally murdered and died in her arms... I couldn't just abandon her. Not when she was pregnant with my child—our blood. But don't ever think my choice was easy. I missed you so goddamn much, Finn."

Sighing, I clench my fists around the comforter. So many years have passed, and this explanation makes more sense now. It shouldn't. It should sound the same, mean the same thing, and feel the same. Yet, it doesn't. If I was in his shoes, I wouldn't have left. But do I really not understand why he made that choice?

I think the reason I've been so angry and hurt over these years is exactly the opposite—I do understand. At least I've grown to understand. But I have no one else to blame, no one else to be angry at. I'm not admitting that to him, though. Turning, I look at my brother, really look at him. Lines have appeared across his features, smile lines under his cheekbones, crow's feet around his eyes, faint creases on his forehead. But his eyes are the same. Calm, hopeful, caring.

I want to punch him harder.

Why couldn't he just be an asshole?

"Come on," I finally say. "Your wife and son are probably waiting for you." I rise and walk away before he answers.

I can't bear to be in this room with him anymore.

"He asks about you, you know," Ronan says behind me.

I stop, but don't turn.

"We show him photos." he continues when I don't answer, "We tell him about you, but he's never satisfied."

"He doesn't even know me, why isn't he satisfied?" I ask.

"Because for the first few years he couldn't understand *why* he didn't know you. Why you didn't want to meet him. We told him your job keeps you away."

"Thanks, I guess." I walk away this time, and he follows, passing with me through the hall, then back in the living area.

"He loved the books."

My steps falter.

"He's read them all. Several times. They're his favorites and he keeps them away from all the others."

I never sent anything to Ronan or Annika. Never spoken with them since they left. Didn't even text. But... I felt bad that I had a nephew out there who would never know me. I wanted a connection, even a faint one. Every once in a while, when Katya sent them a package or met with them, I gave her a book. I told her not to mention they were from me, and she promised she wouldn't. It's possible that she lied... or perhaps Ronan simply knew. Hearing that Aaro loves them makes me feel a certain way.

"There you are." Annika walks in through the patio door, heading straight to her husband, and wrapping her arms around his middle. "The munchkin might need sleep soon. He's wired and smitten, it seems."

Both Ronan and I turn to the patio at the same time. Annika's right. The way the kid looks at Maya is funny and endearing at the same time—he is indeed smitten. Though, he's trying to play it cool. Stealing glances when she's not looking.

"Evelyn said she's leaving, though, so it would be a good idea for us to head out as well," Annika continues.

"Actually, Vincent offered us to stay here. It's safe, there's security patrolling the woods, and it would be better for you and Aaro," my brother answers her.

I could offer his old room in the penthouse, but it feels like a step too far. Too quick. I would rather get him in the ring and smash his face in first. It wouldn't achieve much, but it would certainly make me feel better.

"That's really nice of him. Okay, sounds good to me. I'll ask Katya to bring our stuff from her place."

Katya... I might have to have a word with the woman. I'm not enjoying this secrecy. The fact that she and Carter hid the arrival of my brother doesn't sit right with me. Actually, thinking about it, both of them have been looking at me funny for a few days now. Particularly at Morrigan's birthday party.

"When did you decide you were coming back to Queenscove?" I ask.

"A few weeks ago," Ronan answers.

Huh, okay. "When did you tell Carter about it?"

My brother and his wife exchange brief glances before he answers. "Maybe four days ago."

Oh yes, that timeline fits perfectly. Goddamn it. Though, I do feel better knowing that Carter and Katya haven't been keeping this from me for too long.

"I'm sorry we didn't tell you too. I didn't want to risk it," my brother says.

"Risk what?" I ask.

"Not seeing you, of course."

I'm not sure how to respond to that. Would I have gone away knowing that he was coming specifically to talk to the Sanctum? Maybe. The few times he visited in the past few years, he would go to our parents place and I would make myself busy on missions or going out of town. Any excuse not to be in the same postcode as him.

This was an ambush, and it was the only way for him to see me. I'm bothered that I'm weirdly becoming okay with it.

I nod to my brother. "I understand."

He gives me a faint smile, like he's handling a skittish animal, making sure I don't run away. Christ, have I acted that childish in the last years?

"Excuse me. Nature calls." I didn't need to over-share, but I also didn't want him to think that I'm leaving to end this conversation. Well, I do feel the need to take a break from it, but nature does call.

I walk past the stairs on the narrow corridor to the bathroom, and gentle voices filter through the high, open window—Morrigan and Evelyn.

"It feels... wrong. Dirty."

Those words stop me dead in my tracks, because Evelyn speaks them and my curiosity doesn't just peak. It soars. I'm not proud of it, but I stop walking, hoping there's more to that sentence.

"Have you talked about this with your therapist?" Morrigan asks.

"Not really."

"Why?"

There is a pause. A long one, before Evelyn answers.

"Because I think something's wrong with me. How can someone who went through what I went through still have these thoughts? What if she judges me?"

"Do you think you would be more comfortable talking to me about it?" Morrigan gently speaks the question, making sure there is no demand or expectation.

What the hell are they talking about?

"Oh god. What if you think I'm... wrong?" Evelyn's voice is filled with embarrassment and something that sounds a lot like unease.

"I own a fetish club, Evie. I can assure you, you can share anything."

Wait a damn minute?! What exactly is this conversation about? Evelyn doesn't want to go there. Does she? A burning sense of possessiveness singes through me, and it takes a minute for my brain to catch up. Of course not, the club hasn't been reopened yet after the fire Morrigan's ex started there.

"I guess you're right," Evelyn relents. "If I could talk to anyone about this, it's you and Lulu."

"Exactly! I would never judge, and no matter what it is, I hope I can make you feel more comfortable." Morrigan attempts to soothe her.

There is a brief pause, and my breath is caught in my chest waiting for the intimate confession I should definitely not be listening in on. But I can't help myself, so fuck it. I'm already an asshole.

"After what they did to me, what I feel seems wrong. Inappropriate. Sick. Have you ever felt like you want your partner to just... take? Be at their mercy, sort of? I don't even know how to explain this. Almost like the only consent you give is how turned on you are, but he's already *there* when he discovers this."

"Yes, Evie, I have. There's nothing wrong about that. About giving up control with a person you want, a person you're attracted and connected to."

"But I was raped, Morri. I was forced and they…" she trails off and a burning lump rises up of my throat. "Someone in my situation should not have these kinds of fantasies. It feels sick. What is wrong with me?"

Christ, I want to gather her up in my arms and hold her there. She's not sick. She's so far from that. But it drives me mad thinking that she might end up exploring that kink with someone *else*. Someone who could take advantage of her and not treat her right.

"Many of us who once had the choice stripped away, find solace in the loss of control with a person we trust. A person we want. It's like a different type of therapy. I don't know if it's because the decision to lose control over our body is ours, or maybe it just feels fucking good. Because, let me tell you, it feels so damn good. Fortunately, as you said, your memories of your attack are sparse, and maybe your need for control over it all is even deeper. However, you shouldn't let your fantasies revolve around what happened to you. Let them be. Sometimes a need is just that—a need."

"I never thought of it in this way. Yes, I feel wrong for having these cravings, but they aren't my only ones, nor are they new. I'm questioning them now, their morality, my… mental health, only because of what happened to me."

I am stunned at this conversation. I couldn't move even if someone caught me listening. This insight makes me feel all kinds of wrong. It's utterly intimate and Evelyn would lose her shit knowing that I stole her secret. The worst part of this is that this fantasy of hers is being stored in my mind, like I'm building a list of what would make sweet Evelyn whimper. Should I also add this on the list of all that is wrong about me? Like craving a woman who's barely eighteen?

Yes, I should add it.

"So, it's something you wanted before all of this happened?" Morrigan asks.

There is no answer, but her next words make me think Evelyn probably agreed in a wordless way.

"Then you think it's bad that it hasn't gone away because of the attack."

"It would be the normal expectation, right? And it's not just that, but before it all happened, those types of cravings already felt disturbing. I never had sex before, but all my wet dreams were forceful, raw. I can't believe I just said that." Evelyn's tone raises a few octaves.

I can't either! Jesus, why did she have to say the words *wet dream* and *raw* in the same sentence? I know what I'm dreaming of tonight.

"It's not necessarily the expectation, no. It goes back to the need for control. Fantasizing, living that fantasy in a safe environment gives you your control back. And trust me, Evie, never having sex has nothing to do with what you crave. There are plenty of forty-year-old virgins out there who fantasize about much kinkier things than some dubious consent." Morrigan explains.

"I guess you're right. Thanks Morri, this really helped."

"Do you have someone in mind you would want these fantasies to come to life with?" Morrigan asks her, and I stiffen, eagerly waiting for Evelyn's response.

"I thought I did, but I think I'm going to be seeking someone else."

Oh, hell no! She wants to seek someone else?! Over my dead fucking body! And even then, I'll take the motherfucker down with me.

"Maybe we should do something about it then." Morrigan giggles and I'm ready to burst through that damn window and give her a piece of my mind.

"Shush, Maya's coming," Evelyn alerts her friend, and I take it as my cue to detach myself from this wall.

Through my veins my pulse is rushing so hard, I think my heart's gonna burst out of my fucking chest. It takes more than a few minutes in the bathroom to compose myself finally before coming back into the living area. Ronan gives me a bit of a look when I return, probably wondering why it took me so long to go to the toilet, but I ignore it.

"Say goodbye, Maya." Evelyn's soft, melodic tone, mixed with that sweet brown sugar scent weaves around me just as Aaro darts past and sticks himself against his mom.

"Goodbye..." Maya's little voice sounds shier than usual.

"It was very nice to meet you all. I hope we'll see each other soon," Evelyn says.

"We certainly will. Plus, it was such a nice surprise to have someone in his age range here, it couldn't have worked any better if I planned it."

"It was getting boring with all these adults around." Maya gathers more courage and I stifle a laugh.

"Shush. You love us." Evelyn pats her sister on the top of the head, shaking hers. "We'll see you later then." She moves, now only a few steps away from the front door.

"Wait, who's taking you?" I ask hastily.

She stops but doesn't turn. Not before she takes a few agonizingly slow, deep breaths. The silence is so awkward, Annika took a few quiet steps backwards to remove herself from this. Before I can say something, Evelyn's eyes land on me over her shoulder, and I try to swallow through the sudden dryness in my throat, but it doesn't work. A lump forms, and I swear I can hear her screaming in her mind at me, telling me to mind my own fucking business. Maybe I'm paranoid, maybe I'm just creating fake scenarios in my head, but the annoyance is painted in her furrowed eyebrows.

I deserve this, don't I? I pushed her away yet again and threw the rejection in her face even though my actions don't match my words. I craved opening up to her, craved to share, craved to know more of her, know *everything*, but I don't deserve to know anything at all. I shouldn't. Even if her confession to Morrigan weaves like tendrils of fire through my mind.

She opens her mouth to answer, but another voice pops into the room.

"Okay, I'm done. Let's go." Morrigan wheezes past me and heads straight for the door.

Evelyn says goodbye to everyone, but refuses to acknowledge me anymore. She leaves without a word.

I have a bad feeling about this.

The sparkle in her eyes looked a lot like revenge.

CHAPTER 19
Finnigan

TWO MORE AGONIZING hours passed before I could leave Vin's house. I thought planning and plotting our revenge would do something sweet to my insides, but the opposite happened. All this talk about the man who viciously took the first woman I ever loved away from me stirred a brutal discomfort. It wasn't pain. Not because it didn't hurt, but because the actual pain was reserved for the other reason these hours were agony—Evelyn.

She left in a strange mood, a look of vengeance in her eyes, but resolve too. Resignation. Like she gave up on something and the idea doesn't sit right with me. I don't know why.

Oh, fuck it, of course I know why.

Because it might be me she gave up on, and that makes me all sorts of uncomfortable. Why, I don't know, because I want her to give up. I was the one who chased her away, but not because I didn't want her.

I want her so much I can't breathe properly unless she's around. And when she is, she sucks it out of me, turning into want, need, and something so visceral my heart beats violently in my chest. I crave her starving silver and gold eyes, their invisible touch, the hunger beneath their surface, the demand to live and indulge. To ask for more and feed on the life she never had.

I want *her*.

Knowing she might go out there to seek her desires from someone else fills me with both rage and unfounded jealousy. I might not deserve her, but neither does any other asshole.

Now, I'm standing under the spray of the shower in my penthouse, trying to wash away these conflicting feelings. But I think I'm asking for far too much from mere water. I give it five minutes before I walk out, striding out onto the terrace that overlooks the sea, with nothing but a towel wrapped around my waist. I'm looking for some answers from the calm waves that look too small from this height, but the conflict seems to have the only reply.

The moon has risen, its light brushing over the water, and the calmness unsettles me. It's a sheer contrast to my inner turmoil, because I haven't gone over today's revelation that Bartiste not only is responsible for Evelyn's abduction, but he also *touched* her.

I can't even bring myself to say the true word of what the dead man did to her. I'm a fucking coward. Yet, no matter the word, the reality is the same. I could have lost her to him.

She could have been gone before I had a chance to know her, to witness the woman she's becoming. Admire the strength of her character, of her beautiful mind, experience her transformation, coming into her own. The chance to feel her against me, taste her, and ruin her in the best way possible.

My cock tents against the towel, a soft breeze brushing against it, and I shake my head at the reaction. It's not as involuntary as I would like to believe. Not when it happens every single fucking time I think of Evelyn. It's been going on for weeks, maybe months. Like some teenage goddamn crush or something.

I swipe a hand over my face when I fully acknowledge the word I spoke in my mind—crush.

I'm a twenty-nine year old man... with a crush.

God save me because I'm fucked.

* * *

I didn't make a decision by the time I reached Evelyn's apartment building. But the look in her eyes when she left Vin's house kept resurfacing in my mind, and the nagging sensation that I could be right was agonizing.

Time to find out.

The Sanctum's security is stationed in and around this building too, at Vin's insistence of course, since Morrigan spends a lot of time at her apartment here. I think Madds might have had a say in this too, as he seems oddly focused on the owner of the building—Loreley—though he would never admit it.

One of the guys lets me in and I head straight up to the first floor, my knuckles against the door before my feet halt. Too many moments pass, and just when I'm about to knock again, the door opens.

"Well, hello there."

"Mamaw June," I exclaim, surprised. "Hello."

She chuckles softly and moves to let me in.

"I must admit, I'm not used to you being so disappointed to see me."

"Shit, I'm sorry." I don't even bother to deny it. One does not lie to Mamaw June. The woman has a sixth sense about it.

"It's okay." Her tone is light, amused. "But Evelyn's not here, dear."

I'm too late.

"Do you know where she is?"

"Out. She asked me to look after Maya tonight." She shrugs as she moves toward the living room.

I've never been in this place, but Morrigan's apartment on the floor above has a similar layout. This one has a different personality though, as in it almost lacks it. It looks like it was just about finished, some of the light switches still have the protective film over them. But this old building has so much character with its tall ceilings and intricate coving, that not much needs to be done to it to make it look inviting.

"Finnigan!" A little screech makes me swallow my next question, and a small body slams into me from the side, arms wrapped around my waist.

"Maya. Hello." I greet the cheeky girl. I wonder if she reacts like this to everyone she sees. "You seem cheerful. Aren't you supposed to be in bed?"

She pulls back and steals guilty looks at Mamaw June. "I'm a big girl. I can stay up late."

"It's eight thirty now, I'll give you half an hour and then you're off to bed."

"An hour. Finnigan's here. He can read something to me." She grabs my hand and flashes her doe eyes, clear expectation in them.

"Oh honey, I actually have somewhere—" The words get caught in my throat at the shift in her eyes, sadness slowly seeping into them. "Sure, I'll stay." I can't bring myself to deny her.

She squeals and skips cheerfully to a small bookcase, sliding to her knees and rummages through it.

"Did you have somewhere you needed to be? Because I don't think you're escaping this." The woman chuckles.

I did, but I can't bear the thought of disappointing the little one. Plus, I don't know where I should go.

"Did Evelyn say where she was going?" I ask as I follow toward the sofa.

"She did not, no. And you know me, it's not like I know the *hip* places in town anyway, so it wouldn't matter."

"How about this one?" Maya exclaims and rushes to me, a tattered book in hand.

I sit down on the comfy sofa and grab it from her. *Percy Jackson and the Lighting Thief*. Okay, this is not a bad choice at all. Though this book clearly has seen better times.

"Where did you find this?" I ask Maya as she plops next to me, snuggling against my arm with absolutely no shyness or reservations. Her sister doesn't share the same forward attitude, though... she's the one who came on to me every time. Okay, maybe I am wrong, and she does have the same drive, I'm simply the one to squash it every time.

God, I truly am an asshole.

"One of those cool thrift shops. They have a lot of pretty old things there."

I wonder if Evelyn takes her there out of need or actual pleasure for the cheap, secondhand items. I resign myself to pushing back my plan of finding Evelyn, because there is no way I'm going to break the little girl's heart.

"Can you do something for me, though" I ask her.

"Of course! Anything." She wraps her tiny hands around my bicep and looks at me like I'm about to give her the most important mission in the world.

"Could I have a glass of water, please?"

"Coming right up!" She jumps off the sofa and disappears somewhere behind me.

I chuckle at her enthusiasm, and pull my phone out of my pocket. Before I pop it on the table, I shoot a text to Maddox.

> Have you seen Evelyn? She's not home. Worried about drugs. Can you find out where she is?

He's the only one of us who knows about her previous *adventure* and has been keeping an eye on her. I feel like a dick for using the drugs as an excuse to find out where she is, but the alternative is to tell Maddox that I rejected her attraction to me yet again. Obviously, I can't tell him that.

> On it. I'll text when I find her.

> Thanks.

"Here you go." Maya hands me the glass of water like it's liquid gold, and plops back next to me as I down half of it.

Placing my phone on the wood coffee table before me, I settle in for a reading session. I guess I have to brush off my intonation skills, because I think the little one will demand full immersion in the story.

Yet, even as I start reading, my mind still drifts to one question.

Where the hell is Evelyn?

Evelyn

"GIRL, YOU KNOW you're not gonna find what you're looking for here. Right?" Morrigan's words filter through the loud music as I move my hips on the dance floor of the bar.

It's a busy night, and the man I'm currently swaying my backside against is not the first one this evening. At least this one isn't already drunk, and he seems less handsy than the last one.

"I know. But I can practice." I laugh.

"You sure can. I'm gonna go get a drink. Don't go anywhere." I think that last sentence is for the guy behind me more than for me.

I catch a glimpse of Lulu rolling her hips slowly in the arms of a man who looks ready to kneel at her feet and kiss them. He's a handsome one. Tall and broad enough that you know he's fit underneath his clean-cut clothes, with the face of a clean-shaved lawyer who hikes and goes to the gym in his free time.

Yet, he looks totally wrong for her. But she seems to be enjoying herself.

The guy behind me tightens his hands against my hips and pulls me a little closer.

I don't miss the half-mast rubbing against my ass, and for a moment I want to pull away, run in the opposite direction. But I swallow through the sensation and allow him to hold me, to lead me on the song that everyone on this dance floor seems to enjoy.

"So, what are you doing for the rest of this lovely night?" he asks.

"Exactly this. Dancing. Enjoying myself."

"Here?"

I debate the answer for a moment.

"Oh, yes."

I know I've been dancing with him for quite a few songs. Maybe it was a mistake. It created expectations I didn't foresee. Maybe being as sexually inexperienced as I am, made me more naive than I thought I was.

"I came with my friends, and I'm leaving with them as well," I add. I don't want to hurt the guy.

"Surely they wouldn't mind if you decide you want to *dance* with me at my place." The insinuation is clear in the way he accentuates that word.

"They are very protective of me, so I'm afraid dancing will be limited to this bar." Okay, he's getting a little insistent.

"Well, I'm sure we can find a spot that's a bit more... private."

He attempts to turn me to him, and I resist, attempting to move away instead. But I'm a little unsteady on my feet after four shots and three vodka sours, and the guy isn't even attempting to catch my delicate rejection.

"Actually, I think I'm going to go check on my friend now." I pull away again, but he holds me tighter.

Oh hell, what do I do? I don't want to cause a scene.

"That would be such a shame. Give me one more dance, one more song." He begs and I wonder if that will be the end of it.

I'm a bit too tipsy to protest delicately, so I look for the girls to bail me out instead. I catch Morrigan's flaming red hair, but she's talking to the barman. Turning to Lulu, I see she's preoccupied with the *lawyer* guy, hanging around his neck as he guides her hips against his own. I can't just scream for her, that will cause a scene. But her body stills, bones frozen in place as her gaze fixes on a spot in the distance, and she slowly releases the guy she's with. I follow the direction of her stern gaze, and I'm both annoyed and relieved at what I find there—Maddox. I know why I'm annoyed, but I'm not sure why Lulu reacts like this to the big guy.

"Hey, I think it would be best if we stop dancing now." I warn the man behind me in the most delicate way I can muster right now.

I've grown to view Madds like an older brother, and if he feels the same for me, then I know why he showed up here, and the guy behind me should disappear before he sees him. Madds scans the room, and it takes him three seconds to spot all three of us, his gaze darkening with each one. As he stalks over, I expect him to come straight to me and drag me away, but instead, he stops next to Lulu. Shoulder to shoulder, looking down at her as she scowls up at him. No words are exchanged, only glowers, one more intense than the other. One more possessive than the other. *Holy hell, what is happening over there?*

I'm downright curious and I make a mental note to ask Lulu about it. Or at least

Morri, since I think Lulu will dismiss me. Madds turns his focus on me, and I feel like I got caught doing something I'm not supposed to. Okay, he definitely has big brother attitude.

The guy behind me jerks me against him, and I only blink once and Madds is only two steps away from me.

"Having fun?" he asks, but there's no cheerfulness in his tone.

"Umm, yup." *Yup?* What kind of answer is that?

"Who's this," the guy behind me asks.

"You're done now, right?" Madds asks me, ignoring the guy.

I debate being a brat for a few moments, chewing on the inside of my cheek, but self-preservation wins. Plus, I wanna get rid of this dude.

"I think I want a drink," I answer, because I'm not necessarily done with the night, but I'm done with this guy.

"I'll get you one," he says from behind me, his hands possessive against my hips.

"No. You're good, buddy. I suggest you find someone else."

I laugh at Maddox's words, and I bite my lip to stifle it. He notices but isn't amused as he reaches a hand for me. I grab it, but the guy behind me doesn't let go. Madds notices and steps forward, his six foot and too many inches frame towering over the man.

"Maybe the music is too loud, and you didn't hear me. I said find. Someone. Else." He punctuates each word with another small step until he's crowding us.

With a jerk, the guy releases me, and my back cools—he stepped away. I release a sigh of relief and let Maddox pull me away.

"Have a good evening," I say on a raised tone, turning my head slightly.

There's sarcasm in my voice, but I didn't want to be mean and leave without a word.

When we reach the bar, I slap a hand on Maddox's bicep. "What are you doing here?"

"Rescuing you, clearly."

"Oh, stop it. Seriously, what's with the ambush and the attitude?"

He doesn't answer, just rolls his eyes and ignores me as he pulls his phone out and starts tapping.

"Hey! I'm talking to you." I push the phone down and glimpse at the screen, annoyed that he's ignoring me for it.

Found her. Dancing in Terry's bar with Morrigan and Lulu.

I gasp at the text, clearly about me, but when I catch the first letter of the name at the top of the screen before Madds pulls the phone away, I turn furious.

"Finnigan?! Are you reporting back to him? Did he send you?" Oh, I'm mad. Really mad. The alcohol might have something to do with it too, because I don't usually get so heated.

"He was worried about you."

Those words don't make me feel better in the slightest.

"What right does he have to worry about me? He clearly does not care about me at all. He said that much." I spit back at him, though my words are more directed at Finnigan, even if he's not here.

"Okay, I've kept my questions to myself because prying is not my thing. But what the hell is happening between you and Hennessey?!" Madds crosses his arms against his broad chest, and for a moment there he looks more like a father than a brother.

"I wouldn't mind the answer to that question either." Morri pops up at my side, then joins the scarred man before me.

I roll my eyes at both of them. "Absolutely nothing. Clearly." I want to slap my hand over my mouth because I'm giving far too freaking much away.

They exchange a curious look, and it feels like a silent conversation about me.

"Nothing at all?" the redhead insists.

I'm not quick enough to answer and her brows shoot up, and yet again she exchanges a look with Maddox.

"Hey! Stop that!"

She chuckles at my outburst and shakes her head.

"I knew it. Christ, it's about time. Isn't it?" She looks to Madds for the answer.

He nods and leans against the bar, a thoughtful look in his eyes, like he's drifting somewhere in the past. But then he shakes his head.

"He's a player, Evie. He fucks a new girl every week, sometimes every night. He doesn't date. He's not for you."

"You cannot decide what is and isn't for me," I push back. "If I decide I wish to sleep around with Finnigan Hennessey, I'll do however I please. But just so you know, no, there's nothing going on between the two of us. Nothing at all." *No matter how much I tried.*

Madds is about to argue, but Morri sets a hand over his forearm stopping him. "I hate to tell you, big guy, but Finnigan hasn't fucked around in a while..."

"What?" Both Maddox and I exclaim at the same time, and he scowls.

"It's just an observation. Though, it is coming from me, Vin, and Carter. Finn lacking a woman on his arm every other night is something noticeable." She shrugs. "And I believe the reason he hasn't is standing right in front of me."

"Come to think of it..." Madds trails off. "Oh, for fucks sakes! I'm gonna kill him!" he bursts.

"Oh, settle down. Christ, you really do take your *big brother* duties seriously." Morri laughs.

I feel all fuzzy with affection for the man, but I catch a hint of sadness in his eyes too. It's gone just as fast as it appeared. He mentioned a sister once, but the subject was shut down before it barely started. Maybe one day I'll pry.

"Madds, seriously. There's nothing going on with him and I, he just... pisses me off. Kind of like what you're doing right now." I fold my arms over my chest, cocking my head at him.

Is my act working?

Yet, my mind drifts to their words—Finnigan hasn't been seen with a woman in a long while, which they find abnormal. Something swells inside my chest at the thought that I could be the reason why. Not only that, but there's a hot tingle deep between my legs that revels in the idea of it.

He can reject me all he wants, but the man is lying to himself. And I would smile from ear to freaking ear if it wasn't for these two watching me.

"Should we go home?" I ask, eager to end the night now.

"Great idea," Morri says, downing her drink and setting her glass on the bar.

"Well, I don't know how you feel about this"—Maddox speaks as he looks at his phone, then at me—"but he's there, at your apartment. Waiting for you."

"Excuse me?" I exclaim.

My belly flutters at the sound of it, and I sneak a peek at his screen, then fall back, wobbling a little. I think the alcohol is messing with my head, because the words I read make both annoyance and excitement resonate through me.

WHO THE FUCK WAS SHE DANCING WITH?!

Maybe I'm an idiot for flinging myself at this guy, but I can't explain the pull I have to him. I crave to unravel him, even when his rejections are constant, and his words bite harsher than necessary. After today, I was sure I was ready to give up and move on with my life, but I think all I wanted was a bit of revenge. Rouse him up like a petulant child just to get a reaction.

Well... technically *I* didn't get a reaction. Madds did. But I'll take it, nonetheless.

"Let's get Lulu then," Morri speaks and my attention goes to her.

A rumbling growl mixes with the base of the music, and I narrow my eyes at the sound. *What a strange song.* But then my eyes fall on Madds, and his gaze fixed on the stunning, blonde woman. He watches her with a mix of exasperation, anger, and something that looks a lot like yearning.

Yup, alcohol has certainly affected my perception of reality.

A few minutes later and lots of protest from Lulu, mainly aimed at Madds, and we're out at the front of the bar. He's on the phone telling someone, probably Finnigan, that we're heading home now. I have a gnawing suspicion that he's the reason why Madds came to find us. *No.* Find me. Otherwise, how come Finnigan is at my apartment?

We're in the small parking lot next to the bar, less than twenty feet away from Maddox's SUV, and it takes me too many seconds to realize what an idiot I am.

Once again, I ignore the ominous prickles marring the back of my neck, I don't pay attention to my surroundings, to the faint screech of tires as they stop not far behind me, to the car doors opening, or to the steps nearing us.

I don't pay attention until...

"I've been looking everywhere for you."

That voice seeps out of my nightmares, shattering the silence along with my soul, and I don't know if I'll be able to pick up the pieces this time around.

"Frankie..."

CHAPTER 20
Evelyn

AGAINST MY BETTER judgment, I freeze in place, his voice snaking around my body and holding me pinned. I should run. I have to run. But my mind and body are not in sync, and no matter my internal screams, my legs can't move. My lungs are blocked with ice and no breath seems to penetrate.

"Evelyn!" Someone's bellow pushes through the terror and yanks at me. My instincts kick in and I start fighting against the hold, blinded by the memories.

"It's me, it's Morri! Run, Evelyn, run!"

I faintly register the words and my vision clears enough to see her flaming locks, and air starts to fill my lungs again, pushing through the frost that stalled it. My feet feel like my own again and I push against the asphalt, letting Morri pull me away. The sound of the world explodes around me, and I hear Maddox's rage, the violent commotion, grunts of pain and cracking bones.

Maddox!

I falter for a split moment, turning to see if he's safe, and my nightmares come to life all at once.

"Hello, gorgeous. I like your new hair." Frankie's sleazy face is too close to mine, and his bruising grip circles around my middle.

"Nooo!" The scream rips from the bottom of my lungs as I thrash against him.

"That's it. You know I like it when you fight me."

His lisp makes the memories too real, and thorned vines wrap around my spine, spreading around every bone of my body on a violent tremble, until they reach my fingertips.

But somewhere through the bone-choking panic, Maddox's training comes back to me.

"Get the fuck away from me!" I can hardly believe those words left my mouth, but I'm proud of the confidence in them.

Grabbing one of his fingers splayed over my belly, I twist back until the crunch tears a scream out of the man who raped me. I don't let him dwell on it, whipping my head back until it makes contact. I have no idea what I hit, but the pain in my skull and his curses are enough to tell me my aim was good. His grip falters enough for me to pull out of it, and I swing my elbow back, slamming into his middle, before I whirl and swing my foot at his dick.

I smirk when he doubles over in pain, proud that my actions took him by surprise. I take advantage of the distraction, and uppercut him under his chin while he's bent over his precious balls, then sidekick him to the chest. He lands against one of his men who staggers on his feet, a limp look in his bloody eye, and they both fall to the ground.

My training is still fresh, my body only starting to become stronger, and without the element of surprise, I don't think my moves would have worked this well. Though, a kick in the balls will always work.

I don't dwell. Madds screams at me to get in the car, and I run before he finishes the sentence. Morri shoves me in the back, and we watch as he fights six, crap, no—eight guys. Including Frankie now, who got his bearings and rose. Only, he turns his attention to our car, distracting Madds from the men he's fighting off. Some go down, but—

"Behind you!" I yell, but he can't hear me from the car, and I bang my fists against the window, hoping it will work.

Madds catches Frankie in a headlock, and I take momentary pleasure from his bulging eyes, the pressure in his head likely growing. But in this moment of distraction, another guy punches Madds on the side of his head and Lulu's fear-stricken wail makes me flinch as I suck in a breath.

"I have to help him!" I shout and grab the door handle.

"Evelyn, they could take you again!" Morri holds me in place as we watch Madds grab Frankie and throw him ten feet away like he's nothing but a sack of potatoes, taking two other guys down.

Maddox has blood coming from the back of his head, but ignores it, the look in his eyes feral. In the next moment one of the guys who jumps him is nothing but a crumpled mess on the ground, his head facing the wrong direction, his eyes empty of life.

He expertly beats the shit out of the rest of the men, moving swifter than a man his size should, and just when I think it's all under control, one of the men who was unconscious gets his bearings and rises a few feet behind Madds. He doesn't see him, though, too focused on fighting two of the, surprisingly well trained, men who still stand.

Lulu gasps at the same time I notice the man behind Madds pulling something from his hip as he staggers toward my friend. The scene runs in slow-motion and my stomach drops.

Oh, God, it's a gun!

"Fuck this! Go, go, go!" Morri yells, and I rip open the car door, jumping out as the adrenaline surges through my nerves.

I run as fast as I can toward the man who's about to shoot Madds, my throat aching from a scream I didn't realize is ripping through my throat. He turns to me, an annoyed and confused look in his eyes, but before he can act, I tackle him to the ground.

One single gunshot is fired into the air as his back slams against the concrete on a pain-filled grunt. He grabs me to push me away, but I smash my fist into his face, and he falters.

Then I punch him again. Harder, faster, the crunch of bones cracking the armor I so carefully constructed around myself, holding at bay the person I pretend not to be.

Over and over, I slam my fists in his face.

There is no skill in my hits, only volatile frenzy. My knuckles ache, but adrenaline surges with each strike, urging me on.

Tires screech in the distance, someone curses, but I don't turn. I certainly don't stop. On the contrary, I try to hit harder, wrapping my fist in my other palm and smashing the sides in his face until he goes limp beneath me.

Something grips my shoulders attempting to tug me away, but I resist. I don't stop. I can't. I won't. The grip lowers, sliding under my armpits to lift me off the limp man, but I fight back.

"Evelyn!"

My fists pause midair when the warmth and urgency in that sweet, sweet voice penetrate the frenzy. It's not his touch around my middle though, I would recognize it.

I turn just as Finnigan slams the car door behind him. Strong hands lift me and settle me back on my feet, but I don't move as I watch his curly hair, as wild as the look in his eyes, bounce as he rushes to me.

"Evelyn." He says my name again, but this time there is longing in his voice too, and I want to sink in the warmth of it.

He reaches me with panic in his wide eyes, breaking through my frenzied state completely, his breathing quick and shallow as he pats all over my body.

"Are you hurt?" he asks in a desperate tone as he continues the rapid inspection.

I shake my head, because I don't think I can open my mouth without sobs breaking out.

"Evie, does anything hurt? There's too much blood, I can't tell." The desperation grows in his tone, meeting my eyes, and I realize he didn't see my previous, silent response.

There's blood?

Of course... the man on the ground.

I shake my head again, but my lips quiver.

Something breaks in him then and there, clutching the sides of my head in his warm hands, as he steps even closer, his body lining up with mine. I seize his forearms, holding onto him, this intensity, his fierce gaze with its longing and pain, to his hidden need and demand, like he might run away from me once he realizes what he's doing. What he's revealing.

"Never again." He growls.

I don't know what he means by that, but I feed on each syllable like it gives me life.

"I'm not letting you out of my sight, Evelyn. Ever."

I don't get a chance to agree or protest, because he crushes me against his warm, hard chest, his arms circling my body and wrapping himself around me. The weight I was holding onto, the panic and fear, leave my body in this tight, comforting hold.

"Madds, is Madds okay?"

He doesn't answer, but he tenses against me.

"That guy was about to shoot me from behind. She..." Madds trails off as he explains to Finnigan, and his hold relaxes once more. "I'm okay, Evie."

The safety of him draws my shock to the surface and every bit of my body shakes all at once. I don't realize my fingers are digging into his skin until I feel his touch on my back, rubbing soothingly.

"It's okay, Evie darling, you're safe."

Then the tears come, the damn just at the edge of breaking, but only a few slip through the cracks. I can't allow myself to break, not this hard. I can't be this weak.

"You're safe. I'm here."

He holds me to him, ignoring the pain I'm probably causing with my sharp nails as I force myself to unload the adrenaline without bursting completely.

I'm okay. I'm okay.

It registers in my subconscious that the man I was hitting stopped moving at one point. Yet, I can't bring myself to care that I might have killed him. I should. Right? There's a strong chance I took a life, and it should feel a certain way.

It doesn't.

It never has before.

Not the first time, only months after I became homeless, when a seedy guy accosted me on the street after my dinner shift was over. I lived and worked in the wrong side of town, I knew it was going to happen eventually. He wanted what I was not offering or willing to give. I was easy prey. But he didn't expect the random slat of wood I found on the ground to be smashed in his guts. And I didn't expect the smile that creeped on my lips at the satisfaction I got when he cursed in pain. I hit him until he gave up on me and ran away.

If only I could have done that when Frankie B took my sister.

Wait.

I pull my face away from the comfort of Finnigan's chest and look around. "Where is he?! Where's Frankie?"

"He's gone," Maddox grunts somewhere behind me. "He slid in his car and drove away when the last of his men was going down. I couldn't stop him. I'm sorry."

He's still out there, and he wants me. The thought brings a shudder back into my bones and Finnigan tightens his hold around me once again.

"We're going home. Now." His tone is sharp and low, pulling back to look at me, one hand possessive on the small of my back.

Then he confuses the pants out of me when he pulls his shirt out of his trousers, and brings the bottom of it to my face, wiping it.

"What the... what are you doing?!" If that doesn't wake me out of my stupor, I don't know what would do the job.

"Maya is in the car. I don't want her to see you like this."

"She's here?" I try to break away, but his hold on my back keeps me grounded as he keeps swiping at my face.

"You don't think I would have left her alone with June, do you? She needs to be kept safe, with us."

Delicious warmth spills through my soul at his words, and I feel it deep in my belly. I can't believe he would think of her, of us, like that. When he stops rubbing at my face, his action finally registers as I see his now dirty shirt—blood. A lot of it. Then I dare look down at the man I pummeled as I straddled him, and I fail to recognize any features on his face under all the blood.

Christ, what have I done?

"We'll wash the rest of it at home. You're sure you're not hurt?" he asks, and I give him a quick nod.

Once again, he tugs me against his chest, pressing me against him, like he wants me embedded in his soul. But that warmth leaves me too soon as he steps away and takes my hand instead.

Morri, Lulu, and Madds stand close by, curious looks on all their faces. Maddox raises an eyebrow, but Finnigan warns him off with a growl as he pulls me toward his car.

"Not a fucking word."

His friend doesn't respond, but Morri's features look lighter, amused in a knowing kind of way, and a flush heats my cheeks. How inappropriate of me, considering I just punched a guy to death.

"Call the cleaning crew," Finnigan tells his friend.

"Done. I'll take Morri and Mamaw to Vin."

Just on cue Mamaw June climbs out of the car we're heading to, giving me a kind, worried smile. I mirror that smile in hopes of providing her with a bit of comfort and confirmation that I'm okay. "Thank you for looking after Maya."

"Anytime, sweetheart. Call me later, okay?" God this woman is an angel.

"Keep Lulu with you!" Finnigan turns to Madds as he puts me in the car and straps me in, refusing to let me do it myself.

"The fuck he will!" I hear Lulu's protests.

"Shush, woman. We're not risking any of you," Madds says, and I would laugh if small hands weren't wrapping around my neck from behind, and the car door shuts.

"Evie!" there's such an innocent enthusiasm in Maya's voice.

"Hi honey! Are you okay?"

I avoid turning to her in case there's still blood on my face. She's not going to see the splatters on my blouse, since it's luckily a dark burgundy.

"Yes! I spent the evening with Finnigan. He read to me!" She sounds calm, unaffected. Mamaw June must have shielded her.

"He did?" My gaze wanders to the man in question, who climbed into the driver's seat and slams the door.

He nods as he turns his attention to the road and drives off.

"Yes. He's so good at reading with... what do you call it? Intonation? Can he read me to sleep tonight? Will you let him, Evie? Pleaaase?"

"Oh, honey, I don't think Finnigan—"

"Of course I will." He cuts me off and answers my demanding sister.

"Thank you!" she squeals, excited.

So, I guess he intends to stay over at my apartment until Maya falls asleep. Right, well, that's going to be interesting. Though, the idea makes me feel a lot safer, especially as Frankie B might know where I live, now that he's made his intentions pretty damn clear. We knew he was pissed about his *shipments* being screwed with, but we didn't know I was even on his radar. There's security in Lulu's building, but I'll stay up tonight just in case. There's no way I can sleep, anyway.

I had hopes that I could fake my way through the system and enroll Maya in school, but that is fully squashed now. Not until Frankie is out of the picture and into a grave.

"So, what happened out there? Mamaw June was hugging me, and I couldn't see a thing," my sister asks.

Oh, thank God. Okay, I need to bake Mamaw June the biggest cake ever. The woman is a saint.

"We just needed a little help to go home. Car trouble," I lie to her as I gaze out the window at the pretty streets of Queenscove.

Only, the bar we went to was quite close to our apartment building, and we just drove past it.

"Wait. Finnigan that was—we just passed my street."

He doesn't look at me, his gaze running over all the mirrors, on high alert. It makes me look too, but I don't notice anything out of place. He's probably just checking to make sure we're not being followed.

"We're going to my apartment." He grunts.

"What?" I exclaim but lower my voice so my sister doesn't catch onto my surprise. "Why? We'll be perfectly fine at mine."

"You will be alone," he says with another grunt. "I told you, Evelyn. Never. Again." He punctuates each word with such finality, I'm left with parted lips, unspoken words hanging between them, and a new, burning ache between my legs.

Not again.

Why does this always happen in the most inappropriate moments?

If he notices how I clench my thighs together, or my quickening breaths, he doesn't say a thing. I shut my mouth and settle back in the soft suede seat of his SUV, silently thankful that it's not the normal leather that sticks uncomfortably to my bare skin and wait for this annoying and disturbingly attractive man to take me to his home.

Should I protest more? Probably.

My hands, achy and marked with too much drying blood, tremble, and my legs do the same, for an entirely different reason.

I'm startled when his hand moves from the center console and hovers so close to my thigh. I watch it, silently urging it to drop over my flesh, to clutch it, hold it, anything. Instead, he moves to press a button on the dashboard and warm air blows into the car. I look at him and he steals one short glance at me before occupying himself with the road ahead.

"You looked cold," he explains himself. When I don't answer, he continues, "You're shivering. You should have not worn such a short skirt."

I'm about to say I'm not cold, but I stop myself.

"It's not that short."

Way to make it awkward Evelyn. You could have just said thanks. It's not like you're not silently imagining your sister not being in the car, his hand on your thigh, rubbing down until he finds the seam of your skirt, then runs upward until another seam touches his fingers, and then, without no notice at all, he—

"Are we there yet?"

My sister's excited, high-pitched tone makes me straighten in the seat. This time it doesn't escape Finnigan's notice how I squeeze my thighs together, biting my bottom lip to suppress the need from spilling from my mouth.

Christ, we better be there soon, because this car is starting to feel too small, the air too hot, his proximity too much.

"In a minute."

He takes a familiar turn and there we are, in front of the apartment building where I used to live with Katya. Considering that I was face to face with Frankie B not even an hour ago, it feels like no time has passed at all since I first lived here.

But it has. I'm not the same weak person I was then, and if Frankie B dares to come after me or my sister again, I will be ready.

He will pay.

CHAPTER 21
Evelyn

I WAKE UP with a start, drenched in sweat from the grueling dream I just had. There was nothing violent about it. The nightmare part is waking up from it, unable to feel it any longer, because *he* was in it.

I blink several times, acknowledging my surroundings through the darkness—I'm in Finnigan's spare bedroom and it's still the middle of the night. It doesn't smell like him though, and I feel a touch of sadness at that. The moment I got out of the car my adrenaline crash was so bad, I could barely stand. If I was in my apartment, I would have stayed up, alert, but here... with him... I crashed in his safety. He showed me the bathroom so I could clean up while he looked after my sister, then took me straight to bed, promising to read Maya to sleep in the bedroom next to mine.

The tiredness struck me to the bones, and I went with everything he told me to do. He gave me a small bag Mamaw June apparently packed for me in the few seconds she had before leaving our apartment, and I crawled in bed after changing into a comfy, oversized T-shirt I found in a thrift store. Sleep took me fast.

I turn to my side, shoving my hand under the pillow, and force my eyes closed, urging myself back to sleep. But in this position my thighs press together and the ache that follows between them pulls a dirty gasp out of my mouth. They're so slippery, so hot, so unbearable.

Flipping on my belly, I bury my face in the pillow, and close my eyes. I'm back in that dream, filled with ecstasy and decadence, where Finnigan's hand was clutching my breast, his mouth smothering mine, kissing me deeply, and his cock was sheathed so deep inside me, it ached so good.

I can't bear it anymore!

I turn once again on my back, cursing myself for taking this man's word as law. He told me we can't cross that wretched line of his, he warned me not to try, not to even think about him in *that* way, even when I touched myself. I didn't agree with the man, but for some odd reason, I complied with the order.

Christ, I'm an idiot. He would never know if I did it, if I crossed his damn imaginary line, and he has no control over me. It's not his business what I do between my own sheets.

Only, these are his sheets, not mine. Defying his orders here feels perfect, so much dirtier. My skin turns hotter, the T-shirt too constricting, my drenched cotton panties too tight, and I rip them off and throw them across the room, into the darkness. Now the sheets feel slightly cool against my nakedness, and I sigh at the feel of them.

It feels better. But only for a moment, until I close my eyes and that wretched dream is back, his body over mine, his hands touching me, and I swallow back a moan because now, I'm annoyed. He's so cruel and smug, forbidding me to think of him when I touch myself. He thinks he's doing me a favor, forcing me to distance myself from him and his *line*.

Screw him. There are others out there I can fantasize about as I touch myself, and even if I do choose him, just because he wants to torture himself due to some moral rule he self-imposed, it doesn't mean I have to follow suit.

The fire hums low in my belly, and I press my thighs together once more, hoping to relieve some of that heat. Of course, it burns brighter, my taught nipples grazing against the sheet enhancing the feel of it further.

"Screw this!" I throw the sheet off of me, reveling in the brush of air over my sensitive skin.

I couldn't deny my body any longer even if I tried.

The moment I press my hand over my bare breast, the softest of moans fills the dark bedroom. I splay the other palm on my belly, slowly sliding down, teasing myself with the anticipation that tortures me further. The moment the tips of my fingers reach the hood of my clit, my back arches off the bed and there's nothing soft about the sound escaping from my mouth next.

I rub the bundle of nerves in slow, demanding circles, images of Finnigan flashing through my mind, some out of spite, some because there's no one else I could possibly think of, and the fire begins to rage in my belly.

"Oh... Finnigan," I whisper on a breathless moan as I slide my fingers down, parting myself until I reach that tight opening.

My lips part in a gasp at the flurry of sensations, the ache and emptiness of them all, and I cry out into the darkness.

Then the darkness moves.

I tense, no time to scream or react before it rushes over me and covers my mouth. No time to fight as it rips my hand away from my sleek center, replacing it with his own. I gasp against his hand and the scent of sea salt and dark chocolate melt their way through me. Recognition hits, the scent flowing right out of my dream.

He squeezes my pussy and shame fills me when my back arches involuntarily at the attack. But I still try to fight beneath him, attempting to escape in case my nose betrays me. I try to kick, but he presses harder against me, and I let out a dirty, wanton cry against his palm. Gripping his wrist, I push it away, but it doesn't budge. But I'm not actually that sure if I'm not so much pushing, as I am holding onto him.

I freeze in place as he slides his fingers down the sleek seam of me. It's not panic screaming at me now, it's how wrong I am for getting even wetter.

"I told you..."

All rational thought burns out of my mind when the darkness speaks with the voice from my dream.

"I told you how dangerous it is to cross this line." Finnigan's whisper is heavy, creeping with a decadent darkness.

I can't believe he was in the bedroom. Watching me sleep. Watching me get naked.

"Is this what you were about to do, even when I forbade you to touch yourself with my name on your lips?" One finger pushes inside of me, stretching me too fast. It may actually be more than one.

"So fucking tight." He groans more to himself than me.

But as he pulls out and dives in again even deeper, I release his forearm and grab onto whatever covers his chest, holding on for dear life because I think I'm falling. Falling in this pit of aching need and burning pleasure.

"Is this what you so desperately want, that you can't follow... one. Simple. Order?" He punctuates each word with a hard stroke of his fingers, pulling muffled cries out of me.

"You drive me fucking crazy!"

Thrust.

"So mad that I move through the shadows when I hear your feverish dreams."

Thrust.

"Watching you only to find you moaning my name, not screaming in fear of your nightmares."

Thrust.

He's punishing me with pleasure for his own desires.

"I haven't been able to sleep without knowing you're okay."

Thrust.

"Without knowing you're a good..." *Thrust.* "Fucking..." *Thrust.* "Girl."

I'm losing my mind. Pushed closer to the flaming pit that will change my whole damn life, but not close enough that I feel it's whole destruction.

"Is this why you want to cross the motherfucking line?!"

He curls those digits, touching a part of me I've never been able to find, and my moans turn wild.

"God damn it, Evelyn! How am I ever going to keep my hands away from you now? After feeling how tight, how warm your cunt is? How it responds to me? How fucking ravenous its scent makes me?"

He assaults that spot inside of me with no regard to my cries, my pleas muffled by his palm. He's lost somewhere between my legs like this is his pleasure, not mine.

"What have you done, Evelyn?"

At that same moment he bears down on my clit and pushes me into that flaming pit, burning the world around me. Pleasure sears me from the inside out and I'm sure I would be flying if he didn't hold me down.

What *have I* done?

He releases my mouth and I take shallow, staggered breaths.

How will I go back to how things were? Back to not knowing how his hands truly feel on me?

Was he right all along?

I'm too lost in the aftershock of sensations and burning questions when I realize that he's no longer touching me, because a deep sigh sounds from the shadows, before steps follow, and the door opens. He's in the doorway facing away from me, shoulders dropping as he pulls the door behind himself, uttering the same word I whisper to myself.

"Fuck."

Yes, he was right all along. I can feel it in my gut—there's no going back after crossing this line. I can't help but wonder if he'll try though.

Will he be more successful than I was? I tried to steer myself away from him, my reason not as foolish as his. I don't care that he's eleven or whatever years older than me, though he seems so bothered by it. I thought I needed to get over his promise to me.

We'll get you before anything happens...

He said that before I was returned to that wretched container with the tracker in my mouth. Something did happen, and failing to keep his promise brought so much resentment toward him.

I was blinded. He didn't fail me at all, I simply chose to ignore what I myself asked of him then. The context. I ignored it because it didn't fit my vendetta. The need for a vessel to hone my hate was stronger than the actual truth.

Because the truth is that his promise was a response to my plea. And that plea had nothing to do with me or my safety. I told him I can't fail *her*—my sister—and he answered by telling me that I won't, promising he'll get us out before anything happens. To her. Not to me.

Even now I remember the sorrow in his beautiful azure eyes. He wanted to extend the promise to me too, and the choice of his words told me how much he wished, but he was already unsure if he could even keep the one he made for my sister. It was all out of his control. A sacrifice that was not his to make, but he had to so he could save many. I volunteered for it, knowing the risks.

He gave me exactly what I wanted, what I pleaded for. Madds later told me that it was Finnigan who searched for and carried my sister out. I didn't ask him to save her, I just told him I couldn't bear failing her again. So, he made sure I didn't.

He made sure I kept my own promise to my sister. He made sure I wasn't a liar. That my soul remained intact. Even if my body didn't.

And I responded with disdain and blamed him for the situation I threw myself in. I was a fool.

It kept me away from seeing him for who he is, from my craving for him. And if Finnigan pushes me away because he thinks our age difference wrong, if he villainizes himself for it, then he is a fool too.

There are other differences between us that worry me, that make me feel so inadequate next to him. And sometimes I do wonder if they are the real reason why he pulls away from me so fiercely.

If he has an issue with the fact that I haven't finished my education because I had to take care of my sister, or that I don't come from the same social standing as him, or have money... or a home, then he should say that. Because I can move on from shallowness easily, but not from the ridiculous notion of age.

He will need a better reason than that.

Though, I can't help but ask myself... am I a fool for pursuing this man?

Especially since I have made no final decision about staying in Queenscove?

* * *

I wake up in the morning with surprising ease. My phone says it's seven o'clock, and my limbs are itching to get out of this bed. Though, my thighs say I need to head into a shower, because I swear I can still feel the dampness he left me with last night.

I dreamed of it, of his hand silencing me, the other between my legs, it was more erotic than I expected. I have similar fantasies, but this... it's surpassed them all.

Before I can get myself wet all over again, I jump out of bed and pull my T-shirt on. This room doesn't have an en-suite bathroom, so I open the door peeking out. Okay, I'm on a small corridor, there's bright light at the end of it, and a few more doors here, but all is quiet. There's bound to be a bathroom here. I try the door across from me, pressing the handle slowly.

Warm sea salt and dark chocolate hits me with such ferociousness my mouth is parched in an instant. Though there's nothing but darkness in here, the blinds closed and curtains drawn, I know I'll find no bathroom if I turn the lights on. And yet, my feet seem to have a mind of their own, because they advance in the dark room, leaving the door ajar. A faint trail of light trickles in, right on the strong form sleeping under a thin sheet. The blonde curly strands of his hair brush against his neck, his strong bare back facing me, and I itch to run my hand through those locks and trace his muscles with the tips of my fingers. As I near him, I see a few faint scars on his skin, and I can't help but wonder what dared mark him. My gaze draws down his muscled back, lean and strong, all the way to where the thin sheet barely covers the curve of his ass. And god dammit, what an ass. If only that sheet would magically slide lower.

I have no idea what I'm thinking, if I'm sane at all, because my fingers are now ghosting against his spine. I can't control the need to find out what he feels like. If he's as warm and soft as I imagine him to be. If his muscles feel as magnificent as I think when they flex beneath my palm.

Then his softness tickles my fingertips, and I could groan if I didn't need to hold in my breath. I slowly run them down his spine, and when I reach the middle he flinches, but not startled, more like his spine rolls into my touch. He doesn't stir though, doesn't wake up, his breathing slightly quicker, but I think he's still sleeping. So, I continue my exploration, sliding down his spine until my prize is just about in sight and I can reveal at least a bit of that stunning ass. He feels so good under my touch, I itch to risk it and splay my palm over him, but that would truly be foolish.

Maybe he's a heavy sleeper, and I can get away with it.

Or maybe I should count my blessings and get the heck out of here before the man wakes up and finds me groping him.

I don't get to make my decision.

Like lightning he moves, grabbing my wrist and hauling me up until he can reach my waist, using it to flip me over and slam my back against his soft bed. I only manage a gasp, too stunned to even register my wrists being trapped above my head, held in one of his hands. Or his thigh pinning my legs to the comfortable mattress. Only when his heaving, strong breaths touch my bare skin do I notice my T-shirt is bunched up above my waist, and I'm bared to him. Since I was *technically* going to the bathroom, that's the only thing I pulled on, thinking it's long enough to cover me.

I tug at his hold, urging him to let me go before he notices my exposed core, though only the short curls I refuse to shave are on display, as the hidden part of me is getting increasingly damp at this proximity. At the constraints.

"What do you think you're doing, Evie darling?"

I melt into the bed at his rough, morning voice, tainted with sleep and needy dreams. It takes me a few moments to remember I was supposed to struggle to break free. And yet, I allow a few more moments because his hot breath against my skin feels like summer sun and beautiful beach days.

"Let me go." I tug at his hand, trying to free my own.

I do the same with my legs, but the moment my thighs tighten, I decide against it, only, now I'm all too conscious of the damp patch I might be leaving on his expensive sheets.

"Answer me." He leans in, his nose dangerously close to my cheek.

When I turn my head in the opposite direction, I realize what a huge mistake it was. His hot breath snakes down my throat, settling in the crook of my neck, and nothing can stop the shudder that rattles my skin and spreads goosebumps on every inch of my body.

"I—I was"—*deep inhale*—"looking for the bathroom."

"And you thought that touching me while I slept was going to lead you there?" His breathy voice is even closer, the heat of him brushing over my skin. I'm squirming, but I tell myself it's because I'm trying to break loose.

"It was leading to something," I mutter sarcastically under my breath, and I genuinely want to slap myself for still thinking of his ass.

Such a good ass, though.

"What was that?"

"Nothing," I quip.

"You're playing with fire, Evie darling."

I turn my attention back to him, and even in this darkness, the blue of his eyes shines and I hold onto every speckle. "Let it burn me then, because I'm sick of this aching cold."

He's on me before the next breath reaches my lungs, bracing himself on the arm that holds my wrists trapped. His weight presses me into the mattress, and the thigh that pinned me is now slid under one of my legs, spreading me open.

"Finnigan..." I all but moan.

"Don't, Evelyn. Don't say my name like it's the air that breathes life into you because I'm tainted down to the bone, and my soul will only scorch yours."

"There is nothing left to scorch, Finnigan. I was corrupted long before your soul touched mine. All I can do is burn. Please Finnigan... please—"

He swallows my next words, crushing his lips to mine in the most brutal, shattering kiss. He breathes me in like my life-force is the only thing that can keep his soul alive, and when he pushes his tongue between my lips, nothing can stop the moan that vibrates through my whole flesh.

With a faint growl rumbling in his chest, he deepens the kiss, pressing me harder in the mattress. Our tongues move against each other, chasing the pleasure only the other can give, our lips molding together like two pieces that were once whole and now found their mate again. The only break he takes is to nip at my tongue, or my lips, plunging back in and stealing every single one of my breaths before he feeds them back to me, enriched with all that is him.

I'm lost in the myriad of sensations until a shock of pure pleasure rips through my core. I gasp into his mouth and my hips roll on instinct, to find the source of that rippling pleasure. A satiny, hard length strokes against me, rubbing that charged bundle of nerves, as it grinds up and down. The insight that he sleeps naked brings a hot flush to my cheeks.

A needy mewl rips out of me, but he swallows that too, feeding on my pleasure and pressing harder into me. God, he's so close to where I really need him. All it would take is for him to grind even lower, so the tip of his cock falls between my legs, and then... one *hard* push.

Would it hurt? Considering what happened that wretched night when we first met, it's pretty clear I'm no longer a virgin. Though, I'm thankful my memories are vague. So, all Finnigan would give me now is nothing but pleasure.

I roll my hips harder, urging his cock to find home, but it keeps slipping away from me. Over me. Stroking my clit into an ecstasy filled oblivion distracting me from the task at hand.

"Stop making me fuck you." He grunts against my mouth, still kissing me.

"Never." I moan back at him.

Then his lips leave mine and we're both breathless as we look into each other's eyes.

"I can't be what you need."

This again? Fine.

"Then let me go and leave me the hell alone, Finnigan"—for a moment his grip on me loosens—"and I'll go back to the bar from where you demanded I be retrieved last night, and I'll find someone who will give me *exactly* what I need."

The rumble deep in his chest is what I hoped for as his hold on me tightens once again.

"You think you can go out dressed in your sinful leather outfits or short skirts, driving everyone mad with lust in those filthy bars, and make them think they can wet their dick inside what is..." he trails off.

"What is yours?" I continue for him.

"You can't be mine, damn it!"

"I already am."

That settles it, because in the next breath his mouth is on my throat, biting like he hates every inch of my skin before he licks the slight pain away and brings a different ache to my flesh. It settles deep in my belly and between my legs, and he grounds against me harder. I roll my hips seeking his cock like it can give me life, and he shushes me when I moan too loud, reminding me that we are not alone in this apartment.

Ignoring my silent pleas for his cock, he releases my wrists, pushing my T-shirt all the way up, exposing my breasts to his greedy gaze. His nips and licks follow a trail over each one of them, sucking my nipples into his mouth like his new mission is to dare me to make a sound. But he does it oh so well, licking gently before he scrapes his teeth over the sensitive bud, and I could come right here just from that delicious assault.

He moves in the valley between them before my core can find out if it can find release just from that, following a trail down my body until his chin brushes against my trimmed curls. I'm embarrassed. I imagine the army of women he usually has sex with are waxed from head to toe, sleek and soft.

"I'm sorry, I'm not—"

"You are goddamn perfect." His fingers rake through those curls, as the pad of his palm grounds down against the bundle of nerves, and the shiver breaking through me feels more like a violent tremble.

Then his mouth is on me, and that insecurity disappears with my loud gasp. Finnigan's tongue parts my lips from the bottom to the very top, groaning so low in his chest, I could cry at the sensation. The second time he does it I whimper as he flattens his tongue like he can't bear not having all his taste buds experiencing me. He presses his hands against my thighs and pushes them apart, his tongue delving deeper, circling my entrance and disappointingly moving away from it. The moment it slides over my clit and laps at it like it could give me life, I realize it really could. Because like this, drunk on pleasure in Finnigan's bed, I feel more alive than I ever have. Biting my forearm to muffle a moan, I roll my back as I grind onto his face, seeking my release, and when he sucks that bundle of nerves between his lush lips, I realize the edge is so much closer than I thought it was.

He grunts harsher, displeased, and I feel a tinge of guilt, wondering if he feels ignored. I brace my elbows on the bed and slowly rise, struggling through the onslaught of sensations.

"Did I say I'm done with you?" he hisses.

I yelp as he sits back on his haunches, grabs my ass, and lifts me up to him, circling my belly with one strong, lean arm. I would be upside down if my head and shoulders weren't still on the bed, and when he buries his face between my legs again, I grab onto his thighs and let him drive me off this magnificent cliff.

He gives special attention to my clit, rolling it between his tongue and lips, nipping at it when my pleasure brings me too close to the roaring flames I'm craving. My sexual experience is mostly fictional, or from random conversations with classmates or co-workers, but I was under the impression that men don't have much patience when it comes to giving head, and want to make it quick. But Finnigan, oh my, Finnigan is dragging it out like he finds more pleasure in this than I do.

That would be impossible though, because every time he sucks at me, every time his tongue drags between my folds, every time he teases the entrance, the pleasure grows more than I thought it could be possible.

"Evie?"

We both freeze on the bed, his mouth still on me, my nails digging in his strong thighs. Maya's voice sounded distant beyond Finnigan's door. I start moving my legs and scooting back to get off the bed, but Finnigan tightens his hold.

"Finnigan, Maya's coming," I whisper.

"Then you better hurry, darling."

The grin he gives me before his mouth is on my clit again, melts me back into the soft mattress. I'm about to protest, but his eyes gleam with mischief. His hand joins the feverish assault, and two fingers sink deep into me. My ass buckles and ankles cross as my legs tighten around his neck, pushing him deeper into me. Scorching heat burns inside my core, spreading through my belly, then explodes through every single nerve of my body until the loud cry I'm forcing back has no choice but to come out.

The moment it spills from my lips, Finnigan's large hand covers my mouth and nose and I cry out into his palm, riding this blazing pleasure until my legs go limp around his body.

"Evie?" Maya's voice is closer now and I almost jump out of my skin when Finnigan gives my ass a playful slap to urge me to get off the bed.

Now, that was... strangely intimate. Pair that with his panty-melting grin he's giving me, and I might as well hand him my heart on a platter, because this man is going to take it from me whether I want to or not. Regardless of if he wants it.

And isn't that just terrifying?

I push back the harsh thoughts reminding me that this is not my home, not where my father lives, or that all of this is temporary. I'm going to allow myself to bask in this bubble of pleasure and acceptance for a while longer.

Just a little while longer.

CHAPTER 22
Finnigan

IT TOOK ME much longer to pry myself out of bed than it usually does. Took me even longer to shower, and especially brush my teeth because I couldn't bear washing away Evelyn's taste from my lips. Jesus Christ, that woman tastes like goddamn rainbows. Does that make any logical sense? No, it most definitely does not, but she has a maddening sweet and musty flavor that threatens to drive me mad.

Addicting. So utterly addicting.

The line is well and truly crossed. Seeing her touching herself with my name on her lips threw me straight over it. But having her tight, little cunt around my fingers, breaking apart for me as I was feeding fantasies she doesn't know I'm aware of, pushed me so far away from that line, I'm not even sure anymore if it ever existed. But then I had to taste her pretty pussy too, see her naked beneath me, and that ensured there is no going back.

Question is, how far am I willing to go?

What would happen if I would get to sink my cock in her sweet pussy? Will I ever want to leave? Will I be the same man after?

Already, her strength, her determination, everything she is as a person has been picking away at my constraints. But watching her slip out of my bed, spent and disheveled from pleasure I gave her, cracked something inside me, shackles holding me back. I'm aware of them, but the crack let out shunned feelings. Pain, fear, I was expecting, but the loneliness tasted bitter. Evelyn changes everything, soothes and turns it all to rich sweetness without even knowing.

Twice, I stroked myself in the shower to settle this growing need for her. I came on the wall of it like a fucking teenager.

Finally, I emerge out of my bedroom and the smell hits me straight in the taste buds, making my mouth water. Blueberry and sweetness, warmth and... home. I inhale deep one more time to make sure I'm not making this shit up.

I know Nora didn't cook, because I told both her and George, my permanent house staff, to take paid time off for the foreseeable future. So, Evelyn must be cooking.

Before I even step into the kitchen, a cheerful mini human slams straight into me, oblivious to the fact that her shoulder connected a bit too violently with my balls. I suck in a grunt and power through, because when I look down, Maya's sweet little face is all sunshine and butterflies, her innocence vividly painted in her green eyes.

"Good morning, Finn!" she says with a wide, toothy smile.

"Morning, sweetheart." I bend over and give her a kiss on the top of the head, my voice strained from the ache in my balls.

I rise and catch Evelyn's gaze, brightened with amusement, her lips curled between her teeth as she bites down her laughter. Okay, so she noticed my pain, and this is her response.

Noted.

But noting this is bad, because my retaliation plan involves my tongue, fingers, and her begging me for release for hours.

I'm a doomed man.

She turns to open the oven door, and the delicious scent that fills the penthouse distracts me, so much stronger than before, drawing me in like a moth to a flame.

"I hope this is alright. I was... umm... nervous." she says shyly, wiping her hands on the sides of her black jeans. *She changed.*

"Nervous?" I narrow my eyes and take a seat on the other side of the island from her, at the breakfast bar.

"Yes, sorry. I just like to bake when I'm..."

"Nervous," I finish for her.

She avoids my eyes like this is all so wrong and she regrets saying anything.

"I swim or train with Madds." I throw her a bone, because for some reason I hate seeing her so uncomfortable.

It's also peculiar witnessing this side of her. I've seen her nervous and shy before, but this is coming from a totally different place. I fucked her sweet cunt with my mouth and fingers, and I bet she's picturing it even now as she busies herself with the freshly baked muffins, burning her fingers as she tries to pull them out of the muffin tray I had no idea I own.

"Oh, I like training with Madds." She brightens all over, and a pang of jealousy hits me. "He's really helped me. I'm not sure what I would have done without him. Especially last night..." She trails off and even though that jealousy burns harsher, I'm going to talk to Severin and ask him to train her even harder. Might even give her a gun.

Because she's right—if it wasn't for their training, I wouldn't be staring at her right now. I wouldn't have her taste imprinted in my memory. I wouldn't be smelling these delicious muffins I would have never picked for myself to eat.

"Madds called when I got out of the shower and told me everything. Though I hate that you got involved, you did well. Really well."

She beams at my praise and the manacle fixed in my chest cracks a little further.

Hating that she got involved isn't even close to what I'm still feeling. I was on the phone with Madds when they got attacked. I heard his urgent voice, I heard the screams of the women, I heard the punches, the struggle, I heard it all, because he didn't get a chance to end the call.

Maya was snuggled to my side, snoozing softly after I read to her, and I froze in terror. I heard Frankie's words to Evelyn, probably not all of them, but I heard enough for everything I never knew I wanted, to shatter before me. I was losing her. I was losing her fast, before I even accepted that she's mine, before I told her she is, and the déjà vu crept up on me so fast, the blood stilled in my veins.

I was thrown in the back of that car, eight years ago, when Hanna's pleading voice was begging me to come get her. To find her. Save her. When I implored her to be strong and promised her I would find her. No matter where she was, I would come for her, I would hold her in my arms for the rest of our lives and love her forever. I was back in that moment when all I could hear was the roar of the engine because the call cut off and she was ripped away from me on a heartbreaking cry. I was still there after I hung up, and Maya woke and saw the terror on my features. But I forced my features to smooth and told her we're going to go to my place for the night and pick up her sister on the way.

For the entire way to the bar I prayed to all the gods I could name that those last few words weren't a lie. I prayed history wasn't repeating itself, and Evelyn was still in that parking lot when I got there. But a terrified voice asked a different question inside my head... what if I finally tracked her down and just like Hanna, I would only find a soulless, bloodied body? I urged Mamaw June to pack a quick bag. Very fucking quick. And we were out the door in minutes, forcing myself not to show the emotions that ripped me from the inside out, because I couldn't let Maya see any of them. June was a saint. Kept her occupied and distracted, even if fear shone in her kind eyes.

Mine was bubbling like a volcano inside my veins, and the shock of it was becoming too much. For months I kept Evelyn at arm's length, constantly pushing her away and rejecting her, thinking it would ensure I couldn't get attached to her. How she still burrowed into my soul regardless, I don't know. But she creeped just beneath the shackles and pushed hard enough for a crack to form.

Regardless, the bindings are still there, reminding me what I know to be true—too much of me is broken, and none of me deserves her. I can't be what she wants, because she deserves so much more. Someone whole, someone she could lean on, someone who hasn't fucked half of Queenscove and miles beyond. Someone who can love...

As I look at her now, shyly pottering about my penthouse that seems to smell like a home for the first time in years, if not ever, I realize that letting her go will be much harder than I thought.

And I will have to let her go. Because Evelyn already said she might not stay in Queenscove.

Evelyn

I'M NOT SURE what to make of Finnigan. He looks at me like he found me and lost me all at once. Like I'm here, but just beyond his reach, and I don't know how to take it. Once again that pain I'm becoming so familiar with is back in his bright-blue eyes, and

I itch to reach over and smooth his brow over.

I also want to slap my own hand away because I can deal with the sexual side of things, but getting emotional about the man would be such a huge mistake. Well, getting *more* emotional about him. He's a player, screwing everything in sight and never hanging out with someone more than once or twice, according to Lulu and Morri. Top that off with the fact that I technically have to return to Fleeton, and that he clearly told me he can't do this with me, and I need no further proof that I should guard my heart from him.

Though, I'm not sure that bloody organ is listening.

"Do you want one?" I ask him, holding a warm blueberry muffin to him.

He looks at it like I'm offering him the world in a ring box, then nods finally. "Yes, please."

I pop two on a plate and slide them over, then grab two for me and one for Maya on separate plates. He leans over and picks up my sister's plate, directing her to the sofa in the living area to eat, and turns the TV on for her.

"So we can talk freely," he explains as he sits back down, eying the muffins with more hunger.

He grabs one, taking a tentative bite, and when the flavor hits his tongue, I'm instantly wet at his rumble of pleasure.

"Christ, woman, this is delicious!" He takes another, bigger bite before he even swallows the first, and warmth pools low in my belly.

"Thank you. It's nothing though, only muffins."

"Evelyn, I don't eat muffins. Not because they're sugary and I'm careful about my diet, but muffins, or any other food, is all the same for me. I taste the different flavors, but there aren't any that I like more or less. I eat for nutrition, and that's it. But this"— he looks at that muffin like I baked it with gold and diamonds—"is fucking delicious."

He takes another mouthful, and the azure of his eyes brightens, the pain that was there more distant now.

"I don't know what to say." I genuinely don't. Is he appeasing me or is he truly honest?

"Say you'll bake more for me. Different things too. I want to try more!"

I giggle, reaching for my own breakfast, and notice how he stopped, hand mid-air, his hungry gaze fixed on me. But this hunger is not for food.

"And do that again," he says in a much darker, deeper tone.

Heat gathers between my legs, and now I crave to be that muffin he's munching on, so he can spread me wide on this countertop and eat me out like he's starving. But he shakes his head once and breaks the spell, focusing once again on that lucky muffin.

Waking up in this man's penthouse has been a slight shock to the system. Not just because of the mind-blowing orgasm he gave me last night, or the even dirtier one this morning, but because of his home. I already imagined him in a sleek, luxurious place like this one, floor to ceiling windows everywhere, stainless steel appliances, white walls, and a black and deep gray color scheme. Whether it was based on preconceptions about the playboy with blonde curls and cheeky smile, or it felt like it fit his personality, I don't know.

What I didn't expect was the sheer contrast I was faced with. Against those clean, cold walls, antique paintings are slanted. Everything from oil to acrylic, landscapes to portraits, nudes to tragic battle scenes. And around them... there are books. More books than I can count sit in mismatched bookcases of assorted sizes and wood, and on the floor, in messy stacks gainst the walls and around those paintings. The contrast in styles is staggering. Like this penthouse is but a shell he merely exists in, but those books, those paintings, and the strange little trinkets spread between them, is where he truly lives.

Why doesn't he have matching bookcases? Or neatly stacked books? Why does it look like he's... stuck? Or not settled in yet?

I want to ask him about this discrepancy, but now isn't the right time. There are other questions I have to ask him, and yes, his hands on me were a welcome distraction from what happened last night. He kept me from falling into a panic that wouldn't have helped me. But now, I need to come back down to reality.

Looking around, I make sure Maya's still out of earshot. She's busy with some cartoons on TV, munching happily on her muffin.

"Did they track him down?" I ask Finnigan.

He watches me for a few moments, sighing with disappointment at the change in subject most likely, and shakes his head.

My shoulders slump. "How did he find me, Finnigan? And why? Why did he come for me?"

"I don't know, Evie. What did he tell you last night?"

"How do you know he told me anything?" stupid question. Maddox probably told him.

"I was on the phone with Madds when it all happened. I... heard him." Darkness passes over his eyes, and I can see there's more than just anger there.

Is it unfair that I'm happy he's so affected? That I can see he cares?

"Not much. That he likes my new hair, and... likes it when I fight him." A deep shudder passes through me, turning my blood cold and my spine icy. "And that he's been looking everywhere for me."

That darkness deepens in Finnigan's eyes, his brows narrowed in deep creases. He turned the second muffin into crumbles between his fingers.

"He won't get you, Evelyn. I..." He pauses and shakes his head once. "He won't."

"He might." There is no way he can guarantee my safety. He can't have me by his side at all times.

"I will be with you. He won't get through me. Plus, we are all on high alert now that we know they're bringing the battle here. There will be more security, tightened rules, and eyes everywhere. He will not get to you."

"Security will freak out the customers at the café. Though, I guess you could tell them to act like customers." I think about the table closest to the entrance.

"You're not going back to work. Not now that we know that asshole is after you, determined to get you back."

"Bull—" I shut my mouth and peer around him to make sure Maya is still not listening. "Bullshit," I snap back. "I need to work, Finnigan. Now you know what's at stake for me. I will not risk my father's comfort and health, and you made it pretty clear a while ago that you want me out of Queenscove. So I'm saving money for that, too."

The man inhales so slow and deep, I half expect him to breathe out flames.

"That was then." His answer is short, but heavy with meaning I don't fully grasp.

"Nothing changed. Has it?"

Everything changed. For me at least. But I'm challenging him to face it too.

"I will help you."

"You will do no such thing," I bite back, disappointed at his lack of admission. "I refused your money once, Finnigan, I will do it again. All I need is to work."

He crosses his arms against his expansive chest unfortunately covered by a light-blue T-shirt, and leans back in the bar stool, cocking an eyebrow. "Fine. Call Lulu and see what she says about you going for your next shift."

I frown.

"Please tell me you didn't speak with her. You didn't tell her that I'm not coming back, did you?" I'm braced against the countertop now, leaning in angrily, my tone low and harsh.

He shakes his head. "I didn't, Evie darling, but Lulu loves you, does she not? Do you really think that she would allow you to go out there, in a public place, and work with a target on your head?"

For God's sake. He's right. Lulu wouldn't allow it. She would tell me to hide in the depths of the damn earth with Maya until all this blows over and both Frankie and Vassallo—or Bartiste as they know him—are dead.

"Fuck!" I snap, slapping my hand against my mouth the moment the swear leaves my lips.

Finnigan snickers, his expression lighter. I guess he never hears me swear. Being in Maya's presence constantly, I had to learn to hold back vulgar words and try to be calm all the time.

"Stop laughing," I quip, but even I can't help the smile as I rub my face with both hands and rake my fingers through my hair.

"What's with the hair, Evelyn? Sorry, but I've been dying to ask."

His question surprises me in the middle of this conversation. I shrug. "Needed a change." It's not a lie, but not quite the truth either.

He cocks his head, and I realize something gave me away.

"Very drastic change."

I nod and change the subject. "Were the guys at least able to trace Frankie's car?"

He takes too long to answer, but I don't press. He knows what I'm doing and finally he appeases me.

"They did. It wasn't a rental, which is good. Carter and his team are on it. We'll find him soon. But things will get worse before they get better."

"As long as they get better..."

"They will. Neither of them is gonna touch you ever again."

I nod, even knowing it's not a promise. I wish it was, but that would be very unfair of me.

"How are you feeling after last night? Do you need to talk to someone?" he asks.

I scoff. "Sure, let me go tell my therapist that I bashed someone's head in last night and, probably killed him. I'm sure that won't land me in jail."

"Oh, he's dead." He swipes his hand over his face. "Shit, Evie, I'm sorry. I just... I'm used to—"

"No need to explain. I bet this is just another Tuesday for you."

"It's Sunday, actually."

I glare at him, and the smirk drops off his face.

"It's strange," I finally answer him. "It feels like I was in a trance because I barely remember what happened during. I recall how he raised the gun at Maddox, how I tackled him to the ground, being dragged off of him, and then... you."

"But you saw the aftermath?" I appreciate how he's now trying to be delicate about it.

"Briefly, yes. Though I'm not entirely sure I understood what I was looking at. It didn't feel like I did that, the scene almost looked foreign to me." Though, it's enough to look at my red and bruised knuckles and the sides of my hands to confirm to myself that I was indeed the one who killed that man.

"You can talk to me, you know. What you did, no matter how common it may be for me, it isn't for you. Taking a life is hard, no matter who it is, and it will always take something out of you. I'm here."

I'm not sure what to tell him, because even now I don't know how I feel about it.

"Beyond anything else that's happening between us, I appreciate this. Thank you."

I keep wondering if the ball's going to drop at some point, and then it doesn't. Last night I blamed it on adrenaline and shock, but what excuse do I have now for not reacting like a normal, law-abiding citizen?

I was quick to condemn Finnigan and his Sanctum for their criminal ways, but what does this... and everything from before... make me? Am I at the same level as The Sanctum? Or no better than the people who killed my mother?

CHAPTER 23
Finnigan

"IT'S SETTLED THEN. We raid all three locations at once," Vin confirms as he leans back on the couch.

"We might find more kids." I sigh.

"Good. At least something good will come out of it, since there's no guarantee Frankie or Bartiste will be there," Madds says in an exasperated tone.

There's already been a raid today. Madds and Carter stormed Frankie's location they found after tracking him down, but the bastard slipped through our fingers. Not surprising since he knew we would be on his tail. But Carter already tracked down three more locations connected to him. There's a chance neither him nor his boss will be there, but whatever we find will be useful.

We've gathered at my place. Ronan even brought Annika and Aaro because there was no way he would let them out of his sight. I can't blame him. I feel the same for Evie and Maya, which is why we're all here, even if one isn't my wife and the other not my child. The protectiveness is there though. Mamaw June is entertaining them on the terrace until we finish our conversation.

The plan is clear. We're splitting into three groups and leaving in about an hour or so. Carter has agreed to stay here and keep an eye on cameras, trackers, and whatever else he does. That level of technology baffles me and I'm grateful to have his brain in our ranks. Vin, Madds, and I are taking three teams, and raiding those places. This is not the same as it was all those years before when we went to save Annika and Hanna. We have enough power now that we will demolish them on sight.

We don't need my cousin, Sloan Buchanan, to come from Venator again, like he did last time. However, the moment Ronan mentioned to him that Bartiste is back, the man decided to come and bring an army, regardless. He'll be here in a few days.

There's no escape for Bartiste now. And this time, if he crawls back into whatever hole he went in last time, we will find him. *I* will find him, and he'll eat a whole clip of my gun.

"Are we ready for dinner?" Mamaw June peaks in from the terrace.

We all exchange looks and nod to each other.

"Yeah, we're ready," Vin confirms, and she opens the door fully to let the breeze in and the two kids.

It's been rather interesting seeing Aaro and Maya bond. She's bubbly and bouncy, and Aaro is quiet, broody, yet eager to please. They get along so well. It makes me sad that Ronan and Annika will have to go back to their home once all of this is done and dusted.

Annika has been tense since coming here. Quiet too. She's always been shy, but she hasn't stepped foot in here since they left all those years ago, and her last memories of this penthouse were of tears. So many tears for her lost best friend.

It makes an even bigger bastard out of me, but I'm sort of glad she gets to experience this suffering here, in front of me, because I stayed behind and drowned in it for years. Here, where we brought her and Hanna after we *bonded* on Bovely Island during that terrible storm. We spent our last happy moments in my penthouse, which I used to share with my brother before he left.

I may have lost my first love, but it was a fresh adventure. Annika lost her best friend, her kindred spirit, and she had to watch her be ripped apart by Bartiste's men, then held her as she took her last breath. She's suffered enough.

She looks out past the floor to ceiling windows, her gaze lost somewhere in the horizon, quiet and pensive. I don't miss Evelyn's curious gaze as she studies all of us but pauses just a little longer on my nephew's mom. Everyone rises to go sit at the dinner table, but Annika follows her gaze instead, and walks in the other direction—the terrace. Ronan frowns, a hint of worry shadowing his eyes. He's had his share of sad memories in this penthouse. He never said anything to me. How could he when I was so broken. But I could see it in the way he looked at her through her grief... like he was terrified he would lose her. That she wouldn't come back from the shock she suffered. He takes a step to follow her out on the terrace, but I quickly take two and when he spots me, understanding crosses his features. He nods once, and a hint of a smile dusts over my lips, then I follow his wife outside, closing the door behind me.

It takes two more breaths for me to get the courage to join her where she stands by the railing, her arms wrapped around herself like she's afraid her soul will spill out if she doesn't. She doesn't seem surprised to see me when I finally join her. Setting her gaze on the sunset, she tightens the grip around herself, looking like she wants to talk, but hesitates. Do I make her that uncomfortable?

I take a deep inhale and let out a heavy sigh.

"I'm sorry for how I acted when you left." The words sound awkward, forced, but I hope she can find the genuine feeling underneath all of that.

"I'm sorry we left."

My head whips to her and I suppress the need to press my hand to the spot where my neck just cracked. *She's what?*

"I'm sorry we left *you* when you needed your brother the most," she continues, ignoring my shock.

"I understand why you did it. You needed to protect yourself, your unborn baby, your family."

Then she shakes her head, and I'm even more confused.

"That wasn't the only reason." She turns to me, her eyes glossy, but she fights back the tears. "I had to remove myself from you."

I frown, reigning in what could be a bad reaction.

"Shit, that didn't sound the same as in my head," she says with a sigh and an apologetic look. "I couldn't bear what my presence, my beating heart, was doing to you. I was a constant reminder to you of the cruel unfairness of this world, that two of us were kidnapped that day and only I was lucky enough to return. You deserved to move on, and if I stayed, the pain, the guilt, the anger, would have kept you there... grieving. At least that's what my instinct was telling me. Because every time I looked in a mirror, I saw in my eyes the same guilt, the same anger to this unfairness that looked back at me from yours."

She holds my gaze for a moment longer, then turns back to the burnished sky. So, I do too, leaning my forearms on the railing.

To say I'm surprised is a massive understatement. It was easy to think that they left for themselves, for their baby. It was easy to think that I mattered less. I never allowed myself to think that maybe... just maybe, they did it for me too. I never cared enough to talk to them after that anyway. But many times I wondered if things would have been different if they stayed. I needed comfort, I needed someone to understand my suffering, I needed my brother.

Sighing, I allow myself to accept the acknowledgement waiting in the recesses of my mind—I needed my brother, but I couldn't bear the happiness in his eyes as he looked at his breathing girlfriend. Not then.

Now, I'm holding onto resentment, but beneath that ugly emotion, I find that I'm not bothered by it anymore. Especially not when I catch a glimpse of Aaro, and it dawns on me that the healthy, curious little boy deserved a healthy mother too. Annika was too broken back then.

"You're right," I agree. "I'm not sure how it would have been if I had you here."

"Hard." She answers too quickly, her shoulders falling with the weight of these tough feelings. "I spent many nights on this terrace cursing that I was breathing this pleasantly salty air. Too many times I got close to giving up on myself, and I want to think now that I was so stupid back then for having such thoughts. I want to be embarrassed of myself. But I'm not. There was too much validity in my mindset, in my feelings—and my guilt. Whatever you were thinking about me then, my thoughts were even worse, and that's why I had to leave."

I didn't know her state of mind was so precarious, that she would have gone as far as giving up on life. Fuck, I was never that close. I was grieving, I was sad, but most of all I was angry at my incompetence. I was disappointed in my inability to save Hanna before she was killed. The guilt was eating me from the inside out, but I was never close enough to give up. I'm an even bigger asshole for not noticing how hard Annika was suffering. Though, I'm not sure she would have confessed that to me back then.

I wouldn't have asked anyway, too wrapped up in my own self-loathing. Still am. I am a failure, and it's why I should stay as far away from Evelyn as possible.

What if I fail like that all over again?

What if I lose her too?

Evelyn

THE ATMOSPHERE AT the dinner table is calm, peculiar considering that they plotted three violent raids in the last hour or so. One would think it's so light because two kids are present, but that's not it at all. These men are so nonchalantly comfortable with the destruction they're about to rein down on Frankie and his men, that they are at ease now. Even as they're leaving in a few minutes.

All but Carter, who sits quietly next to me, his back straight, movements eerily fluid as he turns his head, observing, or as he cuts into his last slice of roast ham and steamed vegetables. Every single movement he makes, from the glide of his eyes to the rise of his chest as he breathes, is so controlled. It gives me the impression that he's the most skilled of predators, sitting idly at the top of the food chain, waiting for the prey worth his effort. But sometimes, I also have this urge to poke him to make sure he's real. Weirdly enough, I see some of these traits in Aaro too.

Just like Carter now, I've been observing them in silence since late afternoon. Finn told me everyone was coming over because Carter found something, right as I got out of the shower after my grueling training session with Madds. All three of us went to The Fightclub around midday, Maya included, because I was too anxious to sit around any longer. Once I heard they were coming, I was dying to hear what Carter found. I planned on sitting in the shadow of the corridor and listen in, but no one told me to leave.

Annika and Morrigan came too, and I would have stopped feeling privileged for being allowed to listen in as they planned, if I wasn't the outsider. Which I am. Not a girlfriend, not a mother, definitely not a wife. Yet, no one batted an eyelid at my presence. Not even quiet, eerie, Carter. He is the most curious of them all. He both scares and fascinates me because there's a cold emptiness in his peculiar hazel eyes. There were some emotions, sometimes amusement, sometimes a hint of excitement at the prospect of vengeance and murder, yet there was no warmth. Not the type you expect from a person who has been friends with these people for over a decade. From listening to him talk it's clear he cares. He was the first to push back when something sounded like it could put someone in danger or be an unnecessary risk. Then again, that could come from a practical point of view too. I gathered that he's pretty much a genius, applying his wits in his hacking skills, but I heard him more than once being referred to as *The Carver*, and I shudder to think why that is.

Maya happily munches on the rest of her dinner, her eyes wide as she takes in everyone at the table. There's a pang of sadness in my heart as I realize that she's never experienced anything like this, a big *family* dinner, until we came here. I don't think she remembers us and our parents together at the dinner table, and even so, it wasn't like this. So many chatty people engrossed in different conversations, a little boy she can play with, couples loving on each other. And I'm going to take this away from her. I feel like an asshole. How can I rob my sister of this when she looks like this is where she belongs, just to pull her to our miserable existence back in cold Fleeton, living in a subpar place, hopefully never homeless again, while struggling to feed each other and pay for Dad's care? How can I do that to her?

She looks cheerful and content as she observes Morri and Vin, and Ronan and Annika's sweet gestures to each other, giggling to herself whenever one brushes a hand on the cheek of the other or they steal a kiss. I haven't told her yet that our life here isn't permanent, and I can't predict how she will react when I drop the news that we could be going back to Fleeton. To Dad.

My mind drifts away as the conversation dies down around us, everyone probably thinking more about what's coming once they leave the table.

"Evie?" Maya's voice brings my attention back to her, her voice dragging a bit like it does when she's dying of curiosity.

"Yes?"

"Why don't you have a boyfriend?"

I'm so startled by the question, my gaze shoots around the table just for my cheeks to heat when I notice that most of them have heard the question too. Morri chuckles to herself and I want to throw something at her.

"I don't need one, honey," I answer, praying she's satisfied. "Go on, finish your dinner."

She wipes her face quickly with the napkin, too quickly for me to hope that she's satisfied with my answer.

"But I think you should get one. Find someone to love. Then you'll be happier, and maybe you'll smile more. And bake like you used to."

The innocence in her voice breaks something inside of me. I've been trying so hard to make sure that the cruelty and hardship of our life didn't brush off on her, I made sure not to swear around her, not to yell, get angry or upset, I tried to shield her from it all. I didn't even think to pretend to be happy around her. It's only when I realize just how quiet the space got that my cheeks flame with embarrassment and I want to slide down this chair and hide under the table until everyone leaves.

"I have no interest in a boyfriend. I much like spending my time with you." I smile, brushing my hand over her head. "Now stop asking silly questions or you might not get dessert."

"I like it too, but... I can't love you like that, Evie. I can't love you in that pretty way Daddy loved Mommy."

I choke so hard on my food, Carter pats my back to help me. My sister seems set on embarrassing me and making me cry tonight. What is happening right now? Before I manage to catch my breath, to my freaking horror, she continues.

"Like them." She points to the two couples. "They kiss and hug, and they look at each other like Mommy and Daddy used to. Like Finn looks at you sometimes when you're not paying attention. And like you look at h—"

"Maya! How about you go wash your hands? In the bathroom, now." God almighty, bury me now.

My gaze shoots to Finn. I don't want to look, but there's a twisted desire inside of me that needs to see how Maya's words landed. The man in question is stunned, I'm not even sure he's breathing. Everyone's watching us, but I don't turn. I can't bear to face them, yet. Finn's mood shifts and harsh annoyance strains the strong, beautiful lines of his face. Then he rises and leaves.

The bastard actually leaves.

"Come on! We have work to do!" He shouts for the others to follow.

My gaze finally goes to them, and I have no idea what to think. Madds sighs, annoyed for some reason, Morri looks shocked and amused, Vin shakes his head at her, Carter has this knowing gaze that unsettles me a bit, Mamaw June looks like she's gonna burst from joy, and Ronan and Annika have a mixture of surprise, happiness, and worry on their faces.

"I am going to kill my sister," I mutter to myself, mostly.

Then Morri bursts into laughter, and quickly rises, following the others as they get ready to go out. Only Annika, Mamaw June, Carter, and I remain at the table. Aaro follows after Maya.

"Ignore Morrigan. Her and Vincent drove us mad when they were *courting*." I turn to Carter, checking to make sure that it was he who spoke those words. It was. "Annika even orchestrated a clever riddle and chase to get Ronan. We were all privy to their crazy ways. Some more than others."

Annika chuckles from across the table, but I'm too busy digging through my brain to try to remember if Carter has ever spoken so many words to me before. I'm drawing a blank. The longest conversation we had, which is still one-sided, was when he gave me the tracker before I went back in the container. I think.

"Still, Finnigan and I aren't together. We aren't like that," I counter.

Carter turns his head ever so smoothly toward me and cocks it, his stunning eyes fixed on me. "Are you not?"

There is no missing the slight amusement shining in his eyes. He doesn't want an answer, this question is rhetorical at best. *He knows.*

"Take it from me"—Annika pulls my attention to her—"don't try to pretend, hide, or lie to Carter. The man has a sixth sense."

I would take her words as an eerie warning if it wasn't for the cheeky smile in her eyes, directed at the man next to me. I take it Annika and Ronan tried to downplay their connection then.

"Wait, did you say Annika orchestrated a riddle and a chase?"

"Yes. After she practically conned us of a few million," Carter says in a calm way, like he's telling me about how he went and bought milk this morning.

Annika starts laughing and I turn to her, gob-smacked.

"Hey, I gave it back. Eventually."

Carter chuckles softly and it sounds deeply unnatural. Intriguing, too.

"I'm going to go grab my laptop and things." He rises and leaves the room.

"God, it's so hard to recall good memories from that time." Annika leans back in her chair, crossing her arms against her chest. "The riddle Carter mentioned, brought them to the annual Midsummer party, at the waterfall in the woods, and it was the night that started it all for the two of us. Well, four, really."

Four? I stiffen, pondering the words.

"I was always too withdrawn to do anything out of order. We might have been dealing on the black-market, but Hanna was the salesperson, full of spunk and life. I was just the artist hiding in the background, forging all those paintings. So I wanted to be crazy for once."

I'm sorry, Annika, sweet, kind, shy Annika was a painting forger who sold on the black-market? Oh God, I have so much more to find out about these people.

"When I first saw Ronan, and I realized who we were selling to, I couldn't help myself. I was so drawn to him, like deep down I knew he was *the one*. I know, I know, it sounds insane." She chuckles softly, but then it fades, and her gaze moves somewhere in the distance. "If it wasn't for my obsession, Hanna and I would be retired now. But I stayed, and she insisted on staying with me. Then Bartiste came for us. Sometimes I wonder if we had left after we struck the deal with The Sanctum, would he have found us? Ronan says yes, and the outcome would have been even worse, but it's hard to get over the fact that I lost my best friend, and Finnigan lost his first love."

My mouth falls open, and I fight the gasp too late.

Hanna was his first love?

Annika's eyes widen and she covers her mouth. "You didn't know?"

"Oh, well, I told you, he and I aren't like that. We're not... anything. So, we don't share personal things like this." I try to deflect, but judging by the look in her eyes, I'm not very successful. "I'm sorry for Hanna, losing your best friend must have been terrible."

"It was. The guilt was even worse. I'm almost over mine." She shakes her head, chewing on her lip before she continues. "One day, Finnigan will come to terms with his own guilt too, and when he does, I hope you'll be there next to him."

CHAPTER 24
Evelyn

I'M STARTLED AWAKE by another nightmare. The same memory, the same words spewed by Frankie and Vassallo, or Bartiste, the same slimy sensation lingering. I look around, but Maya is sleeping soundly next to me.

Annika and Aaro took the other bedroom as we waited for the guys to finish the raid. I waited for as long as I could, but in the end, sleep took me. I was hoping, but sleep hasn't settled my anxiety. The guys said that it's likely neither Frankie nor Bartiste will be at the three locations, but I still hope.

More so, I hope Finnigan's okay.

A rumble sounds outside the bedroom, and I hold my breath, listening. It might have been the front door.

Is that him? Is he back?

I slide out of bed, rushing to the door and stepping out, closing it as soft as I can behind me, so as not to wake Maya. The anxiety rushes through my blood and I rush to the living area.

It is him!

"Oh my god, Finnigan!" I slap my hand over my mouth when he turns, and I get a full view of him.

For such a preppy type, the rich, surfer boy looks a lot like a ruthless warrior right now. Blood streaks his blonde curls, his T-shirt is splattered like a Pollock painting, and his knuckles are red, the skin broken on some of them. I might be sick, because this does something so wonderful and insane to me, warmth pooling between my thighs. He looks... vicious. Deliciously so as he beams at me, as happy to see me as I am to see him.

"Are you okay?" I finally reach him, ignoring both Ronan and Carter's raised eyebrows and faint amusement.

"All good, sugar."

"But..." I take his hands in mine, unable to stop myself. "You're hurt."

He removes one hand from mine and brings it up, pinching my chin between his thumb and forefinger, and lifting my gaze to his. "Nothing but scratches."

I nod slowly but can't breathe easier as I imagine how this must look to the others. Awkwardly, I clear my throat and drop his hand, taking a little step back. I'm rewarded with his cheekiest grin, because I know he sees the flush in my cheeks, no way he doesn't when they feel like they're burning.

God, this man's going to ruin me.

"You didn't find him, did you?" I ask, swiping my gaze over to the others.

"No." Ronan's the one who answers.

"It was still productive. We have leads now." Carter shuts the lid to his laptop and tucks it in a bag along with a lot of other technical gear he brought with him.

"Not long. He'll be ours soon enough," Finn adds.

For some odd reason I feel a bit of jealousy. I want to be there when Frankie is caught. I want to be there when he dies. But most of all, I want to be the one who steals his last breath. The Sanctum might be brushing off on me because none of that sounds remotely wrong.

"I'm gonna go wash and crawl in bed with my family. Night!" Ronan says, a satisfied tone in his voice.

"Good night." We all wish him, and my gaze is finally drawn to the window. It's still night, and now I'm so wired up, not sure I can fall back asleep.

"I'm going to take Ronan's old room. It's too late to drive home and still rest." Carter tucks away his gear, so it's not in the way, and waves us good night.

Then there's just me, and my bloodied warrior.

"You're sure you're okay?" I ask again.

"Yes, but I'm tempted to get hurt just so I can have the privilege of being welcomed home like that all over again, with that worried and hungry look in your eyes."

"Um... hungry?" Here's that damn blush again.

"Oh yes. You're looking at me like you want to rip my clothes off and touch every inch of my body to make sure I'm whole. Every. Single. Hard. Inch."

Sweet Mary Mother of Jesus. He did not just say that. And I should definitely not like the sound of it as much as I do.

"Finnigan, I—"

"You should go to bed, Evie darling." His fingers are on my chin again, but only for a brief second, because in the next one, his hand is on the back of my neck, and I'm pulled into the most brutal, demanding, and hungry kiss.

I fist his bloody T-shirt, holding him to me like I'm scared he'll dare break this kiss, but Finnigan has other ideas. His other hand goes to the small of my back, pulling me flush to his body, before his fingers snake further down, pressing into my ass. I moan into his mouth, following the vibrations with the frantic swipes of my tongue against his, and when his clear hard on presses into my lower belly, the urge to climb him like a tree threatens to make a fool out of me.

His previous rejections still stain my memory, but Christ... this starving kiss might just wipe it clean.

With one last bruising press of his lips against mine, he pulls away, that sly grin once again tugging at his lips.

"I wish this wouldn't feel so right."

I frown and open my mouth to spit back at him, but what would I say? Because I wish for the same thing.

"We can allow ourselves to feel right. We deserve as much. Even if there's a time limit on it."

"Time limit?" he asks.

I nod. "You know of my father. I like it here, but this is not about me."

He doesn't look too pleased with my answer, but doesn't argue. "You may be right, we deserve at least a bit of rightness."

He pulls me back to him, kissing me again, only this time the hunger is different. It begs and demands at the same time, it's soft, warm, and intimate, and I find that I like this kiss even more than the one before.

* * *

Three hours I spent in the gym and training ring today. Madds pushed me so much harder, at my request, and taught me some more moves and techniques. Every muscle in my body aches, but it feels so good. I may not be ready to take on Frankie again, but boy do I feel like I could stand against the asshole.

Madds is still upset I jumped out of the car to get the guy who almost shot him, but he hugged me so hard the other day at dinner, I know he's thankful. He's just not the type to spell it out. And the fact that he's eager to train me harder and show me more fighting moves and techniques says a lot. Moreover, I finally regained control of myself. Of my fate. I no longer feel so useless. Madds, The Sanctum, gave me something I never had before—strength. Not just physical, but mental and emotional. I'm more myself than I ever have been before.

"Is it my turn now?" Maya squeals from her seat on the wooden bench far against the back wall.

"You wanna train too?" Maddox asks, amused.

"Yup!" She drops her book and sprints to us. She tries to climb in the ring, but keeps falling on her ass, much to our amusement. She's determined though, and Maddox chuckles as he goes and pulls her up.

"Alright then. While your sister goes and rests, I'll *train* you."

This man takes his role so serious, and sometimes I just want to cry at how amazing he is with her, with us. I never wished for another sibling, and even if I did, they would have paled in comparison to Madds.

He drops to his knees at her level since he's so damn tall. "Show me how you make a fist."

I chuckle and climb out of the ring, starting to unwrap my hands as I head to my gym bag. I don't bother changing, I just pull a pair of joggers over my shorts and stay in my sports bra since I'm too hot. I'll pull a sweatshirt over when we're on our way to Vincent's house. The guys are so worried about me, they keep an eye on me at all times and avoid keeping me in public places for longer than necessary. It's a bit annoying, but then again, I've never felt so protected in my life. I can't complain, not when all that matters is the fact that Maya is safe. Granted, The Fightclub is not a public place, but even the drive from here to the penthouse or Vincent's forest house could be dangerous.

It's been five days since the three raids, and they've all been the same—Finnigan's, baking, gym, worry, sleep.

I could use a drink.

From what I understand, Carter's been baiting the hell out of Frankie and Bartiste. Screwing up their operations, destroying leads and connections, and making sure those assholes aren't welcomed in the underground of Queenscove. This is Sanctum territory, yet those assholes think they can just swoop in and do business here. They'll soon get angry enough that they'll come out and make a mistake. Bloody cowards.

"Hey, Madds? Is Midnight open now?" I raise my voice over Maya's funny grunts as she hits his open palms.

"No. But Carter and Jian or Tina might be there. A bartender, too."

Jian and Tina are two of the hackers from Carter's team. They've been part of it and The Sanctum for years. Brendan is the other, but I rarely see him. He's a proper recluse.

"I'm going to head up there. I need a drink," I let him know as I head toward the stairs that lead up in the secure corridor.

A few weeks ago, Carter set my fingerprint on the access pads and gave me a code so I can go up whenever I felt like having a drink after workouts. He did make sure to tell me to only go if it's not open, though. I didn't ask why, but one can guess.

I swing my bag over my shoulder, and run my fingers through my sweaty, messy bob to make it look a little more decent as I climb the stairs and pass through all the secure doors.

"Hey Carter, is it okay if I come in?" I ask as I peak through the back door and notice him standing at the bar, a laptop in front of him. As always.

"Hi Evelyn. Yes, of course. Actually, can you tell me if you've seen this guy before?" he gestures toward his laptop and waits.

"Oh!" I don't bother hiding the grimace when I see the picture on the screen—a man slumped on the ground in what seems like a dark street of some kind, with a bullet hole in his forehead, his eyes open, but blank.

I swallow a couple of times and take a step closer.

"Actually, yes. He was one of the ones who ushered us into that warehouse or whatever it was. He didn't strike me as a low-ranking guy, but not as important as Frankie. I never heard his name though."

"This helps. I have his phone and can track all his past whereabouts now, and at least I know that I'm not wasting my time. Thank you, Evelyn."

I smile and nod. Once again Carter speaks with me more than just the polite *hello* or *do you want a drink,* and I find it hard to get used to it. Maybe he's not quite as bad as I thought he was.

"Drink?" he asks, and I chuckle to myself as I drop my bag on a chair.

"Yes, please. A strong one, but sweet if possible."

He nods and goes behind the bar himself.

"Oh, sorry, I thought a bartender might be here. I don't want to bother you when you're busy."

"It's no bother. I'm getting one myself too."

I still feel awkward though, but I nod and smile either way.

"Trust me, he'll eat out of the palm of your hand if you do that."

That sweet voice...

When I turn, Finnigan walks in from the back, Tina next to him, and when his eyes land on me, I feel naked. I may be wearing loose joggers and a sports bra, but he watches me with startled hunger, drawing his gaze over me so slowly, I want to spread myself wide for him right here, on this wooden floor. No matter who watches.

"Evie..." he says on a breathy voice, his eyes lingering a bit too long on my breasts before they find my eyes.

Tina walks away and gives me a little wave before she takes a seat at the bar, next to Carter's laptop.

"I was just... I trained downstairs."

Oh my god, I'm mumbling. *Keep it together, Evelyn!*

"Yeah... you did."

Hungry, so very, very hungry.

"Carter's making me a drink."

"You should ask Severin to take you back to the penthouse." He takes a step closer, his heated gaze suggesting he doesn't mean those words.

And I don't want to go yet. "I want a drink first."

"There's alcohol at home."

Home. That sounds awfully familiar, like it's not just *his* home. I'm not going straight there anyway. Maya has an overnight play-date since Annika proposed that the kids should spend as much time together as they can before they'll inevitably have to return home when this whole thing ends.

"I'm getting cabin fever. I'm having a drink here."

Before he can give me another comeback, I move to the bar and climb onto one of the stools, my ass sliding back a bit too far in my attempt to be cocky. But I own it and brace my forearms on the bar, watching Carter's curious eyes on us, a cocked eyebrow showing his amusement as he makes the drinks.

Finnigan shows up to my right, facing me instead of sitting on the stool, and his gaze spreads fire over my body. I dare a peak, and he's watching my arched back, my ass, like he's about to tackle me to the floor and feast on it.

Please, please feast on it!

And I realize, utterly horrified, that I'm going to leave a damp patch on this leather barstool. I have no idea how I'm going to hide it from him. Or the others.

There's no going back now.

"One drink," he says on a low rumble, his tone laced with whiskey and fire, "then I'm getting you home."

My gaze shoots to him, drowning in the promise in his voice, and I know he doesn't miss the hitch in my breath, nor the shift in my thighs as I press them together. I have no drink to fiddle with, only my fingers that are getting increasingly damper, and I'm not sure what to do with myself. Not when he doesn't stop looking at me with azure eyes heavy with unspoken promises, his wide, thick shoulders tensing as he holds himself unusually still. A trickle of sweat runs from beneath my sports bra tickling down my spine, and I shiver at the sensation, my back arching slightly in response. His gaze shoots right there, and I think his hand was about to follow too, but he stops himself, flexing his fist as he follows that drop of sweat disappear in the seam of my leggings.

His eyes are still there, unmoving and tense. "Where's Maya?"

"Downstairs with Maddox. She has a sleepover planned with Aaro after," I say it all in one breath. One hot, heavy breath.

"Where?"

"Vincent's."

He only grunts in response, his gaze still fixed on my skin. Or my ass. Whichever it is, I curse the clothes covering the area, and I curse the company even more.

"Here you go, *Evelyn*."

My eyes snap toward Carter who gives me such a suggestive look, there is no mistaking the fact that he wants me to know that he can tell what's going on. My skin prickles yet again, because yes, Finnigan has eaten my pussy with such hunger, the ghost of his tongue is still there when I close my eyes, and he fingered me with enough expertise, I'm ready to beg him for more. But we haven't spoken about it. He hasn't said a word to me about what we have done. He's giving me enough suggestive looks and considering how hung up he's been on the forbidden side of things, I can certainly call this progress. Even without the verbal acknowledgment.

Where is this going?

How far is he going to allow it to go?

And where will I stop?

Because being here, in Queenscove, among people who have done nothing but protect me and root for me, has been gold dust for my growth. I'm a waitress in a café, but on the inside, I feel like I can take over the damn world.

Only, right now it's not the world I'm craving to tackle, but Finnigan Hennessey. The man with a sharp jaw, an even sharper tongue, and forbidden desire painted vividly in his bright blue eyes. I should care about his previous rejections, they should stir me in the opposite direction, and this might make me stupid, but I crave his acceptance more.

Not because I'm a sucker for punishment, not because I'm a doormat, but because the moment he looked into my eyes when I walked out of that container, I saw a soul drowning in the same pain as mine. A person who couldn't bear to scream his loneliness out loud, their mind breaking with the harrowing noise of it. I saw a man with a broken heart and a broken soul who wanted nothing more than kindred company. And I never said it, never even allowed it to touch on my inner monologue, but deep down I knew that person had to be me.

There are shackles around our hearts, binding our souls in catatonic states of silent despair—and we need each other to break them.

Even if I do leave this beautiful place that gave me my life back, at least I'll leave unshackled. I'll even leave my heart with him if I have to, because at least I'll know that for a moment, I was free. And I'll know that he is too.

I take the glass Carter carefully poured for me, and the first taste warms me with such decadent sweetness, I down three more big sips one after the other, on a groan deep in my throat.

Finnigan's eyes widen, looking at the glass like it offended him somehow. I get only a swift growl in warning as he grabs it and downs it in one go, slamming it back on the bar. One drop glimmers at the corner of his mouth, and when the tip of his tongue reaches to lick it, I'm back in his bedroom, his head between my legs, my cries covered by his hand on my mouth.

God help me...

"Time to go." He grabs my hand in his much larger one and pulls me down from the chair.

"Excuse me?" My protest lands on deaf ears, because he fully ignores me as he drags me back toward the back door.

I barely get to say goodbye as he grabs my hand without even stopping, and ushers me through the corridor I came through. I try to pry myself out of his grip but fail.

"You don't get to say what I do or don't do, Finnigan. If I want to enjoy a drink, I can enjoy a damn—"I run into Finnigan's back as he briefly stops at the top of the stairs.

Warm, wide, strong back I'm dying to rake my nails over. *Christ, what is happening with me?*

"Yo, Severin!" Finnigan calls out for his friend, ignoring me, and then sets off again, walking down the stairs.

"What's up?"

"Are you ready to go now?"

"Yeah, we were just coming up for Evie," he says with a narrowing gaze that drifts to me, then to our joined hands. "Oh, for God's sake."

I force my hand out of Finnigan's hold, furious at his manhandling, because I'm getting tired of his hot and cold behavior. He's reluctant to let go, but I don't give him a choice, then I storm right past him and down the stairs, until I reach Maya quietly lacing one of her shoes.

"Come, sweet girl, let's go see your new friend," I tell her, moving her little hands away and doing up her laces myself so we can get the heck out of here.

"See you later?" Maddox asks, and I know he's addressing Finn.

"Not likely. Busy tonight. See you tomorrow."

He mutters a bye to me, and Maya too, but I let my sister answer, because *busy tonight* for Finnigan Hennessey can only mean one thing—he's going to screw the life out of some random girl tonight.

Something stings behind my eyes, because maybe I was wrong this whole time, maybe I am an idiot, and this man is happy with the manacles binding him. And maybe he doesn't give a shit about me after all.

I twitch when the door slams, and I know he's gone. I thought he was done with his harem of women, even Morri and Madds thought so too, and I wish I wouldn't have read so much into it, because clearly, we were all wrong.

I'm just half a notch on his headboard, the *goth girl* box he probably needed to check off.

I'm just another mark in Finnigan's black book.

CHAPTER 25
Finnigan

I JUMP OUT of my own skin when the front door slams, and spill the glass of vodka sour all over my T-shirt and shorts.

"For fuck's sakes..." I mutter to myself, putting the glass down and rising quickly to see who the hell that was.

As I cross the terrace and head inside, I'm more pissed about my spilled drink than the prospect of someone breaking into my penthouse. Even if this was my third one already. But as I step over the threshold, I see only a blur of a person as they disappear in the corridor.

Evelyn?

I thought she was at Vincent's for that sleepover. I'm annoyed and confused as I storm after her, because I thought I could have some time to breathe. To think. To cool off. She did a fucking number on me, showing up in Midnight in that tight sports bra that pushed her sinful breasts together, her soft skin on display, begging to be touched. I couldn't stop looking at her arched back, her ass pushed out, and all I wanted was to bend her over that bar, press my hand on her back, and sink my cock in her pussy until she vowed never to be touched—or fucking looked at—by any other man ever again.

My possessiveness over this woman is going beyond protecting. Because I want that more than anything, to keep her in a gilded cage away from this cruel world and give her all she's ever wanted on a gold platter. I want to keep her in furs and silk, and make sure no hair on her head will ever fall again, unless it's with her permission. I'm fucking terrified that something could happen to her. Yet, I want to be the one to break that sweet body of hers, and I want her to give me permission to do it. Even as I know now that she wants to fuck without it.

I can smell the ginger and brown sugar scent of her as I follow the trail through the corridor. It reminds me of her tight pussy and how responsive she was to my touch. Even when I came at her in the darkness—especially then. Groaning, I adjust my cock inside my boxers, squeezing it hard into submission.

It doesn't work.

Not when I hear the shower start and all I can imagine is my Evie darling, naked beneath the spray. She's sin and innocence wrapped into one, she's the threat to my heart and the only thing that could save it. And I'm fucking terrified that she'll decide to walk away from Queenscove and leave with it.

But I open the bathroom door anyway, stripping my clothes on the way to the shower she's standing under with her eyes closed, and before I can think too long about that fear, I'm down on my knees behind her, my face buried between her cheeks seeking that hot, delicious center of her as she yelps and attempts to jump away. My arm circles around her before she can move, but doesn't relax even when she realizes it's me.

"Get off me, Finnigan! Why are you here? Weren't you supposed to be *busy*? Buried in some new pus—"

"I lied." I interrupt her with a growl, sinking my teeth in the flesh of her ass cheek. I expect another yelp, but she hisses instead, pushing against me.

"Why?"

"Because the only *pussy* I can bear to think of anymore is yours. And I felt like punishing you for it. Being alone here was safer."

"And now?" She pauses, her muscles finally melting into me as she stifles a mewl. "Do you still want to punish me?"

"I fear I may never stop."

"Don't stop." Evelyn reaches back, raking a hand through my hair, and tugs me into her.

So hungry and demanding. Placing a hand on her back, I push until she's bent over and fully exposed to me, and now... I'm ready to fucking feast.

And feast I do.

I lick her from front to back, paying special attention to her clit, pressing my tongue over the hooded nerve bundle and circling it over and over until she cries out and her legs shake. She's so sensitive, so beautifully responsive, that she doesn't need much attention there to find that coveted peak. And that's why I move to the center of her instead. I know already that she'll be writhing with pleasure when I fuck her with my tongue, swiping on her inner walls like she's the end to my hunger, the cure to my starvation. I'll only bring her to the edge, drive her crazy with pleasure, but not offer enough to topple her over and light that fire she so desperately wants to burn in. I lick and stroke, push and circle, until every muscle in her body is screaming in strain along with her sweet, throaty voice.

Maya's not here, so Evie can be as loud as she craves.

"I can't... I'm going to fall..."

She moans, but I ignore her, because I'm convinced she won't deny herself this pleasure by crumbling to the floor. So I continue, teasing her clit only enough to edge her beautiful soft body, I'm loving more and more each day. Each pound she's been gaining has added to her beauty, because she looks healthier, happier, safer in her own skin, and never did I think that it would stir my cock quite in this way.

Thrusting my tongue in her tight little cunt may just be my new favorite pastime, especially when she bears down on my face seeking more of it.

"Finnigan!" she yells when once again I attack her clit only enough for the flames to lick her skin, but not enough to set her on fire.

"Beg me, Evie darling."

But I only get a broken whimper in response.

"Tell me what you want," I encourage.

"Please..."

"Please what?"

"Please... please make me come."

Music to my fucking ears.

I rise as she cries in frustration, but before the sound finds its end and she rises too, I press my hand to her mouth, pulling her body flush with mine, her back to my front, and reach over to that sensitive bundle of nerves. She's screaming against my hand as I bear down on her clit, then with small circular motions I bring her closer and closer to the roaring fire. My hand on her mouth is a play into her fantasy, not a restriction of her enticing cries, and as her legs begin to shake, her small arms grabbing onto my forearms frantically, I know she loves it. Then I add just a bit more pressure and the minx explodes, delicious whimpers against my palm as her naked flesh shudders against my own.

I let her ride the waves of pleasure, removing my hand from her core when her legs tighten around it, her nerves crying from the sensitivity, but she holds onto me like I'm her lifeline. And Christ, that feels *really* fucking good.

But I'm not done with the minx. When she twists in my arms and jumps me, forcing me to catch her as she wraps her whole body around mine, and straddles my hips, I know she's not done with me either.

I wanna fuck her in this shower, let her body slide onto my cock and take her until there's nothing but our screams keeping this building standing. But Evelyn deserves better than a quick fuck against the cold tiles. She moans my name into my mouth as she kisses me feverishly, and my resolve threatens to break. But I rein it in, kiss her senseless, taking her breath away and replacing it with mine.

The spray of the shower is starting to get in the way of my enjoyment of her, so I walk us out and attempt to put her back down on her feet. But the minx clings to me, refusing to let go, biting my lip and pulling me back in the maddening spell of her lush lips. We're dripping wet, and since I have a feeling she won't let go enough for us to get dry, I prop her ass on the counter and laugh when she yelps at the cold contact. I reach over for the towel hanging on the side, and bring it up to her hair, soaking up the water running down it. She flinches, breaking the kiss, and I want to ask why, but the moment is gone. I'm already moving on to my own hair and she's already distracted.

"Oh..." She presses her pointer finger to her parted lips, gawking down between us.

I don't need to check to know she's looking at my hard cock pressed between our bodies. I don't want to either, because she is so much more interesting to stare at—her body language, her reaction, her innocent doe eyes beaming with lust.

"You are..." She trails off. "Can I touch you?" she asks, hesitation quieting her voice.

"I might die if you don't."

I think she's gonna swipe a finger over the head or something, but when her small hand wraps around me, the feel of her is almost too much. Hissing, I press a hand against her ass and pull her so hard into me, her back arches, head falling back, and I know her clit has made the perfect contact, because she hitches her hips up, seeking the burning sensation that drives her in that sweet oblivion.

I can't fucking take this anymore.

Throwing the towel on the floor, I bring her off the counter as she tightens her legs around my hips, and carry her straight to my bedroom. I throw her on the bed, giving her no time to breathe before I jump on top of her, caging her in as I slide my knees under her legs, and crush my lips to hers.

Sweet moans fill my mouth as she reaches for my back, pulling me down to her. I let her, because her tight nipples against my skin are heaven on earth, and I'm growing addicted to the sensation of her bare skin against my own.

But I break the kiss before my cock can start making decisions for me.

"Evie, please stop me from doing thi—"

"No," she says it before I even finish the sentence.

"I don't want to hurt you."

"I've already been hurt, Finnigan. You'll be the one to wipe away those memories from my body."

Fuck.

I can't bear the thought of Bartiste having touched her, broken her, and marred her flesh and mind with his filth. Evelyn Shaw is mine, and I won't allow the memory of another man to ruin her.

When I press my lips to her now, she sighs and mewls into them, feeling the surrender in my touch.

I can't stop myself. I don't want to anymore.

She wraps her legs around my hips, her pretty cunt pressing against my cock, and I know there's no escape for me. The need to be inside of her prevails over my conscience.

I pull away and reach for my nightstand drawer, finding a condom and ripping the packet with my teeth. I keep waiting for the moment she'll scream me off and tell me she's changed her mind, but it never comes. Even as I sit back on my haunches and roll the rubber over my aching cock, her curious gaze roams over my body, but it's the way she gently bites the side of her bottom lip that turns it lustful.

And yet, she still doesn't change her mind.

When I sink two fingers in her aching, tight cunt, just because I find a twisted comfort in the feel of her, she arches her back and presses into me, seeking more.

And still... she doesn't say *no*.

So I lean over her, braced on one arm as I look into her silver eyes exploding in a gold ray in the center, and drag the tip of my cock down the warm seam of her pussy until I reach the spot that makes her tense the most.

"One last chance, Evie darling."

She grabs me by the sides of my neck, demanding my attention as she holds me into her hypnotic gaze.

"I'll take my chance on you. Fuck me, Finnigan!" And on that sultry, breathy voice, her legs tighten around my hips and with a jolt, she presses me into her, urging me to take what she so willingly offers, stunning the hell out of me.

I let go of my reservations, but my eyes threaten to roll into the back of my head at the vice-like tightness of her. As I groan at the confusing, ridiculous pleasure skirting at the edge of pain, she squeals and stills, nails digging too hard into my back as her whole body goes rigid.

"Evie..." I whisper, my mouth falling open as my mind plays through the myriad of sensations and thoughts.

What the fuck?

I knew she was tight, but this is too much. She's *too* tight.

Her eyes are wide, her breathing quick and shallow, and her mouth fallen open on a silent scream. The shock turns to confusion, then surprise.

Oh my god! My thoughts are catching up to hers.

"Evie darling, I thought... Are you still a virgin?"

CHAPTER 26
Evelyn

AM I STILL a virgin?

My mind is reeling, trying to find the answer. None comes because I don't know what the truth is anymore.

Your body knows, Evelyn.

The sharp pain that tore through me is the answer. The harsh flex of my muscles, my straining lungs, the foreign, aching fullness inside of me, they're all answers. If those aren't enough, Finnigan's gaze, growing increasingly more alarmed, is a definite tell.

"I—I didn't think so. I shouldn't be."

I worked hard to keep the faint memories and flashbacks of the two men on top of me at bay. Now, as my body adjusts to the searing burn and the thick length of Finnigan's cock sheathed deep, I question the little memories I do have.

"I presumed they raped me *here*, too," I whisper, the ache straining my voice.

He cocks one eyebrow, the alarmed expressions shifting to a darker, more possessive direction. *"Here...* too?"

"Well, Frankie B started... umm." Damn, having this conversation now, in this position, is a whole other level of awkward. "You know—*behind*."

Finnigan presses his lips together, swallowing hard. "And you don't remember them touching you... here." He's trying his best to be kind and delicate, but he's not managing to control the horror and anger marring his beautiful features. I could pay for a mirror at this moment, so I can see what look is on mine.

"The memories from after they drugged me are in pieces, so I assumed because of the pain I felt for a while after. Now I presume it was just... general area trauma?" I attempt a shrug but stop myself midway at Finnigan's pained shift in his features. I've adjusted to what happened to me, but I don't think he's processed it.

As the burning between my legs eases, the reality sinks in—*I was still a virgin.* They didn't take this away from me.

Eventually, he nods, expression still unsettled, and shifts slightly. With that simple gesture his whole body moves too, and I gasp at the brief stroke inside of me. I flex my walls too, and he frowns, but the strain in his eyebrows isn't annoyance. It's restraint. What was a burn around my entrance turned into a dull ache, but threads of pleasure are weaving themselves through.

Finnigan is my first. *I'm not completely ruined.*

"Finnigan..."

"Yes?"

"Please move."

And he does. Too fast only the tip of his cock remains inside of me, and I realize as he got there that he misunderstood me. I press my heels into his ass, keeping him from leaving me. "No. Move *inside* of me."

"But you—"

"*I* get a second chance," I interrupt. "I'm not ruined... and there's no way I'm stopping this."

"Ruined? Oh, Evie darling. You are goddamn perfect." He leans in, pressing a bruising kiss to my lips, and I'm not sure if the moan vibrating between us is mine or his.

Then he moves, sliding back inside of me until he finds home, pulling pleasure from my nerves, and I feel like my body is mine again.

"Again..." I beg on a breathy voice, and he responds with a deep rumble in his throat that's much hotter than it should really be.

The man delivers, stroking out of me until I miss the fulness of him, then pushes back in. Only, this time he doesn't wait for me to ask for more. He moves with slow, deliberate thrusts that bring a new flurry of sensations to my core. I'm losing myself in the feverish grinding, but Finnigan brings himself down to earth after each stroke, brows drawn together, as his soft gaze fixes on me. Deep emotions darken his irises, and lips tight like he's holding his breath.

"Let go..." I beg him. "I'm okay, Finnigan. Please, I need more." I wrap my hands around his neck, tugging him to me and clinging desperately until his face is buried in the crook of my neck.

The moment his breath sparks over my skin on his deep groan, and his hand tightens around my thigh, I know his concern is easing.

He settles into a quickening rhythm, driven by my mewls and rolling hips, and my core begins to burn all over again. But, my god, this is a good burn.

No.

An incredible one.

He's touching parts of me that never existed before him, and I'm catching fire with every stroke.

"Jesus Christ, Evie, you feel..." He trails off, rising on one arm braced next to me, gaze heated as it seizes mine.

Sighing, he drives harder into me, yet still holding onto a touch of restraint. I want more. I want it harder, faster, harsher. Yet, his care in these moments makes me trust him with my body more than I trust myself with it. So, I relinquish the control, following his lead, and let him take care of me.

"I feel...?" I urge him to continue.

His hips jerk, and goosebumps spread over my skin at the rush of lightning ripping through my core as a moan fills the air.

"You feel like a dream that should have never come true."

With harsh jerks of his hips, he punctuates the heart-shattering confession, his cock deliciously snug inside of me driving maddening pleasure through my nerves. His movements are more powerful, my body hitching up on the bed, and I brace myself with one hand against the padded headboard.

"Oh god, Finnigan... Yes!" I hold onto the back of his neck with my other hand, anchoring myself as his hips roll in long, hard strokes that threaten to become wilder.

But the threat only lingers, and I'm climbing this mountain of ecstasy, at an excruciatingly steady pace, the pleasure coiling in my core growing stronger.

"More," I demand, choosing to forget about relinquishing that control to him, and slam my hips up to meet his thrust. A hint of discomfort lingers, but I ignore it. I've had my share of pain, and I'm feeding on the control I have over this one. It's finally on my terms.

"You like that, Evie darling?" *Thrust*. "You like my cock filling that sweet"—thrust—"tight pussy of yours?" *Thrust*.

Damn his dirty, dirty mouth.

"I'm not sure *you* do. Do you like filling my pussy, Finnigan? Slick walls strangling your cock? Because you seem... *restrained*." I tease him, challenging his resolve.

"Jesus fuck, Evelyn!" the man growls my name like he's about to devour me whole, the brightness of his eyes smoldering with darkness, "I don't deserve you, but I'm going to keep you anyway."

And then he breaks.

Walls of restraint crumble to the edges of us and there is nothing more keeping us apart, holding us back.

He pulls back on his haunches, grabs my legs, and pins them on his shoulders, slipping his cock out of me in the process. I never thought this type of loss could make me cry out, but it does. He rewards me with a devastating smirk as he holds my legs with one arm, tight against his chest, and lifts me to slide a pillow under my ass. I'm confused, but then he slides his knees to the sides and just like that, we align perfectly. With the other hand he guides his cock back at my entrance and I bite my lip as my walls constrict, begging to be stretched.

The bastard teases me though, rubbing the smooth head up and down through my folds, and when he presses it against my sensitive clit, my back arches on a soft whimper. He picks that moment to thrust back into me, and I think I finally understand what a religious experience is, because this sure as hell feels like one. I reach up, bracing against the headboard just as this devil of a man presses his free hand on my belly. My gaze flies to him, mouth wide on a silent cry as his cock prods against a part of me that threatens to drive me up the walls.

"Finnigan..." I whisper, though it sounds more like I'm praying to him.

"I got you, Evie darling."

And boy, does he.

He glides into me with long, powerful strokes, punctuating each one with a jerk of his hips as his hand presses on my lower belly. He's molten lava inside my core, a blazing ecstasy pushing me deeper into this world where only pleasure exists. We find a maddening rhythm, the shape of him fitting so perfectly around mine, and my heart hurts that we fit together so well. That we will not experience this beautiful collision if I leave.

Those thoughts are drowned by the song of whimpers, growls, and heavy breaths we compose. We lace it with lust that grows stronger. Quicker. Louder. That song vibrates through my flesh, settling in that aching spot inside my core that Finnigan rubs against with each endearingly punishing stroke.

"I can't hold myself back, Evie. You're so—fuck! You're everything."

I cry out when his words land low in my belly, a quake shattering through my core. Even as his tone bears accusations, blame, but I'm not sure if it's for me or him. His eyes though... his eyes are an explosive blaze of need. A primal desire that demands so much more than my pleasure. It wants my soul.

You're everything...

The hunger in his words scrapes against my heart, leaving me breathless with fear.

I don't get a chance to dwell on the feeling when Finnigan's thumb bears down on the aching bundle of nerves at the apex of my folds. He circles it with such deliberate movements, adding just the right amount of pressure for my back to arch, and my legs squeeze around his head. Or neck. I may be suffocating the man, but as long as he fucks me like this through the loss of air, I'm okay with it.

"Oh, Finn—my God, Finnigan I think—" I cry out and cover my mouth with my forearm, biting down.

The roaring ecstasy doesn't come out of nowhere. It blooms deep in my belly, spreading like silk threads weaved with electric fire all through my body. It's an omen of pleasure curling my toes and locking my arched back, and that blaze detonates around his thick, rigid length with such viciousness, stars dance in my vision. The waves of euphoria roll me deeper in this trance where nothing but pleasure and Finnigan exist, his hands stroking my body, his cock jerking violently, turning into molten lava inside my own warmth, his enticing grunts of pleasure... my name on his lips like a chant for more. For everything.

This is it. The culmination of all those aching dreams that made the nightmares harder to remember.

I find my voice again, panting like a wanton whore as my shaking legs fall around him just as he drops on top of my body, caging me in under his satisfying weight. I wrap my arms around him, unwilling to let go of this moment, and hold him as close to me as I can, pushing back the need to crawl under his skin and feed my obsession for this man. He doesn't protest one bit, but peppers soft pecks on my forehead, my temples, the apples of my cheeks.

The intimacy of this moment bears promises of all we're not allowing ourselves to hope for.

It doesn't feel like a beginning, but an end. The end of what we were separately, who we were alone, and what our souls were missing.

CHAPTER 27
Finnigan

IN MY TWENTY-NINE years, I've learned a thing or two about sex. Yet, I've learned nothing about what just happened between Evie and me.

How could I? It's not something I've ever experienced before. This was not sex; this was a collision of two smoldering souls begging for each other.

It truly was *everything*.

And I'm utterly terrified.

"Thank you..."

I pull back when those soft, breathless words tickle my shoulder.

"Did you just thank me?" I bite down the chuckle that would probably ruin this moment.

I can't see the shade of her skin in this dim light, but her little nod makes me wonder if her cheeks are reddening.

"For... sex?" I ask, eyes widening in slight bewilderment.

"For not stopping."

Oh, that makes more sense. "I should have..." Sighing, I lower myself, brushing the tip of my nose against hers, before I trace down her cheeks, around the curve of her jaw, then the slope of her neck.

The satisfied, feather of a gasp she exhales threatens to get me hard all over again. Not that my cock is particularly soft right now. I'm also reluctant to pull out when I found home inside of her. God save me if I'll ever have her wrapped around me without a condom. She'll ruin me. I crave the real feel of her without the barrier, though, I should be thankful for it, because I'm sure I would have blown my load in half a minute without the latex separating us.

I shift up to meet her eyes, and she tightens her grip around me. This time around I do chuckle, and when she attempts to protest my reaction, I press my lips to her swollen ones. Her hold eases and I begin to rise again, breaking the kiss.

"No... don't leave me," she pleads, her voice throaty and low, drunk on pleasure.

"I have to take care of you."

"Leaving me defeats that purpose," she argues.

"Hell, it's hard to argue with that. But you need something else right now."

Before she can protest further, I pull out of her and rise, taking care of the condom when I get in the bathroom. I make quick work of cleaning myself, then soak a clean washcloth under the spray.

"Give me a sec." She slides out of bed on shaky legs, and disappears in the bathroom for less than a minute, before she comes back and lays back down.

"It's going to be cold," I warn Evelyn as I lower myself back onto the bed and give her a few seconds to acknowledge my words before I press the thick cotton onto her. She gasps but doesn't move.

"Alexa, bedroom lights set to soft," I order the speaker, and after she confirms, the two bedside lamps turn on to a very dim, warm light.

"Oh, you can control your lights?" There's such an innocent wonder in her tone as she looks around.

"Yes, it's a voice assistant and speaker. There, on the dresser." I point. "You can ask it all sorts of things."

"I heard of these, but never had the opportunity to try one."

I want to say something to that, but what can I? They've been around for quite a while now, but she's been living in her car or shoddy motels. Not exactly the place for what I now consider basic technology. I turn my attention to her, her swollen pussy looking fucking delectable before me. But now's not the time to feast. I wipe slowly, then fold the cloth to an unused part and press it to her, holding it there as I look up into her eyes.

I fight back a flinch when I'm met with her intense gaze. Jesus fuck, she's beautiful. In this dim light her wild hair in that deep violet looks ethereal, her lips are deliciously swollen, and now I can definitely see a flush on her cheeks.

"Do all men do this to their... umm, after sex."

She corrected herself. To their *what*? Fuck friends? Partners? Girlfriends? What exactly are we?

"I really hope so," I answer, though I feel like an asshole instantly because I haven't done this nearly as often as I should have. But then again, none of the women I've been with were virgins. *Or Evelyn.* "How does it feel?"

She nods and lies back down, making me miss the eye contact. "A bit sore, but good." She says before she lets out a soft sigh. "Really good."

Oh, Christ.

I have to work hard to remind myself that it would be wrong to sink into her again so soon. Even if I only use my tongue or my fingers. I rise and lie next to her before I can convince myself that it would be a good idea, but I make sure to hold the cloth to her.

"No pain?" I ask.

She shakes her head, turning to me, and graces me with those stunning eyes again. Even dark as they are in this dim light, they still work well to shatter my resolve.

"I'm finding it hard to keep my hands off of you right now, Evie darling."

"Then don't." She reaches down, pulls the washcloth from my hand and throws it onto the floor as she turns on her side.

She doesn't hesitate one bit when she throws her leg over my waist, her heel pressing on my ass as she wraps her body around mine. When her small hand brushes the hair from my face, and her breasts press onto my chest, I give in. I grab her ass, loving how my hand covers so much of that plump cheek, and flip onto my back bringing her on top of me.

She yelps then giggles, and I realize that's the sound I want to die hearing. That soft giggle that sounds like birdsong on a lazy autumn day is my death song, and I would slowly drown myself right now so I can hear it on a maddening loop.

Like this, straddling me, she's more sinful than my dominance could ever make her.

She tightens her legs against my hips, and her pussy finds the length of my cock at the same moment her tits brush against my chest, and she crushes her lips against mine. The tips of her bob-cut hair tickle the sides of my face, and I can't help but dig my fingers into her flesh, pushing my ass up so I can press myself against her warm, soft cunt. I drag my other hand up her back, holding her in a possessive grip as she slowly grinds against me, moaning into my mouth as she rolls her tongue around mine.

Her hands are in my hair, tugging at the curls like she's guiding me into the motions she needs me in, and with her soft body rubbing against mine, her pussy getting wetter by the second as it rolls against my cock, I realize that I've never known this type of intimacy. I've done plenty of sexual things, I've explored kinks and even experienced light play in Metamorphosis, Morrigan and Lulu's fetish club. But this feels different. Soft yet intense. Slow yet feverish, and the lack of penetration isn't tainting the moment. Quite the opposite, actually.

She strokes her tongue against mine, pulling away only so she can nip my lips before she dives back in, and my strokes on her back are turning desperate. The feel of her skin is addictive, the warmth, the goosebumps flaring when I touch her waist, it's all so intense. I grab onto the back of her neck, holding her to me as our tongues tangle and the urgency of the kiss grows.

There used to be a line separating Evelyn and I... mere days ago. Now, I can't even distinguish where I end and she begins. I don't want to. Ever again.

Evelyn Shaw is—

"Mine," I growl into her mouth, biting her lower lip before soothing it with my tongue, and dive back into the kiss.

That single word melts her body against mine, and the slickness of her pussy drenching my cock threatens to drive me down a path of madness.

Over and over, we kiss and grind against each other, falling in a beautifully brutal rhythm as we make up a song of mewls and groans. I thrust my hips up as I hold her ass down, and she cries out, throwing her head back. We'll have to do something about that loud mouth of hers when Maya returns, but for now... I want more. I thrust up again, rubbing my length between her wet folds and she meets it with a stroke of her hips, shuddering as she falls back against me. I would call it dry-humping, but there is nothing dry about the drenched seam of Evelyn's pussy.

I run my hand down the length of her spine before returning to the back of her neck, then thread my fingers in her hair, fisting it.

Evelyn yelps, terror breaking that sound as she slaps frantically at my arm and rips her body away from mine. It happens in two seconds flat and I'm too slow and stunned to catch her when she jumps off, cowering as she backs away to the foot of the bed, before she drops off of it.

"Evelyn, darling, I'm sorry I didn't mean to—" The rest of the words catch in my throat when I rise to my knees and see her sitting on the floor.

With knees drawn to her chest, her body shakes uncontrollably as she rakes her fingers through her hair in frantic, trembling motions. Her gaze is unfocused, brows drawn together, and pain weaves with fear on her features.

I drop to my knees on the floor, sliding close to her, careful to not freak her out. "It's okay. It's me, Evie darling, you know I won't hurt you."

She nods with agitated movements, like she knows it to be true, but her body and mind can't fully grasp the truth in the words. She still doesn't look at me, or stop the frenzied combing of her hair.

"You're safe. No one in this life or the next will ever touch you, will ever catch you, will ever hurt you. You belong to yourself and yourself only."

She blinks rapidly, the only indication that those words landed somewhere where she understood them.

I bring myself closer to her, in touching distance, but I don't reach for her.

"Was it the hair?" I ask.

Her movements slow, and I notice the tears brimming her eyes some already streaking down her cheeks. Fury fills me for the men who did this to her, who taught her how to fear, who showed her what pain is. But now is not the time to add to the revenge plot I've been planning for a while. They will pay in blood, and I'll surely make even The Carver himself proud.

Until then... "Can I touch your arm?"

She nods, the gesture still strained with the shuddering of her body. I reach for her upper arm, stroking slowly up and down. She's cold. Like we never even touched for the last hour.

"I'm going to come closer, and hold you to me, okay?"

She takes a few seconds longer to respond now, but then she nods again. I slide closer, but turn my back to the bed, and lean over, wrapping my arms around her. She's stiff even through the shaking but doesn't pull away. So I gather her closer and when she doesn't protest I slide my arm under her knees and lift her to my lap, holding her against my chest as I lean against the bed. With slow, soothing motions I stroke her arm and back, and as her body relaxes, her breathing sounds louder.

I don't speak for a long time because no words should force this situation. I'll be what she needs—warmth, safety, a shoulder to cry on. I'll be anything she wants me to for however long she needs me. I never had the chance the last time I could have been needed like this, when Hanna was dying on that cold concrete floor, and I was there too late. This is it, my second chance. I will not fuck this up.

Her body has softened, her shaking stops, and even her breathing has leveled. But she stays on my lap, sinking just a little deeper into me with every minute that passes.

"I'm sorry..." she whispers.

"Don't you dare apologize for this." I think my tone came through a bit too harsh.

She nods against my shoulder anyway.

"It was the hair," she confirms.

"Can I ask why?"

She breathes in deeply and swallows it before she answers. "It's how they caught me. How they held me, controlled me. It was used against me... viciously. I should have told you I have a thing for..."

"I know now, don't worry. I will never do it again."

She shifts and raises her head to meet my eyes. "Maybe someday," she whispers, sweet hope in her voice.

I smile, because how could I not. She's the strongest person I know, because surviving and moving on with life after what she experienced could break most people.

"Maybe, but only if you do it for yourself, not me. Not anyone else."

She nods, then looks down, a tinge of embarrassment curling her eyebrows.

A thought crosses my mind.

"Is this why you cut your hair?" I ask.

She nods but doesn't meet my eyes this time around. Instead, she lays her head back down on my shoulder, and settles more comfortably into me.

"I would have chopped it all off if I didn't hate short hair on me. This bob haircut felt like a good medium... even if someone caught it, it would be harder to hold it for long, since it can't be wrapped around a fist."

Heat fills my chest and uncomfortable tension pulls at my temples. What a fucked up world we live in where women have to change their bodies to protect themselves. Me and my Sanctum aren't saints, but we understand the sanctity of innocent life.

Which is another reason I shouldn't keep Evelyn. She deserves the simple, calm life, deep in the suburbs with a white picket fence, and cupcakes baking in the oven. Not this, not steeped in crime and constant weariness. We may not deal in human life, but we blackmail, we launder money, we murder. So much murder. We aren't much better, and she deserves better.

"I'm sorry you had to do this to find comfort. Safety."

"It's okay. I love it with this color. I never had the opportunity before, but now... I can finally express myself. Though, the cut was actually Maddox's idea."

Somehow, I'm not surprised it was. After all, he keeps his hair buzz cut for a reason.

"It suits you. Color and all. The clothes too. Of course, you look like a goddamn wet dream in leather trousers, but beyond that, you look like yourself."

She giggles and I swear the sound is music to my fucking ears. She's gonna be okay. I finally breathe easier, I didn't realize how tense my body actually was.

"Thank you," she says. "This has always been the style I've been attracted to. It's quite a privilege to be able to dress like this now. Someday I will have a house lathered in dark walls, maximalist corners drenched in gold frames, plants, and weird art, and a deep-emerald kitchen."

"Really? Is that your dream?"

"Well... actually my dream is to open a bakery."

I pull her away enough for her to see me properly. "That shouldn't be a dream, Evie darling, that should be a plan. You would have Queenscove at your feet with your indulgent cakes."

I catch the soft blush heating her cheeks as she averts her gaze for a moment.

"Thank you. But I'm not sure anyone would actually want my cakes. You see, sunshine and butterflies are not what I like to make."

Well, now I'm intrigued. "What do you like?"

"For lack of a better term, I'd love to own a Gothic bakery. Deep gemstone colors for frostings and icing, intricate designs, anything from lace-work to anatomical hearts and skulls. Of course they can be cute, but... a different kind of cute."

I smile, having absolutely no trouble imagining what a fantastic job she would do. I saw her cake, she might have kept it classic, but her technique looked flawless. Even for my untrained eye. "Your kind of cute," I agree.

"I guess so."

"How about we get back into bed, and you can tell me more about it?"

She beams then, her smile wide, her eyes filled with excitement. I have never seen this look in her gaze before. Like she finally has permission to think and dream for herself, though the limitation is self-imposed. It's intoxicating and infuriating at the same time. She deserves the fucking world, and she deserves to live all her dreams, not avoid conjuring them.

I pull her up with me, settle ourselves in bed, and nestle her in the crook of my arm, so she can share all her dreams with me.

CHAPTER 28
Finnigan

I WAKE UP to an empty bed and a sweet, aromatic scent weaving around through the penthouse, pulling a groan out of me and a growl from my stomach.

I wonder what she baked now.

We stayed up too late as we talked about her bakery dream with a dark, gothic twist, her ideas for the interior, the designs she's been conjuring for years, the flavor combinations that intrigued even me. I was bound to wake up hungry. Though I never crave particular foods, yet now I *need* whatever's cooking in my kitchen.

Rising, I head straight to the walk-in closet to grab a pair of boxers, and stumble around as I slide them up on my way to the kitchen. The scent makes my mouth water, but as Evelyn finally comes into view, it seems to turn bone dry. She's on her bare tiptoes as she sways between the counter and the island on a rock song set on low volume, long, lean legs in full view, and I swallow a curse when my gaze is interrupted by the hem of a long T-shirt that covers her ass and everything above. She used to be concernedly skinny when we brought her to us, but now... there's some meat on her bones, and thanks to Maddox's help, some muscle too. She's still skinny, but Christ, health has never looked so good on a woman.

She glides around my kitchen on the rhythm of the hard guitar strings and the flow of the wind-swept curtains of the open terrace doors, and she looks divinely at home as she pours some dark batter in a baking tin I didn't know I had. George buys all sorts of things when he does his chef duties in my kitchen. Maybe I should actually search these cupboards to see what else I have. *What else Evelyn needs, too.*

I lean against the door frame, crossing my arms against my chest, and watch her. Slender, long fingers wipe the rim of the bowl as she moves further down the tray, and I suck in a groan as she sticks that very finger in her mouth, sucking slowly at it while she keeps pouring that batter. It's not a stretch to imagine something else between those pretty pink lips of hers. She can cover my cock in whatever she wants as long as she sucks on it just like that.

Seemingly satisfied, she grabs the tray and taps it a few times against the counter, before she turns to the oven, drops the door and slides it right in. She doesn't even notice me when she turns after closing the door, taps something on her phone, then goes back to the counter, picking up the same bowl. When she dips in again and swipes at the sides, I suck in a breath, because I know what's about to come. That finger slides between her plump lips, but this time she closes her eyes and the softest of sighs turns my cock so rigid, it almost fucking hurts.

Raking a hand over my face I wonder how long until this woman's going to kill me just by being her own, enticing little self. When she's about to suck on that batter-coated finger again, some of it drips on her chest, staining the T-shirt.

Wait, that's my T-shirt.

Just like that, she turned even hotter, if that was even a possibility.

"Oh no!" She drops the bowl and turns frantically to the sink. "Evelyn, what have you done? You klutz!" She rants at herself as she finds the sponge and attempts to clean it.

I'm behind her in fewer strides than I thought I needed, and when I grab onto the hem of the T-shirt, she jumps, yelping, but I give her no time to protest or fight. I pull it up, forcing it over her head, leaving her arms trapped in it, then I turn her around to face me, grabbing onto the sides of her head.

"Finnigan," she says on a breathy tone that sounds more lustful than startled. "I'm sorry, I—"

But my mouth is crushing hers before she can finish the sentence, her intoxicating ginger and brown sugar scent luring me to dive between her soft lips. I'm careful not to thread my fingers through her hair as I tip her head back, holding her just where I want her, deepening the kiss. A rumble of desire shakes my chest and vibrates straight through hers, drawing a soft cry to fall from her lips, and I swallow those muffled sound-waves like they're the life-force keeping me alive. They might as well do, because the life I used to live before her is done and dusted. Even before I felt her against me, tasted her, swallowed her moans, she tainted my existence with her energy.

There is no going back for me, I'm falling deep into her, and I fear that, once again, I'll be abandoned with a heart I can't put back together myself.

I shake those thoughts away because ignorance truly is bliss, and I release Evelyn so I can pull the T-shirt off of her completely, and bare her naked body to me. Reaching behind her, I turn the tap off, then dip down, and lift her to me. She yelps, but it turns into a giggle as she wraps her legs around my hips, and I walk us to the kitchen island. When her bare behind touches the cold granite, she hisses, I lock my lips onto the crook of her neck, sucking softly at the skin there, and it melts into a feverish cry. Her head falls back, arms settling behind her as she props herself up, and I lick my way down to her breasts, circling one nipple with my tongue, and rewarding it with a soft bite when it hardens to a peak.

Back arching, she pushes her breast against my mouth demanding more attention, and I move to the other one, refusing to leave it waiting for too long. When she moans and sinks her fingers into my hair, all but forcing me where she wants me, I know I'm going to have my hands full. Evelyn might have been a virgin last night, but the way she demands pleasure without speaking a word tells me that she's a greedy little slut in the making, one who has far too many unfulfilled desires that have been piling on for long enough.

But this is my feast, not hers, and I decide what I devour.

A clinking noise sounds as she shifts, and I break away from her enticing skin as it dawns on me that I didn't make sure there aren't any knives sitting on the counter. All I find is a spoon sitting next to a great big bowl. A different one than the one she was licking earlier. Curious, I take a peek.

"Is this icing?"

"Frosting," she corrects on a strained whisper.

"There's a difference?"

She nods, raising an eyebrow as one corner of her lips quirks, her chest rising and falling with heaving breaths, her cheeks deliciously flushed. After the discussion we had last night, I'm intrigued. I swipe my pinkie through the soft, creamy *frosting*, and dip it in my mouth. The dark purple color that matches her hair so well made me think it was going to be sickly sweet, but there's a delicious sourness to it, and I'm compelled to hum in approval. Evelyn's brows furrow with a wanton gaze as she bites into her lower lip.

"What gets you off, Evie darling? Is it me sucking on my finger, or the fact that I'm moaning at the taste of your frosting."

Her brows straighten, as if she only just realized she was lusting over me.

"Come on, don't be shy," I insist.

"Maybe both."

"Maybe? Let's test and find out."

Her doe eyes widen and lips part, but she stays silent. Waiting curiously.

I dip my index finger in the bowl, and suck on it again, this time slower, my eyes fixed on the not-so-innocent-anymore vixen before me. She watches every movement with hawk eyes, and I'm oddly turned on. Not because I'm sucking on my own fucking finger, but because she looks at me like that. Like she could devour me whole, just as I would her. And isn't that just goddamn beautiful?

Returning to the bowl, I pick up more frosting this time, and I go for my mouth slowly, watching how her lips part with the same speed. Only, this time around I drop the cream, letting it fall right on her belly, just above the navel. She gasps and reaches for it, but just as it touches the sweetness, I grab her hand and bring it to my mouth. I lick her finger clean before I place her palm back behind her, then dip down, swiping my tongue over her skin, licking her clean. A soft mewl flexes her belly, and I realize this taste is becoming addictive. Mostly because it pulls those needy sounds out of her.

I grab more frosting, and smear it in a clean line from her navel to the trimmed curls between her legs. Goosebumps spread all over her flesh as she quivers, and there's something addictively beautiful about that. A sort of innocence bread from discovery and I'm going to enjoy helping her find out what makes her wet. I bet she's getting real wet right now. Just as beautiful is the contrast of this dark, violet frosting against her light olive skin. Then again, Evelyn makes everything look beautiful.

When my tongue touches her skin once more, she blatantly moans, her head dropping back as I lick the cream off of her belly, sucking the sensitive flesh.

"I want more." I groan just as I grip her waist, bring her down to her feet, and turn her around, her back to my front.

She doesn't get a chance to lean into me as I press my hand to the middle of her back and bend her over the kitchen island. With a yelp she tries to protest, but I hold her down with one hand and bring the bowl of frosting closer with the other.

"Be a good girl, Evelyn"—I give her right cheek a quick smack, grinning when she yips in shock—"and I might just make you come."

"But I—"

Her protest earns her another slap on the other cheek, and this time her little cry sounds charged. It's not pain twisting on the notes, but something much more carnal. I kick her feet apart, and take half a step back to admire the woman I claimed as mine.

"Fuck me, you have such a pretty cunt." I shake my head, because it should be a crime for that dark-pink slit to look so unbelievably tempting.

Dipping two fingers in the frosting bowl, I scoop a fair amount of it, and she twitches when the cream touches the hood of her clit. When I drag those digits up the seam of her pussy and don't stop when I reach its end, she whips her head around, eyes locking onto mine. I say nothing as I grab the spoon and scoop up more of that cream, holding eye contact with her as I continue spreading it, brushing it over that tight, puckered hole, then up to the top of her ass.

She follows me with her gaze as I dip on one knee, and when I wrap my hands around the tops of her thighs, pulling them apart to better expose her to me, her muscles tense. But then I swipe my tongue over her now even sweeter clit, sucking at that nerve center with newfound fever. Evelyn's head falls against the countertop on a deep sigh, and I lick her slowly, from that sensitive bundle of nerves, through the seam of her delectable pussy, reveling in her shudder and slight yelp as I pass over the tight hole beyond it, and up to the top of her ass.

"This feels... dirty," she says in a throaty voice.

"And yet look how beautifully your flesh trembles when my tongue worships you." Pressing my mouth against her folds, I suck at the sweetness lathered there as she yelps at the contact. "How perfect this frosting looks against your soft skin." I drag my tongue over her ass, insisting on the tight muscle that contracts at the contact. "How responsive even the dirtiest parts of you are to me." I lick between her cheeks, sucking and cleaning every single part of her covered in that tangy sweetness. "I think you like *dirty*. Don't you, Evie darling?"

A soft whimper escapes her throat when I bring my mouth back to her needy clit, rolling the bundle between my tongue and lips as her legs shake ever so gently. I part her with my thumbs, exposing the pink, wet flesh to me and hold her like that for a moment longer, enjoying the magnificent view of her opening gripping on nothing but air. Blowing over the sensitive flesh, I pull a soft groan out of her, but it turns feral when I dive my tongue inside that delicious pussy I made mine mere hours ago. It's only ever been mine, and that thought fills me with a possessiveness I never thought I could feel. I roll my tongue against her walls, fucking her like I'm starving for her essence, and I know just how dirty my sweet Evelyn is when she thrusts into my face, taking what she deserves.

"Oh, Finnigan!"

I want to encourage her, tell her to take everything she needs from me, but she's settling into a rhythm I don't want to disrupt. Not until she comes all over my tongue and face.

So I release one cheek as I keep thrusting into her needy pussy, and bring my other hand to the sensitive bundle of nerves that must be missing the attention. The moment I press the tips of two digits on the hood of it, she cries out and bears down onto my face, rubbing herself against me.

"That's it! Oh my god, Finn, oh my god! I'm going—I'm going to—" But all that comes out next is a lust-tainted scream as her legs shudder, and she gushes her sweet flavor all over my tongue and chin.

She's not exactly a squirter, but feeling how unbelievably wet she gets, I think I could get her there. I hold her up as wave after intense wave of pleasure rolls through her nerves, her pussy spasming around my tongue, and I realize that somehow... I'm still hungry.

I want more.

I *need* more of her.

Something about Evelyn Shaw draws forth addiction.

And I realize that I'll happily turn into a junkie for her.

Evelyn

MY LEGS ARE still shaking by the time Finnigan rises, and when I attempt to peel myself off the kitchen island, he has to catch me, because apparently I can't stand anymore. I can't believe he spread frosting between my ass cheeks and licked me clean. The thought brings a fresh wave of heat to my cheeks.

"That was definitely in violation of some health codes." I snicker as I turn to him.

He laughs in response, filling the space with such casual joy, and Christ, I don't think I've ever seen anything as beautiful. His smile is devastating, but laughter turns this man into a god.

"We'll be more careful when we'll be in your bakery," he says with a wide grin on his lips, and pulls me into a deep kiss like what he just said didn't just shake my entire world and threw it off its axis.

Not only did he imply a future between us two, but my bakery dream isn't an *if* for him, but a *when*. Yes, I opened up to him last night and talked about my dreams, and yes, he did insist on me not calling it a *dream* any longer, but I don't know... I guess I just thought he was indulging me after my panic attack. Or because we just had sex.

But his casual words now don't sound like he was simply indulging me.

I really want to say something, but I'm just going to ruin this amazing bubble we're in right now. I'm not ready to screw it up just yet.

"Now," he starts as he breaks the kiss. "Are you going to tell me why you're baking at this crazy time?"

"It's almost ten a.m.," I say, snickering.

"Is it?! Shit, I don't remember the last time I slept in." He looks around the kitchen, noticing the finished batch of cupcakes cooling on the side. "I hope one of those is mine."

"Yes. They're for all of us. Annika texted me this morning to tell me that they've decided to celebrate Aaro's birthday early, since everyone is here. Plus it would be a nice distraction before the craziness starts. I'm baking these to take over there because the little guy apparently doesn't want cake, he wants cupcakes."

"Oh, so we're doing this today?" he asks.

I nod. "Around lunchtime or just after. Either way, we're supposed to go there for lunch."

"I guess we need to buy a present."

"We?" This time I don't hold back, because there he goes again, using a word that implies so much more about *us*.

"Yes. I'll happily buy something from the three of us. Though, you better ask Maya what she would like to get for her little *boyfriend*."

"Excuse me?!" I squeal, grabbing onto his strong biceps and hold him at arm's length. "My sister does not have a boyfriend. She's just a kid!"

But the pretty, blonde asshole just laughs, shaking his head like I'm being silly.

"I'm serious!" I slap at his shoulder.

"Oh, fuck. Evie darling, come on..."

I give him the most menacing look I can muster in this situation, but he just curls his lips inwards, suppressing more of his amusement.

"You can decide for us two. But Aaro is *not* her boyfriend," I say once more. Though, I must admit, even I don't believe it. Doesn't mean I have to like it.

"Okay. I'll send someone to get the gifts." He pulls out his phone and starts typing.

"We're not going?"

"There's no need. I'll send someone now, and by the time we're ready, they'll bring them to us," he explains.

"But I could go buy the presents myself."

"Out of discussion." He protests before I even finish the sentence. "You know very well you're a target now. Until Bartiste and his organization are crushed, we cannot risk you being out of our sight. I know it sucks, but you have to bear it for a little longer."

I really do want to argue, but this is a stupid hill to die on and he has a point—there's a target on me. Even so, I don't trust Frankie not to follow and *claim* me for himself like apparently, he wishes to do. A shudder rips through me and Finn's expression darkens in response.

"They won't get to you, Evelyn. They will all be dead soon enough, and I'll make sure it's not going to be pretty." He grips my chin between his thumb and forefinger and brings me in for a peck that's much sweeter than it should be from a man of his reputation.

He's a playboy, what is he doing making these kinds of promises to a formerly homeless woman?

"You're so unbothered by talks of gruesome murder." Of course I had nothing smarter to say, Jesus Christ.

Though, I don't seem to be that bothered about it either. I shouldn't be that surprised that my moral compass is so off center. Not after what I've done.

His fingers on my chin tighten, pulling me away from that dark memory.

"You want me to pretend you're some naive bimbo who doesn't understand the world she found herself in? You know what we are, Evelyn, what we do, but I'll sugarcoat it for you in the future if it will make you feel better. However, it doesn't change the fact that for what they've done to you, Bartiste and Frankie will pay in pounds of flesh, and I'll make sure their deaths are slow, excruciating."

CHAPTER 29
Evelyn

AM I REALLY that different from the *bimbos* he's usually with? After all, I lusted for him, wore him down until he slept with me. Surely I don't stand out in that sea of faceless, nameless women.

Yet here I am, listening to his violent words and promises of death like the man is making some sweet, grand gesture I should be swooning over. Who am I kidding? I am swooning over them.

"They've done so much more to so many others. Why take revenge for me?" I blurt out without thinking as he releases my chin.

He frowns, cocking his head. "Because it's you here, standing in my kitchen after sleeping in my bed. It's your taste on my tongue, it's the memory of my cock in your pretty pussy."

"There were countless others before me. Here. In this kitchen."

His hand is on my throat in a flash, the tips of his fingers reaching the back of my neck, he uses his thumb to tilt my head up so I can meet his eyes. The touch is gentle, but so possessive.

"The women who have crossed this threshold, in the last few years, haven't stayed past a few hours. Most have never seen this kitchen. None have slept here. You, Evie darling, are the one and only."

He lets those words linger in the air, their soundless echo licking my skin and penetrating my soul with devastating effect.

The one and only...

I want to ask him why. Demand an explanation. Beg him to make sense of this, because... *why?* Why, damn it? Tension builds between my brows, threatening to turn into a headache. Maybe that pain can make sense of this man, because he's certainly not explaining himself. I don't care why other women haven't been here, I want to know why I am.

But, how can I ask him such a question when the answer might influence my decision about Queenscove and my future? I cannot base my decision on this man.

Asking him about it could break us both.

That question, though, lingers on the tip of my tongue and makes my lips tremble. Finnigan notices, too. He waits. And waits, watching my parted lips with a soft frown between his dark blonde brows. But those bright blue eyes of his carry so much danger, because I swear there's a tinge of hope sparkling in their depths.

"Ask me."

I gasp at his words, but don't speak.

I can't.

"Ask me, Evelyn," he demands, tone darker.

I press my lips together instead, attempting to shake my head, but his grip allows only slight movement.

Finnigan sighs and drops his hand. "Remember when you accused me of being a coward?"

"It's not the same," I snap back.

"Isn't it?"

"This is not just about me."

"*You* came after me, Evelyn. *You* insisted even as I kept repeating that crossing this line is a mistake. *You* pushed. What the fuck did you think would happen once we got here?"

"I..." I don't know.

Maybe I didn't think this far. Because I had it in my mind that Finnigan was different. The perpetual playboy who doesn't get attached.

You lie, Evelyn.

Maybe I thought that at first, but it's not what kept me here, still interested. It was hope that he was the exact opposite of that beneath his charmingly slutty exterior.

"*You* what? Was this all just a game to you?" he asks with both anger and a tinge of disappointment in his tone, and the sound cracks a part of me, making me feel like a terrible person.

"No, it wasn't a game." There's little confidence in my voice.

"Then? What did you expect to find once we came together? What do you want from me, Evelyn? And don't you dare tell me you just wanted to fuck me, because I refuse to believe *you* are the type."

"Maybe you overestimated me," I fight back because there is no way I can get into this now.

I have no answer for him. There is one, weighing my soul deep down, but I can't even acknowledge it for myself.

"Maybe I did."

His words crash down on me, and I swallow the bitter emotions they bring, but I can't hide away from the impact. It's right here, staring at me with sharp eyes, challenging me, and what scares me more is the trace of desire to retreat that gazes back. I'm doing this, I'm responsible for pulling him out of his shell, just to push him back down again.

But this is not all on me. It can't be. He wanted me gone not that long ago, so I'm just giving him what he wanted.

"Staying in Queenscove was never a permanent arrangement, I just needed time.

You know this. After all, you wanted to *help me* leave." There's a clear bite in my tone. It wasn't help he was offering—he was paying me off.

Finnigan narrows his brows, crossing his arms against his chest, and takes a step back. "So that's it then? You decided?"

I stand by the kitchen island, suppressing the need to wrap my arms around myself. "Not yet. There are still things I need to sort first."

"Well, hopefully you'll decide to share with me when you make a fucking decision."

"Why are you acting like you tell me everything, and I'm the bad one who hides stuff from you, Finnigan?"

"What's that supposed to mean?"

"I know I can't be the only one who spent the night. I know that the revenge on Bartiste is not just about what they've done to me! Annika's *friend,* right? That's all she was..." Though I'm sure of the words, they don't taste as good as I thought they would when I speak them. Now, they feel like a low blow.

His arms drop to the sides, his gaze filling with something akin to dismay.

"Since then, Evelyn. Since then there has been no one else. And even then..." He trails off, but those words turn my stomach into a flutter of wings.

"Even then... what?" I ask in a whisper.

He shakes his head and looks away, sighing. "I'm gonna go dress. Be ready in forty minutes." And just like that, he turns to leave.

"No!" I snap back loud enough that his steps stall.

One by one the thick muscles of his back flex and seem to expand, his stance menacingly stern and somehow wider. I urge myself to continue, because if I don't speak now, I might not be able to once he turns around.

"Maybe I've been insisting exactly because of this! I know you want me, I know you like me. You've constantly pushed me away for no rational reason!" That came out much louder than I thought it would, but damn it, I'm pissed.

"Morality, Evelyn!" he shouts as he whips around, drawing his fingers through his hair, his gaze a stormy inner-battle. "You were—*are* too young, and I still have some fucking morals, you know!"

"Don't give me that self-righteous crap again. I thought we passed it. No matter my age, I am the same person I was a month ago, or three, or bloody six. The same one who had to grow up two years ago and learn to both survive and raise a child. Do not dare insult my maturity again, or my ability to make a decision about a man, or my body for that matter." Taking in a deep inhale, I continue, "There's more to your push-back and you know it! Stop blaming it on our age difference."

"Goddamn it, Evelyn, stop it! You don't know anything."

"I know about *her.*"

"You know nothing about Hanna. Nothing!" with clenched fists to the point his knuckles turn white, he storms off, out onto the terrace.

"Then tell me!" I follow him into the humid day, the sun far too cheerful for this conversation.

"What do you want from me? Are you so desperate for me to admit what a fuck up I am? What an utter failure?" The rage in his voice splinters and the pain in it scares me just a little.

"Finn, you're not—"

"But I am! You don't understand." He whips around and startles me when his broken gaze finds mine. "She's dead because of me!"

No, that can't be right.

Annika already told me he's blaming himself for Hanna's death, but this is much more than that.

"That doesn't sound right—"

"No, no, Evie darling, it sounds perfectly right. Because it's true. You wanted to hear it all, so here it fucking is! If my stupid, naive, young ass wouldn't have become infatuated with the older, enticing woman, she would have been far, far away, on the same island my brother and Annika live on. Alive and well even today. She fucking stayed because of me! Bartiste found her here in Queenscove because of me! When he did, I wanted to keep the girls with us, to keep them safe and in our sights, but I let myself be convinced by everyone, including them, that we should separate. Some bullshit about the girls not being a distraction while we went for Bartiste. God, what a fucking stupid mistake that was." He's pacing now, raking his fingers through his hair, his features marred with too much self-hate. "Bartiste was smarter than us back then, he got one of our guys, and found out exactly where the girls were. I had to sit, Evelyn, sit in the back of a car and listen to Hanna's voice pleading with me to get to her in time, unable to do anything about it, as men pounded on her door to get to her. I could hear every single tear fall as shots were fired into that room, and with each word she spoke, I sat there listening to the slithers of hope leaving her. She was strong, but even she couldn't hide the fear from her voice. And I listened to it all."

He stops pacing, gripping the railing and bracing himself as he looks toward the rumbling sea. My heart is caught in my throat, heat simmering behind my eyes as I wrap my arms around my middle.

"I failed," he continues. "Her, myself, Annika... We got there too late. They were gone, and all that was left was a sea of bodies who died because of the same failure. I should have been the one there, protecting her, not our men. So many souls ripped out of this world because I didn't stand firm in front of Hanna, Annika... my brother. By the time we found them, when Bartiste was done with Hanna... she was an empty, bloody shell. They didn't just break her, they fucking decimated her. So much damage, so much blood, cuts and burns... Bartiste used her to punish Annika. Made her watch her best friend get raped and broken, because he was creative in his torture. He knew emotional pain, guilt, can inflict just as much damage. Annika said she begged and begged to take her instead, even as she was pregnant... I can't imagine being restrained and forced to watch a loved one like that."

Finnigan takes a deep staggering breath, as silent tears slide over my cheeks, adding to the ones that have been flowing since he said his men died because of him too.

"She took her last breath seconds before I found them," he continues. "I didn't even get to say I'm sorry. All I could do was carry her empty body out of there."

So much blame... so much sorrow... he can't see past his guilt, and my tears aren't for Hanna, but for him. He didn't fail, he tried so hard, but—

"You couldn't control everything that happened, Finnigan." My voice is soft as I step toward him. "We blame ourselves for things out of our reach, but there are too many battles to fight, and we can't take them all on. She didn't die because of your decision, because you didn't protect her. She died because of a bastard with no soul."

I stop when he shakes his head.

"That's not even my only shame." He takes a deep inhale and breathes it out like fire, "I don't remember what she looks like anymore."

His hands flex around the railing, the confession heavy. He pauses for a long time, but I don't dare interrupt his process.

"I couldn't bear to look at any photos of her, of us, in the last few years. I thought what I did, or failed to do, would keep her imprinted in my mind, but it didn't. The color of her eyes, her general shape, those are still there, but there are no details... only a blur and shadows. She wasn't the love of my life, but I couldn't even give her the courtesy of my memories. How fucked up is that?"

His head drops and I just want to scream. This is exactly what happens when you refuse to talk about how you feel. You hold onto guilt, pain, and turn it into something so deeply ugly.

"Finn... I'm forgetting too."

His shoulders stiffen, head straightening.

"I have nothing of my mother. No photos, no videos, there's nothing left. It's only been two years and yet... I already forgot the shape of her nose, the sweep of her brows. You've kept it all in, and there was no one here to tell you that what you feel, as valid as it is, is normal. Your guilt..." I shake my head, pushing back the rest of the tears. "Your guilt can be healed."

I don't miss the slight sag in his shoulders now. Did I take a weight off of them with my own guilt? Memories are fickle... and they're just another one of those things out of our control.

He looks over his shoulder for a brief moment, the sunshine behind him turning him into a tragic god with his features marred with sorrow. "If I couldn't protect her, how can I protect you? How can I keep you safe if I couldn't before?"

Oh God, this is what he was afraid of?

I'm rushing to him, even if I wasn't that far, and throw my arms around his waist, clutching him tight.

"You are! You're doing so much. You're enough!" I whisper into his bare back I'm staining with my teary cheeks.

Only when he tries to turn do I loosen my grip, and he wraps me in his arms, pressing his lips to the top of my head. "I'll never be enough."

There's so much trauma carried in this salty breeze, too much pain, and unfathomable guilt.

Denying ourselves is only adding to it all.

CHAPTER 30
Evelyn

FINNIGAN'S CONFESSION CLEARED some of the air, but revealing something like that about yourself, by force too, deals damage. We shared a shower in silence as we processed the heavy words. We dressed in silence, stealing stray touches as we passed each other. I put my makeup on in silence as he dealt with the gifts that were bought for us. And now we've been driving to Vincent's in silence. It allowed me to think, maybe too much. He may be the playboy, but I'm the one playing him and I can't believe I didn't see it until now.

Maybe just as worse is that I'm playing myself too. I want this man. As much as I want a good job, a nice house, a better life for my sister and me. I want him there... to share it all with me. A pipe dream. And I can't believe how stupid I was to pursue this without thinking of consequences, without making a decision about our lives first. I've never been selfish, never done anything just for myself, and this was a really, really stupid place to start.

But as I turn slightly, catching sight of the sharp line of his jaw, those almost boyish messy curls brushing against his ear, tense, full lips, and strong hands gripping the steering wheel and gear stick, I can't help but stare. He is... mouthwatering. I know that beneath the cream shirt open at the collar is a strong, wide chest with the finest dusting of blonde hair, taut abs, and arms that beg for my nails to sink into them when he drives into me. But Finnigan Hennessey is so much more than that—he's the man who always takes the time to talk to my sister, who takes care of us, checks on us, he's the man who came after me when he knew my veins itched for poison, who took us in his home crowded with all the books he reads with fervent passion. He's more than I ever gave him credit for.

And he's pissed at me. Not because of the confession I pried out of him, but because he had to share it with someone who might be leaving him.

"Can I ask you something?" Maybe I am wielding that knife after all.

His hand twitches on the gear stick. "Go on."

"Where are your parents? You've only ever mentioned them once."

He frowns and looks at me as if to check that he heard me right, before he turns his attention back on the road.

"I told you before, on their yacht somewhere."

"And you don't care where?"

He sighs. "My parents are... interesting characters. They owned half of Queenscove, if not more, in real estate and other ventures. One day, about ten years ago, they decided they've done enough, sold off most of their businesses, transferred a few to my brother and I, and left to travel."

"And just left you?" I blurt out without thinking.

Finnigan snorts and shakes his head. "My parents did many things without us throughout our lives. Ronan says they love us in their own way, but even he was surprised when they voluntarily showed up at his wedding." He sighs yet again and continues. "Our parents didn't raise us. They provided for us, yes. We had everything we needed and more, we were given anything we wanted if we asked for it, we went to great schools, and had any opportunity, but it wasn't them who raised us. Even if we went on a holiday, it wasn't them who spent time with us outside of meals at restaurants."

I'm not sure how to take this. His upbringing was deeply different from mine. It wasn't great, but it wasn't bad either.

"I know, it sounds a lot like *poor little rich kid*, but it's not money a kid wants, you know?" he says. "We want lo—memories. Memories with our parents, our family. Our grandparents were gone early, our only uncle lived far away, it was just us. Only, it was actually just me, Ronan, babysitters, and housekeepers."

"I'm sorry..." I can't imagine feeling so unloved. My heart breaks for the little boy who just wanted to spend time with his parents.

"I'm not sharing all this for you to feel sorry for me."

"I didn't mean—"

"You didn't, but you still feel sorry for me. Don't. I'm a grown man, Evelyn. I'm over it. I've been over it for a very long time. Long story short, I have no idea where they are. Last month they were somewhere off the West coast. From time to time they return to their house here, check in, spend a few weeks, then leave again."

"Do you miss them?" I know the answer before I finish asking the question.

"No."

My heart squeezes at the nonchalance of that word that should be loaded. He doesn't even speak it in a cold manner, it's just... blatant. I find it hard to imagine what that feels like when I miss my mother so much. My father even more, knowing he's alive, but not... fully there. I yearn for their touch, their hugs, their sweet kisses. Most of all, I miss their laughter. They were amazing separate, but together they were incredible. I can't imagine how Finnigan would have turned out if he had parents like mine. Would his life be different? Would he still be involved in this *business?*

"Do they know about The Sanctum?" Curiosity gets the better of me.

Once again he turns to me, frowning. "They're on a need to know basis," he answers anyway.

"What does that even mean?"

"My parents are businesspeople who built an incredible fortune and managed to retire before they turned forty-five. Not many people manage that by being upstanding citizens. Most of their business ventures were clean, but some... some were just as stained as what I do is. They aren't even the only ones in Queenscove like that. They're just the ones who rose the highest at that time. I'm sure Morrigan told you about her parents? But yes, they've heard enough about The Sanctum."

I'm still reeling in from the information, and it takes me a minute to answer his question.

"Umm... briefly, I guess. I don't think it's necessarily something she likes talking about much."

"Yeah." He scoffs. "The way it ended might not be the type of story you share over brunch."

"What do you mean? How did it end?"

He glances at me, the narrowing eyebrows spelling concern more than annoyance.

"Let's just say... badly for her parents and ex-fiancée, but great for her."

"Why do I feel like you're sparing me from some gruesome details?"

"Because I am. Evelyn, I'm still unsure how much to share with you. How deep you want to be in this world of ours. Especially when you say you don't know if you want to stay. You know so much already."

"So what, you're going to *off me* if I leave and I know too much?" I scowl as I spit those words at him, a bit too much disdain in my voice covering a tinge of fear.

But the man laughs. A sinful rumble that shakes that strong chest of his, messy curls bouncing against his cheek making me want to sink my fingers between them.

"No, Evie darling. Because I don't want you to end up in trouble because you know too much. What you have seen so far scratches the surface. But we deal with threats to our power and people who think they can swoop in and take it from us, constantly. We are masters of blackmail, but there are many who try it on us too. We're trained to deal with this. Our people are trained too. But you, sugar, you're not. And the last thing I intend to do is share too much, get you in too deep, just for you to run away from me and for someone to catch you and hurt you for what you know."

Well, when he puts it that way. My chest relaxes, and I didn't realize how tense the subject made me until the breath left me with a heavy exhale.

"I'm not *running* away, Finn." Though, I'm not sure I believe my words.

In the last few days I've felt like the only way to leave this place, if I do make a decision to do so, is by running away. Not out of fear for them. I'm scared of myself, of allowing the time for goodbyes that I know will threaten to change my mind about the decision. Because deep down I know leaving will be the last thing I'll truly want to do.

"Are you not?" he whispers, but I'm not sure he intended for me to hear him, his head turned to his side window.

I bite my tongue, because I started this conversation in an attempt to smooth things over after upsetting him with the exact same topic.

"I'm sorry for assuming. Thank you for thinking of my safety, I guess."

"It's all I've been thinking about lately." This time he intended for me to hear his whisper, and it brings a heated flush to my cheeks.

"Thank you." I bite my bottom lip and that's the moment he chooses to look at me again, his attention fixed right there.

"What else do you enjoy doing? Besides reading?" I attempt to distract him further.

"What's with all the questions, Evelyn?"

"Well... you've learned so much about me, but I know almost nothing of you."

He sighs again, but it doesn't feel heavy anymore. "Swimming. Not in a pool, but out in the ocean. It helps me clear my head. I like the extremes... the early morning cool water, and the late at night warmth."

Figures. He has a swimmer's body.

"I never heard you mention going swimming." My tone is dreamy, distracted, my imagination filling with strong naked shoulders... the wide expanse of his chest, all wet.

"I haven't done it as often as I wanted to. I've had other... *things* keeping me busy."

"Things... right."

I imagine him looking like a god as he walks out of the sea, ripped lean muscles all over his arms and powerful, long legs, dripping wet. *So, so wet.* And that's not the only thing long about him. I shake my head, squeezing my thighs together at the mental image.

"Are you okay?" he asks.

We've stopped at some traffic lights and he's watching me, but I've lost myself in the image of him naked. His gaze travels down my body, to my joined thighs still tightly pressed together.

"Yes. Sorry, I was just—"

"Imagining me swimming?" he interrupts and heat flares over my cheeks.

"No, of course not! I was just thinking..."

"Thinking. Right." a devastating dimple appears in his right cheek and my god, I want to lean over and kiss it. No, I want to lick it. All of him. Top to bottom.

Jesus Christ, Evelyn!

This is why I'm in this situation. This didn't happen because of my selfishness, but my damn hormones. I let them take over, and now I'm worried his leather seat is going to have a damp spot on it. I always seem to worry about that. I have a problem.

"What else do you think about, Evie darling?"

My gaze whips to him, the change of tone, filled with innuendos, hitting a nerve deep in my core.

"What do you mean?" my voice staggers.

"When it comes to me, what crosses that dirty little mind of yours?"

"What makes you think it's dirty?" I ask, half confused, half intrigued.

He sighs, chewing on his lip for a moment, then wraps his large hand around my thigh, as he starts driving again. The gesture startles me, but I'm sinking into the warmth either way.

"I have a confession to make." He glances over for a second, before turning his gaze on the road, and continues when I don't say anything. "I overheard—purely accidentally—a conversation you were having with Morrigan."

"Umm... what conversation?"

"At Vin's house. I was going to the bathroom and the window on the corridor was open. You were somewhere on the other side of it." He says, squeezing my thigh, the gesture both reassuring and sensual.

"Okay..." This isn't helping.

"You were confessing your fantasy about... control. Or the loss of. Being taken..."

My jaw drops, eyes widening as I attempt to turn in my seat to look at him, gripping the sides. "Oh my god! Finnigan!"

When the ball drops, I'm both mortified and furious, my nails digging into the leather of the seats, and an ache takes root in my temples. I was talking about my dubious consent fantasies.

"How much did you hear?"

"Enough..." He chews on his bottom lip again, turning his gaze on me.

I hate that my core is responding to the roguish look in his eyes, though my heart does too.

"You stayed through it all, didn't you?" I say in disbelief. "You bastard! That was a private conversation!"

"It was and I am sorry. I walked past just as you said something that caught my attention and... I couldn't help myself."

"Oh my god, I can't believe you—"

"I know, it was wrong of me. I honestly admit it. I admitted it then too. Though..."

"What?!" I snap at him.

"I did learn something."

"What, that I have fantasies about being manhandled?!" I can't believe I just said that.

Finnigan smirks, turning to me with a mischievous grin on his beautiful lips. "That too, and I found that information very useful, as you remember."

Images flash through my mind of Finnigan moving through the shadows the first time he *touched* me, and it's probably the hottest thing that has and will ever have happened to me.

"But that's not what I was referring to," he continues. "I learned something valuable about how you feel, or felt, about how you view yourself, and what you struggle with. It didn't help much then, but now that the line is well and truly crossed, I will do anything in my power to make you feel... *right.*"

I remember the words I spoke to Morrigan that day. How I felt wrong for wanting to be in a non-consensual situation considering what I went through. That feeling hasn't left me.

"And what if I don't want you to?" I ask.

This time he doesn't turn, but the hand wrapped around my thigh slides up, reaching the warm place between my thighs. The skirt isn't quite in the way, but I still curse it as he cups me beneath it. As he applies more pressure, I realize the thin cotton of my panties is giving away the effect he has on me.

"Finnigan..." In my mind his name was meant as a protest, but as I grip the sides of the seat, a breath caught in my chest, it came out as nothing more than a desperate, whispered mewl.

"Your body says otherwise, Evie darling."

He drives casually through the outskirts of Queenscove toward Vincent's house in the forest, his eyes fixed on the road, but the tips of his fingers scrape against the fabric covering me. I press my back deeper into the seat, squeezing my thighs together, attempting to trap his hand there, though all I end up doing is press him harder against my aching pussy.

"My body could lie." I finally gather my wits. "It responds, but that doesn't mean it's what I want."

"Stop me then," he says as a finger slides against the seam of my panties, goosebumps exploding over my flesh where he barely just brushes against it.

My thighs stay pressed together, though I don't attempt to stop him further.

"If I say *no*, will you stop?"

"Jesus, Evelyn, of course. Though, I think we can work on your acceptance of yourself and desires, differently." His finger slides over my skin, pushing my panties to the side, and finds the wet seam of my pussy.

I moan and roll my hips against the seat, my nipples hardening at the shudder that rips through me.

"How do you mean?" I ask on a breathy voice.

"Use the word *no* to fuel your fantasy. With me, you can enjoy it, play into it." That wandering digit brushes through my core, and as the car swerves onto a bumpier side road, he drives into me, and a wanton cry spills out. "Relinquish the control and let it drive you deeper into pleasure. And for when you really want me to stop, we'll set a safe word."

"S—safe word." I moan as he adds another finger, pushing into me in a maddening rhythm, not bothering at all to take it slow. Or drive the car slower for that matter, adding to the intense pleasure of it all.

"Yes. Keep it simple and use the word *red*, or choose a different one you prefer better. And if your mouth is covered, snap your fingers." This conversation is slightly surreal with his fingers sunk deep inside of me.

But then they curl, and my thighs slide wide open allowing him all the access he wants and I need.

"Red..." I whisper, my hips bucking against the seat as my hands are desperately searching to grab onto something else.

"Red it is, then." His thrusts grow harsher and my head drops against the headrest, eyes closed as I take his long, thick fingers.

Then the man rolls them, brushing against a part of me that makes my ass shoot up from the seat.

"So damn responsive, Evie darling. And so, so wet." That boyish grin makes another appearance, and I swear I would jump him if it wasn't for the whole driving situation.

The road turns darker, the high trees of the forest sheltering it from most of the sun rays, and I wonder who would hear me if I were to scream my ecstasy out there. It makes me want to do it, but Finnigan strokes me to the cusp of exploding, and not an inch past that threshold. I want to bathe in the pleasure of it all. It burns me from the inside, searing my nerves and turning me into a puddle of need and unbearable cravings.

"Jesus fuck, Evelyn. I could just—"

"I'm so close," I interrupt in a breathy whisper, grabbing onto his forearm and squeezing it to me. "Oh, Finnigan, please..."

"You're so beautiful when you beg. I almost don't want to push you over the edge so I can enjoy it for longer."

"Such a cruel man you are." I moan, as the pad of his palm rubs in a brief, torturous motion over the bundle of nerves crying for his touch.

"Not as cruel as you in that sinful skirt and thigh-high stockings. I swear you dress just to drive me crazy. What I could do to you..."

"Then do it, for the love of god, make me—"

"Not sure you deserve it, Evie darling. Only good girls get to come, but you... you're playing with me. With my desire, my emotions..." His words hold a harsh tone, but his fingers deliver the punishment. Such sweet, cruel punishment, holding me at the precipice of explosive pleasure.

A deep need for revenge for this situation grabs hold of me, and my hand shoots between his own thighs, landing on his stiff cock. He groans at the contact, the car swerving for a split second as he mutters a quick series of curses. We could crash for all I care, and I would still have only one thought in mind—earth shattering release.

I rub him over the trousers, reveling in the way he twitches under my touch, but it doesn't seem like torture yet. I need more. My palm itches for this man and my movements grow urgent, alternating between stroking and gripping him tightly until he hisses under his breath. I like the noises he makes. The slight pain laced with longing. I have to have more of it.

Only, he seems even more determined to punish me, kneading the pad of his palm over my clit, as he finger fucks me with harsh, jerked strokes, threatening to drive me to the brink of lust-filled madness, but holding back just before I reach the precipice.

I retaliate, fumbling with his belt, then his zipper, and finally that one button keeping his beautiful cock away from my itching palm. And damn it how I itch for him. Finnigan is a different type of drug, an addiction I'm scared even he can't keep me away from.

The moment I slide under his boxers and touch the bare, soft skin of his throbbing member, he shifts with a jerk backward in the seat, fisting the steering wheel like the object wronged him in some way. But it's my core he takes vengeance on.

"Evelyn, are you trying to fucking kill me?!"

I stroke my palm up and down his shaft in response, satisfied when a few drops of pre-cum help me along the way. He can make of this what he wants, but he better not die on me, because the feel of him pulsing in my hand, his soft, slippery skin, might just be my new favorite thing. Though the man this cock is currently attached to isn't really my favorite at the moment. Not when he strokes into me with demanding fever, bringing me toward the edge of the cliff that promises unbearable ecstasy, then pulls me right back on the ground before I get to plunge.

So I stroke him harder, faster, with erratic movements I can barely control or focus on as his fervid touch threatens to hypnotize me. But he responds all the same, shifting more and more in his seat, his quickening breaths audible over the roar of the engine.

"You're gonna end us both," he all but growls, though he doesn't sound bothered by the prospect.

Then he pushes a third finger into me, and I cry out as I plant my palm on the ceiling of the car, my back arching from the onslaught of deliciously decadent feelings.

"Such a greedy little cunt you have, Evie darling."

"Stop the damn car, Finn!" I demand, slamming my hand against the dashboard.

"Do you need to use the safe word?" he says, his tone leveling.

"I said, stop the car!" I punctuate the order with a tight stroke of his cock, flicking my wrist at the end, and watching his jaw drop on a sharp inhale, followed by inaudible curses.

The car screeches to a halt on the gravel as he turns his attention on me, his eyes deviously dark, pinning me with a passion that makes me tense and squeeze the fingers stretching me. That shifts something inside of him, his brows furrow, gaze turning feral, and I suck in a breath as the danger rolls off of him in waves. On my protesting whimper, he slides his fingers out of me, and in one swift motion unclips both our seat belts.

"Get the fuck out of the car, Evelyn."

The order rips through me like a lightning bolt, and I'm not sure if I'm in control of my body anymore, because I comply in an instant. Our eyes are fixed on each other as we rush to the front of the car, stray sun rays hitting the blonde man like the gods themselves are licking his skin, and before I can throw myself into his arms, he grips my shoulders and turns me around. He presses my back to his front with his arm over my chest, hand under my chin holding my head tilted to him, and reaches between us until he finds the wet fabric of my panties.

"Is this what you want? Turn me into a feral, uncontrollable creature around you?"

I don't answer, too distracted when he presses his fingers back into me, and I shoot up on my tiptoes, seeking the car to steady myself.

"Because you managed it, Evelyn. I'm fucking feral for you, uncontrollable, only, you're the beautiful creature at my mercy."

He releases my jaw, and before I can complete a gasp, I'm bent over the hood of the car, my skirt thrown over my back, ass up in the air. I hear the faint rustling of a plastic wrapper, then a brief tear, before he pushes my panties aside and runs his fingers through my dripping core.

"Beg me to fuck you. Let me hear how beautiful you pray for my cock to stretch your soft, wet cunt."

His crude words pull the dirtiest of moans out of my throat, and they spill off my lips too loudly, but in the middle of this forest, on Vincent's private road, I don't care.

"Finnigan, please fu—"

I cry out the rest of the word when his cock plunges into me on a harsh stretch. He holds my hips to him as I sink into the pleasure the ache brings.

"Oh God, you feel so good." I moan.

"Like I was made for this tight, little pussy of yours."

He pulls out and pushes back in on a powerful thrust, but this is not like our first time. He doesn't pause. He doesn't linger. He doesn't wait to give me time to adjust. He drives into me in punishing strokes, fingers digging into my flesh as he pulls me to meet his hips each time he slams back in. I have nothing to hold onto, the edge of the hood just out of reach, but it doesn't matter. He uses me like a puppet, controlling my movements or lack thereof, holding me just where he wants me as he fucks into me relentlessly, the rhythm quickening, the slap of skin on skin a depraved anthem that echoes through the trees along with our moans and grunts.

I'm quickly turning into a spent mess, unable to function beyond the ability to take all the pleasure he offers, my brain refusing to acknowledge the existence of anything else beyond the man who fucks me like he owes me punishment.

"I would apologize for how quick this is gonna be"—he says in a breathy grunt—"but you're to blame, dirty Evie. You, with your talented hand, mesmerizing pussy, and sinful eyes."

"Then punish me..." I cry out as he slams into me with enough force to drive me higher onto the hood, the grill pressing against the front of my thighs. My front is too hot from the engine, but it adds to the adrenaline, the intensity of the moment.

"I intend to."

He releases me before his palms land on either side of me with a thud that might have dented his car, and fucks me until I my eyes roll back and my legs shake. There's no space for either of us to reach for my clit, but the heat of the hood, the fabric of my skirt, and the intense friction is more than enough, because in the next moment I cry out, my whole body spasming against him. He thrusts through that orgasm, preying on the sensitivity of my core, even when I feel too tender to keep going.

Finnigan doesn't care. He pistons into me over and over, his movements fast, but so precise. Enough that I feel another orgasm inching in, and I'm still in disbelief when he whispers into my ear.

"One more, my Evie. Come for me again."

I don't know if I can, but for him... I'll try.

This time I force my hand between the car and me, and when I press two fingers to my clit, stars explode behind my eyes, and my body bursts into infinite goosebumps. Finnigan's cock throbs inside of me, suddenly so much warmer, twitching and prolonging my orgasm until I'm entirely limp and spent.

As I lie there, waiting for him to rescue me since there's not enough strength in my muscles to get up and drag myself back in the car, I wonder... how am I supposed to go back to my previous life, when this man is beyond my wildest imagination?

Memories of him will never be enough.

I need the real Finnigan Hennessey in my life.

If he'll take me.

CHAPTER 31
Finnigan

I PULL THE car in next to four others parked in front of Vincent's house, and I'm a bit apprehensive at the sleek, black SUV I don't recognize.

"Looks like we're not the first ones here," Evelyn states, looking over to the row of vehicles, after she closes the mirror she just checked herself in.

She had to fix her makeup after what we did, but the sight of her barely disheveled look made me crave to ruin her even more. An image of my sweet Evelyn, with black makeup running down her cheeks as she chokes on my cock has been floating through my mind incessantly, and at this point, I'm praying that it's a premonition.

"Well, I'm glad they got here before our impromptu stop," I answer, cocking an eyebrow with a grin.

She blushes instantly, and I can't possibly miss how she squeezes her thighs together at the fresh memory imprinted between them. Though, I would much rather it would be me between them right now. Again. And a thousand times after.

I've had more women than I could count, and none out of vanity, but need. Only, that need wasn't physical, it was mental... emotional. The only purpose for it was to distract me from what I really craved, but after the way I lost Hanna, I couldn't allow myself those desires. I plugged in the hole with endless women and none of them ever tempted me to want more from them.

Until Evelyn came along.

She drew me in like no other, preyed on vulnerabilities she didn't know I had, and filled gaps she couldn't possibly know existed. And I rejected it all from the start. I was foolish to think I could resist her, that I was strong enough. Maybe I didn't fight it hard enough, or maybe fate really is a thing.

Only, I don't want to leave the rest to fate.

"Evie"—I shift in the seat and catch the silver and gold of her eyes—"give staying in Queenscove serious thought. For me."

Her eyes widen for one fleeting moment, before slight concern saddens them.

"I am."

"Really? Because you speak more of leaving than of staying, and I need you to give this—Queenscove—a real shot. I've been thinking about it all. Maya will have to be enrolled in school once all is said and done with Bartiste, and it's something I can help with. Give it a chance without having one foot out the door."

"You can't ask this of me, Finnigan."

"I don't want to *ask* this of you; don't you get it? I don't even want to demand it, I want to *take it*. I want to tie you in my penthouse and give you no choice. That's what I actually desire. Which is why I'm holding onto the ounce of self-control I have, and I'm asking you to give it a proper shot."

She's speechless, her lips parted in surprise as she takes in my words and underlying threat.

"You wouldn't," she whispers.

Maybe my glare is answer enough, because I swear there's hope weaved through the shock in her gaze.

"Tell me you will do it, you'll give it a chance. A good one. You've already built a life in Queenscove, Evelyn. There's so much more for you here," I add.

"I will give it a chance. I already am," she finally agrees.

But there's a little voice inside my head that mocks me. It knows what a man of my failures deserves, and it's not a woman like Evelyn. I nod, pensive at the inner turmoil, recognizing the tinge of fear that's been growing inside of me at the same pace as the attachment to this woman.

"I'll grab the cake trays and your things. Get the gift bag, please."

We exit the car simultaneously, but a moment later she's by my side, taking one of the trays from me.

"I can handle it," I argue.

"Me too." She walks away with a strut, but not before cocking an eyebrow and giving me a look more sinful than it should be. I should move, but that damn skirt fluttering with her sway, distracts me. It's not even that short, just above the knees, but knowing she wears thigh-high stockings underneath as well, I want to bend her over and sink into her warm, sweet cunt all over again. She looks like a rock goddess and I get all sorts of ideas of things I want to buy her. Latex bodysuit. Fishnet stockings to rip off. Leather harnesses to frame her waist, or her breasts...

"Coming?" she calls after me, and I have to rush to get to her.

Though, I don't bother pretending to be unaffected by her. I probably should when we get inside. I have a feeling Maddox might demand my head for what I did with the violet-haired woman he's started seeing as a sister. He warned me before to leave her alone, but I think he was thinking more of her emotional state.

She knocks on the door, but I slide in front of her, open it and walk in.

"Vincent has cameras and sensors." I say as I turn her way. "They know we're here."

She shrugs and follows, but once we're in, she's looking somewhere behind me, apprehension in her gaze. I whip around at her slight distress.

"Cousin!" the dark-haired, broad-shouldered man exclaims as he comes toward us.

"Sloan, you've arrived," I greet him, then Morrigan who arrives next to me and helps me with the tray I carry.

I hug my cousin, who left his crime empire for a few days to lend a hand with our Bartiste situation, then step aside to introduce him.

"Evelyn, this is Sloan Buchanan. Our cousin abandoned his hill up in Venator to assist us."

"Your hill?" She looks curious, but a little flustered too. "Sorry, hi, nice to meet you."

"It's great to meet you, too. Though, I feel like I know you already, as I've had the pleasure to meet your sister," Sloan greets her, his stance quite stern, but like always, there's warmth in his eyes and tone. "And yes, my hill. The city of Venator is old. Back in the old days three fortresses were built on its three hills, and it created a bit of a... divide, let's say. One of those hills—Alnit—is my territory."

"Oh, what an interesting name. I know of Venator, but I never looked into its geography. It sounds... familiar," she answers, curious now.

I know Evelyn hasn't finished school after she had to give it all up to take care of her sister. It's a bit of a sore subject with her, mostly because I think she sees it as a flaw, like she's somehow worth less because of it. But I've also noticed her thirst for knowledge. Her sister may be a big fiction reader despite her fragile age, which I thoroughly enjoy. But my Evie has a curiosity like no other, always sifting through my books, and almost every time she chooses non-fiction. Anything from ancient writings to modern history. She never discusses it, though, and always drops the books when I come in the room. One day she'll get over that insecurity, but I won't rush her.

"It comes from Alnitak, one of the stars in Orion's belt," Sloan explains, a little pride in his voice at the interest Evelyn shows.

"That's fascinating." Her gaze drifts, and if I could crack her head open now, I swear I would see the cogs spinning, filing this information for further research. "I would love to hear more about it, but you'll have to excuse me, I need to finish the cupcakes for the birthday boy." She nods to us, her gaze lingering a few moments longer on me, then walks away.

I don't realize I'm still staring after her until Sloan speaks.

"It's good to see you *interested* again."

I turn to him, mouth open ready to bite back, but I have nothing. I can't deny it, but I feel like I have to say something to clarify.

"We're not... together. I guess."

He quirks an eyebrow, challenging my answer.

"She's not sure if she's staying in Queenscove, and we haven't approached the subject about how *interested* we are."

He smirks and shakes his head. "If only relationships were simple."

"What about you?" I ask, trying to deflect.

"I'm doing well. There's some shit stirring up in Venator, but hopefully it won't escalate. It's why Duncan couldn't come, he has to hold down the fort."

"I was asking about your love life," I say, laughing. "But how is your son?"

"Honestly, a bit too good at this *job*, but he's young and his mind is a bit distracted. Money, women, you know the drill. And my love life is just fine."

"*Just fine*. Sounds promising. Duncan will be okay, he'll have a wake-up call soon enough and step up, especially if you say he's talented at the family business," I assure my cousin.

"How are you doing with Bartiste's return and all?"

Sloan was there last time. After the girls were taken, he came to our rescue. We probably would have all been dead without him and his men. He even offered some of them the option to join our Sanctum, to replenish the army we were only just building back then. I inhale deeply and start walking with him, toward the voices I hear outside on the patio.

"Fine. We all really thought he was dead. But it seems my brother and Carter never stopped looking, just in case. But yes, it was all unexpected."

I look at Sloan and his narrowing green eyes scrutinize me. Clearly I didn't answer the question he was truly asking, but getting in the emotional side of things about the PTSD Bartiste left me with isn't going to happen. I haven't gotten into it with my Sanctum brothers, so I'm not doing it with the cousin I see a few times a year.

"He'll be dead soon."

"That he most certainly will. Thank you for joining us in the hunt."

"Believe me man, it's my pleasure." He taps my shoulder and smiles, but it doesn't touch his eyes. They only spell malice.

"Finn," Ronan greets me when we get outside, and Vincent, Carter and Maddox nod toward me, signaling Sloan over.

My brother and I may have started to work through our shit, and I know he really yearns to get closer to me, but I find it somehow difficult. I'm not sure what's holding me back, but I have a feeling it's not to do with him.

"How are you settling back in Queenscove?" I ask as we take a seat next to each other on the outdoor sofa, Sloan moving on to Maddox who looks at me a bit wearily.

"It's... odd. It feels like home, but it also doesn't. I can't explain it. Being on edge doesn't help."

"Are you worried?"

He looks me in the eye like I grew a second head. "Worried? I'm petrified, brother. Bartiste is back. The man who took so much from us." His gaze drifts to his wife who's currently entertaining their son, before returning to me. "I know it's not the same as it was with you; I'm not trying to downplay it in any way. But the fear that it could happen again to Annika, to Aaro, is debilitating."

No, Bartiste didn't take as much from him, but Annika was pregnant when she was kidnapped along with Hanna, and my brother only found out about it over the phone, as she was being taken. There is no way to describe that feeling of helplessness. We couldn't do a thing. It left deep, jagged scars that we share because our trauma is our failure. We failed to protect them.

How can I deserve Evelyn? What if I fail to protect her too? I know Bartiste will be dead at the end of this, I know I will not fail there, but it's her safety I fear up until that point.

"You have a lot to lose now. I understand." I answer finally. "Is this why you came back?"

"Partly. I have hired help at home, but here... I have you and The Sanctum. I knew Annika and Aaro would be safe now. And no matter what happened between us, how you felt about me, there was no chance I wouldn't come for you after realizing Bartiste is back."

It sounds like he didn't care if I wanted him here or not, he was going to be by our—*my* side anyway, through the asshole's return.

"What's the other reason?" I ask.

"I need to see Bartiste dead. I need to make sure."

I nod. No one from our whole group can understand that better than me. I'll treat him like a fucking vampire if I must, and carve his heart out or cut off his head, just to make sure he'll never come back to fucking life.

"Did you find out how the motherfucker lived?" He had a few holes in him, his men couldn't find him either.

"I found a hospital record that matched some of his injuries. He used a different name, so I can't be hundred percent sure, but it sounded like he was found by a random person, half dead. The records were altered though because that's the only thing there. No evidence of surgery, recovery, death, or anything else. He disappeared," Ronan answers.

"I'll make sure he's dust this time around."

He nods in response. It's a certainty for the both of us. For all of us really. Bartiste has been taunting us for long enough, and The Sanctum does not allow errors, let alone failures. We were young when he disappeared on us, but we aren't the same people now. The wheels are in motion, Bartiste is leaving breadcrumbs, and he'll be ours soon enough. The worst thing to admit is that the guy is a master in disappearing and hiding. If he were anyone else, we would admire the talent, but there's nothing to admire about this man.

"You and the girl—" Ronan changes the subject.

"Evelyn," I correct.

"She's young..." His words strike me.

"And that bothers you?"

He takes a deep breath in, then releases it as he ponders, his gaze turning to Annika, still playing with their son.

"She seems mature enough, don't get me wrong. But pulling her into this life at her age seems unfair," he says as he refocuses back on me.

My fists clench and tightness grips my chest. "I know you're not fucking insinuating that I'm forcing her to stay here. That I'm coercing her in some way."

"I'm not, it's just—"

"Evelyn is free to make her own decisions, brother. But I'm not gonna sit idly by and not show her all her options. And *I am* an option. I fucking deserve this too! Fuck knows I've waited long enough." I rise and storm off before he can say anything else.

I'm rounding the house, needing a damn moment to myself before I end up taking my anger out on someone else. But footsteps crunch on the grass behind me, and I whip around, ready to tell them to fuck off.

"Finnigan, sorry, can I talk to you for a moment?"

Loreley.

My warning stops in my throat and I nod, curious. The blonde woman and I don't interact that much, though we are in each other's presence fairly often.

"I know you and Evelyn are getting... close."

"Oh for God's sake, not you too." I step back shaking my head. "Look—"

"No, listen to me. I'm not here about *that*. I want to talk to you about her and Maya. Has she spoken to you about the custody situation?"

This, I didn't expect.

"I tried to approach it once, but she brushed me off and changed the subject. Why?" I ask, fully intrigued now.

"You and I both know she cannot get custody of Maya legally without jumping through enormous hoops that girl can't afford. We spoke of it, she's not really doing anything about it because she's terrified she'll lose Maya to the system until the custody is decided by CPS and a judge." She takes a deep breath and looks behind her, probably making sure Evelyn isn't around. "I offered to help, obviously. But she got really defensive. She's a stubborn one."

"What reason did she give you?" I ask, crossing my arms against my chest.

"She's not comfortable with me doing anything about it because I already helped her so much. I hired her in the café, she lives in my apartment, though she insisted on taking rent out of her salary. You can imagine I barely charge her, but anyway, she fought really hard and actually got angry at me. You probably know as well as me that Evelyn does not get angry. Ever. So I had to back off. I want to speak to Morri about it, ask her to get The Sanctum involved, but I thought I would talk to you first. I see how you look at her..." she ends with a suggestive smile that would make me blush if I wasn't distracted by the custody matter.

"Thanks for coming to me. I'm looking into it."

Loreley's eyes widen as she snaps back. "Really?"

I nod, feeling a bit lighter now. She smiles, a great big smile showing all her perfectly straight white teeth.

"Thank you!" Her shoulders drop on a calming exhale. "And... I probably don't need to say this, but if you hurt that girl, I'll chop your balls off myself and feed them to you."

My brows shoot up as she whips around, her long ponytail brushing against my chest, and walks away. *Jesus Christ.* I kind of believe her though. Loreley is a Dietrich, and that family has quite the reputation in the criminal underworld. She may be out of the family business, but who knows what she learned before. This conversation seems to be what I needed, because I'm calm, another goal added to the list of all that concerns Evelyn.

There's no denying that I would like to keep her, make her stay. Such a contrast to just a few weeks back. I'm still not convinced that I shouldn't just force her hand, but I know what the best decision is—give her all the resources to make her own decision.

I'm about to push that limit though, and I can't anticipate if she's going to take it as an amazing gesture, or manipulation. It's pushing the limit for sure, but I guess I'll find out tomorrow.

"Come, they're going to sing happy birthday to your nephew." Katya appears out of nowhere.

I didn't even realize she was here, and she's gesturing for me to join them where they're all gathered inside. I follow her, and they make room for me around the dining table so I can see Aaro. He's giddily staring at a whole tray of cupcakes with impeccable frosting layered on top, and I have to concentrate not to drift to what we did with the leftovers of that cream earlier today.

Instead of putting only enough candles to cover his age, all the cupcakes have one. There's probably over forty of them and the boy looks just about ready to burst with joy.

If only our lives would just be this... how different we would be.

CHAPTER 32
Evelyn

THIS DAY HAS held a strange normalcy to it. Everything so far has felt surreal. A big happy family celebrating a kid's birthday. Only, this family is the criminal kind, not that you would be able to tell from the way they behave.

The guys have disappeared into Vincent's office a couple of times, likely discussing their businesses, but they returned like nothing happened. Calm and wholly unaffected, carrying on enjoying their family time.

I caught some glimpses of conversations I probably shouldn't have listened in on, like how Bartiste apparently has been taunting The Sanctum, either by trying to send them on fools errands or get them killed. He failed. The Sanctum didn't take the bait, and they were also not weak enough to be touched by his men. Finn and the others apparently are quite pleased with this, because Bartiste is getting bolder and bolder, probably annoyed that all his attempts are being shot down, which means he'll make a mistake soon. From what I heard, he's already made a couple that luckily led to the discovery of two more locations where children were found. They're free now—safe. And Bartiste is angry.

I couldn't take the smile off my face when I overheard this. That bastard needs to rot, and though I want him dead as soon as possible, I can't be mad at this delay when I know that more innocents are being rescued.

Despite all this, today has still felt peculiar. There's a heaviness lingering in the air, and it doesn't seem to go down with the setting sun. On the contrary, it thickens. It turns me restless, threads of anxiety rustling my nerves, and I'm struggling to settle.

From across the garden, flames from the fire pit dance over Finn's features as he talks to his cousin, only, his gaze settles on me with a quiet intensity. My lungs fill with the lightest of air, the relentless buzzing in my ears easing.

I've been thinking about this, his ability to calm my nerves, cool my blood. When I didn't know how to handle myself, what I've been through, and the strange withdrawal from whatever drugs I was injected with, it was him who fed that need. Our rows didn't distract me, they... helped me. It makes no sense when I think about it, and I'm not even sure he knows he's doing it.

Evelyn, that's such a stupidly ridiculous thought.

Of course he doesn't know. He's not damn psychic. Though, I have heard that certain people have a sort of empathy or they read others so well, they can tell when there's a change in blood pressure, or other physical signs. I'm seriously hoping he's one of them, because I don't feel like feeding his ego by actually telling him he's helped me in these ways. I guess I'm holding onto my own ego.

His gaze is still fixed on me, even as his lips move with words clearly directed at Sloan. The intensity of his stare has shifted with the slight narrowing of his eyes, and sparks bloom in my chest, spreading through my body like lightning bolts. This man does things to me. Wild, wicked things.

I've watched him quietly all day. His interactions with the others, the way he carries himself with the kids, noticing the tension in his shoulders easing more and more with each conversation with his brother. But the most noticeable thing is the way he watches me. We've had little physical interaction, but his gaze has constantly made me feel touched. On every single inch of my body. He's not being very inconspicuous about his attention either, and I would rather everyone not know what's going on between us. Though, I'm not entirely sure what that is, and that's my fault, not his. I also think the others might have an inkling about us, after Finnigan arrived when we were attacked in the parking lot.

I rise from the outdoor sofa, feeling the need to flee before someone asks me what's the deal with his stare, and head back inside the house. It's quiet here since everyone's outside, and I head down the corridor toward the bathroom, loving how the moonlight casts its soft light through the high windows.

My next breath is stolen as a hand circles around me and presses over my mouth. I'm snapped back into a strong, taut body, then rushed to the side, into a dark space. I protest against his palm, grabbing at his arms as I struggle to pull away from his hold after he circles my waist with his other arm. With a loud thud, the door closes behind us and pitch-black darkness swallows us as I fight against him, pointlessly screaming against his palm. He manhandles me around, and I can't tell which way is up or down, or where that damn door is, but I forget all those details when my front is slammed against a wall, my cheek pressed against it. An obvious, hard erection pushes against my ass when he lines up his body against mine, and I shudder at the thought, squirming harder to break away.

"No, no, no!" I protest against his hand.

Can he tell what I'm saying?

Hot breath touches my ear, and I think he's going to say something, but instead slickness runs over the edge of it, from the lobe to the top—*he's licking me.* Involuntary heat pools between my legs, shame too.

Goddamn it, this is wrong!

But it has to be Finnigan, right? There's no one else, none of the other guys would do this. I don't know Sloan, but I don't imagine he is that kind of man. I inhale as hard as I can through the restriction, trying to catch Finnigan's scent, but all I'm getting is burnt wood and smoke. The arm wrapped around my waist releases me, and I'm preparing to push as hard as I can against him to get away, when I hear a snapping sound. Then one more.

Oh, he's snapping his fingers—our silent safe word.

It *is* Finnigan.

The sound of a zipper pulls at my anticipation, before he reaches back down around my waist. This time he doesn't wrap around it, but runs his hand down my body. He pushes underneath my skirt, and presses against my pussy at the same time he releases my mouth and grips my throat in his large palm.

"No! No, please!" I beg as I squirm against him, diving deeper into the feelings of unrest that haven't yet left me.

"Beg me all you want, I'm not sparing your little cunt." He all but growls in a low, rumbling tone.

I whimper as his grip tightens against the sides of my throat, a shallow breath catching beneath his fingers just as he dives under my panties and into the sleekness of me.

"Let me go!" I cry out, squirming harder as I reach behind and grab onto his sides.

"Scream louder, sugar, and we'll have an audience to our depravity." He grunts into my ear, his hot breath sending shivers down my spine as a finger, or maybe two, press inside of me.

I'm so wet, the sound coming from between my legs is embarrassing. But it only encourages the man *forcing* himself on me.

"Oh god!" I whimper in a shaky voice, as he hooks his fingers inside of me, pulling me with him when he takes a step back.

"Are you sore?" he asks in a whisper, clearly breaking character.

"Yes."

"I'll st—"

"No!" I interrupt him, squeezing my inner muscles around his fingers, trapping him inside my warmth.

He doesn't say another word. Instead, he bends me over, his hand moving from my throat to my nape, and it happens so fast, I barely have time to brace myself against the wall. His fingers come out, the head of his cock nudges my core for only a moment before he jerks forward, burying himself inside of me to the hilt, and through the slight ache of my former virginity, I draw ecstasy.

"Oh god!" I cry out, struggling to keep my tone low when I realize I can feel *all* of him.

No barrier. No condom. God, it's incredible.

"You keep calling for this *god*, darling, but it's me listening to your prayers."

A wanton shudder rips through my whole body at his sinful words, and since I've never been a religious person, I would happily make him my god. My blue-eyed, murderous god whose maddening cock strokes viciously inside my aching cunt. His hips slap against my ass, the sound so dirty and enticing, I grab onto his side with one hand, urging him to take more. His hand tightens around my throat, pressure growing both in my chest and temples from the air restriction, and I feel like calling for *my* god again, but all that comes out is unintelligible mumbles.

Pressure covers the bundle of nerves at the apex of my slit, his skilled digits circling with precise movements that send burning shocks through my core.

"No, no, no…" I chant, more to myself than him, hating that the heat is taking over me so quickly.

My knees tremble with each slither of pleasure cutting through me, and with one more deep stroke of his cock, I'm breaking apart. He releases my neck and covers my mouth in an instant, pressing over the lust-filled cry shattering through me. But he still fucks me through the orgasm, stroking that pleasure until it's almost unbearable.

When the shaking subsides he pulls out, and I think he's going to allow me a break, but I'm manhandled once more, flipped around, my back slammed against the wall just as soft, demanding lips crash against mine.

He kisses me like he couldn't care if I like it or not, taking his pleasure from me like he has every right to, and something deep in my core contracts in ecstasy at the demand. Only, he's gone before I can deepen the rough kiss, and with quick hands under my ass, I'm hauled up against him, back pressed into the wall for support. On instinct I grab onto his shoulders as I wrap my legs over his hips, and he adjusts me until he's holding me with one hand, the tip of his cock prodding at my entrance once more.

"Christ, you're too light."

I'm about to argue that it's not true, but he lowers me onto his cock, and all I manage is a lustful moan as I tighten my limbs around him. Before I know it, he's not just guiding me up and down, but I'm bouncing onto him too, seeking the delightful pleasure this man gives me with each stroke of his cock. He holds my neck in a comforting possessiveness, and it hits me then… I've never known this type of unconditional safety. Maybe once, amongst my family, but not like this. I could relinquish all control, all sense of self, and I know this man would build a fortress around me to keep me safe, comfortable.

"Please, slide your hand… higher… into my hair." The words are strained with the breathlessness of his thrusts, but also because they're not easy to speak out loud.

His movements falter for a few moments, then he picks up the rhythm again, fingers slowly threading into the hairline of my nape. An icy feeling follows in their wake and deep in my chest freezing stillness grips my lungs.

"Red," I speak quickly. "Just for the fingers. No further, hold them there," I add quickly before Finnigan stops moving altogether.

"Are you sure you want this?" he asks, his thrusts slowing.

I nod, and pull him against me, his chest flush to mine, as I force his lips to meet my own. I kiss him with as much passion as I can muster, because goddamn it, this man deserves it all. His movements quicken once more, his hips jerking upwards as I bounce harder onto him, his cock stroking feverishly against a spot inside of me that makes my muscles shake with each grind. The bones of my back hurt as he crushes me against the wall, his breaths quickening, and his fingers press harder into my scalp, fueling and soothing the panic inside my chest all at the same time.

He breaks the kiss enough to whisper, "Touch yourself, Evie darling."

My cheeks heat in an instant, my mind drunk on pleasure as I try to process what he's asking of me. I do as told, reaching between us until my clit is beneath the tips of two fingers, and I cry out from the sensitivity.

"That's it, my dirty little thing. Make yourself come with my cock stroking every bit of you," he whispers those sinful words on a low rumble.

I speed up the touch, adding more pressure as I assault the bundle of nerves, and threads of ecstasy bloom from that center, bursting all through my body as it shakes and convulses around the man who holds me so tight against him. I come hard enough that stars dance behind my eyes, and I'm worried I drew blood where my nails sank in his shoulder. But he doesn't sound affected. He holds me through it until the shaking stops.

I don't realize I'm smiling until he peppers kisses all over my lips, and the softest of laughs, coming from him, warms my soul. He eases me off of his cock and down to my feet, but he has to hold me through my shaky balance.

"But you, you haven't... finished," I protest when he pulls away, reaching for his cock through the darkness.

There's a pause that lasts too long as I squeeze the hard length that throbs in my hand.

"Make me, then." The grit in his voice turns the words to both an order and a plea, and I get an odd sense of power out of them.

The heat between my legs burns brighter and there's only one thing I crave to do right now. Something I've never done before. I drop to my knees, my hand wrapped around the base of his cock, and when my warm breath touches the tip of it, he mutters a series of curses.

"That's not what I meant, sugar. Jerk me off. You don't have to—"

But the next words lodge in his throat and come out as an unintelligible jumble as I suck the tip of him between my lips, surprised at the saltiness and slight bitterness of his pre-cum. Before he can protest further, I suck him inside my mouth as deep as I can take him, stopping when a strange gag reflex pushes him back out. Then I swallow him back in, curling my lips against my teeth and press my tongue against the underside of his pulsing length.

"Fuck, Evelyn! Goddamn it!" he swears over and over.

"Guide me," I whisper. "I've never done this." Then I swallow him again, bobbing up and down his cock.

"You're doing fucking amazing. *You* could do anything to me, and it would be the best I've ever had."

I whimper around his member at the compliment, and a rumble shakes through him.

"Follow with your hand what your lips can't reach," he says on a throaty whisper, and I comply, running my hand up and down his shaft. "That's it, Evie darling. Fuck, yes."

He's somehow even more rigid between my lips, and I finally understand the *rock hard* expression everyone seems to use.

"Faster," he urges softly.

And I do as told, quickening the rhythm as he struggles not to thrust forward in my mouth, his hips rocking gently.

"Move away now. I'm gonna come!" he warns.

But I've already made up my mind. I want it. I want him to spill into my mouth and drown me in the taste of him. It makes me feel dirty, and god I want to be so damn filthy right now. So I slap a hand over his ass and press him right back into my mouth.

He curses low in his throat as he grips my shoulder and holds me there. I know his instinct craves to grab the back of my head, and the fact that even now he has the self-control to avoid triggering me, makes me want to reward him. So I press him deeper into my mouth, breathing through the gag reflex as the tip of his cock hits the back of my throat, and the sinful grunts that spill from his mouth are followed by the violent twitching of his cock as hot spurts of thick liquid hit my throat. I can't avoid the choking, but he pulls out gently, letting his cum fill my mouth rather than straight down my throat, and I swallow it down the more it comes.

I've never looked at the condoms he threw away after sex, but this seems like a lot of cum. Is it normal? My core tightens when I imagine it filling me, spilling out as he strokes inside of me, and drips down my thighs. I moan as I suck his cock one last time, and he shudders between my lips.

"I can't believe you just did that," he says, breathless. "You swallowed it all?" the man is genuinely surprised.

"Every last drop." I smack my lips together as he helps me up.

"Such a good fucking girl." He growls before he captures my lips with his, and kisses me until I'm panting.

Then he wraps me in his arms, my cheek pressed against his chest, as he rubs my back in slow, soothing motions. We stand like that for long enough that I start to worry what the others are going to say about our absence. Yet, I don't push away. This feels... important. I'm not sure why, but it does.

A few more minutes pass before he finally speaks. "Let's get you cleaned up."

He reaches somewhere to the side and light floods the space. I squeeze my eyes shut, grunting, but accept the fact that this has to happen. Oh, we're in the bathroom. I was so disorientated, I didn't realize this is where he shoved me in.

He moves me to the sink and reaches for some toilet paper he quickly wets and presses between my legs. I wince, but he holds me there as he wipes gently before he throws it in the toilet. He repeats it a few times, and heat flushes me cheeks each time. This is nice... really nice. I fix my makeup and hair in the mirror as he cleans himself, his glorious cock, and this moment is so intimate. It makes me smile. I like it.

"You should go to the toilet," he says.

I cock an eyebrow as I look at him in the mirror.

"I'm serious." He laughs, "After sex, you should always go. Apparently it prevents UTIs."

"I'm not peeing with you here." I smile like an idiot, the prospect sounding ridiculous.

"I licked frosting off your asshole, but we draw the line at you peeing in my presence." He shakes his head, but the smile on his face is devastating. "Very well, my darling Evie." He presses a quick peck to my lips, then quickly straightens his clothes as he walks out of the bathroom, shutting the door behind him.

I drag my fingers through my hair as I focus on myself in the mirror, looking all sexed up and satisfied. At least I'm not going to have to be the one to explain to the others why we both disappeared at the same time. Though the gleam in my eyes might betray us anyway.

CHAPTER 33
Evelyn

EITHER FINNIGAN TALKED to everyone, or they truly don't care, because the moment I return to the terrace, no one even bats an eyelid. They notice me returning but no one focuses on me, their conversations carrying on.

"Evie!" Maya jumps on the sofa next me, grabbing onto my forearm as she lands on her knees, a great big smile on her lips.

"Yes, pretty girl."

"Can I sleep here again tonight?" she asks, grinning from ear to ear.

"Darling, I think we should give them a break tonight."

"Pleeease. I already asked them." She squeezes my arm and throws the best puppy eyes she can pull off.

"She did, indeed." Annika startles me, appearing to my left. "It's honestly fine. No bother at all."

"It's not quite fair to you, Ronan... or Vincent," I whisper to her.

"We're not here for much longer, and we all enjoy her company. From what I heard, you've had your hands full for a while now. You deserve a little break."

"It's not like that, I don't need a break," I say, feeling bad that she thinks she needs to do this for me.

Then her eyes flash somewhere beyond me before returning to mine. I don't know what or who she looked at, but from the heat searing the back of my neck, I can only guess.

"I understand, trust me, but you can still enjoy one," she answers.

"Please, Evie. It's been so fun with Aaro around. And Annika has been teaching me to paint!" Maya squeals.

"Is that right?" I turn to my sister, pleasantly surprised at her words.

"Yes! Wait here, I'll go grab them and I'll show you." She jumps off the sofa and runs away.

I watch her run inside the house, shaking my head and laughing at the girl.

"Look at that energy at this time of night. Are you sure you want to deal with more of that?" I ask Annika.

"It's honestly nothing. Mamaw June has been staying here for safety reasons too, so please, don't worry." She starts moving away, then stops and cocks her head. "So it's a yes, then."

I snort, shaking my head. "You're a saint, you know. Thank you."

She smiles and walks away. I'm going to miss Annika. Her presence here has had an incredible impact on me because it allowed me the space, the time to find out more about myself.

A moment later, my phone that I left on the sofa vibrates, and I fumble for it, noticing text notifications when I pick it up. I know no one here, who texts me? Oh, maybe it's Raven?

I open the notifications just as Maya jumps back on the sofa and I hear the faint rustling of paper being laid on my lap. Only, my gaze can't focus on anything else but the words screaming at me from the screen of my phone.

> Missed me?

> Tell your precious Sanctum about this and I will pull your sister's guts out while she still breathes. But I'll make sure you watch me rip into her first.

What the hell is this? Panic threads through my veins as Maya speaks words I can't hear, excitedly pushing colorful papers in my line of sight.

"Look! It's the forest." She shows me a thick piece of paper covered in various shades of green.

But I'm numb, struggling to pick the dominating emotion ripping through my soul, because I cannot possibly show my fear right now. I feign enthusiasm as my gaze drifts back to my phone and photos appear on the screen. A few dozens of them load, one by one, and as I catch the first few, a chill runs down my spine.

"Evie, are you looking?" I turn back to Maya, the very subject of the photo gallery currently loading on my screen, forcing my staggering breaths to level out as I gush about my sister's works of art.

"I told you! I'm pretty good." She jumps up and down. "Oh, Aaro's calling for me. I'll put these away."

I nod, squeezing her little body to mine. "You're my little genius. I love you, sweet girl."

She frowns for a split second, before kissing my cheek. "I love you, too."

Then she's off as quickly as she came, and I rise from the sofa, walking inside the house as calmly as I could muster at this moment. When I'm out of view, I rush into a guest bedroom, and close the door behind me, unlocking my phone for a better look.

There she is... my sweet sister... under fucking surveillance.

Frankie B has been watching her. Dozens of candid photos of her pop up one after the other. On the beach, in a store, in the back of a car. All in public. Some in front of our apartment building. I'm in there too, Annika, Mamaw June, but neither of us are the focus. Only Maya is. Every muscle shakes beneath my flesh and I drop down to my knees as I scroll through the images of the vulnerable girl lit up on my phone. The one I'm supposed to protect, shield from assholes like him. The words from that text run in a loop in my head, the nonchalant violence bringing bile up my throat.

Another text comes, like the son-of-a-bitch knew I read his messages.

> Midnight, tonight. Dalton Pier. You may not see me, but I will see you every step of the way. And if you're not alone, it won't be just your precious little sister who will suffer.

I stare at my phone in pure disbelief, chest spasming as air fight's to reach my lungs through the staggered breaths I manage. The slither of light creeping through the cracked door blurs before my eyes, but there are no tears brimming them. Only despair. It shatters through the chaos twisting my heart, and the beats bring nothing but pain. It's relentless in its assault, gripping my memories in a sharp vice, and dragging them forward to my present.

I'm back in that dark room of the warehouse, my cheek pressed against the cold, concrete floor as muffled cries of children sound far beyond these walls. But I'm losing them. As poison fills my veins their cries turn too maddening, liquid sounds too distant for their notes to affect me. Except for one—a silent wail from a girl who shares our mother's eyes. Its absence affects me. I know she won't be crying. And she'll be waiting for the sister who will never rescue her, who will lie half unconscious on this stained floor, as the man with a lisp and tar-laced voice takes his pleasure from her pain.

The texture of the concrete scrapes the tips of my fingers as I try to drag myself away from him. I'm questioning my reality.

Maybe I was never saved.

Maybe I'm still lying on that floor. Maybe his dick is still ripping my ass. Maybe I dissociated and made up the last few months of my life.

Maybe Finnigan doesn't even exist.

I'm questioning how deep this panic goes. Which is the lie? The reality?

Laughter somewhere far away cracks the pain and a slither of light breaks through. There is so much effortless joy in that melodic sound, brimming with innocence. Familiar. With aching hands I grip the concrete beneath them harder, trying to drag myself toward that laughter and find out who it belongs to. A visceral need inside of me is screaming of its importance. I have to find out.

Then it comes again, not closer to me, but louder either way. It sounds... small. A tiny voice. Slightly high pitched. A little comical too. Joy blooms in the pit of my stomach. So familiar. The concrete scratches my palms, but I'm pulling away further. Frankie is losing his grip on me. Only, Bartiste appears in my periphery.

You might have to share this one.

His words bring a silent cry to my chest and tears fill my eyes as I struggle to move further away, but I'm not going anywhere. Then the laughter splits the darkness and fills it with colorful light that calls for me—Maya.

I blink frantically as air fills my lungs with vicious force, and fall forward on my hands, heaving. I'm alone, inside the dark, guest bedroom, the door cracked to the dimly lit hallway, and my sister's laughter filters through from somewhere in the distance.

I'm safe.

But she isn't.

My instincts aren't screaming at me, no matter how hard I listen, and I don't know what I should do. The Sanctum can help me. Finnigan can help me. But if what Frankie said is true, that he will see me coming, and considering the surveillance photos he sent me, it's highly likely, then I will be risking Maya's life. How can we protect her if we didn't even know we were being watched?

What if I ask for help... and she will pay for it?

What if I do nothing... and they'll take her from me?

On my phone screen the time seems to scream at me in that bright white—nine forty-eight p.m. I have plenty of time to make a decision, though there's too much time for me to fail to act normal and not get away with it. Maya will get what she asked for and stay here. At least for tonight, Annika and Ronan will watch her.

What about the other nights that will follow? Without me...

Oh, god. I cannot fathom not being part of her life, her growing up without me. Would these people take her in if I'm not here? Would they keep her safe or put her in the system? They wouldn't, would they? No. I can trust them. But I'll leave a note just in case, or maybe I'll text before I meet with Frankie and ask them to take care of her.

Yes. That feels right.

Fuck! No, it doesn't!

None of this is right, but I don't have a choice.

I wrap a strand of my hair around my fingers, nervously rolling it as I force myself not to visualize what consequences I'm going to face. Surrendering myself to Frankie is a terrible idea. Mentally I haven't escaped him yet, but I'm also not trapped in his clutches like I used to be. This will physically bring me right back there. He'll destroy me.

Picking up my phone I go back to his message and the photos of my sister—if I don't do this... he'll destroy *her*. There is no other way, no other choice.

I push myself back up to my feet and walk over to the window, then slowly pull the blind up, revealing the moonlight touching the tops of the trees.

Will I ever see this again if I make this choice? Will I see the outside?

Will I be alive for it?

No!

I cannot think like that. Plan—I need a plan. Finn will want to take me back to the apartment tonight. How am I going to sneak out? There are so many variables, the man has security everywhere in that building, Katya lives there too, people have started knowing me there. However, before they even come into play, it's Finn I have to worry about. There's no way I can sneak out without him hearing, noticing, or searching for me, and I have a feeling he won't be asleep in time for me to leave.

I'll have to sneak out from here. Even with Vincent's cameras or the men patrolling the vicinity and the rest of his forest-covered land, it's not the same as an apartment building. So I tell them I would like to stay tonight with Maya too.

The peculiarity of this situation dawns on me—I'm planning my demise. In my gut I know that this will be my end, because there is no way I will allow a man like Frankie B to own me. No one can own me. I will find a way to escape him, even if it will mean my end.

Now, I just have to act normal in front of the others for another hour and a half.

Deep in my chest a stabbing pain cracks everything I managed to build in the last few months, the shield I formed around the visceral emotions I allowed myself to feel for Finnigan. I love the others too, but Finnigan... what he built inside of me happened gradually. It has a foundation and serrated claws embedded in the edges of my heart, one by one until he became fully seated there. Part of me.

He isn't wrapped around my heart, he *is* part of it. Right next to my smart, silly little sister.

And I'm about to rip my own heart out and abandon them both.

* * *

I counted twelve more breaths after my decision was made, each of them on the rhythm of my slow, dragging steps, but I haven't changed my mind. It's time to walk out of this room so I don't arouse suspicion. Just as I grip the doorknob, steps sound on the other side, on the corridor, and I freeze.

"He's with a woman." That's Carter's calm, leveled voice.

"With a woman?!" Finnigan exclaims.

"That's what I said, yes."

"You can't possibly imply that Frankie is currently on a date. That's not what you're telling me, right?!"

They found him! Pure excitement grips my chest, spilling into goosebumps over my skin, and I cover my mouth to keep from crying out.

"That, or he plans on taking her. It's irrelevant," Carter answers, nonchalant.

"Let's go get him then." *Maddox.*

They're all here, but they're still walking and their voices are starting to lose volume. They must be going into the office at the end of the hallway.

"How many men did he have with him?" Finnigan asks.

"Cameras showed three."

"Three?! Fucking hell, the man is bold. His confidence is ridiculous if he thinks three is enough to protect him. Why the fuck is he feeling so untouchable?" Finn curses.

"The old Dalton Pier isn't exactly populated, as you know. The beach is too close to the industrial area, so he probably thinks he has plenty of privacy there, and it's easy to see someone coming," Carter answers.

Dalton Pier, where he told me to meet him.

Confidence blooms in my veins at the image of the bastard walking calmly on the dark beach, hand in hand with his *date*. Though, I believe in the *victim* theory much more. This is a curveball. But I can catch it. I have to catch it, because this is so much better than the alternative. The result might be the same, and I will probably still end up in his clutches, but... what if I don't? I'll have the element of surprise on my side.

A door closes and snaps me back into the present. Slowly, I open this one to find the corridor empty, and muffled voices coming from Vincent's office. I sneak to the door and listen.

"For what he did to Evelyn he will pay tonight."

"What if it's a trap?" someone asks.

It must be!

It would be perfect timing, taking The Sanctum out before my *meeting* with him. That way, no one would come to my rescue. And if it isn't a trap, I'm still not willing to take the risk.

I'm rushing in the opposite direction before the decision made it into my consciousness. There will be no trap. I refuse to allow these men to fall into one because of me. Even if I have doubts. it is because Frankie just seems like the type of man to have far too much confidence for his own good, I will not risk Finnigan and his Sanctum. I won't risk anyone.

The house is still quiet, voices and laughter only filtering from outside, everyone huddled around the fire pit. My sister too. She's cuddled up on a chair, laughter all gone as she lays there half asleep watching the flame with Aaro. It almost hurts that she looks so at home. So settled.

I want to scream for her, yell my love, but they can't know what I'm about to do. Passing through all of Vincent's security will be hard enough. But they're all distracted now, maybe they won't notice. Or at least not yet, and I'll have a head start.

My bag is still by the front door, and I open it to double check all is still there. Between my wallet, tissue pack, snacks, and random crap, there are two weapons I received as a gift for my protection. Hopefully all this training will mean something and I won't be as vulnerable as last time. I grab the bag and head to the closest room that has windows toward the front, because I know the front door triggers the security system and alerts them. The windows won't. Maybe it's because there is physically no way to open them from the outside, I don't know anything beyond the fact that whenever I've seen someone open a window, nothing has been triggered.

Slowly, I close the door behind me, and head straight to the window, unlatching it. My heart is in my throat as I slowly turn the handle and push it open, listening for the repercussions. None come. So I open it wider, and climb over, dropping outside the house.

I don't waste any time, swing my bag over my shoulder, and bolt through the trees, right at the edge of the road that leads back to the main street. I know there's security patrolling around here, so I stay in the shadows of the trees and run. There is no burn in my lungs, no strain in my muscles, only tension inside of me, questioning my actions tonight. But all I can think about is Maya. My sweet Maya threatened by this revolting asshole. The reservations, insecurities, the fear I had is slowly being replaced by rage. Pure, untapped rage for the man who took so much from me.

I refuse to let him take more.

I have been living in fear that he could be anywhere, lurking, watching, ready to ruin everything for me all over again. So I didn't quite live. His photos are confirmation that he was indeed out there, watching us.

Stopping for a moment, I pull my phone out and book a ride to meet me at the end of this road, beyond the last security camera Vincent has installed here, then I run again. I don't have long before the guys will set off too.

If not for the risk they would fall in a trap, I would let them deal with it. But I refuse to allow anyone to get hurt because of me. And Frankie isn't expecting me so early.

By the time I reach the main road and see the ride waiting for me, the soles of my feet burn from the uneven forest floor, but the adrenaline is keeping me from caring. The older driver gives me a reluctant look when he double checks the destination, but I don't dwell on whatever train of thought he's going through. I have my own to deal with. And currently, my brain is working on a plan for how to go through three men and reach Frankie B.

Fire rushes through my veins, fueling the anger and fear that mixes in a dangerous concoction and are breathing new life into me. My past is about to meet my present, and I pray that the anger will dominate the fear in the end.

I wonder if these men were one of the ones who were with him *that* night... if they were the ones holding me down when Frankie was sticking the needle in my arm? When he pulled my jeans down. Were they the ones who watched? Who laughed? Who cheered him on?

My skin prickles with nerves as the car approaches the destination. There is no going back.

Tonight will end in destruction... and it's likely to be mine.

CHAPTER 34
Evelyn

I'M HIDING BEHIND some crumbling parapet of an old industrial yard, peering over the ledge down to the beach. I agree with Finnigan—what a ridiculous amount of confidence Frankie B must have to think he is safe here. It's quiet, deserted, no soul in sight on the moonlit sand, or beyond. It didn't take long to spot him, even as he is further down the beach now, closer to the pier. From Carter's words I thought he was already at Dalton Pier, but he is actually walking toward it.

Toward our meeting spot, though it's technically supposed to happen in just over an hour.

My fists clench, teeth grinding as I watch him walk with a ridiculous swagger like he owns this beach. This is the man who broke me... how unbearably pathetic. More anger filters through my mind, my body too, fueling my muscles like it's priming them.

He took my sister! He took me! Used me... then passed me right over to his boss.

That anger hits the soles of my feet, my hands clenching around the strap of my small bag I crossed over my body to keep close. Red hot rage fills my vision, my steps quickening with the adrenaline it brings, and not even the constant rumble of the surf soothes me. Before I round the corner I grab my phone and open the text I already wrote on the car ride here—it's short, maybe heartbreaking—but it must be done. I'm ducking behind the parapet, right where it ends and beach sand begins to soften my steps, and I have a clear view of the man who will dictate my fate.

Squatting, I remove the bag off my body, drop my phone inside of it and pull out the knife I got from Maddox, sliding it in my boot. I grab the gun Finnigan gave me for protection, though the silencer I'm currently screwing at the end of it I stole myself from his office. I don't remember why I did it, maybe some unconscious instinct that ironically will come in handy right now.

Shadows swallow me next to this parapet, and Frankie B and his men can't spot me, but I can see them clearly. I waited long enough, checking my surroundings, the vicinity, and none of this looks like a trap for The Sanctum. Maybe I was wrong, maybe we were all wrong. But I'm not backing down. They're maybe fifty yards away from me, enough for clear aim, but the adrenaline coursing through my veins might affect the skills I've honed in the last few months. Maddox is not a huge fan of guns, but he taught me well. I'm not half bad, but tonight... I have to be better. Because there's no way I can stroll down that beach to get to Frankie if his lackeys are still moving.

Ice invades my gut as the realization of my intention hits my rational thoughts—*am I about to kill these men intentionally this time around?* Frowning, I take a moment to acknowledge my feelings, but the ones I'm looking for never come. I feel no apprehension or remorse because the memories of me held down during my assault are filling me with the only emotions that matter right now.

So I lift the gun, aiming it in their direction, bobbing slowly up and down as I follow their movements. The moment one of the men stops walking I squeeze the trigger.

"Fuck!" I curse under my breath when the bullet whizzes past them and hits the sand.

Through the crashing sounds of the waves, only two of them notice the disturbance, but they don't look like they understand what it was. Gripping the bottom of the magazine harder, I inhale deep and aim again releasing it slowly at the same time I squeeze the trigger. The muffled pop is drowned by the rumble of the sea, and one of the men staggers back and reaches for his stomach. I shoot once more, aiming higher, and I expect a scream as he crumbles to the ground, squeezing his chest, but confusion is keeping them silent even as they whirl to look around.

The sea would swallow most of their pointless noises anyway.

As guns are drawn and their gazes search for me, the scene changes from calm to alert, but I force my anxiety back down my throat. I aim once more, not for the head since fifty yards is too far away for me to guarantee the accuracy, but for the chest. Only, the bastard moves just as the bullet flies. Slow panic threatens my muscles and focus, and only one of the next three bullets grazes one of them.

"Just stop moving!" The anger does something to me, and before they can spot my location, I squeeze the trigger once more, and the second man falls back on a piercing shriek. "Finally."

I take my eyes off of them for a moment, searching for the source of that shriek and find the woman Frankie took for a walk, now forcefully trapped in his arms, held away from the gruesome scene.

That brief moment was enough for the third man to spot the general direction the bullets came from, and several shattering pops ripple through the sound waves. I manage to duck before the concrete of the parapet takes the hits. I expected something akin to a boom when they made contact, but it's surprisingly quiet. I rise to find him moving closer, and more bullets strike concrete, one flying just above my head as I duck down.

"This is not how I plan to die." Not before I reach Frankie.

I slide down on my knees and forearms, inching to the edge of the parapet as low as I can go, since the bastard is shooting high. I peer past it as another shot hits the concrete—he's no longer fifty yards away. The sand is slowing him down, but he's covered half the distance to me. *Good.* My aim will be more certain. I squeeze the trigger and the bullet rips through his shoulder on a painful bellow, the sound like music to my ears, but he's not down yet.

"Who the fuck are you?" someone yells from the distance.

That's Frankie B.

I don't answer. He'll find out soon enough.

Pulling the trigger once more, I hit the man's hip, and he staggers, finally falling to the ground. My legs shake as I rise but the early moonlight hits his features, and for a couple grueling seconds I'm pinned in place, panic striking down my nerves.

"I know you." I whisper, focusing my pistol at him. The satisfaction at his fury-twisted pain rippling his features breaks through my fear.

He lifts his own weapon, but I shoot him right in that arm before he can aim, and the gun flies out of his hand.

"You fucking bitch!" he roars, screaming in pain he couldn't possibly hide.

His words don't touch me. I can hear them, but they mean nothing as they float somewhere in the distant places of my consciousness. This feels like a first step, because this bastard was there.

"You held me down." I seethe, stepping closer through the soft sand.

I'm only a few feet away, enough to see the pain-steeped rage marring his features. God, it looks so pretty.

What an odd thought.

Warmth fills my belly, satisfaction turning the adrenaline coursing through my veins into a surge of power.

"Evelyn!"

My gaze whips toward the voice, and I pinpoint Frankie's position—he's farther away than before, arms wrapped tight around the woman who struggles against him. He seems surprised that it's me he's looking at.

"He'll rip you apart," the man on the ground spits, "worse than he did the first time. And then he'll give you to all of us to share and break until all we're fucking is your empty carcass."

I look down at the man crumpled to the ground, spit falling between his thin lips as he attempts a seedy grin when I take aim once more. "But you won't be one of them."

The bullet hits right next to the bridge of his nose, blood and eye matter splattering all around him, and on me too. Then silence comes. Sweet silence amongst the crash of the surf, and when I look up at Frankie B, the smugness is broken by something else. It looks like fascination, but I think there's fear in there too.

Once again, I wait for the guilt and disgust for murdering three people to crash down on me, but nothing comes. All I feel is contentment and can't help but wonder what's wrong with me. As I watch Frankie aim his weapon at me, I do feel a bit of fear too. Still no guilt though...

Is this it, the moment all will be over and he will no longer invade my dreams, turning them into endless nightmares?

I wait a few seconds longer, yet he makes no move to squeeze that trigger. Not even when I begin walking toward him. The blonde woman he forces against his body is shaking silently, trying but failing not to look at the bodies strewn across the beach as dark makeup streams down her pretty face.

I shouldn't waste time, but I'm curious. "How did you know my name?"

He grins and I want to vomit, "You told me. You probably don't remember though, you were off your head impaled on my dick at the time."

Bile lodges in my throat and I tighten my grip around the gun. I shouldn't have asked.

"You're early, *Evelyn*. I wasn't expecting you yet." His lisp grinds my eardrums, and I would gladly make him eat a bullet just so I don't hear it anymore.

"Thought I would surprise you since you wanted me here so badly."

"The plan was to keep you for myself, but considering this"—he waves his gun around the beach and my handy-work—"taming will be necessary. And I'm afraid I'm not good at taming. I tend to kill them, accidentally of course. Lucky for you, I know a few experts at it. I want to say they'll take good care of you before you're returned to me, but the truth is... they'll break you apart. Bit by bit, split your mind in so many pieces, you won't even remember your *Sanctum*, and your body will bear no memory of anything other than their grueling training. You will be pliant, docile. And willing."

I swallow the acidic bile in my throat as I stop not even ten feet away from the man.

"Never." I fume, lining up my gun with his forehead.

I won't miss from this distance, but the asshole yanks the woman in front of him, using her to shield himself as she wails and squirms in his grip.

"Coward," I hiss, keeping my gaze off the intimidating barrel of his gun. "All those threats, just so you can kill me with a gunshot?"

"You stupid fucking girl! Who said anything about killing? I will maim, fix you later, or maybe just partially. Leave you with a limp or something as a constant reminder of your failure."

Failure...

Failure to protect my sister.

Failure to save us.

Failure to avenge us.

I will not be a failure! Not again.

I aim next to the woman's head and pull the trigger. Adrenaline breeds irrational strength, and she cries out, ripping out of his grip and drags herself away.

"Goddamn it!" he yells and shoots at the same time.

Piercing, hot pain slices through my left bicep, and with a shriek spilling off my lips, I squeeze the trigger.

It clicks. Empty.

What the...?

I do it again, but no bullets fly. Then I press it frantically a few more times, keeping my eyes on Frankie.

A sickening grin pulls at his lips, and he bolts toward me. My eyes widen as I step back and throw the useless gun at him. It hits his head but barely slows him down.

The instincts I've been honing in the last few months kick in, and I duck to the right, slamming my right fist in his exposed ribs, then to his head when he bends in pain. He comes for me, staggering on the uneven sand, and I take the opening and kick the gun out his hand. But the asshole is quick, swearing as he throws punches that I manage to intercept and move away from.

I sidekick him low in the gut, then grind my teeth through the ache in my bicep as I throw a quick series of jabs to the throat and head, following him as he stumbles backward. Even so, he lands a couple clumsy but painful punches to my stomach, my legs staggering as I heave, and he takes the opportunity and tackles me to the ground. He doesn't pin me fully, but trying to push him off with that burn in my arm at the same time memories of him on top of me assault me, is almost impossible.

"I missed the feel of you under me," he spits at me with that lisp of his and the seediest of grins pulling at his lips.

When he bends his head to make some sort of contact with mine, I headbutt him with as much force as I can gather in this position. He barks out his anger more than his pain, but at this point I'm deep in a frenzy, half here, half in the memories of him laid over my body, and I use my good arm to land as many punches as I can, blocking his attacks as well. I only pause for one brief moment, but he takes the opportunity and wraps a hand around my throat, squeezing hard enough that pressure builds behind my eyes. I claw at his arms, his shoulder, back, neck, and everything else I can get my hands on, but the man doesn't budge. Instead, he squeezes tighter and panic surges deep in my belly as I bend my legs and plant my feet to try to haul him off.

"That's it, you look so much prettier when hope leaves your eyes and your life is in my hand," he says on a tone he probably thinks sounds seductive, but I want to throw up.

The edges of my vision blur, the haze spilling in further as the air catches in my lungs, but a cold slither of hope presses against my ankle, reminding me it's there, and I reach down to grasp it. A grin pulls at my lips, Frankie frowns, but the confusion turns to a gut-wrenching bellow when the blade of my knife sinks just under his ribs.

He releases my throat to check the wound, but I use his distraction to flip us over, straddling his thighs. I lift my arms high, holding the hilt with both hands, and as his eyes bulge and mouth falls open like a fish out of water, I slam the blade in his stomach with such force, the sides of my fist make him fold over, spitting blood.

The gurgled sounds coming from him scrape against the back of my throat threatening my stomach to turn over, so I pull the knife out and smash it right back in there. But the noise keeps happening, so I repeat the assault.

You're making me sick! Stop!

I slam it in again. Then once more, and the gurgling twists to a whimper. It caresses against my senses, it soothes.

I crawl backwards away from him, my chest tight with unshed tears that burn behind my eyes. He's still, his chest barely moving with weak breaths, mouth agape as he grasps to every ounce of air, and his gaze is fixed on me as he holds his palms over his bleeding abdomen.

"You were wrong... you're the one who looks pretty when hope leaves your eyes, Frankie B." I scoff, shaking my head. "What a stupid fucking name you get to bear while you die."

Utterly ridiculous, like some *guido* who ended up on the wrong side of the tracks. Through blood pouring slowly out of his mouth he manages a weak, taunting laugh.

"You'll die... a horrible death when he finds out," he mutters.

Frowning, I cock my head, but he continues anyway.

"I wanted you to myself... but you're worth less than cattle to him." He takes so long to spit out the words between blood and staggered breaths, I'm losing my patience.

He's referring to his boss, Bartiste. Killing his right-hand man will demand retribution, but The Sanctum is fully prepared to take him on.

"Save your breaths, Frankie. Your threats mean nothing." I gather my knees to my chest as I watch the man who changed my life, waste away. I'll sit here for however long I need to. I need to see this.

"My name…" He coughs, spluttering blood that looks black in the moonlight.

He whispers something, but through his dying breaths and the waves of the sea, I can't make it out. He blinks slowly, eyes staying more closed than open.

I slowly roll onto my knees, getting just a bit closer to the man to see if his moving lips actually spew any relevant words. When his gaze opens to me, I can see the dying light peering back, and I smile. It's the death of my nightmares.

"My name…" he says in a weak whisper, "is Franco *Bartiste*. He's my father."

He exhales one more breath as the light seeps out of his eyes, and my mouth falls open.

"Oh, my god." I just murdered Roberto Bartiste's son.

CHAPTER 35
Finnigan

I LOST COUNT of how many times I called her. How many times I roared in her voicemail, screaming for her to answer her damn phone. Then I pleaded to her...

I prayed to all the gods I stopped believing in that she is okay, that he didn't do anything to her, that she hasn't left me.

But she did. After I bared my pain to her.

The guys and I were in the office, hashing out a quick plan to tackle Frankie, when a few trail cameras and sensors were triggered out in the forest. It's common, there are animals around here, too, and when we couldn't see anything, that's what we thought. But more were triggered, there was movement out of sight, through thick, tall bushes, and our minds were drawn to Bartiste and his men. Annika was already putting the kids to bed at that point, the others were safe tidying up through the house, but our security was on high alert and went to search. When they didn't find anything, Madds, Vin, and I went out there too. We had to be certain since we needed to make sure our family was safe.

But then tires screeched on the road, and Carter called for us. When we joined him, he told us Loreley noticed Evelyn was gone. We thought she was somewhere in the house, just like the others since we had absolutely no reason to think otherwise. Just after, Evelyn texted her, and when Carter showed it to me as we all climbed in his and Ronan's car, my heart sank.

I'm sorry, I wish there was another way, but it's between Maya and I, or you all and I. So, it isn't even a choice at all. I have to protect Maya, and if he is indeed setting a trap for The Sanctum, I can't let them fall in it. Not since it was set so no one could come and save me from him.

I know this could be a mistake, but I can't risk any of you. I hope you'll understand. All of you gave me more than I could ever repay you for, a life beyond my wildest dreams, and I love you for it. If I don't return, please, please make sure Maya is taken care of. I know it's selfish of me, but I can't let him win again.

I'm sorry.

I've re-read that text so many times, it's imprinted in my memory. A jagged claw has been shredding through the depths of my soul, its tip slowly slicing through my heart, and I didn't realize just how much of Evelyn seeped in until now. How much her absence hurts.

In that message she mentions protecting Maya. Us too. Like we've been threatened, being held as leverage over her. Is that the case? She thought her sacrifice would save us? Keep us safe?

The questions run rampant in my mind.

Even with her abandonment, I can't bear the thought of something happening to her. Losing her would be the end of me. I will not survive it. Somewhere through this strange journey we've had, she broke me apart, slicing the edges in patterns only she can match and put back together. And even if anyone but her would dare recognize the shapes, I would rather carve my heart out with bare hands than let them.

Carter weaves through the last of the streets that lead to the desolate beach, tires screeching on the asphalt as he takes that left. He tracked her phone the moment Loreley showed him the text, and knew exactly where she was. And she hasn't moved since. At all. It's both a good and a bad sign, and my stomach lurches with every bump in the road.

Through the whole car ride I wanted to scream at him to hurry the fuck up, but I didn't need to—he drove like a madman, the urgency not lost on him.

"There!" I point to the end of a building, right next to a parapet that edges the beach. "Stop."

I'm out of the car before the others stop behind us, and I duck behind the low wall, rushing to the edge of it. I'm so focused on taking in my surroundings, I almost stumble.

"That's Evelyn's," Maddox whispers behind me as I look down at the small bag dropped at my feet.

I peer in and the first thing I notice is her phone—that's why she hasn't moved. Well, that makes sense, but it doesn't make me feel better. Cocking the gun I peer out, and the first thing I notice is the man splayed out on the sand, dark blood splattered around him.

Did she do this?

Panic grips my insides, wondering how close he got to her. Is she hurt?

More fucking questions I have no answers to.

I look beyond the obviously dead man, down to the bottom of the beach, and mere feet from the crashing of the waves, I catch sight of a slim figure in the bright moonlight. From her hands and knees where she was leaning over the ground, she backs up and falls on her haunches.

Evelyn!

Wait, that's no ground she was leaning over—it's a person.

I'm running before any of these thoughts settle, noticing the other fallen bodies as I speed toward her. There's four in total, including the one she sits by.

She killed.

Again.

But this is not the same as when she protected Madds from getting shot. That was pure instinct, a spur of a moment decision to protect someone, and most of her destruction was driven by fear. Desperation, even. These four men sprawled on the sand weren't killed with the same drive. This was different. Very much intentional. Even premeditated.

I get to her just as she gathers her knees to her chest, staring at the ocean with tense shoulders, and a weak shudder raking through the rest of her body.

"Evelyn!" I shout for her.

But she doesn't even flinch. Maybe over the crashing of the surf she can't hear me.

My feet are sluggish in the soft sand, but I reach her nonetheless, stopping only a few feet behind her, my heart racing as I take in her delicate figure, so vulnerable in this moment. I open my mouth to call for her once more, but no words spill past my lips. Frankie, or better yet, his corpse, lies here, a knife buried to the hilt in his mangled chest. Nowadays, I barely blink when I take a life, so I can't imagine what's going through her mind right now.

But none of that matters right now because she's not gone.

The breath I finally exhale is deeply charged with fear and anxious energy like I've never felt before, and I'm so happy to let it out.

I want to wrap her in my arms and scream at her in equal measures. I want to punish her for her stupidity, for not trusting me, and kiss her because she's still here.

Still alive.

Still *mine*.

Evelyn

THE INCESSANT BUZZING in my brain has quieted. Death brings silence, and not only for the dead. Yet, I find no peace. I feel no better, or worse. No relief...

I won. But no great feeling of victory has taken over me. The stories, the movies— they all lied.

"Evelyn?"

My name sounds distant, slow, like the fog it tries to penetrate is simply too dense to allow it to reach me. Yet it fights through...

"Are you okay?! Evelyn!"

Between each crash of the ocean's waves, the sand beneath my body vibrates. Their rhythm slows as the thumping loudens and the words that filter through the fog soften, carrying something that seems to be missing from my state of mind currently... something strange. Painful.

The vibrations stop as the man who's been soothing my nightmares plunges on his knees in front of me, gripping my shoulders harshly.

"Please, beautiful, please come back to me. Don't leave me again..." The last sentence is spoken in the softest of whispers, carried away on the soft crashes of the waves like it never happened.

Fear.

That's what his words hold. And exactly what stares into my eyes from his striking blue ones.

Did I put that there?

"For the love of god, Evie, please! Are you okay?"

His touch is warm, and tight. He's holding me steady and only now I realize it's because I'm shivering. Am I cold? The salty, strong ocean breeze whips my hair around my face and goosebumps spread over my bare arms. Though, they may be due to Finnigan's possessive touch on me.

He arrived out of nowhere, like I wished him here once the madness ended. Or maybe that's why I took my phone with me, knowing Carter could track it.

I need him.

But will he want me after what I've done?

His eyes roam over my body, pulling at my limbs, petting me, like he's looking for seeping wounds while holding his breath. He hisses when he reaches my bicep, and mutters something about a flesh wound. Watching the foamy waves doing their calm dance as the moonlight shines brighter, higher in the sky than when I came here, I let him do it.

My muscles are weak. My will is even weaker. Numbness seeps through the fibers forming my being, an ominous gloom I can't escape, and they feel a lot like punishment. I deserve it all and not even for what I've done, but for feeling absolutely nothing about it. Nothing at all.

"Oh God, you're okay." He sighs, that sickening fear expelled out of his body as he rips the bottom of his T-shirt and wraps it around my arm.

What's wrong with me? Killing four people should rip my soul apart, should break me, should shred it with guilt. Yet... there's nothing.

"Evie darling, we have to leave."

Why? The salty breeze soothes my skin, and if I don't move, I can keep enjoying it. A pure moment within the destruction I caused.

Not only the one on this beach and the dire consequences it will bring, but what I left behind. The people I so harshly abandoned, even if I did do it to protect them. One of them sits right before me, and I cannot bear acknowledging his presence. I had a tinge of hope that I would survive tonight, but I didn't actually think I would. Do they hate me? Does he hate me?

Distant footsteps shuffle through the sand somewhere behind me, and I flinch, but don't turn. No matter who it is, I know they won't touch me. Not with Finnigan here. He wraps one large hand over my bony knee, narrowing an assessing gaze on me.

"The others are here." He jerks his head toward the source of the shuffling without breaking eye contact. "A cleanup crew is on the way too."

Cleanup crew. Will they scrub my soul too? My thoughts drift somewhere in the distant parts of my mind where they seek the solace that should be there with Frankie's death.

Franco Bartiste actually.

"Are you okay? Say something."

Finnigan's harsher tone forces me to focus and I narrow my gaze on him. Not because of the question, but because of the kindness looking back at me. It holds a tinge of pity.

I don't need his damn pity.

"Christ, listen to me, you've been here for too long. We have to go." His tone grows colder. It doesn't match his expression.

"Go then."

Please don't. I'm scared. But I'm even more scared to be alone with him, to face him properly.

"I'm not fucking playing. Someone could have witnessed this, and if the police were called, you can't risk being seen."

I draw in a deep breath as his eyes narrow on me. He's losing his patience. Oh well. I shrug, but that angers him further.

"Fuck this!" He grips my good arm, pulls me up, and before I can register the movement, he dips down and throws me over his shoulder.

That snaps me right out of my trance, bringing me back to the reality I've been avoiding.

"Son of a—! Put me down, right now!" I smack his lower back, avoiding his annoyingly perfect-shaped ass as he moves to walk away.

"No. If I say we have to go, we have to fucking go."

"I'll walk!" I argue, as I plant my palms on his lower back and push myself up.

But a crack splits through the softening crash of the surf, and a sharp ache heats my right ass cheek.

"You didn't just—" the protest lodges itself in my throat when the last man I killed comes into view, lying on a bed of blood-stained sand with my blade stuck in his gut.

"Ronan, grab that knife."

Even his brother's here?

Embarrassment pools in the pit of my stomach, but I'm unsure why. Maybe it's because I consider the man normal since he's technically not part of this world anymore. And now he's a witness to my sins.

Actually, there's another witness.

"The woman!" I say on a loud gasp.

"We got her. She's fine."

The bobbing around on his shoulder is making me nauseous, and I grab onto him to steady myself.

"What will you do to her?"

"*With*, Evelyn. With her. We're not gonna do anything to her. Carter will question her to find out if she's a threat, and take it from there."

"Carter?!" I all but squeal. "He's going to eat her alive!"

"Only if he has to."

Finnigan ducks down and settles me back onto my unsteady feet, and I'm about to argue that his answer isn't soothing me in any way, but it only reaches his warm palm. Frustration pools in the back of my throat and bleeds through my eyes as the man holds his hand over my mouth.

"I said"—his tone lowers just as his brows do—"we have to leave. Get in the car."

He pushes me backward, and my legs hit something, but there's only empty space behind my ass.

"Le' 'e 'o." I mumble against his skin, and the bastard grins.

He actually grins. So I push my tongue out against his palm, licking it as surprise hits his brows.

"Get in the car, Evelyn." He says it with the softest, most soothing of growls rumbling deep in his chest, and the command spills through my body like syrup, driving my legs to bend and shift until I'm sitting in the car.

A few moments after the door shuts, he slips on the other side of me, and Maddox and Ronan climb in the front at the same time.

Reality sucks the air out of this enclosed space, and only the roar of the engine seems to save me. The man I... like, his brother who has been taking care of my sister, and the giant who has become like a brother to me, sit in an uncomfortable silence as we pull away from the bloodied beach.

I sneak a peek at Finnigan, and his gaze finds mine at the same time. I cannot decipher the range of emotions burning through me. There's too many, too loud, some dark, and others unbearably light. I don't know what to say, if it's the right time to apologize. Will there ever be one?

Pressure builds in my chest and lodges itself in my throat as I lose control of my breathing, and prickles explode beneath every inch of my skin, urging me to scratch it bloody and get them out. Finnigan's gaze widens and his hands rush to me in a split second, just as a broken, sharp cry slips through the dam forming at the back of my tongue. He drags me on his lap, wrapping me in his warm embrace that feels more like home than anything I ever experienced, and presses my cheek in the crook of his neck.

Right here... in the arms of the man I can no longer deny I love, my soul breaks.

The dam opens, and my chest frees the fear and anguish that has plagued me since the moment Franco Bartiste stole me away. He tore so much from me, ripped me open and filled me with malice.

My cries bounce around the car, mixing with the rumble of the engine as I curl deeper into Finnigan's body, folding my arms against my chest as he tightens his hold on me, whispering soothing words against my hair. Even now, he doesn't dare thread his fingers through it—a gesture that would calm any normal person. Instead he keeps to my back, my neck, rubbing in circles.

There's nothing normal about me. I crashed so hard from my high horse, back when I used to judge Finnigan and his Sanctum for their crimes and violent ways. I could blame them for what I've done. For what I've become. But I would be a hypocrite. I was one back then as well.

Because this has been *me* all along.

Their violence hasn't impacted me, they haven't even exposed me to it. It all comes from within, deep in my dark little soul that craves revenge as much as it does the love I feel in this man's touch.

My tears fall in waves, joining the desperate cries I can't control.

"I'm so sorry!" I mutter, repeating those words over and over again praying that the next time they come out, there will be no fear in them.

"Breathe, Evie darling, breathe." He soothes me with soft kisses as I shake against his chest.

Only, I cry harder, nightmares and memories spilling with every tear and broken sob, and through it all I realize… I still feel no remorse for the people I murdered. And the tears seem endless now.

"That's it… let it all out," Finnigan says as he strokes my back gently.

God, it helps. Why does he have this effect on me? I don't know how much time passes, how many roads we've swerved on, or how fast Ronan's been driving, but my chest finally fills with a full breath of air.

"I left!" I blurt out between the last of the sobs.

"You did." He says in such a calm tone, it scares me.

"Why are you…? You're not even upset. You don't care."

The car screeches to a halt at the same time Finnigan pushes me only far enough away that he can look into my eyes, and I hear a muttered *'fuck'* from the front seats.

"I. Don't. Care?"

Oh… I screwed up.

There is no trace of sweet baby blue in his eyes, only the menacing shade of destructive ocean storms, and they're pulling me in their vortex.

"I—"

"Don't!" he interrupts with a raised index finger, silencing me with a deep chill in my bones.

The car moves again and the echo outside of it reminds me of a parking garage. I dare peek past the man who still holds me tight on his lap and confirm it—we're home, in his building.

A few moments later, he maneuvers me out of his hold, then pulls me out of the car after him, but doesn't say a word.

The others are silent too, and even if I was just in the car with him, I dread looking Madds in the eyes. He's probably so pissed at me. When Finn takes a step out of the way, I'm faced with the giant that doesn't look all that gentle right now. Amber eyes regard me with so much fury, it could only be bred from love.

He grips my shoulder, nostrils flaring when he notices the strip of fabric wrapped around my bicep, but doesn't say a thing.

I drop my head, chewing on my lip nervously. "I'm sorry."

"Later," he mutters in response, giving my shoulder a tight squeeze, and I know I'm down for some serious telling-off.

But I guess *later* means he still wants to have me in his line of sight.

A warm hand wraps around mine just as Madds releases me, and I'm pulled away.

"We're going upstairs. Now."

"But—"

"I swear to god, woman." He growls deep in his throat as we hurry over to the elevator, where one of his men is currently waiting, holding it open.

"They're gonna know… about us, now," I whisper.

"That ship fucking sailed, Evelyn," he spits back as the doors close, sealing us in.

I'm left with questions I have no right to demand answers to, and the rest of the ride up to the penthouse is quiet, sizzling with tension, all wrong and right, heavy and soothing. But the anticipation of what's coming is killing me, because no matter what, it's not going to be good.

The *ding* comes too soon, and when the doors open and he steps out, I almost hope he'll leave me in here. But he plants a hand on the frame, and pierces me with his gaze. The order is silent, but I follow it anyway.

The penthouse is bathed in moonlight and the faint glow of two distant lamps, but they're enough to see the tensed, slow rise and fall of Finnigan's shoulder.

"Finnigan, I—"

"I don't care?!" He whips around, rage rolling out of his mouth like a shattering storm as he pins me in place with nothing but his menacing eyes. "You think I don't fucking care about you, Evelyn? Look at me, goddamn it!"

I don't understand, I am looking right at him.

He steps closer, the glow showing him in such an eerie light, he's godlike. Strong. Beautiful. Broken.

Broken.

His heaving breaths, tensed shoulders, fisted hands... oh god, the pain in his features, brimming his eyes, threatens to knock me on my knees.

"You think I'm not upset? Jesus Christ, Evelyn, how could you even say that I don't care?" His steps echo through the vast space as he nears me, and I tense when he grabs the side of my throat, tipping my head back with his thumbs under my chin, forcing my gaze to him. "Is that all you learned in the last few weeks? Hell, in the last few months?! I care, Evelyn. More than I've ever cared for anyone. Ever. I can't fucking breathe knowing I could have lost you before I realized... before I told you that I—I—"

With bruising pressure his lips crush my own, the kiss hungry, demanding, pained, forcing out of me solace and life-force to soothe his own.

I grip his waist, but the moment my fingers sink in, he pushes me away, holding me at arm's length.

"I can't believe you left me. Us. Your sister."

Tears return to my eyes as I gaze back into that pain that I put in his.

"I thought it was the only way. He threatened her. He had her under surveillance."

He shakes his head, releasing my neck, and grabs my hands, holding them between us. "You should have trusted me to help you. To make this right and kill that asshole. Now it's you who carries his blood on your hands."

Literally. As I glance down, my hands and arms are stained with blood, now dry and itchy.

"It will wash off."

He scoffs, shaking his head. "That's not what I mean. This kind of violence is something that stains your soul. You shouldn't have been the one to carry something like this. This was intentional, willing, premeditated, not like when you protected Madds."

I shake my head, tightening my grip on his fingers as I chew on my lip, the words too heavy to be spoken.

"Evie?"

Swallowing the lump in my throat, I take a deep breath and brace myself.

"My soul was stained long before I came to Queenscove."

CHAPTER 36
Evelyn

"WHAT DO YOU mean?"

I shake my head, steering the conversation away. "I'm sorry. I should have trusted you, but he threatened you too. All of you. After he messaged me, I heard you all talk about how you spotted him, that you thought it was a trap. It was the same location where I was supposed to meet him later, and it all sounded too good to be true. Why would he show himself there, just a couple of hours before our meeting, if not..."

"To kill us before he got to you," Finnigan finishes for me.

"It sounds silly now, knowing that it was just his ridiculous confidence, but I couldn't risk it. The thought of anyone dying for me was unbearable. I trust you, god, I trust you with my life. With Maya's life!"

He softens at those last words. He knows I value her much more than I value myself.

"I understand, but please, for the love of god, never. Ever. Do that again. Trust me to protect you both. We haven't exposed you to our *ways* because it wasn't necessary for you to see any of that, but believe me when I tell you, as scary as Bartiste and his men sound, we are scarier. And more than ready to take them."

I sigh, watching him with regret I struggle to hold back. "I can't rationalize it more than I have. Not so deep down I know all of that to be true. But I think the fact that Bartiste has evaded you successfully scared me as well."

"Evie darling, what we share with you is at face value, because you don't need to know every single detail. You shouldn't. But trust me when I say, Bartiste and his men have not evaded us successfully. We are being smart about how we take them down. Bartiste is hiding, but to bring down a kingdom successfully, you start with the army. We've been picking hard at it, and today our soldiers took down more than half of the one he brought here with him. Which is how we found out where Frankie was. Bartiste has experience in hiding, I can admit that no matter how hard it bruises my ego, but he is no longer smarter or stronger than The Sanctum."

My shoulders fall on a relaxing sigh. So many people dead shouldn't be a soothing thought, but alas, they could burn alive in a mass grave for all I care.

Finnigan leads me further in the penthouse, setting me down on the plush sofa, and leaves me to watch the clear, starry sky through the floor to ceiling windows. Water runs in the kitchen, then he returns with a first aid kit and a bowl of water, holding his hand out for mine. I wince when he unwraps the small wound on my bicep, but I can't hold in the smile when pain skirts his eyes. It seems to hurt him more than me, and that does something to my little heart. We don't speak as he cleans the gash. He focuses there and I focus on him, unable to stare anywhere else.

I don't know how to process this. Good things don't happen to me. Instead, everything I touch seems to crumble.

"Okay," he says as he dabs the area. "I'm going to add a few adhesive stitches, but luckily, it's a graze. Albeit a little deeper."

I nod as he rises and disappears again, leaving me with my intrusive thoughts as I stare out the windows. I'm going to miss watching the horizon over the ocean if I do decide to return to Fleeton. This place calls for my soul. A brief time later Finnigan returns with a tray, a bunch of glasses clinking on it as he sets it on the coffee table.

"What's this?"

He points to each of them as he rattles them off. "Whiskey, vodka, rum and coke, vodka lime, water, and orange juice. To cover all… needs."

I puff out a stifled laugh, reach for the vodka lime and down half of it with a groan.

"What did you mean, Evelyn? When you said your soul was already stained before you came here?"

I didn't think I would evade this line of questioning, did I? Hence the variety of drinks.

"Remember what I told you about how I lost my mom?" I wait for his answer, but he frowns in disbelief and nods. "Sorry, I guess I just don't assume you hold onto everything I tell you."

"I remember everything. Go on."

"Maya and I were homeless not long after, but I did my best to keep an ear out for information about her murderer. I found out none of the men responsible were caught. When it comes to gang crime, they rarely are. The thing is… when you live on the streets, even in your car, you hear things. Homeless people are a wealth of information because people don't pay them any mind. They're almost invisible but hear so much. And sometimes they talk. That's how, about ten months or so after we ended up on the streets, I caught wind of this guy, a young one, who was bragging about the night of his gang initiation. Same month, same place, the exact shooting that took my mother. He bragged about how they escaped murder charges, and how *cool* it made him. Raised his street cred."

I pause as Finn wipes a hand over his face, releasing a staggered sigh.

"I followed that *breeze* for a while, until I learned more about him, the gang, who he was, and finally, I saw him. His face is still imprinted in my memory, but after that… I could barely sleep. He plagued my nightmares and pulled my mother into them too. It was always both of them, never just him. A grueling reminder of what he took from me, from us. Then one night, we were staying in this shoddy motel in the bad side of town. One of many, Maya was sleeping in the room, and I went out to get some food.

Then our fates aligned, and I heard him..."

I draw in a deep breath and throw back the rest of the vodka sour. "He was in an alley, on the phone, smoking. All alone. Even through that darkness, I knew it was him. Nothing could have stopped me that night. Not Maya, not my dad, not the police. All I saw was shades of crimson, and all it took was noticing a rusty pipe on the ground. I grabbed it and ran toward him just as he ended the call. He didn't even see me coming. It wouldn't have mattered if he did. No one could have recognized him by the time I stopped. I didn't even scream as I did it. Rage consumed me. I'm not even certain he was dead when I left. He looked dead. Felt dead. What concerned me the most was that I didn't care. Still don't."

Looking at Finn, I expect to see more pity, but it's just sadness gazing back.

"I'm sorry, darling. I really am. That shouldn't have been the aftermath of your mother's murder."

"No. The police should have caught him. All of them. I shouldn't have become a murderer and hated myself for it. But you see, Finn, I blamed you and your criminal world for destroying mine, when in fact... I'm projecting the anger and hate I have for myself. Because all I felt that night was a worrying sense of victory and satisfaction. No remorse. I'm no better, no different."

He watches me calmly, no judgment staining his gaze as he quietly sips his drink, keeping a possessive hold on my thigh.

"In some twisted way I understand. I realized it's what I'm doing with Ronan, and I'm definitely projecting on Aaro." He shakes his head. "And now? Do you have the same feelings about these men?"

I swallow the lump in my throat, questioning if sincerity is the right course of action. He cocks his head ever so slightly, urging me on.

"No," I answer.

He nods once, the movement free of hidden meanings.

"I will bother you with this question, over and over again for a while, Evelyn, and I'm not gonna apologize for it—how are you feeling, are you okay?"

I like that he doesn't dwell on what I've done, on the guilt or lack thereof, he doesn't insist.

"Better, honestly."

I thought I was handling my emotions well, especially with therapy too, but I was wrong. I was just seeping through the seams, letting out only enough to function, and held onto the full brunt of the heartache, pain, and the real tears that come from my hidden scars.

"I know you feel no regret for the men you killed, no matter the impeccable job you did." The little smirk at the end of that gives me an odd sense of pride, "But what you did was still significant, because one of them was Frankie B. Talk to me about it. Don't hide or bottle up any emotions or conflicts you might feel. Something like this, no matter your past, can eat you up from the inside without even realizing. We're not all built to be killers."

Christ, this is a rather odd conversation. The crime lord is basically giving me *murder aftercare*. Well, how can I complain about that?

I nod, and grab the glass of straight-up vodka, drinking a quarter of it, following up with the orange juice to soothe the burn.

"Come here." He drags me against his side before he finishes the request, wrapping his arms around me and burying his nose in my hair.

It takes me a few breaths to relax into his hold. I'm not sure I deserve the comfort, but his warm body against mine feels so right. I wrap one arm around his middle, and when his dark chocolate and sea salt scent invades my senses, I nestle deeper into him.

Mmm... I could make a little tart that tastes like him. Cacao crust, dark chocolate and sea salt cream, piercing blue baroque swirls blooming around a skull in the center, to match his eyes. My mouth already waters. One deep yawn and my eyes drift close. The man is so comfortable. I could climb on top of him and fall asleep.

"I think it's time for a shower and bed." He shifts to rise, but I tighten my hold.

"There's something else." I stop him. "Frankie—it's just a nickname."

"Yes, I know. We haven't found out his real identity yet."

"I did."

With rigid, coiled muscles he leans back and looks down at me, loosening his hold as I tip my head to meet his eyes.

"His real name is Franco *Bartiste*."

Finnigan's eyes widen as his mouth falls open before he spits a long series of vulgar curses.

"I killed Roberto Bartiste's son," I add.

"His son..." he whispers, processing the information. "I guess this is when we find out if Bartiste gave a shit about him or not. It will either drag him out of hiding, or we simply continue with our plan."

He tries to downplay the magnitude, but it shadows over his features still. Before I can say anything else he grabs his phone, typing vigorously, then rises, pulling me with him and toward his bedroom.

I don't protest. My lids weigh heavy, and the dried blood is too itchy on my skin. I need to get rid of it and burn these damn clothes. The last thing I need is more Frankie B on me.

Finnigan

I LAY AWAKE for most of the six hours she slept, watching her like she was going to disappear on me once more if I blinked for too long. I thought I knew fear, experienced the broad spectrum of it, but I was wrong. This isn't fear of loss as I thought, of Evelyn being taken away from me. This is fear of abandonment. She *chose* to leave and take on Frankie B, no matter if she lived or died at the end. No matter if she saw me again. I'm afraid she'll do it again, not forced like this time around, but by her own volition.

That is fear.

Of course I've never felt anything like this before, how could I when I've never experienced this intense, heart-wrenching emotion for someone. I'm afraid to give it a name. What if I do and I'm left with just that... a name? No Evelyn. No object for my desires, for my heart to cling to.

She said she hasn't decided if they're going to stay in Queenscove. I'm struggling to understand why the decision is so hard to make. Do we frighten her so much? Do I? I'm trying to be a good man and allow her space to make her choice, but goddamn it, I'm not a good man! And I certainly don't want to give her a choice in this. She simply cannot leave. Evelyn belongs in Queenscove. With me.

Forcing her hand isn't quite the option, but I can offer an incentive. And it's landing in Queenscove in less than an hour.

I'm about to wake her up when a soft moan passes her lips and hits my cock in an instant. My muscles coil around the sound as a ghost of a strain tightens her eyebrows together. I want to dip right into whatever dreams she's having, because the moment the comforter shifts with her legs squeezing together, I know it's a good one.

Actually, I think I will do just that—dip into her dream and make it a reality. Rising ever so slowly, I climb out of bed, constantly looking back to make sure she doesn't stir or wake up as I go to the walk-in closet, grab a silk tie and carefully climb back into bed. This is going to be a challenge, but I'm intrigued to see if this little minx is a deep sleeper.

She's already laying on her back, only vaguely angled toward the right, so part of the work is already done. With the softest of movements and touches, I bring her wrists together, wrapping the tie around them until they're secure and she's immobilized. I do a quick check of her bullet graze to make sure it's not bleeding, but it all looks good. Reaching over behind the bed, I pull out the strap that hangs there unused since I installed it years and years ago, letting it drape over the padded headboard, the metal ring at the end glinting against the dark blue velvet. I lift Evelyn's arms over her head, the air straining my lungs when she stirs, and I'm expecting her eyes to pop open and see me like this. But she only moans again, her lips parting to let the enticing mewl out.

She's a goddamn dream.

I let her joined wrists rest against the headboard as I loop the remaining length of the tie around the ring, tying it into a bow. Breathing a little easier when she still doesn't wake up, I shift backwards on the bed, pulling the comforter with me, and expose her whole body. She looks so fucking pretty laying here deep in her sleep, completely unaware that she's about to be fucked until her tight little pussy has my name imprinted on its lips. My cock stirs, fully hard as my balls ache with the need to come all over her soft skin. Even in a tank top and underwear she still looks like every bit the sexual creature she's becoming.

She stirs, rubbing her thighs together in the softest of gestures, and the moment her back arches, I strike, covering her mouth with my palm. Her eyes fly wide open, fear laced through the silver and gold, and she shrieks against my skin, kicking her legs in a desperate attempt to free herself once she realizes her arms are bound.

There's only a brief pause in her frenzied writhing and it's the exact moment her gaze shifts, softening with awareness. Yet she holds onto her panic, nurtures it as I yank her tank top up, exposing her breasts to my hungry eyes and even hungrier mouth. I roll one soft bud between my fingers, grinning when she yelps against my palm at the flicker of pain, because her arching back and squirming betrays her pleasure.

"You're fucking beautiful just like this, tied to my bed, your eyes glazed with lust," I tell her as I reach over and start wrenching down her underwear.

She twists to try to stop me, but she exposes her taut ass to me in the process. With a sharp crack of my palm, she yelps again, pausing her writhing enough for me to yank the offending fabric off as she curses against my hand.

"Aaah! Let me go, you ass—!" she screams as I release her mouth, but her insult is muffled by the underwear I shove in her mouth.

"Look at that. How fucking devastating you look, gagged and bound. Can you taste it, Evie darling?" I ask, but she frowns. "Can you taste the sweet wetness on your panties? How fucking drenched you get for me?"

She tries to keep the needy mewl from resonating through her throat, but she fails, and I'm on her in the next second, kneeling over her. She quickly shuffles back, bringing her knees up as she attempts to hide her pretty pussy from me, and my cock responds with a tight jerk. I'm impressed at how good she is at playing into this fantasy.

"You think you can stop me from feasting on that tight little cunt of yours? It's mine, Evelyn. All. Fucking. Mine."

I wrap my hands around her knees and pull her as far down the bed as the strap holding her allows, reveling on her muffled protests and cries. They turn to pure fiery screams when I dip down and suck one nipple into my mouth, nipping just to the edge of pain, as I thrust two fingers in her aching core.

"Your screams might spell *no*, Evie darling, but this pussy is weeping for my fucking cock. Are you gonna be a good girl and take it?" I say with a menacing grin.

She shakes her head in response, her eyes glassy with need.

I slide down in one swift move, enjoying her little cry when my fingers leave her core, but I replace them with my tongue, watching as her head whips back and eyes squeeze shut. She's so fucking sweet, a decadent feast as I roll my tongue inside of her, close to the spot that can tip her over the edge in mere seconds. I have to pin her by the thighs when I move to suck on her clit, because she's just about to shoot off the bed from the onslaught of sensations.

I'm not easing her into it. No, I want her to drown in fucking pleasure, cry out for release and reprieve all at once. So I thrust two digits back into her aching core as I assault her swollen bundle of nerves, sucking hard before I threaten it with my teeth, licking and rolling it between my lips. She's writhing on the bed as her pussy pulses around my fingers, but when it grows in intensity, when she's too close to the cusp of her orgasm, I pull out. She cries out, and I can't help but smirk.

"Change your mind, by any chance? Are you gonna be a good girl and take my cock?"

She frowns, her chest rising and falling with her indecision, then shakes her head, violet hair whipping against her flushed cheeks.

"Okay then," I say as I dip back down, covering her core with my mouth.

Only this time I ignore her clit completely and lap the sweet center of her, massaging her walls as she squirms and whimpers. Words are being muffled by the makeshift gag, and I have a feeling they're all deliciously vulgar, because the woman is rolling her hips against my face, seeking the release she desperately craves. Her pussy tightens around my tongue, my face is drenched in her pleasure, but this is not happening on her terms.

Pressing a palm over her lower belly, I hold her down, but her eyes open so wide, I'm not sure if it's from pleasure or pain. She's not snapping her fingers, so I know she's still into this, but I snap mine with a question in my eyes, just in case she forgot the safe word. A brief shake of her head is my answer.

Licking my way up her body, I latch onto one nipple as I plunge three fingers inside her, smirking when her brows draw together at the stretch. But her body shudders under me and I realize that I never enjoyed holding a woman just at the edge of release, playing with her until she's a begging mess under me. As Evelyn bucks down on my hand, attempting to fuck herself with my fingers, she needs no words to beg, her body does it for her. But I push my fingers in as far as they'll go, pressing my whole hand over her core and pin her down.

"Last goddamn chance." I seethe. "Are you gonna be a good fucking girl and take my cock?"

I see the bratty, challenging denial in her eyes, before the first sweep of her head to one side, but before she can swing it the other way, I'm braced on one hand, my cock is lined up with the hot center of her, and I thrust forward. She cries out, a lust-filled moan as her head rolls back and legs widen to allow me more access.

"Fffuck!" I growl as I drop onto my forearms, caging her soft body beneath me.

I kept her pleasure on the edge, but I should have realized I was holding mine right along with it, because... Christ... I'm gonna come in two strokes. I better make them good ones then.

With harsh bucks of my hips, I fuck into her, turning her little yelps into wanton cries as she wraps her legs around my waist, angling her hips and allowing me deeper. Her muffled cries grow louder with each of my thrusts, but they're not enough for me anymore. So I rip the panties out of her mouth as I roll my hips on a deep stroke, and I almost come at the sound of her lustful moan. Such sweet music to my needy ears.

"Finn... oh god! I think—I think I'm coming," she whispers as she pants.

Meeting each of my thrusts with a harsh buck of her hips, she demands the pleasure she vehemently deserves.

"Eyes on me, Evie darling. Let me see you shatter," I demand when her eyes squeeze closed, and I reach between us to help her off the ledge to oblivion.

A ghost of a touch over her clit and she tumbles over, legs shaking as she holds onto me, pushing me even deeper into her spasming core.

"Fuck, I'm gonna—"

I try to pull away so I don't spill inside of her raw, but she holds me so damn tight, lost in her ecstasy, that I can't possibly get out in time. Not when my own oblivion slams into me with devastating force and pulls me into the depths of pleasure.

When she arches her back and moans as my cum shoots inside her, I swear I come even harder, but I'm hungry for those wanton sounds, and I swallow them with a feral kiss. Pressing her deeper into the pillow as my cum spills in never-ending streams, she meets each thrust of my tongue with her own, stroking me as we both claw our way out of this hypnotizing euphoria.

"God, you're fucking perfect, Evelyn. So goddamn perfect. And mine," I whisper against her mouth.

"All yours," she murmurs, and my heart seems to shatter and piece back together all at once, only it feels different... like it's both mine and hers, and she holds most of the power over it.

All yours...

Maybe there is hope yet.

Maybe she'll stay.

Maybe she'll be *forever* mine.

CHAPTER 37
Evelyn

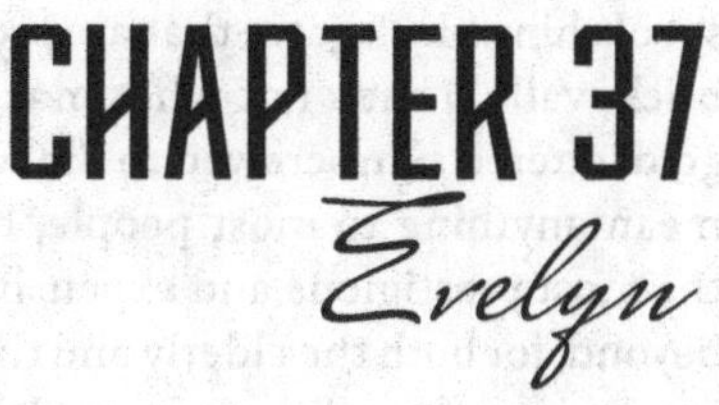

FINNIGAN'S SOFT KISSES still linger on my lips half an hour later, mixed with the words we spoke to each other in the heat of the moment. They sounded more like oaths... vows.

Mine...

All yours...

Until then, I never allowed myself to acknowledge how much I crave exactly that. I want to be his. God, I *need* to be his. Because this infuriatingly gorgeous and smart man has my whole damn heart.

"So you're okay?" Maya's little voice pulls me back into the car as Finn drives us through the bright streets of Queenscove.

"I'm perfectly fine. I'm sorry I didn't wake you up to say goodbye last night." It's a lie since I was gone before she actually fell asleep, but she doesn't need to know that. I'm also wearing a long sleeve shirt so she can't see the bandage wrapped around my arm.

"Okay, then," she says, seemingly satisfied. "So where are we going, Finn?"

"Asking me for the third time is not going to make me tell you, Maya," Finn answers, shaking his head with a smile on those enticing lips. He puts one on mine instantly.

He hasn't told me where we're heading either.

After he screwed my brains out and turned me into a mindless puddle of euphoria, he wrapped my arm and we took a hot shower together before he helped me get dressed. It's just a flesh wound, but he's been fussing over me like a mother hen. It's endearing really. Then he told me he had something to show me. My curiosity spiked since it was barely seven thirty in the morning.

He's been kind of jittery since, flexing his fingers around the steering wheel every time he lets out a heavy, charged breath. He dismissed my questions, insisting it's a surprise for both me *and Maya*, which only spiked my curiosity further. But I relented, it was a lost cause. On our way to pick her up we stopped at the pharmacy to buy the morning-after pill he suggested, and I strongly agreed with since I don't want any *surprises*, and drove to this mysterious location.

I don't know how close or far we are, but he wouldn't be so secretive if it wasn't big. Something about this whole affair both frightens and excites me.

"Are we close?" I give up and ask the question.

He slows down and takes a left on a tree-lined street, but apart from gates at the end of it, there's nothing else.

"We're here," he answers, stealing a glance at me.

My eyes widen and mouth falls open when the car slows down in front of a huge set of shiny black gates that are probably over fifteen-feet tall, surrounded by towering brick walls. That's not what makes my stomach jump with nerves, but the elegant, gold lettered sign screwed to the wall—*Queen Anne Sanctuary*. The cryptic name won't mean anything to most people, but to me, it does. I've looked into it. It's probably the most prestigious and expensive assisted living institute on the South coast, if not beyond, for both the elderly and those who require extra care. Above all, they specialize in a variety of conditions from Alzheimer to MS.

And it's beyond any scope of my imagination in terms of monthly fees. More money that I could ever dream of seeing, not just having.

"Finnigan, what are we doing here?" I ask, unable to keep my eyes off the gate as it opens to what pretty much looks like a well-kept park, filled with tall trees, and flowerbeds flanking the weaving paths that cross through.

I turn to him when no response comes, and he looks at me for a brief moment, then focuses back on the slow drive up the narrow street.

"Wow!" Maya exclaims behind me. "Look at that mansion!"

My head whips back ahead and a beautiful, massive house springs to life through the trees. The façade seems to be built in the same highly decorative period style of Lulu's building, with tall windows, and beautiful iron work. I've seen the place in photos, but it's something else in real life. Finnigan parks right at the front, completely ignoring the *visitors car park* sign that points to the right.

He exits first, signaling me to wait as he walks around the car and opens the doors for us.

I have to ask again. "Seriously, Finnigan, don't mess with me. What are we doing here?"

"Visiting." The cryptic answer spills nonchalantly off of his lips, and I would smack him if my sister wasn't here.

Instead, I follow him through the black double doors looming over the few steps up to them, and we're immediately greeted by a stylish, black-haired woman, wearing a beige skirt suit.

"Mr. Hennessey, lovely to see you again." The woman shakes his hand with a wide smile, way too enthusiastic for my liking, then turns to me. "Miss Shaw, it's a pleasure to welcome you at Queen Anne's." She reaches over, delicately shaking my hand.

She knows my name? What in the hell is going on here?

"Evelyn, this is Ms. Campbell, the director of the institute."

Director? The woman runs the entire place. I nod, forcing myself to remain polite, but a lump quickly makes its way into my throat, urging me to scream my questions.

"Please, follow me." She turns, swiping a card over the access pad of one of the French doors that lead away from this foyer.

I briefly see the reception desk and a few people caught in conversation, but she ushers us through the door she holds open, and I don't have time to process. Dragging Maya along with me, we follow through the corridor lit only by the picture lights above replicas of famous oil paintings, and then through another locked door.

Only, this space is bustling with activity. A large common room with a mixture of normal tables and chairs, comfy sofas and armchairs around coffee tables, with lots of people caught in chatter and laughter as nurses watch over them or help them around. Everyone looks calm and happy. Content.

I can't help the slight smile pulling at the corner of my lips.

"This way."

Ms. Campbell directs us through an open door, down a corridor covered on one side with floor to ceiling windows, and I almost run straight into Finnigan's back when she halts.

"The meeting room is right here and, of course, privacy is ensured."

What in heaven's name is happening? What is this meeting about?

God, I have so many questions.

She points delicately toward an open door, signaling me to walk in. I wait for Finn to take the lead, but he just turns and looks at me.

Laughter echoes past that open door, deep and rich, pure and so damn familiar my heart stops as my mouth falls open, prickles tingling the back of my eyes.

"Daddy!" Maya shouts, pulling free from my hold.

"What did you do?" I whisper to Finnigan, heat filling my chest, spreading through my nerves like wildfire, and I have to clench my fists, digging my nails in my palm to keep from letting it out.

I don't wait for his answer, even as his gaze softens, brows pulling together with a silent apology I can't bear to hear right now. Whipping around, I find my father holding his youngest daughter to his chest with small tears in his eyes as he kisses the top of her head.

Oh god, Daddy.

I'm running to him before I finish the thought, and wrap both of them in my arms, burying my head in the crook of his neck. His scent is so utterly him, even after all this time and through devastating memory loss, he still uses the same aftershave—musk and lemon.

"My sweet Evie, I've missed you so much. You changed your hair!"

"Daddy, are you okay?" I pull back, checking him all over, before I grip his cheeks to hold him to me.

"Perfect now."

His warm smile brings a fresh set of tears to my eyes. He puts Maya down and pulls me in the warmest, tightest hug, dropping sweet kisses on the top of my head.

"I'm okay, my sweet. Thank you for arranging the private plane. Jackie was squealing the whole way, and I think she ate all the peanuts."

Private plane?

"Jackie?"

"Hi, baby girl!" The melodic voice of the older woman sounds from somewhere behind him, and I pull back to find her standing with Maya in her arms, all smiles.

"Oh, Jackie! It's so good to see you!" Daddy lets me go and I rush to her, pulling her in a tight hug. "Are you okay? Is he okay? Were you—" I whisper on a rushed breath.

"We're fine, honey. He's fine too. The trip went by okay, he had a mild sedative at one point when he got a little confused, but it's all good."

I let out a charged breath clutching a hand to my chest.

"What about you?" she asks in a matching whisper. "I was told that it was going to be a surprise for both of you, but I must admit, I fought back quite a bit. At first I thought they wanted to kidnap us."

I stifle an awkward laugh. She has no idea.

"But all the paperwork checked out. I had an interview and everything."

Interview?

"Thank you for looking after him. For keeping him safe," I finally tell her.

"Safe? Evelyn, it was *them* who kept us safe." She nods toward where I know Finnigan stands. "It felt like a presidential escort. And I got a wonderful job thanks to Ms. Campbell."

"You work here now?" I ask much louder, turning to the door where Finnigan and the woman pause their quiet conversation. It explains the interview.

"She came highly recommended. Plus, we heard that your father and her have a great bond, and at Queen Anne Sanctuary we believe in nurturing these connections. They help a great deal in certain cases," the Director confirms.

"Well, I, for one, am happy. Thank you very much for having us in this lovely place." My father nods his head in reverence to the woman. "Sweet Evie, did you see? They even have a fully stocked kitchen, like the ones you see in the movies for cooking courses, for us to use. We can make meringues again."

He's beaming, a smile so wide, I choke up. He's clearly having a good day today, his Alzheimer's allowing us some moments of beautiful clarity.

"Evelyn would love that. She's baking more and more these days." Finn steps up when I can't form any words.

"And who might you be?"

"Finnigan Hennessey, sir." The devastating man sports his softest smile as he extends his hand to my father and they shake. "We saw each other on video call, with the lovely Jackie, a few days ago."

I'm sorry, he did what? I'm going to strangle the man. Not now, though. Not when my dad is next to me. Happy. Safe. Maya clings to him now, looking up at him like he's the moon in the sky.

"Right. And to Evelyn?" my father asks.

"Sorry, sir?"

"Who are you to my sweet Evelyn?"

Finnigan's cheeks turn a lovely shade of pink against his blonde curls, and I'm stepping toward them to intervene.

"Oh, apologies, I'm Evelyn's boyfriend."

I stop dead in my tracks, choking on my own spit when I try to swallow the gasp.

"Need some water, darling?" The man turns to me, a devastating smile dimpling his cheek.

"Finally!" my sister says with a cheeky sigh.

"Maya! I swear... one of these days." I shake my head at her, but she giggles in response and clings tighter to our father.

"Well, it's nice to meet you, son. You're taking care of my girls, yes?"

"Of course. I hope you'll be comfortable at Queen Anne. I've inspected all the facilities and services personally."

"You did?" I ask, unable to hold back anymore of the shock.

"Thoroughly," Ms. Campbell says with a soft chuckle. "We've never been scrutinized quite like this before. Your father is in safe hands. If you'll excuse me, I'll give you some privacy. Please feel free to explore. Jackie here is starting to know her way around, but there are others to assist if you get a little lost. Mr. Hennessey has my contact details if you need anything at all in the future."

"Thank you," I say to the woman, still flabbergasted.

"My pleasure. Welcome to Queen Anne Sanctuary." Her smile is soft and warm as it touches her eyes.

This woman is genuine, and I wonder if she knows how much documentation Finnigan faked to get him here. Dad sits down, pulling Maya on his lap, and they start talking, and I grab Finn's arm and yank him out of earshot.

"What the fuck did you do, Hennessey?" I whisper in a hissed tone.

He cocks his eyebrow, probably at my use of his last name, but amusement brushes his lips.

"I wanted to surprise you—"

"Surprise me?!" I interrupt. "Is that another way of saying that you did something stupid behind my back and without my permission?" My nails dig into his bicep, but it's the only thing keeping me leveled. I don't want to make a scene in front of my father and Jackie.

"Depends how you look at it."

"Is this how you intend on manipulating me into staying in Queenscove?"

His brows lower, gaze darkening at my accusing question.

"Trust me, Evie darling, I have better manipulating techniques than this." He quirks an eyebrow, gaze drawing down my body before it meets my eyes again.

"Don't mess with me; I can see right through you."

He takes a deep, slow breath, cocking his head as he inches closer to me. I tense, but hold strong. Pulling this is completely out of order, though my father's warm laughter filtering through doesn't help my case, especially when it makes me unnaturally giddy.

"Listen to me, Evelyn"—Finn's tone shifts to a low rumble—"I did what I needed to see that beaming smile your father puts on your lips, the tears in your eyes at the sight of his own, and the sheer happiness on your beautiful face, that you can't hide even with your anger. You were devastated, and it broke my fucking heart. After all you've been through, you and Maya did not deserve to suffer through the pain of also being away from your father."

My lips part as I release my hold on his bicep, his declaration leaving me slightly stunned.

"This feels like bribery. I know how much this place costs, and you know for a fact

I cannot afford this."

"Don't you even dare mention money to me right now," he argues as his eyes narrow to a straight line. "You don't understand how much I yearn to make you happy. It's fucking worrying, Evelyn, and I can't make sense of myself. But here I am... trying to make you happy. To make your life easier. Better. You can fight me all you want, but this isn't gonna stop. I'll do whatever I need to do to see that addictive happiness beaming in those gray eyes of yours."

I swallow a lump in my throat as emotions heat their way through my chest at the declaration that feels a lot like he's baring his soul to me. Maybe even his heart.

So many possibilities turn from black and white to full color in my mind, dreams I didn't allow to surface; a high-school degree, my own business, Maya safe in a school, baking with Mamaw June, and regular dinners with all these people who have become family. All of this could happen now.

I just have to allow myself to experience them.

"Finnigan, I—"

"Now is not the time. Go, spend it with your father. Take as long as you want. I'll wait for you in the car."

I drop my gaze, chewing on my lips, and nod. There's plenty of anger and confusion inside of me, but his explanation almost urges me to apologize. Almost.

Turning, I smile once more at the sight of my father and sister beaming as they laugh together, and head over to them. But before I can join them, I halt, and whip back around.

"Stay."

The word spills from my lips like a plea. He answers with the sight of that stunning dimple on his cheek, and a slight nod. I can't deny it, he did make me happy. Devastatingly so because I missed my father more than I allowed him or Maya to know.

"My sweet Evie."

"Daddy," I say, pulling a chair next to his and leaning to press a peck to his cheek. "How about we go for a walk on these beautiful grounds? I have yet to see them."

"Let's go then."

* * *

Apart from Maya's humming in the back seat, the whole ride to Mamaw June's house, to drop her off, was spent in silence.

Now, as he drives us back to his penthouse, the tension in the car is thicker, charged with unspoken words. I hope we're not making a habit of this, though I was purposefully keeping my mouth shut, so I didn't go off at him for crossing this line.

Only, my heart is full after spending all those hours with our dad. We had lunch there, went out to buy him a few things, like clothes, toiletries, and others, since I could barely afford more than thrift-store stuff before. He woke up from his nap and we spent even more time with him until the sun was setting and we could tell that it was becoming a bit too much for him. When the confusion started to hit, we decided it was best to let him rest.

Most of the car ride I spent thinking of when I'll visit him next, instead of being angry at Finn. Because I can do that now, I can see him whenever I want. And he's safe. Happy.

I'm still mad at *my boyfriend*, but I think I'm wishing the sentiment more than actually feeling it, because I think I have to. I should be furious. But the man did all of this for me and my sister. He talked to my father's main caretaker, a woman he knew I trusted, paid off god knows how many people to falsify documents, organized a private plane, and brought my father to one of the leading care homes in the whole country. All at his expense, without even batting an eyelid.

"Come on. Lay it on me. I can't take the damn silence anymore." He huffs, squeezing the steering wheel in his fist as we drive out of the forest road and back into civilization.

I take one deep breath, sifting through all the thoughts and questions I have. But after spending all this time with my dad, some of them don't seem as important anymore. One in particular does weigh on me, though.

"Do you think that by bringing my father here you're going to sway me to decide to stay?"

"No."

"Bullshit," I call out immediately. "You're trying to convince me to stay."

"I definitely *want* you to stay, Evelyn, but it's not why I brought your father. I wanted to eliminate that worry for you. Now that he's here you can focus on what you want for yourself. For Maya. Whether it's work, saving money, baking, or just enjoying yourself, you can do it without missing your father, or worrying about being able to pay for his care."

"You're saying all the right words, Finnigan, but I'm struggling to accept that there are no strings to this. That you're not forcing my hand to stay here."

Realistically, if this is what he was doing, he wouldn't admit it just because I asked. So this is futile. But I can't help but wonder if this gesture is going to sway my decision, regardless. Christ, I'm not even sure a decision was ever necessary. I think I've been governed by fear and lack of options. More and more I feel like there is a world of possibilities here, and it's all due to this man. His Sanctum, too.

But it's him who keeps my soul alive and my heart full.

Him who I want to wake up next to every morning and see each night before I drift off back to sleep.

It's him who I want to share my dreams with and the craziness of raising my little sister.

I want this man by my side.

I want to be his. But most of all, I want him to be mine.

All mine.

After a slow, deep breath, he finally answers, "The spot at the old care home in Fleeton is still reserved for your father. Until you make your decision, it will stay his. So if you wish to return there, he can also return with you without issues. Jackie too, of course."

"Oh, that's..." I trail off.

"Impressive?"

My head whips to him in time to see an annoyingly striking grin pulling at his lips, and I snort, shaking my head.

"Do you not see how worrying it looks to me that you were able to pull this off?"

He shrugs as he drives us through one of Queenscove's main boulevards. "It's nothing."

"Not in my world."

"*Our.*"

"What?" I frown.

"*Our* world, Evie darling. Fight it all you want, but you're one of us. You fit. More importantly," the car stops at some traffic lights, and he turns his gaze to me, "you're mine."

A shudder rips through me as goosebumps bloom over my spine.

"Will I still be yours if I decide to leave?"

His gaze sears through me, but no answer comes. As strange as it seems, I know why. If he answers the question, he'll risk doing just that—manipulate me. Even without trying.

He drives off when the traffic lights turn, and my breaths lighten as his attention shifts.

"Look in the glove box," he tells me.

"For what?"

Is this his answer to my question?

"An envelope. Open it."

Confused, I do as told and pull a large, brown envelope out. Parting the end, I start to pull out a bunch of papers and frown as I look at Finn. Something about the feel of the paper seems a bit too official. A little too thin, yet freshly printed. He nods, signaling me to keep going, even as my hands gently shake. I'm not sure where my reluctance is coming from, but it takes me a few seconds to look over the documents.

I gasp, my hand rushing to my mouth, blinking repeatedly like those words are a mirage and I expect them to disappear any moment now.

"This can't be," I mutter to myself, blinking excessively like that black-on-white ink is going to rearrange itself back to the real words.

Surely this cannot be.

But the words stay put.

Tears brim my eyes as they widen with every new sentence, every set of words, every single time mine and my sister's names are mentioned.

"How?" is all I manage to whisper, as Finn's phone rings, making me jump.

"We have *friends* in high places," he answers as he rejects the call.

I don't even care if what he means is that he blackmailed a bunch of people, or broke some legs, because these documents state, nice and damn clear, that I am Maya's official guardian.

"You did this for me. I have custody," I say in disbelief, heat flooding my soul and wrapping around my heart. *This man...*

His phone rings again, and he mutters curses as he presses a button on his car screen.

"Where are you?"

That sounds like Vincent barking on the other line.

"About a minute away from home."

"Turn the fuck around now! Your building is being stalked. Two of our men are down. They're waiting for you," Vincent urges.

"Shit. Where are you?"

"Loading up, underground. There's something else."

"What?" Finnigan asks, a deep frown settling between his brows.

"It's happening. Bartiste is coming for us."

CHAPTER 38
Finnigan

FUCKING FINALLY!

This bastard evaded us for too long, and no matter how much of his operation we have destroyed so far, the satisfaction is never going to come until Roberto Bartiste is dead.

"Perfect!" I exclaim, stealing a glance at Evelyn who frowns at my reaction, her gaze switching between the phone screen, the paperwork, and me.

"Okay, I'm turning around."

"Morrigan and Loreley are joining Maya." Vin's avoiding saying where. I wonder if he thinks someone could be listening.

"I'm taking *her* too. Text me where to meet you."

"No!" Evelyn's words rush out as I end the call.

"There's no time to debate this."

She's pressed back into the seat as I turn the car around, earning some angry honks from other drivers. I speed up, weaving through the evening traffic, and I head back toward the edge of town.

"Exactly. There is no time. Do not waste it by driving back to Mamaw June's." She shoves the paperwork back in the envelope and pops it back in the glove box.

I clench my fist around the steering wheel and press harder on the gas as I force myself not to raise my tone at her. "That's the best place where you can be right now— safe. With your sister."

"I appreciate that, but it makes no sense. Let's just go meet the others."

"You heard Vin, the others are going there as well," I retort.

"You know I meant Vincent and the others, not the girls! Why are you being like this?"

"I'm not discussing this anymore. There are loads of security around the forest and Mamaw June's, it's safe there."

"Security? I managed to sneak past them."

"Trust me, Vincent almost chopped a few heads because of that. No one goes through anymore."

"Oh, god," she whispers to herself, probably wondering if anyone's hurt because of her, then shakes the thought away. "It's too far, Finn. Please, we have to go after Bartiste." She wraps her small hand around my thigh as her eyes plead with me.

"No, *I* have to go after him. Me, not you!" Holding my tone back didn't last long, not when she insists on being so damn stubborn.

"Finn, plea—"

"Listen to me, Evelyn!" I roar, tires screeching as I pull over, turn in my seat, and grip her sweet face in my hands. "I will not risk your life! Over and over, you underestimate just how much you mean to me. What I'm willing to do to keep you safe. I can't lose you, damn it. Don't you understand? I fucking love you, Evelyn!"

Her plump lips part on a soft gasp, and her eyes are like saucers as she takes in my words.

"You mean too much. So fucking much..." I whisper now, brushing the tip of my nose to hers, and lean my forehead against hers.

"Yo—you love me?"

Pulling back, it's my turn for my eyes to bulge. I did say that, didn't I? Holy shit... I do. I love her.

Fuck me.

"I didn't stand a chance against you, Evie darling. You're a bright fucking star in a soulless world, and you burned right through the shackles that held me back."

Her gaze softens, the words sinking in slowly, caressing her soul as she clutches the back of my head and pulls me in. We kiss feverishly, allowing ourselves these stolen moments before the very thing that brought us together will end.

When we break apart, her eyes seem to sparkle even through this darkness. They spell overwhelming emotions I'm not going to make her put into words right now.

"We have to go, Finn. We have to get him. Please don't waste this shot. If he escapes again—"

"Is this why you're insisting? Evie, darling, he's not getting away. I promise you."

"I want... I have to—damn it!" the struggle is vivid in her features. "I *need* to be there."

Does she not trust me to do this? Or maybe, like me, she needs the visual confirmation that the bastard is dead.

I shake my head, pressing another kiss to her forehead. "Trust me to do this for *us*, Evie. Bartiste will die at my hands. I'll get you all the proof you want, just don't ask me to put you in danger."

Her chest rises on a slow, thoughtful breath, and after her eyes drift off for a moment, she finally nods.

"I trust you."

But no sooner she speaks the words, our world explodes into chaos, splintering pops hitting the trunk of the car.

"Down on the floor!" I shout as I put the car back into gear and drive off, the acceleration pressing me back into the seat.

In the rear-view mirror, headlights approach at dangerous speed. More bullets hit us and the shattering of glass sounds behind us as Evie slides as far down in the footwell as she can.

"Finn!" she yelps, pleading but unsure for what.

"Goddamn it!" I swear as the passenger of the car following us holds a gun out of the side window. "Stay down!"

Another bullet pierces the back window, but this one passes through the front, too close to my head, and I floor it as I speed through the industrial estate. This is gonna be a shitshow. There are still civilians driving on these streets. Granted, not many, but it's enough for one to call the fucking police.

I press a few buttons on the car screen, and after two rings, Carter answers.

"We're taking fire in fucking traffic! Call the Chief to manage this bullshit!"

"Done. Where are you?"

"Edge of the business park in the industrial estate."

"Are you hit?" Carter asks.

"Only the car. I'll get rid of them."

"The plan is in motion, that's why they came for you."

"Shit, I thought I had time to drop her off." Another shot pierces the car body and I swerve, narrowly missing the curb.

"It's sooner than expected, but we're ready."

"Send the feed to my car. I'll meet you as agreed. And Carter..."

No answer comes as he waits.

"Bartiste's head is *mine*!" I warn.

He chuckles then disconnects the call.

"We're not going to June's then?" Evie asks as more bullets snap through the air, grazing the car.

"A bit fucking late now!" I shout over the roar of the engine.

We can't attract attention to Vincent's mom's house. We'll put everyone in danger.

"Where's your gun? I'll try to shoot them." My Evie is brave, but this is not the time.

"Stay down!" CCTV footage shows up on the car screen when I accept the notification that showed up there.

The warehouse is still empty, but not for long.

Tightening my grip on the steering wheel, I take a sharp turn on a high-pitched screech of the tires and Evelyn's yelp, and put my foot down once again, speeding through the quiet street lit by old, yellow lamps. The car behind us follows, but the bullets have paused, and they're further behind.

"Come on you bastard, come on," I mutter under my breath, my gaze snapping between the road ahead and the mirror.

"We're supposed to evade them, not will them closer!" Evelyn shouts from her makeshift hiding place.

"Evade them? I'm not running, darling, I'm fucking hunting!" I roar.

I lift the foot off the gas enough that they're starting to catch up. A few more bullets fly and I know they hit the back seat from the muffled sound.

"What's the plan?" she shouts.

"When I tell you, get up and hold the fuck on!"

She doesn't answer, but from the corner of my eye I can see how she's bracing herself. The road is quieter the deeper we drive into the estate and my gut is beaming with anticipation.

"Now!" I scream.

Evelyn whips out of her hiding place, plants herself in her seat, and manages to strap herself in as I swerve slightly to the left, and plant my foot on the brake. With a shriek, we're right next to the car that followed us, only I let us fall back just enough that my front lines up with their back, and pull a sharp right, catching their back with a crashing jolt.

"Gun in arm rest!" I shout as their car turns perpendicular to ours and I accelerate to carry them forward. The noise of blocked tires against the asphalt grits my eardrums, and I wiggle the steering wheel around to keep them in front of me.

Evelyn complies, and without further instruction, she cocks the weapon, lines it up out the window, and pulls the trigger on a loud pop.

"Good girl!" She hit the driver, and the shooter looks angry now. "Hold on!"

I press the foot on the gas and turn the wheel a few inches to the left, guiding them exactly where I want them, then slam my foot on the brake, screeching to a halt. Their car shifts straight into a concrete wall, windows smashing as it jolts.

Wasting no time, I grab the gun out of Evelyn's hand, and step out. On hurried, unfaltering steps, I reach their car illuminated by my headlights. The shooter attempts to pull himself out through the driver's seat, climbing over the man who's grunting in pain. Not dead yet, then.

Anger-driven adrenaline courses through my veins at the thought that the bastards could have fucking killed Evelyn. On echoing pops, I let two shots fly one after the other, and the men take their last breaths as blood trickles down their foreheads. Without a second thought, I whip around and go right back inside the car.

"What's happening, Finnigan? What are those?" Evelyn asks, eyes fixed on the car screen.

A smirk pulls at my lips as the infrared camera feed shifts between different locations inside the warehouse. Men are strewn all over, standing, sitting, laid down. A small army invades the space through the back entrance, arms drawn. Another group sneaks in through the back, trying to ambush the people already waiting there.

"Seriously, what is this?!"

"Bartiste's men. Coming for us," I answer, a calm quality to my tone.

"No! Finnigan, oh my god! We have to do something!" She shifts in her seat, hands trembling as she presses them to the sides of her head, brows drawn up.

She claims she might want to leave, but she cares so much about men she never met, men she only knows as being part of The Sanctum.

"Watch, darling." I nod toward the screen.

Bright green light flares on the feed as shots are fired, and Evelyn shrieks when the bullets hit the men, one by one caught in a frenzied attack.

"Wait, why aren't they fighting back?" she asks, her tone slow as she stops listening to her emotions and reads the scene before her. "Are they...?"

"Dead," I confirm before the question is asked. "They're shooting their own men. Ones we killed earlier."

"Bait," she whispers.

I nod watching the scene as it calms and confusion sets in. Putting the car back into gear I set off again, and Evelyn gasps just as the camera feed turns white with the flames that engulf the warehouse. Then it all goes black.

"What was that?"

"A culling," I answer. "We planted a seed that we have Frankie B."

"But he's dead."

"Aye. But his dear father has no reason to believe that. The beach was spotless clean within the hour. No bodies, no crime. All he would have known is that he stupidly came to get you, and disappeared. There's not much of a stretch from there to believing we protected you. But this was just a ruse, and we knew Bartiste would know that his son wouldn't be there. He thought he was going to kill us in our own ambush, but we used it to relieve him of some of his army. Sloan's men are in the perimeter, cleaning out the leftovers."

Sirens wail as we turn into another side street on our way out of Queenscove. It sounds like a fire engine, likely going toward the explosion we just caused, but I still don't want to attract attention with all these bullet holes piercing the car and the busted front.

"When we devised the plan, we were worried Bartiste wouldn't give a shit about his son. We didn't know anything about him until you told us. We thought he just popped up in the picture, like some bastard son. If that was the case, his emotional connection to the kid wouldn't have been strong enough. But one of our more recent captives shed some light on the situation after we tempted him with his family's demise. We wouldn't kill innocents unless attacked, but the poor idiot didn't know that."

"Jesus... is he still alive? Actually, never mind. I don't want to know." She exhales a heavy breath and shakes her head. "So what about Frankie?"

"His mother was Bartiste's ex. Not married, but a long-time partner. Abusive relationship from the sounds of it, and she took a page out of her baby daddy's book and disappeared, along with little Frankie. But it turns out that some evil is inherited, because in his early teens, the son forced them out of hiding. He sought his dad and swore his allegiance to him. Bartiste took the mom captive, but apparently was reluctant to trust him. Though, he was also desperate to have his kid back. After all, he was the heir to his disgusting kingdom, and already he showed signs to be as cruel as his daddy. He also became Bartiste's weakness, so he kept him hidden for a long time. This was still happening at the time Bartiste came to Queenscove last time."

She knows which time I mean now, I don't need to explain. Evelyn doesn't say a word, simply waits for me to continue, and I find that, after all I confessed to her, those memories from eight years ago feel... a little more distant. Not like fresh wounds any longer.

"The guy said that Frankie himself told some of his story. He saw what happened to his dad, what we did to him. He was the one who tracked him down in the hospital, he probably knew of the alias his dad would use. That's when the son nursed his broken father back to health, and stepped up in the business. He proved himself to his father, and to cement his commitment to *the cause* he killed his own mother. Stabbed her."

"Christ, that's personal. I mean—" Evelyn sighs. "A gun is quicker."

"Agreed. Frankie didn't just prove himself, he showed his father he's just like him. Which is how we were quite sure our plan would work."

"Rather ironic that Frankie died the same way he killed his mother." There's a tinge of amusement curling her lips. "Why wouldn't Bartiste just think his son is dead, since you captured him?"

"Carter. After planting the seed, Bartiste, or rather one of his men, contacted us. Proof of life was requested, and our resident genius created a deep fake using AI technology, and gave him the proof."

I chuckle at the memory. I saw it. It was fucking good. I didn't even try to understand how Carter did it.

"He can do that? Why does Carter know how to mess with artificial intelligence tech?"

"Amongst other things, for the exact reason why he used it. In case someone does this, or other things, to us, he can learn how to spot it. Reverse the process. Fight back."

"Jesus… I must admit, he does scare me a little." she says running her fingers through her deep violet hair, "I guess we're lucky the man is on our side."

"Yeah. We're all well aware. We're even luckier *The Carver* is on our side."

"That's his nickname, right? What do you mean?"

"The man studies medieval torture methods as light reading. You've seen how brutal, how dangerous Madds can be. Carter is… different. He's silent in his brutality, a different kind of predator, but he feeds on life-force. On screams. On pain. And tears. And as the name suggests… he carves."

She grimaces at the mental image.

"Would he ever betray you since he's so… cold?"

"Never. I'm not sure if he can love. Maybe in his own way. But loyalty is important to him."

"Most times loyalty is better than love… So the agreed location mentioned to him was not this warehouse?" Evelyn asks, pointing to the now black screen.

"No. Different one. We're going there right now."

I grab my phone and shoot a text to Carter.

Still alone?

The response comes within five seconds.

On his way.

Bartiste is nearing. The adrenaline that has been slowly leaving my body as we've been driving, is returning. We were only a few minutes away, but I was anxious that more of Bartiste's men could have followed us. I really wish I could have taken Evelyn to Mamaw June, but it's too late. Too dangerous.

"When we get there, I'm hiding you in a room and you have to stay there. I'm being serious, Evelyn. You cannot. Fucking. Move. Got it?"

I'm focused on the narrowing road as we pass through the old, wrought-iron gates of the abandoned sugar factory, and pull in by an old shed next to another one of our cars. She hasn't answered me.

"You got it, Evie?"

"Yes, yes. Stay hidden. Do not move. Got it." Her tone carries a bit too much stubbornness. I hope it's not a lie. "Why are we parking basically at the front, in plain view?"

I get out of the car and go to grab her. One kiss I steal before I usher her toward the looming, creaky building that hasn't seen much life in the last thirty years.

"Because Carter planted another seed that this is our hiding spot, a temporary center of operations. And also that we're under the impression we've successfully killed Bartiste," I answer with a chuckle.

"He thinks he's ambushing us."

"Exactly."

We pass through a secondary door since we've soldered shut the main one, and after a couple of corridors, we're in the main space of the factory. A projector screen lights up the space and its old machinery, as our men find their positions in the shadows.

"What is that?" Evelyn exclaims, pointing at the video playing on the screen.

I steer her in the other direction, toward the stairs, before she can see the gruesome scene projected there.

"Best not to look at that, Evie."

"This is a fucking bad idea!" Madds rushes to us, Jay, one of our men in tow.

"Trust me, brother. I know. There was no other choice. Jay, take her up to the archive room. It's far enough away, but still in decent reach. Take two more men with you. Protect her at all costs."

"Of course, sir."

Another one of our guys comes over with bulletproof vests for both of us, and I quickly strap Evelyn into hers, then throw mine on.

"No! Finnigan—"

But Maddox pulls her in a crushing hug, his lips a tight line as he looks at me. Yeah buddy, I'm fucking worried out of my mind too. She turns to me once she's released out of his grip.

"I want to stay with you, please Finnigan, I can't… what if something happens?"

I guide her pretty face to mine and press a deep kiss to her lips. When I move away, tears brim her eyes, squeezing my chest. I hope nothing happens to me so I can see her gorgeous face again.

"Jay will keep you safe while I deal with the bastard who wronged you."

"No, I mean what if something happens to *you*? To Madds?"

God, I love her. She's more worried about our safety. Leave it to Evelyn to think of everyone but herself.

"Then you'll nurse me back to health. We'll take Severin to a hospital." I grin, peppering kisses to the tears that are now flowing down her pretty face.

Finally she chuckles. "I'll be very angry and annoying in that case."

"I don't expect any less from you, Evie darling." I pull her in my arms one more time, then reluctantly let go of her. "Now go! Hide! And stay there."

She nods and slowly backs away, giving a chaste smile to Madds as she finally leaves with Jay up the creaky, metal stairs and disappears behind a wall.

"He's passed the gates!" someone's shout echoes through the factory.

We all disperse, hiding in the best spots we've already scouted when we assessed the place. Mine is next to Ronan. All but two access routes have been sealed shut, and blasting through those metal doors will be too much hassle, so we know exactly where Bartiste is coming from. We have the best view of the asshole's face as he'll walk into this space and see exactly what he came here to retrieve.

Maybe the anguish we're hoping for won't mar his features. But if it does, I don't want to miss it.

When the creek of the metal door echoes through the vast space, I know—it's finally time.

CHAPTER 39

Finnigan

I EXPECT THE steps to rush in our direction, but they're careful instead. We don't attack, though. Not until most of them have entered the building. We don't want them to scatter. The snipers stationed out on the building have orders to count to five and if it looks like no one else intends to enter, kill all the ones remaining outside.

Ronan taps me on the shoulder and when I turn to him, he nods toward the left. The moment I look in that direction and aim my gun, watching the first men step in, is the same moment sound trickles in, echoing and bouncing off the heavy metal that forms this space. It's not coming from those men, but from the projector that was just unmuted by Carter.

Oinking and grunting stall their steps and they turn to the screen. Some of them don't react, but others cover their mouths, or turn around, unable to stand the vivid imagery of the *feast*. We wanted to hurt Bartiste, and Carter came up with the best idea how.

"What the fuck is this! It can't be..." Bartiste himself steps in on a slight limp, walking through the several dozen men who have flooded the space, eyes fixed on the screen.

A grin spreads over my lips with the deep shock and hint of sorrow tainting the bastard's features. There's a hint of disgust there too as he watches his one and only son, or better yet his naked corpse, be eaten by pigs. They're in no hurry though, enjoying this feast at a calm, soothing pace.

We don't make a habit of disposing of bodies in this way. Carter reserves his pigs for more *special* kills, and since this one wasn't his, he made an exception. The broken look on Bartiste's face was totally worth it.

"You will pay for this!" he bellows. "You hear me?! You will pay for this!" Spit flies out of his mouth as he turns around the space, blindly trying to find us.

The first shot splits through the sounds of the pigs and one of his men is down. That's our cue. Only a split moment later a shattering bullet-storm assaults my eardrums and Bartiste's men fall like flies around him. Everyone knows not to aim their guns at the man in question. My goal is clear, but it's too early to go straight for him. His men scatter, taking cover behind the old machinery, and I move through the shadows at the edge of the space, taking cover behind the thick concrete columns as I pick them off one by one.

Bullets screech against the metal machinery, howls are pulled when they hit their targets, grunts come from the people now in hand to hand combat, all a cacophony of overwhelming sounds that echo in this vast space. My bullets find home in the neck and forehead of two men who run for me, and before they hit the ground, I look back to where Bartiste was taking cover.

He's not there.

"Watch out! They have armor-piercing rounds!" Vincent shouts from somewhere.

Frantic, I turn around and take cover behind another pillar, desperately looking for Bartiste. My fist clenches, teeth gritting as old memories of the asshole slipping through my fingers, assault me. Our men have strict orders—no one leaves the building. If they do, snipers will take them out. With one deep, slow breath, my pulse calms. Bartiste is not escaping. Even if the finger squeezing the trigger is not mine, he will not escape again.

With that calming thought, I spot him hiding behind some machinery, reloading the clip of his gun. My eyes sweep the perimeter and I jump into a sprint around the edge of the space, taking cover behind the pillars when bullets fly in my direction. It's sad, satisfying, and worrying all at the same time how many bodies I have to jump over to get to the man, praying none of them are ours. Out of nowhere someone leaps in front of me, and my breath whips out of my lungs as he elbows me straight in the sternum. My feet catch onto a body lying on the floor and my gun flies out. His is aimed straight at my head.

But he's too close to me and didn't realize it, so I swing my legs, scissor them around his ankles, and flip him onto the floor. My gun is somewhere behind me, but the time to look for it is not now. I scramble to the guy who's now looking for the same thing as me, but I slam my fist into his stomach, earning a few more seconds to lunge for his gun. Two seconds later, his brain splatters from the right side of his head, and I'm already up, grab my own gun, and rush toward my target.

He can't leave, by now the doors are shut from the outside. We were adamant no one, but us leaves this place tonight. One glance toward the stairs and I stop dead in my tracks—three bulky men rush up them. Aiming my gun, I shoot the one at the top in the back, and a split moment later one of our guys stationed somewhere above puts a hole in his head, and he tumbles back, taking the other two with him down the stairs.

When I turn back for Bartiste, the bastard's gone again, probably hidden somewhere or sick of seeing his son on that screen being eaten by pigs.

"Come the fuck out, Bartiste, you goddamn coward!" I holler, echoing through the sharp pops of guns, and collapsing bodies.

Looking back to the metal stairs, more of his guys rush up. Damn it, they can't get there, they'll be too close to Evelyn. One of them falls with my shots, the other by someone else's bullets.

Taking cover behind another pillar, I look around for Bartiste once more. The factory has turned into a massacre, bodies fallen everywhere, shots still being fired, though less than before, others are just punching or stabbing each other.

Madds is one of them. He prefers hand-to-hand to the bullets, and he's pummeling through men like they're nothing.

Vin is reloading god knows which number magazine into his gun, a devious tug at the corner of his lips. His thing is making people talk with his intimidating demeanor, with secrets and well-chosen words. But as it is with all of us... violence puts such a big fucking smile on his face.

Then there's Carter. His two guns are still fixed in his leather holster, but he's been doing a heck of a lot of damage with his knives. Blood is splattered all over him, and though I can clearly see the disgust contorting his features at the mess, he's fucking relishing in the violence.

But there's still no sign of Bartiste.

"Are you scared, Bartiste? Scared that you're finally going to pay for your sins?" I taunt, my laugh echoing through the vast space.

Goddamn it! Two more men are once again going up the fucking stairs. I aim my weapon but before I can pull the trigger, they're down.

"Take out the ones at the top!" someone shouts the order, and my blood runs cold.

"Where are you, you bastard?"

"Is she up there, *boy*? Is that why you keep taking out everyone who steps up those stairs?"

Oh, that's Bartiste alright. The way he says *boy* brings me back to all those years before, when he kidnapped Annika and Hanna and fucking taunted us. Now he wants Evelyn too? Over my dead-fucking-body and not even then. I'll come out of the goddamn grave and pull him down with me.

"It's me." Ronan alerts me as he slides next to me behind the pillar, taking down two more men. "Don't let him get to you."

"I'm not!" but my tone is snappier than it should be. "Watch out!" I whip my gun over his shoulder and shoot the man who was raising his weapon at him.

"Thanks."

"You need to go, Ronan. Take cover away from this. You have a wife and son at home."

"Now you're getting all protective? I'm not dying today." He grabs the back of my head and brings me down, kissing the top of it. "Besides, you have plenty to lose, too."

I shake my head and turn around.

"Oh fuck no!" I lift the gun, but it's too late. Two of our men stationed at the top fall, the other two take cover as more shots are fired.

Then I catch one more glimpse of Bartiste as he runs from behind one piece of equipment to another, ducking as I let two bullets fly in his direction. The bastard is all the way on the other side of the space, too far for great accuracy, especially since there are no lights there. And I do want to be accurate, since I only want to maim, not kill, just yet.

I go to run, but bullets hit the concrete at my feet and I whip back, crashing against Ronan.

"Goddamn it!" I curse.

But I push away again anyway. And the same thing happens. When my brother tries to move out, bullets fly on his side too.

"They're trying to keep us here."

"Yeah, no shit." I huff out a breath. "Can someone fucking shoot the asshole?" I rage loud enough for the sound to vibrate over the flying bullets.

I can't shoot blindly, as much as it sounds like a pretty damn good idea right now, but I'm not gonna risk accidentally hitting one of our own. I sneak a look, and just as a bullet hits the concrete next to my shoulder, I see a group of Bartiste's men climb up those stairs again. Ice fills my veins as their steps get too close to the top and no one is stopping them. Two finally go down, but the rest turn out of my line of sight and shoot.

My ears ring, and a lump in my throat chokes me. I lunge, but arms catch me in a vice around my middle, pulling me back just as a sharp burn hisses against my forearm.

"They're gonna get to her!" I rage at Ronan's grip.

"You almost got shot, brother! You're no good to her dead."

"Someone go after her!" I shout and hope someone hears me.

I look down at the blood trickling off my forearm—it's just a graze.

A maniacal laugh bounces off the metal walls and I grit my teeth at the sound.

"I'm gonna have her soon!" Bartiste shouts, "Again!" Then the bastard laughs once more.

"Cover me!" I leap out from behind the pillar, sprinting to the next one as bullets fly behind me, but I trust Ronan is taking the opportunity to shoot whoever's aiming their guns at me.

The space has quieted more or less, guns are still fired, but there are enough bodies on the ground to know that there aren't many of Bartiste's men left. Apart from the bastards upstairs.

I have to get to her.

"You're done, Bartiste! You're not getting out of here alive!" I sneak a look and see movement behind some bulky machinery. "Come out, *old man.*"

On careful steps I move from behind the pillar and moments later, the bastard comes out into view too.

"Don't worry now. No one here's going to shoot you." A grin pulls at my lips as I watch the forced expression on his features. "They all know you're mine to kill."

He's trying to cover the fear with made up malice. From the corner of my eyes I spot our men out in the open, guns aimed in several directions—I guess some of the asshole's men are still alive. But my focus is on their boss as more bullets fly and loud thumps hit the ground.

Hopefully those were the last of his men.

I lift my gun, aiming at Bartiste, but a flurry of gunshots split the silence. They're muffled, distant. My breath catches in my lungs—they're coming from upstairs. A heart-wrenching scream splits through the vastness of the space, and my heart stops.

Evelyn!

Evelyn

PAIN AND FURY burst out of me in a bellow that bounces off these metal walls and echoes through my very soul. I took the last man down with the gun Jay threw at me, but not before he put a bullet through his chest. Tears spill freely down my cheeks, and my hand shakes as I brush my palm over Jay's eyes, shutting them. Brinn, his brother, is probably here too. I'll have to be the one to tell him. He died because of me, protecting me.

I wipe a bloody hand over my eyes, brushing the tears away.

"Don't shoot, we're with you." Two men hold their hands up in the doorway. "Finn sent us to protect—"

But I don't hear their words anymore, because others filter through from downstairs.

"Oh, shame. Waste of a good ass. Maybe I should have told them not to kill your bitch. Oops."

Dread spills through my soul at that seedy, disgusting voice that brings terrible memories, but mixed with the poison tainting me already, it turns to rage.

A deep, pained roar reverberates through the whole factory, and I flinch.

"I will string you by your guts through this goddamn factory! It will take you fucking days to die, you goddamn son of a bitch!" Finnigan. Oh god, my Finnigan! The pain in his voice brings me straight to my feet. *"She didn't fucking deserve it!"*

"But you do!" Bartiste shouts. *"You killed my fucking son!"*

I'm running before the thought touches my consciousness, pushing past the men standing by the door, clutching the gun as the metal platform vibrates with each footfall. My gaze finds Finn's wide one as I rush down the steps, shock and relief mixed in his gorgeous blue eyes.

"Nooo!" Finnigan shouts as a loud pop echoes sharply.

Something whizzed past me, but I don't stop even when the second pop sounds, and I slip the last three steps, jumping straight on the ground. I think the second shot came from Ronan who has his gun aimed somewhere behind me, but there's no time to thank him.

"Look at that, the bitch is still alive." The seedy voice still speaks, bile rising up my throat.

"This *bitch* is the one who killed your fucking son, you rapist bastard! I put a blade in his chest, slammed it over and over until he was close enough to death that I could see him try to reach for it and end his wasteful suffering. I watched him drown in his own blood, slow, painful, with a fucking smile on my face!" I rage at Bartiste, then shift my gaze to my gorgeous Finnigan who sprints toward me.

Ronan rushes toward Bartiste and knocks the gun out of his hand, pinning his arms at the back with a feral look on his face. He's holding the man who kidnapped his pregnant wife all those years ago.

"Kill her! Kill her now!" The asshole bellows when he realizes just how fucked he is.

Finnigan stops next to me, grabs my hand as our gazes meet for a relieved moment, then looks over to Bartiste. Only, his eyes fly wide before they land on the bastard. Someone yells. My lungs seize with Finn's coiling muscles. I catch the limping form moving out from behind some machinery, at the same time a boom of a discharged weapon sounds and Finn turns, stepping in front of me.

His brows draw together on a visceral shudder at the same moment his blood splatters all over me and I jerk. Searing rage drives me, the pain ripping through my shoulder not as strong as the one looking back at me from Finn's beautiful gaze, and I step to the side and find the bastard who pulled the trigger before the others can take him away from me. A banshee shriek bounces off the metal walls as I empty the magazine in him, pain tearing through the sound-waves. With the soreness in my throat, I realize the scream was mine.

On unsteady feet, Finn turns around and steps forward, aiming his gun at the man who caused so much sorrow to so many people.

Ronan jumps into a sprint, releasing Bartiste and rushes toward us just like the rest of The Sanctum, wide eyes laced with concern and fear fixed on us.

"Finn," I cry out when he staggers.

But this moment is the culmination of eight grueling years stolen from him by this man, and he pushes forward, steadying the gun with the other hand.

"You'll keep your guts in your belly, *old man*, but I won't grant you a quick death." He unloads the gun twice, in quick succession, and the bellow that follows crawls up my spine uncomfortably.

Bartiste clutches his abdomen, but his bleeding crotch is the wound making me happiest. Like his son before him, he will take a well-deserved long time to die.

But I won't get to watch him. I rip my gaze from him when Finnigan crashes to his knees next to me, and my heart stills in my chest.

"No, no, no! Finnigan, baby!" I follow him to the floor as he falls back, feeling for his chest, but the damn useless vest is in the way.

"He took an armor-piercing one..." someone says behind me.

I fumble around desperately, ignoring my own pain, but large hands push mine away and open the vest to find his shirt soaked in blood.

"Apply pressure!" someone shouts, and those same large hands press over his chest as I move to his face.

"It's gonna be okay, you'll be fine." My voice trembles as I grab him, brushing my thumbs over his eyebrows. "You stupid, stupid man! Why did you have to take the bullet for me?"

My vision clouds with tears I cannot stop from flowing.

"I'll be fine, Evie darling." But his voice is weak. It doesn't match his words, and his piercing blue eyes lost some of their brightness.

"Finn!" Those large hands are replaced by slightly smaller ones, and Ronan appears on the other side of me. "I only just got you back, you're not allowed to fucking bail on me." The concern in his eyes makes me more uneasy.

Finn chuckles, but the noise sounds wrong, gurgled and strained and I want to throw up at how horrific it sounds.

"I'm sorry for the last..." he says to his brother, but the words are slow, forced through the shallow breaths. "Now more than ever, I understand why you left. I regret pushing you away... losing all this time."

"Save it, Finn! Tell me when I can breathe properly, back home. Safe."

But he shakes his head gently. "I'm sorry, Ronan. I was an asshole... you didn't deserve it."

"Stop it, seriously, stop it! Don't talk like you're fucking going anywhere! I refuse to forgive you until we're out of this fucking place."

But Finn just smiles and a cry spills out of me at the lack of hope in his eyes. I want to scream at Ronan to forgive him, but I don't because I agree, Finn is not allowed to go anywhere.

"You're... you're hit." He grunts as his gaze turns to me, looking at my shoulder as he tries to rise.

"I'm fine. Stay down." I push him back.

I'm not fine. The searing pain in my shoulder is almost debilitating as the adrenaline slowly seeps out, but the man I love is dying on the floor before me and my heart hurts more than my flesh.

"I'm sorry..." Finn whispers as the others are trying to figure out how to get him to a hospital and keep his lungs from collapsing on the way.

"Stop, you didn't—"

"I did try to manipulate you... a little bit." He interrupts. "I hoped that... without worrying about... your father, you'll want to stay."

"You asshole! I knew it," I cry, dropping low to press sloppy kisses over his lips. "I never wanted to leave. I was scared, Finn. All I know is tragedy... I thought that leaving before another beautiful thing crumbles around me would be for the best. And now you—"

"You're wrong," he says, coughing weakly. "You... pieced me back together. I love..." His eyes drift closed.

"Finnigan!" I bellow. "Stay with me! Please, oh God, please!" I beg, pressing my forehead to his as my tears stain his beautiful, pale face.

I tap his cheek, gently at first, then harder when his eyes still don't open.

"Brother, wake up!" Ronan's breaking too.

"Do something!" I roar to no one in particular. "Keep him alive or I swear to god..."

The threat dissipates as Finnigan grunts in my hands, and when I look down his eyes try to flutter open.

"Please, baby, stay with me. I promise I won't leave if you don't leave me either..." I'm crying so hard, the surrounding voices are nothing but background noise.

Finnigan's eyes drift close, but this time there's no flutter in his lashes.

"No! Finnigan, come back to me!"

Bellows burn their way through my chest, the pain tearing something embedded so deep inside my soul, it seems to shred every fiber that binds me.

"I'm yours. Forever... Please, come back..."

But there's only darkness, only sorrow, and too much silence.

CHAPTER 40
Evelyn

"DO WE HAVE more bubble wrap?" Maya asks as she walks around the living room, looking between the half-packed boxes.

"Yes, in the corner by that empty bookcase there's a big roll."

She skips with a bit too much enthusiasm in her step for someone who's currently packing moving boxes. There's so much more left to do. I barely packed half the living room, and I'm already bored out of my mind. The ache in my shoulder and limited mobility isn't helping. Maya, though, she's treating it like it's the most fun activity ever.

I must admit it's endearing to see how she treats all these books. Layers upon layers of bubble wrap around them to make sure they reach their destination completely intact. She seems to take greater care of Finnigan's books, picking the older volumes out and wrapping them individually, like she's protecting memories, not bound paper. She insisted that the books are her responsibility, and she's actually made much more progress with them than I've made with the rest of this room.

"When do you think we'll be able to go visit Aaro?" Maya asks in her little voice.

Her friend left with Ronan and Annika only two days ago, returning to their home and leaving an open invitation for us. Considering the photos I've seen of the idyllic island paradise they live in, I'm keen to go as soon as we're settled in our new home and we're free.

"Next school holiday. You're back on a proper schedule, you know that."

"But that's not until Christmas!" she protests. "Ugh, fine... I miss not having to go to school."

"I'm sure you do." I laugh, shaking my head. "Now keep packing."

"Can I help?"

His warm, rich voice fills my chest with comforting heat, and I whip around to find Finnigan leaning against the wall, arms crossed against his chest.

"What are you doing up?" I rise to my feet and rush to him. "You're supposed to be in bed."

I look down at his torso, checking to make sure he's okay and hasn't ripped a stitch.

Three weeks have passed since his surgery, the skin sealed by now, so I'm aware I'm being a bit over the top. It would take much more than rising from bed to tear it open.

"It goes both ways, Evie darling." He brushes his knuckles over my cheek, pulling a smile from my lips. "You know we have people coming who will pack everything."

"I know, but we wanted to focus on the more personal things," I explain.

"Your shoulder needs to heal."

It won't take as long as his lung, but he's not wrong; the bullet that tore through him and lodged in my shoulder did some damage. Those armor-piercing rounds are absolutely ruthless. Madds and the others still feel guilty for missing the guy who shot us, and considering that one of their own almost died, it's probably not going to go away for a while. Finnigan has his own guilt about me, and I'm hoping to squash that soon, because I truly couldn't care less about a wound as long as he's alive and well before me.

Also, there is something creepily romantic about sharing a scar from the same bullet with Finnigan.

After the doctor came out of his surgery and confirmed he's alive, in critical condition but he was going to live, Sloan, Maddox and the rest of the guys apart from Ronan, left Queenscove and decimated what was left of Bartiste's organization. They kept prisoners who gave them all the details they needed, and along with Carter and his hackers, they found what was left of Bartiste's people. Which wasn't much. Turns out that due to the access to the ports in Queenscove, and some of the best trade routes, the asshole was set on taking the city from The Sanctum and establishing his trafficking empire here.

His dream crashed and burned. It died slowly, just like he did, bleeding out on the cold concrete floor while watching the video of his disgusting son being eaten by pigs. By the time we left the warehouse, the pigs were halfway done and Bartiste was dead.

We're free.

I'm free.

"She misses Aaro?" He quirks an eyebrow, gesturing to my sister who's wrapping up books in a corner.

I roll my eyes, shaking my head, "This is not even the first time she mentioned him since we woke up. The kid's only been gone for two days."

"Told you—*boyfriend.*"

He chuckles and I would smack him if he wasn't seriously hurt.

"What about you?" I counter, "Do you miss your brother?"

On a deep sigh his gaze drifts out the windows, but there's no tenseness in his features. That puts a small smile on my lips.

"I think I do. I spent so long punishing him in my mind, blaming him, bashing him, but... it took a simple confrontation to realize it was me I was punishing. Retribution for my own failures. I guess being trapped on a hospital bed for days and not having any choice but to talk to him was all I needed to fully patch up my relationship with him."

I shrug. "Maybe, but it's not just that. You're not the same person you were then, Finn. The pain is not fresh anymore and you're older, more mature. You process these things differently now. Either way, I'm happy you have your brother back."

"Look at you, though." He turns his gaze back to mine. "You're younger now than I was when it all happened to me, but you're ten times more mature."

"Eh, I'm a woman. We're smarter."

He bursts into a full belly laugh, clutching his abdomen, and for a moment I freeze.

"Stop it." I hiss, "You'll hurt yourself. You know you can't strain your lungs."

"Yeah, yeah. Come on, smart-ass." He turns me and smacks my ass, urging me to move, but I don't miss the slight cough. "Come, sit with me."

He guides us on the sofa and pulls me into his side to cuddle me.

"No, I'll hurt you," I protest.

"Stop it, woman. I'm not made of glass. Don't make me ask again."

Reluctantly, I comply and cuddle into his side as he wraps one long, powerful arm around me.

"Are you going to miss this place?" I ask, watching the sheer, white curtains flow in the breeze.

"Probably not. After Ronan moved out, it rarely ever felt like *home*."

I nod because, of course, I understand. After losing mom, Fleeton didn't feel like home, and it had nothing to do with being homeless.

"Are you sure you like the house I found for us?"

Whilst he was recovering in the hospital he was adamant about wanting a fresh start. For all three of us. A place to fill with memories and everything we missed out on. So I went house hunting. Maybe it was luck, maybe it was the hasty, exorbitant offer I made to the couple whose house wasn't even on the market, but it didn't take as long as I thought it would to find the perfect place.

"It's secure, on a private beach where I can go swimming whenever I want, and you assigned a giant room to build a library. What more can I want?"

I chuckle, remembering how his gaze twinkled when I told him about the double height space the owners were using for a tacky games room, which we could turn into a gorgeous library with a small spiral staircase and wrap around balcony. The prospect excited him so much, he told me I'm free to paint every room black and fill it with skulls and oddities, if I want, especially since he noticed I've been exploring my style more and more.

"Are *you* excited? Are you sure it's what you want?"

I snort in response. "I never allowed myself to find out what I want, Finn. This... this is beyond any dreams I ever had."

"You've dreamed of me though." He wiggles his eyebrows.

"Once or twice," I answer, trying to sound nonchalant and failing.

"The kitchen in that house helps, though. Right?" he says with a deep, rumbling chuckle.

"Okay, yeah, the kitchen helps."

It's gorgeous. Large enough to fit a decent size island in the middle, with a huge window stretching almost the entire length of the biggest wall, above the countertop, and two ovens already installed. I have plans to change the color scheme to deep violets and greens, but the configuration is fantastic. I can already see myself baking like a madwoman in there.

"Any reservations?" His tone is lower as he asks the question.

I hesitate for a moment. "It's quite a transition for you. From a 'one night only' kind of guy to living with your girlfriend and a kid. I guess I just wonder if you'll—"

"Stop wondering," he interrupts. "You're mine, Evelyn. Since the moment I laid eyes on you I knew you would be my end. I just didn't know what kind of end. Turns out it was of just... existing. I only ever started truly living once you came into my life. You are everything." He brushes his knuckles down my cheek, stopping under my chin and tipping it up until our mouths align.

His words hit so deep, goosebumps bloom over my skin, bursting from within my chest. He brushes his lips against mine in a ghost of a touch, then presses sweet, soft kisses to them.

"And your sister, she's the bonus I never asked for and could never, ever let go. She's part of you, Evelyn, which makes her part of me too. And I finally have someone to talk books with."

"Thank you." I whisper. My heart swells with his words. His acceptance of my sister, the one who is now officially in my custody because of him, means more than anything. "Though, she might grow out of reading at some point."

"Eh, it will be good for as long as it lasts." He shrugs.

"Are you talking about the new house?" Maya jumps on the opposite end of the sofa and nestles into Finn. No boundaries whatsoever. "I can't wait for my little nook in the library. Can we build a tent? But like, inspired from 'One thousand and one nights', pretty and colorful, with carpets and pillows all over the floor."

"How are you gonna earn the tent?" Finn asks her.

He knows I never give my sister everything she wants unless she earns it. I was never raised spoiled and I don't plan on raising her the same.

She scrunches her eyebrows as she digs for the answer. "Umm... I'll do well in school?"

"You have to do good in school anyway," Finn says with a chuckle.

"Oh, okay. I'll unpack the library after you build it."

Finn turns to me with a surprised expression. "Actually, that's pretty good," he says, laughing.

"Yeah, not going to lie, I never planned on doing that myself. Plus, you know... bad shoulder and all." I shrug, pointing at it.

"Aaah suddenly it's a bad shoulder. Okay, I see how this will be." He shakes his head, but the smile stays on his lips.

"So is that a deal?" Maya pulls at his forearm.

"No. You'll *help me* unpack the library. It's a big, slightly dangerous job, sweet girl. But you'll be my assistant. How about that?"

"Yaaay! Thank you, Finn, thank you!" she wraps her little arms around his neck and hugs him tight, as I'm silently praying she's not going to accidentally fall on his healing chest.

But she pulls away carefully, jumping back off the sofa and disappears somewhere behind us.

Finn chuckles, turning his attention back to me, squeezing me just a little harder.

"Me and her, Evie... it comes effortlessly. Never worry. You gave me something I've been missing for so long, you gave me family. Different from The Sanctum, because you and Maya, you're all mine. Only mine."

"Forever?"

"And beyond."

EPILOGUE
Finnigan

Five months later

BRUSHED BRASS LETTERS shine over matte black background in the early evening light—*The Gothic Bakery*. Evelyn's dream has been slowly taking off.

I trusted her baking and creative skills from the beginning, but I didn't know much about the market to be assured there would be enough clientele for her. Turns out there is. Queenscove's elite especially seems to adore her dark, baroque motifs she makes out of sugar, fondant, and even icing. Her creativity is blooming along with her business, and she had to hire two more staff members, on top of the other two, to keep up.

To say I'm fucking proud of her is an understatement.

I stand outside, leaning against my Mercedes G-class that she pretty much claimed for herself now, waiting and watching as the deep plum walls turn black when she flicks the lights off, then steps out and turns to lock the door behind her.

"Ready?" I ask, extending my hand to her.

"Yup. You're driving, though, I need to retouch my makeup before we get to Midnight."

I nod and open the door, helping her up in the passenger seat.

"How was your dad today?" I ask. I know she went to visit him at lunch.

"Alright, I guess. It was one of those days. Harder. Twice he asked where mom is. But he's okay. Happy."

"I'm sorry." I know he's not been doing all that great, the moments of clarity rarer nowadays.

She shrugs. "He's here, and that's all that matters. Was Maya okay?" she asks.

"Happy to spend the night with Mamaw June, yes. Though she was apparently disappointed that it's too warm now to turn the fireplace on," I answer as I start the car and pull out into traffic.

Evelyn's shop is only a two minute walk away from Midnight. We could have walked there, but she already had the car here. She laughs, a soft melodic sound that always seems to travel straight to my cock.

"It's always too warm in Queenscove. Mamaw June was bloody sweating in January too, but she was still appeasing that stubborn girl."

"She's hard to resist, sugar," I say, snorting.

"Well, people should try harder. Y'all are spoiling her."

I say nothing because it's hundred percent true. Instead, I steal glances as Evelyn taps a small brush over her face, refreshing her extravagant makeup. We are a decadent contrast against each other. Her plum, sleek hair against my wavy, blonde curls, her bold, dark makeup against my golden skin—leather, velvet, and metal against my clean cut clothes. We're perfect. *She's* perfect.

She's a fucking goddess, and she's all mine.

Just as I pull into the secure car park at the back of Midnight, Evelyn's done retouching her makeup and looks at me with a pretty grin on her dark lips.

"Stunning," I say with a smirk. "I can't wait to smudge that lipstick all over your pretty face."

The flush to her cheeks breaks through whatever product she used there and my smirk widens, giving her thigh a squeeze. Exiting the car, I walk to the other side and help her out, then guide her inside the speakeasy.

We're not open for another two hours, so it should only be The Sanctum in here. As we walk inside the main barroom, I find Vin, Morrigan, and Madds lounging on the comfy sofas and armchairs around a coffee table. Low, warm lights illuminate the space, bathing the woodsy bar in a cozy vibe.

I slump into a winged-back armchair, pulling Evie onto my lap, my hand splayed over the fishnet tights barely covering her legs.

"Settle this for us, will you?" Morrigan asks. "Madds is the one who proposed that The Sanctum invest in Metamorphosis after half of it burnt down, and now it's been open for about three months, he has not stepped foot in it. Shouldn't he see what his money bought?"

Metamorphosis, her and Loreley's fetish club, was only open for a couple of months, before an intentional fire burnt down half of it. In the heat of the moment, Madds offered to front them the money to renovate, something that shocked pretty much all of us. I still think there is much more to it. Like the way he looks at Loreley sometimes, with both exasperation and uncomfortable curiosity. She was adamant she didn't want to be indebted to The Sanctum. Luckily, it all worked out, and the club is now reopened and stronger than ever. From what I heard, there's a fight for memberships, as the place is even more desirable now than it was before.

"Why don't you want to go, Madds?" Evelyn asks him.

He shrugs, turning his gaze toward the bar, pretending to focus on something. "I don't need to. It's going great from what I hear."

"It is, but it would be nice if you could see it. Be proud of me and all of that," Morrigan counters.

"I am. I know you both did a great job."

Evie turns to me. "Can we go?"

"No" Madds and I shout simultaneously.

"Hey, that's not fair. I want to see," Evie says.

"Well, other people might want to see *you* and that's a definite no for me."

Morrigan laughs and shakes her head. "Your possessiveness is refreshing, but you know first-hand that no one touches anyone in my club without permission. You know you can just come for a drink. And a show." She wiggles her eyebrows suggestively.

"Maybe just for a little bit." Evelyn leans in, whispering in my ear.

I don't answer, but the look in my eyes might be enough, because a cheeky smile spreads over her face.

"For the love of god, at least don't go when Carter's there," Madds tells her.

"Ever the big brother you are," she says with a chuckle.

"Speaking of the wolf. Where is he?" I ask.

"In the office," Vin answers. "I texted him that you arrived too."

Just on cue, Carter pops in through the back door, as always, dressed in pressed trousers, a light shirt with rolled-up sleeves, and tailored waistcoat. He looks every bit the man who belongs in a speakeasy. Only, there's something different tonight. I can't put my finger on it.

"Carter?" Vin's tone sounds like he's seeing the same thing I am.

"I have to tell you something." Carter releases a slow breath that sounds too much like a sigh. Deeply uncharacteristic for the man.

"What?" I ask.

"I fucked up." His gaze sweeps over each one of us. "About six months ago, when we were looking for Bartiste, I was looking for one of his men, and I went after him myself. I tracked him down one night, cornered him in an alley and after I got what I could out of him... I killed him."

There's a pause. "So?" Vin shrugs.

"Someone saw me."

Vin leans forward in his chair, bracing his elbows on his knees, head cocked, as I guide Evelyn to go sit next to Madds.

"And?" I ask.

"I can't find her."

"*Her?!*" all of us say in unison.

"Sorry, a woman witnessed you killing a man, and in the last six months you haven't been able to find her?" Vin runs through the story.

Carter nods, sliding his hands in his pockets, his expression one of annoyance, and maybe, just maybe, slight embarrassment. Amusement is common on his features, but anything beyond that is extremely rare. Which makes this highly worrying.

"You don't know who she is?" Madds asks.

"No. Couldn't find her. I kept track of reports, of stories, of damn internet posts, and no one has talked about it."

"Maybe she recognized you, she's scared, and knows better than to talk," Vin adds.

"She certainly wasn't scared," Carter mutters under his breath, barely audible.

"What?" Madds asks.

"Nothing."

The others accept his answer and I seem to be the only one who heard what he said.

"Why wait until now to say something?" I ask.

"I thought I would find her by now. The challenge became greater and greater, but nothing popped up."

Vin leans back in his chair, shrugging. "Fine. If nothing has come to light in six months, I'm doubtful it will. I'm sure you'll keep an eye and ear out anyway."

"Yeah." Carter nods slowly, his gaze now fixed on a random glass from the table.

I think he does feel some form of embarrassment. How peculiar. Although, I think the man has an inherent need to know everything. This must be bothering him to no end.

"Was she pretty?"

"Morri, Jesus," Vin says, shaking his head.

Carter scowls in her direction, but she just curls her lips inward, as Evie looks away from him, clearly amused.

"Was she?" I quirk an eyebrow, because now I'm curious.

The Carver sets his gaze on me and I shrug, not even trying to hide my amusement.

"Right, I think it's time for a drink. If you don't mind, Carter, I'll do the honors. I don't trust you won't poison our women, or me, if you make them." I get up and head behind the bar, not missing how the man rolls his eyes before he takes my seat.

As I pour the spirits and mixers in the crystal glasses, I steal glances at my Evie, talking with Madds on the sofa. I know Madds is close with Morrigan; they've known each other since she was sixteen, but his relationship with Evie is completely different. They have a friendship that sometimes is lead in silence, because these two seem to share scars they don't talk about, but understand nonetheless. She had to do a lot of apologizing after the stunt she pulled when she went after Frankie B, but Madds felt so guilty that she got shot during the whole Bartiste thing, that he didn't take long at all to forgive her.

I'm happy for her. She didn't just find a new, better life in Queenscove, or love— she found friendship and family. And knowing that she has others here who are willing to protect her, go through hell and back for her, makes me feel so much better.

I'm shaking a drink when Evie rises from the sofa and my mouth goes dry at the slow, deliberate sway of her hips as her thick soled Doc Martens hit the wooden floor. The minx knows exactly what she's doing with those long legs barely covered in sinful fishnets, the dark green, tight velvet skirt hugging her frame, and the worn band T-shirt she tucked in and cut herself into a V-neck. But she had to add that leather harness over just to drive me crazy.

The tips of her hair graze the sweet spot where the neck meets the shoulder with each step she takes, and I'm jealous, because my tongue and teeth should be doing that.

Propping her forearms on the counter, she leans in, rewarding me with her most sinful smirk.

"So, Mr. Hennessey. Will you take me to Metamorphosis?"

Jesus, she's gonna kill me with that seductive voice. I lean in, grip her chin, and she parts her lips for me, but I barely graze them as I dip to the side, blowing a breath over the side of her neck, before I capture her soft lobe between my teeth, nipping it once.

"Only if you're a good girl. Prove it. Tonight." I brush the tip of my tongue over the sensitive skin just under her ear for a brief moment, before I pull back and continue making the drinks.

"Tonight? What are we doing?" Her flush is evident, even in this dim light.

"Having one stiff drink"—I slide a glass her way—"and then go home."

She cocks her head, biting her lip as she grabs the drink and turns around, her ass swaying as she walks away.

Oh yeah, she'll be a good girl alright.

The next hour goes by excruciatingly slow. No one needs that much time to finish the vodka sour I made, but the minx has been sipping it so fucking slow, each drop of liquid is a pawn in her erotic game. She's deliberate in her torture.

By the time we get in the car, my breathing is strained, just as my damn cock against my trousers is. She grabs my thigh as I'm driving, coaxing me on, but two can play this game. I keep her waiting, *wanting*, on the whole drive home. And since our house is just on the outskirts of Queenscove, down a private road that ends in our own, secluded little bay, the drive isn't all that short.

"Finnigan..." She says my name in a breathy voice that stirs my cock.

"Tsk, tsk, tsk, Evie darling. Good girl, remember?"

"But you like it when I beg," she purrs, sharp nails digging into the top of my thigh.

We reach our gate, secured between two small cliffs, the road looking like it was carved through, and I'm ready to blast through them if they don't fucking open quicker.

"I haven't even touched you yet."

"When has my craving for you ever needed your touch, darling Finnigan?"

Her words hit with a shattering lightning, the current spreading goosebumps through my nerves, urging my foot to press harder on the gas. We're past the gates, and our two story beach villa, lit by beautiful, upturned lights, comes into view. From this distance, against the star-splattered sky and dark sea, it looks like a lighthouse, guiding us home.

Screeching to a halt in front of the detached garage to the right, that's exactly what I want to do—find home. Right inside the pretty pussy of the woman who has flipped my life the right way up, and turned me into a love-sick bastard who can't get enough of her.

With a tight grip on my hand, we rush through the front door and flip the moody lights on. Apparently the ceiling lights are a big no-no, and eventually I had to agree she was right. Funky lamps and picture lights are dotted all around, their glow bouncing off mismatched gold frames and rich-colored paneled walls, giving a deeply cozy quality to our decadent house. We aimed for comfort, and Evelyn added, as she calls it, a Gothic cottage-core vibe to it.

"You know what I've been wanting to do all evening, Evie darling? As you've been sipping that drink at snail speed just to get me all hot and fucking bothered?" I ask as I back her against a wall, caging her in.

She curls her lips inward, swallowing her amusement.

"I don't know what you're talking about." She shakes her head, but I grip her cheeks in my hand, forcing her lips to part as I hold her to me.

"Your pretty makeup running down your face as you choke on my cock."

She gasps, the hitch in her chest pressing her peaked nipples against my shirt, and I shift up just enough to graze them, teasing her.

I swipe my tongue over the dark crimson lipstick, getting a hint of cherries. "Tastes delicious, but I can't wait to see it smeared all over my fucking cock."

"Oh god…" she says in a breathy voice.

Releasing her face, I take a step back, then grip her T-shirt and pull it out from under the hem of the skirt.

"I have to take the harness down," she says pointing to the thick leather straps.

"No." I push her hands away as she rushes to unfasten it.

Ever so fucking slowly, I lift the hem until it passes the horizontal strap rounding her ribs, revealing the soft skin from the underside of her breasts. They're trapped between the leather framing them inside two triangle shapes, meeting over her sternum on a brass metal ring, and disappearing over shoulders. I pull at the side of the T-shirt, guiding her arm through the sleeve, then do the same with the other side at an excruciating pace, grazing the fabric over her hard nipples, relishing in her swallowed cry. Finally, I free her breasts, tugging the T-shirt from under the shoulder straps and over her head, then step back to admire her.

"My goddess…" I whisper.

She blushes a deep berry red that matches her lips so perfectly, her back straightening a fraction.

"Now, Evie darling. On. Your. Knees." She drops before me in an instant, her hands making quick work of the belt, then the buttons of my trousers, freeing my aching cock.

I'm on the larger side, but in her delicate hands it looks damn right huge. It looks even fucking better as she takes me right to the back of her throat in one swift motion.

"Jesus Christ!" I groan, fisting the bottom of my shirt like it can help me hold my balance through the whirlwind of sensations.

She ignores me completely, pulling back to reveal the crimson marks her lipstick left over the veined ridges of my cock, but she takes me deep once more before I can fully admire.

I pull my shirt over my head while I still have enough conscious brain cells to manage the movement, and look down at the pretty sight before me. She swallows me down and I push forward, smirking when she chokes on the tip, spit falling off her lips and over her tits. Finally, tears brim her eyes, starting to mess with her makeup. She hums deep in her throat and the vibrations make my eyes roll back.

"Ready?" I ask.

She looks into my eyes, giving me a slight nod of approval, and I thread my fingers through her plum-colored hair, like we've been practicing for months. With a grin pulling at my lips, I tighten my hold on her as she steadies herself on my thighs, and I pump my cock into her plush mouth.

Tears bring the dark makeup down her cheeks as I fuck between her soft lips, and the sight is enough to make me come right now. Tightening my fist, I dig my nails in my palm at the ecstasy that threatens to bring me to my knees, calling on some pain to keep me from spilling all my pleasure too soon. But God, it feels glorious inside her mouth, with black tears streaming down her face, and red lipstick smudged all over my cock.

"Fuck!" I roar, releasing her in an instant and pulling out of her mouth.

It's too much, too good, but not as good as sinking between her thighs, and it's there where I want to come. I help her up, capturing her lips with mine, our tongues tangling as l walk her backward until her thighs hit the back of the couch.

"You"—I tease a nipple between my thumb and forefinger—"are..."—I nip at her lip, soothing it after with my tongue—"divine."

I fall on one knee, kissing a trail down her bare torso, covered only with that sinful leather harness, and push the skirt over her hips. These fishnet tights are my fucking weakness. Every time she wears them I go feral. She could be dressed like a damn librarian, but if she had these tights underneath, I would still see her as the dirtiest little vixen.

Looking up at her with a smirk, she parts her lips when I grip the flimsy fabric covering her pussy, and pull harshly. She gasps, her brows drawing together, watching intently as I suck on two fingers, push her lace panties to the side then sink them inside her pussy at the same time I cover her clit, pulling it between my lips.

She cries out, the sounds tearing from deep within her chest as she grips my hair and grinds herself on my face. I pump my fingers inside her sopping core, deep and fast, exactly how she likes it, until her knees are shaking and she tightens around me.

"Please, please... Oh, please." She chants between the lust-stained panting, a decadent prayer for the pleasure only I can bring her.

She begs so beautifully. So I give her what she wants, rubbing the sensitive spot inside of her as I suck the bundle of nerves between my lips. She breaks on wanton moans that travel straight to my cock.

Rising, I flip her around while she's still whimpering, bend her over the back of the sofa, and guide the fat tip of my cock through the drenched seam of her pussy. Her spasms turn gentle, the orgasm still vibrating through, so I take my time as I push in to the hilt and absorb every tightening pulse of her sweet cunt.

"Divine..." I whisper, gripping the back of her leather harness as I dig my fingers into her hip, bracing myself.

The first few pumps are dragged and deep, following the rhythm of the soft waves that crash against the sand, beyond the wall of windows before us. I grunt as she whimpers each time my hips meet her ass, drawing out that pleasure from deep inside her as my own seems to coil around the base of my cock.

But it doesn't take long until the surf no longer dictates the speed of my strokes, and the feverish slapping of our skins pulls all matter of lustful sounds from our throats. Each thrust brings bolts of current up my spine, pleasure twisting harder, low in my belly, quickly becoming too much. Too close.

I lift Evie up by the harness, wrapping an arm around her and guiding her lips to meet mine, just as I reach for the needy bundle of nerves between her thighs. She jerks her hips against me at the contact, biting on my lower lip on a lewd whimper when I rub it, my cock stroking madly inside her weeping pussy. Our mouths fuck just as well, licking and stroking, sucking and biting on the thrusting rhythm of our bodies, and when the first spasm of her core chokes my cock, I press harder over the hood of her clit.

The moment she breaks, I swallow her cries, my own orgasm ripping through me with enough strength, my knees go weak for a brief moment. I spill inside of her over and over, wondering just when exactly am I going to stop. It's irrelevant, I'm in no rush to leave her warm core.

"I will never get used to this," she whispers between our slowing kisses.

"This?" I ask, peppering more around her lips, her cheeks, the tip of her curved nose.

"Pleasure." She relaxes into me as I wrap her in my arms. "What you do, what we do, it feels more like worship."

It really does.

"I've only ever worshiped *you*, Evie darling. Pleasure has never felt like this before."

Her cheeks flush and lips pull into a chaste smile.

"Let's clean up. I could do with cooling off with a late night swim."

She nods her answer, pressing another gentle kiss to my lips, and I reluctantly pull out of her, chuckling when she drops down a few inches. She always has to stand on her tiptoes when we fuck like this, and for some odd reason I find it deliciously cute when she dips down to her normal height.

We head to the bathroom, and while I help her clean my cum that's dripping down her thighs, since it's become both my pleasure and my specialty, she removes her messed up makeup.

She's bare-faced now, and she looks so pure, so damn young. I beat myself up for a while, thinking I'm stealing from her years she could be spending making friends her own age, doing all sorts of crazy things, and experimenting like everyone else does at that age. Then I sat back and watched her go through her day-to-day life and those feelings dissipated. Even without me in her life she wouldn't have made those types of choices. Not with Maya by her side. Not with her dad weighing on her. Her personality doesn't fit.

She's different, and she fucking refused to let me go. I suggested it twice—living her youth and all that. The first time, she looked at me like I grew a second head, the second time she threatened me with the knife she was using to slice cake. I was gently advised to shut the fuck up and stop saying stupid things.

"Where did you go?" Her voice filters through the dangerously hot memory of her aiming a buttercream covered knife at me.

"Nowhere, sugar. Come, let's cool off." I lie because I would rather not end up getting stabbed.

We walk stark naked over the wooden patio and onto the soft, warm sand toward the ocean. Most nights, Maya is here and we can't skinny dip, but once in a while Mamaw June takes her for a sleepover and we spend hours out in the calm waters of the bay.

Evelyn hisses when the first slosh of the surf touches her feet and I laugh, shaking my head. "It's pretty damn warm."

"I'm surprised you think so. Your body runs at a hundred degrees. Celsius! This should be ice on your skin." she teases, gritting her teeth as she keeps walking forward.

"Yeah, yeah. You say this every time."

"Yup. Shows that it's true."

I snicker as I dive straight in, stroking underwater and reveling in the feel of it against my skin. When I finally emerge and turn around, Evie is floating on her back, eyes closed as the moonlight shimmers over her wet skin.

Goddess...

This is my life now. Every single day I wake up unable to fully believe that it's not a dream running in a sick loop through my head. It's not *too good to be true*, because we have our share of challenges, our own issues we're working through, failings we haven't fully overcome, but we're doing all of this together.

The two of us... my darling Evie. My moonlit goddess.

"You're doing it again. Losing yourself inside your mind."

Her silver eyes seep into golden sparkles as she turns to me, and I realize I've been drifting over to her without thinking. She drops her legs underwater, swimming gently toward me, and I reach for her. Gripping her waist and guiding her legs over my hips, I tread water for the both of us.

"You're mine..." I whisper, pressing a salty kiss to her lips.

The corner of hers quirks as she brushes the hair back from my face. "You sound surprised."

"Every day." I nod. "I wish you wouldn't have gone through all that pain to get here. I wish I wouldn't either. Yet..." I let the word drift away.

"I know. It's funny, really. We condemn the terrible people who destroy us—our lives. We punish them, hate them, and yet... they created the connection between us, our moment, our opportunity for two to become one. They formed the basis of our love story. Without them I wouldn't have been in that container, and you wouldn't have been on the other side of it. I wouldn't have sacrificed myself for those children, and you wouldn't have looked at me with that gut-wrenching pain in your eyes you didn't even realize you were bleeding all over the room. There wouldn't have been an opportunity for us. We would have never met. This heartbreakingly beautiful, fucked up love would have been wandering all alone, drifting through the universe, crying for a loss that it never gained in the first place. Without the pain they caused us, we wouldn't have felt this... serenity."

I shake my head, a lump in my throat at the harsh words that make so much damn sense. I hate them nonetheless, but they are the harsh truth.

"I can't picture a world without you in it. Without you by my side."

She brushes the tip of her nose against mine, then presses a kiss to my lips.

"You will never have to. You are mine, Finnigan Hennessey."

"All yours, Evie darling."

THE END

BONUS SCENE

Deleted scene between Chapters 39 – 40

Finnigan

PLEASE, BABY...

I won't leave...

Those words don't echo in the darkness threatening to take over; they sink into it, swallowed whole by the terrifying abyss pulling me deeper.

It's her—my Evie. But I can't see her.

She's mine. She's *finally* mine. Yet I'm lost, far into the darkness where pain no longer hurts my body but shreds my soul piece by piece, a ravenous beast devouring its first meal in eons.

Come back to me...

I'm trying, Evie darling, but the shadows are too thick. Molasses against my muscles as I fight toward your light. The pain ripping at my soul isn't mine anymore—it's hers. Through the suffocating dark, fragments of her agonized gaze piercing through, pulling me deeper into her torment.

I'm yours...

Forever...

Don't cry, my love. I'd die a thousand more deaths for you. And a thousand more after that, so long as you keep breathing your sizzling energy into the world.

Forevermore, I love you.

But the shadows suffocate my soul, stall my heart's desperate beats. The darkness swallows her light whole.

* * *

beep *beep* *beep*

Nettles prick my airways, stinging down my throat. The odd sensation leaves me disoriented.

beep *beep* *beep*

The sound is a faint echo, coiling around me like I'm sitting in the middle of the cave, drenched in its darkness.

beep *beep* *beep*

It grows louder. The echo wastes away as I move farther from that cavern. The dark void brightens.

What is that wretched noise?

"Are you sure?"

My heart stalls behind my rib as those melodic soundwaves brush over me. Every muscle in my body seems to awaken all at once. The stinging in my airways grows painful. Vivid. *Alive.*

"Anytime now. Look there, his pulse is speeding up, and his brain activity is intensifying by the moment."

The unfamiliar voice sets me on edge. Who is he? Why is he with her? *My Evelyn.*

Are they alone?

Is she safe?

"Careful. Don't put too much pressure on your shoulder, Miss Shaw. Your ligaments have a lot of healing to do."

Healing? Evelyn needs to heal?

The darkness recedes further as I claw my way out of it, desperate to know what's wrong with her. She's hurt. She's fucking hurt, and I'm not there to protect her.

"It'll take more than a bullet to keep me from him."

Bullet.

Memories crash into me like the violent cascade of the waterfall deep in Queenscove's woods. One after the other, they paint the picture of my last moments. Evie crying over me. Tears drenching her cheeks. Pain. So much pain. Blood soaking her clothes—mine. But hers too.

"You're hurt."

Fire ignites in my chest, raw and unrelenting. *Was that me?* My throat burns as I force a hoarse cough.

"Easy, baby. Don't talk just yet. You're okay. I'm here." Her delicate voice anchors me.

"You're hurt." I rasp, the words scraping their way out.

Petals brush over my cheeks, trapping the next question in my throat as her velvety lips press against my mouth. The world tilts. A groan vibrates, and I think it's mine.

"I'm okay," she whispers against my lips, and I part them, desperate to swallow the same air she breathes.

beep *beep* *beep*

The incessant sound slows, calming, as a crack of light breaks through a crack in the haze.

I blink. Once. Twice. Each time more light seeps in painfully, until violet hues and olive-toned skin come into focus. The third time, her doe eyes fill my vision. Looking at me with more hope and joy than I ever thought possible just from the sight of my sorry ass.

"There you are," she whispers, crinkles crack the soft skin at the corners of her eyes as her lips curl into a smile. "You came back to me."

I think I smile, too, though my muscles feel foreign. But the strain in my cheeks is proof of it. Her widening, bright grin definitely is.

Another figure shifts in the background. My gaze narrows on them.

"Mr. Hennessey, I'm Dr. Lowe, the surgeon who operated on your lungs. Welcome back."

He seems pleasant enough, but the tightness between my brows lingers. Evelyn pulls away and I want to yank her back to me, afraid she'll fall back into that darkness.

Only, I was the one who fell, not her.

She's been right here. Waiting. Hoping.

"Here," she murmurs, slipping her hand beneath my head. Dr. Lowe aids as she brings a straw to my dry lips. "Drink," she urges.

I obey. With one long drag, my eyes drift closed as water rushes down my parched throat, soothing it. The sharp gurgle on an empty glass follows shortly after and the sting in my throat finally eases. My breath seems less painful, too.

"Evie darling," I croak.

"Yes, my love?"

"You're hurt." My gaze drifts to the light blue sling cradling her arm.

"I'm fine. It's already healing."

Already?

"How long have I been out?" I flex my fingers, the dull ache strangely comforting, and try to sit up.

"Stay put, Mr. Hennessey," the doctor commands.

A soft beep signals the motorized bed adjusting, propping me slightly upright. The next breath reaches deeper than the ones before. Painful, but it makes me feel more awake. *Alive.*

I finally see her properly. Dark shadows mar the delicate skin beneath her eyes, her exhaustion palpable. And worry wrinkles the space between her brows. Yet her smile outshines it all.

"Five days," Dr. Lowe explains. "You've been kept in a medically induced coma. The bullet pierced your lung, narrowly missing the main pulmonary artery. You were incredibly lucky, Mr. Hennessey. The damage was extensive, but we repaired it. The rest is up to you. Avoid stress, speaking too much, or any activity that could increase your heart rate. The nurse will also come later to explain your prescription, and to teach you some breathing exercises to help with the healing process."

"When can I go home?"

"Not for at least another five days. Seven is ideal for close monitoring."

"Five it is." My tone brooks no argument. No way I'm staying here, away from Evelyn, for more than necessary.

She flashes a bemused smile, shaking her head. "He'll stay seven, doctor. Thank you."

My jaw drops at her casual dismissal. The doctor departs, leaving us alone.

More maturity than last time I saw her mars her features. It bothers me, because this time it was me who forced her to store away her own pain, her own suffering, for the sake of mine.

"I'm not staying seven days, Evie darling. My place is next to you."

"Watch me tie you to this bed, Finnigan Hennessey. Just *fucking* watch. You're staying until you heal. I didn't almost lose you for you to ruin it by being stubborn."

"But I—"

"I'll gag you if you insist," she interrupts, fire flashing in her eyes.

Suppressing a grin, I raise a brow. I like her like this—assertive. Fierce. An odd sense of pride blooms in the pit of my stomach.

"Come here," I urge, reaching for her hand.

She clasps it without hesitation, brushing a thumb over my palm.

"Sit with me."

"No, Finn. I'll hurt you—"

"I need you, Evie. I can hardly breathe if it's not your air filling my lungs. Come, lay next to me."

I'll crawl to my knees if I have to. I almost died. Almost lost her and changed our forever in the worst of ways. I *must* feel her against me.

"Please, just—"

Emotion glistens in her eyes as she sheepishly climbs in beside me. She curls against my side, careful of her slinged arm as she lays her palm on my belly and head on my shoulder.

With one deep, careful breath, the world steadies. Her warmth the guiding fucking light as it radiates through me, her sugary scent overpowering the sterile hospital air.

No words pass between us—only slowing, contented breaths as our souls align and our future settles on the right path.

I'm still here.

And I'm hers forever.

* * *

Thank you for reading!

**Don't forget to drop a quick review on Amazon and follow Lilith
to keep up with all her new releases!**

ALSO BY THE AUTHOR

SERIES

#1 Dangerous Strokes, a Dark Mafia Romance

#2 Reckless Covenant, a Second Chance Mafia Romance

#3 Manacled Hearts, an Age Gap Mafia Romance

#4 Carved Obsession, a Dark Mafia Romance

#5 Mad Lullaby, a Dark Mafia Romance

STANDALONES

My Kind of Monster, a Dark Contemporary Romance

Even in Death, a Romantic Horror Novella

Blissful Perdition, a Lesbian Romance Short Story

ABOUT THE AUTHOR

Lilith Roman is a romance author who writes stories laced with danger, intense passion, and dark themes—always ending in a happily ever after.

She's an introvert with an addiction to pretty hardbacks she'll never read, anything chocolate, and steamy books. But her love of horror movies and vampire villains has convinced her, without a shadow of a doubt, that even the monster under the bed needs a love story.

For exclusive insights, join her Newsletter, or
Lilith Roman's Corrupted Souls Facebook group.

scan the QR code